# 100 GREAT AMERICAN SHORT STORIES

# 100 GREAT AMERICAN SHORT STORIES

DOVER THRIFT EDITIONS

Edited by
## John Grafton

DOVER PUBLICATIONS, INC.
MINEOLA, NEW YORK

# DOVER THRIFT EDITIONS

General Editor: Susan L. Rattiner
Editor of This Volume: Terri Ann Geus

*Bibliographical Note*

*100 Great American Short Stories*, first published by Dover Publications, Inc., in 2020, is a new anthology of short stories reprinted from standard sources. John Grafton has made the selections and provided a Note specially for this edition. Readers should be forewarned that some stories contain racial and cultural references of the era in which it was written and may be deemed offensive by today's standards. Style inconsistencies are inherent in the original and are sometimes retained for the sake of authenticity.

*Library of Congress Cataloging-in-Publication Data*

Names: Grafton, John, editor.
Title: 100 great American short stories / edited by John Grafton.
Description: Mineola, New York: Dover Publications, Inc., 2020. | Series:
  Dover thrift editions | "100 Great American Short Stories, first
  published by Dover Publications, Inc., in 2020, is a new anthology of
  short stories reprinted from standard sources with a Note by the editor,
  John Grafton"—Title verso.
Identifiers: LCCN 2019025965 | ISBN 9780486831848 (paperback) | ISBN
  0486831841 (paperback)
Subjects: LCSH: Short stories, American—19th century. | Short stories,
  American—20th century.
Classification: LCC PS648.S5 A15 2020 | DDC 813/.0108—dc23
LC record available at https://lccn.loc.gov/2019025965

Manufactured in the United States by LSC Communications
83184101
www.doverpublications.com
2 4 6 8 10 9 7 5 3 1
2020

# Note

---

ARE THERE RULES for writing a good short story? One of the authors featured in this volume, Edgar Allan Poe, absolutely thought there were, and one of his rules seems to be quoted whenever the subject comes up: "A short story must have a single mood, and every sentence must build towards it." Excellent advice no doubt, but, like much excellent advice in many areas of human activity, not for everyone. Another author featured in this collection had a different take on the subject, and was certainly as sure of his ground as Poe was of his. William Sydney Porter (O. Henry) wrote somewhat aggressively: "I'll give you the whole secret to short story writing. Here it is: Write stories that please yourself. There is no Rule 2."

Readers of stories, however, don't have to choose either of these approaches, or any other—we can just enjoy stories of many kinds, by many authors, from many periods. This collection presents a hundred stories which have survived the test of time by American authors who, except for Washington Irving, born in 1783, were all born in the nineteenth century (Ernest Hemingway just makes it, 1899). It includes generous selections of stories by some of the "stars" of that period: Mr. Poe himself, of course, Ambrose Bierce, Jack London, O. Henry, Kate Chopin, and many others, and also includes several stories that may be new discoveries to some readers. There was no hard and fast rule concerning the selections except fine stories by talented writers, and perhaps, something for everyone.

John Grafton

# Contents

## Edith Wharton (1862–1937)

# 100 GREAT AMERICAN SHORT STORIES

# EFFIE WHITTLESY

## George Ade

MRS. WALLACE ASSISTED her husband to remove his overcoat and put her warm palms against his red and wind-beaten cheeks.

"I have good news," said she.

"Another bargain sale?"

"Pshaw, no! A new girl, and I really believe she's a jewel. She isn't young or good-looking, and when I asked her if she wanted any nights off she said she wouldn't go out after dark for anything in the world. What do you think of that?"

"That's too good to be true."

"No, it isn't. Wait and see her. She came here from the intelligence office about two o'clock and said she was willing to 'lick right in.' You wouldn't know the kitchen. She has it as clean as a pin."

"What nationality?"

"None—that is, she's a home product. She's from the country— and *green!* But she's a good soul, I'm sure. As soon as I looked at her, I just felt sure that we could trust her."

"Well, I hope so. If she is all that you say, why, for goodness sake give her any pay she wants—put lace curtains in her room and subscribe for all the story papers on the market."

"Bless you, I don't believe she'd read them. Every time I've looked into the kitchen she's been working like a Trojan and singing 'Beulah Land.'"

"Oh, she sings, does she? I knew there'd be some drawbacks."

"You won't mind that. We can keep the doors closed."

The dinner-table was set in tempting cleanliness. Mrs. Wallace surveyed the arrangement of glass and silver and gave a nod of approval and relief. Then she touched the bell and in a moment the new servant entered.

She was a tall woman who had said her last farewell to girlhood.

Then a very strange thing happened.

Mr. Wallace turned to look at the new girl and his eyes enlarged. He gazed at her as if fascinated either by cap or freckles. An expression of wonderment came to his face and he said, "Well, by George!"

The girl had come very near the table when she took the first overt glance at him. Why did the tureen sway in her hands? She smiled in a frightened way and hurriedly set the tureen on the table.

Mr. Wallace was not long undecided, but during that moment of hesitancy the panorama of his life was rolled backward. He had been reared in the democracy of a small community, and the democratic spirit came uppermost.

"This isn't Effie Whittlesy?" said he.

"For the land's sake!" she exclaimed, backing away, and this was a virtual confession.

"You don't know me."

"Well, if it ain't Ed Wallace!"

Would that words were ample to tell how Mrs. Wallace settled back in her chair blinking first at her husband and then at the new girl, vainly trying to understand what it meant.

She saw Mr. Wallace reach awkwardly across the table and shake hands with the new girl and then she found voice to gasp, "Of all things!"

Mr. Wallace was confused and without a policy. He was wavering between his formal duty as an employer and his natural regard for an old friend. Anyway, it occurred to him that an explanation would be timely.

"This is Effie Whittlesy from Brainerd," said he. "I used to go to school with her. She's been at our house often. I haven't seen her for—I didn't know you were in Chicago," turning to Effie.

"Well, Ed Wallace, you could knock me down with a feather," said Effie, who still stood in a flustered attitude a few paces back from the table. "I had no more idee when I heard the name Wallace that it'd be you, though knowin', of course, you was up here. Wallace is such a common name I never give it a second thought. But the minute I seen you—law! I knew who it was, well enough."

"I thought you were still at Brainerd," said Mr. Wallace, after a pause.

"I left there a year ago November, and come to visit Mort's people. I s'pose you know that Mort has a position with the street-car company. He's doin' *so* well. I didn't want to be no burden on him, so I started out on my own hook, seein' that there was no use of goin' back to Brainerd to slave for two dollars a week. I had a good place with Mr. Sanders, the railroad man on the North Side, but I left becuz they wanted me to serve liquor. I'd about as soon handle a toad as a bottle of beer. Liquor was the ruination of Jesse. He's gone to the dogs—been off with a circus some-wheres for two years."

"The family's all broken up, eh!" asked Mr. Wallace.

"Gone to the four winds since mother died. Of course you know that Lora married Huntford Thomas and is livin' on the old Murphy place. They're doin' about as well as you could expect, with Huntford as lazy as he is."

"Yes? That's good," said Mr. Wallace.

Was this an old settlers' reunion or a quiet family dinner? The soup had been waiting.

Mrs. Wallace came into the breach.

"That will be all for the present, Effie," said she.

Effie gave a startled "Oh!" and vanished into the kitchen.

"It means," said Mr. Wallace, "that we were children together, made mud pies in the same puddle and sat next to each other in the old schoolhouse at Brainerd. She is a Whittlesy. Everybody in Brainerd knew the Whittlesys. Large family, all poor as church mice, but sociable—and freckled. Effie's a good girl."

"Effie! *Effie!* And she called you Ed!"

"My dear, there are no misters in Brainerd. Why shouldn't she call me Ed! She never heard me called anything else."

"She'll have to call you something else here. You tell her so."

"Now, don't ask me to put on any airs with one of the Whittlesys, because they know me from away back. Effie has seen me licked at school. She has been at our house, almost like one of the family, when mother was sick and needed another girl. If my memory serves me right, I've taken her to singing-school and exhibitions. So I'm in no position to lord it over, and I wouldn't do it any way. I'd hate to have her go back to Brainerd and report that she met me here in Chicago and I was too stuck up to remember old times and requested her to address me as 'Mister Wallace.' Now, you never lived in a small town."

"No, I never enjoyed that privilege," said Mrs. Wallace, dryly.

"Well, it is a privilege in some respects, but it carries certain penalties with it, too. It's a very poor schooling for a fellow who wants to be a snob."

"I wouldn't call it snobbishness to correct a servant who addresses me by my first name. 'Ed' indeed! Why, I never dared to call you that."

"No, you never lived in Brainerd."

"And you say you used to take her to singing-school?"

"Yes, ma'am—twenty years ago, in Brainerd. You're not surprised, are you? You knew when you married me that I was a child of the soil, who worked his way through college and came to the city in a suit of store clothes. I'll admit that my past does not exactly qualify me for the Four Hundred, but it will be great if I ever get into politics."

"I don't object to your having a past, but I was just thinking how pleasant it will be when we give a dinner-party to have her come in and address you as 'Ed.'"

Mr. Wallace patted the tablecloth cheerily with both hands and laughed.

"I really don't believe you'd care," said Mrs. Wallace.

"Effie isn't going to demoralize the household," he said, consolingly. "Down in Brainerd we may be a little slack on the by-laws of etiquette, but we can learn in time."

Mrs. Wallace touched the bell and Effie returned.

As she brought in the second course, Mr. Wallace deliberately encouraged her by an amiable smile, and she asked, "Do you get the Brainerd papers?"

"Yes—every week."

"There's been a good deal of sickness down there this winter. Lora wrote to me that your uncle Joe had been kind o' poorly."

"I think he's up and around again."

"That's good."

And she edged back to the kitchen.

With the change for dessert she ventured to say: "Mort was wonderin' about you the other day. He said he hadn't saw you for a long time. My! You've got a nice house here."

After dinner Mrs. Wallace published her edict. Effie would have to go. Mr. Wallace positively forbade the "strong talking-to" which his wife advocated. He said it was better that Effie should go, but she must be sent away gently and diplomatically.

Effie was "doing up" the dishes when Mr. Wallace lounged into the kitchen and began a roundabout talk. His wife, seated in the front room, heard the prolonged murmur. Ed and Effie were going over the family histories of Brainerd and recalling incidents that may have related to mud pies or school exhibitions.

Mrs. Wallace had been a Twombley, of Baltimore, and no Twombley, with relatives in Virginia, could humiliate herself into rivalry with a kitchen girl, or dream of such a thing, so why should Mrs. Wallace be uneasy and constantly wonder what Ed and Effie were talking about?

Mrs. Wallace was faint from loss of pride. The night before they had dined with the Gages. Mr. Wallace, a picture of distinction in his evening clothes, had shown himself the bright light of the seven who sat at the table. She had been proud of him. Twenty-four hours later a servant emerges from the kitchen and hails him as "Ed"!

The low talk in the kitchen continued. Mrs. Wallace had a feverish longing to tiptoe down that way and listen, or else go into the kitchen, sweepingly, and with a few succinct commands, set Miss Whittlesy back into her menial station. But she knew that Mr. Wallace would misinterpret any such move and probably taunt her with joking references to her "jealousy," so she forbore.

Mr. Wallace, with an unlighted cigar in his mouth (Effie had forbidden him to smoke in the kitchen), leaned in the doorway and waited to give the conversation a turn.

At last he said: "Effie, why don't you go down and visit Lora for a month or so? She'd be glad to see you."

"I know, Ed, but I ain't a Rockefeller to lay off work a month at a time an' go around visitin' my relations. I'd like to well enough— but—"

"Oh pshaw! I can get you a ticket to Brainerd tomorrow and it won't cost you anything down there."

"No, it ain't Chicago, that's a fact. A dollar goes a good ways down there. But what'll your wife do? She told me today she'd had an awful time gettin' any help."

"Well—to tell you the truth, Effie, you see—you're an old friend of mine and I don't like the idea of your being here in my house as a—well, as a hired girl."

"No, I guess I'm a servant now. I used to be a hired girl when I worked for your ma, but now I'm a servant. I don't see as it makes any difference what you call me, as long as the work's the same."

"You understand what I mean, don't you? Any time you come here to my house I want you to come as an old acquaintance—a visitor, not a servant."

"Ed Wallace, don't be foolish. I'd as soon work for you as anyone, and a good deal sooner."

"I know, but I wouldn't like to see my wife giving orders to an old friend, as you are. You understand, don't you?"

"I don't know. I'll quit if you say so."

"Tut! tut! I'll get you that ticket and you can start for Brainerd tomorrow. Promise me, now."

"I'll go, and tickled enough, if that's the way you look at it."

"And if you come back, I can get you a dozen places to work."

Next evening Effie departed by carriage, although protesting against the luxury.

"Ed Wallace," she said, pausing in the hallway, "they never will believe me when I tell it in Brainerd."

"Give them my best and tell them I'm about the same as ever."

"I'll do that. Good-bye."

"Good-bye."

Mrs. Wallace, watching from the window, saw Effie disappear into the carriage.

"Thank goodness," said she.

"Yes," said Mr. Wallace, to whom the whole episode had been like a cheering beverage, "I've invited her to call when she comes back."

"To call—here?"

"Most assuredly. I told her you'd be delighted to see her at any time."

"The idea! Did you invite her, really?"

"Of course I did! And I'm reasonably certain that she'll come."

"What shall I do?"

"I think you can manage it, even if you never did live in Brainerd."

Then the revulsion came and Mrs. Wallace, with a return of pride in her husband, said she would try.

# A NIGHT

## Louisa May Alcott

BEING FOND OF the night side of nature, I was soon promoted to the post of night nurse, with every facility for indulging in my favorite pastime of "owling." My colleague, a black-eyed widow, relieved me at dawn, we two taking care of the ward, between us, like the immortal Sairy and Betsey, "turn and turn about." I usually found my boys in the jolliest state of mind their condition allowed; for it was a known fact that Nurse Periwinkle objected to blue devils, and entertained a belief that he who laughed most was surest of recovery. At the beginning of my reign, dumps and dismals prevailed; the nurses looked anxious and tired, the men gloomy or sad; and a general "Hark!-from-the-tombs-a-doleful-sound" style of conversation seemed to be the fashion: a state of things which caused one coming from a merry, social New England town, to feel as if she had got into an exhausted receiver; and the instinct of self-preservation, to say nothing of a philanthropic desire to serve the race, caused a speedy change in Ward No. 1.

More flattering than the most gracefully turned compliment, more grateful than the most admiring glance, was the sight of those rows of faces, all strange to me a little while ago, now lighting up, with smiles of welcome, as I came among them, enjoying that moment heartily, with a womanly pride in their regard, a motherly affection for them all. The evenings were spent in reading aloud, writing letters, waiting on and amusing the men, going the rounds with Dr. P., as he made his second daily survey, dressing my dozen wounds afresh, giving last doses, and making them cozy for the long hours to come, till the nine o'clock bell rang, the gas was turned down, the day nurses went off duty, the night watch came on, and my nocturnal adventure began.

My ward was now divided into three rooms; and, under favor of the matron, I had managed to sort out the patients in such a way that I had what I called, "my duty room," my "pleasure room," and my "pathetic room," and worked for each in a different way. One, I visited, armed with a dressing tray, full of rollers, plasters, and pins; another, with books, flowers, games, and gossip; a third, with teapots, lullabies, consolation, and, sometimes, a shroud.

Wherever the sickest or most helpless man chanced to be, there I held my watch, often visiting the other rooms, to see that the general watchman of the ward did his duty by the fires and the wounds, the latter needing constant wetting. Not only on this account did I meander, but also to get fresher air than the close rooms afforded; for, owing to the stupidity of that mysterious "somebody" who does all the damage in the world, the windows had been carefully nailed down above, and the lower sashes could only be raised in the mildest weather, for the men lay just below. I had suggested a summary smashing of a few panes here and there, when frequent appeals to headquarters had proved unavailing, and daily orders to lazy attendants had come to nothing. No one seconded the motion, however, and the nails were far beyond my reach; for, though belonging to the sisterhood of "ministering angels," I had no wings, and might as well have asked for Jacob's ladder, as a pair of steps, in that charitable chaos.

One of the harmless ghosts who bore me company during the haunted hours, was Dan, the watchman, whom I regarded with a certain awe; for, though so much together, I never fairly saw his face, and, but for his legs, should never have recognized him, as we seldom met by day. These legs were remarkable, as was his whole figure, for his body was short, rotund, and done up in a big jacket, and muffler; his beard hid the lower part of his face, his hat-brim the upper; and all I ever discovered was a pair of sleepy eyes, and a very mild voice. But the legs!—very long, very thin, very crooked and feeble, looking like grey sausages in their tight coverings, without a ray of pegtopishness about them, and finished off with a pair of expansive, green cloth shoes, very like Chinese junks, with the sails down. This figure, gliding noiselessly about the dimly lighted rooms, was strongly suggestive of the spirit of a beer barrel mounted on cork-screws, haunting the old hotel in search of its lost mates, emptied and staved in long ago.

Another goblin who frequently appeared to me, was the attendant of the pathetic room, who, being a faithful soul, was often up to tend two or three men, weak and wandering as babies, after the fever had gone. The amiable creature beguiled the watches of the night by brewing jorums of a fearful beverage, which he called coffee, and insisted on sharing with me; coming in with a great bowl of something like mud soup, scalding hot, guiltless of cream, rich in an all-pervading flavor of molasses, scorch and tin pot. Such an amount of good will and neighborly kindness also went into the mess, that I never could find the heart to refuse, but always received it with thanks, sipped it with hypocritical relish while he remained, and whipped it into the slop-jar the instant he departed, thereby gratifying him, securing one rousing laugh in the doziest hour of the night, and no one was the worse for the transaction but the pigs. Whether they were "cut off untimely in their sins," or not, I carefully abstained from inquiring.

It was a strange life—asleep half the day, exploring Washington the other half, and all night hovering, like a massive cherubim, in a red rigolette, over the slumbering sons of man. I liked it, and found many things to amuse, instruct, and interest me. The snores alone were quite a study, varying from the mild sniff to the stentorian snort, which startled the echoes and hoisted the performer erect to accuse his neighbor of the deed, magnanimously forgive him, and, wrapping the drapery of his couch about him, lie down to vocal slumber. After listening for a week to this band of wind instruments, I indulged in the belief that I could recognize each by the snore alone, and was tempted to join the chorus by breaking out with John Brown's favorite hymn:

"Blow ye the trumpet, blow!"

I would have given much to have possessed the art of sketching, for many of the faces became wonderfully interesting when unconscious. Some grew stern and grim, the men evidently dreaming of war, as they gave orders, groaned over their wounds, or damned the rebels vigorously; some grew sad and infinitely pathetic, as if the pain borne silently all day, revenged itself by now betraying what the man's pride had concealed so well. Often the roughest grew young and pleasant when sleep smoothed the hard lines away, letting the real nature assert itself; many almost seemed to speak, and I learned to know these men better by night than through any intercourse by day. Sometimes they disappointed me, for faces that looked merry and good in the light, grew bad and sly when the shadows came; and though they made no confidences in words, I read their lives, leaving them to wonder at the change of manner this midnight magic wrought in their nurse. A few talked busily; one drummer boy sang sweetly, though no persuasions could win a note from him by day; and several depended on being told what they had talked of in the morning. Even my constitutionals in the chilly halls, possessed a certain charm, for the house was never still. Sentinels tramped round it all night long, their muskets glittering in the wintry moonlight as they walked, or stood before the doors, straight and silent, as figures of stone, causing one to conjure up romantic visions of guarded forts, sudden surprises, and daring deeds; for in these war times the hum drum life of Yankeedom has vanished, and the most prosaic feel some thrill of that excitement which stirs the nation's heart, and makes its capital a camp of hospitals. Wandering up and down these lower halls, I often heard cries from above, steps hurrying to and fro, saw surgeons passing up, or men coming down carrying a stretcher, where lay a long white figure, whose face was shrouded and whose fight was done. Sometimes I stopped to watch the passers in the street, the moonlight shining on the spire opposite, or the gleam of some vessel floating, like a white-winged sea-gull, down the broad Potomac, whose fullest flow can never wash away the red stain of the land.

The night whose events I have a fancy to record, opened with a little comedy, and closed with a great tragedy; for a virtuous and useful life untimely ended is always tragical to those who see not as God sees. My headquarters were beside the bed of a New Jersey boy, crazed by the horrors of that dreadful Saturday. A slight wound in the knee brought him there; but his mind had suffered more than his body; some string of that delicate machine was over strained, and, for days, he had been reliving, in imagination, the scenes he could not forget, till his distress broke out in incoherent ravings, pitiful to hear. As I sat by him, endeavoring to soothe his poor distracted brain by the constant touch of wet hands over his hot forehead, he lay cheering his comrades on, hurrying them back, then counting them as they fell around him, often clutching my arm, to drag me from the vicinity of a bursting shell, or covering up his head to screen himself from a shower of shot; his face brilliant with fever; his eyes restless; his head never still; every muscle strained and rigid; while an incessant stream of defiant shouts, whispered warnings, and broken laments, poured from his lips with that forceful bewilderment which makes such wanderings so hard to overhear.

It was past eleven, and my patient was slowly wearying himself into fitful intervals of quietude, when, in one of these pauses, a curious sound arrested my attention. Looking over my shoulder, I saw a one-legged phantom hopping nimbly down the room; and, going to meet it, recognized a certain Pennsylvania gentleman, whose wound-fever had taken a turn for the worse, and, depriving him of the few wits a drunken campaign had left him, set him literally tripping on the light, fantastic toe "toward home," as he blandly informed me, touching the military cap which formed a striking contrast to the severe simplicity of the rest of his decidedly *undress* uniform. When sane, the least movement produced a roar of pain or a volley of oaths; but the departure of reason seemed to have wrought an agreeable change, both in the man and his manners; for, balancing himself on one leg, like a meditative stork, he plunged into an animated discussion of the war, the President, lager beer, and Enfield rifles, regardless of any suggestions of mine as to the propriety of returning to bed, lest he be court-martialed for desertion.

Anything more supremely ridiculous can hardly be imagined than this figure, scantily draped in white, its one foot covered with a big blue sock, a dingy cap set rakingly askew on its shaven head, and placid satisfaction beaming in its broad red face, as it flourished a mug in one hand, an old boot in the other, calling them canteen and knapsack, while it skipped and fluttered in the most unearthly fashion. What to do with the creature I didn't know; Dan was absent, and if I went to find him, the perambulator might festoon himself out of the window, set his toga on fire, or do some of his neighbors a mischief. The attendant of the room was sleeping like a near relative of the celebrated Seven, and nothing short of pins would rouse him; for he had been out that day, and whiskey asserted its supremacy in balmy whiffs. Still declaiming, in a fine flow of eloquence, the demented gentleman hopped on, blind and deaf to my graspings and entreaties; and I was about to slam the door in his face, and run for help, when a second and saner phantom, "all in white," came to the rescue, in the likeness of a big Prussian, who spoke no English, but divined the crisis, and put an end to it, by bundling the lively monoped into his bed, like a baby, with an authoritative command to "stay put," which received added weight from being delivered in an odd conglomeration of French and German, accompanied by warning wags of a head decorated with a yellow cotton night cap, rendered most imposing by a tassel like a bell-pull. Rather exhausted by his excursion, the member from Pennsylvania subsided; and, after an irrepressible laugh together, my Prussian ally and myself were returning to our places, when the echo of a sob caused us to glance along the beds. It came from one in the corner—such a little bed!—and such a tearful little face looked up at us, as we stopped beside it! The twelve years old drummer boy was not singing now, but sobbing, with a manly effort all the while to stifle the distressful sounds that would break out.

"What is it, Teddy?" I asked, as he rubbed the tears away, and checked himself in the middle of a great sob to answer plaintively:

"I've got a chill, ma'am, but I ain't cryin' for that, 'cause I'm used to it. I dreamed Kit was here, and when I waked up he wasn't, and I couldn't help it, then."

The boy came in with the rest, and the man who was taken dead from the ambulance was the Kit he mourned. Well he might; for, when the wounded were brought from Fredericksburg, the child lay in one of the camps thereabout, and this good friend, though sorely hurt himself, would not leave him to the exposure and neglect of such a time and place; but, wrapping him in his own blanket, carried him in his arms to the transport, tended him during the passage, and only yielded up his charge when Death met him at the door of the hospital which promised care and comfort for the boy. For ten days, Teddy had shivered or burned with fever and ague, pining the while for Kit, and refusing to be comforted, because he had not been able to thank him for the generous protection, which, perhaps, had cost the giver's life. The vivid dream had wrung the childish heart with a fresh pang, and when I tried the solace fitted for his years, the remorseful fear that haunted him found vent in a fresh burst of tears, as he looked at the wasted hands I was endeavoring to warm:

"Oh! if I'd only been as thin when Kit carried me as I am now, maybe he wouldn't have died; but I was heavy, he was hurt worser than we knew, and so it killed him; and I didn't see him, to say good bye."

This thought had troubled him in secret; and my assurances that his friend would probably have died at all events, hardly assuaged the bitterness of his regretful grief.

At this juncture, the delirious man began to shout; the one-legged rose up in his bed, as if preparing for another dart; Teddy bewailed himself more piteously than before: and if ever a woman was at her wit's end, that distracted female was Nurse Periwinkle, during the space of two or three minutes, as she vibrated between the three beds, like an agitated pendulum. Like a most opportune reinforcement, Dan, the bandy, appeared, and devoted himself to the lively party, leaving me free to return to my post; for the Prussian, with a nod and a smile, took the lad away to his own bed, and lulled him to sleep with a soothing murmur, like a mammoth humble bee. I liked that in Fritz, and if he ever wondered afterward at the dainties which sometimes found their way into his rations, or the extra comforts of his bed, he might have found a solution of the mystery in sundry persons' knowledge of the fatherly action of that night.

Hardly was I settled again, when the inevitable bowl appeared, and its bearer delivered a message I had expected, yet dreaded to receive:

"John is going, ma'am, and wants to see you, if you can come."

"The moment this boy is asleep; tell him so, and let me know if I am in danger of being too late."

My Ganymede departed, and while I quieted poor Shaw, I thought of John. He came in a day or two after the others; and, one evening, when I entered my "pathetic room," I found a lately emptied bed occupied by a large, fair man, with a fine face, and the serenest eyes I ever met. One of the earlier comers had often spoken of a friend, who had remained behind, that those apparently worse wounded than himself might reach a shelter first. It seemed a David and Jonathan sort of friendship. The man fretted for his mate, and was never tired of praising John—his courage, sobriety, self-denial, and unfailing kindliness of heart; always winding up with: "He's an out an' out fine feller, ma'am; you see if he ain't."

I had some curiosity to behold this piece of excellence, and when he came, watched him for a night or two, before I made friends with him; for, to tell the truth, I was a little afraid of the stately looking man, whose bed had to be lengthened to accommodate his commanding stature; who seldom spoke, uttered no complaint, asked no sympathy, but tranquilly observed what went on about him; and, as he lay high upon his pillows, no picture of dying statesman or warrior was ever fuller of real dignity than this Virginia blacksmith. A most attractive face he had, framed in brown hair and beard, comely featured and full of vigor, as yet unsubdued by pain; thoughtful and often beautifully mild while watching the afflictions of others, as if entirely forgetful of his own. His mouth was grave and firm, with plenty of will and courage in its lines, but a smile could make it as sweet as any woman's; and his eyes were child's eyes, looking one fairly in the face, with a clear, straightforward glance, which promised well for such as placed their faith in him. He seemed to cling to life, as if it were rich in duties and delights, and he had learned the secret of content. The only time I saw his composure disturbed, was when my surgeon brought another to examine John, who scrutinized their faces with an anxious look, asking of the elder: "Do you think I shall pull through, sir?" "I hope so, my man." And, as the two passed on, John's eye still followed them, with an intentness which would have won a clearer answer from them, had they seen it. A momentary shadow flitted over his face; then came the usual serenity, as if, in that brief eclipse, he had acknowledged the existence of some hard possibility, and, asking nothing yet hoping all things, left the issue in God's hands, with that submission which is true piety.

The next night, as I went my rounds with Dr. P., I happened to ask which man in the room probably suffered most; and, to my great surprise, he glanced at John:

"Every breath he draws is like a stab; for the ball pierced the left lung, broke a rib, and did no end of damage here and there; so the poor lad can find neither forgetfulness nor ease, because he must lie on his wounded back or suffocate. It will be a hard struggle, and a long one, for he possesses great vitality; but even his temperate life can't save him; I wish it could."

"You don't mean he must die, Doctor?"

"Bless you, there's not the slightest hope for him; and you'd better tell him so before long; women have a way of doing such things comfortably, so I leave it to you. He won't last more than a day or two, at furthest."

I could have sat down on the spot and cried heartily, if I had not learned the wisdom of bottling up one's tears for leisure moments. Such an end seemed very hard for such a man, when half a dozen worn out, worthless bodies round him, were gathering up the remnants of wasted lives, to linger on for years perhaps, burdens to others, daily reproaches to themselves. The army needed men like John, earnest, brave, and faithful; fighting for liberty and justice with both heart and hand, true soldiers of the Lord. I could not give him up so soon, or think with any patience of so excellent a nature robbed of its fulfilment, and blundered into eternity by the rashness or stupidity of those at whose hands so many lives may be required. It was an easy thing for Dr. P. to say: "Tell him he must die," but a cruelly hard thing to do, and by no means as "comfortable" as he politely suggested. I had not the heart to do it then, and privately indulged the hope that some change for the better might take place, in spite of gloomy prophesies; so, rendering my task unnecessary. A few minutes later, as I came in again, with fresh rollers, I saw John sitting erect, with no one to support him, while the surgeon dressed his back. I had never hitherto seen it done; for, having simpler wounds to attend to, and knowing the fidelity of the attendant, I had left John to him, thinking it might be more agreeable and safe; for both strength and experience were needed in his case. I had forgotten that the strong man might long for the gentler tendance of a woman's hands, the sympathetic magnetism of a woman's presence, as well as the feebler souls about him. The Doctors words caused me to reproach myself with neglect, not of any real duty perhaps, but of those little cares and kindnesses that solace homesick spirits, and make the heavy hours pass easier. John looked lonely and forsaken just then, as he sat with bent head, hands folded on his knee, and no outward sign of suffering, till, looking nearer, I saw great tears roll down and drop upon the floor. It was a new sight there; for, though I had seen many suffer, some swore, some groaned, most endured silently, but none wept. Yet it did not seem weak, only very touching, and straightway my fear vanished, my heart opened wide and took him in, as, gathering the bent head in my arms, as freely as if he had been a little child, I said, "Let me help you bear it, John."

Never, on any human countenance, have I seen so swift and beautiful a look of gratitude, surprise and comfort, as that which answered me more eloquently than the whispered—

"Thank you, ma'am, this is right good! this is what I wanted!"

"Then why not ask for it before?"

"I didn't like to be a trouble; you seemed so busy, and I could manage to get on alone."

"You shall not want it any more, John."

Nor did he; for now I understood the wistful look that sometimes followed me, as I went out, after a brief pause beside his bed, or merely a passing nod, while busied with those who seemed to need me more than he, because more urgent in their demands; now I knew that to him, as to so many, I was the poor substitute for mother, wife, or sister, and in his eyes no stranger, but a friend who hitherto had seemed neglectful; for, in his modesty, he had never guessed the truth. This was changed now; and, through the tedious operation of probing, bathing, and dressing his wounds, he leaned against me, holding my hand fast, and, if pain wrung further tears from him, no one saw them fall but me. When he was laid down again, I hovered about him, in a remorseful state of mind that would not let me rest, till I had bathed his face, brushed his "bonny brown hair," set all things smooth about him, and laid a knot of heath and heliotrope on his clean pillow. While doing this, he watched me with the satisfied expression I so liked to see; and when I offered the little nosegay, held it carefully in his great hand, smoothed a ruffled leaf or two, surveyed and smelt it with an air of genuine delight, and lay contentedly regarding the glimmer of the sunshine on the green. Although the manliest man among my forty, he said, "Yes, ma'am," like a little boy; received suggestions for his comfort with the quick smile that brightened his whole face; and now and then, as I stood tidying the table by his bed, I felt him softly touch my gown, as if to assure himself that I was there. Anything more natural and frank I never saw, and found this brave John as bashful as brave, yet full of excellencies and fine aspirations, which, having no power to express themselves in words, seemed to have bloomed into his character and made him what he was.

After that night, an hour of each evening that remained to him was devoted to his ease or pleasure. He could not talk much, for breath was precious, and he spoke in whispers; but from occasional conversations, I gleaned scraps of private history which only added to the affection and respect I felt for him. Once he asked me to write a letter, and as I settled pen and paper, I said, with an irrepressible glimmer of feminine curiosity, "Shall it be addressed to wife, or mother, John?"

"Neither, ma'am; I've got no wife, and will write to mother myself when I get better. Did you think I was married because of this?" he asked, touching a plain ring he wore, and often turned thoughtfully on his finger when he lay alone.

"Partly that, but more from a settled sort of look you have, a look which young men seldom get until they marry."

"I don't know that; but I'm not so very young, ma'am, thirty in May, and have been what you might call settled this ten years; for mother's a widow, I'm the oldest child she has, and it wouldn't do for me to marry until Lizzy has a home of her own, and Laurie's learned his trade; for we're not rich, and I must be father to the children and husband to the dear old woman, if I can."

"No doubt but you are both, John; yet how came you to go to war, if you felt so? Wasn't enlisting as bad as marrying?"

"No, ma'am, not as I see it, for one is helping my neighbor, the other pleasing myself. I went because I couldn't help it. I didn't want the glory or the pay; I wanted the right thing done, and people kept saying the men who were in earnest ought to fight. I was in earnest, the Lord knows! but I held off as long as I could, not knowing which was my duty; mother saw the case, gave me her ring to keep me steady, and said 'Go:' so I went."

A short story and a simple one, but the man and the mother were portrayed better than pages of fine writing could have done it.

"Do you ever regret that you came, when you lie here suffering so much?"

"Never, ma'am; I haven't helped a great deal, but I've shown I was willing to give my life, and perhaps I've got to; but I don't blame anybody, and if it was to do over again, I'd do it. I'm a little sorry I wasn't wounded in front; it looks cowardly to be hit in the back, but I obeyed orders, and it don't matter in the end, I know."

Poor John! it did not matter now, except that a shot in front might have spared the long agony in store for him. He seemed to read the thought that troubled me, as he spoke so hopefully when there was no hope, for he suddenly added:

"This is my first battle; do they think it's going to be my last?"

"I'm afraid they do, John."

It was the hardest question I had ever been called upon to answer; doubly hard with those clear eyes fixed on mine, forcing a truthful answer by their own truth. He seemed a little startled at first, pondered over the fateful fact a moment then shook his head, with a glance at the broad chest and muscular limbs stretched out before him:

"I'm not afraid, but it's difficult to believe all at once. I'm so strong it don't seem possible for such a little wound to kill me."

Merry Mercutio's dying words glanced through my memory as he spoke: "'Tis not so deep as a well, nor so wide as a church door, but 'tis enough." And John would have said the same could he have seen the ominous black holes between his shoulders, he never had; and, seeing the ghastly sights about him, could not believe his own wound more fatal than these, for all the suffering it caused him.

"Shall I write to your mother, now?" I asked, thinking that these sudden tidings might change all plans and purposes; but they did not; for the man received the order of the Divine Commander to march with the same unquestioning obedience with which the soldier had received that of the human one, doubtless remembering that the first led him to life, and the last to death.

"No, ma'am; to Laurie just the same; he'll break it to her best, and I'll add a line to her myself when you get done."

So I wrote the letter which he dictated, finding it better than any I had sent; for, though here and there a little ungrammatical or inelegant, each sentence came to me briefly worded, but most expressive; full of excellent counsel to the boy, tenderly bequeathing "mother and Lizzie" to his care, and bidding him good bye in words the sadder for their simplicity. He added a few lines, with steady hand, and, as I sealed it, said, with a patient sort of sigh, "I hope the answer will come in time for me to see it"; then, turning away his face, laid the flowers against his lips, as if to hide some quiver of emotion at the thought of such a sudden sundering of all the dear home ties.

These things had happened two days before; now John was dying, and the letter had not come. I had been summoned to many death beds in my life, but to none that made my heart ache as it did then, since my mother called me to watch the departure of a spirit akin to this in its gentleness and patient strength. As I went in, John stretched out both hands:

"I knew you'd come! I guess I'm moving on, ma'am."

He was; and so rapidly that, even while he spoke, over his face I saw the grey veil falling that no human hand can lift. I sat down by him, wiped the drops from his forehead, stirred the air about him with the slow wave of a fan, and waited to help him die. He stood in sore need of help—and I could do so little; for, as the doctor had foretold, the strong body rebelled against death, and fought every inch of the way, forcing him to draw each breath with a spasm, and clench his hands with an imploring look, as if he asked, "How long must I endure this, and be still!" For hours he suffered dumbly, without a moment's respite, or a moment's murmuring; his limbs grew cold, his face damp, his lips white, and, again and again, he tore the covering off his breast, as if the lightest weight added to his agony; yet through it all, his eyes never lost their perfect serenity, and the man's soul seemed to sit therein, undaunted by the ills that vexed his flesh.

One by one, the men woke, and round the room appeared a circle of pale faces and watchful eyes, full of awe and pity; for, though a stranger, John was beloved by all. Each man there had wondered at his patience, respected his piety, admired his fortitude, and now lamented his hard death; for the influence of an upright nature had made itself deeply felt, even in one little week. Presently, the Jonathan who so loved this comely David, came creeping from his bed for a last look and word. The kind soul was full of trouble, as the choke in his voice, the grasp of his hand, betrayed; but there were no tears, and the farewell of the friends was the more touching for its brevity.

"Old boy, how are you?" faltered the one.

"Most through, thank heaven!" whispered the other.

"Can I say or do anything for you anywheres?"

"Take my things home, and tell them that I did my best."

"I will! I will!"

"Good bye, Ned."

"Good bye, John, good bye!"

They kissed each other, tenderly as women, and so parted, for poor Ned could not stay to see his comrade die. For a little while, there was no sound in the room but the drip of water, from a stump or two, and John's distressful gasps, as he slowly breathed his life away. I thought him nearly gone, and had just laid down the fan, believing its help to be no longer needed, when suddenly he rose up in his bed, and cried out with a bitter cry that broke the silence, sharply startling everyone with its agonized appeal:

"For God's sake, give me air!"

It was the only cry pain or death had wrung from him, the only boon he had asked; and none of us could grant it, for all the airs that blew were useless now. Dan flung up the window. The first red streak of dawn was warming the grey east, a herald of the coming sun; John saw it, and with the love of light which lingers in us to the end, seemed to read in it a sign of hope of help, for, over his whole face there broke that mysterious expression, brighter than any smile, which often comes to eyes that look their last. He laid himself gently down; and, stretching out his strong right arm, as if to grasp and bring the blessed air to his lips in a fuller flow, lapsed into a merciful unconsciousness, which assured us that for him suffering was forever past. He died then; for, though the heavy breaths still tore their way up for a little longer, they were but the waves of an ebbing tide that beat unfelt against the wreck, which an immortal voyager had deserted with a smile. He never spoke again, but to the end held my hand close, so close that when he was asleep at last, I could not draw it away. Dan helped me, warning me as he did so that it was unsafe for dead and living flesh to lie so long together; but though my hand was strangely cold and stiff, and four white marks remained across its back, even when warmth and color had returned elsewhere, I could not but be glad that, through its touch, the presence of human sympathy, perhaps, had lightened that hard hour.

When they had made him ready for the grave, John lay in state for half an hour, a thing which seldom happened in that busy place; but a universal sentiment of reverence and affection seemed to fill the hearts of all who had known or heard of him; and when the rumor of his death went through the house, always astir, many came to see him, and I felt a tender sort of pride in my lost patient; for he looked a most heroic figure, lying there stately and still as the statue of some young knight asleep upon his tomb. The lovely expression which so often beautifies dead faces, soon replaced the marks of pain, and I longed for those who loved him best to see him when half an hour's acquaintance with Death had made them friends. As we stood looking at him, the ward master handed me a letter, saying it had been forgotten the night before. It was John's letter, come just an hour too late to gladden the eyes that had longed and looked for it so eagerly: yet he had it; for, after I had cut some brown locks for his mother, and taken off the ring to send her, telling how well the talisman had done its work, I kissed this good son for her sake, and laid the letter in his hand, still folded as when I drew my own away, feeling that its place was there, and making myself happy with the thought, that, even in his solitary place in the "Government Lot," he would not be without some token of the love which makes life beautiful and outlives death. Then I left him, glad to have known so genuine a man, and carrying with me an enduring memory of the brave Virginia blacksmith, as he lay serenely waiting for the dawn of that long day which knows no night.

# A FORWARD MOVEMENT

## Louisa May Alcott

As TRAVELLERS LIKE to give their own impressions of a journey, though every inch of the way may have been described a half dozen times before, I add some of the notes made by the way, hoping that they will amuse the reader, and convince the skeptical that such a being as Nurse Periwinkle does exist, that she really did go to Washington, and that these Sketches are not romance.

*New York Train—Seven P.M.*—Spinning along to take the boat at New London. Very comfortable; munch gingerbread, and Mrs. C.'s fine pear, which deserves honorable mention, because my first loneliness was comforted by it, and pleasant recollections of both kindly sender and bearer. Look much at Dr. H.'s paper of directions—put my tickets in every conceivable place, that they may be get-at-able, and finish by losing them entirely. Suffer agonies till a compassionate neighbor pokes them out of a crack with his pen-knife. Put them in the inmost corner of my purse, that in the deepest recesses of my pocket, pile a collection of miscellaneous articles atop, and pin up the whole. Just get composed, feeling that I've done my best to keep them safely, when the Conductor appears, and I'm forced to rout them all out again, exposing my precautions, and getting into a flutter at keeping the man waiting. Finally, fasten them on the seat before me, and keep one eye steadily upon the yellow torments, till I forget all about them, in chat with the gentleman who shares my seat. Having heard complaints of the absurd way in which American women become images of petrified propriety, if addressed by strangers, when traveling alone, the inborn perversity of my nature causes me to assume an entirely opposite style of deportment; and, finding my companion hails from Little Athens, is acquainted with several of my three hundred and sixty-five cousins, and in every way a respectable and respectful member of society, I put my bashfulness in my pocket, and plunge into a long conversation on the war, the weather, music, Carlyle, skating, genius, hoops, and the immortality of the soul.

*Ten P.M.*—Very sleepy. Nothing to be seen outside, but darkness made visible; nothing inside but every variety of bunch into which the human form can be twisted, rolled, or "massed," as Miss Prescott says of her jewels. Every man's legs sprawl drowsily, every woman's head (but mine) nods, till it finally settles on somebody's shoulder, a new proof of the truth of the everlasting oak and vine simile; children fret; lovers whisper; old folks snore, and somebody privately imbibes brandy, when the lamps go out. The penetrating perfume rouses the multitude, causing some to start up, like war horses at the smell of powder. When the lamps are relighted, everyone laughs, sniffs, and looks inquiringly at his neighbor—everyone but a stout gentleman, who, with well-gloved hands folded upon his broad-cloth rotundity, sleeps on impressively. Had he been innocent, he would have waked up; for, to slumber in that babe-like manner, with a car full of giggling, staring, sniffing humanity, was simply preposterous. Public suspicion was down upon him at once. I doubt if the appearance of a flat black bottle with a label would have settled the matter more effectually than did the over dignified and profound repose of this short-sighted being. His moral neck-cloth, virtuous boots, and pious attitude availed him nothing, and it was well he kept his eyes shut, for "Humbug!" twinkled at him from every window-pane, brass nail and human eye around him.

*Eleven P.M.*—In the boat "City of Boston," escorted thither by my car acquaintance, and deposited in the cabin. Trying to look as if the greater portion of my life had been passed on board boats, but painfully conscious that I don't know the first thing; so sit bolt upright, and stare about me till I hear one lady say to another—"We must secure our berths at once"; whereupon I dart at one, and, while leisurely taking off my cloak, wait to discover what the second move may be. Several ladies draw the curtains that hang in a semi-circle before each nest—instantly I whisk mine smartly together, and then peep out to see what next. Gradually, on hooks above the blue and yellow drapery, appear the coats and bonnets of my neighbors, while their boots and shoes, in every imaginable attitude, assert themselves below, as if their owners had committed suicide in a body. A violent creaking, scrambling, and fussing, causes the fact that people are going regularly to bed to dawn upon my mind. Of course they are! and so am I—but pause at the seventh pin, remembering that, as I was born to be drowned, an eligible opportunity now presents itself; and, having twice escaped a watery grave, the third immersion will certainly extinguish my vital spark. The boat is new, but if it ever intends to blow up, spring a leak, catch afire, or be run into, it will do the deed tonight, because I'm here to fulfill my destiny. With tragic calmness I resign myself, replace my pins, lash my purse and papers together, with my handkerchief, examine the saving circumference of my hoop, and look about me for any means of deliverance when the moist moment shall arrive; for I've no intention of folding my hands and bubbling to death without an energetic splashing first. Barrels, hen-coops, portable settees, and life-preservers do not adorn the cabin, as they should; and, roving wildly to and fro, my eye sees no ray of hope till it falls upon a plump old lady, devoutly reading in the cabin Bible, and a voluminous night-cap. I remember that, at the swimming school, fat girls always floated best, and in an instant my plan is laid. At the first alarm I firmly attach myself to the plump lady, and cling to her through fire and water; for I feel that my old enemy, the cramp, will seize me by the foot, if I attempt to swim; and, though I can hardly expect to reach Jersey City with myself and my baggage in as good condition as I hoped, I might manage to get picked up by holding to my fat friend; if not it will be a comfort to feel that I've made an effort and shall die in good society. Poor dear woman! how little she dreamed, as she read and rocked, with her cap in a high state of starch, and her feet comfortably cooking at the register, what fell designs were hovering about her, and how intently a small but determined eye watched her, till it suddenly closed.

Sleep got the better of fear to such an extent that my boots appeared to gape, and my bonnet nodded on its peg, before I gave in. Having piled my cloak, bag, rubbers, books and umbrella on the lower shelf, I drowsily swarmed onto the upper one, tumbling down a few times, and excoriating the knobby portions of my frame in the act. A very brief nap on the upper roost was enough to set me gasping as if a dozen feather beds and the whole boat were laid over me. Out I turned; and, after a series of convulsions, which caused my neighbor to ask if I wanted the stewardess, I managed to get my luggage up and myself down. But even in the lower berth, my rest was not unbroken, for various articles kept dropping off the little shelf at the bottom of the bed, and every time I flew up, thinking my hour had come, I bumped my head severely against the little shelf at the top, evidently put there for that express purpose. At last, after listening to the swash of the waves outside, wondering if the machinery usually creaked in that way, and watching a knot-hole in the side of my berth, sure that death would creep in there as soon as I took my eye from it, I dropped asleep, and dreamed of muffins.

*Five A.M.*—On deck, trying to wake up and enjoy an east wind and a morning fog, and a twilight sort of view of something on the shore. Rapidly achieve my purpose, and do enjoy every moment, as we go rushing through the Sound, with steamboats passing up and down, lights dancing on the shore, mist wreaths slowly furling off, and a pale pink sky above us, as the sun comes up.

*Seven A.M.*—In the cars, at Jersey City. Much fuss with tickets, which one man scribbles over, another snips, and a third "makes note on." Partake of refreshment, in the gloom of a very large and dirty depot. Think that my sandwiches would be more relishing without so strong a flavor of napkin, and my gingerbread more easy of consumption if it had not been pulverized by being sat upon. People act as if early traveling didn't agree with them. Children scream and scamper; men smoke and growl; women shiver and fret; porters swear; great truck horses pace up and down with loads of baggage; and everyone seems to get into the wrong car, and come tumbling out again. One man, with three children, a dog, a bird-cage, and several bundles, puts himself and his possessions into every possible place where a man, three children, dog, bird-cage and bundles could be got, and is satisfied with none of them. I follow their movements, with an interest that is really exhausting, and, as they vanish, hope for rest, but don't get it. A strong-minded woman, with a tumbler in her hand, and no cloak or shawl on, comes rushing through the car, talking loudly to a small porter, who lugs a folding bed after her, and looks as if life were a burden to him.

"You promised to have it ready. It is not ready. It must be a car with a water jar, the windows must be shut, the fire must be kept up, the blinds must be down. No, this won't do. I shall go through the whole train, and suit myself, for you promised to have it ready. It is not ready," &c, all through again, like a hand-organ. She haunted the cars, the depot, the office and baggage-room, with her bed, her tumbler, and her tongue, till the train started; and a sense of fervent gratitude filled my soul, when I found that she and her unknown invalid were not to share our car.

*Philadelphia.*—An old place, full of Dutch women, in "bellus top" bonnets, selling vegetables, in long, open markets. Everyone seems to be scrubbing their white steps. All the houses look like tidy jails, with their outside shutters. Several have crape on the door-handles, and many have flags flying from roof or balcony. Few men appear, and the women seem to do the business, which, perhaps, accounts for its being so well done. Pass fine buildings, but don't know what they are. Would like to stop and see my native city; for, having left it at the tender age of two, my recollections are not vivid.

*Baltimore.*—A big, dirty, shippy, shiftless place, full of goats, geese, colored people, and coal, at least the part of it I see. Pass near the spot where the riot took place, and feel as if I should enjoy throwing a stone at somebody, hard. Find a guard at the ferry, the depot, and here and there, along the road. A camp whitens one hill-side, and a cavalry training school, or whatever it should be called, is a very interesting sight, with quantities of horses and riders galloping, marching, leaping, and skirmishing, over all manner of break-neck places. A party of English people get in—the men, with sandy hair and red whiskers, all trimmed alike, to a hair; rough grey coats, very rosy, clean faces, and a fine, full way of speaking, which is particularly agreeable, after our slip-shod American gabble. The two ladies wear funny velvet fur-trimmed hoods; are done up, like compact bundles, in tartan shawls; and look as if bent on seeing everything thoroughly. The devotion of one elderly John Bull to his red-nosed spouse was really beautiful to behold. She was plain and cross, and fussy and stupid, but J. B., Esq., read no papers when she was awake, turned no cold shoulder when she wished to sleep, and cheerfully said, "yes, me dear," to every wish or want the wife of his bosom expressed. I quite warmed to the excellent man, and asked a question or two, as the only means of expressing my good will. He answered very civilly, but evidently hadn't been used to being addressed by strange women in public conveyances; and Mrs. B. fixed her green eyes upon me, as if she thought me a forward hussy, or whatever is good English for a presuming young woman. The pair left their friends before we reached Washington; and the last I saw of them was a vision of a large plaid lady, stalking grimly away, on the arm of a rosy, stout gentleman, loaded with rugs, bags, and books, but still devoted, still smiling, and waving a hearty "Fare ye well! We'll meet ye at Willard's on Chusday."

Soon after their departure we had an accident; for no long journey in America would be complete without one. A coupling iron broke; and, after leaving the last car behind us, we waited for it to come up, which it did, with a crash that knocked everyone forward on their faces, and caused several old ladies to screech dismally. Hats flew off, bonnets were flattened, the stove skipped, the lamps fell down, the water jar turned a somersault, and the wheel just over which I sat received some damage. Of course, it became necessary for all the men to get out, and stand about in everybody's way, while repairs were made; and for the women to wrestle their heads out of the windows, asking ninety-nine foolish questions to one sensible one. A few wise females seized this favorable moment to better their seats, well knowing that few men can face the wooden stare with which they regard the former possessors of the places they have invaded.

The country through which we passed did not seem so very unlike that which I had left, except that it was more level and less wintry. In summer time the wide fields would have shown me new sights, and the way-side hedges blossomed with new flowers; now, everything was sere and sodden, and a general air of shiftlessness prevailed, which would have caused a New England farmer much disgust, and a strong desire to "buckle to," and "right up" things. Dreary little houses, with chimneys built outside, with clay and rough sticks piled crosswise, as we used to build cob towers, stood in barren looking fields, with cow, pig, or mule lounging about the door. We often passed colored people, looking as if they had come out of a picture book, or off the stage, but not at all the sort of people I'd been accustomed to see at the North.

Way-side encampments made the fields and lanes gay with blue coats and the glitter of buttons. Military washes flapped and fluttered on the fences; pots were steaming in the open air; all sorts of tableaux seen through the openings of tents, and everywhere the boys threw up their caps and cut capers as we passed.

*Washington.*—It was dark when we arrived; and, but for the presence of another friendly gentleman, I should have yielded myself a helpless prey to the first overpowering hackman, who insisted that I wanted to go just where I didn't. Putting me into the conveyance I belonged in, my escort added to the obligation by pointing out the objects of interest which we passed in our long drive. Though I'd often been told that Washington was a spacious place, its visible magnitude quite took my breath away, and of course I quoted Randolph's expression, "a city of magnificent distances," as I suppose everyone does when they see it. The Capitol was so like the pictures that hang opposite the staring Father of his Country, in boarding-houses and hotels, that it did not impress me, except to recall the time when I was sure that Cinderella went to housekeeping in just such a place, after she had married the inflammable Prince; though, even at that early period, I had my doubts as to the wisdom of a match whose foundation was of glass.

The White House was lighted up, and carriages were rolling in and out of the great gate. I stared hard at the famous East Room, and would have liked a peep through the crack of the door. My old gentleman was indefatigable in his attentions, and I said "Splendid!" to everything he pointed out, though I suspect I often admired the wrong place, and missed the right. Pennsylvania Avenue, with its bustle, lights, music, and military, made me feel as if I'd crossed the water and landed somewhere in Carnival time. Coming to less noticeable parts of the city, my companion fell silent, and I meditated upon the perfection which Art had attained in America—having just passed a bronze statue of some hero, who looked like a black Methodist minister, in a cocked hat, above the waist, and a tipsy squire below; while his horse stood like an opera dancer, on one leg, in a high, but somewhat remarkable wind, which blew his mane one way and his massive tail the other.

"Hurly-burly House, ma'am!" called a voice, startling me from my reverie, as we stopped before a great pile of buildings, with a flag flying before it, sentinels at the door, and a very trying quantity of men lounging about. My heart beat rather faster than usual, and it suddenly struck me that I was very far from home; but I descended with dignity, wondering whether I should be stopped for want of a countersign, and forced to pass the night in the street. Marching boldly up the steps, I found that no form was necessary, for the men fell back, the guard touched their caps, a boy opened the door, and, as it closed behind me, I felt that I was fairly started, and Nurse Periwinkle's Mission was begun.

# THE OTHER WOMAN

### Sherwood Anderson

"I AM IN love with my wife," he said—a superfluous remark, as I had not questioned his attachment to the woman he had married. We walked for ten minutes and then he said it again. I turned to look at him. He began to talk and told me the tale I am now about to set down.

The thing he had on his mind happened during what must have been the most eventful week of his life. He was to be married on Friday afternoon. On Friday of the week before he got a telegram announcing his appointment to a government position. Something else happened that made him very proud and glad. In secret he was in the habit of writing verses and during the year before several of them had been printed in poetry magazines. One of the societies that give prizes for what they think the best poems published during the year put his name at the head of its list. The story of his triumph was printed in the newspapers of his home city and one of them also printed his picture.

As might have been expected he was excited and in a rather highly strung nervous state all during that week. Almost every evening he went to call on his fiancée, the daughter of a judge. When he got there the house was filled with people and many letters, telegrams and packages were being received. He stood a little to one side and men and women kept coming up to speak to him. They congratulated him upon his success in getting the government position and on his achievement as a poet. Everyone seemed to be praising him and when he went home and to bed he could not sleep. On Wednesday evening he went to the theatre and it seemed to him that people all over the house recognized him. Everyone nodded and smiled. After the first act five or six men and two women left their seats to gather about him. A little group was formed. Strangers sitting along the same row of seats stretched their necks and looked. He had never received so much attention before, and now a fever of expectancy took possession of him.

As he explained when he told me of his experience, it was for him an altogether abnormal time. He felt like one floating in air. When he got into bed after seeing so many people and hearing so many words of praise his head whirled round and round. When he closed his eyes a crowd of people invaded his room. It seemed as though the minds of all the people of his city were centered on himself. The most absurd fancies took possession of him. He imagined himself riding in a carriage through the streets of a city. Windows were thrown open and people ran out at the doors of houses. "There he is. That's him," they shouted, and at the words a glad cry arose. The carriage drove into a street blocked with people. A hundred thousand pairs of eyes looked up at him. "There you are! What a fellow you have managed to make of yourself!" the eyes seemed to be saying.

My friend could not explain whether the excitement of the people was due to the fact that he had written a new poem or whether, in his new government position, he had performed some notable act. The apartment where he lived at that time was on a street perched along the top of a cliff far out at the edge of his city, and from his bedroom window he could look down over trees and factory roofs to a river. As he could not sleep and as the fancies that kept crowding in upon him only made him more excited, he got out of bed and tried to think.

As would be natural under such circumstances, he tried to control his thoughts, but when he sat by the window and was wide awake a most unexpected and humiliating thing happened. The night was clear and fine. There was a moon. He wanted to dream of the woman who was to be his wife, to think out lines for noble poems or make plans that would affect his career. Much to his surprise his mind refused to do anything of the sort.

At a corner of the street where he lived there was a small cigar store and newspaper stand run by a fat man of forty and his wife, a small active woman with bright grey eyes. In the morning he stopped there to buy a paper before going down to the city. Sometimes he saw only the fat man, but often the man had disappeared and the woman waited on him. She was, as he assured me at least twenty times in telling me his tale, a very ordinary person with nothing special or notable about her, but for some reason he could not explain, being in her presence stirred him profoundly. During that week in the midst of his distraction she was the only person he knew who stood out clear and distinct in his mind. When he wanted so much to think noble thoughts he could think only of her. Before he knew what was happening his imagination had taken hold of the notion of having a love affair with the woman.

"I could not understand myself," he declared, in telling me the story. "At night, when the city was quiet and when I should have been asleep, I thought about her all the time. After two or three days of that sort of thing the consciousness of her got into my daytime thoughts. I was terribly muddled. When I went to see the woman who is now my wife I found that my love for her was in no way affected by my vagrant thoughts. There was but one woman in the world I wanted to live with and to be my comrade in undertaking to improve my own character and my position in the world, but for the moment, you see, I wanted this other woman to be in my arms. She had worked her way into my being. On all sides people were saying I was a big man who would do big things, and there I was. That evening when I went to the theatre I walked home because I knew I would be unable to sleep, and to satisfy the annoying impulse in myself I went and stood on the sidewalk before the tobacco shop. It was a two story building, and I knew the woman lived upstairs with her husband. For a long time I stood in the darkness with my body pressed against the wall of the building, and then I thought of the two of them up there and no doubt in bed together. That made me furious.

"Then I grew more furious with myself. I went home and got into bed, shaken with anger. There are certain books of verse and some prose writings that have always moved me deeply, and so I put several books on a table by my bed.

"The voices in the books were like the voices of the dead. I did not hear them. The printed words would not penetrate into my consciousness. I tried to think of the woman I loved, but her figure had also become something far away, something with which I for the moment seemed to have nothing to do. I rolled and tumbled about in the bed. It was a miserable experience.

"On Thursday morning I went into the store. There stood the woman alone. I think she knew how I felt. Perhaps she had been thinking of me as I had been thinking of her. A doubtful hesitating smile played about the corners of her mouth. She had on a dress made of cheap cloth and there was a tear on the shoulder. She must have been ten years older than myself. When I tried to put my pennies on the glass counter, behind which she stood, my hand trembled so that the pennies made a sharp rattling noise. When I spoke the voice that came out of my throat did not sound like anything that had ever belonged to me. It barely arose above a thick whisper. 'I want you,' I said. 'I want you very much. Can't you run away from your husband? Come to me at my apartment at seven tonight.'

"The woman did come to my apartment at seven. That morning she didn't say anything at all. For a minute perhaps we stood looking at each other. I had forgotten everything in the world but just her. Then she nodded her head and I went away. Now that I think of it I cannot remember a word I ever heard her say. She came to my apartment at seven and it was dark. You must understand this was in the month of October. I had not lighted a light and I had sent my servant away.

"During that day I was no good at all. Several men came to see me at my office, but I got all muddled up in trying to talk with them. They attributed my rattle-headedness to my approaching marriage and went away laughing.

"It was on that morning, just the day before my marriage, that I got a long and very beautiful letter from my fiancée. During the night before she also had been unable to sleep and had got out of bed to write the letter. Everything she said in it was very sharp and real, but she herself, as a living thing, seemed to have receded into the distance. It seemed to me that she was like a bird, flying far away in distant skies, and that I was like a perplexed bare-footed boy standing in the dusty road before a farm house and looking at her receding figure. I wonder if you will understand what I mean?

"In regard to the letter. In it she, the awakening woman, poured out her heart. She of course knew nothing of life, but she was a woman. She lay, I suppose, in her bed feeling nervous and wrought up as I had been doing. She realized that a great change was about to take place in her life and was glad and afraid too. There she lay thinking of it all. Then she got out of bed and began talking to me on the bit of paper. She told me how afraid she was and how glad too. Like most young women she had heard things whispered. In the letter she was very sweet and fine. 'For a long time, after we are married, we will forget we are a man and woman,' she wrote. 'We will be human beings. You must remember that I am ignorant and often I will be very stupid. You must love me and be very patient and kind. When I know more, when after a long time you have taught me the way of life, I will try to repay you. I will love you tenderly and passionately. The possibility of that is in me or I would not want to marry at all. I am afraid but I am also happy. O, I am so glad our marriage time is near at hand!"

"Now you see clearly enough what a mess I was in. In my office, after I had read my fiancée's letter, I became at once very resolute and strong. I remember that I got out of my chair and walked about, proud of the fact that I was to be the husband of so noble a woman. Right away I felt concerning her as I had been feeling about myself before I found out what a weak thing I was. To be sure I took a strong resolution that I would not be weak. At nine that evening I had planned to run in to see my fiancée. 'I'm all right now,' I said to myself. 'The beauty of her character has saved me from myself. I will go home now and send the other woman away.' In the morning I had telephoned to my servant and told him that I did not want him to be at the apartment that evening and I now picked up the telephone to tell him to stay at home.

"Then a thought came to me. 'I will not want him there in any event,' I told myself. 'What will he think when he sees a woman coming in my place on the evening before the day I am to be married?' I put the telephone down and prepared to go home. 'If I want my servant out of the apartment it is because I do not want him to hear me talk with the woman. I cannot be rude to her. I will have to make some kind of an explanation,' I said to myself.

"The woman came at seven o'clock, and, as you may have guessed, I let her in and forgot the resolution I had made. It is likely I never had any intention of doing anything else. There was a bell on my door, but she did not ring, but knocked very softly. It seems to me that everything she did that evening was soft and quiet, but very determined and quick. Do I make myself clear? When she came I was standing just within the door where I had been standing and waiting for a half hour. My hands were trembling as they had trembled in the morning when her eyes looked at me and when I tried to put the pennies on the counter in the store. When I opened the door she stepped quickly in and I took her into my arms. We stood together in the darkness. My hands no longer trembled. I felt very happy and strong.

"Although I have tried to make everything clear I have not told you what the woman I married is like. I have emphasized, you see, the other woman. I make the blind statement that I love my wife, and to a man of your shrewdness that means nothing at all. To tell the truth, had I not started to speak of this matter I would feel more comfortable. It is inevitable that I give you the impression that I am in love with the tobacconist's wife. That's not true. To be sure I was very conscious of her all during the week before my marriage, but after she had come to me at my apartment she went entirely out of my mind.

"Am I telling the truth? I am trying very hard to tell what happened to me. I am saying that I have not since that evening thought of the woman who came to my apartment. Now, to tell the facts of the case, that is not true. On that evening I went to my fiancée at nine, as she had asked me to do in her letter. In a kind of way I cannot explain the other woman went with me. This is what I mean—you see I had been thinking that if anything happened between me and the tobacconist's wife I would not be able to go through with my marriage. 'It is one thing or the other with me,' I had said to myself.

"As a matter of fact I went to see my beloved on that evening filled with a new faith in the outcome of our life together. I am afraid I muddle this matter in trying to tell it. A moment ago I said the other woman, the tobacconist's wife, went with me. I do not mean she went in fact. What I am trying to say is that something of her faith in her own desires and her courage in seeing things through went with me. Is that clear to you? When I got to my fiancée's house there was a crowd of people standing about. Some were relatives from distant places I had not seen before. She looked up quickly when I came into the room. My face must have been radiant. I never saw her so moved. She thought her letter had affected me deeply, and of course it had. Up she jumped and ran to meet me. She was like a glad child. Right before the people who turned and looked inquiringly at us, she said the thing that was in her mind. 'O, I am so happy,' she cried. 'You have understood. We will be two human beings. We will not have to be husband and wife.'

"As you may suppose everyone laughed, but I did not laugh. The tears came into my eyes. I was so happy I wanted to shout. Perhaps you understand what I mean. In the office that day when I read the letter my fiancée had written I had said to myself, 'I will take care

of the dear little woman.' There was something smug, you see, about
that. In her house when she cried out in that way, and when everyone
laughed, what I said to myself was something like this: 'We will take
care of ourselves.' I whispered something of the sort into her ears.
To tell you the truth I had come down off my perch. The spirit of
the other woman did that to me. Before all the people gathered about
I held my fiancée close and we kissed. They thought it very sweet
of us to be so affected at the sight of each other. What they would
have thought had they known the truth about me God only knows!

"Twice now I have said that after that evening I never thought of
the other woman at all. That is partially true but, sometimes in the
evening when I am walking alone in the street or in the park as we
are walking now, and when evening comes softly and quickly as it
has come tonight, the feeling of her comes sharply into my body and
mind. After that one meeting I never saw her again. On the next
day I was married and I have never gone back into her street. Often
however as I am walking along as I am doing now, a quick sharp
earthy feeling takes possession of me. It is as though I were a seed in
the ground and the warm rains of the spring had come. It is as though
I were not a man but a tree.

"And now you see I am married and everything is all right. My
marriage is to me a very beautiful fact. If you were to say that
my marriage is not a happy one I could call you a liar and be speaking
the absolute truth. I have tried to tell you about this other woman.
There is a kind of relief in speaking of her. I have never done it
before. I wonder why I was so silly as to be afraid that I would give
you the impression I am not in love with my wife. If I did not
instinctively trust your understanding I would not have spoken. As
the matter stands I have a little stirred myself up. Tonight I shall think
of the other woman. That sometimes occurs. It will happen after I
have gone to bed. My wife sleeps in the next room to mine and the
door is always left open. There will be a moon tonight, and when
there is a moon long streaks of light fall on her bed. I shall awake at
midnight tonight. She will be lying asleep with one arm thrown over
her head.

"What is it that I am now talking about? A man does not speak
of his wife lying in bed. What I am trying to say is that, because of
this talk, I shall think of the other woman tonight. My thoughts will
not take the form they did during the week before I was married. I
still wonder what has become of the woman. For a moment I will
again feel myself holding her close. I will think that for an hour I

was closer to her than I have ever been to anyone else. Then I will think of the time when I will be as close as that to my wife. She is still, you see, an awakening woman. For a moment I will close my eyes and the quick, shrewd, determined eyes of that other woman will look into mine. My head will swim and then I will quickly open my eyes and see again the dear woman with whom I have undertaken to live out my life. Then I will sleep and when I awake in the morning it will be as it was that evening when I walked out of my dark apartment after having had the most notable experience of my life. What I mean to say, you understand is that, for me, when I awake, the other woman will be utterly gone."

# BROTHERS

### Sherwood Anderson

I AM AT my house in the country and it is late October. It rains. Back of my house is a forest and in front there is a road and beyond that open fields. The country is one of low hills, flattening suddenly into plains. Some twenty miles away, across the flat country, lies the huge city Chicago.

On this rainy day the leaves of the trees that line the road before my window are falling like rain, the yellow, red and golden leaves fall straight down heavily. The rain beats them brutally down. They are denied a last golden flash across the sky. In October leaves should be carried away, out over the plains, in a wind. They should go dancing away.

Yesterday morning I arose at daybreak and went for a walk. There was a heavy fog and I lost myself in it. I went down into the plains and returned to the hills, and everywhere the fog was as a wall before me. Out of it trees sprang suddenly, grotesquely, as in a city street late at night people come suddenly out of the darkness into the circle of light under a street lamp. Above there was the light of day forcing itself slowly into the fog. The fog moved slowly. The tops of trees moved slowly. Under the trees the fog was dense, purple. It was like smoke lying in the streets of a factory town.

An old man came up to me in the fog. I know him well. The people here call him insane. "He is a little cracked," they say. He lives alone in a little house buried deep in the forest and has a small dog he carries always in his arms. On many mornings I have met him walking on the road and he has told me of men and women who are his brothers and sisters, his cousins, aunts, uncles, brothers-in-law. It is confusing. He cannot draw close to people near at hand so he gets hold of a name out of a newspaper and his mind plays with it. On one morning he told me he was a cousin to the man named Cox who at the time when I write is a candidate for the presidency. On another morning he told me that Caruso the singer had married a woman who was his sister-in-law. "She is my wife's sister," he said, holding the little dog close. His grey watery eyes looked appealing up to me. He wanted me to believe. "My wife was a sweet slim girl," he declared. "We lived together in a big house and in the morning walked about arm in arm. Now her sister has married Caruso the singer. He is of my family now."

As someone had told me the old man had never married, I went away wondering. One morning in early September I came upon him sitting under a tree beside a path near his house. The dog barked at me and then ran and crept into his arms. At that time the Chicago newspapers were filled with the story of a millionaire who had got into trouble with his wife because of an intimacy with an actress. The old man told me that the actress was his sister. He is sixty years old and the actress whose story appeared in the newspapers is twenty but he spoke of their childhood together. "You would not realize it to see us now but we were poor then," he said. "It's true. We lived in a little house on the side of a hill. Once when there was a storm, the wind nearly swept our house away. How the wind blew! Our father was a carpenter and he built strong houses for other people but our own house he did not build very strong!" He shook his head sorrowfully. "My sister the actress has got into trouble. Our house is not built very strongly," he said as I went away along the path.

\* \* \*

For a month, two months, the Chicago newspapers, that are delivered every morning in our village, have been filled with the story of a murder. A man there has murdered his wife and there seems no reason for the deed. The tale runs something like this—

The man, who is now on trial in the courts and will no doubt be hanged, worked in a bicycle factory where he was a foreman and lived with his wife and his wife's mother in an apartment in Thirty-second Street. He loved a girl who worked in the office of the factory where he was employed. She came from a town in Iowa and when she first came to the city lived with her aunt who has since died.

To the foreman, a heavy stolid looking man with grey eyes, she seemed the most beautiful woman in the world. Her desk was by a window at an angle of the factory, a sort of wing of the building, and the foreman, down in the shop had a desk by another window. He sat at his desk making out sheets containing the record of the work done by each man in his department. When he looked up he could see the girl sitting at work at her desk. The notion got into his head that she was peculiarly lovely. He did not think of trying to draw close to her or of winning her love. He looked at her as one might look at a star or across a country of low hills in October when the leaves of the trees are all red and yellow gold. "She is a pure, virginal thing," he thought vaguely. "What can she be thinking about as she sits there by the window at work."

In fancy the foreman took the girl from Iowa home with him to his apartment in Thirty-second Street and into the presence of his wife and his mother-in-law. All day in the shop and during the evening at home he carried her figure about with him in his mind. As he stood by a window in his apartment and looked out toward the Illinois Central railroad tracks and beyond the tracks to the lake, the girl was there beside him. Down below women walked in the street and in every woman he saw there was something of the Iowa girl. One woman walked as she did, another made a gesture with her hand that reminded him of her. All the women he saw except his wife and his mother-in-law were like the girl he had taken inside himself.

The two women in his own house puzzled and confused him. They became suddenly unlovely and commonplace. His wife in particular was like some strange unlovely growth that had attached itself to his body.

In the evening after the day at the factory he went home to his own place and had dinner. He had always been a silent man and when he did not talk no one minded. After dinner he with his wife went to a picture show. There were two children and his wife expected another. They came into the apartment and sat down. The climb up two flights of stairs had wearied his wife. She sat in a chair beside her mother groaning with weariness.

The mother-in-law was the soul of goodness. She took the place of a servant in the home and got no pay. When her daughter wanted to go to a picture show she waved her hand and smiled. "Go on," she said. "I don't want to go. I'd rather sit here." She got a book and sat reading. The little boy of nine awoke and cried. He wanted to sit on the po-po. The mother-in-law attended to that.

After the man and his wife came home the three people sat in silence for an hour or two before bed time. The man pretended to read a newspaper. He looked at his hands. Although he had washed them carefully grease from the bicycle frames left dark stains under the nails. He thought of the Iowa girl and of her white quick hands playing over the keys of a typewriter. He felt dirty and uncomfortable.

The girl at the factory knew the foreman had fallen in love with her and the thought excited her a little. Since her aunt's death she had gone to live in a rooming house and had nothing to do in the evening. Although the foreman meant nothing to her she could in a way use him. To her he became a symbol. Sometimes he came into the office and stood for a moment by the door. His large hands were covered with black grease. She looked at him without seeing. In his place in her imagination stood a tall slender young man. Of the foreman she saw only the grey eyes that began to burn with a strange fire. The eyes expressed eagerness, a humble and devout eagerness. In the presence of a man with such eyes she felt she need not be afraid.

She wanted a lover who would come to her with such a look in his eyes. Occasionally, perhaps once in two weeks, she stayed a little late at the office, pretending to have work that must be finished. Through the window she could see the foreman waiting. When everyone had gone she closed her desk and went into the street. At the same moment the foreman came out at the factory door.

They walked together along the street a half dozen blocks to where she got aboard her car. The factory was in a place called South Chicago and as they went along evening was coming on. The streets were lined with small unpainted frame houses and dirty faced children ran screaming in the dusty roadway. They crossed over a bridge. Two abandoned coal barges lay rotting in the stream.

He went by her side walking heavily and striving to conceal his hands. He had scrubbed them carefully before leaving the factory but they seemed to him like heavy dirty pieces of waste matter hanging at his side. Their walking together happened but a few times and during one summer. "It's hot," he said. He never spoke to her of anything but the weather. "It's hot," he said. "I think it may rain."

She dreamed of the lover who would some time come, a tall fair young man, a rich man owning houses and lands. The workingman who walked beside her had nothing to do with her conception of love. She walked with him, stayed at the office until the others had gone to walk unobserved with him because of his eyes, because of the eager thing in his eyes that was at the same time humble, that bowed down to her. In his presence there was no danger, could be no danger. He would never attempt to approach too closely, to touch her with his hands. She was safe with him.

In his apartment in the evening the man sat under the electric light with his wife and his mother-in-law. In the next room his two children were asleep. In a short time his wife would have another child. He had been with her to a picture show and in a short time they would get into bed together.

He would lie awake thinking, would hear the creaking of the springs of a bed where, in another room, his mother-in-law was crawling between the sheets. Life was too intimate. He would lie awake eager, expectant—expecting, what?

Nothing. Presently one of the children would cry. It wanted to get out of bed and sit on the po-po. Nothing strange or unusual or lovely would or could happen. Life was too close, intimate. Nothing that could happen in the apartment could in any way stir him; the things his wife might say, her occasional half-hearted outbursts of passion, the goodness of his mother-in-law who did the work of a servant without pay—

He sat in the apartment under the electric light pretending to read a newspaper—thinking. He looked at his hands. They were large, shapeless, a working-man's hands.

The figure of the girl from Iowa walked about the room. With her he went out of the apartment and walked in silence through miles of streets. It was not necessary to say words. He walked with her by a sea, along the crest of a mountain. The night was clear and silent and the stars shone. She also was a star. It was not necessary to say words.

Her eyes were like stars and her lips were like soft hills rising out of dim, star lit plains. "She is unattainable, she is far off like the stars," he thought. "She is unattainable like the stars but unlike the stars she breathes, she lives, like myself she has being."

One evening, some six weeks ago, the man who worked as foreman in the bicycle factory killed his wife and he is now in the courts being tried for murder. Every day the newspapers are filled with the story. On the evening of the murder he had taken his wife as usual to a picture show and they started home at nine. In Thirty-second Street, at a corner near their apartment building, the figure of a man darted suddenly out of an alleyway and then darted back again. The incident may have put the idea of killing his wife into the man's head.

They got to the entrance to the apartment building and stepped into a dark hallway. Then quite suddenly and apparently without thought the man took a knife out of his pocket. "Suppose that man who darted into the alleyway had intended to kill us," he thought. Opening the knife he whirled about and struck at his wife. He struck twice, a dozen times—madly. There was a scream and his wife's body fell.

The janitor had neglected to light the gas in the lower hallway. Afterwards, the foreman decided, that was the reason he did it, that and the fact that the dark slinking figure of a man darted out of an alleyway and then darted back again. "Surely," he told himself, "I could never have done it had the gas been lighted."

He stood in the hallway thinking. His wife was dead and with her had died her unborn child. There was a sound of doors opening in the apartments above. For several minutes nothing happened. His wife and her unborn child were dead—that was all.

He ran upstairs thinking quickly. In the darkness on the lower stairway he had put the knife back into his pocket and, as it turned out later, there was no blood on his hands or on his clothes. The knife he later washed carefully in the bathroom, when the excitement had died down a little. He told everyone the same story. "There has been a holdup," he explained. "A man came slinking out of an alleyway and followed me and my wife home. He followed us into the hallway of the building and there was no light. The janitor has neglected to light the gas." Well—there had been a struggle and in the darkness his wife had been killed. He could not tell how it had happened. "There was no light. The janitor has neglected to light the gas," he kept saying.

For a day or two they did not question him specially and he had time to get rid of the knife. He took a long walk and threw it away into the river in South Chicago where the two abandoned coal barges lay rotting under the bridge, the bridge he had crossed when on the summer evenings he walked to the street car with the girl who was virginal and pure, who was far off and unattainable, like a star and yet not like a star.

And then he was arrested and right away he confessed—told everything. He said he did not know why he killed his wife and was careful to say nothing of the girl at the office. The newspapers tried to discover the motive for the crime. They are still trying. Someone had seen him on the few evenings when he walked with the girl and she was dragged into the affair and had her picture printed in the

papers. That has been annoying for her as of course she has been able
to prove she had nothing to do with the man.

✱   ✱   ✱

Yesterday morning a heavy fog lay over our village here at the edge
of the city and I went for a long walk in the early morning. As I
returned out of the lowlands into our hill country I met the old man
whose family has so many and such strange ramifications. For a time
he walked beside me holding the little dog in his arms. It was cold
and the dog whined and shivered. In the fog the old man's face was
indistinct. It moved slowly back and forth with the fog banks of the
upper air and with the tops of trees. He spoke of the man who has
killed his wife and whose name is being shouted in the pages of the
city newspapers that come to our village each morning. As
he walked beside me he launched into a long tale concerning a life he
and his brother, who has now become a murderer, once lived together.
"He is my brother," he said over and over, shaking his head. He
seemed afraid I would not believe. There was a fact that must be
established. "We were boys together that man and I," he began again.
"You see we played together in a barn back of our father's house.
Our father went away to sea in a ship. That is the way our names
became confused. You understand that. We have different names,
but we are brothers. We had the same father. We played together
in a barn back of our father's house. For hours we lay together in
the hay in the barn and it was warm there."

In the fog the slender body of the old man became like a little
gnarled tree. Then it became a thing suspended in air. It swung back
and forth like a body hanging on the gallows. The face beseeched
me to believe the story the lips were trying to tell. In my mind
everything concerning the relationship of men and women became
confused, a muddle. The spirit of the man who had killed his wife
came into the body of the little old man there by the roadside. It was
striving to tell me the story it would never be able to tell in the court
room in the city, in the presence of the judge. The whole story of
mankind's loneliness, of the effort to reach out to unattainable beauty
tried to get itself expressed from the lips of a mumbling old man,
crazed with loneliness, who stood by the side of a country road on
a foggy morning holding a little dog in his arms.

The arms of the old man held the dog so closely that it began to
whine with pain. A sort of convulsion shook his body. The soul

seemed striving to wrench itself out of the body, to fly away through the fog, down across the plain to the city, to the singer, the politician, the millionaire, the murderer, to its brothers, cousins, sisters, down in the city. The intensity of the old man's desire was terrible and in sympathy my body began to tremble. His arms tightened about the body of the little dog so that it cried with pain. I stepped forward and tore the arms away and the dog fell to the ground and lay whining. No doubt it had been injured. Perhaps ribs had been crushed. The old man stared at the dog lying at his feet as in the hallway of the apartment building the worker from the bicycle factory had stared at his dead wife. "We are brothers," he said again. "We have different names but we are brothers. Our father you understand went off to sea."

*   *   *

I am sitting in my house in the country and it rains. Before my eyes the hills fall suddenly away and there are the flat plains and beyond the plains the city. An hour ago the old man of the house in the forest went past my door and the little dog was not with him. It may be that as we talked in the fog he crushed the life out of his companion. It may be that the dog like the workman's wife and her unborn child is now dead. The leaves of the trees that line the road before my window are falling like rain—the yellow, red and golden leaves fall straight down, heavily. The rain beat them brutally down. They are denied a last golden flash across the sky. In October leaves should be carried away, out over the plains, in a wind. They should go dancing away.

# UNLIGHTED LAMPS

### Sherwood Anderson

MARY COCHRAN WENT out of the rooms where she lived with her father, Doctor Lester Cochran, at seven o'clock on a Sunday evening. It was June of the year nineteen hundred and eight and Mary was eighteen years old. She walked along Tremont to Main Street and across the railroad tracks to Upper Main, lined with small shops and shoddy houses, a rather quiet cheerless place on Sundays when there were few people about. She had told her father she was going to church but did not intend doing anything of the kind. She did not know what she wanted to do. "I'll get off by myself and think," she told herself as she walked slowly along. The night she thought promised to be too fine to be spent sitting in a stuffy church and hearing a man talk of things that had apparently nothing to do with her own problem. Her own affairs were approaching a crisis and it was time for her to begin thinking seriously of her future.

The thoughtful serious state of mind in which Mary found herself had been induced in her by a conversation she had with her father on the evening before. Without any preliminary talk and quite suddenly and abruptly he had told her that he was a victim of heart disease and might die at any moment. He had made the announcement as they stood together in the Doctor's office, back of which were the rooms in which the father and daughter lived.

It was growing dark outside when she came into the office and found him sitting alone. The office and living rooms were on the second floor of an old frame building in the town of Huntersburg, Illinois, and as the Doctor talked he stood beside his daughter near one of the windows that looked down into Tremont Street. The hushed murmur of the town's Saturday night life went on in Main Street just around a corner, and the evening train, bound to Chicago fifty miles to the east, had just passed. The hotel bus came rattling out of Lincoln Street and went through Tremont toward the hotel on Lower Main. A cloud of dust kicked up by the horses' hoofs floated on the quiet air. A straggling group of people followed the bus and the row of hitching posts on Tremont Street was already lined with buggies in which farmers and their wives had driven into town for the evening of shopping and gossip.

After the station bus had passed three or four more buggies were driven into the street. From one of them a young man helped his sweetheart to alight. He took hold of her arm with a certain air of tenderness, and a hunger to be touched thus tenderly by a man's hand, that had come to Mary many times before, returned at almost the same moment her father made the announcement of his approaching death.

As the Doctor began to speak Barney Smithfield, who owned a livery barn that opened into Tremont Street directly opposite the building in which the Cochrans lived, came back to his place of business from his evening meal. He stopped to tell a story to a group of men gathered before the barn door and a shout of laughter arose. One of the loungers in the street, a strongly built young man in a checkered suit, stepped away from the others and stood before the liveryman. Having seen Mary he was trying to attract her attention. He also began to tell a story and as he talked he gesticulated, waved his arms and from time to time looked over his shoulder to see if the girl still stood by the window and if she were watching.

Doctor Cochran had told his daughter of his approaching death in a cold quiet voice. To the girl it had seemed that everything concerning her father must be cold and quiet. "I have a disease of the heart," he said flatly, "have long suspected there was something of the sort the matter with me and on Thursday when I went into Chicago I had myself examined. The truth is I may die at any moment. I would not tell you but for one reason—I will leave little money and you must be making plans for the future."

The Doctor stepped nearer the window where his daughter stood with her hand on the frame. The announcement had made her a little pale and her hand trembled. In spite of his apparent coldness he was touched and wanted to reassure her. "There now," he said hesitatingly, "it'll likely be all right after all. Don't worry. I haven't been a doctor for thirty years without knowing there's a great deal of nonsense about these pronouncements on the part of experts. In a matter like this, that is to say when a man has a disease of the heart, he may putter about for years." He laughed uncomfortably. "I've even heard it said that the best way to insure a long life is to contract a disease of the heart."

With these words the Doctor had turned and walked out of his office, going down a wooden stairway to the street. He had wanted to put his arm about his daughter's shoulder as he talked to her, but never having shown any feeling in his relations with her could not sufficiently release some tight thing in himself.

Mary had stood for a long time looking down into the street. The young man in the checkered suit, whose name was Duke Yetter, had finished telling his tale and a shout of laughter arose. She turned to look toward the door through which her father had passed and dread took possession of her. In all her life there had never been anything warm and close. She shivered although the night was warm and with a quick girlish gesture passed her hand over her eyes.

The gesture was but an expression of a desire to brush away the cloud of fear that had settled down upon her but it was misinterpreted by Duke Yetter who now stood a little apart from the other men before the livery barn. When he saw Mary's hand go up he smiled and turning quickly to be sure he was unobserved began jerking his head and making motions with his hand as a sign that he wished her to come down into the street where he would have an opportunity to join her.

*   *   *

On the Sunday evening Mary, having walked through Upper Main, turned into Wilmott, a street of workmens' houses. During that year the first sign of the march of factories westward from Chicago into the prairie towns had come to Huntersburg. A Chicago manufacturer of furniture had built a plant in the sleepy little farming town, hoping thus to escape the labor organizations that had begun to give him trouble in the city. At the upper end of town, in Wilmott, Swift, Harrison and Chestnut Streets and in cheap, badly-constructed frame houses, most of the factory workers lived. On the warm summer evening they were gathered on the porches at the front of the houses and a mob of children played in the dusty streets. Red-faced men in white shirts and without collars and coats slept in chairs or lay sprawled on strips of grass or on the hard earth before the doors of the houses.

The laborers' wives had gathered in groups and stood gossiping by the fences that separated the yards. Occasionally the voice of one of the women arose sharp and distinct above the steady flow of voices that ran like a murmuring river through the hot little streets.

In the roadway two children had got into a fight. A thick-shouldered red-haired boy struck another boy who had a pale sharp-featured face, a blow on the shoulder. Other children came running. The mother of the red-haired boy brought the promised fight to an end. "Stop it Johnny, I tell you to stop it. I'll break your neck if you don't," the woman screamed.

The pale boy turned and walked away from his antagonist. As he went slinking along the sidewalk past Mary Cochran his sharp little eyes, burning with hatred, looked up at her.

Mary went quickly along. The strange new part of her native town with the hubbub of life always stirring and asserting itself had a strong fascination for her. There was something dark and resentful in her own nature that made her feel at home in the crowded place where life carried itself off darkly, with a blow and an oath. The habitual silence of her father and the mystery concerning the unhappy married life of her father and mother, that had affected the attitude toward her of the people of the town, had made her own life a lonely one and had encouraged in her a rather dogged determination to in some way think her own way through the things of life she could not understand.

And back of Mary's thinking there was an intense curiosity and a courageous determination toward adventure. She was like a little animal of the forest that has been robbed of its mother by the gun of a sportsman and has been driven by hunger to go forth and seek food. Twenty times during the year she had walked alone at evening in the new and fast growing factory district of her town. She was eighteen and had begun to look like a woman, and she felt that other girls of the town of her own age would not have dared to walk in such a place alone. The feeling made her somewhat proud and as she went along she looked boldly about.

Among the workers in Wilmott Street, men and women who had been brought to town by the furniture manufacturer, were many who spoke in foreign tongues. Mary walked among them and liked the sound of the strange voices. To be in the street made her feel that she had gone out of her town and on a voyage into a strange land. In Lower Main Street or in the residence streets in the eastern part of town where lived the young men and women she had always known and where lived also the merchants, the clerks, the lawyers and the more well-to-do American workmen of Huntersburg, she felt always a secret antagonism to herself. The antagonism was not due to anything in her own character. She was sure of that. She had kept so much to herself that she was in fact but little known. "It is because I am the daughter of my mother," she told herself and did not walk often in the part of town where other girls of her class lived.

Mary had been so often in Wilmott Street that many of the people had begun to feel acquainted with her. "She is the daughter of some farmer and has got into the habit of walking into town," they said. A red-haired, broad-hipped woman who came out at the front door of one of the houses nodded to her. On a narrow strip of grass beside another house sat a young man with his back against a tree. He was smoking a pipe, but when he looked up and saw her he took the pipe from his mouth. She decided he must be an Italian, his hair and eyes were so black. "*Ne bella! si fai un onore a passare di qua*[1]," he called waving his hand and smiling.

Mary went to the end of Wilmott Street and came out upon a country road. It seemed to her that a long time must have passed since she left her father's presence although the walk had in fact occupied but a few minutes. By the side of the road and on top of a small hill there was a ruined barn, and before the barn a great hole filled with the charred timbers of what had once been a farmhouse. A pile of stones lay beside the hole and these were covered with creeping vines. Between the site of the house and the barn there was an old orchard in which grew a mass of tangled weeds.

Pushing her way in among the weeds, many of which were covered with blossoms, Mary found herself a seat on a rock that had been rolled against the trunk of an old apple tree. The weeds half concealed her and from the road only her head was visible. Buried away thus in the weeds she looked like a quail that runs in the tall grass and that on hearing some unusual sound, stops, throws up its head and looks sharply about.

The doctor's daughter had been to the decayed old orchard many times before. At the foot of the hill on which it stood the streets of the town began, and as she sat on the rock she could hear faint shouts and cries coming out of Wilmott Street. A hedge separated the orchard

---

[1] *Ne bella! . . . qua*; Italian: No, beautiful! you do an honor to pass this way.

from the fields on the hillside. Mary intended to sit by the tree until darkness came creeping over the land and to try to think out some plan regarding her future. The notion that her father was soon to die seemed both true and untrue, but her mind was unable to take hold of the thought of him as physically dead. For the moment death in relation to her father did not take the form of a cold inanimate body that was to be buried in the ground, instead it seemed to her that her father was not to die but to go away somewhere on a journey. Long ago her mother had done that. There was a strange hesitating sense of relief in the thought. "Well," she told herself, "when the time comes I also shall be setting out, I shall get out of here and into the world." On several occasions Mary had gone to spend a day with her father in Chicago and she was fascinated by the thought that soon she might be going there to live. Before her mind's eye floated a vision of long streets filled with thousands of people all strangers to herself. To go into such streets and to live her life among strangers would be like coming out of a waterless desert and into a cool forest carpeted with tender young grass.

In Huntersburg she had always lived under a cloud and now she was becoming a woman and the close stuffy atmosphere she had always breathed was becoming constantly more and more oppressive. It was true no direct question had ever been raised touching her own standing in the community life, but she felt that a kind of prejudice against her existed. While she was still a baby there had been a scandal involving her father and mother. The town of Huntersburg had rocked with it and when she was a child people had sometimes looked at her with mocking sympathetic eyes. "Poor child! It's too bad," they said. Once, on a cloudy summer evening when her father had driven off to the country and she sat alone in the darkness by his office window, she heard a man and woman in the street mention her name. The couple stumbled along in the darkness on the sidewalk below the office window. "That daughter of Doc Cochran's is a nice girl," said the man. The woman laughed. "She's growing up and attracting men's attention now. Better keep your eyes in your head. She'll turn out bad. Like mother, like daughter," the woman replied.

For ten or fifteen minutes Mary sat on the stone beneath the tree in the orchard and thought of the attitude of the town toward herself and her father. "It should have drawn us together," she told herself, and wondered if the approach of death would do what the cloud that had for years hung over them had not done. It did not at the moment seem to her cruel that the figure of death was soon to visit her father. In a way Death had become for her and for the time a lovely and gracious figure intent upon good. The hand of death was to open the door out of her father's house and into life. With the cruelty of youth she thought first of the adventurous possibilities of the new life.

Mary sat very still. In the long weeds the insects that had been disturbed in their evening song began to sing again. A robin flew into the tree beneath which she sat and struck a clear sharp note of alarm. The voices of people in the town's new factory district came softly up the hillside. They were like bells of distant cathedrals calling people to worship. Something within the girl's breast seemed to break and putting her head into her hands she rocked slowly back and forth. Tears came accompanied by a warm tender impulse toward the living men and women of Huntersburg.

And then from the road came a call. "Hello there kid," shouted a voice, and Mary sprang quickly to her feet. Her mellow mood passed like a puff of wind and in its place hot anger came.

In the road stood Duke Yetter who from his loafing place before the livery barn had seen her set out for the Sunday evening walk and had followed. When she went through Upper Main Street and into the new factory district he was sure of his conquest. "She doesn't want to be seen walking with me," he had told himself, "that's all right. She knows well enough I'll follow but doesn't want me to put in an appearance until she is well out of sight of her friends. She's a little stuck up and needs to be brought down a peg, but what do I care? She's gone out of her way to give me this chance and maybe she's only afraid of her dad."

Duke climbed the little incline out of the road and came into the orchard, but when he reached the pile of stones covered by vines he stumbled and fell. He arose and laughed. Mary had not waited for him to reach her but had started toward him, and when his laugh broke the silence that lay over the orchard she sprang forward and with her open hand struck him a sharp blow on the cheek. Then she turned and as he stood with his feet tangled in the vines ran out to the road. "If you follow or speak to me I'll get someone to kill you," she shouted.

Mary walked along the road and down the hill toward Wilmott Street. Broken bits of the story concerning her mother that had for years circulated in town had reached her ears. Her mother, it was said, had disappeared on a summer night long ago and a young town rough, who had been in the habit of loitering before Barney

Smithfield's Livery Barn, had gone away with her. Now another young rough was trying to make up to her. The thought made her furious.

Her mind groped about striving to lay hold of some weapon with which she could strike a more telling blow at Duke Yetter. In desperation it lit upon the figure of her father already broken in health and now about to die. "My father just wants the chance to kill some such fellow as you," she shouted, turning to face the young man, who having got clear of the mass of vines in the orchard, had followed her into the road. "My father just wants to kill someone because of the lies that have been told in this town about mother."

Having given way to the impulse to threaten Duke Yetter Mary was instantly ashamed of her outburst and walked rapidly along, the tears running from her eyes. With hanging head Duke walked at her heels. "I didn't mean no harm, Miss Cochran," he pleaded. "I didn't mean no harm. Don't tell your father. I was only funning with you. I tell you I didn't mean no harm."

★   ★   ★

The light of the summer evening had begun to fall and the faces of the people made soft little ovals of light as they stood grouped under the dark porches or by the fences in Wilmott Street. The voices of the children had become subdued and they also stood in groups. They became silent as Mary passed and stood with upturned faces and staring eyes. "The lady doesn't live very far. She must be almost a neighbor," she heard a woman's voice saying in English. When she turned her head she saw only a crowd of dark-skinned men standing before a house. From within the house came the sound of a woman's voice singing a child to sleep.

The young Italian, who had called to her earlier in the evening and who was now apparently setting out of his own Sunday evening's adventures, came along the sidewalk and walked quickly away into the darkness. He had dressed himself in his Sunday clothes and had put on a black derby hat and a stiff white collar, set off by a red necktie. The shining whiteness of the collar made his brown skin look almost black. He smiled boyishly and raised his hat awkwardly but did not speak.

Mary kept looking back along the street to be sure Duke Yetter had not followed but in the dim light could see nothing of him. Her angry excited mood went away.

She did not want to go home and decided it was too late to go to church. From Upper Main Street there was a short street that ran eastward and fell rather sharply down a hillside to a creek and a bridge that marked the end of the town's growth in that direction. She went down along the street to the bridge and stood in the failing light watching two boys who were fishing in the creek.

A broad-shouldered man dressed in rough clothes came down along the street and stopping on the bridge spoke to her. It was the first time she had ever heard a citizen of her home town speak with feeling of her father. "You are Doctor Cochran's daughter?" he asked hesitatingly. "I guess you don't know who I am but your father does." He pointed toward the two boys who sat with fishpoles in their hands on the weed-grown bank of the creek. "Those are my boys and I have four other children," he explained. "There is another boy and I have three girls. One of my daughters has a job in a store. She is as old as yourself." The man explained his relations with Doctor Cochran. He had been a farm laborer, he said, and had but recently moved to town to work in the furniture factory. During the previous winter he had been ill for a long time and had no money. While he lay in bed one of his boys fell out of a barn loft and there was a terrible cut in his head.

"Your father came every day to see us and he sewed up my Tom's head." The laborer turned away from Mary and stood with his cap in his hand looking toward the boys. "I was down and out and your father not only took care of me and the boys but he gave my old woman money to buy the things we had to have from the stores in town here, groceries and medicines." The man spoke in such low tones that Mary had to lean forward to hear his words. Her face almost touched the laborer's shoulder. "Your father is a good man and I don't think he is very happy," he went on. "The boy and I got well and I got work here in town but he wouldn't take any money from me. 'You know how to live with your children and with your wife. You know how to make them happy. Keep your money and spend it on them,' that's what he said to me."

The laborer went on across the bridge and along the creek bank toward the spot where his two sons sat fishing and Mary leaned on the railing of the bridge and looked at the slow moving water. It was almost black in the shadows under the bridge and she thought that it was thus her father's life had been lived. "It has been like a stream running always in shadows and never coming out into the sunlight," she thought, and fear that her own life would run on in darkness gripped her. A great new love for her father swept over her and in fancy she felt his arms about her. As a child she had continually dreamed of caresses received at her father's hands and now the dream came back. For a long time she stood looking at the stream and she resolved that the night should not pass without an effort on her part to make the old dream come true. When she again looked up the laborer had built a little fire of sticks at the edge of the stream. "We catch bullheads here," he called. "The light of the fire draws them close to the shore. If you want to come and try your hand at fishing the boys will lend you one of the poles."

"O, I thank you, I won't do it tonight," Mary said, and then fearing she might suddenly begin weeping and that if the man spoke to her again she would find herself unable to answer, she hurried away. "Good bye!" shouted the man and the two boys. The words came quite spontaneously out of the three throats and created a sharp trumpet-like effect that rang like a glad cry across the heaviness of her mood.

★   ★   ★

When his daughter Mary went out for her evening walk Doctor Cochran sat for an hour alone in his office. It began to grow dark and the men who all afternoon had been sitting on chairs and boxes before the livery barn across the street went home for the evening meal. The noise of voices grew faint and sometimes for five or ten minutes there was silence. Then from some distant street came a child's cry. Presently church bells began to ring.

The Doctor was not a very neat man and sometimes for several days he forgot to shave. With a long lean hand he stroked his half grown beard. His illness had struck deeper than he had admitted even to himself and his mind had an inclination to float out of his body. Often when he sat thus his hands lay in his lap and he looked at them with a child's absorption. It seemed to him they must belong to someone else. He grew philosophic. "It's an odd thing about my body. Here I've lived in it all these years and how little use I have had of it. Now it's going to die and decay never having been used. I wonder why it did not get another tenant." He smiled sadly over this fancy but went on with it. "Well I've had thoughts enough concerning people and I've had the use of these lips and a tongue but I've let them lie idle. When my Ellen was here living with me I let her think me cold and unfeeling while something within me was straining and straining trying to tear itself loose."

He remembered how often, as a young man, he had sat in the evening in silence beside his wife in this same office and how his hands had ached to reach across the narrow space that separated them and touch her hands, her face, her hair.

Well, everyone in town had predicted his marriage would turn out badly! His wife had been an actress with a company that came to Huntersburg and got stranded there. At the same time the girl became ill and had no money to pay for her room at the hotel. The young doctor had attended to that and when the girl was convalescent took her to ride about the country in his buggy. Her life had been a hard one and the notion of leading a quiet existence in the little town appealed to her.

And then after the marriage and after the child was born she had suddenly found herself unable to go on living with the silent cold man. There had been a story of her having run away with a young sport, the son of a saloon keeper who had disappeared from town at the same time, but the story was untrue. Lester Cochran had himself taken her to Chicago where she got work with a company going into the far western states. Then he had taken her to the door of her hotel, had put money into her hands and in silence and without even a farewell kiss had turned and walked away.

The Doctor sat in his office living over that moment and other intense moments when he had been deeply stirred and had been on the surface so cool and quiet. He wondered if the woman had known. How many times he had asked himself that question. After he left her that night at the hotel door she never wrote. "Perhaps she is dead," he thought for the thousandth time.

A thing happened that had been happening at odd moments for more than a year. In Doctor Cochran's mind the remembered figure of his wife became confused with the figure of his daughter. When at such moments he tried to separate the two figures, to make them stand out distinct from each other, he was unsuccessful. Turning his head slightly he imagined he saw a white girlish figure coming through a door out of the rooms in which he and his daughter lived. The door was painted white and swung slowly in a light breeze that came in at an open window. The wind ran softly and quietly through the room and played over some papers lying on a desk in a corner. There was a soft swishing sound as of a woman's skirts. The doctor arose and stood trembling. "Which is it? Is it you Mary or is it Ellen?" he asked huskily.

On the stairway leading up from the street there was the sound of heavy feet and the outer door opened. The doctor's weak heart fluttered and he dropped heavily back into his chair.

A man came into the room. He was a farmer, one of the doctor's patients, and coming to the centre of the room he struck a match, held it above his head and shouted. "Hello!" he called. When the doctor arose from his chair and answered he was so startled that the match fell from his hand and lay burning faintly at his feet.

The young farmer had sturdy legs that were like two pillars of stone supporting a heavy building, and the little flame of the match that burned and fluttered in the light breeze on the floor between his feet threw dancing shadows along the walls of the room. The doctor's confused mind refused to clear itself of his fancies that now began to feed upon this new situation.

He forgot the presence of the farmer and his mind raced back over his life as a married man. The flickering light on the wall recalled another dancing light. One afternoon in the summer during the first year after his marriage his wife Ellen had driven with him into the country. They were then furnishing their rooms and at a farmer's house Ellen had seen an old mirror, no longer in use, standing against a wall in a shed. Because of something quaint in the design the mirror had taken her fancy and the farmer's wife had given it to her. On the drive home the young wife had told her husband of her pregnancy and the doctor had been stirred as never before. He sat holding the mirror on his knees while his wife drove and when she announced the coming of the child she looked away across the fields.

How deeply etched, that scene in the sick man's mind! The sun was going down over young corn and oat fields beside the road. The prairie land was black and occasionally the road ran through short lanes of trees that also looked black in the waning light.

The mirror on his knees caught the rays of the departing sun and sent a great ball of golden light dancing across the fields and among the branches of trees. Now as he stood in the presence of the farmer and as the little light from the burning match on the floor recalled that other evening of dancing lights, he thought he understood the failure of his marriage and of his life. On that evening long ago when Ellen had told him of the coming of the great adventure of their marriage he had remained silent because he had thought no words he could utter would express what he felt. There had been a defense for himself built up. "I told myself she should have understood without words and I've all my life been telling myself the same thing about Mary. I've been a fool and a coward. I've always been silent because I've been afraid of expressing myself—like a blundering fool. I've been a proud man and a coward.

"Tonight I'll do it. If it kills me I'll make myself talk to the girl," he said aloud, his mind coming back to the figure of his daughter.

"Hey! What's that?" asked the farmer who stood with his hat in his hand waiting to tell of his mission.

The doctor got his horse from Barney Smithfield's livery and drove off to the country to attend the farmer's wife who was about to give birth to her first child. She was a slender narrow-hipped woman and the child was large, but the doctor was feverishly strong. He worked desperately and the woman, who was frightened, groaned and struggled. Her husband kept coming in and going out of the room and two neighbor women appeared and stood silently about waiting to be of service. It was past ten o'clock when everything was done and the doctor was ready to depart for town.

The farmer hitched his horse and brought it to the door and the doctor drove off feeling strangely weak and at the same time strong. How simple now seemed the thing he had yet to do. Perhaps when he got home his daughter would have gone to bed but he would ask her to get up and come into the office. Then he would tell the whole story of his marriage and its failure sparing himself no humiliation. "There was something very dear and beautiful in my Ellen and I must make Mary understand that. It will help her to be a beautiful woman," he thought, full of confidence in the strength of his resolution.

He got to the door of the livery barn at eleven o'clock and Barney Smithfield with young Duke Yetter and two other men sat talking there. The liveryman took his horse away into the darkness of the barn and the doctor stood for a moment leaning against the wall of the building. The town's night watchman stood with the group by the barn door and a quarrel broke out between him and Duke Yetter, but the doctor did not hear the hot words that flew back and forth or Duke's loud laughter at the night watchman's anger. A queer hesitating mood had taken possession of him. There was something he passionately desired to do but could not remember. Did it have to do with his wife Ellen or Mary his daughter? The figures of the two women were again confused in his mind and to add to the confusion there was a third figure, that of the woman he had just assisted through child birth. Everything was confusion.

He started across the street toward the entrance of the stairway leading to his office and then stopped in the road and stared about. Barney Smithfield having returned from putting his horse in the stall shut the door of the barn and a hanging lantern over the door swung back and forth. It threw grotesque dancing shadows down over the faces and forms of the men standing and quarreling beside the wall of the barn.

★ ★ ★

Mary sat by a window in the doctor's office awaiting his return. So absorbed was she in her own thoughts that she was unconscious of the voice of Duke Yetter talking with the men in the street.

When Duke had come into the street the hot anger of the early part of the evening had returned and she again saw him advancing toward her in the orchard with the look of arrogant male confidence in his eyes but presently she forgot him and thought only of her father. An incident of her childhood returned to haunt her. One afternoon in the month of May when she was fifteen her father had asked her to accompany him on an evening drive into the country. The doctor went to visit a sick woman at a farmhouse five miles from town and as there had been a great deal of rain the roads were heavy. It was dark when they reached the farmer's house and they went into the kitchen and ate cold food off a kitchen table. For some reason her father had, on that evening, appeared boyish and almost gay. On the road he had talked a little. Even at that early age Mary had grown tall and her figure was becoming womanly. After the cold supper in the farm kitchen he walked with her around the house and she sat on a narrow porch. For a moment her father stood before her. He put his hands into his trouser pockets and throwing back his head laughed almost heartily. "It seems strange to think you will soon be a woman," he said. "When you do become a woman what do you suppose is going to happen, eh? What kind of a life will you lead? What will happen to you?"

The doctor sat on the porch beside the child and for a moment she had thought he was about to put his arm around her. Then he jumped up and went into the house leaving her to sit alone in the darkness.

As she remembered the incident Mary remembered also that on that evening of her childhood she had met her father's advances in silence. It seemed to her that she, not her father, was to blame for the life they had led together. The farm laborer she had met on the bridge had not felt her father's coldness. That was because he had himself been warm and generous in his attitude toward the man who had cared for him in his hour of sickness and misfortune. Her father had said that the laborer knew how to be a father and Mary remembered with what warmth the two boys fishing by the creek had called to her as she went away into the darkness. "Their father has known how to be a father because his children have known how to give themselves," she thought guiltily. She also would give herself. Before the night had passed she would do that: On that evening long ago and as she rode home beside her father he had made another unsuccessful effort to break through the wall that separated them. The heavy rains had swollen the streams they had to cross and when they had almost reached town he had stopped the horse on a wooden bridge. The horse danced nervously about and her father held the reins firmly and occasionally spoke to him. Beneath the bridge the swollen stream made a great roaring sound and beside the road in a long flat field there was a lake of flood water. At that moment the moon had come out from behind clouds and the wind that blew across the water made little waves. The lake of flood water was covered with dancing lights. "I'm going to tell you about your mother and myself," her father said huskily, but at that moment the timbers of the bridge began to crack dangerously and the horse plunged forward. When her father had regained control of the frightened beast they were in the streets of the town and his diffident silent nature had reasserted itself.

Mary sat in the darkness by the office window and saw her father drive into the street. When his horse had been put away he did not, as was his custom, come at once up the stairway to the office but lingered in the darkness before the barn door. Once he started to cross the street and then returned into the darkness.

Among the men who for two hours had been sitting and talking quietly a quarrel broke out. Jack Fisher the town nightwatchman had been telling the others the story of a battle in which he had fought during the Civil War and Duke Yetter had begun bantering him. The nightwatchman grew angry. Grasping his nightstick he limped up and down. The loud voice of Duke Yetter cut across the shrill angry voice of the victim of his wit. "You ought to a flanked the fellow, I tell you Jack. Yes sir 'ee, you ought to a flanked that reb and then when you got him flanked you ought to a knocked the stuffings out of the cuss. That's what I would a done," Duke shouted, laughing boisterously. "You would a raised hell, you would," the nightwatchman answered, filled with ineffectual wrath.

The old soldier went off along the street followed by the laughter of Duke and his companions and Barney Smithfield, having put the doctor's horse away, came out and closed the barn door. A lantern hanging above the door swung back and forth. Doctor Cochran again started across the street and when he had reached the foot of the stairway turned and shouted to the men. "Good night," he called cheerfully. A strand of hair was blown by the light summer breeze across Mary's cheek and she jumped to her feet as though she had been touched by a hand reached out to her from the darkness. A hundred times she had seen her father return from drives in the evening but never before had he said anything at all to the loiterers by the barn door. She became half convinced that not her father but some other man was now coming up the stairway.

The heavy dragging footsteps rang loudly on the wooden stairs and Mary heard her father set down the little square medicine case he always carried. The strange cheerful hearty mood of the man continued but his mind was in a confused riot. Mary imagined she could see his dark form in the doorway. "The woman has had a baby," said the hearty voice from the landing outside the door. "Who did that happen to? Was it Ellen or that other woman or my little Mary?"

A stream of words, a protest came from the man's lips. "Who's been having a baby? I want to know. Who's been having a baby? Life doesn't work out. Why are babies always being born?" he asked.

A laugh broke from the doctor's lips and his daughter leaned forward and gripped the arms of her chair. "A babe has been born," he said again. "It's strange eh, that my hands should have helped a baby be born while all the time death stood at my elbow?"

Doctor Cochran stamped upon the floor of the landing. "My feet are cold and numb from waiting for life to come out of life," he said heavily. "The woman struggled and now I must struggle."

Silence followed the stamping of feet and the tired heavy declaration from the sick man's lips. From the street below came another loud shout of laughter from Duke Yetter.

And then Doctor Cochran fell backward down the narrow stairs to the street. There was no cry from him, just the clatter of his shoes upon the stairs and the terrible subdued sound of the body falling.

Mary did not move from her chair. With closed eyes she waited. Her heart pounded. A weakness complete and overmastering had possession of her and from feet to head ran little waves of feeling as though tiny creatures with soft hair-like feet were playing upon her body.

It was Duke Yetter who carried the dead man up the stairs and laid him on a bed in one of the rooms back of the office. One of the men who had been sitting with him before the door of the barn followed lifting his hands and dropping them nervously. Between his fingers he held a forgotten cigarette the light from which danced up and down in the darkness.

# THE UNTOLD LIE

## Sherwood Anderson

RAY PEARSON AND Hal Winters were farm hands employed on a farm three miles north of Winesburg. On Saturday afternoons they came into town and wandered about through the streets with other fellows from the country.

Ray was a quiet, rather nervous man of perhaps fifty with a brown beard and shoulders rounded by too much and too hard labor. In his nature he was as unlike Hal Winters as two men can be unlike.

Ray was an altogether serious man and had a little sharp featured wife who had also a sharp voice. The two, with half a dozen thin legged children, lived in a tumble-down frame house beside a creek at the back end of the Wills farm where Ray was employed.

Hal Winters, his fellow employee, was a young fellow. He was not of the Ned Winters family, who were very respectable people in Winesburg, but was one of the three sons of the old man called Windpeter Winters who had a sawmill near Unionville, six miles away, and who was looked upon by everyone in Winesburg as a confirmed old reprobate.

People from the part of Northern Ohio in which Winesburg lies will remember old Windpeter by his unusual and tragic death. He got drunk one evening in town and started to drive home to Unionville along the railroad tracks. Henry Brattenburg, the butcher, who lived out that way, stopped him at the edge of the town and told him he was sure to meet the down train but Windpeter slashed at him with his whip and drove on. When the train struck and killed him and his two horses a farmer and his wife who were driving home along a nearby road saw the accident. They said that old Windpeter stood up on the seat of his wagon, raving and swearing at the onrushing locomotive, and that he fairly screamed with delight when the team, maddened by his incessant slashing at them, rushed straight ahead to certain death. Boys like young George Willard and Seth Richmond will remember the incident quite vividly because, although everyone in our town said that the old man would go straight to hell and that the community was better off without him, they had a secret conviction that he knew what he was doing and admired his foolish courage. Most boys have seasons of wishing they could die gloriously instead of just being grocery clerks and going on with their humdrum lives.

But this is not the story of Windpeter Winters nor yet of his son Hal who worked on the Wills farm with Ray Pearson. It is Ray's story. It will, however, be necessary to talk a little of young Hal so that you will get into the spirit of it.

Hal was a bad one. Everyone said that. There were three of the Winters boys in that family, John, Hal, and Edward, all broad shouldered big fellows like old Windpeter himself and all fighters and woman-chasers and generally all-around bad ones.

Hal was the worst of the lot and always up to some devilment. He once stole a load of boards from his father's mill and sold them in Winesburg. With the money he bought himself a suit of cheap, flashy clothes. Then he got drunk and when his father came raving into town to find him, they met and fought with their fists on Main Street and were arrested and put into jail together.

Hal went to work on the Wills farm because there was a country school teacher out that way who had taken his fancy. He was only twenty-two then but had already been in two or three of what were spoken of in Winesburg as "women scrapes." Everyone who heard of his infatuation for the school teacher was sure it would turn out badly. "He'll only get her into trouble, you'll see," was the word that went around.

And so these two men, Ray and Hal, were at work in a field on a day in the late October. They were husking corn and occasionally something was said and they laughed. Then came silence. Ray, who was the more sensitive and always minded things more, had chapped hands and they hurt. He put them into his coat pockets and looked away across the fields. He was in a sad distracted mood and was affected by the beauty of the country. If you knew the Winesburg country in the fall and how the low hills are all splashed with yellows and reds you would understand his feeling. He began to think of the time, long ago when he was a young fellow living with his father, then a baker in Winesburg, and how on such days he had wandered away to the woods to gather nuts, hunt rabbits, or just to loaf about and smoke his pipe. His marriage had come about through one of his days of wandering. He had induced a girl who waited on trade in his father's shop to go with him and something had happened. He was thinking of that afternoon and how it had affected his whole life when a spirit of protest awoke in him. He had forgotten about Hal and muttered words. "Tricked by Gad, that's what I was, tricked by life and made a fool of," he said in a low voice.

As though understanding his thoughts, Hal Winters spoke up. "Well, has it been worthwhile? What about it, eh? What about marriage and all that?" he asked and then laughed. Hal tried to keep on laughing but he too was in an earnest mood. He began to talk earnestly. "Has a fellow got to do it?" he asked. "Has he got to be harnessed up and driven through life like a horse?"

Hal didn't wait for an answer but sprang to his feet and began to walk back and forth between the corn shocks. He was getting more and more excited. Bending down suddenly he picked up an ear of the yellow corn and threw it at the fence. "I've got Nell Gunther in trouble," he said. "I'm telling you, but you keep your mouth shut."

Ray Pearson arose and stood staring. He was almost a foot shorter than Hal, and when the younger man came and put his two hands on the older man's shoulders they made a picture. There they stood in the big empty field with the quiet corn shocks standing in rows behind them and the red and yellow hills in the distance, and from being just two indifferent workmen they had become all alive to each other. Hal sensed it and because that was his way he laughed. "Well, old daddy," he said awkwardly, "come on, advise me. I've got Nell in trouble. Perhaps you've been in the same fix yourself. I know what everyone would say is the right thing to do, but what do you say? Shall I marry and settle down? Shall I put myself into the harness to be worn out like an old horse? You know me, Ray. There can't anyone break me but I can break myself. Shall I do it or shall I tell Nell to go to the devil? Come on, you tell me. Whatever you say, Ray, I'll do."

Ray couldn't answer. He shook Hal's hands loose and turning walked straight away toward the barn. He was a sensitive man and there were tears in his eyes. He knew there was only one thing to say to Hal Winters, son of old Windpeter Winters, only one thing that all his own training and all the beliefs of the people he knew would approve, but for his life he couldn't say what he knew he should say.

At half-past four that afternoon Ray was puttering about the barnyard when his wife came up the lane along the creek and called him. After the talk with Hal he hadn't returned to the corn field but worked about the barn. He had already done the evening chores and had seen Hal, dressed and ready for a roistering night in town, come out of the farmhouse and go into the road. Along the path to his own house he trudged behind his wife, looking at the ground and thinking. He couldn't make out what was wrong. Every time he raised his eyes and saw the beauty of the country in the failing light he wanted to do something he had never done before, shout or scream or hit his wife with his fists or something equally unexpected and terrifying. Along the path he went scratching his head and trying to make it out. He looked hard at his wife's back but she seemed all right.

She only wanted him to go into town for groceries and as soon as she had told him what she wanted began to scold. "You're always puttering," she said. "Now I want you to hustle. There isn't anything in the house for supper and you've got to get to town and back in a hurry."

Ray went into his own house and took an overcoat from a hook back of the door. It was torn about the pockets and the collar was shiny. His wife went into the bedroom and presently came out with a soiled cloth in one hand and three silver dollars in the other. Somewhere in the house a child wept bitterly and a dog that had been sleeping by the stove arose and yawned. Again the wife scolded. "The children will cry and cry. Why are you always puttering?" she asked.

Ray went out of the house and climbed the fence into a field. It was just growing dark and the scene that lay before him was lovely. All the low hills were washed with color and even the little clusters of bushes in the corners by the fences were alive with beauty. The whole world seemed to Ray Pearson to have become alive with something just as he and Hal had suddenly become alive when they stood in the corn field staring into each other's eyes.

The beauty of the country about Winesburg was too much for Ray on that fall evening. That is all there was to it. He could not stand it. Of a sudden he forgot all about being a quiet old farm hand and throwing off the torn overcoat began to run across the field. As he ran he shouted a protest against his life, against all life, against everything that makes life ugly. "There was no promise made," he cried into the empty spaces that lay about him. "I didn't promise my Minnie anything and Hal hasn't made any promise to Nell. I know he hasn't. She went into the woods with him because she wanted to go. What he wanted she wanted. Why should I pay? Why should Hal pay? Why should anyone pay? I don't want Hal to become old and worn out. I'll tell him. I won't let it go on. I'll catch Hal before he gets to town and I'll tell him."

Ray ran clumsily and once he stumbled and fell down. "I must catch Hal and tell him," he kept thinking and although his breath came in gasps he kept running harder and harder. As he ran he thought of things that hadn't come into his mind for years—how at the time he married he had planned to go west to his uncle in Portland, Oregon—how he hadn't wanted to be a farm hand, but had thought when he got out west he would go to sea and be a sailor or get a job on a ranch and ride a horse into western towns, shouting and laughing and waking the people in the houses with his wild cries. Then as he ran he remembered his children and in fancy felt their hands clutching at him. All of his thoughts of himself were involved with the thoughts of Hal and he thought the children were clutching at the younger man also. "They are the accidents of life, Hal," he cried. "They are not mine or yours. I had nothing to do with them."

Darkness began to spread over the fields as Ray Pearson ran on and on. His breath came in little sobs. When he came to the fence at the edge of the road and confronted Hal Winters, all dressed up and smoking a pipe as he walked jauntily along, he could not have told what he thought or what he wanted.

Ray Pearson lost his nerve and this is really the end of the story of what happened to him. It was almost dark when he got to the fence and he put his hands on the top bar and stood staring. Hal Winters jumped a ditch and coming up close to Ray put his hands into his pockets and laughed. He seemed to have lost his own sense of what had happened in the corn field and when he put up a strong hand and took hold of the lapel of Ray's coat he shook the old man as he might have shaken a dog that had misbehaved.

"You came to tell me, eh?" he said. "Well, never mind telling me anything. I'm not a coward and I've already made up my mind." He laughed again and jumped back across the ditch. "Nell ain't no fool," he said. "She didn't ask me to marry her. I want to marry her. I want to settle down and have kids."

Ray Pearson also laughed. He felt like laughing at himself and all the world.

As the form of Hal Winters disappeared in the dusk that lay over the road that led to Winesburg, he turned and walked slowly back across the fields to where he had left his torn overcoat. As he went some memory of pleasant evenings spent with the thin-legged children in the tumble-down house by the creek must have come into his mind, for he muttered words. "It's just as well. Whatever I told him would have been a lie," he said softly, and then his form also disappeared into the darkness of the fields.

# PAPER PILLS

## Sherwood Anderson

He was an old man with a white beard and huge nose and hands. Long before the time during which we will know him, he was a doctor and drove a jaded white horse from house to house through the streets of Winesburg. Later he married a girl who had money. She had been left a large fertile farm when her father died. The girl was quiet, tall, and dark, and to many people she seemed very beautiful. Everyone in Winesburg wondered why she married the doctor. Within a year after the marriage she died.

The knuckles of the doctor's hand were extraordinarily large. When the hands were closed they looked like clusters of unpainted wooden balls as large as walnuts fastened together by steel rods. He smoked a cob pipe and after his wife's death sat all day in his empty office close by a window that was covered with cobwebs. He never opened the window. Once on a hot day in August he tried but found it stuck fast and after that he forgot all about it.

Winesburg had forgotten the old man, but in Doctor Reefy there were the seeds of something very fine. Alone in his musty office in the Heffner Block above the Paris Dry Goods Company's Store, he worked ceaselessly, building up something that he himself destroyed. Little pyramids of truth he erected and after erecting knocked them down again that he might have the truths to erect other pyramids.

Doctor Reefy was a tall man who had worn one suit of clothes for ten years. It was frayed at the sleeves and little holes had appeared at the knees and elbows. In the office he wore also a linen duster with huge pockets into which he continually stuffed scraps of paper. After some weeks the scraps of paper became little hard round balls, and when the pockets were filled he dumped them out upon the floor. For ten years he had but one friend, another old man named John Spaniard who owned a tree nursery. Sometimes, in a playful mood, old Doctor Reefy took from his pockets a handful of the paper balls and threw them at the nursery man. "That is to confound you, you blithering old sentimentalist," he cried, shaking with laughter.

The story of Doctor Reefy and his courtship of the tall dark girl who became his wife and left her money to him is a very curious story. It is delicious, like the twisted little apples that grow in the orchards of Winesburg. In the fall one walks in the orchards and the ground is hard with frost underfoot. The apples have been taken from the trees by the pickers. They have been put in barrels and shipped to the cities where they will be eaten in apartments that are filled with books, magazines, furniture, and people. On the trees are only a few gnarled apples that the pickers have rejected. They look like the knuckles of Doctor Reefy's hands. One nibbles at them and they are delicious. Into a little round place at the side of the apple has been gathered all of its sweetness. One runs from tree to tree over the frosted ground picking the gnarled, twisted apples and filling his pockets with them. Only the few know the sweetness of the twisted apples.

The girl and Doctor Reefy began their courtship on a summer afternoon. He was forty-five then and already he had begun the practice of filling his pockets with the scraps of paper that became hard balls and were thrown away. The habit had been formed as he sat in his buggy behind the jaded grey horse and went slowly along country roads. On the papers were written thoughts, ends of thoughts, beginnings of thoughts.

One by one the mind of Doctor Reefy had made the thoughts. Out of many of them he formed a truth that arose gigantic in his mind. The truth clouded the world. It became terrible and then faded away and the little thoughts began again.

The tall dark girl came to see Doctor Reefy because she was in the family way and had become frightened. She was in that condition because of a series of circumstances also curious.

The death of her father and mother and the rich acres of land that had come down to her had set a train of suitors on her heels. For two years she saw suitors almost every evening. Except two they were all alike. They talked to her of passion and there was a strained eager quality in their voices and in their eyes when they looked at her. The two who were different were much unlike each other. One of them, a slender young man with white hands, the son of a jeweler in Winesburg, talked continually of virginity. When he was with her he was never off the subject. The other, a black-haired boy with large ears, said nothing at all but always managed to get her into the darkness where he began to kiss her.

For a time the tall dark girl thought she would marry the jeweler's son. For hours she sat in silence listening as he talked to her and then she began to be afraid of something. Beneath his talk of virginity she began to think there was a lust greater than in all the others. At times it seemed to her that as he talked he was holding her body in his hands. She imagined him turning it slowly about in the white hands and staring at it. At night she dreamed that he had bitten into her body and that his jaws were dripping. She had the dream three times, then she became in the family way to the one who said nothing at all but who in the moment of his passion actually did bite her shoulder so that for days the marks of his teeth showed.

After the tall dark girl came to know Doctor Reefy it seemed to her that she never wanted to leave him again. She went into his office one morning and without her saying anything he seemed to know what had happened to her.

In the office of the doctor there was a woman, the wife of the man who kept the bookstore in Winesburg. Like all old-fashioned country practitioners, Doctor Reefy pulled teeth, and the woman who waited held a handkerchief to her teeth and groaned. Her husband was with her and when the tooth was taken out they both screamed and blood ran down on the woman's white dress. The tall dark girl did not pay any attention. When the woman and the man had gone the doctor smiled. "I will take you driving into the country with me," he said.

For several weeks the tall dark girl and the doctor were together almost every day. The condition that had brought her to him passed in an illness, but she was like one who has discovered the sweetness of the twisted apples, she could not get her mind fixed again upon the round perfect fruit that is eaten in the city apartments. In the fall after the beginning of her acquaintanceship with him she married Doctor Reefy and in the following spring she died. During the winter he read to her all of the odds and ends of thoughts he had scribbled on the bits of paper. After he had read them he laughed and stuffed them away in his pockets to become round hard balls.

# A NIGHT AMONG THE HORSES

## Djuna Barnes

TOWARD DUSK, IN the summer of the year, a man dressed in a frock coat and top hat, and carrying a cane, crept through the underbrush bordering the corral of the Buckler farm.

As he moved small twigs snapped, fell and were silent. His knees were green from wounded shrubbery and grass, and his outspread hands tore unheeded plants. His wrists hurt him and he rested from time to time, always caring for his hat and knotted yellow cane, blowing through his moustache.

Dew had been falling covering the twilight leaves like myriad faces, damp with the perspiration of the struggle for existence, and half a mile away, standing out against the darkness of the night, a grove of white birches shimmered, like teeth in a skull.

He heard the creaking of a gate, and the splashing of late rain into the depths of a dark cistern. His heart ached with the nearness of the earth, the faint murmur of it moving upon itself, like a sleeper who turns to throw an arm about a beloved.

A frog began moaning among the skunk cabbages, and John thrust his hand deep into his bosom.

Something somnolent seemed to be here, and he wondered. It was like a deep, heavy, yet soft prison where, without sin, one may suffer intolerable punishment.

Presently he went on, feeling his way. He reached a high plank fence and sensing it with his fingers, he lay down, resting his head against the ground.

He was tired, he wanted to sleep, but he searched for his hat and cane and straightened out his coat beneath him before he turned his eyes to the stars.

And now he could not sleep, and wondered why he had thought of it; something quick was moving the earth, it seemed to live, to shake with sudden immensity.

He heard a dog barking, and the dim light from a farm window kept winking as the trees swung against its square of light. The odor of daisies came to him, and the assuring, powerful smell of the stables; he opened his mouth and drew in his moustache.

A faint tumult had begun. A tremor ran under the length of his body and trembled off into the earth like a shudder of joy—died down and repeated itself. And presently he began to tremble, answering, throwing out his hands, curling them up weakly, as if the earth were withholding something precious, necessary.

His hat fell off, striking a log with a dull hollow sound, and he pressed his red moustache against the grass weeping.

Again he heard it, felt it; a hundred hoofs beat upon the earth and he knew the horses had gone wild in the corral on the other side of the fence, for animals greet the summer, striking the earth, as friends strike the back of friends. He knew, he understood; a hail to summer, to life, to death.

He drew himself against the bars, pressing his eyes under them, peering, waiting.

He heard them coming up across the heavy turf, rounding the curve in the Willow Road. He opened his eyes and closed them again. The soft menacing sound deepened, as heat deepens, strike through the skin into the very flesh. Head on, with long legs rising, falling, rising again, striking the ground insanely, like needles taking terrible, impossible and purposeless stitches.

He saw their bellies, fawn colored, pitching from side to side. flashing by, straining the fence, and he rose up on his feet and silently, swiftly, fled on beside them.

Something delirious, hysterical, came over him and he fell. Blood trickled into his eyes down from his forehead. It had a fine feeling for a moment, like a mane, like that roan mare's mane that had passed him—red and long and splendid.

He lifted his hand, and closed his eyes once more, but the soft pounding did not cease, though now, in his sitting position, it only jogged him imperceptibly, as a child on a knee.

It seemed to him that he was smothering, and he felt along the side of his face as he had done in youth when they had put a cap on him that was too large. Twining green things, moist with earth-blood, crept over his fingers, the hot, impatient leaves pressed in, and the green of the matted-grass was deathly thick. He had heard about the freeness of nature, thought it was so, and it was not so.

A trailing ground pine had torn up small blades in its journey across the hill, and a vine, wrist-thick, twisted about a pale oak, hideously, gloriously, killing it, dragging it into dust.

A wax Patrick Pipe leaned against his neck, staring with black eyes, and John opened his mouth, running his tongue across his lips snapping it off, sighing.

Move as he would, the grass was always under him, and the crackling of last autumn's leaves and last summer's twigs—minute dead of the infinite greatness—troubled him. Something portentous seemed connected with the patient noises about him. An acorn dropped, striking a thin fine powder out of a frail oak pod. He took it up, tossing it. He had never liked to see things fall.

He sat up, with the dim thunder of the horses far off, but quickening his heart.

He went over the scene he had with Freda Buckler, back there in the house, the long quivering spears of pot-grass standing by the window as she walked up and down, pulling at them, talking to him.

Small, with cunning fiery eyes and a pink and pointed chin. A daughter of a mother who had known too many admirers in her youth; a woman with an ample lap on which she held a Persian kitten or a trifle of fruit. Bounty, avarice, desire, intelligence—both of them had always what they wanted.

He blew down his moustache again thinking of Freda in her floating yellow veil that he had called ridiculous. She had not been angry, he was nothing but a stable boy then. It was the way with those small intriguing women whose nostrils were made delicate through the pain of many generations that they might quiver whenever they caught a whiff of the stables.

"As near as they can get to the earth," he had said and was Freda angry? She stroked his arm always softly, looking away, an inner bitterness drawing down her mouth.

She said, walking up and down quickly, looking ridiculously small:

"I am always gentle John—" frowning, trailing her veil, thrusting out her chin.

He answered: "I liked it better where I was."

"Horses," she said showing sharp teeth, "are nothing for a man with your bile—poy-boy—curry comber, smelling of saddle soap— lovely!" She shrivelled up her nose, touching his arm: "Yes, but better things. I will show you—you shall be a gentleman—fine clothes, you will like them, they feel nice." And laughing she turned on one high heel, sitting down. "I like horses, they make people better; you are amusing, intelligent, you will see—"

"A lackey!" he returned passionately throwing up his arm "what is there in this for you, what are you trying to do to me? The family— askance—perhaps—I don't know."

He sat down pondering. He was getting used to it, or thought he was, all but his wordy remonstrances. He knew better when thinking of his horses, realizing that when he should have married this small, unpleasant and clever woman, he would know them no more.

It was a game between them, which was the shrewder, which would win out? He? A boy of ill breeding, grown from the gutter, fancied by this woman because he had called her ridiculous, or for some other reason that he would never know. This kind of person never tells the truth, and this, more than most things, troubled him. Was he a thing to be played with, debased into something better than he was, than he knew.

Partly because he was proud of himself in the costume of a groom, partly because he was timid, he desired to get away, to go back to the stables. He walked up to the mirrors as if about to challenge them, peering in. He knew he would look absurd, and then knew, with shame, that he looked splendidly better than most of the gentlemen that Freda Buckler knew. He hated himself. A man who had grown out of the city's streets, a fine common thing!

She saw him looking into the mirrors, one after the other, and drew her mouth down. She got up, walking beside him in the end, between him and them, taking his arm.

"You shall enter the army—you shall rise to General, or Lieutenant at least—and there are horses there, and the sound of stirrups—with that physique you will be happy—authority you know," she said shaking her chin, smiling.

"Very well, but a common soldier—"

"As you like—afterward."

"Afterward?"

"Very well, a common soldier."

He sensed something strange in her voice, a sort of irony and it took the patience out of him:

"I have always been common, I could commit crimes, easily, gladly—I'd like to!"

She looked away. "That's natural," she said faintly, "it's an instinct all strong men have—"

She knew what was troubling him, thwarted instincts, common beautiful instincts that he was being robbed of. He wanted to do something final to prove his lower order; caught himself making faces, idiot faces, and she laughed.

"If only your ears stuck out, chin receded," she said, "you might look degenerate, common, but as it is—"

And he would creep away in hat, coat and cane to peer at his horses never daring to go in near them. Sometimes when he wanted to weep he would smear one glove with harness grease, but the other one he held behind his back, pretending one was enough to prove his revolt.

She would torment him with vases, books, pictures, making a fool of him gently, persistently, making him doubt by cruel means, the means of objects he was not used to, eternally taking him out of his sphere.

"We have the best collection of miniatures," she would say with one knee on a low ottoman, bringing them out in her small palm.

"Here, look."

He would put his hands behind him.

"She was a great woman—Lucrezia Borgia—do you know history—" She put it back again because he did not answer, letting his mind, a curious one, torment itself.

"You love things very much, don't you?" she would question because she knew that he had a passion for one thing only. She kept placing new ladders beneath his feet, only to saw them off at the next rung, making him nothing more than a nervous irritable experiment. He was uneasy, like one given food to smell and not to taste, and for a while he had not wanted to taste, and then curiosity began, and he wanted to, and he also wanted to escape, and he could do neither.

Well, after he had married her, what then? Satisfy her whim and where would he be? He would be nothing, neither what he had been nor what other people were. This seemed to him, at times, her wish—a sort of place between lying down and standing up, a cramped position, a slow death. A curious woman.

This same evening he had looked at her attentively for the first time. Her hair was rather pretty, though too mousy, yet just in the nape of the neck, where it met the lawn of the collar it was very attractive. She walked well for a little woman too.

Sometimes she would pretend to be lively, would run a little, catch herself at it, as if she had not intended to do it, and calm down once more, or creeping up to him, stroking his arm, talking to him, she would walk beside him softly, slowly that he might not step out, that he would have to crawl across the carpet.

Once he had thought of trying her with honesty, with the truth of the situation. Perhaps she would give him an honest answer, and he had tried.

"Now Miss Freda—just a word—what are you trying to do? What is it you want? What is there in me that can interest you? I want you to tell me—I want to know—I have got to ask someone, and I haven't anyone to ask but you."

And for a moment she almost relented, only to discover that she could not if she had wished. She did not know always what she meant herself.

"I'll tell you," she said, hoping that this, somehow, might lead her into the truth, for herself, if not for him, but it did not. "You are a little nervous, you will get used to it—you will even grow to like it. Be patient. You will learn soon enough that there is nothing in the world so agreeable as climbing, changing."

"Well," he said trying to read her, "And then?"

"That's all, you will regret the stables in the end—that's all." Her nostrils quivered. A light came into her eyes, a desire to defy, to be defied.

And then on this last night he had done something terrible, he had made a blunder. There had been a party. The guests, a lot of them, were mostly drunk, or touched with drink. And he too had too much. He remembered having thrown his arms about a tall woman, gowned in black with loose shoulder straps, dragging her through a dance. He had even sung a bit of a song, madly, wildly, horribly. And suddenly he had been brought up sharp by the fact that no one thought his behavior strange, that no one thought him presumptuous. Freda's mother had not even moved or dropped the kitten from her lap where it sat, its loud resolute purr shaking the satin of her gown.

And he felt that Freda had got him where she wanted him, between two rungs. Going directly up to her he said:

"You are ridiculous!" and twirled his moustache, spitting into the garden.

And he knew nothing about what happened until he found himself in the shrubbery crawling toward the corral, through the dusk and the dampness of the leaves, carrying his cane, making sure of his hat, looking up at the stars.

And now he knew why he had come. He was with his horses again. His eyes, pressed against the bars, stared in. The black stallion in the lead had been his special pet, a rough animal, but kindly, knowing. And here they were once more, tearing up the grass, galloping about in the night like a ball-room full of real people, people who wanted to do things, who did what they wanted to do.

He began to crawl through the bars, slowly, deftly, and when half way through he paused, thinking.

Presently he went on again, and drawing himself into the corral, his hat and cane thrown in before him, he lay there mouth to the grass.

They were still running, but less madly, one of them had gone up the Willow Road leading into a farther pasture, in a flare of dust, through which it looked immense and faint.

On the top of the hill three or four of the horses were standing, testing the weather. He would mount one, he would ride away, he would escape. And his horses, the things he knew, would be his escape.

Bareback, he thought, would be like the days when he had taken what he could from the rush of the streets, joy, exhilaration, life, and he was not afraid. He wanted to stand up, to cry aloud.

And he saw ten or twelve of them rounding the curve, and he did stand up.

They did not seem to know him, did not seem to know what to make of him, and he stared at them wondering. He did not think of his white shirt front, his sudden arising, the darkness, their excitement. Surely they would know, in a moment more.

Wheeling, flaring their wet nostrils, throwing up their manes, striking the earth in a quandary, they came on, whinnied faintly, and he knew what it was to be afraid.

He had never been afraid and he went down on his knees. With a new horror in his heart he damned them. He turned his eyes up, but he could not open them. He thought rapidly, calling on Freda in his heart, speaking tenderly, promising.

A flare of heat passed his throat and descended into his bosom.

"I want to live. I can do it—damn it—I can do it. I can forge ahead, make my mark."

He forgot where he was for a moment and found new pleasure in this spoken admission, this new rebellion. He moved with the faint shaking of the earth like a child on a woman's lap.

The upraised hoofs of the first horse missed him, but the second did not.

And presently the horses drew apart, nibbling here and there, switching their tails, avoiding a patch of tall grass.

# THE DAMNED THING

### Ambrose Bierce

## 1

## One Does Not Always Eat What Is on the Table

BY THE LIGHT of a tallow candle which had been placed on one end of a rough table a man was reading something written in a book. It was an old account book, greatly worn; and the writing was not, apparently, very legible, for the man sometimes held the page close to the flame of the candle to get a stronger light on it. The shadow of the book would then throw into obscurity a half of the room, darkening a number of faces and figures; for besides the reader, eight other men were present. Seven of them sat against the rough log walls, silent, motionless, and the room being small, not very far from the table. By extending an arm anyone of them could have touched the eighth man, who lay on the table, face upward, partly covered by a sheet, his arms at his sides. He was dead.

The man with the book was not reading aloud, and no one spoke; all seemed to be waiting for something to occur; the dead man only was without expectation. From the blank darkness outside came in, through the aperture that served for a window, all the ever unfamiliar noises of night in the wilderness—the long nameless note of a distant coyote; the stilly pulsing thrill of tireless insects in trees; strange cries of night birds, so different from those of the birds of day; the drone of great blundering beetles, and all that mysterious chorus of small sounds that seem always to have been but half heard when they have suddenly ceased, as if conscious of an indiscretion. But nothing of all this was noted in that company; its members were not overmuch addicted to idle interest in matters of no practical importance; that was obvious in every line of their rugged faces—obvious even in the dim light of the single candle. They were evidently men of the vicinity—farmers and woodsmen.

The person reading was a trifle different; one would have said of him that he was of the world, worldly, albeit there was that in his attire which attested a certain fellowship with the organisms of his environment. His coat would hardly have passed muster in San Francisco; his foot-gear was not of urban origin, and the hat that lay by him on the floor (he was the only one uncovered) was such that if one had considered it as an article of mere personal adornment he would have missed its meaning. In countenance the man was rather prepossessing, with just a hint of sternness; though that he may have assumed or cultivated, as appropriate to one in authority. For he was a coroner. It was by virtue of his office that he had possession of the book in which he was reading; it had been found among the dead man's effects—in his cabin, where the inquest was now taking place.

When the coroner had finished reading he put the book into his breast pocket. At that moment the door was pushed open and a young man entered. He, clearly, was not of mountain birth and breeding: he was clad as those who dwell in cities. His clothing was dusty, however, as from travel. He had, in fact, been riding hard to attend the inquest.

The coroner nodded; no one else greeted him.

"We have waited for you," said the coroner. "It is necessary to have done with this business tonight."

The young man smiled. "I am sorry to have kept you," he said. "I went away, not to evade your summons, but to post to my newspaper an account of what I suppose I am called back to relate."

The coroner smiled.

"The account that you posted to your newspaper," he said, "differs, probably, from that which you will give here under oath."

"That," replied the other, rather hotly and with a visible flush, "is as you please. I used manifold paper and have a copy of what I sent. It was not written as news, for it is incredible, but as fiction. It may go as a part of my testimony under oath."

"But you say it is incredible."

"That is nothing to you, sir, if I also swear that it is true."

The coroner was silent for a time, his eyes upon the floor. The men about the sides of the cabin talked in whispers, but seldom withdrew their gaze from the face of the corpse. Presently the coroner lifted his eyes and said: "We will resume the inquest."

The men removed their hats. The witness was sworn.

"What is your name?" the coroner asked.

"William Harker."

"Age?"

"Twenty-seven."

"You knew the deceased, Hugh Morgan?"

"Yes."

"You were with him when he died?"

"Near him."

"How did that happen—your presence, I mean?"

"I was visiting him at this place to shoot and fish. A part of my purpose, however, was to study him and his odd, solitary way of life. He seemed a good model for a character in fiction. I sometimes write stories."

"I sometimes read them."

"Thank you."

"Stories in general—not yours."

Some of the jurors laughed. Against a sombre background humor shows high lights. Soldiers in the intervals of battle laugh easily, and a jest in the death chamber conquers by surprise.

"Relate the circumstances of this man's death," said the coroner. "You may use any notes or memoranda that you please."

The witness understood. Pulling a manuscript from his breast pocket he held it near the candle and turning the leaves until he found the passage that he wanted began to read.

2

**What May Happen in a Field of Wild Oats**

". . . The sun had hardly risen when we left the house. We were looking for quail, each with a shotgun, but we had only one dog. Morgan said that our best ground was beyond a certain ridge that he pointed out, and we crossed it by a trail through the *chaparral*[1]. On the other side was comparatively level ground, thickly covered with

---

[1] *chaparral*; from Spanish: dwarf evergreen oak.

wild oats. As we emerged from the *chaparral* Morgan was but a few yards in advance. Suddenly we heard, at a little distance to our right and partly in front, a noise as of some animal thrashing about in the bushes, which we could see were violently agitated.

" 'We've started a deer,' I said. 'I wish we had brought a rifle.'

"Morgan, who had stopped and was intently watching the agitated *chaparral,* said nothing, but had cocked both barrels of his gun and was holding it in readiness to aim. I thought him a trifle excited, which surprised me, for he had a reputation for exceptional coolness, even in moments of sudden and imminent peril.

" 'Oh, come,' I said. 'You are not going to fill up a deer with quail-shot, are you?'

"Still he did not reply; but catching sight of his face as he turned it slightly toward me I was struck by the intensity of his look. Then I understood that we had serious business in hand and my first conjecture was that we had 'jumped' a grizzly. I advanced to Morgan's side, cocking my piece as I moved.

"The bushes were now quiet and the sounds had ceased, but Morgan was as attentive to the place as before.

" 'What is it? What the devil is it?' I asked.

" 'That Damned Thing!' he replied, without turning his head. His voice was husky and unnatural. He trembled visibly.

"I was about to speak further, when I observed the wild oats near the place of the disturbance moving in the most inexplicable way. I can hardly describe it. It seemed as if stirred by a streak of wind, which not only bent it, but pressed it down—crushed it so that it did not rise; and this movement was slowly prolonging itself directly toward us.

"Nothing that I had ever seen had affected me so strangely as this unfamiliar and unaccountable phenomenon, yet I am unable to recall any sense of fear. I remember—and tell it here because, singularly enough, I recollected it then—that once in looking carelessly out of an open window I momentarily mistook a small tree close at hand for one of a group of larger trees at a little distance away. It looked the same size as the others, but being more distinctly and sharply defined in mass and detail seemed out of harmony with them. It was a mere falsification of the law of aerial perspective, but it startled, almost terrified me. We so rely upon the orderly operation of familiar natural laws that any seeming suspension of them is noted as a menace to our safety, a warning of unthinkable calamity. So now the apparently causeless movement of the herbage and the slow, undeviating approach of the line of disturbance were distinctly disquieting. My companion appeared actually frightened, and I could hardly credit my senses when I saw him suddenly throw his gun to his shoulder and fire both barrels at the agitated grain! Before the smoke of the discharge had cleared away I heard a loud savage cry—a scream like that of a wild animal—and flinging his gun upon the ground Morgan sprang away and ran swiftly from the spot. At the same instant I was thrown violently to the ground by the impact of something unseen in the smoke—some soft, heavy substance that seemed thrown against me with great force.

"Before I could get upon my feet and recover my gun, which seemed to have been struck from my hands, I heard Morgan crying out as if in mortal agony, and mingling with his cries were such hoarse, savage sounds as one hears from fighting dogs. Inexpressibly terrified, I struggled to my feet and looked in the direction of Morgan's retreat; and may Heaven in mercy spare me from another sight like that! At a distance of less than thirty yards was my friend, down upon one knee, his head thrown back at a frightful angle, hatless, his long hair in disorder and his whole body in violent movement from side to side, backward and forward. His right arm was lifted and seemed to lack the hand—at least, I could see none. The other arm was invisible. At times, as my memory now reports this extraordinary scene, I could discern but a part of his body; it was as if he had been partly blotted out—I cannot otherwise express it—then a shifting of his position would bring it all into view again.

"All this must have occurred within a few seconds, yet in that time Morgan assumed all the postures of a determined wrestler vanquished by superior weight and strength. I saw nothing but him and not always distinctly. During the entire incident his shouts and curses were heard, as if through an enveloping uproar of such sounds of rage and fury as I had never heard from the throat of man or brute!

"For a moment only I stood irresolute, then throwing down my gun I ran forward to my friend's assistance. I had a vague belief that he was suffering from a fit, or some form of convulsion. Before I could reach his side he was down and quiet. All sounds had ceased, but with a feeling of such terror as even these awful events had not inspired I now saw again the mysterious movement of the wild oats, prolonging itself from the trampled area about the prostrate man toward the edge of a wood. It was only when it had reached the wood that I was able to withdraw my eyes and look at my companion. He was dead."

## 3

## A Man Though Naked May Be in Rags

The coroner rose from his seat and stood beside the dead man. Lifting an edge of the sheet he pulled it away, exposing the entire body, altogether naked and showing in the candle-light a clay-like yellow. It had, however, broad maculations of bluish black, obviously caused by extravasated blood from contusions. The chest and sides looked as if they had been beaten with a bludgeon. There were dreadful lacerations; the skin was torn in strips and shreds.

The coroner moved round to the end of the table and undid a silk handkerchief which had been passed under the chin and knotted on the top of the head. When the handkerchief was drawn away it exposed what had been the throat. Some of the jurors who had risen to get a better view repented their curiosity and turned away their faces. Witness Harker went to the open window and leaned out across the sill, faint and sick. Dropping the handkerchief upon the dead man's neck the coroner stepped to an angle of the room and from a pile of clothing produced one garment after another, each of which he held up a moment for inspection. All were torn, and stiff with blood. The jurors did not make a closer inspection. They seemed rather uninterested. They had, in truth, seen all this before; the only thing that was new to them being Harker's testimony.

"Gentlemen," the coroner said, "we have no more evidence, I think. Your duty has been already explained to you; if there is nothing you wish to ask you may go outside and consider your verdict."

The foreman rose—a tall, bearded man of sixty, coarsely clad.

"I shall like to ask one question, Mr. Coroner," he said. "What asylum did this yer last witness escape from?"

"Mr. Harker," said the coroner gravely and tranquilly, "from what asylum did you last escape?"

Harker flushed crimson again, but said nothing, and the seven jurors rose and solemnly filed out of the cabin.

"If you have done insulting me, sir," said Harker, as soon as he and the officer were left alone with the dead man, "I suppose I am at liberty to go?"

"Yes."

Harker started to leave, but paused, with his hand on the door latch. The habit of his profession was strong in him—stronger than his sense of personal dignity. He turned about and said:

"The book you have there—I recognize it as Morgan's diary. You seemed greatly interested in it; you read in it while I was testifying. May I see it? The public would like—"

"The book will cut no figure in this matter," replied the official, slipping it into his coat pocket; "all the entries in it were made before the writer's death."

As Harker passed out of the house the jury reentered and stood about the table, on which the now covered corpse showed under the sheet with sharp definition. The foreman seated himself near the candle, produced from his breast pocket a pencil and scrap of paper and wrote rather laboriously the following verdict, which with various degrees of effort all signed:

"We, the jury, do find that the remains come to their death at the hands of a mountain lion, but some of us thinks, all the same, they had fits."

## 4

## An Explanation from the Tomb

In the diary of the late Hugh Morgan are certain interesting entries having, possibly, a scientific value as suggestions. At the inquest upon his body the book was not put in evidence; possibly the coroner thought it not worthwhile to confuse the jury. The date of the first of the entries mentioned cannot be ascertained; the upper part of the leaf is torn away; the part of the entry remaining follows:

". . . would run in a half-circle, keeping his head turned always toward the centre, and again he would stand still, barking furiously. At last he ran away into the brush as fast as he could go. I thought at first that he had gone mad, but on returning to the house found no other alteration in his manner than what was obviously due to fear of punishment.

"Can a dog see with his nose? Do odours impress some cerebral centre with images of the thing that emitted them? . . .

"Sept. 2.—Looking at the stars last night as they rose above the crest of the ridge east of the house, I observed them successively disappear—from left to right. Each was eclipsed but an instant, and only a few at the same time, but along the entire length of the ridge all that were within a degree or two of the crest were blotted out. It was as if something had passed along between me and them; but I could not see it, and the stars were not thick enough to define its outline. Ugh! don't like this. . . ."

Several weeks' entries are missing, three leaves being torn from the book.

"Sept. 27.—It has been about here again—I find evidences of its presence every day. I watched again all last night in the same cover, gun in hand, double-charged with buckshot. In the morning the fresh footprints were there, as before. Yet I would have sworn that I did not sleep—indeed, I hardly sleep at all. It is terrible, insupportable! If these amazing experiences are real I shall go mad; if they are fanciful I am mad already.

"Oct. 3.—I shall not go—it shall not drive me away. No, this is *my* house, *my* land. God hates a coward. . . .

"Oct. 5.—I can stand it no longer; I have invited Harker to pass a few weeks with me—he has a level head. I can judge from his manner if he thinks me mad.

"Oct. 7.—I have the solution of the mystery; it came to me last night—suddenly, as by revelation. How simple—how terribly simple!

"There are sounds we cannot hear. At either end of the scale are notes that stir no chord of that imperfect instrument, the human ear. They are too high or too grave. I have observed a flock of blackbirds occupying an entire tree-top—the tops of several trees—and all in full song. Suddenly—in a moment—at absolutely the same instant—all spring into the air and fly away. How? They could not all see one another—whole tree-tops intervened. At no point could a leader have been visible to all. There must have been a signal of warning or command, high and shrill above the din, but by me unheard. I have observed, too, the same simultaneous flight when all were silent, among not only blackbirds, but other birds—quail, for example, widely separated by bushes—even on opposite sides of a hill.

"It is known to seamen that a school of whales basking or sporting on the surface of the ocean, miles apart, with the convexity of the earth between, will sometimes dive at the same instant—all gone out of sight in a moment. The signal has been sounded—too grave for the ear of the sailor at the masthead and his comrades on the deck—who nevertheless feel its vibrations in the ship as the stones of a cathedral are stirred by the bass of the organ.

"As with sounds, so with colors. At each end of the solar spectrum the chemist can detect the presence of what are known as 'actinic' rays. They represent colors—integral colors in the composition of light—which we are unable to discern. The human eye is an imperfect instrument; its range is but a few octaves of the real 'chromatic scale.' I am not mad; there are colors that we cannot see.

"And, God help me! the Damned Thing is of such a color!"

# THE BOARDED WINDOW

## Ambrose Bierce

In 1830, ONLY a few miles away from what is now the great city of Cincinnati lay an immense and almost unbroken forest. The whole region was sparsely settled by people of the frontier—restless souls who no sooner had hewn fairly habitable homes out of the wilderness and attained to that degree of prosperity which today we should call indigence than impelled by some mysterious impulse of their nature they abandoned all and pushed farther westward, to encounter new perils and privations in the effort to regain the meagre comforts which they had voluntarily renounced. Many of them had already forsaken that region for the remoter settlements, but among those remaining was one who had been of those first arriving. He lived alone in a house of logs surrounded on all sides by the great forest, of whose gloom and silence he seemed a part, for no one had ever known him to smile nor speak a needless word. His simple wants were supplied by the sale or barter of skins of wild animals in the river town, for not a thing did he grow upon the land which, if needful, he might have claimed by right of undisturbed possession. There were evidences of "improvement"—a few acres of ground immediately about the house had once been cleared of its trees, the decayed stumps of which were half concealed by the new growth that had been suffered to repair the ravage wrought by the ax. Apparently the man's zeal for agriculture had burned with a failing flame, expiring in penitential ashes.

The little log house, with its chimney of sticks, its roof of warping clapboards weighted with traversing poles and its "chinking" of clay, had a single door and, directly opposite, a window. The latter, however, was boarded up—nobody could remember a time when it was not. And none knew why it was so closed; certainly not because of the occupant's dislike of light and air, for on those rare occasions when a hunter had passed that lonely spot the recluse had commonly been seen sunning himself on his doorstep if heaven had provided sunshine for his need. I fancy there are few persons living today who ever knew the secret of that window, but I am one, as you shall see.

The man's name was said to be Murlock. He was apparently seventy years old, actually about fifty. Something besides years had had a hand in his aging. His hair and long, full beard were white, his gray, lustreless eyes sunken, his face singularly seamed with wrinkles which appeared to belong to two intersecting systems. In figure he was tall and spare, with a stoop of the shoulders—a burden bearer. I never saw him; these particulars I learned from my grandfather, from whom also I got the man's story when I was a lad. He had known him when living nearby in that early day.

One day Murlock was found in his cabin, dead. It was not a time and place for coroners and newspapers, and I suppose it was agreed that he had died from natural causes or I should have been told, and should remember. I know only that with what was probably a sense of the fitness of things the body was buried near the cabin, alongside the grave of his wife, who had preceded him by so many years that local tradition had retained hardly a hint of her existence. That closes the final chapter of this true story—excepting, indeed, the circumstance that many years afterward, in company with an equally intrepid spirit, I penetrated to the place and ventured near enough to the ruined cabin to throw a stone against it, and ran away to avoid the ghost which every well-informed boy thereabout knew haunted the spot. But there is an earlier chapter—that supplied by my grandfather.

When Murlock built his cabin and began laying sturdily about with his ax to hew out a farm—the rifle, meanwhile, his means of support—he was young, strong, and full of hope. In that eastern country whence he came he had married, as was the fashion, a young woman in all ways worthy of his honest devotion, who shared the dangers and privations of his lot with a willing spirit and light heart. There is no known record of her name; of her charms of mind and person tradition is silent and the doubter is at liberty to entertain his doubt; but God forbid that I should share it! Of their affection and happiness there is abundant assurance in every added day of the man's widowed life; for what but the magnetism of a blessed memory could have chained that venturesome spirit to a lot like that?

One day Murlock returned from gunning in a distant part of the forest to find his wife prostrate with fever, and delirious. There was no physician within miles, no neighbor; nor was she in a condition to be left, to summon help. So he set about the task of nursing her back to health, but at the end of the third day she fell into unconsciousness and so passed away, apparently, with never a gleam of returning reason.

From what we know of a nature like his we may venture to sketch in some of the details of the outline picture drawn by my grandfather. When convinced that she was dead, Murlock had sense enough to remember that the dead must be prepared for burial. In performance of this sacred duty he blundered now and again, did certain things incorrectly, and others which he did correctly were done over and over. His occasional failures to accomplish some simple and ordinary act filled him with astonishment, like that of a drunken man who wonders at the suspension of familiar natural laws. He was surprised, too, that he did not weep—surprised and a little ashamed; surely it is unkind not to weep for the dead. "Tomorrow," he said aloud, "I shall have to make the coffin and dig the grave; and then I shall miss her, when she is no longer in sight; but now—she is dead, of course, but it is all right—it *must* be all right, somehow. Things cannot be so bad as they seem."

He stood over the body in the fading light, adjusting the hair and putting the finishing touches to the simple toilet, doing all mechanically, with soulless care. And still through his consciousness ran an under-sense of conviction that all was right—that he should have her again as before, and everything explained. He had had no experience in grief; his capacity had not been enlarged by use. His heart could not contain it all, nor his imagination rightly conceive it. He did not know he was so hard struck; *that* knowledge would come later, and never go. Grief is an artist of powers as various as the instruments upon which he plays his dirges for the dead, evoking from some the sharpest, shrillest notes, from others the low, grave chords that throb recurrent like the slow beating of a distant drum. Some natures it startles; some it stupefies. To one it comes like the stroke of an arrow, stinging all the sensibilities to a keener life; to another as the blow of a bludgeon, which in crushing benumbs. We may conceive Murlock to have been that way affected, for (and here we are upon surer ground than that of conjecture) no sooner had he finished his pious work than, sinking into a chair by the side of the table upon which the body lay, and noting how white the profile showed in the deepening gloom, he laid his arms upon the table's edge, and dropped his face into them, tearless yet and unutterably weary. At that moment came in through the open window a long, wailing sound like the cry of a lost child in the far deeps of the darkening wood! But the man did not move. Again, and nearer than before, sounded that unearthly cry upon his failing sense. Perhaps it was a wild beast; perhaps it was a dream. For Murlock was asleep.

Some hours later, as it afterward appeared, this unfaithful watcher awoke and lifting his head from his arms intently listened—he knew not why. There in the black darkness by the side of the dead, recalling all without a shock, he strained his eyes to see—he knew not what. His senses were all alert, his breath was suspended, his blood had stilled its tides as if to assist the silence. Who—what had waked him, and where was it?

Suddenly the table shook beneath his arms, and at the same moment he heard, or fancied that he heard, a light, soft step—another—sounds as of bare feet upon the floor!

He was terrified beyond the power to cry out or move. Perforce he waited—waited there in the darkness through seeming centuries of such dread as one may know, yet live to tell. He tried vainly to speak the dead woman's name, vainly to stretch forth his hand across the table to learn if she were there. His throat was powerless, his arms and hands were like lead. Then occurred something most frightful. Some heavy body seemed hurled against the table with an impetus that pushed it against his breast so sharply as nearly to overthrow him, and at the same instant he heard and felt the fall of something upon the floor with so violent a thump that the whole house was shaken by the impact. A scuffling ensued, and a confusion of sounds impossible to describe. Murlock had risen to his feet. Fear had by excess forfeited control of his faculties. He flung his hands upon the table. Nothing was there!

There is a point at which terror may turn to madness; and madness incites to action. With no definite intent, from no motive but the wayward impulse of a madman, Murlock sprang to the wall, with a little groping seized his loaded rifle, and without aim discharged it. By the flash which lit up the room with a vivid illumination, he saw an enormous panther dragging the dead woman toward the window, its teeth fixed in her throat! Then there were darkness blacker than before, and silence; and when he returned to consciousness the sun was high and the wood vocal with songs of birds.

The body lay near the window, where the beast had left it when frightened away by the flash and report of the rifle. The clothing was deranged, the long hair in disorder, the limbs lay anyhow. From the throat, dreadfully lacerated, had issued a pool of blood not yet entirely coagulated. The ribbon with which he had bound the wrists was broken; the hands were tightly clenched. Between the teeth was a fragment of the animal's ear.

# MY FAVORITE MURDER

## Ambrose Bierce

HAVING MURDERED MY mother under circumstances of singular atrocity, I was arrested and put upon my trial, which lasted seven years. In charging the jury, the judge of the Court of Acquittal remarked that it was one of the most ghastly crimes that he had ever been called upon to explain away.

At this, my attorney rose and said:

"May it please your Honor, crimes are ghastly or agreeable only by comparison. If you were familiar with the details of my client's previous murder of his uncle you would discern in his later offense (if offense it may be called) something in the nature of tender forbearance and filial consideration for the feelings of the victim. The appalling ferocity of the former assassination was indeed inconsistent with any hypothesis but that of guilt; and had it not been for the fact that the honorable judge before whom he was tried was the president of a life insurance company that took risks on hanging, and in which my client held a policy, it is hard to see how he could decently have been acquitted. If your Honor would like to hear about it for instruction and guidance of your Honor's mind, this unfortunate man, my client, will consent to give himself the pain of relating it under oath."

The district attorney said: "Your Honor, I object. Such a statement would be in the nature of evidence, and the testimony in this case is closed. The prisoner's statement should have been introduced three years ago, in the spring of 1881."

"In a statutory sense," said the judge, "you are right, and in the Court of Objections and Technicalities you would get a ruling in your favor. But not in a Court of Acquittal. The objection is overruled."

"I except," said the district attorney.

"You cannot do that," the judge said. "I must remind you that in order to take an exception you must first get this case transferred for a time to the Court of Exceptions on a formal motion duly supported by affidavits. A motion to that effect by your predecessor in office was denied by me during the first year of this trial. Mr. Clerk, swear the prisoner."

The customary oath having been administered, I made the following statement, which impressed the judge with so strong a sense of the comparative triviality of the offense for which I was on trial that he made no further search for mitigating circumstances, but simply instructed the jury to acquit, and I left the court, without a stain upon my reputation:

"I was born in 1856 in Kalamakee, Mich., of honest and reputable parents, one of whom Heaven has mercifully spared to comfort me in my later years. In 1867 the family came to California and settled near Nigger Head, where my father opened a road agency and prospered beyond the dreams of avarice. He was a reticent, saturnine man then, though his increasing years have now somewhat relaxed the austerity of his disposition, and I believe that nothing but his memory of the sad event for which I am now on trial prevents him from manifesting a genuine hilarity.

"Four years after we had set up the road agency an itinerant preacher came along, and having no other way to pay for the night's lodging that we gave him, favored us with an exhortation of such power that, praise God, we were all converted to religion. My father at once sent for his brother, the Hon. William Ridley of Stockton, and on his arrival turned over the agency to him, charging him nothing for the franchise nor plant—the latter consisting of a Winchester rifle, a sawed-off shotgun, and an assortment of masks made out of flour sacks. The family then moved to Ghost Rock and opened a dance house. It was called 'The Saints' Rest Hurdy-Gurdy,' and the proceedings each night began with prayer. It was there that my now sainted mother, by her grace in the dance, acquired the sobriquet of 'The Bucking Walrus.'

"In the fall of '75 I had occasion to visit Coyote, on the road to Mahala, and took the stage at Ghost Rock. There were four other passengers. About three miles beyond Nigger Head, persons whom

I identified as my Uncle William and his two sons held up the stage.
Finding nothing in the express box, they went through the passengers.
I acted a most honorable part in the affair, placing myself in line with
the others, holding up my hands and permitting myself to be deprived
of forty dollars and a gold watch. From my behavior no one could
have suspected that I knew the gentlemen who gave the entertainment.
A few days later, when I went to Nigger Head and asked for the
return of my money and watch my uncle and cousins swore they
knew nothing of the matter, and they affected a belief that my father
and I had done the job ourselves in dishonest violation of commercial
good faith. Uncle William even threatened to retaliate by starting an
opposition dance house at Ghost Rock. As 'The Saints' Rest' had
become rather unpopular, I saw that this would assuredly ruin it and
prove a paying enterprise, so I told my uncle that I was willing to
overlook the past if he would take me into the scheme and keep the
partnership a secret from my father. This fair offer he rejected, and
I then perceived that it would be better and more satisfactory if he
were dead.

"My plans to that end were soon perfected, and communicating
them to my dear parents I had the gratification of receiving their
approval. My father said he was proud of me, and my mother promised
that although her religion forbade her to assist in taking human life
I should have the advantage of her prayers for my success. As a
preliminary measure looking to my security in case of detection I
made an application for membership in that powerful order, the
Knights of Murder, and in due course was received as a member of
the Ghost Rock commandery. On the day that my probation ended
I was for the first time permitted to inspect the records of the order
and learn who belonged to it—all the rites of initiation having been
conducted in masks. Fancy my delight when, in looking over the
roll of membership, I found the third name to be that of my uncle,
who indeed was junior vice-chancellor of the order! Here was an
opportunity exceeding my wildest dreams—to murder I could add
insubordination and treachery. It was what my good mother would
have called 'a special Providence.'

"At about this time something occurred which caused my cup of
joy, already full, to overflow on all sides, a circular cataract of bliss.
Three men, strangers in that locality, were arrested for the stage
robbery in which I had lost my money and watch. They were brought
to trial and, despite my efforts to clear them and fasten the guilt upon
three of the most respectable and worthy citizens of Ghost Rock,

convicted on the clearest proof. The murder would now be as wanton and reasonless as I could wish.

"One morning I shouldered my Winchester rifle, and going over to my uncle's house, near Nigger Head, asked my Aunt Mary, his wife, if he were at home, adding that I had come to kill him. My aunt replied with her peculiar smile that so many gentlemen called on that errand and were afterward carried away without having performed it that I must excuse her for doubting my good faith in the matter. She said I did not look as if I would kill anybody, so, as a proof of good faith I leveled my rifle and wounded a Chinaman who happened to be passing the house. She said she knew whole families that could do a thing of that kind, but Bill Ridley was a horse of another color. She said, however, that I would find him over on the other side of the creek in the sheep lot; and she added that she hoped the best man would win.

"My Aunt Mary was one of the most fair-minded women that I have ever met.

"I found my uncle down on his knees engaged in skinning a sheep. Seeing that he had neither gun nor pistol handy I had not the heart to shoot him, so I approached him, greeted him pleasantly and struck him a powerful blow on the head with the butt of my rifle. I have a very good delivery and Uncle William lay down on his side, then rolled over on his back, spread out his fingers and shivered. Before he could recover the use of his limbs I seized the knife that he had been using and cut his hamstrings. You know, doubtless, that when you sever the *tendo Achillis*[1] the patient has no further use of his leg; it is just the same as if he had no leg. Well, I parted them both, and when he revived he was at my service. As soon as he comprehended the situation, he said:

"'Samuel, you have got the drop on me and can afford to be generous. I have only one thing to ask of you, and that is that you carry me to the house and finish me in the bosom of my family.'

"I told him I thought that a pretty reasonable request and I would do so if he would let me put him into a wheat sack; he would be easier to carry that way and if we were seen by the neighbors en route it would cause less remark. He agreed to that, and going to the barn I got a sack. This, however, did not fit him; it was too short and much wider than he; so I bent his legs, forced his knees up against his breast and got him into it that way, tying the sack above his head.

---

[1] *tendo Achillis*; Latin: Achilles tendon.

He was a heavy man and I had all that I could do to get him on my back, but I staggered along for some distance until I came to a swing that some of the children had suspended to the branch of an oak. Here I laid him down and sat upon him to rest, and the sight of the rope gave me a happy inspiration. In twenty minutes my uncle, still in the sack, swung free to the sport of the wind.

"I had taken down the rope, tied one end tightly about the mouth of the bag, thrown the other across the limb and hauled him up about five feet from the ground. Fastening the other end of the rope also about the mouth of the sack, I had the satisfaction to see my uncle converted into a large, fine pendulum. I must add that he was not himself entirely aware of the nature of the change that he had undergone in his relation to the exterior world, though in justice to a good man's memory I ought to say that I do not think he would in any case have wasted much of my time in vain remonstrance.

"Uncle William had a ram that was famous in all that region as a fighter. It was in a state of chronic constitutional indignation. Some deep disappointment in early life had soured its disposition and it had declared war upon the whole world. To say that it would butt anything accessible is but faintly to express the nature and scope of its military activity: the universe was its antagonist; its methods that of a projectile. It fought like the angels and devils, in mid-air, cleaving the atmosphere like a bird, describing a parabolic curve and descending upon its victim at just the exact angle of incidence to make the most of its velocity and weight. Its momentum, calculated in foot-tons, was something incredible. It had been seen to destroy a four year old bull by a single impact upon that animal's gnarly forehead. No stone wall had ever been known to resist its downward swoop; there were no trees tough enough to stay it; it would splinter them into matchwood and defile their leafy honors in the dust. This irascible and implacable brute—this incarnate thunderbolt—this monster of the upper deep, I had seen reposing in the shade of an adjacent tree, dreaming dreams of conquest and glory. It was with a view to summoning it forth to the field of honor that I suspended its master in the manner described.

"Having completed my preparations, I imparted to the avuncular pendulum a gentle oscillation, and retiring to cover behind a contiguous rock, lifted up my voice in a long rasping cry whose diminishing final note was drowned in a noise like that of a swearing cat, which emanated from the sack. Instantly that formidable sheep was upon its feet and had taken in the military situation at a glance.

In a few moments it had approached, stamping, to within fifty yards of the swinging foeman, who, now retreating and anon advancing, seemed to invite the fray. Suddenly I saw the beast's head drop earthward as if depressed by the weight of its enormous horns; then a dim, white, wavy streak of sheep prolonged itself from that spot in a generally horizontal direction to within about four yards of a point immediately beneath the enemy. There it struck sharply upward, and before it had faded from my gaze at the place whence it had set out I heard a horrid thump and a piercing scream, and my poor uncle shot forward, with a slack rope higher than the limb to which he was attached. Here the rope tautened with a jerk, arresting his flight, and back he swung in a breathless curve to the other end of his arc. The ram had fallen, a heap of indistinguishable legs, wool and horns, but pulling itself together and dodging as its antagonist swept downward it retired at random, alternately shaking its head and stamping its fore-feet. When it had backed about the same distance as that from which it had delivered the assault it paused again, bowed its head as if in prayer for victory and again shot forward, dimly visible as before—a prolonging white streak with monstrous undulations, ending with a sharp ascension. Its course this time was at a right angle to its former one, and its impatience so great that it struck the enemy before he had nearly reached the lowest point of his arc. In consequence he went flying round and round in a horizontal circle whose radius was about equal to half the length of the rope, which I forgot to say was nearly twenty feet long. His shrieks, crescendo in approach and diminuendo in recession, made the rapidity of his revolution more obvious to the ear than to the eye. He had evidently not yet been struck in a vital spot. His posture in the sack and the distance from the ground at which he hung compelled the ram to operate upon his lower extremities and the end of his back. Like a plant that has struck its root into some poisonous mineral, my poor uncle was dying slowly upward.

"After delivering its second blow the ram had not again retired. The fever of battle burned hot in its heart; its brain was intoxicated with the wine of strife. Like a pugilist who in his rage forgets his skill and fights ineffectively at half-arm's length, the angry beast endeavored to reach its fleeting foe by awkward vertical leaps as he passed overhead, sometimes, indeed, succeeding in striking him feebly, but more frequently overthrown by its own misguided eagerness. But as the impetus was exhausted and the man's circles narrowed in scope and diminished in speed, bringing him nearer to the ground, these tactics produced better results, eliciting a superior quality of screams, which I greatly enjoyed.

"Suddenly, as if the bugles had sung truce, the ram suspended hostilities and walked away, thoughtfully wrinkling and smoothing its great aquiline nose, and occasionally cropping a bunch of grass and slowly munching it. It seemed to have tired of war's alarms and resolved to beat the sword into a plowshare and cultivate the arts of peace. Steadily it held its course away from the field of fame until it had gained a distance of nearly a quarter of a mile. There it stopped and stood with its rear to the foe, chewing its cud and apparently half asleep. I observed, however, an occasional slight turn of its head, as if its apathy were more affected than real.

"Meantime Uncle William's shrieks had abated with his motion, and nothing was heard from him but long, low moans, and at long intervals my name, uttered in pleading tones exceedingly grateful to my ear. Evidently the man had not the faintest notion of what was being done to him, and was inexpressibly terrified. When Death comes cloaked in mystery he is terrible indeed. Little by little my uncle's oscillations diminished, and finally he hung motionless. I went to him and was about to give him the *coup de grâce*[2], when I heard and felt a succession of smart shocks which shook the ground like a series of light earthquakes, and turning in the direction of the ram, saw a long cloud of dust approaching me with inconceivable rapidity and alarming effect! At a distance of some thirty yards away it stopped short, and from the near end of it rose into the air what I at first thought a great white bird. Its ascent was so smooth and easy and regular that I could not realize its extraordinary celerity, and was lost in admiration of its grace. To this day the impression remains that it was a slow, deliberate movement, the ram—for it was that animal—being upborne by some power other than its own impetus, and supported through the successive stages of its flight with infinite tenderness and care. My eyes followed its progress through the air with unspeakable pleasure, all the greater by contrast with my former terror of its approach by land. Onward and upward the noble animal sailed, its head bent down almost between its knees, its fore-feet thrown back, its hinder legs trailing to rear like the legs of a soaring heron.

"At a height of forty or fifty feet, as fond recollection presents it to view, it attained its zenith and appeared to remain an instant

---

[2] *coup de grâce*; French: a decisive, finishing blow.

stationary; then, tilting suddenly forward without altering the relative position of its parts, it shot downward on a steeper and steeper course with augmenting velocity, passed immediately above me with a noise like the rush of a cannon shot and struck my poor uncle almost squarely on the top of the head! So frightful was the impact that not only the man's neck was broken, but the rope too; and the body of the deceased, forced against the earth, was crushed to pulp beneath the awful front of that meteoric sheep! The concussion stopped all the clocks between Lone Hand and Dutch Dan's, and Professor Davidson, a distinguished authority in matters seismic, who happened to be in the vicinity, promptly explained that the vibrations were from north to southwest.

"Altogether, I cannot help thinking that in point of artistic atrocity my murder of Uncle William has seldom been excelled."

# THE EYES OF THE PANTHER

### Ambrose Bierce

## I. One Does Not Always Marry When Insane

A MAN AND a woman—nature had done the grouping—sat on a rustic seat, in the late afternoon. The man was middle-aged, slender, swarthy, with the expression of a poet and the complexion of a pirate—a man at whom one would look again. The woman was young, blonde, graceful, with something in her figure and movements suggesting the word "lithe." She was habited in a gray gown with odd brown markings in the texture. She may have been beautiful; one could not readily say, for her eyes denied attention to all else. They were gray-green, long and narrow, with an expression defying analysis. One could only know that they were disquieting. Cleopatra may have had such eyes.

The man and the woman talked.

"Yes," said the woman, "I love you, God knows! But marry you, no. I cannot, will not."

"Irene, you have said that many times, yet always have denied me a reason. I've a right to know, to understand, to feel and prove my fortitude if I have it. Give me a reason."

"For loving you?"

The woman was smiling through her tears and her pallor. That did not stir any sense of humor in the man.

"No; there is no reason for that. A reason for not marrying me. I've a right to know. I must know. I will know!"

He had risen and was standing before her with clenched hands, on his face a frown—it might have been called a scowl. He looked

100

as if he might attempt to learn by strangling her. She smiled no more—merely sat looking up into his face with a fixed, set regard that was utterly without emotion or sentiment. Yet it had something in it that tamed his resentment and made him shiver.

"You are determined to have my reason?" she asked in a tone that was entirely mechanical—a tone that might have been her look made audible.

"If you please—if I'm not asking too much."

Apparently this lord of creation was yielding some part of his dominion over his co-creature.

"Very well, you shall know: I am insane."

The man started, then looked incredulous and was conscious that he ought to be amused. But, again, the sense of humor failed him in his need, and despite his disbelief he was profoundly disturbed by that which he did not believe. Between our convictions and our feelings there is no good understanding.

"That is what the physicians would say," the woman continued—"if they knew. I might myself prefer to call it a case of 'possession.' Sit down and hear what I have to say."

The man silently resumed his seat beside her on the rustic bench by the wayside. Over against them on the eastern side of the valley the hills were already sunset-flushed and the stillness all about was of that peculiar quality that foretells the twilight. Something of its mysterious and significant solemnity had imparted itself to the man's mood. In the spiritual, as in the material world, are signs and presages of night. Rarely meeting her look, and whenever he did so conscious of the indefinable dread with which, despite their feline beauty, her eyes always affected him, Jenner Brading listened in silence to the story told by Irene Marlowe. In deference to the reader's possible prejudice against the artless method of an unpracticed historian the author ventures to substitute his own version for hers.

## II. A Room May Be Too Narrow for Three, Though One Is Outside

In a little log house containing a single room sparely and rudely furnished, crouching on the floor against one of the walls, was a woman, clasping to her breast a child. Outside, a dense unbroken forest extended for many miles in every direction. This was at night and the room was black dark: no human eye could have discerned the woman and the child. Yet they were observed, narrowly, vigilantly, with never even a momentary slackening of attention; and that is the pivotal fact upon which this narrative turns.

Charles Marlowe was of the class, now extinct in this country, of woodmen pioneers—men who found their most acceptable surroundings in sylvan solitudes that stretched along the eastern slope of the Mississippi Valley, from the Great Lakes to the Gulf of Mexico. For more than a hundred years these men pushed ever westward, generation after generation, with rifle and ax, reclaiming from Nature and her savage children here and there an isolated acreage for the plow, no sooner reclaimed than surrendered to their less venturesome but more thrifty successors. At last they burst through the edge of the forest into the open country and vanished as if they had fallen over a cliff. The woodman pioneer is no more; the pioneer of the plains—he whose easy task it was to subdue for occupancy two-thirds of the country in a single generation—is another and interior creation. With Charles Marlowe in the wilderness, sharing the dangers, hardships and privations of that strange, unprofitable life, were his wife and child, to whom, in the manner of his class, in which the domestic virtues were a religion, he was passionately attached. The woman was still young enough to be comely, new enough to the awful isolation of her lot to be cheerful. By withholding the large capacity for happiness which the simple satisfactions of the forest life could not have filled, Heaven had dealt honorably with her. In her light household tasks, her child, her husband and her few foolish books, she found abundant provision for her needs.

One morning in midsummer Marlowe took down his rifle from the wooden hooks on the wall and signified his intention of getting game.

"We've meat enough," said the wife; "please don't go out today. I dreamed last night, O, such a dreadful thing! I cannot recollect it, but I'm almost sure that it will come to pass if you go out."

It is painful to confess that Marlowe received this solemn statement with less of gravity than was due to the mysterious nature of the calamity foreshadowed. In truth, he laughed.

"Try to remember," he said. "Maybe you dreamed that Baby had lost the power of speech."

The conjecture was obviously suggested by the fact that Baby, clinging to the fringe of his hunting-coat with all her ten pudgy thumbs, was at that moment uttering her sense of the situation in a series of exultant goo-goos inspired by sight of her father's raccoon-skin cap.

The woman yielded: lacking the gift of humor she could not hold out against his kindly badinage. So, with a kiss for the mother and a kiss for the child, he left the house and closed the door upon his happiness forever.

At nightfall he had not returned. The woman prepared supper and waited. Then she put Baby to bed and sang softly to her until she slept. By this time the fire on the hearth, at which she had cooked supper, had burned out and the room was lighted by a single candle. This she afterward placed in the open window as a sign and welcome to the hunter if he should approach from that side. She had thoughtfully closed and barred the door against such wild animals as might prefer it to an open window—of the habits of beasts of prey in entering a house uninvited she was not advised, though with true female prevision she may have considered the possibility of their entrance by way of the chimney. As the night wore on she became not less anxious, but more drowsy, and at last rested her arms upon the bed by the child and her head upon the arms. The candle in the window burned down to the socket, sputtered and flared a moment and went out unobserved; for the woman slept and dreamed.

In her dreams she sat beside the cradle of a second child. The first one was dead. The father was dead. The home in the forest was lost and the dwelling in which she lived was unfamiliar. There were heavy oaken doors, always closed, and outside the windows, fastened into the thick stone walls, were iron bars, obviously (so she thought) a provision against Indians. All this she noted with an infinite self-pity, but without surprise—an emotion unknown in dreams. The child in the cradle was invisible under its coverlet which something impelled her to remove. She did so, disclosing the face of a wild animal! In the shock of this dreadful revelation the dreamer awoke, trembling in the darkness of her cabin in the wood.

As a sense of her actual surroundings came slowly back to her she felt for the child that was not a dream, and assured herself by its breathing that all was well with it; nor could she forbear to pass a hand lightly across its face. Then, moved by some impulse for which she probably could not have accounted, she rose and took the sleeping babe in her arms, holding it close against her breast. The head of the child's cot was against the wall to which the woman now turned her back as she stood. Lifting her eyes she saw two bright objects starring the darkness with a reddish-green glow. She took them to be two coals on the hearth, but with her returning sense of direction came the disquieting consciousness that they were not in that quarter of the room, moreover were too high, being nearly at the level of the eyes—of her own eyes. For these were the eyes of a panther.

The beast was at the open window directly opposite and not five paces away. Nothing but those terrible eyes was visible, but in the dreadful tumult of her feelings as the situation disclosed itself to her understanding she somehow knew that the animal was standing on its hinder feet, supporting itself with its paws on the window-ledge. That signified a malign interest—not the mere gratification of an indolent curiosity. The consciousness of the attitude was an added horror, accentuating the menace of those awful eyes, in whose steadfast fire her strength and courage were alike consumed. Under their silent questioning she shuddered and turned sick. Her knees failed her, and by degrees, instinctively striving to avoid a sudden movement that might bring the beast upon her, she sank to the floor, crouched against the wall and tried to shield the babe with her trembling body without withdrawing her gaze from the luminous orbs that were killing her. No thought of her husband came to her in her agony—no hope nor suggestion of rescue or escape. Her capacity for thought and feeling had narrowed to the dimensions of a single emotion—fear of the animal's spring, of the impact of its body, the buffeting of its great arms, the feel of its teeth in her throat, the mangling of her babe. Motionless now and in absolute silence, she awaited her doom, the moments growing to hours, to years, to ages; and still those devilish eyes maintained their watch.

Returning to his cabin late at night with a deer on his shoulders, Charles Marlowe tried the door. It did not yield. He knocked; there was no answer. He laid down his deer and went round to the window. As he turned the angle of the building he fancied he heard a sound as of stealthy footfalls and a rustling in the undergrowth of the forest, but they were too slight for certainty, even to his practiced ear. Approaching the window, and to his surprise finding it open, he threw his leg over the sill and entered. All was darkness and silence. He groped his way to the fire-place, struck a match and lit a candle. Then he looked about. Cowering on the floor against a wall was his wife, clasping his child. As he sprang toward her she rose and broke into laughter, long, loud, and mechanical, devoid of gladness and devoid of sense—the laughter that is not out of keeping with the clanking of a chain. Hardly knowing what he did he extended his arms. She laid the babe in them. It was dead—pressed to death in its mother's embrace.

### III. The Theory of the Defense

That is what occurred during a night in a forest, but not all of it did Irene Marlowe relate to Jenner Brading; not all of it was known to her. When she had concluded, the sun was below the horizon and the long summer twilight had begun to deepen in the hollows of the land. For some moments Brading was silent, expecting the narrative to be carried forward to some definite connection with the conversation introducing it; but the narrator was as silent as he, her face averted, her hands clasping and unclasping themselves as they lay in her lap, with a singular suggestion of an activity independent of her will.

"It is a sad, a terrible story," said Brading at last, "but I do not understand. You call Charles Marlowe father; that I know. That he is old before his time, broken by some great sorrow, I have seen, or thought I saw. But, pardon me, you said that you—that you———"

"That I am insane," said the girl, without a movement of head or body.

"But, Irene, you say—please, dear, do not look away from me— you say that the child was dead, not demented."

"Yes, that one—I am the second. I was born three months after that night, my mother being mercifully permitted to lay down her life in giving me mine."

Brading was again silent; he was a trifle dazed and could not at once think of the right thing to say. Her face was still turned away. In his embarrassment he reached impulsively toward the hands that lay closing and unclosing in her lap, but something—he could not have said what—restrained him. He then remembered, vaguely, that he had never altogether cared to take her hand.

"Is it likely," she resumed, "that a person born under such circumstances is like others—is what you call sane?"

Brading did not reply; he was preoccupied with a new thought that was taking shape in his mind—what a scientist would have called an hypothesis; a detective, a theory. It might throw an added light, albeit a lurid one, upon such doubt of her sanity as her own assertion had not dispelled.

The country was still new and, outside the villages, sparsely populated. The professional hunter was still a familiar figure, and among his trophies were heads and pelts of the larger kinds of game. Tales variously credible of nocturnal meetings with savage animals in lonely roads were sometimes current, passed through the customary stages of growth and decay, and were forgotten. A recent addition to these popular apocrypha, originating, apparently, by spontaneous generation in several households, was of a panther which had frightened some of their members by looking in at windows by night. The yarn had caused its little ripple of excitement—had even attained to the distinction of a place in the local newspaper; but Brading had given it no attention. Its likeness to the story to which he had just listened now impressed him as perhaps more than accidental. Was it not possible that one story had suggested the other—that finding congenial conditions in a morbid mind and a fertile fancy, it had grown to the tragic tale that he had heard?

Brading recalled certain circumstances of the girl's history and disposition, of which, with love's incuriosity, he had hitherto been heedless—such as her solitary life with her father, at whose house no one, apparently, was an acceptable visitor, and her strange fear of the night, by which those who knew her best accounted for her never being seen after dark. Surely in such a mind imagination once kindled might burn with a lawless flame, penetrating and enveloping the entire structure. That she was mad, though the conviction gave him the acutest pain, he could no longer doubt; she had only mistaken an effect of her mental disorder for its cause, bringing into imaginary relation with her own personality the vagaries of the local myth-makers. With some vague intention of testing his new "theory," and no very definite notion of how to set about it, he said, gravely, but with hesitation:

"Irene, dear, tell me—I beg you will not take offence, but tell me—"

"I have told you," she interrupted, speaking with a passionate earnestness that he had not known her to show—"I have already told you that we cannot marry; is anything else worth saying?"

Before he could stop her she had sprung from her seat and without another word or look was gliding away among the trees toward her father's house. Brading had risen to detain her; he stood watching her in silence until she had vanished in the gloom. Suddenly he started as if he had been shot; his face took on an expression of amazement and alarm: in one of the black shadows into which she had disappeared he had caught a quick, brief glimpse of shining eyes! For an instant he was dazed and irresolute; then he dashed into the wood after her, shouting: "Irene, Irene, look out! The panther! The panther!"

In a moment he had passed through the fringe of forest into open ground and saw the girl's gray skirt vanishing into her father's door. No panther was visible.

## IV. An Appeal to the Conscience of God

Jenner Brading, attorney-at-law, lived in a cottage at the edge of the town. Directly behind the dwelling was the forest. Being a bachelor, and therefore, by the Draconian moral code of the time and place denied the services of the only species of domestic servant known thereabout, the "hired girl," he boarded at the village hotel, where also was his office. The woodside cottage was merely a lodging maintained—at no great cost, to be sure—as an evidence of prosperity and respectability. It would hardly do for one to whom the local newspaper had pointed with pride as "the foremost jurist of his time" to be "homeless," albeit he may sometimes have suspected that the words "home" and "house" were not strictly synonymous. Indeed, his consciousness of the disparity and his will to harmonize it were matters of logical inference, for it was generally reported that soon after the cottage was built its owner had made a futile venture in the direction of marriage—had, in truth, gone so far as to be rejected by the beautiful but eccentric daughter of Old Man Marlowe, the recluse. This was publicly believed because he had told it himself and she had not—a reversal of the usual order of things which could hardly fail to carry conviction.

Brading's bedroom was at the rear of the house, with a single window facing the forest. One night he was awakened by a noise at that window; he could hardly have said what it was like. With a little thrill of the nerves he sat up in bed and laid hold of the revolver which, with a forethought most commendable in one addicted to the habit of sleeping on the ground floor with an open window, he had put under his pillow. The room was in absolute darkness, but being unterrified he knew where to direct his eyes, and there he held them, awaiting in silence what further might occur. He could now dimly discern the aperture—a square of lighter black. Presently there appeared at its lower edge two gleaming eyes that burned with a malignant lustre inexpressibly terrible! Brading's heart gave a great jump, then seemed to stand still. A chill passed along his spine and through his hair; he felt the blood forsake his cheeks. He could not have cried out—not to save his life; but being a man of courage he would not, to save his life, have done so if he had been able. Some trepidation his coward body might feel, but his spirit was of sterner stuff. Slowly the shining eyes rose with a steady motion that seemed an approach, and slowly rose Brading's right hand, holding the pistol. He fired!

Blinded by the flash and stunned by the report, Brading nevertheless heard, or fancied that he heard, the wild, high scream of the panther, so human in sound, so devilish in suggestion. Leaping from the bed he hastily clothed himself and, pistol in hand, sprang from the door, meeting two or three men who came running up from the road. A brief explanation was followed by a cautious search of the house. The grass was wet with dew; beneath the window it had been trodden and partly leveled for a wide space, from which a devious trail, visible in the light of a lantern, led away into the bushes. One of the men stumbled and fell upon his hands, which as he rose and rubbed them together were slippery. On examination they were seen to be red with blood.

An encounter, unarmed, with a wounded panther was not agreeable to their taste; all but Brading turned back. He, with lantern and pistol, pushed courageously forward into the wood. Passing through a difficult undergrowth he came into a small opening, and there his courage had its reward, for there he found the body of his victim. But it was no panther. What it was is told, even to this day, upon a weather-worn headstone in the village churchyard, and for many years was attested daily at the graveside by the bent figure and sorrow-seamed face of Old Man Marlowe, to whose soul, and to the soul of his strange, unhappy child, peace. Peace and reparation.

# THE MOONLIT ROAD

## Ambrose Bierce

## I. Statement of Joel Hetman, Jr.

I AM THE most unfortunate of men. Rich, respected, fairly well educated and of sound health—with many other advantages usually valued by those having them and coveted by those who have them not—I sometimes think that I should be less unhappy if they had been denied me, for then the contrast between my outer and my inner life would not be continually demanding a painful attention. In the stress of privation and the need of effort I might sometimes forget the somber secret ever baffling the conjecture that it compels.

I am the only child of Joel and Julia Hetman. The one was a well-to-do country gentleman, the other a beautiful and accomplished woman to whom he was passionately attached with what I now know to have been a jealous and exacting devotion. The family home was a few miles from Nashville, Tennessee, a large, irregularly built dwelling of no particular order of architecture, a little way off the road, in a park of trees and shrubbery.

At the time of which I write I was nineteen years old, a student at Yale. One day I received a telegram from my father of such urgency that in compliance with its unexplained demand I left at once for home. At the railway station in Nashville a distant relative awaited me to apprise me of the reason for my recall: my mother had been barbarously murdered—why and by whom none could conjecture, but the circumstances were these:

My father had gone to Nashville, intending to return the next afternoon. Something prevented his accomplishing the business in hand, so he returned on the same night, arriving just before the dawn. In his testimony before the coroner he explained that having no latchkey and not caring to disturb the sleeping servants, he had, with no clearly defined intention, gone round to the rear of the house. As he turned an angle of the building, he heard a sound as of a door gently closed, and saw in the darkness, indistinctly, the figure of a man, which instantly disappeared among the trees of the lawn. A hasty pursuit and brief search of the grounds in the belief that the trespasser was someone secretly visiting a servant proving fruitless, he entered at the unlocked door and mounted the stairs to my mother's chamber. Its door was open, and stepping into black darkness he fell headlong over some heavy object on the floor. I may spare myself the details; it was my poor mother, dead of strangulation by human hands!

Nothing had been taken from the house, the servants had heard no sound, and excepting those terrible finger-marks upon the dead woman's throat—dear God! that I might forget them!—no trace of the assassin was ever found.

I gave up my studies and remained with my father, who, naturally, was greatly changed. Always of a sedate, taciturn disposition, he now fell into so deep a dejection that nothing could hold his attention, yet anything—a footfall, the sudden closing of a door—aroused in him a fitful interest; one might have called it an apprehension. At any small surprise of the senses he would start visibly and sometimes turn pale, then relapse into a melancholy apathy deeper than before. I suppose he was what is called a "nervous wreck." As to me, I was younger then than now—there is much in that. Youth is Gilead, in which is balm for every wound. Ah, that I might again dwell in that enchanted land! Unacquainted with grief, I knew not how to appraise my bereavement; I could not rightly estimate the strength of the stroke.

One night, a few months after the dreadful event, my father and I walked home from the city. The full moon was about three hours above the eastern horizon; the entire countryside had the solemn stillness of a summer night; our footfalls and the ceaseless song of the katydids were the only sound aloof. Black shadows of bordering trees lay athwart the road, which, in the short reaches between, gleamed a ghostly white. As we approached the gate to our dwelling, whose front was in shadow, and in which no light shone, my father suddenly stopped and clutched my arm, saying, hardly above his breath:

"God! God! what is that?"

"I hear nothing," I replied.

"But see—see!" he said, pointing along the road, directly ahead.

I said: "Nothing is there. Come, father, let us go in—you are ill."

He had released my arm and was standing rigid and motionless in the center of the illuminated roadway, staring like one bereft of sense. His face in the moonlight showed a pallor and fixity inexpressibly distressing. I pulled gently at his sleeve, but he had forgotten my existence. Presently he began to retire backward, step by step, never for an instant removing his eyes from what he saw, or thought he saw. I turned half round to follow, but stood irresolute. I do not recall any feeling of fear, unless a sudden chill was its physical manifestation. It seemed as if an icy wind had touched my face and enfolded my body from head to foot; I could feel the stir of it in my hair.

At that moment my attention was drawn to a light that suddenly streamed from an upper window of the house: one of the servants, awakened by what mysterious premonition of evil who can say, and in obedience to an impulse that she was never able to name, had lit a lamp. When I turned to look for my father he was gone, and in all the years that have passed no whisper of his fate has come across the borderland of conjecture from the realm of the unknown.

## II. Statement of Caspar Grattan

Today I am said to live; tomorrow, here in this room, will lie a senseless shape of clay that all too long was I. If anyone lift the cloth from the face of that unpleasant thing it will be in gratification of a mere morbid curiosity. Some, doubtless, will go further and inquire, "Who was he?" In this writing I supply the only answer that I am able to make—Caspar Grattan. Surely, that should be enough. The name has served my small need for more than twenty years of a life of unknown length. True, I gave it to myself, but lacking another I had the right. In this world one must have a name; it prevents confusion, even when it does not establish identity. Some, though, are known by numbers, which also seem inadequate distinctions.

One day, for illustration, I was passing along a street of a city, far from here, when I met two men in uniform, one of whom, half pausing and looking curiously into my face, said to his companion, "That man looks like 767." Something in the number seemed familiar and horrible. Moved by an uncontrollable impulse, I sprang into a side street and ran until I fell exhausted in a country lane.

I have never forgotten that number, and always it comes to memory attended by gibbering obscenity, peals of joyless laughter, the clang of iron doors. So I say a name, even if self-bestowed, is better than a number. In the register of the potter's field I shall soon have both. What wealth!

Of him who shall find this paper I must beg a little consideration. It is not the history of my life; the knowledge to write that is denied me. This is only a record of broken and apparently unrelated memories, some of them as distinct and sequent as brilliant beads upon a thread, others remote and strange, having the character of crimson dreams with interspaces blank and black—witch-fires glowing still and red in a great desolation.

Standing upon the shore of eternity, I turn for a last look landward over the course by which I came. There are twenty years of footprints fairly distinct, the impressions of bleeding feet. They lead through poverty and pain, devious and unsure, as of one staggering beneath a burden—

> Remote, unfriended, melancholy, slow.

Ah, the poet's prophecy of Me—how admirable, how dreadfully admirable!

Backward beyond the beginning of this *via dolorosa*—this epic of suffering with episodes of sin—I see nothing clearly; it comes out of a cloud. I know that it spans only twenty years, yet I am an old man.

One does not remember one's birth—one has to be told. But with me it was different; life came to me full-handed and dowered me with all my faculties and powers. Of a previous existence I know no more than others, for all have stammering intimations that may be memories and may be dreams. I know only that my first consciousness was of maturity in body and mind—a consciousness accepted without surprise or conjecture. I merely found myself walking in a forest, half-clad, footsore, unutterably weary and hungry. Seeing a farmhouse, I approached and asked for food, which was given me by one who inquired my name. I did not know, yet knew that all had names. Greatly embarrassed, I retreated, and night coming on, lay down in the forest and slept.

The next day I entered a large town which I shall not name. Nor shall I recount further incidents of the life that is now to end—a life of wandering, always and everywhere haunted by an overmastering sense of crime in punishment of wrong and of terror in punishment of crime. Let me see if I can reduce it to narrative.

I seem once to have lived near a great city, a prosperous planter, married to a woman whom I loved and distrusted. We had, it sometimes seems, one child, a youth of brilliant parts and promise. He is at all times a vague figure, never clearly drawn, frequently altogether out of the picture.

One luckless evening it occurred to me to test my wife's fidelity in a vulgar, commonplace way familiar to everyone who has acquaintance with the literature of fact and fiction. I went to the city, telling my wife that I should be absent until the following afternoon. But I returned before daybreak and went to the rear of the house, purposing to enter by a door with which I had secretly so tampered that it would seem to lock, yet not actually fasten. As I approached it, I heard it gently open and close, and saw a man steal away into the darkness. With murder in my heart, I sprang after him, but he had vanished without even the bad luck of identification. Sometimes now I cannot even persuade myself that it was a human being.

Crazed with jealousy and rage, blind and bestial with all the elemental passions of insulted manhood, I entered the house and sprang up the stairs to the door of my wife's chamber. It was closed, but having tampered with its lock also, I easily entered and despite the black darkness soon stood by the side of her bed. My groping hands told me that although disarranged it was unoccupied.

"She is below," I thought, "and terrified by my entrance has evaded me in the darkness of the hall."

With the purpose of seeking her I turned to leave the room, but took a wrong direction—the right one! My foot struck her, cowering in a corner of the room. Instantly my hands were at her throat, stifling a shriek, my knees were upon her struggling body; and there in the darkness, without a word of accusation or reproach, I strangled her till she died!

There ends the dream. I have related it in the past tense, but the present would be the fitter form, for again and again the somber tragedy reenacts itself in my consciousness—over and over I lay the plan, I suffer the confirmation, I redress the wrong. Then all is blank; and afterward the rains beat against the grimy window-panes, or the snows fall upon my scant attire, the wheels rattle in the squalid streets where my life lies in poverty and mean employment. If there is ever sunshine I do not recall it; if there are birds they do not sing.

There is another dream, another vision of the night. I stand among the shadows in a moonlit road. I am aware of another presence, but whose I cannot rightly determine. In the shadow of a great dwelling I catch the gleam of white garments; then the figure of a woman confronts me in the road—my murdered wife! There is death in the face; there are marks upon the throat. The eyes are fixed on mine with an infinite gravity which is not reproach, nor hate, nor menace, nor anything less terrible than recognition. Before this awful apparition I retreat in terror—a terror that is upon me as I write. I can no longer rightly shape the words. See! they—

Now I am calm, but truly there is no more to tell: the incident ends where it began—in darkness and in doubt.

Yes, I am again in control of myself: "the captain of my soul." But that is not respite; it is another stage and phase of expiation. My penance, constant in degree, is mutable in kind: one of its variants is tranquillity. After all, it is only a life-sentence. "To Hell for life"—that is a foolish penalty: the culprit chooses the duration of his punishment. Today my term expires.

To each and all, the peace that was not mine.

### III. Statement of the Late Julia Hetman, Through the Medium Bayrolles

I had retired early and fallen almost immediately into a peaceful sleep, from which I awoke with that indefinable sense of peril which is, I think, a common experience in that other, earlier life. Of its unmeaning character, too, I was entirely persuaded, yet that did not banish it. My husband, Joel Hetman, was away from home; the servants slept in another part of the house. But these were familiar conditions; they had never before distressed me. Nevertheless, the strange terror grew so insupportable that conquering my reluctance to move I sat up and lit the lamp at my bedside. Contrary to my expectation this gave me no relief; the light seemed rather an added danger, for I reflected that it would shine out under the door, disclosing my presence to whatever evil thing might lurk outside. You that are still in the flesh, subject to horrors of the imagination, think what a monstrous fear that must be which seeks in darkness security from malevolent existences of the night. That is to spring to close quarters with an unseen enemy—the strategy of despair!

Extinguishing the lamp I pulled the bedclothing about my head and lay trembling and silent, unable to shriek, forgetful to pray. In this pitiable state I must have lain for what you call hours—with us there are no hours, there is no time.

At last it came—a soft, irregular sound of footfalls on the stairs! They were slow, hesitant, uncertain, as of something that did not see its way; to my disordered reason all the more terrifying for that, as the approach of some blind and mindless malevolence to which is no appeal. I even thought that I must have left the hall lamp burning and the groping of this creature proved it a monster of the night. This was foolish and inconsistent with my previous dread of the light, but what would you have? Fear has no brains; it is an idiot. The dismal witness that it bears and the cowardly counsel that it whispers are unrelated. We know this well, we who have passed into the Realm of Terror, who skulk in eternal dusk among the scenes of our former lives, invisible even to ourselves and one another, yet hiding forlorn in lonely places; yearning for speech with our loved ones, yet dumb, and as fearful of them as they of us. Sometimes the disability is removed, the law suspended: by the deathless power of love or hate we break the spell—we are seen by those whom we would warn, console, or punish. What form we seem to them to bear we know not; we know only that we terrify even those whom we most wish to comfort, and from whom we most crave tenderness and sympathy.

Forgive, I pray you, this inconsequent digression by what was once a woman. You who consult us in this imperfect way—you do not understand. You ask foolish questions about things unknown and things forbidden. Much that we know and could impart in our speech is meaningless in yours. We must communicate with you through a stammering intelligence in that small fraction of our language that you yourselves can speak. You think that we are of another world. No, we have knowledge of no world but yours, though for us it holds no sunlight, no warmth, no music, no laughter, no song of birds, nor any companionship. O God! what a thing it is to be a ghost, cowering and shivering in an altered world, a prey to apprehension and despair!

No, I did not die of fright: the Thing turned and went away. I heard it go down the stairs, hurriedly, I thought, as if itself in sudden fear. Then I rose to call for help. Hardly had my shaking hand found the doorknob when—merciful heaven!—I heard it returning. Its footfalls as it remounted the stairs were rapid, heavy and loud; they shook the house. I fled to an angle of the wall and crouched upon the floor. I tried to pray. I tried to call the name of my dear husband.

Then I heard the door thrown open. There was an interval of unconsciousness, and when I revived I felt a strangling clutch upon my
throat—felt my arms feebly beating against something that bore me
backward—felt my tongue thrusting itself from between my teeth!
And then I passed into this life.

No, I have no knowledge of what it was. The sum of what we
knew at death is the measure of what we know afterward of all that
went before. Of this existence we know many things, but no new
light falls upon any page of that; in memory is written all of it that
we can read. Here are no heights of truth overlooking the confused
landscape of that dubitable domain. We still dwell in the Valley of
the Shadow, lurk in its desolate places, peering from brambles and
thickets at its mad, malign inhabitants. How should we have new
knowledge of that fading past?

What I am about to relate happened on a night. We know when
it is night, for then you retire to your houses and we can venture
from our places of concealment to move unafraid about our old
homes, to look in at the windows, even to enter and gaze upon your
faces as you sleep. I had lingered long near the dwelling where I had
been so cruelly changed to what I am, as we do while any that we
love or hate remain. Vainly I had sought some method of manifestation, some way to make my continued existence and my great love
and poignant pity understood by my husband and son. Always if they
slept they would wake, or if in my desperation I dared approach
them when they were awake, would turn toward me the terrible
eyes of the living, frightening me by the glances that I sought from
the purpose that I held.

On this night I had searched for them without success, fearing to
find them; they were nowhere in the house, nor about the moonlit
lawn. For, although the sun is lost to us forever, the moon, full-orbed
or slender, remains to us. Sometimes it shines by night, sometimes
by day, but always it rises and sets, as in that other life.

I left the lawn and moved in the white light and silence along the
road, aimless and sorrowing. Suddenly I heard the voice of my poor
husband in exclamations of astonishment, with that of my son in
reassurance and dissuasion; and there by the shadow of a group of
trees they stood—near, so near! Their faces were toward me, the
eyes of the elder man fixed upon mine. He saw me—at last, at last,
he saw me! In the consciousness of that, my terror fled as a cruel
dream. The death-spell was broken: Love had conquered Law! Mad
with exultation I shouted—I *must* have shouted, "He sees, he sees:

he will understand!" Then, controlling myself, I moved forward, smiling and consciously beautiful, to offer myself to his arms, to comfort him with endearments, and, with my son's hand in mine, to speak words that should restore the broken bonds between the living and the dead.

Alas! alas! his face went white with fear, his eyes were as those of a hunted animal. He backed away from me, as I advanced, and at last turned and fled into the wood—whither, it is not given to me to know.

To my poor boy, left doubly desolate, I have never been able to impart a sense of my presence. Soon he, too, must pass to this Life Invisible and be lost to me forever.

# JOHN BARTINE'S WATCH

**Ambrose Bierce**

## A Story by a Physician

"The exact time? Good God! my friend, why do you insist? One would think—but what does it matter; it is easily bedtime—isn't that near enough? But, here, if you must set your watch, take mine and see for yourself."

With that he detached his watch—a tremendously heavy, old-fashioned one—from the chain, and handed it to me; then turned away, and walking across the room to a shelf of books, began an examination of their backs. His agitation and evident distress surprised me; they appeared reasonless. Having set my watch by his, I stepped over to where he stood and said, "Thank you."

As he took his timepiece and reattached it to the guard I observed that his hands were unsteady. With a tact upon which I greatly prided myself, I sauntered carelessly to the sideboard and took some brandy and water; then, begging his pardon for my thoughtlessness, asked him to have some and went back to my seat by the fire, leaving him to help himself, as was our custom. He did so and presently joined me at the hearth, as tranquil as ever.

This odd little incident occurred in my apartment, where John Bartine was passing an evening. We had dined together at the club, had come home in a cab and—in short, everything had been done in the most prosaic way; and why John Bartine should break in upon the natural and established order of things to make himself spectacular with a display of emotion, apparently for his own entertainment, I could nowise understand. The more I thought of it, while his brilliant

118

conversational gifts were commending themselves to my inattention, the more curious I grew, and of course had no difficulty in persuading myself that my curiosity was friendly solicitude. That is the disguise that curiosity usually assumes to evade resentment. So I ruined one of the finest sentences of his disregarded monologue by cutting it short without ceremony.

"John Bartine," I said, "you must try to forgive me if I am wrong, but with the light that I have at present I cannot concede your right to go all to pieces when asked the time o' night. I cannot admit that it is proper to experience a mysterious reluctance to look your own watch in the face and to cherish in my presence, without explanation, painful emotions which are denied to me, and which are none of my business."

To this ridiculous speech Bartine made no immediate reply, but sat looking gravely into the fire. Fearing that I had offended I was about to apologize and beg him to think no more about the matter, when looking me calmly in the eyes he said:

"My dear fellow, the levity of your manner does not at all disguise the hideous impudence of your demand; but happily I had already decided to tell you what you wish to know, and no manifestation of your unworthiness to hear it shall alter my decision. Be good enough to give me your attention and you shall hear all about the matter.

"This watch," he said, "had been in my family for three generations before it fell to me. Its original owner, for whom it was made, was my great-grandfather, Bramwell Olcott Bartine, a wealthy planter of Colonial Virginia, and as stanch a Tory as ever lay awake nights contriving new kinds of maledictions for the head of Mr. Washington, and new methods of aiding and abetting good King George. One day this worthy gentleman had the deep misfortune to perform for his cause a service of capital importance which was not recognized as legitimate by those who suffered its disadvantages. It does not matter what it was, but among its minor consequences was my excellent ancestor's arrest one night in his own house by a party of Mr. Washington's rebels. He was permitted to say farewell to his weeping family, and was then marched away into the darkness which swallowed him up forever. Not the slenderest clue to his fate was ever found. After the war the most diligent inquiry and the offer of large rewards failed to turn up any of his captors or any fact concerning his disappearance. He had disappeared, and that was all."

Something in Bartine's manner that was not in his words—I hardly knew what it was—prompted me to ask:

"What is your view of the matter—of the justice of it?"

"My view of it," he flamed out, bringing his clenched hand down upon the table as if he had been in a public house dicing with blackguards—"my view of it is that it was a characteristically dastardly assassination by that damned traitor, Washington, and his ragamuffin rebels!"

For some minutes nothing was said: Bartine was recovering his temper, and I waited. Then I said:

"Was that all?"

"No—there was something else. A few weeks after my great-grandfather's arrest his watch was found lying on the porch at the front door of his dwelling. It was wrapped in a sheet of letter paper bearing the name of Rupert Bartine, his only son, my grandfather. I am wearing that watch."

Bartine paused. His usually restless black eyes were staring fixedly into the grate, a point of red light in each, reflected from the glowing coals. He seemed to have forgotten me. A sudden threshing of the branches of a tree outside one of the windows, and almost at the same instant a rattle of rain against the glass, recalled him to a sense of his surroundings. A storm had risen, heralded by a single gust of wind, and in a few moments the steady plash of the water on the pavement was distinctly heard. I hardly know why I relate this incident; it seemed somehow to have a certain significance and relevancy which I am unable now to discern. It at least added an element of seriousness, almost solemnity. Bartine resumed:

"I have a singular feeling toward this watch—a kind of affection for it; I like to have it about me, though partly from its weight, and partly for a reason I shall now explain, I seldom carry it. The reason is this: Every evening when I have it with me I feel an unaccountable desire to open and consult it, even if I can think of no reason for wishing to know the time. But if I yield to it, the moment my eyes rest upon the dial I am filled with a mysterious apprehension—a sense of imminent calamity. And this is the more insupportable the nearer it is to eleven o'clock—by this watch, no matter what the actual hour may be. After the hands have registered eleven the desire to look is gone; I am entirely indifferent. Then I can consult the thing as often as I like, with no more emotion than you feel in looking at your own. Naturally I have trained myself not to look at that watch in the evening before eleven; nothing could induce me. Your insistence this evening upset me a trifle. I felt very much as I suppose an opium-eater might feel if his yearning for his special and particular kind of hell were re-enforced by opportunity and advice.

"Now that is my story, and I have told it in the interest of your trumpery science; but if on any evening hereafter you observe me wearing this damnable watch, and you have the thoughtfulness to ask me the hour, I shall beg leave to put you to the inconvenience of being knocked down."

His humor did not amuse me. I could see that in relating his delusion he was again somewhat disturbed. His concluding smile was positively ghastly, and his eyes had resumed something more than their old restlessness; they shifted hither and thither about the room with apparent aimlessness and I fancied had taken on a wild expression, such as is sometimes observed in cases of dementia. Perhaps this was my own imagination, but at any rate I was now persuaded that my friend was afflicted with a most singular and interesting monomania. Without, I trust, any abatement of my affectionate solicitude for him as a friend, I began to regard him as a patient, rich in possibilities of profitable study. Why not? Had he not described his delusion in the interest of science? Ah, poor fellow, he was doing more for science than he knew: not only his story but himself was in evidence. I should cure him if I could, of course, but first I should make a little experiment in psychology—nay, the experiment itself might be a step in his restoration.

"That is very frank and friendly of you, Bartine," I said cordially, "and I'm rather proud of your confidence. It is all very odd, certainly. Do you mind showing me the watch?"

He detached it from his waistcoat, chain and all, and passed it to me without a word. The case was of gold, very thick and strong, and singularly engraved. After closely examining the dial and observing that it was nearly twelve o'clock, I opened it at the back and was interested to observe an inner case of ivory, upon which was painted a miniature portrait in that exquisite and delicate manner which was in vogue during the eighteenth century.

"Why, bless my soul!" I exclaimed, feeling a sharp artistic delight—"how under the sun did you get that done? I thought miniature painting on ivory was a lost art."

"That," he replied, gravely smiling, "is not I; it is my excellent great-grandfather, the late Bramwell Olcott Bartine, Esquire, of Virginia. He was younger then than later—about my age, in fact. It is said to resemble me; do you think so?"

"Resemble you? I should say so! Barring the costume, which I supposed you to have assumed out of compliment to the art—or for *vraisemblance*[1], so to say—and the no mustache, that portrait is you in every feature, line, and expression."

No more was said at that time. Bartine took a book from the table and began reading. I heard outside the incessant plash of the rain in the street. There were occasional hurried footfalls on the sidewalks; and once a slower, heavier tread seemed to cease at my door—a policeman, I thought, seeking shelter in the doorway. The boughs of the trees tapped significantly on the window panes, as if asking for admittance. I remember it all through these years and years of a wiser, graver life.

Seeing myself unobserved, I took the old-fashioned key that dangled from the chain and quickly turned back the hands of the watch a full hour; then, closing the case, I handed Bartine his property and saw him replace it on his person.

"I think you said," I began, with assumed carelessness, "that after eleven the sight of the dial no longer affects you. As it is now nearly twelve"—looking at my own timepiece—"perhaps, if you don't resent my pursuit of proof, you will look at it now."

He smiled good-humoredly, pulled out the watch again, opened it, and instantly sprang to his feet with a cry that Heaven has not had the mercy to permit me to forget! His eyes, their blackness strikingly intensified by the pallor of his face, were fixed upon the watch, which he clutched in both hands. For some time he remained in that attitude without uttering another sound; then, in a voice that I should not have recognized as his, he said:

"Damn you! it is two minutes to eleven!"

I was not unprepared for some such outbreak, and without rising replied, calmly enough:

"I beg your pardon; I must have misread your watch in setting my own by it."

He shut the case with a sharp snap and put the watch in his pocket. He looked at me and made an attempt to smile, but his lower lip quivered and he seemed unable to close his mouth. His hands, also, were shaking, and he thrust them, clenched, into the pockets of his sack coat. The courageous spirit was manifestly endeavoring to subdue the coward body. The effort was too great; he began to sway

---

[1]  *vraisemblance*; French: ways in which text are defined in relation to other text to make it intelligible.

from side to side, as from vertigo, and before I could spring from my chair to support him his knees gave way and he pitched awkwardly forward and fell upon his face. I sprang to assist him to rise; but when John Bartine rises we shall all rise.

The postmortem examination disclosed nothing; every organ was normal and sound. But when the body had been prepared for burial a faint dark circle was seen to have developed around the neck; at least I was so assured by several persons who said they saw it, but of my own knowledge I cannot say if that was true.

Nor can I set limitations to the law of heredity. I do not know that in the spiritual world a sentiment or emotion may not survive the heart that held it, and seek expression in a kindred life, ages removed. Surely, if I were to guess at the fate of Bramwell Olcott Bartine, I should guess that he was hanged at eleven o'clock in the evening, and that he had been allowed several hours in which to prepare for the change.

As to John Bartine, my friend, my patient for five minutes, and—Heaven forgive me!—my victim for eternity, there is no more to say. He is buried, and his watch with him—I saw to that. May God rest his soul in Paradise, and the soul of his Virginian ancestor, if, indeed, they are two souls.

# POLLY'S HACK RIDE

## Emma E. Butler

POLLY GRAY HAD lived six and one-half years without ever having enjoyed the luxury of a hack ride.

The little shanty, merely an apology for a house, in which she lived with her parents, sat in a hollow on the main road in the village, at least fifteen feet below the road; and when Polly sat or stood at the front window upstairs, she watched with envy the finely dressed ladies and gentlemen riding by on their way to the big red brick building on the hill.

On several occasions her secret longing got the best of her, and she mustered all the self-control of which her nature boasted to keep from stealing a ride on behind, as she had seen her brothers do on the ice wagon, but the memory of the warm reception usually awaiting the little male Grays, accompanied by predictions of broken necks, arms, legs, etc., caused her little frame to shiver.

Who then could say that Polly was wanting in sisterly love when she exulted in the fact that she was going to a funeral? What did it matter if Ma Gray was heart-broken, and Pa Gray couldn't eat but six biscuits for his supper when he came home and found the long white fringed sash floating from the cracked door knob?

Polly reviewed the events leading up to her present stage of ecstasy: Ma Gray had sent in hot haste for Aunt Betty Williams, who came with question marks stamped on her face, and when she found Ella, the two-year-old pet of the family in the throes of death she was by far too discreet to say so but advised Ma Gray to put her down. Polly had then become afraid and had run downstairs. She felt it—yes, sir—she felt it 'way down in her "stummik!" Something was going to happen, so when Ma Gray appeared at the head of the stairs with eyes swollen, and still a-swellin', and told her in a shaky voice to go to school for the children, she knew it had happened.

She started off at break-neck speed but, undecided just as to the proper gait for one bearing a message of such grave importance, she walked mournfully along for a while, then as the vision of a hack and two white horses arose, she skipped and finally ran again until she reached the school-house.

The afternoon session had just begun, as she timidly knocked on the door of the class-room where the two elder Grays were "get-tin' their schoolin' "; and when the teacher opened the door, she beheld a very dirty little girl blubbering, "Ella's dead; Mamma's cryin'. Kin Bobby and Sally cum home?"

Master Bobby and Miss Sally were dismissed with the reverence due the dignity of their bereavement, and on their way home they proceeded to extract such bits of information as they deemed suitable for the occasion: "Were her eyes open or shut? Had she turned black yet? Did Aunt Betty cry too? Did Mamma fall across the bed as the breath was leaving her body?" Whereupon Miss Polly, being a young lady of a rather keen imagination upon which she drew, and drew heavily in times of need, gave them quite a sensational version of the affair, and by the time they reached home they were fully prepared to grieve with a capital "G." Sally ran to Ma Gray and with a shriek, threw both arms around her neck, while Bobby fell on his knees by the deceased Ella, imploring her to come back and be his baby sister once more.

Aunt Betty told her next door neighbor afterwards that she had her hands full and her heart full too, trying to quiet them. And if the smell of fried liver and onions had not reminded Bobby that it was near dinner time, she really couldn't tell how she should have managed them.

As plateful after plateful of liver, onions and mashed potatoes disappeared, the raging storm of grief subsided in the hearts of the young Grays, and by the time dinner was over Bobby was kept busy unpuckering his lips to suppress a whistle, and Sally had tried several bows of black ribbon on her hair to see which one looked best.

After the dishes were cleared away, and Ma Gray was scouring the floor in a solution of concentrated lye, water and tears, Uncle Bangaway, a retired deacon in the Baptist church, stepped in to pay his respects.

Uncle Bangaway was considered a fine singer in his younger days and was quite proud of the accusation, so he proceeded to express his sympathy for Ma Gray in the words of his favorite hymn, kept in reserve for such occasions:

> "Wasn't my Lord mighty good and kind?
>     O Yeah!
> "Wasn't my Lord mighty good and kind?
>     O Yeah!
> "Wasn't my Lord mighty good and kind
> "To take away the child and leave the mother behind?
>     "O Yeah! O Yeah! O Yeah!"

When he finished singing Ma Gray stopped crying to smile on him. It seemed that the hymn brought to her mind certain facts that were well worth considering.

On the morning of the day appointed for the funeral, a dark cloud hung over the village when Polly awoke, and her heart sank within her. Oh! If it should rain! Every hack she had ever seen on a rainy day had the curtains down, and there was no use riding in a hack if you had to have the curtains down. Anyhow, she began to dress, and before she was half through the sun began to peep through the clouds, and finally it shone brightly; and so did Miss Polly's face.

Who, then, could not pardon the cheerful face she brought downstairs where the funeral party was gathered? Dressed in a new black dress, new shoes, new hair ribbon, even new gloves, and a hack ride scheduled for the next two hours, was enough to make her very soul shine.

She hardly heard the minister as he dwelt at length on the innocence of childhood; nor his reference to Him who suffered the little ones to come unto Him; but the closing strains of "Nearer My God To Thee"[1] seemed to awaken her from pleasant dreams.

When the funeral procession started out Polly felt very sad, but the tears wouldn't come and, of course, "you can't make 'em come, if you ain't got no raw onions."

Now, it fell to her lot to sit in the hack with her great uncle, "Uncle Billings" Ma Gray called him, but Polly often wondered why Pa Gray spoke of him as "Uncle Rummy."

---

[1] "Nearer My God To Thee": a Christian hymn written in the 19th century and based on Genesis 28: 11–19 (the story of Jacob's dream).

One of the many reasons for Polly's aversion to Uncle Billings was because of his prompt appearance before dinner every Sunday, when he would call her mother's attention every time she, Polly, took another doughnut or cookie. So you may be sure her spirits fell when she realized the state of affairs.

On the way to the cemetery neither found much to say to the other, but when they started home Uncle Billings began to lecture Polly concerning her apparent indifference to the family bereavement; during which discourse Polly sat without hearing one word, as her mind was otherwise engaged. She was trying to think of some manner in which to attract the attention of the Higdon girls as she passed the pump; she knew they would be there.

Before her plans were matured, however, the red bonnet of Cecie Higdon loomed up at the corner, and standing right behind her were Bessie and Georgia Higdon and Lucy Matthews.

Now was her chance! Now or never! So she sprang from her seat, leaned far out of the window, and gave one loud "Whee!" to the girls, waving her black-bordered handkerchief meanwhile.

Uncle Billings had just dropped off in a doze, and Polly's whoop brought him out of it so suddenly that he could find nothing more appropriate to say than, "Hush your noise, gal!" when with a sudden jerk the hack stopped and they were home.

As Polly alighted from the hack, she began to realize how, as a mourner, she had lowered her dignity by yelling from the window like a joy-rider, and she was not a little uneasy as to how Ma Gray would consider the matter should old Rummy inform her. So during supper she cautiously avoided meeting his eye, and as soon as she had finished eating she ran upstairs to change her clothes.

Here her mother found her later, with her head resting on the open Bible, and when she tried to awaken her she said, "Yes'm, just tell him not to drive quite so fast."

# LOU, THE PROPHET

## Willa Cather

IT HAD BEEN a very trying summer to everyone, and most of all to Lou. He had been in the West for seven years, but he had never quite gotten over his homesickness for Denmark. Among the northern people who emigrate to the great west, only the children and the old people ever long much for the lands they have left over the water. The men only know that in this new land their plow runs across the field tearing up the fresh, warm earth, with never a stone to stay its course. That if they dig and delve the land long enough, and if they are not compelled to mortgage it to keep body and soul together, some day it will be theirs, their very own. They are not like the southern people; they lose their love for their fatherland quicker and have less of sentiment about them. They have to think too much about how they shall get bread to care much what soil gives it to them. But among even the most blunted, mechanical people, the youths and the aged always have a touch of romance in them.

Lou was only twenty-two; he had been but a boy when his family left Denmark, and had never ceased to remember it. He was a rather simple fellow, and was always considered less promising than his brothers; but last year he had taken up a claim of his own and made a rough dugout upon it and he lived there all alone. His life was that of many another young man in our country. He rose early in the morning, in the summer just before daybreak; in the winter, long before. First he fed his stock, then himself, which was a much less important matter. He ate the same food at dinner that he ate at breakfast, and the same at supper that he ate at dinner. His bill of fare never changed the year round; bread, coffee, beans and sorghum molasses, sometimes a little salt pork. After breakfast he worked until dinner time, ate, and then worked again. He always went to bed soon after the sunset, for he was always tired, and it saved oil. Sometimes, on Sundays, he would go over home after he had done his washing and house cleaning, and sometimes he hunted. His life was as sane and as uneventful as the life of his plow horses, and it was as hard and thankless. He was thrifty for a simple, thickheaded fellow, and in the spring he was to have married Nelse Sorenson's daughter, but he had lost all his cattle during the winter, and was not so prosperous as he had hoped to be; so, instead she married her cousin, who had an "eighty" of his own. That hurt Lou more than anyone ever dreamed.

A few weeks later his mother died. He had always loved his mother. She had been kind to him and used to come over to see him sometimes, and shake up his hard bed for him, and sweep, and make his bread. She had a strong affection for the boy, he was her youngest, and she always felt sorry for him; she had danced a great deal before his birth, and an old woman in Denmark had told her that was the cause of the boy's weak head.

Perhaps the greatest calamity of all was the threatened loss of his corn crop. He had bought a new corn planter on time that spring, and had intended that his corn should pay for it. Now, it looked as though he would not have corn enough to feed his horses. Unless rain fell within the next two weeks, his entire crop would be ruined; it was half gone now. All these things together were too much for poor Lou, and one morning he felt a strange loathing for the bread and sorghum which he usually ate as mechanically as he slept. He kept thinking about the strawberries he used to gather on the mountains after the snows were gone, and the cold water in the mountain streams. He felt hot someway, and wanted cold water. He had no well, and he hauled his water from a neighbor's well every Sunday, and it got warm in the barrels those hot summer days. He worked at his haying all day; at night, when he was through feeding, he stood a long time by the pig stye with a basket on his arm. When the moon came up, he sighed restlessly and tore the buffalo pea flowers with his bare toes. After a while, he put his basket away, and went into his hot, close, little dugout. He did not sleep well, and he dreamed a horrible dream. He thought he saw the Devil and all his angels in the air holding back the rain clouds, and they loosed all the damned in Hell, and they came, poor tortured things, and drank up whole clouds of rain. Then he thought a strange light shone from the south, just over the river bluffs, and the clouds parted, and Christ and all his angels were descending. They were coming, coming, myriads and myriads of them, in a great blaze of glory. Then he felt something give way in his poor, weak head, and with a cry of pain he awoke. He lay shuddering a long time in the dark, then got up and lit his lantern and took from the shelf his mother's Bible. It opened of itself at Revelation, and Lou began to read, slowly indeed, for it was hard work for him. Page by page, he read those burning, blinding, blasting words, and they seemed to shrivel up his poor brain altogether. At last the book slipped from his hands and he sank down upon his knees in prayer, and stayed so until the dull gray dawn stole over the land and he heard the pigs clamoring for their feed.

He worked about the place until noon, and then prayed and read again. So he went on several days, praying and reading and fasting, until he grew thin and haggard. Nature did not comfort him any, he knew nothing about nature, he had never seen her; he had only stared into a black plow furrow all his life. Before, he had only seen in the wide, green lands and the open blue the possibilities of earning his bread; now, he only saw in them a great world ready for the judgment, a funeral pyre ready for the torch.

One morning, he went over to the big prairie dog town, where several little Danish boys herded their fathers' cattle. The boys were very fond of Lou; he never teased them as the other men did, but used to help them with their cattle, and let them come over to his dugout to make sorghum taffy. When they saw him coming, they ran to meet him and asked him where he had been all these days. He did not answer their questions, but said: "Come into the cave, I want to see you."

Some six or eight boys herded near the dog town every summer, and by their combined efforts they had dug a cave in the side of a high bank. It was large enough to hold them all comfortably, and high enough to stand in. There the boys used to go when it rained or when it was cold in the fall. They followed Lou silently and sat down on the floor. Lou stood up and looked tenderly down into the little faces before him. They were old-faced little fellows, though they were not over twelve or thirteen years old, hard work matures boys quickly.

"Boys," he said earnestly, "I have found out why it don't rain, it's because of the sins of the world. You don't know how wicked the world is, it's all bad, all, even Denmark. People have been sinning a long time, but they won't much longer. God has been watching and watching for thousands of years, and filling up the phials of wrath, and now he is going to pour out his vengeance and let Hell loose upon the world. He is burning up our corn now, and worse things will happen; for the sun shall be as sackcloth, and the moon shall be like blood, and the stars of heaven shall fall, and the heavens shall part like a scroll, and the mountains shall be moved out of their places, and the great day of his wrath shall come, against which none may stand. Oh, boys! the floods and the flames shall come down upon us together and the whole world shall perish." Lou paused for breath, and the little boys gazed at him in wonder. The sweat was running down his haggard face, and his eyes were staring wildly. Presently, he resumed in a softer tone, "Boys, if you want rain, there is only one way to get it, by prayer. The people of the world won't pray, perhaps if they did God would not hear them, for they are so wicked; but he will hear you, for you are little children and are likened unto the kingdom of heaven, and he loved ye."

Lou's haggard, unshaven face bent toward them and his blue eyes gazed at them with terrible earnestness.

"Show us how, Lou," said one little fellow in an awed whisper. Lou knelt down in the cave, his long, shaggy hair hung down over his face, and his voice trembled as he spoke:

"Oh God, they call thee many long names in thy book, thy prophets; but we are only simple folk, the boys are all little and I am weak headed ever since I was born, therefore, let us call thee Father, for thy other names are hard to remember. O Father, we are so thirsty, all the world is thirsty; the creeks are all dried up, and the river is so low that the fishes die and rot in it; the corn is almost gone; the hay is light; and even the little flowers are no more beautiful. O God! our corn may yet be saved. O, give us rain! Our corn means so much to us, if it fails, all our pigs and cattle will die, and we ourselves come very near it; but if you do not send rain, O Father, and if the end is indeed come, be merciful to thy great, wicked world. They do many wrong things, but I think they forget thy word, for it is a long book to remember, and some are little and some are born weak headed, like me, and some are born very strong headed, which is near as bad. Oh, forgive them their abominations in all the world, both in Denmark and here, for the fire hurts so, O God! Amen."

The little boys knelt and each said a few blundering words. Outside, the sun shone brightly and the cattle nibbled at the short, dry grass, and the hot wind blew through the shriveled corn; within the cave, they knelt as many another had knelt before them, some in temples, some in prison cells, some in the caves of earth, and One, indeed, in the garden, praying for the sin of the world.

The next day, Lou went to town, and prayed in the streets. When the people saw his emaciated frame and wild eyes, and heard his wild words, they told the sheriff to do his duty, the man must be mad. Then Lou ran away; he ran for miles, then walked and limped and stumbled on, until he reached the cave; there the boys found him in the morning. The officials hunted him for days, but he hid in the cave, and the little Danes kept his secret well. They shared their dinners with him, and prayed with him all day long. They had always liked him, but now they would have gone straight through fire for him, anyone of them, they almost worshipped him. He had about him that mysticism which always appeals so quickly to children. I have always thought that bear story which the Hebrews used to tell their children very improbable. If it was true, then I have my doubts about the prophet; no one in the world will hoot at insincere and affected piety sooner than a child, but no one feels the true prophetic flame quicker, no one is more readily touched by simple goodness. A very young child can tell a sincere man better than any phrenologist.

One morning, he told the boys that he had had another "true dream." He was not going to die like other men, but God was going to take him to himself as he was. The end of the world was close at hand, too very close. He prayed more than usual that day, and when they sat eating their dinner in the sunshine, he suddenly sprang to his feet and stared wildly south, crying, "See, see, it is the great light! the end comes!! and they do not know it; they will keep on sinning, I must tell them, I must!"

"No, no, Lou, they will catch you; they are looking for you, you must not go!"

"I must go, my boys; but first let me speak once more to you. Men would not heed me, or believe me, because my head is weak, but you have always believed in me, that God has revealed his word to me, and I will pray God to take you to himself quickly, for ye are worthy. Watch and pray always, boys, watch the light over the bluffs, it is breaking, breaking, and shall grow brighter. Goodbye, my boys, I must leave ye in the world yet awhile." He kissed them all tenderly and blessed them, and started south. He walked at first, then he ran, faster and faster he went, all the while shouting at the top of his voice, "The sword of the Lord and of Gideon!"

The police officers heard of it, and set out to find him. They hunted the country over and even dragged the river, but they never found him again, living or dead. It is thought that he was drowned and the quicksands of the river sucked his body under. But the little Dane boys in our country firmly believe that he was translated like Enoch of old. On stormy nights, when the great winds sweep down from the north they huddle together in their beds and fancy that in the wind they still hear that wild cry, "The sword of the Lord and of Gideon."

# THE NAMESAKE

## Willa Cather

SEVEN OF US, students, sat one evening in Hartwell's studio on the Boulevard St. Michel. We were all fellow-countrymen; one from New Hampshire, one from Colorado, another from Nevada, several from the farm lands of the Middle West, and I myself from California. Lyon Hartwell, though born abroad, was simply, as everyone knew, "from America." He seemed, almost more than any other one living man, to mean all of it—from ocean to ocean. When he was in Paris, his studio was always open to the seven of us who were there that evening, and we intruded upon his leisure as often as we thought permissible.

Although we were within the terms of the easiest of all intimacies, and although the great sculptor, even when he was more than usually silent, was at all times the most gravely cordial of hosts, yet, on that long remembered evening, as the sunlight died on the burnished brown of the horse-chestnuts below the windows, a perceptible dullness yawned through our conversation.

We were, indeed, somewhat low in spirit, for one of our number, Charley Bentley, was leaving us indefinitely, in response to an imperative summons from home. Tomorrow his studio, just across the hall from Hartwell's, was to pass into other hands, and Bentley's luggage was even now piled in discouraged resignation before his door. The various bales and boxes seemed literally to weigh upon us as we sat in his neighbor's hospitable rooms, drearily putting in the time until he should leave us to catch the ten o'clock express for Dieppe.

The day we had got through very comfortably, for Bentley made it the occasion of a somewhat pretentious luncheon at Maxim's.

There had been twelve of us at table, and the two young Poles were thirsty, the Gascon so fabulously entertaining, that it was near upon five o'clock when we put down our liqueur glasses for the last time, and the red, perspiring waiter, having pocketed the reward of his arduous and protracted services, bowed us affably to the door, flourishing his napkin and brushing back the streaks of wet, black hair from his rosy forehead. Our guests having betaken themselves belated to their respective engagements, the rest of us returned with Bentley—only to be confronted by the depressing array before his door. A glance about his denuded rooms had sufficed to chill the glow of the afternoon, and we fled across the hall in a body and begged Lyon Hartwell to take us in.

Bentley had said very little about it, but we all knew what it meant to him to be called home. Each of us knew what it would mean to himself, and each had felt something of that quickened sense of opportunity which comes at seeing another man in any way counted out of the race. Never had the game seemed so enchanting, the chance to play it such a piece of unmerited, unbelievable good fortune.

It must have been, I think, about the middle of October, for I remember that the sycamores were almost bare in the Luxembourg Gardens that morning, and the terrace about the queens of France were strewn with crackling brown leaves. The fat red roses, out the summer long on the stand of the old flower woman at the corner, had given place to dahlias and purple asters. First glimpses of autumn toilettes flashed from the carriages; wonderful little bonnets nodded at one along the Champs-Elysées; and in the Quarter an occasional feather boa, red or black or white, brushed one's coat sleeve in the gay twilight of the early evening. The crisp, sunny autumn air was all day full of the stir of people and carriages and of the cheer of salutations; greetings of the students, returned brown and bearded from their holiday, gossip of people come back from Trouville, from St. Valery, from Dieppe, from all over Brittany and the Norman coast. Everywhere was the joyousness of return, the taking up again of life and work and play.

I had felt ever since early morning that this was the saddest of all possible seasons for saying good-bye to that old, old city of youth, and to that little corner of it on the south shore which since the Dark Ages themselves—yes, and before—has been so peculiarly the land of the young.

I can recall our very postures as we lounged about Hartwell's rooms that evening, with Bentley making occasional hurried trips to his desolated workrooms across the hall—as if haunted by a feeling of having forgotten something—or stopping to poke nervously at his *perroquets*[1], which he had bequeathed to Hartwell, gilt cage and all. Our host himself sat on the couch, his big, bronze-like shoulders backed up against the window, his shaggy head, beaked nose, and long chin cut clean against the gray light.

Our drowsing interest, in so far as it could be said to be fixed upon anything, was centered upon Hartwell's new figure, which stood on the block ready to be cast in bronze, intended as a monument for some American battlefield. He called it "The Color Sergeant." It was the figure of a young soldier running, clutching the folds of a flag, the staff of which had been shot away. We had known it in all the stages of its growth, and the splendid action and feeling of the thing had come to have a kind of special significance for the half dozen of us who often gathered at Hartwell's rooms—though, in truth, there was as much to dishearten one as to inflame, in the case of a man who had done so much in a field so amazingly difficult; who had thrown up in bronze all the restless, teeming force of that adventurous wave still climbing westward in our own land across the waters. We recalled his "Scout," his "Pioneer," his "Gold Seekers," and those monuments in which he had invested one and another of the heroes of the Civil War with such convincing dignity and power.

"Where in the world does he get the heat to make an idea like that carry?" Bentley remarked morosely, scowling at the clay figure. "Hang me, Hartwell, if I don't think it's just because you're not really an American at all, that you can look at it like that."

The big man shifted uneasily against the window. "Yes," he replied smiling, "perhaps there is something in that. My citizenship was somewhat belated and emotional in its flowering. I've half a mind to tell you about it, Bentley." He rose uncertainly, and, after hesitating a moment, went back into his workroom, where he began fumbling among the litter in the corners.

At the prospect of any sort of personal expression from Hartwell, we glanced questioningly at one another; for although he made us feel that he liked to have us about, we were always held at a distance by a certain diffidence of his. There were rare occasions—when he was in the heat of work or of ideas—when he forgot to be shy, but they

---

[1]  *perroquet*; French: parrot or parakeet.

were so exceptional that no flattery was quite so seductive as being taken for a moment into Hartwell's confidence. Even in the matter of opinions—the commonest of currency in our circle—he was niggardly and prone to qualify. No man ever guarded his mystery more effectually. There was a singular, intense spell, therefore, about those few evenings when he had broken through this excessive modesty, or shyness, or melancholy, and had, as it were, committed himself.

When Hartwell returned from the back room, he brought with him an unframed canvas which he put on an easel near his clay figure. We drew close about it, for the darkness was rapidly coming on. Despite the dullness of the light, we instantly recognized the boy of Hartwell's "Color Sergeant." It was the portrait of a very handsome lad in uniform, standing beside a charger impossibly rearing. Not only in his radiant countenance and flashing eyes, but in every line of his young body there was an energy, a gallantry, a joy of life, that arrested and challenged one.

"Yes, that's where I got the notion," Hartwell remarked, wandering back to his seat in the window. "I've wanted to do it for years, but I've never felt quite sure of myself. I was afraid of missing it. He was an uncle of mine, my father's half-brother, and I was named for him. He was killed in one of the big battles of Sixty-four, when I was a child. I never saw him—never knew him until he had been dead for twenty years. And then, one night, I came to know him as we sometimes do living persons—intimately, in a single moment."

He paused to knock the ashes out of his short pipe, refilled it, and puffed at it thoughtfully for a few moments with his hands on his knees. Then, settling back heavily among the cushions and looking absently out of the window, he began his story. As he proceeded further and further into the experience which he was trying to convey to us, his voice sank so low and was sometimes so charged with feeling, that I almost thought he had forgotten our presence and was remembering aloud. Even Bentley forgot his nervousness in astonishment and sat breathless under the spell of the man's thus breathing his memories out into the dusk.

"It was just fifteen years ago this last spring that I first went home, and Bentley's having to cut away like this brings it all back to me.

"I was born, you know, in Italy. My father was a sculptor, though I dare say you've not heard of him. He was one of those first fellows who went over after Story and Powers—went to Italy for 'Art,' quite simply; to lift from its native bough the willing, iridescent bird. Their story is told, informingly enough, by some of those ingenuous marble things at the Metropolitan. My father came over some time before the outbreak of the Civil War, and was regarded as a renegade by his family because he did not go home to enter the army. His half-brother, the only child of my grandfather's second marriage, enlisted at fifteen and was killed the next year. I was ten years old when the news of his death reached us. My mother died the following winter, and I was sent away to a Jesuit school, while my father, already ill himself, stayed on at Rome, chipping away at his Indian maidens and marble goddesses, still gloomily seeking the thing for which he had made himself the most unhappy of exiles.

"He died when I was fourteen, but even before that I had been put to work under an Italian sculptor. He had an almost morbid desire that I should carry on his work, under, as he often pointed out to me, conditions so much more auspicious. He left me in the charge of his one intimate friend, an American gentleman in the consulate at Rome, and his instructions were that I was to be educated there and to live there until I was twenty-one. After I was of age, I came to Paris and studied under one master after another until I was nearly thirty. Then, almost for the first time, I was confronted by a duty which was not my pleasure.

"My grandfather's death, at an advanced age, left an invalid maiden sister of my father's quite alone in the world. She had suffered for years from a cerebral disease, a slow decay of the faculties which rendered her almost helpless. I decided to go to America and, if possible, bring her back to Paris, where I seemed on my way toward what my poor father had wished for me.

"On my arrival at my father's birthplace, however, I found that this was not to be thought of. To tear this timid, feeble, shrinking creature, doubly aged by years and illness, from the spot where she had been rooted for a lifetime, would have been little short of brutality. To leave her to the care of strangers seemed equally heartless. There was clearly nothing for me to do but to remain and wait for that slow and painless malady to run its course. I was there something over two years.

"My grandfather's home, his father's homestead before him, lay on the high banks of a river in Western Pennsylvania. The little town twelve miles down the stream, whither my great-grandfather used to drive his ox-wagon on market days, had become, in two generations, one of the largest manufacturing cities in the world. For hundreds of miles about us the gentle hill slopes were honeycombed with gas wells and coal shafts; oil derricks creaked in every valley and meadow; the brooks were sluggish and discolored with crude petro-leum, and the air was impregnated by its searching odor. The great glass and iron manufactories had come up and up the river almost to our very door; their smoky exhalations brooded over us, and their crashing was always in our ears. I was plunged into the very incan-descence of human energy. But, though my nerves tingled with the feverish, passionate endeavor which snapped in the very air about me, none of these great arteries seemed to feed me; this tumultuous life did not warm me. On every side were the great muddy rivers, the ragged mountains from which the timber was being ruthlessly torn away, the vast tracts of wild country, and the gulches that were like wounds in the earth; everywhere the glare of that relentless energy which followed me like a searchlight and seemed to scorch and consume me. I could only hide myself in the tangled garden, where the dropping of a leaf or the whistle of a bird was the only incident.

"The Hartwell homestead had been sold away little by little, until all that remained of it was garden and orchard. The house, a square brick structure, stood in the midst of a great garden which sloped toward the river, ending in a grassy bank which fell some forty feet to the water's edge. The garden was now little more than a tangle of neglected shrubbery; damp, rank, and of that intense blue-green peculiar to vegetation in smoky places where the sun shines but rarely, and the mists form early in the evening and hang late in the morning.

"I shall never forget it as I saw it first, when I arrived there in the chill of a backward June. The long, rank grass, thick and soft and falling in billows, was always wet until midday. The gravel walks were bordered with great lilac-bushes, mock-orange, and bridal-wreath. Back of the house was a neglected rose garden, surrounded by a low stone wall over which the long suckers trailed and matted. They had wound their pink, thorny tentacles, layer upon layer, about the lock and the hinges of the rusty iron gate. Even the porches of the house, and the very windows, were damp and heavy with growth: wisteria, clematis, honeysuckle, and trumpet vine. The garden was grown up with trees, especially that part of it which lay above the river. The bark of the old locusts was blackened by the smoke that crept continually up the valley, and their feathery foliage, so merry in its movement and so yellow and joyous in its color, seemed peculiarly precious under that somber sky. There were sycamores and copper beeches; gnarled apple-trees, too old to bear; and fall pear-trees, hung with a sharp, hard fruit in October; all with a leafage singularly rich and luxuriant, and peculiarly vivid in color. The oaks about the house had been old trees when my great-grandfather built his cabin there, more than a century before, and this garden was almost the only spot for miles along the river where any of the original forest growth still survived. The smoke from the mills was fatal to trees of the larger sort, and even these had the look of doomed things—bent a little toward the town and seemed to wait with head inclined before that on-coming, shrieking force.

"About the river, too, there was a strange hush, a tragic submission— it was so leaden and sullen in its color, and it flowed so soundlessly forever past our door.

"I sat there every evening, on the high veranda overlooking it, watching the dim outlines of the steep hills on the other shore, the flicker of the lights on the island, where there was a boat-house, and listening to the call of the boatmen through the mist. The mist came as certainly as night, whitened by moonshine or starshine. The tin water-pipes went splash, splash, with it all evening, and the wind, when it rose at all, was little more than a sighing of the old boughs and a troubled breath in the heavy grasses.

"At first it was to think of my distant friends and my old life that I used to sit there; but after awhile it was simply to watch the days and weeks go by, like the river which seemed to carry them away.

"Within the house I was never at home. Month followed month, and yet I could feel no sense of kinship with anything there. Under the roof where my father and grandfather were born, I remained utterly detached. The somber rooms never spoke to me, the old furniture never seemed tinctured with race. This portrait of my boy uncle was the only thing to which I could draw near, the only link with anything I had ever known before.

"There is a good deal of my father in the face, but it is my father transformed and glorified; his hesitating discontent drowned in a kind of triumph. From my first day in that house, I continually turned to this handsome kinsman of mine, wondering in what terms he had lived and had his hope; what he had found there to look like that, to bound at one, after all those years, so joyously out of the canvas.

"From the timid, clouded old woman over whose life I had come to watch, I learned that in the backyard, near the old rose garden, there was a locust-tree which my uncle had planted. After his death, while it was still a slender sapling, his mother had a seat built round it, and she used to sit there on summer evenings. His grave was under the apple-trees in the old orchard.

"My aunt could tell me little more than this. There were days when she seemed not to remember him at all.

"It was from an old soldier in the village that I learned the boy's story. Lyon was, the old man told me, but fourteen when the first enlistment occurred, but was even then eager to go. He was in the court-house square every evening to watch the recruits at their drill, and when the home company was ordered off he rode into the city on his pony to see the men board the train and to wave them good-bye. The next year he spent at home with a tutor, but when he was fifteen he held his parents to their promise and went into the army. He was color sergeant of his regiment and fell in a charge upon the breastworks of a fort about a year after his enlistment.

"The veteran showed me an account of this charge which had been written for the village paper by one of my uncle's comrades who had seen his part in the engagement. It seems that as his company were running at full speed across the bottom lands toward the fortified hill, a shell burst over them. This comrade, running beside my uncle, saw the colors waver and sink as if falling, and looked to see that the boy's hand and forearm had been torn away by the exploding shrapnel. The boy, he thought, did not realize the extent of his injury, for he laughed, shouted something which his comrade did not catch, caught the flag in his left hand, and ran on up the hill. They went splendidly up over the breastworks, but just as my uncle, his colors flying, reached the top of the embankment, a second shell carried away his left arm at the arm-pit, and he fell over the wall with the flag settling about him.

"It was because this story was ever present with me, because I was unable to shake it off, that I began to read such books as my grandfather had collected upon the Civil War. I found that this war was fought largely by boys, that more men enlisted at eighteen than at any other age. When I thought of those battlefields—and I thought of them much in those days—there was always that glory of youth above them, that impetuous, generous passion stirring the long lines on the march, the blue battalions in the plain. The bugle, whenever I have heard it since, has always seemed to me the very golden throat of that boyhood which spent itself so gaily, so incredibly.

"I used often to wonder how it was that this uncle of mine, who seemed to have possessed all the charm and brilliancy allotted to his family and to have lived up its vitality in one splendid hour, had left so little trace in the house where he was born and where he had awaited his destiny. Look as I would, I could find no letters from him, no clothing or books that might have been his. He had been dead but twenty years, and yet nothing seemed to have survived except the tree he had planted. It seemed incredible and cruel that no physical memory of him should linger to be cherished among his kindred—nothing but the dull image in the brain of that aged sister. I used to pace the garden walks in the evening, wondering that no breath of his, no echo of his laugh, of his call to his pony or his whistle to his dogs, should linger about those shaded paths where the pale roses exhaled their dewy, country smell. Sometimes, in the dim starlight, I have thought that I heard on the grasses beside me the stir of a footfall lighter than my own, and under the black arch of the lilacs I have fancied that he bore me company.

"There was, I found, one day in the year for which my old aunt waited, and which stood out from the months that were all of a sameness to her. On the thirtieth of May she insisted that I should bring down the big flag from the attic and run it up upon the tall flagstaff beside Lyon's tree in the garden. Later in the morning she went with me to carry some of the garden flowers to the grave in the orchard—a grave scarcely larger than a child's.

"I had noticed, when I was hunting for the flag in the attic, a leather trunk with my own name stamped upon it, but was unable to find the key. My aunt was all day less apathetic than usual; she seemed to realize more clearly who I was, and to wish me to be with her. I did not have an opportunity to return to the attic until after dinner that evening, when I carried a lamp upstairs and easily forced the lock of the trunk. I found all the things that I had looked for; put away, doubtless, by his mother, and still smelling faintly of lavender and rose leaves; his clothes, his exercise books, his letters from the army, his first boots, his riding-whip, some of his toys, even. I took them out and replaced them gently. As I was about to shut the lid, I picked up a copy of the Æneid, on the fly-leaf of which was written in a slanting, boyish hand,

Lyon Hartwell, January, 1862.

He had gone to the wars in Sixty-three, I remembered.

"My uncle, I gathered, was none too apt at his Latin, for the pages were dog-eared and rubbed and interlined, the margins mottled with pencil sketches—bugles, stacked bayonets, and artillery carriages. In the act of putting the book down, I happened to run over the pages to the end, and on the fly-leaf at the back I saw his name again, and a drawing—with his initials and a date—of the Federal flag; above it, written in a kind of arch and in the same unformed hand:

"Oh, say, can you see by the dawn's early light
What so proudly we hailed at the twilight's last gleaming?"

It was a stiff, wooden sketch, not unlike a detail from some Egyptian inscription, but, the moment I saw it, wind and color seemed to touch it. I caught up the book, blew out the lamp, and rushed down into the garden.

"I seemed, somehow, at last to have known him; to have been with him in that careless, unconscious moment and to have known him as he was then.

"As I sat there in the rush of this realization, the wind began to rise, stirring the light foliage of the locust over my head and bringing, fresher than before, the woody odor of the pale roses that overran the little neglected garden. Then, as it grew stronger, it brought the sound of something sighing and stirring over my head in the perfumed darkness.

"I thought of that sad one of the Destinies who, as the Greeks believed, watched from birth over those marked for a violent or untimely death. Oh, I could see him, there in the shine of the morning, his book idly on his knee, his flashing eyes looking straight before him, and at his side that grave figure, hidden in her draperies, her eyes following his, but seeing so much farther—seeing what he never saw, that great moment at the end, when he swayed above his comrades on the earthen wall.

"All the while, the bunting I had run up in the morning flapped fold against fold, heaving and tossing softly in the dark—against a sky so black with rain clouds that I could see above me only the blur of something in soft, troubled motion.

"The experience of that night, coming so overwhelmingly to a man so dead, almost rent me in pieces. It was the same feeling that artists know when we, rarely, achieve truth in our work; the feeling of union with some great force, of purpose and security, of being glad that we have lived. For the first time I felt the pull of race and blood and kindred, and felt beating within me things that had not begun with me. It was as if the earth under my feet had grasped and rooted me, and were pouring its essence into me. I sat there until the dawn of morning, and all night long my life seemed to be pouring out of me and running into the ground."

Hartwell drew a long breath that lifted his heavy shoulders, and then let them fall again. He shifted a little and faced more squarely the scattered, silent company before him. The darkness had made us almost invisible to each other, and, except for the occasional red circuit of a cigarette end traveling upward from the arm of a chair, he might have supposed us all asleep.

"And so," Hartwell added thoughtfully, "I naturally feel an interest in fellows who are going home. It's always an experience."

No one said anything, and in a moment there was a loud rap at the door—the concierge, come to take down Bentley's luggage and to announce that the cab was below. Bentley got his hat and coat, enjoined Hartwell to take good care of his *perroquets,* gave each of us a grip of the hand, and went briskly down the long flights of stairs. We followed him into the street, calling our good wishes, and saw him start on his drive across the lighted city to the Gare St. Lazare.

# ON THE GULLS' ROAD

## Willa Cather

### The Ambassador's Story

IT OFTEN HAPPENS that one or another of my friends stops before a red chalk drawing in my study and asks me where I ever found so lovely a creature. I have never told the story of that picture to anyone, and the beautiful woman on the wall, until yesterday, in all these twenty years has spoken to no one but me. Yesterday a young painter, a countryman of mine, came to consult me on a matter of business, and upon seeing my drawing of Alexandra Ebbling, straightway forgot his errand. He examined the date upon the sketch and asked me, very earnestly, if I could tell him whether the lady were still living. When I answered him, he stepped back from the picture and said slowly:

"So long ago? She must have been very young. She was happy?"

"As to that, who can say—about anyone of us?" I replied. "Out of all that is supposed to make for happiness, she had very little."

He shrugged his shoulders and turned away to the window, saying as he did so: "Well, there is very little use in troubling about anything, when we can stand here and look at her, and you can tell me that she has been dead all these years, and that she had very little."

We returned to the object of his visit, but when he bade me goodbye at the door his troubled gaze again went back to the drawing, and it was only by turning sharply about that he took his eyes away from her.

I went back to my study fire, and as the rain kept away less impetuous visitors, I had a long time in which to think of Mrs. Ebbling, I even got out the little box she gave me, which I had not opened for years, and when Mrs. Hemway brought my tea I had barely time to close the lid and defeat her disapproving gaze.

My young countryman's perplexity, as he looked at Mrs. Ebbling, had recalled to me the delight and pain she gave me when I was of his years. I sat looking at her face and trying to see it through his eyes—freshly, as I saw it first upon the deck of the *Germania,* twenty years ago. Was it her loveliness, I often ask myself, or her loneliness, or her simplicity, or was it merely my own youth? Was her mystery only that of the mysterious North out of which she came? I still feel that she was very different from all the beautiful and brilliant women I have known; as the night is different from the day, or as the sea is different from the land. But this is our story, as it comes back to me.

For two years I had been studying Italian and working in the capacity of clerk to the American legation at Rome, and I was going home to secure my first consular appointment. Upon boarding my steamer at Genoa, I saw my luggage into my cabin and then started for a rapid circuit of the deck. Everything promised well. The boat was thinly peopled, even for a July crossing; the decks were roomy; the day was fine; the sea was blue; I was sure of my appointment, and, best of all, I was coming back to Italy. All these things were in my mind when I stopped sharply before a *chaise longue*[1] placed sidewise near the stern. Its occupant was a woman, apparently ill, who lay with her eyes closed, and in her open arm was a chubby little red-haired girl, asleep. I can still remember that first glance at Mrs. Ebbling, and how I stopped as a wheel does when the band slips. Her splendid, vigorous body lay still and relaxed under the loose folds of her clothing, her white throat and arms and red-gold hair were drenched with sunlight. Such hair as it was: wayward as some kind of gleaming seaweed that curls and undulates with the tide. A moment gave me her face; the high cheek-bones, the thin cheeks, the gentle chin, arching back to a girlish throat, and the singular loveliness of the mouth. Even then it flashed through me that the mouth gave the whole face its peculiar beauty and distinction. It was proud and sad and tender, and strangely calm. The curve of the lips could not have been cut more cleanly with the most delicate instrument, and whatever shade of feeling passed over them seemed to partake of their exquisiteness.

---

[1] *chaise longue*; French: a type of couch designed for lying down upon.

But I am anticipating. While I stood stupidly staring (as if, at twenty-five, I had never before beheld a beautiful woman) the whistles broke into a hoarse scream, and the deck under us began to vibrate. The woman opened her eyes, and the little girl struggled into a sitting position, rolled out of her mother's arm, and ran to the deck rail. After putting my chair near the stern, I went forward to see the gang-plank up and did not return until we were dragging out to sea at the end of a long tow-line.

The woman in the *chaise longue* was still alone. She lay there all day, looking at the sea. The little girl, Carin, played noisily about the deck. Occasionally she returned and struggled up into the chair, plunged her head, round and red as a little pumpkin, against her mother's shoulder in an impetuous embrace, and then struggled down again with a lively flourishing of arms and legs. Her mother took such opportunities to pull up the child's socks or to smooth the fiery little braids; her beautiful hands, rather large and very white, played about the riotous little girl with a quieting tenderness. Carin chattered away in Italian and kept asking for her father, only to be told that he was busy.

When any of the ship's officers passed, they stopped for a word with my neighbor, and I heard the first mate address her as Mrs. Ebbling. When they spoke to her, she smiled appreciatively and answered in low, faltering Italian, but I fancied that she was glad when they passed on and left her to her fixed contemplation of the sea. Her eyes seemed to drink the color of it all day long, and after every interruption they went back to it. There was a kind of pleasure in watching her satisfaction, a kind of excitement in wondering what the water made her remember or forget. She seemed not to wish to talk to anyone, but I knew I should like to hear whatever she might be thinking. One could catch some hint of her thoughts, I imagined, from the shadows that came and went across her lips, like the reflection of light clouds. She had a pile of books beside her, but she did not read, and neither could I. I gave up trying at last, and watched the sea, very conscious of her presence, almost of her thoughts. When the sun dropped low and shone in her face, I rose and asked if she would like me to move her chair. She smiled and thanked me, but said the sun was good for her. Her yellow-hazel eyes followed me for a moment and then went back to the sea.

After the first bugle sounded for dinner, a heavy man in uniform came up the deck and stood beside the *chaise longue,* looking down at its two occupants with a smile of satisfied possession. The breast of his trim coat was hidden by waves of soft blond beard, as long and heavy as a woman's hair, which blew about his face in glittering profusion. He wore a large turquoise ring upon the thick hand that he rubbed good-humoredly over the little girl's head. To her he spoke Italian, but he and his wife conversed in some Scandinavian tongue. He stood stroking his fine beard until the second bugle blew, then bent stiffly from his hips, like a soldier, and patted his wife's hand as it lay on the arm of her chair. He hurried down the deck, taking stock of the passengers as he went, and stopped before a thin girl with frizzed hair and a lace coat, asking her a facetious question in thick English. They began to talk about Chicago and went below. Later I saw him at the head of his table in the dining room, the befrizzed Chicago lady on his left. They must have got a famous start at luncheon, for by the end of the dinner Ebbling was peeling figs for her and presenting them on the end of a fork.

The Doctor confided to me that Ebbling was the chief engineer and the dandy of the boat; but this time he would have to behave himself, for he had brought his sick wife along for the voyage. She had a bad heart valve, he added, and was in a serious way.

After dinner Ebbling disappeared, presumably to his engines, and at ten o'clock, when the stewardess came to put Mrs. Ebbling to bed, I helped her to rise from her chair, and the second mate ran up and supported her down to her cabin. About midnight I found the engineer in the card room, playing with the Doctor, an Italian naval officer, and the commodore of a Long Island yacht club. His face was even pinker than it had been at dinner, and his fine beard was full of smoke. I thought a long while about Ebbling and his wife before I went to sleep.

The next morning we tied up at Naples to take on our cargo, and I went on shore for the day. I did not, however, entirely escape the ubiquitous engineer, whom I saw lunching with the Long Island commodore at a hotel in the Santa Lucia. When I returned to the boat in the early evening, the passengers had gone down to dinner, and I found Mrs. Ebbling quite alone upon the deserted deck. I approached her and asked whether she had had a dull day. She looked up smiling and shook her head, as if her Italian had quite failed her. I saw that she was flushed with excitement, and her yellow eyes were shining like two clear topazes.

"Dull? Oh, no! I love to watch Naples from the sea, in this white heat. She has just lain there on her hillside among the vines and laughed for me all day long. I have been able to pick out many of the places I like best."

I felt that she was really going to talk to me at last. She had turned to me frankly, as to an old acquaintance, and seemed not to be hiding from me anything of what she felt, I sat down in a glow of pleasure and excitement and asked her if she knew Naples well.

"Oh, yes! I lived there for a year after I was first married. My husband has a great many friends in Naples. But he was at sea most of the time, so I went about alone. Nothing helps one to know a city like that. I came first by sea, like this. Directly to Naples from Finmark, and I had never been South before." Mrs. Ebbling stopped and looked over my shoulder. Then, with a quick, eager glance at me, she said abruptly: "It was like a baptism of fire. Nothing has ever been quite the same since. Imagine how this bay looked to a Finmark girl. It seemed like the overture to Italy."

I laughed. "And then one goes up the country—song by song and wine by wine."

Mrs. Ebbling sighed. "Ah, yes. It must be fine to follow it. I have never been away from the seaports myself. We live now in Genoa."

The deck steward brought her tray, and I moved forward a little and stood by the rail. When I looked back, she smiled and nodded to let me know that she was not missing anything. I could feel her intentness as keenly as if she were standing beside me.

The sun had disappeared over the high ridge behind the city, and the stone pines stood black and flat against the fires of the afterglow. The lilac haze that hung over the long, lazy slopes of Vesuvius warmed with golden light, and films of blue vapor began to float down toward Baiæ. The sky, the sea, and the city between them turned a shimmering violet, fading grayer as the lights began to glow like luminous pearls along the water-front—the necklace of an irreclaimable queen. Behind me I heard a low exclamation; a slight, stifled sound, but it seemed the perfect vocalization of that weariness with which we at last let go of beauty, after we have held it until the senses are darkened. When I turned to her again, she seemed to have fallen asleep.

That night, as we were moving out to sea and the tail lights of Naples were winking across the widening stretch of black water, I helped Mrs. Ebbling to the foot of the stairway. She drew herself up from her chair with effort and leaned on me wearily. I could have carried her all night without fatigue.

"May I come and talk to you tomorrow?" I asked. She did not reply at once. "Like an old friend?" I added. She gave me her languid hand, and her mouth, set with the exertion of walking, softened altogether. "*Grazia*[2]," she murmured.

I returned to the deck and joined a group of my countrywomen, who, primed with inexhaustible information, were discussing the baseness of Renaissance art. They were intelligent and alert, and as they leaned forward in their deck chairs under the circle of light, their faces recalled to me Rembrandt's picture of a clinical lecture. I heard them through, against my will, and then went to the stern to smoke and to see the last of the island lights. The sky had clouded over, and a soft, melancholy wind was rushing over the sea. I could not help thinking how disappointed I would be if rain should keep Mrs. Ebbling in her cabin tomorrow. My mind played constantly with her image. At one moment she was very clear and directly in front of me; the next she was far away. Whatever else I thought about, some part of my consciousness was busy with Mrs. Ebbling; hunting for her, finding her, losing her, then groping again. How was it that I was so conscious of whatever she might be feeling? that when she sat still behind me and watched the evening sky, I had had a sense of speed and change, almost of danger; and when she was tired and sighed, I had wished for night and loneliness.

## II

Though when we are young we seldom think much about it. there is now and again a golden day when we feel a sudden, arrogant pride in our youth; in the lightness of our feet and the strength of our arms, in the warm fluid that courses so surely within us; when we are conscious of something powerful and mercurial in our breasts, which comes up wave after wave and leaves us irresponsible and free. All the next morning I felt this flow of life, which continually impelled me toward Mrs. Ebbling. After the merest greeting, however, I kept away. I found it pleasant to thwart myself, to measure myself against a current that was sure to carry me with it in the end. I was content to let her watch the sea—the sea that seemed now to have come into me, warm and soft, still and strong. I played shuffleboard with the Commodore, who was anxious to keep down his figure, and ran about the deck with the stout legs of the little pumpkin-colored Carin about my neck. It was not until the child was having her afternoon nap below that I at last came up and stood beside her mother.

---

[2] *grazia*; Italian: thank you.

"You are better today," I exclaimed, looking down at her white gown. She colored unreasonably, and I laughed with a familiarity which she must have accepted as the mere foolish noise of happiness, or it would have seemed impertinent.

We talked at first of a hundred trivial things, and we watched the sea. The coast of Sardinia had lain to our port for some hours and would lie there for hours to come, now advancing in rocky promontories, now retreating behind blue bays. It was the naked south coast of the island, and though our course held very near the shore, not a village or habitation was visible; there was not even a goatherd's hut hidden away among the low pinkish sand hills. Pinkish sand hills and yellow headlands; with dull-colored scrubby bushes massed about their bases and following the dried watercourses. A narrow strip of beach glistened like white paint between the purple sea and the umber rocks, and the whole island lay gleaming in the yellow sunshine and translucent air. Not a wave broke on that fringe of white sand, not the shadow of a cloud played across the bare hills. In the air about us there was no sound but that of a vessel moving rapidly through absolutely still water. She seemed like some great sea-animal, swimming silently, her head well up. The sea before us was so rich and heavy and opaque that it might have been lapis lazuli. It was the blue of legend, simply; the color that satisfies the soul like sleep.

And it was of the sea we talked, for it was the substance of Mrs. Ebbling's story. She seemed always to have been swept along by ocean streams, warm or cold, and to have hovered about the edge of great waters. She was born and had grown up in a little fishing town on the Arctic ocean. Her father was a doctor, a widower, who lived with his daughter and who divided his time between his books and his fishing rod. Her uncle was skipper on a coasting vessel, and with him she had made many trips along the Norwegian coast. But she was always reading and thinking about the blue seas of the South.

"There was a curious old woman in our village, Dame Ericson, who had been in Italy in her youth. She had gone to Rome to study art, and had copied a great many pictures there. She was well connected, but had little money, and as she grew older and poorer she sold her pictures one by one, until there was scarcely a well-to-do family in our district that did not own one of Dame Ericson's paintings. But she brought home many other strange things; a little orange-tree which she cherished until the day of her death, and bits of colored marble, and sea shells and pieces of coral, and a thin flask full of water from the Mediterranean. When I was a little girl she used to show me her things and tell me about the South; about the coral fishers, and the pink islands, and the smoking mountains, and the old, underground Naples. I suppose the water in her flask was like any other, but it never seemed so to me. It looked so elastic and alive, that I used to think if one unsealed the bottle something penetrating and fruitful might leap out and work an enchantment over Finmark."

Lars Ebbling, I learned, was one of her father's friends. She could remember him from the time when she was a little girl and he a dashing young man who used to come home from the sea and make a stir in the village. After he got his promotion to an Atlantic liner and went South, she did not see him until the summer she was twenty, when he came home to marry her. That was five years ago. The little girl, Carin, was three. From her talk, one might have supposed that Ebbling was proprietor of the Mediterranean and its adjacent lands, and could have kept her away at his pleasure. Her own rights in him she seemed not to consider.

But we wasted very little time on Lars Ebbling. We talked, like two very young persons, of arms and men, of the sea beneath us and the shores it washed. We were carried a little beyond ourselves, for we were in the presence of the things of youth that never change; fleeing past them. Tomorrow they would be gone, and no effort of will or memory could bring them back again. All about us was the sea of great adventure, and below us, caught somewhere in its gleaming meshes, were the bones of nations and navies . . . nations and navies that gave youth its hope and made life something more than a hunger of the bowels. The unpeopled Sardinian coast unfolded gently before us, like something left over out of a world that was gone; a place that might well have had no later news since the corn ships brought the tidings of Actium.

"I shall never go to Sardinia," said Mrs. Ebbling. "It could not possibly be as beautiful as this."

"Neither shall I," I replied.

As I was going down to dinner that evening, I was stopped by Lars Ebbling, freshly brushed and scented, wearing a white uniform, and polished and glistening as one of his own engines. He smiled at me with his own kind of geniality. "You have been very kind to talk to my wife," he explained, "It is very bad for her this trip that she speaks no English. I am indebted to you."

I told him curtly that he was mistaken, but my acrimony made no impression upon his blandness. I felt that I should certainly strike the fellow if he stood there much longer, running his blue ring up and down his beard. I should probably have hated any man who was Mrs. Ebbling's husband, but Ebbling made me sick.

### III

The next day I began my drawing of Mrs. Ebbling. She seemed pleased and a little puzzled when I asked her to sit for me. It occurred to me that she had always been among dull people who took her looks as a matter of course, and that she was not at all sure that she was really beautiful. I can see now her quick, confused look of pleasure. I thought very little about the drawing then, except that the making of it gave me an opportunity to study her face; to look as long as I pleased into her yellow eyes, at the noble lines of her mouth, at her splendid, vigorous hair.

"We have a yellow vine at home," I told her, "that is very like your hair. It seems to be growing while one looks at it, and it twines and tangles about itself and throws out little tendrils in the wind."

"Has it any name?"

"We call it love vine."

How little a thing could disconcert her!

As for me, nothing disconcerted me. I awoke every morning with a sense of speed and joy. At night I loved to hear the swish of the water rushing by. As fast as the pistons could carry us, as fast as the water could bear us, we were going forward to something delightful; to something together. When Mrs. Ebbling told me that she and her husband would be five days in the docks in New York and then return to Genoa, I was not disturbed, for I did not believe her. I came and went, and she sat still all day, watching the water. I heard an American lady say that she watched it like one who is going to die, but even that did not frighten me: I somehow felt that she had promised me to live.

All those long blue days when I sat beside her talking about Finmark and the sea, she must have known that I loved her. I sat with my hands idle on my knees and let the tide come up in me. It carried me so swiftly that, across the narrow space of deck between us, it must have swayed her, too, a little. I had no wish to disturb or distress her. If a little, a very little of it reached her, I was satisfied. If it drew her softly, but drew her, I wanted no more. Sometimes

I could see that even the light pressure of my thoughts made her paler. One still evening, after a long talk, she whispered to me, "You must go and walk now, and—don't think about me." She had been held too long and too closely in my thoughts, and she begged me to release her for a little while. I went out into the bow and put her far away, at the sky line, with the faintest star, and thought of her gently across the water. When I went back to her, she was asleep.

But even in those first days I had my hours of misery. Why, for instance, should she have been born in Finmark, and why should Lars Ebbling have been her only door of escape? Why should she be silently taking leave of the world at the age when I was just beginning it, having had nothing, nothing of whatever is worthwhile?

She never talked about taking leave of things, and yet I sometimes felt that she was counting the sunsets. One yellow afternoon, when we were gliding between the shores of Spain and Africa, she spoke of her illness for the first time. I had got some magnolias at Gibraltar, and she wore a bunch of them in her girdle and the rest lay on her lap. She held the cool leaves against her cheek and fingered the white petals. "I can never," she remarked, "get enough of the flowers of the South. They make me breathless, just as they did at first. Because of them I should like to live a long while—almost forever."

I leaned forward and looked at her. "We could live almost forever if we had enough courage. It's of our lives that we die. If we had the courage to change it all, to run away to some blue coast like that over there, we could live on and on, until we were tired."

She smiled tolerantly and looked southward through half shut eyes. "I am afraid I should never have courage enough to go behind that mountain, at least. Look at it, it looks as if it hid horrible things."

A sea mist, blown in from the Atlantic, began to mask the impassive African coast, and above the fog, the grey mountain peak took on the angry red of the sunset. It burned sullen and threatening until the dark land drew the night about her and settled back into the sea. We watched it sink, while under us, slowly but ever increasing, we felt the throb of the Atlantic come and go, the thrill of the vast, untamed waters of that lugubrious and passionate sea. I drew Mrs. Ebbling's wraps about her and shut the magnolias under her cloak. When I left her, she slipped me one warm, white flower.

## IV

From the Straits of Gibraltar we dropped into the abyss, and by morning we were rolling in the trough of a sea that drew us down and held us deep, shaking us gently back and forth until the timbers creaked, and then shooting us out on the crest of a swelling mountain. The water was bright and blue, but so cold that the breath of it penetrated one's bones, as if the chill of the deep under-fathoms of the sea were being loosed upon us. There were not more than a dozen people upon the deck that morning, and Mrs. Ebbling was sheltered behind the stern, muffled in a sea jacket, with drops of moisture upon her long lashes and on her hair. When a shower of icy spray beat back over the deck rail, she took it gleefully.

"After all," she insisted, "this is my own kind of water; the kind I was born in. This is first cousin to the Pole waters, and the sea we have left is only a kind of fairy tale. It's like the burnt out volcanoes; its day is over. This is the real sea now, where the doings of the world go on."

"It is not our reality, at any rate," I answered.

"Oh, yes, it is! These are the waters that carry men to their work, and they will carry you to yours."

I sat down and watched her hair grow more alive and iridescent in the moisture. "You are pleased to take an attitude," I complained.

"No, I don't love realities any more than another, but I admit them, all the same."

"And who are you and I to define the realities?"

"Our minds define them clearly enough, yours and mine, everybody's. Those are the lines we never cross, though we flee from the equator to the Pole. I have never really got out of Finmark, of course. I shall live and die in a fishing town on the Arctic ocean, and the blue seas and the pink islands are as much a dream as they ever were. All the same, I shall continue to dream them."

The Gulf Stream gave us warm blue days again, but pale, like sad memories. The water had faded, and the thin, tepid sunshine made something tighten about one's heart. The stars watched us coldly, and seemed always to be asking me what I was going to do. The advancing line on the chart, which at first had been mere foolishness, began to mean something, and the wind from the west brought disturbing fears and forebodings. I slept lightly, and all day I was restless and uncertain except when I was with Mrs. Ebbling. She quieted me as she did little Carin, and soothed me without saying anything, as she had done that evening at Naples when we watched the sunset. It seemed to me that every day her eyes grew more tender and her lips more calm. A kind of fortitude seemed to be gathering about her mouth, and I dreaded it. Yet when, in an involuntary glance, I put to her the question that tortured me, her eyes always met mine steadily, deep and gentle and full of reassurance. That I had my word at last, happened almost by accident.

On the second night out from shore there was the concert for the Sailors' Orphanage, and Mrs. Ebbling dressed and went down to dinner for the first time, and sat on her husband's right. I was not the only one who was glad to see her. Even the women were pleased. She wore a pale green gown, and she came up out of it regally white and gold. I was so proud that I blushed when anyone spoke of her. After dinner she was standing by her deck-chair talking to her husband when people began to go below for the concert. She took up a long cloak and attempted to put it on. The wind blew the light thing about, and Ebbling chatted and smiled his public smile while she struggled with it. Suddenly his roving eye caught sight of the Chicago girl, who was having a similar difficulty with her draperies, and he pranced half the length of the deck to assist her. I had been watching from the rail, and when she was left alone I threw my cigar away and wrapped Mrs. Ebbling up roughly.

"Don't go down," I begged. "Stay up here. I want to talk to you."

She hesitated a moment and looked at me thoughtfully. Then, with a sigh, she sat down. Everyone hurried down to the saloon, and we were absolutely alone at last, behind the shelter of the stern, with the thick darkness all about us and a warm east wind rushing over the sea. I was too sore and angry to think. I leaned toward her, holding the arm of her chair with both hands, and began anyway.

"You remember those two blue coasts out of Gibraltar? It shall be either one you choose, if you will come with me. I have not much money but we shall get on somehow. There has got to be an end of this. We are neither one of us cowards, and this is humiliating, intolerable."

She sat looking down at her hands, and I pulled her chair impatiently toward me.

"I felt," she said at last, "that you were going to say something like this. You are sorry for me, and I don't wish to be pitied. You think Ebbling neglects me, but you are mistaken. He has had his disappointments, too. He wants children and a gay, hospitable house, and he is tied to a sick woman who cannot get on with people. He has more to complain of than I have, and yet he bears with me. I am grateful to him, and there is no more to be said."

"Oh, isn't there?" I cried, "and I?"

She laid her hand entreatingly upon my arm. "Ah, you! you! Don't ask me to talk about that. *You*—" Her fingers slipped down my coat sleeve to my hand and pressed it. I caught her two hands and held them, telling her I would never let them go.

"And you meant to leave me day after tomorrow, to say goodbye to me as you will to the other people on this boat? You meant to cut me adrift like this, with my heart on fire and all my life unspent in me?"

She sighed despondently. "I am willing to suffer—whatever I must suffer—to have had you," she answered simply. "I was ill—and so lonely—and it came so quickly and quietly. Ah, don't begrudge it to me! Do not leave me in bitterness. If I have been wrong, forgive me." She bowed her head and pressed my fingers entreatingly. A warm tear splashed on my hand. It occurred to me that she bore my anger as she bore little Carin's importunities, as she bore Ebbling. What a circle of pettiness she had about her! I fell back in my chair and my hands dropped at my side. I felt like a creature with its back broken. I asked her what she wished me to do.

"Don't ask me," she whispered. "There is nothing that we can do. I thought you knew that. You forget that—that I am too ill to begin my life over. Even if there were nothing else in the way, that would be enough. And that is what has made it all possible, our loving each other, I mean. If I were well, we couldn't have had even this much. Don't reproach me. Hasn't it been at all pleasant to you to find me waiting for you every morning, to feel me thinking of you when you went to sleep? Every night I have watched the sea for you, as if it were mine and I had made it, and I have listened to the water rushing by you, full of sleep and youth and hope. And everything you had done or said during the day came back to me, and when I went to sleep it was only to feel you more. You see there was never anyone else; I have never thought of anyone in the dark but you." She spoke pleadingly, and her voice had sunk so low that I could scarcely hear her.

"And yet you will do nothing," I groaned. "You will dare nothing. You will give me nothing."

"Don't say that. When I leave you day after tomorrow, I shall have given you all my life. I can't tell you how, but it is true. There is something in each of us that does not belong to the family or to

society, not even to ourselves. Sometimes it is given in marriage, and
sometimes it is given in love, but oftener it is never given at all. We
have nothing to do with giving or withholding it. It is a wild thing
that sings in us once and flies away and never comes back, and mine
has flown to you. When one loves like that, it is enough, somehow.
The other things can go if they must. That is why I can live without
you, and die without you."

I caught her hands and looked into her eyes that shone warm in
the darkness. She shivered and whispered in a tone so different
from any I ever heard from her before or afterward: "Do you grudge
it to me? You are so young and strong, and you have everything
before you. I shall have only a little while to want you in—and I
could want you forever and not weary." I kissed her hair, her
cheeks, her lips, until her head fell forward on my shoulder and
she put my face away with her soft, trembling fingers. She took my
hand and held it close to her, in both her own. We sat silent, and
the moments came and went, bringing us closer and closer, and the
wind and water rushed by us, obliterating our tomorrows and all
our yesterdays.

The next day Mrs. Ebbling kept her cabin, and I sat stupidly by
her chair until dark, with the rugged little girl to keep me company,
and an occasional nod from the engineer.

I saw Mrs. Ebbling again only for a few moments, when we were
coming into the New York harbor. She wore a street dress and a hat,
and these alone would have made her seem far away from me. She
was very pale, and looked down when she spoke to me, as if she had
been guilty of a wrong toward me. I have never been able to remember that interview without heartache and shame, but then I was too
desperate to care about anything. I stood like a wooden post and let
her approach me, let her speak to me, let her leave me. She came up
to me as if it were a hard thing to do, and held out a little package,
timidly, and her gloved hand shook as if she were afraid of me.

"I want to give you something," she said. "You will not want it
now, so I shall ask you to keep it until you hear from me. You gave
me your address a long time ago, when you were making that drawing.
Some day I shall write to you and ask you to open this. You must
not come to tell me goodbye this morning, but I shall be watching
you when you go ashore. Please don't forget that."

I took the little box mechanically and thanked her. I think my
eyes must have filled, for she uttered an exclamation of pity, touched
my sleeve quickly, and left me. It was one of those strange, low,

musical exclamations which meant everything and nothing, like the one that had thrilled me that night at Naples, and it was the last sound I ever heard from her lips.

An hour later I went on shore, one of those who crowded over the gang-plank the moment it was lowered. But the next afternoon I wandered back to the docks and went on board the *Germania*. I asked for the engineer, and he came up in his shirt sleeves from the engine room. He was red and dishevelled, angry and voluble; his bright eye had a hard glint, and I did not once see his masterful smile. When he heard my inquiry he became profane. Mrs. Ebbling had sailed for Bremen on the *Hobenstauffen* that morning at eleven o'clock. She had decided to return by the northern route and pay a visit to her father in Finmark. She was in no condition to travel alone, he said. He evidently smarted under her extravagance. But who, he asked, with a blow of his fist on the rail, could stand between a woman and her whim? She had always been a wilful girl, and she had a doting father behind her. When she set her head with the wind, there was no holding her; she ought to have married the Arctic Ocean. I think Ebbling was still talking when I walked away.

I spent that winter in New York. My consular appointment hung fire (indeed, I did not pursue it with much enthusiasm), and I had a good many idle hours in which to think of Mrs. Ebbling. She had never mentioned the name of her father's village, and somehow I could never quite bring myself to go to the docks when Ebbling's boat was in and ask for news of her. More than once I made up my mind definitely to go to Finmark and take my chance at finding her; the shipping people would know where Ebbling came from. But I never went. I have often wondered why. When my resolve was made and my courage high, when I could almost feel myself approaching her, suddenly everything crumbled under me, and I fell back as I had done that night when I dropped her hands, after telling her, only a moment before, that I would never let them go.

In the twilight of a wet March day, when the gutters were running black outside and the Square was liquefying under crusts of dirty snow, the housekeeper brought me a damp letter which bore a blurred foreign postmark. It was from Niels Nannestad, who wrote that it was his sad duty to inform me that his daughter, Alexandra Ebbling, had died on the second day of February, in the twenty-sixth year of her age. Complying with her request, he enclosed a letter which she had written some days before her death.

I at last brought myself to break the seal of the second letter. It read thus:

> "My Friend:—You may open now the little package I gave you. May I ask you to keep it? I gave it to you because there is no one else who would care about it in just that way. Ever since I left you I have been thinking what it would be like to live a lifetime caring and being cared for like that. It was not the life I was meant to live, and yet, in a way, I have been living it ever since I first knew you.
>
> "Of course you understand now why I could not go with you. I would have spoiled your life for you. Besides that, I was ill—and I was too proud to give you the shadow of myself. I had much to give you, if you had come earlier. As it was, I was ashamed. Vanity sometimes saves us when nothing else will, and mine saved you. Thank you for everything. I hold this to my heart, where I once held your hand,
>
> Alexandra."

The dusk had thickened into night long before I got up from my chair and took the little box from its place in my desk drawer. I opened it and lifted out a thick coil, cut from where her hair grew thickest and brightest. It was tied firmly at one end, and when it fell over my arm it curled and clung about my sleeve like a living thing set free. How it gleamed, how it still gleams in the firelight! It was warm and softly scented under my lips, and stirred under my breath like seaweed in the tide. This, and a withered magnolia flower, and two pink sea shells; nothing more. And it was all twenty years ago!

# THE WIFE OF HIS YOUTH

## Charles Waddell Chesnutt

### I

MR. RYDER WAS going to give a ball. There were several reasons why this was an opportune time for such an event.

Mr. Ryder might aptly be called the dean of the Blue Veins. The original Blue Veins were a little society of colored persons organized in a certain Northern city shortly after the war. Its purpose was to establish and maintain correct social standards among a people whose social condition presented almost unlimited room for improvement. By accident, combined perhaps with some natural affinity, the society consisted of individuals who were, generally speaking, more white than black. Some envious outsider made the suggestion that no one was eligible for membership who was not white enough to show blue veins. The suggestion was readily adopted by those who were not of the favored few, and since that time the society, though possessing a longer and more pretentious name, had been known far and wide as the "Blue Vein Society," and its members as the "Blue Veins."

The Blue Veins did not allow that any such requirement existed for admission to their circle, but, on the contrary, declared that character and culture were the only things considered; and that if most of their members were light-colored, it was because such persons, as a rule, had had better opportunities to qualify themselves for membership. Opinions differed, too, as to the usefulness of the society. There were those who had been known to assail it violently as a glaring example of the very prejudice from which the colored race

161

had suffered most; and later, when such critics had succeeded in getting on the inside, they had been heard to maintain with zeal and earnestness that the society was a lifeboat, an anchor, a bulwark and a shield—a pillar of cloud by day and of fire by night, to guide their people through the social wilderness. Another alleged prerequisite for Blue Vein membership was that of free birth; and while there was really no such requirement, it is doubtless true that very few of the members would have been unable to meet it if there had been. If there were one or two of the older members who had come up from the South and from slavery, their history presented enough romantic circumstances to rob their servile origin of its grosser aspects.

While there were no such tests of eligibility, it is true that the Blue Veins had their notions on these subjects, and that not all of them were equally liberal in regard to the things they collectively disclaimed. Mr. Ryder was one of the most conservative. Though he had not been among the founders of the society, but had come in some years later, his genius for social leadership was such that he had speedily become its recognized adviser and head, the custodian of its standards, and the preserver of its traditions. He shaped its social policy, was active in providing for its entertainment, and when the interest fell off, as it sometimes did, he fanned the embers until they burst again into a cheerful flame.

There were still other reasons for his popularity. While he was not as white as some of the Blue Veins, his appearance was such as to confer distinction upon them. His features were of a refined type, his hair was almost straight; he was always neatly dressed; his manners were irreproachable, and his morals above suspicion. He had come to Groveland a young man, and obtaining employment in the office of a railroad company as messenger had in time worked himself up to the position of stationery clerk, having charge of the distribution of the office supplies for the whole company. Although the lack of early training had hindered the orderly development of a naturally fine mind, it had not prevented him from doing a great deal of reading or from forming decidedly literary tastes. Poetry was his passion. He could repeat whole pages of the great English poets; and if his pronunciation was sometimes faulty, his eye, his voice, his gestures, would respond to the changing sentiment with a precision that revealed a poetic soul and disarmed criticism. He was economical, and had saved money; he owned and occupied a very comfortable house on a respectable street. His residence was handsomely furnished, containing among other things a good library, especially rich in poetry, a piano, and some choice engravings. He generally shared his house with some young couple, who looked after his wants and were company for him; for Mr. Ryder was a single man. In the early days of his connection with the Blue Veins he had been regarded as quite a catch, and young ladies and their mothers had maneuvered with much ingenuity to capture him. Not, however, until Mrs. Molly Dixon visited Groveland had any woman ever made him wish to change his condition to that of a married man.

Mrs. Dixon had come to Groveland from Washington in the spring, and before the summer was over she had won Mr. Ryder's heart. She possessed many attractive qualities. She was much younger than he; in fact, he was old enough to have been her father, though no one knew exactly how old he was. She was whiter than he, and better educated. She had moved in the best colored society of the country, at Washington, and had taught in the schools of the city. Such a superior person had been eagerly welcomed to the Blue Vein Society, and had taken a leading part in its activities. Mr. Ryder had at first been attracted by her charms of person, for she was very good looking and not over twenty-five; then by her refined manners and the vivacity of her wit. Her husband had been a government clerk, and at his death had left a considerable life insurance. She was visiting friends in Groveland, and, finding the town and the people to her liking, had prolonged her stay indefinitely. She had not seemed displeased at Mr. Ryder's attentions, but on the contrary had given him every proper encouragement; indeed, a younger and less cautious man would long since have spoken. But he had made up his mind, and had only to determine the time when he would ask her to be his wife. He decided to give a ball in her honor, and at some time during the evening of the ball to offer her his heart and hand. He had no special fears about the outcome, but, with a little touch of romance, he wanted the surroundings to be in harmony with his own feelings when he should have received the answer he expected.

Mr. Ryder resolved that this ball should mark an epoch in the social history of Groveland. He knew, of course—no one could know better—the entertainments that had taken place in past years, and what must be done to surpass them. His ball must be worthy of the lady in whose honor it was to be given, and must, by the quality of its guests, set an example for the future. He had observed of late a growing liberality, almost a laxity, in social matters, even among members of his own set, and had several times been forced to meet in a social way persons whose complexions and callings in life were hardly up to the standards which he considered proper for the society to maintain. He had a theory of his own.

"I have no race prejudice," he would say, "but we people of mixed blood are ground between the upper and the nether millstone. Our fate lies between absorption by the white race and extinction in the black. The one doesn't want us yet, but may take us in time. The other would welcome us, but it would be for us a backward step. 'With malice toward none, with charity for all,' we must do the best we can for ourselves and those who are to follow us. Self-preservation is the first law of nature."

His ball would serve by its exclusiveness to counteract leveling tendencies, and his marriage with Mrs. Dixon would help to further the upward process of absorption he had been wishing and waiting for.

## II

The ball was to take place on Friday night. The house had been put in order, the carpets covered with canvas, the halls and stairs decorated with palms and potted plants; and in the afternoon Mr. Ryder sat on his front porch, which the shade of a vine running up over a wire netting made a cool and pleasant lounging place. He expected to respond to the toast "The Ladies" at the supper, and from a volume of Tennyson— his favorite poet—was fortifying himself with apt quotations. The volume was open at "A Dream of Fair Women." His eyes fell on these lines, and he read them aloud to judge better of their effect:—

> "At length I saw a lady within call,
>     Stiller than chisell'd marble, standing there;
> A daughter of the gods, divinely tall,
>     And most divinely fair."

He marked the verse, and turning the page read the stanza beginning—

> "O sweet pale Margaret,
> O rare pale Margaret."

He weighed the passage a moment, and decided that it would not do. Mrs. Dixon was the palest lady he expected at the ball, and she was of a rather ruddy complexion, and of lively disposition and buxom build. So he ran over the leaves until his eye rested on the description of Queen Guinevere:—

> "She seem'd a part of joyous Spring:
> A gown of grass-green silk she wore,
> Buckled with golden clasps before;
> A light-green tuft of plumes she bore
> Closed in a golden ring.
>
> •      •      •      •      •      •
>
> "She look'd so lovely, as she sway'd
> The rein with dainty finger-tips,
> A man had given all other bliss,
> And all his worldly worth for this,
> To waste his whole heart in one kiss
> Upon her perfect lips."

As Mr. Ryder murmured these words audibly, with an appreciative thrill, he heard the latch of his gate click, and a light footfall sounding on the steps. He turned his head, and saw a woman standing before his door.

She was a little woman, not five feet tall, and proportioned to her height. Although she stood erect, and looked around her with very bright and restless eyes, she seemed quite old; for her face was crossed and recrossed with a hundred wrinkles, and around the edges of her bonnet could be seen protruding here and there a tuft of short gray wool. She wore a blue calico gown of ancient cut, a little red shawl fastened around her shoulders with an old-fashioned brass brooch, and a large bonnet profusely ornamented with faded red and yellow artificial flowers. And she was very black—so black that her toothless gums, revealed when she opened her mouth to speak, were not red, but blue. She looked like a bit of the old plantation life, summoned up from the past by the wave of a magician's wand, as the poet's fancy had called into being the gracious shapes of which Mr. Ryder had just been reading.

He rose from his chair and came over to where she stood.

"Good-afternoon, madam," he said.

"Good-evenin', suh," she answered, ducking suddenly with a quaint curtsy. Her voice was shrill and piping, but softened somewhat by age. "Is dis yere whar Mistuh Ryduh lib, suh?" she asked, looking around her doubtfully, and glancing into the open windows, through which some of the preparations for the evening were visible.

"Yes," he replied, with an air of kindly patronage, unconsciously flattered by her manner, "I am Mr. Ryder. Did you want to see me?"

"Yas, suh, ef I ain't 'sturbin' of you too much."

"Not at all. Have a seat over here behind the vine, where it is cool. What can I do for you?"

"'Scuse me, suh," she continued, when she had sat down on the edge of a chair, "'scuse me, suh, I's lookin' for my husban'. I heerd you wuz a big man an' had libbed heah a long time, an' I 'lowed you wouldn't min' ef I'd come roun' an' ax you ef you'd ever heerd of a merlatter man by de name er Sam Taylor 'quirin' roun' in de chu'ches ermongs' de people fer his wife 'Liza Jane?"

Mr. Ryder seemed to think for a moment.

"There used to be many such cases right after the war," he said, "but it has been so long that I have forgotten them. There are very few now. But tell me your story, and it may refresh my memory."

She sat back farther in her chair so as to be more comfortable, and folded her withered hands in her lap.

"My name's 'Liza," she began, "'Liza Jane. W'en I wuz young I us'ter b'long ter Marse Bob Smif, down in ole Missoura. I wuz bawn down dere. W'en I wuz a gal I wuz married ter a man named Jim. But Jim died, an' after dat I married a merlatter man named Sam Taylor. Sam wuz free-bawn, but his mammy an' daddy died, an' de w'ite folks 'prenticed him ter my marster fer ter work fer 'im 'tel he wuz growed up. Sam worked in de fiel', an' I wuz de cook. One day Ma'y Ann, ole miss's maid, came rushin' out ter de kitchen, an' says she, 'Liza Jane, ole marse gwine sell yo' Sam down de ribber.'

"'Go way f'm yere,' says I; 'my husban's free!'

"'Don' make no diff'ence. I heerd ole marse tell ole miss he wuz gwine take yo' Sam 'way wid 'im ter-morrow, fer he needed money, an' he knowed whar he could git a t'ousan' dollars fer Sam an' no questions axed.'

"W'en Sam come home f'm de fiel' dat night, I tole him 'bout ole marse gwine steal 'im, an' Sam run erway. His time wuz mos' up, an' he swo' dat w'en he wuz twenty-one he would come back an' he'p me run erway, er else save up de money ter buy my freedom. An' I know he'd 'a' done it, fer he thought a heap er me, Sam did. But w'en he come back he didn' fin' me, fer I wuzn' dere. Ole marse had heerd dat I warned Sam, so he had me whip' an' sol' down de ribber.

"Den de wah broke out, an' w'en it wuz ober de cullud folks wuz scattered. I went back ter de ole home; but Sam wuzn' dere, an' I couldn' l'arn nuffin' 'bout 'im. But I knowed he'd be'n dere to look fer me an' hadn' foun' me, an' had gone erway ter hunt fer me.

"I's be'n lookin' fer 'im eber sence," she added simply, as though twenty-five years were but a couple of weeks, "an' I knows he's be'n lookin' fer me. Fer he sot a heap er sto' by me, Sam did, an' I know he's be'n huntin' fer me all dese years—'less'n he's be'n sick er sump'n, so he couldn' work, er out'n his head, so he couldn' 'member his promise. I went back down de ribber, fer I 'lowed he'd gone down dere lookin' fer me. I's be'n ter Noo Orleens, an' Atlanty, an' Charleston, an' Richmon'; an' w'en I'd be'n all ober de Souf I come ter de Norf. Fer I knows I'll fin' 'im some er dese days," she added softly, "er he'll fin' me, an' den we'll bofe be as happy in freedom as we wuz in de ole days befo' de wah." A smile stole over her withered countenance as she paused a moment, and her bright eyes softened into a far-away look.

This was the substance of the old woman's story. She had wandered a little here and there. Mr. Ryder was looking at her curiously when she finished.

"How have you lived all these years?" he asked.

"Cookin', suh. I's a good cook. Does you know anybody w'at needs a good cook, suh? I's stoppin' wid a cullud fam'ly roun' de corner yonder 'tel I kin git a place."

"Do you really expect to find your husband? He may be dead long ago."

She shook her head emphatically. "Oh no, he ain' dead. De signs an' de tokens tells me. I dremp three nights runnin' on'y dis las' week dat I foun' him."

"He may have married another woman. Your slave marriage would not have prevented him, for you never lived with him after the war, and without that your marriage doesn't count."

"Wouldn' make no diff'ence wid Sam. He wouldn' marry no yuther 'oman 'tel he foun' out 'bout me. I knows it," she added. "Sump'n 's be'n tellin' me all dese years dat I's gwine fin' Sam 'fo' I dies."

"Perhaps he's outgrown you, and climbed up in the world where he wouldn't care to have you find him."

"No, indeed, suh," she replied, "Sam ain' dat kin' er man. He wuz good ter me, Sam wuz, but he wuzn' much good ter nobody e'se, fer he wuz one er de triflin'es' han's on de plantation. I 'spec's ter haf ter suppo't 'im w'en I fin' 'im, fer he nebber would work 'less'n he had ter. But den he wuz free, an' he didn' git no pay fer his work, an' I don' blame 'im much. Mebbe he's done better sence he run erway, but I ain' 'spectin' much."

"You may have passed him on the street a hundred times during the twenty-five years, and not have known him; time works great changes."

She smiled incredulously. "I'd know 'im 'mongs' a hund'ed men. Fer dey wuzn' no yuther merlatter man like my man Sam, an' I couldn' be mistook. I's toted his picture roun' wid me twenty-five years."

"May I see it?" asked Mr. Ryder. "It might help me to remember whether I have seen the original."

As she drew a small parcel from her bosom he saw that it was fastened to a string that went around her neck. Removing several wrappers, she brought to light an old-fashioned daguerreotype in a black case. He looked long and intently at the portrait. It was faded with time, but the features were still distinct, and it was easy to see what manner of man it had represented.

He closed the case, and with a slow movement handed it back to her.

"I don't know of any man in town who goes by that name," he said, "nor have I heard of anyone making such inquiries. But if you will leave me your address, I will give the matter some attention, and if I find out anything I will let you know."

She gave him the number of a house in the neighborhood, and went away, after thanking him warmly.

He wrote the address on the fly-leaf of the volume of Tennyson, and, when she had gone, rose to his feet and stood looking after her curiously. As she walked down the street with mincing step, he saw several persons whom she passed turn and look back at her with a smile of kindly amusement. When she had turned the corner, he went upstairs to his bedroom, and stood for a long time before the mirror of his dressing-case, gazing thoughtfully at the reflection of his own face.

## III

At eight o'clock the ballroom was a blaze of light and the guests had begun to assemble; for there was a literary programme and some routine business of the society to be gone through with before the dancing. A black servant in evening dress waited at the door and directed the guests to the dressing-rooms.

The occasion was long memorable among the colored people of the city; not alone for the dress and display, but for the high average of intelligence and culture that distinguished the gathering as a whole. There were a number of school-teachers, several young doctors, three or four lawyers, some professional singers, an editor, a lieutenant in the United States army spending his furlough in the city, and others in various polite callings; these were colored, though most of them would not have attracted even a casual glance because of any marked difference from white people. Most of the ladies were in evening costume, and dress coats and dancing pumps were the rule among the men. A band of string music, stationed in an alcove behind a row of palms, played popular airs while the guests were gathering.

The dancing began at half past nine. At eleven o'clock supper was served. Mr. Ryder had left the ballroom some little time before the intermission, but reappeared at the supper-table. The spread was worthy of the occasion, and the guests did full justice to it. When the coffee had been served, the toast-master, Mr. Solomon Sadler, rapped for order. He made a brief introductory speech, complimenting host and guests, and then presented in their order the toasts of the evening. They were responded to with a very fair display of after-dinner wit.

"The last toast," said the toast-master, when he reached the end of the list, "is one which must appeal to us all. There is no one of us of the sterner sex who is not at some time dependent upon woman—in infancy for protection, in manhood for companionship, in old age for care and comforting. Our good host has been trying to live alone, but the fair faces I see around me tonight prove that he too is largely dependent upon the gentler sex for most that makes life worth living—the society and love of friends—and rumor is at fault if he does not soon yield entire subjection to one of them. Mr. Ryder will now respond to the toast—The Ladies."

There was a pensive look in Mr. Ryder's eyes as he took the floor and adjusted his eye-glasses. He began by speaking of woman as the gift of Heaven to man, and after some general observations on the relations of the sexes he said: "But perhaps the quality which most distinguishes woman is her fidelity and devotion to those she loves. History is full of examples, but has recorded none more striking than one which only today came under my notice."

He then related, simply but effectively, the story told by his visitor of the afternoon. He gave it in the same soft dialect, which came readily to his lips, while the company listened attentively and sympathetically. For the story had awakened a responsive thrill in many hearts. There were some present who had seen, and others who had heard their fathers and grandfathers tell, the wrongs and sufferings of this past generation, and all of them still felt, in their darker moments, the shadow hanging over them. Mr. Ryder went on:—

"Such devotion and confidence are rare even among women. There are many who would have searched a year, some who would have waited five years, a few who might have hoped ten years; but for twenty-five years this woman has retained her affection for and her faith in a man she has not seen or heard of in all that time.

"She came to me today in the hope that I might be able to help her find this long-lost husband. And when she was gone I gave my fancy rein, and imagined a case I will put to you.

"Suppose that this husband, soon after his escape, had learned that his wife had been sold away, and that such inquiries as he could make brought no information of her whereabouts. Suppose that he was young, and she much older than he; that he was light, and she was black; that their marriage was a slave marriage, and legally binding only if they chose to make it so after the war. Suppose, too, that he made his way to the North, as some of us have done, and there, where he had larger opportunities, had improved them, and had in the course of all these years grown to be as different from the ignorant boy who ran away from fear of slavery as the day is from the night. Suppose, even, that he had qualified himself, by industry, by thrift, and by study, to win the friendship and be considered worthy of the society of such people as these I see around me tonight, gracing my board and filling my heart with gladness; for I am old enough to remember the day when such a gathering would not have been possible in this land. Suppose, too, that, as the years went by, this man's memory of the past grew more and more indistinct, until at last it was rarely, except in his dreams, that any image of this bygone period rose before his mind. And then suppose that accident should bring to his knowledge the fact that the wife of his youth, the wife he had left behind him—not one who had walked by his side and kept pace with him in his upward struggle, but one upon whom advancing years and a laborious life had set their mark—was alive and seeking him, but that he was absolutely safe from recognition or discovery, unless he chose to reveal himself. My friends, what would the man do? I will presume that he was one who loved honor, and tried to deal justly with all men. I will even carry the case further, and suppose that perhaps he had set his heart upon another, whom he had hoped to call his own. What would he do, or rather what ought he to do, in such a crisis of a lifetime?

"It seemed to me that he might hesitate, and I imagined that I was an old friend, a near friend, and that he had come to me for advice; and I argued the case with him. I tried to discuss it impartially. After we had looked upon the matter from every point of view, I said to him, in the words that we all know:—

> "This above all: to thine own self be true,
> And it must follow, as the night the day,
> Thou canst not then be false to any man."

Then, finally, I put the question to him, 'Shall you acknowledge her?'

"And now, ladies and gentlemen, friends and companions, I ask you, what should he have done?"

There was something in Mr. Ryder's voice that stirred the hearts of those who sat around him. It suggested more than mere sympathy with an imaginary situation; it seemed rather in the nature of a personal appeal. It was observed, too, that his look rested more especially upon Mrs. Dixon, with a mingled expression of renunciation and inquiry.

She had listened, with parted lips and streaming eyes. She was the first to speak: "He should have acknowledged her."

"Yes," they all echoed, "he should have acknowledged her."

"My friends and companions," responded Mr. Ryder, "I thank you, one and all. It is the answer I expected, for I knew your hearts."

He turned and walked toward the closed door of an adjoining room, while every eye followed him in wondering curiosity. He came back in a moment, leading by the hand his visitor of the afternoon, who stood startled and trembling at the sudden plunge into this scene of brilliant gayety. She was neatly dressed in gray, and wore the white cap of an elderly woman.

"Ladies and gentlemen," he said, "this is the woman, and I am the man, whose story I have told you. Permit me to introduce to you the wife of my youth."

# MADAME CÉLESTIN'S DIVORCE

## Kate Chopin

MADAME CÉLESTIN ALWAYS wore a neat and snugly fitting calico wrapper when she went out in the morning to sweep her small gallery. Lawyer Paxton thought she looked very pretty in the gray one that was made with a graceful Watteau fold at the back: and with which she invariably wore a bow of pink ribbon at the throat. She was always sweeping her gallery when lawyer Paxton passed by in the morning on his way to his office in St. Denis Street.

Sometimes he stopped and leaned over the fence to say good-morning at his ease; to criticise or admire her rosebushes; or, when he had time enough, to hear what she had to say. Madame Célestin usually had a good deal to say. She would gather up the train of her calico wrapper in one hand, and balancing the broom gracefully in the other, would go tripping down to where the lawyer leaned, as comfortably as he could, over her picket fence.

Of course she had talked to him of her troubles. Everyone knew Madame Célestin's troubles.

"Really, madame," he told her once, in his deliberate, calculating, lawyer-tone, "it's more than human nature—woman's nature—should be called upon to endure. Here you are, working your fingers off"—she glanced down at two rosy finger-tips that showed through the rents in her baggy doeskin gloves—"taking in sewing; giving music lessons; doing God knows what in the way of manual labor to support yourself and those two little ones"—Madame Célestin's pretty face beamed with satisfaction at this enumeration of her trials.

"You right, Judge. Not a picayune, not one, not one, have I lay my eyes on in the pas' fo' months that I can say Célestin give it to me or sen' it to me."

"The scoundrel!" muttered lawyer Paxton in his beard.

"An' *pourtant*,"[1] she resumed, "they say he's making money down roun' Alexandria w'en he wants to work."

"I dare say you haven't seen him for months?" suggested the lawyer.

"It's good six month' since I see a sight of Célestin," she admitted.

"That's it, that's what I say; he has practically deserted you; fails to support you. It wouldn't surprise me a bit to learn that he has ill treated you."

"Well, you know, Judge," with an evasive cough, "a man that drinks—w'at can you expec'? An' if you would know the promises he has made me! Ah, if I had as many dolla' as I had promise from Célestin, I wouldn' have to work, *je vous garantis*."[2]

"And in my opinion, Madame, you would be a foolish woman to endure it longer, when the divorce court is there to offer you redress."

"You spoke about that befo', judge; I'm goin' think about that divo'ce. I believe you right."

Madame Célestin thought about the divorce and talked about it, too; and lawyer Paxton grew deeply interested in the theme.

"You know, about that divo'ce, Judge," Madame Célestin was waiting for him that morning, "I been talking to my family an' my frien's, an' it's me that tells you, they all plumb agains' that divo'ce."

"Certainly, to be sure; that's to be expected, Madame, in this community of Creoles. I warned you that you would meet with opposition, and would have to face it and brave it."

"Oh, don't fear, I'm going to face it! Maman says it's a disgrace like it's neva been in the family. But it's good for Maman to talk, her. W'at trouble she ever had? She says I mus' go by all means consult with Père Duchéron—it's my confessor, you undastan'—Well, I'll go, Judge, to please Maman. But all the confessor' in the worl' ent goin' make me put up with that conduc' of Célestin any longa."

A day or two later, she was there waiting for him again. "You know, Judge, about that divo'ce."

"Yes, yes," responded the lawyer, well pleased to trace a new determination in her brown eyes and in the curves of her pretty

---

[1] *pourtant*; French: yet
[2] *je vous garantis*; French: I can assure you.

mouth. "I suppose you saw Père Duchéron and had to brave it out with him, too."

"Oh, fo' that, a perfec' sermon, I assu' you. A talk of giving scandal an' bad example that I thought would neva en'! He says, fo' him, he wash' his hands; I mus' go see the bishop."

"You won't let the bishop dissuade you, I trust," stammered the lawyer more anxiously than he could well understand.

"You don't know me yet, Judge," laughed Madame Célestin with a turn of the head and a flirt of the broom which indicated that the interview was at an end.

"Well, Madame Célestin! And the bishop!" Lawyer Paxton was standing there holding to a couple of the shaky pickets. She had not seen him. "Oh, it's you, Judge?" and she hastened towards him with an *empressement*[3] that could not but have been flattering.

"Yes, I saw Monseigneur," she began. The lawyer had already gathered from her expressive countenance that she had not wavered in her determination. "Ah, he's a eloquent man. It's not a mo' eloquent man in Natchitoches parish. I was fo'ced to cry, the way he talked to me about my troubles; how he undastan's them, an' feels for me. It would move even you, Judge, to hear how he talk' about that step I want to take; its danga, its temptation. How it is the duty of a Catholic to stan' everything till the las' extreme. An' that life of retirement an' self-denial I would have to lead—he tole me all that."

"But he hasn't turned you from your resolve, I see," laughed the lawyer complacently.

"For that, no," she returned emphatically. "The bishop don't know w'at it is to be married to a man like Célestin, an' have to endu' that conduc' like I have to endu' it. The Pope himse'f can't make me stan' that any longer, if you say I got the right in the law to sen' Célestin sailing."

A noticeable change had come over lawyer Paxton. He discarded his work-day coat and began to wear his Sunday one to the office. He grew solicitous as to the shine of his boots, his collar, and the set of his tie. He brushed and trimmed his whiskers with a care that had not before been apparent. Then he fell into a stupid habit of dreaming as he walked the streets of the old town. It would be very good to take unto himself a wife, he dreamed. And he could dream of no other than pretty Madame Célestin filling that sweet and sacred office as she filled his thoughts, now. Old Natchitoches would not hold

---

[3] *empressement*; French: eagerness.

them comfortably, perhaps; but the world was surely wide enough to live in, outside of Natchitoches town.

His heart beat in a strangely irregular manner as he neared Madame Célestin's house one morning, and discovered her behind the rose-bushes, as usual plying her broom. She had finished the gallery and steps and was sweeping the little brick walk along the edge of the violet border.

"Good-morning, Madame Célestin."

"Ah, it's you, Judge? Good-morning." He waited. She seemed to be doing the same. Then she ventured, with some hesitancy, "You know, Judge, about that divo'ce. 1 been thinking—I reckon you betta neva mine about that divo'ce." She was making deep rings in the palm of her gloved hand with the end of the broomhandle, and looking at them critically. Her face seemed to the lawyer to be unusually rosy; but maybe it was only the reflection of the pink bow at the throat. "Yes, I reckon you needn' mine. You see, Judge, Célestin came home las' night. An' he's promise me on his word an' honor he's going to turn ova a new leaf."

# THE DREAM OF AN HOUR

## Kate Chopin

KNOWING THAT MRS. MALLARD was afflicted with a heart trouble, great care was taken to break to her as gently as possible the news of her husband's death.

It was her sister Josephine who told her, in broken sentences; veiled hints that revealed in half concealing. Her husband's friend Richards was there, too, near her. It was he who had been in the newspaper office when intelligence of the railroad disaster was received, with Brently Mallard's name leading the list of "killed." He had only taken the time to assure himself of its truth by a second telegram, and had hastened to forestall any less careful, less tender friend in bearing the sad message.

She did not hear the story as many women have heard the same, with a paralyzed inability to accept its significance. She wept at once, with sudden, wild abandonment, in her sister's arms. When the storm of grief had spent itself she went away to her room alone. She would have no one follow her.

There stood, facing the open window, a comfortable, roomy armchair. Into this she sank, pressed down by a physical exhaustion that haunted her body and seemed to reach into her soul.

She could see in the open square before her house the tops of trees that were all aquiver with the new spring life. The delicious breath of rain was in the air. In the street below a peddler was crying his wares. The notes of a distant song which someone was singing reached her faintly, and countless sparrows were twittering in the eaves.

There were patches of blue sky showing here and there through the clouds that had met and piled one above the other in the west facing her window.

She sat with her head thrown back upon the cushion of the chair, quite motionless, except when a sob came up into her throat and shook her, as a child who has cried itself to sleep continues to sob in its dreams.

She was young, with a fair, calm face, whose lines bespoke repression and even a certain strength. But now there was a dull stare in her eyes, whose gaze was fixed away off yonder on one of those patches of blue sky. It was not a glance of reflection, but rather indicated a suspension of intelligent thought.

There was something coming to her and she was waiting for it, fearfully. What was it? She did not know; it was too subtle and elusive to name. But she felt it, creeping out of the sky, reaching toward her through the sounds, the scents, the color that filled the air.

Now her bosom rose and fell tumultuously. She was beginning to recognize this thing that was approaching to possess her, and she was striving to beat it back with her will—as powerless as her two white slender hands would have been.

When she abandoned herself a little whispered word escaped her slightly parted lips. She said it over and over under her breath: "free, free, free!" The vacant stare and the look of terror that had followed it went from her eyes. They stayed keen and bright. Her pulses beat fast, and the coursing blood warmed and relaxed every inch of her body.

She did not stop to ask if it were or were not a monstrous joy that held her. A clear and exalted perception enabled her to dismiss the suggestion as trivial.

She knew that she would weep again when she saw the kind, tender hands folded in death; the face that had never looked save with love upon her, fixed and gray and dead. But she saw beyond that bitter moment a long procession of years to come that would belong to her absolutely. And she opened and spread her arms out to them in welcome.

There would be no one to live for her during those coming years; she would live for herself. There would be no powerful will bending hers in that blind persistence with which men and women believe they have a right to impose a private will upon a fellow-creature. A kind intention or a cruel intention made the act seem no less a crime as she looked upon it in that brief moment of illumination.

And yet she had loved him—sometimes. Often she had not. What did it matter! What could love, the unsolved mystery, count for in face of this possession of self-assertion which she suddenly recognized as the strongest impulse of her being!

"Free! Body and soul free!" she kept whispering.

Josephine was kneeling before the closed door with her lips to the key-hole, imploring for admission. "Louise, open the door! I beg; open the door—you will make yourself ill. What are you doing, Louise? For heaven's sake open the door."

"Go away. I am not making myself ill." No; she was drinking in a very elixir of life through that open window.

Her fancy was running riot along those days ahead of her. Spring days, and summer days, and all sorts of days that would be her own. She breathed a quick prayer that life might be long. It was only yesterday she had thought with a shudder that life might be long.

She arose at length and opened the door to her sister's importunities. There was a feverish triumph in her eyes, and she carried herself unwittingly like a goddess of Victory. She clasped her sister's waist, and together they descended the stairs. Richards stood waiting for them at the bottom.

Someone was opening the front door with a latchkey. It was Brently Mallard who entered, a little travel-stained, composedly carrying his grip-sack and umbrella. He had been far from the scene of accident, and did not even know there had been one. He stood amazed at Josephine's piercing cry; at Richards' quick motion to screen him from the view of his wife.

But Richards was too late.

When the doctors came they said she had died of heart disease—of joy that kills.

# A RESPECTABLE WOMAN

## Kate Chopin

MRS. BARODA WAS a little provoked to learn that her husband expected his friend, Gouvernail, up to spend a week or two on the plantation.

They had entertained a good deal during the winter; much of the time had also been passed in New Orleans in various forms of mild dissipation. She was looking forward to a period of unbroken rest, now, and undisturbed tête-à-tête with her husband, when he informed her that Gouvernail was coming up to stay a week or two.

This was a man she had heard much of but never seen. He had been her husband's college friend; was now a journalist, and in no sense a society man or "a man about town," which were, perhaps, some of the reasons she had never met him. But she had unconsciously formed an image of him in her mind. She pictured him tall, slim, cynical; with eye-glasses, and his hands in his pockets; and she did not like him. Gouvernail was slim enough, but he wasn't very tall nor very cynical; neither did he wear eye-glasses nor carry his hands in his pockets. And she rather liked him when he first presented himself.

But why she liked him she could not explain satisfactorily to herself when she partly attempted to do so. She could discover in him none of those brilliant and promising traits which Gaston, her husband, had often assured her that he possessed. On the contrary, he sat rather mute and receptive before her chatty eagerness to make him feel at home and in face of Gaston's frank and wordy hospitality. His manner was as courteous toward her as the most exacting woman could require; but he made no direct appeal to her approval or even esteem.

Once settled at the plantation he seemed to like to sit upon the wide portico in the shade of one of the big Corinthian pillars, smoking his cigar lazily and listening attentively to Gaston's experience as a sugar planter.

"This is what I call living," he would utter with deep satisfaction, as the air that swept across the sugar field caressed him with its warm and scented velvety touch. It pleased him also to get on familiar terms with the big dogs that came about him, rubbing themselves sociably against his legs. He did not care to fish, and displayed no eagerness to go out and kill *grosbecs*[1] when Gaston proposed doing so.

Gouvernail's personality puzzled Mrs. Baroda, but she liked him. Indeed, he was a lovable, inoffensive fellow. After a few days, when she could understand him no better than at first, she gave over being puzzled and remained piqued. In this mood she left her husband and her guest, for the most part, alone together. Then finding that Gouvernail took no manner of exception to her action, she imposed her society upon him, accompanying him in his idle strolls to the mill and walks along the batture. She persistently sought to penetrate the reserve in which he had unconsciously enveloped himself.

"When is he going—your friend?" she one day asked her husband. "For my part, he tires me frightfully."

"Not for a week yet, dear. I can't understand; he gives you no trouble."

"No. I should like him better if he did; if he were more like others, and I had to plan somewhat for his comfort and enjoyment."

Gaston took his wife's pretty face between his hands and looked tenderly and laughingly into her troubled eyes. They were making a bit of toilet sociably together in Mrs. Baroda's dressing-room.

"You are full of surprises, ma belle," he said to her. "Even I can never count upon how you are going to act under given conditions." He kissed her and turned to fasten his cravat before the mirror.

"Here you are," he went on, "taking poor Gouvernail seriously and making a commotion over him, the last thing he would desire or expect."

"Commotion!" she hotly resented. "Nonsense! How can you say such a thing? Commotion, indeed! But, you know, you said he was clever."

"So he is. But the poor fellow is run down by overwork now. That's why I asked him here to take a rest."

---

[1] *grosbecs*; French: a kind of finch with a large heavy bill and short thick neck.

"You used to say he was a man of ideas," she retorted, unconciliated. "I expected him to be interesting, at least. I'm going to the city in the morning to have my spring gowns fitted. Let me know when Mr. Gouvernail is gone; I shall be at my Aunt Octavie's."

That night she went and sat alone upon a bench that stood beneath a live oak tree at the edge of the gravel walk.

She had never known her thoughts or her intentions to be so confused. She could gather nothing from them but the feeling of a distinct necessity to quit her home in the morning.

Mrs. Baroda heard footsteps crunching the gravel; but could discern in the darkness only the approaching red point of a lighted cigar. She knew it was Gouvernail, for her husband did not smoke. She hoped to remain unnoticed, but her white gown revealed her to him. He threw away his cigar and seated himself upon the bench beside her; without a suspicion that she might object to his presence.

"Your husband told me to bring this to you, Mrs. Baroda," he said, handing her a filmy, white scarf with which she sometimes enveloped her head and shoulders. She accepted the scarf from him with a murmur of thanks, and let it lie in her lap.

He made some commonplace observation upon the baneful effect of the night air at that season. Then as his gaze reached out into the darkness, he murmured, half to himself:

> " 'Night of south winds—night of the large few stars!
> Still nodding night—' " [2]

She made no reply to this apostrophe to the night, which indeed, was not addressed to her.

Gouvernail was in no sense a diffident man, for he was not a self-conscious one. His periods of reserve were not constitutional, but the result of moods. Sitting there beside Mrs. Baroda, his silence melted for the time.

He talked freely and intimately in a low, hesitating drawl that was not unpleasant to hear. He talked of the old college days when he and Gaston had been a good deal to each other; of the days of keen and blind ambitions and large intentions. Now there was left with him, at least, a philosophic acquiescence to the existing order—only

---

[2] " '*Night . . . night*—' ": Walt Whitman, Song *of Myself*. Gouvernail appreciates Whitman, a poet widely criticized at the time for immorality.

a desire to be permitted to exist, with now and then a little whiff of genuine life, such as he was breathing now.

Her mind only vaguely grasped what he was saying. Her physical being was for the moment predominant. She was not thinking of his words, only drinking in the tones of his voice. She wanted to reach out her hand in the darkness and touch him with the sensitive tips of her fingers upon the face or the lips. She wanted to draw close to him and whisper against his cheek—she did not care what—as she might have done if she had not been a respectable woman.

The stronger the impulse grew to bring herself near him, the further, in fact, did she draw away from him. As soon as she could do so without an appearance of too great rudeness, she rose and left him there alone.

Before she reached the house, Gouvernail had lighted a fresh cigar and ended his apostrophe to the night.

Mrs. Baroda was greatly tempted that night to tell her husband— who was also her friend—of this folly that had seized her. But she did not yield to the temptation. Beside being a respectable woman she was a very sensible one; and she knew there are some battles in life which a human being must fight alone.

When Gaston arose in the morning, his wife had already departed. She had taken an early morning train to the city. She did not return till Gouvernail was gone from under her roof.

There was some talk of having him back during the summer that followed. That is, Gaston greatly desired it; but this desire yielded to his wife's strenuous opposition.

However, before the year ended, she proposed, wholly from herself, to have Gouvernail visit them again. Her husband was surprised and delighted with the suggestion coming from her.

"I am glad, *chère amie*[3], to know that you have finally overcome your dislike for him; truly he did not deserve it."

"Oh," she told him, laughingly, after pressing a long, tender kiss upon his lips, "I have overcome everything! you will see. This time I shall be very nice to him."

---

[3]  *chère amie*; French: dear friend.

# THE LOCKET

## Kate Chopin

ONE NIGHT IN autumn a few men were gathered about a fire on the slope of a hill. They belonged to a small detachment of Confederate forces and were awaiting orders to march. Their gray uniforms were worn beyond the point of shabbiness. One of the men was heating something in a tin cup over the embers. Two were lying at full length a little distance away, while a fourth was trying to decipher a letter and had drawn close to the light. He had unfastened his collar and a good bit of his flannel shirt front.

"What's that you got around your neck, Ned?" asked one of the men lying in the obscurity.

Ned—or Edmond—mechanically fastened another button of his shirt and did not reply. He went on reading his letter.

"Is it your sweet heart's picture?"

"'Tain't no gal's picture," offered the man at the fire. He had removed his tin cup and was engaged in stirring its grimy contents with a small stick. "That's a charm; some kind of hoodoo business that one o' them priests gave him to keep him out o' trouble. I know them Cath'lics. That's how come Frenchy got permoted an never got a scratch sence he's been in the ranks. Hey, French! ain't I right?" Edmond looked up absently from his letter.

"What is it?" he asked.

"Ain't that a charm you got round your neck?"

"It must be, Nick," returned Edmond with a smile. "I don't know how I could have gone through this year and a half without it."

The letter had made Edmond heart sick and home sick. He stretched himself on his back and looked straight up at the blinking stars. But he was not thinking of them nor of anything but a certain spring day when the bees were humming in the clematis; when a girl was saying good bye to him. He could see her as she unclasped from her neck the locket which she fastened about his own. It was an old fashioned golden locket bearing miniatures of her father and mother with their names and the date of their marriage. It was her most precious earthly possession. Edmond could feel again the folds of the girl's soft white gown, and see the droop of the angel-sleeves as she circled her fair arms about his neck. Her sweet face, appealing, pathetic, tormented by the pain of parting, appeared before him as vividly as life. He turned over, burying his face in his arm and there he lay, still and motionless.

The profound and treacherous night with its silence and semblance of peace settled upon the camp. He dreamed that the fair Octavie brought him a letter. He had no chair to offer her and was pained and embarrassed at the condition of his garments. He was ashamed of the poor food which comprised the dinner at which he begged her to join them.

He dreamt of a serpent coiling around his throat, and when he strove to grasp it the slimy thing glided away from his clutch. Then his dream was clamor.

"Git your duds! you! Frenchy!" Nick was bellowing in his face. There was what appeared to be a scramble and a rush rather than any regulated movement. The hill side was alive with clatter and motion; with sudden up-springing lights among the pines. In the east the dawn was unfolding out of the darkness. Its glimmer was yet dim in the plain below.

"What's it all about?" wondered a big black bird perched in the top of the tallest tree. He was an old solitary and a wise one, yet he was not wise enough to guess what it was all about. So all day long he kept blinking and wondering.

The noise reached far out over the plain and across the hills and awoke the little babes that were sleeping in their cradles. The smoke curled up toward the sun and shadowed the plain so that the stupid birds thought it was going to rain; but the wise one knew better.

"They are children playing a game," thought he. "I shall know more about it if I watch long enough."

At the approach of night they had all vanished away with their din and smoke. Then the old bird plumed his feathers. At last he had understood! With a flap of his great, black wings he shot downward, circling toward the plain.

A man was picking his way across the plain. He was dressed in the garb of a clergyman. His mission was to administer the consolations of religion to any of the prostrate figures in whom there might yet linger a spark of life. A negro accompanied him, bearing a bucket of water and a flask of wine.

There were no wounded here; they had been borne away. But the retreat had been hurried and the vultures and the good Samaritans would have to look to the dead.

There was a soldier—a mere boy—lying with his face to the sky. His hands were clutching the sward on either side and his finger nails were stuffed with earth and bits of grass that he had gathered in his despairing grasp upon life. His musket was gone; he was hatless and his face and clothing were begrimed. Around his neck hung a gold chain and locket. The priest, bending over him, unclasped the chain and removed it from the dead soldier's neck. He had grown used to the terrors of war and could face them unflinchingly; but its pathos, someway, always brought the tears to his old, dim eyes.

The angelus was ringing half a mile away. The priest and the negro knelt and murmured together the evening benediction and a prayer for the dead.

## II

The peace and beauty of a spring day had descended upon the earth like a benediction. Along the leafy road which skirted a narrow, tortuous stream in central Louisiana, rumbled an old fashioned cabriolet, much the worse for hard and rough usage over country roads and lanes. The fat, black horses went in a slow, measured trot, notwithstanding constant urging on the part of the fat, black coachman. Within the vehicle were seated the fair Octavie and her old friend and neighbor, Judge Pillier, who had come to take her for a morning drive.

Octavie wore a plain black dress, severe in its simplicity. A narrow belt held it at the waist and the sleeves were gathered into close fitting wristbands. She had discarded her hoopskirt and appeared not unlike a nun. Beneath the folds of her bodice nestled the old locket. She never displayed it now. It had returned to her sanctified in her eyes; made precious as material things sometimes are by being forever identified with a significant moment of one's existence.

A hundred times she had read over the letter with which the locket had come back to her. No later than that morning she had again pored over it. As she sat beside the window, smoothing the letter out upon her knee, heavy and spiced odors stole in to her with the songs of birds and the humming of insects in the air.

She was so young and the world was so beautiful that there came over her a sense of unreality as she read again and again the priest's letter. He told of that autumn day drawing to its close, with the gold and the red fading out of the west, and the night gathering its shadows to cover the faces of the dead. Oh! She could not believe that one of those dead was her own! with visage uplifted to the gray sky in an agony of supplication. A spasm of resistance and rebellion seized and swept over her. Why was the spring here with its flowers and its seductive breath if he was dead! Why was she here! What further had she to do with life and the living!

Octavie had experienced many such moments of despair, but a blessed resignation had never failed to follow, and it fell then upon her like a mantle and enveloped her.

"I shall grow old and quiet and sad like poor Aunt Tavie," she murmured to herself as she folded the letter and replaced it in the secretary. Already she gave herself a little demure air like her Aunt Tavie. She walked with a slow glide in unconscious imitation of Mademoiselle Tavie whom some youthful affliction had robbed of earthly compensation while leaving her in possession of youth's illusions.

As she sat in the old cabriolet beside the father of her dead lover, again there came to Octavie the terrible sense of loss which had assailed her so often before. The soul of her youth clamored for its rights; for a share in the world's glory and exultation. She leaned back and drew her veil a little closer about her face. It was an old black veil of her Aunt Tavie's. A whiff of dust from the road had blown in and she wiped her cheeks and her eyes with her soft, white handkerchief, a homemade handkerchief, fabricated from one of her old fine muslin petticoats.

"Will you do me the favor, Octavie," requested the judge in the courteous tone which he never abandoned, "to remove that veil which you wear. It seems out of harmony, someway, with the beauty and promise of the day."

The young girl obediently yielded to her old companion's wish and unpinning the cumbersome, sombre drapery from her bonnet, folded it neatly and laid it upon the seat in front of her.

"Ah! that is better; far better!" he said in a tone expressing unbounded relief. "Never put it on again, dear." Octavie felt a little hurt; as if he wished to debar her from share and parcel in the burden of affliction which had been placed upon all of them. Again she drew forth the old muslin handkerchief.

They had left the big road and turned into a level plain which had formerly been an old meadow. There were clumps of thorn trees here and there, gorgeous in their spring radiance. Some cattle were grazing off in the distance in spots where the grass was tall and luscious. At the far end of the meadow was the towering lilac hedge, skirting the lane that led to Judge Pillier's house, and the scent of its heavy blossoms met them like a soft and tender embrace of welcome.

As they neared the house the old gentleman placed an arm around the girl's shoulders and turning her face up to him he said: "Do you not think that on a day like this, miracles might happen? When the whole earth is vibrant with life, does it not seem to you, Octavie, that heaven might for once relent and give us back our dead?" He spoke very low, advisedly, and impressively. In his voice was an old quaver which was not habitual and there was agitation in every line of his visage. She gazed at him with eyes that were full of supplication and a certain terror of joy.

They had been driving through the lane with the towering hedge on one side and the open meadow on the other. The horses had somewhat quickened their lazy pace. As they turned into the avenue leading to the house, a whole choir of feathered songsters fluted a sudden torrent of melodious greeting from their leafy hiding places.

Octavie felt as if she had passed into a stage of existence which was like a dream, more poignant and real than life. There was the old gray house with its sloping eaves. Amid the blur of green, and dimly, she saw familiar faces and heard voices as if they came from far across the fields, and Edmond was holding her. Her dead Edmond; her living Edmond, and she felt the beating of his heart against her and the agonizing rapture of his kisses striving to awake her. It was as if the spirit of life and the awakening spring had given back the soul to her youth and bade her rejoice.

It was many hours later that Octavie drew the locket from her bosom and looked at Edmond with a questioning appeal in her glance.

"It was the night before an engagement," he said. "In the hurry of the encounter, and the retreat next day, I never missed it till the fight was over. I thought of course I had lost it in the heat of the struggle, but it was stolen."

"Stolen," she shuddered, and thought of the dead soldier with his face uplifted to the sky in an agony of supplication.

Edmond said nothing; but he thought of his messmate; the one who had lain far back in the shadow; the one who had said nothing.

# THE NIGHT CAME SLOWLY

## Kate Chopin

I AM LOSING my interest in human beings; in the significance of their lives and their actions. Someone has said it is better to study one man than ten books. I want neither books nor men; they make me suffer. Can one of them talk to me like the night—the Summer night? Like the stars or the caressing wind?

The night came slowly, softly, as I lay out there under the maple tree. It came creeping, creeping stealthily out of the valley, thinking I did not notice. And the outlines of trees and foliage nearby blended in one black mass and the night came stealing out from them, too, and from the east and west, until the only light was in the sky, filtering through the maple leaves and a star looking down through every cranny.

The night is solemn and it means mystery.

Human shapes flitted by like intangible things. Some stole up like little mice to peep at me. I did not mind. My whole being was abandoned to the soothing and penetrating charm of the night.

The katydids began their slumber song: they are at it yet. How wise they are. They do not chatter like people. They tell me only: "sleep, sleep, sleep." The wind rippled the maple leaves like little warm love thrills.

Why do fools cumber the Earth! It was a man's voice that broke the necromancer's spell. A man came today with his "Bible Class." He is detestable with his red cheeks and bold eyes and coarse manner and speech. What does he know of Christ? Shall I ask a young fool who was born yesterday and will die tomorrow to tell me things of Christ? I would rather ask the stars: they have seen him.

# REGRET

## Kate Chopin

MAMZELLE AURÉLIE POSSESSED a good strong figure, ruddy cheeks, hair that was changing from brown to gray, and a determined eye. She wore a man's hat about the farm, and an old blue army overcoat when it was cold, and sometimes top-boots.

Mamzelle Aurélie had never thought of marrying. She had never been in love. At the age of twenty she had received a proposal, which she had promptly declined, and at the age of fifty she had not yet lived to regret it.

So she was quite alone in the world, except for her dog Ponto, and the negroes who lived in her cabins and worked her crops, and the fowls, a few cows, a couple of mules, her gun (with which she shot chicken-hawks), and her religion.

One morning Mamzelle Aurélie stood upon her gallery, contemplating, with arms akimbo, a small band of very small children who, to all intents and purposes, might have fallen from the clouds, so unexpected and bewildering was their coming, and so unwelcome. They were the children of her nearest neighbor, Odile, who was not such a near neighbor, after all.

The young woman had appeared but five minutes before, accompanied by these four children. In her arms she carried little Elodie; she dragged Ti Nomme by an unwilling hand; while Marcéline and Marcélette followed with irresolute steps.

Her face was red and disfigured from tears and excitement. She had been summoned to a neighboring parish by the dangerous illness of her mother; her husband was away in Texas—it seemed to her a million miles away; and Valsin was waiting with the mule-cart to drive her to the station.

"It's no question, Mamzelle Aurélie; you jus' got to keep those youngsters fo' me tell I come back. *Dieu sait*[1], I wouldn' botha you with 'em if it was any otha way to do! Make 'em mine you, Mamzelle Aurélie; don' spare 'em. Me, there, I'm half crazy between the chil'ren, an' Léon not home, an' maybe not even to fine po' maman alive encore!"—a harrowing possibility which drove Odile to take a final hasty and convulsive leave of her disconsolate family.

She left them crowded into the narrow strip of shade on the porch of the long, low house; the white sunlight was beating in on the white old boards; some chickens were scratching in the grass at the foot of the steps, and one had boldly mounted, and was stepping heavily, solemnly, and aimlessly across the gallery. There was a pleasant odor of pinks in the air, and the sound of negroes' laughter was coming across the flowering cotton-field.

Mamzelle Aurélie stood contemplating the children. She looked with a critical eye upon Marcéline, who had been left staggering beneath the weight of the chubby Elodie. She surveyed with the same calculating air Marcélette mingling her silent tears with the audible grief and rebellion of Ti Nomme. During those few contemplative moments she was collecting herself, determining upon a line of action which should be identical with a line of duty. She began by feeding them.

If Mamzelle Aurélie's responsibilities might have begun and ended there, they could easily have been dismissed; for her larder was amply provided against an emergency of this nature. But little children are not little pigs; they require and demand attentions which were wholly unexpected by Mamzelle Aurélie, and which she was ill prepared to give.

She was, indeed, very inapt in her management of Odile's children during the first few days. How could she know that Marcélette always wept when spoken to in a loud and commanding tone of voice? It was a peculiarity of Marcélette's. She became acquainted with Ti Nomme's passion for flowers only when he had plucked all the choicest gardenias and pinks for the apparent purpose of critically studying their botanical construction.

---

[1] *Dieu sait*; French: God knows.

"'Tain't enough to tell 'im, Mamzelle Aurélie," Marcéline instructed her; "you got to tie 'im in a chair. It's w'at maman all time do w'en he's bad: she tie 'im in a chair." The chair in which Mamzelle Aurélie tied Ti Nomme was roomy and comfortable, and he seized the opportunity to take a nap in it, the afternoon being warm.

At night, when she ordered them one and all to bed as she would have shooed the chickens into the hen-house, they stayed uncomprehending before her. What about the little white nightgowns that had to be taken from the pillow-slip in which they were brought over, and shaken by some strong hand till they snapped like ox-whips? What about the tub of water which had to be brought and set in the middle of the floor, in which the little tired, dusty, sunbrowned feet had everyone to be washed sweet and clean? And it made Marcéline and Marcélette laugh merrily—the idea that Mamzelle Aurélie should for a moment have believed that Ti Nomme could fall asleep without being told the story of *Croque-mitaine*[2] or *Loup-garou*[3], or both; or that Elodie could fall asleep at all without being rocked and sung to.

"I tell you, Aunt Ruby," Mamzelle Aurélie informed her cook in confidence; "me, I'd rather manage a dozen plantation' than fo' chil'ren. It's *terrassent!*[4] Bonté! Don't talk to me about chil'ren!"

"'Tain' inspected sich as you would know airy thing 'bout 'em, Mamzelle Aurélie. I see dat plainly yistiddy w'en I spy dat li'le chile playin' wid yo' baskit o' keys. You don' know dat makes chillun grow up hard-headed, to play wid keys? Des like it make 'em teeth hard to look in a lookin'-glass. Them's the things you got to know in the raisin' an' manigement o' chillun."

Mamzelle Aurélie certainly did not pretend or aspire to such subtle and far-reaching knowledge on the subject as Aunt Ruby possessed, who had "raised five an' bared (buried) six" in her day. She was glad enough to learn a few little mother-tricks to serve the moment's need.

Ti Nomme's sticky fingers compelled her to unearth white aprons that she had not worn for years, and she had to accustom herself to his moist kisses—the expressions of an affectionate and exuberant nature. She got down her sewing-basket, which she seldom used, from the top shelf of the armoire, and placed it within the ready and easy reach which torn slips and buttonless waists demanded. It took

---

[2]  *Croque-mitaine*; French: a menacing ghost-like monster in children's stories—the bogeyman

[3]  *Loup-garou*; French: werewolf

[4]  *terrassent*, from the verb *terrasser*; French: to overwhelm

her some days to become accustomed to the laughing, the crying, the chattering that echoed through the house and around it all day long. And it was not the first or the second night that she could sleep comfortably with little Elodie's hot, plump body pressed close against her, and the little one's warm breath beating her cheek like the fanning of a bird's wing.

But at the end of two weeks Mamzelle Aurélie had grown quite used to these things, and she no longer complained.

It was also at the end of two weeks that Mamzelle Aurélie, one evening, looking away toward the crib where the cattle were being fed, saw Valsin's blue cart turning the bend of the road. Odile sat beside the mulatto, upright and alert. As they drew near, the young woman's beaming face indicated that her homecoming was a happy one.

But this coming, unannounced and unexpected, threw Mamzelle Aurélie into a flutter that was almost agitation. The children had to be gathered. Where was Ti Nomme? Yonder in the shed, putting an edge on his knife at the grindstone. And Marcéline and Marcélette? Cutting and fashioning doll-rags in the corner of the gallery. As for Elodie, she was safe enough in Mamzelle Aurélie's arms; and she had screamed with delight at sight of the familiar blue cart which was bringing her mother back to her.

The excitement was all over, and they were gone. How still it was when they were gone! Mamzelle Aurélie stood upon the gallery, looking and listening. She could no longer see the cart; the red sunset and the blue-gray twilight had together flung a purple mist across the fields and road that hid it from her view. She could no longer hear the wheezing and creaking of its wheels. But she could still faintly hear the shrill, glad voices of the children.

She turned into the house. There was much work awaiting her, for the children had left a sad disorder behind them; but she did not at once set about the task of righting it. Mamzelle Aurélie seated herself beside the table. She gave one slow glance through the room, into which the evening shadows were creeping and deepening around her solitary figure. She let her head fall down upon her bended arm, and began to cry. Oh, but she cried! Not softly, as women often do. She cried like a man, with sobs that seemed to tear her very soul. She did not notice Ponto licking her hand.

# THE OPEN BOAT

## Stephen Crane

*A Tale Intended to be after the Fact: Being
the Experience of Four Men from the
Sunk Steamer* COMMODORE

## I

NONE OF THEM knew the color of the sky. Their eyes glanced level, and were fastened upon the waves that swept toward them. These waves were of the hue of slate, save for the tops, which were of foaming white, and all of the men knew the colors of the sea. The horizon narrowed and widened, and dipped and rose, and at all times its edge was jagged with waves that seemed thrust up in points like rocks.

Many a man ought to have a bathtub larger than the boat which here rode upon the sea. These waves were most wrongfully and barbarously abrupt and tall, and each froth-top was a problem in small-boat navigation.

The cook squatted in the bottom, and looked with both eyes at the six inches of gunwale which separated him from the ocean. His sleeves were rolled over his fat forearms, and the two flaps of his unbuttoned vest dangled as he bent to bail out the boat. Often he said, "Gawd! that was a narrow clip." As he remarked it he invariably gazed eastward over the broken sea.

The oiler, steering with one of the two oars in the boat, sometimes raised himself suddenly to keep clear of water that swirled in over the stern. It was a thin little oar, and it seemed often ready to snap.

The correspondent, pulling at the other oar, watched the waves and wondered why he was there.

The injured captain, lying in the bow, was at this time buried in that profound dejection and indifference which comes, temporarily at least, to even the bravest and most enduring when, willy-nilly, the firm fails, the army loses, the ship goes down. The mind of the master of a vessel is rooted deep in the timbers of her, though he command for a day or a decade; and this captain had on him the stern impression of a scene in the grays of dawn of seven turned faces, and later a stump of a topmast with a white ball on it, that slashed to and fro at the waves, went low and lower, and down. Thereafter there was something strange in his voice. Although steady, it was deep with mourning, and of a quality beyond oration or tears.

"Keep'er a little more south, Billie," said he.

"A little more south, sir," said the oiler in the stern.

A seat in this boat was not unlike a seat upon a bucking broncho, and by the same token a broncho is not much smaller. The craft pranced and reared and plunged like an animal. As each wave came, and she rose for it, she seemed like a horse making at a fence outrageously high. The manner of her scramble over these walls of water is a mystic thing, and, moreover, at the top of them were ordinarily these problems in white water, the foam racing down from the summit of each wave requiring a new leap, and a leap from the air. Then, after scornfully bumping a crest, she would slide and race and splash down a long incline, and arrive bobbing and nodding in front of the next menace.

A singular disadvantage of the sea lies in the fact that after successfully surmounting one wave you discover that there is another behind it just as important and just as nervously anxious to do something effective in the way of swamping boats. In a ten-foot dinghy one can get an idea of the resources of the sea in the line of waves that is not probable to the average experience, which is never at sea in a dinghy. As each slaty wall of water approached, it shut all else from the view of the men in the boat, and it was not difficult to imagine that this particular wave was the final outburst of the ocean, the last effort of the grim water. There was a terrible grace in the move of the waves, and they came in silence, save for the snarling of the crests.

In the wan light the faces of the men must have been gray. Their eyes must have glinted in strange ways as they gazed steadily astern.

Viewed from a balcony, the whole thing would doubtless have been weirdly picturesque. But the men in the boat had no time to see it, and if they had had leisure, there were other things to occupy their minds. The sun swung steadily up the sky, and they knew it was broad day because the color of the sea changed from slate to emerald-green streaked with amber lights, and the foam was like tumbling snow. The process of the breaking day was unknown to them. They were aware only of this effect upon the color of the waves that rolled toward them.

In disjointed sentences the cook and the correspondent argued as to the difference between a lifesaving station and a house of refuge. The cook had said: "There's a house of refuge just north of the Mosquito Inlet Light, and as soon as they see us they'll come off in their boat and pick us up."

"As soon as who see us?" said the correspondent.

"The crew," said the cook.

"Houses of refuge don't have crews," said the correspondent. "As I understand them, they are only places where clothes and grub are stored for the benefit of shipwrecked people. They don't carry crews."

"Oh, yes, they do," said the cook.

"No, they don't," said the correspondent.

"Well, we're not there yet, anyhow," said the oiler in the stern.

"Well," said the cook, "perhaps it's not a house of refuge that I'm thinking of as being near Mosquito Inlet Light; perhaps it's a lifesaving station."

"We're not there yet," said the oiler in the stern.

## II

As the boat bounced from the top of each wave the wind tore through the hair of the hatless men, and as the craft plopped her stern down again the spray slashed past them. The crest of each of these waves was a hill, from the top of which the men surveyed for a moment a broad tumultuous expanse, shining and wind-riven. It was probably splendid, it was probably glorious, this play of the free sea, wild with lights of emerald and white and amber.

"Bully good thing it's an onshore wind," said the cook. "If not, where would we be? Wouldn't have a show."

"That's right," said the correspondent.

The busy oiler nodded his assent.

Then the captain, in the bow, chuckled in a way that expressed humor, contempt, tragedy, all in one. "Do you think we've got much of a show now, boys?" said he.

Whereupon the three were silent, save for a trifle of hemming and hawing. To express any particular optimism at this time they felt to be childish and stupid, but they all doubtless possessed this sense of the situation in their minds. A young man thinks doggedly at such times. On the other hand, the ethics of their condition was decidedly against any open suggestion of hopelessness. So they were silent.

"Oh, well," said the captain, soothing his children, "we'll get ashore all right."

But there was that in his tone which made them think; so the oiler quoth, "Yes! if this wind holds."

The cook was bailing. "Yes! if we don't catch hell in the surf."

Canton-flannel gulls flew near and far. Sometimes they sat down on the sea, near patches of brown seaweed that rolled over the waves with a movement like carpets on a line in a gale. The birds sat comfortably in groups, and they were envied by some in the dinghy, for the wrath of the sea was no more to them than it was to a covey of prairie chickens a thousand miles inland. Often they came very close and stared at the men with black bead-like eyes. At these times they were uncanny and sinister in their unblinking scrutiny, and the men hooted angrily at them, telling them to be gone. One came, and evidently decided to alight on the top of the captains head. The bird flew parallel to the boat and did not circle, but made short sidelong jumps in the air in chicken fashion. His black eyes were wistfully fixed upon the captain's head. "Ugly brute," said the oiler to the bird. "You look as if you were made with a jackknife." The cook and the correspondent swore darkly at the creature. The captain naturally wished to knock it away with the end of the heavy painter, but he did not dare do it, because anything resembling an emphatic gesture would have capsized this freighted boat; and so, with his open hand, the captain gently and carefully waved the gull away. After it had been discouraged from the pursuit the captain breathed easier on account of his hair, and others breathed easier because the bird struck their minds at this time as being somehow gruesome and ominous.

In the meantime the oiler and the correspondent rowed. And also they rowed. They sat together in the same seat, and each rowed an oar. Then the oiler took both oars; then the correspondent took both oars; then the oiler; then the correspondent. They rowed and they rowed. The very ticklish part of the business was when the time came for the reclining one in the stern to take his turn at the oars. By the very last star of truth, it is easier to steal eggs from under a hen than it was to change seats in the dinghy. First the man in the stern slid his hand along the thwart and moved with care, as if he were of Sèvres. Then the man in the rowing-seat slid his hand along the other thwart. It was all done with the most extraordinary care. As the two sidled past each other, the whole party kept watchful eyes on the coming wave, and the captain cried: "Look out, now! Steady, there!"

The brown mats of seaweed that appeared from time to time were like islands, bits of earth. They were traveling, apparently, neither one way nor the other. They were, to all intents, stationary. They informed the men in the boat that it was making progress slowly toward the land.

The captain, rearing cautiously in the bow after the dinghy soared on a great swell, said that he had seen the lighthouse at Mosquito Inlet. Presently the cook remarked that he had seen it. The correspondent was at the oars then, and for some reason he too wished to look at the lighthouse; but his back was toward the far shore, and the waves were important, and for some time he could not seize an opportunity to turn his head. But at last there came a wave more gentle than the others, and when at the crest of it he swiftly scoured the western horizon.

"See it?" said the captain.

"No," said the correspondent, slowly; "I didn't see anything."

"Look again," said the captain. He pointed. "It's exactly in that direction."

At the top of another wave the correspondent did as he was bid, and this time his eyes chanced on a small, still thing on the edge of the swaying horizon. It was precisely like the point of a pin. It took an anxious eye to find a lighthouse so tiny.

"Think we'll make it, Captain?"

"If this wind holds and the boat don't swamp, we can't do much else," said the captain.

The little boat, lifted by each towering sea and splashed viciously by the crests, made progress that in the absence of seaweed was not apparent to those in her. She seemed just a wee thing wallowing, miraculously top up, at the mercy of five oceans. Occasionally a great spread of water, like white flames, swarmed into her.

"Bail her, cook," said the captain, serenely.

"All right, Captain," said the cheerful cook.

## III

It would be difficult to describe the subtle brotherhood of men that was here established on the seas. No one said that it was so. No one mentioned it. But it dwelt in the boat, and each man felt it warm him. They were a captain, an oiler, a cook, and a correspondent, and they were friends—friends in a more curiously ironbound degree than may be common. The hurt captain, lying against the water jar in the bow, spoke always in a low voice and calmly; but he could never command a more ready and swiftly obedient crew than the motley three of the dinghy. It was more than a mere recognition of what was best for the common safety. There was surely in it a quality that was personal and heartfelt. And after this devotion to the commander of the boat, there was this comradeship, that the correspondent, for instance, who had been taught to be cynical of men, knew even at the time was the best experience of his life. But no one said that it was so. No one mentioned it.

"I wish we had a sail," remarked the captain. "We might try my overcoat on the end of an oar, and give you two boys a chance to rest." So the cook and the correspondent held the mast and spread wide the overcoat; the oiler steered; and the little boat made good way with her new rig. Sometimes the oiler had to scull sharply to keep a sea from breaking into the boat, but otherwise sailing was a success.

Meanwhile the lighthouse had been growing slowly larger. It had now almost assumed color, and appeared like a little gray shadow on the sky. The man at the oars could not be prevented from turning his head rather often to try for a glimpse of this little gray shadow.

At last, from the top of each wave, the men in the tossing boat could see land. Even as the lighthouse was an upright shadow on the sky, this land seemed but a long black shadow on the sea. It certainly was thinner than paper. "We must be about opposite New Smyrna," said the cook, who had coasted this shore often in schooners. "Captain, by the way, I believe they abandoned that lifesaving station there about a year ago."

"Did they?" said the captain.

The wind slowly died away. The cook and the correspondent were not now obliged to slave in order to hold high the oar. But the waves continued their old impetuous swooping at the dinghy, and the little craft, no longer under way, struggled woundily over them. The oiler or the correspondent took the oars again.

Shipwrecks are apropos of nothing. If men could only train for them and have them occur when the men had reached pink condition, there would be less drowning at sea. Of the four in the dinghy none had slept any time worth mentioning for two days and two nights previous to embarking in the dinghy, and in the excitement of clambering about the deck of a foundering ship they had also forgotten to eat heartily.

For these reasons, and for others, neither the oiler nor the correspondent was fond of rowing at this time. The correspondent wondered ingenuously how in the name of all that was sane could there be people who thought it amusing to row a boat. It was not an amusement; it was a diabolical punishment, and even a genius of mental aberrations could never conclude that it was anything but a horror to the muscles and a crime against the back. He mentioned to the boat in general how the amusement of rowing struck him, and the weary-faced oiler smiled in full sympathy. Previously to the foundering, by the way, the oiler had worked a double watch in the engine room of the ship.

"Take her easy now, boys," said the captain. "Don't spend yourselves. If we have to run a surf you'll need all your strength, because we'll sure have to swim for it. Take your time."

Slowly the land arose from the sea. From a black line it became a line of black and a line of white—trees and sand. Finally the captain said that he could make out a house on the shore. "That's the house of refuge, sure," said the cook. "They'll see us before long, and come out after us."

The distant lighthouse reared high. "The keeper ought to be able to make us out now, if he's looking through a glass," said the captain. "He'll notify the lifesaving people."

"None of those other boats could have got ashore to give word of this wreck," said the oiler, in a low voice, "else the lifeboat would be out hunting us."

Slowly and beautifully the land loomed out of the sea. The wind came again. It had veered from the northeast to the southeast. Finally a new sound struck the ears of the men in the boat. It was the low thunder of the surf on the shore. "We'll never be able to make the lighthouse now," said the captain. "Swing her head a little more north, Billie."

"A little more north, sir," said the oiler.

Whereupon the little boat turned her nose once more down the wind, and all but the oarsman watched the shore grow. Under the influence of this expansion doubt and direful apprehension were leaving the minds of the men. The management of the boat was still most absorbing, but it could not prevent a quiet cheerfulness. In an hour, perhaps, they would be ashore.

Their backbones had become thoroughly used to balancing in the boat, and they now rode this wild colt of a dinghy like circus men. The correspondent thought that he had been drenched to the skin, but happening to feel in the top pocket of his coat, he found therein eight cigars. Four of them were soaked with seawater; four were perfectly scatheless. After a search, somebody produced three dry matches; and thereupon the four waifs rode impudently in their little boat and, with an assurance of an impending rescue shining in their eyes, puffed at the big cigars, and judged well and ill of all men. Everybody took a drink of water.

## IV

"Cook," remarked the captain, "there don't seem to be any signs of life about your house of refuge."

"No," replied the cook. "Funny they don't see us!"

A broad stretch of lowly coast lay before the eyes of the men. It was of low dunes topped with dark vegetation. The roar of the surf was plain, and sometimes they could see the white lip of a wave as it spun up the beach. A tiny house was blocked out black upon the sky. Southward, the slim lighthouse lifted its little gray length.

Tide, wind, and waves were swinging the dinghy northward. "Funny they don't see us," said the men.

The surf's roar was here dulled, but its tone was nevertheless thunderous and mighty. As the boat swam over the great rollers the men sat listening to this roar. "We'll swamp sure," said everybody.

It is fair to say here that there was not a lifesaving station within twenty miles in either direction; but the men did not know this fact, and in consequence they made dark and opprobrious remarks concerning the eyesight of the nation's lifesavers. Four scowling men sat in the dinghy and surpassed records in the invention of epithets.

"Funny they don't see us."

The light-heartedness of a former time had completely faded. To their sharpened minds it was easy to conjure pictures of all kinds of incompetency and blindness and, indeed, cowardice. There was the shore of the populous land, and it was bitter and bitter to them that from it came no sign.

"Well," said the captain, ultimately, "I suppose we'll have to make a try for ourselves. If we stay out here too long, we'll none of us have strength left to swim after the boat swamps."

And so the oiler, who was at the oars, turned the boat straight for the shore. There was a sudden tightening of muscles. There was some thinking.

"If we don't all get ashore," said the captain—"if we don't all get ashore, I suppose you fellows know where to send news of my finish?"

They then briefly exchanged some addresses and admonitions. As for the reflections of the men, there was a great deal of rage in them. Perchance they might be formulated thus: "If I am going to be drowned—if I am going to be drowned—if I am going to be drowned, why, in the name of the seven mad gods who rule the sea, was I allowed to come thus far and contemplate sand and trees? Was I brought here merely to have my nose dragged away as I was about to nibble the sacred cheese of life? It is preposterous. If this old ninny-woman, Fate, cannot do better than this, she should be deprived of the management of men's fortunes. She is an old hen who knows not her intention. If she has decided to drown me, why did she not do it in the beginning and save me all this trouble? The whole affair is absurd. . . . But no; she cannot mean to drown me. She dare not drown me. She cannot drown me. Not after all this work." Afterward the man might have had an impulse to shake his fist at the clouds. "Just you drown me, now, and then hear what I call you!"

The billows that came at this time were more formidable. They seemed always just about to break and roll over the little boat in a turmoil of foam. There was a preparatory and long growl in the speech of them. No mind unused to the sea would have concluded that the dinghy could ascend these sheer heights in time. The shore was still afar. The oiler was a wily surfman. "Boys," he said swiftly, "she won't live three minutes more, and we're too far out to swim. Shall I take her to sea again, Captain?"

"Yes; go ahead!" said the captain.

This oiler, by a series of quick miracles and fast and steady oarsmanship, turned the boat in the middle of the surf and took her safely to sea again.

There was a considerable silence as the boat bumped over the furrowed sea to deeper water. Then somebody in gloom spoke: "Well, anyhow, they must have seen us from the shore by now."

The gulls went in slanting flight up the wind toward the gray, desolate east. A squall, marked by dingy clouds and clouds brick-red, like smoke from a burning building, appeared from the southeast.

"What do you think of those lifesaving people? Ain't they peaches?"

"Funny they haven't seen us."

"Maybe they think we're out here for sport! Maybe they think we're fishin'. Maybe they think we're damned fools."

It was a long afternoon. A changed tide tried to force them southward, but wind and wave said northward. Far ahead, where coastline, sea, and sky formed their mighty angle, there were little dots which seemed to indicate a city on the shore.

"St. Augustine?"

The captain shook his head. "Too near Mosquito Inlet."

And the oiler rowed, and then the correspondent rowed; then the oiler rowed. It was a weary business. The human back can become the seat of more aches and pains than are registered in books for the composite anatomy of a regiment. It is a limited area, but it can become the theater of innumerable muscular conflicts, tangles, wrenches, knots, and other comforts.

"Did you ever like to row, Billie?" asked the correspondent.

"No," said the oiler; "hang it!"

When one exchanged the rowing-seat for a place in the bottom of the boat, he suffered a bodily depression that caused him to be careless of everything save an obligation to wiggle one finger. There was cold seawater swashing to and fro in the boat, and he lay in it. His head, pillowed on a thwart, was within an inch of the swirl of a wave-crest, and sometimes a particularly obstreperous sea came inboard and drenched him once more. But these matters did not annoy him. It is almost certain that if the boat had capsized he would have tumbled comfortably out upon the ocean as if he felt sure that it was a great soft mattress.

"Look! There's a man on the shore!"

"Where?"

"There! See 'im? See 'im?"

"Yes, sure! He's walking along."

"Now he's stopped. Look! He's facing us!"

"He's waving at us!"

"So he is! By thunder!"

"Ah, now we're all right! Now we're all right! There'll be a boat out here for us in half an hour."

"He's going on. He's running. He's going up to that house there."

The remote beach seemed lower than the sea, and it required a searching glance to discern the little black figure. The captain saw a floating stick, and they rowed to it. A bath towel was by some weird chance in the boat, and, tying this on the stick, the captain waved it. The oarsman did not dare turn his head, so he was obliged to ask questions.

"What's he doing now?"

"He's standing still again. He's looking, I think. . . . There he goes again—toward the house. . . . Now he's stopped again."

"Is he waving at us?"

"No, not now; he was, though."

"Look! There comes another man!"

"He's running."

"Look at him go, would you!"

"Why, he's on a bicycle. Now he's met the other man. They're both waving at us. Look!"

"There comes something up the beach."

"What the devil is that thing?"

"Why, it looks like a boat."

"Why, certainly, it's a boat."

"No; it's on wheels."

"Yes, so it is. Well, that must be the lifeboat. They drag them along shore on a wagon."

"That's the lifeboat, sure."

"No, by God, it's—it's an omnibus."

"I tell you it's a lifeboat."

"It is not! It's an omnibus. I can see it plain. See? One of these big hotel omnibuses."

"By thunder, you're right. It's an omnibus, sure as fate. What do you suppose they are doing with an omnibus? Maybe they are going around collecting the life-crew, hey?"

"That's it, likely. Look! There's a fellow waving a little black flag. He's standing on the steps of the omnibus. There come those other two fellows. Now they're all talking together. Look at the fellow with the flag. Maybe he ain't waving it!"

"That ain't a flag, is it? That's his coat. Why, certainly, that's his coat."

"So it is; it's his coat. He's taken it off and is waving it around his head. But would you look at him swing it!"

"Oh, say, there isn't any lifesaving station there. That's just a winter-resort hotel omnibus that has brought over some of the boarders to see us drown."

"What's that idiot with the coat mean? What's he signaling, anyhow?"

"It looks as if he were trying to tell us to go north. There must be a lifesaving station up there."

"No; he thinks we're fishing. Just giving us a merry hand. See? Ah, there, Willie!"

"Well, I wish I could make something out of those signals. What do you suppose he means?"

"He don't mean anything; he's just playing."

"Well, if he'd just signal us to try the surf again, or to go to sea and wait, or go north, or go south, or go to hell, there would be some reason in it. But look at him! He just stands there and keeps his coat revolving like a wheel. The ass!"

"There come more people."

"Now there's quite a mob. Look! Isn't that a boat?"

"Where? Oh, I see where you mean. No, that's no boat."

"That fellow is still waving his coat."

"He must think we like to see him do that. Why don't he quit it? It don't mean anything."

"I don't know. I think he is trying to make us go north. It must be that there's a lifesaving station there somewhere."

"Say, he ain't tired yet. Look at 'im wave!"

"Wonder how long he can keep that up. He's been revolving his coat ever since he caught sight of us. He's an idiot. Why aren't they getting men to bring a boat out? A fishing boat—one of those big yawls—could come out here all right. Why don't he do something?"

"Oh, it's all right now."

"They'll have a boat out here for us in less than no time, now that they've seen us."

A faint yellow tone came into the sky over the low land. The shadows on the sea slowly deepened. The wind bore coldness with it, and the men began to shiver.

"Holy smoke!" said one, allowing his voice to express his impious mood, "if we keep on monkeying out here! If we've got to flounder out here all night!"

"Oh, we'll never have to stay here all night! Don't you worry. They've seen us now, and it won't be long before they'll come chasing out after us."

The shore grew dusky. The man waving a coat blended gradually into this gloom, and it swallowed in the same manner the omnibus and the group of people. The spray, when it dashed uproariously over the side, made the voyagers shrink and swear like men who were being branded.

"I'd like to catch the chump who waved the coat. I feel like socking him one, just for luck."

"Why? What did he do?"

"Oh, nothing, but then he seemed so damned cheerful."

In the meantime the oiler rowed, and then the correspondent rowed, and then the oiler rowed. Gray-faced and bowed forward, they mechanically, turn by turn, plied the leaden oars. The form of the lighthouse had vanished from the southern horizon, but finally a pale star appeared, just lifting from the sea. The streaked saffron in the west passed before the all-merging darkness, and the sea to the east was black. The land had vanished, and was expressed only by the low and drear thunder of the surf.

"If I am going to be drowned—if I am going to be drowned—if I am going to be drowned, why, in the name of the seven mad gods who rule the sea, was I allowed to come thus far and contemplate sand and trees? Was I brought here merely to have my nose dragged away as I was about to nibble the sacred cheese of life?"

The patient captain, drooped over the water jar, was sometimes obliged to speak to the oarsman.

"Keep her head up! Keep her head up!"

"Keep her head up, sir." The voices were weary and low.

This was surely a quiet evening. All save the oarsman lay heavily and listlessly in the boat's bottom. As for him, his eyes were just capable of noting the tall black waves that swept forward in a most sinister silence, save for an occasional subdued growl of a crest.

The cook's head was on a thwart, and he looked without interest at the water under his nose. He was deep in other scenes. Finally he spoke. "Billie," he murmured, dreamfully, "what kind of pie do you like best?"

## V

"Pie!" said the oiler and the correspondent, agitatedly. "Don't talk about those things, blast you!"

"Well," said the cook, "I was just thinking about ham sandwiches, and——"

A night on the sea in an open boat is a long night. As darkness settled finally, the shine of the light, lifting from the sea in the south, changed to full gold. On the northern horizon a new light appeared, a small bluish gleam on the edge of the waters. These two lights were the furniture of the world. Otherwise there was nothing but waves.

Two men huddled in the stern, and distances were so magnificent in the dinghy that the rower was enabled to keep his feet partly warm by thrusting them under his companions. Their legs indeed extended far under the rowing-seat until they touched the feet of the captain forward. Sometimes, despite the efforts of the tired oarsman, a wave came piling into the boat, an icy wave of the night, and the chilling water soaked them anew. They would twist their bodies for a moment and groan, and sleep the dead sleep once more, while the water in the boat gurgled about them as the craft rocked.

The plan of the oiler and the correspondent was for one to row until he lost the ability, and then arouse the other from his sea-water couch in the bottom of the boat.

The oiler plied the oars until his head drooped forward and the overpowering sleep blinded him; and he rowed yet afterward. Then he touched a man in the bottom of the boat, and called his name. "Will you spell me for a little while?" he said meekly.

"Sure, Billie," said the correspondent, awaking and dragging himself to a sitting position. They exchanged places carefully, and the oiler, cuddling down in the sea-water at the cook's side, seemed to go to sleep instantly.

The particular violence of the sea had ceased. The waves came without snarling. The obligation of the man at the oars was to keep the boat headed so that the tilt of the rollers would not capsize her, and to preserve her from filling when the crests rushed past. The black waves were silent and hard to be seen in the darkness. Often one was almost upon the boat before the oarsman was aware.

In a low voice the correspondent addressed the captain. He was not sure that the captain was awake, although this iron man seemed to be always awake. "Captain, shall I keep her making for that light north, sir?"

The same steady voice answered him. "Yes. Keep it about two points off the port bow."

The cook had tied a lifebelt around himself in order to get even the warmth which this clumsy cork contrivance could donate, and he seemed almost stove-like when a rower, whose teeth invariably chattered wildly as soon as he ceased his labor, dropped down to sleep.

The correspondent, as he rowed, looked down at the two men sleeping underfoot. The cook's arm was around the oiler's shoulders, and, with their fragmentary clothing and haggard faces, they were the babes of the sea—a grotesque rendering of the old babes in the wood.

Later he must have grown stupid at his work, for suddenly there was a growling of water, and a crest came with a roar and a swash into the boat, and it was a wonder that it did not set the cook afloat in his lifebelt. The cook continued to sleep, but the oiler sat up, blinking his eyes and shaking with the new cold.

"Oh, I'm awful sorry, Billie," said the correspondent, contritely.

"That's all right, old boy," said the oiler, and lay down again and was asleep.

Presently it seemed that even the captain dozed, and the correspondent thought that he was the one man afloat on all the oceans. The wind had a voice as it came over the waves, and it was sadder than the end.

There was a long, loud swishing astern of the boat, and a gleaming trail of phosphorescence, like blue flame, was furrowed on the black waters. It might have been made by a monstrous knife.

Then there came a stillness, while the correspondent breathed with open mouth and looked at the sea.

Suddenly there was another swish and another long flash of bluish light, and this time it was alongside the boat, and might almost have been reached with an oar. The correspondent saw an enormous fin speed like a shadow through the water, hurling the crystalline spray and leaving the long glowing trail.

The correspondent looked over his shoulder at the captain. His face was hidden, and he seemed to be asleep. He looked at the babes of the sea. They certainly were asleep. So, being bereft of sympathy, he leaned a little way to one side and swore softly into the sea.

But the thing did not then leave the vicinity of the boat. Ahead or astern, on one side or the other, at intervals long or short, fled the long sparkling streak, and there was to be heard the *whirroo* of the dark fin. The speed and power of the thing was greatly to be admired. It cut the water like a gigantic and keen projectile.

The presence of this biding thing did not affect the man with the same horror that it would if he had been a picnicker. He simply looked at the sea dully and swore in an undertone.

Nevertheless, it is true that he did not wish to be alone with the thing. He wished one of his companions to awake by chance and keep him company with it. But the captain hung motionless over the water jar, and the oiler and the cook in the bottom of the boat were plunged in slumber.

## VI

"If I am going to be drowned—if I am going to be drowned—if I am going to be drowned, why, in the name of the seven mad gods who rule the sea, was I allowed to come thus far and contemplate sand and trees?"

During this dismal night, it may be remarked that a man would conclude that it was really the intention of the seven mad gods to drown him, despite the abominable injustice of it. For it was certainly an abominable injustice to drown a man who had worked so hard, so hard. The man felt it would be a crime most unnatural. Other people had drowned at sea since galleys swarmed with painted sails, but still——

When it occurs to a man that nature does not regard him as important, and that she feels she would not maim the universe by disposing of him, he at first wishes to throw bricks at the temple, and he hates deeply the fact that there are no bricks and no temples. Any visible expression of nature would surely be pelleted with his jeers.

Then, if there be no tangible thing to hoot, he feels, perhaps, the desire to confront a personification and indulge in pleas, bowed to one knee, and with hands supplicant, saying, "Yes, but I love myself."

A high cold star on a winter's night is the word he feels that she says to him. Thereafter he knows the pathos of his situation.

The men in the dinghy had not discussed these matters, but each had, no doubt, reflected upon them in silence and according to his mind. There was seldom any expression upon their faces save the general one of complete weariness. Speech was devoted to the business of the boat.

To chime the notes of his emotion, a verse mysteriously entered the correspondent's head. He had even forgotten that he had forgotten this verse, but it suddenly was in his mind.

A soldier of the Legion lay dying in Algiers;
There was lack of woman's nursing, there was dearth of woman's tears;
But a comrade stood beside him, and he took that comrade's hand,
And he said, "I never more shall see my own, my native land."

In his childhood the correspondent had been made acquainted with the fact that a soldier of the Legion lay dying in Algiers, but he had never regarded the fact as important. Myriads of his schoolfellows had informed him of the soldier's plight, but the dinning had naturally ended by making him perfectly indifferent.

He had never considered it his affair that a soldier of the Legion lay dying in Algiers, nor had it appeared to him as a matter for sorrow. It was less to him than the breaking of a pencil's point.

Now, however, it quaintly came to him as a human, living thing. It was no longer merely a picture of a few throes in the breast of a poet, meanwhile drinking tea and warming his feet at the grate; it was an actuality—stern, mournful, and fine.

The correspondent plainly saw the soldier. He lay on the sand with his feet out straight and still. While his pale left hand was upon his chest in an attempt to thwart the going of his life, the blood came between his fingers. In the far Algerian distance, a city of low square forms was set against a sky that was faint with the last sunset hues. The correspondent, plying the oars and dreaming of the slow and slower movements of the lips of the soldier, was moved by a profound and perfectly impersonal comprehension. He was sorry for the soldier of the Legion who lay dying in Algiers.

The thing which had followed the boat and waited had evidently grown bored at the delay. There was no longer to be heard the slash of the cut-water, and there was no longer the flame of the long trail. The light in the north still glimmered, but it was apparently no nearer to the boat. Sometimes the boom of the surf rang in the correspondent's ears, and he turned the craft seaward then and rowed harder. Southward, someone had evidently built a watch fire on the beach. It was too low and too far to be seen, but it made a shimmering, roseate reflection upon the bluff in back of it, and this could be discerned from the boat. The wind came stronger, and sometimes a wave suddenly raged out like a mountain cat, and there was to be seen the sheen and sparkle of a broken crest.

The captain, in the bow, moved on his water jar and sat erect. "Pretty long night," he observed to the correspondent. He looked at the shore. "Those lifesaving people take their time."

"Did you see that shark playing around?"

"Yes, I saw him. He was a big fellow, all right."

"Wish I had known you were awake."

Later the correspondent spoke into the bottom of the boat. "Billie!" There was a slow and gradual disentanglement. "Billie, will you spell me?"

"Sure," said the oiler.

As soon as the correspondent touched the cold, comfortable seawater in the bottom of the boat and had huddled close to the cook's lifebelt he was deep in sleep, despite the fact that his teeth played all the popular airs. This sleep was so good to him that it was but a moment before he heard a voice call his name in a tone that demonstrated the last stages of exhaustion. "Will you spell me?"

"Sure, Billie."

The light in the north had mysteriously vanished, but the correspondent took his course from the wide-awake captain.

Later in the night they took the boat farther out to sea, and the captain directed the cook to take one oar at the stern and keep the boat facing the seas. He was to call out if he should hear the thunder of the surf. This plan enabled the oiler and the correspondent to get respite together. "We'll give those boys a chance to get into shape again," said the captain. They curled down and, after a few preliminary chatterings and trembles, slept once more the dead sleep. Neither knew they had bequeathed to the cook the company of another shark, or perhaps the same shark.

As the boat caroused on the waves, spray occasionally bumped over the side and gave them a fresh soaking, but this had no power to break their repose. The ominous slash of the wind and the water affected them as it would have affected mummies.

"Boys," said the cook, with the notes of every reluctance in his voice, "she's drifted in pretty close. I guess one of you had better take her to sea again." The correspondent, aroused, heard the crash of the toppled crests.

As he was rowing, the captain gave him some whiskey-and-water, and this steadied the chills out of him. "If I ever get ashore and anybody shows me even a photograph of an oar——"

At last there was a short conversation.

"Billie! . . . Billie, will you spell me?"

"Sure," said the oiler.

## VII

When the correspondent again opened his eyes, the sea and the sky were each of the gray hue of the dawning. Later, carmine and gold was painted upon the waters. The morning appeared finally, in its splendor, with a sky of pure blue, and the sunlight flamed on the tips of the waves.

On the distant dunes were set many little black cottages, and a tall white windmill reared above them. No man, nor dog, nor bicycle appeared on the beach. The cottages might have formed a deserted village.

The voyagers scanned the shore. A conference was held in the boat. "Well," said the captain, "if no help is coming, we might better try a run through the surf right away. If we stay out here much longer we will be too weak to do anything for ourselves at all." The others silently acquiesced in this reasoning. The boat was headed for the beach. The correspondent wondered if none ever ascended the tall wind-tower, and if then they never looked seaward. This tower was a giant, standing with its back to the plight of the ants. It represented in a degree, to the correspondent, the serenity of nature amid the struggles of the individual—nature in the wind, and nature in the vision of men. She did not seem cruel to him then, nor beneficent, nor treacherous, nor wise. But she was indifferent, flatly indifferent. It is, perhaps, plausible that a man in this situation, impressed with the unconcern of the universe, should see the innumerable flaws of his life, and have them taste wickedly in his mind, and wish for another chance. A distinction between right and wrong seems absurdly clear to him, then, in this new ignorance of the grave-edge, and he understands that if he were given another opportunity he would mend his conduct and his words, and be better and brighter during an introduction or at a tea.

"Now, boys," said the captain, "she is going to swamp sure. All we can do is to work her in as far as possible, and then when she swamps, pile out and scramble for the beach. Keep cool now, and don't jump until she swamps sure."

The oiler took the oars. Over his shoulders he scanned the surf. "Captain," he said, "I think I'd better bring her about and keep her head-on to the seas and back her in."

"All right, Billie," said the captain. "Back her in." The oiler swung the boat then, and, seated in the stern, the cook and the correspondent were obliged to look over their shoulders to contemplate the lonely and indifferent shore.

The monstrous inshore rollers heaved the boat high until the men were again enabled to see the white sheets of water scudding up the slanted beach. "We won't get in very close," said the captain. Each time a man could wrest his attention from the rollers, he turned his glance toward the shore, and in the expression of the eyes during this contemplation there was a singular quality. The correspondent, observing the others, knew that they were not afraid, but the full meaning of their glances was shrouded.

As for himself, he was too tired to grapple fundamentally with the fact. He tried to coerce his mind into thinking of it, but the mind was dominated at this time by the muscles, and the muscles said they did not care. It merely occurred to him that if he should drown it would be a shame.

There were no hurried words, no pallor, no plain agitation. The men simply looked at the shore. "Now, remember to get well clear of the boat when you jump," said the captain.

Seaward the crest of a roller suddenly fell with a thunderous crash, and the long white comber came roaring down upon the boat.

"Steady now," said the captain. The men were silent. They turned their eyes from the shore to the comber and waited. The boat slid up the incline, leaped at the furious top, bounced over it, and swung down the long back of the wave. Some water had been shipped, and the cook bailed it out.

But the next crest crashed also. The tumbling, boiling flood of white water caught the boat and whirled it almost perpendicular. Water swarmed in from all sides. The correspondent had his hands on the gunwale at this time, and when the water entered at that place he swiftly withdrew his fingers, as if he objected to wetting them.

The little boat, drunken with this weight of water, reeled and snuggled deeper into the sea.

"Bail her out, cook! Bail her out!" said the captain.

"All right, Captain," said the cook.

"Now, boys, the next one will do for us sure," said the oiler. "Mind to jump clear of the boat."

The third wave moved forward, huge, furious, implacable. It fairly swallowed the dinghy, and almost simultaneously the men tumbled into the sea. A piece of lifebelt had lain in the bottom of the boat, and as the correspondent went overboard he held this to his chest with his left hand.

The January water was icy, and he reflected immediately that it was colder than he had expected to find it off the coast of Florida. This appeared to his dazed mind as a fact important enough to be noted at the time. The coldness of the water was sad; it was tragic. This fact was somehow mixed and confused with his opinion of his own situation, so that it seemed almost a proper reason for tears. The water was cold.

When he came to the surface he was conscious of little but the noisy water. Afterward he saw his companions in the sea. The oiler was ahead in the race. He was swimming strongly and rapidly. Off to the correspondent's left, the cook's great white and corked back bulged out of the water; and in the rear the captain was hanging with his one good hand to the keel of the overturned dinghy.

There is a certain immovable quality to a shore, and the correspondent wondered at it amid the confusion of the sea.

It seemed also very attractive; but the correspondent knew that it was a long journey, and he paddled leisurely. The piece of life preserver lay under him, and sometimes he whirled down the incline of a wave as if he were on a hand-sled.

But finally he arrived at a place in the sea where travel was beset with difficulty. He did not pause swimming to inquire what manner of current had caught him, but there his progress ceased. The shore was set before him like a bit of scenery on a stage, and he looked at it and understood with his eyes each detail of it.

As the cook passed, much farther to the left, the captain was calling to him, "Turn over on your back, cook! Turn over on your back and use the oar."

"All right, sir." The cook turned on his back, and, paddling with an oar, went ahead as if he were a canoe.

Presently the boat also passed to the left of the correspondent, with the captain clinging with one hand to the keel. He would have appeared like a man raising himself to look over a board fence if it were not for the extraordinary gymnastics of the boat. The correspondent marveled that the captain could still hold to it.

They passed on nearer to shore—the oiler, the cook, the captain—and following them went the water jar, bouncing gaily over the seas.

The correspondent remained in the grip of this strange new enemy—a current. The shore, with its white slope of sand and its green bluff topped with little silent cottages, was spread like a picture before him. It was very near to him then, but he was impressed as one who, in a gallery, looks at a scene from Brittany or Algiers.

He thought: "I am going to drown? Can it be possible? Can it be possible? Can it be possible?" Perhaps an individual must consider his own death to be the final phenomenon of nature.

But later a wave perhaps whirled him out of this small deadly current, for he found suddenly that he could again make progress toward the shore. Later still he was aware that the captain, clinging with one hand to the keel of the dinghy, had his face turned away from the shore and toward him, and was calling his name. "Come to the boat! Come to the boat!"

In his struggle to reach the captain and the boat, he reflected that when one gets properly wearied drowning must really be a comfortable arrangement—a cessation of hostilities accompanied by a large degree of relief; and he was glad of it, for the main thing in his mind for some moments had been horror of the temporary agony. He did not wish to be hurt.

Presently he saw a man running along the shore. He was undressing with most remarkable speed. Coat, trousers, shirt, everything flew magically off him.

"Come to the boat!" called the captain.

"All right, Captain." As the correspondent paddled, he saw the captain let himself down to bottom and leave the boat. Then the correspondent performed his one little marvel of the voyage. A large wave caught him and flung him with ease and supreme speed completely over the boat and far beyond it. It struck him even then as an event in gymnastics and a true miracle of the sea. An overturned boat in the surf is not a plaything to a swimming man.

The correspondent arrived in water that reached only to his waist, but his condition did not enable him to stand for more than a moment. Each wave knocked him into a heap, and the undertow pulled at him.

Then he saw the man who had been running and undressing, and undressing and running, come bounding into the water. He dragged ashore the cook, and then waded toward the captain; but the captain waved him away and sent him to the correspondent. He was naked—naked as a tree in winter; but a halo was about his head, and he shone like a saint. He gave a strong pull, and a long drag, and a bully heave at the correspondent's hand. The correspondent, schooled in the minor formulæ, said, "Thanks, old man." But suddenly the man cried, "What's that?" He pointed a swift finger. The correspondent said, "Go."

In the shallows, face downward, lay the oiler. His forehead touched sand that was periodically, between each wave, clear of the sea.

The correspondent did not know all that transpired afterward. When he achieved safe ground he fell, striking the sand with each particular part of his body. It was as if he had dropped from a roof, but the thud was grateful to him.

It seems that instantly the beach was populated with men with blankets, clothes, and flasks, and women with coffeepots and all the remedies sacred to their minds. The welcome of the land to the men from the sea was warm and generous; but a still and dripping shape was carried slowly up the beach, and the land's welcome for it could only be the different and sinister hospitality of the grave.

When it came night, the white waves paced to and fro in the moonlight, and the wind brought the sound of the great sea's voice to the men on the shore, and they felt that they could then be interpreters.

# THE BLUE HOTEL

## Stephen Crane

## I

THE PALACE HOTEL at Fort Romper was painted a light blue, a shade that is on the legs of a kind of heron, causing the bird to declare its position against any background. The Palace Hotel, then, was always screaming and howling in a way that made the dazzling winter landscape of Nebraska seem only a gray swampish hush. It stood alone on the prairie, and when the snow was falling the town two hundred yards away was not visible. But when the traveler alighted at the railway station he was obliged to pass the Palace Hotel before he could come upon the company of low clapboard houses which composed Fort Romper, and it was not to be thought that any traveler could pass the Palace Hotel without looking at it. Pat Scully, the proprietor, had proved himself a master of strategy when he chose his paints. It is true that on clear days, when the great transcontinental expresses, long lines of swaying Pullmans, swept through Fort Romper, passengers were overcome at the sight, and the cult that knows the brown-reds and the subdivisions of the dark greens of the East expressed shame, pity, horror, in a laugh. But to the citizens of this prairie town and to the people who would naturally stop there, Pat Scully had performed a feat. With this opulence and splendor, these creeds, classes, egotisms, that streamed through Romper on the rails day after day, they had no color in common.

As if the displayed delights of such a blue hotel were not suffi-ciently enticing, it was Scully's habit to go every morning and evening to meet the leisurely trains that stopped at Romper and work his seductions upon any man that he might see wavering, gripsack in hand.

One morning, when a snow-crusted engine dragged its long string of freight cars and its one passenger coach to the station, Scully performed the marvel of catching three men. One was a shaky and quick-eyed Swede, with a great shining cheap valise; one was a tall bronzed cowboy, who was on his way to a ranch near the Dakota line; one was a little silent man from the East, who didn't look it, and didn't announce it. Scully practically made them prisoners. He was so nimble and merry and kindly that each probably felt it would be the height of brutality to try to escape. They trudged off over the creaking board sidewalks in the wake of the eager little Irishman. He wore a heavy fur cap squeezed tightly down on his head. It caused his two red ears to stick out stiffly, as if they were made of tin.

At last, Scully, elaborately, with boisterous hospitality, conducted them through the portals of the blue hotel. The room which they entered was small. It seemed to be merely a proper temple for an enormous stove, which, in the center, was humming with godlike violence. At various points on its surface the iron had become luminous and glowed yellow from the heat. Beside the stove Scully's son Johnnie was playing High-Five with an old farmer who had whiskers both gray and sandy. They were quarreling. Frequently the old farmer turned his face toward a box of sawdust—colored brown from tobacco juice—that was behind the stove, and spat with an air of great impatience and irritation. With a loud flourish of words Scully destroyed the game of cards, and bustled his son upstairs with part of the baggage of the new guests. He himself conducted them to three basins of the coldest water in the world. The cowboy and the Easterner burnished themselves fiery red with this water, until it seemed to be some kind of metal polish. The Swede, however, merely dipped his fingers gingerly and with trepidation. It was notable that throughout this series of small ceremonies the three travelers were made to feel that Scully was very benevolent. He was conferring great favors upon them. He handed the towel from one to another with an air of philanthropic impulse.

Afterward they went to the first room, and, sitting about the stove, listened to Scully's officious clamor at his daughters, who were preparing the midday meal. They reflected in the silence of experienced men who tread carefully amid new people. Nevertheless, the old farmer, stationary, invincible in his chair near the warmest part of the stove, turned his face from the sawdust box frequently and addressed a glowing commonplace to the strangers. Usually he was answered in short but adequate sentences by either the cowboy or the Easterner. The Swede said nothing. He seemed to be occupied in making furtive estimates of each man in the room. One might have thought that he had the sense of silly suspicion which comes to guilt. He resembled a badly frightened man.

Later, at dinner, he spoke a little, addressing his conversation entirely to Scully. He volunteered that he had come from New York, where for ten years he had worked as a tailor. These facts seemed to strike Scully as fascinating, and afterward he volunteered that he had lived at Romper for fourteen years. The Swede asked about the crops and the price of labor. He seemed barely to listen to Scully's extended replies. His eyes continued to rove from man to man.

Finally, with a laugh and a wink, he said that some of these Western communities were very dangerous; and after his statement he straightened his legs under the table, tilted his head, and laughed again, loudly. It was plain that the demonstration had no meaning to the others. They looked at him wondering and in silence.

## II

As the men trooped heavily back into the front room, the two little windows presented views of a turmoiling sea of snow. The huge arms of the wind were making attempts—mighty, circular, futile—to embrace the flakes as they sped. A gatepost like a still man with a blanched face stood aghast amid this profligate fury. In a hearty voice Scully announced the presence of a blizzard. The guests of the blue hotel, lighting their pipes, assented with grunts of lazy masculine contentment. No island of the sea could be exempt in the degree of this little room with its humming stove. Johnnie, son of Scully, in a tone which defined his opinion of his ability as a card player, challenged the old farmer of both gray and sandy whiskers to a game of High-Five. The farmer agreed with a contemptuous and bitter scoff. They sat close to the stove, and squared their knees under a wide board. The cowboy and the Easterner watched the game with interest. The Swede remained near the window, aloof, but with a countenance that showed signs of an inexplicable excitement.

The play of Johnnie and the graybeard was suddenly ended by another quarrel. The old man arose while casting a look of heated scorn at his adversary. He slowly buttoned his coat, and then stalked with fabulous dignity from the room. In the discreet silence of all other men the Swede laughed. His laughter rang somehow childish. Men by this time had begun to look at him askance, as if they wished to inquire what ailed him.

A new game was formed jocosely. The cowboy volunteered to become the partner of Johnnie, and they all then turned to ask the Swede to throw in his lot with the little Easterner. He asked some questions about the game, and, learning that it wore many names, and that he had played it when it was under an alias, he accepted the invitation. He strode toward the men nervously, as if he expected to be assaulted. Finally, seated, he gazed from face to face and laughed shrilly. This laugh was so strange that the Easterner looked up quickly, the cowboy sat intent and with his mouth open, and Johnnie paused, holding the cards with still fingers.

Afterward there was a short silence. Then Johnnie said, "Well, let's get at it. Come on now!" They pulled their chairs forward until their knees were bunched under the board. They began to play, and their interest in the game caused the others to forget the manner of the Swede.

The cowboy was a board-whacker. Each time that he held superior cards he whanged them, one by one, with exceeding force, down upon the improvised table, and took the tricks with a glowing air of prowess and pride that sent thrills of indignation into the hearts of his opponents. A game with a board-whacker in it is sure to become intense. The countenances of the Easterner and the Swede were miserable whenever the cowboy thundered down his aces and kings, while Johnnie, his eyes gleaming with joy, chuckled and chuckled.

Because of the absorbing play none considered the strange ways of the Swede. They paid strict heed to the game. Finally, during a lull caused by a new deal, the Swede suddenly addressed Johnnie: "I suppose there have been a good many men killed in this room." The jaws of the others dropped and they looked at him.

"What in hell are you talking about?" said Johnnie.

The Swede laughed again his blatant laugh, full of a kind of false courage and defiance. "Oh, you know what I mean all right," he answered.

"I'm a liar if I do!" Johnnie protested. The card was halted, and the men stared at the Swede. Johnnie evidently felt that as the son of the proprietor he should make a direct inquiry. "Now, what might you be drivin' at, mister?" he asked. The Swede winked at him. It was a wink full of cunning. His fingers shook on the edge of the board. "Oh, maybe you think I have been to nowheres. Maybe you think I'm a tenderfoot?"

"I don't know nothin' about you," answered Johnnie, "and I don't give a damn where you've been. All I got to say is that I don't know what you're driving at. There hain't never been nobody killed in this room."

The cowboy, who had been steadily gazing at the Swede, then spoke: "What's wrong with you, mister?"

Apparently it seemed to the Swede that he was formidably menaced. He shivered and turned white near the corners of his mouth. He sent an appealing glance in the direction of the little Easterner. During these moments he did not forget to wear his air of advanced pot-valor. "They say they don't know what I mean," he remarked mockingly to the Easterner.

The latter answered after prolonged and cautious reflection. "I don't understand you," he said, impassively.

The Swede made a movement then which announced that he thought he had encountered treachery from the only quarter where he had expected sympathy, if not help "Oh, I see you are all against me. I see——"

The cowboy was in a state of deep stupefaction. "Say," he cried, as he tumbled the deck violently down upon the board, "say, what are you gittin' at, hey?"

The Swede sprang up with the celerity of a man escaping from a snake on the floor. "I don't want to fight!" he shouted. "I don't want to fight!"

The cowboy stretched his long legs indolently and deliberately. His hands were in his pockets. He spat into the sawdust box. "Well, who the hell thought you did?" he inquired.

The Swede backed rapidly toward a corner of the room. His hands were out protectingly in front of his chest, but he was making an obvious struggle to control his fright. "Gentlemen," he quavered, "I suppose I am going to be killed before I can leave this house! I suppose I am going to be killed before I can leave this house!" In his eyes was the dying-swan look. Through the windows could be seen the snow turning blue in the shadow of dusk. The wind tore at the house, and some loose thing beat regularly against the clapboards like a spirit tapping.

A door opened, and Scully himself entered. He paused in surprise as he noted the tragic attitude of the Swede. Then he said, "What's the matter here?"

The Swede answered him swiftly and eagerly: "These men are going to kill me."

"Kill you!" ejaculated Scully. "Kill you! What are you talkin'?"

The Swede made the gesture of a martyr.

Scully wheeled sternly upon his son. "What is this, Johnnie?"

The lad had grown sullen. "Damned if I know," he answered. "I can't make no sense to it." He began to shuffle the cards, fluttering them together with an angry snap. "He says a good many men have been killed in this room, or something like that. And he says he's goin' to be killed here too. I don't know what ails him. He's crazy, I shouldn't wonder."

Scully then looked for explanation to the cowboy, but the cowboy simply shrugged his shoulders.

"Kill you?" said Scully again to the Swede. "Kill you? Man, you're off your nut."

"Oh, I know," burst out the Swede. "I know what will happen. Yes, I'm crazy—yes. Yes, of course, I'm crazy—yes. But I know one thing——" There was a sort of sweat of misery and terror upon his face. "I know I won't get out of here alive."

The cowboy drew a deep breath, as if his mind was passing into the last stages of dissolution. "Well, I'm doggoned," he whispered to himself.

Scully wheeled suddenly and faced his son. "You've been troublin' this man!"

Johnnie's voice was loud with its burden of grievance. "Why, good Gawd, I ain't done nothin' to 'im."

The Swede broke in. "Gentlemen, do not disturb yourselves. I will leave this house. I will go away, because"—he accused them dramatically with his glance—"because I do not want to be killed."

Scully was furious with his son. "Will you tell me what is the matter, you young divil? What's the matter, anyhow? Speak out!"

"Blame it!" cried Johnnie in despair, "don't I tell you I don't know? He—he says we want to kill him, and that's all I know. I can't tell what ails him."

The Swede continued to repeat: "Never mind, Mr. Scully; never mind. I will leave this house. I will go away, because I do not wish to be killed. Yes, of course, I am crazy—yes. But I know one thing! I will go away. I will leave this house. Never mind, Mr. Scully; never mind. I will go away."

"You will not go 'way," said Scully. "You will not go 'way until I hear the reason of this business. If anybody has troubled you I will take care of him. This is my house. You are under my roof, and I will not allow any peaceable man to be troubled here." He cast a terrible eye upon Johnnie, the cowboy, and the Easterner.

"Never mind, Mr. Scully; never mind. I will go away. I do not wish to be killed." The Swede moved toward the door which opened upon the stairs. It was evidently his intention to go at once for his baggage.

"No, no," shouted Scully peremptorily; but the white-faced man slid by him and disappeared. "Now," said Scully severely, "what does this mane?"

Johnnie and the cowboy cried together: "Why, we didn't do nothin' to 'im!"

Scully's eyes were cold. "No," he said, "you didn't?"

Johnnie swore a deep oath. "Why, this is the wildest loon I ever see. We didn't do nothin' at all. We were jest sittin' here playin' cards, and he——"

The father suddenly spoke to the Easterner. "Mr. Blanc," he asked, "what has these boys been doin'?"

The Easterner reflected again. "I didn't see anything wrong at all," he said at last, slowly.

Scully began to howl. "But what does it mane?" He stared ferociously at his son. "I have a mind to lather you for this, me boy."

Johnnie was frantic. "Well, what have I done?" he bawled at his father.

## III

"I think you are tongue-tied," said Scully finally to his son, the cowboy, and the Easterner; and at the end of this scornful sentence he left the room.

Upstairs the Swede was swiftly fastening the straps of his great valise. Once his back happened to be half turned toward the door, and, hearing a noise there, he wheeled and sprang up, uttering a loud cry. Scully's wrinkled visage showed grimly in the light of the small lamp he carried. This yellow effulgence, streaming upward, colored only his prominent features, and left his eyes, for instance, in mysterious shadow. He resembled a murderer.

"Man! man!" he exclaimed, "have you gone daffy?"

"Oh, no! Oh, no!" rejoined the other. "There are people in this world who know pretty nearly as much as you do—understand?"

For a moment they stood gazing at each other. Upon the Swede's deathly pale cheeks were two spots brightly crimson and sharply edged, as if they had been carefully painted. Scully placed the light on the table and sat himself on the edge of the bed. He spoke ruminatively. "By cracky, I never heard of such a thing in my life. It's a complete muddle. I can't, for the soul of me, think how you ever got this idea into your head." Presently he lifted his eyes and asked: "And did you sure think they were going to kill you?"

The Swede scanned the old man as if he wished to see into his mind. "I did," he said at last. He obviously suspected that this answer might precipitate an outbreak. As he pulled on a strap his whole arm shook, the elbow wavering like a bit of paper.

Scully banged his hand impressively on the footboard of the bed. "Why, man, we're goin' to have a line of ilictric streetcars in this town next spring."

"'A line of electric streetcars,'" repeated the Swede, stupidly.

"And," said Scully, "there's a new railroad goin' to be built down from Broken Arm to here. Not to mintion the four churches and the smashin' big brick schoolhouse. Then there's the big factory, too. Why, in two years Romper'll be a met-tro-*pol*-is."

Having finished the preparation of his baggage, the Swede straightened himself. "Mr. Scully," he said, with sudden hardihood, "how much do I owe you?"

"You don't owe me anythin'," said the old man, angrily.

"Yes, I do," retorted the Swede. He took seventy-five cents from his pocket and tendered it to Scully; but the latter snapped his fingers in disdainful refusal. However, it happened that they both stood gazing in a strange fashion at three silver pieces on the Swede's open palm.

"I'll not take your money," said Scully at last. "Not after what's been goin' on here." Then a plan seemed to strike him. "Here," he cried, picking up his lamp and moving toward the door. "Here! Come with me a minute."

"No," said the Swede, in overwhelming alarm.

"Yes," urged the old man. "Come on! I want you to come and see a picter—just across the hall—in my room."

The Swede must have concluded that his hour was come. His jaw dropped and his teeth showed like a dead man's. He ultimately followed Scully across the corridor, but he had the step of one hung in chains.

Scully flashed the light high on the wall of his own chamber. There was revealed a ridiculous photograph of a little girl. She was leaning against a balustrade of gorgeous decoration, and the formidable bang to her hair was prominent. The figure was as graceful as an upright sledstake, and, withal, it was of the hue of lead. "There," said Scully, tenderly, "that's the picter of my little girl that died. Her name was Carrie. She had the purtiest hair you ever saw! I was that fond of her, she——"

Turning then, he saw that the Swede was not contemplating the picture at all, but, instead, was keeping keen watch on the gloom in the rear.

"Look, man!" cried Scully, heartily. "That's the picter of my little gal that died. Her name was Carrie. And then here's the picter of my oldest boy, Michael. He's a lawyer in Lincoln, an' doin' well. I gave that boy a grand eddication, and I'm glad for it now. He's a fine boy. Look at 'im now. Ain't he bold as blazes, him there in Lincoln, an honored an' respicted gintleman! An honored and respicted gintleman," concluded Scully with a flourish. And, so saying, he smote the Swede jovially on the back.

The Swede faintly smiled.

"Now," said the old man, "there's only one more thing." He dropped suddenly to the floor and thrust his head beneath the bed. The Swede could hear his muffled voice. "I'd keep it under me piller if it wasn't for that boy Johnnie. Then there's the old woman—— Where is it now? I never put it twice in the same place. Ah, now come out with you!"

Presently he backed clumsily from under the bed, dragging with him an old coat rolled into a bundle. "I've fetched him," he muttered. Kneeling on the floor, he unrolled the coat and extracted from its heart a large yellow-brown whiskey bottle.

His first maneuver was to hold the bottle up to the light. Reassured, apparently, that nobody had been tampering with it, he thrust it with a generous movement toward the Swede.

The weak-kneed Swede was about to eagerly clutch this element of strength, but he suddenly jerked his hand away and cast a look of horror upon Scully.

"Drink," said the old man affectionately. He had risen to his feet, and now stood facing the Swede.

There was a silence. Then again Scully said: "Drink!"

The Swede laughed wildly. He grabbed the bottle, put it to his mouth; and as his lips curled absurdly around the opening and his throat worked, he kept his glance, burning with hatred, upon the old man's face.

## IV

After the departure of Scully the three men, with the cardboard still
upon their knees, preserved for a long time an astounded silence.
Then Johnnie said: "That's the doddangedest Swede I ever see."

"He ain't no Swede," said the cowboy, scornfully.

"Well, what is he then?" cried Johnnie. "What is he then?"

"It's my opinion," replied the cowboy deliberately, "he's some
kind of a Dutchman." It was a venerable custom of the country to
entitle as Swedes all light-haired men who spoke with a heavy tongue.
In consequence the idea of the cowboy was not without its daring.
"Yes, sir," he repeated. "It's my opinion this feller is some kind of
a Dutchman."

"Well, he says he's a Swede, anyhow," muttered Johnnie, sulkily.
He turned to the Easterner: "What do you think, Mr. Blanc?"

"Oh, I don't know," replied the Easterner.

"Well, what do you think makes him act that way?" asked the
cowboy.

"Why, he's frightened." The Easterner knocked his pipe against
a rim of the stove. "He's clear frightened out of his boots."

"What at?" cried Johnnie and the cowboy together.

The Easterner reflected over his answer.

"What at?" cried the others again.

"Oh, I don't know, but it seems to me this man has been reading
dime novels, and he thinks he's right out in the middle of it—the
shootin' and stabbin' and all."

"But," said the cowboy, deeply scandalized, "this ain't Wyoming,
ner none of them places. This is Nebrasker."

"Yes," added Johnnie, "an' why don't he wait till he gits *out West?*"

The traveled Easterner laughed. "It isn't different there even—not
in these days. But he thinks he's right in the middle of hell."

Johnnie and the cowboy mused long.

"It's awful funny," remarked Johnnie at last.

"Yes," said the cowboy. "This is a queer game. I hope we don't
git snowed in, because then we'd have to stand this here man bein'
around with us all the time. That wouldn't be no good."

"I wish pop would throw him out," said Johnnie.

Presently they heard a loud stamping on the stairs, accompanied
by ringing jokes in the voice of old Scully, and laughter, evidently
from the Swede. The men around the stove stared vacantly at each
other. "Gosh!" said the cowboy. The door flew open, and old Scully,

flushed and anecdotal, came into the room. He was jabbering at the Swede, who followed him, laughing bravely. It was the entry of two roisterers from a banquet hall.

"Come now," said Scully sharply to the three seated men, "move up and give us a chance at the stove." The cowboy and the Easterner obediently sidled their chairs to make room for the newcomers. Johnnie, however, simply arranged himself in a more indolent attitude, and then remained motionless.

"Come! Git over, there," said Scully.

"Plenty of room on the other side of the stove," said Johnnie.

"Do you think we want to sit in the draught?" roared the father.

But the Swede here interposed with a grandeur of confidence. "No, no. Let the boy sit where he likes," he cried in a bullying voice to the father.

"All right! All right!" said Scully, deferentially. The cowboy and the Easterner exchanged glances of wonder.

The five chairs were formed in a crescent about one side of the stove. The Swede began to talk; he talked arrogantly, profanely, angrily. Johnnie, the cowboy, and the Easterner maintained a morose silence, while old Scully appeared to be receptive and eager, breaking in constantly with sympathetic ejaculations.

Finally the Swede announced that he was thirsty. He moved in his chair, and said that he would go for a drink of water.

"I'll git it for you," cried Scully at once.

"No," said the Swede, contemptuously. "I'll get it for myself." He arose and stalked with the air of an owner off into the executive parts of the hotel.

As soon as the Swede was out of hearing Scully sprang to his feet and whispered intensely to the others: "Upstairs he thought I was tryin' to poison 'im."

"Say," said Johnnie, "this makes me sick. Why don't you throw 'im out in the snow?"

"Why, he's all right now," declared Scully. "It was only that he was from the East, and he thought this was a tough place. That's all. He's all right now."

The cowboy looked with admiration upon the Easterner. "You were straight," he said. "You were on to that there Dutchman."

"Well," said Johnnie to his father, "he may be all right now, but I don't see it. Other time he was scared, but now he's too fresh."

Scully's speech was always a combination of Irish brogue and idiom, Western twang and idiom, and scraps of curiously formal diction taken from the story-books and newspapers. He now hurled a strange mass of language at the head of his son. "What do I keep? What do I keep? What do I keep?" he demanded, in a voice of thunder. He slapped his knee impressively, to indicate that he himself was going to make reply, and that all should heed. "I keep a hotel," he shouted. "A hotel, do you mind? A guest under my roof has sacred privileges. He is to be intimidated by none. Not one word shall he hear that would prijudice him in favor of goin' away. I'll not have it. There's no place in this here town where they can say they iver took in a guest of mine because he was afraid to stay here." He wheeled suddenly upon the cowboy and the Easterner. "Am I right?"

"Yes, Mr. Scully," said the cowboy, "I think you're right."

"Yes, Mr. Scully," said the Easterner, "I think you're right."

## V

At six-o'clock supper, the Swede fizzed like a fire-wheel. He sometimes seemed on the point of bursting into riotous song, and in all his madness he was encouraged by old Scully. The Easterner was encased in reserve; the cowboy sat in wide-mouthed amazement, forgetting to eat, while Johnnie wrathily demolished great plates of food. The daughters of the house, when they were obliged to replenish the biscuits, approached as warily as Indians, and, having succeeded in their purpose, fled with ill-concealed trepidation. The Swede domineered the whole feast, and he gave it the appearance of a cruel bacchanal. He seemed to have grown suddenly taller; he gazed, brutally disdainful, into every face. His voice rang through the room. Once when he jabbed out harpoon-fashion with his fork to pinion a biscuit, the weapon nearly impaled the hand of the Easterner, which had been stretched quietly out for the same biscuit.

After supper, as the men filed toward the other room, the Swede smote Scully ruthlessly on the shoulder. "Well, old boy, that was a good, square meal." Johnnie looked hopefully at his father; he knew that shoulder was tender from an old fall; and, indeed, it appeared for a moment as if Scully was going to flame out over the matter, but in the end he smiled a sickly smile and remained silent. The others understood from his manner that he was admitting his responsibility for the Swede's new viewpoint.

Johnnie, however, addressed his parent in an aside. "Why don't you license somebody to kick you downstairs?" Scully scowled darkly by way of reply.

When they were gathered about the stove, the Swede insisted on another game of High-Five. Scully gently deprecated the plan at first, but the Swede turned a wolfish glare upon him. The old man subsided, and the Swede canvassed the others. In his tone there was always a great threat. The cowboy and the Easterner both remarked indifferently that they would play. Scully said that he would presently have to go to meet the 6:58 train, and so the Swede turned menacingly upon Johnnie. For a moment their glances crossed like blades, and then Johnnie smiled and said, "Yes, I'll play."

They formed a square, with the little board on their knees. The Easterner and the Swede were again partners. As the play went on, it was noticeable that the cowboy was not board-whacking as usual. Meanwhile, Scully, near the lamp, had put on his spectacles and, with an appearance curiously like an old priest, was reading a newspaper. In time he went out to meet the 6:58 train, and, despite his precautions, a gust of polar wind whirled into the room as he opened the door. Besides scattering the cards, it chilled the players to the marrow. The Swede cursed frightfully. When Scully returned, his entrance disturbed a cozy and friendly scene. The Swede again cursed. But presently they were once more intent, their heads bent forward and their hands moving swiftly. The Swede had adopted the fashion of board-whacking.

Scully took up his paper and for a long time remained immersed in matters which were extraordinarily remote from him. The lamp burned badly, and once he stopped to adjust the wick. The newspaper, as he turned from page to page, rustled with a slow and comfortable sound. Then suddenly he heard three terrible words: "You are cheatin'!"

Such scenes often prove that there can be little of dramatic import in environment. Any room can present a tragic front; any room can be comic. This little den was now hideous as a torture chamber. The new faces of the men themselves had changed it upon the instant. The Swede held a huge fist in front of Johnnie's face, while the latter looked steadily over it into the blazing orbs of his accuser. The Easterner had grown pallid; the cowboy's jaw had dropped in that expression of bovine amazement which was one of his important mannerisms. After the three words, the first sound in the room was made by Scully's paper as it floated forgotten to his feet. His spectacles had also fallen from his nose, but by a clutch he had saved them in air. His hand, grasping the spectacles, now remained poised awkwardly and near his shoulder. He stared at the card-players.

Probably the silence was while a second elapsed. Then, if the floor had been suddenly twitched out from under the men they could not have moved quicker. The five had projected themselves headlong toward a common point. It happened that Johnnie, in rising to hurl himself upon the Swede, had stumbled slightly because of his curiously instinctive care for the cards and the board. The loss of the moment allowed time for the arrival of Scully, and also allowed the cowboy time to give the Swede a great push which sent him staggering back. The men found tongue together, and hoarse shouts of rage, appeal, or fear burst from every throat. The cowboy pushed and jostled feverishly at the Swede, and the Easterner and Scully clung wildly to Johnnie; but through the smoky air, above the swaying bodies of the peace-compellers, the eyes of the two warriors ever sought each other in glances of challenge that were at once hot and steely.

Of course the board had been overturned, and now the whole company of cards was scattered over the floor, where the boots of the men trampled the fat and painted kings and queens as they gazed with their silly eyes at the war that was waging above them.

Scully's voice was dominating the yells. "Stop now! Stop, I say! Stop, now——"

Johnnie, as he struggled to burst through the rank formed by Scully and the Easterner, was crying, "Well, he says I cheated! He says I cheated! I won't allow no man to say I cheated! If he says I cheated, he's a————!"

The cowboy was telling the Swede, "Quit, now! Quit, d'ye hear——"

The screams of the Swede never ceased: "He did cheat! I saw him! I saw him——"

As for the Easterner, he was importuning in a voice that was not heeded: "Wait a moment, can't you? Oh, wait a moment. What's the good of a fight over a game of cards? Wait a moment——"

In this tumult no complete sentences were clear. "Cheat"—"Quit"—"He says"—these fragments pierced the uproar and rang out sharply. It was remarkable that, whereas Scully undoubtedly made the most noise, he was the least heard of any of the riotous band.

Then suddenly there was a great cessation. It was as if each man had paused for breath; and although the room was still lighted with the anger of men, it could be seen that there was no danger of immediate conflict, and at once Johnnie, shouldering his way forward, almost succeeded in confronting the Swede. "What did you say I cheated for? What did you say I cheated for? I don't cheat, and I won't let no man say I do!"

The Swede said, "I saw you! I saw you!"

"Well," cried Johnnie, "I'll fight any man what says I cheat!"

"No, you won't," said the cowboy. "Not here."

"Ah, be still, can't you?" said Scully, coming between them.

The quiet was sufficient to allow the Easterner's voice to be heard. He was repeating, "Oh, wait a moment, can't you? What's the good of a fight over a game of cards? Wait a moment!"

Johnnie, his red face appearing above his father's shoulder, hailed the Swede again. "Did you say I cheated?"

The Swede showed his teeth. "Yes."

"Then," said Johnnie, "we must fight."

"Yes, fight," roared the Swede. He was like a demoniac. "Yes, fight! I'll show you what kind of a man I am! I'll show you who you want to fight! Maybe you think I can't fight! Maybe you think I can't! I'll show you, you skin, you card-sharp! Yes, you cheated! You cheated! You cheated!"

"Well, let's go at it, then, mister," said Johnnie, coolly.

The cowboy's brow was beaded with sweat from his efforts in intercepting all sorts of raids. He turned in despair to Scully. "What are you goin' to do now?"

A change had come over the Celtic visage of the old man. He now seemed all eagerness; his eyes glowed.

"We'll let them fight," he answered, stalwartly. "I can't put up with it any longer. I've stood this damned Swede till I'm sick. We'll let them fight."

## VI

The men prepared to go out-of-doors. The Easterner was so nervous that he had great difficulty in getting his arms into the sleeves of his new leather coat. As the cowboy drew his fur cap down over his ears his hands trembled. In fact, Johnnie and old Scully were the only ones who displayed no agitation. These preliminaries were conducted without words.

Scully threw open the door. "Well, come on," he said. Instantly a terrific wind caused the flame of the lamp to struggle at its wick, while a puff of black smoke sprang from the chimney-top. The stove was in mid-current of the blast, and its voice swelled to equal the roar of the storm. Some of the scarred and bedabbled cards were caught up from the floor and dashed helplessly against the farther wall. The men lowered their heads and plunged into the tempest as into a sea.

No snow was falling, but great whirls and clouds of flakes, swept up from the ground by the frantic winds, were streaming southward with the speed of bullets. The covered land was blue with the sheen of an unearthly satin, and there was no other hue save where, at the low, black railway station—which seemed incredibly distant—one light gleamed like a tiny jewel. As the men floundered into a thigh-deep drift, it was known that the Swede was bawling out something. Scully went to him, put a hand on his shoulder, and projected an ear. "What's that you say?" he shouted.

"I say," bawled the Swede again, "I won't stand much show against this gang. I know you'll all pitch on me."

Scully smote him reproachfully on the arm. "Tut, man!" he yelled. The wind tore the words from Scully's lips and scattered them far alee.

"You are all a gang of——" boomed the Swede, but the storm also seized the remainder of this sentence.

Immediately turning their backs upon the wind, the men had swung around a corner to the sheltered side of the hotel. It was the function of the little house to preserve here, amid this great devastation of snow, an irregular V-shape of heavily encrusted grass, which crackled beneath the feet. One could imagine the great drifts piled against the windward side. When the party reached the comparative peace of this spot it was found that the Swede was still bellowing.

"Oh, I know what kind of a thing this is! I know you'll all pitch on me. I can't lick you all!"

Scully turned upon him panther-fashion. "You'll not have to whip all of us. You'll have to whip my son Johnnie. An' the man what troubles you durin' that time will have me to dale with."

The arrangements were swiftly made. The two men faced each other, obedient to the harsh commands of Scully, whose face, in the subtly luminous gloom, could be seen set in the austere impersonal lines that are pictured on the countenances of the Roman veterans. The Easterner's teeth were chattering, and he was hopping up and down like a mechanical toy. The cowboy stood rock-like.

The contestants had not stripped off any clothing. Each was in his ordinary attire. Their fists were up, and they eyed each other in a calm that had the elements of leonine cruelty in it.

During this pause, the Easterner's mind, like a film, took lasting impressions of three men—the iron-nerved master of the ceremony; the Swede, pale, motionless, terrible; and Johnnie, serene yet ferocious, brutish yet heroic. The entire prelude had in it a tragedy greater than the tragedy of action, and this aspect was accentuated by the long, mellow cry of the blizzard, as it sped the tumbling and wailing flakes into the black abyss of the south.

"Now!" said Scully.

The two combatants leaped forward and crashed together like bullocks. There was heard the cushioned sound of blows, and of a curse squeezing out from between the tight teeth of one.

As for the spectators, the Easterner's pent-up breath exploded from him with a pop of relief, absolute relief from the tension of the preliminaries. The cowboy bounded into the air with a yowl. Scully was immovable as from supreme amazement and fear at the fury of the fight which he himself had permitted and arranged.

For a time the encounter in the darkness was such a perplexity of flying arms that it presented no more detail than would a swiftly revolving wheel. Occasionally a face, as if illumined by a flash of light, would shine out, ghastly and marked with pink spots. A moment later, the men might have been known as shadows, if it were not for the involuntary utterance of oaths that came from them in whispers.

Suddenly a holocaust of warlike desire caught the cowboy, and he bolted forward with the speed of a broncho. "Go it, Johnnie! go it! Kill him! Kill him!"

Scully confronted him. "Kape back," he said; and by his glance the cowboy could tell that this man was Johnnie's father.

To the Easterner there was a monotony of unchangeable fighting that was an abomination. This confused mingling was eternal to his sense, which was concentrated in a longing for the end, the priceless end. Once the fighters lurched near him, and as he scrambled hastily backward he heard them breathe like men on the rack.

"Kill him, Johnnie! Kill him! Kill him! Kill him!" The cowboy's face was contorted like one of those agony masks in museums.

"Keep still," said Scully, icily.

Then there was a sudden loud grunt, incomplete, cut short, and Johnnie's body swung away from the Swede and fell with sickening heaviness to the grass. The cowboy was barely in time to prevent the mad Swede from flinging himself upon his prone adversary. "No, you don't," said the cowboy, interposing an arm. "Wait a second."

Scully was at his son's side. "Johnnie! Johnnie, me boy!" His voice had a quality of melancholy tenderness. "Johnnie! Can you go on with it?" He looked anxiously down into the bloody, pulpy face of his son.

There was a moment of silence, and then Johnnie answered in his ordinary voice, "Yes, I—it—yes."

Assisted by his father he struggled to his feet. "Wait a bit now till you git your wind," said the old man.

A few paces away the cowboy was lecturing the Swede. "No, you don't! Wait a second!"

The Easterner was plucking at Scully's sleeve. "Oh, this is enough," he pleaded. "This is enough! Let it go as it stands. This is enough!"

"Bill," said Scully, "git out of the road." The cowboy stepped aside. "Now." The combatants were actuated by a new caution as they advanced toward collision. They glared at each other, and then the Swede aimed a lightning blow that carried with it his entire weight. Johnnie was evidently half stupid from weakness, but he miraculously dodged, and his fist sent the overbalanced Swede sprawling.

The cowboy, Scully, and the Easterner burst into a cheer that was like a chorus of triumphant soldiery, but before its conclusion the Swede had scuffled agilely to his feet and come in berserk abandon at his foe. There was another perplexity of flying arms, and Johnnie's body again swung away and fell, even as a bundle might fall from a roof. The Swede instantly staggered to a little wind-waved tree and leaned upon it, breathing like an engine, while his savage and flame-lit eyes roamed from face to face as the men bent over Johnnie. There was a splendor of isolation in his situation at this time which the Easterner felt once when, lifting his eyes from the man on the ground, he beheld that mysterious and lonely figure, waiting.

"Are you any good yet, Johnnie?" asked Scully in a broken voice.

The son gasped and opened his eyes languidly. After a moment he answered, "No—I ain't—any good—any—more." Then, from shame and bodily ill, he began to weep, the tears furrowing down through the blood-stains on his face. "He was too—too—too heavy for me."

Scully straightened and addressed the waiting figure. "Stranger," he said, evenly, "it's all up with our side." Then his voice changed into that vibrant huskiness which is commonly the tone of the most simple and deadly announcements. "Johnnie is whipped."

Without replying, the victor moved off on the route to the front door of the hotel.

The cowboy was formulating new and unspellable blasphemies. The Easterner was startled to find that they were out in a wind that seemed to come direct from the shadowed arctic floes. He heard again the wail of the snow as it was flung to its grave in the south. He knew now that all this time the cold had been sinking into him deeper and deeper, and he wondered that he had not perished. He felt indifferent to the condition of the vanquished man.

"Johnnie, can you walk?" asked Scully.

"Did I hurt—hurt him any?" asked the son.

"Can you walk, boy? Can you walk?"

Johnnie's voice was suddenly strong. There was a robust impatience in it. "I asked you whether I hurt him any!"

"Yes, yes, Johnnie," answered the cowboy, consolingly; "he's hurt a good deal."

They raised him from the ground, and as soon as he was on his feet he went tottering off, rebuffing all attempts at assistance. When the party rounded the corner they were fairly blinded by the pelting of the snow. It burned their faces like fire. The cowboy carried Johnnie through the drift to the door. As they entered, some cards again rose from the floor and beat against the wall.

The Easterner rushed to the stove. He was so profoundly chilled that he almost dared to embrace the glowing iron. The Swede was not in the room. Johnnie sank into a chair and, folding his arms on his knees, buried his face in them. Scully, warming one foot and then the other at a rim of the stove, muttered to himself with Celtic mournfulness. The cowboy had removed his fur cap, and with a dazed and rueful air he was running one hand through his tousled locks. From overhead they could hear the creaking of boards, as the Swede tramped here and there in his room.

The sad quiet was broken by the sudden flinging open of a door that led toward the kitchen. It was instantly followed by an inrush of women. They precipitated themselves upon Johnnie amid a chorus of lamentation. Before they carried their prey off to the kitchen, there to be bathed and harangued with that mixture of sympathy and abuse which is a feat of their sex, the mother straightened herself and fixed old Scully with an eye of stern reproach. "Shame be upon you, Patrick Scully!" she cried. "Your own son, too. Shame be upon you!"

"There, now! Be quiet, now!" said the old man, weakly.

"Shame be upon you, Patrick Scully!" The girls, rallying to this slogan, sniffed disdainfully in the direction of those trembling accomplices, the cowboy and the Easterner. Presently they bore Johnnie away, and left the three men to dismal reflection.

## VII

"I'd like to fight this here Dutchman myself," said the cowboy, breaking a long silence.

Scully wagged his head sadly. "No, that wouldn't do. It wouldn't be right. It wouldn't be right."

"Well, why wouldn't it?" argued the cowboy. "I don't see no harm in it."

"No," answered Scully, with mournful heroism. "It wouldn't be right. It was Johnnie's fight, and now we mustn't whip the man just because he whipped Johnnie."

"Yes, that's true enough," said the cowboy; "but—he better not get fresh with me, because I couldn't stand no more of it."

"You'll not say a word to him," commanded Scully, and even then they heard the tread of the Swede on the stairs. His entrance was made theatric. He swept the door back with a bang and swaggered to the middle of the room. No one looked at him. "Well," he cried, insolently, at Scully, "I s'pose you'll tell me now how much I owe you?"

The old man remained stolid. "You don't owe me nothin'."

"Huh!" said the Swede, "huh! Don't owe 'im nothin'."

The cowboy addressed the Swede. "Stranger, I don't see how you come to be so gay around here."

Old Scully was instantly alert. "Stop!" he shouted, holding his hand forth, fingers upward. "Bill, you shut up!"

The cowboy spat carelessly into the sawdust box. "I didn't say a word, did I?" he asked.

"Mr. Scully," called the Swede, "how much do I owe you?" It was seen that he was attired for departure, and that he had his valise in his hand.

"You don't owe me nothin'," repeated Scully in the same imperturbable way.

"Huh!" said the Swede. "I guess you're right. I guess if it was any way at all, you'd owe me somethin'. That's what I guess." He turned to the cowboy. "'Kill him! Kill him! Kill him!'" he mimicked, and then guffawed victoriously. "'Kill him!'" He was convulsed with ironical humor.

But he might have been jeering the dead. The three men were immovable and silent, staring with glassy eyes at the stove.

The Swede opened the door and passed into the storm, giving one derisive glance backward at the still group.

As soon as the door was closed, Scully and the cowboy leaped to their feet and began to curse. They trampled to and fro, waving their arms and smashing into the air with their fists. "Oh, but that was a hard minute!" wailed Scully. "That was a hard minute! Him there leerin' and scoffin'! One bang at his nose was worth forty dollars to me that minute! How did you stand it, Bill?"

"How did I stand it?" cried the cowboy in a quivering voice. "How did I stand it? Oh!"

The old man burst into sudden brogue. "I'd loike to take that Swade," he wailed, "and hould 'im down on a shtone flure and bate 'im to a jelly wid a shtick!"

The cowboy groaned in sympathy. "I'd like to git him by the neck and ha-ammer him"—he brought his hand down on a chair with a noise like a pistol-shot—"hammer that there Dutchman until he couldn't tell himself from a dead coyote!"

"I'd bate 'im until he——"

"I'd show *him* some things——"

And then together they raised a yearning, fanatic cry—"Oh-o-oh! If we only could——"

"Yes!"

"Yes!"

"And then I'd——"

"O-o-oh!"

## VIII

The Swede, tightly gripping his valise, tacked across the face of the storm as if he carried sails. He was following a line of little naked, gasping trees which, he knew, must mark the way of the road. His face, fresh from the pounding of Johnnie's fists, felt more pleasure than pain in the wind and the driving snow. A number of square shapes loomed upon him finally, and he knew them as the houses of the main body of the town. He found a street and made travel along it, leaning heavily upon the wind whenever, at a corner, a terrific blast caught him.

He might have been in a deserted village. We picture the world as thick with conquering and elate humanity, but here, with the bugles of the tempest pealing, it was hard to imagine a peopled earth. One viewed the existence of man then as a marvel, and conceded a glamor of wonder to these lice which were caused to cling to a whirling, fire-smitten, ice-locked, disease-stricken, space-lost bulb. The conceit of man was explained by this storm to be the very engine of life. One was a coxcomb not to die in it. However, the Swede found a saloon.

In front of it an indomitable red light was burning, and the snowflakes were made blood-color as they flew through the circumscribed territory of the lamp's shining. The Swede pushed open the door of the saloon and entered A sanded expanse was before him, and at the end of it four men sat about a table drinking. Down one side of the room extended a radiant bar, and its guardian was leaning upon his elbows listening to the talk of the men at the table. The Swede dropped his valise upon the floor and, smiling fraternally upon the barkeeper, said, "Gimme some whiskey, will you?" The man placed a bottle, a whiskey glass, and a glass of ice-thick water upon the bar. The Swede poured himself an abnormal portion of whiskey and drank it in three gulps. "Pretty bad night," remarked the bartender, indifferently. He was making the pretension of blindness which is usually a distinction of his class; but it could have been seen that he was furtively studying the half-erased blood-stains on the face of the Swede. "Bad night," he said again.

"Oh, it's good enough for me," replied the Swede, hardily, as he poured himself some more whiskey. The barkeeper took his coin and maneuvered it through its reception by the highly nickeled cash-machine. A bell rang; a card labeled "20 cts." had appeared.

"No," continued the Swede, "this isn't too bad weather. It's good enough for me."

"So?" murmured the barkeeper, languidly.

The copious drams made the Swede's eyes swim, and he breathed a trifle heavier. "Yes, I like this weather. I like it. It suits me." It was apparently his design to impart a deep significance to these words.

"So?" murmured the bartender again. He turned to gaze dreamily at the scroll-like birds and bird-like scrolls which had been drawn with soap upon the mirrors in back of the bar.

"Well, I guess I'll take another drink," said the Swede, presently. "Have something?"

"No, thanks; I'm not drinkin'," answered the bartender. Afterward he asked, "How did you hurt your face?"

The Swede immediately began to boast loudly. "Why, in a fight. I thumped the soul out of a man down here at Scully's hotel."

The interest of the four men at the table was at last aroused.

"Who was it?" said one.

"Johnnie Scully," blustered the Swede. "Son of the man what runs it. He will be pretty near dead for some weeks, I can tell you. I made a nice thing of him, I did. He couldn't get up. They carried him in the house. Have a drink?"

Instantly the men in some subtle way encased themselves in reserve. "No, thanks," said one. The group was of curious formation. Two were prominent local businessmen; one was the district attorney; and one was a professional gambler of the kind known as "square." But a scrutiny of the group would not have enabled an observer to pick the gambler from the men of more reputable pursuits. He was, in fact, a man so delicate in manner, when among people of fair class, and so judicious in his choice of victims, that in the strictly masculine part of the town's life he had come to be explicitly trusted and admired. People called him a thoroughbred. The fear and contempt with which his craft was regarded were undoubtedly the reason why his quiet dignity shone conspicuous above the quiet dignity of men who might be merely hatters, billiard-markers, or grocery clerks. Beyond an occasional unwary traveler who came by rail, this gambler was supposed to prey solely upon reckless and senile farmers, who, when flush with good crops, drove into town in all the pride and confidence of an absolutely invulnerable stupidity. Hearing at times in circuitous fashion of the despoilment of such a farmer, the important men of Romper invariably laughed in contempt of the victim, and if they thought of the wolf at all, it was with a kind of pride at the knowledge that he would never dare think of attacking their wisdom and courage. Besides, it was popular that this gambler had a real wife and two real children in a neat cottage in a suburb, where he led an exemplary home life; and when anyone even suggested a discrepancy in his character, the crowd immediately vociferated descriptions of this virtuous family circle. Then men who led exemplary home lives, and men who did not lead exemplary home lives, all subsided in a bunch, remarking that there was nothing more to be said.

However, when a restriction was placed upon him—as, for instance, when a strong clique of members of the new Pollywog Club refused to permit him, even as a spectator, to appear in the rooms of the organization—the candor and gentleness with which he accepted the judgment disarmed many of his foes and made his friends more desperately partisan. He invariably distinguished between himself and a respectable Romper man so quickly and frankly that his manner actually appeared to be a continual broadcast compliment.

And one must not forget to declare the fundamental fact of his entire position in Romper. It is irrefutable that in all affairs outside his business, in all matters that occur eternally and commonly between man and man, this thieving card-player was so generous, so just, so moral, that, in a contest, he could have put to flight the consciences of nine tenths of the citizens of Romper.

And so it happened that he was seated in this saloon with the two prominent local merchants and the district attorney.

The Swede continued to drink raw whiskey, meanwhile babbling at the barkeeper and trying to induce him to indulge in potations. "Come on. Have a drink. Come on. What—no? Well, have a little one, then. By gawd, I've whipped a man tonight, and I want to celebrate. I whipped him good, too. Gentlemen," the Swede cried to the men at the table, "have a drink?"

"Ssh!" said the barkeeper.

The group at the table, although furtively attentive, had been pretending to be deep in talk, but now a man lifted his eyes toward the Swede and said, shortly, "Thanks. We don't want any more."

At this reply the Swede ruffled out his chest like a rooster. "Well," he exploded, "it seems I can't get anybody to drink with me in this town. Seems so, don't it? Well!"

"Ssh!" said the barkeeper.

"Say," snarled the Swede, "don't you try to shut me up. I won't have it. I'm a gentleman, and I want people to drink with me. And I want 'em to drink with me now. *Now*—do you understand?" He rapped the bar with his knuckles.

Years of experience had calloused the bartender. He merely grew sulky. "I hear you," he answered.

"Well," cried the Swede, "listen hard then. See those men over there? Well, they're going to drink with me, and don't you forget it. Now you watch."

"Hi!" yelled the barkeeper, "this won't do!"

"Why won't it?" demanded the Swede. He stalked over to the table, and by chance laid his hand upon the shoulder of the gambler. "How about this?" he asked wrathfully. "I asked you to drink with me."

The gambler simply twisted his head and spoke over his shoulder. "My friend, I don't know you."

"Oh, hell!" answered the Swede, "come and have a drink."

"Now, my boy," advised the gambler, kindly, "take your hand off my shoulder and go 'way and mind your own business." He was a little, slim man, and it seemed strange to hear him use this tone of heroic patronage to the burly Swede. The other men at the table said nothing.

"What! You won't drink with me, you little dude? I'll make you, then! I'll make you!" The Swede had grasped the gambler frenziedly at the throat, and was dragging him from his chair. The other men sprang up. The barkeeper dashed around the corner of his bar. There was a great tumult, and then was seen a long blade in the hand of the gambler. It shot forward, and a human body, this citadel of virtue, wisdom, power, was pierced as easily as if it had been a melon. The Swede fell with a cry of supreme astonishment.

The prominent merchants and the district attorney must have at once tumbled out of the place backward. The bartender found himself hanging limply to the arm of a chair and gazing into the eyes of a murderer.

"Henry," said the latter, as he wiped his knife on one of the towels that hung beneath the bar rail, "you tell 'em where to find me. I'll be home, waiting for 'em." Then he vanished. A moment afterward the barkeeper was in the street dinning through the storm for help and, moreover, companionship.

The corpse of the Swede, alone in the saloon, had its eyes fixed upon a dreadful legend that dwelt atop of the cash-machine: "This registers the amount of your purchase."

## IX

Months later, the cowboy was frying pork over the stove of a little ranch near the Dakota line, when there was a quick thud of hoofs outside, and presently the Easterner entered with the letters and the papers.

"Well," said the Easterner at once, "the chap that killed the Swede has got three years. Wasn't much, was it?"

"He has? Three years?" The cowboy poised his pan of pork, while he ruminated upon the news. "Three years. That ain't much."

"No. It was a light sentence," replied the Easterner as he unbuckled his spurs. "Seems there was a good deal of sympathy for him in Romper."

"If the bartender had been any good," observed the cowboy, thoughtfully, "he would have gone in and cracked that there Dutchman on the head with a bottle in the beginnin' of it and stopped all this here murderin'."

"Yes, a thousand things might have happened," said the Easterner, tartly.

The cowboy returned his pan of pork to the fire, but his philosophy continued. "It's funny, ain't it? If he hadn't said Johnnie was cheatin' he'd be alive this minute. He was an awful fool. Game played for fun, too. Not for money. I believe he was crazy."

"I feel sorry for that gambler," said the Easterner.

"Oh, so do I," said the cowboy. "He don't deserve none of it for killin' who he did."

"The Swede might not have been killed if everything had been square."

"Might not have been killed?" exclaimed the cowboy. "Everythin' square? Why, when he said that Johnnie was cheatin' and acted like such a jackass? And then in the saloon he fairly walked up to git hurt?" With these arguments the cowboy browbeat the Easterner and reduced him to rage.

"You're a fool!" cried the Easterner, viciously. "You're a bigger jackass than the Swede by a million majority. Now let me tell you one thing. Let me tell you something. Listen! Johnnie *was* cheating!"

"'Johnnie,'" said the cowboy, blankly. There was a minute of silence, and then he said, robustly, "Why, no. The game was only for fun."

"Fun or not," said the Easterner, "Johnnie was cheating. I saw him. I know it. I saw him. And I refused to stand up and be a man. I let the Swede fight it out alone. And you—you were simply puffing around the place and wanting to fight. And then old Scully himself! We are all in it! This poor gambler isn't even a noun. He is kind of an adverb. Every sin is the result of a collaboration. We, five of us, have collaborated in the murder of this Swede. Usually there are from a dozen to forty women really involved in every murder, but in this case it seems to be only five men—you, I, Johnnie, old Scully; and that fool of an unfortunate gambler came merely as a culmination, the apex of a human movement, and gets all the punishment."

The cowboy, injured and rebellious, cried out blindly into this fog of mysterious theory: "Well, I didn't do anythin', did I?"

# A MYSTERY OF HEROISM

## Stephen Crane

THE DARK UNIFORMS of the men were so coated with dust from the incessant wrestling of the two armies that the regiment almost seemed a part of the clay bank which shielded them from the shells. On the top of the hill a battery was arguing in tremendous roars with some other guns, and to the eye of the infantry, the artillerymen, the guns, the caissons, the horses, were distinctly outlined upon the blue sky. When a piece was fired, a red streak as round as a log flashed low in the heavens, like a monstrous bolt of lightning. The men of the battery wore white duck trousers, which somehow emphasized their legs; and when they ran and crowded in little groups at the bidding of the shouting officers, it was more impressive than usual to the infantry.

Fred Collins, of A Company, was saying: "Thunder! I wisht I had a drink. Ain't there any water round here?" Then somebody yelled, "There goes th' bugler!"

As the eyes of half the regiment swept in one machinelike movement there was an instant's picture of a horse in a great convulsive leap of a death wound and a rider leaning back with a crooked arm and spread fingers before his face. On the ground was the crimson terror of an exploding shell, with fibres of flame that seemed like lances. A glittering bugle swung clear of the rider's back as fell headlong the horse and the man. In the air was an odour as from a conflagration.

Sometimes they of the infantry looked down at a fair little meadow which spread at their feet. Its long, green grass was rippling gently in a breeze. Beyond it was the gray form of a house half torn to pieces by shells and by the busy axes of soldiers who had pursued firewood.

The line of an old fence was now dimly marked by long weeds and by an occasional post. A shell had blown the well-house to fragments. Little lines of gray smoke ribboning upward from some embers indicated the place where had stood the barn.

From beyond a curtain of green woods there came the sound of some stupendous scuffle, as if two animals of the size of islands were fighting. At a distance there were occasional appearances of swift-moving men, horses, batteries, flags, and, with the crashing of infantry volleys were heard, often, wild and frenzied cheers. In the midst of it all Smith and Ferguson, two privates of A Company, were engaged in a heated discussion, which involved the greatest questions of the national existence.

The battery on the hill presently engaged in a frightful duel. The white legs of the gunners scampered this way and that way, and the officers redoubled their shouts. The guns, with their demeanours of stolidity and courage, were typical of something infinitely self-possessed in this clamour of death that swirled around the hill.

One of a "swing" team was suddenly smitten quivering to the ground, and his maddened brethren dragged his torn body in their struggle to escape from this turmoil and danger. A young soldier astride one of the leaders swore and fumed in his saddle, and furiously jerked at the bridle. An officer screamed out an order so violently that his voice broke and ended the sentence in a falsetto shriek.

The leading company of the infantry regiment was somewhat exposed, and the colonel ordered it moved more fully under the shelter of the hill. There was the clank of steel against steel.

A lieutenant of the battery rode down and passed them, holding his right arm carefully in his left hand. And it was as if this arm was not at all a part of him, but belonged to another man. His sober and reflective charger went slowly. The officer's face was grimy and perspiring, and his uniform was tousled as if he had been in direct grapple with an enemy. He smiled grimly when the men stared at him. He turned his horse toward the meadow.

Collins, of A Company, said: "I wisht I had a drink. I bet there's water in that there ol' well yonder!"

"Yes; but how you goin' to git it?"

For the little meadow which intervened was now suffering a terrible onslaught of shells. Its green and beautiful calm had vanished utterly. Brown earth was being flung in monstrous handfuls. And there was a massacre of the young blades of grass. They were being torn, burned, obliterated. Some curious fortune of the battle had made this gentle little meadow the object of the red hate of the shells, and each one as it exploded seemed like an imprecation in the face of a maiden.

The wounded officer who was riding across this expanse said to himself, "Why, they couldn't shoot any harder if the whole army was massed here!"

A shell struck the gray ruins of the house, and as, after the roar, the shattered wall fell in fragments, there was a noise which resembled the flapping of shutters during a wild gale of winter. Indeed, the infantry paused in the shelter of the bank appeared as men standing upon a shore contemplating a madness of the sea. The angel of calamity had under its glance the battery upon the hill. Fewer white-legged men laboured about the guns. A shell had smitten one of the pieces, and after the flare, the smoke, the dust, the wrath of this blow were gone, it was possible to see white legs stretched horizontally upon the ground. And at that interval to the rear, where it is the business of battery horses to stand with their noses to the fight awaiting the command to drag their guns out of the destruction or into it or wheresoever these incomprehensible humans demanded with whip and spur—in this line of passive and dumb spectators, whose fluttering hearts yet would not let them forget the iron laws of man's control of them—in this rank of brute-soldiers there had been relentless and hideous carnage. From the ruck of bleeding and prostrate horses, the men of the infantry could see one animal raising its stricken body with its fore legs, and turning its nose with mystic and profound eloquence toward the sky.

Some comrades joked Collins about his thirst. "Well, if yeh want a drink so bad, why don't yeh go git it!"

"Well, I will in a minnet, if yeh don't shut up!"

A lieutenant of artillery floundered his horse straight down the hill with as great concern as if it were level ground. As he galloped past the colonel of the infantry, he threw up his hand in swift salute. "We've got to get out of that," he roared angrily. He was a black-bearded officer, and his eyes, which resembled beads, sparkled like those of an insane man. His jumping horse sped along the column of infantry.

The fat major, standing carelessly with his sword held horizontally behind him and with his legs far apart, looked after the receding horseman and laughed. "He wants to get back with orders pretty quick, or there'll be no batt'ry left," he observed.

The wise young captain of the second company hazarded to the lieutenant colonel that the enemy's infantry would probably soon attack the hill, and the lieutenant colonel snubbed him.

A private in one of the rear companies looked out over the meadow, and then turned to a companion and said, "Look there, Jim!" It was the wounded officer from the battery, who some time before had started to ride across the meadow, supporting his right arm carefully with his left hand. This man had encountered a shell apparently at a time when no one perceived him, and he could now be seen lying face downward with a stirruped foot stretched across the body of his dead horse. A leg of the charger extended slantingly upward precisely as stiff as a stake. Around this motionless pair the shells still howled.

There was a quarrel in A Company. Collins was shaking his fist in the faces of some laughing comrades. "Dern yeh! I ain't afraid t' go. If yeh say much, I will go!"

"Of course, yeh will! You'll run through that there medder, won't yeh?"

Collins said, in a terrible voice, "You see now!" At this ominous threat his comrades broke into renewed jeers.

Collins gave them a dark scowl and went to find his captain. The latter was conversing with the colonel of the regiment.

"Captain," said Collins, saluting and standing at attention—in those days all trousers bagged at the knees—"captain, I want t' get permission to go git some water from that there well over yonder!"

The colonel and the captain swung about simultaneously and stared across the meadow. The captain laughed. "You must be pretty thirsty, Collins?"

"Yes, sir, I am."

"Well—ah," said the captain. After a moment, he asked, "Can't you wait?"

"No, sir."

The colonel was watching Collins's face. "Look here, my lad," he said, in a pious sort of a voice—"look here, my lad"—Collins was not a lad—"don't you think that's taking pretty big risks for a little drink of water?"

"I dunno," said Collins uncomfortably. Some the resentment toward his companions, which perhaps had forced him into this affair, was beginning to fade. "I dunno wether 'tis."

The colonel and the captain contemplated him for a time.

"Well," said the captain finally.

"Well," said the colonel, "if you want to go, why, go."

Collins saluted. "Much obliged t' yeh."

As he moved away the colonel called after him. "Take some of the other boys' canteens with you an' hurry back now."

"Yes, sir, I will."

The colonel and the captain looked at each other then, for it had suddenly occurred that they could not for the life of them tell whether Collins wanted to go or whether he did not.

They turned to regard Collins, and as they perceived him surrounded by gesticulating comrades, the colonel said: "Well, by thunder! I guess he's going."

Collins appeared as a man dreaming. In the midst of the questions, the advice, the warnings, all the excited talk of his company mates, he maintained a curious silence.

They were very busy in preparing him for his ordeal. When they inspected him carefully it was somewhat like the examination that grooms give a horse before a race; and they were amazed, staggered by the whole affair. Their astonishment found vent in strange repetitions.

"Are yeh sure a–goin'?" they demanded again and again.

"Certainly I am," cried Collins, at last furiously.

He strode sullenly away from them. He was swinging five or six canteens by their cords. It seemed that his cap would not remain firmly on his head, and often he reached and pulled it down over his brow.

There was a general movement in the compact column. The long animal–like thing moved slightly. Its four hundred eyes were turned upon the figure of Collins.

"Well, sir, if that ain't th' derndest thing! I never thought Fred Collins had the blood in him for that kind of business."

"What's he goin' to do, anyhow?"

"He's goin' to that well there after water."

"We ain't dyin' of thirst, are we? That's foolishness."

"Well, somebody put him up to it, an' he's doin' it."

"Say, he must be a desperate cuss."

When Collins faced the meadow and walked away from the regiment, he was vaguely conscious that a chasm, the deep valley of all prides, was suddenly between him and his comrades. It was provisional, but the provision was that he return as a victor. He had blindly been led by quaint emotions, and laid himself under an obligation to walk squarely up to the face of death.

But he was not sure that he wished to make a retraction, even if he could do so without shame. As a matter of truth, he was sure of very little. He was mainly surprised.

It seemed to him supernaturally strange that he had allowed his mind to maneuver his body into such a situation. He understood that it might be called dramatically great.

However, he had no full appreciation of anything, excepting that he was actually conscious of being dazed. He could feel his dulled mind groping after the form and colour of this incident. He wondered why he did not feel some keen agony of fear cutting his sense like a knife. He wondered at this, because human expression had said loudly for centuries that men should feel afraid of certain things, and that all men who did not feel this fear were phenomena—heroes.

He was, then, a hero. He suffered that disappointment which we would all have if we discovered that we were ourselves capable of those deeds which we most admire in history and legend. This, then, was a hero. After all, heroes were not much.

No, it could not be true. He was not a hero. Heroes had no shames in their lives, and, as for him, he remembered borrowing fifteen dollars from a friend and promising to pay it back the next day, and then avoiding that friend for ten months. When at home his mother had aroused him for the early labour of his life on the farm, it had often been his fashion to be irritable, childish, diabolical; and his mother had died since he had come to the war.

He saw that, in this matter of the well, the canteens, the shells, he was an intruder in the land of fine deeds.

He was now about thirty paces from his comrades. The regiment had just turned its many faces toward him.

From the forest of terrific noises there suddenly emerged a little uneven line of men. They fired fiercely and rapidly at distant foliage on which appeared little puffs of white smoke. The spatter of skirmish firing was added to the thunder of the guns on the hill. The little line of men ran forward. A colour sergeant fell flat with his flag as if he had slipped on ice. There was hoarse cheering from this distant field.

Collins suddenly felt that two demon fingers were pressed into his ears. He could see nothing but flying arrows, flaming red. He lurched from the shock of this explosion, but he made a mad rush for the house, which he viewed as a man submerged to the neck in a boiling surf might view the shore. In the air, little pieces of shell howled and the earthquake explosions drove him insane with the menace of their roar. As he ran the canteens knocked together with a rhythmical tinkling.

As he neared the house, each detail of the scene became vivid to him. He was aware of some bricks of the vanished chimney lying on the sod. There was a door which hung by one hinge.

Rifle bullets called forth by the insistent skirmishers came from the far-off bank of foliage. They mingled with the shells and the pieces of shells until the air was torn in all directions by hootings, yells, howls. The sky was full of fiends who directed all their wild rage at his head.

When he came to the well, he flung himself face downward and peered into its darkness. There were furtive silver glintings some feet from the surface. He grabbed one of the canteens and, unfastening its cap, swung it down by the cord. The water flowed slowly in with an indolent gurgle.

And now as he lay with his face turned away he was suddenly smitten with the terror. It came upon his heart like the grasp of claws. All the power faded from his muscles. For an instant he was no more than a dead man.

The canteen filled with a maddening slowness, in the manner of all bottles. Presently he recovered his strength and addressed a screaming oath to it. He leaned over until it seemed as if he intended to try to push water into it with his hands. His eyes as he gazed down into the well shone like two pieces of metal and in their expression was a great appeal and a great curse. The stupid water derided him.

There was the blaring thunder of a shell. Crimson light shone through the swift-boiling smoke and made a pink reflection on part of the wall of the well. Collins jerked out his arm and canteen with the same motion that a man would use in withdrawing his head from a furnace.

He scrambled erect and glared and hesitated. On the ground near him lay the old well bucket, with a length of rusty chain. He lowered it swiftly into the well. The bucket struck the water and then, turning lazily over, sank. When, with hand reaching tremblingly over hand, he hauled it out, it knocked often against the walls of the well and spilled some of its contents.

In running with a filled bucket, a man can adopt but one kind of gait. So through this terrible field over which screamed practical angels of death Collins ran in the manner of a farmer chased out of a dairy by a bull.

His face went staring white with anticipation—anticipation of a blow that would whirl him around and down. He would fall as he had seen other men fall, the life knocked out of them so suddenly that their knees were no more quick to touch the ground than their heads. He saw the long blue line of the regiment, but his comrades were standing looking at him from the edge of an impossible star. He was aware of some deep wheel ruts and hoofprints in the sod beneath his feet.

The artillery officer who had fallen in this meadow had been making groans in the teeth of the tempest of sound. These futile cries, wrenched from him by his agony, were heard only by shells, bullets. When wild-eyed Collins came running, this officer raised himself. His face contorted and blanched from pain, he was about to utter some great beseeching cry. But suddenly his face straightened and he called: "Say, young man, give me a drink of water, will you?"

Collins had no room amid his emotions for surprise. He was mad from the threats of destruction.

"I can't!" he screamed, and in his reply was a full description of his quaking apprehension. His cap was gone and his hair was riotous. His clothes made it appear that he had been dragged over the ground by the heels. He ran on.

The officer's head sank down and one elbow crooked. His foot in its brass-bound stirrup still stretched over the body of his horse and the other leg was under the steed.

But Collins turned. He came dashing back. His face had now turned gray and in his eyes was all terror. "Here it is! here it is!"

The officer was as a man gone in drink. His arm bent like a twig. His head drooped as if his neck were of willow. He was sinking to the ground, to lie face downward.

Collins grabbed him by the shoulder. "Here it is. Here's your drink. Turn over. Turn over, man, for God's sake!"

With Collins hauling at his shoulder, the officer twisted his body and fell with his face turned toward that region where lived the unspeakable noises of the swirling missiles. There was the faintest shadow of a smile on his lips as he looked at Collins. He gave a sigh, a little primitive breath like that from a child.

Collins tried to hold the bucket steadily, but his shaking hands caused the water to splash all over the face of the dying man. Then he jerked it away and ran on.

The regiment gave him a welcoming roar. The grimed faces were wrinkled in laughter.

His captain waved the bucket away. "Give it to the men!"

The two genial, skylarking young lieutenants were the first to gain possession of it. They played over it in their fashion.

When one tried to drink the other teasingly knocked his elbow. "Don't, Billie! You'll make me spill it," said the one. The other laughed.

Suddenly there was an oath, the thud of wood on the ground, and a swift murmur of astonishment among the ranks. The two lieutenants glared at each other. The bucket lay on the ground empty.

# AN EPISODE OF WAR

## Stephen Crane

THE LIEUTENANT'S RUBBER blanket lay on the ground, and upon it he had poured the company's supply of coffee. Corporals and other representatives of the grimy and hot-throated men who lined the breastwork had come for each squad's portion.

The lieutenant was frowning and serious at this task of division. His lips pursed as he drew with his sword various crevices in the heap, until brown squares of coffee, astoundingly equal in size, appeared on the blanket. He was on the verge of a great triumph in mathematics, and the corporals were thronging forward, each to reap a little square, when suddenly the lieutenant cried out and looked quickly at a man near him as if he suspected it was a case of personal assault. The others cried out also when they saw blood upon the lieutenant's sleeve.

He had winced like a man stung, swayed dangerously, and then straightened. The sound of his hoarse breathing was plainly audible. He looked sadly, mystically, over the breastwork at the green face of a wood, where now were many little puffs of white smoke. During this moment the men about him gazed statue-like and silent, astonished and awed by this catastrophe which happened when catastrophes were not expected—when they had leisure to observe it.

As the lieutenant stared at the wood, they too swung their heads, so that for another instant all hands, still silent, contemplated the distant forest as if their minds were fixed upon the mystery of a bullet's journey.

The officer had, of course, been compelled to take his sword into his left hand. He did not hold it by the hilt. He gripped it at

252

the middle of the blade, awkwardly. Turning his eyes from the hostile wood, he looked at the sword as he held it there, and seemed puzzled as to what to do with it, where to put it. In short, this weapon had of a sudden become a strange thing to him. He looked at it in a kind of stupefaction, as if he had been endowed with a trident, a scepter, or a spade.

Finally he tried to sheathe it. To sheathe a sword held by the left hand, at the middle of the blade, in a scabbard hung at the left hip, is a feat worthy of a sawdust ring. This wounded officer engaged in a desperate struggle with the sword and the wobbling scabbard, and during the time of it he breathed like a wrestler.

But at this instant the men, the spectators, awoke from their stonelike poses and crowded forward sympathetically. The orderly-sergeant took the sword and tenderly placed it in the scabbard. At the time, he leaned nervously backward, and did not allow even his finger to brush the body of the lieutenant. A wound gives strange dignity to him who bears it. Well men shy from this new and terrible majesty. It is as if the wounded man's hand is upon the curtain which hangs before the revelations of all existence—the meaning of ants, potentates, wars, cities, sunshine, snow, a feather dropped from a bird's wing; and the power of it sheds radiance upon a bloody form, and makes the other men understand sometimes that they are little. His comrades look at him with large eyes thoughtfully. Moreover, they fear vaguely that the weight of a finger upon him might send him headlong, precipitate the tragedy, hurl him at once into the dim, gray unknown. And so the orderly-sergeant, while sheathing the sword, leaned nervously backward.

There were others who proffered assistance. One timidly presented his shoulder and asked the lieutenant if he cared to lean upon it, but the latter waved him away mournfully. He wore the look of one who knows he is the victim of a terrible disease and understands his helplessness. He again stared over the breastwork at the forest, and then, turning, went slowly rearward. He held his right wrist tenderly in his left hand as if the wounded arm was made of very brittle glass.

And the men in silence stared at the wood, then at the departing lieutenant; then at the wood, then at the lieutenant.

As the wounded officer passed from the line of battle, he was enabled to see many things which as a participant in the fight were unknown to him. He saw a general on a black horse gazing over the lines of blue infantry at the green woods which veiled his problems.

An aide galloped furiously, dragged his horse suddenly to a halt, saluted, and presented a paper. It was, for a wonder, precisely like a historical painting.

To the rear of the general and his staff a group, composed of a bugler, two or three orderlies, and the bearer of the corps standard, all upon maniacal horses, were working like slaves to hold their ground, preserve their respectful interval, while the shells boomed in the air about them, and caused their chargers to make furious quivering leaps.

A battery, a tumultuous and shining mass, was swirling toward the right. The wild thud of hoofs, the cries of the riders shouting blame and praise, menace and encouragement, and, last, the roar of the wheels, the slant of the glistening guns, brought the lieutenant to an intent pause. The battery swept in curves that stirred the heart; it made halts as dramatic as the crash of a wave on the rocks, and when it fled onward this aggregation of wheels, levers, motors had a beautiful unity, as if it were a missile. The sound of it was a war chorus that reached into the depths of man's emotion.

The lieutenant, still holding his arm as if it were of glass, stood watching this battery until all detail of it was lost, save the figures of the riders, which rose and fell and waved lashes over the black mass.

Later, he turned his eyes toward the battle, where the shooting sometimes crackled like bush-fires, sometimes sputtered with exasperating irregularity, and sometimes reverberated like the thunder. He saw the smoke rolling upward and saw crowds of men who ran and cheered, or stood and blazed away at the inscrutable distance.

He came upon some stragglers, and they told him how to find the field hospital. They described its exact location. In fact, these men, no longer having part in the battle, knew more of it than others. They told the performance of every corps, every division, the opinion of every general. The lieutenant, carrying his wounded arm rearward, looked upon them with wonder.

At the roadside a brigade was making coffee and buzzing with talk like a girls' boarding school. Several officers came out to him and inquired concerning things of which he knew nothing. One, seeing his arm, began to scold. "Why, man, that's no way to do. You want to fix that thing." He appropriated the lieutenant and the lieutenant's wound. He cut the sleeve and laid bare the arm, every nerve of which softly fluttered under his touch. He bound his handkerchief over the wound, scolding away in the meantime. His tone allowed one to think that he was in the habit of being wounded every day. The lieutenant hung his head, feeling, in this presence, that he did not know how to be correctly wounded.

The low white tents of the hospital were grouped around an old schoolhouse. There was here a singular commotion. In the foreground two ambulances interlocked wheels in the deep mud. The drivers were tossing the blame of it back and forth, gesticulating and berating, while from the ambulances, both crammed with wounded, there came an occasional groan. An interminable crowd of bandaged men were coming and going. Great numbers sat under the trees nursing heads or arms or legs. There was a dispute of some kind raging on the steps of the schoolhouse. Sitting with his back against a tree a man with a face as gray as a new army blanket was serenely smoking a corncob pipe. The lieutenant wished to rush forward and inform him that he was dying.

A busy surgeon was passing near the lieutenant. "Good morning," he said, with a friendly smile. Then he caught sight of the lieutenant's arm, and his face at once changed. "Well, let's have a look at it." He seemed possessed suddenly of a great contempt for the lieutenant. This wound evidently placed the latter on a very low social plane. The doctor cried out impatiently: "What mutton-head had tied it up that way anyhow?" The lieutenant answered, "Oh, a man."

When the wound was disclosed the doctor fingered it disdainfully. "Humph," he said. "You come along with me and I'll 'tend to you." His voice contained the same scorn as if he were saying: "You will have to go to jail."

The lieutenant had been very meek, but now his face flushed, and he looked into the doctor's eyes. "I guess I won't have it amputated," he said.

"Nonsense, man! Nonsense! Nonsense!" cried the doctor. "Come along, now. I won't amputate it. Come along. Don't be a baby."

"Let go of me," said the lieutenant, holding back wrathfully, his glance fixed upon the door of the old schoolhouse, as sinister to him as the portals of death.

And this is the story of how the lieutenant lost his arm. When he reached home, his sisters, his mother, his wife, sobbed for a long time at the sight of the flat sleeve. "Oh, well," he said, standing shamefaced amid these tears, "I don't suppose it matters so much as all that."

# A DARK-BROWN DOG

## Stephen Crane

A CHILD WAS standing on a street-corner. He leaned with one shoulder against a high board fence and swayed the other to and fro, the while kicking carelessly at the gravel.

Sunshine beat upon the cobbles, and a lazy summer wind raised yellow dust which trailed in clouds down the avenue. Clattering trucks moved with indistinctness through it. The child stood dreamily gazing.

After a time, a little dark-brown dog came trotting with an intent air down the sidewalk. A short rope was dragging from his neck. Occasionally he trod upon the end of it and stumbled.

He stopped opposite the child, and the two regarded each other. The dog hesitated for a moment, but presently he made some little advances with his tail. The child put out his hand and called him. In an apologetic manner the dog came close, and the two had an interchange of friendly pattings and waggles. The dog became more enthusiastic with each moment of the interview, until with his gleeful caperings he threatened to overturn the child. Whereupon the child lifted his hand and struck the dog a blow upon the head.

This thing seemed to overpower and astonish the little dark-brown dog, and wounded him to the heart. He sank down in despair at the child's feet. When the blow was repeated, together with an admonition in childish sentences, he turned over upon his back, and held his paws in a peculiar manner. At the same time with his ears and his eyes he offered a small prayer to the child.

He looked so comical on his back, and holding his paws peculiarly, that the child was greatly amused and gave him little taps repeatedly,

256

to keep him so. But the little dark-brown dog took this chastisement in the most serious way, and no doubt considered that he had committed some grave crime, for he wriggled contritely and showed his repentance in every way that was in his power. He pleaded with the child and petitioned him, and offered more prayers.

At last the child grew weary of this amusement and turned toward home. The dog was praying at the time. He lay on his back and turned his eyes upon the retreating form.

Presently he struggled to his feet and started after the child. The latter wandered in a perfunctory way toward his home, stopping at times to investigate various matters. During one of these pauses he discovered the little dark-brown dog who was following him with the air of a footpad.

The child beat his pursuer with a small stick he had found. The dog lay down and prayed until the child had finished, and resumed his journey. Then he scrambled erect and took up the pursuit again.

On the way to his home the child turned many times and beat the dog, proclaiming with childish gestures that he held him in contempt as an unimportant dog, with no value save for a moment. For being this quality of animal the dog apologized and eloquently expressed regret, but he continued stealthily to follow the child. His manner grew so very guilty that he slunk like an assassin.

When the child reached his doorstep, the dog was industriously ambling a few yards in the rear. He became so agitated with shame when he again confronted the child that he forgot the dragging rope. He tripped upon it and fell forward.

The child sat down on the step and the two had another interview. During it the dog greatly exerted himself to please the child. He performed a few gambols with such abandon that the child suddenly saw him to be a valuable thing. He made a swift, avaricious charge and seized the rope.

He dragged his captive into a hall and up many long stairways in a dark tenement. The dog made willing efforts, but he could not hobble very skilfully up the stairs because he was very small and soft, and at last the pace of the engrossed child grew so energetic that the dog became panic-stricken. In his mind he was being dragged toward a grim unknown. His eyes grew wild with the terror of it. He began to wiggle his head frantically and to brace his legs.

The child redoubled his exertions. They had a battle on the stairs. The child was victorious because he was completely absorbed in his purpose, and because the dog was very small. He dragged his acquirement to the door of his home, and finally with triumph across the threshold.

No one was in. The child sat down on the floor and made overtures to the dog. These the dog instantly accepted. He beamed with affection upon his new friend. In a short time they were firm and abiding comrades.

When the child's family appeared, they made a great row. The dog was examined and commented upon and called names. Scorn was leveled at him from all eyes, so that he became much embarrassed and drooped like a scorched plant. But the child went sturdily to the center of the floor, and, at the top of his voice, championed the dog. It happened that he was roaring protestations, with his arms clasped about the dog's neck, when the father of the family came in from work.

The parent demanded to know what the blazes they were making the kid howl for. It was explained in many words that the infernal kid wanted to introduce a disreputable dog into the family.

A family council was held. On this depended the dog's fate, but he in no way heeded, being busily engaged in chewing the end of the child's dress.

The affair was quickly ended. The father of the family, it appears, was in a particularly savage temper that evening, and when he perceived that it would amaze and anger everybody if such a dog were allowed to remain, he decided that it should be so. The child, crying softly, took his friend off to a retired part of the room to hobnob with him, while the father quelled a fierce rebellion of his wife. So it came to pass that the dog was a member of the household.

He and the child were associated together at all times save when the child slept. The child became a guardian and a friend. If the large folk kicked the dog and threw things at him, the child made loud and violent objections. Once when the child had run, protesting loudly, with tears raining down his face and his arms outstretched, to protect his friend, he had been struck in the head with a very large saucepan from the hand of his father, enraged at some seeming lack of courtesy in the dog. Ever after, the family were careful how they threw things at the dog. Moreover, the latter grew very skilful in avoiding missiles and feet. In a small room containing a stove, a table, a bureau and some chairs, he would display strategic ability of a high order, dodging, feinting and scuttling about among the furniture. He could force three or four people armed with brooms, sticks and handfuls of coal, to use all their ingenuity to get in a blow. And even when they did, it was seldom that they could do him a serious injury or leave any imprint.

But when the child was present these scenes did not occur. It came to be recognized that if the dog was molested, the child would burst into sobs, and as the child, when started, was very riotous and practically unquenchable, the dog had therein a safeguard.

However, the child could not always be near. At night, when he was asleep, his dark-brown friend would raise from some black corner a wild, wailful cry, a song of infinite loneliness and despair, that would go shuddering and sobbing among the buildings of the block and cause people to swear. At these times the singer would often be chased all over the kitchen and hit with a great variety of articles.

Sometimes, too, the child himself used to beat the dog, although it is not known that he ever had what truly could be called a just cause. The dog always accepted these thrashings with an air of admitted guilt. He was too much of a dog to try to look to be a martyr or to plot revenge. He received the blows with deep humility, and furthermore he forgave his friend the moment the child had finished, and was ready to caress the child's hand with his little red tongue.

When misfortune came upon the child, and his troubles overwhelmed him, he would often crawl under the table and lay his small distressed head on the dog's back. The dog was ever sympathetic. It is not to be supposed that at such times he took occasion to refer to the unjust beatings his friend, when provoked, had administered to him.

He did not achieve any notable degree of intimacy with the other members of the family. He had no confidence in them, and the fear that he would express at their casual approach often exasperated them exceedingly. They used to gain a certain satisfaction in underfeeding him, but finally his friend the child grew to watch the matter with some care, and when he forgot it, the dog was often successful in secret for himself.

So the dog prospered. He developed a large bark, which came wondrously from such a small rug of a dog. He ceased to howl persistently at night. Sometimes, indeed, in his sleep, he would utter little yells, as from pain, but that occurred, no doubt, when in his dreams he encountered huge flaming dogs who threatened him direfully.

His devotion to the child grew until it was a sublime thing. He wagged at his approach; he sank down in despair at his departure.

He could detect the sound of the child's step among all the noises of the neighborhood. It was like a calling voice to him.

The scene of their companionship was a kingdom governed by this terrible potentate, the child; but neither criticism nor rebellion ever lived for an instant in the heart of the one subject. Down in the mystic, hidden fields of his little dog-soul bloomed flowers of love and fidelity and perfect faith.

The child was in the habit of going on many expeditions to observe strange things in the vicinity. On these occasions his friend usually jogged aimfully along behind. Perhaps, though, he went ahead. This necessitated his turning around every quarter-minute to make sure the child was coming. He was filled with a large idea of the importance of these journeys. He would carry himself with such an air! He was proud to be the retainer of so great a monarch.

One day, however, the father of the family got quite exceptionally drunk. He came home and held carnival with the cooking utensils, the furniture and his wife. He was in the midst of this recreation when the child, followed by the dark-brown dog, entered the room. They were returning from their voyages.

The child's practised eye instantly noted his father's state. He dived under the table, where experience had taught him was a rather safe place. The dog, lacking skill in such matters, was, of course, unaware of the true condition of affairs. He looked with interested eyes at his friend's sudden dive. He interpreted it to mean: Joyous gambol. He started to patter across the floor to join him. He was the picture of a little dark-brown dog en route to a friend.

The head of the family saw him at this moment. He gave a huge howl of joy, and knocked the dog down with a heavy coffee-pot. The dog, yelling in supreme astonishment and fear, writhed to his feet and ran for cover. The man kicked out with a ponderous foot. It caused the dog to swerve as if caught in a tide. A second blow of the coffeepot laid him upon the floor.

Here the child, uttering loud cries, came valiantly forth like a knight. The father of the family paid no attention to these calls of the child, but advanced with glee upon the dog. Upon being knocked down twice in swift succession, the latter apparently gave up all hope of escape. He rolled over on his back and held his paws in a peculiar manner. At the same time with his eyes and his ears he offered up a small prayer.

But the father was in a mood for having fun, and it occurred to him that it would be a fine thing to throw the dog out of the window.

# HER IS FIRM WITH HIS AILMENTS

## Clarence Day

GOT ANNOYED at us when we didn't stay well. He usually
ell himself and he expected us to be like him, and not faint
np on his hands and thus add to his burdens.
as fearless about disease. He despised it. All this talk about
e said, was merely newfangled nonsense. He said that when
a boy there had been no germs that he knew of. Perhaps
insects existed, but what of it? He was as healthy as they
If any damned germs want to have a try at me," he said,
em on."
Father's point of view, Mother didn't know how to handle
nt. He admired her most of the time and thought there was
like her; he often said to us boys, "Your mother is a wonderful
'; but he always seemed to disapprove of her when she was ill.
er went to bed, for instance, at such times. Yet she didn't
ises. Father heard a little gasping moan sometimes, but she
vant him to hear even that. Consequently he was sure
n't suffering. There was nothing to indicate it, he said.
vorse she felt, the less she ever said about it, and the harder
r him to believe that there was anything really wrong with
e says he can't see why I stay in bed so long," she once wrote
vhen I was away, "but this colitis is a mean affair which keeps
fectly flat. The doctor told him yesterday the meaning of
ut he said he 'had never heard of the damned thing, thank
le feels very abused that he should be 'so upset by people
eer things the matter with them and doctors all over the
(Mother underlined the word "people.")

262

So he reached down and, grabbing the anin
squirming, up. He swung him two or three
his head, and then flung him with great accura

The soaring dog created a surprise in the bl
plants in an opposite window gave an involur
a flower-pot. A man in another window le
watch the flight of the dog. A woman who
clothes in a yard began to caper wildly. Her
clothes-pins, but her arms gave vent to a s
appearance she was like a gagged prisoner. O

The dark-brown body crashed in a heap o
stories below. From thence it rolled to the pa

The child in the room far above burst int
and toddled hastily out of the room. It took h
the alley, because his size compelled him to g
one step at a time, and holding with both ha

When they came for him later, they found
of his dark-brown friend.

**FAT**

FATHER
stayed v
and slur

He v
germs,
he was
invisibl
were. "
"bring

From
an ailme
nobody
woman

Motl
make n
didn't
she was

The
it was f
her. "H
to me,
one pe
colitis,
God.' F
with q
place.''

Even Mother's colds made him fretful. Whenever she had one, she kept going as long as she could, pottering about her room looking white and tired, with a shawl round her shoulders. But sometimes she had to give up and crawl into her bed.

Father pished and poohed to himself about this, and muttered that it was silly. He said Mother was perfectly healthy. When people thought they were ill, he declared it didn't mean that there was anything the matter with them, it was merely a sign of weak character. He often told Mother how weak it was to give in to an ailment, but every time he tried to strengthen her character in this respect, he said she seemed to resent it. He never remembered to try except when she could hardly hold her head up. From his point of view, though, that was the very time that she needed his help.

He needed hers, too, or not exactly her help but her company, and he never hesitated to say so. When she was ill, he felt lost.

He usually came up from his office at about five or six. The first thing he did was to look around the house to find Mother. It made his home feel queer and empty to him when she wasn't there.

One night about six o'clock he opened the door of her bedroom. There was no light except for a struggling little fire which flickered and sank in the grate. A smell of witch–hazel was in the air, mixed with spirits of camphor. On the bed, huddled up under an afghan, Mother lay still, in the dark.

"Are you there, Vinnie?" Father said, in a voice even louder than usual because of his not being sure.

Mother moaned, "Go away."

"What?" he asked, in astonishment.

"Go away. Oh, go 'way."

"Damnation!" he said, marching out.

"Clare!"

"What is it?"

"Won't you *ple-e-ease* shut my door again!"

Father ground his teeth and shut it with such a bang that it made Mother jump.

He told himself she had nothing the matter with her. She'd be all right in the morning. He ate a good dinner. Being lonely, he added an extra glass of claret and some toasted crackers and cheese. He had such a long and dull evening that he smoked two extra cigars.

After breakfast the next morning, he went to her bedroom again. The fire was out. Two worn old slippers lay on a chair. The gray daylight was cheerless. Father stood at the foot of Mother's bed, looking disconsolately at her because she wasn't well yet. He had no one to laugh at or quarrel with; his features were lumpy with gloom.

"What is it?" Mother asked in a whisper, opening her weary eyes.

"Nothing," he said loudly. "Nothing."

"Well, for mercy's sake, don't come in here looking like that, Clare," Mother begged.

"What do you mean? Looking like what?"

"Oh, go away!" Mother shrieked. "When people are sick, they like to see a smile or something. I never will get well if you stand there and stare at me that way! And shut my door quietly this time. And let me alone."

Outside her door, when I asked him how Mother was, he said with a chuckle: "She's all right again. She isn't out of bed yet, but she sounds much better this morning."

Father's own experiences in a sick-room had been very few. When he was in his early thirties, he had an attack of gout which lasted three weeks. From that time until he was seventy-four and had pneumonia, he had no other serious illnesses. He said illnesses were mostly imaginary and he didn't believe in them.

He even declared that his pneumonia was imaginary. "It's only some idea of that doctor's," he said. "Nothing the matter with me but a cold." Our regular physician had died, and this new man and two trained nurses had all they could do, at first, to keep Father in bed.

The new doctor had pale-blue eyes, a slight build, and a way of inwardly smiling at the persons he talked to. He had a strong will in crises, and he was one of the ablest physicians in town. Mother had chosen him, however, chiefly because she liked one of his female cousins.

When Father got worse, the doctor kept warning him that it really *was* pneumonia, and that if he wouldn't be tractable, he might not get over it—especially at seventy-four.

Father lay in bed glowering at him and said: "I didn't send for you, sir. You needn't stand there and tell me what you want me to do. I know all about doctors. They think they know a damned lot. But they don't. Give your pills and things to Mrs. Day—she believes in them. That's all I have to say. There's no need to continue this discussion. There's the door, sir. Goodbye."

But somehow the discussion kept on, and much to his surprise Father at last became convinced he was ill. The doctor, leaving him alone in his bedroom to digest the bad news, came out in the hall, anxious and tired, to have a few words with Mother. As they stood outside Father's door whispering quietly, they heard his voice from within. Apparently, now that he knew he was in trouble, his thoughts had turned to his God. "Have mercy!" they heard him shouting indignantly. "I say have mercy, damn it!"

*　　*　　*

Any sufferings that Father ever had he attributed solely to God. Naturally, he never thought for a moment that God could mean him to suffer. He couldn't imagine God's wishing to punish him either, for his conscience was clear. His explanation seemed to be that God was clumsy, not to say muddle-headed.

However, in spite of God and the doctor, Father got over pneumonia, just as, some forty years before, he had got over his gout. Only, in conquering his gout, he had had the help of a cane and a masseur called Old Lowndes.

While the gout was besieging him, Father sat in a big chair by the fire with his bad foot on a stool, armed with a cane which he kept constantly ready. Not that he used the cane to walk with. When he walked, he hopped around on his other foot, uttering strong howls of fury. But he valued his cane highly, and needed it, too, as a war club. He threatened the whole family with it. When visitors entered the room he brandished it fiercely at them, to keep them away from his toe.

Old Lowndes was allowed to approach nearer than others, but he was warned that if he made any mistakes that cane would come down on his head. Father felt there was no knowing what harm Lowndes might have done if he hadn't shaken his cane at him and made him take care. As it was, owing largely to this useful stick, Father got well.

This experience convinced him that any disease could be conquered by firmness.

*　　*　　*

When he had a cold, his method of dealing with it was to try to clear it out by main force, either by violently blowing his nose or, still better, by sneezing. Mother didn't like him to sneeze, he did it with such a roar. She said she could feel it half across the room, and she was sure it was catching. Father said this was nonsense. He said his sneezes were healthy. And presently we'd hear a hearty, triumphant blast as he sneezed again.

Aside from colds, which he had very seldom, his only foes were sick headaches. He said headaches only came from eating, however. Hence a man who knew enough to stop eating could always get rid of one that way. It took time to starve it out thoroughly. It might take several hours. But as soon as it was gone, he could eat again and enjoy his cigar.

When one of these headaches started, Father lay down and shut his eyes tight and yelled. The severity of a headache could be judged by the volume of sound he put forth. His idea seemed to be to show the headache that he was just as strong as it was, and stronger. When a headache and he went to bed together, they were a noisy pair.

Father's code required him to be game, I suppose. He never spoke or thought of having a code; he wasn't that sort of person; but he denounced men whose standards were low, as to gameness or anything else. It didn't occur to him to conceal his sufferings, however; when he had any pains, he expressed them as fully as he knew how. His way of being brave was not to keep still but to keep on fighting the headache.

Mother used to beg him to be quiet at night, even if he did have a headache, and not wake up the whole house. He never paid the slightest attention to such a request. When she said, "Please don't groan so much, Clare," he'd look at her in disgust, as though he were a warrior being asked to stifle his battle-cries.

One evening he found Mother worrying because Aunt Emma was ill with some disease that was then epidemic.

"Oh, pooh!" Father said. "Nothing the matter with Emma. You can trust people to get any ailment whatever that's fashionable. They hear of a lot of other people having it, and the first thing you know they get scared and think they have it themselves. Then they go to bed, and send for the doctor. The doctor! All poppycock."

"Well, but Clare dear, if you were in charge of them, what would you do instead?"

"Cheer 'em up, that's the way to cure 'em."

"How would you cheer them up, darling?" Mother asked doubtfully.

"I? I'd tell 'em, *'Bah!'*"

# THE LOST PHOEBE

## Theodore Dreiser

THEY LIVED TOGETHER in a part of the country which was not so prosperous as it had once been, about three miles from one of those small towns that, instead of increasing in population, is steadily decreasing. The territory was not very thickly settled; perhaps a house every other mile or so, with large areas of corn—and wheat-land and fallow fields that at odd seasons had been sown to timothy and clover. Their particular house was part log and part frame, the log portion being the old original home of Henry's grandfather. The new portion, of now rain-beaten, time-worn slabs, through which the wind squeaked in the chinks at times, and which several overshadowing elms and a butternut-tree made picturesque and reminiscently pathetic, but a little damp, was erected by Henry when he was twenty-one and just married.

That was forty-eight years before. The furniture inside, like the house outside, was old and mildewy and reminiscent of an earlier day. You have seen the what-not of cherry wood, perhaps, with spiral legs and fluted top. It was there. The old-fashioned four poster bed, with its balllike protuberances and deep curving incisions, was there also, a sadly alienated descendant of an early Jacobean ancestor. The bureau of cherry was also high and wide and solidly built, but faded-looking, and with a musty odor. The rag carpet that underlay all these sturdy examples of enduring furniture was a weak, faded, lead-and-pink-colored affair woven by Phoebe Ann's own hands, when she was fifteen years younger than she was when she died. The creaky wooden loom on which it had been done now stood like a dusty, bony skeleton, along with a broken rocking-chair, a worm-eaten clothes-press—Heaven knows how old—a lime-stained bench that had once been used to keep flowers on outside the door, and other decrepit factors of household utility, in an east room that was a lean-to against this so-called main portion. All sorts of other broken-down furniture were about this place; an antiquated clothes-horse, cracked in two of its ribs; a broken mirror in an old cherry frame, which had fallen from a nail and cracked itself three days before their youngest son, Jerry, died; an extension hat-rack, which once had had porcelain knobs on the ends of its pegs; and a sewing-machine, long since outdone in its clumsy mechanism by rivals of a newer generation.

The orchard to the east of the house was full of gnarled old apple-trees, worm-eaten as to trunks and branches, and fully ornamented with green and white lichens, so that it had a sad, greenish-white, silvery effect in moonlight. The low outhouses, which had once housed chickens, a horse or two, a cow, and several pigs, were covered with patches of moss as to their roof, and the sides had been free of paint for so long that they were blackish gray as to color, and a little spongy. The picket-fence in front, with its gate squeaky and askew, and the side fences of the stake-and-rider type were in an equally run-down condition. As a matter of fact, they had aged synchronously with the persons who lived here, old Henry Reifsneider and his wife Phoebe Ann.

They had lived here, these two, ever since their marriage, forty-eight years before, and Henry had lived here before that from his childhood up. His father and mother, well along in years when he was a boy, had invited him to bring his wife here when he had first fallen in love and decided to marry; and he had done so. His father and mother were the companions of himself and his wife for ten years after they were married, when both died; and then Henry and Phoebe were left with their five children growing lustily apace. But all sorts of things had happened since then. Of the seven children, all told, that had been born to them, three had died; one girl had gone to Kansas; one boy had gone to Sioux Falls, never even to be heard of after; another boy had gone to Washington; and the last girl lived five counties away in the same State, but was so burdened with cares of her own that she rarely gave them a thought. Time and a common-place home life that had never been attractive had weaned them thoroughly, so that, wherever they were, they gave little thought as to how it might be with their father and mother.

Old Henry Reifsneider and his wife Phoebe were a loving couple. You perhaps know how it is with simple natures that fasten themselves like lichens on the stones of circumstance and weather their days to a crumbling conclusion. The great world sounds widely, but it has no call for them. They have no soaring intellect. The orchard, the meadow, the corn-field, the pig-pen, and the chicken-lot measure the range of their human activities. When the wheat is headed it is reaped and threshed; when the corn is browned and frosted it is cut and shocked; when the timothy is in full head it is cut, and the hay-cock erected. After that comes winter, with the hauling of grain to market, the sawing and splitting of wood, the simple chores of fire-building, meal-getting, occasional repairing, and visiting. Beyond these and the changes of weather—the snows, the rains, and the fair days—there are no immediate, significant things. All the rest of life is a far-off, clamorous phantasmagoria, flickering like Northern lights in the night, and sounding as faintly as cow-bells tinkling in the distance.

Old Henry and his wife Phoebe were as fond of each other as it is possible for two old people to be who have nothing else in this life to be fond of. He was a thin old man, seventy when she died, a queer, crotchety person with coarse gray-black hair and beard, quite straggly and unkempt. He looked at you out of dull, fishy, watery eyes that had deep-brown crow's-feet at the sides. His clothes, like the clothes of many farmers, were aged and angular and baggy, standing out at the pockets, not fitting about the neck, protuberant and worn at elbow and knee. Phoebe Ann was thin and shapeless, a very umbrella of a woman, clad in shabby black, and with a black bonnet for her best wear. As time had passed, and they had only themselves to look after, their movements had become slower and slower, their activities fewer and fewer. The annual keep of pigs had been reduced from five to one grunting porker, and the single horse which Henry now retained was a sleepy animal, not over-nourished and not very clean. The chickens, of which formerly there was a large flock, had almost disappeared, owing to ferrets, foxes, and the lack of proper care, which produces disease. The former healthy garden was now a straggling memory of itself, and the vines and flower-beds that formerly ornamented the windows and dooryard had now become choking thickets. A will had been made which divided the small tax-eaten property equally among the remaining four, so that it was really of no interest to any of them. Yet these two lived together in peace and sympathy, only that now and then old Henry would become unduly cranky, complaining almost invariably that something had been neglected or mislaid which was of no importance at all.

"Phoebe, where's my corn-knife? You ain't never minded to let my things alone no more."

"No you hush, Henry," his wife would caution him in a cracked and squeaky voice. "If you don't, I'll leave yuh. I'll git up and walk out of here some day, and then where would y' be? Y' ain't got anybody but me to look after yuh, so yuh just behave yourself. Your corn-knife's on the mantel where it's allus been unless you've gone an' put it summers else."

Old Henry, who knew his wife would never leave him in any circumstances, used to speculate at times as to what he would do if she were to die. That was the one leaving that he really feared. As he climbed on the chair at night to wind the old, long-pendulumed, double-weighted clock, or went finally to the front and the back door to see that they were safely shut in, it was a comfort to know that Phoebe was there, properly ensconced on her side of the bed, and that if he stirred restlessly in the night, she would be there to ask what he wanted.

"Now, Henry, do lie still! You're as restless as a chicken."

"Well, I can't sleep, Phoebe."

"Well, yuh needn't roll so, anyhow. Yuh kin let me sleep."

This usually reduced him to a state of somnolent ease. If she wanted a pail of water, it was a grumbling pleasure for him to get it; and if she did rise first to build the fires, he saw that the wood was cut and placed within easy reach. They divided this simple world nicely between them.

As the years had gone on, however, fewer and fewer people had called. They were well-known for a distance of as much as ten square miles as old Mr. and Mrs. Reifsneider, honest, moderately Christian, but too old to be really interesting any longer. The writing of letters had become an almost impossible burden too difficult to continue or even negotiate via others, although an occasional letter still did arrive from the daughter in Pemberton County. Now and then some old friend stopped with a pie or cake or a roasted chicken or duck, or merely to see that they were well; but even these kindly minded visits were no longer frequent.

One day in the early spring of her sixty-fourth year Mrs. Reifsneider took sick, and from a low fever passed into some indefinable ailment which, because of her age, was no longer curable. Old Henry drove to Swinnerton, the neighboring town, and procured a doctor. Some friends called, and the immediate care of her was taken off his hands. Then one chill spring night she died, and old Henry, in a fog of sorrow and uncertainty, followed her body to the nearest graveyard, an unattractive space with a few pines growing in it. Although he might have gone to the daughter in Pemberton or sent for her, it was really too much trouble and he was too weary and fixed. It was suggested to him at once by one friend and another that he come to stay with them awhile, but he did not see fit. He was so old and so fixed in his notions and so accustomed to the exact surroundings he had known all his days, that he could not think of leaving. He wanted to remain near where they had put his Phoebe: and the fact that he would have to live alone did not trouble him in the least. The living children were notified and the care of him offered if he would leave, but he would not.

"I kin make a shift for myself," he continually announced to old Dr. Morrow, who had attended his wife in this case. "I kin cook a little, and, besides, it don't take much more'n coffee an' bread in the mornin's to satisfy me. I'll get along now well enough. Yuh just let me be." And after many pleadings and proffers of advice, with supplies of coffee and bacon and baked bread duly offered and accepted, he was left to himself. For a while he sat idly outside his door brooding in the spring sun. He tried to revive his interest in farming, and to keep himself busy and free from thought by looking after the fields, which of late had been much neglected. It was a gloomy thing to come in of an evening, however, or in the afternoon and find no shadow of Phoebe where everything suggested her. By degrees he put a few of her things away. At night he sat beside his lamp and read in the papers that were left him occasionally or in a Bible that he had neglected for years, but he could get little solace from these things. Mostly he held his hand over his mouth and looked at the floor as he sat and thought of what had become of her, and how soon he himself would die. He made a great business of making his coffee in the morning and frying himself a little bacon at night; but his appetite was gone. The shell in which he had been housed so long seemed vacant, and its shadows were suggestive of immedicable griefs. So he lived quite dolefully for five long months, and then a change began.

It was one night, after he had looked after the front and the back door, wound the clock, blown out the light, and gone through all the selfsame motions that he had indulged in for years, that he went to bed not so much to sleep as to think. It was a moonlight night. The green–lichen–covered orchard just outside and to be seen from his bed where he now lay was a silvery affair, sweetly spectral.

The moon shone through the east windows, throwing the pattern of the panes on the wooden floor, and making the old furniture, to which he was accustomed, stand out dimly in the room. As usual he had been thinking of Phoebe and the years when they had been young together, and of the children who had gone, and the poor shift he was making of his present days. The house was coming to be in a very bad state indeed. The bed-clothes were in disorder and not clean, for he made a wretched shift of washing. It was a terror to him. The roof leaked, causing things, some of them, to remain damp for weeks at a time, but he was getting into that brooding state where he would accept anything rather than exert himself. He preferred to pace slowly to and fro or to sit and think.

By twelve o'clock of this particular night he was asleep, however, and by two had waked again. The moon by this time had shifted to a position on the western side of the house, and it now shone in through the windows of the living-room and those of the kitchen beyond. A certain combination of furniture—a chair near a table, with his coat on it, the half-open kitchen door casting a shadow, and the position of a lamp near a paper—gave him an exact representation of Phoebe leaning over the table as he had often seen her do in life. It gave him a great start. Could it be she—or her ghost? He had scarcely ever believed in spirits; and still—He looked at her fixedly in the feeble half-light, his old hair tingling oddly at the roots, and then sat up. The figure did not move. He put his thin legs out of the bed and sat looking at her, wondering if this could really be Phoebe. They had talked of ghosts often in their lifetime, of apparitions and omens; but they had never agreed that such things could be. It had never been a part of his wife's creed that she could have a spirit that could return to walk the earth. Her after-world was quite a different affair, a vague heaven, no less, from which the righteous did not trouble to return. Yet here she was now, bending over the table in her black skirt and gray shawl, her pale profile outlined against the moonlight.

"Phoebe," he called, thrilling from head to toe and putting out one bony hand, "have yuh come back?"

The figure did not stir, and he arose and walked uncertainly to the door, looking at it fixedly the while. As he drew near, however, the apparition resolved itself into its primal content—his old coat over the high-backed chair, the lamp by the paper, the half-open door.

"Well," he said to himself, his mouth open, "I thought shore I saw her." And he ran his hand strangely and vaguely through his hair, the while his nervous tension relaxed. Vanished as it had, it gave him the idea that she might return.

Another night, because of this first illusion, and because his mind was now constantly on her and he was old, he looked out of the window that was nearest his bed and commanded a hen–coop and pig-pen and a part of the wagon-shed, and there, a faint mist exuding from the damp of the ground, he thought he saw her again. It was one of those little wisps of mist, one of those faint exhalations of the earth that rise in a cool night after a warm day, and flicker like small white cypresses of fog before they disappear. In life it had been a custom of hers to cross this lot from her kitchen door to the pig-pen to throw in any scrap that was left from her cooking, and here she was again. He sat up and watched it strangely, doubtfully, because of his previous experience, but inclined, because of the nervous titillation that passed over his body, to believe that spirits really were, and that Phoebe, who would be concerned because of his lonely state, must be thinking about him, and hence returning. What other way would she have? How otherwise could she express herself? It would be within the province of her charity so to do, and like her loving interest in him. He quivered and watched it eagerly; but, a faint breath of air stirring, it wound away toward the fence and disappeared.

A third night, as he was actually dreaming, some ten days later, she came to his bedside and put her hand on his head.

"Poor Henry!" she said. "It's too bad."

He roused out of his sleep, actually to see her, he thought, moving from his bed–room into the one living-room, her figure a shadowy mass of black. The weak straining of his eyes caused little points of light to flicker about the outlines of her form. He arose, greatly astonished, walked the floor in the cool room, convinced that Phoebe was coming back to him. If he only thought sufficiently, if he made it perfectly clear by his feeling that he needed her greatly, she would come back, this kindly wife, and tell him what to do. She would perhaps be with him much of the time, in the night, anyhow; and that would make him less lonely, this state more endurable.

In age and with the feeble it is not such a far cry from the subtleties of illusion to actual hallucination, and in due time this transition was made for Henry. Night after night he waited, expecting her return. Once in his weird mood he thought he saw a pale light moving about the room, and another time he thought he saw her walking in the

orchard after dark. It was one morning when the details of his lonely
state were virtually unendurable that he woke with the thought that
she was not dead. How he had arrived at this conclusion it is hard
to say. His mind had gone. In its place was a fixed illusion. He and
Phoebe had had a senseless quarrel. He had reproached her for not
leaving his pipe where he was accustomed to find it, and she had left.
It was an aberrated fulfillment of her old jesting threat that if he did
not behave himself she would leave him.

"I guess I could find yuh ag'in," he had always said. But her cackling
threat had always been:

"Yuh'll not find me if I ever leave yuh. I guess I kin git some place
where yuh can't find me."

This morning when he arose he did not think to build the fire
in the customary way or to grind his coffee and cut his bread, as
was his wont, but solely to meditate as to where he should search
for her and how he should induce her to come back. Recently the
one horse had been dispensed with because he found it cumbersome
and beyond his needs. He took down his soft crush hat after he had
dressed himself, a new glint of interest and determination in his eye,
and taking his black crook cane from behind the door, where he
had always placed it, started out briskly to look for her among
the nearest neighbors. His old shoes clumped soundly in the dust
as he walked, and his gray-black locks, now grown rather long,
straggled out in a dramatic fringe or halo from under his hat. His
short coat stirred busily as he walked, and his hands and face were
peaked and pale.

"Why, hello, Henry! Where're yuh goin' this mornin'?" inquired
Farmer Dodge, who, hauling a load of wheat to market, encountered
him on the public road. He had not seen the aged farmer in months,
not since his wife's death, and he wondered now, seeing him looking
so spry.

"Yuh ain't seen Phoebe, have yuh?" inquired the old man, looking
up quizzically.

"Phoebe who?" inquired Farmer Dodge, not for the moment
connecting the name with Henry's dead wife.

"Why, my wife Phoebe, o' course. Who do yuh s'pose I mean?"
He stared up with a pathetic sharpness of glance from under his
shaggy, gray eyebrows.

"Wall, I'll swan, Henry, yuh ain't jokin', are yuh?" said the solid
Dodge, a pursy man, with a smooth, hard, red face. "It can't be your
wife yuh're talkin' about. She's dead."

"Dead! Shucks!" retorted the demented Reifsneider. "She left me early this mornin', while I was sleepin'. She allus got up to build the fire, but she's gone now. We had a little spat last night, an' I guess that's the reason. But I guess I kin find her. She's gone over to Matilda Race's; that's where she's gone."

He started briskly up the road, leaving the amazed Dodge to stare in wonder after him.

"Well, I'll be switched!" he said aloud to himself. "He's clean out'n his head. That poor old feller's been livin' down there till he's gone outen his mind. I'll have to notify the authorities." And he flicked his whip with great enthusiasm. "Geddap!" he said, and was off.

Reifsneider met no one else in this poorly populated region until he reached the whitewashed fence of Matilda Race and her husband three miles away. He had passed several other houses en route, but these not being within the range of his illusion were not considered. His wife, who had known Matilda well, must be here. He opened the picket-gate which guarded the walk, and stamped briskly up to the door.

"Why, Mr. Reifsneider," exclaimed old Matilda herself, a stout woman, looking out of the door in answer to his knock, "what brings yuh here this mornin'?"

"Is Phoebe here?" he demanded eagerly.

"Phoebe who? What Phoebe?" replied Mrs. Race, curious as to this sudden development of energy on his part.

"Why, my Phoebe, o' course. My wife Phoebe. Who do yuh s'pose? Ain't she here now?"

"Lawsy me!" exclaimed Mrs. Race, opening her mouth. "Yuh pore man! So you're clean out'n your mind now. Yuh come right in and sit down. I'll git yuh a cup o' coffee. O' course your wife ain't here; but yuh come in an' sit down. I'll find her fer yuh after a while. I know where she is."

The old farmer's eyes softened, and he entered. He was so thin and pale a specimen, pantalooned and patriarchal, that he aroused Mrs. Race's extremest sympathy as he took off his hat and laid it on his knees quite softly and mildly.

"We had a quarrel last night, an' she left me," he volunteered.

"Laws! laws!" sighed Mrs. Race, there being no one present with whom to share her astonishment as she went to her kitchen. "The pore man! Now somebody's just got to look after him. He can't be allowed to run around the country this way lookin' for his dead wife. It's turrible."

She boiled him a pot of coffee and brought in some of her new-baked bread and fresh butter. She set out some of her best jam and put a couple of eggs to boil, lying whole-heartedly the while.

"Now yuh stay right there, Uncle Henry, till Jake comes in, an' I'll send him to look for Phoebe. I think it's more'n likely she's over to Swinnerton with some o' her friends. Anyhow, we'll find out. Now yuh just drink this coffee an' eat this bread. Yuh must be tired. Yuh've had a long walk this mornin'." Her idea was to take counsel with Jake, "her man," and perhaps have him notify the authorities.

She bustled about, meditating on the uncertainties of life, while old Reifsneider thrummed on the rim of his hat with his pale fingers and later ate abstractedly of what she offered. His mind was on his wife, however, and since she was not here, or did not appear, it wandered vaguely away to a family by the name of Murray, miles away in another direction. He decided after a time that he would not wait for Jake Race to hunt his wife but would seek her for himself. He must be on, and urge her to come back.

"Well, I'll be goin'," he said, getting up and looking strangely about him. "I guess she didn't come here after all. She went over to the Murrays', I guess. I'll not wait any longer, Mis' Race. There's a lot to do over to the house today." And out he marched in the face of her protests taking to the dusty road again in the warm spring sun, his cane striking the earth as he went.

It was two hours later that this pale figure of a man appeared in the Murrays' doorway, dusty, perspiring, eager. He had tramped all of five miles, and it was noon. An amazed husband and wife of sixty heard his strange query, and realized also that he was mad. They begged him to stay to dinner, intending to notify the authorities later and see what could be done; but though he stayed to partake of a little something, he did not stay long, and was off again to another distant farmhouse, his idea of many things to do and his need of Phoebe impelling him. So it went for that day and the next and the next, the circle of his inquiry ever widening.

The process by which a character assumes the significance of being peculiar, his antics weird, yet harmless, in such a community is often involute and pathetic. This day, as has been said, saw Reifsneider at other doors, eagerly asking his unnatural question, and leaving a trail of amazement, sympathy, and pity in his wake. Although the authorities were informed—the county sheriff, no less—it was not deemed advisable to take him into custody; for when those who knew old Henry, and had for so long, reflected on the condition of the county insane asylum, a place which, because of the poverty of the district, was of staggering aberration and sickening environment, it was decided to let him remain at large; for, strange to relate, it was found on investigation that at night he returned peaceably enough to his lonesome domicile there to discover whether his wife had returned, and to brood in loneliness until the morning. Who would lock up a thin, eager, seeking old man with iron-gray hair and an attitude of kindly, innocent inquiry, particularly when he was well known for a past of only kindly servitude and reliability? Those who had known him best rather agreed that he should be allowed to roam at large. He could do no harm There were many who were willing to help him as to food, old clothes, the odds and ends of his daily life—at least at first. His figure after a time became not so much a common-place as an accepted curiosity, and the replies, "Why, no, Henry; I ain't seen her," or "No, Henry; she ain't been here today," more customary.

For several years thereafter then he was an odd figure in the sun and rain, on dusty roads and muddy ones, encountered occasionally in strange and unexpected places, pursuing his endless search. Undernourishment, after a time, although the neighbors and those who knew his history gladly contributed from their store, affected his body; for he walked much and ate little. The longer he roamed the public highway in this manner, the deeper became his strange hallucination; and finding it harder and harder to return from his more and more distant pilgrimages, he finally began taking a few utensils with him from his home, making a small package of them, in order that he might not be compelled to return. In an old tin coffee-pot of large size he placed a small tin cup, a knife, fork, and spoon, some salt and pepper, and to the outside of it, by a string forced through a pierced hole, he fastened a plate, which could be released, and which was his woodland table. It was no trouble for him to secure the little food that he needed, and with a strange, almost religious dignity, he had no hesitation in asking for that much. By degrees his hair became longer and longer, his once black hat became an earthen brown, and his clothes threadbare and dusty.

For all of three years he walked, and none knew how wide were his perambulations, nor how he survived the storms and cold. They could not see him, with homely rural understanding and forethought, sheltering himself in hay-cocks, or by the sides of cattle, whose warm bodies protected him from the cold, and whose dull understandings were not opposed to his harmless presence. Overhanging rocks and

trees kept him at times from the rain, and a friendly hay-loft or
corn-crib was not above his humble consideration.

The involute progression of hallucination is strange. From asking
at doors and being constantly rebuffed or denied, he finally came to
the conclusion that although his Phoebe might not be in any of the
houses at the doors of which he inquired, she might nevertheless be
within the sound of his voice. And so, from patient inquiry, he began
to call sad, occasional cries, that ever and anon waked the quiet
landscapes and ragged hill regions, and set to echoing his thin "O-o-o
Phoebe! O-o-o Phoebe!" It had a pathetic, albeit insane, ring, and
many a farmer or plowboy came to know it even from afar and say,
"There goes old Reifsneider."

Another thing that puzzled him greatly after a time and after many
hundreds of inquiries was, when he no longer had any particular
dooryard in view and so special inquiry to make, which way to go.
These cross-roads, which occasionally led in four or even six directions, came after a time to puzzle him. But to solve this knotty
problem, which became more and more of a puzzle, there came to
his aid another hallucination. Phoebe's spirit or some power of the
air or wind or nature would tell him. If he stood at the center of
the parting of the ways, closed his eyes, turned thrice about, and
called "O-o-o Phoebe!" twice, and then threw his cane straight
before him, that would surely indicate which way to go for Phoebe,
or one of these mystic powers would surely govern its direction and
fall! In whichever direction it went, even though, as was not
infrequently the case, it took him back along the path he had already
come, or across fields, he was not so far gone in his mind but that
he gave himself ample time to search before he called again. Also the
hallucination seemed to persist that at some time he would surely
find her. There were hours when his feet were sore, and his limbs
weary, when he would stop in the heat to wipe his seamed brow,
or in the cold to beat his arms. Sometimes, after throwing away his
cane, and finding it indicating the direction from which he had just
come, he would shake his head wearily and philosophically, as
if contemplating the unbelievable or an untoward fate, and then start
briskly off. His strange figure came finally to be known in the farthest
reaches of three or four counties. Old Reifsneider was a pathetic
character. His fame was wide.

Near a little town called Watersville, in Green County, perhaps
four miles from that minor center of human activity, there was a
place or precipice locally known as the Red Cliff, a sheer wall of red

sandstone, perhaps a hundred feet high, which raised its sharp face for half a mile or more above the fruitful corn-fields and orchards that lay beneath, and which was surmounted by a thick grove of trees. The slope that slowly led up to it from the opposite side was covered by a rank growth of beech, hickory, and ash, through which threaded a number of wagon-tracks crossing at various angles. In fair weather it had become old Reifsneider's habit, so inured was he by now to the open, to make his bed in some such patch of trees as this to fry his bacon or boil his eggs at the foot of some tree before laying himself down for the night. Occasionally, so light and inconsequential was his sleep, he would walk at night. More often, the moonlight or some sudden wind stirring in the trees or a reconnoitering animal arousing him, he would sit up and think, or pursue his quest in the moonlight or the dark, a strange, unnatural, half wild, half savage-looking but utterly harmless creature, calling at lonely road crossings, staring at dark and shuttered houses, and wondering where, where Phoebe could really be.

That particular lull that comes in the systole-diastole of this earthly ball at two o'clock in the morning invariably aroused him, and though he might not go any farther he would sit up and contemplate the darkness or the stars, wondering. Sometimes in the strange processes of his mind he would fancy that he saw moving among the trees the figure of his lost wife, and then he would get up to follow, taking his utensils, always on a string, and his cane. If she seemed to evade him too easily he would run, or plead, or, suddenly losing track of the fancied figure, stand awed or disappointed, grieving for the moment over the almost insurmountable difficulties of his search.

It was in the seventh year of these hopeless peregrinations, in the dawn of a similar springtime to that in which his wife had died, that he came at last one night to the vicinity of this self-same patch that crowned the rise to the Red Cliff. His far-flung cane, used as a divining-rod at the last cross-roads, had brought him hither. He had walked many, many miles. It was after ten o'clock at night, and he was very weary. Long wandering and little eating had left him but a shadow of his former self. It was a question now not so much of physical strength but of spiritual endurance which kept him up. He had scarcely eaten this day, and now exhausted he set himself down in the dark to rest and possibly to sleep.

Curiously on this occasion a strange suggestion of the presence of his wife surrounded him. It would not be long now, he counseled with himself, although the long months had brought him nothing, until he should see her, talk to her. He fell asleep after a time, his head on his knees. At midnight the moon began to rise, and at two in the morning, his wakeful hour, was a large silver disk shining through the trees to the east. He opened his eyes when the radiance became strong, making a silver pattern at his feet and lighting the woods with strange lusters and silvery, shadowy forms. As usual, his old notion that his wife must be near occurred to him on this occasion, and he looked about him with a speculative, anticipatory eye. What was it that moved in the distant shadows along the path by which he had entered—a pale, flickering will-o'-the-wisp that bobbed gracefully among the trees and riveted his expectant gaze? Moonlight and shadows combined to give it a strange form and a stranger reality, this fluttering of bog-fire or dancing of wandering fire-flies. Was it truly his lost Phoebe? By a circuitous route it passed about him, and in his fevered state he fancied that he could see the very eyes of her, not as she was when he last saw her in the black dress and shawl but now a strangely younger Phoebe, gayer, sweeter, the one whom he had known years before as a girl. Old Reifsneider got up. He had been expecting and dreaming of this hour all these years, and now as he saw the feeble light dancing lightly before him he peered at it questioningly, one thin hand in his gray hair.

Of a sudden there came to him now for the first time in many years the full charm of her girlish figure as he had known it in boyhood, the pleasing, sympathetic smile, the brown hair, the blue sash she had once worn about her waist at a picnic, her gay, graceful movements. He walked around the base of the tree, straining with his eyes, forgetting for once his cane and utensils, and following eagerly after. On she moved before him, a will-o'-the-wisp of the spring, a little flame above her head, and it seemed as though among the small saplings of ash and beech and the thick trunks of hickory and elm that she signaled with a young, a lightsome hand.

"O Phoebe! Phoebe!" he called. "Have yuh really come? Have yuh really answered me?" And hurrying faster, he fell once, scrambling lamely to his feet, only to see the light in the distance dancing illusively on. On and on he hurried until he was fairly running, brushing his ragged arms against the trees, striking his hands and face against impeding twigs. His hat was gone, his lungs were breathless, his reason quite astray, when coming to the edge of the cliff he saw her below among a silvery bed of apple-trees now blooming in the spring.

"O Phoebe!" he called. "O Phoebe! Oh, no, don't leave me!" And feeling the lure of a world where love was young and Phoebe as this vision presented her, a delightful epitome of their quondam youth, he gave a gay cry of "Oh, wait, Phoebe!" and leaped.

Some farmer-boys, reconnoitering this region of bounty and prospect some few days afterward, found first the tin utensils tied together under the tree where he had left them, and then later at the foot of the cliff, pale, broken, but elate, a molded smile of peace and delight upon his lips, his body. His old hat was discovered lying under some low-growing saplings the twigs of which held it back. No one of all the simple population knew how eagerly and joyously he had found his lost mate.

# JESUS CHRIST IN TEXAS

### W. E. B. Du Bois

It was in Waco, Texas.

The convict guard laughed. "I don't know," he said, "I hadn't thought of that." He hesitated and looked at the stranger curiously. In the solemn twilight he got an impression of unusual height and soft, dark eyes. "Curious sort of acquaintance for the colonel," he thought; then he continued aloud: "But that nigger there is bad, a born thief, and ought to be sent up for life; got ten years last time——"

Here the voice of the promoter, talking within, broke in; he was bending over his figures, sitting by the colonel. He was slight, with a sharp nose.

"The convicts," he said, "would cost us $96 a year and board. Well, we can squeeze this so that it won't be over $125 apiece. Now if these fellows are driven, they can build this line within twelve months. It will be running by next April. Freights will fall fifty per cent. Why, man, you'll be a millionaire in less than ten years."

The colonel started. He was a thick, short man, with a clean-shaven face and a certain air of breeding about the lines of his countenance; the word millionaire sounded well to his ears. He thought—he thought a great deal; he almost heard the puff of the fearfully costly automobile that was coming up the road, and he said:

"I suppose we might as well hire them."

"Of course," answered the promoter.

The voice of the tall stranger in the corner broke in here:

"It will be a good thing for them?" he said, half in question.

The colonel moved. "The guard makes strange friends," he thought to himself. "What's this man doing here, anyway?" He looked at him, or rather looked at his eyes, and then somehow he felt a warming toward him. He said:

"Well, at least, it can't harm them; they're beyond that."

"It will do them good, then," said the stranger again.

The promoter shrugged his shoulders. "It will do us good," he said.

But the colonel shook his head impatiently. He felt a desire to justify himself before those eyes, and he answered: "Yes, it will do them good; or at any rate it won't make them any worse than they are." Then he started to say something else, but here sure enough the sound of the automobile breathing at the gate stopped him and they all arose.

"It is settled, then," said the promoter.

"Yes," said the colonel, turning toward the stranger again. "Are you going into town?" he asked with the Southern courtesy of white men to white men in a country town. The stranger said he was. "Then come along in my machine. I want to talk with you about this."

They went out to the car. The stranger as he went turned again to look back at the convict. He was a tall, powerfully built black fellow. His face was sullen, with a low forehead, thick, hanging lips, and bitter eyes. There was revolt written about his mouth despite the hangdog expression. He stood bending over his pile of stones, pounding listlessly. Beside him stood a boy of twelve—yellow, with a hunted, crafty look. The convict raised his eyes and they met the eyes of the stranger. The hammer fell from his hands.

The stranger turned slowly toward the automobile and the colonel introduced him. He had not exactly caught his name, but he mumbled something as he presented him to his wife and little girl, who were waiting.

As they whirled away the colonel started to talk, but the stranger had taken the little girl into his lap and together they conversed in low tones all the way home.

In some way, they did not exactly know how, they got the impression that the man was a teacher and, of course, he must be a foreigner. The long, cloak-like coat told this. They rode in the twilight through the lighted town and at last drew up before the colonel's mansion, with its ghost-like pillars.

The lady in the back seat was thinking of the guests she had invited to dinner and was wondering if she ought not to ask this man to stay.

He seemed cultured and she supposed he was some acquaintance of the colonel's. It would be rather interesting to have him there, with the judge's wife and daughter and the rector. She spoke almost before she thought:

"You will enter and rest awhile?"

The colonel and the little girl insisted. For a moment the stranger seemed about to refuse. He said he had some business for his father, about town. Then for the child's sake he consented.

Up the steps they went and into the dark parlor where they sat and talked a long time. It was a curious conversation. Afterwards they did not remember exactly what was said and yet they all remembered a certain strange satisfaction in that long, low talk.

Finally the nurse came for the reluctant child and the hostess bethought herself:

"We will have a cup of tea; you will be dry and tired."

She rang and switched on a blaze of light. With one accord they all looked at the stranger, for they had hardly seen him well in the glooming twilight. The woman started in amazement and the colonel half rose in anger. Why, the man was a mulatto, surely; even if he did not own the Negro blood, their practised eyes knew it. He was tall and straight and the coat looked like a Jewish gabardine. His hair hung in close curls far down the sides of his face and his face was olive, even yellow.

A peremptory order rose to the colonel's lips and froze there as he caught the stranger's eyes. Those eyes—where had he seen those eyes before? He remembered them long years ago. The soft, tear-filled eyes of a brown girl. He remembered many things, and his face grew drawn and white. Those eyes kept burning into him, even when they were turned half away toward the staircase, where the white figure of the child hovered with her nurse and waved good-night. The lady sank into her chair and thought: "What will the judge's wife say? How did the colonel come to invite this man here? How shall we be rid of him?" She looked at the colonel in reproachful consternation.

Just then the door opened and the old butler came in. He was an ancient black man, with tufted white hair, and he held before him a large, silver tray filled with a china tea service. The stranger rose slowly and stretched forth his hands as if to bless the viands. The old man paused in bewilderment, tottered, and then with sudden gladness in his eyes dropped to his knees, and the tray crashed to the floor.

"My Lord and my God!" he whispered; but the woman screamed: "Mother's china!"

The doorbell rang.

"Heavens! here is the dinner party!" exclaimed the lady. She turned toward the door, but there in the hall, clad in her night clothes, was the little girl. She had stolen down the stairs to see the stranger again, and the nurse above was calling in vain. The woman felt hysterical and scolded at the nurse, but the stranger had stretched out his arms and with a glad cry the child nestled in them. They caught some words about the "Kingdom of Heaven" as he slowly mounted the stairs with his little, white burden.

The mother was glad of anything to get rid of the interloper, even for a moment. The bell rang again and she hastened toward the door, which the loitering black maid was just opening. She did not notice the shadow of the stranger as he came slowly down the stairs and paused by the newel post, dark and silent.

The judge's wife came in. She was an old woman, frilled and powdered into a semblance of youth, and gorgeously gowned. She came forward, smiling with extended hands, but when she was opposite the stranger, somewhere a chill seemed to strike her and she shuddered and cried:

"What a draft!" as she drew a silken shawl about her and shook hands cordially; she forgot to ask who the stranger was. The judge strode in unseeing, thinking of a puzzling case of theft.

"Eh? What? Oh—er—yes—good evening," he said, "good evening." Behind them came a young woman in the glory of youth, and daintily silked, beautiful in face and form, with diamonds around her fair neck. She came in lightly, but stopped with a little gasp; then she laughed gaily and said:

"Why, I beg your pardon. Was it not curious? I thought I saw there behind your man"—she hesitated, but he must be a servant, she argued—"the shadow of great, white wings. It was but the light on the drapery. What a turn it gave me." And she smiled again. With her came a tall, handsome, young naval officer. Hearing his lady refer to the servant, he hardly looked at him, but held his gilded cap carelessly toward him, and the stranger placed it carefully on the rack.

Last came the rector, a man of forty, and well-clothed. He started to pass the stranger, stopped, and looked at him inquiringly.

"I beg your pardon," he said. "I beg your pardon—I think I have met you?"

The stranger made no answer, and the hostess nervously hurried the guests on. But the rector lingered and looked perplexed.

"Surely, I know you. I have met you somewhere," he said, putting his hand vaguely to his head. "You—you remember me, do you not?"

The stranger quietly swept his cloak aside, and to the hostess' unspeakable relief passed out of the door.

"I never knew you," he said in low tones as he went.

The lady murmured some vain excuse about intruders, but the rector stood with annoyance written on his face.

"I beg a thousand pardons," he said to the hostess absently. "It is a great pleasure to be here—somehow I thought I knew that man. I am sure I knew him once."

The stranger had passed down the steps, and as he passed, the nurse, lingering at the top of the staircase, flew down after him, caught his cloak, trembled, hesitated, and then kneeled in the dust.

He touched her lightly with his hand and said: "Go, and sin no more!"

With a glad cry the maid left the house, with its open door, and turned north, running. The stranger turned eastward into the night. As they parted a long, low howl rose tremulously and reverberated through the night. The colonel's wife within shuddered.

"The bloodhounds!" she said.

The rector answered carelessly:

"Another one of those convicts escaped, I suppose. Really, they need severer measures." Then he stopped. He was trying to remember that stranger's name.

The judge's wife looked about for the draft and arranged her shawl. The girl glanced at the white drapery in the hall, but the young officer was bending over her and the fires of life burned in her veins.

Howl after howl rose in the night, swelled, and died away. The stranger strode rapidly along the highway and out into the deep forest. There he paused and stood waiting, tall and still.

A mile up the road behind a man was running, tall and powerful and black, with crime-stained face and convicts' stripes upon him, and shackles on his legs. He ran and jumped, in little, short steps, and his chains rang. He fell and rose again, while the howl of the hounds rang louder behind him.

Into the forest he leapt and crept and jumped and ran, streaming with sweat; seeing the tall form rise before him, he stopped suddenly, dropped his hands in sullen impotence, and sank panting to the earth. A greyhound shot out of the woods behind him, howled, whined, and fawned before the stranger's feet. Hound after hound bayed, leapt, and lay there; then silently, one by one, and with bowed heads, they crept backward toward the town.

The stranger made a cup of his hands and gave the man water to drink, bathed his hot head, and gently took the chains and irons from his feet. By and by the convict stood up. Day was dawning above the treetops. He looked into the stranger's face, and for a moment a gladness swept over the stains of his face.

"Why, you are a nigger, too," he said.

Then the convict seemed anxious to justify himself.

"I never had no chance," he said furtively.

"Thou shalt not steal," said the stranger.

The man bridled.

"But how about them? Can they steal? Didn't they steal a whole year's work, and then when I stole to keep from starving——" He glanced at the stranger.

"No, I didn't steal just to keep from starving. I stole to be stealing. I can't seem to keep from stealing. Seems like when I see things, I just must—but, yes, I'll try!"

The convict looked down at his striped clothes, but the stranger had taken off his long coat; he had put it around him and the stripes disappeared.

In the opening morning the black man started toward the low, log farmhouse in the distance, while the stranger stood watching him. There was a new glory in the day. The black man's face cleared up, and the farmer was glad to get him. All day the black man worked as he had never worked before. The farmer gave him some cold food.

"You can sleep in the barn," he said, and turned away.

"How much do I git a day?" asked the black man.

The farmer scowled.

"Now see here," said he. "If you'll sign a contract for the season, I'll give you ten dollars a month."

"I won't sign no contract," said the black man doggedly.

"Yes, you will," said the farmer, threateningly, "or I'll call the convict guard." And he grinned.

The convict shrank and slouched to the barn. As night fell he looked out and saw the farmer leave the place. Slowly he crept out and sneaked toward the house. He looked through the kitchen door. No one was there, but the supper was spread as if the mistress had laid it and gone out. He ate ravenously. Then he looked into the

front room and listened. He could hear low voices on the porch. On
the table lay a gold watch. He gazed at it, and in a moment he was
beside it—his hands were on it! Quickly he slipped out of the house
and slouched toward the field. He saw his employer coming along
the highway. He fled back in terror and around to the front of the
house, when suddenly he stopped. He felt the great, dark eyes of
the stranger and saw the same dark, cloak-like coat where the stranger
sat on the doorstep talking with the mistress of the house. Slowly,
guiltily, he turned back, entered the kitchen, and laid the watch
stealthily where he had found it; then he rushed wildly back toward
the stranger, with arms outstretched.

The woman had laid supper for her husband, and going down
from the house had walked out toward a neighbor's. She was gone
but a little while, and when she came back she started to see a dark
figure on the doorsteps under the tall, red oak. She thought it was
the new Negro until he said in a soft voice:

"Will you give me bread?"

Reassured at the voice of a white man, she answered quickly in
her soft, Southern tones:

"Why, certainly."

She was a little woman, and once had been pretty; but now her
face was drawn with work and care. She was nervous and always
thinking, wishing, wanting for something. She went in and got him
some corn-bread and a glass of cool, rich buttermilk; then she came
out and sat down beside him. She began, quite unconsciously, to tell
him about herself—the things she had done and had not done and
the things she had wished for. She told him of her husband and this
new farm they were trying to buy. She said it was hard to get niggers
to work. She said they ought all to be in the chain-gang and
made to work. Even then some ran away. Only yesterday one had
escaped, and another the day before.

At last she gossiped of her neighbors, how good they were
and how bad.

"And do you like them all?" asked the stranger.

She hesitated.

"Most of them," she said; and then, looking up into his face and
putting her hand into his, as though he were her father, she said:

"There are none I hate; no, none at all."

He looked away, holding her hand in his, and said dreamily:

"You love your neighbor as yourself?"

She hesitated.

"I try——" she began, and then looked the way he was looking; down under the hill where lay a little, half-ruined cabin.

"They are niggers," she said briefly.

He looked at her. Suddenly a confusion came over her and she insisted, she knew not why.

"But they are niggers!"

With a sudden impulse she arose and hurriedly lighted the lamp that stood just within the door, and held it above her head. She saw his dark face and curly hair. She shrieked in angry terror and rushed down the path, and just as she rushed down, the black convict came running up with hands outstretched. They met in mid-path, and before he could stop he had run against her and she fell heavily to earth and lay white and still. Her husband came rushing around the house with a cry and an oath.

"I knew it," he said. "It's that runaway nigger." He held the black man struggling to the earth and raised his voice to a yell. Down the highway came the convict guard, with hound and mob and gun. They paused across the fields. The farmer motioned to them.

"He—attacked—my wife," he gasped.

The mob snarled and worked silently. Right to the limb of the red oak they hoisted the struggling, writhing black man, while others lifted the dazed woman. Right and left, as she tottered to the house, she searched for the stranger with a yearning, but the stranger was gone. And she told none of her guests.

"No—no, I want nothing," she insisted, until they left her, as they thought, asleep. For a time she lay still, listening to the departure of the mob. Then she rose. She shuddered as she heard the creaking of the limb where the body hung. But resolutely she crawled to the window and peered out into the moonlight; she saw the dead man writhe. He stretched his arms out like a cross, looking upward. She gasped and clung to the window sill. Behind the swaying body, and down where the little, half-ruined cabin lay, a single flame flashed up amid the far-off shout and cry of the mob. A fierce joy sobbed up through the terror in her soul and then sank abashed as she watched the flame rise. Suddenly whirling into one great crimson column it shot to the top of the sky and threw great arms athwart the gloom until above the world and behind the roped and swaying form below hung quivering and burning a great crimson cross.

She hid her dizzy, aching head in an agony of tears, and dared not look, for she knew. Her dry lips moved:

"Despised and rejected of men."

She knew, and the very horror of it lifted her dull and shrinking eyelids. There, heaven-tall, earth-wide, hung the stranger on the crimson cross, riven and bloodstained, with thorn-crowned head and pierced hands. She stretched her arms and shrieked.

He did not hear. He did not see. His calm dark eyes, all sorrowful, were fastened on the writhing, twisting body of the thief, and a voice came out of the winds of the night, saying:

"This day thou shalt be with me in Paradise!"

# THE SCAPEGOAT

## Paul Laurence Dunbar

### I

THE LAW IS usually supposed to be a stern mistress, not to be lightly wooed, and yielding only to the most ardent pursuit. But even law, like love, sits more easily on some natures than on others. This was the case with Mr. Robinson Asbury. Mr. Asbury had started life as a bootblack in the growing town of Cadgers. From this he had risen one step and become porter and messenger in a barber-shop. This rise fired his ambition, and he was not content until he had learned to use the shears and the razor and had a chair of his own. From this, in a man of Robinson's temperament, it was only a step to a shop of his own, and he placed it where it would do the most good.

Fully one-half of the population of Cadgers was composed of Negroes, and with their usual tendency to colonise, a tendency encouraged, and in fact compelled, by circumstances, they had gathered into one part of the town. Here in alleys, and streets as dirty and hardly wider, they thronged like ants.

It was in this place that Mr. Asbury set up his shop, and he won the hearts of his prospective customers by putting up the significant sign, "Equal Rights Barber-Shop." This legend was quite unnecessary, because there was only one race about, to patronise the place. But it was a delicate sop to the people's vanity, and it served its purpose.

Asbury came to be known as a clever fellow, and his business grew. The shop really became a sort of club, and, on Saturday nights especially, was the gathering-place of the men of the whole Negro quarter. He kept the illustrated and race journals there, and those

291

who cared neither to talk nor listen to someone else might see pictured the doings of high society in very short skirts or read in the Negro papers how Miss Boston had entertained Miss Blueford to tea on such and such an afternoon. Also, he kept the policy returns, which was wise, if not moral.

It was his wisdom rather more than his morality that made the party managers after a while cast their glances toward him as a man who might be useful to their interests. It would be well to have a man—a shrewd, powerful man—down in that part of the town who could carry his people's vote in his vest pocket, and who at any time its delivery might be needed, could hand it over without hesitation. Asbury seemed that man, and they settled upon him. They gave him money, and they gave him power and patronage. He took it all silently and he carried out his bargain faithfully. His hands and his lips alike closed tightly when there was anything within them. It was not long before he found himself the big Negro of the district and, of necessity, of the town. The time came when, at a critical moment, the managers saw that they had not reckoned without their host in choosing this barber of the black district as the leader of his people.

Now, so much success must have satisfied any other man. But in many ways Mr. Asbury was unique. For a long time he himself had done very little shaving—except of notes, to keep his hand in. His time had been otherwise employed. In the evening hours he had been wooing the coquettish Dame Law, and, wonderful to say, she had yielded easily to his advances.

It was against the advice of his friends that he asked for admission to the bar. They felt that he could do more good in the place where he was.

"You see, Robinson," said old Judge Davis, "it's just like this: If you're not admitted, it'll hurt you with the people; if you are admitted, you'll move uptown to an office and get out of touch with them."

Asbury smiled an inscrutable smile. Then he whispered something into the judge's ear that made the old man wrinkle from his neck up with appreciative smiles.

"Asbury," he said, "you are—you are—well, you ought to be white, that's all. When we find a black man like you we send him to State's prison. If you were white, you'd go to the Senate."

The Negro laughed confidently.

He was admitted to the bar soon after, whether by merit or by connivance is not to be told.

"Now he will move uptown," said the black community. "Well, that's the way with a coloured man when he gets a start."

But they did not know Asbury Robinson yet. He was a man of surprises, and they were destined to disappointment. He did not move uptown. He built an office in a small open space next his shop, and there hung out his shingle.

"I will never desert the people who have done so much to elevate me," said Mr. Asbury.

"I will live among them and I will die among them."

This was a strong card for the barber-lawyer. The people seized upon the statement as expressing a nobility of an altogether unique brand.

They held a mass meeting and indorsed him. They made resolutions that extolled him, and the Negro band came around and serenaded him, playing various things in varied time.

All this was very sweet to Mr. Asbury, and the party managers chuckled with satisfaction and said, "That Asbury, that Asbury!"

Now there is a fable extant of a man who tried to please everybody, and his failure is a matter of record. Robinson Asbury was not more successful. But be it said that his ill success was due to no fault or shortcoming of his.

For a long time his growing power had been looked upon with disfavour by the coloured law firm of Bingo & Latchett. Both Mr. Bingo and Mr. Latchett themselves aspired to be Negro leaders in Cadgers, and they were delivering Emancipation Day orations and riding at the head of processions when Mr. Asbury was blacking boots. Is it any wonder, then, that they viewed with alarm his sudden rise? They kept their counsel, however, and treated with him, for it was best. They allowed him his scope without open revolt until the day upon which he hung out his shingle. This was the last straw. They could stand no more. Asbury had stolen their other chances from them, and now he was poaching upon the last of their preserves. So Mr. Bingo and Mr. Latchett put their heads together to plan the downfall of their common enemy.

The plot was deep and embraced the formation of an opposing faction made up of the best Negroes of the town. It would have looked too much like what it was for the gentlemen to show themselves in the matter, and so they took into their confidence Mr. Isaac Morton, the principal of the coloured school, and it was under his ostensible leadership that the new faction finally came into being.

Mr. Morton was really an innocent young man, and he had ideals which should never have been exposed to the air. When the wily confederates came to him with their plan he believed that his worth had been recognised, and at last he was to be what Nature destined him for—a leader.

The better class of Negroes—by that is meant those who were particularly envious of Asbury's success—flocked to the new man's standard. But whether the race be white or black, political virtue is always in a minority, so Asbury could afford to smile at the force arrayed against him.

The new faction met together and resolved. They resolved, among other things, that Mr. Asbury was an enemy to his race and a menace to civilisation. They decided that he should be abolished; but, as they couldn't get out an injunction against him, and as he had the whole undignified but still voting black belt behind him, he went serenely on his way.

"They're after you hot and heavy, Asbury," said one of his friends to him.

"Oh, yes," was the reply, "they're after me, but after a while I'll get so far away that they'll be running in front."

"It's all the best people, they say."

"Yes. Well, it's good to be one of the best people, but your vote only counts one just the same."

The time came, however, when Mr. Asbury's theory was put to the test. The Cadgerites celebrated the first of January as Emancipation Day. On this day there was a large procession, with speechmaking in the afternoon and fireworks at night. It was the custom to concede the leadership of the coloured people of the town to the man who managed to lead the procession. For two years past this honour had fallen, of course, to Robinson Asbury, and there had been no disposition on the part of anybody to try conclusions with him.

Mr. Morton's faction changed all this. When Asbury went to work to solicit contributions for the celebration, he suddenly became aware that he had a fight upon his hands. All the better-class Negroes were staying out of it. The next thing he knew was that plans were on foot for a rival demonstration.

"Oh," he said to himself, "that's it, is it? Well, if they want a fight they can have it."

He had a talk with the party managers, and he had another with Judge Davis.

"All I want is a little lift, judge," he said, "and I'll make 'em think the sky has turned loose and is vomiting niggers."

The judge believed that he could do it. So did the party managers. Asbury got his lift. Emancipation Day came.

There were two parades. At least, there was one parade and the shadow of another. Asbury's, however, was not the shadow. There was a great deal of substance about it—substance made up of many people, many banners, and numerous bands. He did not have the best people. Indeed, among his cohorts there were a good many of the pronounced rag-tag and bobtail. But he had noise and numbers. In such cases, nothing more is needed. The success of Asbury's side of the affair did everything to confirm his friends in their good opinion of him.

When he found himself defeated, Mr. Silas Bingo saw that it would be policy to placate his rival's just anger against him. He called upon him at his office the day after the celebration.

"Well, Asbury," he said, "you beat us, didn't you?"

"It wasn't a question of beating," said the other calmly. "It was only an inquiry as to who were the people—the few or the many."

"Well, it was well done, and you've shown that you are a manager. I confess that I haven't always thought that you were doing the wisest thing in living down here and catering to this class of people when you might, with your ability, to be much more to the better class."

"What do they base their claims of being better on?"

"Oh, there ain't any use discussing that. We can't get along without you, we see that. So I, for one, have decided to work with you for harmony."

"Harmony. Yes, that's what we want."

"If I can do anything to help you at any time, why you have only to command me."

"I am glad to find such a friend in you. Be sure, if I ever need you, Bingo, I'll call on you."

"And I'll be ready to serve you."

Asbury smiled when his visitor was gone. He smiled, and knitted his brow. "I wonder what Bingo's got up his sleeve," he said. "He'll bear watching."

It may have been pride at his triumph, it may have been gratitude at his helpers, but Asbury went into the ensuing campaign with reckless enthusiasm. He did the most daring things for the party's sake. Bingo, true to his promise, was ever at his side ready to serve him. Finally, association and immunity made danger less fearsome; the rival no longer appeared a menace.

With the generosity born of obstacles overcome, Asbury determined to forgive Bingo and give him a chance. He let him in on a deal, and from that time they worked amicably together until the election came and passed.

It was a close election and many things had had to be done, but there were men there ready and waiting to do them. They were successful, and then the first cry of the defeated party was, as usual, "Fraud! Fraud!" The cry was taken up by the jealous, the disgruntled, and the virtuous.

Someone remembered how two years ago the registration books had been stolen. It was known upon good authority that money had been freely used. Men held up their hands in horror at the suggestion that the Negro vote had been juggled with, as if that were a new thing. From their pulpits ministers denounced the machine and bade their hearers rise and throw off the yoke of a corrupt municipal government. One of those sudden fevers of reform had taken possession of the town and threatened to destroy the successful party.

They began to look around them. They must purify themselves. They must give the people some tangible evidence of their own yearnings after purity. They looked around them for a sacrifice to lay upon the altar of municipal reform. Their eyes fell upon Mr. Bingo. No, he was not big enough. His blood was too scant to wash away the political stains. Then they looked into each other's eyes and turned their gaze away to let it fall upon Mr. Asbury. They really hated to do it. But there must be a scapegoat. The god from the Machine commanded them to slay him.

Robinson Asbury was charged with many crimes—with all that he had committed and some that he had not. When Mr. Bingo saw what was afoot he threw himself heart and soul into the work of his old rival's enemies. He was of incalculable use to them.

Judge Davis refused to have anything to do with the matter. But in spite of his disapproval it went on. Asbury was indicted and tried. The evidence was all against him, and no one gave more damaging testimony than his friend, Mr. Bingo. The judge's charge was favourable to the defendant, but the current of popular opinion could not be entirely stemmed. The jury brought in a verdict of guilty.

"Before I am sentenced, judge, I have a statement to make to the court. It will take less than ten minutes."

"Go on, Robinson," said the judge kindly.

Asbury started, in a monotonous tone, a recital that brought the prosecuting attorney to his feet in a minute. The judge waved him down, and sat transfixed by a sort of fascinated horror as the convicted man went on. The before-mentioned attorney drew a knife and started for the prisoner's dock. With difficulty he was restrained. A dozen faces in the court-room were red and pale by turns.

"He ought to be killed," whispered Mr. Bingo audibly.

Robinson Asbury looked at him and smiled, and then he told a few things of him. He gave the ins and outs of some of the misdemeanours of which he stood accused. He showed who were the men behind the throne. And still, pale and transfixed, Judge Davis waited for his own sentence.

Never were ten minutes so well taken up. It was a tale of rottenness and corruption in high places told simply and with the stamp of truth upon it.

He did not mention the judge's name. But he had torn the mask from the face of every other man who had been concerned in his downfall. They had shorn him of his strength, but they had forgotten that he was yet able to bring the roof and pillars tumbling about their heads.

The judge's voice shook as he pronounced sentence upon his old ally—a year in State's prison.

Some people said it was too light, but the judge knew what it was to wait for the sentence of doom, and he was grateful and sympathetic.

When the sheriff led Asbury away the judge hastened to have a short talk with him.

"I'm sorry, Robinson," he said, "and I want to tell you that you were no more guilty than the rest of us. But why did you spare me?"

"Because I knew you were my friend," answered the convict.

"I tried to be, but you were the first man that I've ever known since I've been in politics who ever gave me any decent return for friendship."

"I reckon you're about right, judge."

In politics, party reform usually lies in making a scapegoat of someone who is only as criminal as the rest, but a little weaker. Asbury's friends and enemies had succeeded in making him bear the burden of all the party's crimes, but their reform was hardly a success, and their protestations of a change of heart were received with doubt. Already there were those who began to pity the victim and to say that he had been hardly dealt with.

Mr. Bingo was not of these; but he found, strange to say, that his opposition to the idea went but a little way, and that even with Asbury out of his path he was a smaller man than he was before. Fate was strong against him. His poor, prosperous humanity could not enter the lists against a martyr. Robinson Asbury was now a martyr.

## II

A year is not a long time. It was short enough to prevent people from forgetting Robinson, and yet long enough for their pity to grow strong as they remembered. Indeed, he was not gone a year. Good behaviour cut two months off the time of his sentence, and by the time people had come around to the notion that he was really the greatest and smartest man in Cadgers he was at home again.

He came back with no flourish of trumpets, but quietly, humbly. He went back again into the heart of the black district. His business had deteriorated during his absence, but he put new blood and new life into it. He did not go to work in the shop himself, but, taking down the shingle that had swung idly before his office door during his imprisonment, he opened the little room as a news- and cigar-stand.

Here anxious, pitying custom came to him and he prospered again. He was very quiet. Uptown hardly knew that he was again in Cadgers, and it knew nothing whatever of his doings.

"I wonder why Asbury is so quiet," they said to one another. "It isn't like him to be quiet." And they felt vaguely uneasy about him.

So many people had begun to say, "Well, he was a mighty good fellow after all."

Mr. Bingo expressed the opinion that Asbury was quiet because he was crushed, but others expressed doubt as to this. There are calms and calms, some after and some before the storm. Which was this?

They waited a while, and, as no storm came, concluded that this must be the after-quiet. Bingo, reassured, volunteered to go and seek confirmation of this conclusion.

He went, and Asbury received him with an indifferent, not to say, impolite, demeanour.

"Well, we're glad to see you back, Asbury," said Bingo patronisingly. He had variously demonstrated his inability to lead during his rival's absence and was proud of it. "What are you going to do?"

"I'm going to work."

"That's right. I reckon you'll stay out of politics."

"What could I do even if I went in?"

"Nothing now, of course; but I didn't know—"

He did not see the gleam in Asbury's half shut eyes. He only marked his humility, and he went back swelling with the news.

"Completely crushed—all the run taken out of him," was his report.

The black district believed this, too, and a sullen, smouldering anger took possession of them. Here was a good man ruined. Some of the people whom he had helped in his former days—some of the rude, coarse people of the low quarter who were still sufficiently unenlightened to be grateful—talked among themselves and offered to get up a demonstration for him. But he denied them. No, he wanted nothing of the kind. It would only bring him into unfavourable notice. All he wanted was that they would always be his friends and would stick by him.

They would to the death.

There were again two factions in Cadgers. The school-master could not forget how once on a time he had been made a tool of by Mr. Bingo. So he revolted against his rule and set himself up as the leader of an opposing clique. The fight had been long and strong, but had ended with odds slightly in Bingo's favour.

But Mr. Morton did not despair. As the first of January and Emancipation Day approached, he arrayed his hosts, and the fight for supremacy became fiercer than ever. The school-teacher brought the school-children in for chorus singing, secured an able orator, and the best essayist in town. With all this, he was formidable.

Mr. Bingo knew that he had the fight of his life on his hands, and he entered with fear as well as zest. He, too, found an orator, but he was not sure that he was as good as Morton's. There was no doubt but that his essayist was not. He secured a band, but still he felt unsatisfied. He had hardly done enough, and for the schoolmaster to beat him now meant his political destruction.

It was in this state of mind that he was surprised to receive a visit from Mr. Asbury.

"I reckon you're surprised to see me here," said Asbury, smiling.

"I am pleased, I know." Bingo was astute.

"Well, I just dropped in on business."

"To be sure, to be sure, Asbury. What can I do for you?"

"It's more what I can do for you that I came to talk about," was the reply.

"I don't believe I understand you."

"Well, it's plain enough. They say that the school-teacher is giving you a pretty hard fight."

"Oh, not so hard."

"No man can be too sure of winning, though. Mr. Morton once did me a mean turn when he started the faction against me."

Bingo's heart gave a great leap, and then stopped for the fraction of a second.

"You were in it, of course," pursued Asbury, "but I can look over your part in it in order to get even with the man who started it."

It was true, then, thought Bingo gladly. He did not know. He wanted revenge for his wrongs and upon the wrong man. How well the schemer had covered his tracks! Asbury should have his revenge and Morton would be the sufferer.

"Of course, Asbury, you know what I did I did innocently."

"Oh, yes, in politics we are all lambs and the wolves are only to be found in the other party. We'll pass that, though. What I want to say is that I can help you to make your celebration an overwhelming success. I still have some influence down in my district."

"Certainly, and very justly, too. Why, I should be delighted with your aid. I could give you a prominent place in the procession."

"I don't want it; I don't want to appear in this at all. All I want is revenge. You can have all the credit, but let me down my enemy."

Bingo was perfectly willing, and, with their heads close together, they had a long and close consultation. When Asbury was gone, Mr. Bingo lay back in his chair and laughed. "I'm a slick duck," he said.

From that hour Mr. Bingo's cause began to take on the appearance of something very like a boom. More bands were hired. The interior of the State was called upon and a more eloquent orator secured. The crowd hastened to array itself on the growing side.

With surprised eyes, the school-master beheld the wonder of it, but he kept to his own purpose with dogged insistence, even when he saw that he could not turn aside the overwhelming defeat that threatened him. But in spite of his obstinacy, his hours were dark and bitter. Asbury worked like a mole, all underground, but he was indefatigable. Two days before the celebration time everything was perfected for the biggest demonstration that Cadgers had ever known. All the next day and night he was busy among his allies.

On the morning of the great day, Mr. Bingo, wonderfully caparisoned, rode down to the hall where the parade was to form. He was early. No one had yet come. In an hour a score of men all told had collected.

Another hour passed, and no more had come. Then there smote upon his ear the sound of music. They were coming at last. Bringing his sword to his shoulder, he rode forward to the middle of the street. Ah, there they were. But—but—could he believe his eyes? They were going in another direction, and at their head rode—Morton! He gnashed his teeth in fury. He had been led into a trap and betrayed. The procession passing had been his—all his. He heard them cheering, and then, oh! climax of infidelity, he saw his own orator go past in a carriage, bowing and smiling to the crowd.

There was no doubting who had done this thing. The hand of Asbury was apparent in it. He must have known the truth all along, thought Bingo. His allies left him one by one for the other hall, and he rode home in a humiliation deeper than he had ever known before.

Asbury did not appear at the celebration. He was at his little news-stand all day.

In a day or two the defeated aspirant had further cause to curse his false friend. He found that not only had the people defected from him, but that the thing had been so adroitly managed that he appeared to be in fault, and three-fourths of those who knew him were angry at some supposed grievance. His cup of bitterness was full when his partner, a quietly ambitious man, suggested that they dissolve their relations.

His ruin was complete.

The lawyer was not alone in seeing Asbury's hand in his downfall. The party managers saw it too, and they met together to discuss the dangerous factor which, while it appeared to slumber, was so terribly awake. They decided that he must be appeased, and they visited him.

He was still busy at his news-stand. They talked to him adroitly, while he sorted papers and kept an impassive face. When they were all done, he looked up for a moment and replied, "You know, gentlemen, as an ex-convict I am not in politics."

Some of them had the grace to flush.

"But you can use your influence," they said.

"I am not in politics," was his only reply.

And the spring elections were coming on. Well, they worked hard, and he showed no sign. He treated with neither one party nor the other. "Perhaps," thought the managers, "he is out of politics," and they grew more confident.

It was nearing eleven o'clock on the morning of election when a cloud no bigger than a man's hand appeared upon the horizon.

It came from the direction of the black district. It grew, and the managers of the party in power looked at it, fascinated by an ominous dread. Finally it began to rain Negro voters, and as one man they voted against their former candidates. Their organisation was perfect. They simply came, voted, and left, but they overwhelmed everything. Not one of the party that had damned Robinson Asbury was left in power save old Judge Davis. His majority was overwhelming.

The generalship that had engineered the thing was perfect. There were loud threats against the newsdealer. But no one bothered him except a reporter. The reporter called to see just how it was done. He found Asbury very busy sorting papers. To the newspaper man's questions he had only this reply, "I am not in politics, sir." But Cadgers had learned its lesson.

# A CARNIVAL JANGLE

## Alice Moore Dunbar-Nelson

THERE IS A merry jangle of bells in the air, an all-pervading sense of jester's noise, and the flaunting vividness of royal colors; the streets swarm with humanity—humanity in all shapes, manners, forms— laughing, pushing, jostling, crowding, a mass of men and women and children, as varied and as assorted in their several individual peculiarities as ever a crowd that gathered in one locality since the days of Babel.

It is Carnival in New Orleans; a brilliant Tuesday in February, when the very air effervesces an ozone intensely exhilarating—of a nature half spring, half winter—to make one long to cut capers. The buildings are a blazing mass of royal purple and golden yellow, and national flags, bunting and decorations that laugh in the glint of the Midas sun. The streets a crush of jesters and maskers, Jim Crows and clowns, ballet girls and Mephistos, Indians and monkeys; of wild and sudden flashes of music, of glittering pageants and comic ones, of befeathered and belled horses. A madding dream of color and melody and fantasy gone wild in an effervescent bubble of beauty that shifts and changes and passes kaleidoscope-like before the bewildered eye.

A bevy of bright-eyed girls and boys of that uncertainty of age that hovers between childhood and maturity, were moving down Canal Street when there was a sudden jostle with another crowd meeting them. For a minute there was a deafening clamor of laughter, cracking of whips, which all maskers carry, jingle and clatter of carnival bells, and the masked and unmasked extricated themselves and moved from each other's paths. But in the confusion a tall Prince of Darkness had whispered to one of the girls in the unmasked crowd: "You'd better come with us, Flo, you're wasting time in that tame gang. Slip off, they'll never miss you; we'll get you a rig, and show you what life is."

And so it happened that when a half hour passed, and the bright-eyed bevy missed Flo and couldn't find her, wisely giving up the search at last, that she, the quietest and most bashful of the lot, was being initiated into the mysteries of "what life is."

Down Bourbon Street and on Toulouse and St. Peter Streets[1] there are quaint little old-world places, where one may be disguised effectually for a tiny consideration. Thither guided by the shapely Mephisto, and guarded by the team of jockeys and ballet girls, tripped Flo. Into one of the lowest-ceiled, dingiest and most ancient-looking of these disguise shops they stopped.

"A disguise for this demoiselle," announced Mephisto to the woman who met them. She was small and wizened and old, with yellow, flabby jaws and neck like the throat of an alligator, and straight, white hair that stood from her head uncannily stiff.

"But the demoiselle wishes to appear a boy, *un petit garçon*?"[2] she inquired, gazing eagerly at Flo's long, slender frame. Her voice was old and thin, like the high quavering of an imperfect tuning fork, and her eyes were sharp as talons in their grasping glance.

"Mademoiselle does not wish such a costume," gruffly responded Mephisto.

"*Ma foi,*[3] there is no other," said the ancient, shrugging her shoulders. "But one is left now, mademoiselle would make a fine troubadour."

"Flo," said Mephisto, "it's a daredevil scheme, try it; no one will ever know it but us, and we'll die before we tell. Besides, we must; it's late, and you couldn't find your crowd."

And that was why you might have seen a Mephisto and a slender troubadour of lovely form, with mandolin flung across his shoulder, followed by a bevy of jockeys and ballet girls, laughing and singing as they swept down Rampart Street.

When the flash and glare and brilliancy of Canal Street have palled upon the tired eye, and it is yet too soon to go home, and to such a

---

[1]  Bourbon Street and on Toulouse and St. Peter Streets: Famous streets in the French Quarter of New Orleans.

[2]  *un petit garçon*; French: a little boy.

[3]  *Ma foi*; French: My faith; indeed.

prosaic thing as dinner, and one still wishes for novelty, then it is wise to go in the lower districts. Fantasy and fancy and grotesqueness in the costuming and behavior of the maskers run wild. Such dances and whoops and leaps as these hideous Indians and devils do indulge in; such wild curvetings and great walks. And in the open squares, where whole groups do congregate, it is wonderfully amusing. Then, too, there is a ball in every available hall, a delirious ball, where one may dance all day for ten cents; dance and grow mad for joy, and never know who were your companions, and be yourself unknown. And in the exhilaration of the day, one walks miles and miles, and dances and curvets, and the fatigue is never felt.

In Washington Square, away down where Royal Street empties its stream of children and men into the broad channel of Elysian Fields Avenue, there was a perfect Indian dance. With a little imagination one might have willed away the vision of the surrounding houses and fancied one's self again in the forest, where the natives were holding a sacred riot. The square was filled with spectators, masked and unmasked. It was amusing to watch these mimic Redmen, they seemed so fierce and earnest.

Suddenly one chief touched another on the elbow. "See that Mephisto and troubadour over there?" he whispered huskily.

"Yes, who are they?"

"I don't know the devil," responded the other quietly, "but I'd know that other form anywhere. It's Leon, see? I know those white hands like a woman's and that restless head. Ha!"

"But there may be a mistake."

"No. I'd know that one anywhere; I feel it's him. I'll pay him now. Ah, sweetheart, you've waited long, but you shall feast now!" He was caressing something long, and lithe, and glittering beneath his blanket.

In a masked dance it is easy to give a death-blow between the shoulders. Two crowds meet and laugh and shout and mingle almost inextricably, and if a shriek of pain should arise, it is not noticed in the din, and when they part, if one should stagger and fall bleeding to the ground, who can tell who has given the blow? There is naught but an unknown stiletto on the ground, the crowd has dispersed, and masks tell no tales anyway. There is murder, but by whom? for what? *Quien sabe?*[4]

---

[4] *Quien sabe?*; Spanish: Who knows?

And that is how it happened on Carnival night, in the last mad moments of Rex's reign, a broken-hearted woman sat gazing wide-eyed and mute at a horrible something that lay across the bed. Outside the long sweet march music of many bands floated in in mockery, and the flash of rockets and Bengal lights illumined the dead, white face of the girl troubadour.

# MARY ELIZABETH

### Jessie Fauset

MARY ELIZABETH WAS late that morning. As a direct result, Roger left for work without telling me good-bye, and I spent most of the day fighting the headache which always comes if I cry.

For I cannot get a breakfast. I can manage a dinner—one just puts the roast in the oven and takes it out again. And I really excel in getting lunch. There is a good delicatessen near us, and with dainty service and flowers, I get along very nicely. But breakfast! In the first place, it's a meal I neither like nor need. And I never, if I live a thousand years, shall learn to like coffee. I suppose that is why I cannot make it.

"Roger," I faltered, when the awful truth burst upon me and I began to realize that Mary Elizabeth wasn't coming, "Roger, couldn't you get breakfast downtown this morning? You know last time you weren't so satisfied with my coffee."

Roger was hostile. I think he had just cut himself, shaving. Anyway, he was horrid.

"No, I can't get my breakfast downtown!" He actually snapped at me. "Really, Sally, I don't believe there's another woman in the world who would send her husband out on a morning like this on an empty stomach. I don't see how you can be so unfeeling."

Well, it wasn't "a morning like this," for it was just the beginning of November. And I had only proposed his doing what I knew he would have to do eventually.

I didn't say anything more, but started on that breakfast. I don't know why I thought I had to have hot cakes! The breakfast really was awful! The cakes were tough and gummy and got cold one second, exactly, after I took them off the stove. And the coffee boiled, or stewed, or scorched, or did whatever the particular thing is that coffee shouldn't do. Roger sawed at one cake, took one mouthful of the dreadful brew, and pushed away his cup.

"It seems to me you might learn to make a decent cup of coffee," he said icily. Then he picked up his hat and flung out of the house.

I think it is stupid of me, too, not to learn how to make coffee. But, really, I'm no worse than Roger is about lots of things. Take "Five Hundred." Roger knows I love cards, and with the Cheltons right around the corner from us and as fond of it as I am, we could spend many a pleasant evening. But Roger will not learn. Only the night before, after I had gone through a whole hand with him, with hearts as trumps, I dealt the cards around again to imaginary opponents and we started playing. Clubs were trumps, and spades led. Roger, having no spades, played triumphantly a Jack of Hearts and proceeded to take the trick.

"But, Roger," I protested, "you threw off."

"Well," he said, deeply injured, "didn't you say hearts were trumps when you were playing before?"

And when I tried to explain, he threw down the cards and wanted to know what difference it made; he'd rather play casino, anyway! I didn't go out and slam the door.

But I couldn't help from crying this particular morning. I not only value Roger's good opinion, but I hate to be considered stupid.

Mary Elizabeth came in about eleven o'clock. She is a small, weazened woman, very dark, somewhat wrinkled, and a model of self-possession. I wish I could make you see her, or that I could reproduce her accent, not that it is especially colored—Roger's and mine are much more so—but her pronunciation, her way of drawing out her vowels, is so distinctively Mary Elizabethan!

I was ashamed of my red eyes and tried to cover up my embarrassment with sternness.

"Mary Elizabeth," said I, "you are late!" Just as though she didn't know it.

"Yas'm, Mis' Pierson," she said, composedly, taking off her coat. She didn't remove her hat—she never does until she has been in the house some two or three hours. I can't imagine why. It is a small, black, dusty affair, trimmed with black ribbon, some dingy white roses and a sheaf of wheat. I give Mary Elizabeth a dress and hat now and then, but, although I recognize the dress from time to time, I never see any change in the hat. I don't know what she does with my ex-millinery.

"Yas'm," she said again, and looked comprehensively at the untouched breakfast dishes and the awful viands, which were still where Roger had left them.

"Looks as though you'd had to git breakfast yoreself," she observed brightly. And went out in the kitchen and ate all those cakes and drank that unspeakable coffee! Really she did, and she didn't warm them up either.

I watched her miserably, unable to decide whether Roger was too finicky or Mary Elizabeth a natural-born diplomat.

"Mr. Gales led me an awful chase last night," she explained. "When I got home yistiddy evenin', my cousin whut keeps house fer me (!) tole me Mr. Gales went out in the mornin' en hadn't come back."

"Mr. Gales," let me explain, is Mary Elizabeth's second husband, an octogenarian, and the most original person, I am convinced, in existence.

"Yas'm," she went on, eating a final cold hot-cake, "en I went to look fer 'im, en had the whole perlice station out all night huntin' 'im. Look like they wusn't never goin' to find 'im. But I ses, 'Jes' let me look fer enough en long enough en I'll find 'im,' I ses, en I did. Way out Georgy Avenue, with the hat on ole Mis' give 'im. Sent it to 'im all the way fum Chicaga. He's had it fifteen years—high silk beaver. I knowed he wusn't goin' too fer with that hat on.

"I went up to 'im, settin' by a fence all muddy, holdin' his hat on with both hands. En I ses, 'Look here, man, you come erlong home with me, en let me put you to bed.' En he come jest as meek! No-o-me, I knowed he wusn't goin' fer with ole Mis' hat on."

"Who was old 'Mis,' Mary Elizabeth?" I asked her.

"Lady I used to work fer in Noo York," she informed me. "Me en Rosy, the cook, lived with her fer years. Old Mis' was turrible fond of me, though her en Rosy used to querrel all the time. Jes' seemed like they couldn't git erlong. 'Member once Rosy run after her one Sunday with a knife, en I kep 'em apart. Reckon Rosy musta bin right put out with ole Mis' that day. By en by her en Rosy move to Chicaga, en when I married Mr. Gales, she sent 'im that hat. That old white woman shore did like me. It's so late, reckon I'd better put off sweepin' tel termorrer, ma'am."

I acquiesced, following her about from room to room. This was partly to get away from my own doleful thoughts—Roger really had hurt my feelings—but just as much to hear her talk. At first I used not to believe all she said, but after I investigated once and found her truthful in one amazing statement, I capitulated.

She had been telling me some remarkable tale of her first husband and I was listening with the stupefied attention, to which she always reduces me. Remember she was speaking of her first husband.

"En I ses to 'im, I ses, 'Mr. Gale—'"

"Wait a moment, Mary Elizabeth," I interrupted, meanly delighted to have caught her for once. "You mean your first husband, don't you?"

"Yas'm," she replied. "En I ses to 'im, 'Mr. Gale! I ses—'"

"But, Mary Elizabeth," I persisted, "that's your second husband, isn't it—Mr. Gale?"

She gave me her long-drawn "No-o-me! My first husband was Mr. Gale and my second is Mr. *Gales.* He spells his name with a Z, I reckon. I ain't never see it writ. Ez I wus sayin', I ses to Mr. Gale—"

*And it was true!* Since then I have never doubted Mary Elizabeth.

She was loquacious that afternoon. She told me about her sister, "where's got a home in the country and where's got eight children." I used to read Lucy Pratt's stories about little Ephraim or Ezekiel, I forget his name, who always said "where's" instead of "who's," but I never believed it really till I heard Mary Elizabeth use it. For some reason or other she never mentions her sister without mentioning the home, too. "My sister where's got a home in the country" is her unvarying phrase.

"Mary Elizabeth," I asked her once, "does your sister live in the country, or does she simply own a house there?"

"Yas'm," she told me.

She is fond of her sister. "If Mr. Gales wus to die," she told me complacently, "I'd go to live with her."

"If he should die," I asked her idly, "would you marry again?"

"Oh, no-o-me!" She was emphatic. "Though I don't know why I shouldn't, I'd come by it hones'. My father wus married four times."

That shocked me out of my headache. "Four times, Mary Elizabeth, and you had all those stepmothers!" My mind refused to take it in.

"Oh, no-o-me! I always lived with mamma. She was his first wife."

I hadn't thought of people in the state in which I had instinctively placed Mary Elizabeth's father and mother as indulging in divorce, but as Roger says slangily, "I wouldn't know."

Mary Elizabeth took off the dingy hat. "You see, papa and mamma—" the ineffable pathos of hearing this woman of sixty-four, with a husband of eighty, use the old childish terms!

"Papa and mamma wus slaves, you know, Mis' Pierson, and so of course they wusn't exackly married. White folks wouldn't let 'em. But they wus awf'ly in love with each other. Heard mamma tell erbout it lots of times, and how papa wus the han'somest man! Reckon she wus long erbout sixteen or seventeen then. So they jumped over a broomstick, en they wus jes as happy! But not long after I come erlong, they sold papa down South, and mamma never see him no mo' fer years and years. Thought he was dead. So she married again."

"And he came back to her, Mary Elizabeth?" I was overwhelmed with the woefulness of it.

"Yas'm. After twenty-six years. Me and my sister where's got a home in the country    she's really my half-sister, see Mis' Pierson— her en mamma en my step-father en me wus all down in Bumpus, Virginia, workin' fer some white folks, and we used to live in a little cabin, had a front stoop to it. En one day an ole cullud man come by, had a lot o' whiskers. I'd saw him lots of times there in Bumpus, lookin' and peerin' into every cullud woman's face. En jes' then my sister she call out, 'Come here, you Ma'y Elizabeth,' en that old man stopped, en he looked at me en he looked at me, en he ses to me, 'Chile, is yo' name Ma'y Elizabeth?'

"You know, Mis' Pierson, I thought he wus jes' bein' fresh, en I ain't paid no 'tention to 'im. I ain't sed nuthin' ontel he spoke to me three or four times, en then I ses to 'im, 'Go 'way fum here, man, you ain't got no call to be fresh with me. I'm a decent woman. You'd oughta be ashamed of yoreself, an ole man like you.'"

Mary Elizabeth stopped and looked hard at the back of her poor wrinkled hands.

"En he says to me, 'Daughter,' he ses, jes' like that, 'daughter,' he ses, 'hones' I ain't bein' fresh. Is yo' name shore enough Ma'y Elizabeth?'

"En I tole him, 'Yas'r.'

"'Chile,' he ses, 'whar is yo' daddy?'

"'Ain't got no daddy,' I tole him peart-like. 'They done tuk 'im away fum me twenty-six years ago, I wusn't but a mite of a baby. Sol' 'im down the river. My mother often talks about it.' And, oh, Mis' Pierson, you shoulda see the glory come into his face!

"'Yore mother!' he ses, kinda out of breath, 'yore mother! Ma'y Elizabeth, whar is your mother?'

"'Back thar on the stoop,' I tole 'im. 'Why, did you know my daddy?'

"But he didn't pay no 'tention to me, jes' turned and walked up the stoop whar mamma wus settin'! She was feelin' sorta porely that day. En you oughta see me steppin' erlong after 'im.

"He walked right up to her and giv' her one look. 'Oh, Maggie,' he shout out, 'oh, Maggie! Ain't you know me? Maggie, ain't you know me?'

"Mamma look at 'im and riz up outa her cheer. 'Who're you?' she ses kinda trimbly, 'callin' me Maggie thata way? Who're you?'

"He went up real close to her, then, 'Maggie,' he ses jes' like that, kinda sad 'n tender, 'Maggie!' And hel' out his arms.

"She walked right into them. 'Oh,' she ses, 'it's Cassius! It's Cassius! It's my husban' come back to me! It's Cassius!' They wus like two mad people.

"My sister Minnie and me, we jes' stood and gawped at 'em. There they wus, holding on to each other like two pitiful childrun, en he tuk her hands and kissed 'em.

"'Maggie,' he ses, 'you'll come away with me, won't you? You gona take me back, Maggie? We'll go away, you en Ma'y Elizabeth en me. Won't we, Maggie?'

"Reckon my mother clean fergot my stepfather. 'Yes, Cassius,' she ses, 'we'll go away.' And then she sees Minnie, en it all comes back to her. 'Oh, Cassius,' she ses, 'I cain't go with you, I'm married again, en this time fer real. This here gal's mine and three boys, too, and another chile comin' in November!'"

"But she went with him, Mary Elizabeth," I pleaded. "Surely she went with him after all those years. He really was her husband."

I don't know whether Mary Elizabeth meant to be sarcastic or not. "Oh, no-o-me, mamma couldn't a done that. She wus a good woman. Her ole master, whut done sol' my father down river, brung her up too religious fer that, en anyways, papa was married again, too. Had his fourth wife there in Bumpus with 'im."

The unspeakable tragedy of it!

I left her and went up to my room, and hunted out my dark-blue serge dress which I had meant to wear again that winter. But I had to give Mary Elizabeth something, so I took the dress down to her.

She was delighted with it. I could tell she was, because she used her rare and untranslatable expletive.

"Haytian!" she said. "My sister where's got a home in the country, got a dress looks somethin' like this, but it ain't as good. No-o-me. She got hers to wear at a friend's weddin'—gal she was riz up with.

Thet gal married well, too, lemme tell you; her husband's a Sunday School sup'rintender."

I told her she needn't wait for Mr. Pierson, I would put dinner on the table. So off she went in the gathering dusk, trudging bravely back to her Mr. Gales and his high silk hat.

I watched her from the window till she was out of sight. It had been such a long time since I had thought of slavery. I was born in Pennsylvania, and neither my parents nor grandparents had been slaves; otherwise I might have had the same tale to tell as Mary Elizabeth, or worse yet, Roger and I might have lived in those black days and loved and lost each other and futilely, damnably, met again like Cassius and Maggie.

Whereas it was now, and I had Roger and Roger had me.

How I loved him as I sat there in the hazy dusk. I thought of his dear, bronze perfection, his habit of swearing softly in excitement, his blessed stupidity. Just the same I didn't meet him at the door as usual, but pretended to be busy. He came rushing to me with the *Saturday Evening Post,* which is more to me than rubies. I thanked him warmly, but aloofly, if you can get that combination.

We ate dinner almost in silence for my part. But he praised everything—the cooking, the table, my appearance.

After dinner we went up to the little sitting-room. He hoped I wasn't tired—couldn't he fix the pillows for me? So!

I opened the magazine and the first thing I saw was a picture of a woman gazing in stony despair at the figure of a man disappearing around the bend of the road. It was too much. Suppose that were Roger and I! I'm afraid I sniffled. He was at my side in a moment.

"Dear loveliest! Don't cry. It was all my fault. You aren't any worse about coffee than I am about cards! And anyway, I needn't have slammed the door! Forgive me, Sally. I always told you I was hard to get along with. I've had a horrible day—don't stay cross with me, dearest."

I held him to me and sobbed outright on his shoulder. "It isn't you, Roger," I told him, "I'm crying about Mary Elizabeth."

I regret to say he let me go then, so great was his dismay. Roger will never be half the diplomat that Mary Elizabeth is.

"Holy smokes!" he groaned. "She isn't going to leave us for good, is she?"

So then I told him about Maggie and Cassius. "And oh, Roger," I ended futilely, "to think that they had to separate after all those years, when he had come back, old and with whiskers!" I didn't mean to be so banal, but I was crying too hard to be coherent.

Roger had got up and was walking the floor, but he stopped then aghast.

"Whiskers!" he moaned. "My hat! Isn't that just like a woman?" He had to clear his throat once or twice before he could go on, and I think he wiped his eyes.

"Wasn't it the—" I really can't say what Roger said here—"wasn't it the darndest hard luck that when he did find her again, she should be married? She might have waited."

I stared at him astounded. "But, Roger," I reminded him, "he had married three other times, he didn't wait."

"Oh—!" said Roger, unquotably, "married three fiddlesticks! He only did that to try to forget her."

Then he came over and knelt beside me again. "Darling, I do think it is a sensible thing for a poor woman to learn how to cook, but I don't care as long as you love me and we are together. Dear loveliest, if I had been Cassius,"—he caught my hands so tight that he hurt them, "—and I had married fifty times and had come back and found you married to someone else, I'd have killed you, killed you."

Well, he wasn't logical, but he was certainly convincing.

So thus, and not otherwise, Mary Elizabeth healed the breach.

# THE GAY OLD DOG

## Edna Ferber

THOSE OF YOU who have dwelt—or even lingered—in Chicago, Illinois (this is not a humorous story), are familiar with the region known as the Loop. For those others of you to whom Chicago is a transfer point between New York and San Francisco there is presented this brief explanation:

The Loop is a clamorous, smoke-infested district embraced by the iron arms of the elevated tracks. In a city boasting fewer millions, it would be known familiarly as downtown. From Congress to Lake Street, from Wabash almost to the river, those thunderous tracks make a complete circle, or loop. Within it lie the retail shops, the commercial hotels, the theaters, the restaurants. It is the Fifth Avenue (diluted) and the Broadway (deleted) of Chicago. And he who frequents it by night in search of amusement and cheer is known, vulgarly, as a loop-hound.

Jo Hertz was a loop-hound. On the occasion of those sparse first nights granted the metropolis of the Middle West he was always present, third row, aisle, left. When a new loop cafe was opened, Jo's table always commanded an unobstructed view of anything worth viewing. On entering he was wont to say, "Hello, Gus," with careless cordiality to the head-waiter, the while his eye roved expertly from table to table as he removed his gloves. He ordered things under glass, so that his table, at midnight or thereabouts, resembled a hotbed that favors the bell system. The waiters fought for him. He was the kind of man who mixes his own salad dressing. He liked to call for a bowl, some cracked ice, lemon, garlic, paprika, salt, pepper, vinegar and oil, and make a rite of it. People at nearby tables would lay down their knives and forks to watch, fascinated. The secret of it seemed to lie in using all the oil in sight and calling for more.

That was Jo—a plump and lonely bachelor of fifty. A plethoric, roving-eyed and kindly man, clutching vainly at the garments of a youth that had long slipped past him. Jo Hertz, in one of those pinch-waist belted suits and a trench coat and a little green hat, walking up Michigan Avenue of a bright winter's afternoon, trying to take the curb with a jaunty youthfulness against which everyone of his fat-encased muscles rebelled, was a sight for mirth or pity, depending on one's vision.

The gay-dog business was a late phase in the life of Jo Hertz. He had been a quite different sort of canine. The staid and harassed brother of three unwed and selfish sisters is an under dog. The tale of how Jo Hertz came to be a loop-hound should not be compressed within the limits of a short story. It should be told as are the photoplays, with frequent throw-backs and many cut-ins. To condense twenty-three years of a man's life into some five or six thousand words requires a verbal economy amounting to parsimony.

At twenty-seven Jo had been the dutiful, hard-working son (in the wholesale harness business) of a widowed and gummidging mother, who called him Joey. If you had looked close you would have seen that now and then a double wrinkle would appear between Jo's eyes—a wrinkle that had no business there at twenty-seven. Then Jo's mother died, leaving him handicapped by a death-bed promise, the three sisters and a three-story-and-basement house on Calumet Avenue. Jo's wrinkle became a fixture.

Death-bed promises should be broken as lightly as they are seriously made. The dead have no right to lay their clammy fingers upon the living.

"Joey," she had said, in her high, thin voice, "take care of the girls."

"I will, ma," Jo had choked.

"Joey," and the voice was weaker, "promise me you won't marry till the girls are all provided for." Then as Jo had hesitated, appalled: "Joey, it's my dying wish. Promise!"

"I promise, ma," he had said.

Whereupon his mother had died, comfortably, leaving him with a completely ruined life.

They were not bad-looking girls, and they had a certain style, too. That is, Stell and Eva had. Carrie, the middle one, taught school over on the West Side. In those days it took her almost two hours each way. She said the kind of costume she required should have been corrugated steel. But all three knew what was being worn, and they wore it—or fairly faithful copies of it. Eva, the housekeeping sister, had a needle knack. She could skim the State Street windows and come away with a mental photograph of every separate tuck, hem, yoke, and ribbon. Heads of departments showed her the things they kept in drawers, and she went home and reproduced them with the aid of a two–dollar–a–day seamstress. Stell, the youngest, was the beauty. They called her Babe. She wasn't really a beauty, but someone had once told her that she looked like Janice Meredith (it was when that work of fiction was at the height of its popularity). For years afterward, whenever she went to parties, she affected a single, fat curl over her right shoulder, with a rose stuck through it.

Twenty-three years ago one's sisters did not strain at the household leash, nor crave a career. Carrie taught school, and hated it. Eva kept house expertly and complainingly. Babe's profession was being the family beauty, and it took all her spare time. Eva always let her sleep until ten.

This was Jo's household, and he was the nominal head of it. But it was an empty title. The three women dominated his life. They weren't consciously selfish. If you had called them cruel they would have put you down as mad. When you are the lone brother of three sisters, it means that you must constantly be calling for, escorting, or dropping one of them somewhere. Most men of Jo's age were standing before their mirror of a Saturday night, whistling blithely and abstractedly while they discarded a blue polka–dot for a maroon tie, whipped off the maroon for a shot–silk, and at the last moment decided against the shot–silk in favor of a plain black–and–white, because she had once said she preferred quiet ties. Jo, when he should have been preening his feathers for conquest, was saying:

"Well, my God, I *am* hurrying! Give a man time, can't you? I just got home. You girls have been laying around the house all day. No wonder you're ready."

He took a certain pride in seeing his sisters well dressed, at a time when he should have been reveling in fancy waistcoats and brilliant–hued socks, according to the style of that day, and the inalienable right of any unwed male under thirty, in any day. On those rare occasions when his business necessitated an out–of–town trip, he would spend half a day floundering about the shops selecting handkerchiefs, or stockings, or feathers, or fans, or gloves for the girls. They always turned out to be the wrong kind, judging by their reception.

From Carrie, "What in the world do I want of a fan!"

"I thought you didn't have one," Jo would say.

"I haven't. I never go to dances."

Jo would pass a futile hand over the top of his head, as was his way when disturbed. "I just thought you'd like one. I thought every girl liked a fan. Just," feebly, "just to—to have."

"Oh, for pity's sake!"

And from Eva or Babe, "I've *got* silk stockings, Jo." Or, "You brought me handkerchiefs the last time."

There was something selfish in his giving, as there always is in any gift freely and joyfully made. They never suspected the exquisite pleasure it gave him to select these things; these fine, soft, silken things. There were many things about this slow-going, amiable brother of theirs that they never suspected. If you had told them he was a dreamer of dreams, for example, they would have been amused. Sometimes, dead-tired by nine o'clock, after a hard day downtown, he would doze over the evening paper. At intervals he would wake, red-eyed, to a snatch of conversation such as, "Yes, but if you get a blue you can wear it anywhere. It's dressy, and at the same time it's quiet, too." Eva, the expert, wrestling with Carrie over the problem of the new spring dress. They never guessed that the commonplace man in the frayed old smoking-jacket had banished them all from the room long ago; had banished himself, for that matter. In his place was a tall, debonair, and rather dangerously handsome man to whom six o'clock spelled evening clothes. The kind of a man who can lean up against a mantel, or propose a toast, or give an order to a man-servant, or whisper a gallant speech in a lady's ear with equal ease. The shabby old house on Calumet Avenue was transformed into a brocaded and chandeliered rendezvous for the brilliance of the city. Beauty was there, and wit. But none so beautiful and witty as She. Mrs.—er—Jo Hertz. There was wine, of course; but no vulgar display. There was music; the soft sheen of satin; laughter. And he the gracious, tactful host, king of his own domain—

"Jo, for heaven's sake, if you're going to snore go to bed!"

"Why—did I fall asleep?"

"You haven't been doing anything else all evening. A person would think you were fifty instead of thirty."

And Jo Hertz was again just the dull, gray, common-place brother of three well-meaning sisters.

Babe used to say petulantly, "Jo, why don't you ever bring home any of your men friends? A girl might as well not have any brother, all the good you do."

Jo, conscience-stricken, did his best to make amends. But a man who has been petticoat-ridden for years loses the knack, somehow, of comradeship with men. He acquires, too, a knowledge of women, and a distaste for them, equaled only, perhaps, by that of an elevator-starter in a department store.

Which brings us to one Sunday in May. Jo came home from a late Sunday afternoon walk to find company for supper. Carrie often had in one of her schoolteacher friends, or Babe one of her frivolous intimates, or even Eva a staid guest of the old-girl type. There was always a Sunday night supper of potato salad, and cold meat, and coffee, and perhaps a fresh cake. Jo rather enjoyed it, being a hospitable soul. But he regarded the guests with the undazzled eyes of a man to whom they were just so many petticoats, timid of the night streets and requiring escort home. If you had suggested to him that some of his sisters' popularity was due to his own presence, or if you had hinted that the more kittenish of these visitors were palpably making eyes at him, he would have stared in amazement and unbelief.

This Sunday night it turned out to be one of Carrie's friends.

"Emily," said Carrie, "this is my brother, Jo."

Jo had learned what to expect in Carrie's friends. Drab-looking women in the late thirties, whose facial lines all slanted downward.

"Happy to meet you," said Jo, and looked down at a different sort altogether. A most surprisingly different sort, for one of Carrie's friends. This Emily person was very small, and fluffy, and blue-eyed, and sort of—well, crinkly looking. You know. The corners of her mouth when she smiled, and her eyes when she looked up at you, and her hair, which was brown, but had the miraculous effect, somehow, of being golden.

Jo shook hands with her. Her hand was incredibly small, and soft, so that you were afraid of crushing it, until you discovered she had a firm little grip all her own. It surprised and amused you, that grip, as does a baby's unexpected clutch on your patronizing forefinger. As Jo felt it in his own big clasp, the strangest thing happened to him. Something inside Jo Hertz stopped working for a moment, then lurched sickeningly, then thumped like mad. It was his heart. He stood staring down at her, and she up at him, until the others laughed. Then their hands fell apart, lingeringly.

"Are you a school-teacher, Emily?" he said.

"Kindergarten. It's my first year. And don't call me Emily, please."

"Why not? It's your name. I think it's the prettiest name in the world." Which he hadn't meant to say at all. In fact, he was perfectly aghast to find himself saying it. But he meant it.

At supper he passed her things, and stared, until everybody laughed again, and Eva said acidly, "Why don't you feed her?"

It wasn't that Emily had an air of helplessness. She just made you feel you wanted her to be helpless, so that you could help her.

Jo took her home, and from that Sunday night he began to strain at the leash. He took his sisters out, dutifully, but he would suggest, with a carelessness that deceived no one, "Don't you want one of your girl friends to come along? That little What's-her-name—Emily, or something. So long's I've got three of you, I might as well have a full squad."

For a long time he didn't know what was the matter with him. He only knew he was miserable, and yet happy. Sometimes his heart seemed to ache with an actual physical ache. He realized that he wanted to do things for Emily. He wanted to buy things for Emily— useless, pretty, expensive things that he couldn't afford. He wanted to buy everything that Emily needed, and everything that Emily desired. He wanted to marry Emily. That was it. He discovered that one day, with a shock, in the midst of a transaction in the harness business. He stared at the man with whom he was dealing until that startled person grew uncomfortable.

"What's the matter, Hertz?"

"Matter?"

"You look as if you'd seen a ghost or found a gold mine. I don't know which."

"Gold mine," said Jo. And then, "No. Ghost."

For he remembered that high, thin voice, and his promise. And the harness business was slithering downhill with dreadful rapidity, as the automobile business began its amazing climb. Jo tried to stop it. But he was not that kind of business man. It never occurred to him to jump out of the down-going vehicle and catch the up-going one. He stayed on, vainly applying brakes that refused to work.

"You know, Emily, I couldn't support two households now. Not the way things are. But if you'll wait. If you'll only wait. The girls might—that is, Babe and Carrie—"

She was a sensible little thing, Emily. "Of course I'll wait. But we mustn't just sit back and let the years go by. We've got to help."

She went about it as if she were already a little matchmaking matron. She corraled all the men she had ever known and introduced them to Babe, Carrie, and Eva separately, in pairs, and en masse. She arranged parties at which Babe could display the curl. She got up picnics. She stayed home while Jo took the three about. When she was present she tried to look as plain and obscure as possible, so that the sisters should show up to advantage. She schemed, and planned, and contrived, and hoped; and smiled into Jo's despairing eyes.

And three years went by. Three precious years. Carrie still taught school, and hated it. Eva kept house, more and more complainingly as prices advanced and allowance retreated. Stell was still Babe, the family beauty; but even she knew that the time was past for curls. Emily's hair, somehow, lost its glint and began to look just plain brown. Her crinkliness began to iron out.

"Now, look here!" Jo argued, desperately, one night. "We could be happy, anyway. There's plenty of room at the house. Lots of people begin that way. Of course, I couldn't give you all I'd like to at first. But maybe, after a while—"

No dreams of salons, and brocade, and velvet-footed servitors, and satin damask now. Just two rooms, all their own, all alone, and Emily to work for. That was his dream. But it seemed less possible than that other absurd one had been.

You know that Emily was as practical a little thing as she looked fluffy. She knew women. Especially did she know Eva, and Carrie, and Babe. She tried to imagine herself taking the household affairs and the housekeeping pocketbook out of Eva's expert hands. Eva had once displayed to her a sheaf of aigrettes she had bought with what she saved out of the housekeeping money. So then she tried to picture herself allowing the reins of Jo's house to remain in Eva's hands. And everything feminine and normal in her rebelled. Emily knew she'd want to put away her own freshly laundered linen, and smooth it, and pat it. She was that kind of woman. She knew she'd want to do her own delightful haggling with butcher and vegetable peddler. She knew she'd want to muss Jo's hair, and sit on his knee, and even quarrel with him, if necessary, without the awareness of three ever-present pairs of maiden eyes and ears.

"No! No! We'd only be miserable. I know. Even if they didn't object. And they would, Jo. Wouldn't they?"

His silence was miserable assent. Then, "But you do love me, don't you, Emily?"

"I do, Jo. I love you—and love you—and love you. But, Jo, I—can't."

"I know it, dear. I knew it all the time, really. I just thought, maybe, somehow—"

The two sat staring for a moment into space, their hands clasped. Then they both shut their eyes, with a little shudder, as though what they saw was terrible to look upon. Emily's hand, the tiny hand that was so unexpectedly firm, tightened its hold on his, and his crushed the absurd fingers until she winced with pain.

That was the beginning of the end, and they knew it.

Emily wasn't the kind of girl who would be left to pine. There are too many Jo's in the world whose hearts are prone to lurch and then thump at the feel of a soft, fluttering, incredibly small hand in their grip. One year later Emily was married to a young man whose father owned a large, pie-shaped slice of the prosperous state of Michigan.

That being safely accomplished, there was something grimly humorous in the trend taken by affairs in the old house on Calumet. For Eva married. Of all people, Eva! Married well, too, though he was a great deal older than she. She went off in a hat she had copied from a French model at Fields's, and a suit she had contrived with a home dressmaker, aided by pressing on the part of the little tailor in the basement over on Thirty-first Street. It was the last of that, though. The next time they saw her, she had on a hat that even she would have despaired of copying, and a suit that sort of melted into your gaze. She moved to the North Side (trust Eva for that), and Babe assumed the management of the household on Calumet Avenue. It was rather a pinched little household now, for the harness business shrank and shrank.

"I don't see how you can expect me to keep house decently on this!" Babe would say contemptuously. Babe's nose, always a little inclined to sharpness, had whittled down to a point of late. "If you knew what Ben gives Eva."

"It's the best I can do, Sis. Business is something rotten."

"Ben says if you had the least bit of—" Ben was Eva's husband, and quotable, as are all successful men.

"I don't care what Ben says," shouted Jo, goaded into rage. "I'm sick of your everlasting Ben. Go and get a Ben of your own, why don't you, if you're so stuck on the way he does things."

And Babe did. She made a last desperate drive, aided by Eva, and she captured a rather surprised young man in the brokerage way, who had made up his mind not to marry for years and years. Eva wanted to give her her wedding things, but at that Jo broke into sudden rebellion.

"No, sir! No Ben is going to buy my sister's wedding clothes, understand? I guess I'm not broke—yet. I'll furnish the money for her things, and there'll be enough of them, too."

Babe had as useless a trousseau, and as filled with extravagant pink-and-blue and lacy and frilly things as any daughter of doting parents. Jo seemed to find a grim pleasure in providing them. But it left him pretty well pinched. After Babe's marriage (she insisted that they call her Estelle now) Jo sold the house on Calumet. He and Carrie took one of those little flats that were springing up, seemingly over night, all through Chicago's South Side.

There was nothing domestic about Carrie. She had given up teaching two years before, and had gone into Social Service work on the West Side. She had what is known as a legal mind, hard, clear, orderly, and she made a great success of it. Her dream was to live at the Settlement House and give all her time to the work. Upon the little household she bestowed a certain amount of grim, capable attention. It was the same kind of attention she would have given a piece of machinery whose oiling and running had been entrusted to her care. She hated it, and didn't hesitate to say so.

Jo took to prowling about department store basements, and household goods sections. He was always sending home a bargain in a ham, or a sack of potatoes, or fifty pounds of sugar, or a window clamp, or a new kind of paring knife. He was forever doing odd little jobs that the janitor should have done. It was the domestic in him claiming its own.

Then, one night, Carrie came home with a dull glow in her leathery cheeks, and her eyes alight with resolve. They had what she called a plain talk.

"Listen, Jo. They've offered me the job of first assistant resident worker. And I'm going to take it. Take it! I know fifty other girls who'd give their ears for it. I go in next month."

They were at dinner. Jo looked up from his plate, dully. Then he glanced around the little dining-room, with its ugly tan walls and its heavy dark furniture (the Calumet Street pieces fitted cumbersomely into the five-room flat).

"Away? Away from here, you mean—to live?"

Carrie laid down her fork. "Well, really, Jo! After all that explanation."

"But to go over there to live! Why, that neighborhood's full of dirt, and disease, and crime, and the Lord knows what all. I can't let you do that, Carrie."

Carrie's chin came up. She laughed a short little laugh. "Let me! That's eighteenth-century talk, Jo. My life's my own to live. I'm going."

And she went. Jo stayed on in the apartment until the lease was up. Then he sold what furniture he could, stored or gave away the rest, and took a room on Michigan Avenue in one of the old stone mansions whose decayed splendor was being put to such purpose.

Jo Hertz was his own master. Free to marry. Free to come and go. And he found he didn't even think of marrying. He didn't even want to come or go, particularly. A rather frumpy old bachelor, with thinning hair and a thickening neck. Much has been written about the unwed, middle-aged woman; her fussiness, her primness, her angularity of mind and body. In the male that same fussiness develops, and a certain primness, too. But he grows flabby where she grows lean.

Every Thursday evening he took dinner at Eva's, and on Sunday noon at Stell's. He tucked his napkin under his chin and openly enjoyed the home-made soup and the well-cooked meats. After dinner he tried to talk business with Eva's husband, or Stell's. His business talks were the old-fashioned kind, beginning:

"Well, now, looka here. Take, f'rinstance your raw hides and leathers."

But Ben and George didn't want to take f'rinstance your raw hides and leathers. They wanted, when they took anything at all, to take golf, or politics, or stocks. They were the modern type of business man who prefers to leave his work out of his play. Business, with them, was a profession—a finely graded and balanced thing, differing from Jo's clumsy, downhill style as completely as does the method of a great criminal detective differ from that of a village constable. They would listen, restively, and say, "Uh-uh," at intervals, and at the first chance they would sort of fade out of the room, with a meaning glance at their wives. Eva had two children now. Girls. They treated Uncle Jo with good-natured tolerance. Stell had no children. Uncle Jo degenerated, by almost imperceptible degrees, from the position of honored guest, who is served with white meat, to that of one who is content with a leg and one of those obscure and bony sections which, after much turning with a bewildered and investigating knife and fork, leave one baffled and unsatisfied.

Eva and Stell got together and decided that Jo ought to marry.

"It isn't natural," Eva told him. "I never saw a man who took so little interest in women."

"Me!" protested Jo, almost shyly. "Women!"

"Yes. Of course. You act like a frightened school boy."

So they had in for dinner certain friends and acquaintances of fitting age. They spoke of them as "splendid girls." Between thirty-six and forty. They talked awfully well, in a firm, clear way, about civics, and classes, and politics, and economics, and boards. They rather terrified Jo. He didn't understand much that they talked about, and he felt humbly inferior, and yet a little resentful, as if something had passed him by. He escorted them home, dutifully, though they told him not to bother, and they evidently meant it. They seemed capable, not only of going home quite unattended, but of delivering a pointed lecture to any highwayman or brawler who might molest them.

The following Thursday Eva would say, "How did you like her, Jo?"

"Like who?" Jo would spar feebly.

"Miss Matthews."

"Who's she?"

"Now, don't be funny, Jo. You know very well I mean the girl who was here for dinner. The one who talked so well on the emigration question."

"Oh, her! Why, I liked her, all right. Seems to be a smart woman."

"Smart! She's a perfectly splendid girl."

"Sure," Jo would agree cheerfully.

"But didn't you like her?"

"I can't say I did, Eve. And I can't say I didn't. She made me think a lot of a teacher I had in the fifth reader. Name of Himes. As I recall her, she must have been a fine woman. But I never thought of her as a woman at all. She was just Teacher."

"You make me tired," snapped Eva impatiently. "A man of your age. You don't expect to marry a girl, do you? A child!"

"I don't expect to marry anybody," Jo had answered.

And that was the truth, lonely though he often was.

The following year Eva moved to Winnetka. Anyone who got the meaning of the Loop knows the significance of a move to a north shore suburb, and a house. Eva's daughter, Ethel, was growing up, and her mother had an eye on society.

That did away with Jo's Thursday dinner. Then Stell's husband bought a car. They went out into the country every Sunday. Stell said it was getting so that maids objected to Sunday dinners, anyway. Besides, they were unhealthy, old-fashioned things. They always meant to ask Jo to come along, but by the time their friends were placed, and the lunch, and the boxes, and sweaters, and George's camera, and everything, there seemed to be no room for a man of Jo's bulk. So that eliminated the Sunday dinners.

"Just drop in any time during the week," Stell said, "for dinner. Except Wednesday—that's our bridge night—and Saturday. And, of course, Thursday. Cook is out that night. Don't wait for me to 'phone."

And so Jo drifted into that sad-eyed, dyspeptic family made up of those you see dining in second-rate restaurants, their paper propped up against the bowl of oyster crackers, munching solemnly and with indifference to the stare of the passer-by surveying them through the brazen plate-glass window.

And then came the War. The war that spelled death and destruction to millions. The war that brought a fortune to Jo Hertz, and transformed him, over night, from a baggy-kneed old bachelor whose business was a failure to a prosperous manufacturer whose only trouble was the shortage in hides for the making of his product— leather! The armies of Europe called for it. Harnesses! More harnesses! Straps! Millions of straps! More! More!

The musty old harness business over on Lake Street was magically changed from a dust-covered, dead-alive concern to an orderly hive that hummed and glittered with success. Orders poured in. Jo Hertz had inside information on the War. He knew about troops and horses. He talked with French and English and Italian buyers—noblemen, many of them—commissioned by their countries to get American-made supplies. And now, when he said to Ben or George, "Take f'rinstance your raw hides and leathers," they listened with respectful attention.

And then began the gay dog business in the life of Jo Hertz. He developed into a loop-hound, ever keen on the scent of fresh plea-sure. That side of Jo Hertz which had been repressed and crushed and ignored began to bloom, unhealthily. At first he spent money on his rather contemptuous nieces. He sent them gorgeous fans, and watch bracelets, and velvet bags. He took two expensive rooms at a downtown hotel, and there was something more tear-compelling than grotesque about the way he gloated over the luxury of a separate ice-water tap in the bathroom. He explained it.

"Just turn it on. Ice-water! Any hour of the day or night."

He bought a car. Naturally. A glittering affair; in color a bright blue, with pale-blue leather straps and a great deal of gold fittings and wire wheels. Eva said it was the kind of a thing a soubrette would use, rather than an elderly business man. You saw him driving about in it, red-faced and rather awkward at the wheel. You saw him, too, in the Pompeiian room at the Congress Hotel of a Saturday afternoon when doubtful and roving-eyed matrons in kolinsky capes are wont to congregate to sip pale amber drinks. Actors grew to recognize the semi-bald head and the shining, round, good-natured face looming out at them from the dim well of the parquet, and sometimes, in a musical show, they directed a quip at him, and he liked it. He could pick out the critics as they came down the aisle, and even had a nodding acquaintance with two of them.

"Kelly, of the *Herald*," he would say carelessly. "Bean, of the *Trib*. They're all afraid of him."

So he frolicked, ponderously. In New York he might have been called a Man About Town.

And he was lonesome. He was very lonesome. So he searched about in his mind and brought from the dim past the memory of the luxuriously furnished establishment of which he used to dream in the evenings when he dozed over his paper in the old house on Calumet. So he rented an apartment, many-roomed and expensive, with a man-servant in charge, and furnished it in styles and periods ranging through all the Louis. The living room was mostly rose color. It was like an unhealthy and bloated boudoir. And yet there was nothing sybaritic or uncleanly in the sight of this paunchy, middle-aged man sinking into the rosy-cushioned luxury of his ridiculous home. It was a frank and naive indulgence of long-starved senses, and there was in it a great resemblance to the rolling-eyed ecstasy of a school-boy smacking his lips over an all-day sucker.

The War went on, and on, and on. And the money continued to roll in—a flood of it. Then, one afternoon, Eva, in town on shopping bent, entered a small, exclusive, and expensive shop on Michigan Avenue. Exclusive, that is, in price. Eva's weakness, you may remember, was hats. She was seeking a hat now. She described what she sought with a languid conciseness, and stood looking about her after the saleswoman had vanished in quest of it. The room was becomingly rose-illumined and somewhat dim, so that some minutes had passed before she realized that a man seated on a raspberry brocade settee not five feet away—a man with a walking stick, and yellow gloves, and tan spats, and a check suit—was her brother Jo. From him Eva's wild-eyed glance leaped to the woman who was trying on hats before one of the many long mirrors. She was seated, and a saleswoman was exclaiming discreetly at her elbow.

Eva turned sharply and encountered her own saleswoman returning, hat-laden. "Not today," she gasped. "I'm feeling ill. Suddenly." And almost ran from the room.

That evening she told Stell, relating her news in that telephone pidgin-English devised by every family of married sisters as protection against the neighbors and Central. Translated, it ran thus:

"He looked straight at me. My dear, I thought I'd die! But at least he had sense enough not to speak. She was one of those limp, willowy creatures with the greediest eyes that she tried to keep softened to a baby stare, and couldn't, she was so crazy to get her hands on those hats. I saw it all in one awful minute. You know the way I do. I suppose some people would call her pretty. I don't. And her color! Well! And the most expensive-looking hats. Aigrettes, and paradise, and feathers. Not one of them under seventy-five. Isn't it disgusting! At his age! Suppose Ethel had been with me!"

The next time it was Stell who saw them. In a restaurant. She said it spoiled her evening. And the third time it was Ethel. She was one of the guests at a theater party given by Nicky Overton II. You know. The North Shore Overtons. Lake Forest. They came in late, and occupied the entire third row at the opening performance of "Believe Me!" And Ethel was Nicky's partner. She was glowing like a rose. When the lights went up after the first act Ethel saw that her uncle Jo was seated just ahead of her with what she afterward described as a Blonde. Then her uncle had turned around, and seeing her, had been surprised into a smile that spread genially all over his plump arid rubicund face. Then he had turned to face forward again, quickly.

"Who's the old bird?" Nicky had asked. Ethel had pretended not to hear, so he had asked again.

"My uncle," Ethel answered, and flushed all over her delicate face, and down to her throat. Nicky had looked at the Blonde, and his eyebrows had gone up ever so slightly.

It spoiled Ethel's evening. More than that, as she told her mother of it later, weeping, she declared it had spoiled her life.

Ethel talked it over with her husband in that intimate, kimonoed hour that precedes bedtime. She gesticulated heatedly with her hair brush.

"It's disgusting, that's what it is. Perfectly disgusting. There's no fool like an old fool. Imagine! A creature like that. At his time of life."

There exists a strange and loyal kinship among men. "Well, I don't know," Ben said now, and even grinned a little. "I suppose a boy's got to sow his wild oats some time."

"Don't be any more vulgar than you can help," Eva retorted. "And I think you know, as well as I, what it means to have that Overton boy interested in Ethel."

"If he's interested in her," Ben blundered, "I guess the fact that Ethel's uncle went to the theater with someone who wasn't Ethel's aunt won't cause a shudder to run up and down his frail young frame, will it?"

"All right," Eva had retorted. "If you're not man enough to stop it, I'll have to, that's all. I'm going up there with Stell this week."

They did not notify Jo of their coming. Eva telephoned his apartment when she knew he would be out, and asked his man if he expected his master home to dinner that evening. The man had said yes. Eva arranged to meet Stell in town. They would drive to Jo's apartment together, and wait for him there.

When she reached the city Eva found turmoil there. The first of the American troops to be sent to France were leaving. Michigan Boulevard was a billowing, surging mass: Flags, pennants, bands, crowds. All the elements that make for demonstration. And over the whole—quiet. No holiday crowd, this. A solid, determined mass of people waiting patient hours to see the khaki-clads go by. Three years of indefatigable reading had brought them to a clear knowledge of what these boys were going to.

"Isn't it dreadful!" Stell gasped.

"Nicky Overton's only nineteen, thank goodness."

Their car was caught in the jam. When they moved at all it was by inches. When at last they reached Jo's apartment they were flushed, nervous, apprehensive. But he had not yet come in. So they waited.

No, they were not staying to dinner with their brother, they told the relieved houseman. Jo's home has already been described to you. Stell and Eva, sunk in rose-colored cushions, viewed it with disgust, and some mirth. They rather avoided each other's eyes.

"Carrie ought to be here," Eva said. They both smiled at the thought of the austere Carrie in the midst of those rosy cushions, and hangings, and lamps. Stell rose and began to walk about, restlessly. She picked up a vase and laid it down; straightened a picture. Eva got up, too, and wandered into the hall. She stood there a moment, listening. Then she turned and passed into Jo's bedroom. And there you knew Jo for what he was.

This room was as bare as the other had been ornate. It was Jo, the clean-minded and simple-hearted, in revolt against the cloying luxury

with which he had surrounded himself. The bedroom, of all rooms
in any house, reflects the personality of its occupant. True, the actual
furniture was paneled, cupid-surmounted, and ridiculous. It had been
the fruit of Jo's first orgy of the senses. But now it stood out in that
stark little room with an air as incongruous and ashamed as that of a
pink tarleton danseuse who finds herself in a monk's cell. None of
those wall-pictures with which bachelor bedrooms are reputed to be
hung. No satin slippers. No scented notes. Two plain-backed military
brushes on the chiffonier (and he so nearly hairless!). A little orderly
stack of books on the table near the bed. Eva fingered their titles and
gave a little gasp. One of them was on gardening. "Well, of all things!"
exclaimed Stell. A book on the War, by an Englishman. A detective
story of the lurid type that lulls us to sleep. His shoes ranged in a
careful row in the closet, with shoe-trees in everyone of them. There
was something speaking about them. They looked so human. Eva
shut the door on them, quickly. Some bottles on the dresser. A jar
of pomade. An ointment such as a man uses who is growing bald
and is panic-stricken too late. An insurance calendar on the wall.
Some rhubarb-and-soda mixture on the shelf in the bathroom, and
a little box of pepsin tablets.

"Eats all kinds of things at all hours of the night," Eva said, and
wandered out into the rose-colored front room again with the air of
one who is chagrined at her failure to find what she has sought. Stell
followed her, furtively.

"Where do you suppose he can be?" she demanded. "It's—" she
glanced at her wrist, "why, it's after six!"

And then there was a little click. The two women sat up, tense.
The door opened. Jo came in. He blinked a little. The two women
in the rosy room stood up.

"Why—Eve! Why, Babe! Well! Why didn't you let me know?"

"We were just about to leave. We thought you weren't coming
home."

Jo came in, slowly. "I was in the jam on Michigan, watching the
boys go by." He sat down, heavily. The light from the window fell
on him. And you saw that his eyes were red.

And you'll have to learn why. He had found himself one of the
thousands in the jam on Michigan Avenue, as he said. He had a place
near the curb, where his big frame shut off the view of the unfortunates
behind him. He waited with the placid interest of one who has
subscribed to all the funds and societies to which a prosperous,
middle-aged business man is called upon to subscribe in war time.

Then, just as he was about to leave, impatient at the delay, the crowd had cried, with a queer dramatic, exultant note in its voice, "Here they come! Here come the boys!"

Just at that moment two little, futile, frenzied fists began to beat a mad tattoo on Jo Hertz's broad back. Jo tried to turn in the crowd, all indignant resentment. "Say, looka here!"

The little fists kept up their frantic beating and pushing. And a voice—a choked, high little voice—cried, "Let me by! I can't see! You man, you! You big fat man! My boy's going by—to war—and I can't see! Let me by!"

Jo scrooged around, still keeping his place. He looked down. And upturned to him in agonized appeal was the face of little Emily. They stared at each other for what seemed a long, long time. It was really only the fraction of a second. Then Jo put one great arm firmly around Emily's waist and swung her around in front of him. His great bulk protected her. Emily was clinging to his hand. She was breathing rapidly, as if she had been running. Her eyes were straining up the street.

"Why, Emily, how in the world!—"

"I ran away. Fred didn't want me to come. He said it would excite me too much."

"Fred?"

"My husband. He made me promise to say good-bye to Jo at home."

"Jo?"

"Jo's my boy. And he's going to war. So I ran away. I had to see him. I had to see him go."

She was dry-eyed. Her gaze was straining up the street.

"Why, sure," said Jo. "Of course you want to see him." And then the crowd gave a great roar. There came over Jo a feeling of weakness. He was trembling. The boys went marching by.

"There he is," Emily shrilled, above the din. "There he is! There he is! There he—" And waved a futile little hand. It wasn't so much a wave as a clutching. A clutching after something beyond her reach.

"Which one? Which one, Emily?"

"The handsomeone. The handsomeone. There!" Her voice quavered and died.

Jo put a steady hand on her shoulder. "Point him out," he commanded. "Show me." And the next instant. "Never mind. I see him."

Somehow, miraculously, he had picked him from among the hundreds. Had picked him as surely as his own father might have. It was Emily's boy. He was marching by, rather stiffly. He was nineteen, and fun-loving, and he had a girl, and he didn't particularly want to go to France and—to go to France. But more than he had hated going, he had hated not to go. So he marched by, looking straight ahead, his jaw set so that his chin stuck out just a little. Emily's boy.

Jo looked at him, and his face flushed purple. His eyes, the hard-boiled eyes of a loop-hound, took on the look of a sad old man. And suddenly he was no longer Jo, the sport; old J. Hertz, the gay dog. He was Jo Hertz, thirty, in love with life, in love with Emily, and with the stinging blood of young manhood coursing through his veins.

Another minute and the boy had passed on up the broad street—the fine, flag-bedecked street—just one of a hundred service-hats bobbing in rhythmic motion like sandy waves lapping a shore and flowing on.

Then he disappeared altogether.

Emily was clinging to Jo. She was mumbling something over and over. "I can't. I can't. Don't ask me to. I can't let him go. Like that. I can't."

Jo said a queer thing.

"Why, Emily! We wouldn't have him stay home, would we? We wouldn't want him to do anything different, would we? Not our boy. I'm glad he volunteered. I'm proud of him. So are you, glad."

Little by little he quieted her. He took her to the car that was waiting, a worried chauffeur in charge. They said good-bye, awkwardly. Emily's face was a red, swollen mass.

So it was that when Jo entered his own hallway half an hour later he blinked, dazedly, and when the light from the window fell on him you saw that his eyes were red.

Eva was not one to beat about the bush. She sat forward in her chair, clutching her bag rather nervously.

"Now, look here, Jo. Stell and I are here for a reason. We're here to tell you that this thing's got to stop."

"Thing? Stop?"

"You know very well what I mean. You saw me at the milliner's that day. And night before last, Ethel. We're all disgusted. If you must go about with people like that, please have some sense of decency."

Something gathering in Jo's face should have warned her. But he was slumped down in his chair in such a huddle, and he looked so old and fat that she did not heed it. She went on. "You've got us to consider. Your sisters. And your nieces. Not to speak of your own—"

But he got to his feet then, shaking, and at what she saw in his face even Eva faltered and stopped. It wasn't at all the face of a fat, middle-aged sport. It was a face Jovian, terrible.

"You!" he began, low-voiced, ominous. "You!" He raised a great fist high. "You two murderers! You didn't consider me, twenty years ago. You come to me with talk like that. Where's my boy! You killed him, you two, twenty years ago. And now he belongs to somebody else. Where's my son that should have gone marching by today?" He flung his arms out in a great gesture of longing. The red veins stood out on his forehead. "Where's my son! Answer me that, you two selfish, miserable women. Where's my son!" Then, as they huddled together, frightened, wild eyed. "Out of my house! Out of my house! Before I hurt you!"

They fled, terrified. The door banged behind them.

Jo stood, shaking, in the center of the room. Then he reached for a chair, gropingly, and sat down. He passed one moist, flabby hand over his forehead and it came away wet. The telephone rang. He sat still. It sounded far away and unimportant, like something forgotten. I think he did not even hear it with his conscious ear. But it rang and rang insistently. Jo liked to answer his telephone when at home.

"Hello!" He knew instantly the voice at the other end.

"That you, Jo?" it said.

"Yes."

"How's my boy?"

"I'm—all right."

"Listen, Jo. The crowd's coming over tonight. I've fixed up a little poker game for you. Just eight of us."

"I can't come tonight, Gert."

"Can't! Why not?"

"I'm not feeling so good."

"You just said you were all right."

"I *am* all right. Just kind of tired."

The voice took on a cooing note. "Is my Joey tired? Then he shall be all comfy on the sofa, and he doesn't need to play if he don't want to. No, sir."

Jo stood staring at the black mouth-piece of the telephone. He was seeing a procession go marching by. Boys, hundreds of boys, in khaki.

"Hello! Hello!" the voice took on an anxious note. "Are you there?"

"Yes," wearily.

"Jo, there's something the matter. You're sick. I'm coming right over."

"No!"

"Why not? You sound as if you'd been sleeping. Look here—"

"Leave me alone!" cried Jo, suddenly, and the receiver clacked onto the hook. "Leave me alone. Leave me alone." Long after the connection had been broken.

He stood staring at the instrument with unseeing eyes. Then he turned and walked into the front room. All the light had gone out of it. Dusk had come on. All the light had gone out of everything. The zest had gone out of life. The game was over—the game he had been playing against loneliness and disappointment. And he was just a tired old man. A lonely, tired old man in a ridiculous, rose-colored room that had grown, all of a sudden, drab.

# ROAST BEEF, MEDIUM

## Edna Ferber

THERE IS A journey compared to which the travels of Bunyan's hero were a summer-evening's stroll. The Pilgrims by whom this forced march is taken belong to a maligned fraternity, and are known as traveling men. Sample-case in hand, trunk key in pocket, cigar in mouth, brown derby atilt at an angle of ninety, each young and untried traveler starts on his journey down that road which leads through morasses of chicken *à la* Creole, over greasy mountains of queen fritters made doubly perilous by slippery glaciers of rum sauce, into formidable jungles of breaded veal chops threaded by sanguine and deadly streams of tomato gravy, past sluggish mires of dreadful things *en casserole,* over hills of corned-beef hash, across shaking quagmires of veal glacé, plunging into sloughs of slaw, until, haggard, weary, digestion shattered, complexion gone, he reaches the safe haven of roast beef, medium. Once there, he never again strays, although the pompadoured, white-aproned siren sing-songs in his ear the praises of Irish stew, and pork with apple sauce.

Emma McChesney was eating her solitary supper at the Berger house at Three Rivers, Michigan. She had arrived at the Roast Beef haven many years before. She knew the digestive perils of a small town hotel dining-room as a guide on the snow-covered mountain knows each treacherous pitfall and chasm. Ten years on the road had taught her to recognize the deadly snare that lurks in the seemingly calm bosom of minced chicken with cream sauce. Not for her the impenetrable mysteries of a hamburger and onions. It had been a struggle, brief but terrible, from which Emma McChesney had emerged triumphant, her complexion and figure saved.

No more metaphor. On with the story, which left Emma at her safe and solitary supper.

She had the last number of the *Dry Goods Review* propped up against the vinegar cruet, and the Worcestershire, and the salt shaker. Between conscientious, but disinterested mouthfuls of medium roast beef, she was reading the snappy ad set forth by her firm's bitterest competitors, the Strauss Sans-silk Skirt Company. It was a good reading ad. Emma McChesney, who had forgotten more about petticoats than the average skirt salesman ever knew, presently allowed her luke-warm beef to grow cold and flabby as she read. Somewhere in her subconscious mind she realized that the lanky head waitress had placed someone opposite her at the table. Also, subconsciously, she heard him order liver and bacon, with onions. She told herself that as soon as she reached the bottom of the column she'd look up to see who the fool was. She never arrived at the column's end.

"I just hate to tear you away from that love lyric; but if I might trouble you for the vinegar—"

Emma groped for it back of her paper and shoved it across the table without looking up.

"—and the Worcester—"

One eye on the absorbing column, she passed the tall bottle. But at its removal her prop was gone. The *Dry Goods Review* was too weighty for the salt shaker alone.

"—and the salt. Thanks. Warm, isn't it?"

There was a double vertical frown between Emma McChesney's eyes as she glanced up over the top of her *Dry Goods Review*. The frown gave way to a half smile. The glance settled into a stare.

"But then, anybody would have stared. He expected it," she said, afterwards, in telling about it. "I've seen matinée idols, and tailors' supplies salesmen, and Julian Eltinge, but this boy had any male professional beauty I ever saw, looking as handsome and dashing as a bowl of cold oatmeal. And he knew it."

Now, in the ten years that she had been out representing T. A. Buck's Featherloom Petticoats, Emma McChesney had found it necessary to make a rule or two for herself. In the strict observance of one of these she had become past mistress in the fine art of congealing the warm advances of fresh and friendly salesmen of the opposite sex. But this case was different, she told herself. The man across the table was little more than a boy—an amazingly handsome, astonishingly impudent, cockily confident boy, who was staring with insolent approval at Emma McChesney's trim, shirt-waisted figure, and her fresh, attractive coloring, and her well-cared-for hair beneath the smart summer hat.

"It isn't in human nature to be as good-looking as you are," spake Emma McChesney, suddenly, being a person who never trifled with half-way measures. "I'll bet you have bad teeth, or an impediment in your speech."

The gorgeous young man smiled. His teeth were perfect. "Peter Piper picked a peck of pickled peppers," he announced, glibly. "Nothing missing there, is there?"

"Must be your morals then," retorted Emma McChesney. "My! My! And on the road! Why, the trail of bleeding hearts that you must leave all the way from Maine to California would probably make the Red Sea turn white with envy."

The Fresh Young Kid speared a piece of liver and looked soulfully up into the adoring eyes of the waitress who was hovering over him.

"Got any nice hot biscuits tonight, girlie?" he inquired.

"I'll get you some; sure," wildly promised his handmaiden, and disappeared kitchenward.

"Brand new to the road, aren't you?" observed Emma McChesney, cruelly.

"What makes you think—"

"Liver and bacon, hot biscuits, Worcestershire," elucidated she. "No old-timer would commit suicide that way. After you've been out for two or three years you'll stick to the Rock of Gibraltar—roast beef, medium. Oh, I get wild now and then, and order eggs if the girl says she knows the hen that layed 'em, but plain roast beef, unchloroformed, is the one best bet. You can't go wrong if you stick to it."

The god-like young man leaned forward, forgetting to eat.

"You don't mean to tell me you're on the road!"

"Why not?" demanded Emma McChesney, briskly.

"Oh, fie, fie!" said the handsome youth, throwing her a languishing look. "Any woman as pretty as you are, and with those eyes, and that hair, and figure—Say, Little One, what are you going to do tonight?"

Emma McChesney sugared her tea, and stirred it, slowly. Then she looked up. "Tonight, you fresh young kid, you!" she said calmly, "I'm going to dictate two letters, explaining why business was rotten last week, and why it's going to pick up next week, and then I'm going to keep an engagement with a nine-hour beauty sleep."

"Don't get sore at a fellow. You'd take pity on me if you knew how I have to work to kill an evening in one of these little town-pump burgs. Kill 'em! It can't be done. They die harder than the heroine in a ten, twenty, thirty. From supper to bedtime is twice as long as from breakfast to supper. Honest!"

But Emma McChesney looked inexorable, as women do just before they relent. Said she: "Oh, I don't know. By the time I get through trying to convince a bunch of customers that T. A. Buck's Featherloom Petticoat has every other skirt in the market looking like a piece of Fourth of July bunting that's been left out in the rain, I'm about ready to turn down the spread and leave a call for six-thirty."

"Be a good fellow," pleaded the unquenchable one. "Let's take in all the nickel shows, and then see if we can't drown our sorrows in—er—"

Emma McChesney slipped a coin under her plate, crumpled her napkin, folded her arms on the table, and regarded the boy across the way with what our best talent calls a long, level look. It was so long and so level that even the airiness of the buoyant youngster at whom it was directed began to lessen perceptibly, long before Emma began to talk.

"Tell me, young 'un, did anyone ever refuse you anything? I thought not. I should think that when you realize what you've got to learn it would scare you to look ahead. I don't expect you to believe me when I tell you I never talk to fresh guys like you, but it's true. I don't know why I'm breaking my rule for you, unless it's because you're so unbelievably good-looking that I'm anxious to know where the blemish is. The Lord don't make 'em perfect, you know. I'm going to get out those letters, and then, if it's just the same to you, we'll take a walk. These nickel shows are getting on my nerves. It seems to me that if I have to look at one more Western picture about a fool girl with her hair in a braid riding a show horse in the wilds of Clapham Junction and being rescued from a band of almost-Indians by the handsome, but despised Eastern tenderfoot, or if I see one more of those historical pictures, with the women wearing costumes that are a pass between early Egyptian and late State Street, I know I'll get hysterics and have to be carried shrieking, up the aisle. Let's walk down Main Street and look in the store windows, and up as far as the park and back."

"Great!" assented he. "Is there a park?"

"I don't know," replied Emma McChesney, "but there is. And for your own good I'm going to tell you a few things. There's more to this traveling game than just knocking down on expenses, talking to every pretty woman you meet, and learning to ask for fresh white-bread heels at the Palmer House in Chicago. I'll meet you in the lobby at eight."

Emma McChesney talked steadily, and evenly, and generously, from eight until eight-thirty. She talked from the great storehouse of practical knowledge which she had accumulated in her ten years on the road. She told the handsome young cub many things for which he should have been undyingly thankful. But when they reached the park—the cool, dim, moon-silvered park, its benches dotted with glimpses of white showing close beside a blur of black, Emma McChesney stopped talking. Not only did she stop talking, but she ceased to think of the boy seated beside her on the bench.

In the band-stand, under the arc-light, in the center of the pretty little square, some neighborhood children were playing a noisy game, with many shrill cries, and much shouting and laughter. Suddenly, from one of the houses across the way, a woman's voice was heard, even above the clamor of the children.

"Fred-dee!" called the voice. "Maybelle! Come, now."

And a boy's voice answered, as boys' voices have since Cain was a child playing in the Garden of Eden, and as boys' voices will as long as boys are:

"Aw, ma, I ain't a bit sleepy. We just begun a new game, an' I'm leader. Can't we just stay out a couple of minutes more?"

"Well, five minutes," agreed the voice. "But don't let me call you again."

Emma McChesney leaned back on the rustic bench and clasped her strong, white hands behind her head, and stared straight ahead into the soft darkness. And if it had been light you could have seen that the bitter lines showing faintly about her mouth were outweighed by the sweet and gracious light which was glowing in her eyes.

"Fred-dee!" came the voice of command again. "May-belle! This minute, now!"

One by one the flying little figures under the arc-light melted away in the direction of the commanding voice and home and bed. And Emma McChesney forgot all about fresh young kids and featherloom petticoats and discounts and bills of lading and sample-cases and grouchy buyers. After all, it had been her protecting maternal

instinct which had been aroused by the boy at supper, although she
had not known it then. She did not know it now, for that matter.
She was busy remembering just such evenings in her own life—
summer evenings, filled with the high, shrill laughter of children at
play. She too, had stood in the doorway, making a funnel of her
hands, so that her clear call through the twilight might be heard
above the cries of the boys and girls. She had known how loath the
little feet had been to leave their play, and how they had lagged up
the porch stairs, and into the house. Years, whose memory she had
tried to keep behind her, now suddenly loomed before her in the
dim quiet of the little flower-scented park.

A voice broke the silence, and sent her dream-thoughts scattering
to the winds.

"Honestly, kid," said the voice, "I could be crazy about you, if
you'd let me."

The forgotten figure beside her woke into sudden life. A strong
arm encircled her shoulders. A strong hand seized her own, which
were clasped behind her head. Two warm, eager lips were pressed
upon her lips, checking the little cry of surprise and wrath that rose
in her throat.

Emma McChesney wrenched herself free with a violent jerk,
and pushed him from her. She did not storm. She did not even
rise. She sat very quietly, breathing fast. When she turned at last to
look at the boy beside her it seemed that her white profile cut the
darkness. The man shrank a little, and would have stammered
something, but Emma McChesney checked him.

"You nasty, good-for-nothing, handsome young devil, you!" she
said. "So you're married."

He sat up with a jerk. "How did you—what makes you think so?"

"That was a married kiss—a two-year-old married kiss, at least.
No boy would get as excited as that about kissing an old stager like
me. The chances are you're out of practise. I knew that if it wasn't
teeth or impediment it must be morals. And it is."

She moved over on the bench until she was close beside him.
"Now, listen to me, boy." She leaned forward, impressively. "Are
you listening?"

"Yes," answered the handsome young devil, sullenly.

"What I've got to say to you isn't so much for your sake, as for
your wife's. I was married when I was eighteen, and stayed married
eight years. I've had my divorce ten years, and my boy is seventeen
years old. Figure it out. How old is Ann?"

"I don't believe it," he flashed back. "You're not a day over twenty-six—anyway, you don't look it. I—"

"Thanks," drawled Emma. "That's because you've never seen me in negligée. A woman's as old as she looks with her hair on the dresser and bed only a few minutes away. Do you know why I was decent to you in the first place? Because I was foolish enough to think that you reminded me of my own kid. Every fond mama is gump enough to think that every Greek god she sees looks like her own boy, even if her own happens to squint and have two teeth missing—which mine hasn't, thank the Lord! He's the greatest young—Well, now, look here, young 'un. I'm going to return good for evil. Traveling men and geniuses should never marry. But as long as you've done it, you might as well start right. If you move from this spot till I get through with you, I'll yell police and murder. Are you ready?"

"I'm dead sorry, on the square, I am—"

"Ten minutes late," interrupted Emma McChesney. "I'm dishing up a sermon, hot, for one, and you've got to choke it down. Whenever I hear a traveling man howling about his lonesome evenings, and what a dog's life it is, and no way for a man to live, I always wonder what kind of a summer picnic he thinks it is for his wife. She's really a widow seven months in the year, without any of a widow's privileges. Did you ever stop to think what she's doing evenings? No, you didn't. Well, I'll tell you. She's sitting home, night after night, probably embroidering monograms on your shirt sleeves by way of diversion. And on Saturday night, which is the night when every married woman has the inalienable right to be taken out by her husband, she can listen to the woman in the flat upstairs getting ready to go to the theater. The fact that there's a ceiling between 'em doesn't prevent her from knowing just where they're going, and why he has worked himself into a rage over his white lawn tie, and whether they're taking a taxi or the car and who they're going to meet afterward at supper. Just by listening to them coming downstairs she can tell how much Mrs. Third Flat's silk stockings cost, and if she's wearing her new La Valliere or not. Women have that instinct, you know. Or maybe you don't. There's so much you've missed."

"Say, look here—" broke from the man beside her. But Emma McChesney laid her cool fingers on his lips.

"Nothing from the side-lines, please," she said. "After they've gone she can go to bed, or she can sit up, pretending to read, but really wondering if that squeaky sound coming from the direction of the kitchen is a loose screw in the storm door, or if it's someone trying to break into the flat. And she'd rather sit there, scared green, than go back through that long hall to find out. And when Tillie comes home with her young man at eleven o'clock, though she promised not to stay out later than ten, she rushes back to the kitchen and falls on her neck, she's so happy to see her. Oh, it's a gay life. You talk about the heroism of the early Pilgrim mothers! I'd like to know what they had on the average traveling man's wife."

"Bess goes to the matinée every Saturday," he began, in feeble defense.

"Matinée!" scoffed Emma McChesney. "Do you think any woman goes to matinée by preference? Nobody goes but girls of sixteen, and confirmed old maids without brothers, and traveling men's wives. Matinée! Say, would you ever hesitate to choose between an all-day train and a sleeper? It's the same idea. What a woman calls going to the theater is something very different. It means taking a nap in the afternoon, so her eyes will be bright at night, and then starting at about five o'clock to dress, and lay her husband's clean things out on the bed. She loves it. She even enjoys getting his bath towels ready, and putting his shaving things where he can lay his hands on 'em, and telling the girl to have dinner ready promptly at six-thirty. It means getting out her good dress that hangs in the closet with a cretonne bag covering it, and her black satin coat, and her hat with the paradise aigrettes that she bought with what she saved out of the housekeeping money. It means her best silk stockings, and her diamond sunburst that he's going to have made over into a La Valliere just as soon as business is better. She loves it all, and her cheeks get pinker and pinker, so that she really doesn't need the little dash of rouge that she puts on 'because everybody does it, don't you know?' She gets ready, all but her dress, and then she puts on a kimono and slips out to the kitchen to make the gravy for the chicken because the girl never can get it as smooth as he likes it. That's part of what she calls going to the theater, and having a husband. And if there are children—"

There came a little, inarticulate sound from the boy. But Emma's quick ear caught it.

"No? Well, then, we'll call that one black mark less for you. But if there are children—and for her sake I hope there will be—she's father and mother to them. She brings them up, single-handed, while he's on the road. And the worst she can do is to say to them, 'Just wait until your father gets home. He'll hear of this.' But shucks!

When he comes home he can't whip the kids for what they did seven weeks before, and that they've forgotten all about, and for what he never saw, and can't imagine. Besides, he wants his comfort when he gets home. He says he wants a little rest and peace, and he's darned if he's going to run around evenings. Not much, he isn't! But he doesn't object to her making a special effort to cook all those little things that he's been longing for on the road. Oh, there'll be a seat in Heaven for every traveling man's wife—though at that, I'll bet most of 'em will find themselves stuck behind a post."

"You're all right!" exclaimed Emma McChesney's listener, suddenly. "How a woman like you can waste her time on the road is more than I can see. And I want to thank you. I'm not such a fool—"

"I haven't let you finish a sentence so far, and I'm not going to yet. Wait a minute. There's one more paragraph to this sermon. You remember what I told you about old stagers, and the roast beef diet? Well, that applies right through life. It's all very well to trifle with the little side-dishes at first, but there comes a time when you've got to quit fooling with the minced chicken, and the imitation lamb chops of this world, and settle down to plain, everyday, roast beef, medium. That other stuff may tickle your palate for a while, but sooner or later it will turn on you, and ruin your moral digestion. You stick to roast beef, medium. It may sound prosaic, and unimaginative and dry, but you'll find that it wears in the long run. You can take me over to the hotel now. I've lost an hour's sleep, but I don't consider it wasted. And you'll oblige me by putting the stopper on any conversation that may occur to you between here and the hotel. I've talked until I'm so low on words that I'll probably have to sell featherlooms in sign language tomorrow."

They walked to the very doors of the Berger House in silence. But at the foot of the stairs that led to the parlor floor he stopped, and looked into Emma McChesney's face. His own was rather white and tense.

"Look here," he said. "I've got to thank you. That sounds idiotic, but I guess you know what I mean. And I won't ask you to forgive a hound like me. I haven't been so ashamed of myself since I was a kid. Why, if you knew Bess—if you knew—"

"I guess I know Bess, all right. I used to be a Bess, myself. Just because I'm a traveling man it doesn't follow that I've forgotten the Bess feeling. As far as that goes, I don't mind telling you that I've got neuralgia from sitting in that park with my feet in the damp grass. I can feel it in my back teeth, and by eleven o'clock it will be camping over my left eye, with its little brothers doing a war dance up the side of my face. And, boy, I'd give last week's commissions if there was someone to whom I had the right to say: 'Henry, will you get up and get me a hot-water bag for my neuralgia? It's something awful. And just open the left-hand lower drawer of the chiffonier and get out one of those gauze vests and then get me a safety pin from the tray on my dresser. I'm going to pin it around my head.'"

# THE SMILERS

## F. Scott Fitzgerald

## I

WE ALL HAVE that exasperated moment!

There are times when you almost tell the harmless old lady next door what you really think of her face—that it ought to be on a night-nurse in a house for the blind; when you'd like to ask the man you've been waiting ten minutes for if he isn't all over-heated from racing the postman down the block; when you nearly say to the waiter that if they deducted a cent from the bill for every degree the soup was below tepid the hotel would owe you half a dollar; when—and this is the infallible earmark of true exasperation—a smile affects you as an oil-baron's undershirt affects a cow's husband.

But the moment passes. Scars may remain on your dog or your collar or your telephone receiver, but your soul has slid gently back into its place between the lower edge of your heart and the upper edge of your stomach, and all is at peace.

But the imp who turns on the shower-bath of exasperation apparently made it so hot one time in Sylvester Stockton's early youth that he never dared dash in and turn it off—in consequence no first old man in an amateur production of a Victorian comedy was ever more pricked and prodded by the daily phenomena of life than was Sylvester at thirty.

Accusing eyes behind spectacles—suggestion of a stiff neck—this will have to do for his description, since he is not the hero of this story. He is the plot. He is the factor that makes it one story instead of three stories. He makes remarks at the beginning and end.

The late afternoon sun was loitering pleasantly along Fifth Avenue when Sylvester, who had just come out of that hideous public library where he had been consulting some ghastly book, told his impossible chauffeur (it is true that I am following his movements through his own spectacles) that he wouldn't need his stupid, incompetent services any longer. Swinging his cane (which he found too short) in his left hand (which he should have cut off long ago since it was constantly offending him), he began walking slowly down the Avenue.

When Sylvester walked at night he frequently glanced behind and on both sides to see if anyone was sneaking up on him. This had become a constant mannerism. For this reason he was unable to pretend that he didn't see Betty Tearle sitting in her machine in front of Tiffany's.

Back in his early twenties he had been in love with Betty Tearle. But he had depressed her. He had misanthropically dissected every meal, motor trip and musical comedy that they attended together, and on the few occasions when she had tried to be especially nice to him—from a mother's point of view he had been rather desirable—he had suspected hidden motives and fallen into a deeper gloom than ever. Then one day she told him that she would go mad if he ever again parked his pessimism in her sun-parlour.

And ever since then she had seemed to be smiling—uselessly, insultingly, charmingly smiling.

"Hello, Sylvo," she called.

"Why—how do, Betty." He wished she wouldn't call him Sylvo—it sounded like a—like a darn monkey or something.

"How goes it?" she asked cheerfully. "Not very well, I suppose."

"Oh, yes," he answered stiffly, "I manage."

"Taking in the happy crowd?"

"Heavens, yes." He looked around him. "Betty, why are they happy? What are they smiling at? What do they find to smile at?"

Betty flashed at him a glance of radiant amusement.

"The women may smile because they have pretty teeth, Sylvo."

"You smile," continued Sylvester cynically, "because you're comfortably married and have two children. You imagine you're happy, so you suppose everyone else is."

Betty nodded.

"You may have hit it, Sylvo—" The chauffeur glanced around and she nodded at him. "Good-bye."

Sylvo watched with a pang of envy which turned suddenly to exasperation as he saw she had turned and smiled at him once more.

Then her car was out of sight in the traffic, and with a voluminous sigh he galvanized his cane into life and continued his stroll.

At the next corner he stopped in at a cigar store and there he ran into Waldron Crosby. Back in the days when Sylvester had been a prize pigeon in the eyes of debutantes he had also been a game partridge from the point of view of promoters. Crosby, then a young bond salesman, had given him much safe and sane advice and saved him many dollars. Sylvester liked Crosby as much as he could like anyone. Most people did like Crosby.

"Hello, you old bag of 'nerves,'" cried Crosby genially, "come and have a big gloom-dispelling Corona."

Sylvester regarded the cases anxiously. He knew he wasn't going to like what he bought.

"Still out at Larchmont, Waldron?" he asked.

"Right-o."

"How's your wife?"

"Never better."

"Well," said Sylvester suspiciously, "you brokers always look as if you're smiling at something up your sleeve. It must be a hilarious profession."

Crosby considered.

"Well," he admitted, "it varies—like the moon and the price of soft drinks—but it has its moments."

"Waldron," said Sylvester earnestly, "you're a friend of mine—please do me the favour of not smiling when I leave you. It seems like a—like a mockery."

A broad grin suffused Crosby's countenance.

"Why, you crabbed old son-of-a-gun!"

But Sylvester with an irate grunt had turned on his heel and disappeared.

He strolled on. The sun finished its promenade and began calling in the few stray beams it had left among the westward streets. The Avenue darkened with black bees from the department stores; the traffic swelled in to an interlaced jam; the buses were packed four deep like platforms above the thick crowd; but Sylvester, to whom the daily shift and change of the city was a matter only of sordid monotony, walked on, taking only quick sideward glances through his frowning spectacles.

He reached his hotel and was elevated to his four-room suite on the twelfth floor.

"If I dine downstairs," he thought, "the orchestra will play either 'Smile, Smile, Smile' or 'The Smiles That You Gave To Me.' But then if I go to the Club I'll meet all the cheerful people I know, and if I go somewhere else where there's no music, I won't get anything fit to eat."

He decided to have dinner in his rooms.

An hour later, after disparaging some broth, a squab and a salad, he tossed fifty cents to the room-waiter, and then held up his hand warningly.

"Just oblige me by not smiling when you say thanks?"

He was too late. The waiter had grinned.

"Now, will you please tell me," asked Sylvester peevishly, "what on earth you have to smile about?"

The waiter considered. Not being a reader of the magazines he was not sure what was characteristic of waiters, yet he supposed something characteristic was expected of him.

"Well, Mister," he answered, glancing at the ceiling with all the ingenuousness he could muster in his narrow, sallow countenance, "it's just something my face does when it sees four bits comin'."

Sylvester waved him away.

"Waiters are happy because they've never had anything better," he thought. "They haven't enough imagination to want anything."

At nine o'clock from sheer boredom he sought his expressionless bed.

## II

As Sylvester left the cigar store, Waldron Crosby followed him out, and turning off Fifth Avenue down a cross street entered a brokerage office. A plump man with nervous hands rose and hailed him.

"Hello, Waldron."

"Hello, Potter—I just dropped in to hear the worst."

The plump man frowned.

"We've just got the news," he said.

"Well, what is it? Another drop?"

"Closed at seventy-eight. Sorry, old boy."

"Whew!"

"Hit pretty hard?"

"Cleaned out!"

The plump man shook his head, indicating that life was too much for him, and turned away.

Crosby sat there for a moment without moving. Then he rose, walked into Potter's private office and picked up the phone.

"Gi'me Larchmont 838."

In a moment he had his connection.

"Mrs. Crosby there?"

A man's voice answered him.

"Yes; this you, Crosby? This is Doctor Shipman."

"Dr. Shipman?" Crosby's voice showed sudden anxiety.

"Yes—I've been trying to reach you all afternoon. The situation's changed and we expect the child tonight."

"Tonight?"

"Yes. Everything's O.K. But you'd better come right out."

"I will. Good-bye."

He hung up the receiver and started out the door, but paused as an idea struck him. He returned, and this time called a Manhattan number.

"Hello, Donny, this is Crosby."

"Hello, there, old boy. You just caught me; I was going—"

"Say, Donny, I want a job right away, quick."

"For whom?"

"For me."

"Why, what's the—"

"Never mind. Tell you later. Got one for me?"

"Why, Waldron, there's not a blessed thing here except a clerkship. Perhaps next—"

"What salary goes with the clerkship?"

"Forty—say forty-five a week."

"I've got you. I start tomorrow."

"All right. But say, old man—"

"Sorry, Donny, but I've got to run."

Crosby hurried from the brokerage office with a wave and a smile at Potter. In the street he took out a handful of small change and after surveying it critically hailed a taxi.

"Grand Central—quick!" he told the driver.

### III

At six o'clock Betty Tearle signed the letter, put it into an envelope and wrote her husband's name upon it. She went into his room and after a moment's hesitation set a black cushion on the bed and laid the white letter on it so that it could not fail to attract his attention when he came in. Then with a quick glance around the room she walked into the hall and upstairs to the nursery.

"Clare," she called softly.

"Oh, Mummy!" Clare left her doll's house and scurried to her mother.

"Where's Billy, Clare?"

Billy appeared eagerly from under the bed.

"Got anything for me?" he inquired politely.

His mother's laugh ended in a little catch and she caught both her children to her and kissed them passionately. She found that she was crying quietly and their flushed little faces seemed cool against the sudden fever racing through her blood.

"Take care of Clare—always—Billy darling—"

Billy was puzzled and rather awed.

"You're crying," he accused gravely.

"I know—I know I am—"

Clare gave a few tentative sniffles, hesitated, and then clung to her mother in a storm of weeping.

"I d-don't feel good, Mummy—I don't feel good."

Betty soothed her quietly.

"We won't cry any more, Clare dear—either of us."

But as she rose to leave the room her glance at Billy bore a mute appeal, too vain, she knew, to be registered on his childish consciousness.

Half an hour later as she carried her travelling bag to a taxi-cab at the door she raised her hand to her face in mute admission that a veil served no longer to hide her from the world.

"But I've chosen," she thought dully.

As the car turned the corner she wept again, resisting a temptation to give up and go back.

"Oh, my God!" she whispered. "What am I doing? What have I done? What have I done?"

## IV

When Jerry, the sallow, narrow-faced waiter, left Sylvester's rooms he reported to the head-waiter, and then checked out for the day.

He took the subway south and alighting at Williams Street walked a few blocks and entered a billiard parlour.

An hour later he emerged with a cigarette drooping from his bloodless lips, and stood on the sidewalk as if hesitating before making a decision. He set off eastward.

As he reached a certain corner his gait suddenly increased and then quite as suddenly slackened. He seemed to want to pass by, yet some magnetic attraction was apparently exerted on him, for with a sudden face-about he turned in at the door of a cheap restaurant—half-cabaret, half chop-suey parlour—where a miscellaneous assortment gathered nightly.

Jerry found his way to a table situated in the darkest and most obscure corner. Seating himself with a contempt for his surroundings that betokened familiarity rather than superiority he ordered a glass of claret.

The evening had begun. A fat woman at the piano was expelling the last jauntiness from a hackneyed foxtrot, and a lean, dispirited male was assisting her with lean, dispirited notes from a violin. The attention of the patrons was directed at a dancer wearing soiled stockings and done largely in peroxide and rouge who was about to step upon a small platform, meanwhile exchanging pleasantries with a fat, eager person at the table beside her who was trying to capture her hand.

Over in the corner Jerry watched the two by the platform and, as he gazed, the ceiling seemed to fade out, the walls growing into tall buildings and the platform becoming the top of a Fifth Avenue bus on a breezy spring night three years ago. The fat, eager person disappeared, the short skirt of the dancer rolled down and the rouge faded from her cheeks—and he was beside her again in an old delirious ride, with the lights blinking kindly at them from the tall buildings beside and the voices of the street merging into a pleasant somnolent murmur around them.

"Jerry," said the girl on top of the bus, "I've said that when you were gettin' seventy-five I'd take a chance with you. But, Jerry, I can't wait forever."

Jerry watched several street numbers sail by before he answered.

"I don't know what's the matter," he said helplessly, "they won't raise me. If I can locate a new job——"

"You better hurry, Jerry," said the girl; "I'm gettin' sick of just livin' along. If I can't get married I got a couple of chances to work in a cabaret—get on the stage maybe."

"You keep out of that," said Jerry quickly. "There ain't no need, if you just wait about another month or two."

"I can't wait forever, Jerry," repeated the girl. "I'm tired of stayin' poor alone."

"It won't be so long," said Jerry clenching his free hand, "I can make it somewhere, if you'll just wait."

But the bus was fading out and the ceiling was taking shape and the murmur of the April streets was fading into the rasping whine of the violin—for that was all three years before and now he was sitting here.

The girl glanced up on the platform and exchanged a metallic impersonal smile with the dispirited violinist, and Jerry shrank farther back in his corner watching her with burning intensity.

"Your hands belong to anybody that wants them now," he cried silently and bitterly. "I wasn't man enough to keep you out of that— not man enough, by God, by God!"

But the girl by the door still toyed with the fat man's clutching fingers as she waited for her time to dance.

## V

Sylvester Stockton tossed restlessly upon his bed. The room, big as it was, smothered him, and a breeze drifting in and bearing with it a rift of moon seemed laden only with the cares of the world he would have to face next day.

"They don't understand," he thought. "They don't see, as I do, the underlying misery of the whole damn thing. They're hollow optimists. They smile because they think they're always going to be happy.

"Oh, well," he mused drowsily, "I'll run up to Rye tomorrow and endure more smiles and more heat. That's all life is—just smiles and heat, smiles and heat."

# TARQUIN OF CHEAPSIDE

### F. Scott Fitzgerald

## I

RUNNING FOOTSTEPS—LIGHT, soft-soled shoes made of curious leathery cloth brought from Ceylon setting the pace; thick flowing boots, two pairs, dark blue and gilt, reflecting the moonlight in blunt gleams and splotches, following a stone's throw behind.

Soft Shoes flashes through a patch of moonlight, then darts into a blind labyrinth of alleys and becomes only an intermittent scuffle ahead somewhere in the enfolding darkness. In go Flowing Boots, with short swords lurching and long plumes awry, finding a breath to curse God and the black lanes of London.

Soft Shoes leaps a shadowy gate and crackles through a hedgerow. Flowing Boots leap the gate and crackle through the hedgerow—and there, startlingly, is the watch ahead—two murderous pikemen of ferocious cast of mouth acquired in Holland and the Spanish marches.

But there is no cry for help. The pursued does not fall panting at the feet of the watch, clutching a purse; neither do the pursuers raise a hue and cry. Soft Shoes goes by in a rush of swift air. The watch curse and hesitate, glance after the fugitive, and then spread their pikes grimly across the road and wait for Flowing Boots. Darkness, like a great hand, cuts off the even flow of the moon.

The hand moves off the moon whose pale caress finds again the eaves and lintels, and the watch, wounded and tumbled in the dust. Up the street one of Flowing Boots leaves a black trail of spots until he binds himself, clumsily as he runs, with fine lace caught from his throat.

It was no affair for the watch: Satan was at large tonight and Satan seemed to be he who appeared dimly in front, heel over gate, knee over fence. Moreover, the adversary was obviously travelling near home or at least in that section of London consecrated to his coarser whims, for the street narrowed like a road in a picture and the houses bent over further and further, cooping in natural ambushes suitable for murder and its histrionic sister, sudden death.

Down long and sinuous lanes twisted the hunted and the harriers, always in and out of the moon in a perpetual queen's move over a checker-board of glints and patches. Ahead, the quarry, minus his leather jerkin now and half blinded by drips of sweat, had taken to scanning his ground desperately on both sides. As a result he suddenly slowed short, and retracing his steps a bit scooted up an alley so dark that it seemed that here sun and moon had been in eclipse since the last glacier slipped roaring over the earth. Two hundred yards down he stopped and crammed himself into a niche in the wall where he huddled and panted silently, a grotesque god without bulk or outline in the gloom.

Flowing Boots, two pairs, drew near, came up, went by, halted twenty yards beyond him, and spoke in deep-lunged, scanty whispers:

"I was attune to that scuffle; it stopped."

"Within twenty paces."

"He's hid."

"Stay together now and we'll cut him up."

The voice faded into a low crunch of a boot, nor did Soft Shoes wait to hear more—he sprang in three leaps across the alley, where he bounded up, flapped for a moment on the top of the wall like a huge bird, and disappeared, gulped down by the hungry night at a mouthful.

## II

*"He read at wine, he read in bed,*
*He read, aloud, had he the breath,*
*His every thought was with the dead,*
*And so he read himself to death."*

Any visitor to the old James the First graveyard near Peat's Hill may spell out this bit of doggerel, undoubtedly one of the worst recorded of an Elizabethan, on the tomb of Wessel Caxter.

This death of his, says the antiquary, occurred when he was thirty-seven, but as this story is concerned with the night of a certain chase through darkness, we find him still alive, still reading. His eyes were somewhat dim, his stomach somewhat obvious—he was a misbuilt man and indolent—oh, Heavens! But an era is an era, and in the reign of Elizabeth, by the grace of Luther, Queen of England, no man could help but catch the spirit of enthusiasm. Every loft in Cheapside published its *Magnum Folium* (or magazine) of the new blank verse; the Cheapside Players would produce anything on sight as long as it "got away from those reactionary miracle plays," and the English Bible had run through seven "very large" printings in as many months.

So Wessel Caxter (who in his youth had gone to sea) was now a reader of all on which he could lay his hands—he read manuscripts in holy friendship; he dined rotten poets; he loitered about the shops where the *Magna Folia* were printed, and he listened tolerantly while the young playwrights wrangled and bickered among themselves, and behind each other's backs made bitter and malicious charges of plagiarism or anything else they could think of.

Tonight he had a book, a piece of work which, though inordinately versed, contained, he thought, some rather excellent political satire. "The Faerie Queene" by Edmund Spenser lay before him under the tremulous candle-light. He had ploughed through a canto; he was beginning another:

### The Legend of Britomartis or of Chastity

*It falls me here to write of Chastity.*
*The fayrest vertue, far above the rest. . . .*

A sudden rush of feet on the stairs, a rusty swing-open of the thin door, and a man thrust himself into the room, a man without a jerkin, panting, sobbing, on the verge of collapse.

"Wessel," words choked him, "stick me away somewhere, love of Our Lady!"

Caxter rose, carefully closing his book, and bolted the door in some concern.

"I'm pursued," cried out Soft Shoes. "I vow there's two short-witted blades trying to make me into mincemeat and near succeeding. They saw me hop the back wall!"

"It would need," said Wessel, looking at him curiously, "several battalions armed with blunderbusses, and two or three Armadas, to keep you reasonably secure from the revenges of the world."

Soft Shoes smiled with satisfaction. His sobbing gasps were giving way to quick, precise breathing; his hunted air had faded to a faintly perturbed irony.

"I feel little surprise," continued Wessel.

"They were two such dreary apes."

"Making a total of three."

"Only two unless you stick me away. Man, man, come alive; they'll be on the stairs in a spark's age."

Wessel took a dismantled pike-staff from the corner, and raising it to the high ceiling, dislodged a rough trap-door opening into a garret above.

"There's no ladder."

He moved a bench under the trap, upon which Soft Shoes mounted, crouched, hesitated, crouched again, and then leaped amazingly upward. He caught at the edge of the aperture and swung back and forth for a moment, shifting his hold; finally doubled up and disappeared into the darkness above. There was a scurry, a migration of rats, as the trapdoor was replaced; . . . silence.

Wessel returned to his reading-table, opened to the Legend of Britomartis or of Chastity—and waited. Almost a minute later there was a scramble on the stairs and an intolerable hammering at the door. Wessel sighed and, picking up his candle, rose.

"Who's there?"

"Open the door!"

"Who's there?"

An aching blow frightened the frail wood, splintered it around the edge. Wessel opened it a scarce three inches, and held the candle high. His was to play the timorous, the super-respectable citizen, disgracefully disturbed.

"One small hour of the night for rest. Is that too much to ask from every brawler and———"

"Quiet, gossip! Have you seen a perspiring fellow?"

The shadows of two gallants fell in immense wavering outlines over the narrow stairs; by the light Wessel scrutinized them closely. Gentlemen, they were, hastily but richly dressed—one of them wounded severely in the hand, both radiating a sort of furious horror. Waving aside Wessel's ready miscomprehension, they pushed by him into the room and with their swords went through the business of poking carefully into all suspected dark spots in the room, further extending their search to Wessel's bedchamber.

"Is he hid here?" demanded the wounded man fiercely.

"Is who here?"

"Any man but you."

"Only two others that I know of."

For a second Wessel feared that he had been too damned funny, for the gallants made as though to prick him through.

"I heard a man on the stairs," he said hastily, "full five minutes ago, it was. He most certainly failed to come up."

He went on to explain his absorption in "The Faerie Queene" but, for the moment at least, his visitors, like the great saints, were anæsthetic to culture.

"What's been done?" inquired Wessel.

"Violence!" said the man with the wounded hand. Wessel noticed that his eyes were quite wild. "My own sister. Oh, Christ in heaven, give us this man!"

Wessel winced.

"Who is the man?"

"God's word! We know not even that. What's that trap up there?" he added suddenly.

"It's nailed down. It's not been used for years." He thought of the pole in the corner and quailed in his belly, but the utter despair of the two men dulled their astuteness.

"It would take a ladder for anyone not a tumbler," said the wounded man listlessly.

His companion broke into hysterical laughter.

"A tumbler. Oh, a tumbler. Oh——"

Wessel stared at them in wonder.

"That appeals to my most tragic humor," cried the man, "that no one—oh, no one—could get up there but a tumbler."

The gallant with the wounded hand snapped his good fingers impatiently.

"We must go next door—and then on——"

Helplessly they went as two walking under a dark and storm-swept sky.

Wessel closed and bolted the door and stood a moment by it, frowning in pity.

A low-breathed "Ha!" made him look up. Soft Shoes had already raised the trap and was looking down into the room, his rather elfish face squeezed into a grimace, half of distaste, half of sardonic amusement.

"They take off their heads with their helmets," he remarked in a whisper, "but as for you and me, Wessel, we are two cunning men."

"Now you be cursed," cried Wessel vehemently. "I knew you for a dog, but when I hear even the half of a tale like this, I know you for such a dirty cur that I am minded to club your skull."

Soft Shoes stared at him, blinking.

"At all events," he replied finally, "I find dignity impossible in this position."

With this he let his body through the trap, hung for an instant, and dropped the seven feet to the floor.

"There was a rat considered my ear with the air of a gourmet," he continued, dusting his hands on his breeches. "I told him in the rat's peculiar idiom that I was deadly poison, so he took himself off."

"Let's hear of this night's lechery!" insisted Wessel angrily.

Soft Shoes touched his thumb to his nose and wiggled the fingers derisively at Wessel.

"Street gamin!" muttered Wessel.

"Have you any paper?" demanded Soft Shoes irrelevantly, and then rudely added, "or can you write?"

"Why should I give you paper?"

"You wanted to hear of the night's entertainment. So you shall, and you give me pen, ink, a sheaf of paper, and a room to myself."

Wessel hesitated.

"Get out!" he said finally.

"As you will. Yet you have missed a most intriguing story."

Wessel wavered—he was soft as taffy, that man—gave in. Soft Shoes went into the adjoining room with the begrudged writing materials and precisely closed the door. Wessel grunted and returned to "The Faerie Queene"; so silence came once more upon the house.

### III

Three o'clock went into four. The room paled, the dark outside was shot through with damp and chill, and Wessel, cupping his brain in his hands, bent low over his table, tracing through the pattern of knights and fairies and the harrowing distresses of many girls. There were dragons chortling along the narrow street outside; when the sleepy armorer's boy began his work at half-past five the heavy clink and chank of plate and linked mail swelled to the echo of a marching cavalcade.

A fog shut down at the first flare of dawn, and the room was grayish yellow at six when Wessel tiptoed to his cupboard bedchamber and pulled open the door. His guest turned on him a face pale as parchment in which two distraught eyes burned like great red letters. He had drawn a chair close to Wessel's *prie-dieu*[1] which he was using as a desk; and on it was an amazing stack of closely written pages. With a long sigh Wessel withdrew and returned to his siren, calling himself fool for not claiming his bed here at dawn.

The clump of boots outside, the croaking of old beldames from attic to attic, the dull murmur of morning, unnerved him, and, dozing, he slumped in his chair, his brain, overladen with sound and color, working intolerably over the imagery that stacked it. In this restless dream of his he was one of a thousand groaning bodies crushed near the sun, a helpless bridge for the strong-eyed Apollo. The dream tore at him, scraped along his mind like a ragged knife. When a hot hand touched his shoulder, he awoke with what was nearly a scream to find the fog thick in the room and his guest, a gray ghost of misty stuff, beside him with a pile of paper in his hand.

"It should be a most intriguing tale, I believe, though it requires some going over. May I ask you to lock it away, and in God's name let me sleep?"

He waited for no answer, but thrust the pile at Wessel, and literally poured himself like stuff from a suddenly inverted bottle upon a couch in the corner; slept, with his breathing regular, but his brow wrinkled in a curious and somewhat uncanny manner.

Wessel yawned sleepily and, glancing at the scrawled, uncertain first page, he began reading aloud very softly:

### The Rape of Lucrece

"*From the besieged Ardea all in post,*
*Borne by the trustless wings of false desire,*
*Lust-breathing Tarquin leaves the Roman host——*"

---

[1] *prie-dieu;* French: a kneeling bench with a shelf on which to rest one's elbows designed for prayer.

# BABES IN THE WOODS

## F. Scott Fitzgerald

### I

AT THE TOP of the stairs she paused. The emotions of divers on spring-boards, leading-ladies on opening nights, and lumpy, bestriped young men on the day of the Big Game, crowded through her. She felt as if she should have descended to a burst of drums or to a discordant blend of gems from Thaïs and Carmen. She had never been so worried about her appearance, she had never been so satisfied with it. She had been sixteen years old for two months.

"Isabelle!" called Elaine from her doorway.

"I'm ready," she caught a slight lump of nervousness in her throat.

"I've got on the wrong slippers and stockings—you'll have to wait a minute."

Isabelle started toward Elaine's door for a last peek at a mirror, but something decided her to stand there and gaze down the stairs. They curved tantalizingly and she could just catch a glimpse of two pairs of masculine feet in the hall below. Pump-shod in uniform black they gave no hint of identity, but eagerly she wondered if one pair were attached to Kenneth Powers. This young man, as yet unmet, had taken up a considerable part of her day—the first day of her arrival. Going up in the machine from the station Elaine had volunteered, amid a rain of questions and comment, revelation and exaggeration—

"Kenneth Powers is simply *mad* to meet you. He's stayed over a day from college and he's coming tonight. He's heard so much about you—"

It had pleased her to know this. It put them on more equal terms, although she was accustomed to stage her own romances with or without a send-off. But following her delighted tremble of anticipation came a sinking sensation which made her ask:

"How do you mean he's heard about me? What sort of things?"

Elaine smiled—she felt more or less in the capacity of a showman with her more exotic guest.

"He knows you're good looking and all that." She paused—"I guess he knows you've been kissed."

Isabelle had shuddered a bit under the fur robe. She was accustomed to be followed by this, but it never failed to arouse in her the same feeling of resentment; yet in a strange town it was an advantage. She was a speed, was she? Well? Let them find out. She wasn't quite old enough to be sorry nor nearly old enough to be glad.

"Anne (this was another schoolmate) told him, I didn't—I knew you wouldn't like it." Elaine had gone on naively. "She's coming over tonight to the dinner."

Out the window Isabelle watched the high-piled snow glide by in the frosty morning. It was ever so much colder here than in Pittsburg; the glass of the side door was iced and the windows were shirred with snow in the corners. Her mind played still with the one subject. Did he dress like that boy there who walked calmly down what was evidently a bustling business street, in moccasins and winter-carnival costume? How very *western!* Of course he wasn't that way: he went to college, was a freshman or something. Really she had no distinct idea of him. A two year back picture had not impressed her except by the big eyes, which he had probably grown up to by now. However in the last two weeks at school, when her Christmas visit to Elaine had been decided on, he had assumed the proportions of a worthy adversary. Children, the most astute of matchmakers, plot and plan quickly and Elaine had cleverly played a word sonata to Isabelle's excitable temperament. Isabelle was and had been for some time capable of very strong, if not very transient emotions.

They drew up at a spreading red stone building, set back from the snowy street. Mrs. Terrell greeted her rather impersonally and Elaine's various younger brothers were produced from the corners where they skulked politely. Isabelle shook hands most tactfully. At her best she allied all with whom she came in contact, except older girls and some women. All the impressions that she made were conscious.

The half dozen girls she met that morning were all rather impressed—and as much by her direct personality as by her reputation. Kenneth Powers seemed an unembarrassed subject of conversation. Evidently he was a bit light of love. He was neither popular nor unpopular. Every girl there seemed to have had an affair with him at some time or other, but no one volunteered any really useful information. He was going to fall for her . . . Elaine had issued that statement to her young set and they were retailing it back to Elaine as fast as they set eyes on Isabelle. Isabelle resolved mentally, that if necessary, she would force herself to like him—she owed it to Elaine. What if she were terribly disappointed. Elaine had painted him in such glowing colors—he was good looking, had a "line" and was properly inconstant. In fact he summed up all the romance that her age and environment led her to desire. Were those his dancing shoes that fox-trotted tentatively around the soft rug below?

All impressions and in fact all ideas were terribly kaleidoscopic to Isabelle. She had that curious mixture of the social and artistic temperaments, found often in two classes, society women and actors. Her education, or rather her sophistication, had been absorbed from the boys who had dangled upon her favor, her tact was instinctive and her capacity for love affairs was limited only by the number of boys she met. Flirt smiled from her large, black-brown eyes and figured in her intense physical magnetism.

So she waited at the head of the stairs that evening while slippers and stockings were changed. Just as she was getting impatient Elaine came out beaming with her accustomed good nature and high spirits. Together they descended the broad stairs while the nervous searchlight of Isabelle's mind flashed on two ideas. She was glad she had high color tonight and she wondered if he danced well.

Downstairs the girls she had met in the afternoon surrounded her for a moment, looking unbelievably changed by the soft yellow light; then she heard Elaine's voice repeating a cycle of names and she found herself bowing to a sextette of black and white and terribly stiff figures. The name Powers figured somewhere, but she did not place him at first. A confused and very juvenile moment of awkward backings and bumpings, and everyone found themselves arranged talking to the very persons they least desired to. Isabelle maneuvered herself and Peter Carroll, a sixth-former from Hotchkiss whom she had met that afternoon, to a seat at the piano. A reference, supposedly humorous, to the afternoon, was all she needed. What Isabelle could do socially with one idea was remarkable.

First she repeated it rapturously in an enthusiastic contralto; then she held it off at a distance and smiled at it—her wonderful smile; then she delivered it in variations and played a sort of mental catch with it, all this in the nominal form of dialogue. Peter was fascinated and totally unconscious that this was being done not for him but for the black eyes that glistened under the shining, carefully watered hair a little to her left. As an actor even in the fullest flush of his own conscious magnetism gets a lasting impression of most of the people in the front row, so Isabelle sized up Kenneth Powers. First, he was of middle height, and from her feeling of disappointment, she knew that she had expected him to be tall and of Vernon Castle-ish slenderness. His hair and eyes were his most noticeable possessions—they were black and they fairly glittered. For the rest, he had rather dark skin with a faint flush, and a straight romantic profile, the effect set off by a close-fitting dress suit and a silk ruffled shirt of the kind that women still delight in on men, but men were just beginning to get tired of.

Kenneth was just quietly smiling.

"Don't *you* think so?" she said suddenly, turning to him innocent eyed.

There was a stir near the door and Elaine led the way to dinner. Kenneth struggled to her side and whispered:

"You're my dinner partner—Isabelle."

Isabelle gasped—this was rather quick work. Of course it made it more interesting, but really she felt as if a good line had been taken from the star and given to a minor character. She mustn't lose the leadership a bit. The dinner table glittered with laughter at the confusion of getting places and then curious eyes were turned on her, sitting near the head. She was enjoying this immensely, and Peter Carroll was so engrossed with the added sparkle of her rising color that he forgot to pull out Elaine's chair and fell into a dim confusion. Kenneth was on the other side, full of confidence and vanity, looking at her most consciously. He started directly and so did Peter.

"I've heard a lot about you—"

"Wasn't it funny this afternoon—"

Both stopped. Isabelle turned to Kenneth shyly. Her face was always enough answer for anyone, but she decided to speak.

"How—who from?"

"From everybody—for years." She blushed appropriately. On her right Peter was hors-de-combat already, although he hadn't quite realized it.

"I'll tell you what I thought about you when I first saw you," Kenneth continued. She leaned slightly toward him and looked modestly at the celery before her. Peter sighed—he knew Kenneth and the situations that Kenneth was born to handle. He turned to Elaine and asked her when she was going back to school.

## II

Isabelle and Kenneth were distinctly not innocent, nor were they particularly hardened. Morover, amateur standing had very little value in the game they were beginning to play. They were simply very sophisticated, very calculating and finished, young actors, each playing a part that they had played for years. They had both started with good looks and excitable temperaments and the rest was the result of certain accessible popular novels, and dressing-room conversation culled from a slightly older set. When Isabelle's eyes, wide and innocent, proclaimed the ingenue most, Kenneth was proportionally less deceived. He waited for the mask to drop off, but at the same time he did not question her right to wear it. She, on her part, was not impressed by his studied air of blase sophistication. She came from a larger city and had slightly an advantage in range. But she accepted his pose. It was one of the dozen little conventions of this kind of affair. He was aware that he was getting this particular favor now because she had been coached. He knew that he stood for merely the best thing in sight, and that he would have to improve his opportunity before he lost his advantage. So they proceeded, with an infinite guile that would have horrified the parents of both.

After dinner the party swelled to forty and there was dancing in a large ex-play-room downstairs. Everything went smoothly—boys cut in on Isabelle every few feet and then squabbled in the corners with: "You might let me get more than an *inch*," and "She didn't like it either—she told me so next time I cut in." It was true—she told everyone so, and gave every hand a parting pressure that said "You know that your dances are *making* my evening."

But time passed, two hours of it and the less subtle beaux had better learned to focus their pseudo-passionate glances elsewhere for eleven o'clock found Isabelle and Kenneth on a leather lounge in a little den off the music-room. She was conscious that they were a handsome pair and seemed to belong distinctively on this leather lounge while lesser lights fluttered and chattered down stairs. Boys who passed the door looked in enviously—girls who passed only laughed and frowned, and grew wise within themselves.

They had now reached a very definite stage. They had traded ages, eighteen and sixteen. She had listened to much that she had heard before. He was a freshman at college, sang in the glee club and expected to make the freshman hockey-team. He had learned that some of the boys she went with in Pittsburg were "terrible speeds" and came to parties intoxicated—most of them were nineteen or so, and drove alluring Stutzes. A good half of them seemed to have already flunked out of various boarding schools and colleges, but some of them bore good collegiate names that made him feel rather young. As a matter of fact Isabelle's acquaintance with college boys was mostly through older cousins. She had bowing acquaintance with a lot of young men who thought she was "a pretty kid" and "worth keeping an eye on." But Isabelle strung the names into a fabrication of gaiety that would have dazzled a Viennese nobleman. Such is the power of young contralto voices on leather sofas.

I have said that they had reached a very definite stage—nay more—a very critical stage. Kenneth had stayed over a day to meet her and his train left at twelve-eighteen that night. His trunk and suitcase awaited him at the station and his watch was already beginning to worry him and hang heavy in his pocket.

"Isabelle," he said suddenly. "I want to tell you something." They had been talking lightly about "that funny look in her eyes," and on the relative merits of dancing and sitting out, and Isabelle knew from the change in his manner exactly what was coming—indeed she had been wondering how soon it would come. Kenneth reached above their heads and turned out the electric light so that they were in the dark except for the glow from the red lamps that fell through the door from the music room. Then he began:

"I don't know—I don't know whether or not you know what you—what I'm going to say. Lordy Isabelle—this sounds like a line but it isn't."

"I know," said Isabelle softly.

"I may never see you again—I have darned hard luck sometimes." He was leaning away from her on the other arm of the lounge, but she could see his black eyes plainly in the dark.

"You'll see me again—silly." There was just the slightest emphasis on the last word—so that it became almost a term of endearment. He continued a bit huskily:

"I've fallen for a lot of people—girls—and I guess you have too—boys, I mean but honestly you—" he broke off suddenly and leaned forward, chin on his hands, a favorite and studied gesture. "Oh what's the use, you'll go your way and I suppose I'll go mine."

Silence for a moment. Isabelle was quite stirred—she wound her handkerchief into a tight ball and by the faint light that streamed over her, dropped it deliberately on the floor. Their hands touched for an instant but neither spoke. Silences were becoming more frequent and more delicious. Outside another stray couple had come up and were experimenting on the piano. After the usual preliminary of "chopsticks," one of them started "Babes in the Woods" and a light tenor carried the words into the den—

> "Give me your hand
> I'll understand
> We're off to slumberland."

Isabelle hummed it softly and trembled as she felt Kenneth's hand close over hers.

"Isabelle," he whispered. "You know I'm mad about you. You *do* give a darn about me."

"Yes."

"How much do you care—do you like anyone better?"

"No." He could scarcely hear her, although he bent so near that he felt her breath against his cheek.

"Isabelle, we're going back to school for six long months and why shouldn't we—if I could only just have one thing to remember you by—"

"Close the door." Her voice had just stirred so that he half wondered whether she had spoken at all. As he swung the door softly shut, the music seemed quivering just outside.

> "Moonlight is bright
> Kiss me good-night."

What a wonderful song she thought—everything was wonderful tonight, most of all this romantic scene in the den with their hands clinging and the inevitable looming charmingly close. The future vista of her life seemed an unended succession of scenes like this, under moonlight and pale starlight, and in the backs of warm limousines and in low cosy roadsters stopped under sheltering trees—only the boy might change, and this one was so nice.

"Isabelle!" His whisper blended in the music and they seemed to float nearer together. Her breath came faster. "Can't I kiss you Isabelle—Isabelle?" Lips half parted, she turned her head to him in the dark. Suddenly the ring of voices, the sound of running footsteps surged toward them. Like a flash Kenneth reached up and turned on the light and when the door opened and three boys, the wrathy and dance-craving Peter among them, rushed in, he was turning over the magazines on the table, while she sat, without moving, serene and unembarrassed, and even greeted them with a welcoming smile. But her heart was beating wildly and she felt somehow as if she had been deprived.

It was evidently over. There was a clamour for a dance, there was a glance that passed between them, on his side, despair, on hers, regret, and then the evening went on, with the reassured beaux and the eternal cutting in.

At quarter to twelve Kenneth shook hands with her gravely, in a crowd assembled to wish him good-speed. For an instant he lost his poise and she felt slightly foolish, when a satirical voice from a concealed wit on the edge of the company cried:

"Take her outside, Kenneth." As he took her hand he pressed it a little and she returned the pressure as she had done to twenty hands that evening—that was all.

At two o'clock upstairs Elaine asked her if she and Kenneth had had a "time" in the den. Isabelle turned to her quietly. In her eyes was the light of the idealist, the inviolate dreamer of Joan-like dreams.

"No!" she answered. "I don't do that sort of thing any more—he asked me to, but I said 'No.'"

As she crept into bed she wondered what he'd say in his special delivery tomorrow. He had such a good looking mouth—would she ever—?

"Fourteen angels were watching over them" sang Elaine sleepily from the next room.

"Damn!" muttered Isabelle and punched the pillow into a luxurious lump—"Damn!"

# THE REVOLT OF "MOTHER"

### Mary E. Wilkins Freeman

"Father!"

"What is it?"

"What are them men diggin' over there in the field for?"

There was a sudden dropping and enlarging of the lower part of the old man's face, as if some heavy weight had settled therein; he shut his mouth tight, and went on harnessing the great bay mare. He hustled the collar on to her neck with a jerk.

"Father!"

The old man slapped the saddle upon the mare's back.

"Look here, father, I want to know what them men are diggin' over in the field for, an' I'm goin' to know."

"I wish you'd go into the house, mother, an' 'tend to your own affairs," the old man said then. He ran his words together, and his speech was almost as inarticulate as a growl.

But the woman understood; it was her most native tongue. "I ain't goin' into the house till you tell me what them men are doin' over there in the field," said she.

Then she stood waiting. She was a small woman, short and straight-waisted like a child in her brown cotton gown. Her forehead was mild and benevolent between the smooth curves of gray hair; there were meek downward lines about her nose and mouth; but her eyes, fixed upon the old man, looked as if the meekness had been the result of her own will, never of the will of another.

They were in the barn, standing before the wide-open doors. The spring air, full of the smell of growing grass and unseen blossoms, came in their faces. The deep yard in front was littered with farm-wagons and piles of wood; on the edges, close to the fence and the house, the grass was a vivid green, and there were some dandelions.

The old man glanced doggedly at his wife as he tightened the last buckles on the harness. She looked as immovable to him as one of the rocks in his pasture-land, bound to the earth with generations of blackberry vines. He slapped the reins over the horse, and started forth from the barn.

"*Father!*" said she.

The old man pulled up. "What is it?"

"I want to know what them men are diggin' over there in that field for."

"They're diggin' a cellar, I s'pose, if you've got to know."

"A cellar for what?"

"A barn."

"A barn? You ain't goin' to build a barn over there where we was goin' to have a house, father?"

The old man said not another word. He hurried the horse into the farm wagon, and clattered out of the yard, jouncing as sturdily on his seat as a boy.

The woman stood a moment looking after him, then she went out of the barn across a corner of the yard to the house. The house, standing at right angles with the great barn and a long reach of sheds and out-buildings, was infinitesimal compared with them. It was scarcely as commodious for people as the little boxes under the barn eaves were for doves.

A pretty girl's face, pink and delicate as a flower, was looking out of one of the house windows. She was watching three men who were digging over in the field which bounded the yard near the road line. She turned quietly when the woman entered.

"What are they digging for, mother?" said she. "Did he tell you?"

"They're diggin' for—a cellar for a new barn."

"Oh, mother, he ain't going to build another barn?"

"That's what he says."

A boy stood before the kitchen glass combing his hair. He combed slowly and painstakingly, arranging his brown hair in a smooth hillock over his forehead. He did not seem to pay any attention to the conversation.

"Sammy, did you know father was going to build a new barn?" asked the girl.

The boy combed assiduously.

"Sammy!"

He turned, and showed a face like his father's under his smooth crest of hair. "Yes, I s'pose I did," he said, reluctantly.

"How long have you known it?" asked his mother.

"'Bout three months, I guess."

"Why didn't you tell of it?"

"Didn't think 'twould do no good."

"I don't see what father wants another barn for," said the girl, in her sweet, slow voice. She turned again to the window, and stared out at the digging men in the field. Her tender, sweet face was full of a gentle distress. Her forehead was as bald and innocent as a baby's, with the light hair strained back from it in a row of curl-papers. She was quite large, but her soft curves did not look as if they covered muscles.

Her mother looked sternly at the boy. "Is he goin' to buy more cows?" said she.

The boy did not reply; he was tying his shoes.

"Sammy, I want you to tell me if he's goin' to buy more cows."

"I s'pose he is."

"How many?"

"Four, I guess."

His mother said nothing more. She went into the pantry and there was a clatter of dishes. The boy got his cap from a nail behind the door, took an old arithmetic from the shelf, and started for school. He was lightly built, but clumsy. He went out of the yard with a curious spring in the hips, that made his loose home-made jacket tilt up in the rear.

The girl went to the sink, and began to wash the dishes that were piled up there. Her mother came promptly out of the pantry, and shoved her aside. "You wipe 'em," said she; "I'll wash. There's a good many this mornin'."

The mother plunged her hands vigorously into the water, the girl wiped the plates slowly and dreamily. "Mother," said she, "don't you think it's too bad father's going to build that new barn, much as we need a decent house to live in?"

Her mother scrubbed a dish fiercely. "You ain't found out yet we're women-folks, Nanny Penn," said she. "You ain't seen enough of men-folks yet to. One of these days you'll find it out, an' then you'll know that we know only what men-folks think we do, so far as any use of it goes, an' how we'd ought to reckon men-folks in with Providence an' not complain of what they do any more than we do of the weather."

"I don't care; I don't believe George is anything like that, anyhow," said Nanny. Her delicate face flushed pink, her lips pouted softly, as if she were going to cry.

"You wait an' see. I guess George Eastman ain't no better than other men. You hadn't ought to judge father, though. He can't help it, 'cause he don't look at things jest the way we do. An' we've been pretty comfortable here, after all. The roof don't leak—ain't never but once—that's one thing. Father's kept it shingled right up."

"I do wish we had a parlor."

"I guess it won't hurt George Eastman any to come to see you in a nice clean kitchen. I guess a good many girls don't have as good a place as this. Nobody's ever heard me complain."

"I ain't complained either, mother."

"Well, I don't think you'd better, a good father an' a good home as you've got. S'pose your father made you go out an' work for your livin'? Lots of girls have to that ain't no stronger an' better able to than you be."

Sarah Penn washed the frying-pan with a conclusive air. She scrubbed the outside of it as faithfully as the inside. She was a masterly keeper of her box of a house. Her one living-room never seemed to have in it any of the dust which the friction of life with inanimate matter produces. She swept, and there seemed to be no dirt to go before the broom; she cleaned, and one could see no difference. She was like an artist so perfect that he has apparently no art. Today she got out a mixing bowl and a board, and rolled some pies, and there was no more flour upon her than upon her daughter who was doing finer work. Nanny was to be married in the fall, and she was sewing on some white cambric and embroidery. She sewed industriously while her mother cooked, her soft milk-white hands and wrists showed whiter than her delicate work.

"We must have the stove moved out in the shed before long," said Mrs. Penn. "Talk about not havin' things, it's been a real blessin' to be able to put a stove up in that shed in hot weather. Father did one good thing when he fixed that stove-pipe out there."

Sarah Penn's face as she rolled her pies had that expression of meek vigor which might have characterized one of the New Testament saints. She was making mince-pies. Her husband, Adoniram Penn, liked them better than any other kind. She baked twice a week. Adoniram often liked a piece of pie between meals. She hurried this morning. It had been later than usual when she began, and she wanted to have a pie baked for dinner. However deep a resentment she might be forced to hold against her husband, she would never fail in sedulous attention to his wants.

Nobility of character manifests itself at loop-holes when it is not provided with large doors. Sarah Penn's showed itself today in flaky dishes of pastry. So she made the pies faithfully, while across the table she could see, when she glanced up from her work, the sight that rankled in her patient and steadfast soul—the digging of the cellar of the new barn in the place where Adoniram forty years ago had promised her their new house should stand.

The pies were done for dinner. Adoniram and Sammy were home a few minutes after twelve o'clock. The dinner was eaten with serious haste. There was never much conversation at the table in the Penn family. Adoniram asked a blessing, and they ate promptly, then rose up and went about their work.

Sammy went back to school, taking soft sly lopes out of the yard like a rabbit. He wanted a game of marbles before school, and feared his father would give him some chores to do. Adoniram hastened to the door and called after him, but he was out of sight.

"I don't see what you let him go for, mother," said he. "I wanted him to help me unload that wood."

Adoniram went to work out in the yard unloading wood from the wagon. Sarah put away the dinner dishes, while Nanny took down her curl-papers and changed her dress. She was going down to the store to buy some more embroidery and thread.

When Nanny was gone, Mrs. Penn went to the door. "Father!" she called.

"Well, what is it?"

"I want to see you jest a minute, father."

"I can't leave this wood nohow. I've got to git it unloaded an' go for a load of gravel afore two o'clock. Sammy had ought to helped me. You hadn't ought to let him go to school so early."

"I want to see you jest a minute."

"I tell ye I can't, nohow, mother."

"Father, you come here." Sarah Penn stood in the door like a queen; she held her head as if it bore a crown; there was that patience which makes authority royal in her voice. Adoniram went.

Mrs. Penn led the way into the kitchen, and pointed to a chair. "Sit down, father," said she; "I've got somethin' I want to say to you."

He sat down heavily; his face was quite stolid, but he looked at her with restive eyes. "Well, what is it, mother?"

"I want to know what you're buildin' that new barn for, father?"

"I ain't got nothin' to say about it."

"It can't be you think you need another barn?"

"I tell ye I ain't got nothin' to say about it, mother; an' I ain't goin' to say nothin'."

"Be you goin' to buy more cows?"

Adoniram did not reply; he shut his mouth tight.

"I know you be, as well as I want to. Now, father, look here"—Sarah Penn had not sat down; she stood before her husband in the humble fashion of a Scripture woman—"I'm goin' to talk real plain to you: I never have sence I married you, but I'm goin' to now. I ain't never complained, an' I ain't goin' to complain now, but I'm goin' to talk plain. You see this room here, father; you look at it well. You see there ain't no carpet on the floor, an' you see the paper is all dirty, an' droppin' off the walls. We ain't had no new paper on it for ten year, an' then I put it on myself an' it didn't cost but ninepence a roll. You see this room, father; it's all the one I've had to work in an' eat in an' sit in since we was married. There ain't another woman in the whole town whose husband ain't got half the means you have but what's got better. It's all the room Nanny's got to have her company in; an' there ain't one of her mates but what's got better, an' their fathers not so able as hers is. It's all the room she'll have to be married in. What would you have thought, father, if we had had our weddin' in a room no better than this? I was married in my mother's parlor, with a carpet on the floor, an' stuffed furniture, an' a mahogany card-table. An' this is all the room my daughter will have to be married in. Look here, father!"

Sarah Penn went across the room as though it were a tragic stage. She flung open a door and disclosed a tiny bedroom, only large enough for a bed and bureau, with a path between. "There, father," said she—"there's all the room I've had to sleep in forty year. All my children were born there—the two that died, an' the two that's livin'. I was sick with a fever there."

She stepped to another door and opened it. It led into the small, ill-lighted pantry. "Here," said she, "is all the buttery I've got—every place I've got for my dishes, to set away my victuals in, an' to keep my milk-pans in. Father, I've been takin' care of the milk of six cows in this place, an' now you're goin' to build a new barn, an' keep more cows, an' give me more to do in it."

She threw open another door. A narrow crooked flight of stairs wound upward from it. "There, father," said she; "I want you to look at the stairs that go up to them two unfinished chambers that are all the places our son an' daughter have had to sleep in all their lives. There ain't a prettier girl in town nor a more ladylike one than Nanny, an' that's the place she has to sleep in. It ain't so good as your horse's stall; it ain't so warm an' tight."

Sarah Penn went back and stood before her husband. "Now, father," said she, "I want to know if you think you're doin' right an' accordin' to what you profess. Here, when we was married, forty year ago, you promised me faithful that we should have a new house built in that lot over in the field before the year was out. You said you had money enough, an' you wouldn't ask me to live in no such place as this. It is forty year now, an' you've been makin' more money, an' I've been savin' of it for you ever since, an' you ain't built no house yet. You've built sheds an' cowhouses an' one new barn, an' now you're goin' to build another. Father, I want to know if you think it's right. You're lodgin' your dumb beasts better than you are your own flesh an' blood. I want to know if you think it's right."

"I ain't got nothin' to say."

"You can't say nothin' without ownin' it ain't right, father. An' there's another thing—I ain't complained; I've got along forty year, an' I s'pose I should forty more, if it wa'n't for that—if we don't have another house. Nanny she can't live with us after she's married. She'll have to go somewheres else to live away from us, an' it don't seem as if I could have it so, noways, father. She wa'n't ever strong. She's got considerable color, but there wa'n't ever any backbone to her. I've always took the heft of everything off her, an' she ain't fit to keep house an' do everything herself. She'll be all worn out inside of a year. Think of her doin' all the washin' an' ironin' an' bakin' with them soft white hands an' arms, an' sweepin'! I can't have it so, noways, father."

Mrs. Penn's face was burning; her mild eyes gleamed. She had pleaded her little cause like a Webster; she had ranged from severity to pathos; but her opponent employed that obstinate silence which makes eloquence futile with mocking echoes. Adoniram arose clumsily.

"Father, ain't you got nothin' to say?" said Mrs. Penn.

"I've got to go off after that load of gravel. I can't stan' here talkin' all day."

"Father, won't you think it over, an' have a house built there instead of a barn?"

"I ain't got nothin' to say."

Adoniram shuffled out. Mrs. Penn went into her bedroom. When she came out, her eyes were red. She had a roll of unbleached cotton cloth. She spread it out on the kitchen table, and began cutting out some shirts for her husband. The men over in the field had a team to help them this afternoon; she could hear their halloos. She had a scanty pattern for the shirts; she had to plan and piece the sleeves.

Nanny came home with her embroidery, and sat down with her needle-work. She had taken down her curl-papers, and there was a soft roll of fair hair like an aureole over her forehead; her face was as delicately fine and clear as porcelain. Suddenly she looked up, and the tender red flamed all over her face and neck. "Mother," said she.

"What say?"

"I've been thinking—I don't see how we're goin' to have any— wedding in this room. I'd be ashamed to have his folks come if we didn't have anybody else."

"Mebbe we can have some new paper before then; I can put it on. I guess you won't have no call to be ashamed of your belongin's."

"We might have the wedding in the new barn," said Nanny, with gentle pettishness. "Why, mother, what makes you look so?"

Mrs. Penn had started, and was staring at her with a curious expression. She turned again to her work, and spread out a pattern carefully on the cloth. "Nothin'," said she.

Presently Adoniram clattered out of the yard in his two-wheeled dump cart, standing as proudly upright as a Roman charioteer. Mrs. Penn opened the door and stood there a minute looking out; the halloos of the men sounded louder.

It seemed to her all through the spring months that she heard nothing but the halloos and the noises of saws and hammers. The new barn grew fast. It was a fine edifice for this little village. Men came on pleasant Sundays, in their meeting suits and clean shirt bosoms, and stood around it admiringly. Mrs. Penn did not speak of it, and Adoniram did not mention it to her, although sometimes, upon a return from inspecting it, he bore himself with injured dignity.

"It's a strange thing how your mother feels about the new barn," he said, confidentially, to Sammy one day.

Sammy only grunted after an odd fashion for a boy: he had learned it from his father.

The barn was all completed ready for use by the third week in July. Adoniram had planned to move his stock in on Wednesday; on Tuesday he received a letter which changed his plans. He came in with it early in the morning. "Sammy's been to the post-office," said he, "an' I've got a letter from Hiram." Hiram was Mrs. Penn's brother, who lived in Vermont.

"Well," said Mrs. Penn, "what does he say about the folks?"

"I guess they're all right. He says he thinks if I come up country right off there's a chance to buy jest the kind of a horse I want." He stared reflectively out of the window at the new barn.

Mrs. Penn was making pies. She went on clapping the rolling-pin into the crust, although she was very pale, and her heart beat loudly.

"I dun' know but what I'd better go," said Adoniram. "I hate to go off jest now, right in the midst of hayin', but the ten-acre lot's cut, an' I guess Rufus an' the others can git along without me three or four days. I can't get a horse round here to suit me, nohow, an' I've got to have another for all that wood-haulin' in the fall. I told Hiram to watch out, an' if he got wind of a good horse to let me know. I guess I'd better go."

"I'll get out your clean shirt an' collar," said Mrs. Penn calmly.

She laid out Adoniram's Sunday suit and his clean clothes on the bed in the little bedroom. She got his shaving-water and razor ready. At last she buttoned on his collar and fastened his black cravat.

Adoniram never wore his collar and cravat except on extra occasions. He held his head high, with a rasped dignity. When he was all ready, with his coat and hat brushed, and a lunch of pie and cheese in a paper bag, he hesitated on the threshold of the door. He looked at his wife, and his manner was defiantly apologetic. "*If* them cows come today, Sammy can drive 'em into the new barn," said he; "an' when they bring the hay up, they can pitch it in there."

"Well," replied Mrs. Penn.

Adoniram set his shaven face ahead and started. When he had cleared the door-step, he turned and looked back with a kind of nervous solemnity. "I shall be back by Saturday if nothin' happens," said he.

"Do be careful, father," returned his wife.

She stood in the door with Nanny at her elbow and watched him out of sight. Her eyes had a strange, doubtful expression in them; her peaceful forehead was contracted. She went in, and about her baking again. Nanny sat sewing. Her wedding-day was drawing nearer, and she was getting pale and thin with her steady sewing. Her mother kept glancing at her.

"Have you got that pain in your side this mornin'?" she asked.

"A little."

Mrs. Penn's face, as she worked, changed, her perplexed forehead smoothed, her eyes were steady, her lips firmly set. She formed a maxim for herself, although incoherently with her unlettered thoughts. "Unsolicited opportunities are the guide-posts of the Lord to the new roads of life," she repeated in effect, and she made up her mind to her course of action.

"S'posin' I *had* wrote to Hiram," she muttered once, when she was in the pantry—"s'posin' I had wrote, an' asked him if he knew of any horse? But I didn't, an' father's goin' wa'n't none of my doin'. It looks like a providence." Her voice rang out quite loud at the last.

"What you talkin' about, mother?" called Nanny.

"Nothin'."

Mrs. Penn hurried her baking; at eleven o'clock it was all done. The load of hay from the west field came slowly down the cart track, and drew up at the new barn. Mrs. Penn ran out. "Stop!" she screamed—"stop!"

The men stopped and looked; Sammy upreared from the top of the load, and stared at his mother.

"Stop!" she cried out again. "Don't you put the hay in that barn; put it in the old one."

"Why, he said to put it in here," returned one of the haymakers, wonderingly. He was a young man, a neighbor's son, whom Adoniram hired by the year to help on the farm.

"Don't you put the hay in the new barn; there's room enough in the old one, ain't there?" said Mrs. Penn.

"Room enough," returned the hired man, in his thick, rustic tones. "Didn't need the new barn, nohow, far as room's concerned. Well, I s'pose he changed his mind." He took hold of the horses' bridles.

Mrs. Penn went back to the house. Soon the kitchen windows were darkened, and a fragrance like warm honey came into the room.

Nanny laid down her work. "I thought father wanted them to put the hay into the new barn?" she said, wonderingly.

"It's all right," replied her mother.

Sammy slid down from the load of hay, and came in to see if dinner was ready.

"I ain't goin' to get a regular dinner today, as long as father's gone," said his mother. "I've let the fire go out. You can have some bread an' milk an' pie. I thought we could get along." She set out some bowls of milk, some bread, and a pie on the kitchen table. "You'd better eat your dinner now," said she. "You might jest as well get through with it. I want you to help me afterward."

Nanny and Sammy stared at each other. There was something strange in their mother's manner. Mrs. Penn did not eat anything herself. She went into the pantry, and they heard her moving dishes while they ate. Presently she came out with a pile of plates. She got the clothes-basket out of the shed, and packed them in it. Nanny and Sammy watched. She brought out cups and saucers, and put them in with the plates.

"What you goin' to do, mother?" inquired Nanny, in a timid voice. A sense of something unusual made her tremble, as if it were a ghost. Sammy rolled his eyes over his pie.

"You'll see what I'm goin' to do," replied Mrs. Penn. "If you're through, Nanny, I want you to go upstairs an' pack up your things; an' I want you, Sammy, to help me take down the bed in the bedroom."

"Oh, mother, what for?" gasped Nanny.

"You'll see."

During the next few hours a feat was performed by this simple, pious New England mother which was equal in its way to Wolfe's storming of the Heights of Abraham. It took no more genius and audacity of bravery for Wolfe to cheer his wondering soldiers up those steep precipices, under the sleeping eyes of the enemy, than for Sarah Penn, at the head of her children, to move all their little household goods into the new barn while her husband was away.

Nanny and Sammy followed their mother's instructions without a murmur; indeed, they were overawed. There is a certain uncanny and superhuman quality about all such purely original undertakings as their mother's was to them. Nanny went back and forth with her light loads, and Sammy tugged with sober energy.

At five o'clock in the afternoon the little house in which the Penns had lived for forty years had emptied itself into the new barn.

Every builder builds somewhat for unknown purposes, and is in a measure a prophet. The architect of Adoniram Penn's barn, while he designed it for the comfort of four-footed animals, had planned better than he knew for the comfort of humans. Sarah Penn saw at a glance its possibilities. Those great box-stalls, with quilts hung before them, would make better bedrooms than the one she had occupied for forty years, and there was a tight carriage-room. The harness-room, with its chimney and shelves, would make a kitchen of her dreams. The great middle space would make a parlor, by-and-by, fit for a palace. Upstairs there was as much room as down. With partitions and windows, what a house would there be! Sarah looked at the row of stanchions before the allotted space for cows, and reflected that she would have her front entry there.

At six o'clock the stove was up in the harness-room, the kettle was boiling, and the table set for tea. It looked almost as home-like as the abandoned house across the yard had ever done. The young hired man milked, and Sarah directed him calmly to bring the milk to the new barn. He came gaping, dropping little blots of foam from the brimming pails on the grass. Before the next morning he had spread the story of Adoniram Penn's wife moving into the new barn all over the little village. Men assembled in the store and talked it over, women with shawls over their heads scuttled into each other's houses before their work was done. Any deviation from the ordinary course of life in this quiet town was enough to stop all progress in it. Everybody paused to look at the staid, independent figure on the side track. There was a difference of opinion with regard to her. Some held her to be insane; some, of a lawless and rebellious spirit.

Friday the minister went to see her. It was in the forenoon, and she was at the barn door shelling pease for dinner. She looked up and returned his salutation with dignity, then she went on with her work. She did not invite him in. The saintly expression of her face remained fixed, but there was an angry flush over it.

The minister stood awkwardly before her, and talked. She handled the pease as if they were bullets. At last she looked up, and her eyes showed the spirit that her meek front had covered for a lifetime.

"There ain't no use talkin', Mr. Hersey," said she. "I've thought it all over an' over, an' I believe I'm doin' what's right. I've made it the subject of prayer, an' it's betwixt me an' the Lord an' Adoniram. There ain't no call for nobody else to worry about it."

"Well, of course, if you have brought it to the Lord in prayer, and feel satisfied that you are doing right, Mrs. Penn," said the minister, helplessly. His thin gray-bearded face was pathetic. He was a sickly man; his youthful confidence had cooled; he had to scourge himself up to some of his pastoral duties as relentlessly as a Catholic ascetic, and then he was prostrated by the smart.

"I think it's right jest as much as I think it was right for our forefathers to come over from the old country 'cause they didn't have what belonged to 'em," said Mrs. Penn. She arose. The barn threshold might have been Plymouth Rock from her bearing. "I don't doubt you mean well, Mr. Hersey," said she, "but there are things people hadn't ought to interfere with. I've been a member of the church for over forty year. I've got my own mind an' my own feet, an' I'm goin' to think my own thoughts an' go my own ways, an' nobody but the Lord is goin' to dictate to me unless I've a mind to have him. Won't you come in an' set down? How is Mis' Hersey?"

"She is well, I thank you," replied the minister. He added some more perplexed apologetic remarks; then he retreated.

He could expound the intricacies of every character study in the Scriptures, he was competent to grasp the Pilgrim Fathers and all historical innovators, but Sarah Penn was beyond him. He could deal with primal cases, but parallel ones worsted him. But, after all, although it was aside from his province, he wondered more how Adoniram Penn would deal with his wife than how the Lord would. Everybody shared the wonder. When Adoniram's four new cows arrived, Sarah ordered three to be put in the old barn, the other in the house shed where the cooking-stove had stood. That added to the excitement. It was whispered that all four cows were domiciled in the house.

Toward sunset on Saturday, when Adoniram was expected home, there was a knot of men in the road near the new barn. The hired man had milked, but he still hung around the premises. Sarah Penn had supper all ready. There were brown-bread and baked beans and a custard pie; it was the supper that Adoniram loved on a Saturday night. She had on a clean calico, and she bore herself imperturbably. Nanny and Sammy kept close at her heels. Their eyes were large, and Nanny was full of nervous tremors. Still there was to them more pleasant excitement than anything else. An inborn confidence in their mother over their father asserted itself.

Sammy looked out of the harness-room window. "There he is," he announced, in an awed whisper. He and Nanny peeped around the casing. Mrs. Penn kept on about her work. The children watched Adoniram leave the new horse standing in the drive while he went to the house door. It was fastened. Then he went around to the shed. That door was seldom locked, even when the family was away. The thought how her father would be confronted by the cow flashed upon Nanny. There was a hysterical sob in her throat. Adoniram emerged from the shed and stood looking about in a dazed fashion. His lips moved; he was saying something, but they could not hear what it was. The hired man was peeping around a corner of the old barn, but nobody saw him.

Adoniram took the new horse by the bridle and led him across the yard to the new barn. Nanny and Sammy slunk close to their mother. The barn doors rolled back, and there stood Adoniram, with the long mild face of the great Canadian farm horse looking over his shoulder.

Nanny kept behind her mother, but Sammy stepped suddenly forward, and stood in front of her.

Adoniram stared at the group. "What on airth you all down here for?" said he. "What's the matter over to the house?"

"We've come here to live, father," said Sammy. His shrill voice quavered out bravely.

"What"—Adoniram sniffed—"what is it smells like cookin'?" said he. He stepped forward and looked in the open door of the harness-room. Then he turned to his wife. His old bristling face was pale and frightened. "What on airth does this mean, mother?" he gasped.

"You come in here, father," said Sarah. She led the way into the harness-room and shut the door. "Now, father," said she, "you needn't be scared. I ain't crazy. There ain't nothin' to be upset over. But we've come here to live, an' we're goin' to live here. We've got jest as good a right here as new horses an' cows. The house wa'n't fit for us to live in any longer, an' I made up my mind I wa'n't goin' to stay there. I've done my duty by you forty year, an' I'm goin' to do it now; but I'm goin' to live here. You've got to put in some windows and partitions; an' you'll have to buy some furniture."

"Why, mother!" the old man gasped.

"You'd better take your coat off an' get washed—there's the wash-basin—an' then we'll have supper."

"Why, mother!"

Sammy went past the window, leading the new horse to the old barn. The old man saw him, and shook his head speechlessly. He tried to take off his coat, but his arms seemed to lack the power. His wife helped him. She poured some water into the tin basin, and put in a piece of soap. She got the comb and brush, and smoothed his thin gray hair after he had washed. Then she put the beans, hot bread, and tea on the table. Sammy came in, and the family drew up. Adoniram sat looking dazedly at his plate, and they waited.

"Ain't you goin' to ask a blessin', father?" said Sarah.

And the old man bent his head and mumbled.

All through the meal he stopped eating at intervals, and stared furtively at his wife; but he ate well. The home food tasted good to him, and his old frame was too sturdily healthy to be affected by his mind. But after supper he went out, and sat down on the step of the smaller door at the right of the barn, through which he had meant his Jerseys to pass in stately file, but which Sarah designed for her front house-door, and he leaned his head on his hands.

After the supper dishes were cleared away and the milk-pans washed, Sarah went out to him. The twilight was deepening. There was a clear green glow in the sky. Before them stretched the smooth level of field; in the distance was a cluster of hay-stacks like the huts of a village; the air was very cool and calm and sweet. The landscape might have been an ideal one of peace.

Sarah bent over and touched her husband on one of his thin, sinewy shoulders. "Father!"

The old man's shoulders heaved: he was weeping.

"Why, don't do so, father," said Sarah.

"I'll—put up the—partitions, an'—everything you—want, mother."

Sarah put her apron up to her face; she was overcome by her own triumph.

Adoniram was like a fortress whose walls had no active resistance, and went down the instant the right besieging tools were used. "Why, mother," he said, hoarsely, "I hadn't no idee you was so set on't as all this comes to."

# OLD WOMAN MAGOUN

### Mary E. Wilkins Freeman

THE HAMLET OF Barry's Ford is situated in a sort of high valley among the mountains. Below it the hills lie in moveless curves like a petrified ocean; above it they rise in green-cresting waves which never break. It is *Barry's* Ford because at one time the Barry family was the most important in the place, and *Ford* because just at the beginning of the hamlet the little turbulent Barry River is fordable. There is, however, now a rude bridge across the river.

Old Woman Magoun was largely instrumental in bringing the bridge to pass. She haunted the miserable little grocery, wherein whiskey and hands of tobacco were the most salient features of the stock in trade, and she talked much. She would elbow herself into the midst of a knot of idlers and talk.

"That bridge ought to be built this very summer," said Old Woman Magoun. She spread her strong arms like wings, and sent the loafers, half laughing, half angry, flying in every direction. "If I were a *man*," said she, "I'd go out this very minute and lay the fust log. If I were a passel of lazy men layin' round, I'd start up for once in my life, I would." The men cowered visibly—all except Nelson Barry; he swore under his breath and strode over to the counter.

Old Woman Magoun looked after him majestically. "You can cuss all you want to, Nelson Barry," said she; "I ain't afraid of you. I don't expect you to lay ary log of the bridge, but I'm goin' to have it built this very summer." She did. The weakness of the masculine element in Barry's Ford was laid low before such strenuous feminine assertion.

Old Woman Magoun and some other women planned a treat—two sucking pigs, and pies, and sweet cake—for a reward after the bridge should be finished. They even viewed leniently the increased consumption of ardent spirits.

"It seems queer to me," Old Woman Magoun said to Sally Jinks, "that men can't do nothin' without havin' to drink and chew to keep their sperits up. Lord! I've worked all my life and never done nuther."

"Men is different," said Sally Jinks.

"Yes, they be," assented Old Woman Magoun, with open contempt.

The two women sat on a bench in front of Old Woman Magoun's house, and little Lily Barry, her granddaughter, sat holding her doll on a small mossy stone nearby. From where they sat they could see the men at work on the new bridge. It was the last day of the work.

Lily clasped her doll—a poor old rag thing—close to her childish bosom, like a little mother, and her face, round which curled her long yellow hair, was fixed upon the men at work. Little Lily had never been allowed to run with the other children of Barry's Ford. Her grandmother had taught her everything she knew—which was not much, but tending at least to a certain measure of spiritual growth—for she, as it were, poured the goodness of her own soul into this little receptive vase of another. Lily was firmly grounded in her knowledge that it was wrong to lie or steal or disobey her grandmother. She had also learned that one should be very industrious. It was seldom that Lily sat idly holding her doll-baby, but this was a holiday because of the bridge. She looked only a child, although she was nearly fourteen; her mother had been married at sixteen. That is, Old Woman Magoun said that her daughter, Lily's mother, had married at sixteen; there had been rumors, but no one had dared openly gainsay the old woman. She said that her daughter had married Nelson Barry, and he had deserted her. She had lived in her mother's house, and Lily had been born there, and she had died when the baby was only a week old. Lily's father, Nelson Barry, was the fairly dangerous degenerate of a good old family. Nelson's father before him had been bad. He was now the last of the family, with the exception of a sister of feeble intellect, with whom he lived in the old Barry house. He was a middle-aged man, still handsome. The shiftless population of Barry's Ford looked up to him as to an evil deity. They wondered how Old Woman Magoun dared brave him as she did. But Old Woman Magoun had within her a mighty sense of reliance upon herself as being on the right track in the midst of a maze of evil, which gave her courage. Nelson Barry had manifested no interest whatever in his daughter. Lily seldom saw her father. She did not often go to the store which was his favorite haunt. Her grandmother took care that she should not do so.

However, that afternoon she departed from her usual custom and sent Lily to the store.

She came in from the kitchen, whither she had been to baste the roasting pig. "There's no use talkin'," said she, "I've got to have some more salt. I've jest used the very last I had to dredge over that pig. I've got to go to the store."

Sally Jinks looked at Lily. "Why don't you send her?" she asked.

Old Woman Magoun gazed irresolutely at the girl. She was herself very tired. It did not seem to her that she could drag herself up the dusty hill to the store. She glanced with covert resentment at Sally Jinks. She thought that she might offer to go. But Sally Jinks said again, "Why don't you let her go?" and looked with a languid eye at Lily holding her doll on the stone.

Lily was watching the men at work on the bridge, with her childish delight in a spectacle of any kind, when her grandmother addressed her.

"Guess I'll let you go down to the store an' git some salt, Lily," said she.

The girl turned uncomprehending eyes upon her grandmother at the sound of her voice. She had been filled with one of the innocent reveries of childhood. Lily had in her the making of an artist or a poet. Her prolonged childhood went to prove it, and also her retrospective eyes, as clear and blue as blue light itself, which seemed to see past all that she looked upon. She had not come of the old Barry family for nothing. The best of the strain was in her, along with the splendid stanchness in humble lines which she had acquired from her grandmother.

"Put on your hat," said Old Woman Magoun; "the sun is hot, and you might git a headache." She called the girl to her, and put back the shower of fair curls under the rubber band which confined the hat. She gave Lily some money, and watched her knot it into a corner of her little cotton handkerchief. "Be careful you don't lose it," said she, "and don't stop to talk to anybody, for I am in a hurry for that salt. Of course, if anybody speaks to you answer them polite, and then come right along."

Lily started, her pocket-handkerchief weighted with the small silver dangling from one hand, and her rag doll carried over her shoulder like a baby. The absurd travesty of a face peeped forth from Lily's yellow curls. Sally Jinks looked after her with a sniff.

"She ain't goin' to carry that rag doll to the store?" said she.

"She likes to," replied Old Woman Magoun, in a half-shamed yet defiantly extenuating voice.

"Some girls at her age is thinkin' about beaux instead of rag dolls," said Sally Jinks.

The grandmother bristled. "Lily ain't big nor old for her age," said she. "I ain't in any hurry to have her git married. She ain't none too strong."

"She's got a good color," said Sally Jinks. She was crocheting white cotton lace, making her thick fingers fly. She really knew how to do scarcely anything except to crochet that coarse lace; somehow her heavy brain or her fingers had mastered that.

"I know she's got a beautiful color," replied Old Woman Magoun, with an odd mixture of pride and anxiety, "but it comes an' goes."

"I've heard that was a bad sign," remarked Sally Jinks, loosening some thread from her spool.

"Yes, it is," said the grandmother. "She's nothin' but a baby, though she's quicker than most to learn."

Lily Barry went on her way to the store. She was clad in a scanty short frock of blue cotton; her hat was tipped back, forming an oval frame for her innocent face. She was very small, and walked like a child, with the clap-clap of little feet of babyhood. She might have been considered, from her looks, under ten.

Presently she heard footsteps behind her; she turned around a little timidly to see who was coming. When she saw a handsome, well-dressed man, she felt reassured. The man came alongside and glanced down carelessly at first, then his look deepened. He smiled, and Lily saw he was very handsome indeed, and that his smile was not only reassuring but wonderfully sweet and compelling.

"Well, little one," said the man, "where are you bound, you and your dolly?"

"I am going to the store to buy some salt for grandma," replied Lily, in her sweet treble. She looked up in the man's face, and he fairly started at the revelation of its innocent beauty. He regulated his pace by hers, and the two went on together. The man did not speak again at once. Lily kept glancing timidly up at him, and every time that she did so the man smiled and her confidence increased.

Presently when the man's hand grasped her little childish one hanging by her side, she felt a complete trust in him. Then she smiled up at him. She felt glad that this nice man had come along, for just here the road was lonely.

After a while the man spoke. "What is your name, little one?" he asked, caressingly.

"Lily Barry."

The man started. "What is your father's name?"

"Nelson Barry," replied Lily.

The man whistled. "Is your mother dead?"

"Yes, sir."

"How old are you, my dear?"

"Fourteen," replied Lily.

The man looked at her with surprise. "As old as that?"

Lily suddenly shrank from the man. She could not have told why. She pulled her little hand from his, and he let it go with no remonstrance. She clasped both her arms around her rag doll, in order that her hand should not be free for him to grasp again.

She walked a little farther away from the man, and he looked amused. "You still play with your doll?" he said, in a soft voice.

"Yes, sir," replied Lily. She quickened her pace and reached the store.

When Lily entered the store, Hiram Gates, the owner, was behind the counter. The only man besides in the store was Nelson Barry. He sat tipping his chair back against the wall; he was half asleep, and his handsome face was bristling with a beard of several days' growth and darkly flushed. He opened his eyes when Lily entered, the strange man following. He brought his chair down on all fours, and he looked at the man—not noticing Lily at all—with a look compounded of defiance and uneasiness.

"Hullo, Jim!" he said.

"Hullo, old man!" returned the stranger.

Lily went over to the counter and asked for the salt, in her pretty little voice. When she had paid for it and was crossing the store, Nelson Barry was on his feet.

"Well, how are you, Lily? It is Lily, isn't it?" he said.

"Yes, sir," replied Lily, faintly.

Her father bent down and, for the first time in her life, kissed her, and the whiskey odor of his breath came into her face.

Lily involuntarily started, and shrank away from him. Then she rubbed her mouth violently with her little cotton handkerchief, which she held gathered up with the rag doll.

"Damn it all! I believe she is afraid of me," said Nelson Barry, in a thick voice.

"Looks a little like it," said the other man, laughing.

"It's that damned old woman," said Nelson Barry. Then he smiled again at Lily. "I didn't know what a pretty little daughter I was blessed with," said he, and he softly stroked Lily's pink cheek under her hat.

Now Lily did not shrink from him. Hereditary instincts and nature itself were asserting themselves in the child's innocent, receptive breast.

Nelson Barry looked curiously at Lily. "How old are you, anyway, child?" he asked.

"I'll be fourteen in September," replied Lily.

"But you still play with your doll?" said Barry, laughing kindly down at her.

Lily hugged her doll more tightly, in spite of her father's kind voice. "Yes, sir," she replied.

Nelson glanced across at some glass jars filled with sticks of candy. "See here, little Lily, do you like candy?" said he.

"Yes, sir."

"Wait a minute."

Lily waited while her father went over to the counter. Soon he returned with a package of the candy.

"I don't see how you are going to carry so much," he said, smiling. "Suppose you throw away your doll?"

Lily gazed at her father and hugged the doll tightly, and there was all at once in the child's expression something mature. It became the reproach of a woman. Nelson's face sobered.

"Oh, it's all right, Lily," he said; "keep your doll. Here, I guess you can carry this candy under your arm."

Lily could not resist the candy. She obeyed Nelson's instructions for carrying it, and left the store laden. The two men also left, and walked in the opposite direction, talking busily.

When Lily reached home, her grandmother, who was watching for her, spied at once the package of candy.

"What's that?" she asked, sharply.

"My father gave it to me," answered Lily, in a faltering voice. Sally regarded her with something like alertness.

"Your father?"

"Yes, ma'am."

"Where did you see him?"

"In the store."

"He gave you this candy?"

"Yes, ma'am."

"What did he say?"

"He asked me how old I was, and—"

"And what?"

"I don't know," replied Lily; and it really seemed to her that she did not know, she was so frightened and bewildered by it all, and, more than anything else, by her grandmother's face as she questioned her.

Old Woman Magoun's face was that of one upon whom a long-anticipated blow had fallen. Sally Jinks gazed at her with a sort of stupid alarm.

Old Woman Magoun continued to gaze at her grandchild with that look of terrible solicitude, as if she saw the girl in the clutch of a tiger. "You can't remember what else he said?" she asked, fiercely, and the child began to whimper softly.

"No, ma'am," she sobbed. "I—don't know, and—"

"And what? Answer me."

"There was another man there. A real handsome man."

"Did he speak to you?" asked Old Woman Magoun.

"Yes, ma'am; he walked along with me a piece," confessed Lily, with a sob of terror and bewilderment.

"What did *he* say to you?" asked Old Woman Magoun, with a sort of despair.

Lily told, in her little, faltering, frightened voice, all of the conversation which she could recall. It sounded harmless enough, but the look of the realization of a long-expected blow never left her grandmother's face.

The sun was getting low, and the bridge was nearing completion. Soon the workmen would be crowding into the cabin for their promised supper. There became visible in the distance, far up the road, the heavily plodding figure of another woman who had agreed to come and help. Old Woman Magoun turned again to Lily.

"You go right upstairs to your own chamber now," said she.

"Good land! Ain't you goin' to let that poor child stay up and see the fun?" said Sally Jinks.

"You jest mind your own business," said Old Woman Magoun, forcibly, and Sally Jinks shrank. "You go right up there now, Lily," said the grandmother, in a softer tone, "and grandma will bring you up a nice plate of supper."

"When be you goin' to let that girl grow up?" asked Sally Jinks, when Lily had disappeared.

"She'll grow up in the Lord's good time," replied Old Woman Magoun, and there was in her voice something both sad and threatening. Sally Jinks again shrank a little.

Soon the workmen came flocking noisily into the house. Old Woman Magoun and her two helpers served the bountiful supper. Most of the men had drunk as much as, and more than, was good for them, and Old Woman Magoun had stipulated that there was to be no drinking of anything except coffee during supper.

"I'll git you as good a meal as I know how," she said, "but if I see ary one of you drinkin' a drop, I'll run you all out. If you want anything to drink, you can go up to the store afterward. That's the place for you to go to, if you've got to make hogs of yourselves. I ain't goin' to have no hogs in my house."

Old Woman Magoun was implicitly obeyed. She had a curious authority over most people when she chose to exercise it. When the supper was in full swing, she quietly stole upstairs and carried some food to Lily. She found the girl, with the rag doll in her arms, crouching by the window in her little rocking-chair—a relic of her infancy, which she still used.

"What a noise they are makin', grandma!" she said, in a terrified whisper, as her grandmother placed the plate before her on a chair.

"They've 'most all of 'em been drinkin'. They air a passel of hogs," replied the old woman.

"Is the man that was with—with my father down there?" asked Lily, in a timid fashion. Then she fairly cowered before the look in her grandmother's eyes.

"No, he ain't; and what's more, he never will be down there if I can help it," said Old Woman Magoun, in a fierce whisper. "I know who he is. They can't cheat me. He's one of them Willises—that family the Barrys married into. They're worse than the Barrys, ef they *have* got money. Eat your supper, and put him out of your mind, child."

It was after Lily was asleep, when Old Woman Magoun was alone, clearing away her supper dishes, that Lily's father came. The door was closed, and he knocked, and the old woman knew at once who was there. The sound of that knock meant as much to her as the whir of a bomb to the defender of a fortress. She opened the door, and Nelson Barry stood there.

"Good-evening, Mrs. Magoun," he said.

Old Woman Magoun stood before him, filling up the doorway with her firm bulk.

"Good-evening, Mrs. Magoun," said Nelson Barry again.

"I ain't got no time to waste," replied the old woman, harshly. "I've got my supper dishes to clean up after them men."

She stood there and looked at him as she might have looked at a rebellious animal which she was trying to tame. The man laughed.

"It's no use," said he. "You know me of old. No human being can turn me from my way when I am once started in it. You may as well let me come in."

Old Woman Magoun entered the house, and Barry followed her. Barry began without any preface. "Where is the child?" asked he.

"Upstairs. She has gone to bed."

"She goes to bed early."

"Children ought to," returned the old woman, polishing a plate.

Barry laughed. "You are keeping her a child a long while," he remarked, in a soft voice which had a sting in it.

"She *is* a child," returned the old woman, defiantly.

"Her mother was only three years older when Lily was born."

The old woman made a sudden motion toward the man which seemed fairly menacing. Then she turned again to her dish-washing.

"I want her," said Barry.

"You can't have her," replied the old woman, in a still stern voice.

"I don't see how you can help yourself. You have always acknowledged that she was my child."

The old woman continued her task, but her strong back heaved. Barry regarded her with an entirely pitiless expression.

"I am going to have the girl, that is the long and short of it," he said, "and it is for her best good, too. You are a fool, or you would see it."

"Her best good?" muttered the old woman.

'Yes, her best good. What are you going to do with her, anyway? The girl is a beauty, and almost a woman grown, although you try to make out that she is a baby. You can't live forever."

"The Lord will take care of her," replied the old woman, and again she turned and faced him, and her expression was that of a prophetess.

"Very well, let Him," said Barry, easily. "All the same I'm going to have her, and I tell you it is for her best good. Jim Willis saw her this afternoon, and—"

Old Woman Magoun looked at him. "Jim Willis!" she fairly shrieked.

"Well, what of it?"

"One of them Willises!" repeated the old woman, and this time her voice was thick. It seemed almost as if she were stricken with paralysis. She did not enunciate clearly.

The man shrank a little. "Now what is the need of your making such a fuss?" he said. "I will take her, and Isabel will look out for her."

"Your half-witted sister?" said Old Woman Magoun.

"Yes, my half-witted sister. She knows more than you think."

"More wickedness."

"Perhaps. Well, a knowledge of evil is a useful thing. How are you going to avoid evil if you don't know what it is like? My sister and I will take care of my daughter."

The old woman continued to look at the man, but his eyes never fell. Suddenly her gaze grew inconceivably keen. It was as if she saw through all externals.

"I know what it is!" she cried. "You have been playing cards and you lost, and this is the way you will pay him."

Then the man's face reddened, and he swore under his breath.

"Oh, my God!" said the old woman; and she really spoke with her eyes aloft as if addressing something outside of them both. Then she turned again to her dish-washing.

The man cast a dogged look at her back. "Well, there is no use talking. I have made up my mind," said he, "and you know me and what that means. I am going to have the girl."

"When?" said the old woman, without turning around.

"Well, I am willing to give you a week. Put her clothes in good order before she comes."

The old woman made no reply. She continued washing dishes. She even handled them so carefully that they did not rattle.

"You understand," said Barry. "Have her ready a week from today."

"Yes," said Old Woman Magoun, "I understand."

Nelson Barry, going up the mountain road, reflected that Old Woman Magoun had a strong character, that she understood much better than her sex in general the futility of withstanding the inevitable.

"Well," he said to Jim Willis when he reached home, "the old woman did not make such a fuss as I expected."

"Are you going to have the girl?"

"Yes; a week from today. Look here, Jim; you've got to stick to your promise."

"All right," said Willis. "Go you one better."

The two were playing at cards in the old parlor, once magnificent, now squalid, of the Barry house. Isabel, the half-witted sister, entered, bringing some glasses on a tray. She had learned with her feeble intellect some tricks, like a dog. One of them was the mixing of sundry drinks. She set the tray on a little stand near the two men, and watched them with her silly simper.

"Clear out now and go to bed," her brother said to her, and she obeyed.

Early the next morning Old Woman Magoun went up to Lily's little sleeping-chamber, and watched her a second as she lay asleep, with her yellow locks spread over the pillow. Then she spoke. "Lily," said she—"Lily, wake up. I am going to Greenham across the new bridge, and you can go with me."

Lily immediately sat up in bed and smiled at her grandmother. Her eyes were still misty, but the light of awakening was in them.

"Get right up," said the old woman. "You can wear your new dress if you want to."

Lily gurgled with pleasure like a baby. "And my new hat?" asked she.

"I don't care."

Old Woman Magoun and Lily started for Greenham before Barry's Ford, which kept late hours, was fairly awake. It was three miles to Greenham. The old woman said that, since the horse was a little lame, they would walk. It was a beautiful morning, with a diamond radiance of dew over everything. Her grandmother had curled Lily's hair more punctiliously than usual. The little face peeped like a rose out of two rows of golden spirals. Lily wore her new muslin dress with a pink sash, and her best hat of a fine white straw trimmed with a wreath of rosebuds; also the neatest black open-work stockings and pretty shoes. She even had white cotton gloves. When they set out, the old, heavily stepping woman, in her black gown and cape and bonnet, looked down at the little pink fluttering figure. Her face was full of the tenderest love and admiration, and yet there was something terrible about it. They crossed the new bridge—a primitive structure built of logs in a slovenly fashion. Old Woman Magoun pointed to a gap.

"Jest see that," said she. "That's the way men work."

"Men ain't very nice, be they?" said Lily, in her sweet little voice.

"No, they ain't, take them all together," replied her grandmother.

"That man that walked to the store with me was nicer than some, I guess," Lily said, in a wishful fashion. Her grandmother reached down and took the child's hand in its small cotton glove. "You hurt me, holding my hand so tight," Lily said presently, in a deprecatory little voice.

The old woman loosened her grasp. "Grandma didn't know how tight she was holding your hand," said she. "She wouldn't hurt you for nothin', except it was to save your life, or somethin' like that." She spoke with an undertone of tremendous meaning which the girl was too childish to grasp. They walked along the country road. Just before they reached Greenham they passed a stone wall overgrown with blackberry-vines, and, an unusual thing in that vicinity, a lusty spread of deadly nightshade full of berries.

"Those berries look good to eat, grandma," Lily said.

At that instant the old woman's face became something terrible to see. "You can't have any now," she said, and hurried Lily along.

"They look real nice," said Lily.

When they reached Greenham, Old Woman Magoun took her way straight to the most pretentious house there, the residence of the lawyer, whose name was Mason. Old Woman Magoun bade Lily wait in the yard for a few moments, and Lily ventured to seat herself on a bench beneath an oak-tree; then she watched with some wonder her grandmother enter the lawyer's office door at the right of the house. Presently the lawyer's wife came out and spoke to Lily under the tree. She had in her hand a little tray containing a plate of cake, a glass of milk, and an early apple. She spoke very kindly to Lily; she even kissed her, and offered her the tray of refreshments, which Lily accepted gratefully. She sat eating, with Mrs. Mason watching her, when Old Woman Magoun came out of the lawyer's office with a ghastly face.

"What are you eatin'?" she asked Lily, sharply. "Is that a sour apple?"

"I thought she might be hungry," said the lawyer's wife, with loving, melancholy eyes upon the girl.

Lily had almost finished the apple. "It's real sour, but I like it; it's real nice, grandma," she said.

"You ain't been drinkin' milk with a sour apple?"

"It was real nice milk, grandma."

"You ought never to have drunk milk and eat a sour apple," said her grandmother. "Your stomach was all out of order this mornin', an' sour apples and milk is always apt to hurt anybody."

"I don't know but they are," Mrs. Mason said, apologetically, as she stood on the green lawn with her lavender muslin sweeping around her. "I am real sorry, Mrs. Magoun. I ought to have thought. Let me get some soda for her."

"Soda never agrees with her," replied the old woman, in a harsh voice. "Come," she said to Lily, "it's time we were goin' home."

After Lily and her grandmother had disappeared down the road, Lawyer Mason came out of his office and joined his wife, who had seated herself on the bench beneath the tree. She was idle, and her face wore the expression of those who review joys forever past. She had lost a little girl, her only child, years ago, and her husband always knew when she was thinking about her. Lawyer Mason looked older than his wife; he had a dry, shrewd, slightly one-sided face.

"What do you think, Maria?" he said. "That old woman came to me with the most pressing entreaty to adopt that little girl."

"She is a beautiful little girl," said Mrs. Mason, in a slightly husky voice.

"Yes, she is a pretty child," assented the lawyer, looking pityingly at his wife; "but it is out of the question, my dear. Adopting a child is a serious measure, and in this case a child who comes from Barry's Ford."

"But the grandmother seems a very good woman," said Mrs. Mason.

"I rather think she is. I never heard a word against her. But the father! No, Maria, we cannot take a child with Barry blood in her veins. The stock has run out; it is vitiated physically and morally. It won't do, my dear."

"Her grandmother had her dressed up as pretty as a little girl could be," said Mrs. Mason, and this time the tears welled into her faithful, wistful eyes.

"Well, we can't help that," said the lawyer, as he went back to his office.

Old Woman Magoun and Lily returned, going slowly along the road to Barry's Ford. When they came to the stone wall where the blackberry-vines and the deadly nightshade grew, Lily said she was tired, and asked if she could not sit down for a few minutes. The strange look on her grandmother's face had deepened. Now and then Lily glanced at her and had a feeling as if she were looking at a stranger.

"Yes, you can set down if you want to," said Old Woman Magoun, deeply and harshly.

Lily started and looked at her, as if to make sure that it was her grandmother who spoke. Then she sat down on a stone which was comparatively free of the vines.

"Ain't you goin' to set down, grandma?" Lily asked, timidly.

"No; I don't want to get into that mess," replied her grandmother. "I ain't tired. I'll stand here."

Lily sat still; her delicate little face was flushed with heat. She extended her tiny feet in her best shoes and gazed at them. "My shoes are all over dust," said she.

"It will brush off," said her grandmother, still in that strange voice.

Lily looked around. An elm-tree in the field behind her cast a spray of branches over her head; a little cool puff of wind came on her face. She gazed at the low mountains on the horizon, in the midst of which she lived, and she sighed, for no reason that she knew. She began idly picking at the blackberry-vines; there were no berries on them; then she put her little fingers on the berries of the deadly nightshade. "These look like nice berries," she said.

Old Woman Magoun, standing stiff and straight in the road, said nothing.

"They look good to eat," said Lily.

Old Woman Magoun still said nothing, but she looked up into the ineffable blue of the sky, over which spread at intervals great white clouds shaped like wings.

Lily picked some of the deadly nightshade berries and ate them. "Why, they are real sweet," said she. "They are nice." She picked some more and ate them.

Presently her grandmother spoke. "Come," she said, "it is time we were going. I guess you have set long enough."

Lily was still eating the berries when she slipped down from the wall and followed her grandmother obediently up the road.

Before they reached home, Lily complained of being very thirsty. She stopped and made a little cup of a leaf and drank long at a mountain brook. "I am dreadful dry, but it hurts me to swallow," she said to her grandmother when she stopped drinking and joined the old woman waiting for her in the road. Her grandmother's face seemed strangely dim to her. She took hold of Lily's hand as they went on. "My stomach burns," said Lily, presently. "I want some more water."

"There is another brook a little farther on," said Old Woman Magoun, in a dull voice.

When they reached that brook, Lily stopped and drank again, but she whimpered a little over her difficulty in swallowing. "My stomach burns, too," she said, walking on, "and my throat is so dry, grandma." Old Woman Magoun held Lily's hand more tightly. "You hurt me holding my hand so tight, grandma," said Lily, looking up at her grandmother, whose face she seemed to see through a mist, and the old woman loosened her grasp.

When at last they reached home, Lily was very ill. Old Woman Magoun put her on her own bed in the little bedroom out of the kitchen. Lily lay there and moaned, and Sally Jinks came in.

"Why, what ails her?" she asked. "She looks feverish."

Lily unexpectedly answered for herself. "I ate some sour apples and drank some milk," she moaned.

"Sour apples and milk are dreadful apt to hurt anybody," said Sally Jinks. She told several people on her way home that Old Woman Magoun was dreadful careless to let Lily eat such things.

Meanwhile Lily grew worse. She suffered cruelly from the burning in her stomach, the vertigo, and the deadly nausea. "I am so sick, I am so sick, grandma," she kept moaning. She could no longer see her grandmother as she bent over her, but she could hear her talk.

Old Woman Magoun talked as Lily had never heard her talk before, as nobody had ever heard her talk before. She spoke from the depths of her soul; her voice was as tender as the coo of a dove, and it was grand and exalted. "You'll feel better very soon, little Lily," said she.

"I am so sick, grandma."

"You will feel better very soon, and then—"

"I am sick."

"You shall go to a beautiful place."

Lily moaned.

"You shall go to a beautiful place," the old woman went on.

"Where?" asked Lily, groping feebly with her cold little hands. Then she moaned again.

"A beautiful place, where the flowers grow tall."

"What color? Oh, grandma, I am so sick."

"A blue color," replied the old woman. Blue was Lily's favorite color. "A beautiful blue color, and as tall as your knees, and the flowers always stay there, and they never fade."

"Not if you pick them, grandma? Oh!"

"No, not if you pick them; they never fade, and they are so sweet you can smell them a mile off; and there are birds that sing, and all the roads have gold stones in them, and the stone walls are made of gold."

"Like the ring grandpa gave you? I am so sick, grandma."

"Yes, gold like that. And all the houses are built of silver and gold, and the people all have wings, so when they get tired walking they can fly, and—"

"I am so sick, grandma."

"And all the dolls are alive," said Old Woman Magoun. "Dolls like yours can run, and talk, and love you back again."

Lily had her poor old rag doll in bed with her, clasped close to her agonized little heart. She tried very hard with her eyes, whose pupils were so dilated that they looked black, to see her grandmother's face when she said that, but she could not. "It is dark," she moaned, feebly.

"There where you are going it is always light," said the grandmother, "and the commonest things shine like that breastpin Mrs. Lawyer Mason had on today."

Lily moaned pitifully, and said something incoherent. Delirium was commencing. Presently she sat straight up in bed and raved; but even then her grandmother's wonderful compelling voice had an influence over her.

"You will come to a gate with all the colors of the rainbow," said her grandmother; "and it will open, and you will go right in and walk up the gold street, and cross the field where the blue flowers come up to your knees, until you find your mother, and she will take you home where you are going to live. She has a little white room all ready for you, white curtains at the windows, and a little white looking-glass, and when you look in it you will see—"

"What will I see? I am so sick, grandma."

"You will see a face like yours, only it's an angel's; and there will be a little white bed, and you can lay down an' rest."

"Won't I be sick, grandma?" asked Lily. Then she moaned and babbled wildly, although she seemed to understand through it all what her grandmother said.

"No, you will never be sick any more. Talkin' about sickness won't mean anything to you."

It continued. Lily talked on wildly, and her grandmother's great voice of soothing never ceased, until the child fell into a deep sleep, or what resembled sleep; but she lay stiffly in that sleep, and a candle flashed before her eyes made no impression on them.

Then it was that Nelson Barry came. Jim Willis waited outside the door. When Nelson entered he found Old Woman Magoun on her knees beside the bed, weeping with dry eyes and a might of agony which fairly shook Nelson Barry, the degenerate of a fine old race.

"Is she sick?" he asked, in a hushed voice.

Old Woman Magoun gave another terrible sob, which sounded like the gasp of one dying.

"Sally Jinks said that Lily was sick from eating milk and sour apples," said Barry, in a tremulous voice. "I remember that her mother was very sick once from eating them."

Lily lay still, and her grandmother on her knees shook with her terrible sobs.

Suddenly Nelson Barry started. "I guess I had better go to Greenham for a doctor if she's as bad as that," he said. He went close to the bed and looked at the sick child. He gave a great start. Then he felt of her hands and reached down under the bedclothes for her little feet. "Her hands and feet are like ice," he cried out. "Good God! Why didn't you send for someone—for me before? Why, she's dying; she's almost gone!"

Barry rushed out and spoke to Jim Willis, who turned pale and came in and stood by the bedside.

"She's almost gone," he said, in a hushed whisper.

"There's no use going for the doctor; she'd be dead before he got here," said Nelson, and he stood regarding the passing child with a strange, sad face—unutterably sad, because of his incapability of the truest sadness.

"Poor little thing, she's past suffering, anyhow," said the other man, and his own face also was sad with a puzzled, mystified sadness.

Lily died that night. There was quite a commotion in Barry's Ford until after the funeral, it was all so sudden, and then everything went on as usual. Old Woman Magoun continued to live as she had done before. She supported herself by the produce of her tiny farm; she was very industrious, but people said that she was a trifle touched, since every time she went over the log bridge with her eggs or her garden vegetables to sell in Greenham, she carried with her, as one might have carried an infant, Lily's old rag doll.

# ONE GOOD TIME

## Mary E. Wilkins Freeman

RICHARD STONE WAS nearly seventy-five years old when he died, his wife was over sixty, and his daughter Narcissa past middle age. Narcissa Stone had been very pretty, and would have been pretty still had it not been for those lines, as distinctly garrulous of discontent and worry as any words of mouth, which come so easily in the face of a nervous, delicate-skinned woman. They were around Narcissa's blue eyes, her firmly closed lips, her thin nose; a frown like a crying repetition of some old anxiety and indecision was on her forehead; and she had turned her long neck so much to look over her shoulder for new troubles on her track that the lines of fearful expectation had settled there. Narcissa had yet her beautiful thick hair, which the people in the village had never quite liked because it was red, her cheeks were still pink, and she stooped only a little from her slender height when she walked. Some people said that Narcissa Stone would be quite good-looking now if she had a decent dress and bonnet. Neither she nor her mother had any clothes which were not deemed shabby, even by the humbly attired women in the little mountain village. "Mis' Richard Stone, she ain't had a new silk dress since Narcissa was born," they said; "and as for Narcissa, she ain't never had anything that looked fit to wear to meeting."

When Richard Stone died, people wondered if his widow and Narcissa would not have something new. Mrs. Nathan Wheat, who was a third cousin to Richard Stone, went, the day before the funeral, a half-mile down the brook road to see Hannah Turbin, the dressmaker. The road was little travelled; she walked through an undergrowth of late autumn flowers, and when she reached the Turbins' house her black thibet gown was gold-powdered and white-flecked to the knees with pollen and winged seeds of passed flowers.

Hannah Turbin's arm, brown and wrinkled like a monkey's, in its woollen sleeve, described arcs of jerky energy past the window, and never ceased when Mrs. Wheat came up the path and entered the house. Hannah herself scarcely raised her seamy brown face from her work.

"Good-afternoon," said Mrs. Wheat.

Hannah nodded. "Good-afternoon," she responded then, as if words were an afterthought.

Mrs. Wheat shook her black skirts vigorously. "I'm all over dust from them yaller weeds," said she. "Well, I don't care about this old thibet." She pulled a rocking-chair forward and seated herself. "Warm for this time of year," said she.

Hannah drew her thread through her work. "Yes, 'tis," she returned, with a certain pucker of scorn, as if the utter foolishness of allusions to obvious conditions of nature struck her. Hannah Turbin was not a favorite in the village, but she was credited with having much common-sense, and people held her in somewhat distant respect.

"Guess it's Injun summer," remarked Mrs. Wheat.

Hannah Turbin said nothing at all to that. Mrs. Wheat cast furtive glances around the room as she swayed in her rocking-chair. Everything was very tidy, and there were few indications of its owner's calling. A number of fashion papers were neatly piled on a bureau in the corner, and some nicely folded breadths of silk lay beside them. There was not a scrap or shred of cloth upon the floor; not a thread, even. Hannah was basting a brown silk basque. Mrs. Wheat could see nowhere the slightest evidence of what she had come to ascertain, so was finally driven to inquiry, still, however, by devious windings.

"Seems sad about Richard," she said.

"Yes," returned Hannah, with a sudden contraction of her brown face, which seemed to flash a light over a recollection in Mrs. Wheat's mind. She remembered that there was a time, years ago, when Richard Stone had paid some attention to Hannah Turbin, and people had thought he might marry her instead of Jane Basset. However, it had happened so long ago that she did not really believe that Hannah dwelt upon it, and it faded immediately from her own mind.

"Well," said she, with a sigh, "it is a happy release, after all, he's been such a sufferer so long. It's better for him, and it's better for

Jane and Narcissa. He's left 'em comfortable; they've got the farm, and his life's insured, you know. Besides, I suppose Narcissa'll marry William Crane now. Most likely they'll rent the farm, and Jane will go and live with Narcissa when she's married. I want to know—"

Hannah Turbin sewed.

"I was wondering," continued Mrs. Wheat, "if Jane and Narcissa wasn't going to have some new black dresses for the funeral. They ain't got a thing that's fit to wear, I know. I don't suppose they've got much money on hand now except what little Richard saved up for his funeral expenses. I know he had a little for that because he told me so, but the life-insurance is coming in, and anybody would trust them. There's a nice piece of black cashmere down to the store, a dollar a yard. I didn't know but they'd get dresses off it; but Jane she never tells me anything—anybody'd think she might, seeing as I was poor Richard's cousin; and as for Narcissa, she's as close as her mother."

Hannah Turbin sewed.

"Ain't Jane and Narcissa said anything to you about making them any new black dresses to wear to the funeral?" asked Mrs. Wheat, with desperate directness.

"No, they ain't," replied Hannah Turbin.

"Well, then, all I've got to say is they'd ought to be ashamed of themselves. There they've got fourteen if not fifteen hundred dollars coming in from poor Richard's insurance money, and they ain't even going to get decent clothes to wear to his funeral out of it. They ain't made any plans for new bonnets, I know. It ain't showing proper respect to the poor man. Don't you say so?"

"I suppose folks are their own best judges," said Hannah Turbin, in her conclusive, half-surly fashion, which intimidated most of her neighbors. Mrs. Wheat did not stay much longer. When she went home through the ghostly weeds and grasses of the country road she was almost as indignant with Hannah Turbin as with Jane Stone and Narcissa. "Never saw anybody so close in my life," said she to herself. "Needn't talk if she don't want to. Dun'no' as thar's any harm in my wanting to know if my own third cousin is going to have mourning wore for him."

Mrs. Wheat, when she reached home, got a black shawl which had belonged to her mother out of the chest, where it had lain in camphor, and hung it on the clothesline to air. She also removed a spray of bright velvet flowers from her bonnet, and sewed in its place a black ostrich feather. She found an old crape veil too, and steamed it into stiffness. "I'm going to go to that funeral looking decent, if his own wife and daughter ain't," she told her husband.

"If I wa'n't along, folks would take you for the widder," said Nathan Wheat, with a chuckle. Nathan Wheat was rather inclined to be facetious with his wife.

However, Mrs. Wheat was not the only person who attended poor Richard Stone's funeral in suitable attire. Hannah Turbin was black from head to foot; the material, it is true, was not of the conventional mourning kind, but the color was. She wore a black silk gown, a black ladies'-cloth mantle, a black velvet bonnet trimmed with black flowers, and a black lace veil.

"Hannah Turbin looked as if she was dressed in second mourning," Mrs. Wheat said to her husband after the funeral. "I should have thought she'd most have worn some color, seeing as some folks might remember she was disappointed about Richard Stone; but, anyway, it was better than to go looking the way Jane and Narcissa did. There was Jane in that old brown dress, and Narcissa in her green, with a blue flower in her bonnet. I think it was dreadful, and poor Richard leaving them all that money through his dying, too."

In truth, all the village was scandalized at the strange attire of the widow and daughter of Richard Stone at his funeral, except William Crane. He could not have told what Mrs. Stone wore, through scarcely admitting her in any guise into his inmost consciousness, and as for Narcissa, he admitted her so fully that he could not see her robes at all in such a dazzlement of vision.

"William Crane never took his eyes off Narcissa Stone all through the funeral; shouldn't be surprised if he married her in a month or six weeks," people said.

William Crane took Jane and Narcissa to the grave in his covered wagon, keeping his old white horse at a decorous jog behind the hearse in the little funeral procession, and people noted that. They wondered if he would go over to the Stones' that evening, and watched, but he did not. He left the mother and daughter to their close communion of grief that night, but the next the neighbors saw him in his best suit going down the road before dark. "Must have done up his chores early to get started soon as this," they said.

William Crane was about Narcissa's age but he looked older. His gait was shuffling, his hair scanty and gray, and, moreover, he had that expression of patience which comes only from long abiding, both of body and soul. He went through the south yard to the side door of the house, stepping between the rocks. The yard abounded in mossy slopes of half-sunken rocks, as did the entire farm. Folks often remarked of Richard Stone's place, as well as himself, "Stone by name, and stone by nature." Underneath nearly all his fields, cropping plentifully to the surface, were rock ledges. The grass could be mown only by hand. As for this south yard, it required skilful maneuvering to drive a team through it. When William Crane knocked that evening, Narcissa opened the door. "Oh, it's you!" she said. "How do you do?"

"How do you do, Narcissa?" William responded, and walked in. He could have kissed his old love in the gloom of the little entry, but he did not think of that. He looked at her anxiously with his soft, patient eyes. "How are you gettin' on?" he asked.

"Well as can be expected," replied Narcissa.

"How's your mother?"

"She's well as can be expected."

William followed Narcissa, who led the way, not into the parlor, as he had hoped, but into the kitchen. The kitchen's great interior of smoky gloom was very familiar to him, but tonight it looked strange. For one thing, the arm-chair to which Richard Stone had been bound with his rheumatism for the last fifteen years was vacant, and pushed away into a corner. William looked at it, and it seemed to him that he must see the crooked, stern old figure in it, and hear again the peremptory tap of the stick which he kept always at his side to summon assistance. After his first involuntary glance at the dead man's chair, William saw his widow coming forward out of her bedroom with a great quilt over her arm.

"Good-evenin', William," she said, with faint melancholy, then lapsed into feeble weeping.

"Now, mother, you said you wouldn't; you know it don't do any good, and you'll be sick," Narcissa cried out, impatiently.

"I know it, Narcissa, but I can't help it, I can't. I'm dreadful upset! Oh, William, I'm dreadful upset! It ain't his death alone—it's—"

"Mother, I'd rather tell him myself," interrupted Narcissa. She took the quilt from her mother, and drew the rocking-chair towards her. "Do sit down and keep calm, mother," said she.

But it was not easy for the older woman, in her bewilderment of grief and change, to keep calm.

"Oh, William, do you know what we're goin' to do?" she wailed, yet seating herself obediently in the rocking-chair. "We're goin' to New York. Narcissa says so. We're goin' to take the insurance money, when we get it, an' we're goin' to New York. I tell her we hadn't ought to, but she won't listen to it! There's the trunk. Look at there, William! She dragged it down from the garret this forenoon. Look at there, William!"

William's startled eyes followed the direction of Mrs. Stone's wavering index finger, and saw a great ancient trunk lined with blue-and-white wall-paper, standing open against the opposite wall.

"She dragged it down from the garret this forenoon," continued Mrs. Stone, in the same tone of unfaltering tragedy, while Narcissa, her delicate lips pursed tightly, folded up the bed-quilt which her mother had brought. "It bumped so hard on those garret stairs I thought she'd break it, or fall herself, but she wouldn't let me help her. Then she cleaned it, an' made some paste, an' lined it with some of the parlor paper. There ain't any key to it—I never remember none. The trunk was in this house when I come here. Richard had it when he went West before we were married. Narcissa she says she is goin' to tie it up with the clothes-line. William, can't you talk to her? Seems to me I can't go to New York nohow."

William turned then to Narcissa, who was laying the folded bed-quilt in the trunk. He looked pale and bewildered, and his voice trembled when he spoke. "This ain't true, is it, Narcissa?" he said.

"Yes, it is," she replied, shortly, still bending over the trunk.

"We ain't goin' for a month," interposed her mother again; "we can't get the insurance money before then, Lawyer Maxham says; but she says she's goin' to have the trunk standin' there, an' put things in when she thinks of it, so she won't forget nothin'. She says we'd better take one bed-quilt with us, in case they don't have 'nough clothes on the bed. We've got to stay to a hotel. Oh, William, can't you say anything to stop her?"

"This ain't true, Narcissa?" William repeated, helplessly.

Narcissa raised herself and faced him. Her cheeks were red, her blue eyes glowing, her hair tossing over her temples in loose waves. She looked as she had when he first courted her. "Yes, it is, William Crane," she cried. "Yes, it is."

William looked at her so strangely and piteously that she softened a little. "I've got my reasons," said she. "Maybe I owe it to you to tell them. I suppose you were expecting something different." She hesitated a minute, looking at her mother, who cried out again:

"Oh, William, say somethin' to stop her! Can't you say somethin' to stop her?"

Then Narcissa motioned to him resolutely. "Come into the parlor, William," said she, and he followed her out across the entry.

The parlor was chilly; the chairs stood as they had done at the funeral, primly against the walls glimmering faintly in the dusk with blue-and-white paper like the trunk lining. Narcissa stood before William and talked with feverish haste. "I'm going," said she—"I'm going to take that money and go with mother to New York, and you mustn't try to stop me, William. I know what you've been expecting. I know, now father's gone, you think there ain't anything to hinder our getting married; you think we'll rent this house, and mother and me will settle down in yours for the rest of our lives. I know you ain't counting on that insurance money; it ain't like you."

"The Lord knows it ain't, Narcissa," William broke out with pathetic pride.

"I know that as well as you do. You thought we'd put it in the bank for a rainy day, in case mother got feeble, or anything, and that is all you did think. Maybe I'd ought to. I s'pose I had, but I ain't going to. I ain't never done anything my whole life that I thought I ought not to do, but now I'm going to. I'm going to if it's wicked. I've made up my mind. I ain't never had one good time in my whole life, and now I'm going to, even if I have to suffer for it afterwards.

"I ain't never had anything like other women. I've never had any clothes nor gone anywhere. I've just stayed at home here and drudged. I've done a man's work on the farm. I've milked and made butter and cheese; I've waited on father; I've got up early and gone to bed late. I've just drudged, drudged, ever since I can remember. I don't know anything about the world nor life. I don't know anything but my own old tracks, and—I'm going to get out of them for a while, whether or no."

"How long are you calculating to stay?"

"I don't know."

"I've been thinking," said William, "I'd have some new gilt paper on the sitting-room at my house, and a new stove in the kitchen. I thought—"

"I know what you thought," interrupted Narcissa, still trembling and glowing with nervous fervor. "And you're real good, William. It ain't many men would have waited for me as you've done, when father wouldn't let me get married as long as he lived. I know by good rights I hadn't ought to keep you waiting, but I'm going to, and it ain't because I don't think enough of you—it ain't that; I can't help it. If you give up having me at all, if you think you'd rather marry somebody else, I can't help it; I won't blame you—"

"Maybe you want me to, Narcissa," said William, with a sad dignity. "If you do, if you want to get rid of me, if that's it—"

Narcissa started. "That ain't it," said she. She hesitated, and added, with formal embarrassment—she had the usual reticence of a New England village woman about expressions of affection, and had never even told her lover in actual words that she loved him—"My feelings towards you are the same as they have always been, William."

It was almost dark in the parlor. They could see only each other's faces gleaming as with pale light. "It would be a blow to me if I thought they wa'n't, Narcissa," William returned, simply.

"They are."

William put his arm around her waist, and they stood close together for a moment. He stroked back her tumbled red hair with clumsy tenderness. "You have had a hard time, Narcissa," he whispered, brokenly. "If you want to go, I ain't going to say anything against it. I ain't going to deny I'm kind of disappointed. I've been living alone so long, and I feel kind of sore sometimes with waitin', but—"

"I shouldn't make you any kind of a wife if I married you now, without waiting," Narcissa said, in a voice at once stern and tender. She stood apart from him, and put up her hand with a sort of involuntary maiden primness to smooth her hair where his had stroked it awry. "If," she went on, "I had to settle down in your house, as I have done in father's, and see the years stretching ahead like a long road without any turn, and nothing but the same old dog-trot of washing and ironing and scrubbing and cooking and sewing and washing dishes till I drop into my grave, I should hate you, William Crane."

"I could fetch an' carry all the water for the washin', Narcissa, and I could wash the dishes," said William, with humble beseeching.

"It ain't that. I know you'd do all you could. It's—Oh, William! I've got to have a break; I've got to have one good time. I—like you, and—I liked father; but love ain't enough sometimes when it ties anybody. Everybody has got their own feet and their own wanting to use 'em, and sometimes when love comes in the way of that, it ain't anything but a dead wall. Once we had a black heifer that would jump all the walls; we had to sell her. She always made me think of myself. I tell you, William, I've got to jump my wall, and I've got to have one good time."

William Crane nodded his gray head in patient acquiescence. His forehead was knitted helplessly; he could not in the least understand what his sweetheart meant; in her present mood she was in altogether a foreign language for him, but still the unintelligible sound of her was sweet as a song to his ears. This poor village lover had at least gained the crown of absolute faith through his weary years of waiting; the woman he loved was still a star, and her rays not yet resolved into human reachings and graspings.

"How long do you calculate to be gone, Narcissa?" he asked again.

"I don't know," she replied. "Fifteen hundred dollars is a good deal of money. I s'pose it'll take us quite a while to spend it, even if we ain't very saving."

"You ain't goin' to spend it all, Narcissa!" William gave a little dismayed gasp in spite of himself.

"Land, no! we couldn't, unless we stayed three years, an' I ain't calculating to be gone as long as that. I'm going to bring home what we don't want, and put it in the bank; but—I shouldn't be surprised if it took 'most a year to spend what I've laid out to."

"'Most a year!"

"Yes; I've got to buy us both new clothes for one thing. We ain't neither of us got anything fit to wear, and ain't had for years. We didn't go to the funeral lookin' decent, and I know folks talked. Mother felt bad about it, but I couldn't help it. I wa'n't goin' to lay out money foolish and get things here when I was going to New York and could have others the way they ought to be. I'm going to buy us some jewelry too; I ain't never had a good breastpin even; and as for mother, father never even bought her a ring when they were married. I ain't saying anything against him; it wa'n't the fashion so much in those days."

"I was calculatin'—" William stammered, blushing. "I always meant to, Narcissa."

"Yes, I know you have; but you mustn't lay out too much on it, and I don't care anything about a stone ring—just a plain gold one. There's another thing I'm going to have, too, an' that's a gold watch. I've wanted one all my life."

"Mebbe—" began William, painfully.

"No!" cried Narcissa, peremptorily. "I don't want you to buy me one. I ain't ever thought of it. I'm going to buy it myself. I'm going to buy mother a real cashmere shawl, too, like the one that New York lady had that came to visit Lawyer Maxham's wife. I've got a list of things written down on paper. I guess I'll have to buy another trunk in New York to put them in."

"Well," said William, with a great sigh, "I guess I'd better be goin'. I hope you'll have as good a time as you're countin' on, Narcissa."

"It's the first good time I ever did count on, and I'd ought to," said Narcissa. "I'm going to take mother to the theatre, too. I don't know but it's wicked, but I'm going to." Narcissa fluttered out of the parlor and William shuffled after her. He would not go into the kitchen again.

"Well, good-night," said Narcissa, and William also said good-night, with another heavy sigh. "Look out for them rocks going out of the yard, an' don't tumble over 'em," she called after him.

"I'm used to 'em," he answered back, sadly, from the darkness.

Narcissa shut and bolted the door. "He don't like it; he feels real bad about it; but I can't help it—I'm going."

Through the next few weeks Narcissa Stone's face looked strange to those who had known her from childhood. While the features were the same, her soul informed them with a new purpose, which overlighted all the old ones of her life, and even the simple village folks saw the effect, though with no understanding. Soon the news that Narcissa and her mother were going to New York was abroad. On the morning they started, in the three-seated open wagon which served as stage to connect the little village with the railroad ten miles away, all the windows were set with furtively peering faces.

"There they go," the women told one another. "Narcissa an' her mother an' the trunk. Wonder if Narcissa's got that money put away safe? They're wearin' the same old clothes. S'pose we sha'n't know 'em when they get back. Heard they was goin' to stay a year. Guess old Mr. Stone would rise up in his grave if he knew it. Lizzy saw William Crane a-helpin' Narcissa h'ist the trunk out ready for the stage. I wouldn't stan' it if I was him. Ten chances to one Narcissa'll pick up somebody down to New York, with all that money. She's good-lookin', an' she looks better since her father died."

Narcissa, riding out of her native village to those unknown fields in which her imagination had laid the scene of the one good time of her life, regarded nothing around her. She sat straight, her slender body resisting stiffly the jolt of the stage. She said not a word, but looked ahead with shining eyes. Her mother wept, a fold of her old shawl before her face. Now and then she lamented aloud, but softly, lest the driver hear. "Goin' away from the place where I was born an' married, an' have lived ever since I knew anything, to stay a year. I can't stan' it, I can't."

"Hush, mother! You'll have a real good time."

"No, I sha'n't, I sha'n't. Goin'—to stay a whole—year. I—can't, nohow."

"S'pose we sha'n't see you back in these parts for some time," the stage-driver said, when he helped them out at the railroad station. He was an old man, and had known Narcissa since her childhood.

"Most likely not," she replied. Her mother's face was quite stiff with repressed emotion when the stage-driver lifted her out. She did not want him to report in the village that she was crying when she started for New York. She had some pride in spite of her distress.

"Well, I'll be on the lookout for ye a year from today," said the stage-driver, with a jocular twist of his face. There were no passengers for his village on the in-coming train, so he had to drive home alone through the melancholy autumn woods. The sky hung low with pale, freezing clouds; over everything was that strange hush which prevails before snow. The stage-driver, holding the reins loosely over his tramping team, settled forward with elbows on his knees, and old brows bent with aimless brooding. Over and over again his brain worked the thought, like a peaceful cud of contemplation. "They're goin' to be gone a year. Narcissa Stone an' her mother are goin' to be gone a year, afore I'll drive 'em home."

So little imagination had the routine of his life fostered that he speculated not, even upon the possible weather of that far-off day, or the chances of his living to see it. It was simply, "They're goin' to be gone a year afore I'll drive 'em home."

So fixed was his mind upon that one outcome of the situation that when Narcissa and her mother reappeared in less than one week—in six days—he could not for a moment bring his mind intelligently to bear upon it. The old stage-driver may have grown something like his own horses through his long sojourn in their company, and his intelligence, like theirs, been given to only the halts and gaits of its first breaking.

For a second he had a bewildered feeling that time had flown fast, that a week was a year. Everybody in the village had said the travellers would not return for a year. He hoisted the ancient paper-lined trunk into his stage, then a fine new one, nailed and clamped with shining brass, then a number of packages, all the time with puzzled eyes askant upon Narcissa and her mother. He would scarcely have known them, as far as their dress was concerned. Mrs. Stone wore a fine black satin gown; her perturbed old face looked out of luxurious environments of fur and lace and rich black plumage. As for Narcissa, she was almost regal. The old stage-driver backed and ducked awkwardly, as if she were a stranger, when she approached. Her fine skirts flared imposingly, and rustled with unseen silk; her slender shoulders were made shapely by the graceful spread of rich fur, her red hair shone under a hat fit for a princess, and there was about her a faint perfume of violets which made the stage-driver gaze confusedly at the snowy ground under the trees when they had started on the homeward road. "Seems as if I smelt posies, but I know there ain't none hereabouts this time of year," he remarked, finally, in a tone of mild ingratiation, as if more to himself than to his passengers.

"It's some perfumery Narcissa's got on her pocket-handkerchief that she bought in New York," said Mrs. Stone, with a sort of sad pride. She looked worn and bewildered, ready to weep at the sight of familiar things, and yet distinctly superior to all such weakness. As for Narcissa, she looked like a child thrilled with scared triumph at getting its own way, who rejoices even in the midst of correction at its own assertion of freedom.

"That so?" said the stage-driver, admiringly. Then he added, doubtfully, bringing one white-browed eye to bear over his shoulder, "Didn't stay quite so long as you calculated on?"

"No, we didn't," replied Narcissa, calmly. She nudged her mother with a stealthy, firm elbow, and her mother understood well that she was to maintain silence.

"I ain't going to tell a living soul about it but William Crane; I owe it to him," Narcissa had said to her mother before they started on their homeward journey. "The other folks sha'n't know. They can guess and surmise all they want to, but they sha'n't know. I sha'n't tell; and William, he's as close-mouthed as a rock; and as for you, mother, you always did know enough to hold your tongue when you made up your mind to it."

Mrs. Stone had compressed her mouth until it looked like her daughter's. She nodded. "Yes," said she; "I know some things that I ain't never told you, Narcissa."

The stage passed William Crane's house. He was shuffling around to the side door from the barn, with a milk-pail in each hand, when they reached it.

"Stop a minute," Narcissa said to the driver. She beckoned to William, who stared, standing stock-still, holding his pails. Narcissa beckoned again imperatively. Then William set the pails down on the snowy ground and came to the fence. He looked over it, quite pale, and gaping.

"We've got home," said Narcissa.

William nodded; he could not speak.

"Come over by-and-by," said Narcissa.

William nodded.

"I'm ready to go now," Narcissa said to the stage-driver. "That's all."

That evening, when William Crane reached his sweetheart's house, a bright light shone on the road from the parlor windows. Narcissa opened the door. He stared at her open-mouthed. She wore a gown the like of which he had never seen before—soft lengths of blue silk and lace trailed about her, blue ribbons fluttered.

"How do you do?" said she.

William nodded solemnly.

Come in.

William followed her into the parlor, with a wary eye upon his feet, lest they trample her trailing draperies. Narcissa settled gracefully into the rocking-chair; William sat opposite and looked at her. Narcissa was a little pale, still her face wore that look of insistent triumph.

"Home quicker'n you expected," William said, at length.

"Yes," said Narcissa. There was a wonderful twist on her red hair, and she wore a high shell comb. William's dazzled eyes noted something sparkling in the laces at her throat; she moved her hand, and something on that flashed like a point of white flame. William remembered vaguely how, often in the summer-time when he had opened his house-door in the sunny morning, the dewdrops on the grass had flashed in his eyes. He had never seen diamonds.

"What started you home so much sooner than you expected?" he asked, after a little.

"I spent—all the money—"

"All—that money?"

"Yes."

"Fifteen hundred dollars in less 'n a week?"

"I spent more'n that."

"More'n that?" William could scarcely bring out the words. He was very white.

"Yes," said Narcissa. She was paler than when he had entered, but she spoke quite decidedly. "I'm going to tell you all about it, William. I ain't going to make a long story of it. If after you've heard it you think you'd rather not marry me, I sha'n't blame you. I sha'n't have anything to say against it. I'm going to tell you just what I've been doing; then you can make up your mind.

"Today's Tuesday, and we went away last Thursday. We've been gone just six days. Mother an' me got to New York Thursday night, an' when we got out of the cars the men come round hollering this hotel an' that hotel. I picked out a man that looked as if he didn't drink and would drive straight, an' he took us to an elegant carriage, an' mother an' me got in. Then we waited till he got the trunk an' put it up on the seat with him where he drove. Mother she hollered to him not to let it fall off.

"We went to a beautiful hotel. There was a parlor with a red velvet carpet and red stuffed furniture, and a green sitting-room, and a blue one. The ceilin' had pictures on it. There was a handsome young gentleman downstairs at a counter in the room where we went first, and mother asked him, before I could stop her, if the folks in the hotel was all honest. She'd been worrying all the way for fear somebody'd steal the money.

"The gentleman said—he was real polite—if we had any money or valuables, we had better leave them with him, and he would put them in the safe. So we did. Then a young man with brass buttons on his coat took us to the elevator and showed us our rooms. We had a parlor with a velvet carpet an' stuffed furniture and a gilt clock on the mantel-shelf, two bed-rooms, and a bath-room. There ain't anything in town equal to it. Lawyer Maxham ain't got anything to come up to it. The young man offered to untie the rope on the trunk, so I let him. He seemed real kind about it.

"Soon's the young man went I says to mother, 'We ain't going down to get any tea tonight.'

"'Why not?' says she.

"'I ain't going down a step in this old dress,' says I, 'an' you ain't going in yours.'

"Mother didn't like it very well. She said she was faint to her stomach, and wanted some tea, but I made her eat some gingerbread we'd brought from home, an' get along. The young man with the brass buttons come again after a while an' asked if there was anything we wanted, but I thanked him an' told him there wasn't.

"I would have asked him to bring up mother some tea and a hot biscuit, but I didn't know but what it would put 'em out; it was after seven o'clock then. So we got along till morning.

"The next morning mother an' me went out real early, an' went into a bakery an' bought some cookies. We ate 'em as we went down the street, just to stay our stomachs; then we went to buying. I'd taken some of the money in my purse, an' I got mother an' me, first of all, two handsome black silk dresses, and we put 'em on as soon as we got back to the hotel, and went down to breakfast.

"You never see anythin' like the dining-room, and the kinds of things to eat. We couldn't begin to eat 'em all. There were men standin' behind our chairs to wait on us all the time.

"Right after breakfast mother an' me put our rooms to rights; then we went out again and bought things at the stores. Everybody was buying Christmas presents, an' the stores were all trimmed with evergreen—you never see anything like it. Mother an' me never had any Christmas presents, an' I told her we'd begin, an' buy 'em for each other. When the money I'd taken with us was gone, I sent things to the hotel for the gentleman at the counter to pay, the way he'd told me to. That day we bought our breastpins and this ring, an' mother's and my gold watch, an'—I got one for you too, William. Don't you say anything—it's your Christmas present. That afternoon we went to Central Park, an' that evenin' we went to the theatre. The next day we went to the stores again, an' I bought mother a black satin dress, and me a green one. I got this I've got on, too. It's what they call a tea-gown. I always wore it to tea in the hotel after I got it. I got a hat, too, an' mother a bonnet; an' I got a fur cape, and mother a cloak with fur on the neck an' all around it. That evening mother an' me went to the opera; we sat in something they call a box. I wore my new green silk and breastpin, an' mother wore her black satin. We both of us took our bonnets off. The music was splendid; but I wouldn't have young folks go to it much.

"The next day was Sunday. Mother an' me went to meeting in a splendid church, and wore our new black silks. They gave us seats way up in front, an' there was a real good sermon, though mother thought it wa'n't very practical, an' folks got up an' sat down more'n we do. Mother an' me set still, for fear we'd get up an' down in the wrong place. That evening we went to a sacred concert. Everywhere we went we rode in a carriage. They invited us to at the hotel, an' I s'posed it was free, but it wa'n't, I found out afterwards.

"The next day was Monday—that's yesterday. Mother an' me went out to the stores again. I bought a silk bed-quilt, an' some handsome vases, an' some green an' gilt teacups setting in a tray to match. I've got 'em home without breaking. We got some silk stockings, too, an' some shoes, an' some gold-bowed spectacles for mother, an' two more silk dresses, an' mother a real cashmere shawl. Then we went to see some wax-works, and the pictures and curiosities in the Art Museum; then in the afternoon we went to ride again, and we were goin' to the theatre in the evening; but the gentleman at the counter called out to me when I was going past an' said he wanted to speak to me a minute.

"Then I found out we'd spent all that fifteen hundred dollars, an' more too. We owed 'em 'most ten dollars at the hotel; an' that wa'n't the worst of it—we didn't have enough money to take us home.

"Mother she broke right down an' cried, an' said it was all we had in the world besides the farm, an' it was poor father's insurance money, an' we couldn't get home, an' we'd have to go to prison.

"Folks come crowding around, an' I couldn't stop her. I don't know what I did do myself; I felt kind of dizzy, an' things looked dark. A lady come an' held a smelling-bottle to my nose, an' the gentleman at the counter sent a man with brass buttons for some wine.

"After I felt better an' could talk steady they questioned me up pretty sharp, an' I told 'em the whole story—about father an' his rheumatism, an' everything, just how I was situated, an' I must say they treated us like Christian folks, though, after all, I don't know as we were much beholden to 'em. We never begun to eat all there was on the list, an' we were real careful of the furniture; we didn't really get our money's worth after all was said. But they said the rest of our bill to them was no matter, an' they gave us our tickets to come home."

There was a pause. William looked at Narcissa in her blue gown as if she were a riddle whose answer was lost in his memory. His honest eyes were fairly pitiful from excess of questioning.

"Well," said Narcissa, "I've come back, an' I've spent all that money. I've been wasteful an' extravagant an'—There was a gentleman beautifully dressed who sat at our table, an' he talked real pleasant about the weather, an'—I got to thinking about him a little. Of course I didn't like him as well as you, William, for what comes first comes last with all our folks, but somehow he seemed to be kind of a part of the good time. I sha'n't never see him again, an' all there was betwixt us was his saying twice it was a pleasant day, an' once it was cold, an' me saying yes; but I'm going to tell you the whole. I've been an' wasted fifteen hundred dollars; I've let my thoughts wander from you; an' that ain't all. I've had a good time, an' I can't say I ain't. I've had one good time, an'—I ain't sorry. You can—do just what you think best, William, an'—I won't blame you."

William Crane went over to the window. When he turned round and looked at Narcissa his eyes were full of tears and his wide mouth was trembling. "Do you think you can be contented to—stay on my side of the wall now, Narcissa?" he said, with a sweet and pathetic dignity.

Narcissa in her blue robes went over to him, and put, for the first time of her own accord, an arm around his faithful neck. "I wouldn't go out again if the bars were down," said she.

# A VILLAGE SINGER

## Mary E. Wilkins Freeman

THE TREES WERE in full leaf, a heavy south wind was blowing, and
there was a loud murmur among the new leaves. The people
noticed it, for it was the first time that year that the trees had so
murmured in the wind. The spring had come with a rush during
the last few days.

The murmur of the trees sounded loud in the village church,
where the people sat waiting for the service to begin. The windows
were open; it was a very warm Sunday for May.

The church was already filled with this soft sylvan music—the
tender harmony of the leaves and the south wind, and the sweet,
desultory whistles, of birds—when the choir arose and began
to sing.

In the centre of the row of women singers stood Alma Way.
All the people stared at her, and turned their ears critically. She was
the new leading soprano. Candace Whitcomb, the old one, who
had sung in the choir for forty years, had lately been given her
dismissal. The audience considered that her voice had grown too
cracked and uncertain on the upper notes. There had been much
complaint, and after long deliberation the church-officers had made
known their decision as mildly as possible to the old singer. She
had sung for the last time the Sunday before, and Alma Way had
been engaged to take her place. With the exception of the organist,
the leading soprano was the only paid musician in the large choir.
The salary was very modest, still the village people considered it
large for a young woman. Alma was from the adjoining village of
East Derby; she had quite a local reputation as a singer.

Now she fixed her large solemn blue eyes; her long, delicate face, which had been pretty, turned paler; the blue flowers on her bonnet trembled; her little thin gloved hands, clutching the singing-book, shook perceptibly; but she sang out bravely. That most formidable mountain-height of the world, self-distrust and timidity, arose before her, but her nerves were braced for its ascent. In the midst of the hymn she had a solo; her voice rang out piercingly sweet; the people nodded admiringly at each other; but suddenly there was a stir; all the faces turned toward the windows on the south side of the church. Above the din of the wind and the birds, above Alma Way's sweetly straining tones, arose another female voice, singing another hymn to another tune.

"It's her," the women whispered to each other; they were half aghast, half smiling.

Candace Whitcomb's cottage stood close to the south side of the church. She was playing on her parlor organ, and singing, to drown out the voice of her rival.

Alma caught her breath; she almost stopped; the hymn-book waved like a fan; then she went on. But the long husky drone of the parlor organ and the shrill clamor of the other voice seemed louder than anything else.

When the hymn was finished, Alma sat down. She felt faint; the woman next her slipped a peppermint into her hand. "It ain't worth minding," she whispered, vigorously. Alma tried to smile; down in the audience a young man was watching her with a kind of fierce pity.

In the last hymn Alma had another solo. Again the parlor organ droned above the carefully delicate accompaniment of the church organ, and again Candace Whitcomb's voice clamored forth in another tune.

After the benediction, the other singers pressed around Alma. She did not say much in return for their expressions of indignation and sympathy. She wiped her eyes furtively once or twice, and tried to smile. William Emmons, the choir leader, elderly, stout, and smooth-faced, stood over her, and raised his voice. He was the old musical dignitary of the village, the leader of the choral club and the singing-schools. "A most outrageous proceeding," he said. People had coupled his name with Candace Whitcomb's. The old bachelor tenor and old maiden soprano had been wont to walk together to her home next door after the Saturday night rehearsals, and they had sung duets to the parlor organ. People had watched sharply her old face, on which the blushes of youth sat pitifully, when William Emmons entered the singing-seats. They wondered if he would ever ask her to marry him.

And now he said further to Alma Way that Candace Whitcomb's voice had failed utterly of late, that she sang shockingly, and ought to have had sense enough to know it.

When Alma went down into the audience-room, in the midst of the chattering singers, who seemed to have descended, like birds, from song flights to chirps, the minister approached her. He had been waiting to speak to her. He was a steady-faced, fleshy old man, who had preached from that one pulpit over forty years. He told Alma, in his slow way, how much he regretted the annoyance to which she had been subjected, and intimated that he would endeavor to prevent a recurrence of it. "Miss Whitcomb—must be—reasoned with," said he; he had a slight hesitation of speech, not an impediment. It was as if his thoughts did not slide readily into his words, although both were present. He walked down the aisle with Alma, and bade her good-morning when he saw Wilson Ford waiting for her in the doorway. Everybody knew that Wilson Ford and Alma were lovers; they had been for the last ten years.

Alma colored softly, and made a little imperceptible motion with her head; her silk dress and the lace on her mantle fluttered, but she did not speak. Neither did Wilson, although they had not met before that day. They did not look at each other's faces—they seemed to see each other without that—and they walked along side by side.

They reached the gate before Candace Whitcomb's little house. Wilson looked past the front yard, full of pink and white spikes on flowering bushes, at the lace-curtained windows; a thin white profile, stiffly inclined, apparently over a book, was visible at one of them. Wilson gave his head a shake. He was a stout man, with features so strong that they overcame his flesh. "I'm going up home with you, Alma," said he; "and then—I'm coming back, to give Aunt Candace one blowing up."

"Oh, don't, Wilson."

"Yes, I shall. If you want to stand this kind of a thing you may; I sha'n't."

"There's no need of your talking to her. Mr. Pollard's going to."

"Did he say he was?"

"Yes. I think he's going in before the afternoon meeting, from what he said."

"Well, there's one thing about it, if she does that thing again this afternoon, I'll go in there and break that old organ up into kindling-wood." Wilson set his mouth hard, and shook his head again.

Alma gave little side glances up at him, her tone was deprecatory, but her face was full of soft smiles. "I suppose she does feel dreadfully about it," said she. "I can't help feeling kind of guilty, taking her place."

"I don't see how you're to blame. It's outrageous, her acting so."

"The choir gave her a photograph album last week, didn't they?"

"Yes. They went there last Thursday night, and gave her an album and a surprise-party. She ought to behave herself."

"Well, she's sung there so long, I suppose it must be dreadful hard for her to give it up."

Other people going home from church were very near Wilson and Alma. She spoke softly that they might not hear; he did not lower his voice in the least. Presently Alma stopped before a gate.

"What are you stopping here for?" asked Wilson.

"Minnie Lansing wanted me to come and stay with her this noon."

"You're going home with me."

"I'm afraid I'll put your mother out."

"Put mother out! I told her you were coming, this morning. She's got all ready for you. Come along; don't stand here."

He did not tell Alma of the pugnacious spirit with which his mother had received the announcement of her coming, and how she had stayed at home to prepare the dinner, and make a parade of her hard work and her injury.

Wilson's mother was the reason why he did not marry Alma. He would not take his wife home to live with her, and was unable to support separate establishments. Alma was willing enough to be married and put up with Wilson's mother, but she did not complain of his decision. Her delicate blond features grew sharper, and her blue eyes more hollow. She had had a certain fine prettiness, but now she was losing it, and beginning to look old, and there was a prim, angular, old maiden carriage about her narrow shoulders.

Wilson never noticed it, and never thought of Alma as not possessed of eternal youth, or capable of losing or regretting it.

"Come along, Alma," said he; and she followed meekly after him down the street.

Soon after they passed Candace Whitcomb's house, the minister went up the front walk and rang the bell. The pale profile at the window had never stirred as he opened the gate and came up the walk.

However, the door was promptly opened, in response to his ring. "Good-morning, Miss Whitcomb," said the minister.

"*Good*-morning." Candace gave a sweeping toss of her head as she spoke. There was a fierce upward curl to her thin nostrils and her lips, as if she scented an adversary. Her black eyes had two tiny cold sparks of fury in them, like an enraged bird's. She did not ask the minister to enter, but he stepped lumberingly into the entry, and she retreated rather than led the way into her little parlor. He settled into the great rocking-chair and wiped his face. Candace sat down again in her old place by the window. She was a tall woman, but very slender and full of pliable motions, like a blade of grass.

"It's a—very pleasant day," said the minister.

Candace made no reply. She sat still, with her head drooping. The wind stirred the looped lace-curtains; a tall rose-tree outside the window waved; soft shadows floated through the room. Candace's parlor organ stood in front of an open window that faced the church; on the corner was a pitcher with a bunch of white lilacs. The whole room was scented with them. Presently the minister looked over at them and sniffed pleasantly.

"You have—some beautiful—lilacs there."

Candace did not speak. Every line of her slender figure looked flexible, but it was a flexibility more resistant than rigor.

The minister looked at her. He filled up the great rocking-chair; his arms in his shiny black coat-sleeves rested squarely and comfortably upon the hair-cloth arms of the chair.

"Well, Miss Whitcomb, I suppose I—may as well come to—the point. There was—a little—matter I wished to speak to you about. I don't suppose you were—at least I can't suppose you were—aware of it, but—this morning, during the singing by the choir, you played and—sung a little too—loud. That is, with—the windows open. It—disturbed us—a little. I hope you won't feel hurt—my dear Miss Candace, but I knew you would rather I would speak of it, for I knew—you would be more disturbed than anybody else at the idea of such a thing."

Candace did not raise her eyes; she looked as if his words might sway her through the window. "I ain't disturbed at it," said she. "I did it on purpose; I meant to."

The minister looked at her.

"You needn't look at me. I know jest what I'm about. I sung the way I did on purpose, an' I'm goin' to do it again, an' I'd like to see you stop me. I guess I've got a right to set down to my own organ, an' sing a psalm tune on a Sabbath day, 'f I want to; an' there ain't no amount of talkin' an' palaverin' a-goin' to stop me. See there!" Candace swung aside her skirts a little. "Look at that!"

The minister looked. Candace's feet were resting on a large red-plush photograph album.

"Makes a nice footstool, don't it?" said she.

The minister looked at the album, then at her; there was a slowly gathering alarm in his face; he began to think she was losing her reason.

Candace had her eyes full upon him now, and her head up. She laughed, and her laugh was almost a snarl. "Yes; I thought it would make a beautiful footstool," said she. "I've been wantin' one for some time." Her tone was full of vicious irony.

"Why, miss—" began the minister; but she interrupted him:

"I know what you're a-goin' to say, Mr. Pollard, an' now I'm goin' to have my say; I'm a-goin' to speak. I want to know what you think of folks that pretend to be Christians treatin' anybody the way they've treated me? Here I've sung in those singin'-seats forty year. I ain't never missed a Sunday, except when I've been sick, an' I've gone an' sung a good many times when I'd better been in bed, an' now I'm turned out without a word of warnin'. My voice is jest as good as ever 'twas; there can't anybody say it ain't. It wa'n't ever quite so high-pitched as that Way girl's, mebbe; but she flats the whole durin' time. My voice is as good an' high today as it was twenty year ago; an' if it wa'n't, I'd like to know where the Christianity comes in. I'd like to know if it wouldn't be more to the credit of folks in a church to keep an old singer an' an old minister, if they didn't sing an' hold forth quite so smart as they used to, ruther than turn 'em off an' hurt their feelin's. I guess it would be full as much to the glory of God. S'pose the singin' an' the preachin' wa'n't quite so good, what difference would it make? Salvation don't hang on anybody's hittin' a high note, that I ever heard of. Folks are gettin' as high-steppin' an' fussy in a meetin'-house as they are in a tavern, nowadays. S'pose they should turn you off, Mr. Pollard, come an' give you a photograph album, an' tell you to clear out, how'd you like it? I ain't findin' any fault with your preachin'; it was always good enough to suit me; but it don't stand to reason folks'll be as took up with your sermons as when you was a young man. You can't expect it. S'pose they should turn you out in your old age, an' call in some young bob squirt, how'd you feel? There's William Emmons, too; he's three years older'n I am, if he does lead the choir an' run all the singin' in town. If my voice has gi'en out, it stan's to reason his has. It ain't, though. William Emmons sings jest as well as he ever did. Why don't they turn him out the way they have me, an' give him a photograph album? I dun know but it would be a good idea to send everybody, as soon as they get a little old an' gone by, an' young folks begin to push, onto some desert island, an' give 'em each a photograph album. Then they can sit down an' look at pictures the rest of their days. Mebbe government'll take it up.

"There they come here last week Thursday, all the choir, jest about eight o'clock in the evenin', an' pretended they'd come to give me a nice little surprise. Surprise! h'm! Brought cake an' oranges, an' was jest as nice as they could be, an' I was real tickled. I never had a surprise-party before in my life. Jenny Carr she played, an' they wanted me to sing alone, an' I never suspected a thing. I've been mad ever since to think what a fool I was, an' how they must have laughed in their sleeves.

"When they'd gone I found this photograph album on the table, all done up as nice as you please, an' directed to Miss Candace Whitcomb from her many friends, an' I opened it, an' there was the letter inside givin' me notice to quit.

"If they'd gone about it any decent way, told me right out honest that they'd got tired of me, an' wanted Alma Way to sing instead of me, I wouldn't minded so much; I should have been hurt 'nough, for I'd felt as if some that had pretended to be my friends wa'n't; but it wouldn't have been as bad as this. They said in the letter that they'd always set great value on my services, an' it wa'n't from any lack of appreciation that they turned me off, but they thought the duty was gettin' a little too arduous for me. I I'm! I hadn't complained. If they'd turned me right out fair an' square, showed me the door, an' said, 'Here, you get out,' but to go an' spill molasses, as it were, all over the threshold, tryin' to make me think it's all nice an' sweet—

"I'd sent that photograph album back quick's I could pack it, but I didn't know who started it, so I've used it for a footstool. It's all it's good for, 'cordin' to my way of thinkin'. An' I ain't been particular to get the dust off my shoes before I used it neither."

Mr. Pollard, the minister, sat staring. He did not look at Candace; his eyes were fastened upon a point straight ahead. He had a look of helpless solidity, like a block of granite. This country minister, with his steady, even temperament, treading with heavy precision his one track for over forty years, having nothing new in his life except the new sameness of the seasons, and desiring nothing new, was incapable of understanding a woman like this, who had lived as quietly as he, and all the time held within herself the elements of revolution. He could not account for such violence, such extremes, except in a loss of reason. He had a conviction that Candace was getting beyond herself. He himself was not a typical New-Englander; the national elements of character were not pronounced in him. He was aghast and bewildered at this outbreak, which was tropical, and more than tropical, for a New England nature has a floodgate, and the power which it releases is an accumulation. Candace Whitcomb had been a quiet woman, so delicately resolute that the quality had been scarcely noticed in her, and her ambition had been unsuspected. Now the resolution and the ambition appeared raging over her whole self.

She began to talk again. "I've made up my mind that I'm goin' to sing Sundays the way I did this mornin', an' I don't care what folks say," said she. "I've made up my mind that I'm goin' to take matters into my own hands. I'm goin' to let folks see that I ain't trod down quite flat, that there's a little rise left in me. I ain't goin' to give up beat yet a while; an' I'd like to see anybody stop me. If I ain't got a right to play a psalm tune on my organ an' sing, I'd like to know. If you don't like it, you can move the meetin'-house."

Candace had had an inborn reverence for clergymen. She had always treated Mr. Pollard with the utmost deference. Indeed, her manner toward all men had been marked by a certain delicate stiffness and dignity. Now she was talking to the old minister with the homely freedom with which she might have addressed a female gossip over the back fence. He could not say much in return. He did not feel competent to make headway against any such tide of passion; all he could do was to let it beat against him. He made a few expostulations, which increased Candace's vehemence; he expressed his regret over the whole affair, and suggested that they should kneel and ask the guidance of the Lord in the matter, that she might be led to see it all in a different light.

Candace refused flatly. "I don't see any use prayin' about it," said she. "I don't think the Lord's got much to do with it, anyhow."

It was almost time for the afternoon service when the minister left. He had missed his comfortable noontide rest, through this encounter with his revolutionary parishioner. After the minister had gone, Candace sat by the window and waited. The bell rang, and she watched the people file past. When her nephew Wilson Ford with Alma appeared, she grunted to herself. "She's thin as a rail," said she;

"guess there won't be much left of her by the time Wilson gets her. Little soft-spoken nippin' thing, she wouldn't make him no kind of a wife, anyway. Guess it's jest as well."

When the bell had stopped tolling, and all the people entered the church, Candace went over to her organ and seated herself. She arranged a singing-book before her, and sat still, waiting. Her thin, colorless neck and temples were full of beating pulses; her black eyes were bright and eager; she leaned stiffly over toward the music-rack, to hear better. When the church organ sounded out she straightened herself; her long skinny fingers pressed her own organ-keys with nervous energy. She worked the pedals with all her strength; all her slender body was in motion. When the first notes of Alma's solo began, Candace sang. She had really possessed a fine voice, and it was wonderful how little she had lost it. Straining her throat with jealous fury, her notes were still for the main part true. Her voice filled the whole room; she sang with wonderful fire and expression. That, at least, mild little Alma Way could never emulate. She was full of steadfastness and unquestioning constancy, but there were in her no smouldering fires of ambition and resolution. Music was not to her what it had been to her older rival. To this obscure woman, kept relentlessly by circumstances in a narrow track, singing in the village choir had been as much as Italy was to Napoleon—and now on her island of exile she was still showing fight.

After the church service was done, Candace left the organ and went over to her old chair by the window. Her knees felt weak, and shook under her. She sat down, and leaned back her head. There were red spots on her cheeks. Pretty soon she heard a quick slam of her gate, and an impetuous tread on the gravel-walk. She looked up, and there was her nephew Wilson Ford hurrying up to the door. She cringed a little, then she settled herself more firmly in her chair.

Wilson came into the room with a rush. He left the door open, and the wind slammed it to after him.

"Aunt Candace, where are you?" he called out, in a loud voice.

She made no reply. He looked around fiercely, and his eyes seemed to pounce upon her.

"Look here, Aunt Candace," said he, "are you crazy?" Candace said nothing. "Aunt Candace!" She did not seem to see him. "If you don't answer me," said Wilson, "I'll just go over there and pitch that old organ out of the window!"

"Wilson Ford!" said Candace, in a voice that was almost a scream.

"Well, what say! What have you got to say for yourself, acting the way you have? I tell you what 'tis, Aunt Candace, I won't stand it."

"I'd like to see you help yourself."

"I will help myself. I'll pitch that old organ out of the window, and then I'll board up the window on that side of your house. Then we'll see."

"It ain't your house, and it won't never be."

"Who said it was my house? You're my aunt, and I've got a little lookout for the credit of the family. Aunt Candace, what are you doing this way for?"

"It don't make no odds what I'm doin' so for. I ain't bound to give my reasons to a young fellar like you, if you do act so mighty toppin'. But I'll tell you one thing, Wilson Ford, after the way you've spoke today, you sha'n't never have one cent of my money, an' you can't never marry that Way girl if you don't have it. You can't never take her home to live with your mother, an' this house would have been mighty nice an' convenient for you some day. Now you won't get it. I'm goin' to make another will. I'd made one, if you did but know it. Now you won't get a cent of my money, you nor your mother neither. An' I ain't goin' to live a dreadful while longer, neither. Now I wish you'd go home; I want to lay down. I'm 'bout sick."

Wilson could not get another word from his aunt. His indignation had not in the least cooled. Her threat of disinheriting him did not cow him at all; he had too much rough independence, and indeed his aunt Candace's house had always been too much of an air-castle for him to contemplate seriously. Wilson, with his burly frame and his headlong common-sense, could have little to do with air-castles, had he been hard enough to build them over graves. Still, he had not admitted that he never could marry Alma. All his hopes were based upon a rise in his own fortunes, not by some sudden convulsion, but by his own long and steady labor. Some time, he thought, he should have saved enough for the two homes.

He went out of his aunt's house still storming. She arose after the door had shut behind him, and got out into the kitchen. She thought that she would start a fire and make a cup of tea. She had not eaten anything all day. She put some kindling-wood into the stove and touched a match to it; then she went back to the sitting-room, and settled down again into the chair by the window. The fire in the kitchen-stove roared, and the light wood was soon burned out. She thought no more about it. She had not put on the teakettle. Her head ached, and once in a while she shivered. She sat at the window while the afternoon waned and the dusk came on. At seven o'clock the meeting bell rang again, and the people flocked by. This time she did not stir. She had shut her parlor organ. She did not need to out-sing her rival this evening; there was only congregational singing at the Sunday-night prayer-meeting.

She sat still until it was nearly time for meeting to be done; her head ached harder and harder, and she shivered more. Finally she arose. "Guess I'll go to bed," she muttered. She went about the house, bent over and shaking, to lock the doors. She stood a minute in the back door, looking over the fields to the woods. There was a red light over there. "The woods are on fire," said Candace. She watched with a dull interest the flames roll up, withering and destroying the tender green spring foliage. The air was full of smoke, although the fire was half a mile away.

Candace locked the door and went in. The trees with their delicate garlands of new leaves, with the new nests of song birds, might fall, she was in the roar of an in-tenser fire; the growths of all her springs and the delicate wontedness of her whole life were going down in it. Candace went to bed in her little room off the parlor, but she could not sleep. She lay awake all night. In the morning she crawled to the door and hailed a little boy who was passing. She bade him go for the doctor as quickly as he could, then to Mrs. Ford's, and ask her to come over. She held on to the door while she was talking. The boy stood staring wonderingly at her. The spring wind fanned her face. She had drawn on a dress skirt and put her shawl over her shoulders, and her gray hair was blowing over her red cheeks.

She shut the door and went back to her bed. She never arose from it again. The doctor and Mrs. Ford came and looked after her, and she lived a week. Nobody but herself thought until the very last that she would die; the doctor called her illness merely a light run of fever; she had her senses fully.

But Candace gave up at the first. "It's my last sickness," she said to Mrs. Ford that morning when she first entered; and Mrs. Ford had laughed at the notion; but the sick woman held to it. She did not seem to suffer much physical pain; she only grew weaker and weaker, but she was distressed mentally. She did not talk much, but her eyes followed everybody with an agonized expression.

On Wednesday William Emmons came to inquire for her. Candace heard him out in the parlor. She tried to raise herself on one elbow that she might listen better to his voice.

"William Emmons come in to ask how you was," Mrs. Ford said, after he was gone.

"I—heard him," replied Candace. Presently she spoke again. "Nancy," said she, "where's that photograph album?"

"On the table," replied her sister, hesitatingly.

"Mebbe—you'd better—brush it up a little."

"Well."

Sunday morning Candace wished that the minister should be asked to come in at the noon intermission. She had refused to see him before. He came and prayed with her, and she asked his forgiveness for the way she had spoken the Sunday before. "I—hadn't ought to—spoke so," said she. "I was—dreadful wrought up."

"Perhaps it was your sickness coming on," said the minister, soothingly.

Candace shook her head. "No—it wa'n't. I hope the Lord will—forgive me."

After the minister had gone, Candace still appeared unhappy. Her pitiful eyes followed her sister everywhere with the mechanical persistency of a portrait.

"What is it you want, Candace?" Mrs. Ford said at last. She had nursed her sister faithfully, but once in a while her impatience showed itself.

"Nancy!"

"What say?"

"I wish—you'd go out when—meetin's done, an'—head off Alma an' Wilson, an'—ask 'em to come in. I feel as if—I'd like to—hear her sing."

Mrs. Ford stared. "Well," said she.

The meeting was now in session. The windows were all open, for it was another warm Sunday. Candace lay listening to the music when it began, and a look of peace came over her face. Her sister had smoothed her hair back, and put on a clean cap. The white curtain in the bedroom window waved in the wind like a white sail. Candace almost felt as if she were better, but the thought of death seemed easy.

Mrs. Ford at the parlor window watched for the meeting to be out. When the people appeared, she ran down the walk and waited for Alma and Wilson. When they came she told them what Candace wanted, and they all went in together.

"Here's Alma an' Wilson, Candace," said Mrs. Ford, leading them to the bedroom door.

Candace smiled. "Come in," she said, feebly. And Alma and Wilson entered and stood beside the bed. Candace continued to look at them, the smile straining her lips.

"Wilson!"

"What is it, Aunt Candace?"

"I ain't altered that—will. You an' Alma can—come here an'—live—when I'm—gone. Your mother won't mind livin' alone. Alma can have—all—my things."

"Don't, Aunt Candace." Tears were running over Wilson's cheeks, and Alma's delicate face was all of a quiver.

"I thought—maybe—Alma 'd be willin' to—sing for me," said Candace.

"What do you want me to sing?" Alma asked, in a trembling voice.

"'Jesus, lover of my soul.'"

Alma, standing there beside Wilson, began to sing. At first she could hardly control her voice, then she sang sweetly and clearly.

Candace lay and listened. Her face had a holy and radiant expression. When Alma stopped singing it did not disappear, but she looked up and spoke, and it was like a secondary glimpse of the old shape of a forest tree through the smoke and flame of the transfiguring fire the instant before it falls. "You flatted a little on—soul," said Candace.

# MRS. RIPLEY'S TRIP

## Hamlin Garland

THE NIGHT WAS in windy November, and the blast, threatening rain, roared around the poor little shanty of "Uncle Ripley," set like a chicken-trap on the vast Iowa prairie. Uncle Ethan was mending his old violin, with many York State "dums!" and "I gol darns!" totally oblivious of his tireless old wife, who, having "finished the supper-dishes," sat knitting a stocking evidently for the little grandson who lay before the stove like a cat. Neither of the old people wore glasses, and their light was a tallow candle; they couldn't afford "none o' them new-fangled lamps." The room was small, the chairs wooden, and the walls bare—a home where poverty was a never-absent guest. The old lady looked pathetically little, weazened and hopeless in her ill-fitting garments (whose original color had long since vanished), intent as she was on the stocking in her knotted, stiffened fingers, but there was a peculiar sparkle in her little black eyes, and an unusual resolution in the straight lines of her withered and shapeless lips. Suddenly she paused, stuck a needle in the spare knob of hair at the back of her head, and, looking at Ripley, said decisively: "Ethan Ripley, you'll haff to do your own cooking from now on to New Year's; I'm goin' back to Yaark State."

The old man's leather-brown face stiffened into a look of quizzical surprise for a moment; then he cackled, incredulously: "Ho! Ho! har! Sho! be y', now? I want to know if y' be."

"Well, you'll find out."

"Goin' to start tomorrow, mother?"

"No, sir, I ain't; but I am on Thursday. I want to get to Sally's by Sunday, sure, an' to Silas's on Thanks-givin'."

There was a note in the old woman's voice that brought genuine stupefaction into the face of Uncle Ripley. Of course in this case, as in all others, the money consideration was uppermost.

"Howgy 'spect to get the money, mother? Anybody died an' left yeh a pile?"

"Never you mind where I get the money so's't *you* don't haff to bear it. The land knows, if I'd a-waited for *you* to pay my way—"

"You needn't twit me of bein' poor, old woman," said Ripley, flaming up after the manner of many old people. "I've done *my* part t' get along. I've worked day in and day out—"

"Oh! *I* ain't done no work, have I?" snapped she, laying down the stocking and levelling a needle at him, and putting a frightful emphasis on "I."

"I didn't say you hadn't done no work."

"Yes, you did!"

"I didn't, neither. I said—"

"I *know* what you said."

"I said I'd done *my part!*" roared the husband, dominating her as usual by superior lung power. "I didn't *say* you hadn't done your part," he added, with an unfortunate touch of emphasis on "say."

"I know y' didn't *say* it, but y' meant it. I don't know what y' call doin' my part, Ethan Ripley; but if cookin' for a drove of harvest hands and thrashin' hands, takin' care o' the eggs and butter, 'n' diggin' taters an' milkin', ain't *my* part, I don't never expect to do my part, 'n' you might as well know it fust 's last. I'm sixty years old," she went on, with a little break in her harsh voice, dominating him now by woman's logic, "an' I've never had a day to myself, not even Fourth of July. If I've went a-visitin' 'r to a picnic, I've had to come home an' milk 'n' get supper for you men-folks. I ain't been away t' stay overnight for thirteen years in this house, 'n' it was just so in Davis County for ten more. For twenty-three years, Ethan Ripley, I've stuck right to the stove an' churn without a day or a night off." Her voice choked again, but she rallied, and continued impressively, "And now I'm a-goin' back to Yaark State."

Ethan was vanquished. He stared at her in speechless surprise, his jaw hanging. It was incredible.

"For twenty-three years," she went on, musingly, "I've just about promised myself every year I'd go back an' see my folks." She was distinctly talking to herself now, and her voice had a touching, wistful cadence. "I've wanted to go back an' see the old folks, an' the hills where we played, an' eat apples off the old tree down by the old well. I've had them trees an' hills in my mind days and days—nights too—an' the girls I used to know, an' my own folks—"

She fell into a silent muse, which lasted so long that the ticking of the clock grew loud as a gong in the man's ears, and the wind outside seemed to sound drearier than usual. He returned to the money problem, kindly, though.

"But how y' goin' t' raise the money? I ain't got no extra cash this time. Agin Roach is paid an' the mortgage interest paid we ain't got no hundred dollars to spare, Jane, not by a jugful."

"Waal, don't you lay awake nights studyin' on where I'm a-goin' to get the money," said the old woman, taking delight in mystifying him. She had him now, and he couldn't escape. He strove to show his indifference, however, by playing a tune or two on the violin.

"Come, Tukey, you better climb the wooden hill," Mrs. Ripley said, a half-hour later, to the little chap on the floor, who was beginning to get drowsy under the influence of his grandpa's fiddling. "Pa, you had orta 'a put that string in the clock today—on the 'larm side the string is broke," she said, upon returning from the boy's bedroom. "I orta get up extra early tomorrow, to get some sewin' done. Land knows, I can't fix up much, but they is a leetle I c'n do. I want to look decent."

They were alone now, and they both sat expectantly.

"You 'pear to think, mother, that I'm agin yer goin'."

"Waal, it would kinder seem as if y' hadn't hustled yerself any t' help me git off."

He was smarting under the sense of being wronged. "Wa'al, I'm jest as willin' you should go as I am for myself; but if I ain't got no money I don't see how I'm goin' to send—"

"I don' want ye to send; nobody ast ye to, Ethan Ripley. I guess if I had what I've earnt since we came on this farm I'd have enough to go to Jericho with."

"You've got as much out of it as I have. You talk about your goin' back. Ain't I been wantin' to go back myself? And ain't I kep' still 'cause I see it wa'n't no use? I guess I've worked jest as long an' as hard as you, an' in storms an' wind an' heat, ef it comes t' that."

The woman was staggered, but she wouldn't give up; she must get in one more thrust.

"Wa'al, if you'd'a managed as well as I have, you'd have some money to go with." And she rose, and went to mix her bread, and set it "raisin'." He sat by the fire twanging his fiddle softly. He was plainly thrown into gloomy retrospection, something quite unusual for him. But his fingers picking out the bars of a familiar tune set him to smiling, and whipping his bow across the strings, he forgot all about his wife's resolutions and his own hardships. Trouble always slid off his back like "punkins off a haystack" anyway.

The old man still sat fiddling softly after his wife disappeared in the hot and stuffy little bedroom off the kitchen. His shaggy head bent lower over his violin. He heard her shoes *drop—one, two*. Pretty soon she called.

"Come, put up that squeakin' old fiddle, and go to bed. Seems as if you orta have sense enough not to set there keepin' everybody in the house awake."

"You hush up," retorted he. "I'll come when I git ready, not till. I'll be glad when you're gone—"

"Yes, I warrant *that.*"

With which amiable good-night they went off to sleep, or at least she did, while he lay awake, pondering on "where under the sun she was goin' t' raise that money."

The next day she was up bright and early, working away on her own affairs, ignoring Ripley totally, the fixed look of resolution still on her little old wrinkled face. She killed a hen and dressed and baked it. She fixed up a pan of doughnuts and made a cake. She was engaged on the doughnuts when a neighbor came in, one of those women who take it as a personal affront when anyone in the neighborhood does anything without asking their advice. She was fat, and could talk a man blind in three minutes by the watch.

"What's this I hear, Mis' Ripley?"

"I dun know. I expect you hear about all they is goin' on in this neighborhood," replied Mrs. Ripley, with crushing bluntness; but the gossip did not flinch.

"Well, Sett Turner told *me* that her husband told *her* that Ripley told *him* that you was goin' back East on a visit."

"Waal, what of it?"

"Well, air yeh?"

"The Lord willin' an' the weather permittin', I expect to be."

"Good land, I want to know! Well, well! I never was so astonished in my life. I said, ses I, 'It can't be.' 'Well,' ses 'e, 'tha's what *she* told me,' ses 'e. 'But,' ses I, 'she is the last woman in the world to go gallivantin' off East,' ses I. 'Well, then, it must be so,' ses I. But, land sakes! do tell me all about it. How come you to make up your mind? All these years you've been kind a-talkin' it over, an' now y'r actshelly goin'—Waal, *I never!* 'I 'spose Ripley furnishes the money,' ses I to him. 'Well, no,' ses 'e. 'Ripley says he'll be blowed if he sees where the money's comin' from,' ses 'e; and ses I, 'But maybe she's jest jokin',' ses I. 'Not much,' he says. Ses 'e: 'Ripley believes she's goin' fast enough. He's just as anxious to find out as we be—' "

Here Mrs. Doudney paused for breath; she had walked so fast and had rested so little that her interminable flood of "ses I's" and "ses he's" ceased necessarily. She had reached, moreover, the point of most vital interest—the money.

"An' you'll find out jest 'bout as soon as he does," was the dry response from the figure hovering over the stove, and with all her maneuvering that was all she got.

All day Ripley went about his work exceedingly thoughtful for him. It was cold, blustering weather. The wind rustled among the cornstalks with a wild and mournful sound, the geese and ducks went sprawling down the wind, and horses' coats were ruffled and backs raised.

The old man was husking corn alone in the field, his spare form rigged out in two or three ragged coats, his hands inserted in a pair of gloves minus nearly all the fingers, his thumbs done up in "stalls," and his feet thrust into huge coarse boots. During the middle of the day the frozen ground thawed, and the mud stuck to his boots, and the "down ears" wet and chapped his hands, already worn to the quick. Toward night it grew cold and threatened snow. In spite of all these attacks he kept his cheerfulness and, though he was very tired, he was softened in temper.

Having plenty of time to think matters over, he had come to the conclusion "that the old woman needed a play-spell. I ain't likely to be no richer next year than I am this one; if I wait till I'm able to send her she won't never go. I calc'late I c'n git enough out o' them shoats to send her. I'd kind a'lotted on eat'n' them pigs done up into sassengers, but if the ol' woman goes East, Tukey an' me'll kind a haff to pull through without 'em. We'll have a turkey f'r Thanksgivin' an' a chicken once'n a while. Lord! but we'll miss the gravy on the flap-jacks. A-men!" (He smacked his lips over the thought of the lost dainty.) "But let 'er rip! We can stand it. Then there is my buffalo overcoat. I'd kind a calc'lated on havin' a buffalo—but that's gone up the spout along with them sassengers."

These heroic sacrifices having been determined upon, he put them into effect at once.

This he was able to do, for his corn-rows ran alongside the road leading to Cedarville, and his neighbors were passing almost all hours of the day.

It would have softened Jane Ripley's heart could she have seen his bent and stiffened form amid the corn-rows, the cold wind piercing to the bone through his threadbare and insufficient clothing. The rising wind sent the snow rattling among the moaning stalks at intervals. The cold made his poor dim eyes water, and he had to stop now and then to swing his arms about his chest to warm them. His voice was hoarse with shouting at the shivering team.

That night as Mrs. Ripley was clearing the dishes away, she got to thinking about the departure of the next day, and she began to soften. She gave way to a few tears when little Tewksbury Gilchrist, her grandson, came up and stood beside her.

"Gran'ma, you ain't goin' to stay away always, are yeh?"

"Why, course not, Tukey. What made y' think that?"

"Well, y' ain't told us nawthin' 'tall about it. An' yeh kind o' look 's if yeh was mad."

"Well, I ain't mad; I'm jest a-thinkin', Tukey. Y'see I come away from them hills when I was a little girl a'most; before I married y'r granddad. And I ain't never been back. 'Most all my folks is there, sonny, an' we've been s' poor all these years I couldn't seem t' never get started. Now, when I'm 'most ready t' go, I feel kind a queer— 'sif I'd cry."

And cry she did, while little Tewksbury stood patting her trembling hands. Hearing Ripley's step on the porch, she rose hastily, and drying her eyes, plunged at the work again. Ripley came in with a big armful of wood, which he rolled into the woodbox with a thundering crash. Then he pulled off his mittens, slapped them together to knock off the ice and snow, and laid them side by side under the stove. He then removed cap, coat, blouse and boots, which last he laid upon the woodbox, the soles turned toward the stove-pipe.

As he sat down without speaking, he opened the front doors of the stove, and held the palms of his stiffened hands to the blaze. The light brought out a thoughtful look on his large, uncouth, yet kindly visage. Life had laid hard lines on his brown skin, but it had not entirely soured a naturally kind and simple nature. It had made him penurious and dull and iron-muscled; had stifled all the slender flowers of his nature; yet there was warm soil somewhere hid in his heart.

"It's snowin' like all p'sessed," he remarked, finally, "I guess we'll have a sleigh-ride tomorrow. I calc'late t' drive y' daown in scrumptious style. If yeh must leave, why, we'll give yeh a whoopin' old send-off, won't we, Tukey?"

"I ben a-thinkin' things over kind o' t' day, mother, an' I've come t' the conclusion that we *have* been kind a hard on yeh, without knowin' it, y' see. Y' see I'm kind a easy-goin', an' little Tuke he's only a child, an' we ain't c'nsidered how you felt."

She didn't appear to be listening, but she was, and he didn't appear, on his part, to be talking to her, and he kept his voice as hard and as dry as he could.

"An' I was tellin' Tukey t' day that it was a dum shame our crops hadn't turned out better. An' when I saw ol' Hatfield go by I hailed him, an' asked him what he'd gimme fer two o' m' shoats. Waal, the upshot is, I sent t' town for some things I calc'lated ye'd need. An' here's a ticket to Georgetown, and ten dollars. Why, ma, what's up?"

Mrs. Ripley broke down, and with her hands all wet with dishwater, as they were, covered her face and sobbed. She felt like kissing him, but she didn't. Tewksbury began to whimper too; but the old man was astonished. His wife had not wept for years (before him). He rose and walked clumsily up to her and timidly touching her hair—

"Why, mother! What's the matter? What 'v' I done now? I was calc'latin' to sell them pigs anyway. Hatfield jest advanced the money on 'em."

She hopped up and dashed into the bedroom, and in a few minutes returned with a yarn mitten, tied around the wrist, which she laid on the table with a thump, saying: "I don't want yer money. There's money enough to take me where I want to go."

"Whee-ew! Thunder and gimpsum root! Where'd ye git that? Didn't dig it out of a hole?"

"No, I jest saved it—a dime at a time—see?" Here she turned it out on the table—some bills, but mostly silver dimes and quarters.

"Thunder and scissors! Must be two er three hundred dollars there," stared he.

"They's jest seventy-five dollars and thirty cents; jest about enough to go back on. Tickets is fifty-five dollars, goin' an' comin'. That leaves twenty dollars for other expenses, not countin' what I've already spent, which is six-fifty," said she, recovering her self-possession. "It's plenty."

"But y' ain't calc'lated on no sleepers nor hotel bills."

"I ain't goin' on no sleeper. Mis' Doudney says it's jest scandalous the way things is managed on them cars. I'm goin' on the old-fashioned cars, where they ain't no half-dressed men runnin' around."

"But *you* needn't be afraid of them, mother, at your age—"

"There! you needn't throw my age an' homeliness into my face, Ethan Ripley. If I hadn't waited an' tended on you so long, I'd look a little more's I did when I married yeh."

Ripley gave it up in despair. He didn't realize fully enough how the proposed trip had unsettled his wife's nerves. She didn't realize it herself.

"As for the hotel bills, they won't be none. I ain't a-goin' to pay them pirates as much for a day's board as we'd charge for a week's, an' have nawthin' to eat but dishes. I'm goin' to take a chicken an' some hard-boiled eggs, an' I'm goin' right through to Georgetown."

"Well, all right; but here's the ticket I got."

"I don't want yer ticket."

"But you've got to take it."

"Waal, I hain't."

"Why, yes, ye have. It's bought, an' they won't take it back."

"Won't they?" She was staggered again.

"Not much they won't. I ast 'em. A ticket sold is sold."

"Waal, if they won't—"

"You bet they won't."

"I s'pose I'll haff to use it"; and that ended it.

They were a familiar sight as they rode down the road toward town next day. As usual, Mrs. Ripley sat up straight and stiff as "a half-drove wedge in a white-oak log." The day was cold and raw. There was some snow on the ground, but not enough to warrant the use of sleighs. It was "Neither sleddin' nor wheelin'." The old people sat on a board laid across the box, and had an old quilt or two drawn up over their knees. Tewksbury lay in the back part of the box (which was filled with hay), where he jounced up and down, in company with a queer old trunk and a brand-new imitation-leather hand-bag. There is no ride quite so desolate and uncomfortable as a ride in a lumber wagon on a cold day in autumn, when the ground is frozen, and the wind is strong and raw with threatening snow. The wagon wheels grind along in the snow, the cold gets in under the seat at the calves of one's legs, and the ceaseless bumping of the bottom of the box on the feet is frightful.

There was not much talk on the way down, and what little there was related mainly to certain domestic regulations to be strictly followed, regarding churning, pickles, pancakes, etc. Mrs. Ripley wore a shawl over her head, and carried her queer little black bonnet in her hand. Tewksbury was also wrapped in a shawl. The boy's teeth were pounding together like castanets by the time they reached Cedarville, and every muscle ached with the fatigue of shaking. After a few purchases they drove down to the railway station, a frightful little den (common in the West), which was always too hot or too cold. It happened to be hot just now—a fact which rejoiced little Tewksbury.

"Now git my trunk *stamped* 'r *fixed,* 'r whatever they call it," she said to Ripley, in a commanding tone, which gave great delight to the inevitable crowd of loafers beginning to assemble. "Now remember, Tukey, have grandad kill that biggest turkey right before Thanksgivin', an' then you run right over to Mis' Doudney's—she's got an awful tongue, but she can bake a turkey first-rate—an' she'll fix up some squash-pies for yeh. You can warm up one o' them mince-pies. I wish ye could be with me, but ye can't, so do the best ye can.

Ripley returning now, she said: "Waal, now, I've fixed things up the best I could. I've baked bread enough to last a week, an' Mis' Doudney has promised to bake for yeh."

"I don't like her bakin'."

"Waal, you'll haff to stand it till I get back, 'n' you'll find a jar o' sweet pickles an' some crabapple sauce down suller, 'n' you'd better melt up brown sugar for 'lasses, 'n' for goodness' sake don't eat all them mince-pies up the fust week, 'n' see that Tukey ain't froze goin' to school. An' now you'd better get out for home. Good-bye, an' remember them pies."

As they were riding home, Ripley roused up after a long silence. "Did she—a—kiss you good-bye, Tukey?"

"No, sir," piped Tewksbury.

"Thunder! didn't she?" After a silence. "She didn't me, neither. I guess she kind a sort a forgot it, bein' so flustrated, y' know."

One cold, windy, intensely bright day, Mrs. Stacey, who lives about two miles from Cedarville, looking out of the window, saw a queer little figure struggling along the road, which was blocked here and there with drifts. It was an old woman laden with a good half-dozen parcels, anyone of which was a load, which the wind seemed determined to wrench from her. She was dressed in black, with a full skirt, and her cloak being short, the wind had excellent opportunity to inflate her garments and sail her off occasionally into the deep snow outside the track, but she held on bravely till she reached the gate. As she turned in, Mrs. Stacey cried:

"Why! it's Gran'ma Ripley. Just getting back from her trip. Why! how do you do? Come in. Why! you must be nearly frozen. Let me take off your hat and veil."

"No, thank ye kindly, but I can't stop. I must be gittin' back to Ripley. I expec' that man has jest let ev'rything go six ways f'r Sunday."

"Oh, you must sit down just a minute and warm."

"Waal, I will, but I've got to git home by sundown, sure. I don' suppose they's a thing in the house to eat."

"Oh dear! I wish Stacey was here, so he could take you home. An' the boys at school."

"Don't need any help, if 'twa'nt for these bundles an' things. I guess I'll jest leave some of 'em here, an'—Here! take one of them apples. I brought 'em from Lizy Jane's suller, back to Yaark State."

"Oh! they're delicious! You must have had a lovely time."

"Pretty good. But I kep' thinkin' o' Ripley an' Tukey all the time. I s'pose they have had a gay time of it" (she meant the opposite of gay). "Waal, as I told Lizy Jane, I've had my spree, an' now I've got to git back to work. They ain't no rest for such as we are. I told Lizy Jane them folks in the big houses have Thanks-givin' dinner every day uv their lives, and men an' women in splendid clo's to wait on 'em, so't Thanks-givin' don't mean anything to 'em; but we poor critters, we make a great to-do if we have a good dinner oncet a year. I've saw a pile o' this world, Mrs. Stacey—a pile of it! I didn't think they was so many big houses in the world as I saw b'tween here an' Chicago. Waal, I can't set here gabbin'; I must git home to Ripley. Jest kinder stow them bags away. I'll take two an' leave them three others. Good-bye, I must be gittin' home to Ripley. He'll want his supper on time." And off up the road the indomitable little figure trudged, head held down to the cutting blast. Little snow-fly, a speck on a measureless expanse, crawling along with painful breathing and slipping, sliding steps—"Gittin' home to Ripley an' the boy."

Ripley was out to the barn when she entered, but Tewksbury was building a fire in the old cook-stove. He sprang up with a cry of joy, and ran to her. She seized him and kissed him, and it did her so much good she hugged him close, and kissed him again and again, crying hysterically.

"Oh, gran'ma, I'm so glad to see you! We've had an awful time since you've ben gone."

She released him and looked around. A lot of dirty dishes were on the table, the table-cloth was a "sight to behold," and so was the stove—kettle-marks all over the table-cloth, splotches of pancake batter all over the stove.

"Waal, I sh'd say as much," she dryly vouchsafed, untying her bonnet strings.

When Ripley came in she had on her regimentals, the stove was brushed, the room swept, and she was elbow-deep in the dish-pan. "Hullo, mother! Got back, hev yeh?"

"I sh'd say it was about time," she replied briefly, without looking up or ceasing work. "Has ol' 'Grumpy' dried up yit?" This was her greeting.

Her trip was a fact now; no chance could rob her of it. She had looked forward twenty-three years toward it, and now she could look back at it accomplished. She took up her burden again, never more thinking to lay it down.

# A DAY'S PLEASURE

## Hamlin Garland

WHEN MARKHAM CAME in from shoveling his last wagon-load of corn into the crib, he found that his wife had put the children to bed, and was kneading a batch of dough with the dogged action of a tired and sullen woman.

He slipped his soggy boots off his feet and, having laid a piece of wood on top of the stove, put his heels on it comfortably. His chair squeaked as he leaned back on its hind legs, but he paid no attention; he was used to it, exactly as he was used to his wife's lameness and ceaseless toil.

"That closes up my corn," he said after a silence. "I guess I'll go to town tomorrow to git my horses shod."

"I guess I'll git ready and go along," said his wife in a sorry attempt to be firm and confident of tone.

"What do you want to go to town fer?" he grumbled.

"What does anybody want to go to town fer?" she burst out, facing him. "I ain't been out o' this house fer six months, while you go an' go!"

"Oh, it ain't six months. You went down that day I got the mower."

"When was that? The tenth of July, and you know it."

"Well, mebbe 'twas. I didn't think it was so long ago. I ain't no objection to your goin', only I'm goin' to take a load of wheat."

"Well, jest leave off a sack, an' that'll balance me an' the baby," she said spiritedly.

"All right," he replied good-naturedly, seeing she was roused. "Only that wheat ought to be put up tonight if you're goin'. You won't have

441

any time to hold sacks for me in the morning with them young ones to get off to school."

"Well, let's go do it then," she said, sullenly resolute.

"I hate to go out agin; but I s'pose we'd better."

He yawned dismally and began pulling his boots on again, stamping his swollen feet into them with grunts of pain. She put on his coat and one of the boy's caps, and they went out to the granary. The night was cold and clear.

"Don't look so much like snow as it did last night," said Sam. "It may turn warm."

Laying out the sacks in the light of the lantern, they sorted out those which were whole, and Sam climbed into the bin with a tin pail in his hand, and the work began.

He was a sturdy fellow, and he worked desperately fast; the shining tin pail dived deep into the cold wheat and dragged heavily on the woman's tired hands as it came to the mouth of the sack, and she trembled with fatigue, but held on and dragged the sacks away when filled, and brought others, till at last Sam climbed out, puffing and wheezing, to tie them up.

"I guess I'll load 'em in the morning," he said. "You needn't wait fer me. I'll tie 'em up alone."

"Oh, I don't mind," she replied, feeling a little touched by his unexpectedly easy acquiescence to her request. When they went back to the house the moon had risen.

It had scarcely set when they were wakened by the crowing roosters. The man rolled stiffly out of bed and began rattling at the stove in the dark, cold kitchen.

His wife arose lamer and stiffer than usual and began twisting her thin hair into a knot.

Sam did not stop to wash, but went out to the barn. The woman, however, hastily soused her face into the hard limestone water at the sink and put the kettle on. Then she called the children. She knew it was early, and they would need several callings. She pushed breakfast forward, running over in her mind the things she must have: two spools of thread, six yards of cotton flannel, a can of coffee, and mittens for Kitty. These she must have—there were oceans of things she needed.

The children soon came scudding down out of the darkness of the upstairs to dress tumultuously at the kitchen stove. They humped and shivered, holding up their bare feet from the cold floor, like chickens in new fallen snow. They were irritable, and snarled and snapped and struck like cats and dogs. Mrs. Markham stood it for a while with mere commands to "hush up," but at last her patience gave out, and she charged down on the struggling mob and cuffed them right and left.

They ate their breakfast by lamplight, and when Sam went back to his work around the barnyard it was scarcely dawn. The children, left alone with their mother, began to tease her to let them go to town also.

"No, sir—nobody goes but baby. Your father's goin' to take a load of wheat."

She was weak with the worry of it all when she had sent the older children away to school, and the kitchen work was finished. She went into the cold bedroom off the little sitting room and put on her best dress. It had never been a good fit, and now she was getting so thin it hung in wrinkled folds everywhere about the shoulders and waist. She lay down on the bed a moment to ease that dull pain in her back. She had a moment's distaste for going out at all. The thought of sleep was more alluring. Then the thought of the long, long day, and the sickening sameness of her life, swept over her again, and she rose and prepared the baby for the journey.

It was but little after sunrise when Sam drove out into the road and started for Belleplain. His wife sat perched upon the wheat-sacks behind him, holding the baby in her lap, a cotton quilt under her, and a cotton horse-blanket over her knees.

Sam was disposed to be very good-natured, and he talked back at her occasionally, though she could only understand him when he turned his face toward her. The baby stared out at the passing fence-posts, and wiggled his hands out of his mittens at every opportunity. He was merry at least.

It grew warmer as they went on, and a strong south wind arose. The dust settled upon the woman's shawl and hat. Her hair loosened and blew unkemptly about her face. The road which led across the high, level prairie was quite smooth and dry, but still it jolted her, and the pain in her back increased. She had nothing to lean against, and the weight of the child grew greater, till she was forced to place him on the sacks beside her, though she could not loose her hold for a moment.

The town drew in sight—a cluster of small frame houses and stores on the dry prairie beside a railway station. There were no trees yet which could be called shade trees. The pitilessly severe light of the sun flooded everything. A few teams were hitched about, and in the lee of the stores a few men could be seen seated comfortably, their broad hat-rims flopping up and down, their faces brown as leather.

Markham put his wife out at one of the grocery-stores, and drove off down toward the elevators to sell his wheat.

The grocer greeted Mrs. Markham in a perfunctorily kind manner, and offered her a chair, which she took gratefully. She sat for a quarter of an hour almost without moving, leaning against the back of the high chair. At last the child began to get restless and troublesome, and she spent half an hour helping him amuse himself around the nail-kegs.

At length she rose and went out on the walk, carrying the baby. She went into the dry-goods store and took a seat on one of the little revolving stools. A woman was buying some woolen goods for a dress. It was worth twenty-seven cents a yard, the clerk said, but he would knock off two cents if she took ten yards. It looked warm, and Mrs. Markham wished she could afford it for Mary.

A pretty young girl came in, and laughed and chatted with the clerk, and bought a pair of gloves. She was the daughter of the grocer. Her happiness made the wife and mother sad. When Sam came back she asked him for some money.

"What you want to do with it?" he asked.

"I want to spend it," she said.

She was not to be trifled with, so he gave her a dollar.

"I need a dollar more."

"Well, I've got to go take up that note at the bank."

"Well, the children's got to have some new underclo'es," she said.

He handed her a two-dollar bill and then went out to pay his note.

She bought her cotton flannel and mittens and thread, and then sat leaning against the counter. It was noon, and she was hungry. She went out to the wagon, got the lunch she had brought, and took it into the grocery to eat it—where she could get a drink of water.

The grocer gave the baby a stick of candy and handed the mother an apple.

"It'll kind o' go down with your doughnuts," he said.

After eating her lunch she got up and went out. She felt ashamed to sit there any longer. She entered another dry-goods store, but when the clerk came toward her saying, "Anything today, Mrs. ——?" she answered, "No, I guess not," and turned away with foolish face.

She walked up and down the street, desolately homeless. She did not know what to do with herself. She knew no one except the grocer. She grew bitter as she saw a couple of ladies pass, holding their demi-trains in the latest city fashion. Another woman went by pushing a baby carriage, in which sat a child just about as big as her own. It was bouncing itself up and down on the long slender springs, and laughing and shouting. Its clean round face glowed from its pretty fringed hood. She looked down at the dusty clothes and grimy face of her own little one and walked on savagely.

She went into the drug store where the soda fountain was, but it made her thirsty to sit there, and she went out on the street again. She heard Sam laugh, and saw him in a group of men over by the blacksmith shop. He was having a good time and had forgotten her.

Her back ached so intolerably that she concluded to go in and rest once more in the grocer's chair. The baby was growing cross and fretful. She bought five cents' worth of candy to take home to the children and gave baby a little piece to keep him quiet. She wished Sam would come. It must be getting late. The grocer said it was not much after one. Time seemed terribly long. She felt that she ought to do something while she was in town. She ran over her purchases— yes, that was all she had planned to buy. She fell to figuring on the things she needed. It was terrible. It ran away up into twenty or thirty dollars at the least. Sam, as well as she, needed underwear for the cold winter, but they would have to wear the old ones, even if they were thin and ragged. She would not need a dress, she thought bitterly, because she never went anywhere. She rose, and went out on the street once more, and wandered up and down, looking at everything in the hope of enjoying something.

A man from Boon Creek backed a load of apples up to the sidewalk, and as he stood waiting for the grocer he noticed Mrs. Markham and the baby, and gave the baby an apple. This was a pleasure. He had such a hearty way about him. He on his part saw an ordinary farmer's wife with dusty dress, unkempt hair, and tired face. He did not know exactly why she appealed to him, but he tried to cheer her up.

The grocer was familiar with these bedraggled and weary wives. He was accustomed to see them sit for hours in his big wooden chair and nurse tired and fretful children. Their forlorn, aimless, pathetic wandering up and down the street was a daily occurrence, and had never possessed any special meaning to him.

## II

In a cottage around the corner from the grocery store two men and a woman were finishing a dainty luncheon. The woman was dressed in cool, white garments, and she seemed to make the day one of perfect comfort.

The home of the Honorable Mr. Hall was by no means the costliest in the town, but his wife made it the most attractive. He was one of the leading lawyers of the county, and a man of culture and progressive views. He was entertaining a friend who had lectured the night before in the Congregational church.

They were by no means in serious discussion. The talk was rather frivolous. Hall had the ability to caricature men with a few gestures and attitudes, and was giving to his Eastern friend some descriptions of the old-fashioned Western lawyers he had met in his practice. He was very amusing, and his guest laughed heartily for a time.

But suddenly Hall became aware that Otis was not listening. Then he perceived that he was peering out of the window at someone, and that on his face a look of bitter sadness was falling.

Hall stopped. "What do you see, Otis?"

Otis replied, "I see a forlorn, weary woman."

Mrs. Hall rose and went to the window. Mrs. Markham was walking by the house, her baby in her arms. Savage anger and weeping were in her eyes and on her lips, and there was hopeless tragedy in her shambling walk and weak back.

In the silence Otis went on: "I saw the poor, dejected creature twice this morning. I couldn't forget her."

"Who is she?" asked Mrs. Hall very softly.

"Her name is Markham; she's Sam Markham's wife," said Hall.

The young wife led the way into the sitting room, and the men took seats and lit their cigars. Hall was meditating a diversion when Otis resumed suddenly:

"That woman came to town today to get a change, to have a little play-spell, and she's wandering around like a starved and weary cat. I wonder if there is a woman in this town with sympathy enough and courage enough to go out and help that woman? The saloonkeepers, the politicians, and the grocers make it pleasant for the man—so pleasant that he forgets his wife. But the wife is left without a word."

Mrs. Hall's work dropped, and on her pretty face was a look of pain. The man's harsh words had wounded her—and wakened her.

She took up her hat and hurried out on the walk. The men looked
at each other, and then the husband said:

"It's going to be a little sultry for the men around these diggings.
Suppose we go out for a walk."

Delia felt a hand on her arm as she stood at the corner.

"You look tired, Mrs. Markham; won't you come in a little while?
I'm Mrs. Hall."

Mrs. Markham turned with a scowl on her face and a biting word
on her tongue, but something in the sweet, round little face of the
other woman silenced her, and her brow smoothed out.

"Thank you kindly, but it's most time to go home. I'm looking
fer Mr. Markham now."

"Oh, come in a little while; the baby is cross and tried out;
please do."

Mrs. Markham yielded to the friendly voice, and together the two
women reached the gate just as two men hurriedly turned the other
corner.

"Let me relieve you," said Mrs. Hall.

The mother hesitated: "He's so dusty."

"Oh, that won't matter. Oh, what a big fellow he is! I haven't any
of my own," said Mrs. Hall, and a look passed like an electric spark
between the two women, and Delia was her willing guest from that
moment.

They went into the little sitting room, so dainty and lovely to the
farmer's wife, and as she sank into an easy-chair she was faint and
drowsy with the pleasure of it. She submitted to being brushed. She
gave the baby into the hands of the Swedish girl, who washed its
face and hands and sang it to sleep, while its mother sipped some tea.
Through it all she lay back in her easy-chair, not speaking a word,
while the ache passed out of her back, and her hot, swollen head
ceased to throb.

But she saw everything—the piano, the pictures, the curtains,
the wall-paper, the little tea-stand. They were almost as grateful to
her as the food and fragrant tea. Such housekeeping as this she had
never seen. Her mother had worn her kitchen floor thin as brown
paper in keeping a speckless house, and she had been in houses that
were larger and costlier, but something of the charm of her hostess
was in the arrangement of vases, chairs, or pictures. It was tasteful.

Mrs. Hall did not ask about her affairs. She talked to her about the
sturdy little baby and about the things upon which Delia's eyes dwelt.
If she seemed interested in a vase she was told what it was and where

it was made. She was shown all the pictures and books. Mrs. Hall seemed to read her visitor's mind. She kept as far from the farm and her guest's affairs as possible, and at last she opened the piano and sang to her—not slow-moving hymns, but catchy love-songs full of sentiment, and then played some simple melodies, knowing that Mrs. Markham's eyes were studying her hands, her rings, and the flash of her fingers on the keys—seeing more than she heard—and through it all Mrs. Hall conveyed the impression that she, too, was having a good time.

The rattle of the wagon outside roused them both. Sam was at the gate for her. Mrs. Markham rose hastily. "Oh, it's almost sundown!" she gasped in astonishment as she looked out of the window.

"Oh, that won't kill anybody," replied her hostess. "Don't hurry. Carrie, take the baby out to the wagon for Mrs. Markham while I help her with her things."

"Oh, I've had such a good time," Mrs. Markham said as they went down the little walk.

"So have I," replied Mrs. Hall. She took the baby a moment as her guest climbed in. "Oh, you big, fat fellow!" she cried as she gave him a squeeze. "You must bring your wife in oftener, Mr. Markham," she said as she handed the baby up.

Sam was staring with amazement.

"Thank you, I will," he finally managed to say.

"Good-night," said Mrs. Markham.

"Good-night, dear," called Mrs. Hall, and the wagon began to rattle off.

The tenderness and sympathy in her voice brought the tears to Delia's eyes—not hot nor bitter tears, but tears that cooled her eyes and cleared her mind.

The wind had gone down, and the red sunlight fell mistily over the world of corn and stubble. The crickets were still chirping, and the feeding cattle were drifting toward the farmyards. The day had been made beautiful by human sympathy.

# A JURY OF HER PEERS

### Susan Glaspell

WHEN MARTHA HALE opened the storm-door and got a cut of the north wind, she ran back for her big woolen scarf. As she hurriedly wound that round her head her eye made a scandalized sweep of her kitchen. It was no ordinary thing that called her away—it was probably farther from ordinary than anything that had ever happened in Dickson County. But what her eye took in was that her kitchen was in no shape for leaving: her bread all ready for mixing, half the flour sifted and half unsifted.

She hated to see things half done; but she had been at that when the team from town stopped to get Mr. Hale, and then the sheriff came running in to say his wife wished Mrs. Hale would come too—adding, with a grin, that he guessed she was getting scared and wanted another woman along. So she had dropped everything right where it was.

"Martha!" now came her husband's impatient voice. "Don't keep folks waiting out here in the cold."

She again opened the storm-door, and this time joined the three men and the one woman waiting for her in the big two-seated buggy.

After she had the robes tucked around her she took another look at the woman who sat beside her on the back seat. She had met Mrs. Peters the year before at the county fair, and the thing she remembered about her was that she didn't seem like a sheriff's wife. She was small and thin and didn't have a strong voice. Mrs. Gorman, the sheriff's wife before Gorman went out and Peters came in, had a voice that somehow seemed to be backing up the law with every word. But if Mrs. Peters didn't look like a sheriff's wife, Peters made it up in looking like a sheriff. He was to a dot the kind of man who could get himself elected sheriff—a heavy man with a big voice, who was particularly genial with the law-abiding, as if to make it plain that he knew the difference between criminals and non-criminals. And right there it came into Mrs. Hale's mind, with a stab, that this man who was so pleasant and lively with all of them was going to the Wrights' now as a sheriff.

"The country's not very pleasant this time of year," Mrs. Peters at last ventured, as if she felt they ought to be talking as well as the men.

Mrs. Hale scarcely finished her reply, for they had gone up a little hill and could see the Wright place now, and seeing it did not make her feel like talking. It looked very lonesome this cold March morning. It had always been a lonesome-looking place. It was down in a hollow, and the poplar trees around it were lonesome-looking trees. The men were looking at it and talking about what had happened. The county attorney was bending to one side of the buggy, and kept looking steadily at the place as they drew up to it.

"I'm glad you came with me," Mrs. Peters said nervously, as the two women were about to follow the men in through the kitchen door.

Even after she had her foot on the door-step, her hand on the knob, Martha Hale had a moment of feeling she could not cross that threshold. And the reason it seemed she couldn't cross it now was simply because she hadn't crossed it before. Time and time again it had been in her mind, "I ought to go over and see Minnie Foster"— she still thought of her as Minnie Foster, though for twenty years she had been Mrs. Wright. And then there was always something to do and Minnie Foster would go from her mind. But *now* she could come.

The men went over to the stove. The women stood close together by the door. Young Henderson, the county attorney, turned around and said:

"Come up to the fire, ladies."

Mrs. Peters took a step forward, then stopped. "I'm not—cold," she said.

The men talked for a minute about what a good thing it was the sheriff had sent his deputy out that morning to make a fire for them, and then Sheriff Peters stepped back from the stove, unbuttoned his outer coat, and leaned his hands on the kitchen table in a way that seemed to mark the beginning of official business. "Now, Mr. Hale," he said in a sort of semi-official voice, "before we move things about, you tell Mr. Henderson just what it was you saw when you came here yesterday morning."

The county attorney was looking around the kitchen.

"By the way," he said, "has anything been moved?" He turned to the sheriff. "Are things just as you left them yesterday?"

Peters looked from cupboard to sink; from that to a small worn rocker a little to one side of the kitchen table.

"It's just the same."

"Somebody should have been left here yesterday," said the county attorney.

"Oh—yesterday," returned the sheriff, with a little gesture as of yesterday having been more than he could bear to think of. "When I had to send Frank to Morris Center for that man who went crazy—let me tell you, I had my hands full *yesterday*. I knew you could get back from Omaha by today, George, and as long as I went over everything here myself—"

"Well, Mr. Hale," said the county attorney, in a way of letting what was past and gone go, "tell just what happened when you came here yesterday morning."

Mrs. Hale, still leaning against the door, had that sinking feeling of the mother whose child is about to speak a piece. Lewis often wandered along and got things mixed up in a story. She hoped he would tell this straight and plain, and not say unnecessary things that would just make things harder for Minnie Foster. He didn't begin at once, and she noticed that he looked queer—as if standing in that kitchen and having to tell what he had seen there yesterday morning made him almost sick.

"Harry and I had started to town with a load of potatoes," Mrs. Hale's husband began.

Harry was Mrs. Hale's oldest boy. He wasn't with them now, for the very good reason that those potatoes never got to town yesterday and he was taking them this morning, so he hadn't been home when the sheriff stopped to say he wanted Mr. Hale to come over to the Wright place and tell the county attorney his story there, where he could point it all out.

"We came along this road," Hale was going on, with a motion of his hand to the road over which they had just come, "and as we got in sight of the house I says to Harry, 'I'm goin' to see if I can't get John Wright to take a telephone.' You see," he explained to Henderson, "unless I can get somebody to go in with me they won't come out this branch road except for a price *I* can't pay. I'd spoke to Wright about it once before; but he put me off, saying folks talked too much anyway, and all he asked was peace and quiet—guess you know about how much he talked himself. But I thought maybe if I went to the house and talked about it before his wife, and said all the women-folks liked the telephones, and that in this lonesome stretch of road it would be a good thing—well, I said to Harry that that was what I was going to say—though I said at the same time that I didn't know as what his wife wanted made much difference to John—"

Now, there he was!—saying things he didn't need to say. Mrs. Hale tried to catch her husband's eye, but fortunately the county attorney interrupted with:

"Let's talk about that a little later, Mr. Hale. I do want to talk about that, but I'm anxious now to get along to just exactly what happened when you got here."

When he began this time, it was very deliberately and carefully:

"I didn't see or hear anything. I knocked at the door. And still it was all quiet inside. I knew they must be up—it was past eight o'clock. So I knocked again, louder, and I thought I heard somebody say, 'Come in.' I wasn't sure—I'm not sure yet. But I opened the door— this door," jerking a hand toward the door by which the two women stood, "and there, in that rocker"—pointing to it—"sat Mrs. Wright."

Everyone in the kitchen looked at the rocker. It came into Mrs. Hale's mind that that rocker didn't look in the least like Minnie Foster—the Minnie Foster of twenty years before. It was a dingy red, with wooden rungs up the back, and the middle rung was gone, and the chair sagged to one side.

"How did she—look?" the county attorney was inquiring.

"Well," said Hale, "she looked—queer."

"How do you mean—queer?"

As he asked it he took out a notebook and pencil. Mrs. Hale did not like the sight of that pencil. She kept her eye fixed on her husband, as if to keep him from saying unnecessary things that would go into that notebook and make trouble.

Hale did speak guardedly, as if the pencil had affected him too.

"Well, as if she didn't know what she was going to do next. And kind of—done up."

"How did she seem to feel about your coming?"

"Why, I don't think she minded—one way or other. She didn't pay much attention. I said, 'Ho' do, Mrs. Wright? It's cold, ain't it?' And she said, 'Is it?'—and went on pleatin' at her apron.

"Well, I was surprised. She didn't ask me to come up to the stove, or to sit down, but just set there, not even lookin' at me. And so I said: 'I want to see John.' And then she laughed. I guess you would call it a laugh.

"I thought of Harry and the team outside, so I said, a little sharp, 'Can I see John?' 'No,' says she—kind of dull like. 'Ain't he home?' says I. Then she looked at me. 'Yes,' says she, 'he's home.' 'Then why can't I see him?' I asked her, out of patience with her now. ''Cause he's dead,' says she, just as quiet and dull—and fell to pleatin' her apron. 'Dead?' says I, like you do when you can't take in what you've heard.

"She just nodded her head, not getting a bit excited, but rockin' back and forth.

"'Why—where is he?' says I, not knowing *what* to say.

"She just pointed upstairs—like this"—pointing to the room above.

"I got up, with the idea of going up there myself. By this time I—didn't know what to do. I walked from there to here; then I says: 'Why, what did he die of?'

"'He died of a rope round his neck,' says she; and just went on pleatin' at her apron."

Hale stopped speaking, and stood staring at the rocker, as if he were still seeing the woman who had sat there the morning before. Nobody spoke; it was as if everyone were seeing the woman who had sat there the morning before.

"And what did you do then?" the county attorney at last broke the silence.

"I went out and called Harry. I thought I might—need help. I got Harry in, and we went upstairs." His voice fell almost to a whisper. "There he was—lying over the—"

"I think I'd rather have you go into that upstairs," the attorney interrupted, "where you can point it all out. Just go on now with the rest of the story."

"Well, my first thought was to get that rope off. It looked—"

He stopped, his face twitching.

"But Harry, he went up to him, and he said, 'No, he's dead all right, and we'd better not touch anything.' So we went downstairs. She was still sitting that same way. 'Has anybody been notified?' I asked. 'No,' said she, unconcerned.

"'Who did this, Mrs. Wright?' said Harry. He said it business-like, and she stopped pleatin' at her apron. 'I don't know,' she says. 'You don't *know*?' says Harry. 'Weren't you sleepin' in the bed with him?' 'Yes,' says she, 'but I was on the inside.' 'Somebody slipped a rope round his neck and strangled him, and you didn't wake up?' says Harry. 'I didn't wake up,' she said after him.

"We may have looked as if we didn't see how that could be, for after a minute she said, 'I sleep sound.'

"Harry was going to ask her more questions, but I said maybe that weren't our business; maybe we ought to let her tell her story first to the coroner or the sheriff. So Harry went fast as he could over to High Road—the Rivers' place, where there's a telephone."

"And what did she do when she knew you had gone for the coroner?" The attorney got his pencil in his hand all ready for writing.

"She moved from that chair to this one over here"—Hale pointed to a small chair in the corner—"and just sat there with her hands held together and looking down. I got a feeling that I ought to make some conversation, so I said I had come in to see if John wanted to put in a telephone; and at that she started to laugh, and then she stopped and looked at me—scared."

At the sound of a moving pencil the man who was telling the story looked up.

"I dunno—maybe it wasn't scared," he hastened; "I wouldn't like to say it was. Soon Harry got back, and then Dr. Lloyd came, and you, Mr. Peters, and so I guess that's all I know that you don't."

He said that last with relief, and moved a little, as if relaxing. Everyone moved a little. The county attorney walked toward the stair door.

"I guess we'll go upstairs first—then out to the barn and around."

He paused and looked around the kitchen.

"You're convinced there was nothing important here?" he asked the sheriff. "Nothing that would—point to any motive?"

The sheriff too looked all around, as if to re-convince himself.

"Nothing here but kitchen things," he said, with a little laugh for the insignificance of kitchen things.

The county attorney was looking at the cupboard—a peculiar, ungainly structure, half closet and half cupboard, the upper part of it being built in the wall, and the lower part just the old-fashioned kitchen cupboard. As if its queerness attracted him, he got a chair and opened the upper part and looked in. After a moment he drew his hand away sticky.

"Here's a nice mess," he said resentfully.

The two women had drawn nearer, and now the sheriff's wife spoke.

"Oh—her fruit," she said, looking to Mrs. Hale for sympathetic understanding. She turned back to the county attorney and explained: "She worried about that when it turned so cold last night. She said the fire would go out and her jars burst."

Mrs. Peters' husband broke into a laugh.

"Well, can you beat the women! Held for murder, and worrying about her preserves!

The young attorney set his lips.

"I guess before we're through she may have something more serious than preserves to worry about."

"Oh, well," said Mrs. Hale's husband, with good-natured superiority, "women are used to worrying over trifles."

The two women moved a little closer together. Neither of them spoke. The county attorney seemed suddenly to remember his manners—and think of his future.

"And yet," said he, with the gallantry of a young politician, "for all their worries, what would we do without the ladies?"

The women did not speak, did not unbend. He went to the sink and began washing his hands. He turned to wipe them on the roller towel—whirled it for a cleaner place.

"Dirty towels! Not much of a housekeeper, would you say, ladies?"

He kicked his foot against some dirty pans under the sink.

"There's a great deal of work to be done on a farm," said Mrs. Hale stiffly.

"To be sure. And yet"—with a little bow to her—"I know there are some Dickson County farm-houses that do not have such roller towels."

"Those towels get dirty awful quick. Men's hands aren't always as clean as they might be."

"Ah, loyal to your sex, I see," he laughed. He stopped and gave her a keen look. "But you and Mrs. Wright were neighbors. I suppose you were friends, too."

Martha Hale shook her head.

"I've seen little enough of her of late years. I've not been in this house—it's more than a year."

"And why was that? You didn't like her?"

"I liked her well enough," she replied with spirit. "Farmers' wives have their hands full, Mr. Henderson. And then—" She looked around the kitchen.

"Yes?" he encouraged.

"It never seemed a very cheerful place," said she, more to herself than to him.

"No," he agreed; "I don't think anyone would call it cheerful. I shouldn't say she had the home-making instinct."

"Well, I don't know as Wright had, either," she muttered.

"You mean they didn't get on very well?" he was quick to ask.

"No; I don't mean anything," she answered, with decision. As she turned a little away from him, she added: "But I don't think a place would be any the cheerfuller for John Wright's bein' in it."

"I'd like to talk to you about that a little later, Mrs. Hale," he said. "I'm anxious to get the lay of things upstairs now."

He moved toward the stair door, followed by the two men.

"I suppose anything Mrs. Peters does'll be all right?" the sheriff inquired. "She was to take in some clothes for her, you know—and a few little things. We left in such a hurry yesterday."

The county attorney looked at the two women whom they were leaving alone there among the kitchen things.

"Yes—Mrs. Peters," he said, his glance resting on the woman who was not Mrs. Peters, the big farmer woman who stood behind the sheriff's wife. "Of course Mrs. Peters is one of us," he said, in a manner of entrusting responsibility. "And keep your eye out, Mrs. Peters, for anything that might be of use. No telling; you women might come upon a clue to the motive—and that's the thing we need."

Mr. Hale rubbed his face after the fashion of a showman getting ready for a pleasantry.

"But would the women know a clue if they did come upon it?" he said; and, having delivered himself of this, he followed the others through the stair door.

The women stood motionless and silent, listening to the footsteps, first upon the stairs, then in the room above.

Then, as if releasing herself from something strange, Mrs. Hale began to arrange the dirty pans under the sink, which the county attorney's disdainful push of the foot had deranged.

"I'd hate to have men comin' into my kitchen," she said testily—"snoopin' round and criticizin'.."

"Of course it's no more than their duty," said the sheriff's wife, in her manner of timid acquiescence.

"Duty's all right," replied Mrs. Hale bluffly; "but I guess that deputy sheriff that come out to make the fire might have got a little of this on." She gave the roller towel a pull. "Wish I'd thought of that sooner! Seems mean to talk about her for not having things slicked up, when she had to come away in such a hurry."

She looked around the kitchen. Certainly it was not "slicked up." Her eye was held by a bucket of sugar on a low shelf. The cover was off the wooden bucket, and beside it was a paper bag—half full.

Mrs. Hale moved toward it.

"She was putting this in there," she said to herself—slowly.

She thought of the flour in her kitchen at home—half sifted. She had been interrupted, and had left things half done. What had interrupted Minnie Foster? Why had that work been left half done? She made a move as if to finish it—unfinished things always bothered her—and then she glanced around and saw that Mrs. Peters was watching her—and she didn't want Mrs. Peters to get that feeling she had got of work begun and then—for some reason—not finished.

"It's a shame about her fruit," she said, and walked toward the cupboard that the county attorney had opened, and got on the chair, murmuring: "I wonder if it's all gone."

It was a sorry enough looking sight, but "Here's one that's all right," she said at last. She held it toward the light. "This is cherries, too." She looked again. "I declare I believe that's the only one."

With a sigh, she got down from the chair, went to the sink, and wiped off the bottle.

"She'll feel awful bad, after all her hard work in the hot weather. I remember the afternoon I put up my cherries last summer."

She set the bottle on the table, and, with another sigh, started to sit down in the rocker. But she did not sit down. Something kept her from sitting down in that chair. She straightened—stepped back, and, half turned away, stood looking at it, seeing the woman who had sat there "pleatin' at her apron."

The thin voice of the sheriff's wife broke in upon her: "I must be getting those things from the front room closet." She opened the door into the other room, started in, stepped back. "You coming with me, Mrs. Hale?" she asked nervously. "You—you could help me get them."

They were soon back—the stark coldness of that shut-up room was not a thing to linger in.

"My!" said Mrs. Peters, dropping the things on the table and hurrying to the stove.

Mrs. Hale stood examining the clothes the woman who was being detained in town had said she wanted.

"Wright was close!" she exclaimed, holding up a shabby black skirt that bore the marks of much making over. "I think maybe that's why she kept so much to herself. I s'pose she felt she couldn't do her part; and then, you don't enjoy things when you feel shabby. She used to wear pretty clothes and be lively—when she was Minnie Foster, one of the town girls, singing in the choir. But that—oh, that was twenty years ago."

With a carefulness in which there was something tender, she folded the shabby clothes and piled them at one corner of the table. She looked up at Mrs. Peters, and there was something in the other woman's look that irritated her.

"She don't care," she said to herself. "Much difference it makes to her whether Minnie Foster had pretty clothes when she was a girl."

Then she looked again, and she wasn't so sure; in fact, she hadn't at any time been perfectly sure about Mrs. Peters. She had that shrinking manner, and yet her eyes looked as if they could see a long way into things.

"This all you was to take in?" asked Mrs. Hale.

"No," said the sheriff's wife; "she said she wanted an apron. Funny thing to want," she ventured in her nervous little way, "for there's not much to get you dirty in jail, goodness knows. But I suppose just to make her feel more natural. If you're used to wearing an apron—. She said they were in the bottom drawer of this cupboard. Yes—here they are. And then her little shawl that always hung on the stair door."

She took the small gray shawl from behind the door leading upstairs.

Suddenly Mrs. Hale took a quick step toward the other woman.

"Mrs. Peters!"

"Yes, Mrs. Hale?"

"Do you think she—did it?"

A frightened look blurred the other thing in Mrs. Peters' eyes.

"Oh, I don't know," she said, in a voice that seemed to shrink away from the subject.

"Well, I don't think she did," affirmed Mrs. Hale stoutly. "Asking for an apron, and her little shawl. Worryin' about her fruit."

"Mr. Peters says—." Footsteps were heard in the room above; she stopped, looked up, then went on in a lowered voice: "Mr. Peters says—it looks bad for her. Mr. Henderson is awful sarcastic in a speech, and he's going to make fun of her saying she didn't—wake up."

For a moment Mrs. Hale had no answer. Then, "Well, I guess John Wright didn't wake up—when they was slippin' that rope under his neck," she muttered.

"No, it's *strange,*" breathed Mrs. Peters. "They think it was such a—funny way to kill a man."

"That's just what Mr. Hale said," said Mrs. Hale, in a resolutely natural voice. "There was a gun in the house. He says that's what he can't understand."

"Mr. Henderson said, coming out, that what was needed for the case was a motive. Something to show anger—or sudden feeling."

"Well, I don't see any signs of anger around here," said Mrs. Hale. "I don't—"

She stopped. It was as if her mind tripped on something. Her eye was caught by a dish-towel in the middle of the kitchen table. Slowly she moved toward the table. One half of it was wiped clean, the other half messy. Her eyes made a slow, almost unwilling turn to the bucket of sugar and the half empty bag beside it. Things begun—and not finished.

After a moment she stepped back, and said, in that manner of releasing herself: "Wonder how they're finding things upstairs? I hope she had it a little more red up there. You know"—she paused, and feeling gathered—"it seems kind of *sneaking:* locking her up in town and coming out here to get her own house to turn against her!"

"But, Mrs. Hale," said the sheriff's wife, "the law is the law."

"I s'pose 'tis," answered Mrs. Hale shortly.

She turned to the stove, worked with it a minute, and when she straightened up she said aggressively:

"The law is the law—and a bad stove is a bad stove. How'd you like to cook on this?"—pointing with the poker to the broken lining. She opened the oven door and started to express her opinion of the oven; but she was swept into her own thoughts, thinking of what it would mean, year after year, to have that stove to wrestle with. The thought of Minnie Foster trying to bake in that oven—and the thought of her never going over to see Minnie Foster—

She was startled by hearing Mrs. Peters say:

"A person gets discouraged—and loses heart."

The sheriff's wife had looked from the stove to the pail of water which had been carried in from outside. The two women stood there silent, above them the footsteps of the men who were looking for evidence against the woman who had worked in that kitchen. That look of seeing into things, of seeing through a thing to something else, was in the eyes of the sheriff's wife now. When Mrs. Hale next spoke to her, it was gently:

"Better loosen up your things, Mrs. Peters. We'll not feel them when we go out."

Mrs. Peters went to the back of the room to hang up the fur tippet she was wearing. A moment later she exclaimed, "Why, she was piecing a quilt," and held up a large sewing basket piled high with quilt pieces.

Mrs. Hale spread some of the blocks out on the table.

"It's log-cabin pattern," she said, putting several of them together. "Pretty, isn't it?"

They were so engaged with the quilt that they did not hear the footsteps on the stairs. Just as the stair door opened Mrs. Hale was saying:

"Do you suppose she was going to quilt it or just knot it?"

The sheriff threw up his hands.

"They wonder whether she was going to quilt it or just knot it!" he cried.

There was a laugh for the ways of women, a warming of hands over the stove, and then the county attorney said briskly:

"Well, let's go right out to the barn and get that cleared up."

"I don't see as there's anything so strange," Mrs. Hale said resentfully, after the outside door had closed on the three men—"our taking up our time with little things while we're waiting for them to get the evidence. I don't see as it's anything to laugh about."

"Of course they've got awful important things on their minds," said the sheriff's wife apologetically.

They returned to an inspection of the block for the quilt. Mrs. Hale was looking at the fine, even sewing, and preoccupied with thoughts of the woman who had done that sewing, when she heard the sheriff's wife say, in a queer tone:

"Why, look at this one."

She turned to take the block held out to her.

"The sewing," said Mrs. Peters, in a troubled way. "All the rest of them have been so nice and even—but—this one. Why, it looks as if she didn't know what she was about!"

Their eyes met—something flashed to life, passed between them; then, as if with an effort, they seemed to pull away from each other. A moment Mrs. Hale sat there, her hands folded over that sewing which was so unlike all the rest of the sewing. Then she had pulled a knot and drawn the threads.

"Oh, what are you doing, Mrs. Hale?" asked the sheriff's wife.

"Just pulling out a stitch or two that's not sewed very good," said Mrs. Hale mildly.

"I don't think we ought to touch things," Mrs. Peters said, a little helplessly.

"I'll just finish up this end," answered Mrs. Hale, still in that mild, matter-of-fact fashion.

She threaded a needle and started to replace bad sewing with good. For a little while she sewed in silence. Then, in that thin, timid voice, she heard:

"Mrs. Hale!"

"Yes, Mrs. Peters?"

"What do you suppose she was so—nervous about?"

"Oh, *I* don't know," said Mrs. Hale, as if dismissing a thing not important enough to spend much time on. "I don't know as she was—nervous. I sew awful queer sometimes when I'm just tired."

She cut a thread, and out of the corner of her eye looked up at Mrs. Peters. The small, lean face of the sheriff's wife seemed to have tightened up. Her eyes had that look of peering into something. But next moment she moved, and said in her indecisive way:

"Well, I must get those clothes wrapped. They may be through sooner than we think. I wonder where I could find a piece of paper— and string."

"In that cupboard, maybe," suggested Mrs. Hale, after a glance around.

One piece of the crazy sewing remained unripped. Mrs. Peter's back turned, Martha Hale now scrutinized that piece, compared it with the dainty, accurate sewing of the other blocks. The difference was startling. Holding this block made her feel queer, as if the distracted thoughts of the woman who had perhaps turned to it to try and quiet herself were communicating themselves to her.

Mrs. Peters' voice roused her.

"Here's a bird-cage," she said. "Did she have a bird, Mrs. Hale?"

"Why, I don't know whether she did or not." She turned to look at the cage Mrs. Peters was holding up. "I've not been here in so long." She sighed. "There was a man last year selling canaries cheap— but I don't know as she took one. Maybe she did. She used to sing real pretty herself."

"Seems kind of funny to think of a bird here." She half laughed— an attempt to put up a barrier. "But she must have had one—or why would she have a cage? I wonder what happened to it."

"I suppose maybe the cat got it," suggested Mrs. Hale, resuming her sewing.

"No; she didn't have a cat. She's got that feeling some people have about cats—being afraid of them. When they brought her to our house yesterday, my cat got in the room, and she was real upset and asked me to take it out."

"My sister Bessie was like that," laughed Mrs. Hale.

The sheriff's wife did not reply. The silence made Mrs. Hale turn around. Mrs. Peters was examining the bird-cage.

"Look at this door," she said slowly. "It's broke. One hinge has been pulled apart."

Mrs. Hale came nearer.

"Looks as if someone must have been—rough with it."

Again their eyes met—startled, questioning, apprehensive. For a moment neither spoke nor stirred. Then Mrs. Hale, turning away, said brusquely:

"If they're going to find any evidence, I wish they'd be about it. I don't like this place."

"But I'm awful glad you came with me, Mrs. Hale." Mrs. Peters put the bird-cage on the table and sat down. "It would be lonesome for me—sitting here alone."

"Yes, it would, wouldn't it?" agreed Mrs. Hale, a certain very determined naturalness in her voice. She had picked up the sewing, but now it dropped in her lap, and she murmured in a different voice: "But I tell you what I *do* wish, Mrs. Peters. I wish I had come over sometimes when she was here. I wish—I had."

"But of course you were awful busy, Mrs. Hale. Your house—and your children."

"I could've come," retorted Mrs. Hale shortly. "I stayed away because it weren't cheerful—and that's why I ought to have come. I"—she looked around—"I've never liked this place. Maybe because it's down in a hollow and you don't see the road. I don't know what it is, but it's a lonesome place, and always was. I wish I had come over to see Minnie Foster sometimes. I can see now—" She did not put it into words.

"Well, you mustn't reproach yourself," counseled Mrs. Peters. "Somehow, we just don't see how it is with other folks till—something comes up."

"Not having children makes less work," mused Mrs. Hale, after a silence, "but it makes a quiet house—and Wright out to work all day—and no company when he did come in. Did you know John Wright, Mrs. Peters?"

"Not to know him. I've seen him in town. They say he was a good man."

"Yes—good," conceded John Wright's neighbor grimly. "He didn't drink, and kept his word as well as most, I guess, and paid his debts. But he was a hard man, Mrs. Peters. Just to pass the time of day with him—" She stopped, shivered a little. "Like a raw wind that gets to the bone." Her eyes fell upon the cage on the table before her, and she added, almost bitterly: "I should think she would've wanted a bird!"

Suddenly she leaned forward, looking intently at the cage. "But what do you s'pose went wrong with it?"

"I don't know," returned Mrs. Peters; "unless it got sick and died."

But after she said it she reached over and swung the broken door. Both women watched it as if somehow held by it.

"You didn't know—her?" Mrs. Hale asked, a gentler note in her voice.

"Not till they brought her yesterday," said the sheriff's wife.

"She—come to think of it, she was kind of like a bird herself. Real sweet and pretty, but kind of timid and—fluttery. How—she—did—change."

That held her for a long time. Finally, as if struck with a happy thought and relieved to get back to everyday things, she exclaimed:

"Tell you what, Mrs. Peters, why don't you take the quilt in with you? It might take up her mind."

"Why, I think that's a real nice idea, Mrs. Hale," agreed the sheriff's wife, as if she too were glad to come into the atmosphere of a simple kindness. "There couldn't possibly be any objection to that, could there? Now, just what will I take? I wonder if her patches are in here—and her things."

They turned to the sewing basket.

"Here's some red," said Mrs. Hale, bringing out a roll of cloth. Underneath that was a box. "Here, maybe her scissors are in here—and her things." She held it up. "What a pretty box! I'll warrant that was something she had a long time ago—when she was a girl."

She held it in her hand a moment; then, with a little sigh, opened it. Instantly her hand went to her nose.

"Why—!"

Mrs. Peters drew nearer—then turned away.

"There's something wrapped up in this piece of silk," faltered Mrs. Hale.

Her hand not steady, Mrs. Hale raised the piece of silk. "Oh, Mrs. Peters!" she cried, "it's—"

Mrs. Peters bent closer.

"It's the bird," she whispered.

"But, Mrs. Peters!" cried Mrs. Hale. *"Look* at it! Its *neck*—look at its neck! It's all—other side *to."*

The sheriff's wife again bent closer.

"Somebody wrung its neck," said she, in a voice that was slow and deep.

And then again the eyes of the two women met—this time clung together in a look of dawning comprehension, of growing horror. Mrs. Peters looked from the dead bird to the broken door of the cage. Again their eyes met. And just then there was a sound at the outside door.

Mrs. Hale slipped the box under the quilt pieces in the basket, and sank into the chair before it. Mrs. Peters stood holding to the table. The county attorney and the sheriff came in.

"Well, ladies," said the county attorney, as one turning from serious things to little pleasantries, "have you decided whether she was going to quilt it or knot it?"

"We think," began the sheriff's wife in a flurried voice, "that she was going to—knot it."

He was too preoccupied to notice the change that came in her voice on that last.

"Well, that's very interesting, I'm sure," he said tolerantly. He caught sight of the cage. "Has the bird flown?"

"We think the cat got it," said Mrs. Hale in a voice curiously even.

He was walking up and down, as if thinking something out.

"Is there a cat?" he asked absently.

Mrs. Hale shot a look up at the sheriff's wife.

"Well, not *now,"* said Mrs. Peters. "They're superstitious, you know; they leave."

The county attorney did not heed her. "No sign at all of anyone having come in from the outside," he said to Peters, in the manner of continuing an interrupted conversation. "Their own rope. Now let's go upstairs again and go over it, piece by piece. It would have to have been someone who knew just the—"

The stair door closed behind them and their voices were lost.

The two women sat motionless, not looking at each other, but as if peering into something and at the same time holding back. When they spoke now it was as if they were afraid of what they were saying, but as if they could not help saying it.

"She liked the bird," said Martha Hale, low and slowly. "She was going to bury it in that pretty box."

"When I was a girl," said Mrs. Peters, under her breath, "my kitten—there was a boy took a hatchet, and before my eyes—before I could get there—" She covered her face an instant. "If they hadn't held me back I would have"—she caught herself, looked upstairs where footsteps were heard, and finished weakly—"hurt him."

Then they sat without speaking or moving.

"I wonder how it would seem," Mrs. Hale at last began, as if feeling her way over strange ground—"never to have had any children around." Her eyes made a slow sweep of the kitchen, as if seeing what that kitchen had meant through all the years. "No, Wright wouldn't like the bird," she said after that—"a thing that sang. She used to sing. He killed that too." Her voice tightened.

Mrs. Peters moved easily.

"Of course we don't know who killed the bird."

"I knew John Wright," was Mrs. Hale's answer.

"It was an awful thing was done in this house that night, Mrs. Hale," said the sheriff's wife. "Killing a man while he slept—slipping a thing round his neck that choked the life out of him."

Mrs. Hale's hand went out to the bird-cage.

"His neck. Choked the life out of him."

"We don't *know* who killed him," whispered Mrs. Peters wildly. "We don't *know*."

Mrs. Hale had not moved. "If there had been years and years of—nothing, then a bird to sing to you, it would be awful—still—after the bird was still."

It was as if something within her not herself had spoken, and it found in Mrs. Peters something she did not know as herself.

"I know what stillness is," she said, in a queer, monotonous voice. "When we homesteaded in Dakota, and my first baby died—after he was two years old—and me with no other then—"

Mrs. Hale stirred.

"How soon do you suppose they'll be through looking for the evidence?"

"I know what stillness is," repeated Mrs. Peters, in just that same way. Then she too pulled back. "The law has got to punish crime, Mrs. Hale," she said in her tight little way.

"I wish you'd seen Minnie Foster," was the answer, "when she wore a white dress with blue ribbons, and stood up there in the choir and sang."

The picture of that girl, the fact that she had lived neighbor to that girl for twenty years, and had let her die for lack of life, was suddenly more than she could bear.

"Oh, I *wish* I'd come over here once in a while!" she cried. "That was a crime! That was a crime! Who's going to punish that?"

"We mustn't take on," said Mrs. Peters, with a frightened look toward the stairs.

"I might 'a' *known* she needed help! I tell you, it's *queer,* Mrs. Peters. We live close together, and we live far apart. We all go through the same things—it's all just a different kind of the same thing! If it weren't—why do you and I *understand?* Why do we *know*—what we know this minute?"

She dashed her hand across her eyes. Then, seeing the jar of fruit on the table, she reached for it and choked out:

"If I was you I wouldn't *tell* her her fruit was gone! Tell her it *ain't.* Tell her it's all right—all of it. Here—take this in to prove it to her! She—she may never know whether it was broke or not."

Mrs. Peters reached out for the bottle of fruit as if she were glad to take it—as if touching a familiar thing, having something to do, could keep her from something else. She got up, looked about for something to wrap the fruit in, took a petticoat from the pile of clothes she had brought from the front room, and nervously started winding that round the bottle.

"My!" she began, in a high, false voice, "it's a good thing the men couldn't hear us! Getting all stirred up over a little thing like a—dead canary." She hurried over that. "As if that could have anything to do with—with—My, wouldn't they *laugh?*"

Footsteps were heard on the stairs.

"Maybe they would," muttered Mrs. Hale—"maybe they wouldn't."

"No, Peters," said the county attorney incisively; "it's all perfectly clear, except the reason for doing it. But you know juries when it comes to women. If there was some definite thing—something to show. Something to make a story about. A thing that would connect up with this clumsy way of doing it."

In a covert way Mrs. Hale looked at Mrs. Peters. Mrs. Peters was looking at her. Quickly they looked away from each other. The outer door opened and Mr. Hale came in.

"I've got the team round now," he said. "Pretty cold out there."

"I'm going to stay here awhile by myself," the county attorney suddenly announced. "You can send Frank out for me, can't you?"

he asked the sheriff. "I want to go over everything. I'm not satisfied we can't do better."

Again, for one brief moment, the two women's eyes found one another.

The sheriff came up to the table.

"Did you want to see what Mrs. Peters was going to take in?"

The county attorney picked up the apron. He laughed. "Oh, I guess they're not very dangerous things the ladies have picked out."

Mrs. Hale's hand was on the sewing basket in which the box was concealed. She felt that she ought to take her hand off the basket. She did not seem able to. He picked up one of the quilt blocks which she had piled on to cover the box. Her eyes felt like fire. She had a feeling that if he took up the basket she would snatch it from him.

But he did not take it up. With another little laugh, he turned away.

"No; Mrs. Peters doesn't need supervising. For that matter, a sheriff's wife is married to the law. Ever think of it that way, Mrs. Peters?"

Mrs. Peters was standing beside the table. Mrs. Hale shot a look up at her; but she could not see her face. Mrs. Peters had turned away. When she spoke, her voice was muffled.

"Not—just that way," she said.

"Married to the law!" chuckled Mrs. Peters' husband. He moved toward the door into the front room, and said to the county attorney:

"I just want you to come in here a minute, George. We ought to take a look at these windows."

"Oh—windows," said the county attorney scoffingly.

"We'll be right out, Mr. Hale," said the sheriff to the farmer.

Hale went to look after the horses. The sheriff followed the county attorney into the other room. Again—for one final moment—the two women were alone in that kitchen.

Martha Hale sprang up, her hands tight together, looking at that other woman, with whom it rested. At first she could not see her eyes, for the sheriff's wife had not turned back since she turned away at that suggestion of being married to the law. But now Mrs. Hale made her turn back. Her eyes made her turn back. Slowly, unwillingly, Mrs. Peters turned her head until her eyes met the eyes of the other woman. There was a moment when they held each other in a steady, burning look in which there was no evasion nor flinching.

Then Martha Hale's eyes pointed the way to the basket in which was hidden the thing that would make certain the conviction of the other woman—that woman who was not there and yet who had been there with them all through that hour.

For a moment Mrs. Peters did not move. And then she did it. With a rush forward, she threw back the quilt pieces, got the box, tried to put it in her handbag. It was too big. Desperately she opened it, started to take the bird out. But there she broke—she could not touch the bird. She stood there helpless, foolish.

There was the sound of a knob turning in the inner door. Martha Hale snatched the box from the sheriffs wife, and got it in the pocket of her big coat just as the sheriff and the county attorney came back.

"Well, Henry," said the county attorney facetiously, "at least we found out that she was not going to quilt it. She was going to—what is it you call it, ladies?"

Mrs. Hale's hand was against the pocket of her coat.

"We call it—knot it, Mr. Henderson."

# THE OUTCASTS OF POKER FLAT

### Bret Harte

As MR. JOHN OAKHURST, gambler, stepped into the main street of Poker Flat on the morning of the twenty-third of November, 1850, he was conscious of a change in its moral atmosphere since the preceding night. Two or three men, conversing earnestly together, ceased as he approached, and exchanged significant glances. There was a Sabbath lull in the air, which, in a settlement unused to Sabbath influences, looked ominous.

Mr. Oakhurst's calm, handsome face betrayed small concern in these indications. Whether he was conscious of any predisposing cause, was another question. "I reckon they're after somebody," he reflected; "likely it's me." He returned to his pocket the handkerchief with which he had been whipping away the red dust of Poker Flat from his neat boots, and quietly discharged his mind of any further conjecture.

In point of fact, Poker Flat was "after somebody." It had lately suffered the loss of several thousand dollars, two valuable horses, and a prominent citizen. It was experiencing a spasm of virtuous reaction, quite as lawless and ungovernable as any of the acts that had provoked it. A secret committee had determined to rid the town of all improper persons. This was done permanently in regard of two men who were then hanging from the boughs of a sycamore in the gulch, and temporarily in the banishment of certain other objectionable characters. I regret to say that some of these were ladies. It is but due to the sex, however, to state that their impropriety was professional, and it was only in such easily established standards of evil that Poker Flat ventured to sit in judgment.

Mr. Oakhurst was right in supposing that he was included in this category. A few of the committee had urged hanging him as a possible example, and a sure method of reimbursing themselves from his pockets of the sums he had won from them. "It's agin justice," said Jim Wheeler, "to let this yer young man from Roaring Camp—an entire stranger—carry away our money." But a crude sentiment of equity residing in the breasts of those who had been fortunate enough to win from Mr. Oakhurst overruled this narrower local prejudice.

Mr. Oakhurst received his sentence with philosophic calmness, none the less coolly that he was aware of the hesitation of his judges. He was too much of a gambler not to accept Fate. With him life was at best an uncertain game, and he recognized the usual percentage in favor of the dealer.

A party of armed men accompanied the deported wickedness of Poker Flat to the outskirts of the settlement. Besides Mr. Oakhurst, who was known to be a coolly desperate man, and for whose intimidation the armed escort was intended, the expatriated party consisted of a young woman familiarly known as "The Duchess"; another, who had bore the title of "Mother Shipton"; and "Uncle Billy," a suspected sluice-robber and confirmed drunkard. The cavalcade provoked no comments from the spectators, nor was any word uttered by the escort. Only when the gulch which marked the uttermost limit of Poker Flat was reached, the leader spoke briefly and to the point. The exiles were forbidden to return at the peril of their lives.

As the escort disappeared, their pent-up feelings found vent in a few hysterical tears from the Duchess, some bad language from Mother Shipton, and a Parthian volley of expletives from Uncle Billy. The philosophic Oakhurst alone remained silent. He listened calmly to Mother Shipton's desire to cut somebody's heart out, to the repeated statements of the Duchess that she would die in the road, and to the alarming oaths that seemed to be bumped out of Uncle Billy as he rode forward. With the easy good-humor characteristic of his class, he insisted upon exchanging his own riding-horse, "Five Spot," for the sorry mule which the Duchess rode. But even this act did not draw the party into any closer sympathy. The young woman read-justed her somewhat draggled plumes with a feeble, faded coquetry; Mother Shipton eyed the possessor of "Five Spot" with malevolence; and Uncle Billy included the whole party in one sweeping anathema.

The road to Sandy Bar—a camp that, not having as yet experienced the regenerating influences of Poker Flat, consequently seemed to offer some invitation to the emigrants—lay over a steep mountain range. It was distant a day's severe travel. In that advanced season, the party soon passed out of the moist, temperate regions of the foot-hills into the dry, cold, bracing air of the Sierras. The trail was narrow and difficult. At noon the Duchess, rolling out of her saddle upon the ground, declared her intention of going no farther, and the party halted.

The spot was singularly wild and impressive. A wooded amphitheatre, surrounded on three sides by precipitous cliffs of naked granite, sloped gently towards the crest of another precipice that overlooked the valley. It was, undoubtedly, the most suitable spot for a camp, had camping been advisable. But Mr. Oakhurst knew that scarcely half the journey to Sandy Bar was accomplished, and the party were not equipped or provisioned for delay. This fact he pointed out to his companions curtly, with a philosophic commentary on the folly of "throwing up their hand before the game was played out." But they were furnished with liquor, which in this emergency stood them in place of food, fuel, rest, and prescience. In spite of his remonstrances, it was not long before they were more or less under its influence. Uncle Billy passed rapidly from a bellicose state into one of stupor, the Duchess became maudlin, and Mother Shipton snored. Mr. Oakhurst alone remained erect, leaning against a rock, calmly surveying them.

Mr. Oakhurst did not drink. It interfered with a profession which required coolness, impassiveness, and presence of mind, and, in his own language, he "couldn't afford it." As he gazed at his recumbent fellow-exiles, the loneliness begotten of his pariah-trade, his habits of life, his very vices, for the first time seriously oppressed him. He bestirred himself in dusting his black clothes, washing his hands and face, and other acts characteristic of his studiously neat habits, and for a moment forgot his annoyance. The thought of deserting his weaker and more pitiable companions never perhaps occurred to him. Yet he could not help feeling the want of that excitement which, singularly enough, was most conducive to that calm equanimity for which he was notorious. He looked at the gloomy walls that rose a thousand feet sheer above the circling pines around him; at the sky, ominously clouded; at the valley below, already deepening into shadow. And, doing so, suddenly he heard his own name called.

A horseman slowly ascended the trail. In the fresh, open face of the new-comer, Mr. Oakhurst recognized Tom Simson, otherwise known as "The Innocent" of Sandy Bar. He had met him some months before over a "little game," and had, with perfect equanimity, won the entire fortune—amounting to some forty dollars—of that guileless youth. After the game was finished, Mr. Oakhurst drew the youthful speculator behind the door, and thus addressed him: "Tommy, you're a good little man, but you can't gamble worth a cent. Don't try it over again." He then handed him his money back, pushed him gently from the room, and so made a devoted slave of Tom Simson.

There was a remembrance of this in his boyish and enthusiastic greeting of Mr. Oakhurst. He had started, he said, to go to Poker Flat to seek his fortune. "Alone?" No, not exactly alone; in fact (a giggle), he had run away with Piney Woods. Didn't Mr. Oakhurst remember Piney? She that used to wait on the table at the Temperance House? They had been engaged a long time, but old Jake Woods had objected, and so they had run away, and were going to Poker Flat to be married; and here they were. And they were tired out, and how lucky it was they had found a place to camp and company. All this the Innocent delivered rapidly, while Piney, a stout, comely damsel of fifteen, emerged from behind the pine-tree, where she had been blushing unseen, and rode to the side of her lover.

Mr. Oakhurst seldom troubled himself with sentiment, still less with propriety; but he had a vague idea that the situation was not fortunate. He retained, however, his presence of mind sufficiently to kick Uncle Billy, who was about to say something, and Uncle Billy was sober enough to recognize in Mr. Oakhurst's kick a superior power that would not bear trifling. He then endeavored to dissuade Tom Simson from delaying further, but in vain. He even pointed out the fact that there was no provision, nor means of making a camp. But, unluckily, the Innocent met this objection by assuring the party that he was provided with an extra mule loaded with provisions, and by the discovery of a rude attempt at a log-house near the trail. "Piney can stay with Mrs. Oakhurst," said the Innocent, pointing to the Duchess, "and I can shift for myself."

Nothing but Mr. Oakhurst's admonishing foot saved Uncle Billy from bursting into a roar of laughter. As it was, he felt compelled to retire up the cañon until he could recover his gravity. There he confided the joke to the tall pine-trees, with many slaps of his leg, contortions of his face, and the usual profanity. But when he returned to the party, he found them seated by a fire—for the air had grown strangely chill, and the sky overcast—in apparently amicable conversation. Piney was actually talking in an impulsive, girlish fashion to the Duchess, who was listening with an interest and animation she had not shown for many days. The Innocent was holding forth, apparently with equal effect, to Mr. Oakhurst and Mother Shipton, who was actually relaxing into amiability. "Is this yer a d—d pic-nic?" said Uncle Billy, with inward scorn, as he surveyed the sylvan group, the glancing firelight, and the tethered animals in the foreground. Suddenly an idea mingled with the alcoholic fumes that disturbed his brain. It was apparently of a jocular nature, for he felt impelled to slap his leg again and cram his fist into his mouth.

As the shadows crept slowly up the mountain, a slight breeze rocked the tops of the pine-trees, and moaned through their long and gloomy aisles. The ruined cabin, patched and covered with pine-boughs, was set apart for the ladies. As the lovers parted, they unaffectedly exchanged a kiss, so honest and sincere that it might have been heard above the swaying pines. The frail Duchess and the malevolent Mother Shipton were probably too stunned to remark upon this last evidence of simplicity, and so turned without a word to the hut. The fire was replenished, the men lay down before the door, and in a few minutes were asleep.

Mr. Oakhurst was a light sleeper. Toward morning he awoke benumbed and cold. As he stirred the dying fire, the wind, which was now blowing strongly, brought to his cheek that which caused the blood to leave it—snow!

He started to his feet with the intention of awakening the sleepers, for there was no time to lose. But turning to where Uncle Billy had been lying, he found him gone. A suspicion leaped to his brain and a curse to his lips. He ran to the spot where the mules had been tethered; they were no longer there. The tracks were already rapidly disappearing in the snow.

The momentary excitement brought Mr. Oakhurst back to the fire with his usual calm. He did not waken the sleepers. The Innocent slumbered peacefully, with a smile on his good-humored, freckled face; the virgin Piney slept beside her frailer sisters as sweetly as though attended by celestial guardians, and Mr. Oakhurst, drawing his blanket over his shoulders, stroked his mustaches and waited for the dawn. It came slowly in a whirling mist of snow-flakes, that dazzled and confused the eye. What could be seen of the landscape appeared magically changed. He looked over the valley, and summed up the present and future in two words—"snowed in!"

A careful inventory of the provisions, which, fortunately for the party, had been stored within the hut, and so escaped the felonious fingers of Uncle Billy, disclosed the fact that with care and prudence they might last ten days longer. "That is," said Mr. Oakhurst, *sotto voce*[1] to the Innocent, "if you're willing to board us. If you ain't—and perhaps you'd better not—you can wait till Uncle Billy gets back with provisions." For some occult reason Mr. Oakhurst could not bring himself to disclose Uncle Billy's rascality, and so offered the hypothesis that he had wandered from the camp and had accidentally stampeded the animals. He dropped a warning to the Duchess and Mother Shipton, who of course knew the facts of their associate's defection. "They'll find out the truth about us *all* when they find out anything," he added significantly, "and there's no good frightening them now."

Tom Simson not only put all his worldly store at the disposal of Mr. Oakhurst, but seemed to enjoy the prospect of their enforced seclusion. "We'll have a good camp for a week, and then the snow'll melt, and we'll all go back together." The cheerful gaiety of the young man, and Mr. Oakhurst's calm, infected the others. The Innocent, with the aid of pine-boughs, extemporized a thatch for the roofless cabin, and the Duchess directed Piney in the rearrangement of the interior with a taste and tact that opened the blue eyes of that provincial maiden to their fullest extent. "I reckon now you're used to fine things at Poker Flat," said Piney. The Duchess turned away sharply to conceal something that reddened her cheeks through its professional tint, and Mother Shipton requested Piney not to "chatter." But when Mr. Oakhurst returned from a weary search for the trail, he heard the sound of happy laughter echoed from the rocks. He stopped in some alarm, and his thoughts first naturally reverted to the whiskey, which he had prudently cached. "And yet it don't somehow sound like whiskey," said the gambler. It was not until he caught sight of the blazing fire through the still blinding storm and the group around it, that he settled to the conviction that it was "square fun."

Whether Mr. Oakhurst had cached his cards with the whiskey as something debarred the free access of the community, I cannot say. It was certain that, in Mother Shipton's words, he "didn't say cards once" during that evening. Haply the time was beguiled by an accordion, produced somewhat ostentatiously by Tom Simson from his pack. Notwithstanding some difficulties attending the manipulation of this instrument, Piney Woods managed to pluck several reluctant melodies from its keys, to an accompaniment by the Innocent on a pair of bone castanets. But the crowning festivity of the evening was

---

[1] *sotto voce*; Italian: in a soft voice so as not to be overheard.

reached in a rude camp-meeting hymn, which the lovers, joining hands, sang with great earnestness and vociferation. I fear that a certain defiant tone and Covenanter's swing to its chorus, rather than any devotional quality, caused it speedily to infect the others, who at last joined in the refrain:—

> "I'm proud to live in the service of the Lord,
> And I'm bound to die in His army."

The pines rocked, the storm eddied and whirled above the miserable group, and the flames of their altar leaped heavenward, as if in token of the vow.

At midnight the storm abated, the rolling clouds parted, and the stars glittered keenly above the sleeping camp. Mr. Oakhurst, whose professional habits had enabled him to live on the smallest possible amount of sleep, in dividing the watch with Tom Simson, somehow managed to take upon himself the greater part of that duty. He excused himself to the Innocent by saying that he had "often been a week without sleep." "Doing what?" asked Tom. "Poker!" replied Oakhurst, sententiously; "when a man gets a streak of luck—nigger-luck—he don't get tired. The luck gives in first. Luck," continued the gambler, reflectively, "is a mighty queer thing. All you know about it for certain is that it's bound to change. And it's finding out when it's going to change that makes you. We've had a streak of bad luck since we left Poker Flat—you come along, and slap you get into it, too. If you can hold your cards right along you're all right. For," added the gambler, with cheerful irrelevance—

> "'I'm proud to live in the service of the Lord,
> And I'm bound to die in His army.'"

The third day came, and the sun, looking through the white-curtained valley, saw the outcasts divide their slowly decreasing store of provisions for the morning meal. It was one of the peculiarities of that mountain climate that its rays diffused a kindly warmth over the wintry landscape, as if in regretful commiseration of the past. But it revealed drift on drift of snow piled high around the hut—a hopeless, uncharted, trackless sea of white lying below the rocky shores to which the castaways still clung. Through the marvellously clear air the smoke of the pastoral village of Poker Flat rose miles away. Mother Shipton saw it, and from a remote pinnacle of her rocky fastness, hurled in that direction a final malediction. It was her last vituperative attempt, and perhaps for that reason was invested with a certain degree of sublimity. It did her good, she privately informed the Duchess. "Just you go out there and cuss, and see." She then set herself to the task of amusing "the child," as she and the Duchess were pleased to call Piney. Piney was no chicken, but it was a soothing and original theory of the pair thus to account for the fact that she didn't swear and wasn't improper.

When night crept up again through the gorges, the reedy notes of the accordion rose and fell in fitful spasms and long-drawn gasps by the flickering camp-fire. But music failed to fill entirely the aching void left by insufficient food, and a new diversion was proposed by Piney—storytelling. Neither Mr. Oakhurst nor his female companions caring to relate their personal experiences, this plan would have failed, too, but for the Innocent. Some months before he had chanced upon a stray copy of Mr. Pope's ingenious translation of the Iliad. He now proposed to narrate the principal incidents of that poem—having thoroughly mastered the argument and fairly forgotten the words— in the current vernacular of Sandy Bar. And so for the rest of that night the Homeric demigods again walked the earth. Trojan bully and wily Greek wrestled in the winds, and the great pines in the cañon seemed to bow to the wrath of the son of Peleus. Mr. Oakhurst listened with quiet satisfaction. Most especially was he interested in the fate of "Ash-heels," as the Innocent persisted in denominating the "swift-footed Achilles."

So with small food and much of Homer and the accordion, a week passed over the heads of the outcasts. The sun again forsook them, and again from leaden skies the snow-flakes were sifted over the land. Day by day closer around them drew the snowy circle, until at last they looked from their prison over drifted walls of drizzling white, that towered twenty feet above their heads. It became more and more difficult to replenish their fires, even from the fallen trees beside them, now half hidden in the drifts. And yet no one complained. The lovers turned from the dreary prospect, and looked into each other's eyes, and were happy. Mr. Oakhurst settled himself coolly to the losing game before him. The Duchess, more cheerful than she had been, assumed the care of Piney. Only Mother Shipton— once the strongest of the party—seemed to sicken and fade. At midnight on the tenth day she called Oakhurst to her side. "I'm going," she said, in a voice of querulous weakness, "but don't say anything about it. Don't waken the kids. Take the bundle from under my head and open it." Mr. Oakhurst did so. It contained Mother Shipton's rations for the last week, untouched. "Give 'em to the child," she said, pointing to the sleeping Piney. "You've starved yourself," said the gambler. "That's what they call it," said the woman, querulously, as she lay down again, and, turning her face to the wall, passed quietly away.

The accordion and the bones were put aside that day, and Homer was forgotten. When the body of Mother Shipton had been committed to the snow, Mr. Oakhurst took the Innocent aside, and showed him a pair of snow-shoes, which he had fashioned from the old pack-saddle. "There's one chance in a hundred to save her yet," he said, pointing to Piney; "but it's there," he added, pointing toward Poker Flat. "If you can reach there in two days she's safe." "And you?" asked Tom Simson. "I'll stay here," was the curt reply.

The lovers parted with a long embrace. "You are not going, too?" said the Duchess, as she saw Mr. Oakhurst apparently waiting to accompany him. "As far as the cañon," he replied. He turned suddenly, and kissed the Duchess, leaving her pallid face aflame, and her trembling limbs rigid with amazement.

Night came, but not Mr. Oakhurst. It brought the storm again and the whirling snow. Then the Duchess, feeding the fire, found that someone had quietly piled beside the hut enough fuel to last a few days longer. The tears rose to her eyes, but she hid them from Piney.

The women slept but little. In the morning, looking into each other's faces, they read their fate. Neither spoke; but Piney, accepting the position of the stronger, drew near and placed her arm around the Duchess's waist. They kept this attitude for the rest of the day. That night the storm reached its greatest fury, and, rending asunder the protecting pines, invaded the very hut.

Toward morning they found themselves unable to feed the fire, which gradually died away. As the embers slowly blackened, the Duchess crept closer to Piney, and broke the silence of many hours: "Piney, can you pray?" "No, dear," said Piney, simply. The Duchess, without knowing exactly why, felt relieved, and, putting her head upon Piney's shoulder, spoke no more. And so reclining, the younger and purer pillowing the head of her soiled sister upon her virgin breast, they fell asleep.

The wind lulled as if it feared to waken them. Feathery drifts of snow, shaken from the long pine-boughs, flew like white-winged birds, and settled about them as they slept. The moon through the rifted clouds looked down upon what had been the camp. But all human stain, all trace of earthly travail, was hidden beneath the spotless mantle mercifully flung from above.

They slept all that day and the next, nor did they waken when voices and footsteps broke the silence of the camp. And when pitying fingers brushed the snow from their wan faces, you could scarcely have told, from the equal peace that dwelt upon them, which was she that had sinned. Even the law of Poker Flat recognized this, and turned away, leaving them still locked in each other's arms.

But at the head of the gulch, on one of the largest pine-trees, they found the deuce of clubs pinned to the bark with a bowie-knife. It bore the following, written in pencil, in a firm hand:—

†

BENEATH THIS TREE

LIES THE BODY

OF

JOHN OAKHURST,

WHO STRUCK A STREAK OF BAD LUCK

ON THE 23RD OF NOVEMBER, 1850,

AND

HANDED IN HIS CHECKS

ON THE 7TH DECEMBER, 1850.

†

And pulseless and cold, with a Derringer by his side and a bullet in his heart, though still calm as in life, beneath the snow lay he who was at once the strongest and yet the weakest of the outcasts of Poker Flat.

# TENNESSEE'S PARTNER

## Bret Harte

I DO NOT think that we ever knew his real name. Our ignorance of it certainly never gave us any social inconvenience, for at Sandy Bar in 1854 most men were christened anew. Sometimes these appellatives were derived from some distinctiveness of dress, as in the case of "Dungaree Jack"; or from some peculiarity of habit, as shown in "Saleratus Bill," so called from an undue proportion of that chemical in his daily bread; or from some unlucky slip, as exhibited in "The Iron Pirate," a mild, inoffensive man, who earned that baleful title by his unfortunate mispronunciation of the term "iron pyrites." Perhaps this may have been the beginning of a rude heraldry; but I am constrained to think that it was because a man's real name in that day rested solely upon his own unsupported statement. "Call yourself Clifford, do you?" said Boston, addressing a timid new-comer with infinite scorn; "hell is full of such Cliffords!" He then introduced the unfortunate man, whose name happened to be really Clifford, as "Jay-bird Charley,"—an unhallowed inspiration of the moment, that clung to him ever after.

But to return to Tennessee's Partner, whom we never knew by any other than this relative title; that he had ever existed as a separate and distinct individuality we only learned later. It seems that in 1853 he left Poker Flat to go to San Francisco, ostensibly to procure a wife. He never got any farther than Stockton. At that place he was attracted by a young person who waited upon the table at the hotel where he took his meals. One morning he said something to her which caused her to smile not unkindly, to somewhat coquettishly break a plate of toast over his upturned, serious, simple face, and to retreat to the kitchen. He followed her, and emerged a few moments later, covered with more toast and victory. That day week they were married by a Justice of the Peace, and returned to Poker Flat. I am aware that something more might be made of this episode, but I prefer to tell it as it was current at Sandy Bar—in the gulches and bar-rooms—where all sentiment was modified by a strong sense of humor.

Of their married felicity but little is known, perhaps for the reason that Tennessee, then living with his partner, one day took occasion to say something to the bride on his own account, at which, it is said, she smiled not unkindly and chastely retreated—this time as far as Marysville, where Tennessee followed her, and where they went to housekeeping without the aid of a Justice of the Peace. Tennessee's Partner took the loss of his wife simply and seriously, as was his fashion. But to everybody's surprise, when Tennessee one day returned from Marysville, without his partner's wife—she having smiled and retreated with somebody else—Tennessee's Partner was the first man to shake his hand and greet him with affection. The boys who had gathered in the cañon to see the shooting were naturally indignant. Their indignation might have found vent in sarcasm but for a certain look in Tennessee's Partner's eye that indicated a lack of humorous appreciation. In fact, he was a grave man, with a steady application to practical detail which was unpleasant in a difficulty.

Meanwhile a popular feeling against Tennessee had grown up on the Bar. He was known to be a gambler; he was suspected to be a thief. In these suspicions Tennessee's Partner was equally compromised; his continued intimacy with Tennessee after the affair above quoted could only be accounted for on the hypothesis of a copartnership of crime. At last Tennessee's guilt became flagrant. One day he overtook a stranger on his way to Red Dog. The stranger afterward related that Tennessee beguiled the time with interesting anecdote and reminiscence, but illogically concluded the interview in the following words: "And now, young man, I'll trouble you for your knife, your pistols, and your money. You see your weppings might get you into trouble at Red Dog, and your money's a temptation to the evilly disposed. I think you said your address was San Francisco. I shall endeavor to call." It may be stated here that Tennessee had a fine flow of humor, which no business preoccupation could wholly subdue.

This exploit was his last. Red Dog and Sandy Bar made common cause against the highwayman. Tennessee was hunted in very much the same fashion as his prototype, the grizzly. As the toils closed around him, he made a desperate dash through the Bar, emptying his revolver at the crowd before the Arcade Saloon, and so on up Grizzly Cañon; but at its farther extremity he was stopped by a small man on a gray horse. The men looked at each other a moment in silence. Both were fearless, both self-possessed and independent; and both types of a civilization that in the seventeenth century would have been called heroic, but, in the nineteenth, simply "reckless." "What have you got there?—I call," said Tennessee, quietly. "Two bowers and an ace," said the stranger, as quietly, showing two revolvers and a bowie knife. "That takes me," returned Tennessee; and with this gambler's epigram, he threw away his useless pistol, and rode back with his captor.

It was a warm night. The cool breeze which usually sprang up with the going down of the sun behind the *chaparral*-crested mountain was that evening withheld from Sandy Bar. The little cañon was stifling with heated resinous odors, and the decaying drift-wood on the Bar sent forth faint, sickening exhalations. The feverishness of day, and its fierce passions, still filled the camp. Lights moved restlessly along the bank of the river, striking no answering reflection from its tawny current. Against the blackness of the pines the windows of the old loft above the express-office stood out staringly bright; and through their curtainless panes the loungers below could see the forms of those who were even then deciding the fate of Tennessee. And above all this, etched on the dark firmament, rose the Sierra, remote and passionless, crowned with remoter passionless stars.

The trial of Tennessee was conducted as fairly as was consistent with a judge and jury who felt themselves to some extent obliged to justify, in their verdict, the previous irregularities of arrest and indictment. The law of Sandy Bar was implacable, but not vengeful. The excitement and personal feeling of the chase were over; with Tennessee safe in their hands they were ready to listen patiently to any defense, which they were already satisfied was insufficient. There being no doubt in their own minds, they were willing to give the prisoner the benefit of any that might exist. Secure in the hypothesis that he ought to be hanged, on general principles, they indulged him with more latitude of defense than his reckless hardihood seemed to ask. The Judge appeared to be more anxious than the prisoner, who, otherwise unconcerned, evidently took a grim pleasure in the responsibility he had created. "I don't take any hand in this yer game," had been his invariable, but good-humored reply to all questions. The Judge—who was also his captor—for a moment vaguely regretted that he had not shot him "on sight," that morning, but presently dismissed this human weakness as unworthy of the judicial mind. Nevertheless, when there was a tap at the door, and it was said that Tennessee's Partner was there on behalf of the prisoner, he was admitted at once without question. Perhaps the younger members of the jury, to whom the proceedings were becoming irksomely thoughtful, hailed him as a relief.

For he was not, certainly, an imposing figure. Short and stout, with a square face, sunburned into a preternatural redness, clad in a loose duck "jumper," and trousers streaked and splashed with red soil, his aspect under any circumstances would have been quaint, and was now even ridiculous. As he stooped to deposit at his feet a heavy carpet-bag he was carrying, it became obvious, from partially developed regions and inscriptions, that the material with which his trousers had been patched had been originally intended for a less ambitious covering. Yet he advanced with great gravity, and after having shaken the hand of each person in the room with labored cordiality, he wiped his serious, perplexed face on a red bandanna handkerchief, a shade lighter than his complexion, laid his powerful hand upon the table to steady himself, and thus addressed the Judge:—

"I was passin' by," he began, by way of apology, "and I thought I'd just step in and see how things was gittin' on with Tennessee thar—my pardner. It's a hot night. I disremember any sich weather before on the Bar."

He paused a moment, but nobody volunteering any other meteorological recollection, he again had recourse to his pocket-handkerchief, and for some moments mopped his face diligently.

"Have you anything to say in behalf of the prisoner?" said the Judge, finally.

"Thet's it," said Tennessee's Partner, in a tone of relief. "I come yar as Tennessee's pardner—knowing him nigh on four years, off and on, wet and dry, in luck and out o' luck. His ways ain't allers my ways, but thar ain't any p'ints in that young man, thar ain't any liveliness as he's been up to, as I don't know. And you sez to me, sez you—confidential-like, and between man and man—sez you, 'Do you know anything in his behalf?' and I sez to you, sez I—confidential-like, as between man and man—'What should a man know of his pardner?'"

"Is this all you have to say?" asked the Judge, impatiently, feeling, perhaps, that a dangerous sympathy of humor was beginning to humanize the Court.

"Thet's so," continued Tennessee's Partner. "It ain't for me to say anything agin' him. And now what's the case? Here's Tennessee wants money, wants it bad, and doesn't like to ask it of his old pardner. Well, what does Tennessee do? He lays for a stranger, and he fetches that stranger. And you lays for *him,* and you fetches *him;* and the honors is easy. And I put it to you, bein' a far-minded man, and to you, gentlemen, all, as far-minded men, ef this isn't so."

"Prisoner," said the Judge, interrupting, "have you any questions to ask this man?"

"No! no!" continued Tennessee's Partner, hastily. "I play this yer hand alone. To come down to the bed-rock, it's just this: Tennessee, thar, has played it pretty rough and expensive-like on a stranger, and on this yer camp. And now, what's the fair thing? Some would say more; some would say less. Here's seventeen hundred dollars in coarse gold and a watch—it's about all my pile—and call it square!" And before a hand could be raised to prevent him, he had emptied the contents of the carpet-bag upon the table.

For a moment his life was in jeopardy. One or two men sprang to their feet, several hands groped for hidden weapons, and a suggestion to "throw him from the window" was only overridden by a gesture from the Judge. Tennessee laughed. And apparently oblivious of the excitement, Tennessee's Partner improved the opportunity to mop his face again with his handkerchief.

When order was restored, and the man was made to understand, by the use of forcible figures and rhetoric, that Tennessee's offense could not be condoned by money, his face took a more serious and sanguinary hue, and those who were nearest to him noticed that his rough hand trembled slightly on the table. He hesitated a moment as he slowly returned the gold to the carpet-bag, as if he had not yet entirely caught the elevated sense of justice which swayed the tribunal, and was perplexed with the belief that he had not offered enough. Then he turned to the Judge, and saying, "This yer is a lone hand, played alone, and without my pardner," he bowed to the jury and was about to withdraw, when the Judge called him back. "If you have anything to say to Tennessee, you had better say it now." For the first time that evening the eyes of the prisoner and his strange advocate met. Tennessee smiled, showed his white teeth, and saying,

"Euchred, old man!" held out his hand. Tennessee's Partner took it in his own, and saying, "I just dropped in as I was passin' to see how things was gettin' on," let the hand passively fall, and adding that "it was a warm night," again mopped his face with his handkerchief, and without another word withdrew.

The two men never again met each other alive. For the unparalleled insult of a bribe offered to Judge Lynch—who, whether bigoted, weak, or narrow, was at least incorruptible—firmly fixed in the mind of that mythical personage any wavering determination of Tennessee's fate; and at the break of day he was marched, closely guarded, to meet it at the top of Marley's Hill.

How he met it, how cool he was, how he refused to say anything, how perfect were the arrangements of the committee, were all duly reported, with the addition of a warning moral and example to all future evil-doers, in the Red Dog Clarion, by its editor, who was present, and to whose vigorous English I cheerfully refer the reader. But the beauty of that midsummer morning, the blessed amity of earth and air and sky, the awakened life of the free woods and hills, the joyous renewal and promise of Nature, and above all, the infinite Serenity that thrilled through each, was not reported, as not being a part of the social lesson. And yet, when the weak and foolish deed was done, and a life, with its possibilities and responsibilities, had passed out of the misshapen thing that dangled between earth and sky, the birds sang, the flowers bloomed, the sun shone, as cheerily as before; and possibly the Red Dog Clarion was right.

Tennessee's Partner was not in the group that surrounded the ominous tree. But as they turned to disperse, attention was drawn to the singular appearance of a motionless donkey-cart halted at the side of the road. As they approached, they at once recognized the venerable "Jenny" and the two-wheeled cart as the property of Tennessee's Partner—used by him in carrying dirt from his claim; and a few paces distant the owner of the equipage himself, sitting under a buckeye-tree, wiping the perspiration from his glowing face. In answer to an inquiry, he said he had come for the body of the "diseased" "if it was all the same to the committee." He didn't wish to "hurry anything"; he could "wait." He was not working that day; and when the gentlemen were done with the "diseased," he would take him. "Ef thar is any present," he added, in his simple, serious way, "as would care to jine in the fun'l, they kin come." Perhaps it was from a sense of humor, which I have already intimated was a feature of Sandy Bar—perhaps it was from something even better than that; but two-thirds of the loungers accepted the invitation at once.

It was noon when the body of Tennessee was delivered into the hands of his partner. As the cart drew up to the fatal tree, we noticed that it contained a rough oblong box, apparently made from a section of sluicing—and half filled with bark and the tassels of pine The cart was further decorated with slips of willow, and made fragrant with buckeye-blossoms. When the body was deposited in the box, Tennessee's Partner drew over it a piece of tarred canvas, and gravely mounting the narrow seat in front, with his feet upon the shafts, urged the little donkey forward. The equipage moved slowly on, at that decorous pace which was habitual with "Jenny," even under less solemn circumstances. The men—half-curiously, half-jestingly, but all good-humoredly—strolled along beside the cart; some in advance, some a little in the rear of the homely catafalque. But, whether from the narrowing of the road or some present sense of decorum, as the cart passed on the company fell to the rear in couples, keeping step, and otherwise assuming the external show of a formal procession. Jack Folinsbee, who had at the outset played a funeral march in dumb show upon an imaginary trombone, desisted, from a lack of sympathy and appreciation—not having, perhaps, your true humorist's capacity to be content with the enjoyment of his own fun.

The way led through Grizzly Cañon—by this time clothed in funereal drapery and shadows. The red-woods, burying their moccasined feet in the red soil, stood in Indian file along the track, trailing an uncouth benediction from their bending boughs upon the passing bier. A hare, surprised into helpless activity, sat upright and pulsating in the ferns by the roadside as the *cortége*[1] went by. Squirrels hastened to gain a secure outlook from higher boughs; and the blue-jays, spreading their wings, fluttered before them like out-riders, until the outskirts of Sandy Bar were reached, and the solitary cabin of Tennessee's Partner.

Viewed under more favorable circumstances, it would not have been a cheerful place. The unpicturesque site, the rude and unlovely outlines, the unsavory details, which distinguish the nest-building of the California miner, were all here, with the dreariness of decay superadded. A few paces from the cabin there was a rough enclosure, which, in the brief days of Tennessee's Partner's matrimonial felicity,

---

[1] *cortége*; French: a solemn procession.

had been used as a garden, but was now overgrown with fern. As we approached it, we were surprised to find that what we had taken for a recent attempt at cultivation was the broken soil about an open grave.

The cart was halted before the enclosure; and rejecting the offers of assistance with the same air of simple self-reliance he had displayed throughout, Tennessee's Partner lifted the rough coffin on his back, and deposited it, unaided, within the shallow grave. He then nailed down the board which served as a lid; and mounting the little mound of earth beside it, took off his hat, and slowly mopped his face with his handkerchief. This the crowd felt was a preliminary to speech; and they disposed themselves variously on stumps and boulders, and sat expectant.

"When a man," began Tennessee's Partner, slowly, "has been running free all day, what's the natural thing for him to do? Why, to come home. And if he ain't in a condition to go home, what can his best friend do? Why, bring him home! And here's Tennessee has been running free, and we brings him home from his wandering." He paused, and picked up a fragment of quartz, rubbed it thoughtfully on his sleeve, and went on: "It ain't the first time that I've packed him on my back, as you see'd me now. It ain't the first time that I brought him to this yer cabin when he couldn't help himself; it ain't the first time that I and 'Jinny' have waited for him on yon hill, and picked him up and so fetched him home, when he couldn't speak, and didn't know me. And now that it's the last time, why——" he paused, and rubbed the quartz gently on his sleeve—"you see it's a sort of rough on his partner. And now, gentlemen," he added, abruptly, picking up his long-handled shovel, "the fun'l's over; and my thanks, and Tennessee's thanks to you for your trouble."

Resisting any proffers of assistance, he began to fill in the grave, turning his back upon the crowd, that after a few moments' hesitation gradually withdrew. As they crossed the little ridge that hid Sandy Bar from view, some, looking back, thought they could see Tennessee's Partner, his work done, sitting upon the grave, his shovel between his knees, and his face buried in his red bandanna handkerchief. But it was argued by others that you couldn't tell his face from his handkerchief at that distance; and this point remained undecided.

In the reaction that followed the feverish excitement of that day, Tennessee's Partner was not forgotten. A secret investigation had cleared him of any complicity in Tennessee's guilt, and left only a suspicion of his general sanity. Sandy Bar made a point of calling on him, and proffering various uncouth, but well-meant kindnesses. But from that day his rude health and great strength seemed visibly to decline; and when the rainy season fairly set in, and the tiny grass-blades were beginning to peep from the rocky mound above Tennessee's grave, he took to his bed.

One night, when the pines beside the cabin were swaying in the storm, and trailing their slender fingers over the roof, and the roar and rush of the swollen river were heard below, Tennessee's Partner lifted his head from the pillow, saying, "It is time to go for Tennessee; I must put 'Jinny' in the cart"; and would have risen from his bed but for the restraint of his attendant. Struggling, he still pursued his singular fancy: "There, now, steady, 'Jinny,'—steady, old girl. How dark it is! Look out for the ruts—and look out for him, too, old gal. Sometimes, you know, when he's blind drunk, he drops down right in the trail. Keep on straight up to the pine on the top of the hill. Thar—I told you so!—thar he is—coming this way, too—all by himself, sober, and his face a-shining. Tennessee! Pardner!"

And so they met.

# AN INGÉNUE OF THE SIERRAS

Bret Harte

## One

WE ALL HELD our breath as the coach rushed through the semidarkness
of Galloper's Ridge. The vehicle itself was only a huge lumbering
shadow; its side lights were carefully extinguished, and Yuba Bill had
just politely removed from the lips of an outside passenger even the
cigar with which he had been ostentatiously exhibiting his coolness.
For it had been rumored that the Ramon Martinez gang of "road
agents" were "laying" for us on the second grade, and would time the
passage of our lights across Galloper's in order to intercept us in the
"brush" beyond. If we could cross the ridge without being seen, and
so get through the brush before they reached it, we were safe. If they
followed, it would only be a stern chase with the odds in our favor.

The huge vehicle swayed from side to side, rolled, dipped, and
plunged, but Bill kept the track, as if, in the whispered words of the
expressman, he could "feel and smell" the road he could no longer
see. We knew that at times we hung perilously over the edge of slopes
that eventually dropped a thousand feet sheer to the tops of the sugar
pines below, but we knew that Bill knew it also. The half visible
heads of the horses, drawn wedgewise together by the tightened reins,
appeared to cleave the darkness like a plowshare, held between his
rigid hands. Even the hoofbeats of the six horses had fallen into a
vague, monotonous, distant roll. Then the ridge was crossed, and we
plunged into the still blacker obscurity of the brush. Rather we no
longer seemed to move—it was only the phantom night that rushed
by us. The horses might have been submerged in some swift Lethean

488

stream; nothing but the top of the coach and the rigid bulk of Yuba
Bill arose above them. Yet even in that awful moment our speed was
unslackened; it was as if Bill cared no longer to *guide* but only to drive,
or as if the direction of his huge machine was determined by other
hands than his. An incautious whisperer hazarded the paralyzing
suggestion of our "meeting another team." To our great astonishment
Bill overheard it; to our greater astonishment he replied. "It 'ud be
only a neck and neck race which would get to h——ll first," he said
quietly. But we were relieved—for he had *spoken!* Almost simultaneously
the wider turnpike began to glimmer faintly as a visible track before
us; the wayside trees fell out of line, opened up, and dropped off one
after another; we were on the broader tableland, out of danger, and
apparently unperceived and unpursued.

Nevertheless in the conversation that broke out again with the
relighting of the lamps, and the comments, congratulations, and
reminiscences that were freely exchanged, Yuba Bill preserved a
dissatisfied and even resentful silence. The most generous praise of
his skill and courage awoke no response. "I reckon the old man waz
just spilin' for a fight, and is feelin' disappointed," said a passenger.
But those who knew that Bill had the true fighter's scorn for any
purely purposeless conflict were more or less concerned and watchful
of him. He would drive steadily for four or five minutes with
thoughtfully knitted brows, but eyes still keenly observant under his
slouched hat, and then, relaxing his strained attitude, would give way
to a movement of impatience. "You ain't uneasy about anything,
Bill, are you?" asked the expressman confidentially. Bill lifted his
eyes with a slightly contemptuous surprise. "Not about anything ter
*come*. It's what *hez* happened that I don't exackly *sabe*[1]. I don't see
no signs of Ramon's gang ever havin' been out at all, and ef they
were out I don't see why they didn't go for us."

"The simple fact is that our ruse was successful," said an outside
passenger. "They waited to see our lights on the ridge, and not seeing
them, missed us until we had passed. That's my opinion."

"You ain't puttin' any price on that opinion, air ye?" inquired Bill
politely.

"No."

" 'Cos thar's a comic paper in 'Frisco pays for them things, and
I've seen worse things in it."

---

[1]  *sabe*, from the verb *saber*; Spanish: to know, understand.

"Come off, Bill," retorted the passenger, slightly nettled by the tittering of his companions. "Then what did you put out the lights for?"

"Well," returned Bill grimly, "it mout have been because I didn't keer to hev you chaps blazin' away at the first bush you *thought* you saw move in your skeer, and bringin' down their fire on us."

The explanation, though unsatisfactory, was by no means an improbable one, and we thought it better to accept it with a laugh. Bill, however, resumed his abstracted manner.

"Who got in at the Summit?" he at last asked abruptly of the expressman.

"Derrick and Simpson of Cold Spring, and one of the 'Excelsior' boys," responded the expressman.

"And that Pike County girl from Dow's Flat, with her bundles. Don't forget her," added the outside passenger ironically.

"Does anybody here know her?" continued Bill, ignoring the irony.

"You'd better ask Judge Thompson; he was mighty attentive to her; gettin' her a seat by the off window, and lookin' after her bundles and things."

"Gettin' her a seat by the *window*?" repeated Bill.

"Yes, she wanted to see everything, and wasn't afraid of the shooting."

"Yes," broke in a third passenger, "and he was so d—d civil that when she dropped her ring in the straw, he struck a match agin all your rules, you know, and held it for her to find it. And it was just as we were crossin' through the brush, too. I saw the hull thing through the window, for I was hanging over the wheels with my gun ready for action. And it wasn't no fault of Judge Thompson's if his d—d foolishness hadn't shown us up, and got us a shot from the gang."

Bill gave a short grunt, but drove steadily on without further comment or even turning his eyes to the speaker.

We were now not more than a mile from the station at the crossroads where we were to change horses. The lights already glimmered in the distance, and there was a faint suggestion of the coming dawn on the summits of the ridge to the west. We had plunged into a belt of timber, when suddenly a horseman emerged at a sharp canter from a trail that seemed to be parallel with our own. We were all slightly startled, Yuba Bill alone preserving his moody calm.

"Hullo!" he said.

The stranger wheeled to our side as Bill slackened his speed. He seemed to be a "packer" or freight muleteer.

"Ye didn't get 'held up' on the Divide?" continued Bill cheerfully.

"No," returned the packer, with a laugh; "*I* don't carry treasure. But I see you're all right, too. I saw you crossin' over Galloper's."

"*Saw* us?" said Bill sharply. "We had our lights out."

"Yes, but there was suthin' white—a handkerchief or woman's veil, I reckon—hangin' from the window. It was only a movin' spot agin the hillside, but ez I was lookin' out for ye I knew it was you by that. Good night!"

He cantered away. We tried to look at each other's faces, and at Bill's expression in the darkness, but he neither spoke nor stirred until he threw down the reins when we stopped before the station. The passengers quickly descended from the roof; the expressman was about to follow, but Bill plucked his sleeve.

"I'm goin' to take a look over this yer stage and these yer passengers with ye, afore we start."

"Why, what's up?"

"Well," said Bill, slowly disengaging himself from one of his enormous gloves, "when we waltzed down into the brush up there I saw a man, ez plain ez I see you, rise up from it. I thought our time had come and the band was goin' to play, when he sorter drew back, made a sign, and we just scooted past him."

"Well?"

"Well," said Bill, "it means that this yer coach was *passed through free* tonight."

"You don't object to *that*—surely? I think we were deucedly lucky."

Bill slowly drew off his other glove. "I've been riskin' my everlastin' life on this d—d line three times a week," he said with mock humility, "and I'm allus thankful for small mercies. *But*," he added grimly, "when it comes down to being passed free by some pal of a hoss thief, and thet called a speshal Providence, *I ain't in it!* No, sir, I ain't in it!"

## Two

It was with mixed emotions that the passengers heard that a delay of fifteen minutes to tighten certain screw bolts had been ordered by the autocratic Bill. Some were anxious to get their breakfast at Sugar Pine, but others were not averse to linger for the daylight that promised greater safety on the road. The expressman, knowing the real cause of Bill's delay, was nevertheless at a loss to understand the object of it. The passengers were all well-known; any idea of complicity with the road agents was wild and impossible, and even if there was a confederate of the gang among them, he would have been more likely to precipitate a robbery than to check it. Again, the discovery of such a confederate—to whom they clearly owed their safety—and his arrest would have been quite against the Californian sense of justice, if not actually illegal. It seemed evident that Bill's quixotic sense of honor was leading him astray.

The station consisted of a stable, a wagon shed, and a building containing three rooms. The first was fitted up with "bunks" or sleeping berths for the employees; the second was the kitchen; and the third and larger apartment was dining room or sitting room, and was used as general waiting room for the passengers. It was not a refreshment station, and there was no "bar." But a mysterious command from the omnipotent Bill produced a demijohn of whiskey, with which he hospitably treated the company. The seductive influence of the liquor loosened the tongue of the gallant Judge Thompson. He admitted to having struck a match to enable the fair Pike Countian to find her ring, which, however, proved to have fallen in her lap. She was "a fine, healthy young woman—a type of the Far West, sir; in fact, quite a prairie blossom! yet simple and guileless as a child." She was on her way to Marysville, he believed, "although she expected to meet friends—a friend, in fact—later on." It was her first visit to a large town—in fact, any civilized center—since she crossed the plains three years ago. Her girlish curiosity was quite touching, and her innocence irresistible. In fact, in a country whose tendency was to produce "frivolity and forwardness in young girls, he found her a most interesting young person." She was even then out in the stable yard watching the horses being harnessed, "preferring to indulge a pardonable healthy young curiosity than to listen to the empty compliments of the younger passengers."

The figure which Bill saw thus engaged, without being otherwise distinguished, certainly seemed to justify the Judge's opinion. She appeared to be a well-matured country girl, whose frank gray eyes and large laughing mouth expressed a wholesome and abiding gratification in her life and surroundings. She was watching the replacing of luggage in the boot. A little feminine start, as one of her own parcels was thrown somewhat roughly on the roof, gave Bill his opportunity. "Now there," he growled to the helper, "ye ain't carting stone! Look out, will yer! Some of your things, miss?" he added, with gruff courtesy, turning to her. "These yer trunks, for instance?"

She smiled a pleasant assent, and Bill, pushing aside the helper, seized a large square trunk in his arms. But from excess of zeal, or some other mischance, his foot slipped, and he came down heavily, striking the corner of the trunk on the ground and loosening its hinges and fastenings. It was a cheap, common-looking affair, but the accident discovered in its yawning lid a quantity of white, lace-edged feminine apparel of an apparently superior quality. The young lady uttered another cry and came quickly forward, but Bill was profuse in his apologies, himself girded the broken box with a strap, and declared his intention of having the company "make it good" to her with a new one. Then he casually accompanied her to the door of the waiting room, entered, made a place for her before the fire by simply lifting the nearest and most youthful passenger by the coat collar from the stool that he was occupying, and having installed the lady in it, displaced another man who was standing before the chimney, and drawing himself up to his full six feet of height in front of her, glanced down upon his fair passenger as he took his waybill from his pocket.

"Your name is down here as Miss Mullins?" he said.

She looked up, became suddenly aware that she and her questioner were the center of interest to the whole circle of passengers, and with a slight rise of color, returned, "Yes."

"Well, Miss Mullins, I've got a question or two to ask ye. I ask it straight out afore this crowd. It's in my rights to take ye aside and ask it—but that ain't my style; I'm no detective. I needn't ask it at all, but act as ef I knowed the answer, or I might leave it to be asked by others. Ye needn't answer it ef ye don't like; ye've got a friend over ther—Judge Thompson—who is a friend to ye, right or wrong, jest as any other man here is—as though ye'd packed your own jury. Well, the simple question I've got to ask ye is *this:* Did you signal to anybody from the coach when we passed Galloper's an hour ago?"

We all thought that Bill's courage and audacity had reached its climax here. To openly and publicly accuse a "lady" before a group of chivalrous Californians, and that lady possessing the further attractions of youth, good looks, and innocence, was little short of desperation. There was an evident movement of adhesion towards the fair stranger, a slight muttering broke out on the right, but the very boldness of the act held them in stupefied surprise. Judge Thompson, with a bland propitiatory smile began: "Really, Bill, I must protest on behalf of this young lady"—when the fair accused, raising her eyes to her accuser, to the consternation of everybody answered with the slight but convincing hesitation of conscientious truthfulness:

"*I did.*"

"Ahem!" interposed the Judge hastily, "er—that is—er—you allowed your handkerchief to flutter from the window—I noticed it myself—casually—one might say even playfully—but without any particular significance."

The girl, regarding her apologist with a singular mingling of pride and impatience, returned briefly:

"I signaled."

"Who did you signal to?" asked Bill gravely.

"The young gentleman I'm going to marry."

A start, followed by a slight titter from the younger passengers, was instantly suppressed by a savage glance from Bill.

"What did you signal to him for?" he continued.

"To tell him I was here, and that it was all right," returned the young girl, with a steadily rising pride and color.

"Wot was all right?" demanded Bill.

"That I wasn't followed, and that he could meet me on the road beyond Cass's Ridge Station." She hesitated a moment, and then, with a still greater pride, in which a youthful defiance was still mingled, said: "I've run away from home to marry him. And I mean to! No one can stop me. Dad didn't like him just because he was poor, and dad's got money. Dad wanted me to marry a man I hate, and got a lot of dresses and things to bribe me."

"And you're taking them in your trunk to the other feller?" said Bill grimly.

"Yes, he's poor," returned the girl defiantly.

"Then your father's name is Mullins?" asked Bill.

"It's not Mullins. I—I—took that name," she hesitated, with her first exhibition of self-consciousness.

"Wot is his name?"

"Eli Hemmings."

A smile of relief and significance went round the circle. The fame of Eli or "Skinner" Hemmings as a notorious miser and usurer had passed even beyond Galloper's Ridge.

"The step that you're taking, Miss Mullins, I need not tell you, is one of great gravity," said Judge Thompson, with a certain paternal seriousness of manner, in which, however, we were glad to detect a glaring affectation; "and I trust that you and your affianced have fully weighed it. Far be it from me to interfere with or question the natural affections of two young people, but may I ask you what you know of the—er—young gentleman for whom you are sacrificing so much, and perhaps imperiling your whole future? For instance, have you known him long?"

The slightly troubled air of trying to understand—not unlike the vague wonderment of childhood—with which Miss Mullins had received the beginning of this exordium, changed to a relieved smile of comprehension as she said quickly, "Oh yes, nearly a whole year."

"And," said the Judge, smiling, "has he a vocation—is he in business?"

"Oh yes," she returned; "he's a collector."

"A collector?"

"Yes; he collects bills, you know—money," she went on, with childish eagerness, "not for himself—*he* never has any money, poor Charley—but for his firm. It's dreadful hard work, too; keeps him out for days and nights, over bad roads and baddest weather. Sometimes, when he's stole over to the ranch just to see me, he's been so bad he could scarcely keep his seat in the saddle, much less stand. And he's got to take mighty big risks, too. Times the folks are cross with him and won't pay; once they shot him in the arm, and he came to me, and I helped do it up for him. But he don't mind. He's real brave—jest as brave as he's good." There was such a wholesome ring of truth in this pretty praise that we were touched in sympathy with the speaker.

"What firm does he collect for?" asked the Judge gently.

"I don't know exactly—he won't tell me; but I think it's a Spanish firm. You see—" she took us all into her confidence with a sweeping smile of innocent yet half-mischievous artfulness—"I only know because I peeped over a letter he once got from his firm, telling him he must hustle up and be ready for the road the next day; but I think the name was Martinez—yes, Ramon Martinez."

In the dead silence that ensued—a silence so profound that we could hear the horses in the distant stable yard rattling their harness—one of the younger "Excelsior" boys burst into a hysteric laugh, but the fierce eye of Yuba Bill was down upon him, and seemed to instantly stiffen him into a silent, grinning mask. The young girl, however, took no note of it. Following out, with loverlike diffusiveness, the reminiscences thus awakened, she went on:

"Yes, it's mighty hard work, but he says it's all for me, and as soon as we're married he'll quit it. He might have quit it before, but he won't take no money of me, nor what I told him I could get out of dad! That ain't his style. He's mighty proud—if he is poor—is Charley. Why, thar's all ma's money which she left me in the Savin's Bank that I wanted to draw out—for I had the right—and give it to him, but he wouldn't hear of it! Why, he wouldn't take one of the things I've got with me, if he knew it. And so he goes on ridin' and ridin', here and there and everywhere, and gettin' more and more played out and sad, and thin and pale as a spirit, and always so uneasy about his business, and startin' up at times when we're meetin' out in the South Woods or in the far clearin', and sayin': 'I must be goin' now, Polly,' and yet always tryin' to be chiffle and chipper afore me. Why, he must have rid miles and miles to have watched for me thar in the brush at the foot of Gallopers tonight, jest to see if all was safe; and Lordy! I'd have given him the signal and showed a light if I'd died for it the next minit. There! That's what I know of Charley—that's what I'm running away from home for—that's what I'm running to him for, and I don't care who knows it! And I only wish I'd done it afore—and I would—if—if—if—he'd only *asked me*! There now!" She stopped, panted, and choked. Then one of the sudden transitions of youthful emotion overtook the eager, laughing face; it clouded up with the swift change of childhood, a lightning quiver of expression broke over it, and—then came the rain!

I think this simple act completed our utter demoralization! We smiled feebly at each other with that assumption of masculine superiority which is miserably conscious of its own helplessness at such moments. We looked out of the window, blew our noses, said: "Eh—what?" and "I say," vaguely to each other, and were greatly relieved, and yet apparently astonished, when Yuba Bill, who had turned his back upon the fair speaker, and was kicking the logs in the fireplace, suddenly swept down upon us and bundled us all into the road, leaving Miss Mullins alone. Then he walked aside with Judge Thompson for a few moments; returned to us, autocratically demanded of the party a complete reticence towards Miss Mullins on the subject matter under discussion, reentered the station, reappeared with the young lady, suppressed a faint idiotic cheer which broke from us at the spectacle of her innocent face once more cleared and rosy, climbed the box, and in another moment we were under way.

"Then she don't know what her lover is yet?" asked the expressman eagerly.

"No."

"Are *you* certain it's one of the gang?"

"Can't say *for sure*. It mout be a young chap from Yolo who bucked again the tiger[2] at Sacramento, got regularly cleaned out and busted, and joined the gang for a flier. They say thar was a new hand in that job over at Keeley's—and a mighty game one, too; and ez there was some buckshot onloaded that trip, he might hev got his share, and that would tally with what the girl said about his arm. See! Ef that's the man, I've heered he was the son of some big preacher in the States, and a college sharp to boot, who ran wild in 'Frisco, and played himself for all he was worth. They're the wust kind to kick when they once get a foot over the traces. For stiddy, comf'ble kempany," added Bill reflectively, "give *me* the son of a man that was *hanged!*"

"But what are you going to do about this?"

"That depends upon the feller who comes to meet her."

"But you ain't going to try to take him? That would be playing it pretty low down on them both."

"Keep your hair on, Jimmy! The Judge and me are only going to rastle with the sperrit of that gay young galoot when he drops down for his girl—and exhort him pow'ful! Ef he allows he's convicted of sin and will find the Lord, we'll marry him and the gal offhand at the next station, and the Judge will officiate himself for nothin'. We're goin' to have this yer elopement done on the square—and our waybill clean—you bet!"

"But you don't suppose he'll trust himself in your hands?"

"Polly will signal to him that it's all square."

"Ah!" said the expressman. Nevertheless in those few moments the men seemed to have exchanged dispositions. The expressman looked doubtfully, critically, and even cynically before him. Bill's face had relaxed, and something like a bland smile beamed across it, as he drove confidently and unhesitatingly forward.

Day, meantime, although full blown and radiant on the mountain summits around us, was yet nebulous and uncertain in the valleys into which we were plunging. Lights still glimmered in the cabins and few ranch buildings which began to indicate the thicker settlements. And the shadows were heaviest in a little copse, where a note from Judge Thompson in the coach was handed up to Yuba Bill, who at once slowly began to draw up his horses. The coach stopped finally near the junction of a small crossroad. At the same

---

[2] Gambled at faro.

moment Miss Mullins slipped down from the vehicle, and with a parting wave of her hand to the Judge, who had assisted her from the steps, tripped down the crossroad, and disappeared in its semiobscurity. To our surprise the stage waited, Bill holding the reins listlessly in his hands. Five minutes passed—an eternity of expectation, and as there was that in Yuba Bill's face which forbade idle questioning, an aching void of silence also! This was at last broken by a strange voice from the road:

"Go on—we'll follow."

The coach started forward. Presently we heard the sound of other wheels behind us. We all craned our necks backward to get a view of the unknown, but by the growing light we could only see that we were followed at a distance by a buggy with two figures in it. Evidently Polly Mullins and her lover! We hoped that they would pass us. But the vehicle, although drawn by a fast horse, preserved its distance always, and it was plain that its driver had no desire to satisfy our curiosity. The expressman had recourse to Bill.

"Is it the man you thought of?" he asked eagerly.

"I reckon," said Bill briefly.

"But," continued the expressman, returning to his former skepticism, "what's to keep them both from levanting together now?"

Bill jerked his hand towards the boot with a grim smile.

"Their baggage."

"Oh!" said the expressman.

"Yes," continued Bill. "We'll hang on to that gal's little frills and fixin's until this yer job's settled and the ceremony's over, jest as ef we waz her own father. And, what's more, young man," he added, suddenly turning to the expressman, "*you'll* express them trunks of hers *through to Sacramento* with your kempany's labels, and hand her the receipts and checks for them so she *can get 'em there.* That'll keep *him* outer temptation and the reach o' the gang, until they get away among white men and civilization again. When your hoary-headed ole grandfather, or to speak plainer, that partikler old whiskey-soaker known as Yuba Bill, wot sits on this box," he continued, with a diabolical wink at the expressman, "waltzes in to pervide for a young couple jest startin' in life, thar's nothin' mean about his style, you bet. He fills the bill every time! Speshul Providences take a back seat when he's around."

When the station hotel and straggling settlement of Sugar Pine, now distinct and clear in the growing light, at last rose within rifleshot on the plateau, the buggy suddenly darted swiftly by us, so swiftly that the faces of the two occupants were barely distinguishable as they passed, and keeping the lead by a dozen lengths, reached the door of the hotel. The young girl and her companion leaped down and vanished within as we drew up. They had evidently determined to elude our curiosity, and were successful.

But the material appetites of the passengers, sharpened by the keen mountain air, were more potent than their curiosity, and as the breakfast bell rang out at the moment the stage stopped, a majority of them rushed into the dining room and scrambled for places without giving much heed to the vanished couple or to the Judge and Yuba Bill, who had disappeared also. The through coach to Marysville and Sacramento was likewise waiting, for Sugar Pine was the limit of Bill's ministration, and the coach which we had just left went no farther. In the course of twenty minutes, however, there was a slight and somewhat ceremonious bustling in the hall and on the veranda, and Yuba Bill and the Judge reappeared. The latter was leading, with some elaboration of manner and detail, the shapely figure of Miss Mullins, and Yuba Bill was accompanying her companion to the buggy. We all rushed to the windows to get a good view of the mysterious stranger and probable ex-brigand whose life was now linked with our fair fellow passenger. I am afraid, however, that we all participated in a certain impression of disappointment and doubt. Handsome and even cultivated-looking, he assuredly was—young and vigorous in appearance. But there was a certain half-shamed, half-defiant suggestion in his expression, yet coupled with a watchful, lurking uneasiness which was not pleasant and hardly becoming in a bridegroom—and the possessor of such a bride. But the frank, joyous, innocent face of Polly Mullins, resplendent with a simple, happy confidence, melted our hearts again, and condoned the fellow's shortcomings. We waved our hands; I think we would have given three rousing cheers as they drove away if the omnipotent eye of Yuba Bill had not been upon us. It was well, for the next moment we were summoned to the presence of that soft-hearted autocrat.

We found him alone with the Judge in a private sitting room, standing before a table on which there were a decanter and glasses. As we filed expectantly into the room and the door closed behind us, he cast a glance of hesitating tolerance over the group.

"Gentlemen," he said slowly, "you was all present at the beginnin' of a little game this mornin', and the Judge thar thinks that you oughter be let in at the finish. *I* don't see that it's any of *your* d—d business—so to speak; but ez the Judge here allows you're all in the secret, I've called you in to take a partin' drink to the health of Mr. and Mrs. Charley Byng—ez is now comf'ably off on their bridal tower. What *you* know or what you suspects of the young galoot that's married the gal ain't worth shucks to anybody, and I wouldn't give it to a yaller pup to play with, but the Judge thinks you ought all to promise right here that you'll keep it dark. That's his opinion. Ez far as my opinion goes, gen'l'men," continued Bill, with greater blandness and apparent cordiality, "I wanter simply remark, in a keerless, offhand gin'ral way, that ef I ketch any God-forsaken, lop-eared, chuckle-headed blatherin' idjet airin' *his* opinion—"

"One moment, Bill," interposed Judge Thompson with a grave smile; "let me explain. You understand, gentlemen," he said, turning to us, "the singular, and I may say affecting, situation which our good-hearted friend here has done so much to bring to what we hope will be a happy termination. I want to give here, as my professional opinion, that there is nothing in his request which, in your capacity as good citizens and law-abiding men, you may not grant. I want to tell you, also, that you are condoning no offense against the statutes; that there is not a particle of legal evidence before us of the criminal antecedents of Mr. Charles Byng, except that which has been told you by the innocent lips of his betrothed, which the law of the land has now sealed forever in the mouth of his wife, and that our own actual experience of his acts has been in the main exculpatory of any previous irregularity—if not incompatible with it. Briefly, no judge would charge, no jury convict, on such evidence. When I add that the young girl is of legal age, that there is no evidence of any previous undue influence, but rather of the reverse, on the part of the bridegroom, and that I was content, as a magistrate, to perform the ceremony, I think you will be satisfied to give your promise, for the sake of the bride, and drink a happy life to them both."

I need not say that we did this cheerfully, and even extorted from Bill a grunt of satisfaction. The majority of the company, however, who were going with the through coach to Sacramento, then took their leave, and as we accompanied them to the veranda, we could see that Miss Polly Mullins's trunks were already transferred to the other vehicle under the protecting seals and labels of the all-potent Express Company. Then the whip cracked, the coach rolled away, and the last traces of the adventurous young couple disappeared in the hanging red dust of its wheels.

But Yuba Bill's grim satisfaction at the happy issue of the episode seemed to suffer no abatement. He even exceeded his usual deliberately regulated potations, and standing comfortably with his back to the center of the now deserted bar-room, was more than usually loquacious with the expressman. "You see," he said, in bland reminiscence, "when your old Uncle Bill takes hold of a job like this, he puts it straight through without changin' hosses. Yet thar was a moment, young feller, when I thought I was stompt! It was when we'd made up our mind to make that chap tell the gal fust all what he was! Ef she'd rared or kicked in the traces, or hung back only ez much ez that, we'd hev given him jest five minits' law to get up and get and leave her, and we'd hev toted that gal and her fixin's back to her dad again! But she jest gave a little scream and start, and then went off inter hysterics, right on his buzzum, laughin' and cryin' and sayin' that nothin' should part 'em. Gosh! if I didn't think *he* woz more cut up than she about it; a minit it looked as ef *he* didn't allow to marry her arter all, but that passed, and they was married hard and fast—you bet! I reckon he's had enough of stayin' out o' nights to last him, and ef the valley settlements hevn't got hold of a very shinin' member, at least the foothills hev got shut of one more of the Ramon Martinez gang."

"What's that about the Ramon Martinez gang?" said a quiet potential voice.

Bill turned quickly. It was the voice of the Divisional Superintendent of the Express Company—a man of eccentric determination of character, and one of the few whom the autocratic Bill recognized as an equal—who had just entered the barroom. His dusty pongee cloak and soft hat indicated that he had that morning arrived on a round of inspection.

"Don't care if I do, Bill," he continued, in response to Bill's invitatory gesture, walking to the bar. "It's a little raw out on the road. Well, what were you saying about Ramon Martinez gang? You haven't come across one of 'em, have you?"

"No," said Bill, with a slight blinking of his eye, as he ostentatiously lifted his glass to the light.

"And you *won't*," added the Superintendent, leisurely sipping his liquor. "For the fact is, the gang is about played out. Not from want of a job now and then, but from the difficulty of disposing of the results of their work. Since the new instructions to the agents to identify and trace all dust and bullion offered to them went into force, you see, they can't get rid of their swag. All the gang are spotted at the offices, and it costs too much for them to pay a fence or a middleman of any standing. Why, all that flaky river gold they took from the Excelsior Company can be identified as easy as if it was stamped with the company's mark. They can't melt it down themselves; they can't get others to do it for them; they can't ship it to the mint or assay offices in Marysville and 'Frisco, for they won't take it without our certificate and seals; and *we* don't take any undeclared freight *within* the lines that we've drawn around their beat, except from people and agents known. Why, *you* know that well enough, Jim," he said, suddenly appealing to the expressman, "don't you?"

Possibly the suddenness of the appeal caused the expressman to swallow his liquor the wrong way, for he was overtaken with a fit of coughing, and stammered hastily as he laid down his glass, "Yes—of course—certainly."

"No, sir," resumed the Superintendent cheerfully, "they're pretty well played out. And the best proof of it is that they've lately been robbing ordinary passengers' trunks. There was a freight wagon held up' near Dow's Flat the other day, and a lot of baggage gone through. I had to go down there to look into it. Darned if they hadn't lifted a lot o' woman's wedding things from that rich couple who got married the other day out at Marysville. Looks as if they were playing it rather low-down, don't it? Coming down to hardpan and the bedrock—eh?"

The expressman's face was turned anxiously towards Bill, who, after a hurried gulp of his remaining liquor, still stood staring at the window. Then he slowly drew on one of his large gloves. "Ye didn't," he said, with a slow, drawling, but perfectly distinct, articulation, "happen to know old 'Skinner' Hemmings when you were over there?"

"Yes."

"And his daughter?"

"He hasn't got any."

"A sort o' mild, innocent, guileless child of nature?" persisted Bill, with a yellow face, a deadly calm, and Satanic deliberation.

"No. I tell you he *hasn't* any daughter. Old man Hemmings is a confirmed old bachelor. He's too mean to support more than one."

"And you didn't happen to know any o' that gang, did ye?" continued Bill, with infinite protraction.

"Yes. Knew 'em all. There was French Pete, Cherokee Bob, Kanaka Joe, One-eyed Stillson, Softy Brown, Spanish Jack, and two or three Greasers."

"And ye didn't know a man by the name of Charley Byng?"

"No," returned the Superintendent, with a slight suggestion of weariness and a distraught glance towards the door.

"A dark, stylish chap, with shifty black eyes and a curled-up merstache?" continued Bill, with dry, colorless persistence.

"No. Look here, Bill, I'm in a little bit of a hurry—but I suppose you must have your little joke before we part. Now, what *is* your little game?"

"Wot you mean?" demanded Bill, with sudden brusqueness.

"Mean? Well, old man, you know as well as I do. You're giving me the very description of Ramon Martinez himself, ha! ha! No—Bill! You didn't play me this time. You're mighty spry and clever, but you didn't catch on just then."

He nodded and moved away with a light laugh. Bill turned a stony face to the expressman. Suddenly a gleam of mirth came into his gloomy eyes. He bent over the young man, and said in a hoarse, chuckling whisper:

"But I got even after all!"

"How?"

"He's tied up to that lying little she-devil, hard and fast!"

# THE MINISTER'S BLACK VEIL

## Nathaniel Hawthorne

### A Parable[1]

THE SEXTON STOOD in the porch of Milford meeting-house, pulling lustily at the bell-rope. The old people of the village came stooping along the street. Children, with bright faces, tript merrily beside their parents, or mimicked a graver gait, in the conscious dignity of their Sunday clothes. Spruce bachelors looked sidelong at the pretty maidens, and fancied that the Sabbath sunshine made them prettier than on weekdays. When the throng had mostly streamed into the porch, the sexton began to toll the bell, keeping his eye on the Reverend Mr. Hooper's door. The first glimpse of the clergyman's figure was the signal for the bell to cease its summons.

"But what has good Parson Hooper got upon his face?" cried the sexton in astonishment.

All within hearing immediately turned about, and beheld the semblance of Mr. Hooper, pacing slowly his meditative way towards the meeting-house. With one accord they started, expressing more wonder than if some strange minister were coming to dust the cushions of Mr. Hooper's pulpit.

---

[1] Another clergyman in New England, Mr. Joseph Moody, of York, Maine, who died about eighty years since, made himself remarkable by the same eccentricity that is here related of the Reverend Mr. Hooper. In his case, however, the symbol had a different import. In early life he had accidentally killed a beloved friend; and from that day till the hour of his own death, he hid his face from men.

"Are you sure it is our parson?" inquired Goodman Gray of the sexton.

"Of a certainty it is good Mr. Hooper," replied the sexton. "He was to have exchanged pulpits with Parson Shute of Westbury; but Parson Shute sent to excuse himself yesterday, being to preach a funeral sermon."

The cause of so much amazement may appear sufficiently slight. Mr. Hooper, a gentlemanly person of about thirty, though still a bachelor, was dressed with due clerical neatness, as if a careful wife had starched his band, and brushed the weekly dust from his Sunday's garb. There was but one thing remarkable in his appearance. Swathed about his forehead, and hanging down over his face, so low as to be shaken by his breath, Mr. Hooper had on a black veil. On a nearer view, it seemed to consist of two folds of crape, which entirely concealed his features, except the mouth and chin, but probably did not intercept his sight, farther than to give a darkened aspect to all living and inanimate things. With this gloomy shade before him, good Mr. Hooper walked onward, at a slow and quiet pace, stooping somewhat and looking on the ground, as is customary with abstracted men, yet nodding kindly to those of his parishioners who still waited on the meeting-house steps. But so wonder-struck were they, that his greeting hardly met with a return.

"I can't really feel as if good Mr. Hooper's face was behind that piece of crape," said the sexton.

"I don't like it," muttered an old woman, as she hobbled into the meeting-house. "He has changed himself into something awful, only by hiding his face."

"Our parson has gone mad!" cried Goodman Gray, following him across the threshold.

A rumor of some unaccountable phenomenon had preceded Mr. Hooper into the meeting-house, and set all the congregation astir. Few could refrain from twisting their heads towards the door; many stood upright, and turned directly about; while several little boys clambered upon the seats, and came down again with a terrible racket. There was a general bustle, a rustling of the women's gowns and shuffling of the men's feet, greatly at variance with that hushed repose which should attend the entrance of the minister. But Mr. Hooper appeared not to notice the perturbation of his people. He entered with an almost noiseless step, bent his head mildly to the pews on each side, and bowed as he passed his oldest parishioner, a white-haired great-grandsire, who occupied an armchair in the centre of the aisle. It was strange to observe, how slowly this venerable man became conscious of something singular in the appearance of his pastor. He seemed not fully to partake of the prevailing wonder, till Mr. Hooper had ascended the stairs, and showed himself in the pulpit, face to face with his congregation, except for the black veil. That mysterious emblem was never once withdrawn. It shook with his measured breath as he gave out the psalm; it threw its obscurity between him and the holy page, as he read the Scriptures; and while he prayed, the veil lay heavily on his uplifted countenance. Did he seek to hide it from the dread Being whom he was addressing?

Such was the effect of this simple piece of crape, that more than one woman of delicate nerves was forced to leave the meeting-house. Yet perhaps the pale-faced congregation was almost as fearful a sight to the minister, as his black veil to them.

Mr. Hooper had the reputation of a good preacher, but not an energetic one: he strove to win his people heavenward, by mild persuasive influences, rather than to drive them thither, by the thunders of the Word. The sermon which he now delivered, was marked by the same characteristics of style and manner, as the general series of his pulpit oratory. But there was something, either in the sentiment of the discourse itself, or in the imagination of the auditors, which made it greatly the most powerful effort that they had ever heard from their pastor's lips. It was tinged, rather more darkly than usual, with the gentle gloom of Mr. Hooper's temperament. The subject had reference to secret sin, and those sad mysteries which we hide from our nearest and dearest, and would fain conceal from our own consciousness, even forgetting that the Omniscient can detect them. A subtle power was breathed into his words. Each member of the congregation, the most innocent girl, and the man of hardened breast, felt as if the preacher had crept upon them, behind his awful veil, and discovered their hoarded iniquity of deed or thought. Many spread their clasped hands on their bosoms. There was nothing terrible in what Mr. Hooper said; at least, no violence; and yet, with every tremor of his melancholy voice, the hearers quaked. An unsought pathos came hand in hand with awe. So sensible were the audience of some unwonted attribute in their minister, that they longed for a breath of wind to blow aside the veil, almost believing that a stranger's visage would be discovered, though the form, gesture, and voice were those of Mr. Hooper.

At the close of the services, the people hurried out with indecorous confusion, eager to communicate their pent-up amazement, and conscious of lighter spirits, the moment they lost sight of the black veil. Some gathered in little circles, huddled closely together, with their mouths all whispering in the centre; some went homeward alone, wrapt in silent meditation; some talked loudly, and profaned the Sabbath-day with ostentatious laughter. A few shook their sagacious heads, intimating that they could penetrate the mystery; while one or two affirmed that there was no mystery at all, but only that Mr. Hooper's eyes were so weakened by the midnight lamp, as to require a shade. After a brief interval, forth came good Mr. Hooper also, in the rear of his flock. Turning his veiled face from one group to another, he paid due reverence to the hoary heads, saluted the middle-aged with kind dignity, as their friend and spiritual guide, greeted the young with mingled authority and love, and laid his hands on the little children's heads to bless them. Such was always his custom on the Sabbath-day. Strange and bewildered looks repaid him for his courtesy. None, as on former occasions, aspired to the honor of walking by their pastor's side. Old Squire Saunders, doubtless by an accidental lapse of memory, neglected to invite Mr. Hooper to his table, where the good clergyman had been wont to bless the food, almost every Sunday since his settlement. He returned, therefore, to the parsonage, and, at the moment of closing the door, was observed to look back upon the people, all of whom had their eyes fixed upon the minister. A sad smile gleamed faintly from beneath the black veil, and flickered about his mouth, glimmering as he disappeared.

"How strange," said a lady, "that a simple black veil, such as any woman might wear on her bonnet, should become such a terrible thing on Mr. Hooper's face!"

"Something must surely be amiss with Mr. Hooper's intellects," observed her husband, the physician of the village. "But the strangest part of the affair is the effect of this vagary, even on a sober-minded man like myself. The black veil, though it covers only our pastor's face, throws its influence over his whole person, and makes him ghost-like from head to foot. Do you not feel it so?"

"Truly do I," replied the lady; "and I would not be alone with him for the world. I wonder he is not afraid to be alone with himself!"

"Men sometimes are so," said her husband.

The afternoon service was attended with similar circumstances. At its conclusion, the bell tolled for the funeral of a young lady. The relatives and friends were assembled in the house, and the more distant acquaintances stood about the door, speaking of the good qualities of the deceased, when their talk was interrupted by the appearance of Mr. Hooper, still covered with his black veil. It was now an appropriate emblem. The clergyman stepped into the room where the corpse was laid, and bent over the coffin, to take a last farewell of his deceased parishioner. As he stooped, the veil hung straight down from his forehead, so that, if her eye-lids had not been closed for ever, the dead maiden might have seen his face. Could Mr. Hooper be fearful of her glance, that he so hastily caught back the black veil? A person, who watched the interview between the dead and living, scrupled not to affirm, that, at the instant when the clergyman's features were disclosed, the corpse had slightly shuddered, rustling the shroud and muslin cap, though the countenance retained the composure of death. A superstitious old woman was the only witness of this prodigy. From the coffin, Mr. Hooper passed into the chamber of the mourners, and thence to the head of the staircase, to make the funeral prayer. It was a tender and heart-dissolving prayer, full of sorrow, yet so imbued with celestial hopes, that the music of a heavenly harp, swept by the fingers of the dead, seemed faintly to be heard among the saddest accents of the minister. The people trembled, though they but darkly understood him, when he prayed that they, and himself, and all of mortal race, might be ready, as he trusted this young maiden had been, for the dreadful hour that should snatch the veil from their faces. The bearers went heavily forth, and the mourners followed, saddening all the street, with the dead before them, and Mr. Hooper in his black veil behind.

"Why do you look back?" said one in the procession to his partner.

"I had a fancy," replied she, "that the minister and the maiden's spirit were walking hand in hand."

"And so had I, at the same moment," said the other.

That night, the handsomest couple in Milford village were to be joined in wedlock. Though reckoned a melancholy man, Mr. Hooper had a placid cheerfulness for such occasions, which often excited a sympathetic smile, where livelier merriment would have been thrown away. There was no quality of his disposition which made him more beloved than this. The company at the wedding awaited his arrival with impatience, trusting that the strange awe, which had gathered over him throughout the day, would now be dispelled. But such was not the result. When Mr. Hooper came, the first thing that their eyes rested on was the same horrible black veil, which had added deeper gloom to the funeral, and could portend nothing but evil to the wedding. Such was its immediate effect on the guests, that a cloud seemed to have rolled duskily from beneath the black crape, and dimmed the light of the candles. The bridal pair stood up before the minister. But the bride's cold fingers quivered in the tremulous hand of the bridegroom, and her death-like paleness caused a whisper, that the maiden who had been buried a few hours before, was come from her grave to be married. If ever another wedding were so dismal, it was that famous one, where they tolled the wedding-knell. After performing the ceremony, Mr. Hooper raised a glass of wine to his lips, wishing happiness to the new-married couple, in a strain of mild pleasantry that ought to have brightened the features of the guests, like a cheerful gleam from the hearth. At that instant, catching a glimpse of his figure in the looking-glass, the black veil involved his own spirit in the horror with which it overwhelmed all others. His frame shuddered—his lips grew white—he spilt the untasted wine upon the carpet—and rushed forth into the darkness. For the Earth, too, had on her Black Veil.

The next day, the whole village of Milford talked of little else than Parson Hooper's black veil. That, and the mystery concealed behind it, supplied a topic for discussion between acquaintances meeting in the street, and good women gossiping at their open windows. It was the first item of news that the tavern-keeper told to his guests. The children babbled of it on their way to school. One imitative little imp covered his face with an old black handkerchief, thereby so affrighting his playmates, that the panic seized himself, and he well nigh lost his wits by his own waggery.

It was remarkable, that, of all the busy-bodies and impertinent people in the parish, not one ventured to put the plain question to Mr. Hooper, wherefore he did this thing. Hitherto, whenever there appeared the slightest call for such interference, he had never lacked advisers, nor shown himself averse to be guided by their judgment. If he erred at all, it was by so painful a degree of self-distrust, that even the mildest censure would lead him to consider an indifferent action as a crime. Yet, though so well acquainted with this amiable weakness, no individual among his parishioners chose to make the black veil a subject of friendly remonstrance. There was a feeling of dread, neither plainly confessed nor carefully concealed, which caused each to shift the responsibility upon another, till at length it was found expedient to send a deputation of the church, in order to deal with Mr. Hooper about the mystery, before it should grow into a scandal. Never did an embassy so ill discharge its duties. The minister received them with friendly courtesy, but became silent, after they were seated, leaving to his visiters the whole burthen of introducing their important business. The topic, it might be supposed, was obvious enough. There was the black veil, swathed round Mr. Hooper's forehead, and concealing every feature above his placid mouth, on which, at times, they could perceive the glimmering of a melancholy smile. But that piece of crape, to their imagination, seemed to hang down before his heart, the symbol of a fearful secret between him and them. Were the veil but cast aside, they might speak freely of it, but not till then. Thus they sat a considerable time, speechless, confused, and shrinking uneasily from Mr. Hooper's eye, which they felt to be fixed upon them with an invisible glance. Finally, the deputies returned abashed to their constituents, pronouncing the matter too weighty to be handled, except by a council of the churches, if, indeed, it might not require a general synod.

But there was one person in the village, unappalled by the awe with which the black veil had impressed all beside herself. When the deputies returned without an explanation, or even venturing to demand one, she, with the calm energy of her character, determined to chase away the strange cloud that appeared to be settling round Mr. Hooper, every moment more darkly than before. As his plighted wife, it should be her privilege to know what the black veil concealed. At the minister's first visit, therefore, she entered upon the subject, with a direct simplicity, which made the task easier both for him and her. After he had seated himself, she fixed her eyes steadfastly upon the veil, but could discern nothing of the dreadful gloom that had so overawed the multitude: it was but a double fold of crape, hanging down from his forehead to his mouth, and slightly stirring with his breath.

"No," said she aloud, and smiling, "there is nothing terrible in this piece of crape, except that it hides a face which I am always glad to look upon. Come, good sir, let the sun shine from behind the cloud. First lay aside your black veil: then tell me why you put it on."

Mr. Hooper's smile glimmered faintly.

"There is an hour to come," said he, "when all of us shall cast aside our veils. Take it not amiss, beloved friend, if I wear this piece of crape till then."

"Your words are a mystery too," returned the young lady. "Take away the veil from them, at least."

"Elizabeth, I will," said he, "so far as my vow may suffer me. Know, then, this veil is a type and a symbol, and I am bound to wear it ever, both in light and darkness, in solitude and before the gaze of multitudes, and as with strangers, so with my familiar friends. No mortal eye will see it withdrawn. This dismal shade must separate me from the world: even you, Elizabeth, can never come behind it!"

"What grievous affliction hath befallen you," she earnestly inquired, "that you should thus darken your eyes for ever?"

"If it be a sign of mourning," replied Mr. Hooper, "I, perhaps, like most other mortals, have sorrows dark enough to be typified by a black veil."

"But·what if the world will not believe that it is the type of an innocent sorrow?" urged Elizabeth. "Beloved and respected as you are, there may be whispers, that you hide your face under the consciousness of secret sin. For the sake of your holy office, do away this scandal!"

The color rose into her cheeks, as she intimated the nature of the rumors that were already abroad in the village. But Mr. Hooper's mildness did not forsake him. He even smiled again—that same sad smile, which always appeared like a faint glimmering of light, proceeding from the obscurity beneath the veil.

"If I hide my face for sorrow, there is cause enough," he merely replied; "and if I cover it for secret sin, what mortal might not do the same?"

And with this gentle, but unconquerable obstinacy, did he resist all her entreaties. At length Elizabeth sat silent. For a few moments she appeared lost in thought, considering, probably, what new methods might be tried, to withdraw her lover from so dark a fantasy, which, if it had no other meaning, was perhaps a symptom of mental disease. Though of a firmer character than his own, the tears rolled down her cheeks. But, in an instant, as it were, a new feeling took the place of sorrow: her eyes were fixed insensibly on the black veil, when, like a sudden twilight in the air, its terrors fell around her. She arose, and stood trembling before him.

"And do you feel it then at last?" said he mournfully.

She made no reply, but covered her eyes with her hand, and turned to leave the room. He rushed forward and caught her arm.

"Have patience with me, Elizabeth!" cried he passionately. "Do not desert me, though this veil must be between us here on earth. Be mine, and hereafter there shall be no veil over my face, no darkness between our souls! It is but a mortal veil—it is not for eternity! Oh! you know not how lonely I am, and how frightened to be alone behind my black veil. Do not leave me in this miserable obscurity for ever!"

"Lift the veil but once, and look me in the face," said she.

"Never! It cannot be!" replied Mr. Hooper.

"Then, farewell!" said Elizabeth.

She withdrew her arm from his grasp, and slowly departed, pausing at the door, to give one long, shuddering gaze, that seemed almost to penetrate the mystery of the black veil. But, even amid his grief, Mr. Hooper smiled to think that only a material emblem had separated him from happiness, though the horrors which it shadowed forth, must be drawn darkly between the fondest of lovers.

From that time no attempts were made to remove Mr. Hooper's black veil, or, by a direct appeal, to discover the secret which it was supposed to hide. By persons who claimed a superiority to popular prejudice, it was reckoned merely an eccentric whim, such as often mingles with the sober actions of men otherwise rational, and tinges them all with its own semblance of insanity. But with the multitude, good Mr. Hooper was irreparably a bugbear. He could not walk the streets with any peace of mind, so conscious was he that the gentle and timid would turn aside to avoid him, and that others would make it a point of hardihood to throw themselves in his way. The impertinence of the latter class compelled him to give up his customary walk, at sunset, to the burial ground, for when he leaned pensively over the gate, there would always be faces behind the grave-stones, peeping at his black veil. A fable went the rounds, that the stare of the dead people drove him thence. It grieved him, to the very depth of his kind heart, to observe how the children fled from his approach, breaking up their merriest sports, while his melancholy figure was yet afar off. Their instinctive dread caused him to feel, more strongly than aught else, that a preternatural horror was interwoven with the threads of the black crape. In truth, his own antipathy to the veil was known to be so great, that he never willingly passed before a mirror, nor stooped to drink at a still fountain, lest, in its peaceful bosom, he should be affrighted by himself. This was what gave plausibility to the whispers, that Mr. Hooper's conscience tortured him for some great crime, too horrible to be entirely concealed, or otherwise than so obscurely intimated. Thus, from beneath the black veil, there rolled a cloud into the sunshine, an ambiguity of sin or sorrow, which enveloped the poor minister, so that love or sympathy could never reach him. It was said, that ghost and fiend consorted with him there. With self-shudderings and outward terrors, he walked continually in its shadow, groping darkly within his own soul, or gazing through a medium that saddened the whole world. Even the lawless wind, it was believed, respected his dreadful secret, and never blew aside the veil. But still good Mr. Hooper sadly smiled, at the pale visages of the worldly throng as he passed by.

Among all its bad influences, the black veil had the one desirable effect, of making its wearer a very efficient clergyman. By the aid of his mysterious emblem—for there was no other apparent cause—he became a man of awful power, over souls that were in agony for sin. His converts always regarded him with a dread peculiar to themselves, affirming, though but figuratively, that, before he brought them to celestial light, they had been with him behind the black veil. Its gloom, indeed, enabled him to sympathize with all dark affections. Dying sinners cried aloud for Mr. Hooper, and would not yield their breath till he appeared; though ever, as he stooped to whisper consolation, they shuddered at the veiled face so near their own. Such were the terrors of the black veil, even when Death had bared his visage! Strangers came long distances to attend service at his church, with the mere idle purpose of gazing at his figure, because it was forbidden them to behold his face. But many were made to quake ere they departed! Once, during Governor Belcher's administration, Mr. Hooper was appointed to preach the election sermon. Covered with his black veil, he stood before the chief magistrate, the council, and the representatives, and wrought so deep an impression, that the legislative measures of that year, were characterized by all the gloom and piety of our earliest ancestral sway.

In this manner Mr. Hooper spent a long life, irreproachable in outward act, yet shrouded in dismal suspicions; kind and loving, though unloved, and dimly feared; a man apart from men, shunned in their health and joy, but ever summoned to their aid in mortal anguish. As years wore on, shedding their snows above his sable veil, he acquired a name throughout the New-England churches, and they called him Father Hooper. Nearly all his parishioners, who were of mature age when he was settled, had been borne away by many a funeral: he had one congregation in the church, and a more crowded one in the church-yard; and having wrought so late into the evening, and done his work so well, it was now good Father Hooper's turn to rest.

Several persons were visible by the shaded candlelight, in the death-chamber of the old clergyman. Natural connections he had none. But there was the decorously grave, though unmoved physician, seeking only to mitigate the last pangs of the patient whom he could not save. There were the deacons, and other eminently pious members of his church. There, also, was the

Reverend Mr. Clark, of Westbury, a young and zealous divine, who had ridden in haste to pray by the bedside of the expiring minister. There was the nurse, no hired handmaiden of death, but one whose calm affection had endured thus long, in secresy, in solitude, amid the chill of age, and would not perish, even at the dying hour. Who, but Elizabeth! And there lay the hoary head of good Father Hooper upon the death-pillow, with the black veil still swathed about his brow and reaching down over his face, so that each more difficult gasp of his faint breath caused it to stir. All through life that piece of crape had hung between him and the world: it had separated him from cheerful brotherhood and woman's love, and kept him in that saddest of all prisons, his own heart; and still it lay upon his face, as if to deepen the gloom of his darksome chamber, and shade him from the sunshine of eternity.

For some time previous, his mind had been confused, wavering doubtfully between the past and the present, and hovering forward, as it were, at intervals, into the indistinctness of the world to come. There had been feverish turns, which tossed him from side to side, and wore away what little strength he had. But in his most convulsive struggles, and in the wildest vagaries of his intellect, when no other thought retained its sober influence, he still showed an awful solicitude lest the black veil should slip aside. Even if his bewildered soul could have forgotten, there was a faithful woman at his pillow, who, with averted eyes, would have covered that aged face, which she had last beheld in the comeliness of manhood. At length the death-stricken old man lay quietly in the torpor of mental and bodily exhaustion, with an imperceptible pulse, and breath that grew fainter and fainter, except when a long, deep, and irregular inspiration seemed to prelude the flight of his spirit.

The minister of Westbury approached the bedside.

"Venerable Father Hooper," said he, "the moment of your release is at hand. Are you ready for the lifting of the veil, that shuts in time from eternity?"

Father Hooper at first replied merely by a feeble motion of his head; then, apprehensive, perhaps, that his meaning might be doubtful, he exerted himself to speak.

"Yea," said he, in faint accents, "my soul hath a patient weariness until that veil be lifted."

"And is it fitting," resumed the Reverend Mr. Clark, "that a man so given to prayer, of such a blameless example, holy in deed and thought, so far as mortal judgment may pronounce; is it fitting that a father in the church should leave a shadow on his memory, that may seem to blacken a life so pure? I pray you, my venerable brother, let not this thing be! Suffer us to be gladdened by your triumphant aspect, as you go to your reward. Before the veil of eternity be lifted, let me cast aside this black veil from your face!"

And thus speaking, the Reverend Mr. Clark bent forward to reveal the mystery of so many years. But, exerting a sudden energy, that made all the beholders stand aghast, Father Hooper snatched both his hands from beneath the bedclothes, and pressed them strongly on the black veil, resolute to struggle, if the minister of Westbury would contend with a dying man.

"Never!" cried the veiled clergyman. "On earth, never!"

"Dark old man!" exclaimed the affrighted minister, "with what horrible crime upon your soul are you now passing to the judgment?"

Father Hooper's breath heaved; it rattled in his throat; but, with a mighty effort, grasping forward with his hands, he caught hold of life, and held it back till he should speak. He even raised himself in bed; and there he sat, shivering with the arms of death around him, while the black veil hung down, awful, at that last moment, in the gathered terrors of a life-time. And yet the faint, sad smile, so often there, now seemed to glimmer from its obscurity, and linger on Father Hooper's lips.

"Why do you tremble at me alone?" cried he, turning his veiled face round the circle of pale spectators. "Tremble also at each other! Have men avoided me, and women shown no pity, and children screamed and fled, only for my black veil? What, but the mystery which it obscurely typifies, has made this piece of crape so awful? When the friend shows his inmost heart to his friend; the lover to his best-beloved; when man does not vainly shrink from the eye of his Creator, loathsomely treasuring up the secret of his sin; then deem me a monster, for the symbol beneath which I have lived, and die! I look around me, and, lo! on every visage a Black Veil!"

While his auditors shrank from one another, in mutual affright, Father Hooper fell back upon his pillow, a veiled corpse, with a faint smile lingering on the lips. Still veiled, they laid him in his coffin, and a veiled corpse they bore him to the grave. The grass of many years has sprung up and withered on that grave, the burial-stone is moss-grown, and good Mr. Hooper's face is dust; but awful is still the thought, that it mouldered beneath the Black Veil!

# THE WIVES OF THE DEAD

## Nathaniel Hawthorne

THE FOLLOWING STORY, the simple and domestic incidents of which
may be deemed scarcely worth relating, after such a lapse of time,
awakened some degree of interest, a hundred years ago, in a principal
seaport of the Bay Province. The rainy twilight of an autumn day;
a parlor on the second floor of a small house, plainly furnished, as
beseemed the middling circumstances of its inhabitants, yet decorated
with little curiosities from beyond the sea, and a few delicate specimens
of Indian manufacture—these are the only particulars to be premised
in regard to scene and season. Two young and comely women sat
together by the fireside, nursing their mutual and peculiar sorrows.
They were the recent brides of two brothers, a sailor and a landsman,
and two successive days had brought tidings of the death of each, by
the chances of Canadian warfare, and the tempestuous Atlantic. The
universal sympathy excited by this bereavement, drew numerous
condoling guests to the habitation of the widowed sisters. Several,
among whom was the minister, had remained till the verge of evening;
when one by one, whispering many comfortable passages of Scripture,
that were answered by more abundant tears, they took their leave
and departed to their own happier homes. The mourners, though
not insensible to the kindness of their friends, had yearned to be left
alone. United, as they had been, by the relationship of the living,
and now more closely so by that of the dead, each felt as if whatever
consolation her grief admitted, were to be found in the bosom of
the other. They joined their hearts, and wept together silently. But
after an hour of such indulgence, one of the sisters, all of whose
emotions were influenced by her mild, quiet, yet not feeble character,

516

began to recollect the precepts of resignation and endurance, which piety had taught her, when she did not think to need them. Her misfortune, besides, as earliest known, should earliest cease to interfere with her regular course of duties; accordingly, having placed the table before the fire, and arranged a frugal meal, she took the hand of her companion.

"Come, dearest sister; you have eaten not a morsel today," she said. "Arise, I pray you, and let us ask a blessing on that which is provided for us."

Her sister-in-law was of a lively and irritable temperament, and the first pangs of her sorrow had been expressed by shrieks and passionate lamentation. She now shrunk from Mary's words, like a wounded sufferer from a hand that revives the throb.

"There is no blessing left for me, neither will I ask it," cried Margaret, with a fresh burst of tears. "Would it were His will that I might never taste food more."

Yet she trembled at these rebellious expressions, almost as soon as they were uttered, and, by degrees, Mary succeeded in bringing her sister's mind nearer to the situation of her own. Time went on, and their usual hour of repose arrived. The brothers and their brides, entering the married state with no more than the slender means which then sanctioned such a step, had confederated themselves in one household, with equal rights to the parlor, and claiming exclusive privileges in two sleeping rooms contiguous to it. Thither the widowed ones retired, after heaping ashes upon the dying embers of their fire, and placing a lighted lamp upon the hearth. The doors of both chambers were left open, so that a part of the interior of each, and the beds with their unclosed curtains, were reciprocally visible. Sleep did not steal upon the sisters at one and the same time. Mary experienced the effect often consequent upon grief quietly borne, and soon sunk into temporary forgetfulness, while Margaret became more disturbed and feverish, in proportion as the night advanced with its deepest and stillest hours. She lay listening to the drops of rain, that came down in monotonous succession, unswayed by a breath of wind; and a nervous impulse continually caused her to lift her head from the pillow, and gaze into Mary's chamber and the intermediate apartment. The cold light of the lamp threw the shadows of the furniture up against the wall, stamping them immoveably there, except when they were shaken by a sudden flicker of the flame. Two vacant arm-chairs were in their old positions on opposite sides of the hearth, where the brothers had been wont to sit in young and laughing dignity, as heads of families; two humbler seats were near them, the true thrones of that little empire, where Mary and herself had exercised in love, a power that love had won. The cheerful radiance of the fire had shone upon the happy circle, and the dead glimmer of the lamp might have befitted their reunion now. While Margaret groaned in bitterness, she heard a knock at the street-door.

"How would my heart have leapt at that sound but yesterday!" thought she, remembering the anxiety with which she had long awaited tidings from her husband. "I care not for it now; let them begone, for I will not arise."

But even while a sort of childish fretfulness made her thus resolve, she was breathing hurriedly, and straining her ears to catch a repetition of the summons. It is difficult to be convinced of the death of one whom we have deemed another self. The knocking was now renewed in slow and regular strokes, apparently given with the soft end of a doubled fist, and was accompanied by words, faintly heard through several thicknesses of wall. Margaret looked to her sister's chamber, and beheld her still lying in the depths of sleep. She arose, placed her foot upon the floor, and slightly arrayed herself, trembling between fear and eagerness as she did so.

"Heaven help me!" sighed she. "I have nothing left to fear, and methinks I am ten times more a coward than ever."

Seizing the lamp from the hearth, she hastened to the window that overlooked the street-door. It was a lattice, turning upon hinges; and having thrown it back, she stretched her head a little way into the moist atmosphere. A lantern was reddening the front of the house, and melting its light in the neighboring puddles, while a deluge of darkness overwhelmed every other object. As the window grated on its hinges, a man in a broad brimmed hat and blanket-coat, stepped from under the shelter of the projecting story, and looked upward to discover whom his application had aroused. Margaret knew him as a friendly innkeeper of the town.

"What would you have, Goodman Parker?" cried the widow.

"Lack-a-day, is it you, Mistress Margaret?" replied the innkeeper. "I was afraid it might be your sister Mary; for I hate to see a young woman in trouble, when I haven't a word of comfort to whisper her."

"For Heaven's sake, what news do you bring?" screamed Margaret.

"Why, there has been an express through the town within this half hour," said Goodman Parker, "travelling from the eastern jurisdiction with letters from the governor and council. He tarried at my house to refresh himself with a drop and a morsel, and I asked him what tidings on the frontiers. He tells me we had the better in the skirmish you wot of, and that thirteen men reported slain are well and sound, and your husband among them. Besides, he is appointed of the escort to bring the captivated Frenchers and Indians home to the province jail. I judged you wouldn't mind being broke of your rest, and so I stept over to tell you. Good night."

So saying, the honest man departed; and his lantern gleamed along the street, bringing to view indistinct shapes of things, and the fragments of a world, like order glimmering through chaos, or memory roaming over the past. But Margaret staid not to watch these picturesque effects. Joy flashed into her heart, and lighted it up at once, and breathless, and with winged steps, she flew to the bedside of her sister. She paused, however, at the door of the chamber, while a thought of pain broke in upon her.

"Poor Mary!" said she to herself. "Shall I waken her, to feel her sorrow sharpened by my happiness? No; I will keep it within my own bosom till the morrow."

She approached the bed to discover if Mary's sleep were peaceful. Her face was turned partly inward to the pillow, and had been hidden there to weep; but a look of motionless contentment was now visible upon it, as if her heart, like a deep lake, had grown calm because its dead had sunk down so far within. Happy is it, and strange, that the lighter sorrows are those from which dreams are chiefly fabricated. Margaret shrunk from disturbing her sister-in-law, and felt as if her own better fortune, had rendered her involuntarily unfaithful, and as if altered and diminished affection must be the consequence of the disclosure she had to make. With a sudden step, she turned away. But joy could not long be repressed, even by circumstances that would have excited heavy grief at another moment. Her mind was thronged with delightful thoughts, till sleep stole on and transformed them to visions, more delightful and more wild, like the breath of winter, (but what a cold comparison!) working fantastic tracery upon a window.

When the night was far advanced, Mary awoke with a sudden start. A vivid dream had latterly involved her in its unreal life, of which, however, she could only remember that it had been broken in upon at the most interesting point. For a little time, slumber hung about her like a morning mist, hindering her from perceiving the distinct outline of her situation. She listened with imperfect consciousness to two or three volleys of a rapid and eager knocking; and first she deemed the noise a matter of course, like the breath she drew; next, it appeared a thing in which she had no concern; and lastly, she became aware that it was a summons necessary to be obeyed. At the same moment, the pang of recollection darted into her mind; the pall of sleep was thrown back from the face of grief; the dim light of the chamber, and the objects therein revealed, had retained all her suspended ideas, and restored them as soon as she unclosed her eyes. Again, there was a quick peal upon the street-door. Fearing that her sister would also be disturbed, Mary wrapped herself in a cloak and hood, took the lamp from the hearth, and hastened to the window. By some accident, it had been left unhasped, and yielded easily to her hand.

"Who's there?" asked Mary, trembling as she looked forth.

The storm was over, and the moon was up; it shone upon broken clouds above, and below upon houses black with moisture, and upon little lakes of the fallen rain, curling into silver beneath the quick enchantment of a breeze. A young man in a sailor's dress, wet as if he had come out of the depths of the sea, stood alone under the window. Mary recognized him as one whose livelihood was gained by short voyages along the coast; nor did she forget, that, previous to her marriage, he had been an unsuccessful wooer of her own.

"What do you seek here, Stephen?" said she.

"Cheer up, Mary, for I seek to comfort you," answered the rejected lover. "You must know I got home not ten minutes ago, and the first thing my good mother told me was the news about your husband. So, without saying a word to the old woman, I clapt on my hat, and ran out of the house. I couldn't have slept a wink before speaking to you, Mary, for the sake of old times."

"Stephen, I thought better of you!" exclaimed the widow, with gushing tears, and preparing to close the lattice; for she was no whit inclined to imitate the first wife of Zadig.

"But stop, and hear my story out," cried the young sailor. "I tell you we spoke a brig yesterday afternoon, bound in from Old England. And who do you think I saw standing on deck, well and hearty, only a bit thinner than he was five months ago?"

Mary leaned from the window, but could not speak.

"Why, it was your husband himself," continued the generous seaman. "He and three others saved themselves on a spar, when the Blessing turned bottom upwards. The brig will beat into the bay by daylight, with this wind, and you'll see him here tomorrow. There's the comfort I bring you, Mary, and so good night."

He hurried away, while Mary watched him with a doubt of waking reality, that seemed stronger or weaker as he alternately entered the shade of the houses, or emerged into the broad streaks of moonlight. Gradually, however, a blessed flood of conviction swelled into her heart, in strength enough to overwhelm her, had its increase been more abrupt. Her first impulse was to rouse her sister-in-law, and communicate the new-born gladness. She opened the chamber-door, which had been closed in the course of the night, though not latched, advanced to the bedside, and was about to lay her hand upon the slumberer's shoulder. But then she remembered that Margaret would awake to thoughts of death and woe, rendered not the less bitter by their contrast with her own felicity. She suffered the rays of the lamp to fall upon the unconscious form of the bereaved one. Margaret lay in unquiet sleep, and the drapery was displaced around her; her young cheek was rosy-tinted, and her lips half opened in a vivid smile; an expression of joy, debarred its passage by her sealed eyelids, struggled forth like incense from the whole countenance.

"My poor sister! you will waken too soon from that happy dream," thought Mary.

Before retiring, she set down the lamp and endeavored to arrange the bed-clothes, so that the chill air might not do harm to the feverish slumberer. But her hand trembled against Margaret's neck, a tear also fell upon her cheek, and she suddenly awoke.

# THE AMBITIOUS GUEST

## Nathaniel Hawthorne

ONE SEPTEMBER NIGHT, a family had gathered round their hearth, and piled it high with the drift-wood of mountain-streams, the dry cones of the pine, and the splintered ruins of great trees, that had come crashing down the precipice. Up the chimney roared the fire, and brightened the room with its broad blaze. The faces of the father and mother had a sober gladness; the children laughed; the eldest daughter was the image of Happiness at seventeen; and the aged grandmother, who sat knitting in the warmest place, was the image of Happiness grown old. They had found the "herb, heart's ease," in the bleakest spot of all New-England. This family were situated in the Notch of the White Hills, where the wind was sharp throughout the year, and pitilessly cold in the winter—giving their cottage all its fresh inclemency, before it descended on the valley of the Saco. They dwelt in a cold spot and a dangerous one; for a mountain towered above their heads, so steep, that the stones would often rumble down its sides, and startle them at midnight.

The daughter had just uttered some simple jest, that filled them all with mirth, when the wind came through the Notch and seemed to pause before their cottage—rattling the door, with a sound of wailing and lamentation, before it passed into the valley. For a moment, it saddened them, though there was nothing unusual in the tones. But the family were glad again, when they perceived that the latch was lifted by some traveller, whose footsteps had been unheard amid the dreary blast, which heralded his approach, and wailed as he was entering, and went moaning away from the door.

Though they dwelt in such a solitude, these people held daily converse with the world. The romantic pass of the Notch is a great artery, through which the life-blood of internal commerce is continually throbbing, between Maine, on one side, and the Green Mountains and the shores of the St. Lawrence on the other. The stage-coach always drew up before the door of the cottage. The wayfarer, with no companion but his staff, paused here to exchange a word, that the sense of loneliness might not utterly overcome him, ere he could pass through the cleft of the mountain, or reach the first house in the valley. And here the teamster, on his way to Portland market, would put up for the night—and, if a bachelor, might sit an hour beyond the usual bed-time, and steal a kiss from the mountain-maid, at parting. It was one of those primitive taverns, where the traveller pays only for food and lodging, but meets with a homely kindness, beyond all price. When the footsteps were heard, therefore, between the outer door and the inner one, the whole family rose up, grandmother, children, and all, as if about to welcome someone who belonged to them, and whose fate was linked with theirs.

The door was opened by a young man. His face at first wore the melancholy expression, almost despondency, of one who travels a wild and bleak road, at night-fall and alone, but soon brightened up, when he saw the kindly warmth of his reception. He felt his heart spring forward to meet them all, from the old woman, who wiped a chair with her apron, to the little child that held out its arms to him. One glance and smile placed the stranger on a footing of innocent familiarity with the eldest daughter.

"Ah, this fire is the right thing!" cried he; "especially when there is such a pleasant circle round it. I am quite benumbed; for the Notch is just like the pipe of a great pair of bellows; it has blown a terrible blast in my face, all the way from Bartlett."

"Then you are going towards Vermont?" said the master of the house, as he helped to take a light knapsack off the young man's shoulders.

"Yes; to Burlington, and far enough beyond," replied he. "I meant to have been at Ethan Crawford's, tonight; but a pedestrian lingers along such a road as this. It is no matter; for, when I saw this good fire, and all your cheerful faces, I felt as if you had kindled it on purpose for me, and were waiting my arrival. So I shall sit down among you, and make myself at home."

The frank-hearted stranger had just drawn his chair to the fire, when something like a heavy footstep was heard without, rushing down the steep side of the mountain, as with long and rapid strides, and taking such a leap, in passing the cottage, as to strike the opposite precipice. The family held their breath, because they knew the sound, and their guest held his, by instinct.

"The old Mountain has thrown a stone at us, for fear we should forget him," said the landlord, recovering himself. "He sometimes nods his head, and threatens to come down; but we are old neighbors, and agree together pretty well, upon the whole. Besides, we have a sure place of refuge, hard by, if he should be coming in good earnest."

Let us now suppose the stranger to have finished his supper of bear's meat; and, by his natural felicity of manner, to have placed himself on a footing of kindness with the whole family—so that they talked as freely together, as if he belonged to their mountain brood. He was of a proud, yet gentle spirit—haughty and reserved among the rich and great; but ever ready to stoop his head to the lowly cottage door, and be like a brother or a son at the poor man's fireside. In the household of the Notch, he found warmth and simplicity of feeling, the pervading intelligence of New-England, and a poetry, of native growth, which they had gathered, when they little thought of it, from the mountain-peaks and chasms, and at the very threshold of their romantic and dangerous abode. He had travelled far and alone; his whole life, indeed, had been a solitary path; for, with the lofty caution of his nature, he had kept himself apart from those who might otherwise have been his companions. The family, too, though so kind and hospitable, had that consciousness of unity among themselves, and separation from the world at large, which, in every domestic circle, should still keep a holy place, where no stranger may intrude. But, this evening, a prophetic sympathy impelled the refined and educated youth to pour out his heart before the simple mountaineers, and constrained them to answer him with the same free confidence. And thus it should have been. Is not the kindred of a common fate a closer tie than that of birth?

The secret of the young man's character was, a high and abstracted ambition. He could have borne to live an undistinguished life, but not to be forgotten in the grave. Yearning desire had been transformed to hope; and hope, long cherished, had become like certainty, that, obscurely as he journeyed now, a glory was to beam on all his pathway—though not, perhaps, while he was treading it. But, when posterity should gaze back into the gloom of what was now the present, they would trace the brightness of his footsteps, brightening as meaner glories faded, and confess, that a gifted one had passed from his cradle to his tomb, with none to recognize him.

"As yet," cried the stranger—his cheek glowing and his eye flashing with enthusiasm—"as yet, I have done nothing. Were I to vanish from the earth tomorrow, none would know so much of me as you; that a nameless youth came up, at nightfall, from the valley of the Saco, and opened his heart to you in the evening, and passed through the Notch, by sunrise, and was seen no more. Not a soul would ask—'Who was he?—Whither did the wanderer go?' But, I cannot die till I have achieved my destiny. Then, let Death come! I shall have built my monument!"

There was a continual flow of natural emotion, gushing forth amid abstracted reverie, which enabled the family to understand this young man's sentiments, though so foreign from their own. With quick sensibility of the ludicrous, he blushed at the ardor into which he had been betrayed.

"You laugh at me," said he, taking the eldest daughter's hand, and laughing himself. "You think my ambition as nonsensical as if I were to freeze myself to death on the top of Mount Washington, only that people might spy at me from the country roundabout. And truly, that would be a noble pedestal for a man's statue!"

"It is better to sit here, by this fire," answered the girl, blushing, "and be comfortable and contented, though nobody thinks about us."

"I suppose," said her father, after a fit of musing, "there is something natural in what the young man says; and if my mind had been turned that way, I might have felt just the same. It is strange, wife, how his talk has set my head running on things, that are pretty certain never to come to pass."

"Perhaps they may," observed the wife. "Is the man thinking what he will do when he is a widower?"

"No, no!" cried he, repelling the idea with reproachful kindness. "When I think of your death, Esther, I think of mine, too. But I was wishing we had a good farm, in Bartlett, or Bethlehem, or Littleton, or some other township round the White Mountains; but not where they could tumble on our heads. I should want to stand well with my neighbors, and be called 'Squire, and sent to General Court, for a term or two; for a plain, honest man may do as much good there as a lawyer. And when I should be grown quite an old man, and you an old woman, so as not to be long apart, I might die happy enough in my bed, and leave you all crying around me. A slate grave-stone would suit me as well as a marble one—with just my name and age, and a verse of a hymn, and something to let people know, that I lived an honest man and died a Christian."

"There now!" exclaimed the stranger; "it is our nature to desire a monument, be it slate, or marble, or a pillar of granite, or a glorious memory in the universal heart of man."

"We're in a strange way, tonight," said the wife, with tears in her eyes. "They say it's a sign of something, when folks' minds go a wandering so. Hark to the children!"

They listened accordingly. The younger children had been put to bed in another room, but with an open door between, so that they could be heard talking busily among themselves. One and all seemed to have caught the infection from the fireside circle, and were outvying each other, in wild wishes, and childish projects of what they would do, when they came to be men and women. At length, a little boy, instead of addressing his brothers and sisters, called out to his mother.

"I'll tell you what I wish, mother," cried he. "I want you and father and grandma'm, and all of us, and the stranger too, to start right away, and go and take a drink out of the basin of the Flume!"

Nobody could help laughing at the child's notion of leaving a warm bed, and dragging them from a cheerful fire, to visit the basin of the Flume—a brook, which tumbles over the precipice, deep within the Notch. The boy had hardly spoken, when a wagon rattled along the road, and stopped a moment before the door. It appeared to contain two or three men, who were cheering their hearts with the rough chorus of a song, which resounded, in broken notes, between the cliffs, while the singers hesitated whether to continue their journey, or put up here for the night.

"Father," said the girl, "they are calling you by name."

But the good man doubted whether they had really called him, and was unwilling to show himself too solicitous of gain, by inviting people to patronize his house. He therefore did not hurry to the door; and the lash being soon applied, the travellers plunged into the Notch, still singing and laughing, though their music and mirth came back drearily from the heart of the mountain.

"There, mother!" cried the boy, again. "They'd have given us a ride to the Flume."

Again they laughed at the child's pertinacious fancy for a night-ramble. But it happened, that a light cloud passed over the daughter's spirit; she looked gravely into the fire, and drew a breath that was almost a sigh. It forced its way, in spite of a little struggle to repress it. Then starting and blushing, she looked quickly round the circle, as if they had caught a glimpse into her bosom. The stranger asked what she had been thinking of.

"Nothing," answered she, with a downcast smile. "Only I felt lonesome just then."

"Oh, I have always had a gift of feeling what is in other people's hearts," said he, half seriously. "Shall I tell the secrets of yours? For I know what to think, when a young girl shivers by a warm hearth, and complains of lonesomeness at her mother's side. Shall I put these feelings into words?"

"They would not be a girl's feelings any longer, if they could be put into words," replied the mountain-nymph, laughing, but avoiding his eye.

All this was said apart. Perhaps a germ of love was springing in their hearts, so pure that it might blossom in Paradise, since it could not be matured on earth; for women worship such gentle dignity as his; and the proud, contemplative, yet kindly soul is oftenest captivated by simplicity like hers. But, while they spoke softly, and he was watching the happy sadness, the lightsome shadows, the shy yearnings of a maiden's nature, the wind, through the Notch, took a deeper and drearier sound. It seemed, as the fanciful stranger said, like the choral strain of the spirits of the blast, who, in old Indian times, had their dwelling among these mountains, and made their heights and recesses a sacred region. There was a wail, along the road, as if a funeral were passing. To chase away the gloom, the family threw pine branches on their fire, till the dry leaves crackled and the flame arose, discovering once again a scene of peace and humble happiness. The light hovered about them fondly, and caressed them all. There were the little faces of the children, peeping from their bed apart, and here the father's frame of strength, the mother's subdued and careful mien, the high-browed youth, the budding girl, and the good old grandam, still knitting in the warmest place. The aged woman looked up from her task, and, with fingers ever busy, was the next to speak.

"Old folks have their notions," said she, "as well as young ones. You've been wishing and planning; and letting your heads run on one thing and another, till you've set my mind a wandering too. Now what should an old woman wish for, when she can go but a step or two before she comes to her grave? Children, it will haunt me night and day, till I tell you."

"What is it, mother?" cried the husband and wife, at once.

Then the old woman, with an air of mystery, which drew the circle closer round the fire, informed them that she had provided her grave-clothes some years before—a nice linen shroud, a cap with a muslin ruff, and everything of a finer sort than she had worn since her wedding-day. But, this evening, an old superstition had strangely recurred to her. It used to be said, in her younger days, that, if anything were amiss with a corpse, if only the ruff were not smooth, or the cap did not set right, the corpse, in the coffin and beneath the clods, would strive to put up its cold hands and arrange it. The bare thought made her nervous.

"Don't talk so, grandmother!" said the girl, shuddering.

"Now,"—continued the old woman, with singular earnestness, yet smiling strangely at her own folly—"I want one of you, my children—when your mother is drest, and in the coffin—I want one of you to hold a looking-glass over my face. Who knows but I may take a glimpse at myself, and see whether all's right?"

"Old and young, we dream of graves and monuments," murmured the stranger-youth. "I wonder how mariners feel, when the ship is sinking, and they, unknown and undistinguished, are to be buried together in the ocean—that wide and nameless sepulchre!"

For a moment, the old woman's ghastly conception so engrossed the minds of her hearers, that a sound, abroad in the night, rising like the roar of a blast, had grown broad, deep, and terrible, before the fated group were conscious of it. The house, and all within it, trembled; the foundations of the earth seemed to be shaken, as if this awful sound were the peal of the last trump. Young and old exchanged one wild glance, and remained an instant, pale, affrighted, without utterance, or power to move. Then the same shriek burst simultaneously from all their lips.

"The Slide! The Slide!"

The simplest words must intimate, but not portray, the unutterable horror of the catastrophe. The victims rushed from their cottage, and sought refuge in what they deemed a safer spot—where, in contemplation of such an emergency, a sort of barrier had been reared. Alas! they had quitted their security, and fled right into the pathway of destruction. Down came the whole side of the mountain, in a cataract of ruin. Just before it reached the house, the stream broke into two branches—shivered not a window there, but overwhelmed the whole vicinity, blocked up the road, and annihilated everything in its dreadful course. Long ere the thunder of that great

Slide had ceased to roar among the mountains, the mortal agony had been endured, and the victims were at peace. Their bodies were never found.

The next morning, the light smoke was seen stealing from the cottage-chimney, up the mountain-side. Within, the fire was yet smouldering on the hearth, and the chairs in a circle round it, as if the inhabitants had but gone forth to view the devastation of the Slide, and would shortly return, to thank Heaven for their miraculous escape. All had left separate tokens, by which those, who had known the family, were made to shed a tear for each. Who has not heard their name? The story had been told far and wide, and will forever be a legend of these mountains. Poets have sung their fate.

There were circumstances, which led some to suppose that a stranger had been received into the cottage on this awful night, and had shared the catastrophe of all its inmates. Others denied that there were sufficient grounds for such a conjecture. Wo, for the high-souled youth, with his dream of Earthly Immortality! His name and person utterly unknown; his history, his way of life, his plans, a mystery never to be solved; his death and his existence, equally a doubt! Whose was the agony of that death-moment?

# DAVID SWAN

## Nathaniel Hawthorne

### A Fantasy

WE CAN BE but partially acquainted even with events which actually influence our course through life, and our final destiny. There are innumerable other events, if such they may be called, which come close upon us, yet pass away without actual results, or even betraying their near approach, by the reflection of any light or shadow across our minds. Could we know all the vicissitudes of our fortunes, life would be too full of hope and fear, exultation or disappointment, to afford us a single hour of true serenity. This idea may be illustrated by a page from the secret history of David Swan.

We have nothing to do with David, until we find him, at the age of twenty, on the high road from his native place to the city of Boston, where his uncle, a small dealer in the grocery line, was to take him behind the counter. Be it enough to say, that he was a native of New Hampshire, born of respectable parents, and had received an ordinary school education, with a classic finish by a year at Gilmanton academy. After journeying on foot, from sunrise till nearly noon of a summer's day, his weariness and the increasing heat determined him to sit down in the first convenient shade, and await the coming up of the stage coach. As if planted on purpose for him, there soon appeared a little tuft of maples, with a delightful recess in the midst, and such a fresh bubbling spring, that it seemed never to have sparkled for any wayfarer but David Swan. Virgin or not, he kissed it with his thirsty lips, and then flung himself along the brink, pillowing his head upon some shirts and a pair of pantaloons, tied up in a striped cotton handkerchief.

The sunbeams could not reach him; the dust did not yet rise from the road, after the heavy rain of yesterday; and his grassy lair suited the young man better than a bed of down. The spring murmured drowsily beside him; the branches waved dreamily across the blue sky, overhead; and a deep sleep, perchance hiding dreams within its depths, fell upon David Swan. But we are to relate events which he did not dream of.

While he lay sound asleep in the shade, other people were wide awake, and passed to and fro, a-foot, on horseback, and in all sorts of vehicles, along the sunny road by his bed-chamber. Some looked neither to the right hand nor to the left, and knew not that he was there; some merely glanced that way, without admitting the slumberer among their busy thoughts; some laughed to see how soundly he slept; and several, whose hearts were brimming full of scorn, ejected their venomous superfluity on David Swan. A middle aged widow, when nobody else was near, thrust her head a little way into the recess, and vowed that the young fellow looked charming in his sleep. A temperance lecturer saw him, and wrought poor David into the texture of his evening's discourse, as an awful instance of dead drunkenness by the road-side. But, censure, praise, merriment, scorn, and indifference, were all one, or rather all nothing, to David Swan.

He had slept only a few moments, when a brown carriage, drawn by a handsome pair of horses, bowled easily along, and was brought to a stand-still, nearly in front of David's resting place. A linch pin had fallen out, and permitted one of the wheels to slide off. The damage was slight, and occasioned merely a momentary alarm to an elderly merchant and his wife, who were returning to Boston in the carriage. While the coachman and a servant were replacing the wheel, the lady and gentleman sheltered themselves beneath the maple trees, and there espied the bubbling fountain, and David Swan asleep beside it. Impressed with the awe which the humblest sleeper usually sheds around him, the merchant trod as lightly as the gout would allow; and his spouse took good heed not to rustle her silk gown, lest David should start up, all of a sudden.

"How soundly he sleeps!" whispered the old gentleman. "From what a depth he draws that easy breath! Such sleep as that, brought on without an opiate, would be worth more to me than half my income; for it would suppose health, and an untroubled mind."

"And youth, besides," said the lady. "Healthy and quiet age does not sleep thus. Our slumber is no more like his, than our wakefulness."

The longer they looked, the more did this elderly couple feel interested in the unknown youth, to whom the way side and the maple shade were as a secret chamber, with the rich gloom of damask curtains brooding over him. Perceiving that a stray sunbeam glimmered down upon his face, the lady contrived to twist a branch aside, so as to intercept it. And having done this little act of kindness, she began to feel like a mother to him.

"Providence seems to have laid him here," whispered she to her husband, "and to have brought us hither to find him, after our disappointment in our cousin's son. Methinks I can see a likeness to our departed Henry. Shall we waken him?"

"To what purpose?" said the merchant, hesitating. "We know nothing of the youth's character."

"That open countenance!" replied his wife, in the same hushed voice, yet earnestly. "This innocent sleep!"

While these whispers were passing, the sleeper's heart did not throb, nor his breath become agitated, nor his features betray the least token of interest.—Yet Fortune was bending over him, just ready to let fall a burthen of gold. The old merchant had lost his only son, and had no heir to his wealth, except a distant relative, with whose conduct he was dissatisfied. In such cases, people sometimes do stranger things than to act the magician, and awaken a young man to splendor, who fell asleep in poverty.

"Shall we not waken him?" repeated the lady, persuasively.

"The coach is ready, Sir," said the servant, behind.

The old couple started, reddened, and hurried away, mutually wondering, that they should ever have dreamed of doing any thing so very ridiculous. The merchant threw himself back in the carriage, and occupied his mind with the plan of a magnificent asylum for unfortunate men of business. Meanwhile, David Swan enjoyed his nap.

The carriage could not have gone above a mile or two, when a pretty young girl came along, with a tripping pace, which shewed precisely how her little heart was dancing in her bosom. Perhaps it was this merry kind of motion that caused—is there any harm in saying it?—her garter to slip its knot. Conscious that the silken girth, if silk it were, was relaxing its hold, she turned aside into the shelter of the maple trees, and there found a young man asleep by the spring! Blushing, as red as any rose, that she should have intruded into a gentleman's bed-chamber, and for such a purpose too, she was about to make her escape on tiptoe. But, there was peril near the sleeper.

A monster of a bee had been wandering overhead—buzz, buzz, buzz—now among the leaves, now flashing through the strips of sunshine, and now lost in the dark shade, till finally he appeared to be settling on the eyelid of David Swan. The sting of a bee is sometimes deadly. As freehearted as she was innocent, the girl attacked the intruder with her handkerchief, brushed him soundly, and drove him from beneath the maple shade. How sweet a picture! This good deed accomplished, with quickened breath, and a deeper blush, she stole a glance at the youthful stranger, for whom she had been battling with a dragon in the air.

"He is handsome!" thought she, and blushed redder yet.

How could it be that no dream of bliss grew so strong within him, that, shattered by its very strength, it should part asunder, and allow him to perceive the girl among its phantoms? Why, at least, did no smile of welcome brighten upon his face? She was come, the maid whose soul, according to the old and beautiful idea, had been severed from his own, and whom, in all his vague but passionate desires, he yearned to meet. Her, only, could he love with a perfect love—him, only, could she receive into the depths of her heart—and now her image was faintly blushing in the fountain, by his side; should it pass away, its happy lustre would never gleam upon his life again.

"How sound he sleeps!" murmured the girl.

She departed, but did not trip along the road so lightly as when she came.

Now, this girl's father was a thriving country merchant in the neighbourhood, and happened, at that identical time, to be looking out for just such a young man as David Swan. Had David formed a way side acquaintance with the daughter, he would have become the father's clerk, and all else in natural succession. So here, again, had good fortune—the best of fortunes—stolen so near, that her garments brushed against him; and he knew nothing of the matter.

The girl was hardly out of sight, when two men turned aside beneath the maple shade. Both had dark faces, set off by cloth caps, which were drawn down aslant over their brows. Their dresses were shabby, yet had a certain smartness. These were a couple of rascals, who got their living by whatever the devil sent them, and now, in the interim of other business, had staked the joint profits of their next piece of villany on a game of cards, which was to have been decided here under the trees. But, finding David asleep by the spring, one of the rogues whispered to his fellow,

"Hist!—Do you see that bundle under his head?"

The other villain nodded, winked, and leered.

"I'll bet you a horn of brandy," said the first, "that the chap has either a pocket book, or a snug little hoard of small change, stowed away amongst his shirts. And if not there, we shall find it in his pantaloons pocket."

"But how if he wakes?" said the other.

His companion thrust aside his waistcoat, pointed to the handle of a dirk, and nodded.

"So be it!" muttered the second villain.

They approached the unconscious David, and, while one pointed the dagger towards his heart, the other began to search the bundle beneath his head. Their two faces, grim, wrinkled, and ghastly with guilt and fear, bent over their victim, looking horrible enough to be mistaken for fiends, should he suddenly awake. Nay, had the villains glanced aside into the spring, even they would hardly have known themselves, as reflected there. But David Swan had never worn a more tranquil aspect, even when asleep on his mother's breast.

"I must take away the bundle," whispered one.

"If he stirs, I'll strike," muttered the other.

But, at this moment, a dog, scenting along the ground, came in beneath the maple trees, and gazed alternately at each of these wicked men, and then at the quiet sleeper. He then lapped out of the fountain.

"Pshaw!" said one villain. "We can do nothing now. The dog's master must be close behind."

"Let's take a drink, and be off," said the other.

The man, with the dagger, thrust back the weapon into his bosom, and drew forth a pocket pistol, but not of that kind which kills by a single discharge. It was a flask of liquor, with a block tin tumbler screwed upon the mouth. Each drank a comfortable dram, and left the spot, with so many jests, and such laughter at their unaccomplished wickedness, that they might be said to have gone on their way rejoicing. In a few hours, they had forgotten the whole affair, nor once imagined that the recording angel had written down the crime of murder against their souls, in letters as durable as eternity. As for David Swan, he still slept quietly, neither conscious of the shadow of death when it hung over him, nor of the glow of renewed life, when that shadow was withdrawn.

He slept, but no longer so quietly as at first. An hour's repose had snatched, from his elastic frame, the weariness with which many hours of toil had burthened it. Now, he stirred—now, moved his lips, without a sound—now, talked, in an inward tone, to the noon-day spectres of his dream. But a noise of wheels came rattling louder and louder along the road, until it dashed through the dispersing mist of David's slumber—and there was the stage coach. He started up, with all his ideas about him.

"Halloo, driver!—Take a passenger?" shouted he.

"Room on top!" answered the driver.

Up mounted David, and bowled away merrily towards Boston, without so much as a parting glance at that fountain of dreamlike vicissitude. He knew not that a phantom of Wealth had thrown a golden hue upon its waters—nor that one of Love had sighed softly to their murmur—nor that one of Death had threatened to crimson them with his blood—all, in the brief hour since he lay down to sleep. Sleeping or waking, we hear not the airy footsteps of the strange things that almost happen. Does it not argue a superintending Providence, that, while viewless and unexpected events thrust themselves continually athwart our path, there should still be regularity enough, in mortal life, to render foresight even partially available?

# UP IN MICHIGAN

## Ernest Hemingway

JIM GILMORE CAME to Hortons Bay from Canada. He bought the blacksmith shop from old man Horton. Jim was short and dark with big mustaches and big hands. He was a good horse-shoer and did not look much like a blacksmith even with his leather apron on. He lived upstairs above the blacksmith shop and took his meals at A. J. Smith's.

Liz Coates worked for Smith's. Mrs. Smith, who was a very large clean woman, said Liz Coates was the neatest girl she'd ever seen. Liz had good legs and always wore clean gingham aprons and Jim noticed that her hair was always neat behind. He liked her face because it was so jolly but he never thought about her.

Liz liked Jim very much. She liked it the way he walked over from the shop and often went to the kitchen door to watch for him to start down the road. She liked it about his mustache. She liked it about how white his teeth were when he smiled. She liked it very much that he didn't look like a blacksmith. She liked it how much A. J. Smith and Mrs. Smith liked Jim. One day she found that she liked it the way the hair was black on his arms and how white they were above the tanned line when he washed up in the washbasin outside the house. Liking that made her feel funny.

Hortons Bay, the town, was only five houses on the main road between Boyne City and Charlevoix. There was the general store and post office with a high false front and maybe a wagon hitched out in front, Smith's house, Stroud's house, Fox's house, Horton's house and Van Hoosen's house. The houses were in a big grove of elm trees and the road was very sandy. There was farming country and timber each way up the road. Up the road a ways was the Methodist church and down the road the other direction was the township school. The blacksmith shop was painted red and faced the school.

A steep sandy road ran down the hill to the bay through the timber. From Smith's back door you could look out across the woods that ran down to the lake and across the bay. It was very beautiful in the spring and summer, the bay blue and bright and usually whitecaps on the lake out beyond the point from the breeze blowing from Charlevoix and Lake Michigan. From Smith's back door Liz could see ore barges way out in the lake going toward Boyne City. When she looked at them they didn't seem to be moving at all but if she went in and dried some more dishes and then came out again they would be out of sight beyond the point.

All the time now Liz was thinking about Jim Gilmore. He didn't seem to notice her much. He talked about the shop to A. J. Smith and about the Republican Party and about James G. Blaine. In the evenings he read the Toledo Blade and the Grand Rapids paper by the lamp in the front room or went out spearing fish in the bay with a jacklight with A. J. Smith. In the fall he and Smith and Charley Wyman took a wagon and tent, grub, axes, their rifles and two dogs and went on a trip to the pine plains beyond Vanderbilt deer hunting. Liz and Mrs. Smith were cooking for four days for them before they started. Liz wanted to make something special for Jim to take but she didn't finally because she was afraid to ask Mrs. Smith for the eggs and flour and afraid if she bought them Mrs. Smith would catch her cooking. It would have been all right with Mrs. Smith but Liz was afraid.

All the time Jim was gone on the deer hunting trip Liz thought about him. It was awful while he was gone. She couldn't sleep well from thinking about him but she discovered it was fun to think about him too. If she let herself go it was better. The night before they were to come back she didn't sleep at all, that is she didn't think she slept because it was all mixed up in a dream about not sleeping and really not sleeping. When she saw the wagon coming down the road she felt weak and sick sort of inside. She couldn't wait till she saw Jim and it seemed as though everything would be all right when he came. The wagon stopped outside under the big elm and Mrs. Smith and Liz went out. All the men had beards and there were three deer in the back of the wagon, their thin legs sticking stiff over the edge of the wagon box. Mrs. Smith kissed Alonzo and he hugged her. Jim said "Hello Liz," and grinned. Liz hadn't known just what would happen when Jim got back but she was sure it would be something. Nothing had happened. The men were just home that was all. Jim pulled the burlap sacks off the deer and Liz looked at them. One was a big buck. It was stiff and hard to lift out of the wagon.

"Did you shoot it Jim?" Liz asked.

"Yeah. Ain't it a beauty?" Jim got it onto his back to carry to the smokehouse.

That night Charley Wyman stayed to supper at Smith's. It was too late to get back to Charlevoix. The men washed up and waited in the front room for supper.

"Ain't there something left in that crock Jimmy?" A. J. Smith asked and Jim went out to the wagon in the barn and fetched in the jug of whiskey the men had taken hunting with them. It was a four gallon jug and there was quite a little slopped back and forth in the bottom. Jim took a long pull on his way back to the house. It was hard to lift such a big jug up to drink out of it. Some of the whiskey ran down on his shirt front. The two men smiled when Jim came in with the jug. A. J. Smith sent for glasses and Liz brought them. A. J. poured out three big shots.

"Well here's looking at you A. J." said Charley Wyman.

"That damn big buck Jimmy." said A. J.

"Here's all the ones we missed A. J." said Jim and downed his liquor.

"Tastes good to a man."

"Nothing like it this time of year for what ails you."

"How about another boys?"

"Here's how A. J."

"Down the creek boys."

"Here's to next year."

Jim began to feel great. He loved the taste and the feel of whisky. He was glad to be back to a comfortable bed and warm food and the shop. He had another drink. The men came in to supper feeling hilarious but acting very respectable. Liz sat at the table after she put on the food and ate with the family. It was a good dinner. The men ate seriously. After supper they went into the front room again and Liz cleaned off with Mrs. Smith. Then Mrs. Smith went upstairs and pretty soon Smith came out and went upstairs too. Jim and Charley were still in the front room. Liz was sitting in the kitchen next to the stove pretending to read a book and thinking about Jim.

She didn't want to go to bed yet because she knew Jim would be coming out and she wanted to see him as he went out so she could take the way he looked up to bed with her.

She was thinking about him hard and then Jim came out. His eyes were shining and his hair was a little rumpled. Liz looked down at her book. Jim came over back of her chair and stood there and she could feel him breathing and then he put his arms around her. Her breasts felt plump and firm and the nipples were erect under his hands. Liz was terribly frightened, no one had ever touched her, but she thought, "He's come to me finally. He's really come."

She held herself stiff because she was so frightened and did not know anything else to do and then Jim held her tight against the chair and kissed her. It was such a sharp, aching, hurting feeling that she thought she couldn't stand it. She felt Jim right through the back of the chair and she couldn't stand it and then something clicked inside of her and the feeling was warmer and softer. Jim held her tight hard against the chair and she wanted it now and Jim whispered, "Come on for a walk."

Liz took her coat off the peg on the kitchen wall and they went out the door. Jim had his arm around her and every little way they stopped and pressed against each other and Jim kissed her. There was no moon and they walked ankle deep in the sandy road through the trees down to the dock and the warehouse on the bay. The water was lapping in the piles and the point was dark across the bay. It was cold but Liz was hot all over from being with Jim. They sat down in the shelter of the warehouse and Jim pulled Liz close to him. She was frightened. One of Jim's hands went inside her dress and stroked over her breast and the other hand was in her lap, She was very frightened and didn't know how he was going to go about things but she snuggled close to him. Then the hand that felt so big in her lap went away and was on her leg and started to move up it.

"Don't Jim." Liz said. Jim slid the hand further up.

"You musn't Jim. You musn't." Neither Jim nor Jim's big hand paid any attention to her.

The boards were hard. Jim had her dress up and was trying to do something to her. She was frightened but she wanted it. She had to have it but it frightened her.

"You musn't do it Jim. You musn't."

"I got to. I'm going to. You know we got to."

"No we haven't Jim. We ain't got to. Oh it isn't right. Oh it's so big and it hurts so. You can't. Oh Jim. Jim. Oh."

The hemlock planks of the dock were hard and splintery and cold and Jim was heavy on her and he had hurt her. Liz pushed him, she was so uncomfortable and cramped. Jim was asleep. He wouldn't move. She worked out from under him and sat up and straightened her skirt and coat and tried to do something with her hair. Jim was sleeping with his mouth a little open. Liz leaned over and kissed him on the cheek. He was still asleep. She lifted his head a little and shook it. He rolled his head over and swallowed. Liz started to cry. She walked over to the edge of the dock and looked down to the water. There was a mist coming up from the bay. She was cold and miserable and everything felt gone. She walked back to where Jim was lying and shook him once more to make sure. She was crying.

"Jim" she said, "Jim. Please Jim."

Jim stirred and curled a little tighter. Liz took off her coat and leaned over and covered him with it. She tucked it around him neatly and carefully. Then she walked across the dock and up the steep sandy road to go to bed. A cold mist was coming up through the woods from the bay.

# OUT OF SEASON

## Ernest Hemingway

ON THE FOUR lira he had earned by spading the hotel garden
quite drunk. He saw the young gentleman coming down th
and spoke to him mysteriously. The young gentleman said h
not eaten yet but would be ready to go as soon as lunch was fini
Forty minutes or an hour.

At the cantina near the bridge they trusted him for three m
grappas because he was so confident and mysterious about his
for the afternoon. It was a windy day with the sun coming out fr
behind clouds and then going under in sprinkles of rain. A wonde
ful day for trout fishing.

The young gentleman came out of the hotel and asked him abou
the rods. Should his wife come behind with the rods? Yes, said Peduzzi
let her follow us. The young gentleman went back into the hotel and
spoke to his wife. He and Peduzzi started down the road. The young
gentleman had a musette over his shoulder. Peduzzi saw the wife, who
looked as young as the young gentleman and was wearing mountain
boots and a blue beret, start out to follow them down the road carrying
the fishing rods unjointed one in each hand. Peduzzi didn't like her
to be way back there. Signorina, he called, winking at the young
gentleman, come up here and walk with us. Signora come up here.
Let us all walk together. Peduzzi wanted them all three to walk down
the street of Cortina together.

The wife stayed behind, following rather sullenly. Signorina,
Peduzzi called tenderly, come up here with us. The young gentleman
looked back and shouted something. The wife stopped lagging behind
and walked up.

ı the main street of the town
/ *Arturo*! Tipping his hat. The
ɔr of the Fascist café. Groups of
ıt of the shops stared at the three.
wdered jackets working on the
ıoked up as they passed. Nobody
ı except the town beggar, lean and
ırd, who lifted his hat as they passed.
a store with the window full of bottles
a bottle from an inside pocket of his old
ı, some marsala for the Signora, something,
ıstured with the bottle. It was a wonderful
ırsala, Signorina? A little marsala?
ıly. You'll have to play up to this, she said. I
ıd he says. He's drunk isn't he?
man appeared not to hear Peduzzi. He was
ell makes him say marsala. That's what Max

*he got*
*e path*
*e had*
*ıhed.*

aid finally, taking hold of the young gentleman's
ımiled reluctant to press the subject but needing to
*ore*
*iob* ɡ gentleman into action.
*ɔm* gentleman took out his pocket book and gave him a
*ır-* Peduzzi went up the steps to the door of the Speciality
and Foreign Wines shop. It was locked.
*t* ːd until two, someone passing in the street said scornfully.
ıme down the steps. He felt hurt. Never mind, he said, we
ı at the Concordia.
walked down the road to the Concordia three abreast. On
ıch of the Concordia where the rusty bobsleds were stacked the
ɡ gentleman said, *Was wollen sie?*[1] Peduzzi handed him the ten
ıote folded over and over. Nothing, he said, Anything. He was
ıbarrassed. Marsala maybe. I don't know. Marsala?
The door of the Concordia shut on the young gentleman and the
ᴡife. Three marsalas, said the y. g. to the girl behind the pastry counter.
Two you mean? she asked. No, he said, one for a *vecchio*[2]. Oh, she
said, a *vecchio,* and laughed getting down the bottle. She poured out
the three muddy looking drinks into three glasses. The wife was sitting
at a table under the line of newspapers on sticks. The y. g. put one of

---

[1]   *Was wollen sie?*; German: What do you want?

[2]   *vecchio*; Italian: old man

the marsalas in front of her. You might as well drink it,
it'll make you feel better. She sat and looked at the g
went outside the door with a glass for Peduzzi but coul

I don't know where he is, he said coming back i
room carrying the glass.

He wanted a quart of it, said the wife.

How much is a quarter litre, the y. g. asked the girl.

Of the bianco? One lira.

No, of the marsala. Put these two in too, he said giv
own glass and the one poured for Peduzzi. She filled the q
wine measure with a funnel. A bottle to carry it, said the

She went to hunt for a bottle. It all amused her.

I'm sorry you feel so rotten Tiny, he said, I'm sorry I t
way I did at lunch. We were both getting at the same th
different angles.

It doesn't make any difference, she said. None of it ma
difference.

Are you too cold, he asked. I wish you'd worn another sw

I've got on three sweaters.

The girl came in with a very slim brown bottle and poure
marsala into it. The y. g. paid five lira more. They went o
the door. The girl was amused. Peduzzi was walking up and d
at the other end out of the wind and holding the rods.

Come on, he said, I will carry the rods. What difference do
make if anybody sees them. No one will trouble us. No one will m
any trouble for me in Cortina. I know them at the *municipio*[3]. I ha
been a soldier. Everybody in this town likes me. I sell frogs. What
it is forbidden to fish? Not a thing. Nothing. No trouble. Big trout
tell you. Lots of them.

They were walking down the hill toward the river. The town wa
in back of them. The sun had gone under and it was sprinkling rain.
There, said Peduzzi, pointing to a girl in the doorway of a house
they passed. My daughter.

His doctor, the wife said, has he got to show us his doctor?

He said his daughter, said the y. g.

The girl went into the house as Peduzzi pointed.

They walked down the hill across the fields and then turned to
follow the river bank. Peduzzi talked rapidly with much winking
and knowingness. As they walked three abreast the wife caught

---

[3]   *municipio*; Italian: city hall.

he said. Maybe
...lass. The y. g.
...d not see him.
...to the pastry

...udged her in the ribs. Part
...o dialect and sometimes in
...t make out which the young
...od the best so he was being
...man said *Ja Ja*[4] Peduzzi decided
...young gentleman and the wife

...us going through with these rods.
...by the game police now. I wish we
...This damned old fool is so drunk too.
...the guts to just go back, said the wife.
...n.

Go on back Tiny.

...you. If you go to jail we might as well

...ing her his
...uarter litre
y. g.

...own the bank and Peduzzi stood his coat
...sturing at the river. It was brown and muddy.
...was a dump heap.
...ian, said the young gentleman.

...lked the
...ng from

...a d' un' mezz' ora.

...st a half an hour more. Go on back Tiny. You're
...anyway. It's a rotten day and we aren't going to
...way.

...kes any
...eater.

...said, and climbed up the grassy bank.
...down at the river and did not notice her till she was
...sight over the crest. *Frau!*[5] he shouted. *Frau! Fraulein!*[6]
...oing? She went on over the crest of the hill.

...d the
...ut of
...own

...e! said Peduzzi. It shocked him.
...off the rubber bands that held the rod segments together
...ienced to joint up one of the rods.
...u said it was half an hour further.
...es. It is good half an hour down. It is good here too.
...ly?

...s it
...ke
...ve
...if
I

...course. It is good here and good there too.
...ie y. g. sat down on the bank and jointed up a rod, put on the
...and threaded the line through the guides. He felt uncomfortable
...d afraid that any minute a gamekeeper or a posse of citizens would

*Ja Ja*; German: Yes Yes.
5  *frau*; German: woman, Mrs.
6  *fraulein*; German: young lady, Miss.

come over the bank from the town. He could see the houses of the town and the campanile over the edge of the hill. He opened his leader box. Peduzzi leaned over and dug his flat hard thumb and forefinger in and tangled the moistened leaders.

Have you some lead?

No.

You must have some lead. Peduzzi was excited. You must have *piombo*[7]. *Piombo*. A little *piombo*. Just here. Just above the hook or your bait will float on the water. You must have it. Just a little *piombo*.

Have you got some?

No. He looked through all his pockets desperately. Sifting through the cloth dirt in the linings of his inside military pockets. I haven't any. We must have *piombo*.

We can't fish then, said the y. g. and unjointed the rod, reeling the line back through the guides. We'll get some *piombo* and fish tomorrow.

But listen *caro*[8], you must have *piombo*. The line will lie flat on the water. Peduzzi's day was going to pieces before his eyes. You must have *piombo*. A little is enough. Your stuff is all clean and new but you have no lead. I would have brought some. You said you had everything.

The y. g. looked at the stream discoloured by the melting snow. I know, he said, we'll get some *piombo* and fish tomorrow.

At what hour in the morning? Tell me that.

At seven.

The sun came out. It was warm and pleasant. The young gentleman felt relieved. He was no longer breaking the law. Sitting on the bank he took the bottle of marsala out of his pocket and passed it to Peduzzi. Peduzzi passed it back. The y. g. took a drink of it and passed it to Peduzzi again. Peduzzi passed it back again. Drink, he said, drink. It's your marsala. After another short drink the y. g. handed the bottle over. Peduzzi had been watching it closely. He took the bottle very hurriedly and tipped it up. The grey hairs in the folds of his neck oscillated as he drank, his eyes fixed on the end of the narrow brown bottle. He drank it all. The sun shone while he drank. It was wonderful. This was a great day after all. A wonderful day.

---

[7] *piombo*; Italian: lead (the metal).
[8] *caro*; Italian: dear.

*Senta caro!*[9] In the morning at seven. He had called the young gentleman *caro* several times and nothing had happened. It was good marsala. His eyes glistened. Days like this stretched out ahead. It would begin again at seven in the morning.

They started to walk up the hill toward the town. The y. g. went on ahead. He was quite a way up the hill. Peduzzi called to him.

Listen *caro* can you let me take five lira for a favour?

For today? asked the young gentleman frowning.

No, not today. Give it to me today for tomorrow. I will provide everything for tomorrow. *Pane, salami, formaggio,*[10] good stuff for all of us. You and I and the signora. Bait for fishing, minnows, not worms only. Perhaps I can get some marsala. All for five lira. Five lira for a favour.

The young gentleman looked through his pocket book and took out a two lira note and two ones.

Thank you *caro*. Thank you, said Peduzzi in the tone of one member of the Carleton Club accepting the Morning Post from another. This was living. He was through with the hotel garden, breaking up frozen manure with a dung fork. Life was opening out.

Until seven o'clock then *caro*, he said, slapping the y. g. on the back. Promptly at seven.

I may not be going, said the young gentleman putting his purse back in his pocket.

What, said Peduzzi. I will have minnows Signor. *Salami*, everything. You and I and the Signora. The three of us.

I may not be going, said the y. g., very probably not. I will leave word with the padrone at the hotel office.

---

[9]  *Senta caro*; Italian: listen dear.
[10]  *Pane, salami, formaggio*; Italian: bread, salami, and cheese.

# MY OLD MAN

## Ernest Hemingway

I GUESS LOOKING at it now my old man was cut out for a fat guy, one of those regular little roly fat guys you see around, but he sure never got that way, except a little toward the last, and then it wasn't his fault, he was riding over the jumps only and he could afford to carry plenty of weight then. I remember the way he'd pull on a rubber shirt over a couple of jerseys and a big sweat shirt over that and get me to run with him in the forenoon in the hot sun. He'd have maybe taken a trial trip with one of Razzo's skins early in the morning after just getting in from Torino at four o'clock in the morning and beating it out to the stables in a cab and then with the dew all over everything and the sun just starting to get going I'd help him pull off his boots and he'd get into a pair of sneakers and all these sweaters and we'd start out.

"Come on kid" he'd say, stepping up and down on his toes in front of the jock's dressing room, "let's get moving."

Then we'd start off jogging around the infield once maybe with him ahead running nice and then turn out the gate and along one of those roads with all the trees along both sides of them that run out from San Siro. I'd go ahead of him when we hit the road and I could run pretty stout and I'd look around and he'd be jogging easy just behind me and after a little while I'd look around again and he'd begun to sweat. Sweating heavy and he'd just be dogging it along with his eyes on my back, but when he'd catch me looking at him he'd grin and say, "Sweating plenty?" When my old man grinned nobody could help but grin too. We'd keep right on running out toward the mountains and then my old man would yell "Hey Joe!"

and I'd look back and he'd be sitting under a tree with a towel he'd had around his waist wrapped around his neck.

I'd come back and sit down beside him and he'd pull a rope out of his pocket and start skipping rope out in the sun with the sweat pouring off his face and him skipping rope out in the white dust with the rope going cloppetty cloppety clop clop clop and the sun hotter and him working harder up and down a patch of the road. Say it was a treat to see my old man skip rope too. He could whirr it fast or lop it slow and fancy. Say you ought to have seen wops look at us sometimes when they'd come by going into town walking along with big white steers hauling the cart. They sure looked as though they thought the old man was nuts. He'd start the rope whirring till they'd stop dead still and watch him, then give the steers a cluck and a poke with the goad and get going again.

When I'd sit watching him working out in the hot sun I sure felt fond of him. He sure was fun and he done his work so hard and he'd finish up with a regular whirring that'd drive the sweat out on his face like water and then sling the rope at the tree and come over and sit down with me and lean back against the tree with the towel and a sweater wrapped around his neck.

"Sure is hell keeping it down, Joe" he'd say and lean back and shut his eyes and breathe long and deep, "it ain't like when you're a kid." Then he'd get up before he started to cool and we'd jog along back to the stables. That's the way it was keeping down to weight. He was worried all the time. Most jocks can just about ride off all they want to. A jock loses about a kilo every time he rides, but my old man was sort of dried out and he couldn't keep down his kilos without all that running.

I remember once at San Siro, Regoli, a little wop that was riding for Buzoni came out across the paddock going to the bar for something cool and flicking his boots with his whip, after he'd just weighed in and my old man had just weighed in too and came out with the saddle under his arm looking red faced and tired and too big for his silks and he stood there looking at young Regoli standing up to the outdoors bar cool and kid looking and I says, "What's the matter Dad?" cause I thought maybe Regoli had bumped him or something and he just looked at Regoli and said, "Oh to hell with it" and went on to the dressing room.

Well it would have been all right maybe if we'd stayed in Milan and ridden at Milan and Torino cause if there ever were any easy courses it's those two. "Pianola, Joe," my old man said when he dismounted in the winning stall after what the wops thought was a hell of a steeplechase. I asked him once, "This course rides its-self. It's the pace you're going at that makes riding the jumps dangerous Joe. We ain't going any pace here, and they ain't any really bad jumps either. But it's the pace always—not the jumps that makes the trouble."

San Siro was the swellest course I'd ever seen but the old man said it was a dog's life. Going back and forth between Mirafiore and San Siro and riding just about every day in the week with a train ride every other night.

I was nuts about the horses too. There's something about it when they come out and go up the track to the post. Sort of dancy and tight looking with the jock keeping a tight hold on them and maybe easing off a little and letting them run a little going up. Then once they were at the barrier it got me worse than anything. Especially at San Siro with that big green infield and the mountains way off and the fat wop starter with his big whip and the jocks fiddling them around and then the barrier snapping up and that bell going off and them all getting off in a bunch and then commencing to string out. You know the way a bunch of skins gets off. If you're up in the stand with a pair of glasses all you see is them plunging off and then that bell goes off and it seems like it rings for a thousand years and then they come sweeping round the turn. There wasn't ever anything like it for me.

But my old man said one day in the dressing room when he was getting into his street clothes, "None of these things are horses Joe. They'd kill that bunch of skates for their hides and hoofs up at Paris." That was the day he'd won the Premio Commercio with Lantorna shooting her out of the field the last hundred meters like pulling a cork out of a bottle.

It was right after the Premio Commercio that we pulled out and left Italy. My old man and Holbrook and a fat wop in a straw hat that kept wiping his face with a handkerchief were having an argument at a table in the Galleria. They were all talking French and the two of them were after my old man about something. Finally he didn't say anything any more but just sat there and looked at Holbrook and the two of them kept after him, first one talking and then the other and the fat wop always butting in on Holbrook.

"You go out and buy me a Sportsman, will you Joe?" my old man said and handed me a couple of *soldi*[1] without looking away from Holbrook.

---

[1] *soldi*; Italian: a monetary unit in Italy.

So I went out of the Galleria and walked over to in front of the Scala and bought a paper and came back and stood a little way away because I didn't want to butt in and my old man was sitting back in his chair looking down at his coffee and fooling with a spoon and Holbrook and the big wop were standing and the big wop was wiping his face and shaking his head. And I came up and my old man acted just as though the two of them weren't standing there and said, "Want an ice Joe?" Holbrook looked down at my old man and said slow and careful, "You son of a bitch" and he and the fat wop went out through the tables.

My old man sat there and sort of smiled at me but his face was white and he looked sick as hell and I was scared and felt sick inside because I knew something had happened and I didn't see how anybody could call my old man a son of a bitch and get away with it. My old man opened up the Sportsman and studied the handicaps for a while and then he said, "You got to take a lot of things in this world Joe." And three days later we left Milan for good on the Turin train for Paris after an auction sale out in front of Turner's stables of everything we couldn't get into a trunk and a suit case.

We got into Paris early in the morning in a long dirty station the old man told me was the Gare de Lyon. Paris was an awful big town after Milan. Seems like in Milan everybody is going somewhere and all the trams run somewhere and there ain't any sort of a mixup, but Paris is all balled up and they never do straighten it out. I got to like it though, part of it anyway, and say it's got the best race courses in the world. Seems as though that were the thing that keeps it all going and about the only thing you can figure on is that every day the buses will be going out to whatever track they're running at going right out through everything to the track. I never really got to know Paris well because I just came in about once or twice a week with the old man from Maisons and he always sat at the Café de la Paix on the Opera side with the rest of the gang from Maisons and I guess that's one of the busiest parts of the town. But say it is funny that a big town like Paris wouldn't have a Galleria isn't it?

Well, we went out to live at Maisons-Lafitte, where just about everybody lives except the gang at Chantilly, with a Mrs. Meyers that runs a boarding house. Maisons is about the swellest place to live I've ever seen in all my life. The town ain't so much, but there's a lake and a swell forest that we used to go off bumming in all day, a couple of us kids, and my old man made me a sling shot and we got a lot of things with it but the best one was a magpie. Young

Dick Atkinson shot a rabbit with it one day and we put it under a tree and were all sitting around and Dick had some cigarettes and all of a sudden the rabbit jumped up and beat it into the brush and we chased it but we couldn't find it. Gee we had fun at Maisons. Mrs. Meyers used to give me lunch in the morning and I'd be gone all day. I learned to talk French quick. It's an easy language.

As soon as we got to Maisons my old man wrote to Milan for his license and he was pretty worried till it came. He used to sit around the Café de Paris in Maisons with the gang there, there were lots of guys he'd known when he rode up at Paris before the war lived at Maisons, and there's a lot of time to sit around because the work around a racing stable for the jocks that is, is all cleaned up by nine o'clock in the morning. They take the first batch of skins out to gallop them at 5:30 in the morning and they work the second lot at 8 o'clock. That means getting up early all right and going to bed early too. If a jock's riding for somebody too he can't go boozing around because the trainer always has an eye on him if he's a kid and if he ain't a kid he's always got an eye on himself. So mostly if a jock ain't working he sits around the Café de Paris with the gang and they can all sit around about two or three hours in front of some drink like a vermouth and seltz and they talk and tell stories and shoot pool and it's sort of like a club or the Galleria in Milan. Only it ain't really like the Galleria because there everybody is going by all the time and there's everybody around at the tables.

Well my old man got his license all right. They sent it through to him without a word and he rode a couple of times. Amiens, up country and that sort of thing, but he didn't seem to get any engagement. Everybody liked him and whenever I'd come in to the Café in the forenoon I'd find somebody drinking with him because my old man wasn't tight like most of these jockeys that have got the first dollar they made riding at the World's Fair in St. Louis in Nineteen ought four. That's what my old man would say when he'd kid George Burns. But it seemed like everybody steered clear of giving my old man any mounts.

We went out to wherever they were running every day with the car from Maisons and that was the most fun of all. I was glad when the horses came back from Deauville and the summer. Even though it meant no more bumming in the woods, cause then we'd ride to Enghien or Tremblay or St. Cloud and watch them from the trainers' and jockeys' stand. I sure learned about racing from going out with that gang and the fun of it was going every day.

I remember once out at St. Cloud. It was a big two hundred thousand franc race with seven entries and Kzar a big favourite. I went around to the paddock to see the horses with my old man and you never saw such horses. This Kzar is a great big yellow horse that looks like just nothing but run. I never saw such a horse. He was being led around the paddock with his head down and when he went by me I felt all hollow inside he was so beautiful. There never was such a wonderful, lean, running built horse. And he went around the paddock putting his feet just so and quiet and careful and moving easy like he knew just what he had to do and not jerking and standing up on his legs and getting wild eyed like you see these selling platers with a shot of dope in them. The crowd was so thick I couldn't see him again except just his legs going by and some yellow and my old man started out through the crowd and I followed him over to the jock's dressing room back in the trees and there was a big crowd around there too but the man at the door in a derby nodded to my old man and we got in and everybody was sitting around and getting dressed and pulling shirts over their heads and pulling boots on and it all smelled hot and sweaty and linimenty and outside was the crowd looking in.

The old man went over and sat down beside George Gardner that was getting into his pants and said, "What's the dope George?" just in an ordinary tone of voice cause there ain't any use him feeling around because George either can tell him or he can't tell him.

"He won't win" George says very low, leaning over and buttoning the bottoms of his pants.

"Who will" my old man says leaning over close so nobody can hear.

"Kircubbin" George says, "And if he does, save me a couple of tickets."

My old man says something in a regular voice to George and George says, "Don't ever bet on anything I tell you" kidding like and we beat it out and through all the crowd that was looking in over to the 100 franc mutuel machine. But I knew something big was up because George is Kzar's jockey. On the way he gets one of the yellow odds sheets with the starting prices on and Kzar is only paying 5 for 10, Cefisidote is next at 3 to 1 and fifth down the list this Kircubbin at 8 to 1. My old man bets five thousand on Kircubbin to win and puts on a thousand to place and we went around back of the grandstand to go up the stairs and get a place to watch the race.

We were jammed in tight and first a man in a long coat with a
grey tall hat and a whip folded up in his hand came out and then one
after another the horses, with the jocks up and a stable boy holding
the bridle on each side and walking along, followed the old guy.
That big yellow horse Kzar came first. He didn't look so big when
you first looked at him until you saw the length of his legs and the
whole way he's built and the way he moves. Gosh I never saw such
a horse. George Gardner was riding him and they moved along slow,
back of the old guy in the gray tall hat that walked along like he was
the ring master in a circus. Back of Kzar, moving along smooth and
yellow in the sun, was a good looking black with a nice head with
Tommy Archibald riding him and after the black was a string of five
more horses all moving along slow in a procession past the grandstand
and the pesage. My old man said the black was Kircubbin and I took
a good look at him and he was a nice looking horse all right but
nothing like Kzar.

Everybody cheered Kzar when he went by and he sure was
one swell looking horse. The procession of them went around on
the other side past the pelouse and then back up to the near end
of the course and the circus master had the stable boys turn them
loose one after another so they could gallop by the stands on their
way up to the post and let everybody have a good look at them.
They weren't at the post hardly any time at all when the gong started
and you could see them way off across the infield all in a bunch
starting on the first swing like a lot of little toy horses. I was watching
them through the glasses and Kzar was running well back with one
of the bays making the pace. They swept down and around and
came pounding past and Kzar was way back when they passed us
and this Kircubbin horse in front and going smooth. Gee it's awful
when they go by you and then you have to watch them go farther
away and get smaller and smaller and then all bunched up on the
turns and then come around towards into the stretch and you feel
like swearing and goddaming worse and worse. Finally they made
the last turn and came into the straightaway with this Kircubbin
horse way out in front. Everybody was looking funny and saying
"Kzar" in sort of a sick way and they pounding nearer down the
stretch, and then something came out of the pack right into my
glasses like a horse-headed yellow streak and everybody began to
yell "Kzar" as though they were crazy. Kzar came on faster than I'd
ever seen anything in my life and pulled up on Kircubbin that was
going fast as any black horse could go with the jock flogging hell

out of him with the gad and they were right dead neck and neck for a second but Kzar seemed going about twice as fast with those great jumps and that head out—but it was while they were neck and neck that they passed the winning post and when the numbers went up in the slots the first one was 2 and that meant Kircubbin had won.

I felt all trembly and funny inside, and then we were all jammed in with the people going downstairs to stand in front of the board where they'd post what Kircubbin paid. Honest watching the race I'd forgot how much my old man had bet on Kircubbin. I'd wanted Kzar to win so damned bad. But now it was all over it was swell to know we had the winner.

"Wasn't it a swell race Dad?" I said to him.

He looked at me sort of funny with his derby on the back of his head, "George Gardner's a swell jockey all right," he said, "It sure took a great jock to keep that Kzar horse from winning."

Of course I knew it was funny all the time. But my old man saying that right out like that sure took the kick all out of it for me and I didn't get the real kick back again ever, even when they posted the numbers up on the board and the bell rang to pay off and we saw that Kircubbin paid 67.50 for 10. All around people were saying "Poor Kzar. Poor Kzar!" And I thought, I wish I were a jockey and could have rode him instead of that son of a bitch. And that was funny, thinking of George Gardner as a son of a bitch because I'd always liked him and besides he'd given us the winner, but I guess that's what he is all right.

My old man had a big lot of money after that race and he took to coming into Paris oftener. If they raced at Tremblay he'd have them drop him in town on their way back to Maisons and he and I'd sit out in front of the Café de la Paix and watch the people go by. It's funny sitting there. There's streams of people going by and all sorts of guys come up and want to sell you things and I loved to sit there with my old man. That was when we'd have the most fun. Guys would come by selling funny rabbits that jumped if you squeezed a bulb and they'd come up to us and my old man would kid with them. He could talk French just like English and all those kind of guys knew him cause you can always tell a jockey—and then we always sat at the same table and they got used to seeing us there. There were guys selling matrimonial papers and girls selling rubber eggs that when you squeezed them a rooster came out of

them and one old wormy looking guy that went by with post cards
of Paris showing them to everybody, and of course nobody ever
bought any and then he would come back and show the under side
of the pack and they would all be smutty post cards and lots of
people would dig down and buy them.

Gee I remember the funny people that used to go by. Girls around
supper time looking for somebody to take them out to eat and they'd
speak to my old man and he'd make some joke at them in French
and they'd pat me on the head and go on. Once there was an American
woman sitting with her kid daughter at the next table to us and they
were both eating ices and I kept looking at the girl and she was
awfully good looking and I smiled at her and she smiled at me but
that was all that ever came of it because I looked for her mother and
her every day and I made up ways that I was going to speak to her
and I wondered if I got to know her if her mother would let me take
her out to Auteuil or Tremblay but I never saw either of them again.
Anyway I guess it wouldn't have been any good anyway because
looking back on it I remember the way I thought out would be best
to speak to her was to say, "Pardon me, but perhaps I can give you
a winner at Enghien today?" and after all maybe she would have
thought I was a tout instead of really trying to give her a winner.

We'd sit at the Café de la Paix, my old man and me, and we had
a big drag with the waiter because my old man drank whisky and it
cost five francs and that meant a good tip when the saucers were
counted up. My old man was drinking more than I'd ever seen him,
but he wasn't riding at all now and besides he said that whiskey kept
his weight down. But I noticed he was putting it on all right just the
same. He'd busted away from his old gang out at Maisons and seemed
to like just sitting around on the boulevard with me. But he was
dropping money every day at the track. He'd feel sort of doleful after
the last race, if he'd lost on the day, until we'd get to our table and
he'd have his first whiskey and then he'd be fine.

He'd be reading the Paris-Sport and he'd look over at me and say,
"Where's your girl Joe?" to kid me on account I had told him about
the girl that day at the next table. And I'd get red but I liked being
kidded about her. It gave me a good feeling. "Keep your eye peeled
for her Joe." he'd say, "She'll be back."

He'd ask me questions about things and some of the things I'd say
he'd laugh. And then he'd get started talking about things. About
riding down in Egypt, or at St. Moritz on the ice before my mother

died, and about during the war when they had regular races down in the south of France without any purses, or betting or crowd or anything just to keep the breed up. Regular races with the jocks riding hell out of the horses. Gee I could listen to my old man talk by the hour, especially when he'd had a couple or so of drinks. He'd tell me about when he was a boy in Kentucky and going coon hunting and the old days in the states before everything went on the bum there. And he'd say, "Joe, when we've got a decent stake, you're going back there to the States and go to school."

"What've I got to go back there to go to school for when everything's on the bum there?" I'd ask him.

"That's different." he'd say and get the waiter over and pay the pile of saucers and we'd get a taxi to the Gare St. Lazare and get on the train out to Maisons.

One day at Auteuil after a selling steeplechase my old man bought in the winner for 30.000 francs. He had to bid a little to get him but the stable let the horse go finally and my old man had his permit and his colors in a week. Gee I felt proud when my old man was an owner. He fixed it up for stable space with Charles Drake and cut out coming in to Paris and started his running and sweating out again and him and I were the whole stable gang. Our horse's name was Gillford, he was Irish bred and a nice sweet jumper. My old man figured that training him and riding him himself he was a good investment. I was proud of everything and I thought Gillford was as good a horse as Kzar. He was a good solid jumper, a bay, with plenty of speed on the flat if you asked him for it and he was a nice looking horse too.

Gee I was fond of him. The first time he started with my old man up he finished third in a 2.500 meter hurdle race and when my old man got off him, all sweating and happy in the place stall and went in to weigh I felt as proud of him as though it was the first race he'd ever placed in. You see when a guy ain't been riding for a long time you can't make yourself really believe that he has ever rode. The whole thing was different now cause down in Milan even big races never seemed to make any difference to my old man, if he won he wasn't ever excited or anything, and now it was so I couldn't hardly sleep the night before a race and I knew my old man was excited too even if he didn't show it. Riding for yourself makes an awful difference.

Second time Gillford and my old man started was a rainy Sunday at Auteuil in the Prix du Marat, a 4.500 meter steeplechase. As soon as he'd gone out I beat it up in the stand with the new glasses my old man had bought for me to watch them. They started way over at the far end of the course and there was some trouble at the barrier. Something with goggle blinders on was making a great fuss and rearing around and busted the barrier once but I could see my old man in our black jacket with a white cross and a black cap sitting up on Gillford and patting him with his hand. Then they were off in a jump and out of sight behind the trees and the gong going for dear life and the pari mutuel wickets rattling down. Gosh I was so excited I was afraid to look at them but I fixed the glasses on the place where they would come out back of the trees and then out they came with the old black jacket going third and they all sailing over the jump like birds. Then they went out of sight again and then they came pounding out and down the hill and all going nice and sweet and easy and taking the fence smooth in a bunch and moving away from us all solid. Looked as though you could walk across on their backs they were all so bunched and going so smooth, then they bellied over the big double Bullfinch and something came down. I couldn't see who it was but in a minute the horse was up and galloping free and the field, all bunched still, sweeping around the long left turn into the straightaway. They jumped the stone wall and came jammed down the stretch toward the big water jump right in front of the stands. I saw them coming and hollered at my old man as he went by and he was leading by about a length and riding way out over and light as a monkey and they were racing for the water jump. They took off over the big hedge of the water jump in a pack and then there was a crash and two horses pulled sideways out off it and kept on going and three others were piled up. I couldn't see my old man anywhere. One horse knee-ed himself up and the jock had hold of the bridle and mounted and went slamming on after the place money. The other horse was up and away by himself, jerking his head and galloping with the bridle rein hanging and the jock staggered over to one side of the track against the fence. Then Gillford rolled over to one side off my old man and got up and started to run on three legs with his off hoof dangling and there was my old man lying there on the grass flat out with his face up and blood all over the side of his head. I ran down the stand and bumped into a jam of people and got to the rail and a cop grabbed me and held me and two big stretcher bearers were going out after my old man and around on the other side of the course I saw three horses, strung way out, coming out of the trees and taking the jump.

My old man was dead when they brought him in and while a doctor was listening to his heart with a thing plugged in his ears I heard a shot up the track that meant they'd killed Gillford. I lay down beside my old man when they carried the stretcher into the hospital room and hung onto the stretcher and cried and cried and he looked so white and gone and so awfully dead and I couldn't help feeling that if my old man was dead maybe they didn't need to have shot Gillford. His hoof might have got well. I don't know. I loved my old man so much.

Then a couple of guys came in and one of them patted me on the back and then went over and looked at my old man and then pulled a sheet off the cot and and spread it over him; and the other was telephoning in French for them to send the ambulance to take him out to Maisons. And I couldn't stop crying, crying and choking, sort of, and George Gardner came in and sat down beside me on the floor and put his arm around me and says, "Come on Joe old boy. Get up and we'll go out and wait for the ambulance."

George and I went out to the gate and I was trying to stop bawling and George wiped off my face with his handkerchief and we were standing back a little ways while the crowd was going out of the gate and a couple of guys stopped near us while we were waiting for the crowd to get through the gate and one of them was counting a bunch of mutuel tickets and he said, "Well Butler got his all right."

The other guy said, "I don't give a good goddam if he did, the crook. He had it coming to him on the stuff he's pulled."

"I'll say he had," said the other guy and tore the bunch of tickets in two.

And George Gardner looked at me to see if I'd heard and I had all right and he said, "Don't you listen to what those bums said Joe. Your old man was one swell guy."

But I don't know. Seems like when they get started they don't leave a guy nothing.

# THE COP AND THE ANTHEM

### O. Henry

ON HIS BENCH in Madison Square Soapy moved uneasily. When wild geese honk high of nights, and when women without sealskin coats grow kind to their husbands, and when Soapy moves uneasily on his bench in the park, you may know that winter is near at hand.

A dead leaf fell in Soapy's lap. That was Jack Frost's card. Jack is kind to the regular denizens of Madison Square, and gives fair warning of his annual call. At the corners of four streets he hands his pasteboard to the North Wind, footman of the mansion of All Outdoors, so that the inhabitants thereof may make ready.

Soapy's mind became cognizant of the fact that the time had come for him to resolve himself into a singular Committee of Ways and Means to provide against the coming rigor. And therefore he moved uneasily on his bench.

The hibernatorial ambitions of Soapy were not of the highest. In them there were no considerations of Mediterranean cruises, of soporific Southern skies or drifting in the Vesuvian Bay. Three months on the Island was what his soul craved. Three months of assured board and bed and congenial company, safe from Boreas and bluecoats, seemed to Soapy the essence of things desirable.

For years the hospitable Blackwell's had been his winter quarters. Just as his more fortunate fellow New Yorkers had bought their tickets to Palm Beach and the Riviera each winter, so Soapy had made his humble arrangements for his annual hegira to the Island. And now the time was come. On the previous night three Sabbath newspapers, distributed beneath his coat, about his ankles and over his lap, had failed to repulse the cold as he slept on his bench near the spurting fountain in the ancient square. So the Island loomed big and timely in Soapy's mind. He scorned the provisions made in the name of charity for the city's dependents. In Soapy's opinion the Law was more benign than Philanthropy. There was an endless round of institutions, municipal and eleemosynary, on which he might set out and receive lodging and food accordant with the simple life. But to one of Soapy's proud spirit the gifts of charity are encumbered. If not in coin you must pay in humiliation of spirit for every benefit received at the hands of philanthropy. As Caesar had his Brutus, every bed of charity must have its toll of a bath, every loaf of bread its compensation of a private and personal inquisition. Wherefore it is better to be a guest of the law, which, though conducted by rules, does not meddle unduly with a gentleman's private affairs.

Soapy, having decided to go to the Island, at once set about accomplishing his desire. There were many easy ways of doing this. The pleasantest was to dine luxuriously at some expensive restaurant; and then, after declaring insolvency, be handed over quietly and without uproar to a policeman. An accommodating magistrate would do the rest.

Soapy left his bench and strolled out of the square and across the level sea of asphalt, where Broadway and Fifth Avenue flow together. Up Broadway he turned, and halted at a glittering café, where are gathered together nightly the choicest products of the grape, the silkworm, and the protoplasm.

Soapy had confidence in himself from the lowest button of his vest upward. He was shaven, and his coat was decent and his neat black, ready-tied four-in-hand had been presented to him by a lady missionary on Thanksgiving Day. If he could reach a table in the restaurant unsuspected success would be his. The portion of him that would show above the table would raise no doubt in the waiter's mind. A roasted mallard duck, thought Soapy, would be about the thing—with a bottle of Chablis, and then Camembert, a demi-tasse and a cigar. One dollar for the cigar would be enough. The total would not be so high as to call forth any supreme manifestation of revenge from the café management; and yet the meat would leave him filled and happy for the journey to his winter refuge.

But as Soapy set foot inside the restaurant door the head waiter's eye fell upon his frayed trousers and decadent shoes. Strong and ready hands turned him about and conveyed him in silence and haste to the sidewalk and averted the ignoble fate of the menaced mallard.

Soapy turned off Broadway. It seemed that his route to the coveted Island was not to be an epicurean one. Some other way of entering limbo must be thought of.

At a corner of Sixth Avenue electric lights and cunningly displayed wares behind plate-glass made a shop window conspicuous. Soapy took a cobblestone and dashed it through the glass. People came running around the corner, a policeman in the lead. Soapy stood still, with his hands in his pockets, and smiled at the sight of brass buttons.

"Where's the man that done that?" inquired the officer, excitedly.

"Don't you figure out that I might have had something to do with it?" said Soapy, not without sarcasm, but friendly, as one greets good fortune.

The policeman's mind refused to accept Soapy even as a clue. Men who smash windows do not remain to parley with the law's minions. They take to their heels. The policeman saw a man halfway down the block running to catch a car. With drawn club he joined in the pursuit. Soapy, with disgust in his heart, loafed along, twice unsuccessful.

On the opposite side of the street was a restaurant of no great pretensions. It catered to large appetites and modest purses. Its crockery and atmosphere were thick; its soup and napery thin. Into this place Soapy took his accusive shoes and telltale trousers without challenge. At a table he sat and consumed beefsteak, flapjacks, doughnuts and pie. And then to the waiter he betrayed the fact that the minutest coin and himself were strangers.

"Now, get busy and call a cop," said Soapy. "And don't keep a gentleman waiting."

"No cops for youse," said the waiter, with a voice like butter cakes and an eye like the cherry in a Manhattan cocktail. "Hey, Con!"

Neatly upon his left ear on the callous pavement two waiters pitched Soapy. He arose joint by joint, as a carpenter's rule opens, and beat the dust from his clothes. Arrest seemed but a rosy dream. The Island seemed very far away. A policeman who stood before a drug store two doors away laughed and walked down the street.

Five blocks Soapy travelled before his courage permitted him to woo capture again. This time the opportunity presented what he fatuously termed to himself a "cinch." A young woman of a modest and pleasing guise was standing before a show window gazing with sprightly interest at its display of shaving mugs and inkstands, and two yards from the window a large policeman of severe demeanor leaned against a water plug.

It was Soapy's design to assume the role of the despicable and execrated "masher." The refined and elegant appearance of his victim and the contiguity of the conscientious cop encouraged him to believe that he would soon feel the pleasant official clutch upon his arm that would insure his winter quarters on the right little, tight little isle.

Soapy straightened the lady missionary's ready-made tie, dragged his shrinking cuffs into the open, set his hat at a killing cant and sidled toward the young woman. He made eyes at her, was taken with sudden coughs and "hems," smiled, smirked and went brazenly through the impudent and contemptible litany of the "masher." With half an eye Soapy saw that the policeman was watching him fixedly. The young woman moved away a few steps, and again bestowed her absorbed attention upon the shaving mugs. Soapy followed, boldly stepping to her side, raised his hat and said:

"Ah there, Bedelia! Don't you want to come and play in my yard?"

The policeman was still looking. The persecuted young woman had but to beckon a finger and Soapy would be practically en route for his insular haven. Already he imagined he could feel the cozy warmth of the station-house. The young woman faced him and, stretching out a hand, caught Soapy's coat sleeve.

"Sure, Mike," she said joyfully, "if you'll blow me to a pail of suds. I'd have spoke to you sooner, but the cop was watching."

With the young woman playing the clinging ivy to his oak Soapy walked past the policeman overcome with gloom. He seemed doomed to liberty.

At the next corner he shook off his companion and ran. He halted in the district where by night are found the lightest streets, hearts, vows and librettos. Women in furs and men in greatcoats moved gaily in the wintry air. A sudden fear seized Soapy that some dreadful enchantment had rendered him immune to arrest. The thought brought a little of panic upon it, and when he came upon another policeman lounging grandly in front of a transplendent theatre he caught at the immediate straw of "disorderly conduct."

On the sidewalk Soapy began to yell drunken gibberish at the top of his harsh voice. He danced, howled, raved, and otherwise disturbed the welkin.

The policeman twirled his club, turned his back to Soapy and remarked to a citizen.

"'Tis one of them Yale lads celebratin' the goose egg they give to the Hartford College. Noisy; but no harm. We've instructions to lave them be."

Disconsolate, Soapy ceased his unavailing racket. Would never a policeman lay hands on him? In his fancy the Island seemed an unattainable Arcadia. He buttoned his thin coat against the chilling wind.

In a cigar store he saw a well-dressed man lighting a cigar at a swinging light. His silk umbrella he had set by the door on entering. Soapy stepped inside, secured the umbrella and sauntered off with it slowly. The man at the cigar light followed hastily.

"My umbrella," he said, sternly.

"Oh, is it?" sneered Soapy, adding insult to petit larceny. "Well, why don't you call a policeman? I took it. Your umbrella! Why don't you call a cop? There stands one on the corner."

The umbrella owner slowed his steps. Soapy did likewise, with a presentiment that luck would again run against him. The policeman looked at the two curiously.

"Of course," said the umbrella man—"that is—well, you know how these mistakes occur—I—if it's your umbrella I hope you'll excuse me—I picked it up this morning in a restaurant—If you recognize it as yours, why—I hope you'll—"

"Of course it's mine," said Soapy, viciously.

The ex-umbrella man retreated. The policeman hurried to assist a tall blonde in an opera cloak across the street in front of a street car that was approaching two blocks away.

Soapy walked eastward through a street damaged by improvements. He hurled the umbrella wrathfully into an excavation. He muttered against the men who wear helmets and carry clubs. Because he wanted to fall into their clutches, they seemed to regard him as a king who could do no wrong.

At length Soapy reached one of the avenues to the east where the glitter and turmoil was but faint. He set his face down this toward Madison Square, for the homing instinct survives even when the home is a park bench.

But on an unusually quiet corner Soapy came to a standstill. Here was an old church, quaint and rambling and gabled. Through one violet-stained window a soft light glowed, where, no doubt, the organist loitered over the keys, making sure of his mastery of the coming Sabbath anthem. For there drifted out to Soapy's ears sweet music that caught and held him transfixed against the convolutions of the iron fence.

The moon was above, lustrous and serene; vehicles and pedestrians were few; sparrows twittered sleepily in the eaves—for a little while the scene might have been a country churchyard. And the anthem that the organist played cemented Soapy to the iron fence, for he had known it well in the days when his life contained such things as mothers and roses and ambitions and friends and immaculate thoughts and collars.

The conjunction of Soapy's receptive state of mind and the influences about the old church wrought a sudden and wonderful change in his soul. He viewed with swift horror the pit into which he had tumbled, the degraded days, unworthy desires, dead hopes, wrecked faculties and base motives that made up his existence.

And also in a moment his heart responded thrillingly to this novel mood. An instantaneous and strong impulse moved him to battle with his desperate fate. He would pull himself out of the mire; he would make a man of himself again; he would conquer the evil that had taken possession of him. There was time; he was comparatively young yet: he would resurrect his old eager ambitions and pursue them without faltering. Those solemn but sweet organ notes had set up a revolution in him. Tomorrow he would go into the roaring downtown district and find work. A fur importer had once offered him a place as driver. He would find him tomorrow and ask for the position. He would be somebody in the world. He would—

Soapy felt a hand laid on his arm. He looked quickly around into the broad face of a policeman.

"What are you doin' here?" asked the officer.

"Nothin'," said Soapy.

"Then come along," said the policeman.

"Three months on the Island," said the Magistrate in the Police Court the next morning.

# THE RANSOM OF RED CHIEF

## O. Henry

IT LOOKED LIKE a good thing: but wait till I tell you. We were down South, in Alabama—Bill Driscoll and myself—when this kidnapping idea struck us. It was, as Bill afterward expressed it, "during a moment of temporary mental apparition"; but we didn't find that out till later.

There was a town down there, as flat as a flannel-cake, and called Summit, of course. It contained inhabitants of as undeleterious and self-satisfied a class of peasantry as ever clustered around a Maypole.

Bill and me had a joint capital of about six hundred dollars, and we needed just two thousand dollars more to pull off a fraudulent town-lot scheme in Western Illinois with. We talked it over on the front steps of the hotel. Philoprogenitiveness, says we, is strong in semi-rural communities; therefore, and for other reasons, a kidnapping project ought to do better there than in the radius of newspapers that send reporters out in plain clothes to stir up talk about such things. We knew that Summit couldn't get after us with anything stronger than constables and, maybe, some lackadaisical bloodhounds and a diatribe or two in the *Weekly Farmers' Budget*. So, it looked good.

We selected for our victim the only child of a prominent citizen named Ebenezer Dorset. The father was respectable and tight, a mortgage fancier and a stern, upright collection-plate passer and forecloser. The kid was a boy of ten, with bas-relief freckles, and hair the color of the cover of the magazine you buy at the newsstand when you want to catch a train. Bill and me figured that Ebenezer would melt down for a ransom of two thousand dollars to a cent. But wait till I tell you.

About two miles from Summit was a little mountain, covered with a dense cedar brake. On the rear elevation of this mountain was a cave. There we stored provisions.

One evening after sundown, we drove in a buggy past old Dorset's house. The kid was in the street, throwing rocks at a kitten on the opposite fence.

"Hey, little boy!" says Bill, "would you like to have a bag of candy and a nice ride?"

The boy catches Bill neatly in the eye with a piece of brick.

"That will cost the old man an extra five hundred dollars," says Bill, climbing over the wheel.

That boy put up a fight like a welter-weight cinnamon bear; but, at last, we got him down in the bottom of the buggy and drove away. We took him up to the cave, and I hitched the horse in the cedar brake. After dark I drove the buggy to the little village, three miles away, where we had hired it, and walked back to the mountain.

Bill was pasting court-plaster over the scratches and bruises on his features. There was a fire burning behind the big rock at the entrance of the cave, and the boy was watching a pot of boiling coffee, with two buzzard tail-feathers stuck in his red hair. He points a stick at me when I come up, and says:

"Ha! cursed paleface, do you dare to enter the camp of Red Chief, the terror of the plains?"

"He's all right now," says Bill, rolling up his trousers and examining some bruises on his shins. "We're playing Indian. We're making Buffalo Bill's show look like magic-lantern views of Palestine in the town hall. I'm Old Hank, the Trapper, Red Chief's captive, and I'm to be scalped at daybreak. By Geronimo! that kid can kick hard."

Yes, sir, that boy seemed to be having the time of his life. The fun of camping out in a cave had made him forget that he was a captive himself. He immediately christened me Snake-eye, the Spy, and announced that, when his braves returned from the warpath, I was to be broiled at the stake at the rising of the sun.

Then we had supper; and he filled his mouth full of bacon and bread and gravy, and began to talk. He made a during-dinner speech something like this:

"I like this fine. I never camped out before; but I had a pet 'possum once, and I was nine last birthday. I hate to go to school. Rats ate up sixteen of Jimmy Talbot's aunt's speckled hen's eggs. Are there any real Indians in these woods? I want some more gravy. Does the trees moving make the wind blow? We had five puppies. What makes your nose so red, Hank? My father has lots of money. Are the stars hot? I whipped Ed Walker twice, Saturday. I don't like girls. You dassent catch toads unless with a string. Do oxen make any noise? Why are oranges round? Have you got beds to sleep on in this cave? Amos Murray has got six toes. A parrot can talk, but a monkey or a fish can't. How many does it take to make twelve?"

Every few minutes he would remember that he was a pesky redskin, and pick up his stick rifle and tiptoe to the mouth of the cave to rubber for the scouts of the hated paleface. Now and then he would let out a war-whoop that made Old Hank the Trapper shiver. That boy had Bill terrorized from the start.

"Red Chief," says I to the kid, "would you like to go home?"

"Aw, what for?" says he. "I don't have any fun at home. I hate to go to school. I like to camp out. You won't take me back home again, Snake-eye, will you?"

"Not right away," says I. "We'll stay here in the cave awhile."

"All right!" says he. "That'll be fine. I never had such fun in all my life."

We went to bed about eleven o'clock. We spread down some wide blankets and quilts and put Red Chief between us. We weren't afraid he'd run away. He kept us awake for three hours, jumping up and reaching for his rifle and screeching: "Hist! pard," in mine and Bill's ears, as the fancied crackle of a twig or the rustle of a leaf revealed to his young imagination the stealthy approach of the outlaw band. At last, I fell into a troubled sleep, and dreamed that I had been kidnapped and chained to a tree by a ferocious pirate with red hair.

Just at daybreak, I was awakened by a series of awful screams from Bill. They weren't yells, or howls, or shouts, or whoops, or yawps, such as you'd expect from a manly set of vocal organs—they were simply indecent, terrifying, humiliating screams, such as women emit when they see ghosts or caterpillars. It's an awful thing to hear a strong, desperate, fat man scream incontinently in a cave at daybreak.

I jumped up to see what the matter was. Red Chief was sitting on Bill's chest, with one hand twined in Bill's hair. In the other he had the sharp case-knife we used for slicing bacon; and he was industriously and realistically trying to take Bill's scalp, according to the sentence that had been pronounced upon him the evening before.

I got the knife away from the kid and made him lie down again. But, from that moment, Bill's spirit was broken. He laid down on his side of the bed, but he never closed an eye again in sleep as long as that boy was with us. I dozed off for a while, but along toward sun-up I remembered that Red Chief had said I was to be burned at the stake at the rising of the sun. I wasn't nervous or afraid; but I sat up and lit my pipe and leaned against a rock.

"What you getting up so soon for, Sam?" asked Bill.

"Me?" says I. "Oh, I got a kind of a pain in my shoulder. I thought sitting up would rest it."

"You're a liar!" says Bill. "You're afraid. You was to be burned at sunrise, and you was afraid he'd do it. And he would, too, if he could find a match. Ain't it awful, Sam? Do you think anybody will pay out money to get a little imp like that back home?"

"Sure," said I. "A rowdy kid like that is just the kind that parents dote on. Now, you and the Chief get up and cook breakfast, while I go up on the top of this mountain and reconnoitre."

I went up on the peak of the little mountain and ran my eye over the contiguous vicinity. Over towards Summit I expected to see the sturdy yeomanry of the village armed with scythes and pitchforks beating the countryside for the dastardly kidnappers. But what I saw was a peaceful landscape dotted with one man ploughing with a dun mule. Nobody was dragging the creek; no couriers dashed hither and yon, bringing tidings of no news to the distracted parents. There was a sylvan attitude of somnolent sleepiness pervading that section of the external outward surface of Alabama that lay exposed to my view. "Perhaps," says I to myself, "it has not yet been discovered that the wolves have borne away the tender lambkin from the fold. Heaven help the wolves!" says I, and I went down the mountain to breakfast.

When I got to the cave I found Bill backed up against the side of it, breathing hard, and the boy threatening to smash him with a rock half as big as a cocoanut.

"He put a red-hot boiled potato down my back," explained Bill, "and then mashed it with his foot; and I boxed his ears. Have you got a gun about you, Sam?"

I took the rock away from the boy and kind of patched up the argument. "I'll fix you," says the kid to Bill. "No man ever yet struck the Red Chief but he got paid for it. You better beware!"

After breakfast the kid takes a piece of leather with strings wrapped around it out of his pocket and goes outside the cave unwinding it.

"What's he up to now?" says Bill, anxiously. "You don't think he'll run away, do you, Sam?"

"No fear of it," says I. "He don't seem to be much of a home body. But we've got to fix up some plan about the ransom. There don't seem to be much excitement around Summit on account of his disappearance; but maybe they haven't realized yet that he's gone. His folks may think he's spending the night with Aunt Jane or one of the neighbors. Anyhow, he'll be missed today. Tonight we must get a message to his father demanding the two thousand dollars for his return."

Just then we heard a kind of war-whoop, such as David might have emitted when he knocked out the champion Goliath. It was a sling that Red Chief had pulled out of his pocket, and he was whirling it around his head.

I dodged, and heard a heavy thud and a kind of a sigh from Bill, like a horse gives out when you take his saddle off. A niggerhead rock the size of an egg had caught Bill just behind his left ear. He loosened himself all over and fell in the fire across the frying pan of hot water for washing the dishes. I dragged him out and poured cold water on his head for half an hour.

By and by, Bill sits up and feels behind his ear and says: "Sam, do you know who my favorite Biblical character is?"

"Take it easy," says I. "You'll come to your senses presently."

"King Herod," says he. "You won't go away and leave me here alone, will you, Sam?"

I went out and caught that boy and shook him until his freckles rattled.

"If you don't behave," says I, "I'll take you straight home. Now, are you going to be good, or not?"

"I was only funning," says he sullenly. "I didn't mean to hurt Old Hank. But what did he hit me for? I'll behave, Snake-eye, if you won't send me home, and if you'll let me play the Black Scout today."

"I don't know the game," says I. "That's for you and Mr. Bill to decide. He's your playmate for the day. I'm going away for a while, on business. Now, you come in and make friends with him and say you are sorry for hurting him, or home you go, at once."

I made him and Bill shake hands, and then I took Bill aside and told him I was going to Poplar Grove, a little village three miles from the cave, and find out what I could about how the kidnapping had been regarded in Summit. Also, I thought it best to send a peremptory letter to old man Dorset that day, demanding the ransom and dictating how it should be paid.

"You know, Sam," says Bill, "I've stood by you without batting an eye in earthquakes, fire and flood—in poker games, dynamite outrages, police raids, train robberies, and cyclones. I never lost my nerve yet till we kidnapped that two-legged skyrocket of a kid. He's got me going. You won't leave me long with him, will you, Sam?"

"I'll be back some time this afternoon," says I. "You must keep the boy amused and quiet till I return. And now we'll write the letter to old Dorset."

Bill and I got paper and pencil and worked on the letter while Red Chief, with a blanket wrapped around him, strutted up and down, guarding the mouth of the cave. Bill begged me tearfully to make the ransom fifteen hundred dollars instead of two thousand. "I ain't attempting," says he, "to decry the celebrated moral aspect of parental affection, but we're dealing with humans, and it ain't human for anybody to give up two thousand dollars for that forty-pound chunk of freckled wildcat. I'm willing to take a chance at fifteen hundred dollars. You can charge the difference up to me."

So, to relieve Bill, I acceded, and we collaborated a letter that ran this way:

Ebenezer Dorset, Esq.:

We have your boy concealed in a place far from Summit. It is useless for you or the most skilful detectives to attempt to find him. Absolutely, the only terms on which you can have him restored to you are these: We demand fifteen hundred dollars in large bills for his return: the money to be left at midnight tonight at the same spot and in the same box as your reply—as hereinafter described. If you agree to these terms, send your answer in writing by a solitary messenger tonight at half-past eight o'clock. After crossing Owl Creek on the road to Poplar Grove the fence of the wheat field on the right-hand side. At the bottom of the fence-post, opposite the third tree, will be found a small pasteboard box.

The messenger will place the answer in this box and return immediately to Summit.

If you attempt any treachery or fail to comply with our demand as stated, you will never see your boy again.

If you pay the money as demanded, he will be returned to you safe and well within three hours. These terms are final, and if you do not accede to them no further communication will be attempted.

                                                        *Two Desperate Men*

I addressed this letter to Dorset, and put it in my pocket. As I was about to start, the kid comes up to me and says:

"Aw, Snake-eye, you said I could play the Black Scout while you was gone."

"Play it, of course," says I. "Mr. Bill will play with you. What kind of a game is it?"

"I'm the Black Scout," says Red Chief, "and I have to ride to the stockade to warn the settlers that the Indians are coming. I'm tired of playing Indian myself. I want to be the Black Scout."

"All right," says I. "It sounds harmless to me. I guess Mr. Bill will help you foil the pesky savages."

"What am I to do?" asks Bill, looking at the kid suspiciously.

"You are the hoss," says Black Scout. "Get down on your hands and knees. How can I ride to the stockade without a hoss?"

"You'd better keep him interested," said I, "till we get the scheme going. Loosen up."

Bill gets down on his all fours, and a look comes in his eye like a rabbit's when you catch it in a trap.

"How far is it to the stockade, kid?" he asks, in a husky manner of voice.

"Ninety miles," says the Black Scout. "And you have to hump yourself to get there on time. Whoa, now!"

The Black Scout jumps on Bill's back and digs his heels in his side.

"For Heaven's sake," says Bill, "hurry back, Sam, as soon as you can. I wish we hadn't made the ransom more than a thousand. Say, you quit kicking me or I'll get up and warm you good."

I walked over to Poplar Grove and sat around the post-office and store, talking with the chaw-bacons that came in to trade. One whiskerando says that he hears Summit is all upset on account of Elder Ebenezer Dorset's boy having been lost or stolen. That was all I wanted to know. I bought some smoking tobacco, referred casually to the price of black-eyed peas, posted my letter surreptitiously, and came away. The post-master said the mail-carrier would come by in an hour to take the mail to Summit.

When I got back to the cave Bill and the boy were not to be found. I explored the vicinity of the cave, and risked a yodel or two, but there was no response.

So I lighted my pipe and sat down on a mossy bank to await developments.

In about half an hour I heard the bushes rustle, and Bill wabbled out into the little glade in front of the cave. Behind him was the kid, stepping softly like a scout, with a broad grin on his face.

Bill stopped, took off his hat, and wiped his face with a red handkerchief. The kid stopped about eight feet behind him.

"Sam," says Bill, "I suppose you'll think I'm a renegade, but I couldn't help it. I'm a grown person with masculine proclivities and habits of self-defense, but there is a time when all systems of egotism and predominance fail. The boy is gone. I have sent him home. All is off. There was martyrs in old times," goes on Bill, "that suffered death rather than give up the particular graft they enjoyed. None of 'em ever was subjugated to such supernatural tortures as I have been. I tried to be faithful to our articles of depredation; but there came a limit."

"What's the trouble, Bill?" I asks him.

"I was rode," says Bill, "the ninety miles to the stockade, not barring an inch. Then, when the settlers was rescued, I was given oats. Sand ain't a palatable substitute. And then, for an hour I had to try to explain to him why there was nothin' in holes, how a road can run both ways, and what makes the grass green. I tell you, Sam, a human can only stand so much. I takes him by the neck of his clothes and drags him down the mountain. On the way he kicks my legs black and blue from the knees down; and I've got to have two or three bites on my thumb and hand cauterized.

"But he's gone"—continues Bill—"gone home. I showed him the road to Summit and kicked him about eight feet nearer there at one kick. I'm sorry we lose the ransom; but it was either that or Bill Driscoll to the madhouse."

Bill is puffing and blowing, but there is a look of ineffable peace and growing content on his rose-pink features.

"Bill," says I, "there isn't any heart disease in your family, is there?"

"No," says Bill, "nothing chronic except malaria and accidents. Why?"

"Then you might turn around," says I, "and have a look behind you."

Bill turns and sees the boy, and loses his complexion and sits down plump on the ground and begins to pluck aimlessly at grass and little sticks. For an hour I was afraid of his mind. And then I told him that my scheme was to put the whole job through immediately and that we would get the ransom and be off with it by midnight if old Dorset fell in with our proposition. So Bill braced up enough to give the kid a weak sort of a smile and a promise to play the Russian in a Japanese war with him as soon as he felt a little better.

I had a scheme for collecting that ransom without danger of being caught by counterplots that ought to commend itself to professional kidnappers. The tree under which the answer was to be left—and the money later on—was close to the road fence with big, bare fields on all sides. If a gang of constables should be watching for anyone to come for the note, they could see him a long way off crossing the fields or in the road. But no, sirree! At half-past eight I was up in that tree as well hidden as a tree toad, waiting for the messenger to arrive.

Exactly on time, a half-grown boy rides up the road on a bicycle, locates the pasteboard box at the foot of the fence-post, slips a folded piece of paper into it, and pedals away again back toward Summit.

I waited an hour and then concluded the thing was square. I slid down the tree, got the note, slipped along the fence till I struck the woods, and was back at the cave in another half an hour. I opened the note, got near the lantern, and read it to Bill. It was written with a pen in a crabbed hand, and the sum and substance of it was this:

Two Desperate Men:

   Gentlemen: I received your letter today by post, in regard to the ransom you ask for the return of my son. I think you are a little high in your demands, and I hereby make you a counter-proposition, which I am inclined to believe you will accept. You bring Johnny home and pay me two hundred and fifty dollars in cash, and I agree to take him off your hands. You had better come at night, for the neighbors believe he is lost, and I couldn't be responsible for what they would do to anybody they saw bringing him back.

Very respectfully,
*Ebenezer Dorset*

"Great pirates of Penzance," says I; "of all the impudent—"

But I glanced at Bill, and hesitated. He had the most appealing look in his eyes I ever saw on the face of a dumb or a talking brute.

"Sam," says he, "what's two hundred and fifty dollars, after all? We've got the money. One more night of this kid will send me to a bed in Bedlam. Besides being a thorough gentleman, I think Mr. Dorset is a spendthrift for making us such a liberal offer. You ain't going to let the chance go, are you?"

"Tell you the truth, Bill," says I, "this little he ewe lamb has somewhat got on my nerves too. We'll take him home, pay the ransom, and make our getaway."

We took him home that night. We got him to go by telling him that his father had bought a silver-mounted rifle and a pair of moccasins for him, and we were going to hunt bears the next day.

It was just twelve o'clock when we knocked at Ebenezer's front door. Just at the moment when I should have been abstracting the fifteen hundred dollars from the box under the tree, according to the original proposition, Bill was counting out two hundred and fifty dollars into Dorset's hand.

When the kid found out we were going to leave him at home he started up a howl like a calliope and fastened himself as tight as a leech to Bill's leg. His father peeled him away gradually, like a porous plaster.

"How long can you hold him?" asks Bill.

"I'm not as strong as I used to be," says old Dorset, "but I think I can promise you ten minutes."

"Enough," says Bill. "In ten minutes I shall cross the Central, Southern and Middle Western States, and be legging it trippingly for the Canadian border."

And, as dark as it was, and as fat as Bill was, and as good a runner as I am, he was a good mile and a half out of Summit before I could catch up with him.

# MASTERS OF ARTS

## O. Henry

A TWO-INCH STUB of a blue pencil was the wand with which Keogh performed the preliminary acts of his magic. So, with this he covered paper with diagrams and figures while he waited for the United States of America to send down to Coralio a successor to Atwood, resigned.

The new scheme that his mind had conceived, his stout heart indorsed, and his blue pencil corroborated, was laid around the characteristics and human frailties of the new president of Anchuria. These characteristics, and the situation out of which Keogh hoped to wrest a golden tribute, deserve chronicling contributive to the clear order of events.

President Losada—many called him Dictator—was a man whose genius would have made him conspicuous even among Anglo-Saxons, had not that genius been intermixed with other traits that were petty and subversive. He had some of the lofty patriotism of Washington (the man he most admired), the force of Napoleon, and much of the wisdom of the sages. These characteristics might have justified him in the assumption of the title of "The Illustrious Liberator," had they not been accompanied by a stupendous and amazing vanity that kept him in the less worthy ranks of the dictators.

Yet he did his country great service. With a mighty grasp he shook it nearly free from the shackles of ignorance and sloth and the vermin that fed upon it, and all but made it a power in the council of nations. He established schools and hospitals, built roads, bridges, railroads and palaces, and bestowed generous subsidies upon the arts and sciences. He was the absolute despot and the idol of his people. The wealth of the country poured into his hands. Other presidents had

575

been rapacious without reason. Losada amassed enormous wealth, but his people had their share of the benefits.

The joint in his armour was his insatiate passion for monuments and tokens commemorating his glory. In every town he caused to be erected statues of himself bearing legends in praise of his greatness. In the walls of every public edifice, tablets were fixed reciting his splendour and the gratitude of his subjects. His statuettes and portraits were scattered throughout the land in every house and hut. One of the sycophants in his court painted him as St. John, with a halo and a train of attendants in full uniform. Losada saw nothing incongruous in this picture, and had it hung in a church in the capital. He ordered from a French sculptor a marble group including himself with Napoleon, Alexander the Great, and one or two others whom he deemed worthy of the honour.

He ransacked Europe for decorations, employing policy, money and intrigue to cajole the orders he coveted from kings and rulers. On state occasions his breast was covered from shoulder to shoulder with crosses, stars, golden roses, medals and ribbons. It was said that the man who could contrive for him a new decoration, or invent some new method of extolling his greatness, might plunge a hand deep into the treasury.

This was the man upon whom Billy Keogh had his eye. The gentle buccaneer had observed the rain of favours that fell upon those who ministered to the president's vanities, and he did not deem it his duty to hoist his umbrella against the scattering drops of liquid fortune.

In a few weeks the new consul arrived, releasing Keogh from his temporary duties. He was a young man fresh from college, who lived for botany alone. The consulate at Coralio gave him the opportunity to study tropical flora. He wore smoked glasses, and carried a green umbrella. He filled the cool, back porch of the consulate with plants and specimens so that space for a bottle and chair was not to be found. Keogh gazed on him sadly, but without rancour, and began to pack his gripsack. For his new plot against stagnation along the Spanish Main required of him a voyage overseas.

Soon came the *Karlsefin* again—she of the trampish habits—gleaning a cargo of cocoanuts for a speculative descent upon the New York market. Keogh was booked for a passage on the return trip.

"Yes, I'm going to New York," he explained to the group of his countrymen that had gathered on the beach to see him off. "But I'll be back before you miss me. I've undertaken the art education of this piebald country, and I'm not the man to desert it while it's in the early throes of tintypes."

With this mysterious declaration of his intentions Keogh boarded the *Karlsefin*.

Ten days later, shivering, with the collar of his thin coat turned high, he burst into the studio of Carolus White at the top of a tall building in Tenth Street, New York City.

Carolus White was smoking a cigarette and frying sausages over an oil stove. He was only twenty-three, and had noble theories about art.

"Billy Keogh!" exclaimed White, extending the hand that was not busy with the frying pan. "From what part of the uncivilized world, I wonder!"

"Hello, Carry," said Keogh, dragging forward a stool, and holding his fingers close to the stove. "I'm glad I found you so soon. I've been looking for you all day in the directories and art galleries. The free-lunch man on the corner told me where you were, quick. I was sure you'd be painting pictures yet."

Keogh glanced about the studio with the shrewd eye of a connoisseur in business.

"Yes, you can do it," he declared, with many gentle nods of his head. "That big one in the corner with the angels and green clouds and band-wagon is just the sort of thing we want. What would you call that, Carry—scene from Coney Island, ain't it?"

"That," said White, "I had intended to call 'The Translation of Elijah,' but you may be nearer right than I am."

"Name doesn't matter," said Keogh, largely; "it's the frame and the varieties of paint that does the trick. Now, I can tell you in a minute what I want. I've come on a little voyage of two thousand miles to take you in with me on a scheme. I thought of you as soon as the scheme showed itself to me. How would you like to go back with me and paint a picture? Ninety days for the trip, and five thousand dollars for the job."

"Cereal food or hair-tonic posters?" asked White.

"It isn't an ad."

"What kind of a picture is it to be?"

"It's a long story," said Keogh.

"Go ahead with it. If you don't mind, while you talk I'll just keep my eye on these sausages. Let 'em get one shade deeper than a Vandyke brown and you spoil 'em."

Keogh explained his project. They were to return to Coralio, where White was to pose as a distinguished American portrait painter who was touring in the tropics as a relaxation from his arduous and remunerative professional labours. It was not an unreasonable hope, even to those who trod in the beaten paths of business, that an artist with so much prestige might secure a commission to perpetuate upon canvas the lineaments of the president, and secure a share of the *pesos* that were raining upon the caterers to his weaknesses.

Keogh had set his price at ten thousand dollars. Artists had been paid more for portraits. He and White were to share the expenses of the trip, and divide the possible profits. Thus he laid the scheme before White, whom he had known in the West before one declared for Art and the other became a Bedouin.

Before long the two machinators abandoned the rigour of the bare studio for a snug corner of a café. There they sat far into the night, with old envelopes and Keogh's stub of blue pencil between them.

At twelve o'clock White doubled up in his chair, with his chin on his fist, and shut his eyes at the unbeautiful wallpaper.

"I'll go you, Billy," he said, in the quiet tones of decision. "I've got two or three hundred saved up for sausages and rent; and I'll take the chance with you. Five thousand! It will give me two years in Paris and one in Italy. I'll begin to pack tomorrow."

"You'll begin in ten minutes," said Keogh. "It's tomorrow now. The *Karlsefin* starts back at four P.M. Come on to your painting shop, and I'll help you."

For five months in the year Coralio is the Newport of Anchuria. Then only does the town possess life. From November to March it is practically the seat of government. The president with his official family sojourns there; and society follows him. The pleasure-loving people make the season one long holiday of amusement and rejoicing. *Fiestas,* balls, games, sea bathing, processions and small theatres contribute to their enjoyment. The famous Swiss band from the capital plays in the little plaza every evening, while the fourteen carriages and vehicles in the town circle in funereal but complacent procession. Indians from the interior mountains, looking like prehistoric stone idols, come down to peddle their handiwork in the streets. The people throng the narrow ways, a chattering, happy, careless stream of buoyant humanity. Preposterous children rigged out with the shortest of ballet skirts and gilt wings, howl, underfoot, among the effervescent crowds. Especially is the arrival of the presidential party, at the opening of the season, attended with pomp, show and patriotic demonstrations of enthusiasm and delight.

When Keogh and White reached their destination, on the return trip of the *Karlsefin,* the gay winter season was well begun. As they stepped upon the beach they could hear the band playing in the plaza. The village maidens, with fireflies already fixed in their dark locks, were gliding, barefoot and coy-eyed, along the paths. Dandies in white linen, swinging their canes, were beginning their seductive strolls. The air was full of human essence, of artificial enticement, of coquetry, indolence, pleasure—the man-made sense of existence.

The first two or three days after their arrival were spent in preliminaries. Keogh escorted the artist about town, introducing him to the little circle of English-speaking residents and pulling whatever wires he could to effect the spreading of White's fame as a painter. And then Keogh planned a more spectacular demonstration of the idea he wished to keep before the public.

He and White engaged rooms in the Hotel de los Estranjeros. The two were clad in new suits of immaculate duck, with American straw hats, and carried canes of remarkable uniqueness and inutility. Few caballeros in Coralio—even the gorgeously uniformed officers of the Anchurian army—were as conspicuous for ease and elegance of demeanour as Keogh and his friend, the great American painter, Señor White.

White set up his easel on the beach and made striking sketches of the mountain and sea views. The native population formed at his rear in a vast, chattering semicircle to watch his work. Keogh, with his care for details, had arranged for himself a pose which he carried out with fidelity. His role was that of friend to the great artist, a man of affairs and leisure. The visible emblem of his position was a pocket camera.

"For branding the man who owns it," said he, "a genteel dilettante with a bank account and an easy conscience, a steam-yacht ain't in it with a camera. You see a man doing nothing but loafing around making snap-shots, and you know right away he reads up well in 'Bradstreet.' You notice these old millionaire boys—soon as they get through taking everything else in sight they go to taking photographs. People are more impressed by a kodak than they are by a title or a four-carat scarf-pin." So Keogh strolled blandly about Coralio, snapping the scenery and the shrinking señoritas, while White posed conspicuously in the higher regions of art.

Two weeks after their arrival, the scheme began to bear fruit. An aide-de-camp of the president drove to the hotel in a dashing victoria.

The president desired that Señor White come to the Casa Morena for an informal interview.

Keogh gripped his pipe tightly between his teeth. "Not a cent less than ten thousand," he said to the artist—"remember the price. And in gold or its equivalent—don't let him stick you with this bargain-counter stuff they call money here."

"Perhaps it isn't that he wants," said White.

"Get out!" said Keogh, with splendid confidence. "I know what he wants. He wants his picture painted by the celebrated young American painter and filibuster now sojourning in his down-trodden country. Off you go."

The victoria sped away with the artist. Keogh walked up and down, puffing great clouds of smoke from his pipe, and waited. In an hour the victoria swept again to the door of the hotel, deposited White, and vanished. The artist dashed up the stairs, three at a step. Keogh stopped smoking, and became a silent interrogation point.

"Landed," exclaimed White, with his boyish face flushed with elation. "Billy, you are a wonder. He wants a picture. I'll tell you all about it. By Heavens! that dictator chap is a corker! He's a dictator clear down to his finger-ends. He's a kind of combination of Julius Cæsar, Lucifer and Chauncey Depew done in sepia. Polite and grim—that's his way. The room I saw him in was about ten acres big, and looked like a Mississippi steamboat with its gilding and mirrors and white paint. He talks English better than I can ever hope to. The matter of the price came up. I mentioned ten thousand. I expected him to call the guard and have me taken out and shot. He didn't move an eyelash. He just waved one of his chestnut hands in a careless way, and said, 'Whatever you say.' I am to go back tomorrow and discuss with him the details of the picture."

Keogh hung his head. Self-abasement was easy to read in his downcast countenance.

"I'm failing, Carry," he said, sorrowfully. "I'm not fit to handle these man's-size schemes any longer. Peddling oranges in a push-cart is about the suitable graft for me. When I said ten thousand, I swear I thought I had sized up that brown man's limit to within two cents. He'd have melted down for fifteen thousand just as easy. Say— Carry—you'll see old man Keogh safe in some nice, quiet idiot asylum, won't you, if he makes a break like that again?"

The Casa Morena, although only one story in height, was a building of brown stone, luxurious as a palace in its interior. It stood on a low hill in a walled garden of splendid tropical flora at the upper edge of Coralio. The next day the president's carriage came again for the artist. Keogh went out for a walk along the beach, where he and his "picture box" were now familiar sights. When he returned to the hotel White was sitting in a steamer-chair on the balcony.

"Well," said Keogh, "did you and His Nibs decide on the kind of a chromo he wants?"

White got up and walked back and forth on the balcony a few times. Then he stopped, and laughed strangely. His face was flushed, and his eyes were bright with a kind of angry amusement.

"Look here, Billy," he said, somewhat roughly, "when you first came to me in my studio and mentioned a picture, I thought you wanted a Smashed Oats or a Hair Tonic poster painted on a range of mountains or the side of a continent. Well, either of those jobs would have been Art in its highest form compared to the one you've steered me against. I can't paint that picture, Billy. You've got to let me out. Let me try to tell you what that barbarian wants. He had it all planned out and even a sketch made of his idea. The old boy doesn't draw badly at all. But, ye goddesses of Art! listen to the monstrosity he expects me to paint. He wants himself in the centre of the canvas, of course. He is to be painted as Jupiter sitting on Olympus, with the clouds at his feet. At one side of him stands George Washington, in full regimentals, with his hand on the president's shoulder. An angel with outstretched wings hovers overhead, and is placing a laurel wreath on the president's head, crowning him—Queen of the May, I suppose. In the background is to be cannon, more angels and soldiers. The man who would paint that picture would have to have the soul of a dog, and would deserve to go down into oblivion without even a tin can tied to his tail to sound his memory."

Little beads of moisture crept out all over Billy Keogh's brow. The stub of his blue pencil had not figured out a contingency like this. The machinery of his plan had run with flattering smoothness until now. He dragged another chair upon the balcony, and got White back to his seat. He lit his pipe with apparent calm.

"Now, sonny," he said, with gentle grimness, "you and me will have an Art to Art talk. You've got your art and I've got mine. Yours is the real Pierian stuff that turns up its nose at bock-beer signs and oleographs of the Old Mill. Mine's the art of Business. This was my scheme, and it worked out like two-and-two. Paint that president man as Old King Cole, or Venus, or a landscape, or a fresco, or a bunch of lilies, or anything he thinks he looks like. But get the paint on the canvas and collect the spoils. You wouldn't throw me down, Carry, at this stage of the game. Think of that ten thousand."

"I can't help thinking of it," said White, "and that's what hurts. I'm tempted to throw every ideal I ever had down in the mire, and steep my soul in infamy by painting that picture. That five thousand meant three years of foreign study to me, and I'd almost sell my soul for that."

"Now it ain't as bad as that," said Keogh, soothingly. "It's a business proposition. It's so much paint and time against money. I don't fall in with your idea that that picture would so everlastingly jolt the art side of the question. George Washington was all right, you know, and nobody could say a word against the angel. I don't think so bad of that group. If you was to give Jupiter a pair of epaulets and a sword, and kind of work the clouds around to look like a blackberry patch, it wouldn't make such a bad battle scene. Why, if we hadn't already settled on the price, he ought to pay an extra thousand for Washington, and the angel ought to raise it five hundred."

"You don't understand, Billy," said White, with an uneasy laugh. "Some of us fellows who try to paint have big notions about Art. I wanted to paint a picture some day that people would stand before and forget that it was made of paint. I wanted it to creep into them like a bar of music and mushroom there like a soft bullet. And I wanted 'em to go away and ask, 'What else has he done?' And I didn't want 'em to find a thing; not a portrait nor a magazine cover nor an illustration nor a drawing of a girl—nothing but *the* picture. That's why I've lived on fried sausages, and tried to keep true to myself. I persuaded myself to do this portrait for the chance it might give me to study abroad. But this howling, screaming caricature! Good Lord! can't you see how it is?"

"Sure," said Keogh, as tenderly as he would have spoken to a child, and he laid a long forefinger on White's knee. "I see. It's bad to have your art all slugged up like that. I know. You wanted to paint a big thing like the panorama of the battle of Gettysburg. But let me kalsomine you a little mental sketch to consider. Up to date we're out $385.50 on this scheme. Our capital took every cent both of us could raise. We've got about enough left to get back to New York on. I need my share of that ten thousand. I want to work a copper deal in Idaho, and make a hundred thousand. That's the business end of the thing. Come down off your art perch, Carry, and let's land that hatful of dollars."

"Billy," said White, with an effort, "I'll try. I won't say I'll do it, but I'll try. I'll go at it, and put it through if I can."

"That's business," said Keogh, heartily. "Good boy! Now, here's another thing—rush that picture—crowd it through as quick as you can. Get a couple of boys to help you mix the paint if necessary. I've picked up some pointers around town. The people here are beginning to get sick of Mr. President. They say he's been too free with concessions; and they accuse him of trying to make a dicker with England to sell out the country. We want that picture done and paid for before there's any row."

In the great patio of Casa Morena, the president caused to be stretched a huge canvas. Under this White set up his temporary studio. For two hours each day the great man sat to him.

White worked faithfully. But, as the work progressed, he had seasons of bitter scorn, of infinite self-contempt, of sullen gloom and sardonic gaiety. Keogh, with the patience of a great general, soothed, coaxed, argued—kept him at the picture.

At the end of a month White announced that the picture was completed—Jupiter, Washington, angels, clouds, cannon and all. His face was pale and his mouth drawn straight when he told Keogh. He said the president was much pleased with it. It was to be hung in the National Gallery of Statesmen and Heroes. The artist had been requested to return to Casa Morena on the following day to receive payment. At the appointed time he left the hotel, silent under his friend's joyful talk of their success.

An hour later he walked into the room where Keogh was waiting, threw his hat on the floor, and sat upon the table.

"Billy," he said, in strained and labouring tones, "I've a little money out West in a small business that my brother is running. It's what I've been living on while I've been studying art. I'll draw out my share and pay you back what you've lost on this scheme."

"Lost!" exclaimed Keogh, jumping up. "Didn't you get paid for the picture?"

"Yes, I got paid," said White. "But just now there isn't any picture, and there isn't any pay. If you care to hear about it, here are the edifying details. The president and I were looking at the painting. His secretary brought a bank draft on New York for ten thousand dollars and handed it to me. The moment I touched it I went wild. I tore it into little pieces and threw them on the floor. A workman was repainting the pillars inside the *patio*. A bucket of his paint happened to be convenient. I picked up his brush and slapped a quart of blue paint all over that ten-thousand-dollar nightmare. I bowed, and walked out. The president didn't move or speak. That was one time he was taken by surprise. It's tough on you, Billy, but I couldn't help it."

There seemed to be excitement in Coralio. Outside there was a confused, rising murmur pierced by high-pitched cries. "*Bajo el traidor—Muerte el traidor!*"[1] were the words they seemed to form.

"Listen to that!" exclaimed White, bitterly; "I know that much Spanish. They're shouting, 'Down with the traitor!' I heard them before. I felt that they meant me. I was a traitor to Art. The picture had to go."

" 'Down with the blank fool' would have suited your case better," said Keogh, with fiery emphasis. "You tear up ten thousand dollars like an old rag because the way you've spread on five dollars' worth of paint hurts your conscience. Next time I pick a side-partner in a scheme the man has got to go before a notary and swear he never even heard the word 'ideal' mentioned."

Keogh strode from the room, white-hot. White paid little attention to his resentment. The scorn of Billy Keogh seemed a trifling thing beside the greater self-scorn he had escaped.

In Coralio the excitement waxed. An outburst was imminent. The cause of this demonstration of displeasure was the presence in the town of a big, pink-cheeked Englishman, who, it was said, was an agent of his government come to clinch the bargain by which the president placed his people in the hands of a foreign power. It was charged that not only had he given away priceless concessions, but that the public debt was to be transferred into the hands of the English, and the custom-houses turned over to them as a guarantee. The long-enduring people had determined to make their protest felt.

On that night, in Coralio and in other towns, their ire found vent. Yelling mobs, mercurial but dangerous, roamed the streets. They overthrew the great bronze statue of the president that stood in the centre of the plaza, and hacked it to shapeless pieces. They tore from public buildings the tablets set there proclaiming the glory of the "Illustrious Liberator." His pictures in the government offices were demolished. The mobs even attacked the Casa Morena, but were driven away by the military, which remained faithful to the executive. All the night terror reigned.

The greatness of Losada was shown by the fact that by noon the next day order was restored, and he was still absolute. He issued proclamations denying positively that any negotiation of any kind

---

[1]  *Bajo . . . traidor;* Spanish: down with the traitor—kill the traitor.

had been entered into with England. Sir Stafford Vaughn, the pink-cheeked Englishman, also declared in placards and in public print that his presence there had no international significance. He was a traveller without guile. In fact (so he stated), he had not even spoken with the president or been in his presence since his arrival.

During this disturbance, White was preparing for his homeward voyage in the steamship that was to sail within two or three days. About noon, Keogh, the restless, took his camera out with the hope of speeding the lagging hours. The town was now as quiet as if peace had never departed from her perch on the red-tiled roofs.

About the middle of the afternoon, Keogh hurried back to the hotel with something decidedly special in his air. He retired to the little room where he developed his pictures.

Later on he came out to White on the balcony, with a luminous, grim, predatory smile on his face.

"Do you know what that is?" he asked, holding up a 4 × 5 photograph mounted on cardboard.

"Snap-shot of a señorita sitting in the sand—alliteration unintentional," guessed White, lazily.

"Wrong," said Keogh with shining eyes. "It's a slung-shot. It's a can of dynamite. It's a gold mine. It's a sight-draft on your president man for twenty thousand dollars—yes, sir—twenty thousand this time, and no spoiling the picture. No ethics of art in the way. Art! You with your smelly little tubes! I've got you skinned to death with a kodak. Take a look at that."

White took the picture in his hand, and gave a long whistle.

"Jove!" he exclaimed, "but wouldn't that stir up a row in town if you let it be seen. How in the world did you get it, Billy?"

"You know that high wall around the president man's back garden? I was up there trying to get a bird's-eye of the town. I happened to notice a chink in the wall where a stone and a lot of plaster had slid out. Thinks I, I'll take a peep through to see how Mr. President's cabbages are growing. The first thing I saw was him and this Sir Englishman sitting at a little table about twenty feet away. They had the table all spread over with documents, and they were hobnobbing over them as thick as two pirates. 'Twas a nice corner of the garden, all private and shady with palms and orange trees, and they had a pail of champagne set by handy in the grass. I knew then was the time for me to make my big hit in Art. So I raised the machine up to the crack, and pressed the button. Just as I did so them old boys shook hands on the deal—you see they took that way in the picture."

Keogh put on his coat and hat.

"What are you going to do with it?" asked White.

"Me," said Keogh in a hurt tone, "why, I'm going to tie a pink ribbon to it and hang it on the what-not, of course. I'm surprised at you. But while I'm out you just try to figure out what gingercake potentate would be most likely to want to buy this work of art for his private collection—just to keep it out of circulation."

The sunset was reddening the tops of the cocoanut palms when Billy Keogh came back from Casa Morena. He nodded to the artist's questioning gaze; and lay down on a cot with his hands under the back of his head.

"I saw him. He paid the money like a little man. They didn't want to let me in at first. I told 'em it was important. Yes, that president man is on the plenty-able list. He's got a beautiful business system about the way he uses his brains. All I had to do was to hold up the photograph so he could see it, and name the price. He just smiled, and walked over to a safe and got the cash. Twenty one-thousand-dollar brand-new United States Treasury notes he laid on the table, like I'd pay out a dollar and a quarter. Fine notes, too—they crackled with a sound like burning the brush off a ten-acre lot."

"Let's try the feel of one," said White, curiously. "I never saw a thousand-dollar bill." Keogh did not immediately respond.

"Carry," he said, in an absent-minded way, "you think a heap of your art, don't you?"

"More," said White, frankly, "than has been for the financial good of myself and my friends."

"I thought you were a fool the other day," went on Keogh, quietly, "and I'm not sure now that you wasn't. But if you was, so am I. I've been in some funny deals, Carry, but I've always managed to scramble fair, and match my brains and capital against the other fellow's. But when it comes to—well, when you've got the other fellow cinched, and the screws on him, and he's got to put up—why, it don't strike me as being a man's game. They've got a name for it, you know; it's—confound you, don't you understand. A fellow feels—it's something like that blamed art of yours—he—well, I tore that photograph up and laid the pieces on that stack of money and shoved the whole business back across the table. 'Excuse me, Mr. Losada,' I said, 'but I guess I've made a mistake in the price. You get the photo for nothing.' Now, Carry, you get out the pencil, and we'll do some more figuring. I'd like to save enough out of our capital for you to have some fried sausages in your joint when you get back to New York."

# A MUNICIPAL REPORT

## O. Henry

The cities are full of pride,
    Challenging each to each—
This from her mountainside,
    That from her burthened beach.

R. KIPLING

Fancy a novel about Chicago or Buffalo, let us say, of Nashville, Tennessee! There are just three big cities in the United States that are "story cities"—New York, of course, New Orleans, and, best of the lot, San Francisco.

—FRANK NORRIS

EAST IS EAST, and West is San Francisco, according to Californians. Californians are a race of people; they are not merely inhabitants of a State. They are the Southerners of the West. Now, Chicagoans are no less loyal to their city; but when you ask them why, they stammer and speak of lake fish and the new Odd Fellows Building. But Californians go into detail.

Of course they have, in the climate, an argument that is good for half an hour while you are thinking of your coal bills and heavy under-wear. But as soon as they come to mistake your silence for conviction, madness comes upon them, and they picture the city of the Golden Gate as the Bagdad of the New World. So far, as a matter of opinion, no refutation is necessary. But dear cousins all (from Adam and Eve descended), it is a rash one who will lay his finger on the map and say: "In this town there can be no romance—what could happen here?" Yes, it is a bold and a rash deed to challenge in one sentence history, romance, and Rand and McNally.

NASHVILLE.—A city, port of delivery, and the capital of the State of Tennessee, is on the Cumberland River and on the N. C. & St. L. and the L. & N. railroads. This city is regarded as the most important educational centre in the South.

I stepped off the train at 8 P.M. Having searched the thesaurus in vain for adjectives, I must, as a substitution, hie me to comparison in the form of a recipe.

Take a London fog 30 parts; malaria 10 parts; gas leaks 20 parts; dewdrops gathered in a brick yard at sunrise, 25 parts; odor of honeysuckle 15 parts. Mix.

The mixture will give you an approximate conception of a Nashville drizzle. It is not so fragrant as a moth-ball nor as thick as pea-soup; but 'tis enough—'twill serve.

I went to a hotel in a tumbril. It required strong self-suppression for me to keep from climbing to the top of it and giving an imitation of Sidney Carton. The vehicle was drawn by beasts of a bygone era and driven by something dark and emancipated.

I was sleepy and tired, so when I got to the hotel I hurriedly paid it the fifty cents it demanded (with approximate lagniappe, I assure you). I knew its habits; and I did not want to hear it prate about its old "marster" or anything that happened "befo' de wah."

The hotel was one of the kind described as "renovated." That means $20,000 worth of new marble pillars, tiling, electric lights and brass cuspidors in the lobby, and a new L. & N. time table and a lithograph of Lookout Mountain in each one of the great rooms above. The management was without reproach, the attention full of exquisite Southern courtesy, the service as slow as the progress of a snail and as good-humored as Rip Van Winkle. The food was worth traveling a thousand miles for. There is no other hotel in the world where you can get such chicken livers *en brochette*.

At dinner I asked a Negro waiter if there was anything doing in town. He pondered gravely for a minute, and then replied: "Well, boss, I don't really reckon there's anything at all doin' after sundown."

Sundown had been accomplished; it had been drowned in the drizzle long before. So that spectacle was denied me. But I went forth upon the streets in the drizzle to see what might be there.

It is built on undulating grounds; and the streets are lighted by electricity at a cost of $32,470 per annum.

As I left the hotel there was a race riot. Down upon me charged a company of freedmen, or Arabs, or Zulus, armed with—no, I saw with relief that they were not rifles, but whips. And I saw dimly a caravan of black, clumsy vehicles; and at the reassuring shouts, "Kyar you anywhere in the town, boss, fuh fifty cents," I reasoned that I was merely a "fare" instead of a victim.

I walked through long streets, all leading uphill. I wondered how those streets ever came down again. Perhaps they didn't until they were "graded." On a few of the "main streets" I saw lights in stores here and there; saw street cars go by conveying worthy burghers hither and yon; saw people pass engaged in the art of conversation, and heard a burst of semi-lively laughter issuing from a soda-water and ice-cream parlor. The streets other than "main" seemed to have enticed upon their borders houses consecrated to peace and domesticity. In many of them lights shone behind discreetly drawn window shades, in a few pianos tinkled orderly and irreproach-able music. There was, indeed, little "doing." I wished I had come before sundown. So I returned to my hotel.

In November, 1864, the Confederate General Hood advanced against Nashville, where he shut up a National force under General Thomas. The latter then sallied forth and defeated the Confederates in a terrible conflict.

All my life I have heard of, admired, and witnessed the fine marksmanship of the South in its peaceful conflicts in the tobacco-chewing regions. But in my hotel a surprise awaited me. There were twelve bright, new, imposing, capacious brass cuspidors in the great lobby, tall enough to be called urns and so wide-mouthed that the crack pitcher of a lady baseball team should have been able to throw a ball into one of them at five paces distant. But, although a terrible battle had raged and was still raging, the enemy had not suffered. Bright, new, imposing, capacious, untouched, they stood. But, shades of Jefferson Brick! the tile floor—the beautiful tile floor! I could not avoid thinking of the battle of Nashville, and trying to draw, as is my foolish habit, some deductions about hereditary marksmanship.

Here I first saw Major (by misplaced courtesy) Wentworth Caswell. I knew him for a type the moment my eyes suffered from the sight of him. A rat has no geographical habitat. My old friend, A. Tennyson, said, as he so well said almost everything:

> Prophet, curse me the blabbing lip,
> And curse me the British vermin, the rat.

Let us regard the word "British" as interchangeable *ad lib*. A rat is a rat.

This man was hunting about the hotel lobby like a starved dog that had forgotten where he had buried a bone. He had a face of great acreage, red, pulpy, and with a kind of sleepy massiveness like that of Buddha. He possessed one single virtue—he was very smoothly shaven. The mark of the beast is not indelible upon a man until he goes about with a stubble. I think that if he had not used his razor that day I would have repulsed his advances, and the criminal calendar of the world would have been spared the addition of one murder.

I happened to be standing within five feet of a cuspidor when Major Caswell opened fire upon it. I had been observant enough to percieve that the attacking force was using Gatlings instead of squirrel rifles, so I sidestepped so promptly that the major seized the opportunity to apologize to a noncombatant. He had the blabbing lip. In four minutes he had become my friend and had dragged me to the bar.

I desire to interpolate here that I am a Southerner. But I am not one by profession or trade. I eschew the string tie, the slouch hat, the Prince Albert, the number of bales of cotton destroyed by Sherman, and plug chewing. When the orchestra plays "Dixie" I do not cheer. I slide a little lower on the leather-cornered seat and, well, order another Würzburger and wish that Longstreet had—but what's the use?

Major Caswell banged the bar with his fist, and the first gun at Fort Sumter re-echoed. When he fired the last one at Appomattox I began to hope. But then he began on family trees, and demonstrated that Adam was only a third cousin of a collateral branch of the Caswell family. Genealogy disposed of, he took up, to my distaste, his private family matters. He spoke of his wife, traced her descent back to Eve, and profanely denied any possible rumor that she may have had relations in the land of Nod.

By this time I began to suspect that he was trying to obscure by noise the fact that he had ordered the drinks, on the chance that I would be bewildered into paying for them. But when they were down he crashed a silver dollar loudly upon the bar. Then, of course, another serving was obligatory. And when I had paid for that I took leave of him brusquely; for I wanted no more of him. But before I had obtained my release he had prated loudly of an income that his wife received, and showed a handful of silver money.

When I got my key at the desk the clerk said to me courteously: "If that man Caswell has annoyed you, and if you would like to make a complaint, we will have him ejected. He is a nuisance, a loafer, and without any known means of support, although he seems to have some money most the time. But we don't seem to be able to hit upon any means of throwing him out legally."

"Why, no," said I, after some reflection; "I don't see my way clear to making a complaint. But I would like to place myself on record as asserting that I do not care for his company. Your town," I continued, "seems to be a quiet one. What manner of entertainment, adventure, or excitement, have you to offer to the stranger within your gates?"

"Well, sir," said the clerk, "there will be a show here next Thursday. It is—I'll look it up and have the announcement sent up to your room with the ice water. Good-night."

After I went up to my room I looked out the window. It was only about ten o'clock, but I looked upon a silent town. The drizzle continued, spangled with dim lights, as far apart as currants in a cake sold at the Ladies' Exchange.

"A quiet place," I said to myself, as my first shoe struck the ceiling of the occupant of the room beneath mine. "Nothing of the life here that gives color and good variety to the cities in the East and West. Just a good, ordinary, humdrum, business town."

Nashville occupies a foremost place among the manufacturing centres of the country. It is the fifth boot and shoe market in the United States, the largest candy and cracker manufacturing city in the South, and does an enormous wholesale drygoods, grocery, and drug business.

I must tell you how I came to be in Nashville, and I assure you the digression brings as much tedium to me as it does to you. I was traveling elsewhere on my own business, but I had a commission from a Northern literary magazine to stop over there and establish a personal connection between the publication and one of its contributors, Azalea Adair.

Adair (there was no clue to the personality except the handwriting) had sent in some essays (lost art!) and poems that had made the editors

swear approvingly over their one o'clock luncheon. So they had
commissioned me to round up said Adair and corner by contract his
or her output at two cents a word before some other publisher offered
her ten or twenty.

At nine o'clock the next morning, after my chicken livers *en
brochette*[1] (try them if you can find that hotel), I strayed out into the
drizzle, which was still on for an unlimited run. At the first corner I
came upon Uncle Cæsar. He was a stalwart Negro, older than the
pyramids, with gray wool and a face that reminded me of Brutus,
and a second afterwards of the late King Cettiwayo. He wore the
most remarkable coat that I ever had seen or expect to see. It reached
to his ankles and had once been a Confederate gray in colors. But
rain and sun and age had so variegated it that Joseph's coat, beside
it, would have faded to a pale monochrome. I must linger with that
coat, for it has to do with the story—the story that is so long in
coming, because you can hardly expect anything to happen
in Nashville.

Once it must have been the military coat of an officer. The cape
of it had vanished, but all adown its front it had been frogged and
tasseled magnificently. But now the frogs and tassels were gone. In
their stead had been patiently stitched (I surmised by some surviving
"black mammy") new frogs made of cunningly twisted common
hempen twine. This twine was frayed and disheveled. It must have
been added to the coat as a substitute for vanished splendors, with
tasteless but painstaking devotion, for it followed faithfully the
curves of the long-missing frogs. And, to complete the comedy and
pathos of the garment, all its buttons were gone save one. The
second button from the top alone remained. The coat was fastened
by other twine strings tied through the buttonholes and other holes
rudely pierced in the opposite side. There was never such a weird
garment so fantastically bedecked and of so many mottled hues.
The lone button was the size of a half-dollar, made of yellow horn
and sewed on with coarse twine.

This Negro stood by a carriage so old that Ham himself might
have started a hack line with it after he left the ark with the two
animals hitched to it. As I approached he threw open the door, drew
out a feather duster, waved it without using it, and said in deep,
rumbling tones:

---

[1] *en brochette*; French: on a skewer.

"Step right in, suh; ain't a speck of dust in it—jus' got back from a funeral, suh."

I inferred that on such gala occasions carriages were given an extra cleaning. I looked up and down the street and perceived that there was little choice among the vehicles for hire that lined the curb. I looked in my memorandum book for the address of Azalea Adair.

"I want to go to 861 Jessamine Street," I said, and was about to step into the hack. But for an instant the thick, long, gorilla-like arm of the Negro barred me. On his massive and saturnine face a look of sudden suspicion and enmity flashed for a moment. Then, with quickly returning conviction, he asked, blandishingly: "What are you gwine there for, boss?"

"What is it to you?" I asked, a little sharply.

"Nothin', suh, jus' nothin'. Only it's a lonesome kind of part of town and few folks ever has business out there. Step right in. The seats is clean—jes' got back from a funeral, suh."

A mile and a half it must have been to our journey's end. I could hear nothing but the fearful rattle of the ancient hack over the uneven brick paving; I could smell nothing but the drizzle, now further flavored with coal smoke and something like a mixture of tar and oleander blossoms. All I could see through the streaming windows were two rows of dim houses.

The city has an area of 10 square miles; 181 miles of streets, of which 137 miles are paved; a system of waterworks that cost $2,000,000, with 77 miles of mains.

Eight-sixty-one Jessamine Street was a decayed mansion. Thirty yards back from the street it stood, outmerged in a splendid grove of trees and untrimmed shrubbery. A row of box bushes overflowed and almost hid the paling fence from sight; the gate was kept closed by a rope noose that encircled the gate post and the first paling of the gate. But when you got inside you saw that 861 was a shell, a shadow, a ghost of former grandeur and excellence. But in the story, I have not yet got inside.

When the hack had ceased from rattling and the weary quadrupeds came to a rest I handed my jehu his fifty cents with an additional quarter, feeling a glow of conscious generosity as I did so. He refused it.

"It's two dollars, suh," he said.

"How's that?" I asked. "I plainly heard you call out at the hotel. 'Fifty cents to any part of the town.'"

"It's two dollars, suh," he repeated obstinately. "It's a long ways from the hotel."

"It is within the city limits and well within them," I argued. "Don't think that you have picked up a greenhorn Yankee. Do you see those hills over there?" I went on, pointing toward the east (I could not see them, myself, for the drizzle); "well, I was born and raised on their other side. You old fool nigger, can't you tell people from other people when you see 'em?"

The grim face of King Cettiwayo softened. "Is you from the South, suh? I reckon it was them shoes of yourn fooled me. They is somethin' sharp in the toes for a Southern gen'l'man to wear."

"Then the charge is fifty cents, I suppose?" said I, inexorably.

His former expression, a mingling of cupidity and hostility, returned, remained ten seconds, and vanished.

"Boss," he said, "fifty cents is right; but I *needs* two dollars, suh; I'm *obleeged* to have two dollars. I ain't *demandin'* it now, suh; after I knows whar you's from; I'm jus sayin' that I *has* to have two dollars tonight and business is mighty po'."

Peace and confidence settled upon his heavy features. He had been luckier than he had hoped. Instead of having picked up a greenhorn, ignorant of rates, he had come upon an inheritance.

"You confounded old rascal," I said, reaching down to my pocket, "you ought to be turned over to the police."

For the first time I saw him smile. He knew; *he knew;* HE KNEW.

I gave him two one-dollar bills. As I handed them over I noticed that one of them had seen parlous times. Its upper right-hand corner was missing, and it had been torn through in the middle, but joined again. A strip of blue tissue paper, pasted over the split, preserved its negotiability.

Enough of the African bandit for the present: I left him happy, lifted the rope, and opened the creaky gate.

The house, as I said, was a shell. A paint brush had not touched it in twenty years. I could not see why a strong wind should not have bowled it over like a house of cards until I looked again at the trees that hugged it close—the trees that saw the battle of Nashville and still drew their protecting branches around it against storm and enemy and cold.

Azalea Adair, fifty years old, white-haired, a descendant of the cavaliers, as thin and frail as the house she lived in, robed in the cheapest and cleanest dress I ever saw, with an air as simple as a queen's, received me.

The reception room seemed a mile square, because there was nothing in it except some rows of books, on unpainted white-pine bookshelves, a cracked marble-topped table, a rag rug, a hairless horsehair sofa, and two or three chairs. Yes, there was a picture on the wall, a colored crayon drawing of a cluster of pansies. I looked around for the portrait of Andrew Jackson and the pine-cone hanging basket but they were not there.

Azalea Adair and I had conversation, a little of which will be repeated to you. She was a product of the old South, gently nurtured in the sheltered life. Her learning was not broad, but was deep and of splendid originality in its somewhat narrow scope. She had been educated at home, and her knowledge of the world was derived from inference and by inspiration. Of such is the precious, small group of essayists made. While she talked to me I kept brushing my fingers, trying, unconsciously, to rid them guiltily of the absent dust from the half-calf backs of Lamb, Chaucer, Hazlitt, Marcus Aurelius, Montaigne, and Hood. She was exquisite, she was a valuable discovery. Nearly everybody nowadays knows too much—oh, so much too much—of real life.

I could perceive clearly that Azalea Adair was very poor. A house and a dress she had, not much else, I fancied. So, divided between my duty to the magazine and my loyalty to the poets and essayists who fought Thomas in the valley of the Cumberland, I listened to her voice which was like a harpsichord's, and found that I could not speak of contracts. In the presence of the nine Muses and the three Graces one hesitated to lower the topic to two cents. There would have to be another colloquy after I had regained my commercialism. But I spoke of my mission, and three o'clock of the next afternoon was set for the discussion of the business proposition.

"Your town," I said, as I began to make ready to depart (which is the time for smooth generalities) "seems to be a quiet, sedate place. A home town, I should say, where few things out of the ordinary ever happen."

It carries on an extensive trade in stoves and hollow ware with the West and South, and its flouring mills have a daily capacity of more than 2,000 barrels.

Azalea Adair seemed to reflect.

"I have never thought of it that way," she said, with a kind of sincere intensity that seemed to belong to her. "Isn't it in the still, quiet places that things do happen? I fancy that when God began to create the earth on the first Monday morning one could have leaned out one's window and heard the drops of mud splashing from His trowel as He built up the everlasting hills. What did the noisiest project in the world—I mean the building of the Tower of Babel—result in finally? A page and a half of Esperanto in the *North American Review*."

"Of course," said I, platitudinously, "human nature is the same everywhere; but there is more color—er—more drama and movement and—er—romance in some cities than in others."

"On the surface," said Azalea Adair. "I have traveled many times around the world in a golden airship wafted on two wings—print and dreams. I have seen (on one of my imaginary tours) the Sultan of Turkey bowstring with his own hands one of his wives who had uncovered her face in public. I have seen a man in Nashville tear up his theatre tickets because his wife was going out with her face covered—with rice powder. In San Francisco's Chinatown I saw the slave girl Sing Yee dipped slowly, inch by inch, in boiling almond oil to make her swear she would never see her American lover again. She gave in when the boiling oil had reached three inches above her knee. At a euchre party in East Nashville the other night I saw Kitty Morgan cut dead by seven of her schoolmates and lifelong friends because she had married a house painter. The boiling oil was sizzling as high as her heart; but I wish you could have seen the fine little smile that she carried from table to table. Oh, yes, it is a humdrum town. Just a few miles of red brick houses and mud and stores and lumber yards."

Someone had knocked hollowly at the back of the house. Azalea Adair breathed a soft apology and went to investigate the sound. She came back in three minutes with brightened eyes, a faint flush on her cheeks, and ten years lifted from her shoulders.

"You must have a cup of tea before you go," she said, "and a sugar cake."

She reached and shook a little iron bell. In shuffled a small Negro girl about twelve, barefoot, not very tidy, glowering at me with thumb in mouth and bulging eyes.

Azalea Adair opened a tiny, worn purse and drew out a dollar bill, a dollar bill with the upper right-hand corner missing, torn in two pieces and pasted together again with a strip of blue tissue paper. It was one of those bills I had given the piratical Negro—there was no doubt of it.

"Go up to Mr. Baker's store on the corner, Impy," she said, handing the girl the dollar bill, "and get a quarter of a pound of tea—the kind he always sends me—and ten cents' worth of sugar cakes. Now, hurry. The supply of tea in the house happens to be exhausted," she explained to me.

Impy left by the back way. Before the scrape of her hard, bare feet had died away on the back porch, a wild shriek—I was sure it was hers—filled the hollow house. Then the deep, gruff tones of an angry man's voice mingled with the girl's further squeals and unintelligible words.

Azalea Adair rose without surprise or emotion and disappeared. For two minutes I heard the hoarse rumble of the man's voice; then something like an oath and a slight scuffle, and she returned calmly to her chair.

"This is a roomy house," she said, "and I have a tenant for part of it. I am sorry to have to rescind my invitation to tea. It is impossible to get the kind I always use at the store. Perhaps tomorrow Mr. Baker will be able to supply me."

I was sure that Impy had not had time to leave the house. I inquired concerning street-car lines and took my leave. After I was well on my way I remembered that I had not learned Azalea Adair's name. But tomorrow would do.

That same day I started in on the course of iniquity that this uneventful city forced upon me. I was in the town only two days, but in that time I managed to lie shamelessly by telegraph, and to be an accomplice—after the fact, if that is the correct legal term—to a murder.

As I rounded the corner nearest my hotel the Afrite coachman of the polychromatic, non pareil coat seized me, swung open the dungeony door of his peripatetic sarcophagus, flirted his feather duster and began his ritual: "Step right in, boss. Carriage is clean—jus' got back from a funeral. Fifty cents to any——"

And then he knew me and grinned broadly. "'Scuse me, boss; you is de gen'l'man what rid out with me dis mawnin'. Thank you kindly, suh."

"I am going out to 861 again tomorrow afternoon at three," said I, "and if you will be here, I'll let you drive me. So you know Miss Adair?" I concluded, thinking of my dollar bill.

"I belonged to her father, Judge Adair, suh," he replied.

"I judge that she is pretty poor," I said. "She hasn't much money to speak of, has she?"

For an instant I looked again at the fierce countenance of King Cettiwayo, and then he changed back to an extortionate old Negro hack driver.

"She ain't gwine to starve, suh," he said, slowly. "She has reso'ces, suh; she has reso'ces."

"I shall pay you fifty cents for the trip," said I.

"Dat is puffeckly correct, suh," he answered, humbly. "I jus' *had* to have dat two dollars dis mawnin', boss."

I went to the hotel and lied by electricity. I wired the magazine: "A. Adair holds out for eight cents a word."

The answer that came back was: "Give it to her quick, you duffer."

Just before dinner "Major" Wentworth Caswell bore down upon me with the greetings of a long-lost friend. I have seen few men whom I have so instantaneously hated, and of whom it was so difficult to be rid. I was standing at the bar when he invaded me; therefore I could not wave the white ribbon in his face. I would have paid gladly for the drinks, hoping, thereby, to escape another; but he was one of those despicable, roaring, advertising bibbers who must have brass bands and fireworks attend upon every cent that they waste in their follies.

With an air of producing millions he drew two one-dollar bills from a pocket and dashed one of them upon the bar. I looked once more at the dollar bill with the upper right-hand corner missing, torn through the middle, and patched with a strip of blue tissue paper. It was my dollar bill again. It could have been no other.

I went up to my room. The drizzle and the monotony of a dreary, eventless Southern town had made me tired and listless. I remember that just before I went to bed I mentally disposed of the mysterious dollar bill (which might have formed the clue to a tremendously fine detective story of San Francisco) by saying to myself sleepily: "Seems as if a lot of people here own stock in the Hack-Drivers' Trust. Pays dividends promptly, too. Wonder if——" Then I fell asleep.

King Cettiwayo was at his post the next day, and rattled my bones over the stones out to 861. He was to wait and rattle me back again when I was ready.

Azalea Adair looked paler and cleaner and frailer than she had looked on the day before. After she had signed the contract at eight cents per word she grew still paler and began to slip out of her chair.

Without much trouble I managed to get her up on the antediluvian horse-hair sofa and then I ran out to the sidewalk and yelled to the coffee-colored Pirate to bring a doctor. With a wisdom that I had not suspected in him, he abandoned his team and struck off up the street afoot, realizing the value of speed. In ten minutes he returned with a grave, gray-haired, and capable man of medicine. In a few words (worth much less than eight cents each) I explained to him my presence in the hollow house of mystery. He bowed with stately understanding, and turned to the old Negro.

"Uncle Cæsar," he said, calmly, "run up to my house and ask Miss Lucy to give you a cream pitcher full of fresh milk and half a tumbler of port wine. And hurry back. Don't drive—run. I want you to get back sometime this week."

It occurred to me that Dr. Merriman also felt a distrust as to the speeding powers of the land-pirate's steeds. After Uncle Cæsar was gone, lumberingly, but swiftly, up the street, the doctor looked me over with great politeness and as much careful calculation until he had decided that I might do.

"It is only a case of insufficient nutrition," he said. "In other words, the result of poverty, pride, and starvation. Mrs. Caswell has many devoted friends who would be glad to aid her, but she will accept nothing except from that old Negro, Uncle Cæsar, who was once owned by her family."

"Mrs. Caswell!" said I, in surprise. And then I looked at the contract and saw that she had signed it "Azalea Adair Caswell."

"I thought she was Miss Adair," I said.

"Married to a drunken, worthless loafer, sir," said the doctor. "It is said that he robs her even of the small sums that her old servant contributes toward her support."

When the milk and wine had been brought the doctor soon revived Azalea Adair. She sat up and talked of the beauty of the autumn leaves that were then in season and their height of color. She referred lightly to her fainting seizure as the outcome of an old palpitation of the heart. Impy fanned her as she lay on the sofa. The doctor was due elsewhere, and I followed him to the door. I told him that it was within my power and intentions to make a reasonable advance of money to Azalea Adair on future contributions to the magazine, and he seemed pleased.

"By the way," he said, "perhaps you would like to know that you have had royalty for a coachman. Old Cæsar's grandfather was a king in Congo. Cæsar himself has royal ways, as you may have observed."

As the doctor was moving off I heard Uncle Cæsar's voice inside: "Did he git bofe of dem two dollars from you, Mis' Zalea?"

"Yes, Cæsar," I heard Azalea Adair answer weakly. And then I went in and concluded business negotiations with our contributor. I assumed the responsibility of advancing fifty dollars, putting it as a necessary formality in binding our bargain. And then Uncle Cæsar drove me back to the hotel.

Here ends all of the story as far as I can testify as a witness. The rest must be only bare statements of facts.

At about six o'clock I went out for a stroll. Uncle Cæsar was at his corner. He threw open the door of his carriage, flourished his duster, and began his depressing formula: "Step right in, suh. Fifty cents to anywhere in the city—hack's puffickly clean, suh—jus' got back from a funeral——"

And then he recognized me. I think his eyesight was getting bad. His coat had taken on a few more faded shades of color, the twine strings were more frayed and ragged, the last remaining button—the button of yellow horn—was gone. A motley descendant of kings was Uncle Cæsar!

About two hours later I saw an excited crowd besieging the front of a drug store. In a desert where nothing happens this was manna; so I wedged my way inside. On an extemporized couch of empty boxes and chairs was stretched the mortal corporeality of Major Wentworth Caswell. A doctor was testing him for the mortal ingredient. His decision was that it was conspicuous by its absence.

The erstwhile Major had been found dead on a dark street and brought by curious and ennuied citizens to the drug store. The late human being had been engaged in terrific battle—the details showed that. Loafer and reprobate though he had been, he had been also a warrior. But he had lost. His hands were yet clinched so tightly that his fingers would not be opened. The gentle citizens who had known him stood about and searched their vocabularies to find some good words, if it were possible, to speak of him. One kind-looking man said, after much thought: "When 'Cas' was about fo'teen he was one of the best spellers in the school."

While I stood there the fingers of the right hand of "the man that was," which hung down the side of a white pine box, relaxed, and dropped something at my feet. I covered it with one foot quietly, and a little later on I picked it up and pocketed it. I reasoned that in his last struggle his hand must have seized that object unwittingly and held it in a death grip.

At the hotel that night the main topic of conversation, with the possible exceptions of politics and prohibition, was the demise of Major Caswell. I heard one man say to a group of listeners:

"In my opinion, gentlemen, Caswell was murdered by some of these no-account niggers for his money. He had fifty dollars this afternoon which he showed to several gentlemen in the hotel. When he was found the money was not on his person."

I left the city the next morning at nine, and as the train was crossing the bridge over the Cumberland River I took out of my pocket a yellow horn overcoat button the size of a fifty-cent piece, with frayed ends of coarse twine hanging from it, and cast it out of the window into the slow, muddy waters below.

*I wonder what's doing in Buffalo!*

# A NEWSPAPER STORY

## O. Henry

AT 8 A.M. it lay on Giuseppi's news-stand, still damp from the presses. Giuseppi, with the cunning of his ilk, philandered on the opposite corner leaving his patrons to help themselves, no doubt on a theory related to the hypothesis of the watched pot.

This particular newspaper was, according to its custom and design, an educator, a guide, a monitor, a champion, and a household counsellor and *vade mecum*.[1]

From its many excellencies might be selected three editorials. One was in simple and chaste but illuminating language directed to parents and teachers, deprecating corporal punishment for children.

Another was an accusive and significant warning addressed to a notorious labor leader who was on the point of instigating his clients to a troublesome strike.

The third was an eloquent demand that the police force be sustained and aided in everything that tended to increase its efficiency as public guardians and servants.

Besides these more important chidings and requisitions upon the store of good citizenship was a wise prescription or form of procedure laid out by the editor of the heart-to-heart column in the specific case of a young man who had complained of the obduracy of his lady love, teaching him how he might win her.

Again, there was, on the beauty page, a complete answer to a young lady inquirer who desired admonition toward the securing of bright eyes, rosy cheeks, and a beautiful countenance.

---

[1] *vade mecum*; Latin: handbook.

One other item requiring special cognizance was a brief "personal," running thus:

Dear Jack:—Forgive me. You were right. Meet me at corner of Madison and —th at 8:30 this morning. We leave at noon.

Penitent

At 8 o'clock a young man with a haggard look and the feverish gleam of unrest in his eye dropped a penny and picked up the top paper as he passed Giuseppi's stand. A sleepless night had left him a late riser. There was an office to be reached by nine, and a shave and a hasty cup of coffee to be crowded into the interval.

He visited his barber shop and then hurried on his way. He pocketed his paper, meditating a belated perusal of it at the luncheon hour. At the next corner it fell from his pocket, carrying with it his pair of new gloves. Three blocks he walked, missed the gloves and turned back fuming.

Just on the half-hour he reached the corner where lay the gloves and paper. But he strangely ignored that which he had come to seek. He was holding two little hands as tightly as ever he could and looking into two penitent brown eyes, while joy rioted in his heart.

"Dear Jack," she said, "I knew you would be here on time."

"I wonder what she means by that," he was saying to himself; "but it's all right, it's all right."

A big wind puffed out of the west, picked up the paper from the sidewalk, opened it and sent it flying and whirling down a side street. Up that street was driving a skittish bay to a spider-wheel buggy the young man who had written to the heart-to-heart editor for a recipe that he might win her for whom he sighed.

The wind, with a prankish flurry, flapped the flying newspaper against the face of the skittish bay. There was a lengthened streak of bay mingled with the red of running gear that stretched itself out for four blocks. Then a water-hydrant played its part in the cosmogony, the buggy became match wood as foreordained, and the driver rested very quietly where he had been flung on the asphalt in front of a certain brownstone mansion.

They came out and had him inside very promptly. And there was one who made herself a pillow for his head, and cared for no curious eyes, bending over and saying, "Oh, it was you; it was you all the time, Bobby! Couldn't you see it? And if you die, why, so must I, and——"

But in all this wind we must hurry to keep in touch with our paper.

Policeman O'Brine arrested it as a character dangerous to traffic. Straightening its dishevelled leaves with his big, slow fingers, he stood a few feet from the family entrance of the Shandon Bells Café. One headline he spelled out ponderously. "The Papers to the Front in a Move to Help the Police."

But, whist! The voice of Danny, the head bartender, through the crack of the door: "Here's a nip for ye, Mike, ould man."

Behind the widespread, amicable columns of the press Policeman O'Brine receives swiftly his nip of the real stuff. He moves away, stalwart, refreshed, fortified, to his duties. Might not the editor man view with pride the early, the spiritual, the literal fruit that had blessed his labors.

Policeman O'Brine folded the paper and poked it playfully under the arm of a small boy that was passing. That boy was named Johnny, and he took the paper home with him. His sister was named Gladys, and she had written to the beauty editor of the paper asking for the practicable touchstone of beauty. That was weeks ago, and she had ceased to look for an answer. Gladys was a pale girl, with dull eyes and a discontented expression. She was dressing to go up to the avenue to get some braid. Beneath her skirt she pinned two leaves of the paper Johnny had brought. When she walked the rustling sound was an exact imitation of the real thing.

On the street she met the Brown girl from the flat below and stopped to talk. The Brown girl turned green. Only silk at $5 a yard could make the sound that she heard when Gladys moved. The Brown girl, consumed by jealousy, said something spiteful and went her way, with pinched lips.

Gladys proceeded towards the avenue. Her eyes now sparkled like jagerfonteins. A rosy bloom visited her cheeks; a triumphant, subtle, vivifying smile transfigured her face. She was beautiful. Could the beauty editor have seen her then! There was something in her answer in the paper, I believe, about cultivating a kind feeling towards others in order to make plain features attractive.

The labor leader against whom the paper's solemn and weighty editorial injunction was laid was the father of Gladys and Johnny. He picked up the remains of the journal from which Gladys had ravished a cosmetic of silken sounds. The editorial did not come under his eye, but instead it was greeted by one of those ingenious and specious puzzle problems that enthrall alike the simpleton and the sage.

The labor leader tore off half of the page, provided himself with table, pencil, and paper and glued himself to the puzzle.

Three hours later, after waiting vainly for him at the appointed place, other more conservative leaders declared and ruled in favor of arbitration, and the strike with its attendant dangers was averted. Subsequent editions of the paper referred, in colored inks, to the clarion tone of its successful denunciation of the labor leader's intended designs.

The remaining leaves of the active journal also went loyally to the proving of its potency.

When Johnny returned from school he sought a secluded spot and removed the missing columns from the inside of his clothing, where they had been artfully distributed so as to successfully defend such areas as are generally attacked during scholastic castigations. Johnny attended a private school and had had trouble with his teacher. As has been said, there was an excellent editorial against corporal punishment in that morning's issue, and no doubt it had its effect.

After this can anyone doubt the power of the press?

# EDITHA

## William Dean Howells

THE AIR WAS thick with the war feeling, like the electricity of a storm which has not yet burst. Editha sat looking out into the hot spring afternoon, with her lips parted, and panting with the intensity of the question whether she could let him go. She had decided that she could not let him stay, when she saw him at the end of the still leafless avenue, making slowly up towards the house, with his head down and his figure relaxed. She ran impatiently out on the veranda, to the edge of the steps, and imperatively demanded greater haste of him with her will before she called aloud to him: "George!"

He had quickened his pace in mystical response to her mystical urgence, before he could have heard her; now he looked up and answered, "Well?"

"Oh, how united we are!" she exulted, and then she swooped down the steps to him. "What is it?" she cried.

"It's war," he said, and he pulled her up to him and kissed her.

She kissed him back intensely, but irrelevantly, as to their passion, and uttered from deep in her throat. "How glorious!"

"It's war," he repeated, without consenting to her sense of it; and she did not know just what to think at first. She never knew what to think of him; that made his mystery, his charm. All through their courtship, which was contemporaneous with the growth of the war feeling, she had been puzzled by his want of seriousness about it. He seemed to despise it even more than he abhorred it. She could have understood his abhorring any sort of bloodshed; that would have been a survival of his old life when he thought he would be a minister, and before he changed and took up the law. But making light of a cause so high and noble seemed to show a want of earnestness at the core of his being. Not but that she felt herself able to cope with a congenital defect of that sort, and make his love for her save him from himself. Now perhaps the miracle was already wrought in him. In the presence of the tremendous fact that he announced, all triviality seemed to have gone out of him; she began to feel that. He sank down on the top step, and wiped his forehead with his handkerchief, while she poured out upon him her question of the origin and authenticity of his news.

All the while, in her duplex emotioning, she was aware that now at the very beginning she must put a guard upon herself against urging him, by any word or act, to take the part that her whole soul willed him to take, for the completion of her ideal of him. He was very nearly perfect as he was, and he must be allowed to perfect himself. But he was peculiar, and he might very well be reasoned out of his peculiarity. Before her reasoning went her emotioning: her nature pulling upon his nature, her womanhood upon his manhood, without her knowing the means she was using to the end she was willing. She had always supposed that the man who won her would have done something to win her; she did not know what, but something. George Gearson had simply asked her for her love, on the way home from a concert, and she gave her love to him, without, as it were, thinking. But now, it flashed upon her, if he could do something worthy to *have* won her—be a hero, *her* hero—it would be even better than if he had done it before asking her; it would be grander. Besides, she had believed in the war from the beginning.

"But don't you see, dearest," she said, "that it wouldn't have come to this if it hadn't been in the order of Providence? And I call any war glorious that is for the liberation of people who have been struggling for years against the cruelest oppression. Don't you think so, too?"

"I suppose so," he returned, languidly. "But war! Is it glorious to break the peace of the world?"

"That ignoble peace! It was no peace at all, with that crime and shame at our very gates." She was conscious of parroting the current phrases of the newspapers, but it was no time to pick and choose her words. She must sacrifice anything to the high ideal she had for him, and after a good deal of rapid argument she ended with the climax: "But now it doesn't matter about the how or why. Since the war has come, all that is gone. There are no two sides any more. There is nothing now but our country."

He sat with his eyes closed and his head leant back against the veranda, and he remarked, with a vague smile, as if musing aloud, "Our country—right or wrong."

"Yes, right or wrong!" she returned, fervidly. "I'll go and get you some lemonade." She rose rustling, and whisked away, when she came back with two tall glasses of clouded liquid on a tray, and the ice clucking in them, he still sat as she had left him, and she said, as if there had been no interruption: "But there is no question of wrong in this ease. I call it a sacred war. A war for liberty and humanity, if ever there was one. And I know you will see it just as I do, yet."

He took half the lemonade at a gulp, and he answered as he set the glass down: "I know you always have the highest ideal. When I differ from you I ought to doubt myself."

A generous sob rose in Editha's throat for the humility of a man, so very nearly perfect, who was willing to put himself below her.

Besides, she felt, more subliminally, that he was never so near slipping through her fingers as when he took that meek way.

"You shall not say that! Only, for once I happen to be right." She seized his hand in her two hands, and poured her soul from her eyes into his. "Don't you think so?" she entreated him.

He released his hand and drank the rest of his lemonade, and she added, "Have mine, too," but he shook his head in answering, "I've no business to think so, unless I act so, too."

Her heart stopped a beat before it pulsed on with leaps that she felt in her neck. She had noticed that strange thing in men: they seemed to feel bound to do what they believed, and not think a thing was finished when they said it, as girls did. She knew what was in his mind, but she pretended not, and she said, "Oh, I am not sure," and then faltered.

He went on as if to himself, without apparently heeding her: "There's only one way of proving one's faith in a thing like this."

She could not say that she understood, but she did understand.

He went on again. "If I believed—if I felt as you do about this war—Do you wish me to feel as you do?"

Now she was really not sure; so she said: "George, I don't know what you mean."

He seemed to muse away from her as before. "There is a sort of fascination in it. I suppose that at the bottom of his heart every man would like at times to have his courage tested, to see how he would act."

"How can you talk in that ghastly way?"

"It *is* rather morbid. Still, that's what it comes to, unless you're swept away by ambition or driven by conviction. I haven't the conviction or the ambition, and the other thing is what it comes to with me. I ought to have been a preacher, after all; then I couldn't have asked it of myself, as I must, now I'm a lawyer. And you believe it's a holy war, Editha?" he suddenly addressed her. "Oh, I know you do! But you wish me to believe so, too?"

She hardly knew whether he was mocking or not, in the ironical way he always had with her plainer mind. But the only thing was to be outspoken with him.

"George, I wish you to believe whatever you think is true, at any and every cost. If I've tried to talk you into anything, I take it all back."

"Oh, I know that, Editha. I know how sincere you are, and how— I wish I had your undoubting spirit! I'll think it over; I'd like to believe as you do. But I don't, now; I don't, indeed. It isn't this war alone; though this seems peculiarly wanton and needless; but it's every war—so stupid; it makes me sick. Why shouldn't this thing have been settled reasonably?"

"Because," she said, very throatily again, "God meant it to be war."

"You think it was God? Yes, I suppose that is what people will say."

"Do you suppose it would have been war if God hadn't meant it?"

"I don't know. Sometimes it seems as if God had put this world into men's keeping to work it as they pleased."

"Now, George, that is blasphemy."

"Well, I won't blaspheme. I'll try to believe in your pocket Providence," he said, and then he rose to go.

"Why don't you stay to dinner?" Dinner at Balcom's Works was at one o'clock.

"I'll come back to supper, if you'll let me. Perhaps I shall bring you a convert."

"Well, you may come back, on that condition."

"All right. If I don't come, you'll understand."

He went away without kissing her, and she felt it a suspension of their engagement. It all interested her intensely; she was undergoing a tremendous experience, and she was being equal to it. While she stood looking after him, her mother came out through one of the long windows onto the veranda, with a catlike softness and vagueness.

"Why didn't he stay to dinner?"

"Because—because—war has been declared," Editha pronounced, without turning.

Her mother said, "Oh, my!" and then said nothing more until she had sat down in one of the large Shaker chairs and rocked herself for some time. Then she closed whatever tacit passage of thought there had been in her mind with the spoken words: "Well, I hope *he* won't go."

"And *I* hope he *will,*" the girl said, and confronted her mother with a stormy exaltation that would have frightened any creature less unimpressionable than a cat.

Her mother rocked herself again for an interval of cogitation. What she arrived at in speech was: "Well, I guess you've done a wicked thing, Editha Balcom."

The girl said, as she passed indoors through the same window her mother had come out by: "I haven't done anything—yet."

In her room, she put together all her letters and gifts from Gearson, down to the withered petals of the first flower he had offered, with that timidity of his veiled in that irony of his. In the heart of the packet she enshrined her engagement ring which she had restored to the pretty box he had brought it her in. Then she sat down, if not calmly yet strongly, and wrote:

"GEORGE:—I understood when you left me. But I think we had better emphasize your meaning that if we cannot be one in everything we had better be one in nothing. So I am sending these things for your keeping till you have made up your mind.

"I shall always love you, and therefore I shall never marry anyone else. But the man I marry must love his country first of all, and be able to say to me,

> "'I could not love thee, dear, so much,
> Loved I not honor more.'

"There is no honor above America with me. In this great hour there is no other honor.

"Your heart will make my words clear to you. I had never expected to say so much, but it has come upon me that I must say the utmost.
                                                                    "EDITHA."

She thought she had worded her letter well, worded it in a way that could not be bettered; all had been implied and nothing expressed.

She had it ready to send with the packet she had tied with red, white, and blue ribbon, when it occurred to her that she was not just to him, that she was not giving him a fair chance. He had said he would go and think it over, and she was not waiting. She was pushing, threatening, compelling. That was not a woman's part. She must leave him free, free, free. She could not accept for her country or herself a forced sacrifice.

In writing her letter she had satisfied the impulse from which it sprang; she could well afford to wait till he had thought it over. She put the packet and the letter by, and rested serene in the consciousness of having done what was laid upon her by her love itself to do, and yet used patience, mercy, justice.

She had her reward. Gearson did not come to tea, but she had given him till morning, when, late at night there came up from the village the sound of a fife and drum, with a tumult of voices, in shouting, singing, and laughing. The noise drew nearer and nearer; it reached the street end of the avenue; there it silenced itself, and one voice, the voice she knew best, rose over the silence. It fell; the air was filled with cheers; the fife and drum struck up, with the shouting, singing, and laughing again, but now retreating; and a single figure came hurrying up the avenue.

She ran down to meet her lover and clung to him. He was very gay, and he put his arm round her with a boisterous laugh. "Well, you must call me Captain now; or Cap, if you prefer; that's what the boys call me. Yes, we've had a meeting at the town-hall, and everybody has volunteered; and they selected me for captain, and I'm going to the war, the big war, the glorious war, the holy war ordained by the pocket Providence that blesses butchery. Come along; let's tell the whole family about it. Call them from their downy beds, father, mother, Aunt Hitty, and all the folks!"

But when they mounted the veranda steps he did not wait for a larger audience; he poured the story out upon Editha alone.

"There was a lot of speaking, and then some of the fools set up a shout for me. It was all going one way, and I thought it would be a good joke to sprinkle a little cold water on them. But you can't do that with a crowd that adores you. The first thing I knew I was sprinkling hell-fire on them. 'Cry havoc, and let slip the dogs of war.' That was the style. Now that it had come to the fight, there were no two parties; there was one country, and the thing was to fight to a finish as quick as possible. I suggested volunteering then and there, and I wrote my name first of all on the roster. Then they elected me—that's all. I wish I had some ice-water."

She left him walking up and down the veranda, while she ran for the ice-pitcher and a goblet, and when she came back he was still walking up and down, shouting the story he had told her to her father and mother, who had come out more sketchily dressed than they commonly were by day. He drank goblet after goblet of the ice-water without noticing who was giving it, and kept on talking, and laughing through his talk wildly. "It's astonishing," he said, "how well the worse reason looks when you try to make it appear the better. Why, I believe I was the first convert to the war in that crowd tonight! I never thought I should like to kill a man; but now I shouldn't care; and the smokeless powder lets you see the man drop that you kill. It's all for the country! What a thing it is to have a country that *can't* be wrong, but if it is, is right, anyway!"

Editha had a great, vital thought, an inspiration. She set down the ice-pitcher on the veranda floor, and ran upstairs and got the letter she had written him. When at last he noisily bade her father and mother, "Well, good-night. I forgot I woke you up; I sha'n't want any sleep myself," she followed him down the avenue to the gate. There, after the whirling words that seemed to fly away from her thoughts and refuse to serve them, she made a last effort to solemnize the moment that seemed so crazy, and pressed the letter she had written upon him.

"What's this?" he said. "Want me to mail it?"

"No, no. It's for you. I wrote it after you went this morning. Keep it—keep it—and read it sometime—" She thought, and then her inspiration came: "Read it if ever you doubt what you've done, or fear that I regret your having done it. Read it after you've started."

They strained each other in embraces that seemed as ineffective as their words, and he kissed her face with quick, hot breaths that were so unlike him, that made her feel as if she had lost her old lover and found a stranger in his place. The stranger said: "What a gorgeous flower you are, with your red hair, and your blue eyes that look black now, and your face with the color painted out by the white moonshine! Let me hold you under the chin, to see whether I love blood, you tiger-lily!" Then he laughed Gearson's laugh, and released her, scared and giddy. Within her wilfulness she had been frightened by a sense of subtler force in him, and mystically mastered as she had never been before.

She ran all the way back to the house, and mounted the steps panting. Her mother and father were talking of the great affair. Her mother said: "Wa'n't Mr. Gearson in rather of an excited state of mind? Didn't you think he acted curious?"

"Well, not for a man who'd just been elected captain and had set 'em up for the whole of Company A," her father chuckled back.

"What in the world do you mean, Mr. Balcom? Oh! There's Editha!" She offered to follow the girl indoors.

"Don't come, mother!" Editha called, vanishing.

Mrs. Balcom remained to reproach her husband. "I don't see much of anything to laugh at."

"Well, it's catching. Caught it from Gearson. I guess it won't be much of a war, and I guess Gearson don't think so, either. The other fellows will back down as soon as they see we mean it. I wouldn't lose any sleep over it. I'm going back to bed, myself."

Gearson came again next afternoon, looking pale and rather sick, but quite himself, even to his languid irony. "I guess I'd better tell you, Editha, that I consecrated myself to your god of battles last night by pouring too many libations to him down my own throat. But I'm all right now. One has to carry off the excitement, somehow."

"Promise me," she commanded, "that you'll never touch it again!"

"What! Not let the cannikin clink? Not let the soldier drink? Well, I promise."

"You don't belong to yourself now; you don't even belong to *me*. You belong to your country, and you have a sacred charge to keep yourself strong and well for your country's sake. I have been thinking, thinking all night and all day long."

"You look as if you had been crying a little, too," he said, with his queer smile.

"That's all past. I've been thinking, and worshipping *you*. Don't you suppose I know all that you've been through, to come to this? I've followed you every step from your old theories and opinions."

"Well, you've had a long row to hoe."

"And I know you've done this from the highest motives—"

"Oh, there won't be much pettifogging to do till this cruel war is—"

"And you haven't simply done it for my sake. I couldn't respect you if you had."

"Well, then we'll say I haven't. A man that hasn't got his own respect intact wants the respect of all the other people he can corner.

But we won't go into that. I'm in for the thing now, and we've got to face our future. My idea is that this isn't going to be a very protracted struggle; we shall just scare the enemy to death before it comes to a fight at all. But we must provide for contingencies, Editha. If anything happens to me—"

"Oh, George!" She clung to him, sobbing.

"I don't want you to feel foolishly bound to my memory. I should hate that, wherever I happened to be."

"I am yours, for time and eternity—time and eternity." She liked the words; they satisfied her famine for phrases.

"Well, say eternity; that's all right; but time's another thing; and I'm talking about time. But there is something! My mother! If anything happens—"

She winced, and he laughed. "You're not the bold soldier-girl of yesterday!" Then he sobered. "If anything happens, I want you to help my mother out. She won't like my doing this thing. She brought me up to think war a fool thing as well as a bad thing. My father was in the Civil War; all through it; lost his arm in it." She thrilled with the sense of the arm round her; what if that should be lost? He laughed as if divining her: "Oh, it doesn't run in the family, as far as I know!" Then he added, gravely: "He came home with misgivings about war, and they grew on him. I guess he and mother agreed between them that I was to be brought up in his final mind about it; but that was before my time. I only knew him from my mother's report of him and his opinions; I don't know whether they were hers first; but they were hers last. This will be a blow to her. I shall have to write and tell her—"

He stopped, and she asked: "Would you like me to write, too, George?"

"I don't believe that would do. No, I'll do the writing. She'll understand a little if I say that I thought the way to minimize it was to make war on the largest possible scale at once—that I felt I must have been helping on the war somehow if I hadn't helped keep it from coming, and I knew I hadn't; when it came, I had no right to stay out of it."

Whether his sophistries satisfied him or not, they satisfied her. She clung to his breast, and whispered, with closed eyes and quivering lips: "Yes, yes, yes!"

"But if anything should happen, you might go to her and see what you could do for her. You know? It's rather far off; she can't leave her chair—"

"Oh, I'll go, if it's the ends of the earth! But nothing will happen! Nothing *can!* I—"

She felt herself lifted with his rising, and Gearson was saying, with his arm still round her, to her father: "Well, we're off at once, Mr. Balcom. We're to be formally accepted at the capital, and then bunched up with the rest somehow, and sent into camp somewhere, and got to the front as soon as possible. We all want to be in the van, of course; we're the first company to report to the Governor. I came to tell Editha, but I hadn't got round to it."

She saw him again for a moment at the capital, in the station, just before the train started southward with his regiment. He looked well, in his uniform, and very soldierly, but somehow girlish, too, with his clean-shaven face and slim figure. The manly eyes and the strong voice satisfied her, and his preoccupation with some unexpected details of duty flattered her. Other girls were weeping and bemoaning themselves, but she felt a sort of noble distinction in the abstraction, the almost unconsciousness, with which they parted. Only at the last moment he said: "Don't forget my mother. It mayn't be such a walk-over as I supposed," and he laughed at the notion.

He waved his hand to her as the train moved off—she knew it among a score of hands that were waved to other girls from the platform of the car, for it held a letter which she knew was hers. Then he went inside the car to read it, doubtless, and she did not see him again. But she felt safe for him through the strength of what she called her love. What she called her God, always speaking the name in a deep voice and with the implication of a mutual understanding, would watch over him and keep him and bring him back to her. If with an empty sleeve, then he should have three arms instead of two, for both of hers should be his for life. She did not see, though, why she should always be thinking of the arm his father had lost.

There were not many letters from him, but they were such as she could have wished, and she put her whole strength into making hers such as she imagined he could have wished, glorifying and supporting him. She wrote to his mother glorifying him as their hero, but the brief answer she got was merely to the effect that Mrs. Gearson was not well enough to write herself, and thanking her for her letter by the hand of someone who called herself "Yrs truly, Mrs. W. J. Andrews."

Editha determined not to be hurt, but to write again quite as if the answer had been all she expected. Before it seemed as if she could have written, there came news of the first skirmish, and in the list of the killed, which was telegraphed as a trifling loss on our side, was Gearson's name. There was a frantic time of trying to make out that it might be, must be, some other Gearson; but the name and the company and the regiment and the State were too definitely given.

Then there was a lapse into depths out of which it seemed as if she never could rise again; then a lift into clouds far above all grief, black clouds, that blotted out the sun, but where she soared with him, with George—George! She had the fever that she expected of herself, but she did not die in it; she was not even delirious, and it did not last long. When she was well enough to leave her bed, her one thought was of George's mother, of his strangely worded wish that she should go to her and see what she could do for her. In the exaltation of the duty laid upon her—it buoyed her up instead of burdening her—she rapidly recovered.

Her father went with her on the long railroad journey from northern New York to western Iowa; he had business out at Davenport, and he said he could just as well go then as any other time; and he went with her to the little country town where George's mother lived in a little house on the edge of the illimitable cornfields, under trees pushed to a top of the rolling prairie. George's father had settled there after the Civil War, as so many other old soldiers had done; but they were Eastern people, and Editha fancied touches of the East in the June rose overhanging the front door, and the garden with early summer flowers stretching from the gate of the paling fence.

It was very low inside the house, and so dim, with the closed blinds, that they could scarcely see one another: Editha tall and black in her crapes which filled the air with the smell of their dyes; her father standing decorously apart with his hat on his forearm, as at funerals; a woman rested in a deep arm-chair, and the woman who had let the strangers in stood behind the chair.

The seated woman turned her head round and up, and asked the woman behind her chair: "*Who* did you say?"

Editha, if she had done what she expected of herself, would have gone down on her knees at the feet of the seated figure and said, "I am George's Editha," for answer.

But instead of her own voice she heard that other woman's voice, saying: "Well, I don't know as I *did* get the name just right. I guess I'll have to make a little more light in here," and she went and pushed two of the shutters ajar.

Then Editha's father said, in his public will–now–address–a–few–remarks tone: "My name is Balcom, ma'am—Junius H. Balcom, of Balcom's Works, New York; my daughter—"

"Oh!" the seated woman broke in, with a powerful voice, the voice that always surprised Editha from Gearson's slender frame. "Let me see you. Stand round where the light can strike on your face," and Editha dumbly obeyed. "So, you're Editha Balcom," she sighed.

"Yes," Editha said, more like a culprit than a comforter.

"What did you come for?" Mrs. Gearson asked.

Editha's face quivered and her knees shook. "I came—because—because George—" She could go no further.

"Yes," the mother said, "he told me he had asked you to come if he got killed. You didn't expect that, I suppose, when you sent him."

"I would rather have died myself than done it!" Editha said, with more truth in her deep voice than she ordinarily found in it. "I tried to leave him free—"

"Yes, that letter of yours, that came back with his other things, left him free."

Editha saw now where George's irony came from.

"It was not to be read before—unless—until—I told him so," she faltered.

"Of course, he wouldn't read a letter of yours, under the circumstances, till he thought you wanted him to. Been sick?" the woman abruptly demanded.

"Very sick," Editha said, with self-pity.

"Daughter's life," her father interposed, "was almost despaired of, at one time."

Mrs. Gearson gave him no heed. "I suppose you would have been glad to die, such a brave person as you! I don't believe *he* was glad to die. He was always a timid boy, that way; he was afraid of a good many things; but if he was afraid he did what he made up his mind to. I suppose he made up his mind to go, but I knew what it cost him by what it cost me when I heard of it. I had been through *one* war before. When you sent him you didn't expect he would get killed."

The voice seemed to compassionate Editha, and it was time. "No," she huskily murmured.

"No, girls don't; women don't, when they give their men up to their country. They think they'll come marching back, somehow, just as gay as they went, or if it's an empty sleeve, or even an empty pantaloon, it's all the more glory, and they're so much the prouder of them, poor things!"

The tears began to run down Editha's face; she had not wept till then; but it was now such a relief to be understood that the tears came.

"No, you didn't expect him to get killed," Mrs. Gearson repeated, in a voice which was startlingly like George's again. "You just expected him to kill someone else, some of those foreigners, that weren't there because they had any say about it, but because they had to be there, poor wretches—conscripts, or whatever they call 'em. You thought it would be all right for my George, *your* George, to kill the sons of those miserable mothers and the husbands of those girls that you would never see the faces of." The woman lifted her powerful voice in a psalmlike note. "I thank my God he didn't live to do it! I thank my God they killed him first, and that he ain't livin' with their blood on his hands!" She dropped her eyes, which she had raised with her voice, and glared at Editha. "What you got that black on for?" She lifted herself by her powerful arms so high that her helpless body seemed to hang limp its full length. "Take it off, take it off, before I tear it from your back!"

The lady who was passing the summer near Balcom's Works was sketching Editha's beauty, which lent itself wonderfully to the effects of a colorist. It had come to that confidence which is rather apt to grow between artist and sitter, and Editha had told her everything.

"To think of your having such a tragedy in your life!" the lady said. She added: "I suppose there are people who feel that way about war. But when you consider the good this war has done—how much it has done for the country! I can't understand such people, for my part. And when you had come all the way out there to console her—got up out of a sick-bed! Well!"

"I think," Editha said, magnanimously, "she wasn't quite in her right mind; and so did papa."

"Yes," the lady said, looking at Editha's lips in nature and then at her lips in art, and giving an empirical touch to them in the picture. "But how dreadful of her! How perfectly—excuse me—how *vulgar!*"

A light broke upon Editha in the darkness which she felt had been without a gleam of brightness for weeks and months. The mystery that had bewildered her was solved by the word; and from that moment she rose from grovelling in shame and self-pity, and began to live again in the ideal.

# SWEAT

## Zora Neale Hurston

### I

IT WAS ELEVEN o'clock of a Spring night in Florida. It was Sunday. Any other night, Delia Jones would have been in bed for two hours by this time. But she was a washwoman, and Monday morning meant a great deal to her. So she collected the soiled clothes on Saturday when she returned the clean things. Sunday night after church, she sorted and put the white things to soak. It saved her almost a half-day's start. A great hamper in the bedroom held the clothes that she brought home. It was so much neater than a number of bundles lying around.

She squatted on the kitchen floor beside the great pile of clothes, sorting them into small heaps according to color, and humming a song in a mournful key, but wondering through it all where Sykes, her husband, had gone with her horse and buckboard.

Just then something long, round, limp and black fell upon her shoulders and slithered to the floor beside her. A great terror took hold of her. It softened her knees and dried her mouth so that it was a full minute before she could cry out or move. Then she saw that it was the big bull whip her husband liked to carry when he drove.

She lifted her eyes to the door and saw him standing there bent over with laughter at her fright. She screamed at him.

"Sykes, what you throw dat whip on me like dat? You know it would skeer me—looks just like a snake, an' you knows how skeered Ah is of snakes."

"Course Ah knowed it! That's how come Ah done it." He slapped his leg with his hand and almost rolled on the ground in his mirth. "If you such a big fool dat you got to have a fit over a earth worm or a string, Ah don't keer how bad Ah skeer you."

"You ain't got no business doing it. Gawd knows it's a sin. Some day Ah'm gointuh drop dead from some of yo' foolishness. 'Nother thing, where you been wid mah rig? Ah feeds dat pony. He ain't fuh you to be drivin' wid no bull whip."

"You sho' is one aggravatin' nigger woman!" he declared and stepped into the room. She resumed her work and did not answer him at once. "Ah done tole you time and again to keep them white folks' clothes outa dis house."

He picked up the whip and glared at her. Delia went on with her work. She went out into the yard and returned with a galvanized tub and set it on the washbench. She saw that Sykes had kicked all of the clothes together again, and now stood in her way truculently, his whole manner hoping, *praying,* for an argument. But she walked calmly around him and commenced to re-sort the things.

"Next time, Ah'm gointer kick 'em outdoors," he threatened as he struck a match along the leg of his corduroy breeches.

Delia never looked up from her work, and her thin, stooped shoulders sagged further.

"Ah ain't for no fuss t'night Sykes. Ah just come from taking sacrament at the church house."

He snorted scornfully. "Yeah, you just come from de church house on a Sunday night, but heah you is gone to work on them clothes. You ain't nothing but a hypocrite. One of them amen-corner Christians—sing, whoop, and shout, then come home and wash white folks' clothes on the Sabbath."

He stepped roughly upon the whitest pile of things, kicking them helter-skelter as he crossed the room. His wife gave a little scream of dismay, and quickly gathered them together again.

"Sykes, you quit grindin' dirt into these clothes! How can Ah git through by Sat'day if Ah don't start on Sunday?"

"Ah don't keer if you never git through. Anyhow, Ah done promised Gawd and a couple of other men, Ah ain't gointer have it in mah house. Don't gimme no lip neither, else Ah'll throw 'em out and put mah fist up side yo' head to boot."

Delia's habitual meekness seemed to slip from her shoulders like a blown scarf. She was on her feet; her poor little body, her bare knuckly hands bravely defying the strapping hulk before her.

heah, Sykes, you done gone too fu.
fur fifteen years, and Ah been takin' in wash.
Sweat, sweat, sweat! Work and sweat, cry and sweat,

"What's that got to do with me?" he asked brutal.

"What's it got to do with you, Sykes? Mah tub of .
yo' belly with vittles more times than yo' hands is filled it. r
is done paid for this house and Ah reckon Ah kin keep on s
in it."

She seized the iron skillet from the stove and struck a defens.
pose, which act surprised him greatly, coming from her. It cowec
him and he did not strike her as he usually did.

"Naw you won't," she panted, "that ole snaggle-toothed black
woman you runnin' with ain't comin' heah to pile up on *mah* sweat
and blood. You ain't paid for nothin' on this place, and Ah'm gointer
stay right heah till Ah'm toted out foot foremost."

"Well, you better quit gittin' me riled up, else they'll be totin'
you out sooner than you expect. Ah'm so tired of you Ah don't
know whutto do. Gawd! How Ah hates skinny wimmen!"

A little awed by this new Delia, he sidled out of the door and
slammed the back gate after him. He did not say where he had gone,
but she knew too well. She knew very well that he would not return
until nearly daybreak also. Her work over, she went on to bed but
not to sleep at once. Things had come to a pretty pass!

She lay awake, gazing upon the debris that cluttered their matrimonial
trail. Not an image left standing along the way. Anything like flowers
had long ago been drowned in the salty stream that had been pressed
from her heart. Her tears, her sweat, her blood. She had brought love
to the union and he had brought a longing after the flesh. Two months
after the wedding, he had given her the first brutal beating. She had
the memory of his numerous trips to Orlando with all of his wages
when he had returned to her penniless, even before the first year had
passed. She was young and soft then, but now she thought of her
knotty, muscled limbs, her harsh knuckly hands, and drew herself up
into an unhappy little ball in the middle of the big feather bed. Too
late now to hope for love, even if it were not Bertha it would be
someone else. This case differed from the others only in that she was
bolder than the others. Too late for everything except her little home.
She had built it for her old days, and planted one by one the trees
and flowers there. It was lovely to her, lovely.

Somehow, before sleep came, she found herself saying aloud: "Oh
well, whatever goes over the Devil's back, is got to come under his

...uther, Sykes, like everybody else, is gointer reap
...r that she was able to build a spiritual earthworks
...oand. His shells could no longer reach her. AMEN. She
...p and slept until he announced his presence in bed by
...r feet and rudely snatching the covers away.

...me come kivah heah, an' git yo' damn foots over on yo'
...de! Ah oughter mash you in yo' mouf fuh drawing dat skillet
...me."

Delia went clear to the rail without answering him. A triumphant
indifference to all that he was or did.

## II

The week was as full of work for Delia as all other weeks, and Saturday
found her behind her little pony, collecting and delivering clothes.

It was a hot, hot day near the end of July. The village men on Joe
Clarke's porch even chewed cane listlessly. They did not hurl the
cane-knots as usual. They let them dribble over the edge of the porch.
Even conversation had collapsed under the heat.

"Heah come Delia Jones," Jim Merchant said, as the shaggy pony
came 'round the bend of the road toward them. The rusty buckboard
was heaped with baskets of crisp, clean laundry.

"Yep," Joe Lindsay agreed. "Hot or col', rain or shine, jes' ez reg'lar
ez de weeks roll roun' Delia carries 'em an' fetches 'em on Sat'day."

"She better if she wanter eat," said Moss. "Syke Jones ain't wuth
de shot an' powder hit would tek tuh kill 'em. Not to *huh* he ain't."

"He sho' ain't," Walter Thomas chimed in. "It's too bad, too,
cause she wuz a right pretty li'l trick when he got huh. Ah'd uh
mah'ied huh mahself if he hadnter beat me to it."

Delia nodded briefly at the men as she drove past.

"Too much knockin' will ruin *any* 'oman. He done beat huh
'nough tuh kill three women, let 'lone change they looks," said Elijah
Moseley. "How Syke kin stommuck dat big black greasy Mogul he's
layin' roun' wid, gits me. Ah swear dat eight-rock couldn't kiss a
sardine can Ah done thowed out de back do' 'way las' yeah."

"Aw, she's fat, thass how come. He's allus been crazy 'bout fat
women," put in Merchant. "He'd a' been tied up wid one long time
ago if he could a' found one tuh have him. Did Ah tell yuh 'bout
him come sidlin' roun' *mah* wife—bringin' her a basket uh peecans
outa his yard fuh a present? Yessir, mah wife! She tol' him tuh take
'em right straight back home, 'cause Delia works so hard ovah dat

washtub she reckon everything on de place taste lak sweat an' soapsuds. Ah jus' wisht Ah'd a' caught 'im 'roun' dere! Ah'd a' made his hips ketch on fiah down dat shell road."

"Ah know he done it, too. Ah sees 'im grinnin' at every 'oman dat passes," Walter Thomas said. "But even so, he useter eat some mighty big hunks uh humble pie tuh git dat li'l 'oman he got. She wuz ez pritty ez a speckled pup! Dat wuz fifteen years ago. He useter be so skeered uh losin' huh, she could make him do some parts of a husband's duty. Dey never wuz de same in de mind."

"There oughter be a law about him," said Lindsay. "He ain't fit tuh carry guts tuh a bear."

Clarke spoke for the first time. "'Tain't no law on earth dat kin make a man be decent if it ain't in 'im. There's plenty men dat takes a wife lak dey do a joint uh sugar-cane. It's round, juicy an' sweet when dey gits it. But dey squeeze an' grind, squeeze an' grind an' wring tell dey wring every drop uh pleasure dat's in 'em out. When dey's satisfied dat dey is wrung dry, dey treats 'em jes' lak dey do a cane-chew. Dey thows 'em away. Dey knows whut dey is doin' while dey is at it, an' hates theirselves fuh it but they keeps on hangin' after huh tell she's empty. Den dey hates huh fuh bein' a cane-chew an' in de way."

"We oughter take Syke an' dat stray 'oman uh his'n down in Lake Howell swamp an' lay on de rawhide till they cain't say Lawd a' mussy. He allus wuz uh ovahbearin' niggah, but since dat white 'oman from up north done teached 'im how to run a automobile, he done got too beggety to live—an' we oughter kill 'im," Old Man Anderson advised.

A grunt of approval went around the porch. But the heat was melting their civic virtue and Elijah Moseley began to bait Joe Clarke.

"Come on, Joe, git a melon outa dere an' slice it up for yo' customers. We'se all sufferin' wid de heat. De bear's done got *me!*"

"Thass right, Joe, a watermelon is jes' whut Ah needs tuh cure de eppizudicks," Walter Thomas joined forces with Moseley. "Come on dere, Joe. We all is steady customers an' you ain't set us up in a long time. Ah chooses dat long, bowlegged Floridy favorite."

"A god, an' be dough. You all gimme twenty cents and slice away," Clarke retorted. "Ah needs a col' slice m'self. Heah, everybody chip in. Ah'll lend y'all mah meat knife."

The money was all quickly subscribed and the huge melon brought forth. At that moment, Sykes and Bertha arrived. A determined silence fell on the porch and the melon was put away again.

Merchant snapped down the blade of his jackknife and moved toward the store door.

"Come on in, Joe, an' gimme a slab uh sow belly an' uh pound uh coffee—almost fuhgot 'twas Sat'day. Got to git on home." Most of the men left also.

Just then Delia drove past on her way home, as Sykes was ordering magnificently for Bertha. It pleased him for Delia to see.

"Git whutsoever yo' heart desires, Honey. Wait a minute, Joe. Give huh two bottles uh strawberry soda-water, uh quart parched ground-peas, an' a block uh chewin' gum."

With all this they left the store, with Sykes reminding Bertha that this was his town and she could have it if she wanted it.

The men returned soon after they left, and held their watermelon feast.

"Where did Syke Jones git da 'oman from nohow?" Lindsay asked.

"Ovah Apopka. Guess dey musta been cleanin' out de town when she lef'. She don't look lak a thing but a hunk uh liver wid hair on it."

"Well, she sho' kin squall," Dave Carter contributed. "When she gits ready tuh laff, she jes' opens huh mouf an' latches it back tuh de las' notch. No ole granpa alligator down in Lake Bell ain't got nothin' on huh."

### III

Bertha had been in town three months now. Sykes was still paying her room-rent at Delia Lewis'—the only house in town that would have taken her in. Sykes took her frequently to Winter Park to 'stomps'. He still assured her that he was the swellest man in the state.

"Sho' you kin have dat li'l ole house soon's Ah git dat 'oman outa dere. Everything b'longs tuh me an' you sho' kin have it. Ah sho' 'bominates uh skinny 'oman. Lawdy, you sho' is got one portly shape on you! You kin git *anything* you wants. Dis is *mah* town an' you sho' kin have it."

Delia's work-worn knees crawled over the earth in Gethsemane and up the rocks of Calvary many, many times during these months. She avoided the villagers and meeting places in her efforts to be blind and deaf. But Bertha nullified this to a degree, by coming to Delia's house to call Sykes out to her at the gate.

Delia and Sykes fought all the time now with no peaceful interludes. They slept and ate in silence. Two or three times Delia had attempted a timid friendliness, but she was repulsed each time. It was plain that the breaches must remain agape.

The sun had burned July to August. The heat streamed down like a million hot arrows, smiting all things living upon the earth. Grass withered, leaves browned, snakes went blind in shedding and men and dogs went mad. Dog days!

Delia came home one day and found Sykes there before her. She wondered, but started to go on into the house without speaking, even though he was standing in the kitchen door and she must either stoop under his arm or ask him to move. He made no room for her. She noticed a soap box beside the steps, but paid no particular attention to it, knowing that he must have brought it there. As she was stooping to pass under his outstretched arm, he suddenly pushed her backward, laughingly.

"Look in de box dere Delia, Ah done brung yuh somethin'!"

She nearly fell upon the box in her stumbling, and when she saw what it held, she all but fainted outright.

"Syke! Syke, mah Gawd! You take dat rattlesnake 'way from heah! You *gottuh*. Oh, Jesus, have mussy!"

"Ah ain't got tuh do nuthin' uh de kin'—fact is Ah ain't got tuh do nothin' but die. 'Tain't no use uh you puttin' on airs makin' out lak you skeered uh dat snake—he's gointer stay right heah tell he die. He wouldn't bite me cause Ah knows how tuh handle 'im. Nohow he wouldn't risk breakin' out his fangs 'gin *yo* skinny laigs."

"Naw, now Syke, don't keep dat thing 'round tryin' tuh skeer me tuh death. You knows Ah'm even feared uh earth worms. Thass de biggest snake Ah evah did see. Kill 'im Syke, please."

"Doan ast me tuh do nothin' fuh yuh. Goin' 'round tryin' tuh be so damn asterperious. Naw, Ah ain't gonna kill it. Ah think uh damn sight mo' uh him dan you! Dat's a nice snake an' anybody doan lak 'im kin jes' hit de grit."

The village soon heard that Sykes had the snake, and came to see and ask questions.

"How de hen-fire did you ketch dat six-foot rattler, Syke?" Thomas asked.

"He's full uh frogs so he cain't hardly move, thass how Ah eased up on 'm. But Ah'm a snake charmer an' knows how tuh handle 'em. Shux, dat ain't nothin'. Ah could ketch one eve'y day if Ah so wanted tuh."

"Whut he needs is a heavy hick'ry club leaned real heavy on his head. Dat's de bes' way tuh charm a rattlesnake."

"Naw, Walt, y'all jes' don't understand dese diamon' backs lak Ah do," said Sykes in a superior tone of voice.

The village agreed with Walter, but the snake stayed on. His box remained by the kitchen door with its screen wire covering. Two or three days later it had digested its meal of frogs and literally came to life. It rattled at every movement in the kitchen or the yard. One day as Delia came down the kitchen steps she saw his chalky-white fangs curved like scimitars hung in the wire meshes. This time she did not run away with averted eyes as usual. She stood for a long time in the doorway in a red fury that grew bloodier for every second that she regarded the creature that was her torment.

That night she broached the subject as soon as Sykes sat down to the table.

"Syke, Ah wants you tuh take dat snake 'way fum heah. You done starved me an' Ah put up widcher, you done beat me and Ah took dat, but you done kilt all mah insides bringin' dat varmint heah."

Sykes poured out a saucer full of coffee and drank it deliberately before he answered her.

"A whole lot Ah keer 'bout how you feels inside uh out. Dat snake ain't goin' no damn wheah till Ah gits ready fuh 'im tuh go. So fur as beatin' is concerned, yuh ain't took near all dat you gointer take ef yuh stay 'round *me*."

Delia pushed back her plate and got up from the table. "Ah hates you, Syke," she said calmly. "Ah hates you tuh de same degree dat Ah useter love yuh. Ah done took an' took till mah belly is full up tuh mah neck. Dat's de reason Ah got mah letter fum de church an' moved mah membership tuh Woodbridge—so Ah don't haftuh take no sacrament wid yuh. Ah don't wantuh see yuh 'round me atall. Lay 'round wid dat 'oman all yuh wants tuh, but gwan 'way fum me an' mah house. Ah hates yuh lak uh suck-egg dog."

Sykes almost let the huge wad of corn bread and collard greens he was chewing fall out of his mouth in amazement. He had a hard time whipping himself up to the proper fury to try to answer Delia.

"Well, Ah'm glad you does hate me. Ah'm sho' tiahed uh you hangin' ontuh me. Ah don't want yuh. Look at yuh stringey ole neck! Yo' rawbony laigs an' arms is enough tuh cut uh man tuh death. You looks jes' lak de devvul's doll-baby tuh *me*. You cain't hate me no worse dan Ah hates you. Ah been hatin' you fuh years."

"Yo' ole black hide don't look lak nothin' tuh me, but uh passle uh wrinkled up rubber, wid yo' big ole yeahs flappin' on each side lak uh paih uh buzzard wings. Don't think Ah'm gointuh be run 'way fum mah house neither. Ah'm goin' tuh de white folks 'bout *you,* mah young man, de very nex' time you lay yo' han's on me. Mah cup is done run ovah." Delia said this with no signs of fear and Sykes departed from the house, threatening her, but made not the slightest move to carry out any of them.

That night he did not return at all, and the next day being Sunday, Delia was glad she did not have to quarrel before she hitched up her pony and drove the four miles to Woodbridge.

She stayed to the night service—'love feast'—which was very warm and full of spirit. In the emotional winds her domestic trials were borne far and wide so that she sang as she drove homeward,

> Jurden water, black an' col
> Chills de body, not de soul
> An' Ah wantah cross Jurden in uh calm time.

She came from the barn to the kitchen door and stopped.

"Whut's de mattah, ol' Satan, you ain't kickin' up yo' racket?" She addressed the snake's box. Complete silence. She went on into the house with a new hope in its birth struggles. Perhaps her threat to go to the white folks had frightened Sykes! Perhaps he was sorry! Fifteen years of misery and suppression had brought Delia to the place where she would hope *anything* that looked toward a way over or through her wall of inhibitions.

She felt in the match-safe behind the stove at once for a match. There was only one there.

"Dat niggah wouldn't fetch nothin' heah tuh save his rotten neck, but he kin run thew whut Ah brings quick enough. Now he done toted off nigh on tuh haff uh box uh matches. He done had dat 'oman heah in mah house, too."

Nobody but a woman could tell how she knew this even before she struck the match. But she did and it put her into a new fury.

Presently she brought in the tubs to put the white things to soak. This time she decided she need not bring the hamper out of the bedroom; she would go in there and do the sorting. She picked up the pot-bellied lamp and went in. The room was small and the hamper stood hard by the foot of the white iron bed. She could sit and reach through the bedposts—resting as she worked.

*"Ah wantah cross Jurden in uh calm time."* She was singing again. The mood of the 'love feast' had returned. She threw back the lid of the basket almost gaily. Then, moved by both horror and terror,

she sprang back toward the door. *There lay the snake in the basket!*
He moved sluggishly at first, but even as she turned round and
round, jumped up and down in an insanity of fear, he began to stir
vigorously. She saw him pouring his awful beauty from the basket
upon the bed, then she seized the lamp and ran as fast as she could
to the kitchen. The wind from the open door blew out the light
and the darkness added to her terror. She sped to the darkness of
the yard, slamming the door after her before she thought to set
down the lamp. She did not feel safe even on the ground, so she
climbed up in the hay barn.

There for an hour or more she lay sprawled upon the hay a gibbering
wreck.

Finally she grew quiet, and after that came coherent thought. With
this stalked through her a cold, bloody rage. Hours of this. A period
of introspection, a space of retrospection, then a mixture of both.
Out of this an awful calm.

"Well, Ah done de bes' Ah could. If things ain't right, Gawd
knows 'tain't mah fault."

She went to sleep—a twitch sleep—and woke up to a faint gray
sky. There was a loud hollow sound below. She peered out. Sykes
was at the wood-pile, demolishing a wire-covered box.

He hurried to the kitchen door, but hung outside there some
minutes before he entered, and stood some minutes more inside
before he closed it after him.

The gray in the sky was spreading. Delia descended without fear
now, and crouched beneath the low bedroom window. The drawn
shade shut out the dawn, shut in the night. But the thin walls held
back no sound.

"Dat ol' scratch is woke up now!" She mused at the tremendous
whirr inside, which every woodsman knows, is one of the sound
illusions. The rattler is a ventriloquist. His whirr sounds to the right,
to the left, straight ahead, behind, close under foot—everywhere but
where it is. Woe to him who guesses wrong unless he is prepared to
hold up his end of the argument! Sometimes he strikes without
rattling at all.

Inside, Sykes heard nothing until he knocked a pot lid off the stove
while trying to reach the match-safe in the dark. He had emptied
his pockets at Bertha's.

The snake seemed to wake up under the stove and Sykes made a
quick leap into the bedroom. In spite of the gin he had had, his head
was clearing now.

"Mah Gawd!" he chattered, "ef Ah could on'y strack uh light!"

The rattling ceased for a moment as he stood paralyzed. He waited. It seemed that the snake waited also.

"Oh, fuh de light! Ah thought he'd be too sick"—Sykes was muttering to himself when the whirr began again, closer, right underfoot this time. Long before this, Sykes' ability to think had been flattened down to primitive instinct and he leaped—onto the bed.

Outside Delia heard a cry that might have come from a maddened chimpanzee, a stricken gorilla. All the terror, all the horror, all the rage that man possibly could express, without a recognizable human sound.

A tremendous stir inside there, another series of animal screams, the intermittent whirr of the reptile. The shade torn violently down from the window, letting in the red dawn, a huge brown hand seizing the window stick, great dull blows upon the wooden floor punctuating the gibberish of sound long after the rattle of the snake had abruptly subsided. All this Delia could see and hear from her place beneath the window, and it made her ill. She crept over to the four-o'clocks and stretched herself on the cool earth to recover.

She lay there. "Delia, Delia!" She could hear Sykes calling in a most despairing tone as one who expected no answer. The sun crept on up, and he called. Delia could not move—her legs had gone flabby. She never moved, he called, and the sun kept rising.

"Mah Gawd!" She heard him moan, "Mah Gawd fum Heben!" She heard him stumbling about and got up from her flower-bed. The sun was growing warm. As she approached the door she heard him call out hopefully, "Delia, is dat you Ah heah?"

She saw him on his hands and knees as soon as she reached the door. He crept an inch or two toward her—all that he was able, and she saw his horribly swollen neck and his one open eye shining with hope. A surge of pity too strong to support bore her away from that eye that must, could not, fail to see the tubs. He would see the lamp. Orlando with its doctors was too far. She could scarcely reach the chinaberry tree, where she waited in the growing heat while inside she knew the cold river was creeping up and up to extinguish that eye which must know by now that she knew.

# ADVENTURE OF THE
# GERMAN STUDENT

## Washington Irving

ON A STORMY night, in the tempestuous times of the French revolution, a young German was returning to his lodgings, at a late hour, across the old part of Paris. The lightning gleamed, and the loud claps of thunder rattled through the lofty narrow streets—but I should first tell you something about this young German.

Gottfried Wolfgang was a young man of good family. He had studied for some time at Göttingen, but being of a visionary and enthusiastic character, he had wandered into those wild and speculative doctrines which have so often bewildered German students. His secluded life, his intense application, and the singular nature of his studies, had an effect on both mind and body. His health was impaired; his imagination diseased. He had been indulging in fanciful speculations on spiritual essences, until, like Swedenborg, he had an ideal world of his own around him. He took up a notion, I do not know from what cause, that there was an evil influence hanging over him; an evil genius or spirit seeking to ensnare him and ensure his perdition. Such an idea working on his melancholy temperament, produced the most gloomy effects. He became haggard and desponding. His friends discovered the mental malady preying upon him, and determined that the best cure was a change of scene; he was sent, therefore, to finish his studies amidst the splendors and gayeties of Paris.

Wolfgang arrived at Paris at the breaking out of the revolution. The popular delirium at first caught his enthusiastic mind, and he was captivated by the political and philosophical theories of the day: but the scenes of blood which followed shocked his sensitive nature, disgusted him with society and the world, and made him more than ever a recluse. He shut himself up in a solitary apartment in the *Pays Latin,* the quarter of students. There, in a gloomy street not far from the monastic walls of the Sorbonne, he pursued his favorite speculations. Sometimes he spent hours together in the great libraries of Paris, those catacombs of departed authors, rummaging among their hoards of dusty and obsolete works in quest of food for his unhealthy appetite. He was, in a manner, a literary ghoul, feeding in the charnel-house of decayed literature.

Wolfgang, though solitary and recluse, was of an ardent temperament, but for a time it operated merely upon his imagination. He was too shy and ignorant of the world to make any advances to the fair, but he was a passionate admirer of female beauty, and in his lonely chamber would often lose himself in reveries on forms and faces which he had seen, and his fancy would deck out images of loveliness far surpassing the reality.

While his mind was in this excited and sublimated state, a dream produced an extraordinary effect upon him. It was of a female face of transcendent beauty. So strong was the impression made, that he dreamt of it again and again. It haunted his thoughts by day, his slumbers by night; in fine, he became passionately enamoured of this shadow of a dream. This lasted so long that it became one of those fixed ideas which haunt the minds of melancholy men, and are at times mistaken for madness.

Such was Gottfried Wolfgang, and such his situation at the time I mentioned. He was returning home late one stormy night, through some of the old and gloomy streets of the *Marais,* the ancient part of Paris. The loud claps of thunder rattled among the high houses of the narrow streets. He came to the Place de Grève, the square where public executions are performed. The lightning quivered about the pinnacles of the ancient Hôtel de Ville, and shed flickering gleams over the open space in front. As Wolfgang was crossing the square, he shrank back with horror at finding himself close by the guillotine. It was the height of the reign of terror, when this dreadful instrument of death stood ever ready, and its scaffold was continually running with the blood of the virtuous and the brave. It had that very day been actively employed in the work of carnage, and there it stood in grim array, amidst a silent and sleeping city, waiting for fresh victims.

Wolfgang's heart sickened within him, and he was turning shuddering from the horrible engine, when he beheld a shadowy form, cowering as it were at the foot of the steps which led up to the scaffold. A succession of vivid flashes of lightning revealed it more distinctly. It was a female figure, dressed in black. She was seated on one of the lower steps of the scaffold, leaning forward, her face hid in her lap; and her long dishevelled tresses hanging to the ground, streaming with the rain which fell in torrents. Wolfgang paused. There was something awful in this solitary monument of woe. The female had the appearance of being above the common order. He knew the times to be full of vicissitude, and that many a fair head, which had once been pillowed on down, now wandered houseless. Perhaps this was some poor mourner whom the dreadful axe had rendered desolate, and who sat here heart-broken on the strand of existence, from which all that was dear to her had been launched into eternity.

He approached, and addressed her in the accents of sympathy. She raised her head and gazed wildly at him. What was his astonishment at beholding, by the bright glare of the lightning, the very face which had haunted him in his dreams. It was pale and disconsolate, but ravishingly beautiful.

Trembling with violent and conflicting emotions, Wolfgang again accosted her. He spoke something of her being exposed at such an hour of the night, and to the fury of such a storm, and offered to conduct her to her friends. She pointed to the guillotine with a gesture of dreadful signification.

"I have no friend on earth!" said she.

"But you have a home," said Wolfgang.

"Yes—in the grave!"

The heart of the student melted at the words.

"If a stranger dare make an offer," said he, "without danger of being misunderstood, I would offer my humble dwelling as a shelter; myself as a devoted friend. I am friendless myself in Paris, and a stranger in the land; but if my life could be of service, it is at your disposal, and should be sacrificed before harm or indignity should come to you."

There was an honest earnestness in the young man's manner that had its effect. His foreign accent, too, was in his favor; it showed him not to be a hackneyed inhabitant of Paris. Indeed, there is an eloquence in true enthusiasm that is not to be doubted. The homeless stranger confided herself implicitly to the protection of the student.

He supported her faltering steps across the Pont Neuf, and by the place where the statue of Henry the Fourth had been overthrown by the populace. The storm had abated, and the thunder rumbled at a distance. All Paris was quiet; that great volcano of human passion slumbered for a while, to gather fresh strength for the next day's eruption. The student conducted his charge through the ancient streets of the *Pays Latin,* and by the dusky walls of the Sorbonne, to the great dingy hotel which he inhabited. The old portress who admitted them stared with surprise at the unusual sight of the melancholy Wolfgang with a female companion.

On entering his apartment, the student, for the first time, blushed at the scantiness and indifference of his dwelling. He had but one chamber—an old-fashioned saloon—heavily carved, and fantastically furnished with the remains of former magnificence, for it was one of those hotels in the quarter of the Luxembourg palace, which had once belonged to nobility. It was lumbered with books and papers, and all the usual apparatus of a student, and his bed stood in a recess at one end.

When lights were brought, and Wolfgang had a better opportunity of contemplating the stranger, he was more than ever intoxicated by her beauty. Her face was pale, but of a dazzling fairness, set off by a profusion of raven hair that hung clustering about it. Her eyes were large and brilliant, with a singular expression approaching almost to wildness. As far as her black dress permitted her shape to be seen, it was of perfect symmetry. Her whole appearance was highly striking, though she was dressed in the simplest style. The only thing approaching to an ornament which she wore, was a broad black band round her neck, clasped by diamonds.

The perplexity now commenced with the student how to dispose of the helpless being thus thrown upon his protection. He thought of abandoning his chamber to her, and seeking shelter for himself elsewhere. Still, he was so fascinated by her charms, there seemed to be such a spell upon his thoughts and senses, that he could not tear himself from her presence. Her manner, too, was singular and unaccountable. She spoke no more of the guillotine. Her grief had abated. The attentions of the student had first won her confidence, and then, apparently, her heart. She was evidently an enthusiast like himself, and enthusiasts soon understand each other.

In the infatuation of the moment, Wolfgang avowed his passion for her. He told her the story of his mysterious dream, and how she had possessed his heart before he had even seen her. She was strangely affected by his recital, and acknowledged to have felt an impulse towards him equally unaccountable. It was the time for wild theory and wild actions. Old prejudices and superstitions were done away; everything was under the sway of the "Goddess of Reason." Among other rubbish of the old times, the forms and ceremonies of marriage began to be considered superfluous bonds for honorable minds. Social compacts were the vogue. Wolfgang was too much of a theorist not to be tainted by the liberal doctrines of the day.

"Why should we separate?" said he: "our hearts are united; in the eye of reason and honor we are as one. What need is there of sordid forms to bind high souls together?"

The stranger listened with emotion: she had evidently received illumination at the same school.

"You have no home or family," continued he: "let me be everything to you, or rather let us be everything to one another. If form is necessary, form shall be observed—there is my hand. I pledge myself to you forever."

"Forever?" said the stranger, solemnly.

"Forever!" repeated Wolfgang.

The stranger clasped the hand extended to her: "Then I am yours," murmured she, and sank upon his bosom.

The next morning the student left his bride sleeping, and sallied forth at an early hour to seek more spacious apartments suitable to the change in his situation. When he returned, he found the stranger lying with her head hanging over the bed, and one arm thrown over it. He spoke to her, but received no reply. He advanced to awaken her from her uneasy posture. On taking her hand, it was cold—there was no pulsation—her face was pallid and ghastly. In a word, she was a corpse.

Horrified and frantic, he alarmed the house. A scene of confusion ensued. The police were summoned. As the officer of police entered the room, he started back on beholding the corpse.

"Great heaven!" cried he, "how did this woman come here?"

"Do you know anything about her?" said Wolfgang eagerly.

"Do I?" exclaimed the officer: "she was guillotined yesterday."

He stepped forward; undid the black collar round the neck of the corpse, and the head rolled on the floor!

The student burst into a frenzy. "The fiend! the fiend has gained possession of me!" shrieked he: "I am lost forever."

They tried to soothe him, but in vain. He was possessed with the frightful belief that an evil spirit had reanimated the dead body to ensnare him. He went distracted, and died in a mad-house.

Here the old gentleman with the haunted head finished his narrative.

"And is this really a fact?" said the inquisitive gentleman.

"A fact not to be doubted," replied the other. "I had it from the best authority. The student told it to me himself. I saw him in a madhouse in Paris."

# THE WIDOW AND HER SON

## Washington Irving

Pittie olde age, within whose silver haires
Honour and reverence evermore have rain'd.
　　　　　　　　Marlowe's *Tamburlaine*

THOSE WHO ARE in the habit of remarking such matters must have noticed the passive quiet of an English landscape on Sunday. The clacking of the mill, the regularly recurring stroke of the flail, the din of the blacksmith's hammer, the whistling of the ploughman, the rattling of the cart, and all other sounds of rural labor are suspended. The very farm-dogs bark less frequently, being less disturbed by passing travellers. At such times I have almost fancied the wind sunk into quiet, and that the sunny landscape, with its fresh green tints melting into blue haze, enjoyed the hallowed calm.

Sweet day, so pure, so calm, so bright
The bridal of the earth and sky.[1]

Well was it ordained that the day of devotion should be a day of rest. The holy repose which reigns over the face of nature has its moral influence; every restless passion is charmed down, and we feel the natural religion of the soul gently springing up within us. For my part, there are feelings that visit me, in a country church, amid the beautiful serenity of nature, which I experience nowhere else;

---

[1] From a poem called "Virtue," by George Herbert (1593–1633).

and if not a more religious, I think I am a better man on Sunday than on any other day of the seven.

During my recent residence in the country, I used frequently to attend at the old village church. Its shadowy aisles, its mouldering monuments, its dark oaken panelling, all reverend with the gloom of departed years, seemed to fit it for the haunt of solemn meditation; but, being in a wealthy, aristocratic neighborhood, the glitter of fashion penetrated even into the sanctuary; and I felt myself continually thrown back upon the world by the frigidity and pomp of the poor worms around me. The only being in the whole congregation who appeared thoroughly to feel the humble and prostrate piety of a true Christian was a poor decrepit old woman, bending under the weight of years and infirmities. She bore the traces of something better than abject poverty. The lingerings of decent pride were visible in her appearance. Her dress, though humble in the extreme, was scrupulously clean. Some trivial respect, too, had been awarded her, for she did not take her seat among the village poor, but sat alone on the steps of the altar. She seemed to have survived all love, all friendship, all society, and to have nothing left her but the hopes of heaven. When I saw her feebly rising and bending her aged form in prayer; habitually conning her prayer-book, which her palsied hand and failing eyes could not permit her to read, but which she evidently knew by heart, I felt persuaded that the faltering voice of that poor woman arose to heaven far before the responses of the clerk, the swell of the organ, or the chanting of the choir.

I am fond of loitering about country churches, and this was so delightfully situated that it frequently attracted me. It stood on a knoll, round which a small stream made a beautiful bend, and then wound its way through a long reach of soft meadow scenery. The church was surrounded by yew trees, which seemed almost coeval with itself. Its tall Gothic spire shot up lightly from among them, with rooks and crows generally wheeling about it. I was seated there one still sunny morning watching two laborers who were digging a grave. They had chosen one of the most remote and neglected corners of the churchyard, where, from the number of nameless graves around, it would appear that the indigent and friendless were huddled into the earth. I was told that the new-made grave was for the only son of a poor widow. While I was meditating on the distinctions of worldly rank, which extend thus down into the very dust, the toll of the bell announced the approach of the funeral. They were the obsequies of poverty, with which pride had nothing to do. A coffin of the plainest materials, without pall or other covering, was borne by some of the villagers. The sexton walked before with an air of cold indifference. There were no mock mourners in the trappings of affected woe, but there was one real mourner who feebly tottered after the corpse. It was the aged mother of the deceased, the poor old woman whom I had seen seated on the steps of the altar. She was supported by a humble friend, who was endeavoring to comfort her. A few of the neighboring poor had joined the train, and some children of the village were running hand in hand, now shouting with unthinking mirth, and now pausing to gaze, with childish curiosity, on the grief of the mourner.

As the funeral train approached the grave, the parson issued from the church porch, arrayed in the surplice, with prayer-book in hand, and attended by the clerk. The service, however, was a mere act of charity. The deceased had been destitute, and the survivor was penniless. It was shuffled through, therefore, in form, but coldly and unfeelingly. The well-fed priest moved but a few steps from the church door; his voice could scarcely be heard at the grave; and never did I hear the funeral service—that sublime and touching ceremony—turned into such a frigid mummery of words.

I approached the grave. The coffin was placed on the ground. On it were inscribed the name and age of the deceased—"George Somers, aged twenty-six years." The poor mother had been assisted to kneel down at the head of it. Her withered hands were clasped, as if in prayer; but I could perceive, by a feeble rocking of the body and a convulsive motion of the lips, that she was gazing on the last relics of her son with the yearnings of a mother's heart.

Preparations were made to deposit the coffin in the earth. There was that bustling stir, which breaks so harshly on the feelings of grief and affection; directions given in the cold tones of business; the striking of spades into sand and gravel; which, at the grave of those we love, is, of all sounds, the most withering. The bustle around seemed to waken the mother from a wretched reverie. She raised her glazed eyes and looked about with a faint wildness. As the men approached with cords to lower the coffin into the grave, she wrung her hands and broke into an agony of grief. The poor woman who attended her took her by the arm, endeavoring to raise her from the earth, and to whisper something like consolation: "Nay, now—nay, now—don't take it so sorely to heart." She could only shake her head and wring her hands, as one not to be comforted.

As they lowered the body into the earth, the creaking of the cords seemed to agonize her; but when, on some accidental obstruction, there was a jostling of the coffin, all the tenderness of the mother burst forth, as if any harm could come to him who was far beyond the reach of worldly suffering.

I could see no more—my heart swelled into my throat—my eyes filled with tears; I felt as if I were acting a barbarous part in standing by and gazing idly on this scene of maternal anguish. I wandered to another part of the churchyard, where I remained until the funeral train had dispersed.

When I saw the mother slowly and painfully quitting the grave, leaving behind her the remains of all that was dear to her on earth, and returning to silence and destitution, my heart ached for her. What, thought I, are the distresses of the rich? They have friends to soothe—pleasures to beguile—a world to divert and dissipate their griefs. What are the sorrows of the young? Their growing minds soon close above the wound—their elastic spirits soon rise beneath the pressure—their green and ductile affections soon twine round new objects. But the sorrows of the poor, who have no outward appliances to soothe—the sorrows of the aged, with whom life at best is but a wintry day, and who can look for no after-growth of joy—the sorrows of a widow, aged, solitary, destitute, mourning over an only son, the last solace of her years—these are indeed sorrows which make us feel the impotency of consolation.

It was some time before I left the churchyard. On my way homeward, I met with the woman who had acted as comforter: she was just returning from accompanying the mother to her lonely habitation, and I drew from her some particulars connected with the affecting scene I had witnessed.

The parents of the deceased had resided in the village from childhood. They had inhabited one of the neatest cottages, and by various rural occupations, and the assistance of a small garden, had supported themselves creditably and comfortably, and led a happy and blameless life. They had one son, who had grown up to be the staff and pride of their age. "Oh, sir!" said the good woman, "he was such a comely lad, so sweet-tempered, so kind to everyone around him, so dutiful to his parents! It did one's heart good to see him of a Sunday, dressed out in his best, so tall, so straight, so cheery, supporting his old mother to church; for she was always fonder of leaning on George's arm than on her good man's; and, poor soul, she might well be proud of him, for a finer lad there was not in the country round."

Unfortunately, the son was tempted, during a year of scarcity and agricultural hardship, to enter into the service of one of the small craft that plied on a neighboring river. He had not been long in this employ, when he was entrapped by a press-gang and carried off to sea. His parents received tidings of his seizure, but beyond that they could learn nothing. It was the loss of their main prop. The father, who was already infirm, grew heartless and melancholy and sunk into his grave. The widow, left lonely in her age and feebleness, could no longer support herself, and came upon the parish. Still there was a kind feeling toward her throughout the village, and a certain respect as being one of the oldest inhabitants. As no one applied for the cottage in which she had passed so many happy days, she was permitted to remain in it, where she lived solitary and almost helpless. The few wants of nature were chiefly supplied from the scanty productions of her little garden, which the neighbors would now and then cultivate for her. It was but a few days before the time at which these circumstances were told me that she was gathering some vegetables for her repast when she heard the cottage-door, which faced the garden, suddenly open. A stranger came out, and seemed to be looking eagerly and wildly around. He was dressed in seamen's clothes, was emaciated and ghastly pale, and bore the air of one broken by sickness and hardships. He saw her and hastened toward her, but his steps were faint and faltering; he sank on his knees before her and sobbed like a child. The poor woman gazed upon him with a vacant and wandering eye. "Oh, my dear, dear mother! don't you know your son? your poor boy, George?" It was, indeed, the wreck of her once noble lad, who shattered by wounds, by sickness and foreign imprisonment, had at length dragged his wasted limbs homeward, to repose among the scenes of his childhood.

I will not attempt to detail the particulars of such a meeting, where sorrow and joy were so completely blended: still, he was alive! he was come home! he might yet live to comfort and cherish her old age! Nature, however, was exhausted in him; and if anything had been wanting to finish the work of fate, the desolation of his native cottage would have been sufficient. He stretched himself on the pallet on which his widowed mother had passed many a sleepless night, and he never rose from it again.

The villagers, when they heard that George Somers had returned, crowded to see him, offering every comfort and assistance that their humble means afforded. He was too weak, however, to talk—he could only look his thanks. His mother was his constant attendant, and he seemed unwilling to be helped by any other hand.

There is something in sickness that breaks down the pride of manhood, that softens the heart, and brings it back to the feelings of infancy. Who that has languished, even in advanced life, in sickness and despondency, who that has pined on a weary bed in the neglect and loneliness of a foreign land, but has thought on the mother "that looked on his childhood," that smoothed his pillow, and administered to his helplessness? Oh, there is an enduring tenderness in the love of a mother to a son that transcends all other affections of the heart. It is neither to be chilled by selfishness, nor daunted by danger, nor weakened by worthlessness, nor stifled by ingratitude. She will sacrifice every comfort to his convenience; she will surrender every pleasure to his enjoyment; she will glory in his fame and exult in his prosperity; and, if misfortune overtakes him, he will be the dearer to her from misfortune; and if disgrace settles upon his name, she will still love and cherish him in spite of his disgrace; and if all the world beside cast him off, she will be all the world to him.

Poor George Somers had known what it was to be in sickness, and none to soothe—lonely and in prison, and none to visit him. He could not endure his mother from his sight; if she moved away, his eyes would follow her. She would sit for hours by his bed watching him as he slept. Sometimes he would start from a feverish dream and look anxiously up until he saw her bending over him; when he would take her hand, lay it on his bosom, and fall asleep with the tranquillity of a child. In this way he died.

My first impulse on hearing this humble tale of affliction was to visit the cottage of the mourner, and administer pecuniary assistance, and, if possible, comfort. I found, however, on inquiry, that the good feelings of the villagers had prompted them to do everything that the case admitted; and as the poor know best how to console each other's sorrows, I did not venture to intrude.

The next Sunday I was at the village church, when, to my surprise, I saw the poor old woman tottering down the aisle to her accustomed seat on the steps of the altar.

She had made an effort to put on something like mourning for her son; and nothing could be more touching than this struggle between pious affection and utter poverty—a black ribbon or so, a faded black handkerchief, and one or two more such humble attempts to express by outward signs that grief which passes show. When I looked round upon the storied monuments, the stately hatchments, the cold marble pomp with which grandeur mourned magnificently over departed pride, and turned to this poor widow, bowed down by age and sorrow at the altar of her God, and offering up the prayers and praises of a pious though a broken heart, I felt that this living monument of real grief was worth them all.

I related her story to some of the wealthy members of the congregation, and they were moved by it. They exerted themselves to render her situation more comfortable and to lighten her afflictions. It was, however, but smoothing a few steps to the grave. In the course of a Sunday or two after, she was missed from her usual seat at church, and before I left the neighborhood I heard, with a feeling of satisfaction, that she had quietly breathed her last and had gone to rejoin those she loved, in that world where sorrow is never known and friends are never parted.

# BROOKSMITH

## Henry James

WE ARE SCATTERED now, the friends of the late Mr. Oliver Offord; but whenever we chance to meet I think we are conscious of a certain esoteric respect for each other. "Yes, you too have been in Arcadia," we seem not too grumpily to allow. When I pass the house in Mansfield Street I remember that Arcadia was there. I don't know who has it now, and I don't want to know; it's enough to be so sure that if I should ring the bell there would be no such luck for me as that Brooksmith should open the door. Mr. Offord, the most agreeable, the most lovable of bachelors, was a retired diplomatist, living on his pension, confined by his infirmities to his fireside and delighted to be found there any afternoon in the year by such visitors as Brooksmith allowed to come up. Brooksmith was his butler and his most intimate friend, to whom we all stood, or I should say sat, in the same relation in which the subject of the sovereign finds himself to the prime minister. By having been for years, in foreign lands, the most delightful Englishman anyone had ever known, Mr. Offord had, in my opinion, rendered signal service to his country. But I suppose he had been too much liked—liked even by those who didn't like *it*—so that as people of that sort never get titles or dotations for the horrid things they have *not* done, his principal reward was simply that we went to see him.

Oh, we went perpetually, and it was not our fault if he was not over-welmed with this particular honour. Any visitor who came once came again—to come merely once was a slight which nobody, I am sure, had ever put upon him. His circle, therefore, was essentially composed of *habitués*,[1] who were *habitués* for each other as well as for him, as those of a happy salon should be. I remember vividly every element of the place, down to the intensely Londonish look of the grey opposite houses, in the gap of the white curtains of the high windows, and the exact spot where, on a particular afternoon, I put down my tea-cup for Brooksmith, lingering an instant, to gather it up as if he were plucking a flower. Mr. Offord's drawing-room was indeed Brooksmith's garden, his pruned and tended human *parterre*,[2] and if we all flourished there and grew well in our places it was largely owing to his supervision.

Many persons have heard much, though most have doubtless seen little, of the famous institution of the salon, and many are born to the depression of knowing that this finest flower of social life refuses to bloom where the English tongue is spoken. The explanation is usually that our women have not the skill to cultivate it—the art to direct, between suggestive shores, the course of the stream of talk. My affectionate, my pious memory of Mr. Offord contradicts this induction only, I fear, more insidiously to confirm it. The very sallow and slightly smoked drawing-room in which he spent so large a portion of the last years of his life certainly deserved the distinguished name; but on the other hand it could not be said at all to owe its stamp to the soft pressure of the indispensable sex. The dear man had indeed been capable of one of those sacrifices to which women are deemed peculiarly apt; he had recognised (under the influence, in some degree, it is true, of physical infirmity), that if you wished people to find you at home you must manage not to be out. He had in short accepted the fact which many dabblers in the social art are slow to learn, that you must really, as they say, take a line and that the only way to be at home is to stay at home. Finally his own fireside had become a summary of his habits. Why should he ever have left it?—since this would have been leaving what was notoriously pleasantest in London, the compact charmed cluster (thinning away indeed into casual couples), round the fine old last century chimney-piece which, with the exception of the remarkable collection of miniatures, was the best thing the place contained. Mr. Offord was not rich; he had nothing but his pension and the use for life of the somewhat superannuated house.

---

[1] *habitué*; French: a person who frequents a certain establishment or type of establishment.

[2] *parterre*; French: an ornamental arrangement of flower beds.

When I am reminded by some uncomfortable contrast of today how perfectly we were all handled there I ask myself once more what had been the secret of such perfection. One had taken it for granted at the time, for anything that is supremely good produces more acceptance than surprise. I felt we were all happy, but I didn't consider how our happiness was managed. And yet there were questions to be asked, questions that strike me as singularly obvious now that there is nobody to answer them. Mr. Offord had solved the insoluble; he had, without feminine help (save in the sense that ladies were dying to come to him and he saved the lives of several), established a salon; but I might have guessed that there was a method in his madness—a law in his success. He had not hit it off by a mere fluke. There was an art in it all, and how was the art so hidden? Who, indeed, if it came to that, was the occult artist? Launching this inquiry the other day, I had already got hold of the tail of my reply. I was helped by the very wonder of some of the conditions that came back to me— those that used to seem as natural as sunshine in a fine climate.

How was it, for instance, that we never were a crowd, never either too many or too few, always the right people *with* the right people (there must really have been no wrong people at all), always coming and going, never sticking fast nor overstaying, yet never popping in or out with an indecorous familiarity? How was it that we all sat where we wanted and moved when we wanted and met whom we wanted and escaped whom we wanted; joining, according to the accident of inclination, the general circle or falling in with a single talker on a convenient sofa? Why were all the sofas so convenient, the accidents so happy, the talkers so ready, the listeners so willing, the subjects presented to you in a rotation as quickly fore-ordained as the courses at dinner? A dearth of topics would have been as unheard of as a lapse in the service. These speculations couldn't fail to lead me to the fundamental truth that Brooksmith had been somehow at the bottom of the mystery. If he had not established the salon at least he had carried it on. Brooksmith, in short, was the artist!

We felt this, covertly, at the time, without formulating it, and were conscious, as an ordered and prosperous community, of his evenhanded justice, untainted with flunkeyism. He had none of that vulgarity—his touch was infinitely fine. The delicacy of it was clear to me on the first occasion my eyes rested, as they were so often to rest again, on the domestic revealed, in the turbid light of the street, by the opening of the house-door. I saw on the spot that though he had plenty of school he carried it without arrogance—he had remained articulate and human. *L'Ecole Anglaise*[3], Mr. Offord used to call him, laughing, when, later, it happened more than once that we had some conversation about him. But I remember accusing Mr. Offord of not doing him quite ideal justice. That he was not one of the giants of the school, however, my old friend, who really understood him perfectly and was devoted to him, as I shall show, quite admitted; which doubtless poor Brooksmith had himself felt, to his cost, when his value in the market was originally determined. The utility of his class in general is estimated by the foot and the inch, and poor Brooksmith had only about five feet two to put into circulation. He acknowledged the inadequacy of this provision, and I am sure was penetrated with the everlasting fitness of the relation between service and stature. If *he* had been Mr. Offord he certainly would have found Brooksmith wanting, and indeed the laxity of his employer on this score was one of many things which he had had to condone and to which he had at last indulgently adapted himself.

I remember the old man's saying to me: "Oh, my servants, if they can live with me a fortnight they can live with me for ever. But it's the first fortnight that tries 'em." It was in the first fortnight, for instance, that Brooksmith had had to learn that he was exposed to being addressed as "my dear fellow" and "my poor child." Strange and deep must such a probation have been to him, and he doubtless emerged from it tempered and purified. This was written to a certain extent in his appearance; in his spare, brisk little person, in his cloistered white face and extraordinarily polished hair, which told of responsibility, looked as if it were kept up to the same high standard as the plate; in his small, clear, anxious eyes, even in the permitted, though not exactly encouraged tuft on his chin. "He thinks me rather mad, but I've broken him in, and now he likes the place, he likes the company," said the old man. I embraced this fully after I had become aware that Brooksmith's main characteristic was a deep and shy refinement, though I remember I was rather puzzled when, on another occasion, Mr. Offord remarked: "What he likes is the talk—mingling in the conversation." I was conscious that I had never seen Brooksmith permit himself this freedom, but I guessed in a moment that what Mr. Offord alluded to was a participation more intense than any speech could have represented—that of being perpetually present on a hundred legitimate pretexts, errands, necessities, and breathing the

---

[3] *L'Ecole Anglaise*; French: The English School.

very atmosphere of criticism, the famous criticism of life. "Quite an education, sir, isn't it, sir?" he said to me one day at the foot of the stairs, when he was letting me out; and I have always remembered the words and the tone as the first sign of the quickening drama of poor Brooksmith's fate. It was indeed an education, but to what was this sensitive young man of thirty-five, of the servile class, being educated?

Practically and inevitably, for the time, to companionship, to the perpetual, the even exaggerated reference and appeal of a person brought to dependence by his time of life and his infirmities and always addicted moreover (this was the exaggeration) to the art of giving you pleasure by letting you do things for him. There were certain things Mr. Offord was capable of pretending he liked you to do, even when he didn't, if he thought *you* liked them. If it happened that you didn't either (this was rare, but it might be), of course there were cross-purposes; but Brooksmith was there to prevent their going very far. This was precisely the way he acted as moderator: he averted misunderstandings or cleared them up. He had been capable, strange as it may appear, of acquiring for this purpose an insight into the French tongue, which was often used at Mr. Offord's; for besides being habitual to most of the foreigners, and they were many, who haunted the place or arrived with letters (letters often requiring a little worried consideration, of which Brooksmith always had cognisance), it had really become the primary language of the master of the house. I don't know if all the *malentendus*[4] were in French, but almost all the explanations were, and this didn't a bit prevent Brooksmith from following them. I know Mr. Offord used to read passages to him from Montaigne and Saint-Simon, for he read perpetually when he was alone—when they were alone, I should say—and Brooksmith was always about. Perhaps you'll say no wonder Mr. Offord's butler regarded him as "rather mad." However, if I'm not sure what he thought about Montaigne I'm convinced he admired Saint-Simon. A certain feeling for letters must have rubbed off on him from the mere handling of his master's books, which he was always carrying to and fro and putting back in their places.

I often noticed that if an anecdote or a quotation, much more a lively discussion, was going forward, he would, if busy with the fire or the curtains, the lamp or the tea, find a pretext for remaining in the room till the point should be reached. If his purpose was to catch

---

[4] *malentendus*; French: misunderstandings.

it you were not discreet to call him off, and I shall never forget a
look, a hard, stony stare (I caught it in its passage), which, one day
when there were a good many people in the room, he fastened upon
the footman who was helping him in the service and who, in an
undertone, had asked him some irrelevant question. It was the only
manifestation of harshness that I ever observed on Brooksmith's part,
and at first I wondered what was the matter. Then I became conscious
that Mr. Offord was relating a very curious anecdote, never before
perhaps made so public, and imparted to the narrator by an eye-witness
of the fact, bearing upon Lord Byron's life in Italy. Nothing would
induce me to reproduce it here; but Brooksmith had been in danger
of losing it. If I ever should venture to reproduce it I shall feel how
much I lose in not having my fellow-auditor to refer to.

The first day Mr. Offord's door was closed was therefore a dark
date in contemporary history. It was raining hard and my umbrella
was wet, but Brooksmith took it from me exactly as if this were a
preliminary for going upstairs. I observed however that instead of
putting it away he held it poised and trickling over the rug, and then
I became aware that he was looking at me with deep, acknowledging
eyes—his air of universal responsibility. I immediately understood;
there was scarcely need of the question and the answer that passed
between us. When I did understand that the old man had given up,
for the first time, though only for the occasion, I exclaimed dolefully:
"What a difference it will make—and to how many people!"

"I shall be one of them, sir!" said Brooksmith; and that was
the beginning of the end.

Mr. Offord came down again, but the spell was broken, and the
great sign of it was that the conversation was, for the first time, not
directed. It wandered and stumbled, a little frightened, like a lost
child—it had let go the nurse's hand. "The worst of it is that now we
shall talk about my health—*c'est la fin de tout*,[5]" Mr. Offord said, when
he reappeared; and then I recognised what a sign of change that would
be—for he had never tolerated anything so provincial. The talk became
ours, in a word—not his; and as ours, even when *he* talked, it could
only be inferior. In this form it was a distress to Brooksmith, whose
attention now wandered from it altogether: he had so much closer a
vision of his master's intimate conditions than our superficialities
represented. There were better hours, and he was more in and out
of the room, but I could see that he was conscious that the great

---

[5]   *c'est . . . tout*; French: it's the end of everything.

institution was falling to pieces. He seemed to wish to take counsel with me about it, to feel responsible for its going on in some form or other. When for the second period—the first had lasted several days— he had to tell me that our old friend didn't receive, I half expected to hear him say after a moment: "Do you think I ought to, sir, in his place?"—as he might have asked me, with the return of autumn, if I thought he had better light the drawing-room fire.

He had a resigned philosophic sense of what his guests—our guests, as I came to regard them in our colloquies—would expect. His feeling was that he wouldn't absolutely have approved of himself as a substitute for the host; but he was so saturated with the religion of habit that he would have made, for our friends, the necessary sacrifice to the divinity. He would take them on a little further, till they could look about them. I think I saw him also mentally confronted with the opportunity to deal—for once in his life—with some of his own dumb preferences, his limitations of sympathy, *weeding* a little, in prospect, and returning to a purer tradition. It was not unknown to me that he considered that toward the end of Mr. Offord's career a certain laxity of selection had crept in.

At last it came to be the case that we all found the closed door more often than the open one; but even when it was closed Brooksmith managed a crack for me to squeeze through; so that practically I never turned away without having paid a visit. The difference simply came to be that the visit was to Brooksmith. It took place in the hall, at the familiar foot of the stairs, and we didn't sit down—at least Brooksmith didn't; moreover it was devoted wholly to one topic and always had the air of being already over—beginning, as it were, at the end. But it was always interesting—it always gave me something to think about. It is true that the subject of my meditation was ever the same—ever "It's all very well, but what *will* become of Brooksmith?" Even my private answer to this question left me still unsatisfied. No doubt Mr. Offord would provide for him, but *what* would he provide? that was the great point. He couldn't provide society; and society had become a necessity of Brooksmith's nature. I must add that he never showed a symptom of what I may call sordid solicitude—anxiety on his own account. He was rather livid and intensely grave, as befitted a man before whose eyes the "shade of that which once was great" was passing away. He had the solemnity of a person winding up, under depressing circumstances, a long established and celebrated business; he was a kind of social executor or liquidator. But his manner seemed to testify exclusively to the uncertainty of *our* future. I couldn't in those days have afforded it—I lived in two rooms in Jermyn Street and didn't "keep a man"; but even if my income had permitted I shouldn't have ventured to say to Brooksmith (emulating Mr. Offord), "My dear fellow, I'll take you on." The whole tone of our intercourse was so much more an implication that it was *I* who should now want a lift. Indeed there was a tacit assurance in Brooksmith's whole attitude that he would have me on his mind.

One of the most assiduous members of our circle had been Lady Kenyon, and I remember his telling me one day that her ladyship had, in spite of her own infirmities, lately much aggravated, been in person to inquire. In answer to this I remarked that she would feel it more than anyone. Brooksmith was silent a moment; at the end of which he said, in a certain tone (there is no reproducing some of his tones), "I'll go and see her." I went to see her myself, and I learned that he had waited upon her; but when I said to her, in the form of a joke but with a core of earnest, that when all was over some of us ought to combine, to club together to set Brooksmith up on his own account, she replied a trifle disappointingly: "Do you mean in a public-house?" I looked at her in a way that I think Brooksmith himself would have approved, and then I answered: "Yes, the Offord Arms." What I had meant, of course, was that, for the love of art itself, we ought to look to it that such a peculiar faculty and so much acquired experience should not be wasted. I really think that if we had caused a few black-edged cards to be struck off and circulated—"Mr. Brooksmith will continue to receive on the old premises from four to seven; business carried on as usual during the alterations"—the majority of us would have rallied.

Several times he took me upstairs—always by his own proposal—and our dear old friend, in bed, in a curious flowered and brocaded *casaque*[6] which made him, especially as his head was tied up in a handkerchief to match, look, to my imagination, like the dying Voltaire, held for ten minutes a sadly shrunken little salon. I felt indeed each time, as if I were attending the last *coucher*[7] of some social sovereign. He was royally whimsical about his sufferings and not at all concerned—quite as if the Constitution provided for the case—about his successor. He glided over *our* sufferings charmingly, and none of his jokes—it was a gallant abstention, some of them would

---

[6]   *casaque*; French: a long, close-fitting garment typically worn by clergy members—a cassock.

[7]   *coucher*; French: sleep.

have been so easy—were at our expense. Now and again, I confess,
there was one at Brooksmith's, but so pathetically sociable as to make
the excellent man look at me in a way that seemed to say: "Do
exchange a glance with me, or I sha'n't be able to stand it." What
he was not able to stand was not what Mr. Offord said about him,
but what he wasn't able to say in return. His notion of conversation,
for himself, was giving you the convenience of speaking to him; and
when he went to "see" Lady Kenyon, for instance, it was to carry
her the tribute of his receptive silence. Where would the speech of
his betters have been if proper service had been a manifestation of
sound? In that case the fundamental difference would have had to
be shown by *their* dumbness, and many of them, poor things, were
dumb enough without that provision. Brooksmith took an unfailing
interest in the preservation of the fundamental difference; it was the
thing he had most on his conscience.

What had become of it, however, when Mr. Offord passed away
like any inferior person—was relegated to eternal stillness like a
butler upstairs? His aspect for several days after the expected event
may be imagined, and the multiplication by funereal observance of
the things he didn't say. When everything was over—it was late the
same day—I knocked at the door of the house of mourning as I so
often had done before. I could never call on Mr. Offord again, but
I had come, literally, to call on Brooksmith. I wanted to ask him if
there was anything I could do for him, tainted with vagueness as this
inquiry could only be. My wild dream of taking him into my own
service had died away: my service was not worth his being taken
into. My offer to him could only be to help him to find another
place, and yet there was an indelicacy, as it were, in taking for granted
that his thoughts would immediately be fixed on another. I had a
hope that he would be able to give his life a different form—though
certainly not the form, the frequent result of such bereavements, of
his setting up a little shop. That would have been dreadful; for I
should have wished to further any enterprise that he might embark
in, yet how could I have brought myself to go and pay him shillings
and take back coppers over a counter? My visit then was simply an
intended compliment. He took it as such, gratefully and with all the
tact in the world. He knew I really couldn't help him and that I knew
he knew I couldn't; but we discussed the situation—with a good
deal of elegant generality—at the foot of the stairs, in the hall already
dismantled, where I had so often discussed other situations with him.
The executors were in possession, as was still more apparent when

he made me pass for a few minutes into the dining-room, where various objects were muffled up for removal.

Two definite facts, however, he had to communicate; one being that he was to leave the house for ever that night (servants, for some mysterious reason, seem always to depart by night), and the other— he mentioned it only at the last, with hesitation—that he had already been informed his late master had left him a legacy of eighty pounds. "I'm very glad," I said, and Brooksmith rejoined: "It was so like him to think of me." This was all that passed between us on the subject, and I know nothing of his judgment of Mr. Offord's memento. Eighty pounds are always eighty pounds, and no one has ever left *me* an equal sum; but, all the same, for Brooksmith, I was disappointed. I don't know what I had expected—in short I was disappointed. Eighty pounds might stock a little shop—a *very* little shop; but, I repeat, I couldn't bear to think of that. I asked my friend if he had been able to save a little, and he replied: "No, sir; I have had to do things." I didn't inquire what things he had had to do; they were his own affair, and I took his word for them as assentingly as if he had had the greatness of an ancient house to keep up; especially as there was something in his manner that seemed to convey a prospect of further sacrifice.

"I shall have to turn round a bit, sir—I shall have to look about me," he said; and then he added, indulgently, magnanimously: "If you should happen to hear of anything for me——"

I couldn't let him finish; this was, in its essence, too much in the really grand manner. It would be a help to my getting him off my mind to be able to pretend I *could* find the right place, and that help he wished to give me, for it was doubtless painful to him to see me in so false a position. I interposed with a few words to the effect that I was well aware that wherever he should go, whatever he should do, he would miss our old friend terribly—miss him even more than I should, having been with him so much more. This led him to make the speech that I have always remembered as the very text of the whole episode.

"Oh, sir, it's sad for *you*, very sad, indeed, and for a great many gentlemen and ladies; that it is, sir. But for me, sir, it is, if I may say so, still graver even than that: it's just the loss of something that was everything. For me, sir," he went on, with rising tears, "he was just *all*, if you know what I mean, sir. You have others, sir, I daresay— not that I would have you understand me to speak of them as in any way tantamount. But you have the pleasures of society, sir; if it's only in talking about him, sir, as I daresay you do freely—for all his blessed memory has to fear from it—with gentlemen and ladies who have had the same honour. That's not for me, sir, and I have to keep my associations to myself. Mr. Offord was *my* society, and now I have no more. You go back to conversation, sir, after all, and I go back to my place," Brooksmith stammered, without exaggerated irony or dramatic bitterness, but with a flat, unstudied veracity and his hand on the knob of the street-door. He turned it to let me out and then he added: "I just go downstairs, sir, again, and I stay there."

"My poor child," I replied, in my emotion, quite as Mr. Offord used to speak, "my dear fellow, leave it to me; we'll look after you, we'll all do something for you."

"Ah, if you could give me someone *like* him! But there ain't two in the world," said Brooksmith as we parted.

He had given me his address—the place where he would be to be heard of. For a long time I had no occasion to make use of the information; for he proved indeed, on trial, a very difficult case. In a word the people who knew him and had known Mr. Offord, didn't want to take him, and yet I couldn't bear to try to thrust him among people who didn't know him. I spoke to many of our old friends about him, and I found them all governed by the odd mixture of feelings of which I myself was conscious, and disposed, further, to entertain a suspicion that he was "spoiled," with which I then would have nothing to do. In plain terms a certain embarrassment, a sensible awkwardness, when they thought of it, attached to the idea of using him as a menial: they had met him so often in society. Many of them would have asked him, and did ask him, or rather did ask me to ask him, to come and see them; but a mere visiting-list was not what I wanted for him. He was too short for people who were very particular; nevertheless I heard of an opening in a diplomatic household which led me to write him a note, though I was looking much less for something grand than for something human. Five days later I heard from him. The secretary's wife had decided, after keeping him waiting till then, that she couldn't take a servant out of a house in which there had not been a lady. The note had a P.S.: "It's a good job there wasn't, sir, such a lady as some."

A week later he came to see me and told me he was "suited"—committed to some highly respectable people (they were something very large in the City), who lived on the Bayswater side of the Park. "I daresay it will be rather poor, sir," he admitted; "but I've seen the fireworks, haven't I, sir?—it can't be fireworks *every* night. After

Mansfield Street there ain't much choice." There was a certain amount, however, it seemed; for the following year, going one day to call on a country cousin, a lady of a certain age who was spending a fortnight in town with some friends of her own, a family unknown to me and resident in Chester Square, the door of the house was opened, to my surprise and gratification, by Brooksmith in person. When I came out I had some conversation with him, from which I gathered that he had found the large City people too dull for endurance, and I guessed, though he didn't say it, that he had found them vulgar as well. I don't know what judgment he would have passed on his actual patrons if my relative had not been their friend; but under the circumstances he abstained from comment.

None was necessary, however, for before the lady in question brought her visit to a close they honoured me with an invitation to dinner, which I accepted. There was a largeish party on the occasion, but I confess I thought of Brooksmith rather more than of the seated company. They required no depth of attention—they were all referable to usual, irredeemable, inevitable types. It was the world of cheerful commonplace and conscious gentility and prosperous density, a full-fed, material, insular world, a world of hideous florid plate and ponderous order and thin conversation. There was not a word said about Byron. Nothing would have induced me to look at Brooksmith in the course of the repast, and I felt sure that not even my overturning the wine would have induced him to meet my eye. We were in intellectual sympathy—we felt, as regards each other, a kind of social responsibility. In short we had been in Arcadia together, and we had both come to *this!* No wonder we were ashamed to be confronted. When he helped on my overcoat, as I was going away, we parted, for the first time since the earliest days in Mansfield Street, in silence. I thought he looked lean and wasted, and I guessed that his new place was not more "human" than his previous one. There was plenty of beef and beer, but there was no reciprocity. The question for him to have asked before accepting the position would have been not "How many footmen are kept?" but "How much imagination?"

The next time I went to the house—I confess it was not very soon—I encountered his successor, a personage who evidently enjoyed the good fortune of never having quitted his natural level. Could any be higher? he seemed to ask—over the heads of three footmen and even of some visitors. He made me feel as if Brooksmith were dead; but I didn't dare to inquire—I couldn't have borne his "I haven't the least idea, sir." I despatched a note to the address

Brooksmith had given me after Mr. Offord's death, but I received no answer. Six months later, however, I was favoured with a visit from an elderly, dreary, dingy person, who introduced herself to me as Mr. Brooksmith's aunt and from whom I learned that he was out of place and out of health and had allowed her to come and say to me that if I could spare half-an-hour to look in at him he would take it as a rare honour.

I went the next day—his messenger had given me a new address—and found my friend lodged in a short sordid street in Marylebone, one of those corners of London that wear the last expression of sickly meanness. The room into which I was shown was above the small establishment of a dyer and cleaner who had inflated kid gloves and discoloured shawls in his shop-front. There was a great deal of grimy infant life up and down the place, and there was a hot, moist smell within, as of the "boiling" of dirty linen. Brooksmith sat with a blanket over his legs at a clean little window, where, from behind stiff bluish-white curtains, he could look across at a huckster's and a tinsmith's and a small greasy public-house. He had passed through an illness and was convalescent, and his mother, as well as his aunt, was in attendance on him. I liked the mother, who was bland and intensely humble, but I didn't much fancy the aunt, whom I connected, perhaps unjustly, with the opposite public-house (she seemed somehow to be greasy with the same grease), and whose furtive eye followed every movement of my hand, as if to see if it were not going into my pocket. It didn't take this direction—I couldn't, unsolicited, put myself at that sort of ease with Brooksmith. Several times the door of the room opened, and mysterious old women peeped in and shuffled back again. I don't know who they were; poor Brooksmith seemed encompassed with vague, prying, beery females.

He was vague himself, and evidently weak, and much embarrassed, and not an allusion was made between us to Mansfield Street. The vision of the salon of which he had been an ornament hovered before me, however, by contrast, sufficiently. He assured me that he was really getting better, and his mother remarked that he would come round if he could only get his spirits up. The aunt echoed this opinion, and I became more sure that in her own case she knew where to go for such a purpose. I'm afraid I was rather weak with my old friend, for I neglected the opportunity, so exceptionally good, to rebuke the levity which had led him to throw up honourable positions—fine, stiff, steady berths, with morning prayers, as I knew, attached to one of them—in Bayswater and Belgravia. Very likely his reasons had been profane and sentimental; he didn't want morning prayers, he wanted to be somebody's dear fellow; but I couldn't be the person to rebuke him. He shuffled these episodes out of sight—I saw that he had no wish to discuss them. I perceived further, strangely enough, that it would probably be a questionable pleasure for him to see me again: he doubted now even of my power to condone his aberrations. He didn't wish to have to explain; and his behaviour, in future, was likely to need explanation. When I bade him farewell he looked at me a moment with eyes that said everything: "How can I talk about those exquisite years in this place, before these people, with the old women poking their heads in? It was very good of you to come to see me—it wasn't my idea; *she* brought you. We've said everything; it's over; you'll lose all patience with me, and I'd rather you shouldn't see the rest." I sent him some money, in a letter, the next day, but I saw the rest only in the light of a barren sequel.

A whole year after my visit to him I became aware once, in dining out, that Brooksmith was one of the several servants who hovered behind our chairs. He had not opened the door of the house to me, and I had not recognised him in the cluster of retainers in the hall. This time I tried to catch his eye, but he never gave me a chance, and when he handed me a dish I could only be careful to thank him audibly. Indeed I partook of two entrées of which I had my doubts, subsequently converted into certainties, in order not to snub him. He looked well enough in health, but much older, and wore, in an exceptionally marked degree, the glazed and expressionless mask of the British domestic *de race*[8]. I saw with dismay that if I had not known him I should have taken him, on the showing of his countenance, for an extravagant illustration of irresponsive servile gloom. I said to myself that he had become a reactionary, gone over to the Philistines, thrown himself into religion, the religion of his "place," like a foreign lady *sur le retour*[9]. I divined moreover that he was only engaged for the evening—he had become a mere waiter, had joined the band of the white-waistcoated who "go out." There was something pathetic in this fact, and it was a terrible vulgarisation of Brooksmith. It was the mercenary prose of butlerhood; he had given up the struggle for the poetry. If reciprocity was what he had missed, where was the reciprocity now? Only in the bottoms of the wine-glasses and the five shillings (or whatever they get), clapped into his hand

---

[8]   *de race*; French: of race.
[9]   *sur le retour*; French: on the way back.

by the permanent man. However, I supposed he had taken up a precarious branch of his profession because after all it sent him less downstairs. His relations with London society were more superficial, but they were of course more various. As I went away, on this occasion, I looked out for him eagerly among the four or five attendants whose perpendicular persons, fluting the walls of London passages, are supposed to lubricate the process of departure; but he was not on duty. I asked one of the others if he were not in the house, and received the prompt answer: "Just left, sir. Anything I can do for you, sir?" I wanted to say "Please give him my kind regards"; but I abstained; I didn't want to compromise him, and I never came across him again.

Often and often, in dining out, I looked for him, sometimes accepting invitations on purpose to multiply the chances of my meeting him. But always in vain; so that as I met many other members of the casual class over and over again, I at last adopted the theory that he always procured a list of expected guests beforehand and kept away from the banquets which he thus learned I was to grace. At last I gave up hope, and one day, at the end of three years, I received another visit from his aunt. She was drearier and dingier, almost squalid, and she was in great tribulation and want. Her sister, Mrs. Brooksmith, had been dead a year, and three months later her nephew had disappeared. He had always looked after her a bit—since her troubles; I never knew what her troubles had been—and now she hadn't so much as a petticoat to pawn. She had also a niece, to whom she had been everything, before her troubles, but the niece had treated her most shameful. These were details; the great and romantic fact was Brooksmith's final evasion of his fate. He had gone out to wait one evening, as usual, in a white waistcoat she had done up for him with her own hands, being due at a large party up Kensington way. But he had never come home again, and had never arrived at the large party, or at any party that anyone could make out. No trace of him had come to light—no gleam of the white waistcoat had pierced the obscurity of his doom. This news was a sharp shock to me, for I had my ideas about his real destination. His aged relative had promptly, as she said, guessed the worst. Somehow and somewhere he had got out of the way altogether, and now I trust that, with characteristic deliberation, he is changing the plates of the immortal gods. As my depressing visitant also said, he never *had* got his spirits up. I was fortunately able to dismiss her with her own somewhat improved. But the dim ghost of poor Brooksmith is one of those that I see. He had indeed been spoiled.

# THE TWO FACES

### Henry James

THE SERVANT, WHO, in spite of his sealed stamped look, appeared to have his reasons, stood there for instruction in a manner not quite usual after announcing the name. Mrs. Grantham, however, took it up—"Lord Gwyther?"—with a quick surprise that for an instant justified him even to the small scintilla in the glance she gave her companion, which might have had exactly the sense of the butler's hesitation. This companion, a shortish fairish youngish man, clean-shaven and keen-eyed, had, with a promptitude that would have struck an observer—which the butler indeed was—sprung to his feet and moved to the chimney-piece, though his hostess herself meanwhile managed not otherwise to stir. "Well?" she said as for the visitor to advance; which she immediately followed with a sharper "He's not there?"

"Shall I show him up, ma'am?"

"But of course!" The point of his doubt made her at last rise for impatience, and Bates, before leaving the room, might still have caught the achieved irony of her appeal to the gentleman into whose communion with her he had broken. "Why in the world not—? What a way—!" she exclaimed as Sutton felt beside his cheek the passage of her eyes to the glass behind him.

"He wasn't sure you'd see anyone."

"I don't see 'anyone,' but I see individuals."

"That's just it—and sometimes you don't see them."

"Do you mean ever because of *you?*" she asked as she touched into place a tendril of hair. "That's just his impertinence, as to which I shall speak to him."

657

"Don't," said Shirley Sutton. "Never notice anything."

"That's nice advice from you," she laughed, "who notice everything!"

"Ah but I speak of nothing."

She looked at him a moment. "You're still more impertinent than Bates. You'll please not budge," she went on.

"Really? I must sit him out?" he continued as, after a minute, she had not again spoken—only glancing about, while she changed her place, partly for another look at the glass and partly to see if she could improve her seat. What she felt was rather more than, clever and charming though she was, she could hide. "If you're wondering how you seem I can tell you. Awfully cool and easy."

She gave him another stare. She was beautiful and conscious. "And if you're wondering *how you* seem—"

"Oh I'm not!" he laughed from before the fire. "I always perfectly know."

"How you seem," she retorted, "is as if you didn't!"

Once more for a little he watched her. "You're looking lovely for him—extraordinarily lovely, within the marked limits of your range. But that's enough. Don't be clever."

"Then who *will* be?"

"There you are!" he sighed with amusement.

"Do you know him?" she asked as, through the door left open by Bates, they heard steps on the landing.

Sutton had to think an instant, and produced a "No" just as Lord Gwyther was again announced, which gave an unexpectedness to the greeting offered him a moment later by this personage—a young man, stout and smooth and fresh, but not at all shy, who, after the happiest rapid passage with Mrs. Grantham, put out a hand with a straight free "How d' ye do?"

"Mr. Shirley Sutton," Mrs. Grantham explained.

"Oh yes," said her second visitor quite as if he knew; which, as he couldn't have known, had for her first the interest of confirming a perception that his lordship would be—no, not at all, in general, embarrassed, only was now exceptionally and especially agitated. As it is, for that matter, with Sutton's total impression that we are particularly and almost exclusively concerned, it may be further mentioned that he was not less clear as to the really handsome way in which the young man kept himself together and little by little—though with all proper aid indeed—finally found his feet. All sorts of things, for the twenty minutes, occurred to Sutton, though one of them was certainly not that it would, after all, be better he should go. One of them was that their hostess was doing it in perfection—simply, easily, kindly, yet with something the least bit queer in her wonderful eyes; another was that if he had been recognised without the least ground it was through a tension of nerves on the part of his fellow guest that produced inconsequent motions; still another was that, even had departure been indicated, he would positively have felt dissuasion in the rare promise of the scene. This was in especial after Lord Gwyther not only had announced that he was now married, but had mentioned that he wished to bring his wife to Mrs. Grantham for the benefit so certain to be derived. It was the passage immediately produced by that speech that provoked in Sutton the intensity, as it were, of his arrest. He already knew of the marriage as well as Mrs. Grantham herself, and as well also as he knew of some other things; and this gave him doubtless the better measure of what took place before him and the keener consciousness of the quick look that, at a marked moment—though it was not absolutely meant for him any more than for his companion—Mrs. Grantham let him catch.

She smiled, but it had a gravity. "I think, you know, you ought to have told me before."

"Do you mean when I first got engaged? Well, it all took place so far away, and we really told, at home, so few people."

Oh there might have been reasons; but it had not been quite right. "You were married at Stuttgart? That wasn't too far for *my* interest, at least, to reach."

"Awfully kind of you—and of course one knew you *would* be kind. But it wasn't at Stuttgart; it was over there, but quite in the country. We should have managed it in England but that her mother naturally wished to be present, yet wasn't in health to come. So it was really, you see, a sort of little hole-and-corner German affair."

This didn't in the least check Mrs. Grantham's claim, but it started a slight anxiety. "Will she be—a—then German?"

Sutton knew her to know perfectly what Lady Gwyther would "be," but he had by this time, while their friend explained, his independent interest. "Oh dear no! My father-in-law has never parted with the proud birthright of a Briton. But his wife, you see, holds an estate in Würtemberg from *her* mother, Countess Kremnitz, on which, with the awful condition of his English property, you know, they've found it for years a tremendous saving to live. So that though Valda was luckily born at home she has practically spent her life over there."

"Oh I see." Then, after a slight pause, "Is Valda her pretty name?" Mrs. Grantham asked.

"Well," said the young man, only wishing, in his candour, it was clear, to be drawn out—"well, she has, in the manner of her mother's people, about thirteen; but that's the one we generally use."

Mrs. Grantham waited but an instant. "Then may *I* generally use it?"

"It would be too charming of you; and nothing would give her— as I assure you nothing would give *me*—greater pleasure." Lord Gwyther quite glowed with the thought.

"Then I think that instead of coming alone you might have brought her to see me."

"It's exactly what," he instantly replied, "I came to ask your leave to do." He explained that for the moment Lady Gwyther was not in town, having as soon as she arrived gone down to Torquay to put in a few days with one of her aunts, also her godmother, to whom she was an object of great interest. She had seen no one yet, and no one—not that *that* mattered—had seen her; she knew nothing whatever of London and was awfully frightened at facing it and at what (however little) might be expected of her. "She wants someone," he said, "someone who knows the whole thing, don't you see? and who's thoroughly kind and clever, as you would be, if I may say so, to take her by the hand." It was at this point and on these words that the eyes of Lord Gwyther's two auditors inevitably and wonderfully met. But there was nothing in the way he kept it up to show he caught the encounter. "She wants, if I may tell you so, a real friend for the great labyrinth; and asking myself what I could do to make things ready for her, and who would be absolutely the best woman in London—"

"You thought naturally of *me?*" Mrs. Grantham had listened with no sign but the faint flash just noted; now, however, she gave him the full light of her expressive face—which immediately brought Shirley Sutton, looking at his watch, once more to his feet.

"She *is* the best woman in London!" He addressed himself with a laugh to the other visitor, but offered his hand in farewell to their hostess.

You're going?"

"I must," he said without scruple.

"Then we do meet at dinner?"

"I hope so." On which, to take leave, he returned with interest to Lord Gwyther the friendly clutch he had a short time before received.

## II

They did meet at dinner, and if they were not, as it happened, side by side, they made that up afterwards in the happiest angle of a drawing-room that offered both shine and shadow and that was positively much appreciated, in the circle in which they moved, for the favourable "corners" created by its shrewd mistress. Mrs. Grantham's face, charged with something produced in it by Lord Gwyther's visit, had been with him so constantly for the previous hours that, when she instantly challenged him on his "treatment" of her in the afternoon, he was on the point of naming it as his reason for not having remained with her. Something new had quickly come into her beauty; he couldn't as yet have said what, nor whether on the whole to its advantage or its loss. Till he should see this clearer, at any rate he would say nothing; so that he found with sufficient presence of mind a better excuse. If in short he had in defiance of her particular request left her alone with Lord Gwyther it was simply because the situation had suddenly turned so exciting that he had fairly feared the contagion of it—the temptation of its making him, most improperly, put in his word.

They could now talk of these things at their ease. Other couples, ensconced and scattered, enjoyed the same privilege, and Sutton had more and more the profit, such as it was, of feeling that his interest in Mrs. Grantham had become—what was the luxury of so high a social code—an acknowledged and protected relation. He knew his London well enough to know that he was on the way to be regarded as her main source of consolation for the trick Lord Gwyther had several months before publicly played her. Many persons had not held that, by the high social code in question, his lordship could have "reserved the right" to turn up that way, from one day to another, engaged to be married. For himself London took, with its short cuts and its cheap psychology, an immense deal for granted. To his own sense he was never—could in the nature of things never be—any man's "successor." Just what had constituted the predecessorship of other men was apparently that they had been able to make up their mind. He, worse luck, was at the mercy of her face, and more than ever at the mercy of it now, which meant moreover not that it made a slave of him, but that it made, disconcertingly, a sceptic. It was the absolute perfection of the handsome, but things had a way of coming into it. "I felt," he said, "that you were there together at a point at which you had a right to the ease the absence of a listener would give. I was sure that when you made me promise to stay you hadn't guessed—"

"That he could possibly have come to me on such an extraordinary errand? No, of course I hadn't guessed. Who *would?* But didn't you see how little I was upset by it?"

Sutton demurred. Then with a smile: "I think *he* saw how little."

"You yourself didn't then?"

He again held back, but not, after all, to answer. "He was wonderful, wasn't he?"

"I think he was," she returned after a moment. To which she added: "Why did he pretend that way he knew you?"

"He didn't pretend. He somehow felt on the spot that I was 'in it.'" Sutton had found this afterwards and found it to represent a reality. "It was an effusion of cheer and hope. He was so glad to see me there and to find you happy."

"Happy?"

"Happy. Aren't you?"

"Because of *you?*"

"Well—according to the impression he received as he came in."

"That was sudden then," she asked, "and unexpected?"

Her companion thought. "Prepared in some degree, but confirmed by the sight of us, there together, so awfully jolly and sociable over your fire."

Mrs. Grantham turned this round. "If he knew I was 'happy' then—which, by the way, is none of his business, nor of yours either—why in the world did he come?"

"Well, for good manners, and for his idea," said Sutton.

She took it in, appearing to have no hardness of rancour that could bar discussion. "Do you mean by his idea his proposal that I should grandmother his wife? And if you do is the proposal your reason for calling him wonderful?"

Sutton laughed. "Pray what's yours?" As this was a question, however, that she took her time to answer or not to answer—only appearing interested for a moment in a combination that had formed itself on the other side of the room—he presently went on. "What's *his?*—that would seem to be the point. His, I mean, for having decided on the extraordinary step of throwing his little wife, bound hands and feet, into your arms. Intelligent as you are, and with these three or four hours to have thought it over, I yet don't see how that can fail still to mystify you."

She continued to watch their opposite neighbours. " 'Little,' you call her. Is she so very small?"

"Tiny, tiny—she *must* be; as different as possible in every way—of necessity—from you. They always *are* the opposite pole, you know," said Shirley Sutton.

She glanced at him now. "You strike me as of an impudence—!"

"No, no. I only like to make it out with you."

She looked away again and after a little went on. "I'm sure she's charming, and only hope one isn't to gather he's already tired of her."

"Not a bit! He's tremendously in love, and he'll remain so."

"So much the better. And if it's a question," said Mrs. Grantham, "of one's doing what one can for her, he has only, as I told him when you had gone, to give me the chance."

"Good! So he *is* to commit her to you?"

"You use extraordinary expressions, but it's settled that he brings her."

"And you'll really and truly help her?"

"Really and truly?" said Mrs. Grantham with her eyes again on him. "Why not? For what do you take me?"

"Ah isn't that just what I still have the discomfort, every day I live, of asking myself?"

She had made, as she spoke, a movement to rise, which, as if she was tired of his tone, his last words appeared to determine. But, also getting up, he held her, when they were on their feet, long enough to hear the rest of what he had to say. "If you do help her, you know, you'll show him you've understood."

"Understood what?"

"Why, his idea—the deep acute train of reasoning that has led him to take, as one may say, the bull by the horns; to reflect that as you might, as you probably *would,* in any case, get at her, he plays the wise game, as well as the bold one, by treating your generosity as a real thing and placing himself publicly under an obligation to you."

Mrs. Grantham showed not only that she had listened, but that she had for an instant considered. "What is it you elegantly describe as my getting 'at' her?"

"He takes his risk, but puts you, you see, on your honour."

She thought a moment more. "What profundities indeed then over the simplest of matters! And if your idea is," she went on, "that if I do help her I shall show him I've understood them, so it will be that if I don't—"

"You'll show him"—Sutton took her up—"that you haven't? Precisely. But in spite of not wanting to appear to have understood *too* much—"

"I may still be depended on to do what I can? Quite certainly. You'll see what I may still be depended on to do." And she moved away.

## III

It was not, doubtless, that there had been anything in their rather sharp separation at that moment to sustain or prolong the interruption; yet it definitely befell that, circumstances aiding, they practically failed to meet again before the great party at Burbeck. This occasion was to gather in some thirty persons from a certain Friday to the following Monday, and it was on the Friday that Sutton went down. He had known in advance that Mrs. Grantham was to be there, and this perhaps, during the interval of hindrance, had helped him a little to be patient. He had before him the certitude of a real full cup—two days brimming over with the sight of her. He found, however, on his arrival that she was not yet in the field, and presently learned that her place would be in a small contingent that was to join the party on the morrow. This knowledge he extracted from Miss Banker, who was always the first to present herself at any gathering that was to enjoy her, and whom moreover—partly on that very account—the wary not less than the speculative were apt to hold themselves well-advised to engage with at as early as possible a stage of the business. She was stout red rich mature universal—a massive much-fingered volume, alphabetical wonderful indexed, that opened of itself at the right place. She opened for Sutton instinctively at G——, which happened to be remarkably convenient. "What she's really waiting over for is to bring down Lady Gwyther."

"Ah the Gwythers are coming?"

"Yes; caught, through Mrs. Grantham, just in time. *She'll* be the feature—everyone wants to see her."

Speculation and wariness met and combined at this moment in Shirley Sutton. "Do you mean—a—Mrs. Grantham?"

"Dear no! Poor little Lady Gwyther, who, but just arrived in England, appears now literally for the first time in her life in any society whatever, and whom (don't you know the extraordinary story? you ought to—*you!)* she, of all people, has so wonderfully taken up. It will be quite—here—as if she were 'presenting' her."

Sutton of course took in more things than even appeared. "I never know what I ought to know; I only know, inveterately, what I oughtn't. So what *is* the extraordinary story?"

"You really haven't heard?"

"Really," he replied without winking.

"It happened indeed but the other day," said Miss Banker, "yet everyone's already wondering. Gwyther has thrown his wife on her mercy—but I won't believe you if you pretend to me you don't know why he shouldn't."

Sutton asked himself then what he *could* pretend. "Do you mean because she's merciless?"

She hesitated. "If you don't know perhaps I oughtn't to tell you."

He liked Miss Banker and found just the right tone to plead. "*Do* tell me."

"Well," she sighed, "it will be your own fault—! They have been such friends that there could have been but one name for the crudity of his original *procédé*[1]. When I was a girl we used to call it throwing over. They call it in French to *lâcher*[2]. But I refer not so much to the act itself as to the manner of it, though you may say indeed of course that there's in such cases after all only one manner. Least said soonest mended."

Sutton seemed to wonder. "Oh he said too much?"

"He said nothing. That was it."

Sutton kept it up. "But was *what?*"

"Why, what she must, like any woman in her shoes, have felt to be his perfidy. He simply went and *did* it—took to himself this child, that is, without the preliminary of a scandal or a rupture—before she could turn round."

"I follow you. But it would appear from what you say that she *has* turned round now."

"Well," Miss Banker laughed, "we shall see for ourselves how far. It will be what everyone will try to see."

---

[1] *procédé;* French: process.
[2] *lâcher;* French: release.

"Oh then we've work cut out!" And Sutton certainly felt that he himself had—an impression that lost nothing from a further talk with Miss Banker in the course of a short stroll in the grounds with her the next day. He spoke as one who had now considered many things.

"Did I understand from you yesterday that Lady Gwyther's a 'child'?"

"Nobody knows. It's prodigious the way she has managed."

"The way Lady Gwyther has—?"

"No, the way May Grantham has kept her till this hour in her pocket."

He was quick at his watch. "Do you mean by 'this hour' that they're due now?"

"Not till tea. All the others arrive together in time for that." Miss Banker had clearly, since the previous day, filled in gaps and become, as it were, revised and enlarged. "She'll have kept a cat from seeing her, so as to produce her entirely herself."

"Well," Sutton mused, "that will have been a very noble sort of return—"

"For Gwyther's behaviour? Very. Yet I feel creepy."

"Creepy?"

"Because so much depends for the girl—in the way of the right start or the wrong start—on the signs and omens of this first appearance. It's a great house and a great occasion, and we're assembled here, it strikes me, very much as the Roman mob at the circus used to be to see the next Christian maiden brought out to the tigers."

"Oh if she *is* a Christian maiden—!" Sutton murmured. But he stopped at what his imagination called up.

It perhaps fed that faculty a little that Miss Banker had the effect of making out that Mrs. Grantham might individually be, in any case, something of a Roman matron. "She has kept her in the dark so that we may only take her from her hand. She'll have formed her for us."

"In so few days?"

"Well, she'll have prepared her—decked her for the sacrifice with ribbons and flowers."

"Ah if you only mean that she'll have taken her to her dressmaker—!" And it came to Sutton, at once as a new light and as a check, almost, to anxiety, that this was all poor Gwyther, mistrustful probably of a taste formed by Stuttgart, might have desired of their friend.

There were usually at Burbeck many things taking place at once; so that wherever else, on such occasions, tea might be served, it went forward with matchless pomp, weather permitting, on a shaded stretch of one of the terraces and in presence of one of the prospects. Shirley Sutton, moving, as the afternoon waned, more restlessly about and mingling in dispersed groups only to find they had nothing to keep him quiet, came upon it as he turned a corner of the house—saw it seated there in all its state. It might be said that at Burbeck it was, like everything else, made the most of. It constituted immediately, with multiplied tables and glittering plate, with rugs and cushions and ices and fruit and wonderful porcelain and beautiful women, a scene of splendour, almost an incident of grand opera. One of the beautiful women might quite have been expected to rise with a gold cup and a celebrated song.

One of them did rise, as happened, while Sutton drew near, and he found himself a moment later seeing nothing and nobody but Mrs. Grantham. They met on the terrace, just away from the others, and the movement in which he had the effect of arresting her might have been that of withdrawal. He quickly saw, however, that if she had been about to pass into the house it was only on some errand— to get something or to call someone—that would immediately have restored her to her public. It somehow struck him on the spot—and more than ever yet, though the impression was not wholly new to him—that she felt herself a figure for the forefront of the stage and indeed would have been recognised by anyone at a glance as the *prima donna assoluta*[3]. She caused, in fact, during the few minutes he stood talking to her, an extraordinary series of waves to roll extraordinarily fast over his sense, not the least mark of the matter being that the appearance with which it ended was again the one with which it had begun. "The face—the face," as he kept dumbly repeating; that was at last, as at first, all he could clearly see. She had a perfection resplendent, but what in the world had it done, this perfection, to her beauty? It was her beauty doubtless that looked out at him, but it was into something else that, as their eyes met, he strangely found himself looking.

It was as if something had happened in consequence of which she had changed, and there was that in this swift perception that made him glance eagerly about for Lady Gwyther. But as he took in the recruited group—identities of the hour added to those of the previous twenty-four—he saw, among his recognitions, one of which was the husband of the person missing, that Lady Gwyther

---

[3]  *prima donna assoluta*; Italian: the absolute principal female singer of an opera company.

was not there. Nothing in the whole business was more singular than his consciousness that, as he came back to his interlocutress after the nods and smiles and hand-waves he had launched, she knew what had been his thought. She knew for whom he had looked without success; but why should this knowledge visibly have hardened and sharpened her, and precisely at a moment when she was unprecedentedly magnificent? The indefinable apprehension that had somewhat sunk after his second talk with Miss Banker and then had perversely risen again—this nameless anxiety now produced on him, with a sudden sharper pinch, the effect of a great suspense. The action of that, in turn, was to show him that he hadn't yet fully known how much he had at stake on a final view. It was revealed to him for the first time that he "really cared" whether Mrs. Grantham were a safe nature. It was too ridiculous by what a thread it hung, but something was certainly in the air that would definitely tell him.

What was in the air descended the next moment to earth. He turned round as he caught the expression with which her eyes attached themselves to something that approached. A little person, very young and very much dressed, had come out of the house, and the expression in Mrs. Grantham's eyes was that of the artist confronted with her work and interested, even to impatience, in the judgement of others. The little person drew nearer, and though Sutton's companion, without looking at him now, gave it a name and met it, he had jumped for himself at certitude. He saw many things—too many, and they appeared to be feathers, frills, excrescences of silk and lace— massed together and conflicting, and after a moment also saw struggling out of them a small face that struck him as either scared or sick. Then, with his eyes again returning to Mrs. Grantham, he saw another.

He had no more talk with Miss Banker till late that evening—an evening during which he had felt himself too noticeably silent; but something had passed between this pair, across dinner-table and drawing-room, without speech, and when they at last found words it was in the needed ease of a quiet end of the long, lighted gallery, where she opened again at the very paragraph.

"You were right—that *was* it. She did the only thing that, at such short notice, she *could* do. She took her to her dressmaker."

Sutton, with his back to the reach of the gallery, had, as if to banish a vision, buried his eyes for a minute in his hands. "And oh the face—the face!"

"Which?" Miss Banker asked.

"Whichever one looks at."

"But May Grantham's glorious. She has turned herself out—"

"With a splendour of taste and a sense of effect, eh? Yes." Sutton showed he saw far.

"She *has* the sense of effect. The sense of effect as exhibited in Lady Gwyther's clothes—!" was something Miss Banker failed of words to express. "Everybody's overwhelmed. Here, you know, that sort of thing's grave. The poor creature's lost."

"Lost?"

"Since on the first impression, as we said, so much depends. The first impression's made—oh made! I defy her now ever to unmake it. Her husband, who's proud, won't like her the better for it. And I don't see," Miss Banker went on, "that her prettiness *was* enough—a mere little feverish frightened freshness; what *did* he see in her?—to be so blasted. It has been done with an atrocity of art—"

"That supposes the dressmaker then also a devil?"

"Oh your London women and their dressmakers!" Miss Banker laughed.

"But the face—the face!" Sutton woefully repeated.

"May's?"

"The little girl's. It's exquisite."

"Exquisite?"

"For unimaginable pathos."

"Oh!" Miss Banker dropped.

"She has at last begun to see." Sutton showed again how far *he* saw. "It glimmers upon her innocence, she makes it dimly out—what has been done with her. She's even worse this evening—the way, my eye, she looked at dinner!—than when she came. Yes"—he was confident—"it has dawned (how couldn't it, out of all of you?) and she knows."

"She ought to have known before!" Miss Banker intelligently sighed.

"No; she wouldn't in that case have been so beautiful."

"Beautiful?" cried Miss Banker; "overloaded like a monkey in a show!"

"The face, yes; which goes to the heart. It's that that makes it," said Shirley Sutton. "And it's that"—he thought it out—"that makes the other."

"I see. Conscious?"

"Horrible!"

"You take it hard," said Miss Banker.

Lord Gwyther, just before she spoke, had come in sight and now was near them. Sutton on this, appearing to wish to avoid him, reached, before answering his companion's observation, a door that opened close at hand. "So hard," he replied from that point, "that I shall be off tomorrow morning."

"And not see the rest?" she called after him.

But he had already gone, and Lord Gwyther, arriving, amiably took up her question. "The rest of what?"

Miss Banker looked him well in the eyes. "Of Mrs. Grantham's clothes."

# THE COURTING OF SISTER WISBY

## Sarah Orne Jewett

ALL THE MORNING there had been an increasing temptation to take
an outdoor holiday, and early in the afternoon the temptation outgrew
my power of resistance. A far away pasture on the long southwestern
slope of a high hill was persistently present to my mind, yet there
seemed to be no particular reason why I should think of it. I was not
sure that I wanted anything from the pasture, and there was no sign,
except the temptation, that the pasture wanted anything of me. But
I was on the farther side of as many as three fences before I stopped
to think again where I was going, and why.

There is no use in trying to tell another person about that afternoon
unless he distinctly remembers weather exactly like it. No number
of details concerning an Arctic ice blockade will give a single shiver
to a child of the tropics. This was one of those perfect New England
days in late summer, when the spirit of autumn takes a first stealthy
flight, like a spy, through the ripening countryside, and, with feigned
sympathy for those who droop with August heat, puts her cool cloak
of bracing air about leaf and flower and human shoulders. Every
living thing grows suddenly cheerful and strong; it is only when you
catch sight of a horror-stricken little maple in swampy soil—a little
maple that has second-sight and fore-knowledge of coming disaster
to her race—only then does a distrust of autumn's friendliness dim
your joyful satisfaction.

In the midwinter there is always a day when one has the first
foretaste of spring; in late August there is a morning when the air
is for the first time autumn-like. Perhaps it is a hint to the squirrels
to get in their first supplies for the winter hoards, or a reminder

that summer will soon end, and everybody had better make the most of it. We are always looking forward to the passing and ending of winter, but when summer is here it seems as if summer must always last. As I went across the fields that day, I found myself half lamenting that the world must fade again, even that the best of her budding and bloom was only a preparation for another springtime, for an awakening beyond the coming winter's sleep.

The sun was slightly veiled; there was a chattering group of birds, which had gathered for a conference about their early migration. Yet, oddly enough, I heard the voice of a belated bobolink, and presently saw him rise from the grass and hover leisurely, while he sang a brief tune. He was much behind time if he were still a housekeeper; but as for the other birds who listened, they cared only for their own notes. An old crow went sagging by, and gave a croak at his despised neighbor, just as a black reviewer croaked at Keats— so hard it is to be just to one's contemporaries. The bobolink was indeed singing out of season, and it was impossible to say whether he really belonged most to this summer or to the next. He might have been delayed on his northward journey; at any rate, he had a light heart now, to judge from his song, and I wished that I could ask him a few questions—how he liked being the last man among the bobolinks, and where he had taken singing lessons in the South.

Presently I left the lower fields, and took a path that led higher, where I could look beyond the village to the northern country mountainward. Here the sweet fern grew thick and fragrant, and I also found myself heedlessly treading on pennyroyal. Nearby, in a field corner, I long ago made a most comfortable seat by putting a stray piece of board and bit of rail across the angle of the fences. I have spent many a delightful hour there, in the shade and shelter of a young pitch pine and a wild cherry tree, with a lovely outlook toward the village, just far enough away beyond the green slopes and tall elms of the lower meadows. But that day I still had the feeling of being outward bound, and did not turn aside nor linger. The high pasture land grew more and more enticing.

I stopped to pick some blackberries that twinkled at me like beads among their dry vines, and two or three yellow-birds fluttered up from the leaves of a thistle and then came back again, as if they had complacently discovered that I was only an overgrown yellowbird, in strange disguise but perfectly harmless. They made me feel as if I were an intruder, though they did not offer to peck at me, and we parted company very soon. It was good to stand at last on the great shoulder of the hill. The wind was coming in from the sea, there was a fine fragrance from the pines, and the air grew sweeter every moment. I took new pleasure in the thought that in a piece of wild pasture land like this one may get closest to Nature, and subsist upon what she gives of her own free will. There have been no drudging, heavy-shod ploughmen to overturn the soil, and vex it into yielding artificial crops. Here one has to take just what Nature is pleased to give, whether one is a yellowbird or a human being. It is very good entertainment for a summer wayfarer, and I am asking my reader now to share the winter provision which I harvested that day. Let us hope that the small birds are also faring well after their fashion, but I give them an anxious thought while the snow goes hurrying in long waves across the buried fields, this windy winter night.

I next went farther down the hill, and got a drink of fresh cool water from the brook, and pulled a tender sheaf of sweet flag beside it. The mossy old fence just beyond was the last barrier between me and the pasture which had sent an invisible messenger earlier in the day, but I saw that somebody else had come first to the rendezvous: there was a brown gingham cape-bonnet and a sprigged shoulder-shawl bobbing up and down, a little way off among the junipers. I had taken such uncommon pleasure in being alone that I instantly felt a sense of disappointment; then a warm glow of pleasant satisfaction rebuked my selfishness. This could be no one but dear old Mrs. Goodsoe, the friend of my childhood and fond dependence of my maturer years. I had not seen her for many weeks, but here she was, out on one of her famous campaigns for herbs, or perhaps just returning from a blueberrying expedition. I approached with care, so as not to startle the gingham bonnet; but she heard the rustle of the bushes against my dress, and looked up quickly, as she knelt, bending over the turf. In that position she was hardly taller than the luxuriant junipers themselves.

"I'm a-gittin' in my mulleins," she said briskly, "an' I've been thinking o' you these twenty times since I come out o' the house. I begun to believe you must ha' forgot me at last."

"I have been away from home," I explained. "Why don't you get in your pennyroyal too? There's a great plantation of it beyond the next fence but one."

"Pennyr'yal!" repeated the dear little old woman, with an air of compassion for inferior knowledge; "'tain't the right time, darlin'. Pennyr'yal's too rank now. But for mulleins this day is prime. I've got a dreadful graspin' fit for 'em this year; seems if I must be goin to need 'em extry. I feel like the squirrels must when they know a hard winter's comin'." And Mrs. Goodsoe bent over her work again, while I stood by and watched her carefully cut the best full-grown leaves with a clumsy pair of scissors, which might have served through at least half a century of herb-gathering. They were fastened to her apron strings by a long piece of list.

"I'm going to take my jack-knife and help you," I suggested, with some fear of refusal. "I just passed a flourishing family of six or seven heads that must have been growing on purpose for you."

"Now be keerful, dear heart," was the anxious response; "choose 'em well. There's odds in mulleins same's there is in angels. Take a plant that's all run up to stalk, and there ain't but little goodness in the leaves. This one I'm at now must ha' been stepped on by some creatur and blighted of its bloom, and the leaves is han'some! When I was small I used to have a notion that Adam an' Eve must ha' took mulleins fer their winter wear. Ain't they just like flannel, for all the world? I've had experience, and I know there's plenty of sickness might be saved to folks if they'd quit horse-radish and such fiery, exasperating things, and use mullein drarves in proper season. Now I shall spread these an' dry 'em nice on my spare floor in the garrit, an' come to steam 'em for use along in the winter there'll be the valley of the whole summer's goodness in 'em, sartin." And she snipped away with the dull scissors while I listened respectfully, and took great pains to have my part of the harvest present a good appearance.

"This is most too dry a head," she added presently, a little out of breath. "There! I can tell you there's win'rows o' young doctors, bilin' over with book-larnin', that is truly ignorant of what to do for the sick, or how to p'int out those paths that well people foller toward sickness. Book-fools I call 'em, them young men, an' some on 'em never'll live to know much better, if they git to be Methuselahs. In my time every middle-aged woman who had brought up a family had some proper ideas of dealin' with complaints. I won't say but there was some fools amongst *them,* but I'd rather take my chances, unless they'd forsook herbs and gone to dealin' with patent stuff. Now my mother really did sense the use of herbs and roots. I never see anybody that come up to her. She was a meek-looking woman, but very understandin', mother was."

"Then that's where you learned so much yourself, Mrs. Goodsoe," I ventured to say.

"Bless your heart, I don't hold a candle to her; 'tis but little I can ·ecall of what she used to say. No, her larnin' died with her," said my friend, in a self-deprecating tone. "Why, there was as many as twenty kinds of roots alone that she used to keep by her, that I forgot the use of; an' I'm sure I shouldn't know where to find the most of 'em, any. There was an herb"—*airb* she called it—"an herb called Pennsylvany; and she used to think everything of nobleliverwort, but I never could seem to get the right effects from it, as she could. Though I don't know as she ever really did use masterwort where somethin' else wouldn't ha' served. She had a cousin married out in Pennsylvany that used to take pains to get it to her every year or two, and so she felt 'twas important to have it. Some set more by such things as come from a distance, but I rec'lect mother always used to maintain that folks was meant to be doctored with the stuff that grew right about 'em; 'twas sufficient, an' so ordered. That was before the whole population took to livin' on wheels, the way they do now. 'Twas never my idee that we was meant to know what's goin' on all over the world to once. There's goin' to be some sort of a set-back one o' these days, with these telegraphs an' things, an' letters comin' every hand's turn, and folks leavin' their proper work to answer 'em. I may not live to see it. 'Twas allowed to be difficult for folks to git about in old times, or to git word across the country, and they stood in their lot an' place, and weren't all just alike, either, same as pine-spills."

We were kneeling side by side now, as if in penitence for the march of progress, but we laughed as we turned to look at each other.

"Do you think it did much good when everybody brewed a cracked quart mug of herb-tea?" I asked, walking away on my knees to a new mullein.

"I've always lifted my voice against the practice, far's I could," declared Mrs. Goodsoe; "an' I won't deal out none o' the herbs I save for no such nonsense. There was three houses along our road—I call no names—where you couldn't go into the livin' room without findin' a mess o' herb-tea drorin' on the stove or side o' the fireplace, winter or summer, sick or well. One was thoroughwut, one would be camomile, and the other, like as not, yellow dock; but they all used to put in a little new rum to git out the goodness, or keep it from spilin'." (Mrs. Goodsoe favored me with a knowing smile.) "Land, how mother used to laugh! But, poor creatures, they had to work hard, and I guess it never done 'em a mite o' harm; they was all good herbs. I wish you could hear the quawkin' there used to b when they was indulged with a real case o' sickness. Everybo would collect from far an' near; you'd see 'em coming along the r and across the pastures then; everybody clamorin' that nothin' would do no kind o' good but her choice o' teas or drarves to the feet. I wonder there was a babe lived to grow up in the whole lower part o' the town; an' if nothin' else 'peared to ail 'em, word was passed about that 'twas likely Mis' So-and-So's last young one was goin' to be foolish. Land, how they'd gather! I know one day the doctor come to Widder Peck's and the house was crammed so't he could scercely git inside the door; and he says, just as polite, 'Do send for some of the neighbors!' as if there wa'n't a soul to turn to, right or left. You'd ought to seen 'em begin to scatter."

"But don't you think the cars and telegraphs have given people more to interest them, Mrs. Goodsoe? Don't you believe people's lives were narrower then, and more taken up with little things?" I asked, unwisely, being a product of modern times.

"Not one mite, dear," said my companion stoutly. "There was as big thoughts then as there is now; these times was born o' them. The difference is in folks themselves; but now, instead o' doin' their own housekeepin' and watchin' their own neighbors—though that was carried to excess—they git word that a niece's child is ailin' the other side o' Massachusetts, and they drop everything and git on their best clothes, and off they jiggit in the cars. 'Tis a bad sign when folks wear out their best clothes faster 'n they do their everyday ones. The other side o' Massachusetts has got to look after itself by rights. An' besides that, Sunday-keepin's all gone out o' fashion. Some lays it to one thing an' some another, but some o' them old ministers that folks are all a-sighin' for did preach a lot o' stoff that wa'n't nothin' but chaff; 'twa'n't the word o' God out o' either Old Testament or New. But everybody went to meetin' and heard it, and come home, and was set to fightin' with their next door neighbor over it. Now I'm a believer, and I try to live a Christian life, but I'd as soon hear a surveyor's book read out, figgers an' all, as try to get any simple truth out o' most sermons. It's them as is most to blame."

"What was the matter that day at Widow Peck's?" I hastened to ask, for I knew by experience that the good, clear minded soul beside me was apt to grow unduly vexed and distressed when she contemplated the state of religious teaching.

"Why, there wa'n't nothin' the matter, only a gal o' Miss Peck's had met with a dis'pintment and had gone into screechin' fits. 'Twas rovin' creatur that had come along hayin' time, and he'd gone off a' forsook her betwixt two days; nobody ever knew what become him. Them Pecks was 'Good Lord, anybody!' kind o' gals, an took up with whoever they could get. One of 'em married Heron, the Irishman; they lived in that little house that was burnt this summer, over on the edge o' the plains. He was a good-hearted creatur, with a laughin' eye and a clever word for everybody. He was the first Irishman that ever came this way, and we was all for gettin' a look at him, when he first used to go by. Mother's folks was what they call Scotch-Irish, though; there was an old race of 'em settled about here. They could foretell events, some on 'em, and had second-sight. I know folks used to say mother's grandmother had them gifts, but mother was never free to speak about it to us. She remembered her well, too."

"I suppose that you mean old Jim Heron, who was such a famous fiddler?" I asked with great interest, for I am always delighted to know more about that rustic hero, parochial Orpheus that he must have been!

"Now, dear heart, I suppose you don't remember him, do you?" replied Mrs. Goodsoe, earnestly. "Fiddle! He'd about break your heart with them tunes of his, or else set your heels flyin' up the floor in a jig, though you was minister o' the First Parish and all wound up for a funeral prayer. I tell ye there win't no tunes sounds like them used to. It used to seem to me summer nights when I was comin' along the plains road, and he set by the window playin', as if there was a bewitched human creatur in that old red fiddle o' his. He could make it sound just like a woman's voice tellin' somethin' over and over, as if folks could help her out o' her sorrows if she could only make 'em understand. I've set by the stone wall and cried as if my heart was broke, and dear knows it wa'n't in them days. How he would twirl off them jigs and dance tunes! He used to make somethin' han'some out of 'em in fall an' winter, playin' at huskins and dancin' parties; but he was unstiddy by spells, as he got along in years, and never knew what it was to be forehanded. Everybody felt bad when he died; you couldn't help likin' the creatur. He'd got the gift—that's all you could say about it.

"There was a Mis' Jerry Foss, that lived over by the brook bridge, on the plains road, that had lost her husband early, and was left with three chil'n. She set the world by 'em, and was a real pleasant, ambitious little woman, and was workin' on as best she could with that little farm, when there come a rage o' scarlet fever, and her boy and two girls was swept off and laid dead within the same week. Everyone o' the neighbors did what they could, but she'd had no sleep since they was taken sick, and after the funeral she set ther

just like a piece o' marble, and would only shake her head when
you spoke to her. They all thought her reason would go; and
'twould certain, if she couldn't have shed tears. An' one o' the
neighbors—'twas like mother's sense, but it might have been somebody else—spoke o' Jim Heron. Mother an' one or two o' the
women that knew her best was in the house with her. 'Twas right
in the edge o' the woods and some of us younger ones was over
by the wall on the other side of the road where there was a couple
of old willows—I remember just how the brook damp felt—and
we kept quiet's we could, and some other folks come along down
the road, and stood waitin' on the little bridge, hopin' somebody'd
come out, I suppose, and they'd git news. Everybody was wrought
up, and felt a good deal for her, you know. By an' by Jim Heron
come stealin' right out o' the shadows an' set down on the doorstep,
an' 'twas a good while before we heard a sound; then, oh, dear me!
'twas what the whole neighborhood felt for that mother all spoke
in the notes, an' they told me afterwards that Mis' Foss's face changed
in a minute, and she come right over 'n got into my mother's
lap—she was a little woman—an' laid her head down, and there
she cried herself into a blessed sleep. After awhile one o' the other
women stole out an' told the folks, and we all went home. He only
played that one tune.

"But there!" resumed Mrs. Goodsoe, after a silence, during which
my eyes were filled with tears. "His wife always complained that the
fiddle made her nervous. She never 'peared to think nothin' o' poor
Heron after she'd once got him."

"That's often the way," I said, with harsh cynicism, though I had
no guilty person in my mind at the moment; and we went straying
off, not very far apart, up through the pasture. Mrs. Goodsoe cautioned
me that we must not get so far off that we could not get back the
same day. The sunshine began to feel very hot on our backs, and we
both turned toward the shade. We had already collected a large bundle of mullein leaves, which were carefully laid into a clean, calico
apron, held together by the four corners, and proudly carried by me,
though my companion regarded them with anxious eyes. We sat
down together at the edge of the pine woods, and Mrs. Goodsoe
proceeded to fan herself with her limp cape-bonnet.

"I declare, how hot it is! The east wind's all gone again," she said.
"It felt so cool this forenoon that I overburdened myself with as thick
a petticoat as any I've got. I'm despri't afeared of having a chill, now
that I ain't so young as once. I hate to be housed up."

"It's only August, after all," I assured her unnecessarily, confirming my statement by taking two peaches out of my pocket, and laying them side by side on the brown pine needles between us.

"Dear sakes alive!" exclaimed the old lady, with evident pleasure. "Where did you get them, now? Doesn't anything taste twice better out-o'-doors? I ain't had such a peach for years. Do le's keep the stones, an' I'll plant 'em; it only takes four years for a peach pit to come to bearing, an' I guess I'm good for four years, 'thout I meet with some accident."

I could not help agreeing, or taking a fond look at the thin little figure, and her winkled brown face and kind, twinkling eyes. She looked as if she had properly dried herself, by mistake, with some of her mullein leaves, and was likely to keep her goodness, and to last the longer in consequence. There never was a truer, simple-hearted soul made out of the old-fashioned country dust than Mrs. Goodsoe. I thought, as I looked away from her across the wide country, that nobody was left in any of the farmhouses so original, so full of rural wisdom and reminiscence, so really able and dependable, as she. And nobody had made better use of her time in a world foolish enough to sometimes undervalue medicinal herbs.

When we had eaten our peaches we still sat under the pines, and I was not without pride when I had poked about in the ground with a little twig, and displayed to my crony a long fine root, bright yellow to the eye, and a wholesome bitter to the taste.

"Yis, dear, goldthread," she assented indulgently. "Seems to me there's more of it than anything except grass an' hardtack. Good for canker, but no better than two or three other things I can call to mind; but I always lay in a good wisp of it, for old times' sake. Now, I want to know why you should ha' bit it, and took away all the taste o' your nice peach? I was just thinkin' what a han'some entertainment we've had. I've got so I 'sociate certain things with certain folks, and goldthread was somethin' Lizy Wisby couldn't keep house without, no ways whatever. I believe she took so much it kind o' puckered her disposition."

"Lizy Wisby?" I repeated inquiringly.

"You knew her, if ever, by the name of Mis' Deacon Brimblecom," answered my friend, as if this were only a brief preface to further information, so I waited with respectful expectation: Mrs. Goodsoe had grown tired out in the sun, and a good story would be an excuse for sufficient rest. It was a most lovely place where we sat, halfway up the long hillside; for my part, I was perfectly contented and happy

"You've often heard of Deacon Brimblecom?" she asked, as if a great deal depended upon his being properly introduced.

"I remember him," said I. "They called him Deacon Brimfull, you know, and he used to go about with a witch-hazel branch to show people where to dig wells."

"That's the one," said Mrs. Goodsoe, laughing. "I didn't know's you could go so far back. I'm always divided between whether you can remember everything I can, or are only a babe in arms."

"I have a dim recollection of there being something strange about their marriage," I suggested, after a pause, which began to appear dangerous. I was so much afraid the subject would be changed.

"I can tell you all about it," I was quickly answered. "Deacon Brimblecom was very pious accordin' to his lights in his early years. He lived way back in the country then, and there come a rovin' preacher along, and set everybody up that way all by the ears. I've heard the old folks talk it over, but I forget most of his doctrine, except some of his followers was persuaded they could dwell among the angels while yet on airth, and this Deacon Brimfull, as you call him, felt sure he was called by the voice of a spirit bride. So he left a good, deservin' wife he had, an' four children, and built him a new house over to the other side of the land he'd had from his father. They didn't take much pains with the buildin', because they expected to be translated before long, and then the spirit brides and them folks was goin' to appear and divide up the airth amongst 'em, and the world's folks and on-believers was goin' to serve 'em or be sent to torments. They had meetin's about in the schoolhouses, an' all sorts o' goin's on; some on 'em went crazy, but the deacon held on to what wits he had, an' by an' by the spirit bride didn't turn out to be much of a housekeeper, an' he had always been used to good livin', so he sneaked home ag'in. One o' mother's sisters married up to Ash Hill, where it all took place; that's how I come to have the particulars."

"Then how did he come to find his Eliza Wisby?" I inquired. "Do tell me the whole story; you've got mullein leaves enough."

"There's all yisterday's at home, if I haven't," replied Mrs. Goodsoe. "The way he come a-courtin' o' Sister Wisby was this: she went a-courtin' o' him.

"There was a spell he lived to home, and then his poor wife died, and he had a spirit bride in good earnest, an' the child'n was placed about with his folks and hers, for they was both out o' good fami- ies; and I don't know what come over him, but he had another pious fit that looked for all the world like the real thing. He hadn't no family cares, and he lived with his brother's folks, and turned his land in with theirs. He used to travel to every meetin' an' conference that was within reach of his old sorrel hoss's feeble legs; he j'ined the Christian Baptists that was just in their early prime, and he was a great exhorter, and got to be called deacon, though I guess he wa'n't deacon, 'less it was for a spare hand when deacon times was scercer'n usual. An' one time there was a four-days' protracted meetin' to the church in the lower part of the town. 'Twas a real solemn time; somethin' more'n usual was goin' forward, an' they collected from the whole country round. Women folks liked it, an' the men too; it give 'em a change, an' they was quartered round free, same as conference folks now. Some on 'em, for a joke, sent Silas Brimblecom up to Lizy Wisby's, though she'd give out she couldn't accommodate nobody, because of expectin' her cousin's folks. Everybody knew 'twas a lie; she was amazin' close considerin' she had plenty to do with. There was a streak that wa'n't just right somewheres in Lizy's wits, I always thought. She was very kind in case o' sickness, I'll say that for her.

"You know where the house is, over there on what they call Windy Hill? There the deacon went, all unsuspectin', and 'stead o' Lizy's resentin' of him she put in her own hoss, and they come back together to evenin' meetin'. She was prominent among the sect herself, an' he bawled and talked, and she bawled and talked, an' took up more'n the time allotted in the exercises, just as if they was showin' off to each what they was able to do at expoundin'. Everybody was laughin' at 'em after the meetin' broke up, and that next day an' the next, an' all through, they was constant, and seemed to be havin' a beautiful occasion. Lizy had always give out she scorned the men, but when she got a chance at a particular one 'twas altogether different, and the deacon seemed to please her somehow or 'nother, and—There! you don't want to listen to this old stuff that's past an' gone?"

"Oh, yes, I do," said I.

"I run on like a clock that's onset her striking hand," said Mrs. Goodsoe mildly. "Sometimes my kitchen timepiece goes on half the forenoon, and I says to myself the day before yesterday I would let it be a warnin', and keep it in mind for a check on my own speech. The next news that was heard was that the deacon an' Lizy—well, opinions differed which of 'em had spoke first, but them fools settled it before the protracted meetin' was over, and give away their hearts before he started for home. They considered 'twould be wise, though, considerin' their short acquaintance, to take one another on trial a spell; 'twas Lizy's notion, and she asked him why he wouldn't come over and stop with her till spring, and then, if both continued to like, they could git married any time 'twas convenient. Lizy, she come and talked it over with mother, and mother disliked to offend her, but she spoke pretty plain; and Lizy felt hurt, an' thought they was showin' excellent judgment, so much harm come from hasty unions and folks comin' to a realizin' sense of each other's failin's when 'twas too late.

"So one day our folks saw Deacon Brimfull a-ridin' by with a gre't coopful of hens in the back o' his wagon, and bundles o' stuff tied to top and hitched to the exes underneath; and he riz a hymn just as he passed the house, and was speedin' the old sorrel with a willer switch. 'Twas most Thanksgivin' time, an' sooner'n she expected him. New Year's was the time she set; but he thought he'd come while the roads was fit for wheels. They was out to meetin' together Thanksgivin' Day, an' that used to be a gre't season for marryin'; so the young folks nudged each other, and some on 'em ventured to speak to the couple as they come down the aisle. Lizy carried it off real well; she wa'n't afraid o' what nobody said or thought, and so home they went. They'd got out her yaller sleigh and her hoss; she never would ride after the deacon's poor old creatur, and I believe it died long o' the winter from stiffenin' up.

"Yes," said Mrs. Goodsoe, emphatically, after we had silently considered the situation for a short space of time, "yes, there was consider'ble talk, now I tell you! The raskil boys pestered 'em just about to death for a while. They used to collect up there an' rap on the winders, and they'd turn out all the deacon's hens 'long at nine o'clock o' night, and chase 'em all over the dingle; an' one night they even lugged the pig right out o' the sty, and shoved it into the back entry, an' run for their lives. They'd stuffed its mouth full o' somethin,' so it couldn't squeal till it got there. There wa'n't a sign o' nobody to be seen when Lizy hasted out with the light, and she an' the deacon had to persuade the creatur back as best they could; 'twas a cold night, and they said it took 'em till towards mornin'. You see the deacon was just the kind of a man that a hog wouldn't budge for; it takes a masterful man to deal with a hog. Well, there was no end to the works nor the talk, but Lizy left 'em pretty much alone. She did 'pear kind of dignified about it, I must say!"

"And then, were they married in the spring?"

"I was tryin' to remember whether it was just before Fast Day or just after," responded my friend, with a careful look at the sun, which was nearer the west than either of us had noticed. "I think likely 'twas along in the last o' April, anyway some of us looked out o' the window one Monday mornin' early, and says, 'For goodness' sake! Lizy's sent the deacon home again!' His old sorrel havin' passed away, he was ridin' in Ezry Welsh's hoss-cart, with his hen-coop and more bundles than he had when he come, and looked as meechin' as ever you see. Ezry was drivin', and he let a glance fly swiftly round to see if any of us was lookin' out; an' then I declare if he didn't have the malice to turn right in towards the barn, where he see my oldest brother, Joshuay, an' says he real natural, 'Joshuay, just step out with your wrench. I believe I hear my kingbolt rattlin' kind o' loose.' Brother, he went out an' took in the sitooation, an' the deacon bowed kind of stiff. Joshuay was so full o' laugh, and Ezry Welsh, that they couldn't look one another in the face. There wa'n't nothing ailed the kingbolt, you know, an' when Josh riz up he says, 'Goin' up country for a spell, Mr. Brimblecom?'

"'I be,' says the deacon, lookin' dreadful mortified and cast down.

"'Ain't things turned out well with you an' Sister Wisby?' says Joshuay. 'You had ought to remember that the woman is the weaker vessel.'

"'Hang her, let her carry less sail, then!' the deacon bu'st out, and he stood right up an' shook his fist there by the hencoop, he was so mad; an' Ezry's hoss was a young creatur, an' started up and set the deacon right over backwards into the chips. We didn't know but he'd broke his neck; but when he see the women folks runnin' out he jumped up quick as a cat, an' clim into the cart, an' off they went. Ezry said he told him that he couldn't git along with Lizy, she was so fractious in thundery weather; if there was a rumble in the daytime she must go right to bed an' screech, and 'twas night she must git right up an' go an' call him out of a sound sleep. But everybody knew he'd never gone home unless she'd sent him.

"Somehow they made it up ag'in, him an' Lizy, and she had him back. She's been countin' all along on not havin' to hire nobidy to work about the gardin' an' so on, an' she said she wa'nt' goin' to let him have a whole winter's board for nothin'. So the old hens was moved back, and they was married right off fair an' square, an' I don't know but they got along well as most folks. He brought his youngest girl down to live with 'em after a while, an' she was a real treasure to Lizy; everybody spoke well o' Phœbe Brimblecom. The deacon got over his pious fit, and there was consider'ble work in him if you kept right after him. He was an amazin' cider-drinker, and he airnt the name you know him by in his latter days. Lizy never trusted him with nothin', but she kep' him well. She left everything she owned to Phœbe, when she died, 'cept somethin' to satisfy the law. There, they're all gone now; seems to me sometimes, when I get thinkin', as if I'd lived a thousand years!"

I laughed, but I found Mrs. Goodsoe's thoughts had taken a serious turn.

"There, I come by some old graves down here in the lower edge of the pasture," she said as we rose to go. "I couldn't help thinking how I should like to be laid right out in the pasture ground, when my time comes; it looked sort o' comfortable, and I have ranged these slopes so many summers. Seems as if I could see right up through the turf and tell when the weather was pleasant, and get the goodness o' the sweet fern. Now, dear, just hand me my apernful o' mulleins out o' the shade. I hope you won't come to need none this winter, but I'll dry some special for you."

"I'm going by the road," said I, "or else by the path across the meadows, so I will walk as far as the house with you. Aren't you pleased with my company?" for she demurred at my going the least bit out of the way.

So we strolled towards the little gray house, with our plunder of mullein leaves slung on a stick which we carried between us. Of course I went in to make a call, as if I had not seen my hostess before; she is the last maker of muster-gingerbread, and before I came away I was kindly measured for a pair of mittens.

"You'll be sure to come an' see them two peach trees after I get 'em well growin'?" Mrs. Goodsoe called after me when I had said good-bye, and was almost out of hearing down the road.

# SANCTUARY

## Nella Larsen

## I

ON THE SOUTHERN coast, between Merton and Shawboro, there is a strip of desolation some half a mile wide and nearly ten miles long between the sea and old fields of ruined plantations. Skirting the edge of this narrow jungle is a partly grown-over road, which still shows traces of furrows made by the wheels of wagons that have long since rotted away or been cut into firewood. This road is little used, now that the state has built its new highway a bit to the west and wagons are less numerous than automobiles.

In the forsaken road a man was walking swiftly. But in spite of his hurry, at every step he set down his feet with infinite care, for the night was windless and the heavy silence intensified each sound; even the breaking of a twig could be plainly heard. And the man had need of caution as well as haste.

Before a lonely cottage that shrank timidly back from the road the man hesitated a moment, then struck out across the patch of green in front of it. Stepping behind a clump of bushes close to the house, he looked in through the lighted window at Annie Poole, standing at her kitchen table mixing the supper biscuits.

He was a big black man with pale brown eyes in which there was an odd mixture of fear and amazement. The light showed streaks of gray soil on his heavy, sweating face and great hands, and on his torn clothes. In his woolly hair clung bits of dried leaves and dead grass.

He made a gesture as if to tap on the window, but turned away to the door instead. Without knocking he opened it and went in.

## II

The woman's brown gaze was immediately on him, though she did not move. She said, "You ain't in no hurry, is you, Jim Hammer?" It wasn't, however, entirely a question.

"Ah's in trubble, Mis' Poole," the man explained, his voice shaking, his fingers twitching.

"W'at you done done now?"

"Shot a man, Mis' Poole."

"Trufe?" The woman seemed calm. But the word was spat out.

"Yas'm. Shot 'im." In the man's tone was something of wonder, as if he himself could not quite believe that he had really done this thing which he affirmed.

"Daid?"

"Dunno, Mis' Poole. Dunno."

"White man o' niggah?"

"Cain't say, Mis' Poole. White man, Ah reckons."

Annie Poole looked at him with cold contempt. She was a tiny, withered woman—fifty, perhaps—with a wrinkled face the color of old copper, framed by a crinkly mass of white hair. But about her small figure was some quality of hardness that belied her appearance of frailty. At last she spoke, boring her sharp little eyes into those of the anxious creature before her.

"An' w'at am you lookin' foh me to do 'bout et?"

"Jes' lemme stop till dey's gone by. Hide me till dey passes. Reckon dey ain't fur off now." His begging voice changed to a frightened whimper. "Foh de Lawd's sake, Mis' Poole, lemme stop."

And why, the woman inquired caustically, should she run the dangerous risk of hiding him?

"Obadiah, he'd lemme stop ef he was to home," the man whined.

Annie Poole sighed. "Yas," she admitted slowly, reluctantly, "Ah spec' he would. Obadiah, he's too good to youall no 'count trash." Her slight shoulders lifted in a hopeless shrug. "Yas, Ah reckon he'd do et. Emspecial' seein' how he allus set such a heap o' store by you. Cain't see w'at foh, mahse'f. Ah shuah don' see nuffin' in you but a heap o' dirt."

But a look of irony, of cunning, of complicity passed over her face. She went on, "Still, 'siderin' all an' all, how Obadiah's right fon' o' you, an' how white folks is white folks, Ah'm a-gwine hide you dis one time."

Crossing the kitchen, she opened a door leading into a small bedroom, saying, "Git yo'se'f in dat dere feather baid an' Ah'm a-gwine put de clo's on de top. Don' reckon dey'll fin' you ef dey does look foh you in mah house. An Ah don' spec' dey'll go foh to do dat. Not lessen you been keerless an' let 'em smell you out gittin' hyah." She turned on him a withering look. "But you allus been triflin'. Cain't do nuffin' propah. An' Ah'm a-tellin' you ef dey warn't white folks an' you a po' niggah, Ah shuah wouldn't be lettin' you mess up mah feather baid dis ebenin', 'cose Ah jes' plain don' want you hyah. Ah done kep' mahse'f outen trubble all mah life. So's Obadiah."

"Ah's powahful 'bliged to you, Mis' Poole. You shuah am one good 'oman. De Lawd'll mos' suttinly—"

Annie Poole cut him off. "Dis ain't no time foh all dat kin' o' fiddle-de-roll. Ah does mah duty as Ah sees et 'thout no thanks from you. Ef de Lawd had gib you a white face 'stead o' dat dere black one, Ah shuah would turn you out. Now hush yo' mouf an' git yo'se'f in. An' don' git movin' and scrunchin' undah dose covahs and git yo'se'f kotched in mah house."

Without further comment the man did as he was told. After he had laid his soiled body and grimy garments between her snowy sheets, Annie Poole carefully rearranged the covering and placed piles of freshly laundered linen on top. Then she gave a pat here and there, eyed the result, and, finding it satisfactory, went back to her cooking.

## III

Jim Hammer settled down to the racking business of waiting until the approaching danger should have passed him by. Soon savory odors seeped in to him and he realized that he was hungry. He wished that Annie Poole would bring him something to eat. Just one biscuit. But she wouldn't, he knew. Not she. She was a hard one, Obadiah's mother.

By and by he fell into a sleep from which he was dragged back by the rumbling sound of wheels in the road outside. For a second, fear clutched so tightly at him that he almost leaped from the suffocating shelter of the bed in order to make some active attempt to escape the horror that his capture meant. There was a spasm at his heart, a pain so sharp, so slashing that he had to suppress an impulse to cry out. He felt himself falling. Down, down, down . . . Everything grew dim and very distant in his memory . . . Vanished . . . Came rushing back.

Outside there was silence. He strained his ears. Nothing. No footsteps. No voices. They had gone on then. Gone without even stopping to ask Annie Poole if she had seen him pass that way. A sigh of relief slipped from him. His thick lips curled in an ugly, cunning smile. It had been smart of him to think of coming to Obadiah's mother's to hide. She was an old demon, but he was safe in her house.

He lay a short while longer, listening intently, and, hearing nothing, started to get up. But immediately he stopped, his yellow eyes glowing like pale flames. He had heard the unmistakable sound of men coming toward the house. Swiftly he slid back into the heavy, hot stuffiness of the bed and lay listening fearfully.

The terrifying sounds drew nearer. Slowly. Heavily. Just for a moment he thought they were not coming in—they took so long. But there was a light knock and the noise of a door being opened. His whole body went taut. His feet felt frozen, his hands clammy, his tongue like a weighted, dying thing. His pounding heart made it hard for his straining ears to hear what they were saying out there.

"Ebenin', Mistah Lowndes." Annie Poole's voice sounded as it always did, sharp and dry.

There was no answer. Or had he missed it? With slow care he shifted his position, bringing his head nearer the edge of the bed. Still he heard nothing. What were they waiting for? Why didn't they ask about him?

Annie Poole, it seemed, was of the same mind. "Ah don' reckon you all done traipsed 'way out hyah jes' foh yo' healf," she hinted.

"There's bad news for you, Annie, I'm 'fraid." The sheriff's voice was low and queer.

Jim Hammer visualized him standing out there—a tall, stooped man, his white tobacco-stained mustache drooping limply at the ends, his nose hooked and sharp, his eyes blue and cold. Bill Lowndes was a hard one too. And white.

"W'atall bad news, Mistah Lowndes?" The woman put the question quietly, directly.

"Obadiah—" the sheriff began—hesitated—began again. "Oba-diah—ah—er, he's outside, Annie. I'm 'fraid—"

"Shucks! You done missed. Obadiah, he ain't done nuffin', Mistah Lowndes. Obadiah!" she called stridently. "Obadiah! git hyah an' splain yo'se'f."

But Obadiah didn't answer, didn't come in. Other men came in. Came in with steps that dragged and halted. No one spoke. Not even Annie Poole. Something was laid carefully upon the floor.

"Obadiah, chile," his mother said softly, "Obadiah, chile." Then, with sudden alarm, "He ain't daid, is he? Mistah Lowndes! Obadiah, he ain't daid?"

Jim Hammer didn't catch the answer to that pleading question. A new fear was stealing over him.

"There was a to-do, Annie," Bill Lowndes explained gently, "at the garage back o' the factory. Fellow tryin' to steal tires. Obadiah heerd a noise an' run out with two or three others. Scared the rascal, all right. Fired off his gun an' run. We allow et to be Jim Hammer. Picked up his cap back there. Never was no 'count. Thievin' an' sly. But we'll git 'im, Annie. We'll git 'im."

The man huddled in the feather bed prayed silently. "Oh, Lawd! Ah didn't go to do et. Not Obadiah, Lawd. You knows dat. You knows et." And into his frenzied brain came the thought that it would be better for him to get up and go out to them before Annie Poole gave him away. For he was lost now. With all his great strength he tried to get himself out of the bed. But he couldn't.

"Oh, Lawd!" he moaned. "Oh, Lawd!" His thoughts were bitter and they ran through his mind like panic. He knew that it had come to pass as it said somewhere in the Bible about the wicked. The Lord had stretched out his hand and smitten him. He was paralyzed. He couldn't move hand or foot. He moaned again. It was all there was left for him to do. For in the terror of this new calamity that had come upon him, he had forgotten the waiting danger which was so near out there in the kitchen.

His hunters, however, didn't hear him. Bill Lowndes was saying, "We been a-lookin' for Jim out along the old road. Figured he'd make tracks for Shawboro. You ain't noticed anybody pass this evenin', Annie?"

The reply came promptly, unwaveringly. "No, Ah ain't sees nobody pass. Not yet."

## IV

Jim Hammer caught his breath.

"Well," the sheriff concluded, "we'll be gittin' along. Obadiah was a mighty fine boy. Ef they was all like him—I'm sorry, Annie. Anything I c'n do, let me know."

"Thank you, Mistah Lowndes."

With the sound of the door closing on the departing men, power to move came back to the man in the bedroom. He pushed his dirt-caked feet out from the covers and rose up, but crouched down again. He wasn't cold now, but hot all over and burning. Almost he wished that Bill Lowndes and his men had taken him with them.

Annie Poole had come into the room.

It seemed a long time before Obadiah's mother spoke. When she did there were no tears, no reproaches; but there was a raging fury in her voice as she lashed out. "Git outen mah feather baid, Jim Hammer, an' outen mah house, an' don' nevah stop thankin' you' Jesus he done gib you dat black face."

# LITTLE SELVES

## Mary Lerner

MARGARET O'BRIEN, A great-aunt and seventy-five, knew she was near the end. She did not repine, for she had had a long, hard life and she was tired. The young priest who brought her communion had administered the last rites—holy oils on her eyelids (Lord, forgive her the sins of seeing!); holy oils on her lips (Lord, forgive her the sins of speaking!), on her ears, on her knotted hands, on her weary feet. Now she was ready, though she knew the approach of the dread presence would mean greater suffering. So she folded quiet hands beneath her heart, there where no child had ever lain, yet where now something grew and fattened on her strength. And she seemed given over to pleasant revery.

Neighbors came in to see her, and she roused herself and received them graciously, with a personal touch for each.—"And has your Julia gone to New York, Mrs. Carty? Nothing would do her but she must be going, I suppose. 'T was the selfsame way with me, when I was coming out here from the old country. Full of money the streets were, I used to be thinking. Well, well; the hills far away are green."

Or to Mrs. Devlin: "Terence is at it again, I see by the look of you. Poor man! There's no holding him? Eh, woman dear! Thirst is the end of drinking and sorrow is the end of love."

If her visitors stayed longer than a few minutes, however, her attention wandered; her replies became cryptic. She would murmur something about "all the seven parishes," or the Wicklow hills, or "the fair cove of Cork tippytoe into the ocean"; then fall into silence, smiling, eyes closed, yet with a singular look of attention.

At such times her callers would whisper: "Glory b' t' God! she's so near it there's no fun in it," and slip out soberly into the kitchen.

Her niece, Anna Lennan, mother of a fine brood of children, would stop work for the space of a breath and enjoy a bit of conversation.

"Ain't she failing, though, the poor afflicted creature?" Mrs. Hanley cried one day. "Her mind is going back on her already."

"Are you of that opinion? I'm thinking she's mind enough yet, when she wants to attend; but mostly she's just drawn into herself, as busy as a bee about something, whatever it is that she's turning over in her head day-in, day-out. She sleeps scarce a wink for all she lies there so quiet, and, in the night, my man and I hear her talking to herself. 'No, no,' she'll say. 'I've gone past. I must be getting back to the start.' Or, another time, 'This is it, now. If I could be stopping!'"

"And what do you think she is colloguing about?"

"There's no telling. Himself does be saying it's in an elevator she is, but that's because he puts in the day churning up and down in one of the same. What else can you expect? 'T is nothing but 'Going up! going down!' with him all night as it is. Betune the two of them they have me fair destroyed with their traveling. 'Are you lacking anything, Aunt Margaret?' I call out to her. 'I am not,' she answers, impatient-like. 'Don't be ever fussing and too-ing, will you?'"

"Tch! tch!"

"And do you suppose the children are a comfort to her? Sorra bit. Just a look at them and she wants to be alone. 'Take them away, let you,' says she, shutting her eyes. 'The others is realer.'"

"And you think she's in her right mind all the same?"

"I do. 'T is just something she likes to be thinking over—something she's fair dotty about. Why, it's the same when Father Flint is here. Polite and riverintial at the first, then impatient, and, if the poor man doesn't be taking the hint, she just closes up shop and off again into her whimsies. You'd swear she was in fear of missing something."

The visitor, being a young wife, had an explanation to hazard. "If she was a widow woman, now, or married—perhaps she had a liking for somebody once. Perhaps she might be trying to imagine them young days over again. Do you think could it be that?"

Anna shook her head. "My mother used to say she was a born old maid. All *she* wanted was work and saving her bit of money, and to church every minute she could be sparing."

"Still, you can't be telling. 'T is often that kind weeps sorest when 't is too late. My own old aunt used to cry, 'If I could be twenty-five again, wouldn't I do different!'"

"Maybe, maybe, though I doubt could it be so."

Nor was it so. The old woman, lying back so quietly among her pillows with closed eyes, yet with that look of singular intentness and concentration, was seeking no lover of her youth; though, indeed, she had had one once, and from time to time he did enter her revery, try as she would to prevent him. At that point, she always made the singular comment, "Gone past! I must be getting back to the beginning," and, pressing back into her earliest consciousness, she would remount the flooding current of the years. Each time, she hoped to get further—though remoter shapes were illusive, and, if approached too closely, vanished— for, once embarked on her river of memories, the descent was relentlessly swift. How tantalizing that swiftness! However she yearned to linger, she was rushed along till, all too soon, she sailed into the common light of day. At that point, she always put about, and laboriously recommenced the ascent.

Today, something her niece had said about Donnybrook Fair—for Anna, too, was a child of the old sod—seemed to swell out with a fair wind the sails of her visionary bark. She closed her mind to all familiar shapes and strained back—way, way back, concentrating all her powers in an effort of will. For a bit she seemed to hover in populous space. This did not disturb her; she had experienced the same thing before. It simply meant she had mounted pretty well up to the fountainhead. The figures, when they did come, would be the ones she most desired.

At last, they began to take shape, tenuously at first, then of fuller body, each bringing its own setting, its own atmospheric suggestion— whether of dove-feathered Irish cloud and fresh greensward, of sudden downpour, or equally sudden clearing, with continual leafy drip, drip, drip, in the midst of brilliant sunshine.

For Margaret O'Brien, ardent summer sunlight seemed suddenly to pervade the cool, orderly little bedchamber. Then, "Here she is!" and a wee girl of four danced into view, wearing a dress of pink print, very tight at the top and very full at the bottom. She led the way to a tiny new house whence issued the cheery voice of hammers. Lumber and tools were lying round; from within came men's voices. The small girl stamped up the steps and looked in. Then she made for the narrow stair.

"Where's Margaret gone to?" said one of the men. "The upper floor's not finished. It's falling through the young one will be."

"Peggy!" called the older man. "Come down here with you."

There was a delighted squeal. The pink dress appeared at the head of the stairs. "Oh, the funny little man, daddy! Such a funny little old man with a high hat! Come quick, let you, and see him."

The two men ran to the stairs.

"Where is he?"

She turned back and pointed. Then her face fell.

"Gone! the little man is gone!"

Her father laughed and picked her up in his arms. "How big was he, Peg? As big as yourself, I wonder?"

"No, no! Small."

"As big as the baby?"

She considered a moment. "Yes, just as big as that. But a man, da."

"Well, why aren't you after catching him and holding him for ransom? 'T is pots and pots o' gold they've hidden away, the little people, and will be paying a body what he asks to let them go."

She pouted, on the verge of tears. "I want him to come back."

"I mistrust he won't be doing that, the leprechaun. Once you take your eye away, it's off with him for good and all."

Margaret O'Brien hugged herself with delight. *That* was a new one; she had never got back that far before. Yet how well she remembered it all! She seemed to smell the woody pungency of the lumber, the limy odor of whitewash from the field-stone cellar.

The old woman's dream went on. Out of the inexhaustible storehouse of the past, she summoned, one by one, her much-loved memories. There was a pigtailed Margaret in bonnet and shawl, trudging to school one wintry day. She had seen many wintry school-days, but this one stood out by reason of the tears she had shed by the way. She saw the long benches, the slates, the charts, the tall teacher at his desk. With a swelling of the throat, she saw the little girl sob out her declaration: "I'm not for coming no more, Mr. Wilde."

"What's that, Margaret? And why not? Haven't I been good to you?"

Tears choked the child. "Oh, Mr. Wilde, it's just because you're so terrible good to me. They say you are trying to make a Protestant out of me. So I'll not be coming no more."

The tall man drew the little girl to his knee and reassured her. Margaret O'Brien could review that scene with tender delight now. She had not been forced to give up her beloved school. Mr. Wilde had explained to her that her brothers were merely teasing her because she was so quick and such a favorite.

A little Margaret knelt on the cold stone floor at church and stared at the pictured saints or heard the budding branches rustle in the orchard outside. Another Margaret, a little taller, begged for a new sheet of ballads every time her father went to the fair.—There were the long flimsy sheets, with closely printed verses. These you must adapt to familiar tunes. This Margaret, then, swept the hearth and stacked the turf and sang from her bench in the chimney-corner. Sometimes it was something about "the little old red coat me father wore," which was "All buttons, buttons, buttons, buttons; all buttons down before"; or another beginning "Oh, dear, what can the matter be? Johnny's so long at the fair! He promised to buy me a knot of blue ribbon to tie up my bonnie brown hair."

Then there was a picture of the time the fairies actually bewitched the churn, and, labor as you might, no butter would form, not the least tiny speck. Margaret and her mother took the churn apart and examined every part of it. Nothing out of the way. "'T is the fairies is in it," her mother said. "All Souls' Day a-Friday. Put out a saucer of cream the night for the little people, let you." A well-grown girl in a blue cotton frock, the long braids of her black hair whipping about her in the windy evening, set out the cream on the stone flags before the low doorway, wasting no time in getting in again. The next day, how the butter "came!" Hardly started they were, when they could feel it forming. When Margaret washed the dasher, she "kept an eye out" for the dark corners of the room, for the air seemed thronged and murmurous.

After this picture, came always the same tall girl still in the same blue frock, this time with a shawl on her head. She brought in potatoes from the sheltered heaps that wintered out in the open. From one pailful she picked out a little flat stone, rectangular and smoother and more evenly proportional than any stone she had ever seen.

"What a funny stone!" she said to her mother.

Her mother left carding her wool to look. "You may well say so. 'T is one of the fairies' tables. Look close and you'll be turning up their little chairs as well."

It was as her mother said. Margaret found four smaller stones of like appearance, which one might well imagine to be stools for tiny dolls.

"Shall I be giving them to little Bee for playthings?"

"You will not. You'll be putting them outside. In the morning, though you may be searching the countryside, no trace of them will you find, for the fairies will be taking them again."

So Margaret stacked the fairy table and chairs outside. Next morning, she ran out half reluctantly, for she was afraid she would find them and that would spoil the story. But, no! they were gone. She never saw them again, though she searched in all imaginable places. Nor was that the last potato heap to yield these mysterious stones.

Margaret, growing from scene to scene, appeared again in a group of laughing boys and girls.

"What'll we play now?"

"Let's write the ivy test."

"Here's leaves."

Each wrote a name on a leaf and dropped it into a jar of water. Next morning, Margaret, who had misgivings, stole down early and searched for her leaf. Yes, the die was cast! At the sight of its bruised surface, ready tears flooded her eyes. She had written the name of her little grandmother, and the condition of the leaf foretold death within the year. The other leaves were unmarred. She quickly destroyed the ill-omened bit of ivy and said nothing about it, though the children clamored. "There's one leaf short. Whose is gone?" "Mine is there!" "Is it yours, John?" "Is it yours, Esther?" But Margaret kept her counsel, and, within the year, the little grandmother was dead. Of course, she was old, though vigorous; yet Margaret would never play that game again. It was like gambling with fate.

And still the girls kept swinging past. Steadily, all too swiftly, Margaret shot up to a woman's stature; her skirts crept down, her braids ought to have been bobbed up behind. She let them hang, however, and still ran with the boys, questing the bogs, climbing the apple trees, storming the wind-swept hills. Her mother would point to her sister Mary, who, though younger, sat now by the fire with her "spriggin'" [embroidery] for "the quality." Mary could crochet, too, and had a fine range of "shamrogue" patterns. So the mother would chide Margaret.

"What kind of a girl are you, at all, to be ever leping and tearing like a redshanks [deer]? 'T is high time for you to be getting sensible and learning something. Whistles and scouting-guns is all you're good for, and there's no silver in them things as far as I can see."

What fine whistles she contrived out of the pithy willow shoots in the spring! And the scouting-guns hollowed out of elder-stalks, which they charged with water from the brook by means of wadded sticks, working piston-wise! They would hide behind a hedge and bespatter enemies and friends alike. Many's the time they got their ears warmed in consequence or went supperless to bed, pretending not to see the table spread with baked potatoes—"laughing potatoes," they called them, because they were ever splitting their sides—besides delicious buttermilk, new-laid eggs, oat-cakes and fresh butter. "A child without supper is two to breakfast," their mother would say, smiling, when she saw them "tackle" their stirabout the next day.

How full of verve and life were all these figures! That glancing creature grow old? How could such things be! The sober pace of maturity even seemed out of her star. Yet here she was, growing up, for all her reluctance. An awkward gossoon leaned over the gate in the moonlight, though she was indoors, ready to hide. But nobody noticed her alarm.

"There's that long-legged McMurray lad again; scouting after Mary, I'll be bound," said her mother, all unawares.

But it was not Mary that he came for, though she married him just the same, and came out to America with their children some years after her sister's lone pilgrimage.

The intrusion of Jerry McMurray signaled the grounding of her dream bark on the shoals of reality. Who cared about the cut-and-dried life of a grown woman? Enchantment now lay behind her, and, if the intervals between periods of pain permitted, she again turned an expectant face toward the old childish visions. Sometimes she could make the trip twice over without being overtaken by suffering. But her intervals of comfort grew steadily shorter; frequently she was interrupted before she could get rightly launched on her delight. And always there seemed to be one vision more illusive than the rest which she particularly longed to recapture. At last, chance words of Anna's put her on its trail in this wise.

When she was not, as her niece said, "in her trance, wool-gathering," Anna did her best to distract her, sending the children in to ask "would she have a sup of tea now," or a taste of wine jelly. One day, after the invalid had spent a bad night, she brought in her new long silk coat for her aunt's inspection, for the old woman had always been "tasty" and "dressy," and had made many a fine gown in her day. The sharp old eyes lingered on the rich and truly striking braid ornament that secured the loose front of the garment.

"What's that plaster?" she demanded, disparagingly.

Anna, inclined to be wroth, retorted; "I suppose you'd be preferring one o' them tight ganzy [sweater] things that fit the figger like a jersey, all buttoned down before."

A sudden light flamed in the old face. "I have it!" she cried. "'T is what I've been seeking this good while. 'T will come now—the red coat! I must be getting back to the beginning."

With that, she was off, relaxing and composing herself, as if surrendering to the spell of a hypnotist.

To reach any desired picture in her gallery, she must start at the outset. Then they followed on, in due order—all that procession of little girls: pink clad, blue-print clad, bare-legged or brogan-shod; flirting their short skirts, plaiting their heavy braids. About half way along, a new figure asserted itself—a girl of nine or ten, who twisted this way and that before a blurred bit of mirror and frowned at the red coat that flapped about her heels—bought oversize, you may be sure, so that she shouldn't grow out of it too soon. The sleeves swallowed her little brown hands, the shoulders and back were grotesquely sack-like, the front had a puss [pout] on it.

"'T is the very fetch of Paddy the gander I am in it. I'll not be wearing it so." She frowned with sudden intentness. "Could I be fitting it a bit, I wonder, the way mother does cut down John's coats for Martin?"

With needle, scissors and thread, she crept up to her little chamber under the eaves. It was early in the forenoon when she set to work ripping. The morning passed, and the dinner hour.

"Peggy! Where's the girl gone to, I wonder?"

"To Aunt Theresa's, I'm thinking."

"Well, it's glad I am she's out o' my sight, for my hands itched to be shaking her. Stand and twist herself inside out she did, fussing over the fit of the good coat I'm after buying her. The little fustherer!"

For the small tailoress under the roof, the afternoon sped on winged feet: pinning, basting, and stitching; trying on, ripping out again, and re-fitting. "I'll be taking it in a wee bit more." She had to crowd up to the window to catch the last of the daylight. At dusk, she swept her dark hair from her flushed cheeks and forced her sturdy body into the red coat. It was a "fit," believe you me! Modeled on the lines of the riding-habit of a full-figured lady she had seen hunting about the countryside, it buttoned up tight over her flat, boyish chest and bottled up her squarish little waist. About her narrow hips, it rippled out in a short "frisk." Beneath, her calico skirt, and bramble-scratched brown legs.

Warmed with triumph, she flew downstairs. Her mother and a neighbor were sitting in the glow of the peat fire. She tried to meet them with assurance, but, at sight of their altered faces, misgiving clutched her. She pivoted before the mirror.

"Holy hour!" cried her mother "What sausage-skin is that you've got into?" Then, as comprehension grew: "Glory b' t' God, Ellen! 't is the remains of the fine new coat I'm after buying her, large enough to last her the next five years!"

"'T was too large!" the child whimpered. "A gander I looked in it!" Then, cajolingly, "I'm but after taking it in a bit, ma. 'T will do grand now, and maybe I'll not be getting much fatter. Look at the fit of it, just!"

"Fit! God save the mark!" cried her mother.

"Is the child after making that jacket herself?" asked the neighbor.

"I am," Margaret spoke up, defiantly. "I cut it and shaped it and put it together. It has even a frisk to the tail."

"Maggie," said the neighbor to Margaret's mother. "'T is as good a piece o' work for a child of her years as ever I see. You ought not to be faulting her, she's done that well. And," bursting into irrepressible laughter, "it's herself will have to be wearing it, woman dear! All she needs now is a horse and a side-saddle to be an equeestrieen!"

So the wanton destruction of the good red coat—in that house where good coats were sadly infrequent—ended with a laugh after all. How long she wore that tight jacket, and how grand she felt in it, let the other children laugh as they would!

What joy the old woman took in this incident! With its fullness of detail, it achieved a delicious suggestion of permanence, in contrast to the illusiveness of other isolated moments. Margaret O'Brien *saw* all these other figures, but she really *was* the child with the red coat. In the long years between, she had fashioned many fine dresses—gowned gay girls for their conquests and robed fair brides for the altar. Of all these, nothing now remained; but she could feel the good stuff of the red kersey under her little needle-scratched fingers, and see the glow of its rich color against her wind-kissed brown cheek.

"To the life!" she exclaimed aloud, exultantly. "To the very life!"

"What life, Aunt Margaret?" asked Anna, with gentle solicitude. "Is it afraid of the end you are, darling?"

"No, no, asthore. I've resigned myself long since, though 't was bitter knowledge at the outset. Well, well, God is good and we can't live forever.

Her eyes, opening to the two flaring patent gas-burners, winked as if she had dwelt long in a milder light. "What's all this glare about?" she asked playfully. "I guess the chandler's wife is dead. Snuff out the whole of them staring candles, let you. 'T is daylight yet; just the time o' day I always did like the best."

Anna obeyed and sat down beside the bed in the soft spring dusk. A little wind crept in under the floating white curtains, bringing with it the sweetness of new grass and pear-blossoms from the trim yard. It seemed an interval set apart from the hurrying hours of the busy day for rest and thought and confidences—an open moment. The old woman must have felt its invitation, for she turned her head and held out a shy hand to her niece.

"Anna, my girl, you imagine 't is the full o' the moon with me, I'm thinking. But, no, never woman was more in her right mind than I. Do you want I should be telling you what I've been hatching these many long days and nights? 'T will be a good laugh for you, I'll go bail."

And, as best she could, she gave the trend of her imaginings. Anna did not laugh, however. Instead, with the ever-ready sympathy and comprehension of the Celt, she showed brimming eyes. "'T is a thought I've often myself, let me tell you," she admitted. "Of all the little girls that were me, and now can be living no longer."

"You've said it!" cried the old woman, delighted at her unexpected responsiveness. "Only with me, 't is fair pit'yus. There's all those poor dear lasses there's nobody but me left to remember, and soon there'll not be even that. Sometimes they seem to be pleading just not to be forgotten, so I have to be keeping them alive in my head. I'm succeeding, too, and, if you'll believe me, 't is them little whips seem to be the real ones, and the live children here the shadders." Her voice choked with sudden tears. "They're all the children ever I had. My grief! that I'll have to be leaving them! They'll die now, for no man lives who can remember them any more."

Anna's beauty, already fading with the cares of house and children, seemed to put on all its former fresh charm. She leaned forward with girlish eagerness. "Auntie Margaret," she breathed, with new tenderness, "there's many a day left you yet. I'll be sitting here aside of you every evening at twilight just, and you can be showing me the lasses you have in mind. Many's the time my mother told me of the old place, and I can remember it well enough myself, though I was the youngest of the lot. So you can be filling it with all of our people—Mary and Margaret, John, Martin and Esther, Uncle Sheamus and the rest. I'll see them just as clear as yourself, for I've a place in my head where pictures come as thick and sharp as stars on a frosty night, when I get thinking. Then, with me ever calling them up, they'll be dancing and stravaging about till doomsday."

So the old woman had her heart's desire. She recreated her earlier selves and passed them on, happy in the thought that she was saving them from oblivion. "Do you mind that bold lass clouting her pet bull, now?" she would ask, with delight, speaking more and more as if of a third person. "And that other hussy that's after making a ganzy out of her good coat? I'd admire to have the leathering of that one."

Still the old woman lingered, a good month beyond her allotted time. As spring ripened, the days grew long. In the slow-fading twilights, the two women set their stage, gave cues for entrances and exits. Over the white counterpane danced the joyous figures, so radiant, so incredibly young, the whole cycle of a woman's girlhood. Grown familiar now, they came of their own accord, soothing her hours of pain with their laughing beauty, or, suddenly contemplative, assisting with seemly decorum at her devotional ecstasies.

"A saintly woman," the young priest told Anna on one of the last days. "She will make a holy end. Her meditations must be beautiful, for she has the true light of Heaven on her face. She looks as if she heard already the choiring of the angels."

And Anna, respectfully agreeing, kept her counsel. He was a good and sympathetic man and a priest of God, but, American-born, he was, like her stolid, kindly husband, outside the magic circle of comprehension. "He sees nothing, poor man," she thought, indulgently. "But he does mean well." So she set her husband to "mind" the young ones, and, easily doffing the sordid preoccupations of every day, slipped back into the enchanted ring.

# WAR

## Jack London

## I

HE WAS A young man, not more than twenty-four or five, and he might have sat his horse with the careless grace of his youth had he not been so catlike and tense. His black eyes roved everywhere, catching the movements of twigs and branches where small birds hopped, questing ever onward through the changing vistas of trees and brush, and returning always to the clumps of undergrowth on either side. And as he watched, so did he listen, though he rode on in silence, save for the boom of heavy guns from far to the west. This had been sounding monotonously in his ears for hours, and only its cessation could have aroused his notice. For he had business closer to hand. Across his saddle-bow was balanced a carbine.

So tensely was he strung, that a bunch of quail, exploding into flight from under his horse's nose, startled him to such an extent that automatically, instantly, he had reined in and fetched the carbine halfway to his shoulder. He grinned sheepishly, recovered himself, and rode on. So tense was he, so bent upon the work he had to do, that the sweat stung his eyes unwiped, and unheeded rolled down his nose and spattered his saddle pommel. The band of his cavalryman's hat was fresh-stained with sweat. The roan horse under him was likewise wet. It was high noon of a breathless day of heat. Even the birds and squirrels did not dare the sun, but sheltered in shady hiding places among the trees.

Man and horse were littered with leaves and dusted with yellow pollen, for the open was ventured no more than was compulsory.

They kept to the brush and trees, and invariably the man halted and peered out before crossing a dry glade or naked stretch of upland pasturage. He worked always to the north, though his way was devious, and it was from the north that he seemed most to apprehend that for which he was looking. He was no coward, but his courage was only that of the average civilized man, and he was looking to live, not die.

Up a small hillside he followed a cowpath through such dense scrub that he was forced to dismount and lead his horse. But when the path swung around to the west, he abandoned it and headed to the north again along the oak-covered top of the ridge.

The ridge ended in a steep descent—so steep that he zigzagged back and forth across the face of the slope, sliding and stumbling among the dead leaves and matted vines and keeping a watchful eye on the horse above that threatened to fall down upon him. The sweat ran from him, and the pollen-dust, settling pungently in mouth and nostrils, increased his thirst. Try as he would, nevertheless the descent was noisy, and frequently he stopped, panting in the dry heat and listening for any warning from beneath.

At the bottom he came out on a flat, so densely forested that he could not make out its extent. Here the character of the woods changed, and he was able to remount. Instead of the twisted hillside oaks, tall straight trees, big-trunked and prosperous, rose from the damp fat soil. Only here and there were thickets, easily avoided, while he encountered winding, park-like glades where the cattle had pastured in the days before war had run them off.

His progress was more rapid now, as he came down into the valley, and at the end of half an hour he halted at an ancient rail fence on the edge of a clearing. He did not like the openness of it, yet his path lay across to the fringe of trees that marked the banks of the stream. It was a mere quarter of a mile across that open, but the thought of venturing out in it was repugnant. A rifle, a score of them, a thousand, might lurk in that fringe by the stream.

Twice he essayed to start, and twice he paused. He was appalled by his own loneliness. The pulse of war that beat from the West suggested the companionship of battling thousands; here was naught but silence, and himself, and possible death-dealing bullets from a myriad ambushes. And yet his task was to find what he feared to find. He must go on, and on, till somewhere, some time, he encountered another man, or other men, from the other side, scouting, as he was scouting, to make report, as he must make report, of having come in touch.

Changing his mind, he skirted inside the woods for a distance, and again peeped forth. This time, in the middle of the clearing, he saw a small farmhouse. There were no signs of life. No smoke curled from the chimney, not a barnyard fowl clucked and strutted. The kitchen door stood open, and he gazed so long and hard into the black aperture that it seemed almost that a farmer's wife must emerge at any moment.

He licked the pollen and dust from his dry lips, stiffened himself, mind and body, and rode out into the blazing sunshine. Nothing stirred. He went on past the house, and approached the wall of trees and bushes by the river's bank. One thought persisted maddeningly. It was of the crash into his body of a high-velocity bullet. It made him feel very fragile and defenseless, and he crouched lower in the saddle.

Tethering his horse in the edge of the wood, he continued a hundred yards on foot till he came to the stream. Twenty feet wide it was, without perceptible current, cool and inviting, and he was very thirsty. But he waited inside his screen of leafage, his eyes fixed on the screen on the opposite side. To make the wait endurable, he sat down, his carbine resting on his knees. The minutes passed, and slowly his tenseness relaxed. At last he decided there was no danger; but just as he prepared to part the bushes and bend down to the water, a movement among the opposite bushes caught his eye.

It might be a bird. But he waited. Again there was an agitation of the bushes, and then, so suddenly that it almost startled a cry from him, the bushes parted and a face peered out. It was a face covered with several weeks' growth of ginger-colored beard. The eyes were blue and wide apart, with laughter-wrinkles in the corners that showed despite the tired and anxious expression of the whole face.

All this he could see with microscopic clearness, for the distance was no more than twenty feet. And all this he saw in such brief time, that he saw it as he lifted his carbine to his shoulder. He glanced along the sights, and knew that he was gazing upon a man who was as good as dead. It was impossible to miss at such point blank range.

But he did not shoot. Slowly he lowered the carbine and watched. A hand, clutching a water-bottle, became visible and the ginger beard bent downward to fill the bottle. He could hear the gurgle of the water. Then arm and bottle and ginger beard disappeared behind the closing bushes. A long time he waited, when, with thirst unslaked, he crept back to his horse, rode slowly across the sun-washed clearing, and passed into the shelter of the woods beyond.

## II

Another day, hot and breathless. A deserted farmhouse, large, with many outbuildings and an orchard, standing in a clearing. From the woods, on a roan horse, carbine across pommel, rode the young man with the quick black eyes. He breathed with relief as he gained the house. That a fight had taken place here earlier in the season was evident. Clips and empty cartridges, tarnished with verdigris, lay on the ground, which, while wet, had been torn up by the hoofs of horses. Hard by the kitchen garden were graves, tagged and numbered. From the oak tree by the kitchen door, in tattered, weather-beaten garments, hung the bodies of two men. The faces, shriveled and defaced, bore no likeness to the faces of men. The roan horse snorted beneath them, and the rider caressed and soothed it and tied it farther away.

Entering the house, he found the interior a wreck. He trod on empty cartridges as he walked from room to room to reconnoiter from the windows. Men had camped and slept everywhere, and on the floor of one room he came upon stains unmistakable where the wounded had been laid down.

Again outside, he led the horse around behind the barn and invaded the orchard. A dozen trees were burdened with ripe apples. He filled his pockets, eating while he picked. Then a thought came to him, and he glanced at the sun, calculating the time of his return to camp. He pulled off his shirt, tying the sleeves and making a bag. This he proceeded to fill with apples.

As he was about to mount his horse, the animal suddenly pricked up its ears. The man, too, listened, and heard, faintly, the thud of hoofs on soft earth. He crept to the corner of the barn and peered out. A dozen mounted men, strung out loosely, approaching from the opposite side of the clearing, were only a matter of a hundred yards or so away. They rode on to the house. Some dismounted, while others remained in the saddle as an earnest that their stay would be short. They seemed to be holding a council, for he could hear them talking excitedly in the detested tongue of the alien invader. The time passed, but they seemed unable to reach a decision. He put the carbine away in its boot, mounted, and waited impatiently, balancing the shirt of apples on the pommel.

He heard footsteps approaching, and drove his spurs so fiercely into the roan as to force a surprised groan from the animal as it leaped forward. At the corner of the barn he saw the intruder, a mere boy of nineteen or twenty for all of his uniform, jump back to escape being run down. At the same moment the roan swerved, and its rider caught a glimpse of the aroused men by the house. Some were springing from their horses, and he could see the rifles going to their shoulders. He passed the kitchen door and the dried corpses swinging in the shade, compelling his foes to run around the front of the house. A rifle cracked, and a second, but he was going fast, leaning forward, low in the saddle, one hand clutching the shirt of apples, the other guiding the horse.

The top bar of the fence was four feet high, but he knew his roan and leaped it at full career to the accompaniment of several scattered shots. Eight hundred yards straight away were the woods, and the roan was covering the distance with mighty strides. Every man was now firing. They were pumping their guns so rapidly that he no longer heard individual shots. A bullet went through his hat, but he was unaware, though he did know when another tore through the apples on the pommel. And he winced and ducked even lower when a third bullet, fired low, struck a stone between his horse's legs and ricochet-ted off through the air, buzzing and humming like some incredible insect.

The shots died down as the magazines were emptied, until, quickly, there was no more shooting. The young man was elated. Through that astonishing fusillade he had come unscathed. He glanced back. Yes, they had emptied their magazines. He could see several reloading. Others were running back behind the house for their horses. As he looked, two already mounted, came back into view around the corner, riding hard. And at the same moment, he saw the man with the unmistakable ginger beard kneel down on the ground, level his gun, and coolly take his time for the long shot.

The young man threw his spurs into the horse, crouched very low, and swerved in his flight in order to distract the other's aim. And still the shot did not come. With each jump of the horse, the woods sprang nearer. They were only two hundred yards away, and still the shot was delayed.

And then he heard it, the last thing he was to hear, for he was dead ere he hit the ground in the long crashing fall from the saddle. And they, watching at the house, saw him fall, saw his body bounce when it struck the earth, and saw the burst of red-cheeked apples that rolled about him. They laughed at the unexpected eruption of apples, and clapped their hands in applause of the long shot by the man with the ginger beard.

# TO THE MAN ON TRAIL

## Jack London

"Dump it in."

"But I say, Kid, isn't that going it a little too strong? Whisky and alcohol's bad enough; but when it comes to brandy and pepper-sauce and"—

"Dump it in. Who's making this punch, anyway?" And Malemute Kid smiled benignantly through the clouds of steam. "By the time you've been in this country as long as I have, my son, and lived on rabbit-tracks and salmon-belly, you'll learn that Christmas comes only once per annum. And a Christmas without punch is sinking a hole to bedrock with nary a pay-streak."

"Stack up on that fer a high cyard," approved Big Jim Belden, who had come down from his claim on Mazy May to spend Christmas, and who, as everyone knew, had been living the two months past on straight moose-meat. "Hain't fergot the *hooch* we-uns made on the Tanana, hev yeh?"

"Well, I guess yes. Boys, it would have done your hearts good to see that whole tribe fighting drunk—and all because of a glorious ferment of sugar and sour dough. That was before your time," Malemute Kid said as he turned to Stanley Prince, a young mining expert who had been in two years. "No white women in the country then, and Mason wanted to get married. Ruth's father was chief of the Tananas, and objected, like the rest of the tribe. Stiff? Why, I used my last pound of sugar; finest work in that line I ever did in my life. You should have seen the chase, down the river and across the portage."

"But the squaw?" asked Louis Savoy, the tall French-Canadian, becoming interested; for he had heard of this wild deed, when at Forty Mile the preceding winter.

Then Malemute Kid, who was a born raconteur, told the unvarnished tale of the Northland Lochinvar. More than one rough adventurer of the North felt his heartstrings draw closer, and experienced vague yearnings for the sunnier pastures of the Southland, where life promised something more than a barren struggle with cold and death.

"We struck the Yukon just behind the first ice run," he concluded, "and the tribe only a quarter of an hour behind. But that saved us; for the second run broke the jam above and shut them out. When they finally got into Nuklukyeto, the whole Post was ready for them. And as to the foregathering, ask Father Roubeau here: he performed the ceremony."

The Jesuit took the pipe from his lips, but could only express his gratification with patriarchal smiles, while Protestant and Catholic vigorously applauded.

"By gar!" ejaculated Louis Savoy, who seemed overcome by the romance of it. "La petite squaw; mon Mason brav. By gar!"

Then, as the first tin cups of punch went round, Bettles the Unquenchable sprang to his feet and struck up his favorite drinking song:—

> "There's Henry Ward Beecher
> And Sunday-school teachers,
>     All drink of the sassafras root;
> But you bet all the same,
> If it had its right name,
>     It's the juice of the forbidden fruit."

> "Oh the juice of the forbidden fruit,"

roared out the Bacchanalian chorus—

> "Oh the juice of the forbidden fruit;
>     But you bet all the same,
>     If it had its right name,
> It's the juice of the forbidden fruit."

Malemute Kid's frightful concoction did its work; the men of the camps and trails unbent in its genial glow, and jest and song and tales of past adventure went round the board. Aliens from a dozen lands, they toasted each and all. It was the Englishman, Prince, who pledged "Uncle Sam, the precocious infant of the New World"; the Yankee, Bettles, who drank to "The Queen, God bless her"; and together, Savoy and Meyers, the German trader, clanged their cups to Alsace and Lorraine.

Then Malemute Kid arose, cup in hand, and glanced at the greased-paper window, where the frost stood full three inches thick. "A health to the man on trail this night; may his grub hold out; may his dogs keep their legs; may his matches never miss fire."

★  ★  ★

Crack! Crack!—they heard the familiar music of the dogwhip, the whining howl of the Malemutes, and the crunch of a sled as it drew up to the cabin. Conversation languished while they waited the issue.

"An old-timer; cares for his dogs and then himself," whispered Malemute Kid to Prince, as they listened to the snapping jaws and the wolfish snarls and yelps of pain which proclaimed to their practiced ears that the stranger was beating back their dogs while he fed his own.

Then came the expected knock, sharp and confident, and the stranger entered. Dazzled by the light, he hesitated a moment at the door, giving to all a chance for scrutiny. He was a striking personage, and a most picturesque one, in his Arctic dress of wool and fur. Standing six foot two or three, with proportionate breadth of shoulders and depth of chest, his smooth-shaven face nipped by the cold to a gleaming pink, his long lashes and eyebrows white with ice, and the ear and neck flaps of his great wolfskin cap loosely raised, he seemed, of a verity, the Frost King, just stepped in out of the night. Clasped outside his mackinaw jacket, a beaded belt held two large Colt's revolvers and a hunting-knife, while he carried, in addition to the inevitable dogwhip, a smokeless rifle of the largest bore and latest pattern. As he came forward, for all his step was firm and elastic, they could see that fatigue bore heavily upon him.

An awkward silence had fallen, but his hearty "What cheer, my lads?" put them quickly at ease, and the next instant Malemute Kid and he had gripped hands. Though they had never met, each had heard of the other, and the recognition was mutual. A sweeping introduction and a mug of punch were forced upon him before he could explain his errand.

"How long since that basket-sled, with three men and eight dogs, passed?" he asked.

"An even two days ahead. Are you after them?"

"Yes; my team. Run them off under my very nose, the cusses. I've gained two days on them already—pick them up on the next run."

"Reckon they'll show spunk?" asked Belden, in order to keep up the conversation, for Malemute Kid already had the coffee-pot on and was busily frying bacon and moose-meat.

The stranger significantly tapped his revolvers.

"When'd yeh leave Dawson?"

"Twelve o'clock."

"Last night?"— as a matter of course.

"Today."

A murmur of surprise passed round the circle. And well it might; for it was just midnight, and seventy-five miles of rough river trail was not to be sneered at for a twelve hours' run.

The talk soon became impersonal, however, harking back to the trails of childhood. As the young stranger ate of the rude fare, Malemute Kid attentively studied his face. Nor was he long in deciding that it was fair, honest, and open, and that he liked it. Still youthful, the lines had been firmly traced by toil and hardship. Though genial in conversation, and mild when at rest, the blue eyes gave promise of the hard steel-glitter which comes when called into action, especially against odds. The heavy jaw and square-cut chin demonstrated rugged pertinacity and indomitability. Nor, though the attributes of the lion were there, was there wanting the certain softness, the hint of womanliness, which bespoke the emotional nature.

"So thet's how me an' the ol' woman got spliced," said Belden, concluding the exciting tale of his courtship. "'Here we be, dad,' sez she. 'An' may yeh be damned,' sez he to her, an' then to me, 'Jim, yeh—yeh git outen them good duds o' yourn; I want a right peart slice o' thet forty acre ploughed 'fore dinner.' An' then he turns on her an' sez, 'An' yeh, Sal; yeh sail inter them dishes.' An' then he sort o' sniffled an' kissed her. An' I was thet happy—but he seen me an' roars out, 'Yeh, Jim!' An' yeh bet I dusted fer the barn."

"Any kids waiting for you back in the States?" asked the stranger.

"Nope; Sal died 'fore any come. Thet's why I'm here." Belden abstractedly began to light his pipe, which had failed to go out, and then brightened up with, "How 'bout yerself, stranger— married man?"

For reply, he opened his watch, slipped it from the thong which served for a chain, and passed it over. Belden pricked up the slush-lamp, surveyed the inside of the case critically, and swearing admiringly to himself, handed it over to Louis Savoy. With numerous "By gars!" he finally surrendered it to Prince, and they noticed that his hands trembled and his eyes took on a peculiar softness. And so it passed from horny hand to horny hand—the pasted photograph of a woman, the clinging kind that such men fancy, with a babe at the breast. Those who had not yet seen the wonder were keen with curiosity; those who had, became silent and retrospective. They could face the pinch of famine, the grip of scurvy, or the quick death by field or flood; but the pictured semblance of a stranger woman and child made women and children of them all.

"Never have seen the youngster yet—he's a boy, she says, and two years old," said the stranger as he received the treasure back. A lingering moment he gazed upon it, then snapped the case and turned away, but not quick enough to hide the restrained rush of tears.

Malemute Kid led him to a bunk and bade him turn in.

"Call me at four, sharp. Don't fail me," were his last words, and a moment later he was breathing in the heaviness of exhausted sleep.

"By Jove! he's a plucky chap," commented Prince. "Three hours' sleep after seventy-five miles with the dogs, and then the trail again. Who is he, Kid?"

"Jack Westondale. Been in going on three years, with nothing but the name of working like a horse, and any amount of bad luck to his credit. I never knew him, but Sitka Charley told me about him."

"It seems hard that a man with a sweet young wife like his should be putting in his years in this God-forsaken hole, where every year counts two on the outside."

"The trouble with him is clean grit and stubbornness. He's cleaned up twice with a stake, but lost it both times."

Here the conversation was broken off by an uproar from Bettles, for the effect had begun to wear away. And soon the bleak years of monotonous grub and deadening toil were being forgotten in rough merriment. Malemute Kid alone seemed unable to lose himself, and cast many an anxious look at his watch. Once he put on his mittens and beaver-skin cap, and leaving the cabin, fell to rummaging about in the cache.

Nor could he wait the hour designated; for he was fifteen minutes ahead of time in rousing his guest. The young giant had stiffened badly, and brisk rubbing was necessary to bring him to his feet. He tottered painfully out of the cabin, to find his dogs harnessed and everything ready for the start. The company wished him good luck and a short chase, while Father Roubeau, hurriedly blessing him, led the stampede for the cabin; and small wonder, for it is not good to face seventy-four degrees below zero with naked ears and hands.

Malemute Kid saw him to the main trail, and there, gripping his hand heartily, gave him advice.

"You'll find a hundred pounds of salmon-eggs on the sled," he said. "The dogs will go as far on that as with one hundred and fifty of fish, and you can't get dog-food at Pelly, as you probably expected." The stranger started, and his eyes flashed, but he did not interrupt. "You can't get an ounce of food for dog or man till you reach Five Fingers, and that's a stiff two hundred miles. Watch out for open water on the Thirty Mile River, and be sure you take the big cut-off above Le Barge."

"How did you know it? Surely the news can't be ahead of me already?"

"I don't know it; and what's more, I don't want to know it. But you never owned that team you're chasing. Sitka Charley sold it to them last spring. But he sized you up to me as square once, and I believe him. I've seen your face; I like it. And I've seen—why, damn you, hit the high places for salt water and that wife of yours, and"— Here the Kid unmittened and jerked out his sack.

"No; I don't need it," and the tears froze on his cheeks as he convulsively gripped Malemute Kid's hand.

"Then don't spare the dogs; cut them out of the traces as fast as they drop; buy them, and think they're cheap at ten dollars a pound. You can get them at Five Fingers, Little Salmon, and the Hootalinqua. And watch out for wet feet," was his parting advice. "Keep a-traveling up to twenty-five, but if it gets below that, build a fire and change your socks."

★   ★   ★

Fifteen minutes had barely elapsed when the jingle of bells announced new arrivals. The door opened, and a mounted policeman of the

Northwest Territory entered, followed by two half-breed dog-drivers.
Like Westondale, they were heavily armed and showed signs of
fatigue. The half-breeds had been born to the trail, and bore it easily;
but the young policeman was badly exhausted. Still, the dogged
obstinacy of his race held him to the pace he had set, and would hold
him till he dropped in his tracks.

"When did Westondale pull out?" he asked. "He stopped here,
didn't he?" This was supererogatory, for the tracks told their own
tale too well.

Malemute Kid had caught Belden's eye, and he, scenting the wind,
replied evasively, "A right peart while back."

"Come, my man; speak up," the policeman admonished.

"Yeh seem to want him right smart. Hez he ben gittin' cantankerous
down Dawson way?"

"Held up Harry McFarland's for forty thousand; exchanged it at
the P. C. store for a check on Seattle; and who's to stop the cashing
of it if we don't overtake him? When did he pull out?"

Every eye suppressed its excitement, for Malemute Kid had
given the cue, and the young officer encountered wooden faces
on every hand.

Striding over to Prince, he put the question to him. Though it
hurt him, gazing into the frank, earnest face of his fellow countryman,
he replied inconsequentially on the state of the trail.

Then he espied Father Roubeau, who could not lie. "A quarter
of an hour ago," the priest answered; "but he had four hours' rest
for himself and dogs."

"Fifteen minutes' start, and he's fresh! My God!" The poor fellow
staggered back, half fainting from exhaustion and disappointment,
murmuring something about the run from Dawson in ten hours and
the dogs being played out.

Malemute Kid forced a mug of punch upon him; then he turned
for the door, ordering the dog-drivers to follow. But the warmth
and promise of rest were too tempting, and they objected strenuously.
The Kid was conversant with their French patois, and followed it
anxiously.

They swore that the dogs were gone up; that Siwash and Babette
would have to be shot before the first mile was covered; that the
rest were almost as bad; and that it would be better for all hands to
rest up.

"Lend me five dogs?" he asked, turning to Malemute Kid.

But the Kid shook his head.

"I'll sign a check on Captain Constantine for five thousand—here's my papers—I'm authorized to draw at my own discretion."

Again the silent refusal.

"Then I'll requisition them in the name of the Queen."

Smiling incredulously, the Kid glanced at his well-stocked arsenal, and the Englishman, realizing his impotency, turned for the door. But the dog-drivers still objecting, he whirled upon them fiercely, calling them women and curs. The swart face of the older half-breed flushed angrily, as he drew himself up and promised in good, round terms that he would travel his leader off his legs, and would then be delighted to plant him in the snow.

The young officer—and it required his whole will—walked steadily to the door, exhibiting a freshness he did not possess. But they all knew and appreciated his proud effort; nor could he veil the twinges of agony that shot across his face. Covered with frost, the dogs were curled up in the snow, and it was almost impossible to get them to their feet. The poor brutes whined under the stinging lash, for the dog-drivers were angry and cruel; nor till Babette, the leader, was cut from the traces, could they break out the sled and get under way.

"A dirty scoundrel and a liar!" "By gar! him no good!" "A thief!" "Worse than an Indian!" It was evident that they were angry—first, at the way they had been deceived; and second, at the outraged ethics of the Northland, where honesty, above all, was man's prime jewel. "An' we gave the cuss a hand, after knowin' what he'd did." All eyes were turned accusingly upon Malemute Kid, who rose from the corner where he had been making Babette comfortable, and silently emptied the bowl for a final round of punch.

"It's a cold night, boys—a bitter cold night," was the irrelevant commencement of his defense. "You've all traveled trail, and know what that stands for. Don't jump a dog when he's down. You've only heard one side. A whiter man than Jack Westondale never ate from the same pot nor stretched blanket with you or me. Last fall he gave his whole clean-up, forty thousand, to Joe Castrell, to buy in on Dominion. Today he'd be a millionaire. But while he stayed behind at Circle City, taking care of his partner with the scurvy, what does Castrell do? Goes into McFarland's, jumps the limit, and drops the whole sack. Found him dead in the snow the next day. And poor Jack laying his plans to go out this winter to his wife and the boy he's never seen. You'll notice he took exactly what his partner lost, forty thousand. Well, he's gone out; and what are you going to do about it?"

The Kid glanced round the circle of his judges, noted the softening of their faces, then raised his mug aloft. "So a health to the man on trail this night; may his grub hold out; may his dogs keep their legs; may his matches never miss fire. God prosper him; good luck go with him; and"—

"Confusion to the Mounted Police!" cried Bettles, to the crash of the empty cups.

# IN A FAR COUNTRY

## Jack London

WHEN A MAN journeys into a far country, he must be prepared to forget many of the things he has learned, and to acquire such customs as are inherent with existence in the new land; he must abandon the old ideals and the old gods, and oftentimes he must reverse the very codes by which his conduct has hitherto been shaped. To those who have the protean faculty of adaptability, the novelty of such change may even be a source of pleasure; but to those who happen to be hardened to the ruts in which they were created, the pressure of the altered environment is unbearable, and they chafe in body and in spirit under the new restrictions which they do not understand. This chafing is bound to act and react, producing divers evils and leading to various misfortunes. It were better for the man who cannot fit himself to the new groove to return to his own country; if he delay too long, he will surely die.

The man who turns his back upon the comforts of an elder civilization, to face the savage youth, the primordial simplicity of the North, may estimate success at an inverse ratio to the quantity and quality of his hopelessly fixed habits. He will soon discover, if he be a fit candidate, that the material habits are the less important. The exchange of such things as a dainty menu for rough fare, of the stiff leather shoe for the soft, shapeless moccasin, of the feather bed for a couch in the snow, is after all a very easy matter. But his pinch will come in learning properly to shape his mind's attitude toward all things, and especially toward his fellow man. For the courtesies of ordinary life, he must substitute unselfishness, forbearance, and tolerance. Thus, and thus only, can he gain that pearl of great price—true comradeship.

He must not say "Thank you"; he must mean it without opening his mouth, and prove it by responding in kind. In short, he must substitute the deed for the word, the spirit for the letter.

When the world rang with the tale of Arctic gold, and the lure of the North gripped the heartstrings of men, Carter Weatherbee threw up his snug clerkship, turned the half of his savings over to his wife, and with the remainder bought an outfit. There was no romance in his nature—the bondage of commerce had crushed all that; he was simply tired of the ceaseless grind, and wished to risk great hazards in view of corresponding returns. Like many another fool, disdaining the old trails used by the Northland pioneers for a score of years, he hurried to Edmonton in the spring of the year; and there, unluckily for his soul's welfare, he allied himself with a party of men.

There was nothing unusual about this party, except its plans. Even its goal, like that of all other parties, was the Klondike. But the route it had mapped out to attain that goal took away the breath of the hardiest native, born and bred to the vicissitudes of the Northwest. Even Jacques Baptiste, born of a Chippewa woman and a renegade *voyageur*[1] (having raised his first whimpers in a deerskin lodge north of the sixty-fifth parallel, and had the same hushed by blissful sucks of raw tallow), was surprised. Though he sold his services to them and agreed to travel even to the never-opening ice, he shook his head ominously whenever his advice was asked.

Percy Cuthfert's evil star must have been in the ascendant, for he, too, joined this company of argonauts. He was an ordinary man, with a bank account as deep as his culture, which is saying a good deal. He had no reason to embark on such a venture—no reason in the world, save that he suffered from an abnormal development of sentimentality. He mistook this for the true spirit of romance and adventure. Many another man has done the like, and made as fatal a mistake.

The first break-up of spring found the party following the ice-run of Elk River. It was an imposing fleet, for the outfit was large, and they were accompanied by a disreputable contingent of half-breed *voyageurs* with their women and children. Day in and day out, they labored with the bateaux and canoes, fought mosquitoes and other kindred pests, or sweated and swore at the portages. Severe toil like this lays a man naked to the very roots of his soul, and ere Lake Athabasca was lost in the south, each member of the party had hoisted his true colors.

---

[1]  *voyageur*, in Canada: an expert woodsman, boatman, and guide in remote regions.

The two shirks and chronic grumblers were Carter Weatherbee and Percy Cuthfert. The whole party complained less of its aches and pains than did either of them. Not once did they volunteer for the thousand and one petty duties of the camp. A bucket of water to be brought, an extra armful of wood to be chopped, the dishes to be washed and wiped, a search to be made through the outfit for some suddenly indispensable article—and these two effete scions of civilization discovered sprains or blisters requiring instant attention. They were the first to turn in at night, with a score of tasks yet undone; the last to turn out in the morning, when the start should be in readiness before the breakfast was begun. They were the first to fall to at meal-time, the last to have a hand in the cooking; the first to dive for a slim delicacy, the last to discover they had added to their own another man's share. If they toiled at the oars, they slyly cut the water at each stroke and allowed the boat's momentum to float up the blade. They thought nobody noticed; but their comrades swore under their breaths and grew to hate them, while Jacques Baptiste sneered openly and damned them from morning till night. But Jacques Baptiste was no gentleman.

At the Great Slave, Hudson Bay dogs were purchased, and the fleet sank to the guards with its added burden of dried fish and pemmican. Then canoe and bateau answered to the swift current of the Mackenzie, and they plunged into the Great Barren Ground. Every likely-looking "feeder" was prospected, but the elusive "pay-dirt" danced ever to the north. At the Great Bear, overcome by the common dread of the Unknown Lands, their *voyageurs* began to desert, and Fort of Good Hope saw the last and bravest bending to the tow-lines as they bucked the current down which they had so treacherously glided. Jacques Baptiste alone remained. Had he not sworn to travel even to the never-opening ice?

The lying charts, compiled in main from hearsay, were now constantly consulted. And they felt the need of hurry, for the sun had already passed its northern solstice and was leading the winter south again. Skirting the shores of the bay, where the Mackenzie disembogues into the Arctic Ocean, they entered the mouth of the Little Peel River. Then began the arduous upstream toil, and the two Incapables fared worse than ever. Tow-line and pole, paddle and tump-line, rapids and portages—such tortures served to give the one a deep disgust for great hazards, and printed for the other a fiery text on the true romance of adventure. One day they waxed mutinous, and being vilely cursed by Jacques Baptiste, turned, as worms sometimes will.

But the half-breed thrashed the twain, and sent them, bruised and bleeding, about their work. It was the first time either had been man-handled.

Abandoning their river craft at the headwaters of the Little Peel, they consumed the rest of the summer in the great portage over the Mackenzie watershed to the West Rat. This little stream fed the Porcupine, which in turn joined the Yukon where that mighty highway of the North countermarches on the Arctic Circle. But they had lost in the race with winter, and one day they tied their rafts to the thick eddy-ice and hurried their goods ashore. That night the river jammed and broke several times; the following morning it had fallen asleep for good.

"We can't be more 'n four hundred miles from the Yukon," concluded Sloper, multiplying his thumb nails by the scale of the map. The council, in which the two Incapables had whined to excellent disadvantage, was drawing to a close.

"Hudson Bay Post, long time ago. No use um now." Jacques Baptiste's father had made the trip for the Fur Company in the old days, incidentally marking the trail with a couple of frozen toes.

"Sufferin' cracky!" cried another of the party. "No whites?"

"Nary white," Sloper sententiously affirmed; "but it's only five hundred more up the Yukon to Dawson. Call it a rough thousand from here."

Weatherbee and Cuthfert groaned in chorus.

"How long'll that take, Baptiste?"

The half-breed figured for a moment. "Workum like hell, no man play out, ten—twenty—forty—fifty days. Um babies come" (designating the Incapables), "no can tell. Mebbe when hell freeze over; mebbe not then."

The manufacture of snowshoes and moccasins ceased. Somebody called the name of an absent member, who came out of an ancient cabin at the edge of the camp-fire and joined them. The cabin was one of the many mysteries which lurk in the vast recesses of the North. Built when and by whom, no man could tell. Two graves in the open, piled high with stones, perhaps contained the secret of those early wanderers. But whose hand had piled the stones?

The moment had come. Jacques Baptiste paused in the fitting of a harness and pinned the struggling dog in the snow. The cook made mute protest for delay, threw a handful of bacon into a noisy pot of beans, then came to attention. Sloper rose to his feet. His body was a ludicrous contrast to the healthy physiques of the Incapables. Yellow and weak, fleeing from a South American fever-hole, he had not broken his flight across the zones, and was still able to toil with men. His weight was probably ninety pounds, with the heavy hunting-knife thrown in, and his grizzled hair told of a prime which had ceased to be. The fresh young muscles of either Weatherbee or Cuthfert were equal to ten times the endeavor of his; yet he could walk them into the earth in a day's journey. And all this day he had whipped his stronger comrades into venturing a thousand miles of the stiffest hardship man can conceive. He was the incarnation of the unrest of his race, and the old Teutonic stubbornness, dashed with the quick grasp and action of the Yankee, held the flesh in the bondage of the spirit.

"All those in favor of going on with the dogs as soon as the ice sets, say ay."

"Ay!" rang out eight voices—voices destined to string a trail of oaths along many a hundred miles of pain.

"Contrary minded?"

"No!" For the first time the Incapables were united without some compromise of personal interests.

"And what are you going to do about it?" Weatherbee added belligerently.

"Majority rule! Majority rule!" clamored the rest of the party.

"I know the expedition is liable to fall through if you don't come," Sloper replied sweetly; "but I guess, if we try real hard, we can manage to do without you. What do you say, boys?"

The sentiment was cheered to the echo.

"But I say, you know," Cuthfert ventured apprehensively; "what's a chap like me to do?"

"Ain't you coming with us?"

"No-o."

"Then do as you damn well please. We won't have nothing to say."

"Kind o' calkilate yuh might settle it with that canoodlin' pardner of yourn," suggested a heavy-going Westerner from the Dakotas, at the same time pointing out Weatherbee. "He'll be shore to ask yuh what yur a-goin' to do when it comes to cookin' an' gatherin' the wood."

"Then we'll consider it all arranged," concluded Sloper. "We'll pull out tomorrow, if we camp within five miles- —just to get everything in running order and remember if we've forgotten anything."

The sleds groaned by on their steel-shod runners, and the dogs strained low in the harnesses in which they were born to die. Jacques Baptiste paused by the side of Sloper to get a last glimpse of the cabin. The smoke curled up pathetically from the Yukon stovepipe. The two Incapables were watching them from the doorway.

Sloper laid his hand on the other's shoulder.

"Jacques Baptiste, did you ever hear of the Kilkenny cats?"

The half-breed shook his head.

"Well, my friend and good comrade, the Kilkenny cats fought till neither hide, nor hair, nor yowl, was left. You understand?—till nothing was left. Very good. Now, these two men don't like work. They won't work. We know that. They'll be all alone in that cabin all winter—a mighty long, dark winter. Kilkenny cats—well?"

The Frenchman in Baptiste shrugged his shoulders, but the Indian in him was silent. Nevertheless, it was an eloquent shrug, pregnant with prophecy.

Things prospered in the little cabin at first. The rough badinage of their comrades had made Weatherbee and Cuthfert conscious of the mutual responsibility which had devolved upon them; besides, there was not so much work after all for two healthy men. And the removal of the cruel whip-hand, or in other words the bulldozing half-breed, had brought with it a joyous reaction. At first, each strove to outdo the other, and they performed petty tasks with an unction which would have opened the eyes of their comrades who were now wearing out bodies and souls on the Long Trail.

All care was banished. The forest, which shouldered in upon them from three sides, was an inexhaustible woodyard. A few yards from their door slept the Porcupine, and a hole through its winter robe formed a bubbling spring of water, crystal clear and painfully cold. But they soon grew to find fault with even that. The hole would persist in freezing up, and thus gave them many a miserable hour of ice-chopping. The unknown builders of the cabin had extended the side-logs so as to support a cache at the rear. In this was stored the bulk of the party's provisions. Food there was, without stint, for three times the men who were fated to live upon it. But the most of it was of the kind which built up brawn and sinew, but did not tickle the palate. True, there was sugar in plenty for two ordinary men; but these two were little else than children. They early discovered the virtues of hot water judiciously saturated with sugar, and they prodigally swam their flapjacks and soaked their crusts in the rich, white syrup. Then coffee and tea, and especially the dried fruits, made disastrous inroads upon it. The first words they had were over the sugar question. And it is a really serious thing when two men, wholly dependent upon each other for company, begin to quarrel.

Weatherbee loved to discourse blatantly on politics, while Cuthfert, who had been prone to clip his coupons and let the commonwealth jog on as best it might, either ignored the subject or delivered himself of startling epigrams. But the clerk was too obtuse to appreciate the clever shaping of thought, and this waste of ammunition irritated Cuthfert. He had been used to blinding people by his brilliancy, and it worked him quite a hardship, this loss of an audience. He felt personally aggrieved and unconsciously held his mutton-head companion responsible for it.

Save existence, they had nothing in common—came in touch on no single point. Weatherbee was a clerk who had known naught but clerking all his life; Cuthfert was a master of arts, a dabbler in oils, and had written not a little. The one was a lower-class man who considered himself a gentleman, and the other was a gentleman who knew himself to be such. From this it may be remarked that a man can be a gentleman without possessing the first instinct of true comradeship. The clerk was as sensuous as the other was aesthetic, and his love adventures, told at great length and chiefly coined from his imagination, affected the supersensitive master of arts in the same way as so many whiffs of sewer gas. He deemed the clerk a filthy, uncultured brute, whose place was in the muck with the swine, and told him so; and he was reciprocally informed that he was a milk-and-water sissy and a cad. Weatherbee could not have defined "cad" for his life; but it satisfied its purpose, which after all seems the main point in life.

Weatherbee flatted every third note and sang such songs as "The Boston Burglar" and "The Handsome Cabin Boy," for hours at a time, while Cuthfert wept with rage, till he could stand it no longer and fled into the outer cold. But there was no escape. The intense frost could not be endured for long at a time, and the little cabin crowded them—beds, stove, table, and all—into a space of ten by twelve. The very presence of either became a personal affront to the other, and they lapsed into sullen silences which increased in length and strength as the days went by. Occasionally, the flash of an eye or the curl of a lip got the better of them, though they strove to wholly ignore each other during these mute periods. And a great wonder sprang up in the breast of each, as to how God had ever come to create the other.

With little to do, time became an intolerable burden to them. This naturally made them still lazier. They sank into a physical lethargy which there was no escaping, and which made them rebel at the performance of the smallest chore. One morning when it was his turn to cook the common breakfast, Weatherbee rolled out of his blankets, and to the snoring of his companion, lighted first the slush-lamp and then the fire. The kettles were frozen hard, and there was no water in the cabin with which to wash. But he did not mind that. Waiting for it to thaw, he sliced the bacon and plunged into the hateful task of bread-making. Cuthfert had been slyly watching through his half-closed lids. Consequently there was a scene, in which they fervently blessed each other, and agreed, thenceforth, that each do his own cooking. A week later, Cuthfert neglected his morning ablutions, but none the less complacently ate the meal which he had cooked. Weatherbee grinned. After that the foolish custom of washing passed out of their lives.

As the sugar-pile and other little luxuries dwindled, they began to be afraid they were not getting their proper shares, and in order that they might not be robbed, they fell to gorging themselves. The luxuries suffered in this gluttonous contest, as did also the men. In the absence of fresh vegetables and exercise, their blood became impoverished, and a loathsome, purplish rash crept over their bodies. Yet they refused to heed the warning. Next, their muscles and joints began to swell, the flesh turning black, while their mouths, gums, and lips took on the color of rich cream. Instead of being drawn together by their misery, each gloated over the other's symptoms as the scurvy took its course.

They lost all regard for personal appearance, and for that matter, common decency. The cabin became a pigpen, and never once were the beds made or fresh pine boughs laid underneath. Yet they could not keep to their blankets, as they would have wished; for the frost was inexorable, and the fire box consumed much fuel. The hair of their heads and faces grew long and shaggy, while their garments would have disgusted a ragpicker. But they did not care. They were sick, and there was no one to see; besides, it was very painful to move about.

To all this was added a new trouble—the Fear of the North. This Fear was the joint child of the Great Cold and the Great Silence, and was born in the darkness of December, when the sun dipped below the southern horizon for good. It affected them according to their natures. Weatherbee fell prey to the grosser superstitions, and did his best to resurrect the spirits which slept in the forgotten graves. It was a fascinating thing, and in his dreams they came to him from out of the cold, and snuggled into his blankets, and told him of their toils and troubles ere they died. He shrank away from the clammy contact as they drew closer and twined their frozen limbs about him, and when they whispered in his ear of things to come, the cabin rang with his frightened shrieks. Cuthfert did not understand—for they no longer spoke—and when thus awakened he invariably grabbed for his revolver. Then he would sit up in bed, shivering nervously, with the weapon trained on the unconscious dreamer. Cuthfert deemed the man going mad, and so came to fear for his life.

His own malady assumed a less concrete form. The mysterious artisan who had laid the cabin, log by log, had pegged a wind-vane to the ridge-pole. Cuthfert noticed it always pointed south, and one day, irritated by its steadfastness of purpose, he turned it toward the east. He watched eagerly, but never a breath came by to disturb it. Then he turned the vane to the north, swearing never again to touch it till the wind did blow. But the air frightened him with its unearthly calm, and he often rose in the middle of the night to see if the vane had veered—ten degrees would have satisfied him. But no, it poised above him as unchangeable as fate. His imagination ran riot, till it became to him a fetich. Sometimes he followed the path it pointed across the dismal dominions, and allowed his soul to become saturated with the Fear. He dwelt upon the unseen and the unknown till the burden of eternity appeared to be crushing him. Everything in the Northland had that crushing effect—the absence of life and motion; the darkness; the infinite peace of the brooding land; the ghastly silence, which made the echo of each heart-beat a sacrilege; the solemn forest which seemed to guard an awful, inexpressible something, which neither word nor thought could compass.

The world he had so recently left, with its busy nations and great enterprises, seemed very far away. Recollections occasionally obtruded—recollections of marts and galleries and crowded thoroughfares, of evening dress and social functions, of good men and dear women he had known—but they were dim memories of a life he had lived long centuries agone, on some other planet. This phantasm was the Reality. Standing beneath the wind-vane, his eyes fixed on the polar skies, he could not bring himself to realize that the Southland really existed, that at that very moment it was a-roar with life and action. There was no Southland, no men being born of women, no giving and taking in marriage. Beyond his bleak sky-line there stretched vast solitudes, and beyond these still vaster solitudes. There were no lands of sunshine, heavy with the perfume of flowers. Such things were only old dreams of paradise. The sunlands of the West and the spicelands of the East, the smiling Arcadias and blissful Islands of the Blest—ha! ha! His laughter split the void and shocked him with its unwonted sound. There was no sun. This was the Universe, dead and cold and dark, and he its only citizen. Weatherbee? At such moments Weatherbee did not count. He was a Caliban, a monstrous phantom, fettered to him for untold ages, the penalty of some forgotten crime.

He lived with Death among the dead, emasculated by the sense of his own insignificance, crushed by the passive mastery of the slumbering ages. The magnitude of all things appalled him. Everything partook of the superlative save himself—the perfect cessation of wind and motion, the immensity of the snow-covered wilderness, the height of the sky and the depth of the silence. That wind-vane—if it would only move. If a thunderbolt would fall, or the forest flare up in flame. The rolling up of the heavens as a scroll, the crash of Doom—anything, anything! But no, nothing moved; the Silence crowded in, and the Fear of the North laid icy fingers on his heart.

Once, like another Crusoe, by the edge of the river he came upon a track—the faint tracery of a snowshoe rabbit on the delicate snow-crust. It was a revelation. There was life in the Northland. He would follow it, look upon it, gloat over it. He forgot his swollen muscles, plunging through the deep snow in an ecstasy of anticipation. The forest swallowed him up, and the brief midday twilight vanished; but he pursued his quest till exhausted nature asserted itself and laid him helpless in the snow. There he groaned and cursed his folly, and knew the track to be the fancy of his brain; and late that night he dragged himself into the cabin on hands and knees, his cheeks frozen and a strange numbness about his feet. Weatherbee grinned malevolently, but made no offer to help him. He thrust needles into his toes and thawed them out by the stove. A week later mortification set in.

But the clerk had his own troubles. The dead men came out of their graves more frequently now, and rarely left him, waking or sleeping. He grew to wait and dread their coming, never passing the twin cairns without a shudder. One night they came to him in his sleep and led him forth to an appointed task. Frightened into inarticulate horror, he awoke between the heaps of stones and fled wildly to the cabin. But he had lain there for some time, for his feet and cheeks were also frozen.

Sometimes he became frantic at their insistent presence, and danced about the cabin, cutting the empty air with an axe, and smashing everything within reach. During these ghostly encounters, Cuthfert huddled into his blankets and followed the madman about with a cocked revolver, ready to shoot him if he came too near. But, recovering from one of these spells, the clerk noticed the weapon trained upon him. His suspicions were aroused, and thenceforth he, too, lived in fear of his life. They watched each other closely after that, and faced about in startled fright whenever either passed behind the other's back. This apprehensiveness became a mania which controlled them even in their sleep. Through mutual fear they tacitly let the slush-lamp burn all night, and saw to a plentiful supply of bacon-grease before retiring. The slightest movement on the part of one was sufficient to arouse the other, and many a still watch their gazes countered as they shook beneath their blankets with fingers on the trigger-guards.

What with the Fear of the North, the mental strain, and the ravages of the disease, they lost all semblance of humanity, taking on the appearance of wild beasts, hunted and desperate. Their cheeks and noses, as an aftermath of the freezing, had turned black. Their frozen toes had begun to drop away at the first and second joints. Every movement brought pain, but the fire box was insatiable, wringing a ransom of torture from their miserable bodies. Day in, day out, it demanded its food —a veritable pound of flesh—and they dragged themselves into the forest to chop wood on their knees. Once, crawling thus in search of dry sticks, unknown to each other they entered a thicket from opposite sides. Suddenly, without warning, two peering death's-heads confronted each other. Suffering had so transformed them that recognition was impossible. They sprang to their feet, shrieking with terror, and dashed away on their mangled stumps; and falling at the cabin door, they clawed and scratched like demons till they discovered their mistake.

Occasionally they lapsed normal, and during one of these sane intervals, the chief bone of contention, the sugar, had been divided equally between them. They guarded their separate sacks, stored up in the cache, with jealous eyes; for there were but a few cupfuls left, and they were totally devoid of faith in each other. But one day Cuthfert made a mistake. Hardly able to move, sick with pain, with his head swimming and eyes blinded, he crept into the cache, sugar canister in hand, and mistook Weatherbee's sack for his own.

January had been born but a few days when this occurred. The sun had some time since passed its lowest southern declination, and at meridian now threw flaunting streaks of yellow light upon the northern sky. On the day following his mistake with the sugar-bag, Cuthfert found himself feeling better, both in body and in spirit. As noontime drew near and the day brightened, he dragged himself outside to feast on the evanescent glow, which was to him an earnest of the sun's future intentions. Weatherbee was also feeling somewhat better, and crawled out beside him. They propped themselves in the snow beneath the moveless wind-vane, and waited.

The stillness of death was about them. In other climes, when nature falls into such moods, there is a subdued air of expectancy, a waiting for some small voice to take up the broken strain. Not so in the North. The two men had lived seeming aeons in this ghostly peace. They could remember no song of the past; they could conjure no song of the future. This unearthly calm had always been—the tranquil silence of eternity.

Their eyes were fixed upon the north. Unseen, behind their backs, behind the towering mountains to the south, the sun swept toward the zenith of another sky than theirs. Sole spectators of the mighty canvas, they watched the false dawn slowly grow. A faint flame began to glow and smoulder. It deepened in intensity, ringing the changes of reddish-yellow, purple, and saffron. So bright did it become that Cuthfert thought the sun must surely be behind it—a miracle, the sun rising in the north! Suddenly, without warning and without fading, the canvas was swept clean. There was no color in the sky. The light had gone out of the day. They caught their breaths in half-sobs. But lo! the air was a-glint with particles of scintillating frost, and there, to the north, the wind-vane lay in vague outline on the snow. A shadow! A shadow! It was exactly midday. They jerked their heads hurriedly to the south. A golden rim peeped over the mountain's snowy shoulder, smiled upon them an instant, then dipped from sight again.

There were tears in their eyes as they sought each other. A strange softening came over them. They felt irresistibly drawn toward each other. The sun was coming back again. It would be with them tomorrow, and the next day, and the next. And it would stay longer every visit, and a time would come when it would ride their heaven day and night, never once dropping below the sky-line. There would be no night. The ice-locked winter would be broken; the winds would blow and the forests answer; the land would bathe in the blessed sunshine, and life renew. Hand in hand, they would quit this horrid dream and journey back to the Southland. They lurched blindly forward, and their hands met—their poor maimed hands, swollen and distorted beneath their mittens.

But the promise was destined to remain unfulfilled. The Northland is the Northland, and men work out their souls by strange rules, which other men, who have not journeyed into far countries, cannot come to understand.

An hour later, Cuthfert put a pan of bread into the oven, and fell to speculating on what the surgeons could do with his feet when he got back. Home did not seem so very far away now. Weatherbee was rummaging in the cache. Of a sudden, he raised a whirlwind of blasphemy, which in turn ceased with startling abruptness. The other man had robbed his sugar-sack. Still, things might have happened differently, had not the two dead men come out from under the stones and hushed the hot words in his throat. They led him quite gently from the cache, which he forgot to close. That consummation was reached; that something they had whispered to him in his dreams was about to happen. They guided him gently, very gently, to the woodpile, where they put the axe in his hands. Then they helped him shove open the cabin door, and he felt sure they shut it after him—at least he heard it slam and the latch fall sharply into place. And he knew they were waiting just without, waiting for him to do his task.

"Carter! I say, Carter!"

Percy Cuthfert was frightened at the look on the clerk's face, and he made haste to put the table between them.

Carter Weatherbee followed, without haste and without enthusiasm. There was neither pity nor passion in his face, but rather the patient, stolid look of one who has certain work to do and goes about it methodically.

"I say, what's the matter?"

The clerk dodged back, cutting off his retreat to the door, but never opening his mouth.

"I say, Carter, I say; let's talk. There's a good chap."

The master of arts was thinking rapidly, now, shaping a skillful flank movement on the bed where his Smith & Wesson lay. Keeping his eyes on the madman, he rolled backward on the bunk, at the same time clutching the pistol.

"Carter!"

The powder flashed full in Weatherbee's face, but he swung his weapon and leaped forward. The axe bit deeply at the base of the spine, and Percy Cuthfert felt all consciousness of his lower limbs leave him. Then the clerk fell heavily upon him, clutching him by the throat with feeble fingers. The sharp bite of the axe had caused Cuthfert to drop the pistol, and as his lungs panted for release, he fumbled aimlessly for it among the blankets. Then he remembered. He slid a hand up the clerk's belt to the sheath-knife; and they drew very close to each other in that last clinch.

Percy Cuthfert felt his strength leave him. The lower portion of his body was useless. The inert weight of Weatherbee crushed him—crushed him and pinned him there like a bear under a trap. The cabin became filled with a familiar odor, and he knew the bread to be burning. Yet what did it matter? He would never need it. And there were all of six cupfuls of sugar in the cache—if he had foreseen this he would not have been so saving the last several days. Would the wind-vane ever move? It might even be veering now. Why not? Had he not seen the sun today? He would go and see. No; it was impossible to move. He had not thought the clerk so heavy a man.

How quickly the cabin cooled! The fire must be out. The cold was forcing in. It must be below zero already, and the ice creeping up the inside of the door. He could not see it, but his past experience enabled him to gauge its progress by the cabin's temperature. The lower hinge must be white ere now. Would the tale of this ever reach the world? How would his friends take it? They would read it over their coffee, most likely, and talk it over at the clubs. He could see them very clearly. "Poor Old Cuthfert," they murmured; "not such a bad sort of a chap, after all." He smiled at their eulogies, and passed on in search of a Turkish bath. It was the same old crowd upon the streets. Strange, they did not notice his moosehide moccasins and tattered German socks! He would take a cab. And after the bath a shave would not be bad. No; he would eat first. Steak, and potatoes, and green things—how fresh it all was! And what was that? Squares of honey, streaming liquid amber! But why did they bring so much? Ha! ha! he could never eat it all. Shine! Why certainly. He put his foot on the box. The bootblack looked curiously up at him, and he remembered his moosehide moccasins and went away hastily.

Hark! The wind-vane must be surely spinning. No; a mere singing in his ears. That was all—a mere singing. The ice must have passed the latch by now. More likely the upper hinge was covered. Between the moss-chinked roof-poles, little points of frost began to appear. How slowly they grew! No; not so slowly. There was a new one, and there another. Two—three—four; they were coming too fast to count. There were two growing together. And there, a third had joined them. Why, there were no more spots. They had run together and formed a sheet.

Well, he would have company. If Gabriel ever broke the silence of the North, they would stand together, hand in hand, before the great White Throne. And God would judge them, God would judge them!

Then Percy Cuthfert closed his eyes and dropped off to sleep.

# TO BUILD A FIRE

## Jack London

DAY HAD BROKEN cold and gray, exceedingly cold and gray, when the man turned aside from the main Yukon trail and climbed the high earth-bank, where a dim and little-travelled trail led eastward through the fat spruce timberland. It was a steep bank, and he paused for breath at the top, excusing the act to himself by looking at his watch. It was nine o'clock. There was no sun nor hint of sun, though there was not a cloud in the sky. It was a clear day, and yet there seemed an intangible pall over the face of things, a subtle gloom that made the day dark, and that was due to the absence of sun. This fact did not worry the man. He was used to the lack of sun. It had been days since he had seen the sun, and he knew that a few more days must pass before that cheerful orb, due south, would just peep above the skyline and dip immediately from view.

The man flung a look back along the way he had come. The Yukon lay a mile wide and hidden under three feet of ice. On top of this ice were as many feet of snow. It was all pure white, rolling in gentle undulations where the ice-jams of the freeze-up had formed. North and south, as far as his eye could see, it was unbroken white, save for a dark hair-line that curved and twisted from around the spruce-covered island to the south, and that curved and twisted away into the north, where it disappeared behind another spruce-covered island. This dark hair-line was the trail—the main trail—that led south five hundred miles to the Chilcoot Pass, Dyea, and salt water; and that led north seventy miles to Dawson, and still on to the north a thousand miles to Nulato, and finally to St. Michael on Bering Sea, a thousand miles and half a thousand more.

But all this—the mysterious, far-reaching hair-line trail, the absence of sun from the sky, the tremendous cold, and the strangeness and weirdness of it all—made no impression on the man. It was not because he was long used to it. He was a newcomer in the land, a *chechaquo*, and this was his first winter. The trouble with him was that he was without imagination. He was quick and alert in the things of life, but only in the things, and not in the significances. Fifty degrees below zero meant eighty-odd degrees of frost. Such fact impressed him as being cold and uncomfortable, and that was all. It did not lead him to meditate upon his frailty as a creature of temperature, and upon man's frailty in general, able only to live within certain narrow limits of heat and cold; and from there on it did not lead him to the conjectural field of immortality and man's place in the universe. Fifty degrees below zero stood for a bite of frost that hurt and that must be guarded against by the use of mittens, ear-flaps, warm moccasins, and thick socks. Fifty degrees below zero was to him just precisely fifty degrees below zero. That there should be anything more to it than that was a thought that never entered his head.

As he turned to go on, he spat speculatively. There was a sharp, explosive crackle that startled him. He spat again. And again, in the air, before it could fall to the snow, the spittle crackled. He knew that at fifty below spittle crackled on the snow, but this spittle had crackled in the air. Undoubtedly it was colder than fifty below—how much colder he did not know. But the temperature did not matter. He was bound for the old claim on the left fork of Henderson Creek, where the boys were already. They had come over across the divide from the Indian Creek country, while he had come the roundabout way to take a look at the possibilities of getting out logs in the spring from the islands in the Yukon. He would be in to camp by six o'clock; a bit after dark, it was true, but the boys would be there, a fire would be going, and a hot supper would be ready. As for lunch, he pressed his hand against the protruding bundle under his jacket. It was also under his shirt, wrapped up in a handkerchief and lying against the naked skin. It was the only way to keep the biscuits from freezing. He smiled agreeably to himself as he thought of those biscuits, each cut open and sopped in bacon grease, and each enclosing a generous slice of fried bacon.

He plunged in among the big spruce trees. The trail was faint. A foot of snow had fallen since the last sled had passed over, and he was glad he was without a sled, travelling light. In fact, he carried nothing but the lunch wrapped in the handkerchief. He was surprised, however, at the cold. It certainly was cold, he concluded, as he rubbed his numb nose and cheek-bones with his mittened hand. He was a warm-whiskered man, but the hair on his face did not protect the high cheek-bones and the eager nose that thrust itself aggressively into the frosty air.

At the man's heels trotted a dog, a big native husky, the proper wolf-dog, gray-coated and without any visible or temperamental difference from its brother, the wild wolf. The animal was depressed by the tremendous cold. It knew that it was no time for travelling. Its instinct told it a truer tale than was told to the man by the man's judgment. In reality, it was not merely colder than fifty below zero; it was colder than sixty below, than seventy below. It was seventy-five below zero. Since the freezing-point is thirty-two above zero, it meant that one hundred and seven degrees of frost obtained. The dog did not know anything about thermometers. Possibly in its brain there was no sharp consciousness of a condition of very cold such as was in the man's brain. But the brute had its instinct. It experienced a vague but menacing apprehension that subdued it and made it slink along at the man's heels, and that made it question eagerly every unwonted movement of the man as if expecting him to go into camp or to seek shelter somewhere and build a fire. The dog had learned fire, and it wanted fire, or else to burrow under the snow and cuddle its warmth away from the air.

The frozen moisture of its breathing had settled on its fur in a fine powder of frost, and especially were its jowls, muzzle, and eyelashes whitened by its crystalled breath. The man's red beard and mustache were likewise frosted, but more solidly, the deposit taking the form of ice and increasing with every warm, moist breath he exhaled. Also, the man was chewing tobacco, and the muzzle of ice held his lips so rigidly that he was unable to clear his chin when he expelled the juice. The result was that a crystal beard of the color and solidity of amber was increasing its length on his chin. If he fell down it would shatter itself, like glass, into brittle fragments. But he did not mind the appendage. It was the penalty all tobacco-chewers paid in that country, and he had been out before in two cold snaps. They had not been so cold as this, he knew, but by the spirit thermometer at Sixty Mile he knew they had been registered at fifty below and at fifty-five.

He held on through the level stretch of woods for several miles, crossed a wide flat of niggerheads, and dropped down a bank to the frozen bed of a small stream. This was Henderson Creek, and he knew he was ten miles from the forks. He looked at his watch. It was ten o'clock. He was making four miles an hour, and he calculated that he would arrive at the forks at half past twelve. He decided to celebrate that event by eating his lunch there.

The dog dropped in again at his heels, with a tail drooping discouragement, as the man swung along the creek-bed. The furrow of the old sled-trail was plainly visible, but a dozen inches of snow covered the marks of the last runners. In a month no man had come up or down that silent creek. The man held steadily on. He was not much given to thinking, and just then particularly he had nothing to think about save that he would eat lunch at the forks and that at six o'clock he would be in camp with the boys. There was nobody to talk to, and, had there been, speech would have been impossible because of the ice-muzzle on his mouth. So he continued monotonously to chew tobacco and to increase the length of his amber beard.

Once in a while the thought reiterated itself that it was very cold and that he had never experienced such cold. As he walked along he rubbed his cheek-bones and nose with the back of his mittened hand. He did this automatically, now and again changing hands. But rub as he would, the instant he stopped his cheek-bones went numb, and the following instant the end of his nose went numb. He was sure to frost his cheeks; he knew that, and experienced a pang of regret that he had not devised a nose-strap of the sort Bud wore in cold snaps. Such a strap passed across the cheeks, as well, and saved them. But it didn't matter much, after all. What were frosted cheeks? A bit painful, that was all; they were never serious.

Empty as the man's mind was of thoughts, he was keenly observant, and he noticed the changes in the creek, the curves and bends and timber-jams, and always he sharply noted where he placed his feet. Once, coming around a bend, he shied abruptly, like a startled horse, curved away from the place where he had been walking, and retreated several paces back along the trail. The creek he knew was frozen clear to the bottom—no creek could contain water in that arctic winter—but he knew also that there were springs that bubbled out from the hillsides and ran along under the snow and on top the ice of the creek. He knew that the coldest snaps never froze these springs, and he knew likewise their danger. They were traps. They hid pools of water under the snow that might be three inches deep, or three feet. Sometimes a skin of ice half an inch thick covered them, and in turn was covered by the snow. Sometimes there were alternate layers of water and ice-skin, so that when one broke through he kept on breaking through for a while, sometimes wetting himself to the waist.

That was why he had shied in such panic. He had felt the give under his feet and heard the crackle of a snow-hidden ice-skin. And to get his feet wet in such a temperature meant trouble and danger. At the very least it meant delay, for he would be forced to stop and build a fire, and under its protection to bare his feet while he dried his socks and moccasins. He stood and studied the creek-bed and its banks, and decided that the flow of water came from the right. He reflected awhile, rubbing his nose and cheeks, then skirted to the left, stepping gingerly and testing the footing for each step. Once clear of the danger, he took a fresh chew of tobacco and swung along at his four-mile gait.

In the course of the next two hours he came upon several similar traps. Usually the snow above the hidden pools had a sunken, candied appearance that advertised the danger. Once again, however, he had a close call; and once, suspecting danger, he compelled the dog to go on in front. The dog did not want to go. It hung back until the man shoved it forward, and then it went quickly across the white, unbroken surface. Suddenly it broke through, floundered to one side, and got away to firmer footing. It had wet its forefeet and legs, and almost immediately the water that clung to it turned to ice. It made quick efforts to lick the ice off its legs, then dropped down in the snow and began to bite out the ice that had formed between the toes. This was a matter of instinct. To permit the ice to remain would mean sore feet. It did not know this. It merely obeyed the mysterious prompting that arose from the deep crypts of its being. But the man knew, having achieved a judgment on the subject, and he removed the mitten from his right hand and helped tear out the ice-particles. He did not expose his fingers more than a minute, and was astonished at the swift numbness that smote them. It certainly was cold. He pulled on the mitten hastily, and beat the hand savagely across his chest.

At twelve o'clock the day was at its brightest. Yet the sun was too far south on its winter journey to clear the horizon. The bulge of the earth intervened between it and Henderson Creek, where the man walked under a clear sky at noon and cast no shadow. At half-past twelve, to the minute, he arrived at the forks of the creek. He was pleased at the speed he had made. If he kept it up, he would certainly be with the boys by six. He unbuttoned his jacket and shirt and drew forth his lunch. The action consumed no more than a quarter of a minute, yet in that brief moment the numbness laid hold of the exposed fingers. He did not put the mitten on, but, instead, struck the fingers a dozen sharp smashes against his leg. Then he sat down on a snow-covered log to eat. The sting that followed upon the striking of his fingers against his leg ceased so quickly that he was startled. He had had no chance to take a bite of biscuit. He struck the fingers repeatedly and returned them to the mitten, baring the other hand for the purpose of eating. He tried to take a mouthful, but the ice-muzzle prevented. He had forgotten to build a fire and thaw out. He chuckled at his foolishness, and as he chuckled he noted the numbness creeping into the exposed fingers. Also, he noted that the stinging which had first come to his toes when he sat down was already passing away. He wondered whether the toes were warm or numb. He moved them inside the moccasins and decided that they were numb.

He pulled the mitten on hurriedly and stood up. He was a bit frightened. He stamped up and down until the stinging returned into the feet. It certainly was cold, was his thought. That man from Sulphur Creek had spoken the truth when telling how cold it sometimes got in the country. And he had laughed at him at the time! That showed one must not be too sure of things. There was no mistake about it, it *was* cold. He strode up and down, stamping his feet and threshing his arms, until reassured by the returning warmth. Then he got out matches and proceeded to make a fire. From the undergrowth, where high water of the previous spring had lodged a supply of seasoned twigs, he got his fire-wood. Working carefully from a small beginning, he soon had a roaring fire, over which he thawed the ice from his face and in the protection of which he ate his biscuits. For the moment the cold of space was outwitted. The dog took satisfaction in the fire, stretching out close enough for warmth and far enough away to escape being singed.

When the man had finished, he filled his pipe and took his comfortable time over a smoke. Then he pulled on his mittens, settled the ear-flaps of his cap firmly about his ears, and took the creek trail up the left fork. The dog was disappointed and yearned back toward the fire. This man did not know cold. Possibly all the generations of his ancestry had been ignorant of cold, of real cold, of cold one hundred and seven degrees below freezing-point. But the dog knew; all its ancestry knew, and it had inherited the knowledge. And it knew that it was not good to walk abroad in such fearful cold. It was the time to lie snug in a hole in the snow and wait for a curtain of cloud to be drawn across the face of outer space whence this cold came. On the other hand, there was no keen intimacy between the dog and the man. The one was the toil-slave of the other, and the only caresses it had ever received were the caresses of the whip-lash and of harsh and menacing throat-sounds that threatened the whip-lash. So the dog made no effort to communicate its apprehension to the man. It was not concerned in the welfare of the man; it was for its own sake that it yearned back toward the fire. But the man whistled, and spoke to it with the sound of whip-lashes, and the dog swung in at the man's heels and followed after.

The man took a chew of tobacco and proceeded to start a new amber beard. Also, his moist breath quickly powdered with white his mustache, eyebrows, and lashes. There did not seem to be so many springs on the left fork of the Henderson, and for half an hour the man saw no signs of any. And then it happened. At a place where there were no signs, where the soft, unbroken snow seemed to advertise solidity beneath, the man broke through. It was not deep. He wet himself halfway to the knees before he floundered out to the firm crust.

He was angry, and cursed his luck aloud. He had hoped to get into camp with the boys at six o'clock, and this would delay him an hour, for he would have to build a fire and dry out his foot-gear. This was imperative at that low temperature—he knew that much; and he turned aside to the bank, which he climbed. On top, tangled in the underbrush about the trunks of several small spruce trees, was a high-water deposit of dry fire-wood—sticks and twigs, principally, but also larger portions of seasoned branches and fine, dry, last-year's grasses. He threw down several large pieces on top of the snow. This served for a foundation and prevented the young flame from drowning itself in the snow it otherwise would melt. The flame he got by touching a match to a small shred of birch-bark that he took from his pocket. This burned even more readily than paper. Placing it on the foundation, he fed the young flame with wisps of dry grass and with the tiniest dry twigs.

He worked slowly and carefully, keenly aware of his danger. Gradually, as the flame grew stronger, he increased the size of the twigs with which he fed it. He squatted in the snow, pulling the twigs out from their entanglement in the brush and feeding directly to the flame. He knew there must be no failure. When it is seventy-five below zero, a man must not fail in his first attempt to build a fire—that is, if his feet are wet. If his feet are dry, and he fails, he can run along the trail for half a mile and restore his circulation. But the circulation of wet and freezing feet cannot be restored by running when it is seventy-five below. No matter how fast he runs, the wet feet will freeze the harder.

All this the man knew. The old-timer on Sulphur Creek had told him about it the previous fall, and now he was appreciating the advice. Already all sensation had gone out of his feet. To build the fire he had been forced to remove his mittens, and the fingers had quickly gone numb. His pace of four miles an hour had kept his heart pumping blood to the surface of his body and to all the extremities. But the instant he stopped, the action of the pump eased down. The cold of space smote the unprotected tip of the planet, and he, being on that unprotected tip, received the full force of the blow. The blood of his body recoiled before it. The blood was alive, like the dog, and like the dog it wanted to hide away and cover itself up from the fearful cold. So long as he walked four miles an hour, he pumped that blood, willy-nilly, to the surface; but now it ebbed away and sank down into the recesses of his body. The extremities were the first to feel its absence. His wet feet froze the faster, and his exposed fingers numbed the faster, though they had not yet begun to freeze. Nose and cheeks were already freezing, while the skin of all his body chilled as it lost its blood.

But he was safe. Toes and nose and cheeks would be only touched by the frost, for the fire was beginning to burn with strength. He was feeding it with twigs the size of his finger. In another minute he would be able to feed it with branches the size of his wrist, and then he could remove his wet foot-gear, and, while it dried, he could keep his naked feet warm by the fire, rubbing them at first, of course, with snow. The fire was a success. He was safe. He remembered the advice of the old-timer on Sulphur Creek, and smiled. The old-timer had been very serious in laying down the law that no man must travel alone in the Klondike after fifty below. Well, here he was; he had had the accident; he was alone; and he had saved himself. Those old-timers were rather womanish, some of them, he thought. All a man had to do was to keep his head, and he was all right. Any man who was a man could travel alone. But it was surprising, the rapidity with which his cheeks and nose were freezing. And he had not thought his fingers could go lifeless in so short a time. Lifeless they were, for he could scarcely make them move together to grip a twig, and they seemed remote from his body and from him. When he touched a twig, he had to look and see whether or not he had hold of it. The wires were pretty well down between him and his finger-ends.

All of which counted for little. There was the fire, snapping and crackling and promising life with every dancing flame. He started to untie his moccasins. They were coated with ice; the thick German socks were like sheaths of iron halfway to the knees; and the moccasin strings were like rods of steel all twisted and knotted as by some conflagration. For a moment he tugged with his numb fingers, then, realizing the folly of it, he drew his sheath-knife.

But before he could cut the strings, it happened. It was his own fault or, rather, his mistake. He should not have built the fire under the spruce tree. He should have built it in the open. But it had been easier to pull the twigs from the brush and drop them directly on the fire. Now the tree under which he had done this carried a weight of snow on its boughs. No wind had blown for weeks, and each bough was fully freighted. Each time he had pulled a twig he had communicated a slight agitation to the tree—an imperceptible agitation, so far as he was concerned, but an agitation sufficient to bring about the disaster. High up in the tree one bough capsized its load of snow. This fell on the boughs beneath, capsizing them. This process continued, spreading out and involving the whole tree. It grew like an avalanche, and it descended without warning upon the man and the fire, and the fire was blotted out! Where it had burned was a mantle of fresh and disordered snow.

The man was shocked. It was as though he had just heard his own sentence of death. For a moment he sat and stared at the spot where the fire had been. Then he grew very calm. Perhaps the old-timer on Sulphur Creek was right. If he had only had a trail-mate he would have been in no danger now. The trail-mate could have built the fire. Well, it was up to him to build the fire over again, and this second time there must be no failure. Even if he succeeded, he would most likely lose some toes. His feet must be badly frozen by now, and there would be some time before the second fire was ready.

Such were his thoughts, but he did not sit and think them. He was busy all the time they were passing through his mind. He made a new foundation for a fire, this time in the open, where no treacherous tree could blot it out. Next, he gathered dry grasses and tiny twigs from the high-water flotsam. He could not bring his fingers together to pull them out, but he was able to gather them by the handful. In this way he got many rotten twigs and bits of green moss that were undesirable, but it was the best he could do. He worked methodically, even collecting an armful of the larger branches to be used later when the fire gathered strength. And all the while the dog sat and watched him, a certain yearning wistfulness in its eyes, for it looked upon him as the fire-provider, and the fire was slow in coming.

When all was ready, the man reached in his pocket for a second piece of birch-bark. He knew the bark was there, and, though he could not feel it with his fingers, he could hear its crisp rustling as he fumbled for it. Try as he would, he could not clutch hold of it. And all the time, in his consciousness, was the knowledge that each instant his feet were freezing. This thought tended to put him in a panic, but he fought against it and kept calm. He pulled on his mittens with his teeth, and threshed his arms back and forth, beating his hands with all his might against his sides. He did this sitting down, and he stood up to do it; and all the while the dog sat in the snow, its wolf-brush of a tail curled around warmly over its forefeet, its sharp wolf-ears pricked forward intently as it watched the man. And the man, as he beat and threshed with his arms and hands, felt a great surge of envy as he regarded the creature that was warm and secure in its natural covering.

After a time he was aware of the first faraway signals of sensation in his beaten fingers. The faint tingling grew stronger till it evolved into a stinging ache that was excruciating, but which the man hailed with satisfaction. He stripped the mitten from his right hand and fetched forth the birch-bark. The exposed fingers were quickly going numb again. Next he brought out his bunch of sulphur matches. But the tremendous cold had already driven the life out of his fingers. In his effort to separate one match from the others, the whole bunch fell in the snow. He tried to pick it out of the snow, but failed. The dead fingers could neither touch nor clutch. He was very careful. He drove the thought of his freezing feet, and nose, and cheeks, out of his mind, devoting his whole soul to the matches. He watched, using the sense of vision in place of that of touch, and when he saw his fingers on each side the bunch, he closed them—that is, he willed to close them, for the wires were down, and the fingers did not obey. He pulled the mitten on the right hand, and beat it fiercely against his knee. Then, with both mittened hands, he scooped the bunch of matches, along with much snow, into his lap. Yet he was no better off.

After some manipulation he managed to get the bunch between the heels of his mittened hands. In this fashion he carried it to his mouth. The ice crackled and snapped when by a violent effort he opened his mouth. He drew the lower jaw in, curled the upper lip out of the way, and scraped the bunch with his upper teeth in order to separate a match. He succeeded in getting one, which he dropped on his lap. He was no better off. He could not pick it up. Then he devised a way. He picked it up in his teeth and scratched it on his leg. Twenty times he scratched before he succeeded in lighting it. As it flamed he held it with his teeth to the birch-bark. But the burning brimstone went up his nostrils and into his lungs, causing him to cough spasmodically. The match fell into the snow and went out.

The old-timer on Sulphur Creek was right, he thought in the moment of controlled despair that ensued: after fifty below, a man should travel with a partner. He beat his hands, but failed in exciting any sensation. Suddenly he bared both hands, removing the mittens with his teeth. He caught the whole bunch between the heels of his hands. His arm-muscles not being frozen enabled him to press the hand-heels tightly against the matches. Then he scratched the bunch along his leg. It flared into flame, seventy sulphur matches at once! There was no wind to blow them out. He kept his head to one side to escape the strangling fumes, and held the blazing bunch to the birch-bark. As he so held it, he became aware of sensation in his hand. His flesh was burning. He could smell it. Deep down below the surface he could feel it. The sensation developed into pain that grew acute. And still he endured it, holding the flame of the matches clumsily to the bark that would not light readily because his own burning hands were in the way, absorbing most of the flame.

At last, when he could endure no more, he jerked his hands apart. The blazing matches fell sizzling into the snow, but the birch-bark was alight. He began laying dry grasses and the tiniest twigs on the flame. He could not pick and choose, for he had to lift the fuel between the heels of his hands. Small pieces of rotten wood and green moss clung to the twigs, and he bit them off as well as he could with his teeth. He cherished the flame carefully and awkwardly. It meant life, and it must not perish. The withdrawal of blood from the surface of his body now made him begin to shiver, and he grew more awkward. A large piece of green moss fell squarely on the little fire. He tried to poke it out with his fingers, but his shivering frame made him poke too far, and he disrupted the nucleus of the little fire, the burning grasses and tiny twigs separating and scattering. He tried to poke them together again, but in spite of the tenseness of the effort, his shivering got away with him, and the twigs were hopelessly scattered. Each twig gushed a puff of smoke and went out. The fire-provider had failed. As he looked apathetically about him, his eyes chanced on the dog, sitting across the ruins of the fire from him, in the snow, making restless, hunching movements, slightly lifting one forefoot and then the other, shifting its weight back and forth on them with wistful eagerness.

The sight of the dog put a wild idea into his head. He remembered the tale of the man, caught in a blizzard, who killed a steer and crawled inside the carcass, and so was saved. He would kill the dog and bury his hands in the warm body until the numbness went out of them. Then he could build another fire. He spoke to the dog, calling it to him; but in his voice was a strange note of fear that frightened the animal, who had never known the man to speak in such way before. Something was the matter, and its suspicious nature sensed danger—it knew not what danger, but somewhere, somehow, in its brain arose an apprehension of the man. It flattened its ears down at the sound of the man's voice, and its restless, hunching movements and the liftings and shiftings of its forefeet became more pronounced; but it would not come to the man. He got on his hands and knees and crawled toward the dog. This unusual posture again excited suspicion, and the animal sidled mincingly away.

The man sat up in the snow for a moment and struggled for calmness. Then he pulled on his mittens, by means of his teeth, and got upon his feet. He glanced down at first in order to assure himself that he was really standing up, for the absence of sensation in his feet left him unrelated to the earth. His erect position in itself started to drive the webs of suspicion from the dog's mind; and when he spoke peremptorily, with the sound of whip-lashes in his voice, the dog rendered its customary allegiance and came to him. As it came within reaching distance, the man lost his control. His arms flashed out to the dog, and he experienced genuine surprise when he discovered that his hands could not clutch, that there was neither bend nor feeling in the fingers. He had forgotten for the moment that they were frozen and that they were freezing more and more. All this happened quickly, and before the animal could get away, he encircled its body with his arms. He sat down in the snow, and in this fashion held the dog, while it snarled and whined and struggled.

But it was all he could do, hold its body encircled in his arms and sit there. He realized that he could not kill the dog. There was no way to do it. With his helpess hands he could neither draw nor hold his sheath-knife nor throttle the animal. He released it, and it plunged wildly away, with tail between its legs, and still snarling. It halted forty feet away and surveyed him curiously, with ears sharply pricked forward. The man looked down at his hands in order to locate them, and found them hanging on the ends of his arms. It struck him as curious that one should have to use his eyes in order to find out where his hands were. He began threshing his arms back and forth, beating the mittened hands against his sides. He did this for five minutes, violently, and his heart pumped enough blood up to the surface to put a stop to his shivering. But no sensation was aroused in the hands. He had an impression that they hung like weights on the ends of his arms, but when he tried to run the impression down, he could not find it.

A certain fear of death, dull and oppressive, came to him. This fear quickly became poignant as he realized that it was no longer a mere matter of freezing his fingers and toes, or of losing his hands and feet, but that it was a matter of life and death with the chances against him. This threw him into a panic, and he turned and ran up the creek-bed along the old, dim trail. The dog joined in behind and kept up with him. He ran blindly, without intention, in fear such as he had never known in his life. Slowly, as he ploughed and floundered through the snow, he began to see things again—the banks of the creek, the old timber-jams, the leafless aspens, and the sky. The running made him feel better. He did not shiver. Maybe, if he ran on, his feet would thaw out; and, anyway, if he ran far enough, he would reach camp and the boys. Without doubt he would lose some fingers and toes and some of his face; but the boys would take care of him, and save the rest of him when he got there. And at the same time there was another thought in his mind that said he would never get to the camp and the boys; that it was too many miles away, that the freezing had too great a start on him, and that he would soon be stiff and dead. This thought he kept in the background and refused to consider. Sometimes it pushed itself forward and demanded to be heard, but he thrust it back and strove to think of other things.

It struck him as curious that he could run at all on feet so frozen that he could not feel them when they struck the earth and took the weight of his body. He seemed to himself to skim along above the surface, and to have no connection with the earth. Somewhere he had once seen a winged Mercury, and he wondered if Mercury felt as he felt when skimming over the earth.

His theory of running until he reached camp and the boys had one flaw in it. he lacked the endurance. Several times he stumbled, and finally he tottered, crumpled up, and fell. When he tried to rise, he failed. He must sit and rest, he decided, and next time he would merely walk and keep on going. As he sat and regained his breath, he noted that he was feeling quite warm and comfortable. He was not shivering, and it even seemed that a warm glow had come to his chest and trunk. And yet, when he touched his nose or cheeks, there was no sensation. Running would not thaw them out. Nor would it thaw out his hands and feet. Then the thought came to him that the frozen portions of his body must be extending. He tried to keep this thought down, to forget it, to think of something else; he was aware of the panicky feeling that it caused, and he was afraid of the panic. But the thought asserted itself, and persisted, until it produced a vision of his body totally frozen. This was too much, and he made another wild run along the trail. Once he slowed down to a walk, but the thought of the freezing extending itself made him run again.

And all the time the dog ran with him, at his heels. When he fell down a second time, it curled its tail over its forefeet and sat in front of him, facing him, curiously eager and intent. The warmth and security of the animal angered him, and he cursed it till it flattened down its ears appeasingly. This time the shivering came more quickly upon the man. He was losing in his battle with the frost. It was creeping into his body from all sides. The thought of it drove him on, but he ran no more than a hundred feet, when he staggered and pitched headlong. It was his last panic. When he had recovered his breath and control, he sat up and entertained in his mind the conception of meeting death with dignity. However, the conception did not come to him in such terms. His idea of it was that he had been making a fool of himself, running around like a chicken with its head cut off—such was the simile that occurred to him. Well, he was bound to freeze anyway, and he might as well take it decently. With this newfound peace of mind came the first glimmerings of drowsiness. A good idea, he thought, to sleep off to death. It was like taking an anæsthetic. Freezing was not so bad as people thought. There were lots worse ways to die.

He pictured the boys finding his body next day. Suddenly he found himself with them, coming along the trail and looking for himself.

And, still with them, he came around a turn in the trail and found himself lying in the snow. He did not belong with himself any more, for even then he was out of himself, standing with the boys and looking at himself in the snow. It certainly was cold, was his thought. When he got back to the States he could tell the folks what real cold was. He drifted on from this to a vision of the old-timer on Sulphur Creek. He could see him quite clearly, warm and comfortable, and smoking a pipe.

"You were right, old hoss; you were right," the man mumbled to the old-timer of Sulphur Creek.

Then the man drowsed off into what seemed to him the most comfortable and satisfying sleep he had ever known. The dog sat facing him and waiting. The brief day drew to a close in a long, slow twilight. There were no signs of a fire to be made, and, besides, never in the dog's experience had it known a man to sit like that in the snow and make no fire. As the twilight drew on, its eager yearning for the fire mastered it, and with a great lifting and shifting of forefeet, it whined softly, then flattened its ears down in anticipation of being chidden by the man. But the man remained silent. Later, the dog whined loudly. And still later it crept close to the man and caught the scent of death. This made the animal bristle and back away. A little longer it delayed, howling under the stars that leaped and danced and shone brightly in the cold sky. Then it turned and trotted up the trail in the direction of the camp it knew, where were the other food-providers and fire-providers.

# THE LAW OF LIFE

## Jack London

OLD KOSKOOSH LISTENED greedily. Though his sight had long since faded, his hearing was still acute, and the slightest sound penetrated to the glimmering intelligence which yet abode behind the withered forehead, but which no longer gazed forth upon the things of the world. Ah! that was Sit-cum-to-ha, shrilly anathematizing the dogs as she cuffed and beat them into the harnesses. Sit-cum-to-ha was his daughter's daughter, but she was too busy to waste a thought upon her broken grandfather, sitting alone there in the snow, forlorn and helpless. Camp must be broken. The long trail waited while the short day refused to linger. Life called her, and the duties of life, not death. And he was very close to death now.

The thought made the old man panicky for the moment, and he stretched forth a palsied hand which wandered tremblingly over the small heap of dry wood beside him. Reassured that it was indeed there, his hand returned to the shelter of his mangy furs, and he again fell to listening. The sulky crackling of half-frozen hides told him that the chief's moose-skin lodge had been struck, and even then was being rammed and jammed into portable compass. The chief was his son, stalwart and strong, head man of the tribesmen, and a mighty hunter. As the women toiled with the camp luggage, his voice rose, chiding them for their slowness. Old Koskoosh strained his ears. It was the last time he would hear that voice. There went Geehow's lodge! And Tusken's! Seven, eight, nine; only the shaman's could be still standing. There! They were at work upon it now. He could hear the shaman grunt as he piled it on the sled. A child whimpered, and a woman soothed it with soft, crooning gutturals Little Koo-tee, the old man thought, a fretful child, and not overstrong. It would die soon, perhaps, and they would burn a hole through the frozen tundra and pile rocks above to keep the wolverines away. Well, what did it matter? A few years at best, and as many an empty belly as a full one. And in the end, Death waited, ever-hungry and hungriest of them all.

What was that? Oh, the men lashing the sleds and drawing tight the thongs. He listened, who would listen no more. The whip-lashes snarled and bit among the dogs. Hear them whine! How they hated the work and the trail! They were off! Sled after sled churned slowly away into the silence. They were gone. They had passed out of his life, and he faced the last bitter hour alone. No. The snow crunched beneath a moccasin; a man stood beside him; upon his head a hand rested gently. His son was good to do this thing. He remembered other old men whose sons had not waited after the tribe. But his son had. He wandered away into the past, till the young man's voice brought him back.

"Is it well with you?" he asked.

And the old man answered, "It is well."

"There be wood beside you," the younger man continued, "and the fire burns bright. The morning is gray, and the cold has broken. It will snow presently. Even now is it snowing."

"Ay, even now is it snowing."

"The tribesmen hurry. Their bales are heavy, and their bellies flat with lack of feasting. The trail is long and they travel fast. I go now. It is well?"

"It is well. I am as a last year's leaf, clinging lightly to the stem. The first breath that blows, and I fall. My voice is become like an old woman's. My eyes no longer show me the way of my feet, and my feet are heavy, and I am tired. It is well."

He bowed his head in content till the last noise of the complaining snow had died away, and he knew his son was beyond recall. Then his hand crept out in haste to the wood. It alone stood between him and the eternity that yawned in upon him. At last the measure of his life was a handful of fagots. One by one they would go to feed the fire, and just so, step by step, death would creep upon him. When the last stick had surrendered up its heat, the frost would begin to gather strength. First his feet would yield, then his hands; and the numbness would travel, slowly, from the extremities to the body. His head would fall forward upon his knees, and he would rest. It was easy. All men must die.

He did not complain. It was the way of life, and it was just. He had been born close to the earth, close to the earth had he lived, and the law thereof was not new to him. It was the law of all flesh. Nature was not kindly to the flesh. She had no concern for that concrete thing called the individual. Her interest lay in the species, the race. This was the deepest abstraction old Koskoosh's barbaric mind was capable of, but he grasped it firmly. He saw it exemplified in all life. The rise of the sap, the bursting greenness of the willow bud, the fall of the yellow leaf—in this alone was told the whole history. But one task did Nature set the individual. Did he not perform it, he died. Did he perform it, it was all the same, he died. Nature did not care; there were plenty who were obedient, and it was only the obedience in this matter, not the obedient, which lived and lived always. The tribe of Koskoosh was very old. The old men he had known when a boy, had known old men before them. Therefore it was true that the tribe lived, that it stood for the obedience of all its members, way down into the forgotten past, whose very resting-places were unremembered. They did not count; they were episodes. They had passed away like clouds from a summer sky. He also was an episode, and would pass away. Nature did not care. To life she set one task, gave one law. To perpetuate was the task of life, its law was death. A maiden was a good creature to look upon, full-breasted and strong, with spring to her step and light in her eyes. But her task was yet before her. The light in her eyes brightened, her step quickened, she was now bold with the young men, now timid, and she gave them of her own unrest. And ever she grew fairer and yet fairer to look upon, till some hunter, able no longer to withhold himself, took her to his lodge to cook and toil for him and to become the mother of his children. And with the coming of her offspring her looks left her. Her limbs dragged and shuffled, her eyes dimmed and bleared, and only the little children found joy against the withered cheek of the old squaw by the fire. Her task was done. But a little while, on the first pinch of famine or the first long trail, and she would be left, even as he had been left, in the snow, with a little pile of wood. Such was the law.

He placed a stick carefully upon the fire and resumed his meditations. It was the same everywhere, with all things. The mosquitoes vanished with the first frost. The little tree-squirrel crawled away to die. When age settled upon the rabbit it became slow and heavy, and could no longer outfoot its enemies. Even the big bald-face grew clumsy and blind and quarrelsome, in the end to be dragged down by a handful of yelping huskies. He remembered how he had abandoned his own father on an upper reach of the Klondike one winter, the winter before the missionary came with his talk-books and his box of medicines. Many a time had Koskoosh smacked his lips over the recollection of that box, though now his mouth refused to moisten. The "painkiller" had been especially good. But the missionary was a bother after all, for he brought no meat into the camp, and he ate heartily, and the hunters grumbled. But he chilled his lungs on the divide by the Mayo, and the dogs afterwards nosed the stones away and fought over his bones.

Koskoosh placed another stick on the fire and harked back deeper into the past. There was the time of the Great Famine, when the old men crouched empty-bellied to the fire, and let fall from their lips dim traditions of the ancient day when the Yukon ran wide open for three winters, and then lay frozen for three summers. He had lost his mother in that famine. In the summer the salmon run had failed, and the tribe looked forward to the winter and the coming of the caribou. Then the winter came, but with it there were no caribou. Never had the like been known, not even in the lives of the old men. But the caribou did not come, and it was the seventh year, and the rabbits had not replenished, and the dogs were naught but bundles of bones. And through the long darkness the children wailed and died, and the women, and the old men; and not one in ten of the tribe lived to meet the sun when it came back in the spring. That *was* a famine!

But he had seen times of plenty, too, when the meat spoiled on their hands, and the dogs were fat and worthless with overeating—times when they let the game go unkilled, and the women were fertile, and the lodges were cluttered with sprawling men-children and women-children. Then it was the men became high-stomached, and revived ancient quarrels, and crossed the divides to the south to kill the Pellys, and to the west that they might sit by the dead fires of the Tananas. He remembered, when a boy, during a time of plenty, when he saw a moose pulled down by the wolves. Zing-ha lay with him in the snow and watched—Zing-ha, who later became the craftiest of hunters, and who, in the end, fell through an air-hole on the Yukon. They found him, a month afterward, just as he had crawled halfway out and frozen stiff to the ice.

But the moose. Zing-ha and he had gone out that day to play at hunting after the manner of their fathers. On the bed of the creek they struck the fresh track of a moose, and with it the tracks of many wolves. "An old one," Zing-ha, who was quicker at reading the sign, said—"an old one who cannot keep up with the herd. The wolves have cut him out from his brothers, and they will never leave him." And it was so. It was their way. By day and by night, never resting, snarling on his heels, snapping at his nose, they would stay by him to the end. How Zing-ha and he felt the blood-lust quicken! The finish would be a sight to see!

Eager-footed, they took the trail, and even he, Koskoosh, slow of sight and an unversed tracker, could have followed it blind, it was so wide. Hot were they on the heels of the chase, reading the grim tragedy, fresh-written, at every step. Now they came to where the moose had made a stand. Thrice the length of a grown man's body, in every direction, had the snow been stamped about and uptossed. In the midst were the deep impressions of the splay-hoofed game, and all about, everywhere, were the lighter footmarks of the wolves. Some, while their brothers harried the kill, had lain to one side and rested. The full-stretched impress of their bodies in the snow was as perfect as though made the moment before. One wolf had been caught in a wild lunge of the maddened victim and trampled to death. A few bones, well picked, bore witness.

Again, they ceased the uplift of their snowshoes at a second stand. Here the great animal had fought desperately. Twice had he been dragged down, as the snow attested, and twice had he shaken his assailants clear and gained footing once more. He had done his task long since, but none the less was life dear to him. Zing-ha said it was a strange thing, a moose once down to get free again; but this one certainly had. The shaman would see signs and wonders in this when they told him.

And yet again, they come to where the moose had made to mount the bank and gain the timber. But his foes had laid on from behind, till he reared and fell back upon them, crushing two deep into the snow. It was plain the kill was at hand, for their brothers had left them untouched. Two more stands were hurried past, brief in time-length and very close together. The trail was red now, and the clean stride of the great beast had grown short and slovenly. Then they heard the first sounds of the battle—not the full-throated chorus of the chase, but the short, snappy bark which spoke of close quarters and teeth to flesh. Crawling up the wind, Zing-ha bellied it through the snow, and with him crept he, Koskoosh, who was to be chief of the tribesmen in the years to come. Together they shoved aside the under branches of a young spruce and peered forth. It was the end they saw.

The picture, like all of youth's impressions, was still strong with him, and his dim eyes watched the end played out as vividly as in that far-off time. Koskoosh marvelled at this, for in the days which followed, when he was a leader of men and a head of councillors, he had done great deeds and made his name a curse in the mouths of the Pellys, to say naught of the strange white man he had killed, knife to knife, in open fight.

For long he pondered on the days of his youth, till the fire died down and the frost bit deeper. He replenished it with two sticks this time, and gauged his grip on life by what remained. If Sit-cum-to-ha had only remembered her grandfather, and gathered a larger armful, his hours would have been longer. It would have been easy. But she was ever a careless child, and honored not her ancestors from the time the Beaver, son of the son of Zing-ha, first cast eyes upon her. Well, what mattered it? Had he not done likewise in his own quick youth? For a while he listened to the silence. Perhaps the heart of his son might soften, and he would come back with the dogs to take his old father on with the tribe to where the caribou ran thick and the fat hung heavy upon them.

He strained his ears, his restless brain for the moment stilled. Not a stir, nothing. He alone took breath in the midst of the great silence. It was very lonely. Hark! What was that? A chill passed over his body. The familiar, long-drawn howl broke the void, and it was close at hand. Then on his darkened eyes was projected the vision of the moose—the old bull moose—the torn flanks and bloody sides, the riddled mane, and the great branching horns, down low and tossing to the last. He saw the flashing forms of gray, the gleaming eyes, the lolling tongues, the slavered fangs. And he saw the inexorable circle close in till it became a dark point in the midst of the stamped snow.

A cold muzzle thrust against his cheek, and at its touch his soul leaped back to the present. His hand shot into the fire and dragged out a burning faggot. Overcome for the nonce by his hereditary fear of man, the brute retreated, raising a prolonged call to his brothers; and greedily they answered, till a ring of crouching, jaw-slobbered gray was stretched round about. The old man listened to the drawing in of this circle. He waved his brand wildly, and sniffs turned to snarls; but the panting brutes refused to scatter. Now one wormed his chest forward, dragging his haunches after, now a second, now a third; but never a one drew back. Why should he cling to life? he asked, and dropped the blazing stick into the snow. It sizzled and went out. The circle grunted uneasily, but held its own. Again he saw the last stand of the old bull moose, and Koskoosh dropped his head wearily upon his knees. What did it matter after all? Was it not the law of life?

# THE HAPPY FAILURE

## Herman Melville

THE APPOINTMENT WAS that I should meet my elderly uncle at the river-side, precisely at nine in the morning. The skiff was to be ready, and the apparatus to be brought down by his grizzled old black man. As yet, the nature of the wonderful experiment remained a mystery to all but the projector.

I was first on the spot. The village was high up the river, and the inland summer sun was already oppressively warm. Presently I saw my uncle advancing beneath the trees, hat off, and wiping his brow; while far behind staggered poor old Yorpy, with what seemed one of the gates of Gaza on his back.

"Come, hurrah, stump along, Yorpy!" cried my uncle, impatiently turning round every now and then.

Upon the black's staggering up to the skiff, I perceived that the great gate of Gaza was transformed into a huge, shabby, oblong box, hermetically sealed. The sphinx-like blankness of the box quadrupled the mystery in my mind.

"Is *this* the wonderful apparatus?" said I, in amazement. "Why, it's nothing but a battered old dry-goods box, nailed up. And is *this* the thing, uncle, that is to make you a million of dollars ere the year be out? What a forlorn-looking, lack-lustre, old ash-box it is."

"Put it into the skiff!" roared my uncle to Yorpy, without heeding my boyish disdain. "Put it in, you grizzle-headed cherub—put it in carefully, carefully! If the box bursts, my everlasting fortune collapses."

"Bursts?—collapses?" cried I, in alarm. "It ain't full of combustibles? Quick! let me go to the further end of the boat!"

"Sit still, you simpleton!" cried my uncle again. "Jump in, Yorpy, and hold on to the box like grim death while I shove off. Carefully! carefully! you dunderheaded black! Mind t'other side of the box, I say! Do you mean to destroy the box?"

"Duyvel take de pox!" muttered old Yorpy, who was a sort of Dutch African. "De pox has been my cuss for de ten long 'ear."

"Now, then, we're off—take an oar, youngster; you, Yorpy, clinch the box fast. Here we go now. Carefully! carefully! You, Yorpy, stop shaking the box! Easy! easy! there's a big snag. Pull now. Hurrah! deep water at last! Now give way, youngster, and away to the island."

"The island!" said I. "There's no island hereabouts."

"There is ten miles above the bridge, though," said my uncle, determinately.

"Ten miles off! Pull that old dry-goods box ten miles up the river in this blazing sun!"

"All that I have to say," said my uncle, firmly, "is that we are bound to Quash Island."

"Mercy, uncle! If I had known of this great long pull of ten mortal miles in this fiery sun, you wouldn't have juggled *me* into the skiff so easy. What's *in* that box?—paving-stones? See how the skiff settles down under it. I won't help pull a box of paving-stones ten miles. What's the use of pulling 'em?"

"Look you, simpleton," quoth my uncle, pausing upon his suspended oar. "Stop rowing, will ye! Now then, if you don't want to share in the glory of my experiment; if you are wholly indifferent to halving its immortal renown; I say, sir, if you care not to be present at the first trial of my Great Hydraulic-Hydrostatic Apparatus for draining swamps and marshes, and converting them, at the rate of one acre the hour, into fields more fertile than those of the Genessee; if you care not, I repeat, to have this proud thing to tell—in far future days, when poor old I shall have been long dead and gone, boy—to your children, and your children's children; in that case, sir, you are free to land forthwith."

"Oh, uncle! I did not mean—"

"No words, sir! Yorpy, take his oar, and help pull him ashore."

"But, my dear uncle; I declare to you that—"

"Not a syllable, sir; you have cast open scorn upon the Great Hydraulic-Hydrostatic Apparatus. Yorpy, put him ashore, Yorpy. It's shallow here again. Jump out, Yorpy, and wade with him ashore."

"Now, my dear, good, kind uncle, do but pardon me this one time, and I will say just nothing about the apparatus."

"Say nothing about it! When it is my express end and aim it shall be famous! Put him ashore, Yorpy."

"Nay, uncle, I *will* not give up my oar. I have an oar in this matter, and I mean to keep it. You shall not cheat me out of my share of your glory."

"Ah, now there—that's sensible. You may stay, youngster. Pull again now."

We were all silent for a time, steadily plying our way. At last I ventured to break water once more.

"I am glad, dear uncle, you have revealed to me at last the nature and end of your great experiment. It is the effectual draining of swamps; an attempt, dear uncle, in which, if you do but succeed (as I know you will), you will earn the glory denied to a Roman emperor. He tried to drain the Pontine marsh, but failed."

"The world has shot ahead the length of its own diameter since then," quoth my uncle, proudly. "If that Roman emperor were here, I'd show him what can be done in the present enlightened age."

Seeing my good uncle so far mollified now as to be quite self-complacent, I ventured another remark.

"This is a rather severe, hot pull, dear uncle."

"Glory is not to be gained, youngster, without pulling hard for it—against the stream, too, as we do now. The natural tendency of man, in the mass, is to go down with the universal current into oblivion."

"But why pull so far, dear uncle, upon the present occasion? Why pull ten miles for it? You do but propose, as I understand it, to put to the actual test this admirable invention of yours. And could it not be tested almost anywhere?"

"Simple boy," quoth my uncle, "would you have some malignant spy steal from me the fruits of ten long years of high-hearted, persevering endeavor? Solitary in my scheme, I go to a solitary place to test it. If I fail—for all things are possible—no one out of the family will know it. If I succeed, secure in the secrecy of my invention, I can boldly demand any price for its publication."

"Pardon me, dear uncle; you are wiser than I."

"One would think years and gray hairs should bring wisdom, boy."

"Yorpy there, dear uncle; think you his grizzled locks thatch a brain improved by long life?"

"Am I Yorpy, boy? Keep to your oar!"

Thus padlocked again, I said no further word till the skiff grounded on the shallows, some twenty yards from the deep-wooded isle.

"Hush!" whispered my uncle, intensely; "not a word now!" and he sat perfectly still, slowly sweeping with his glance the whole country around, even to both banks of the here wide-expanded stream.

"Wait till that horseman, yonder, passes!" he whispered again, pointing to a speck moving along a lofty river-side road, which perilously wound on midway up a long line of broken bluffs and cliffs. "There—he's out of sight now, behind the copse. Quick! Yorpy! Carefully, though! Jump overboard, and shoulder the box, and—Hold!"

We were all mute and motionless again.

"Ain't that a boy, sitting like Zacchæus in yonder tree of the orchard on the other bank? Look, youngster—young eyes are better than old—don't you see him?"

"Dear uncle, I see the orchard, but I can't see any boy."

"He's a spy—I know he is," suddenly said my uncle, disregardful of my answer, and intently gazing, shading his eyes with his flattened hand. "Don't touch the box, Yorpy. Crouch! crouch down, all of ye!"

"Why, uncle—there—see—the boy is only a withered white bough. I see it very plainly now."

"You don't see the tree I mean," quoth my uncle, with a decided air of relief, "but never mind; I defy the boy. Yorpy, jump out, and shoulder the box. And now then, youngster, off with your shoes and stockings, roll up your trowsers legs, and follow me. Carefully, Yorpy, carefully. That's more precious than a box of gold, mind."

"Heavy as de gelt, anyhow," growled Yorpy, staggering and splashing in the shallows beneath it.

"There, stop under the bushes there—in among the flags—so— gently, gently—there, put it down just there. Now, youngster, are you ready? Follow—tiptoes, tiptoes!"

"I can't wade in this mud and water on my tiptoes, uncle; and I don't see the need of it either."

"Go ashore, sir—instantly!"

"Why, uncle, I *am* ashore."

"Peace! follow me, and no more."

Crouching in the water in complete secrecy, beneath the bushes and among the tall flags, my uncle now stealthily produced a hammer and wrench from one of his enormous pockets, and presently tapped the box. But the sound alarmed him.

"Yorpy," he whispered, "go you off to the right, behind the bushes, and keep watch. If you see anyone coming, whistle softly. Youngster, you do the same to the left."

We obeyed; and presently, after considerable hammering and supplemental tinkering, my uncle's voice was heard in the utter solitude, loudly commanding our return.

Again we obeyed, and now found the cover of the box removed. All eagerness, I peeped in, and saw a surprising multiplicity of convoluted metal pipes and syringes of all sorts and varieties, all sizes and calibres, inextricably inter-wreathed together in one gigantic coil. It looked like a huge nest of anacondas and adders.

"Now then, Yorpy," said my uncle, all animation, and flushed with the foretaste of glory, "do you stand this side, and be ready to tip when I give the word. And do you, youngster, stand ready to do as much for the other side. Mind, don't budge it the fraction of a barley-corn till I say the word. All depends on a proper adjustment."

"No fear, uncle. I will be careful as a lady's tweezers."

"I s'ant lift de heavy pox," growled old Yorpy, "till de wort pe given; no fear o' dat."

"Oh boy," said my uncle now, upturning his face devotionally, while a really noble gleam irradiated his gray eyes, locks, and wrinkles; "oh boy! this, *this* is the hour which for ten long years has, in the prospect, sustained me through all my painstaking obscurity. Fame will be the sweeter because it comes at the last; the truer, because it comes to an old man like me, not to a boy like you. Sustainer! I glorify Thee."

He bowed over his venerable head, and—as I live—something like a shower-drop somehow fell from my face into the shallows.

"Tip!"

We tipped.

"A little more!"

We tipped a little more.

"A *leetle* more!"

We tipped a *leetle* more.

"Just a *leetle*, very *leetle* bit more."

With great difficulty we tipped just a *leetle*, very *leetle* more.

All this time my uncle was diligently stooping over, and striving to peep in, up, and under the box where the coiled anacondas and adders lay; but the machine being now fairly immersed, the attempt was wholly vain.

He rose erect, and waded slowly all round the box; his countenance firm and reliant, but not a little troubled and vexed.

It was plain something or other was going wrong. But as I was left in utter ignorance as to the mystery of the contrivance, I could not tell where the difficulty lay, or what was the proper remedy.

Once more, still more slowly, still more vexedly, my uncle waded round the box, the dissatisfaction gradually deepening, but still controlled, and still with hope at the bottom of it.

Nothing could be more sure than that some anticipated effect had, as yet, failed to develop itself. Certain I was, too, that the waterline did not lower about my legs.

"Tip it a *leetle* bit—very *leetle* now."

"Dear uncle, it is tipped already as far as it can be. Don't you see it rests now square on its bottom?"

"You, Yorpy, take your black hoof from under the box!"

This gust of passion on the part of my uncle made the matter seem still more dubious and dark. It was a bad symptom, I thought.

"Surely you *can* tip it just a *leetle* more!"

"Not a hair, uncle."

"Blast and blister the cursed box, then!" roared my uncle, in a terrific voice, sudden as a squall. Running at the box, he dashed his bare foot into it, and with astonishing power all but crushed in the side. Then, seizing the whole box, he disemboweled it of all its anacondas and adders, and, tearing and wrenching them, flung them right and left over the water.

"Hold, hold, my dear, dear uncle!—do, for Heaven's sake, desist. Don't destroy so, in one frantic moment, all your long calm years of devotion to one darling scheme. Hold, I conjure!"

Moved by my vehement voice and uncontrollable tears, he paused in his work of destruction, and stood steadfastly eying me, or rather blankly staring at me, like one demented.

"It is not yet wholly ruined, dear uncle; come put it together now. You have hammer and wrench; put it together again, and try it once more. While there is life there is hope."

"While there is life hereafter there is *despair*," he howled.

"Do, do now, dear uncle—here, here, put these pieces together; or, if that can't be done without more tools, try a *section* of it—that will do just as well. Try it once; try, uncle."

My persistent persuasiveness told upon him. The stubborn stump of hope, plowed at and uprooted in vain, put forth one last miraculous green sprout.

Steadily and carefully culling out of the wreck some of the more curious-looking fragments, he mysteriously involved them together, and then, clearing out the box, slowly inserted them there, and ranging Yorpy and me as before, bade us tip the box once again.

We did so; and as no perceptible effect yet followed, I was each moment looking for the previous command to tip the box over yet more, when, glancing into my uncle's face, I started aghast. It seemed pinched, shriveled into mouldy whiteness, like a mildewed grape. I dropped the box, and sprang toward him just in time to prevent his fall.

Leaving the woeful box where we had dropped it, Yorpy and I helped the old man into the skiff, and silently pulled from Quash Isle.

How swiftly the current now swept us down! How hardly before had we striven to stem it! I thought of my poor uncle's saying, not an hour gone by, about the universal drift of the mass of humanity toward utter oblivion.

"Boy!" said my uncle at last, lifting his head.

I looked at him earnestly, and was gladdened to see that the terrible blight of his face had almost departed.

"Boy, there's not much left in an old world for an old man to invent."

I said nothing.

"Boy, take my advice, and never try to invent anything but—happiness."

I said nothing.

"Boy, about ship, and pull back for the box."

"Dear uncle!"

"It will make a good wood-box, boy. And faithful old Yorpy can sell the old iron for tobacco-money."

"Dear massa! dear old massa! dat be very fust time in de ten long 'ear yoo hab mention kindly old Yorpy. I tank yoo, dear old massa; I tank yoo so kindly. Yoo is yourself again in de ten long 'ear."

"Aye, long ears enought," sighed my uncle; "Æsopian ears. But it's all over now. Boy, I'm glad I've failed. I say, boy, failure has made a good old man of me. It was horrible at first, but I'm glad I've failed. Praise be to God for the failure!"

His face kindled with a strange, rapt earnestness. I have never forgotten that look. If the event made my uncle a good old man, as he called it, it made me a wise young one. Example did for me the work of experience.

When some years had gone by, and my dear old uncle began to fail, and, after peaceful days of autumnal content, was gathered gently to his fathers—faithful old Yorpy closing his eyes—as I took my last look at his venerable face, the pale resigned lips seemed to move. I seemed to hear again his deep, fervent cry—"Praise be to God for the failure!"

# THE BELL-TOWER

## Herman Melville

*Like negroes, these powers own man sullenly;*
*mindful of their higher master; while serving,*
*plot revenge.*

*The world is apoplectic with high-living of*
*ambition; and apoplexy has its fall.*

*Seeking to conquer a larger liberty, man but*
*extends the empire of necessity.*
*from a private MS.*

IN THE SOUTH of Europe, nigh a once frescoed capital, now with dank mould cankering its bloom, central in a plain, stands what, at distance, seems the black mossed stump of some immeasurable pine, fallen, in forgotten days, with Anak and the Titan.

As all along where the pine tree falls, its dissolution leaves a mossy mound—last-flung shadow of the perished trunk; never lengthening, never lessening; unsubject to the fleet falsities of the sun; shade immutable, and true gauge which cometh by prostration—so westward from what seems the stump, one steadfast spear of lichened ruin veins the plain.

From that tree-top, what birded chimes of silver throats had rung. A stone pine; a metallic aviary in its crown: the Bell-Tower, built by the great mechanician, the unblest foundling, Bannadonna.

Like Babel's, its base was laid in a high hour of renovated earth, following the second deluge, when the waters of the Dark Ages had dried up, and once more the green appeared. No wonder that, after so long and deep submersion, the jubilant expectation of the race should, as with Noah's sons, soar into Shinar aspiration.

In firm resolve, no man in Europe at that period went beyond Bannadonna. Enriched through commerce with the Levant, the state in which he lived voted to have the noblest Bell-Tower in Italy. His repute assigned him to be architect.

Stone by stone, month by month, the tower rose. Higher, higher; snaillike in pace, but torch or rocket in its pride.

After the masons would depart, the builder, standing alone upon its ever-ascending summit, at close of every day, saw that he overtopped still higher walls and trees. He would tarry till a late hour there, wrapped in schemes of other and still loftier piles. Those who of saints' days thronged the spot—hanging to the rude poles of scaffolding, like sailors on yards, or bees on boughs, unmindful of lime and dust, and falling chips of stone—their homage not the less inspirited him to self-esteem.

At length the holiday of the Tower came. To the sound of viols, the climax-stone slowly rose in air, and, amid the firing of ordnance, was laid by Bannadonna's hands upon the final course. Then mounting it, he stood erect, alone, with folded arms, gazing upon the white summits of blue inland Alps, and whiter crests of bluer Alps off-shore— sights invisible from the plain. Invisible, too, from thence was that eye he turned below, when, like the cannon booms, came up to him the people's combustions of applause.

That which stirred them so was, seeing with what serenity the builder stood three hundred feet in the air, upon an unrailed perch. This none but he durst do. But his periodic standing upon the pile, in each stage of its growth—such discipline had its last result.

Little remained now but the bells. These, in all respects, must correspond with their receptacle.

The minor ones were prosperously cast. A highly enriched one followed, of a singular make, intended for suspension in a manner before unknown. The purpose of this bell, its rotary motion and connection with the clock-work, also executed at the time, will, in the sequel, receive mention.

In the one erection, bell-tower and clock-tower were united, though, before that period, such structures had commonly been built distinct; as the Campanile and Torre dell' Orologio of St. Mark to this day attest.

But it was upon the great state bell that the founder lavished his more daring skill. In vain did some of the less elated magistrates here caution him; saying that though truly the tower was Titanic, yet limit should be set to the dependent weight of its swaying masses. But undeterred, he prepared his mammoth mold, dented with mythological devices; kindled his fires of balsamic firs; melted his tin and copper, and, throwing in much plate, contributed by the public spirit of the nobles, let loose the tide.

The unleashed metals bayed like hounds. The workmen shrunk. Through their fright, fatal harm to the bell was dreaded. Fearless as Shadrach, Bannadonna, rushing through the glow, smote the chief culprit with his ponderous ladle. From the smitten part, a splinter was dashed into the seething mass, and at once was melted in.

Next day a portion of the work was heedfully uncovered. All seemed right. Upon the third morning, with equal satisfaction, it was bared still lower. At length, like some old Theban king, the whole cooled casting was disinterred. All was fair except in one strange spot. But as he suffered no one to attend him in these inspections, he concealed the blemish by some preparation which none knew better to devise.

The casting of such a mass was deemed no small triumph for the caster; one, too, in which the state might not scorn to share. The homicide was overlooked. By the charitable that deed was but imputed to sudden transports of esthetic passion, not to any flagitious quality. A kick from an Arabian charger; not sign of vice, but blood.

His felony remitted by the judge, absolution given him by the priest, what more could even a sickly conscience have desired!

Honoring the tower and its builder with another holiday, the republic witnessed the hoisting of the bells and clock-work amid shows and pomps superior to the former.

Some months of more than usual solitude on Bannadonna's part ensued. It was not unknown that he was engaged upon something for the belfry, intended to complete it, and surpass all that had gone before. Most people imagined that the design would involve a casting like the bells. But those who thought they had some further insight, would shake their heads, with hints, that not for nothing did the mechanician keep so secret. Meantime, his seclusion failed not to invest his work with more or less of that sort of mystery pertaining to the forbidden.

Ere long he had a heavy object hoisted to the belfry, wrapped in a dark sack or cloak—a procedure sometimes had in the case of an elaborate piece of sculpture, or statue, which, being intended to grace the front of a new edifice, the architect does not desire exposed to critical eyes, till set up, finished, in its appointed place. Such was the impression now. But, as the object rose, a statuary present observed, or thought he did, that it was not entirely rigid, but was, in a manner, pliant. At last, when the hidden thing had attained its final height, and, obscurely seen from below, seemed almost of itself to step into the belfry, as if with little assistance from the crane, a shrewd old blacksmith present ventured the suspicion that it was but a living man. This surmise was thought a foolish one, while the general interest failed not to augment.

Not without demur from Bannadonna, the chief magistrate of the town, with an associate—both elderly men—followed what seemed the image up the tower. But, arrived at the belfry, they had little recompense. Plausibly entrenching himself behind the conceded mysteries of his art, the mechanician withheld present explanation. The magistrates glanced toward the cloaked object, which, to their surprise, seemed now to have changed its attitude, or else had before been more perplexingly concealed by the violent muffling action of the wind without. It seemed now seated upon some sort of frame, or chair, contained within the domino. They observed that nigh the top, in a sort of square, the web of the cloth, either from accident or design, had its warp partly withdrawn, and the cross threads plucked out here and there, so as to form a sort of woven grating. Whether it were the low wind or no, stealing through the stone lattice-work, or only their own perturbed imaginations, is uncertain, but they thought they discerned a slight sort of fitful, spring-like motion in the domino. Nothing, however incidental or insignificant, escaped their uneasy eyes. Among other things, they pried out, in a corner, an earthen cup, partly corroded and partly encrusted, and one whispered to the other, that this cup was just such a one as might, in mockery, be offered to the lips of some brazen statue, or, perhaps, still worse.

But, being questioned, the mechanician said, that the cup was simply used in his founder's business, and described the purpose; in short, a cup to test the condition of metals in fusion. He added, that it had got into the belfry by the merest chance.

Again, and again they gazed at the domino, as at some suspicious incognito at a Venetian masque. All sorts of vague apprehensions stirred them. They even dreaded lest, when they should descend, the mechanician, though without a flesh and blood companion, for all that, would not be left alone.

Affecting some merriment at their disquietude, he begged to relieve them, by extending a coarse sheet of workman's canvas between them and the object.

Meantime he sought to interest them in his other work; nor, now that the domino was out of sight, did they long remain insensible to the artistic wonders lying round them; wonders hitherto beheld but in their unfinished state; because, since hoisting the bells, none but the caster had entered within the belfry. It was one trait of his, that, even in details, he would not let another do what he could, without too great loss of time, accomplish for himself. So, for several preceding weeks, whatever hours were unemployed in his secret design, had been devoted to elaborating the figures on the bells.

The clock-bell, in particular, now drew attention. Under a patient chisel, the latent beauty of its enrichments, before obscured by the cloudings incident to casting, that beauty in its shyest grace, was now revealed. Round and round the bell, twelve figures of gay girls, garlanded, hand-in-hand, danced in a choral ring—the embodied hours.

"Bannadonna," said the chief, "this bell excels all else. No added touch could here improve. Hark!" hearing a sound, "was that the wind?"

"The wind, Excellenza," was the light response. "But the figures, they are not yet without their faults. They need some touches yet. When those are given, and the—block yonder," pointing towards the canvas screen, "when Haman there, as I merrily call him—him? *it*, I mean—when Haman is fixed on this, his lofty tree, then, gentlemen, will I be most happy to receive you here again."

The equivocal reference to the object caused some return of restlessness. However, on their part, the visitors forbore further allusion to it, unwilling, perhaps, to let the foundling see how easily it lay within his plebeian art to stir the placid dignity of nobles.

"Well, Bannadonna," said the chief, "how long ere you are ready to set the clock going, so that the hour shall be sounded? Our interest in you, not less than in the work itself, makes us anxious to be assured of your success. The people, too—why, they are shouting now. Say the exact hour when you will be ready."

"Tomorrow, Excellenza, if you listen for it—or should you not, all the same—strange music will be heard. The stroke of one shall be the first from yonder bell," pointing to the bell, adorned with girls and garlands, "that stroke shall fall there, where the hand of Una clasps Dua's. The stroke of one shall sever that loved clasp. Tomorrow, then, at one o'clock, as struck here, precisely here," advancing and placing his finger upon the clasp, "the poor mechanic will be most happy once more to give you liege audience, in this his littered shop. Farewell till then, illustrious magnificoes, and hark ye for your vassal's stroke."

His still, Vulcanic face hiding its burning brightness like a forge, he moved with ostentatious deference towards the scuttle, as if so far to escort their exit. But the junior magistrate, a kind-hearted man, troubled at what seemed to him a certain sardonical disdain, lurking beneath the foundling's humble mien, and in Christian sympathy more distressed at it on his account than on his own, dimly surmising what might be the final fate of such a cynic solitaire, nor perhaps uninfluenced by the general strangeness of surrounding things, this good magistrate had glanced sadly, sideways from the speaker, and thereupon his foreboding eye had started at the expression of the unchanging face of the Hour Una.

"How is this, Bannadonna?" he lowly asked, "Una looks unlike her sisters."

"In Christ's name, Bannadonna," impulsively broke in the chief, his attention for the first attracted to the figure, by his associate's remark, "Una's face looks just like that of Deborah, the prophetess, as painted by the Florentine, Del Fonca."

"Surely, Bannadonna," lowly resumed the milder magistrate, "you meant the twelve should wear the same jocundly abandoned air. But see, the smile of Una seems but a fatal one. 'Tis different."

While his mild associate was speaking, the chief glanced, inquiringly from him to the caster, as if anxious to mark how the discrepancy would be accounted for. As the chief stood, his advanced foot was on the scuttle's curb.

Bannadonna spoke:

"Excellenza, now that, following your keener eye, I glance upon the face of Una, I do, indeed perceive some little variance. But look all round the bell, and you will find no two faces entirely correspond. Because there is a law in art——but the cold wind is rising more; these lattices are but a poor defense. Suffer me, magnificoes, to conduct you, at least, partly on your way. Those in whose well-being there is a public stake, should be heedfully attended."

"Touching the look of Una, you were saying, Bannadonna, that there was a certain law in art," observed the chief, as the three now descended the stone shaft, "pray, tell me, then—— "

"Pardon; another time, Excellenza;—the tower is damp."

"Nay, I must rest, and hear it now. Here—here is a wide landing, and through this leeward slit, no wind, but ample light. Tell us of your law; and at large."

"Since, Excellenza, you insist, know that there is a law in art, which bars the possibility of duplicates. Some years ago, you may remember, I graved a small seal for your republic, bearing, for its chief device, the head of your own ancestor, its illustrious founder. It becoming necessary, for the customs' use, to have innumerable impressions for bales and boxes, I graved an entire plate, containing one hundred of the seals. Now, though, indeed, my object was to have those hundred heads identical, and though, I dare say, people think them so, yet, upon closely scanning an uncut impression from the plate, no two of those five-score faces, side by side, will be found alike. Gravity is the air of all; but, diversified in all. In some, benevolent; in some, ambiguous; in two or three, to a close scrutiny, all but incipiently malign, the variation of less than a hair's breadth in the linear shadings round the mouth sufficing to all this. Now, Excellenza, transmute that general gravity into joyousness, and subject it to twelve of those variations I have described, and tell me, will you not have my hours here, and Una one of them? But I like——."

"Hark! is that—a footfall above?"

"Mortar, Excellenza; sometimes it drops to the belfry-floor from the arch where the stonework was left undressed. I must have it seen to. As I was about to say: for one, I like this law forbidding duplicates. It evokes fine personalities. Yes, Excellenza, that strange, and—to you—uncertain smile, and those fore-looking eyes of Una, suit Bannadonna very well."

"Hark!—sure we left no soul above?"

"No soul, Excellenza; rest assured, no *soul*.—Again the mortar."

"It fell not while we were there."

"Ah, in your presence, it better knew its place, Excellenza," blandly bowed Bannadonna.

"But Una," said the milder magistrate, "she seemed intently gazing on you; one would have almost sworn that she picked you out from among us three."

"If she did, possibly, it might have been her finer apprehension, Excellenza."

"How, Bannadonna? I do not understand you."

"No consequence, no consequence, Excellenza—but the shifted wind is blowing through the slit. Suffer me to escort you on, and then, pardon, but the toiler must to his tools."

"It may be foolish, Signor," said the milder magistrate, as, from the third landing, the two now went down unescorted, "but, somehow, our great mechanician moves me strangely. Why, just now, when he so superciliously replied, his walk seemed Sisera's, God's vain foe, in Del Fonca's painting. And that young, sculptured Deborah, too. Aye, and that——."

"Tush, tush, Signor!" returned the chief. "A passing whim. Deborah?—Where's Jael, pray?"

"Ah," said the other, as they now stepped upon the sod, "ah, Signor, I see you leave your fears behind you with the chill and gloom; but mine, even in this sunny air, remain. Hark!"

It was a sound from just within the tower door, whence they had emerged. Turning, they saw it closed.

"He has slipped down and barred us out," smiled the chief; "but it is his custom."

Proclamation was now made, that the next day, at one hour after meridian, the clock would strike, and—thanks to the mechanician's powerful art—with unusual accompaniments. But what those should be, none as yet could say. The announcement was received with cheers.

By the looser sort, who encamped about the tower all night, lights were seen gleaming through the topmost blind-work, only disappearing with the morning sun. Strange sounds, too, were heard, or were thought to be, by those whom anxious watching might not have left mentally undisturbed—sounds, not only of some ringing implement, but also—so they said—half-suppressed screams and plainings, such as might have issued from some ghostly engine, overplied.

Slowly the day drew on; part of the concourse chasing the weary time with songs and games, till, at last, the great blurred sun rolled, like a football, against the plain.

At noon, the nobility and principal citizens came from the town in cavalcade; a guard of soldiers, also, with music, the more to honor the occasion.

Only one hour more. Impatience grew. Watches were held in hands of feverish men, who stood, now scrutinizing their small dial-plates, and then, with neck thrown back, gazing toward the belfry, as if the eve might foretell that which could only be made sensible to the ear; for, as yet, there was no dial to the tower-clock.

The hour-hands of a thousand watches now verged within a hair's breadth of the figure I. A silence, as of the expectation of some Shiloh, pervaded the swarming plain. Suddenly a dull, mangled sound—naught ringing in it; scarcely audible, indeed, to the outer circles of the people—that dull sound dropped heavily from the belfry. At the same moment, each man stared at his neighbor blankly. All watches were upheld. All hour-hands were at—had passed—the figure I. No bell-stroke from the tower. The multitude became tumultuous.

Waiting a few moments, the chief magistrate, commanding silence, hailed the belfry, to know what thing unforeseen had happened there.

No response.

He hailed again and yet again.

All continued hushed.

By his order, the soldiers burst in the tower-door; when, stationing guards to defend it from the now surging mob, the chief, accompanied by his former associate, climbed the winding stairs. Half-way up, they stopped to listen. No sound. Mounting faster, they reached the belfry; but, at the threshold, started at the spectacle disclosed. A spaniel, which, unbeknown to them, had followed them thus far, stood shivering as before some unknown monster in a brake: or, rather, as if it snuffed footsteps leading to some other world.

Bannadonna lay, prostrate and bleeding, at the base of the bell which was adorned with girls and garlands. He lay at the feet of the hour Una; his head coinciding, in a vertical line, with her left hand, clasped by the hour Dua. With downcast face impending over him, like Jael over nailed Sisera in the tent, was the domino; now no more becloaked.

It had limbs, and seemed clad in a scaly mail, lustrous as a dragon-beetle's. It was manacled, and its clubbed arms were uplifted, as if, with its manacles, once more to smite its already smitten victim. One advanced foot of it was inserted beneath the dead body, as if in the act of spurning it.

Uncertainty falls on what now followed.

It were but natural to suppose that the magistrates would, at first, shrink from immediate personal contact with what they saw. At the least, for a time, they would stand in involuntary doubt; it may be, in more or less of horrified alarm. Certain it is, that an arquebuss was called for from below. And some add, that its report, followed by a fierce whiz, as of the sudden snapping of a main-spring, with a steely din, as if a stack of sword-blades should be dashed upon a pavement, these blended sounds came ringing to the plain, attracting every eye far upward to the belfry, whence, through the lattice-work, thin wreaths of smoke were curling.

Some averred that it was the spaniel, gone mad by fear, which was shot. This, others denied. True it was, the spaniel never more was seen; and, probably, for some unknown reason, it shared the burial now to be related of the domino. For, whatever the preceding circumstances may have been, the first instinctive panic over, or else all ground of reasonable fear removed, the two magistrates, by themselves, quickly rehooded the figure in the dropped cloak wherein it had been hoisted. The same night, it was secretly lowered to the ground, smuggled to the beach, pulled far out to sea, and sunk. Nor to any after urgency, even in free convivial hours, would the twain ever disclose the full secrets of the belfry.

From the mystery unavoidably investing it, the popular solution of the foundling's fate involved more or less of supernatural agency. But some few less unscientific minds pretended to find little difficulty in otherwise accounting for it. In the chain of circumstantial inferences drawn, there may, or may not, have been some absent or defective links. But, as the explanation in question is the only one which tradition has explicitly preserved, in dearth of better, it will here be given. But, in the first place, it is requisite to present the supposition entertained as to the entire motive and mode, with their origin, of the secret design of Bannadonna; the minds above-mentioned assuming to penetrate as well into his soul as into the event. The disclosure will indirectly involve reference to peculiar matters, none of the clearest, beyond the immediate subject.

At that period, no large bell was made to sound otherwise than as at present, by agitation of a tongue within, by means of ropes, or percussion from without, either from cumbrous machinery, or stalwart watchmen, armed with heavy hammers, stationed in the belfry, or in sentry-boxes on the open roof, according as the bell was sheltered or exposed.

It was from observing these exposed bells, with their watchmen, that the foundling, as was opined, derived the first suggestion of his scheme. Perched on a great mast or spire, the human figure, viewed from below, undergoes such a reduction in its apparent size, as to obliterate its intelligent features. It evinces no personality. Instead of bespeaking volition, its gestures rather resemble the automatic ones of the arms of a telegraph.

Musing, therefore, upon the purely Punchinello aspect of the human figure thus beheld, it had indirectly occurred to Bannadonna to devise some metallic agent, which should strike the hour with its mechanic hand, with even greater precision than the vital one. And, moreover, as the vital watchman on the roof, sallying from his retreat at the given periods, walked to the bell with uplifted mace, to smite it, Bannadonna had resolved that his invention should likewise possess the power of locomotion, and, along with that, the appearance, at least, of intelligence and will.

If the conjectures of those who claimed acquaintance with the intent of Bannadonna be thus far correct, no unenterprising spirit could have been his. But they stopped not here; intimating that though, indeed, his design had, in the first place, been prompted by the sight of the watchman, and confined to the devising of a subtle substitute for him: yet, as is not seldom the case with projectors, by insensible gradations, proceeding from comparatively pigmy aims to titanic ones, the original scheme had, in its anticipated eventualities, at last, attained to an unheard-of degree of daring. He still bent his efforts upon the locomotive figure for the belfry, but only as a partial type of an ulterior creature, a sort of elephantine Helot, adapted to further, in a degree scarcely to be imagined, the universal conveniences and glories of humanity; supplying nothing less than a supplement to the Six Days' Work; stocking the earth with a new serf, more useful than the ox, swifter than the dolphin, stronger than the lion, more cunning than the ape, for industry an ant, more fiery than serpents, and yet, in patience, another ass. All excellences of all God-made creatures, which served man, were here to receive advancement, and then to be combined in one. Talus was to have been the all-accomplished Helot's name. Talus, iron slave to Bannadonna, and, through him, to man.

Here, it might well be thought that, were these last conjectures as to the foundling's secrets not erroneous, then must he have been hopelessly infected with the craziest chimeras of his age; far outgoing Albert Magus and Cornelius Agrippa. But the contrary was averred. However marvelous his design, however apparently transcending not alone the bounds of human invention, but those of divine creation, yet the proposed means to be employed were alleged to have been confined within the sober forms of sober reason. It was affirmed that, to a degree of more than skeptic scorn, Bannadonna had been without sympathy for any of the vain-glorious irrationalities of his time. For example, he had not concluded, with the visionaries among the metaphysicians, that between the finer mechanic forces and the ruder animal vitality some germ of correspondence might prove discoverable.

As little did his scheme partake of the enthusiasm of some natural philosophers, who hoped, by physiological and chemical inductions, to arrive at a knowledge of the source of life, and so qualify themselves to manufacture and improve upon it. Much less had he aught in common with the tribe of alchemists, who sought, by a species of incantations to evoke some surprising vitality from the laboratory. Neither had he imagined, with certain sanguine theosophists, that, by faithful adoration of the Highest, unheard of powers would be vouchsafed to man. A practical materialist, what Bannadonna had aimed at was to have been reached, not by logic, not by crucible, not by conjuration, not by altars; but by plain vise-bench and hammer. In short, to solve nature, to steal into her, to intrigue beyond her, to procure someone else to bind her to his hand; these, one and all, had not been his objects; but, asking no favors from any element or any being, of himself, to rival her, outstrip her, and rule her. He stooped to conquer. With him, common sense was theurgy; machinery, miracle; Prometheus, the heroic name for machinist; man, the true God.

Nevertheless, in his initial step, so far as the experimental automaton for the belfry was concerned, he allowed fancy some little play; or, perhaps, what seemed his fancifulness was but his utilitarian ambition collaterally extended. In figure, the creature for the belfry should not be likened after the human pattern, nor any animal one, nor after the ideals, however wild, of ancient fable, but equally in aspect as in organism be an original production; the more terrible to behold, the better.

Such, then, were the suppositions as to the present scheme, and the reserved intent. How, at the very threshold, so unlooked-for a catastrophe overturned all, or rather, what was the conjecture here, is now to be set forth.

It was thought that on the day preceding the fatality, his visitors having left him, Bannadonna had unpacked the belfry image, adjusted it, and placed it in the retreat provided—a sort of sentry-box in one corner of the belfry; in short, through-out the night, and for some part of the ensuing morning, he had been engaged in arranging everything connected with the domino; the issuing from the sentry-box each sixty minutes; sliding along a grooved way, like a railway; advancing to the clock-bell, with uplifted manacles; striking it at one of the twelve junctions of the four-and-twenty hands; then wheeling, circling the bell and retiring to its post, there to bide for another sixty minutes, when the same process was to be repeated; the bell, by a cunning mechanism, meantime turning on its vertical axis, so as to present, to the descending mace, the clasped hands of the next two figures, when it would strike two, three, and so on, to the end. The musical metal in this time-bell being so managed in the fusion, by some art, perishing with its originator, that each of the clasps of the four-and-twenty hands should give forth its own peculiar resonance when parted.

But on the magic metal, the magic and metallic stranger never struck but that one stroke, drove but that one nail, severed but that one clasp, by which Bannadonna clung to his ambitious life. For, after winding up the creature in the sentry-box, so that, for the present, skipping the intervening hours, it should not emerge till the hour of one, but should then infallibly emerge, and, after deftly oiling the grooves whereon it was to slide, it was surmised that the mechanician must then have hurried to the bell, to give his final touches to its sculpture. True artist, he here became absorbed; and absorption still further intensified, it may be, by his striving to abate that strange look of Una; which, though, before others, he had treated with such unconcern, might not, in secret, have been without its thorn.

And so, for the interval, he was oblivious of his creature; which, not oblivious of him, and true to its creation, and true to its heedful winding up, left its post precisely at the given moment; along its well-oiled route, slid noiselessly towards its mark; and, aiming at the hand of Una, to ring one clangorous note, dully smote the intervening brain of Bannadonna, turned backwards to it; the manacled arms then instantly up-springing to their hovering poise. The falling body clogged the thing's return; so, there it stood, still impending over Bannadonna, as if whispering some post-mortem terror. The chisel lay dropped from the hand, but beside the hand; the oil-flask spilled across the iron track.

In his unhappy end, not unmindful of the rare genius of the mechanician, the republic decreed him a stately funeral. It was resolved that the great bell—the one whose casting had been jeopardized through the timidity of the ill-starred workman—should be rung upon the entrance of the bier into the cathedral. The most robust man of the country round was assigned the office of bell-ringer.

But as the pall-bearers entered the cathedral porch, naught but a broken and disastrous sound, like that of some lone Alpine land-slide, fell from the tower upon their ears. And then all was hushed.

Glancing backwards, they saw the groined belfry crashed sideways in. It afterwards appeared that the powerful peasant, who had the bell-rope in charge, wishing to test at once the full glory of the bell, had swayed down upon the rope with one concentrate jerk. The mass of quaking metal, too ponderous for its frame, and strangely feeble somewhere at its top, loosed from its fastening, tore sideways down, and tumbling in one sheer fall, three hundred feet to the soft sward below, buried itself inverted and half out of sight.

Upon its disinterment, the main fracture was found to have started from a small spot in the ear; which, being scraped, revealed a defect, deceptively minute, in the casting; which defect must subsequently have been pasted over with some unknown compound.

The remolten metal soon reassumed its place in the tower's repaired superstructure. For one year the metallic choir of birds sang musically in its belfry bough-work of sculptured blinds and traceries. But on the first anniversary of the tower's completion—at early dawn, before the concourse had surrounded it—an earthquake came; one loud crash was heard. The stone-pine, with all its bower of songsters, lay overthrown upon the plain.

So the blind slave obeyed its blinder lord; but, in obedience, slew him. So the creator was killed by the creature. So the bell was too heavy for the tower. So the bell's main weakness was where man's blood had flawed it. And so pride went before the fall.

# THE FIDDLER

### Herman Melville

So MY POEM is damned, and immortal fame is not for me! I am nobody forever and ever. Intolerable fate!

Snatching my hat, I dashed down the criticism, and rushed out into Broadway, where enthusiastic throngs were crowding to a circus in a side-street nearby, very recently started, and famous for a capital clown.

Presently my old friend Standard rather boisterously accosted me.

"Well met, Helmstone, my boy! Ah! what's the matter? Haven't been committing murder? Ain't flying justice? You look wild!"

"You have seen it, then?" said I, of course referring to the criticism.

"Oh yes; I was there at the morning performance. Great clown, I assure you. But here comes Hautboy. Hautboy—Helmstone."

Without having time or inclination to resent so mortifying a mistake, I was instantly soothed as I gazed on the face of the new acquaintance so unceremoniously introduced. His person was short and full, with a juvenile, animated cast to it. His complexion rurally ruddy; his eye sincere, cheery, and gray. His hair alone betrayed that he was not an overgrown boy. From his hair I set him down as forty or more.

"Come, Standard," he gleefully cried to my friend, "are you not going to the circus? The clown is inimitable, they say. Come; Mr. Helmstone, too—come both; and circus over, we'll take a nice stew and punch at Taylor's."

The sterling content, good humor, and extraordinary ruddy, sincere expression of this most singular new acquaintance acted upon me like magic. It seemed mere loyalty to human nature to accept an invitation from so unmistakably kind and honest a heart.

During the circus performance I kept my eye more on Hautboy than on the celebrated clown. Hautboy was the sight for me. Such genuine enjoyment as his struck me to the soul with a sense of the reality of the thing called happiness. The jokes of the clown he seemed to roll under his tongue as ripe magnum bonums. Now the foot, now the hand, was employed to attest his grateful applause. If any hit more than ordinary, he turned upon Standard and me to see if his rare pleasure was shared. In a man of forty I saw a boy of twelve; and this too without the slightest abatement of my respect. Because all was so honest and natural, every expression and attitude so graceful with genuine good nature, that the marvelous juvenility of Hautboy assumed a sort of divine and immortal air, like that of some forever youthful god of Greece.

But much as I gazed upon Hautboy, and much as I admired his air, yet that desperate mood in which I had first rushed from the house had not so entirely departed as not to molest me with momentary returns. But from these relapses I would rouse myself, and swiftly glance round the broad amphitheatre of eagerly interested and all-applauding human faces. Hark! claps, thumps, deafening huzzas; the vast assembly seemed frantic with acclamation; and what, mused I, has caused all this? Why, the clown only comically grinned with one of his extra grins.

Then I repeated in my mind that sublime passage in my poem, in which Cleothemes the Argive vindicates the justice of the war. Aye, aye, thought I to myself, did I now leap into the ring there, and repeat that identical passage, nay, enact the whole tragic poem before them, would they applaud the poet as they applaud the clown? No! They would hoot me, and call me doting or mad. Then what does this prove? Your infatuation or their insensibility? Perhaps both; but indubitably the first. But why wail? Do you seek admiration from the admirers of a buffoon? Call to mind the saying of the Athenian, who, when the people vociferously applauded in the forum, asked his friend in a whisper what foolish thing had he said?

Again my eye swept the circus, and fell on the ruddy radiance of the countenance of Hautboy. But its clear honest cheeriness disdained my disdain. My intolerant pride was rebuked. And yet Hautboy dreamed not what magic reproof to a soul like mine sat on his laughing brow. At the very instant I felt the dart of the censure, his eye twinkled, his hand waved, his voice was lifted in jubilant delight at another joke of the inexhaustible clown.

Circus over, we went to Taylor's. Among crowds of others, we sat down to our stews and punches at one of the small marble tables. Hautboy sat opposite to me. Though greatly subdued from its former hilarity, his face still shone with gladness. But added to this was a quality not so prominent before: a certain serene expression of leisurely, deep good sense. Good sense and good humor in him joined hands. As the conversation proceeded between the brisk Standard and him— for I said little or nothing—I was more and more struck with the excellent judgment he evinced. In most of his remarks upon a variety of topics Hautboy seemed intuitively to hit the exact line between enthusiasm and apathy. It was plain that while Hautboy saw the world pretty much as it was, yet he did not theoretically espouse its bright side nor its dark side. Rejecting all solutions, he but acknowledged facts. What was sad in the world he did not superficially gainsay; what was glad in it he did not cynically slur; and all which was to him personally enjoyable, he gratefully took to his heart. It was plain, then—so it seemed at that moment, at least—that his extraordinary cheerfulness did not arise either from deficiency of feeling or thought.

Suddenly remembering an engagement, he took up his hat, bowed pleasantly, and left us.

"Well, Helmstone," said Standard, inaudibly drumming on the slab, "what do you think of your new acquaintance?"

The two last words tingled with a peculiar and novel significance.

"New acquaintance indeed," echoed I. "Standard, I owe you a thousand thanks for introducing me to one of the most singular men I have ever seen. It needed the optical sight of such a man to believe in the possibility of his existence."

"You rather like him, then," said Standard, with ironical dryness.

"I hugely love and admire him, Standard. I wish I were Hautboy."

"Ah? That's a pity, now. There's only one Hautboy in the world."

This last remark set me to pondering again, and somehow it revived my dark mood.

"His wonderful cheerfulness, I suppose," said I, sneering with spleen, "originates not less in a felicitous fortune than in a felicitous temper. His great good sense is apparent; but great good sense may exist without sublime endowments. Nay, I take it, in certain cases, that good sense is simply owing to the absence of those. Much more, cheerfulness. Unpossessed of genius, Hautboy is eternally blessed."

"Ah? You would not think him an extraordinary genius, then?"

"Genius? What! such a short, fat fellow a genius! Genius, like Cassius, is lank."

"Ah? But could you not fancy that Hautboy might formerly have had genius, but luckily getting rid of it, at last fatted up?"

"For a genius to get rid of his genius is as impossible as for a man in the galloping consumption to get rid of that."

"Ah? You speak very decidedly."

"Yes, Standard," cried I, increasing in spleen, "your cheery Hautboy, after all, is no pattern, no lesson for you and me. With average abilities; opinions clear, because circumscribed; passions docile, because they are feeble; a temper hilarious, because he was born to it—how can your Hautboy be made a reasonable example to a heady fellow like you, or an ambitious dreamer like me? Nothing tempts him beyond common limit; in himself he has nothing to restrain. By constitution he is exempted from all moral harm. Could ambition but prick him; had he but once heard applause, or endured contempt, a very different man would your Hautboy be. Acquiescent and calm from the cradle to the grave, he obviously slides through the crowd."

"Ah?"

"Why do you say Ah to me so strangely whenever I speak?"

"Did you ever hear of Master Betty?"

"The great English prodigy, who long ago ousted the Siddons and the Kembles from Drury Lane, and made the whole town run mad with acclamation?"

"The same," said Standard, once more inaudibly drumming on the slab.

I looked at him perplexed. He seemed to be holding the master-key of our theme in mysterious reserve; seemed to be throwing out his Master Betty, too, to puzzle me only the more.

"What under heaven can Master Betty, the great genius and prodigy, an English boy twelve years old, have to do with the poor commonplace plodder, Hautboy, an American of forty?"

"Oh, nothing in the least. I don't imagine that they ever saw each other. Besides, Master Betty must be dead and buried long ere this."

"Then why cross the ocean, and rifle the grave to drag his remains into this living discussion?"

"Absent-mindedness, I suppose. I humbly beg pardon. Proceed with your observations on Hautboy. You think he never had genius, quite too contented, and happy and fat for that—ah? You think him no pattern for men in general? affording no lesson of value to neglected merit, genius ignored, or impotent presumption rebuked?—all of which three amount to much the same thing. You admire his cheerfulness, while scorning his commonplace soul. Poor Hautboy, how sad that your very cheerfulness should, by a by-blow, bring you despite!"

"I don't say I scorn him; you are unjust. I simply declare that he is no pattern for me."

A sudden noise at my side attracted my ear. Turning, I saw Hautboy again, who very blithely reseated himself on the chair he had left.

"I was behind time with my engagement," said Hautboy, "so thought I would run back and rejoin you. But come, you have sat long enough here. Let us go to my rooms. It is only a five minutes' walk."

"If you will promise to fiddle for us, we will," said Standard.

Fiddle! thought I—he's a jiggumbob *fiddler*, then? No wonder genius declines to measure its pace to a fiddler's bow. My spleen was very strong on me now.

"I will gladly fiddle you your fill," replied Hautboy to Standard. "Come on."

In a few minutes we found ourselves in the fifth story of a sort of storehouse, in a lateral street to Broadway. It was curiously furnished with all sorts of odd furniture which seemed to have been obtained, piece by piece, at auctions of old-fashioned household stuff. But all was charmingly clean and cozy.

Pressed by Standard, Hautboy forthwith got out his dented old fiddle and, sitting down on a tall rickety stool, played away right merrily at "Yankee Doodle" and other off-handed, dashing, and disdainfully care-free airs. But common as were the tunes, I was transfixed by something miraculously superior in the style. Sitting there on the old stool, his rusty hat sideways cocked on his head, one foot dangling adrift, he plied the bow of an enchanter. All my moody discontent, every vestige of peevishness, fled. My whole splenetic soul capitulated to the magical fiddle.

"Something of an Orpheus, ah?" said Standard, archly nudging me beneath the left rib.

"And I, the charmed Bruin," murmured I.

The fiddle ceased. Once more, with redoubled curiosity, I gazed upon the easy, indifferent Hautboy. But he entirely baffled inquisition.

When, leaving him, Standard and I were in the street once more, I earnestly conjured him to tell me who, in sober truth, this marvelous Hautboy was.

"Why, haven't you seen him? And didn't you yourself lay his whole anatomy open on the marble slab at Taylor's? What more can you possibly learn? Doubtless, your own masterly insight has already put you in possession of all."

"You mock me, Standard. There is some mystery here. Tell me, I entreat you, who is Hautboy?"

"An extraordinary genius, Helmstone," said Standard, with sudden ardor, "who in boyhood drained the whole flagon of glory; whose going from city to city was a going from triumph to triumph. One who has been an object of wonder to the wisest, been caressed by the loveliest, received the open homage of thousands on thousands of the rabble. But today he walks Broadway and no man knows him. With you and me, the elbow of the hurrying clerk, and the pole of the remorseless omnibus, shove him. He who has a hundred times been crowned with laurels, now wears, as you see, a bunged beaver. Once fortune poured showers of gold into his lap, as showers of laurel leaves upon his brow. Today, from house to house he hies, teaching fiddling for a living. Crammed once with fame, he is now hilarious without it. *With* genius and *without* fame, he is happier than a king. More a prodigy now than ever."

"His true name?"

"Let me whisper it in your ear."

"What! Oh, Standard, myself, as a child, have shouted myself hoarse applauding that very name in the theatre."

"I have heard your poem was not very handsomely received," said Standard, now suddenly shifting the subject.

"Not a word of that, for Heaven's sake!" cried I. "If Cicero, traveling in the East, found sympathetic solace for his grief in beholding the arid overthrow of a once gorgeous city, shall not my petty affair be as nothing, when I behold in Hautboy the vine and the rose climbing the shattered shafts of his tumbled temple of Fame?"

Next day I tore all my manuscripts, bought me a fiddle, and went to take regular lessons of Hautboy.

# WHAT WAS IT?

## Fitz-James O'Brien

It is, I confess, with considerable diffidence that I approach the strange narrative which I am about to relate. The events which I purpose detailing are of so extraordinary a character that I am quite prepared to meet with an unusual amount of incredulity and scorn. I accept all such beforehand. I have, I trust, the literary courage to face unbelief. I have, after mature consideration, resolved to narrate, in as simple and straightforward a manner as I can compass, some facts that passed under my observation, in the month of July last, and which, in the annals of the mysteries of physical science, are wholly unparalleled.

I live at No.—Twenty-sixth Street, in New York. The house is in some respects a curious one. It has enjoyed for the last two years the reputation of being haunted. It is a large and stately residence, surrounded by what was once a garden, but which is now only a green enclosure used for bleaching clothes. The dry basin of what has been a fountain, and a few fruit trees ragged and unpruned, indicate that this spot in past days was a pleasant, shady retreat, filled with fruits and flowers and the sweet murmur of waters.

The house is very spacious. A hall of noble size leads to a large spiral staircase winding through its centre, while the various apartments are of imposing dimensions. It was built some fifteen or twenty years since by Mr. A——, the well-known New York merchant, who five years ago threw the commercial world into convulsions by a stupendous bank fraud. Mr. A——, as everyone knows, escaped to Europe, and died not long after, of a broken heart. Almost immediately after the news of his decease reached this country and was verified, the report spread in Twenty-sixth Street that No.—was haunted. Legal measures had dispossessed the widow of its former owner, and it was inhabited merely by a caretaker and his wife, placed there by the house agent into whose hands it had passed for purposes of renting or sale. These people declared that they were troubled with unnatural noises. Doors were opened without any visible agency. The remnants of furniture scattered through the various rooms, were, during the night, piled one upon the other by unknown hands. Invisible feet passed up and down the stairs in broad daylight, accompanied by the rustle of unseen silk dresses, and the gliding of viewless hands along the massive balusters. The caretaker and his wife declared they would live there no longer. The house agent laughed, dismissed them, and put others in their place. The noises and supernatural manifestations continued. The neighborhood caught up the story, and the house remained untenanted for three years. Several persons negotiated for it; but, somehow, always before the bargain was closed they heard the unpleasant rumors and declined to treat any further.

It was in this state of things that my landlady, who at that time kept a boarding-house in Bleecker Street, and who wished to move further up town, conceived the bold idea of renting No.—Twenty-sixth Street. Happening to have in her house rather a plucky and philosophical set of boarders, she laid her scheme before us, stating candidly everything she had heard respecting the ghostly qualities of the establishment to which she wished to remove us. With the exception of two timid persons—a sea-captain and a returned Californian, who immediately gave notice that they would leave—all of Mrs. Moffat's guests declared that they would accompany her in her chivalric incursion into the abode of spirits.

Our removal was effected in the month of May, and we were charmed with our new residence. The portion of Twenty-sixth Street where our house is situated, between Seventh and Eighth Avenues, is one of the pleasantest localities in New York. The gardens back of the houses, running down nearly to the Hudson, form, in the summer time, a perfect avenue of verdure. The air is pure and invigorating, sweeping, as it does, straight across the river from the Weehawken heights, and even the ragged garden which surrounded the house, although displaying on washing days rather too much clothesline, still gave us a piece of greensward to look at, and a cool retreat in the summer evenings, where we smoked our cigars in the dusk, and watched the fireflies flashing their dark lanterns in the long grass.

Of course we had no sooner established ourselves at No.—than we began to expect the ghosts. We absolutely awaited their advent with eagerness. Our dinner conversation was supernatural. One of the boarders, who had purchased Mrs. Crowe's "Night Side of Nature" for his own private delectation, was regarded as a public enemy by the entire household for not having bought twenty copies. The man led a life of supreme wretchedness while he was reading this volume. A system of espionage was established, of which he was the victim. If he incautiously laid the book down for an instant and left the room, it was immediately seized and read aloud in secret places to a select few. I found myself a person of immense importance, it having leaked out that I was tolerably well versed in the history of supernaturalism, and had once written a story the foundation of which was a ghost. If a table or a wainscot panel happened to warp when we were assembled in the large drawing-room, there was an instant silence, and everyone was prepared for an immediate clanking of chains and a spectral form.

After a month of psychological excitement, it was with the utmost dissatisfaction that we were forced to acknowledge that nothing in the remotest degree approaching the supernatural had manifested itself. Once the black butler asseverated that his candle had been blown out by some invisible agency while he was undressing himself for the night; but as I had more than once discovered this colored gentleman in a condition when one candle must have appeared to him like two, I thought it possible that, by going a step further in his potations, he might have reversed this phenomenon, and seen no candle at all where he ought to have beheld one.

Things were in this state when an incident took place so awful and inexplicable in its character that my reason fairly reels at the bare memory of the occurrence. It was the tenth of July. After dinner was over I repaired, with my friend Dr. Hammond, to the garden to smoke my evening pipe. Independent of certain mental sympathies which existed between the Doctor and myself, we were linked together by a vice. We both smoked opium. We knew each other's secret, and respected it. We enjoyed together that wonderful expansion of thought, that marvellous intensifying of the perceptive faculties, that boundless feeling of existence when we seem to have points of contact with the whole universe—in short, that unimaginable spiritual bliss, which I would not surrender for a throne, and which I hope you, reader, will never—never taste.

Those hours of opium happiness which the Doctor and I spent together in secret were regulated with a scientific accuracy. We did not blindly smoke the drug of paradise, and leave our dreams to chance. While smoking, we carefully steered our conversation through the brightest and calmest channels of thought. We talked of the East, and endeavored to recall the magical panorama of its glowing scenery. We criticised the most sensuous poets—those who painted life ruddy with health, brimming with passion, happy in the possession of youth and strength and beauty. If we talked of Shakespeare's "Tempest," we lingered over Ariel, and avoided Caliban. Like the Guebers, we turned our faces to the east, and saw only the sunny side of the world.

This skillful coloring of our train of thought produced in our subsequent visions a corresponding tone. The splendors of Arabian fairyland dyed our dreams. We paced that narrow strip of grass with the tread and port of kings. The song of the *rana arborea*[1], while he clung to the bark of the ragged plum tree, sounded like the strains of divine musicians. Houses, walls, and streets melted like rain clouds, and vistas of unimaginable glory stretched away before us. It was a rapturous companionship. We enjoyed the vast delight more perfectly because, even in our most ecstatic moments, we were conscious of each other's presence. Our pleasures, while individual, were still twin, vibrating and moving in musical accord.

On the evening in question, the tenth of July, the Doctor and myself drifted into an unusually metaphysical mood. We lit our large meerschaums, filled with fine Turkish tobacco, in the core of which burned a little black nut of opium, that, like the nut in the fairy tale, held within its narrow limits wonders beyond the reach of kings; we paced to and fro, conversing. A strange perversity dominated the currents of our thought. They would *not* flow through the sun-lit channels into which we strove to divert them. For some unaccountable reason, they constantly diverged into dark and lonesome beds, where a continual gloom brooded. It was in vain that, after our old fashion, we flung ourselves on the shores of the East, and talked of its gay bazaars, of the splendors of the time of Haroun, of harems and golden palaces. Black afreets continually arose from the depths of our talk, and expanded, like the one the fisherman released from the copper vessel, until they blotted everything bright from our vision. Insensibly, we yielded to the occult force that swayed us, and indulged in gloomy speculation. We had talked some time upon the proneness of the human mind to mysticism, and the almost universal love of the terrible

---

[1] *rana arborea*; Italian: a small tree frog found in Europe, Asia, and parts of Africa.

when Hammond suddenly said to me, "What do you consider to be the greatest element of terror?"

The question puzzled me. That many things were terrible, I knew. Stumbling over a corpse in the dark; beholding, as I once did, a woman floating down a deep and rapid river, with wildly lifted arms, and awful, upturned face, uttering, as she drifted, shrieks that rent one's heart, while we, the spectators, stood frozen at a window which overhung the river at a height of sixty feet, unable to make the slightest effort to save her, but dumbly watching her last supreme agony and her disappearance. A shattered wreck, with no life visible, encountered floating listlessly on the ocean, is a terrible object, for it suggests a huge terror, the proportions of which are veiled. But it now struck me, for the first time, that there must be one great and ruling embodiment of fear—a King of Terrors, to which all others must succumb. What might it be? To what train of circumstances would it owe its existence?

"I confess, Hammond," I replied to my friend, "I never considered the subject before. That there must be one Something more terrible than any other thing, I feel. I cannot attempt, however, even the most vague definition."

"I am somewhat like you, Harry," he answered. "I feel my capacity to experience a terror greater than anything yet conceived by the human mind—something combining in fearful and unnatural amalgamation hitherto supposed incompatible elements. The calling of the voices in Brockden Brown's novel of 'Wieland' is awful; so is the picture of the Dweller of the Threshold, in Bulwer's 'Zanoni'; but," he added, shaking his head gloomily, "there is something more horrible still than these."

"Look here, Hammond," I rejoined, "let us drop this kind of talk, for heaven's sake! We shall suffer for it, depend on it."

"I don't know what's the matter with me tonight," he replied, "but my brain is running upon all sorts of weird and awful thoughts. I feel as if I could write a story like Hoffman, tonight, if I were only master of a literary style."

"Well, if we are going to be Hoffmanesque in our talk, I'm off to bed. Opium and nightmares should never be brought together. How sultry it is! Good-night, Hammond."

"Good-night, Harry. Pleasant dreams to you."

"To you, gloomy wretch, afreets, ghouls, and enchanters."

We parted, and each sought his respective chamber. I undressed quickly and got into bed, taking with me, according to my usual custom, a book, over which I generally read myself to sleep. I opened the volume as soon as I had laid my head upon the pillow, and instantly flung it to the other side of the room. It was Goudon's "History of Monsters," a curious French work, which I had lately imported from Paris, but which, in the state of mind I had then reached, was anything but an agreeable companion. I resolved to go to sleep at once; so, turning down my gas until nothing but a little blue point of light glimmered on the top of the tube, I composed myself to rest.

The room was in total darkness. The atom of gas that still remained alight did not illuminate a distance of three inches round the burner. I desperately drew my arm across my eyes, as if to shut out even the darkness, and tried to think of nothing. It was in vain. The confounded themes touched on by Hammond in the garden kept obtruding themselves on my brain. I battled against them. I erected ramparts of would-be blankness of intellect to keep them out. They still crowded upon me. While I was lying still as a corpse, hoping that by a perfect physical inaction I should hasten mental repose, an awful incident occurred. A Something dropped, as it seemed, from the ceiling, plumb upon my chest, and the next instant I felt two bony hands encircling my throat, endeavoring to choke me.

I am no coward, and am possessed of considerable physical strength. The suddenness of the attack, instead of stunning me, strung every nerve to its highest tension. My body acted from instinct, before my brain had time to realize the terrors of my position. In an instant I wound two muscular arms around the creature, and squeezed it, with all the strength of despair, against my chest. In a few seconds the bony hands that had fastened on my throat loosened their hold, and I was free to breathe once more. Then commenced a struggle of awful intensity. Immersed in the most profound darkness, totally ignorant of the nature of the Thing by which I was so suddenly attacked, finding my grasp slipping every moment, by reason, it seemed to me, of the entire nakedness of my assailant, bitten with sharp teeth in the shoulder, neck, and chest, having every moment to protect my throat against a pair of sinewy, agile hands, which my utmost efforts could not confine—these were a combination of circumstances to combat which required all the strength, skill, and courage that I possessed.

At last, after a silent, deadly, exhausting struggle, I got my assailant under by a series of incredible efforts of strength. Once pinned, with my knee on what I made out to be its chest, I knew that I was victor.

I rested for a moment to breathe. I heard the creature beneath me panting in the darkness, and felt the violent throbbing of a heart. It was apparently as exhausted as I was; that was one comfort. At this moment I remembered that I usually placed under my pillow, before going to bed, a large yellow silk pocket handkerchief. I felt for it instantly; it was there. In a few seconds more I had, after a fashion, pinioned the creature's arms.

I now felt tolerably secure. There was nothing more to be done but to turn on the gas, and, having first seen what my midnight assailant was like, arouse the household. I will confess to being actuated by a certain pride in not giving the alarm before; I wished to make the capture alone and unaided.

Never losing my hold for an instant, I slipped from the bed to the floor, dragging my captive with me. I had but a few steps to make to reach the gas burner; these I made with the greatest caution, holding the creature in a grip like a vise. At last I got within arm's length of the tiny speck of blue light which told me where the gas burner lay. Quick as lightning I released my grasp with one hand and let on the full flood of light. Then I turned to look at my captive.

I cannot even attempt to give any definition of my sensations the instant after I turned on the gas. I suppose I must have shrieked with terror, for in less than a minute afterward my room was crowded with the inmates of the house. I shudder now as I think of that awful moment. *I saw nothing!* Yes; I had one arm firmly clasped round a breathing, panting, corporeal shape, my other hand gripped with all its strength a throat as warm, and apparently fleshly, as my own; and yet, with this living substance in my grasp, with its body pressed against my own, and all in the bright glare of a large jet of gas, I absolutely beheld nothing! Not even an outline—a vapor!

I do not, even at this hour, realize the situation in which I found myself. I cannot recall the astounding incident thoroughly. Imagination in vain tries to compass the awful paradox.

It breathed. I felt its warm breath upon my cheek. It struggled fiercely. It had hands. They clutched me. Its skin was smooth, like my own. There it lay, pressed close up against me, solid as stone—and yet utterly invisible!

I wonder that I did not faint or go mad on the instant. Some wonderful instinct must have sustained me; for, absolutely, in place of loosening my hold on the terrible Enigma, I seemed to gain an additional strength in my moment of horror, and tightened my grasp with such wonderful force that I felt the creature shivering with agony.

Just then Hammond entered my room at the head of the household. As soon as he beheld my face—which, I suppose, must have been an awful sight to look at—he hastened forward, crying, "Great heaven, Harry! what has happened?"

"Hammond! Hammond!" I cried, "come here. O, this is awful! I have been attacked in bed by something or other, which I have hold of; but I can't see it—I can't see it!"

Hammond, doubtless struck by the unfeigned horror expressed in my countenance, made one or two steps forward with an anxious yet puzzled expression. A very audible titter burst from the remainder of my visitors. This suppressed laughter made me furious. To laugh at a human being in my position! It was the worst species of cruelty. *Now,* I can understand why the appearance of a man struggling violently, as it would seem, with an airy nothing, and calling for assistance against a vision, should have appeared ludicrous. *Then,* so great was my rage against the mocking crowd that had I the power I would have stricken them dead where they stood.

"Hammond! Hammond!" I cried again, despairingly, "for God's sake come to me. I can hold the—the Thing but a short while longer. It is overpowering me. Help me! Help me!"

"Harry," whispered Hammond, approaching me, "you have been smoking too much opium."

"I swear to you, Hammond, that this is no vision," I answered, in the same low tone. "Don't you see how it shakes my whole frame with its struggles? If you don't believe me, convince yourself. Feel it—touch it."

Hammond advanced and laid his hand in the spot I indicated. A wild cry of horror burst from him. He had felt it!

In a moment he had discovered somewhere in my room a long piece of cord, and was the next instant winding it and knotting it about the body of the unseen being that I clasped in my arms.

"Harry," he said, in a hoarse, agitated voice, for, though he preserved his presence of mind, he was deeply moved, "Harry, it's all safe now. You may let go, old fellow, if you're tired. The Thing can't move."

I was utterly exhausted, and I gladly loosed my hold.

Hammond stood holding the ends of the cord that bound the Invisible, twisted round his hand, while before him, self supporting as it were, he beheld a rope laced and interlaced, and stretching tightly around a vacant space. I never saw a man look so thoroughly stricken with awe. Nevertheless his face expressed all the courage and determination which I knew him to possess. His lips, although white, were set firmly, and one could perceive at a glance that, although stricken with fear, he was not daunted.

The confusion that ensued among the guests of the house who were witnesses of this extraordinary scene between Hammond and myself—who beheld the pantomime of binding this struggling Something—who beheld me almost sinking from physical exhaustion when my task of jailer was over—the confusion and terror that took possession of the bystanders, when they saw all this, was beyond description. The weaker ones fled from the apartment. The few who remained clustered near the door and could not be induced to approach Hammond and his Charge. Still incredulity broke out through their terror. They had not the courage to satisfy themselves, and yet they doubted. It was in vain that I begged of some of the men to come near and convince themselves by touch of the existence in that room of a living being which was invisible. They were incredulous, but did not dare to undeceive themselves. How could a solid, living, breathing body be invisible, they asked. My reply was this. I gave a sign to Hammond, and both of us—conquering our fearful repugnance to touch the invisible creature—lifted it from the ground, manacled as it was, and took it to my bed. Its weight was about that of a boy of fourteen.

"Now, my friends," I said, as Hammond and myself held the creature suspended over the bed, "I can give you self-evident proof that here is a solid, ponderable body, which, nevertheless, you cannot see. Be good enough to watch the surface of the bed attentively."

I was astonished at my own courage in treating this strange event so calmly; but I had recovered from my first terror, and felt a sort of scientific pride in the affair, which dominated every other feeling.

The eyes of the bystanders were immediately fixed on my bed. At a given signal Hammond and I let the creature fall. There was the dull sound of a heavy body alighting on a soft mass. The timbers of the bed creaked. A deep impression marked itself distinctly on the pillow, and on the bed itself. The crowd who witnessed this gave a low cry, and rushed from the room. Hammond and I were left alone with our Mystery.

We remained silent for some time, listening to the low, irregular breathing of the creature on the bed, and watching the rustle of the bedclothes as it impotently struggled to free itself from confinement. Then Hammond spoke.

"Harry, this is awful."

"Ay, awful."

"But not unaccountable."

"Not unaccountable! What do you mean? Such a thing has never occurred since the birth of the world. I know not what to think, Hammond. God grant that I am not mad, and that this is not an insane fantasy!"

"Let us reason a little, Harry. Here is a solid body which we touch, but which we cannot see. The fact is so unusual that it strikes us with terror. Is there no parallel, though, for such a phenomenon? Take a piece of pure glass. It is tangible and transparent. A certain chemical coarseness is all that prevents its being so entirely transparent as to be totally invisible. It is not *theoretically impossible,* mind you, to make a glass which shall not reflect a single ray of light— a glass so pure and homogeneous in its atoms that the rays from the sun will pass through it as they do through the air, refracted but not reflected. We do not see the air, and yet we feel it."

"That's all very well, Hammond, but these are inanimate substances. Glass does not breathe, air does not breathe. *This* thing has a heart that palpitates—a will that moves it—lungs that play and inspire and respire."

"You forget the phenomena of which we have so often heard of late," answered the Doctor, gravely. "At the meetings called 'spirit circles,' invisible hands have been thrust into the hands of those persons round the table—warm, fleshly hands that seemed to pulsate with mortal life."

"What? Do you think, then, that this thing is—"

"I don't know what it is," was the solemn reply; "but please the gods I will, with your assistance, thoroughly investigate it."

We watched together, smoking many pipes, all night long, by the bedside of the unearthly being that tossed and panted until it was apparently wearied out. Then we learned by the low, regular breathing that it slept.

The next morning the house was all astir. The boarders congregated on the landing outside my room, and Hammond and myself were lions. We had to answer a thousand questions as to the state of our extraordinary prisoner, for as yet not one person in the house except ourselves could be induced to set foot in the apartment.

The creature was awake. This was evidenced by the convulsive manner in which the bedclothes were moved in its effort to escape. There was something truly terrible in beholding, as it were, those second-hand indications of the terrible writhings and agonized struggles for liberty which themselves were invisible.

Hammond and myself had racked our brains during the long night to discover some means by which we might realize the shape and general appearance of the Enigma. As well as we could make out by passing our hands over the creature's form, its outlines and lineaments were human. There was a mouth; a round, smooth head without hair; a nose, which, however, was little elevated above the cheeks; and its hands and feet felt like those of a boy. At first we thought of placing the being on a smooth surface and tracing its outline with chalk, as shoemakers trace the outline of the foot. This plan was given up as being of no value. Such an outline would give not the slightest idea of its conformation.

A happy thought struck me. We would take a cast of it in plaster of Paris. This would give us the solid figure, and satisfy all our wishes. But how to do it? The movements of the creature would disturb the setting of the plastic covering, and distort the mould. Another thought. Why not give it chloroform? It had respiratory organs—that was evident by its breathing. Once reduced to a state of insensibility, we could do with it what we would. Doctor X——was sent for; and after the worthy physician had recovered from the first shock of amazement, he proceeded to administer the chloroform. In three minutes afterward we were enabled to remove the fetters from the creature's body, and a modeller was busily engaged in covering the invisible form with the moist clay. In five minutes more we had a mould, and before evening a rough facsimile of the Mystery. It was shaped like a man—distorted, uncouth, and horrible, but still a man. It was small, not over four feet and some inches in height, and its limbs revealed a muscular development that was unparalleled. Its face surpassed in hideousness anything I had ever seen. Gustave Doré, or Callot, or Tony Johannot never conceived anything so horrible. There is a face in one of the latter's illustrations to *Un Voyage où il vous plaira,* which somewhat approaches the countenance of this creature, but does not equal it. It was the physiognomy of what I should fancy a ghoul might be. It looked as if it was capable of feeding on human flesh.

Having satisfied our curiosity, and bound everyone in the house to secrecy, it became a question what was to be done with our

Enigma? It was impossible that we should keep such a horror in our house; it was equally impossible that such an awful being should be let loose upon the world. I confess that I would have gladly voted for the creature's destruction. But who would shoulder the responsibility? Who would undertake the execution of this horrible semblance of a human being? Day after day this question was deliberated gravely. The boarders all left the house. Mrs. Moffat was in despair, and threatened Hammond and myself with all sorts of legal penalties if we did not remove the Horror. Our answer was, "We will go if you like, but we decline taking this creature with us. Remove it yourself if you please. It appeared in your house. On you the responsibility rests." To this there was, of course, no answer. Mrs. Moffat could not obtain for love or money a person who would even approach the Mystery.

The most singular part of the affair was that we were entirely ignorant of what the creature habitually fed on. Everything in the way of nutriment that we could think of was placed before it, but was never touched. It was awful to stand by, day after day, and see the clothes toss, and hear the hard breathing, and know that it was starving.

Ten, twelve days, a fortnight passed, and it still lived. The pulsations of the heart, however, were daily growing fainter, and had now nearly ceased. It was evident that the creature was dying for want of sustenance. While this terrible life struggle was going on, I felt miserable. I could not sleep. Horrible as the creature was, it was pitiful to think of the pangs it was suffering.

At last it died. Hammond and I found it cold and stiff one morning in the bed. The heart had ceased to beat, the lungs to inspire. We hastened to bury it in the garden. It was a strange funeral, the dropping of that viewless corpse into the damp hole. The cast of its form I gave to Doctor X—,who keeps it in his museum in Tenth Street.

As I am on the eve of a long journey from which I may not return, I have drawn up this narrative of an event the most singular that has ever come to my knowledge.

# MS. FOUND IN A BOTTLE

### Edgar Allan Poe

> *Qui n'a plus qu'un moment à vivre*
> *N'a plus rien à dissimuler.*[1]
> —*Quinault*—ATYS

OF MY COUNTRY and of my family I have little to say. Ill usage and length of years have driven me from the one, and estranged me from the other. Hereditary wealth afforded me an education of no common order, and a contemplative turn of mind enabled me to methodise the stores which early study very diligently garnered up. Beyond all things, the works of the German moralists gave me great delight; not from any ill-advised admiration of their eloquent madness, but from the ease with which my habits of rigid thought enabled me to detect their falsities. I have often been reproached with the aridity of my genius; a deficiency of imagination has been imputed to me as a crime; and the Pyrrhonism of my opinions has at all times rendered me notorious. Indeed, a strong relish for physical philosophy has, I fear, tinctured my mind with a very common error of this age—I mean the habit of referring occurrences, even the least susceptible of such reference, to the principles of that science. Upon the whole, no person could be less liable than myself to be led away from the severe precincts of truth by the *ignes fatui*[2] of superstition. I have thought proper to premise thus much, lest

---

[1] *Qui . . . dissimuler*; Latin: The man who has only a moment to live has nothing to hide.
[2] *ignes fatui*; Latin: will-o'-the-wisps.

the incredible tale I have to tell should be considered rather the raving of a crude imagination, than the positive experience of a mind to which the reveries of fancy have been a dead letter and a nullity.

After many years spent in foreign travel, I sailed in the year 18—, from the port of Batavia, in the rich and populous island of Java, on a voyage to the Archipelago of the Sunda islands. I went as passenger— having no other inducement than a kind of nervous restlessness which haunted me as a fiend.

Our vessel was a beautiful ship of about four hundred tons, copper-fastened, and built at Bombay of Malabar teak. She was freighted with cotton-wool and oil, from the Lachadive islands. We had also on board coir, jaggeree, ghee, cocoa-nuts, and a few cases of opium. The stowage was clumsily done, and the vessel consequently crank.

We got under way with a mere breath of wind, and for many days stood along the eastern coast of Java, without any other incident to beguile the monotony of our course than the occasional meeting with some of the small grabs of the Archipelago to which we were bound.

One evening, leaning over the taffrail, I observed a very singular, isolated cloud, to the N. W. It was remarkable, as well for its color, as from its being the first we had seen since our departure from Batavia. I watched it attentively until sunset, when it spread all at once to the eastward and westward, girting in the horizon with a narrow strip of vapor, and looking like a long line of low beach. My notice was soon afterwards attracted by the dusky-red appearance of the moon, and the peculiar character of the sea. The latter was undergoing a rapid change, and the water seemed more than usually transparent. Although I could distinctly see the bottom, yet, heaving the lead, I found the ship in fifteen fathoms. The air now became intolerably hot, and was loaded with spiral exhalations similar to those arising from heated iron. As night came on, every breath of wind died away, and a more entire calm it is impossible to conceive. The flame of a candle burned upon the poop without the least percep- tible motion, and a long hair, held between the finger and thumb, hung without the possibility of detecting a vibration. However, as the captain said he could perceive no indication of danger, and as we were drifting in bodily to shore, he ordered the sails to be furled, and the anchor let go. No watch was set, and the crew, consisting principally of Malays, stretched themselves deliberately

upon deck. I went below—not without a full presentiment of evil.
Indeed, every appearance warranted me in apprehending a Simoon.
I told the captain my fears; but he paid no attention to what I said,
and left me without deigning to give a reply. My uneasiness, however,
prevented me from sleeping, and about midnight I went upon deck.—
As I placed my foot upon the upper step of the companion-ladder,
I was startled by a loud, humming noise, like that occasioned by the
rapid revolution of a mill-wheel, and before I could ascertain its
meaning, I found the ship quivering to its centre. In the next instant,
a wilderness of foam hurled us upon our beam-ends, and rushing
over us fore and aft, swept the entire decks from stem to stern.

The extreme fury of the blast proved, in a great measure, the
salvation of the ship. Although completely water-logged, yet, as her
masts had gone by the board, she rose, after a minute, heavily from
the sea, and, staggering awhile beneath the immense pressure of the
tempest, finally righted.

By what miracle I escaped destruction, it is impossible to say.
Stunned by the shock of the water, I found myself, upon recovery,
jammed in between the stern-post and rudder. With great difficulty
I gained my feet, and looking dizzily around, was at first struck
with the idea of our being among breakers; so terrific, beyond the
wildest imagination, was the whirlpool of mountainous and foaming
ocean within which we were engulfed. After a while, I heard the
voice of an old Swede, who had shipped with us at the moment
of our leaving port. I hallooed to him with all my strength, and
presently he came reeling aft. We soon discovered that we were
the sole survivors of the accident. All on deck, with the exception
of ourselves, had been swept overboard; the captain and mates
must have perished as they slept, for the cabins were deluged with
water. Without assistance, we could expect to do little for the
security of the ship, and our exertions were at first paralyzed by
the momentary expectation of going down. Our cable had, of
course, parted like pack-thread, at the first breath of the hurricane,
or we should have been instantaneously overwhelmed. We scudded
with frightful velocity before the sea, and the water made clear
breaches over us. The framework of our stern was shattered
excessively, and, in almost every respect, we had received considerable injury; but to our extreme joy we found the pumps unchoked,
and that we had made no great shifting of our ballast. The main
fury of the blast had already blown over, and we apprehended
little danger from the violence of the wind; but we looked forward

to its total cessation with dismay; well believing, that in our shattered condition, we should inevitably perish in the tremendous
swell which would ensue. But this very just apprehension seemed
by no means likely to be soon verified. For five entire days and
nights—during which our only subsistence was a small quantity of
jaggeree, procured with great difficulty from the forecastle—the
hulk flew at a rate defying computation, before rapidly succeeding
flaws of wind, which, without equalling the first violence of the
Simoon, were still more terrific than any tempest I had before
encountered. Our course for the first four days was, with trifling
variations, S. E. and by S.; and we must have run down the coast
of New Holland.—On the fifth day the cold became extreme,
although the wind had hauled round a point more to the northward. The sun arose with a sickly yellow lustre, and clambered a
very few degrees above the horizon—emitting no decisive light.
There were no clouds apparent, yet the wind was upon the increase,
and blew with a fitful and unsteady fury. About noon, as nearly as
we could guess, our attention was again arrested by the appearance
of the sun. It gave out no light, properly so called, but a dull and
sullen glow without reflection, as if all its rays were polarized. Just
before sinking within the turgid sea, its central fires suddenly went
out, as if hurriedly extinguished by some unaccountable power. It
was a dim, silver-like rim, alone, as it rushed down the unfathomable
ocean.

We waited in vain for the arrival of the sixth day—that day to me
has not arrived—to the Swede, never did arrive. Thenceforward
we were enshrouded in pitchy darkness, so that we could not have
seen an object at twenty paces from the ship. Eternal night continued
to envelop us, all unrelieved by the phosphoric sea-brilliancy to which
we had been accustomed in the tropics. We observed too, that,
although the tempest continued to rage with unabated violence, there
was no longer to be discovered the usual appearance of surf, or foam,
which had hitherto attended us. All around were horror, and thick
gloom, and a black sweltering desert of ebony.—Superstitious terror
crept by degrees into the spirit of the old Swede, and my own soul
was wrapped up in silent wonder. We neglected all care of the ship,
as worse than useless, and securing ourselves, as well as possible, to
the stump of the mizzen-mast, looked out bitterly into the world of
ocean. We had no means of calculating time, nor could we form any
guess of our situation. We were, however, well aware of having
made farther to the southward than any previous navigators, and felt

great amazement at not meeting with the usual impediments of ice. In the meantime every moment threatened to be our last—every mountainous billow hurried to overwhelm us. The swell surpassed anything I had imagined possible, and that we were not instantly buried is a miracle. My companion spoke of the lightness of our cargo, and reminded me of the excellent qualities of our ship; but I could not help feeling the utter hopelessness of hope itself, and prepared myself gloomily for that death which I thought nothing could defer beyond an hour, as, with every knot of way the ship made, the swelling of the black stupendous seas became more dismally appalling. At times we gasped for breath at an elevation beyond the albatross—at times became dizzy with the velocity of our descent into some watery hell, where the air grew stagnant, and no sound disturbed the slumbers of the kraken.

We were at the bottom of one of these abysses, when a quick scream from my companion broke fearfully upon the night. "See! see!" cried he, shrieking in my ears, "Almighty God! see! see!" As he spoke, I became aware of a dull, sullen glare of red light which streamed down the sides of the vast chasm where we lay, and threw a fitful brilliancy upon our deck. Casting my eyes upwards, I beheld a spectacle which froze the current of my blood. At a terrific height directly above us, and upon the very verge of the precipitous descent, hovered a gigantic ship, of perhaps four thousand tons. Although upreared upon the summit of a wave more than a hundred times her own altitude, her apparent size still exceeded that of any ship of the line or East Indiaman in existence. Her huge hull was of a deep dingy black, unrelieved by any of the customary carvings of a ship. A single row of brass cannon protruded from her open ports, and dashed from their polished surfaces the fires of innumerable battle-lanterns, which swung to and fro about her rigging. But what mainly inspired us with horror and astonishment, was that she bore up under a press of sail in the very teeth of that supernatural sea, and of that ungovernable hurricane. When we first discovered her, her bows were alone to be seen, as she rose slowly from the dim and horrible gulf beyond her. For a moment of intense terror she paused upon the giddy pinnacle, as if in contemplation of her own sublimity, then trembled and tottered, and—came down.

At this instant, I know not what sudden self-possession came over my spirit. Staggering as far aft as I could, I awaited fearlessly the ruin that was to overwhelm. Our own vessel was at length ceasing from her struggles, and sinking with her head to the sea. The shock of the descending mass struck her, consequently, in that portion of her frame which was already under water, and the inevitable result was to hurl me, with irresistible violence, upon the rigging of the stranger.

As I fell, the ship hove in stays, and went about; and to the confusion ensuing I attributed my escape from the notice of the crew. With little difficulty I made my way, unperceived, to the main hatchway, which was partially open, and soon found an opportunity of secreting myself in the hold. Why I did so I can hardly tell. An indefinite sense of awe, which at first sight of the navigators of the ship had taken hold of my mind, was perhaps the principle of my concealment. I was unwilling to trust myself with a race of people who had offered, to the cursory glance I had taken, so many points of vague novelty, doubt, and apprehension. I therefore thought proper to contrive a hiding-place in the hold. This I did by removing a small portion of the shifting-boards, in such a manner as to afford me a convenient retreat between the huge timbers of the ship.

I had scarcely completed my work, when a footstep in the hold forced me to make use of it. A man passed by my place of concealment with a feeble and unsteady gait. I could not see his face, but had an opportunity of observing his general appearance. There was about it an evidence of great age and infirmity. His knees tottered beneath a load of years, and his entire frame quivered under the burthen. He muttered to himself, in a low broken tone, some words of a language which I could not understand, and groped in a corner among a pile of singular-looking instruments, and decayed charts of navigation. His manner was a wild mixture of the peevishness of second childhood, and the solemn dignity of a God. He at length went on deck, and I saw him no more.

*   *   *

A feeling, for which I have no name, has taken possession of my soul—a sensation which will admit of no analysis, to which the lessons of bygone times are inadequate, and for which I fear futurity itself will offer me no key. To a mind constituted like my own, the latter consideration is an evil. I shall never—I know that I shall never—be satisfied with regard to the nature of my conceptions. Yet it is not wonderful that these conceptions are indefinite, since they

have their origin in sources so utterly novel. A new sense—a new
entity is added to my soul.

★  ★  ★

It is long since I first trod the deck of this terrible ship, and the rays
of my destiny are, I think, gathering to a focus. Incomprehensible
men! Wrapped up in meditations of a kind which I cannot divine,
they pass me by unnoticed. Concealment is utter folly on my part,
for the people *will not* see. It was but just now that I passed directly
before the eyes of the mate; it was no long while ago that I ventured
into the captain's own private cabin, and took thence the materials
with which I write, and have written. I shall from time to time
continue this journal. It is true that I may not find an opportunity
of transmitting it to the world, but I will not fail to make the endeav-
our. At the last moment I will enclose the MS. in a bottle, and cast
it within the sea.

★  ★  ★

An incident has occurred which has given me new room for meditation. Are such things the operation of ungoverned chance? I had
ventured upon deck and thrown myself down, without attracting
any notice, among a pile of ratlin-stuff and old sails, in the bottom
of the yawl. While musing upon the singularity of my fate, I unwittingly daubed with a tar-brush the edges of a neatly-folded studding-sail
which lay near me on a barrel. The studding-sail is now bent upon
the ship, and the thoughtless touches of the brush are spread out
into the word DISCOVERY.

I have made many observations lately upon the structure of the
vessel. Although well armed, she is not, I think, a ship of war. Her
rigging, build, and general equipment, all negative a supposition of
this kind. What she *is not,* I can easily perceive; what she *is,* I fear it
is impossible to say. I know not how it is, but in scrutinizing her
strange model and singular cast of spars, her huge size and overgrown
suits of canvass, her severely simple bow and antiquated stern, there
will occasionally flash across my mind a sensation of familiar things,
and there is always mixed up with such indistinct shadows of
recollection, an unaccountable memory of old foreign chronicles and
ages long ago. ★ ★ ★ ★ ★ ★ ★

I have been looking at the timbers of the ship. She is built of a material to which I am a stranger. There is a peculiar character about the wood which strikes me as rendering it unfit for the purpose to which it has been applied. I mean its extreme *porousness*, considered independently of the worm-eaten condition which is a consequence of navigation in these seas, and apart from the rottenness attendant upon age. It will appear perhaps an observation somewhat over-curious, but this wood would have every characteristic of Spanish oak, if Spanish oak were distended by any unnatural means.

In reading the above sentence a curious apothegm of an old weather-beaten Dutch navigator comes full upon my recollection. "It is as sure," he was wont to say, when any doubt was entertained of his veracity, "as sure as there is a sea where the ship itself will grow in bulk like the living body of the seaman." ★ ★ ★ ★ ★ ★ ★ ★ ★ ★

About an hour ago, I made bold to thrust myself among a group of the crew. They paid me no manner of attention, and, although I stood in the very midst of them all, seemed utterly unconscious of my presence. Like the one I had at first seen in the hold, they all bore about them the marks of a hoary old age. Their knees trembled with infirmity; their shoulders were bent double with decrepitude; their shrivelled skins rattled in the wind; their voices were low, tremulous, and broken; their eyes glistened with the rheum of years; and their gray hairs streamed terribly in the tempest. Around them, on every part of the deck, lay scattered mathematical instruments of the most quaint and obsolete construction.

★   ★   ★

I mentioned, some time ago, the bending of a studding-sail. From that period, the ship, being thrown dead off the wind, has continued her terrific course due south, with every rag of canvass packed upon her, from her trucks to her lower studding-sail booms, and rolling every moment her top-gallant yard-arms into the most appalling hell of water which it can enter into the mind of man to imagine. I have just left the deck, where I find it impossible to maintain a footing, although the crew seem to experience little inconvenience. It appears to me a miracle of miracles that our enormous bulk is not swallowed up at once and for ever. We are surely doomed to hover continually upon the brink of eternity, without taking a final plunge into the abyss. From billows a thousand times more stupendous than any I have ever seen, we glide away with the facility of the arrowy sea-gull; and the colossal waters rear their heads above us like demons of the deep, but like demons confined to simple threats, and forbidden to destroy. I am led to attribute these frequent escapes to the only natural cause which can account for such effect. I must suppose the ship to be within the influence of some strong current, or impetuous under-tow. * * *

I have seen the captain face to face, and in his own cabin—but, as I expected, he paid me no attention. Although in his appearance there is, to a casual observer, nothing which might bespeak him more or less than man, still, a feeling of irrepressible reverence and awe mingled with the sensation of wonder with which I regarded him. In stature, he is nearly my own height; that is, about five feet eight inches, He is of a well-knit and compact frame of body, neither robust nor remarkably otherwise. But it is the singularity of the expression which reigns upon the face—it is the intense, the wonderful, the thrilling evidence of old age, so utter, so extreme, which excites within my spirit a sense—a sentiment ineffable. His forehead, although little wrinkled, seems to bear upon it the stamp of a myriad of years. His gray hairs are records of the past, and his grayer eyes are sybils of the future. The cabin floor was thickly strewn with strange, iron-clasped folios, and mouldering instruments of science, and obsolete long-forgotten charts. His head was bowed down upon his hands, and he pored, with a fiery unquiet eye, over a paper which I took to be a commission, and which, at all events, bore the signature of a monarch. He muttered to himself—as did the first seaman whom I saw in the hold, some low peevish syllables of a foreign tongue; and although the speaker was close at my elbow, his voice seemed to reach my ears from the distance of a mile. * * * * * * * * * * *

The ship and all in it are imbued with the spirit of Eld. The crew glide to and fro like the ghosts of buried centuries; their eyes have an eager and uneasy meaning; and when their fingers fall athwart my path in the wild glare of the battle-lanterns, I feel as I have never felt before, although I have been all my life a dealer in antiquities, and have imbibed the shadows of fallen columns at Balbec, and Tadmor, and Persepolis, until my very soul has become a ruin. * * * *

When I look around me, I feel ashamed of my former apprehensions. If I trembled at the blast which has hitherto attended us, shall I not stand aghast at a warring of wind and ocean, to convey any idea of which, the words tornado and simoon are trivial and ineffective? All in the immediate vicinity of the ship, is the blackness of eternal night, and a chaos of foamless water; but, about a league on either side of us, may be seen, indistinctly and at intervals, stupendous ramparts of ice, towering away into the desolate sky, and looking like the walls of the universe. ★ ★ ★ ★ ★ ★

As I imagined, the ship proves to be in a current—if that appellation can properly be given to a tide which, howling and shrieking by the white ice, thunders on to the southward with a velocity like the headlong dashing of a cataract.

★   ★   ★

To conceive the horror of my sensations is, I presume, utterly impossible; yet a curiosity to penetrate the mysteries of these awful regions, predominates even over my despair, and will reconcile me to the most hideous aspect of death. It is evident that we are hurrying onwards to some exciting knowledge—some never-to-be-imparted secret, whose attainment is destruction. Perhaps this current leads us to the southern pole itself. It must be confessed that a supposition apparently so wild has every probability in its favor.

★   ★   ★

The crew pace the deck with unquiet and tremulous step; but there is upon their countenances an expression more of the eagerness of hope than of the apathy of despair.

In the meantime the wind is still in our poop, and, as we carry a crowd of canvass, the ship is at times lifted bodily from out the sea! Oh, horror upon horror!—the ice opens suddenly to the right, and to the left, and we are whirling dizzily, in immense concentric circles, round and round the borders of a gigantic amphitheatre, the summit of whose walls is lost in the darkness and the distance. But little time will be left me to ponder upon my destiny! The circles rapidly grow small—we are plunging madly within the grasp of the whirlpool—and amid a roaring, and bellowing, and thundering of ocean and of tempest, the ship is quivering—oh God! and—going down!

*Note*—The "MS. Found in a Bottle" was originally published in 1831 [sic]; and it was not until many years afterwards that I became acquainted with the maps of Mercator, in which the ocean is represented as rushing, by four mouths, into the (northern) Polar Gulf, to be absorbed into the bowels of the earth; the Pole itself being represented by a black rock, towering to a prodigious height. [The Author]

# THE OBLONG BOX

### Edgar Allan Poe

SOME YEARS AGO, I engaged passage from Charleston, S. C., to the
city of New York, in the fine packet-ship "Independence," Captain
Hardy. We were to sail on the fifteenth of the month (June), weather
permitting; and, on the fourteenth, I went on board to arrange some
matters in my stateroom.

I found that we were to have a great many passengers, including
a more than usual number of ladies. On the list were several of my
acquaintances; and, among other names, I was rejoiced to see that
of Mr. Cornelius Wyatt, a young artist, for whom I entertained
feelings of warm friendship. He had been with me a fellow-student
at C— University, where we were very much together. He had the
ordinary temperament of genius, and was a compound of misanthropy,
sensibility, and enthusiasm. To these qualities he united the warmest
and truest heart which ever beat in a human bosom.

I observed that his name was carded upon *three* staterooms; and,
upon again referring to the list of passengers, I found that he had
engaged passage for himself, wife, and two sisters—his own. The
staterooms were sufficiently roomy, and each had two berths, one
above the other. These berths, to be sure, were so exceedingly narrow
as to be insufficient for more than one person; still, I could not
comprehend why there were *three* staterooms for these four persons.
I was, just at that epoch, in one of those moody frames of mind which
make a man abnormally inquisitive about trifles; and I confess, with
shame, that I busied myself in a variety of ill-bred and preposterous
conjectures about this matter of the supernumerary stateroom. It was
no business of mine, to be sure; but with none the less pertinacity

did I occupy myself in attempts to resolve the enigma. At last I reached
a conclusion which wrought in me great wonder why I had not
arrived at it before. "It is a servant, of course," I said; "what a fool I
am, not sooner to have thought of so obvious a solution!" And then
I again repaired to the list—but here I saw distinctly that *no* servant
was to come with the party; although, in fact, it had been the original
design to bring one—for the words "and servant" had been first
written and then overscored. "Oh, extra baggage to be sure," I now
said to myself—"something he wishes not to be put in the hold—
something to be kept under his own eye—ah, I have it—a painting
or so—and this is what he has been bargaining about with Nicolino,
the Italian Jew." This idea satisfied me, and I dismissed my curiosity
for the nonce.

Wyatt's two sisters I knew very well, and most amiable and clever
girls they were. His wife he had newly married, and I had never yet
seen her. He had often talked about her in my presence, however,
and in his usual style of enthusiasm. He described her as of surpassing
beauty, wit, and accomplishment. I was, therefore, quite anxious to
make her acquaintance.

On the day in which I visited the ship (the fourteenth), Wyatt and
party were also to visit it—so the captain informed me—and I waited
on board an hour longer than I had designed, in hope of being presented to the bride; but then an apology came. "Mrs. W. was a little
indisposed, and would decline coming on board until tomorrow, at
the hour of sailing."

The morrow having arrived, I was going from my hotel to the
wharf, when Captain Hardy met me and said that, "owing to
circumstances" (a stupid but convenient phrase), "he rather thought
the 'Independence' would not sail for a day or two, and that when
all was ready, he would send up and let me know." This I thought
strange, for there was a stiff southerly breeze; but as "the circumstances" were not forthcoming, although I pumped for them with
much perseverance, I had nothing to do but to return home and
digest my impatience at leisure.

I did not receive the expected message from the captain for nearly
a week. It came at length, however, and I immediately went on board.
The ship was crowded with passengers, and everything was in the
bustle attendant upon making sail. Wyatt's party arrived in about ten
minutes after myself. There were the two sisters, the bride, and the
artist—the latter in one of his customary fits of moody misanthropy.
I was too well used to these, however, to pay them any especial

attention. He did not even introduce me to his wife;—this courtesy devolving, perforce, upon his sister Marian—a very sweet and intelligent girl, who, in a few hurried words, made us acquainted.

Mrs. Wyatt had been closely veiled; and when she raised her veil, in acknowledging my bow, I confess that I was very profoundly astonished. I should have been much more so, however, had not long experience advised me not to trust, with too implicit a reliance, the enthusiastic descriptions of my friend, the artist, when indulging in comments upon the loveliness of woman. When beauty was the theme, I well knew with what facility he soared into the regions of the purely ideal.

The truth is, I could not help regarding Mrs. Wyatt as a decidedly plain-looking woman. If not positively ugly, she was not, I think, very far from it. She was dressed, however, in exquisite taste—and then I had no doubt that she had captivated my friend's heart by the more enduring graces of the intellect and soul. She said very few words, and passed at once into her stateroom with Mr. W.

My old inquisitiveness now returned. There was *no* servant—*that* was a settled point. I looked, therefore, for the extra baggage. After some delay, a cart arrived at the wharf, with an oblong pine box, which was everything that seemed to be expected. Immediately upon its arrival we made sail, and in a short time were safely over the bar and standing out to sea.

The box in question was, as I say, oblong. It was about six feet in length by two and a half in breadth;—I observed it attentively, and like to be precise. Now this shape was *peculiar;* and no sooner had I seen it, than I took credit to myself for the accuracy of my guessing. I had reached the conclusion, it will be remembered, that the extra baggage of my friend, the artist, would prove to be pictures, or at least a picture; for I knew he had been for several weeks in conference with Nicolino:—and now here was a box which, from its shape, *could* possibly contain nothing in the world but a copy of Leonardo's "Last Supper"; and a copy of this very "Last Supper," done by Rubini the younger, at Florence, I had known, for some time, to be in the possession of Nicolino. This point, therefore, I considered as sufficiently settled. I chuckled excessively when I thought of my acumen. It was the first time I had ever known Wyatt to keep from me any of his artistical secrets; but here he evidently intended to steal a march upon me, and smuggle a fine picture to New York, under my very nose; expecting me to know nothing of the matter. I resolved to quiz him *well,* now and hereafter.

One thing, however, annoyed me not a little. The box did *not* go into the extra stateroom. It was deposited in Wyatt's own; and there, too, it remained, occupying very nearly the whole of the floor—no doubt to the exceeding discomfort of the artist and his wife;—this the more especially as the tar or paint with which it was lettered in sprawling capitals, emitted a strong, disagreeable, and, to *my* fancy, a peculiarly disgusting odor. On the lid were painted the words— *"Mrs. Adelaide Curtis, Albany, New York. Charge of Cornelius Wyatt, Esq. This side up. To be handled with care."*

Now, I was aware that Mrs. Adelaide Curtis, of Albany, was the artist's wife's mother;—but then I looked upon the whole address as a mystification, intended especially for myself. I made up my mind, of course, that the box and contents would never get farther north than the studio of my misanthropic friend, in Chambers Street, New York.

For the first three or four days we had fine weather, although the wind was dead ahead; having chopped round to the northward, immediately upon our losing sight of the coast. The passengers were, consequently, in high spirits and disposed to be social. I *must* except, however, Wyatt and his sisters, who behaved stiffly, and, I could not help thinking, uncourteously to the rest of the party. *Wyatt's* conduct I did not so much regard. He was gloomy, even beyond his usual habit—in fact he was *morose*—but in him I was prepared for eccentricity. For the sisters, however, I could make no excuse. They secluded themselves in their staterooms during the greater part of the passage, and absolutely refused, although I repeatedly urged them, to hold communication with any person on board.

Mrs. Wyatt herself, was far more agreeable. That is to say, she was *chatty;* and to be chatty is no slight recommendation at sea. She became *excessively* intimate with most of the ladies; and, to my profound astonishment, evinced no equivocal disposition to coquet with the men. She amused us all very much. I say *"amused"*—and scarcely know how to explain myself. The truth is, I soon found that Mrs. W. was far oftener laughed *at* than *with.* The gentlemen said little about her; but the ladies, in a little while, pronounced her "a good-hearted thing, rather indifferent-looking, totally uneducated, and decidedly vulgar." The great wonder was, how Wyatt had been entrapped into such a match. Wealth was the general solution—but this I knew to be no solution at all; for Wyatt had told me that she neither brought him a dollar nor had any expectations from any source whatever. "He had married," he said, "for love, and for love only; and his bride was far more than worthy of his love." When I thought of these expressions, on the part of my friend, I confess that I felt indescribably puzzled. Could it be possible that he was taking leave of his senses? What else could I think? *He*, so refined, so intellectual, so fastidious, with so exquisite a perception of the faulty, and so keen an appreciation of the beautiful! To be sure, the lady seemed especially fond of *him*—particularly so in his absence—when she made herself ridiculous by frequent quotations of what had been said by her "beloved husband, Mr. Wyatt." The word "husband" seemed forever—to use one of her own delicate expressions—forever "on the tip of her tongue." In the mean time, it was observed by all on board, that he avoided *her* in the most pointed manner, and, for the most part, shut himself up alone in his stateroom, where, in fact, he might have been said to live altogether, leaving his wife at full liberty to amuse herself as she thought best, in the public society of the main cabin.

My conclusion, from what I saw and heard, was, that the artist, by some unaccountable freak of fate, or perhaps in some fit of enthusiastic and fanciful passion, had been induced to unite himself with a person altogether beneath him, and that the natural result, entire and speedy disgust, had ensued. I pitied him from the bottom of my heart—but could not, for that reason, quite forgive his incommunicativeness in the matter of the "Last Supper." For this I resolved to have my revenge.

One day he came upon deck, and, taking his arm as had been my wont, I sauntered with him backwards and forwards. His gloom, however (which I considered quite natural under the circumstances), seemed entirely unabated. He said little, and that moodily, and with evident effort. I ventured a jest or two, and he made a sickening attempt at a smile. Poor fellow!—as I thought of *his wife,* I wondered that he could have heart to put on even the semblance of mirth. At last I ventured a home thrust. I determined to commence a series of covert insinuations, or innuendoes, about the oblong box—just to let him perceive, gradually, that I was *not* altogether the butt, or victim, of his little bit of pleasant mystification. My first observation was by way of opening a masked battery. I said something about the "peculiar shape of *that* box"; and, as I spoke the words, I smiled knowingly, winked, and touched him gently with my fore finger in the ribs.

The manner in which Wyatt received this harmless pleasantry, convinced me, at once, that he was mad. At first he stared at me as if he found it impossible to comprehend the witticism of my remark; but as its point seemed slowly to make its way into his brain, his eyes, in the same proportion, seemed protruding from their sockets. Then he grew very red—then hideously pale—then, as if highly amused with what I had insinuated, he began a loud and boisterous laugh, which, to my astonishment, he kept up, with gradually increasing vigor, for ten minutes or more. In conclusion, he fell flat and heavily upon the deck. When I ran to uplift him, to all appearance he was *dead*.

I called assistance, and, with much difficulty, we brought him to himself. Upon reviving he spoke incoherently for some time. At length we bled him and put him to bed. The next morning he was quite recovered, so far as regarded his mere bodily health. Of his mind I say nothing, of course. I avoided him during the rest of the passage, by advice of the captain, who seemed to coincide with me altogether in my views of his insanity, but cautioned me to say nothing on this head to any person on board.

Several circumstances occurred immediately after this fit of Wyatt's, which contributed to heighten the curiosity with which I was already possessed. Among other things, this: I had been nervous—drank too much strong green tea, and slept ill at night—in fact, for two nights I could not be properly said to sleep at all. Now, my stateroom opened into the main cabin, or dining-room, as did those of all the single men on board. Wyatt's three rooms were in the after-cabin, which was separated from the main one by a slight sliding door, never locked even at night. As we were almost constantly on a wind, and the breeze was not a little stiff, the ship heeled to leeward very considerably; and whenever her starboard side was to leeward, the sliding door between the cabins slid open, and so remained, nobody taking the trouble to get up and shut it. But my berth was in such a position, that when my own stateroom door was open, as well as the sliding door in question (and my own door was *always* open on account of the heat), I could see into the after-cabin quite distinctly, and just at that portion of it, too, where were situated the staterooms of Mr. Wyatt. Well, during two nights *(not* consecutive) while I lay awake, I clearly saw Mrs. W., about eleven o'clock upon each night, steal cautiously from the stateroom of Mr. W. and enter the extra room, where she remained until daybreak, when she was called by her husband and went back. That they were virtually separated was clear. They had separate apartments—no doubt in contemplation of a more permanent divorce; and here, after all, I thought, was the mystery of the extra stateroom.

There was another circumstance, too, which interested me much. During the two wakeful nights in question, and immediately after the disappearance of Mrs. Wyatt into the extra stateroom, I was attracted by certain singular, cautious, subdued noises in that of her husband. After listening to them for some time, with thoughtful attention, I at length succeeded perfectly in translating their import. They were sounds occasioned by the artist in prying open the oblong box, by means of a chisel and mallet—the latter being apparently muffled, or deadened, by some soft woollen or cotton substance in which its head was enveloped.

In this manner I fancied I could distinguish the precise moment when he fairly disengaged the lid—also, that I could determine when he removed it altogether, and when he deposited it upon the lower berth in his room; this latter point I knew, for example, by certain slight taps which the lid made in striking against the wooden edges of the berth, as he endeavored to lay it down *very* gently—there being no room for it on the floor. After this there was a dead stillness, and I heard nothing more, upon either occasion, until nearly daybreak; unless, perhaps, I may mention a low sobbing, or murmuring sound, so very much suppressed as to be nearly inaudible—if, indeed, the whole of this latter noise were not rather produced by my own imagination. I say it seemed to *resemble* sobbing or sighing—but, of course, it could not have been either. I rather think it was a ringing in my own ears. Mr. Wyatt, no doubt, according to custom, was merely giving the rein to one of his hobbies—indulging in one of his fits of artistic enthusiasm. He had opened his oblong box, in order to feast his eyes on the pictorial treasure within. There was nothing in this, however, to make him *sob*. I repeat therefore, that it must have been simply a freak of my own fancy, distempered by good Captain Hardy's green tea. Just before dawn, on each of the two nights of which I speak, I distinctly heard Mr. Wyatt replace the lid upon the oblong box, and force the nails into their old places by means of the muffled mallet. Having done this, he issued from his stateroom, fully dressed, and proceeded to call Mrs. W. from hers.

We had been at sea seven days, and were now off Cape Hatteras, when there came a tremendously heavy blow from the southwest. We were, in a measure, prepared for it, however, as the weather had been holding out threats for some time. Everything was made snug, alow and aloft; and as the wind steadily freshened, we lay to, at length, under spanker and foretopsail, both double-reefed.

In this trim, we rode safely enough for forty-eight hours—the ship proving herself an excellent sea boat, in many respects, and shipping no water of any consequence. At the end of this period, however, the gale had freshened into a hurricane, and our after-sail split into ribbons, bringing us so much in the trough of the water that we shipped several prodigious seas, one immediately after the other. By this accident we lost three men overboard, with the caboose, and nearly the whole of the larboard bulwarks. Scarcely had we recovered our senses, before the foretopsail went into shreds, when we got up a storm stay-sail, and with this did pretty well for some hours, the ship heading the seas much more steadily than before.

The gale still held on, however, and we saw no signs of its abating. The rigging was found to be ill-fitted, and greatly strained; and on the third day of the blow, about five in the afternoon, our mizzen-mast, in a heavy lurch to windward, went by the board. For an hour or more, we tried in vain to get rid of it, on account of the prodigious rolling of the ship; and, before we had succeeded, the carpenter came aft and announced four feet water in the hold. To add to our dilemma, we found the pumps choked and nearly useless.

All was now confusion and despair—but an effort was made to lighten the ship by throwing overboard as much of her cargo as could be reached, and by cutting away the two masts that remained. This we at last accomplished—but we were still unable to do anything at the pumps; and, in the mean time, the leak gained on us very fast.

At sundown, the gale had sensibly diminished in violence, and, as the sea went down with it, we still entertained faint hopes of saving ourselves in the boats. At eight, P. M., the clouds broke away to windward, and we had the advantage of a full moon—a piece of good fortune which served wonderfully to cheer our drooping spirits.

After incredible labor we succeeded, at length, in getting the longboat over the side without material accident, and into this we crowded the whole of the crew and most of the passengers. This party made off immediately, and, after undergoing much suffering, finally arrived, in safety, at Ocracoke Inlet, on the third day after the wreck.

Fourteen passengers, with the captain, remained on board, resolving to trust their fortunes to the jolly-boat at the stern. We lowered it without difficulty, although it was only by a miracle that we prevented it from swamping as it touched the water. It contained, when afloat, the captain and his wife, Mr. Wyatt and party, a Mexican officer, wife, four children, and myself, with a negro valet.

We had no room, of course, for anything except a few positively necessary instruments, some provision, and the clothes upon our backs. No one had thought of even attempting to save anything more. What must have been the astonishment of all then, when, having proceeded a few fathoms from the ship, Mr. Wyatt stood up in the stern-sheets, and coolly demanded of Captain Hardy that the boat should be put back for the purpose of taking in his oblong box!

"Sit down, Mr. Wyatt," replied the Captain, somewhat sternly; "you will capsize us if you do not sit quite still. Our gunwale is almost in the water now."

"The box!" vociferated Mr. Wyatt, still standing—"the box, I say! Captain Hardy, you cannot, you *will* not refuse me. Its weight will be but a trifle—it is nothing—mere nothing. By the mother who bore you—for the love of Heaven—by your hope of salvation, I *implore* you to put back for the box!"

The captain, for a moment, seemed touched by the earnest appeal of the artist, but he regained his stern composure, and merely said—

"Mr. Wyatt, you are *mad*. I cannot listen to you. Sit down, I say, or you will swamp the boat. Stay—hold him—seize him!—he is about to spring overboard! There—I knew it—he is over!"

As the Captain said this, Mr. Wyatt, in fact, sprang from the boat, and, as we were yet in the lee of the wreck, succeeded, by almost superhuman exertion, in getting hold of a rope which hung from the fore-chains. In another moment he was on board, and rushing frantically down into the cabin.

In the meantime, we had been swept astern of the ship, and being quite out of her lee, were at the mercy of the tremendous sea which was still running. We made a determined effort to put back, but our little boat was like a feather in the breath of the tempest. We saw at a glance that the doom of the unfortunate artist was sealed.

As our distance from the wreck rapidly increased, the madman (for as such only could we regard him) was seen to emerge from the companion-way, up which, by dint of a strength that appeared gigantic, he dragged, bodily, the oblong box. While we gazed in the extremity of astonishment, he passed, rapidly, several turns of a three-inch rope, first around the box and then around his body.

In another instant both body and box were in the sea—disappearing suddenly, at once and forever.

We lingered awhile sadly upon our oars, with our eyes riveted upon the spot. At length we pulled away. The silence remained unbroken for an hour. Finally, I hazarded a remark.

"Did you observe, Captain, how suddenly they sank? Was not that an exceedingly singular thing? I confess that I entertained some feeble hope of his final deliverance, when I saw him lash himself to the box, and commit himself to the sea."

"They sank, as a matter of course," replied the Captain, "and that like a shot. They will soon rise again, however—but *not till the salt melts.*"

"The salt!" I ejaculated.

"Hush!" said the Captain, pointing to the wife and sisters of the deceased. "We must talk of these things at some more appropriate time."

We suffered much, and made a narrow escape; but fortune befriended *us,* as well as our mates in the long boat. We landed, in fine, more dead than alive, after four days of intense distress, upon the beach opposite Roanoke Island. We remained here a week, were not ill-treated by the wreckers, and at length obtained a passage to New York.

About a month after the loss of the "Independence," I happened to meet Captain Hardy in Broadway. Our conversation turned, naturally, upon the disaster, and especially upon the sad fate of poor Wyatt. I thus learned the following particulars.

The artist had engaged passage for himself, wife, two sisters and a servant. His wife was, indeed, as she had been represented, a most lovely, and most accomplished woman. On the morning of the fourteenth of June (the day in which I first visited the ship), the lady suddenly sickened and died. The young husband was frantic with grief—but circumstances imperatively forbade the deferring his voyage to New York. It was necessary to take to her mother the corpse of his adored wife, and, on the other hand, the universal prejudice which would prevent his doing so openly, was well known. Nine-tenths of the passengers would have abandoned the ship rather than take passage with a dead body.

In this dilemma, Captain Hardy arranged that the corpse, being first partially embalmed, and packed, with a large quantity of salt, in a box of suitable dimensions, should be conveyed on board as merchandise. Nothing was to be said of the lady's decease; and, as it was well understood that Mr. Wyatt had engaged passage for his wife, it became necessary that some person should personate her during the voyage. This the deceased's lady's-maid was easily prevailed on to do. The extra stateroom, originally engaged for this girl, during her mistress' life, was now merely retained. In this stateroom the pseudo wife slept, of course, every night. In the day-time she performed, to the best of her ability, the part of her mistress—whose person, it had been carefully ascertained, was unknown to any of the passengers on board.

My own mistakes arose, naturally enough, through too careless, too inquisitive, and too impulsive a temperament. But of late, it is a rare thing that I sleep soundly at night. There is a countenance which haunts me, turn as I will. There is an hysterical laugh which will forever ring within my ears.

# THE FALL OF THE HOUSE OF USHER

## Edgar Allan Poe

*Son cœur est un luth suspendu;*
*Sitôt qu'on le touche il résonne*[1].
—DE BÉRANGER

DURING THE WHOLE of a dull, dark, and soundless day in the autumn of the year, when the clouds hung oppressively low in the heavens, I had been passing alone, on horseback, through a singularly dreary tract of country; and at length found myself, as the shades of the evening drew on, within view of the melancholy House of Usher. I know not how it was—but, with the first glimpse of the building, a sense of insufferable gloom pervaded my spirit. I say insufferable; for the feeling was unrelieved by any of that half-pleasurable, because poetic, sentiment, with which the mind usually receives even the sternest natural images of the desolate or terrible. I looked upon the scene before me—upon the mere house, and the simple land-scape features of the domain—upon the bleak walls—upon the vacant eye-like windows—upon a few rank sedges—and upon a few white trunks of decayed trees—with an utter depression of soul which I can compare to no earthly sensation more properly than to the after-dream of the reveller upon opium—the bitter lapse into everyday life—the hideous dropping off of the veil. There was an iciness, a sinking, a sickening of the heart—an unredeemed dreari-ness of thought which no goading of the imagination could torture

---

[1] *Son . . . résonne;* French: His/her heart is a poised lute; as soon as it is touched, it resounds."

into aught of the sublime. What was it—I paused to think—what was it that so unnerved me in the contemplation of the House of Usher? It was a mystery all insoluble; nor could I grapple with the shadowy fancies that crowded upon me as I pondered. I was forced to fall back upon the unsatisfactory conclusion, that while, beyond doubt, there *are* combinations of very simple natural objects which have the power of thus affecting us, still the analysis of this power lies among considerations beyond our depth. It was possible, I reflected, that a mere different arrangement of the particulars of the scene, of the details of the picture, would be sufficient to modify, or perhaps to annihilate its capacity for sorrowful impression; and, acting upon this idea, I reined my horse to the precipitous brink of a black and lurid tarn that lay in unruffled lustre by the dwelling, and gazed down—but with a shudder even more thrilling than before—upon the remodelled and inverted images of the gray sedge, and the ghastly tree-stems, and the vacant and eye-like windows.

Nevertheless, in this mansion of gloom I now proposed to myself a sojourn of some weeks. Its proprietor, Roderick Usher, had been one of my boon companions in boyhood; but many years had elapsed since our last meeting. A letter, however, had lately reached me in a distant part of the country—a letter from him—which, in its wildly importunate nature, had admitted of no other than a personal reply. The MS. gave evidence of nervous agitation. The writer spoke of acute bodily illness—of a mental disorder which oppressed him—and of an earnest desire to see me, as his best, and indeed his only personal friend, with a view of attempting, by the cheerfulness of my society, some alleviation of his malady. It was the manner in which all this, and much more, was said—it was the apparent *heart* that went with his request—which allowed me no room for hesitation; and I accordingly obeyed forthwith what I still considered a very singular summons.

Although, as boys, we had been even intimate associates, yet I really knew little of my friend. His reserve had been always excessive and habitual. I was aware, however, that his very ancient family had been noted, time out of mind, for a peculiar sensibility of temperament, displaying itself, through long ages, in many works of exalted art, and manifested, of late, in repeated deeds of munificent yet unobtrusive charity, as well as in a passionate devotion to the intricacies, perhaps even more than to the orthodox and easily recognisable beauties, of musical science. I had learned, too, the very remarkable fact, that the stem of the Usher race, all time-honoured as it was, had put forth, at no period, any enduring branch; in other words, that the entire family lay in the direct line of descent, and had always, with very trifling and very temporary variation, so lain. It was this deficiency, I considered, while running over in thought the perfect keeping of the character of the premises with the accredited character of the people, and while speculating upon the possible influence which the one, in the long lapse of centuries, might have exercised upon the other—it was this deficiency, perhaps, of collateral issue, and the consequent undeviating transmission, from sire to son, of the patrimony with the name, which had, at length, so identified the two as to merge the original title of the estate in the quaint and equivocal appellation of the "House of Usher"—an appellation which seemed to include, in the minds of the peasantry who used it, both the family and the family mansion.

I have said that the sole effect of my somewhat childish experiment—that of looking down within the tarn—had been to deepen the first singular impression. There can be no doubt that the consciousness of the rapid increase of my superstition—for why should I not so term it?—served mainly to accelerate the increase itself. Such, I have long known, is the paradoxical law of all sentiments having terror as a basis. And it might have been for this reason only, that, when I again uplifted my eyes to the house itself, from its image in the pool, there grew in my mind a strange fancy—a fancy so ridiculous, indeed, that I but mention it to show the vivid force of the sensations which oppressed me. I had so worked upon my imagination as really to believe that about the whole mansion and domain there hung an atmosphere peculiar to themselves and their immediate vicinity—an atmosphere which had no affinity with the air of heaven, but which had reeked up from the decayed trees, and the gray wall, and the silent tarn—a pestilent and mystic vapour, dull, sluggish, faintly discernible, and leaden-hued.

Shaking off from my spirit what *must* have been a dream, I scanned more narrowly the real aspect of the building. Its principal feature seemed to be that of an excessive antiquity. The discoloration of ages had been great. Minute fungi overspread the whole exterior, hanging in a fine tangled web-work from the eaves. Yet all this was apart from any extraordinary dilapidation. No portion of the masonry had fallen; and there appeared to be a wild inconsistency between its still perfect adaptation of parts, and the crumbling condition of the individual stones. In this there was much that reminded me of the specious totality of old wood-work which has rotted for long years in some neglected vault, with no disturbance from the breath of the external air. Beyond this indication of extensive decay, however, the fabric gave little token of instability. Perhaps the eye of a scrutinising observer might have discovered a barely perceptible fissure, which, extending from the roof of the building in front, made its way down the wall in a zigzag direction, until it became lost in the sullen waters of the tarn.

Noticing these things, I rode over a short causeway to the house. A servant in waiting took my horse, and I entered the Gothic archway of the hall. A valet, of stealthy step, thence conducted me, in silence, through many dark and intricate passages in my progress to the *studio* of his master. Much that I encountered on the way contributed, I know not how, to heighten the vague sentiments of which I have already spoken. While the objects around me—while the carvings of the ceilings, the sombre tapestries of the walls, the ebon blackness of the floors, and the phantasmagoric armorial trophies which rattled as I strode, were but matters to which, or to such as which, I had been accustomed from my infancy—while I hesitated not to acknowledge how familiar was all this—I still wondered to find how unfamiliar were the fancies which ordinary images were stirring up. On one of the staircases, I met the physician of the family. His countenance, I thought, wore a mingled expression of low cunning and perplexity. He accosted me with trepidation and passed on. The valet now threw open a door and ushered me into the presence of his master.

The room in which I found myself was very large and lofty. The windows were long, narrow, and pointed, and at so vast a distance from the black oaken floor as to be altogether inaccessible from within. Feeble gleams of encrimsoned light made their way through the trellised panes, and served to render sufficiently distinct the more prominent objects around; the eye, however, struggled in vain to reach the remoter angles of the chamber, or the recesses of the vaulted and fretted ceiling. Dark draperies hung upon the walls. The general furniture was profuse, comfortless, antique, and tattered. Many books and musical instruments lay scattered about, but failed to give any vitality to the scene. I felt that I breathed an atmosphere of sorrow. An air of stern, deep, and irredeemable gloom hung over and pervaded all.

Upon my entrance, Usher arose from a sofa on which he had been lying at full length, and greeted me with a vivacious warmth which had much in it, I at first thought, of an overdone cordiality—of the

constrained effort of the *ennuyé*[2] man of the world. A glance, however, at his countenance, convinced me of his perfect sincerity. We
sat down; and for some moments, while he spoke not, I gazed upon
him with a feeling half of pity, half of awe. Surely, a man had never
before so terribly altered, in so brief a period, as had Roderick Usher!
It was with difficulty that I could bring myself to admit the identity
of the wan being before me with the companion of my early boyhood.
Yet the character of his face had been at all times remarkable. A
cadaverousness of complexion; an eye large, liquid, and luminous
beyond comparison; lips somewhat thin and very pallid, but of a
surpassingly beautiful curve; a nose of a delicate Hebrew model, but
with a breadth of nostril unusual in similar formations; a finely
moulded chin, speaking, in its want of prominence, of a want of
moral energy; hair of a more than web-like softness and tenuity;
these features, with an inordinate expansion above the regions of
the temple, made up altogether a countenance not easily to be
forgotten. And now in the mere exaggeration of the prevailing
character of these features, and of the expression they were wont to
convey, lay so much of change that I doubted to whom I spoke.
The now ghastly pallor of the skin, and the now miraculous lustre
of the eye, above all things startled and even awed me. The silken
hair, too, had been suffered to grow all unheeded, and as, in its wild
gossamer texture, it floated rather than fell about the face, I could
not, even with effort, connect its arabesque expression with any idea
of simple humanity.

  In the manner of my friend I was at once struck with an
incoherence—an inconsistency; and I soon found this to arise from
a series of feeble and futile struggles to overcome an habitual
trepidancy—an excessive nervous agitation. For something of this
nature I had indeed been prepared, no less by his letter, than by
reminiscences of certain boyish traits, and by conclusions deduced
from his peculiar physical conformation and temperament. His action
was alternately vivacious and sullen. His voice varied rapidly from a
tremulous indecision (when the animal spirits seemed utterly in
abeyance) to that species of energetic concision—that abrupt, weighty,
unhurried, and hollow-sounding enunciation—that leaden, self-
balanced and perfectly modulated guttural utterance, which may be
observed in the lost drunkard, or the irreclaimable eater of opium,
during the periods of his most intense excitement.

---

[2]  *ennuyé*; French: bored.

It was thus that he spoke of the object of my visit, of his earnest desire to see me, and of the solace he expected me to afford him. He entered, at some length, into what he conceived to be the nature of his malady. It was, he said, a constitutional and a family evil, and one for which he despaired to find a remedy—a mere nervous affection, he immediately added, which would undoubtedly soon pass off. It displayed itself in a host of unnatural sensations. Some of these, as he detailed them, interested and bewildered me; although, perhaps, the terms, and the general manner of the narration had their weight. He suffered much from a morbid acuteness of the senses; the most insipid food was alone endurable; he could wear only garments of certain texture; the odours of all flowers were oppressive; his eyes were tortured by even a faint light; and there were but peculiar sounds, and these from stringed instruments, which did not inspire him with horror.

To an anomalous species of terror I found him a bounden slave. "I shall perish," said he, "I *must* perish in this deplorable folly. Thus, thus, and not otherwise, shall I be lost. I dread the events of the future, not in themselves, but in their results. I shudder at the thought of any, even the most trivial, incident, which may operate upon this intolerable agitation of soul. I have, indeed, no abhorrence of danger, except in its absolute effect—in terror. In this unnerved—in this pitiable condition—I feel that the period will sooner or later arrive when I must abandon life and reason together, in some struggle with the grim phantasm, FEAR."

I learned, moreover, at intervals, and through broken and equivocal hints, another singular feature of his mental condition. He was enchained by certain superstitious impressions in regard to the dwelling which he tenanted, and whence, for many years, he had never ventured forth—in regard to an influence whose supposititious force was conveyed in terms too shadowy here to be re-stated—an influence which some peculiarities in the mere form and substance of his family mansion, had, by dint of long sufferance, he said, obtained over his spirit—an effect which the *physique* of the gray walls and turrets, and of the dim tarn into which they all looked down, had, at length, brought about upon the *morale* of his existence.

He admitted, however, although with hesitation, that much of the peculiar gloom which thus afflicted him could be traced to a more natural and far more palpable origin—to the severe and long-continued illness—indeed to the evidently approaching dissolution—of a tenderly beloved sister—his sole companion for long years—his last and only relative on earth. "Her decease," he said, with a bitterness which I can never forget, "would leave him (him the hopeless and the frail) the last of the ancient race of the Ushers." While he spoke, the lady Madeline (for so was she called) passed slowly through a remote portion of the apartment, and, without having noticed my presence, disappeared. I regarded her with an utter astonishment not unmingled with dread—and yet I found it impossible to account for such feelings. A sensation of stupor oppressed me, as my eyes followed her retreating steps. When a door, at length, closed upon her, my glance sought instinctively and eagerly the countenance of the brother—but he had buried his face in his hands, and I could only perceive that a far more than ordinary wanness had overspread the emaciated fingers through which trickled many passionate tears.

The disease of the lady Madeline had long baffled the skill of her physicians. A settled apathy, a gradual wasting away of the person, and frequent although transient affections of a partially cataleptical character, were the unusual diagnosis. Hitherto she had steadily borne up against the pressure of her malady, and had not betaken herself finally to bed; but, on the closing in of the evening of my arrival at the house, she succumbed (as her brother told me at night with inexpressible agitation) to the prostrating power of the destroyer; and I learned that the glimpse I had obtained of her person would thus probably be the last I should obtain—that the lady, at least while living, would be seen by me no more.

For several days ensuing, her name was unmentioned by either Usher or myself: and during this period I was busied in earnest endeavours to alleviate the melancholy of my friend. We painted and read together; or I listened, as if in a dream, to the wild improvisations of his speaking guitar. And thus, as a closer and still closer intimacy admitted me more unreservedly into the recesses of his spirit, the more bitterly did I perceive the futility of all attempt at cheering a mind from which darkness, as if an inherent positive quality, poured forth upon all objects of the moral and physical universe, in one unceasing radiation of gloom.

I shall ever bear about me a memory of the many solemn hours I thus spent alone with the master of the House of Usher. Yet I should fail in any attempt to convey an idea of the exact character of the studies, or of the occupations, in which he involved me, or led me the way. An excited and highly distempered ideality threw a sulphureous lustre over all. His long improvised dirges will ring forever in my ears. Among other things, I hold painfully in mind a certain singular perversion and amplification of the wild air of the last waltz of Von Weber. From the paintings over which his elaborate fancy brooded, and which grew, touch by touch, into vaguenesses at which I shuddered the more thrillingly, because I shuddered knowing not why;—from these paintings (vivid as their images now are before me) I would in vain endeavor to educe more than a small portion which should lie within the compass of merely written words. By the utter simplicity, by the nakedness of his designs, he arrested and overawed attention. If ever mortal painted an idea, that mortal was Roderick Usher. For me at least—in the circumstances then surrounding me—there arose out of the pure abstractions which the hypochondriac contrived to throw upon his canvas, an intensity of intolerable awe, no shadow of which felt I ever yet in the contemplation of the certainly glowing yet too concrete reveries of Fuseli.

One of the phantasmagoric conceptions of my friend, partaking not so rigidly of the spirit of abstraction, may be shadowed forth, although feebly, in words. A small picture presented the interior of an immensely long and rectangular vault or tunnel, with low walls, smooth, white, and without interruption or device. Certain accessory points of the design served well to convey the idea that this excavation lay at an exceeding depth below the surface of the earth. No outlet was observed in any portion of its vast extent, and no torch, or other artificial source of light was discernible; yet a flood of intense rays rolled throughout, and bathed the whole in a ghastly and inappropriate splendour.

I have just spoken of that morbid condition of the auditory nerve which rendered all music intolerable to the sufferer, with the exception of certain effects of stringed instruments. It was, perhaps, the narrow limits to which he thus confined himself upon the guitar, which gave birth, in great measure, to the fantastic character of his performances. But the fervid *facility* of his *impromptus* could not be so accounted for. They must have been, and were, in the notes, as well as in the words of his wild fantasias (for he not unfrequently accompanied himself with rhymed verbal improvisations), the result of that intense mental collectedness and concentration to which I have previously alluded as observable only in particular moments of the highest artificial excitement. The words of one of these rhapsodies I have easily remembered. I was, perhaps, the more forcibly impressed with it, as he gave it, because, in the under or mystic current of its meaning, I fancied that I perceived, and for the first time, a full consciousness on the part of Usher, of the tottering of his lofty reason upon her throne. The verses, which were entitled "The Haunted Palace," ran very nearly, if not accurately, thus:

### I

In the greenest of our valleys,
     By good angels tenanted,
Once a fair and stately palace—
     Radiant palace—reared its head.
In the monarch Thought's dominion—
     It stood there!
Never seraph spread a pinion
     Over fabric half so fair.

### II

Banners yellow, glorious, golden,
     On its roof did float and flow;
(This—all this—was in the olden
     Time long ago)
And every gentle air that dallied,
     In that sweet day,
Along the ramparts plumed and pallid,
     A winged odour went away.

### III

Wanderers in that happy valley
     Through two luminous windows saw
Spirits moving musically
     To a lute's well-tuned law,
Round about a throne, where sitting
     (Porphyrogene!)
In state his glory well befitting,
     The ruler of the realm was seen.

### IV

And all with pearl and ruby glowing
     Was the fair palace door,

Through which came flowing, flowing, flowing
    And sparkling evermore,
A troop of Echoes whose sweet duty
    Was but to sing,
In voices of surpassing beauty,
    The wit and wisdom of their king.

### V

But evil things, in robes of sorrow.
    Assailed the monarch's high estate;
(Ah, let us mourn, for never morrow
    Shall dawn upon him, desolate!)
And, round about his home, the glory
    That blushed and bloomed
Is but a dim-remembered story
    Of the oldtime entombed.

### VI

And travellers now within that valley,
    Through the red-litten windows, see
Vast forms that move fantastically
    To a discordant melody;
While, like a rapid ghastly river,
    Through the pale door,
A hideous throng rush out forever,
    And laugh—but smile no more.

I well remember that suggestions arising from this ballad led us into a train of thought wherein there became manifest an opinion of Usher's, which I mention not so much on account of its novelty (for other men have thought thus) as on account of the pertinacity with which he maintained it. This opinion, in its general form, was that of the sentience of all vegetable things. But, in his disordered fancy, the idea had assumed a more daring character, and trespassed, under certain conditions, upon the kingdom of inorganization. I lack words to express the full extent, of the earnest *abandon* of his persuasion. The belief, however, was connected (as I have previously hinted) with the gray stones of the home of his forefathers. The conditions of the sentience had been here, he imagined, fulfilled in the method of collocation of these stones—in the order of their arrangement, as well as in that of the many *fungi* which overspread them, and of the decayed trees which stood around—above all, in the long undisturbed endurance of this arrangement, and in its reduplication in the still waters of the tarn. Its evidence—the evidence of the sentience—was to be seen, he said (and I here started as he spoke), in the gradual yet certain condensation of an atmosphere of their own about the waters and the walls. The result was discoverable, he added, in that silent, yet importunate and terrible influence which for centuries had moulded the destinies of his family, and which made *him* what I now saw him—what he was. Such opinions need no comment, and I will make none.

Our books—the books which, for years, had formed no small portion of the mental existence of the invalid—were, as might be supposed, in strict keeping with this character of phantasm. We pored together over such works as the Ververt et Chartreuse of Gresset; the Belphegor of Machiavelli; the Heaven and Hell of Swedenborg; the Subterranean Voyage of Nicholas Klimm by Holberg; the Chiromancy of Robert Flud, of Jean D'Indaginé, and of De la Chambre; the Journey into the Blue Distance of Tieck; and the City of the Sun of Campanella. One favourite volume was a small octavo edition of the *Directorium Inquisitorum,* by the Dominican Eymeric de Gironne; and there were passages in Pomponius Mela, about the old African Satyrs and Ægipans, over which Usher would sit dreaming for hours. His chief delight, however, was found in the perusal of an exceedingly rare and curious book in quarto Gothic— the manual of a forgotten church—the *Vigiliae Mortuorum secundum Chorum Ecclesiae Maguntinae.*

I could not help thinking of the wild ritual of this work, and of its probable influence upon the hypochondriac, when, one evening, having informed me abruptly that the lady Madeline was no more, he stated his intention of preserving her corpse for a fortnight (previously to its final interment), in one of the numerous vaults within the main walls of the building. The worldly reason, however, assigned for this singular proceeding, was one which I did not feel at liberty to dispute. The brother had been led to his resolution (so he told me) by consideration of the unusual character of the malady of the deceased, of certain obtrusive and eager inquiries on the part of her medical men, and of the remote and exposed situation of the burial-ground of the family. I will not deny that when I called to mind the sinister countenance of the person whom I met upon the staircase, on the day of my arrival at the house, I had no desire to oppose what I regarded as at best but a harmless, and by no means an unnatural, precaution.

At the request of Usher, I personally aided him in the arrangements for the temporary entombment. The body having been encoffined, we two alone bore it to its rest. The vault in which we placed it (and which had been so long unopened that our torches, half smothered in its oppressive atmosphere, gave us little opportunity for investigation) was small, damp, and entirely without means of admission for light; lying, at great depth, immediately beneath that portion of the building in which was my own sleeping apartment. It had been used, apparently, in remote feudal times, for the worst purposes of a donjon-keep, and, in later days, as a place of deposit for powder, or some other highly combustible substance, as a portion of its floor, and the whole interior of a long archway through which we reached it, were carefully sheathed with copper. The door, of massive iron, had been, also, similarly protected. Its immense weight caused an unusually sharp grating sound, as it moved upon its hinges.

Having deposited our mournful burden upon tressels within this region of horror, we partially turned aside the yet unscrewed lid of the coffin, and looked upon the face of the tenant. A striking similitude between the brother and sister now first arrested my attention; and Usher, divining, perhaps, my thoughts, murmured out some few words from which I learned that the deceased and himself had been twins, and that sympathies of a scarcely intelligible nature had always existed between them. Our glances, however, rested not long upon the dead—for we could not regard her unawed. The disease which had thus entombed the lady in the maturity of youth, had left, as usual in all maladies of a strictly cataleptical character, the mockery of a faint blush upon the bosom and the face, and that suspiciously lingering smile upon the lip which is so terrible in death. We replaced and screwed down the lid, and, having secured the door of iron, made our way, with toil, into the scarcely less gloomy apartments of the upper portion of the house.

And now, some days of bitter grief having elapsed, an observable change came over the features of the mental disorder of my friend. His ordinary manner had vanished. His ordinary occupations were neglected or forgotten. He roamed from chamber to chamber with hurried, unequal, and objectless step. The pallor of his countenance had assumed, if possible, a more ghastly hue—but the luminousness of his eye had utterly gone out. The once occasional huskiness of his tone was heard no more; and a tremulous quaver, as if of extreme terror, habitually characterized his utterance. There were times, indeed, when I thought his unceasingly agitated mind was labouring with some oppressive secret, to divulge which he struggled for the necessary courage. At times, again, I was obliged to resolve all into the mere inexplicable vagaries of madness, for I beheld him gazing upon vacancy for long hours, in an attitude of the profoundest attention, as if listening to some imaginary sound. It was no wonder that his condition terrified—that it infected me. I felt creeping upon me, by slow yet certain degrees, the wild influences of his own fantastic yet impressive superstitions.

It was, especially, upon retiring to bed late in the night of the seventh or eighth day after the placing of the lady Madeline within the donjon, that I experienced the full power of such feelings. Sleep came not near my couch—while the hours waned and waned away. I struggled to reason off the nervousness which had dominion over me. I endeavoured to believe that much, if not all of what I felt, was due to the bewildering influence of the gloomy furniture of the room—of the dark and tattered draperies, which, tortured into motion by the breath of a rising tempest, swayed fitfully to and fro upon the walls, and rustled uneasily about the decorations of the bed. But my efforts were fruitless. An irrepressible tremour gradually pervaded my frame; and, at length, there sat upon my very heart an incubus of utterly causeless alarm. Shaking this off with a gasp and a struggle, I uplifted myself upon the pillows, and, peering earnestly within the intense darkness of the chamber, hearkened—I know not why, except that an instinctive spirit prompted me—to certain low and indefinite sounds which came, through the pauses of the storm, at long intervals, I knew not whence. Overpowered by an intense sentiment of horror, unaccountable yet unendurable, I threw on my clothes with haste (for I felt that I should sleep no more during the night), and endeavoured to arouse myself from the pitiable condition into which I had fallen, by pacing rapidly to and fro through the apartment.

I had taken but few turns in this manner, when a light step on an adjoining staircase arrested my attention. I presently recognized it as that of Usher. In an instant afterward he rapped, with a gentle touch, at my door, and entered, bearing a lamp. His countenance was, as usual, cadaverously wan—but, moreover, there was a species of mad hilarity in his eyes—an evidently restrained *hysteria* in his whole demeanour. His air appalled me—but anything was preferable to the solitude which I had so long endured, and I even welcomed his presence as a relief.

"And you have not seen it?" he said abruptly, after having stared about him for some moments in silence—"you have not then seen it?—but, stay! you shall." Thus speaking, and having carefully shaded his lamp, he hurried to one of the casements, and threw it freely open to the storm.

The impetuous fury of the entering gust nearly lifted us from our feet. It was, indeed, a tempestuous yet sternly beautiful night, and one wildly singular in its terror and its beauty. A whirlwind had apparently collected its force in our vicinity; for there were frequent and violent alterations in the direction of the wind; and the exceeding density of the clouds (which hung so low as to press upon the turrets of the house) did not prevent our perceiving the lifelike velocity with which they flew careering from all points against each other, without passing away into the distance. I say that even their exceeding density did not prevent our perceiving this—yet we had no glimpse of the moon or stars—nor was there any flashing forth of the lightning. But the under surfaces of the huge masses of agitated vapour, as well as all terrestrial objects immediately around us, were glowing in the unnatural light of a faintly luminous and distinctly visible gaseous exhalation which hung about and enshrouded the mansion.

"You must not—you shall not behold this!" said I, shudderingly, to Usher, as I led him, with a gentle violence, from the window to a seat. "These appearances, which bewilder you, are merely electrical phenomena not uncommon—or it may be that they have their ghastly origin in the rank miasma of the tarn. Let us close this casement;—the air is chilling and dangerous to your frame. Here is one of your favourite romances. I will read, and you shall listen;—and so we will pass away this terrible night together."

The antique volume which I had taken up was the "Mad Trist" of Sir Launcelot Canning; but I had called it a favourite of Usher's more in sad jest than in earnest; for, in truth, there is little in its uncouth and unimaginative prolixity which could have had interest for the lofty and spiritual ideality of my friend. It was, however, the only book immediately at hand; and I indulged a vague hope that the excitement which now agitated the hypochondriac, might find relief (for the history of mental disorder is full of similar anomalies) even in the extremeness of the folly which I should read. Could I have judged, indeed, by the wild overstrained air of vivacity with which he hearkened, or apparently hearkened, to the words of the tale, I might well have congratulated myself upon the success of my design.

I had arrived at that well-known portion of the story where Ethelred, the hero of the Trist, having sought in vain for peaceable admission into the dwelling of the hermit, proceeds to make good an entrance by force. Here, it will be remembered, the words of the narrative run thus:

"And Ethelred, who was by nature of a doughty heart, and who was now mighty withal, on account of the powerfulness of the wine which he had drunken, waited no longer to hold parley with the hermit, who, in sooth, was of an obstinate and maliceful turn, but, feeling the rain upon his shoulders, and fearing the rising of the tempest, uplifted his mace outright, and, with blows, made quickly room in the plankings of the door for his gauntleted hand; and now pulling therewith sturdily, he so cracked, and ripped, and tore all asunder, that the noise of the dry and hollow-sounding wood alarumed and reverberated throughout the forest."

At the termination of this sentence I started, and for a moment, paused; for it appeared to me (although I at once concluded that my excited fancy had deceived me)—it appeared to me that, from some very remote portion of the mansion, there came, indistinctly, to my ears, what might have been, in its exact similarity of character, the echo (but a stifled and dull one certainly) of the very cracking and ripping sound which Sir Launcelot had so particularly described. It was, beyond doubt, the coincidence alone which had arrested my attention; for, amid the rattling of the sashes of the casements, and the ordinary commingled noises of the still increasing storm, the sound, in itself, had nothing, surely, which should have interested or disturbed me. I continued the story:

"But the good champion Ethelred, now entering within the door, was sore enraged and amazed to perceive no signal of the maliceful hermit; but, in the stead thereof, a dragon of a scaly and prodigious demeanour, and of a fiery tongue, which sate in guard before a palace of gold, with a floor of silver; and upon the wall there hung a shield of shining brass with this legend enwritten—

> Who entereth herein, a conqueror hath bin;
> Who slayeth the dragon, the shield he shall win;

And Ethelred uplifted his mace, and struck upon the head of the dragon, which fell before him, and gave up his pesty breath, with a shriek so horrid and harsh, and withal so piercing, that Ethelred had fain to close his ears with his hands against the dreadful noise of it, the like whereof was never before heard."

Here again I paused abruptly, and now with a feeling of wild amazement—for there could be no doubt whatever that, in this instance, I did actually hear (although from what direction it proceeded I found it impossible to say) a low and apparently distant, but harsh, protracted, and most unusual screaming or grating sound—the exact counterpart of what my fancy had already conjured up for the dragon's unnatural shriek as described by the romancer.

Oppressed, as I certainly was, upon the occurrence of the second and most extraordinary coincidence, by a thousand conflicting sensations, in which wonder and extreme terror were predominant, I still retained sufficient presence of mind to avoid exciting, by any observation, the sensitive nervousness of my companion. I was by no means certain that he had noticed the sounds in question; although, assuredly, a strange alteration had, during the last few minutes, taken place in his demeanour. From a position fronting my own, he had gradually brought round his chair, so as to sit with his face to the door of the chamber; and thus I could but partially perceive his features, although I saw that his lips trembled as if he were murmuring inaudibly. His head had dropped upon his breast—yet I knew that he was not asleep, from the wide and rigid opening of the eye as I caught a glance of it in profile. The motion of his body, too, was at variance with this idea—for he rocked from side to side with a gentle yet constant and uniform sway. Having rapidly taken notice of all this, I resumed the narrative of Sir Launcelot, which thus proceeded:

"And now, the champion, having escaped from the terrible fury of the dragon, bethinking himself of the brazen shield, and of the breaking up of the enchantment which was upon it, removed the carcass from out of the way before him, and approached valorously over the silver pavement of the castle to where the shield was upon the wall; which in sooth tarried not for his full coming, but fell down at his feet upon the silver floor, with a mighty great and terrible ringing sound."

No sooner had these syllables passed my lips, than—as if a shield of brass had indeed, at the moment, fallen heavily upon a floor of silver—I became aware of a distinct, hollow, metallic, and clangorous, yet apparently muffled reverberation. Completely unnerved, I leaped to my feet, but the measured rocking movement of Usher was undisturbed. I rushed to the chair in which he sat. His eyes were bent fixedly before him, and throughout his whole countenance there reigned a stony rigidity. But, as I placed my hand upon his shoulder, there came a strong shudder over his whole person; a sickly smile quivered about his lips; and I saw that he spoke in a low, hurried, and gibbering murmur, as if unconscious of my presence. Bending closely over him, I at length drank in the hideous import of his words.

"Not hear it?—yes, I hear it, and *have* heard it. Long—long— long—many minutes, many hours, many days, have I heard it—yet I dared not—oh, pity me, miserable wretch that I am!—I dared not—I *dared* not speak! *We have put her living in the tomb!* Said I not that my senses were acute? I *now* tell you that I heard her first feeble movements in the hollow coffin. I heard them—many, many days ago—yet I dared not—*I dared not speak!* And now—tonight— Ethelred—ha! ha!—the breaking of the hermit's door, and the death-cry of the dragon, and the clangour of the shield!—say, rather, the rending of her coffin, and the grating of the iron hinges of her prison, and her struggles within the coppered archway of the vault! Oh whither shall I fly? Will she not be here anon? Is she not hurrying to upbraid me for my haste? Have I not heard her footstep on the stair? Do I not distinguish that heavy and horrible beating of her heart? MADMAN!" here he sprang furiously to his feet, and shrieked out his syllables, as if in the effort he were giving up his soul— "MADMAN! I TELL YOU THAT SHE NOW STANDS WITHOUT THE DOOR!"

As if in the superhuman energy of his utterance there had been found the potency of a spell—the huge antique panels to which the speaker pointed, threw slowly back, upon the instant, their ponderous and ebony jaws. It was the work of the rushing gust—but then without those doors there DID stand the lofty and enshrouded figure of the lady Madeline of Usher. There was blood upon her white robes, and the evidence of some bitter struggle upon every portion of her emaciated frame. For a moment she remained trembling and reeling to and fro upon the threshold, then, with a low moaning cry, fell heavily inward upon the person of her brother, and in her violent and now final death-agonies, bore him to the floor a corpse, and a victim to the terrors he had anticipated.

From that chamber, and from that mansion, I fled aghast. The storm was still abroad in all its wrath as I found myself crossing the old causeway. Suddenly there shot along the path a wild light, and I turned to see whence a gleam so unusual could have issued; for the vast house and its shadows were alone behind me. The radiance was that of the full, setting, and blood-red moon which now shone vividly through that once barely-discernible fissure of which I have before spoken as extending from the roof of the building, in a zigzag direction, to the base. While I gazed, this fissure rapidly widened— there came a fierce breath of the whirlwind—the entire orb of the satellite burst at once upon my sight—my brain reeled as I saw the mighty walls rushing asunder—there was a long tumultuous shouting sound like the voice of a thousand waters—and the deep and dank tarn at my feet closed sullenly and silently over the fragments of the "HOUSE OF USHER."

# THE BLACK CAT

## Edgar Allan Poe

FOR THE MOST wild, yet most homely narrative which I am about to pen, I neither expect nor solicit belief. Mad indeed would I be to expect it, in a case where my very senses reject their own evidence. Yet, mad am I not—and very surely do I not dream. But tomorrow I die, and today I would unburthen my soul. My immediate purpose is to place before the world, plainly, succinctly, and without comment, a series of mere household events. In their consequences, these events have terrified—have tortured—have destroyed me. Yet I will attempt to expound them. To me, they have presented little but Horror—to many they will seem less terrible than *baroques*. Hereafter, perhaps, some intellect may be found which will reduce my phantasm to the common-place—some intellect more calm, more logical, and far less excitable than my own, which will perceive, in the circumstances I detail with awe, nothing more than an ordinary succession of very natural causes and effects.

From my infancy I was noted for the docility and humanity of my disposition. My tenderness of heart was even so conspicuous as to make me the jest of my companions. I was especially fond of animals, and was indulged by my parents with a great variety of pets. With these I spent most of my time, and never was so happy as when feeding and caressing them. This peculiarity of character grew with my growth, and, in my manhood, I derived from it one of my principal sources of pleasure. To those who have cherished an affection for a faithful and sagacious dog, I need hardly be at the trouble of explaining the nature or the intensity of the gratification thus derivable. There is something in the unselfish and self-sacrificing love of a brute, which goes directly to the heart of him who has had frequent occasion to test the paltry friendship and gossamer fidelity of mere *Man*.

I married early, and was happy to find in my wife a disposition not uncongenial with my own. Observing my partiality for domestic pets, she lost no opportunity of procuring those of the most agreeable kind. We had birds, gold fish, a fine dog, rabbits, a small monkey, and *a cat*.

This latter was a remarkably large and beautiful animal, entirely black, and sagacious to an astonishing degree. In speaking of his intelligence, my wife, who at heart was not a little tinctured with superstition, made frequent allusion to the ancient popular notion, which regarded all black cats as witches in disguise. Not that she was ever *serious* upon this point—and I mention the matter at all for no better reason than that it happens, just now, to be remembered.

Pluto—this was the cat's name—was my favorite pet and playmate. I alone fed him, and he attended me wherever I went about the house. It was even with difficulty that I could prevent him from following me through the streets.

Our friendship lasted, in this manner, for several years, during which my general temperament and character—through the instrumentality of the Fiend Intemperance—had (I blush to confess it) experienced a radical alteration for the worse. I grew, day by day, more moody, more irritable, more regardless of the feelings of others. I suffered myself to use intemperate language to my wife. At length, I even offered her personal violence. My pets, of course, were made to feel the change in my disposition. I not only neglected, but ill-used them. For Pluto, however, I still retained sufficient regard to restrain me from maltreating him, as I made no scruple of maltreating the rabbits, the monkey, or even the dog, when by accident, or through affection, they came in my way. But my disease grew upon me—for what disease is like Alcohol!—and at length even Pluto, who was now becoming old, and consequently somewhat peevish—even Pluto began to experience the effects of my ill temper.

One night, returning home, much intoxicated, from one of my haunts about town, I fancied that the cat avoided my presence. I seized him; when, in his fright at my violence, he inflicted a slight wound upon my hand with his teeth. The fury of a demon instantly possessed me. I knew myself no longer. My original soul seemed, at once, to take its flight from my body; and a more than fiendish malevolence, gin-nurtured, thrilled every fibre of my frame. I took from my waistcoat-pocket a pen-knife, opened it, grasped the poor beast by the throat, and deliberately cut one of its eyes from the socket! I blush, I burn, I shudder, while I pen the damnable atrocity.

When reason returned with the morning—when I had slept off the fumes of the night's debauch—I experienced a sentiment half of horror, half of remorse, for the crime of which I had been guilty; but it was, at best, a feeble and equivocal feeling, and the soul remained untouched. I again plunged into excess, and soon drowned in wine all memory of the deed.

In the meantime the cat slowly recovered. The socket of the lost eye presented, it is true, a frightful appearance, but he no longer appeared to suffer any pain. He went about the house as usual, but, as might be expected, fled in extreme terror at my approach. I had so much of my old heart left, as to be at first grieved by this evident dislike on the part of a creature which had once so loved me. But this feeling soon gave place to irritation. And then came, as if to my final and irrevocable overthrow, the spirit of PERVERSENESS. Of this spirit philosophy takes no account. Yet I am not more sure that my soul lives, than I am that perverseness is one of the primitive impulses of the human heart—one of the indivisible primary faculties, or sentiments, which give direction to the character of Man. Who has not, a hundred times, found himself committing a vile or a silly action, for no other reason than because he knows he should *not*? Have we not a perpetual inclination, in the teeth of our best judgment, to violate that which is *Law,* merely because we understand it to be such? This spirit of perverseness, I say, came to my final overthrow. It was this unfathomable longing of the soul *to vex itself*—to offer violence to its own nature—to do wrong for the wrong's sake only— that urged me to continue and finally to consummate the injury I had inflicted upon the unoffending brute. One morning, in cool blood, I slipped a noose about its neck and hung it to the limb of a tree;—hung it with the tears streaming from my eyes, and with the bitterest remorse at my heart;—hung it *because* I knew that it had loved me, and *because* I felt it had given me no reason of offence;— hung it *because* I knew that in so doing I was committing a sin—a deadly sin that would so jeopardize my immortal soul as to place it—if such a thing were possible—even beyond the reach of the infinite mercy of the Most Merciful and Most Terrible God.

On the night of the day on which this cruel deed was done, I was aroused from sleep by the cry of fire. The curtains of my bed were in flames. The whole house was blazing. It was with great difficulty that my wife, a servant, and myself, made our escape from the conflagration. The destruction was complete. My entire worldly wealth was swallowed up, and I resigned myself thenceforward to despair.

I am above the weakness of seeking to establish a sequence of cause and effect, between the disaster and the atrocity. But I am detailing a chain of facts—and wish not to leave even a possible link imperfect. On the day succeeding the fire, I visited the ruins. The walls, with one exception, had fallen in. This exception was found in a compartment wall, not very thick, which stood about the middle of the house, and against which had rested the head of my bed. The plastering had here, in great measure, resisted the action of the fire—a fact which I attributed to its having been recently spread. About this wall a dense crowd were collected, and many persons seemed to be examining a particular portion of it with very minute and eager attention. The words "strange!" "singular!" and other similar expressions, excited my curiosity. I approached and saw, as if graven in *bas relief* upon the white surface, the figure of a gigantic *cat*. The impression was given with an accuracy truly marvellous. There was a rope about the animal's neck.

When I first beheld this apparition—for I could scarcely regard it as less—my wonder and my terror were extreme. But at length reflection came to my aid. The cat, I remembered, had been hung in a garden adjacent to the house. Upon the alarm of fire, this garden had been immediately filled by the crowd—by someone of whom the animal must have been cut from the tree and thrown, through an open window, into my chamber. This had probably been done with the view of arousing me from sleep. The falling of other walls had compressed the victim of my cruelty into the substance of the freshly-spread plaster; the lime of which, with the flames, and the *ammonia* from the carcass, had then accomplished the portraiture as I saw it.

Although I thus readily accounted to my reason, if not altogether to my conscience, for the startling fact just detailed, it did not the less fail to make a deep impression upon my fancy. For months I could not rid myself of the phantasm of the cat; and, during this period, there came back into my spirit a half-sentiment that seemed, but was not, remorse. I went so far as to regret the loss of the animal, and to look about me, among the vile haunts which I now habitually frequented, for another pet of the same species, and of somewhat similar appearance, with which to supply its place.

One night as I sat, half stupefied, in a den of more than infamy, my attention was suddenly drawn to some black object, reposing upon the head of one of the immense hogsheads of Gin, or of Rum, which constituted the chief furniture of the apartment. I had been looking steadily at the top of this hogshead for some minutes, and what now caused me surprise was the fact that I had not sooner perceived the object thereupon. I approached it, and touched it with my hand. It was a black cat—a very large one—fully as large as Pluto, and closely resembling him in every respect but one. Pluto had not a white hair upon any portion of his body; but this cat had a large, although indefinite splotch of white, covering nearly the whole region of the breast.

Upon my touching him, he immediately arose, purred loudly, rubbed against my hand, and appeared delighted with my notice. This, then, was the very creature of which I was in search. I at once offered to purchase it of the landlord; but this person made no claim to it—knew nothing of it—had never seen it before.

I continued my caresses, and, when I prepared to go home, the animal evinced a disposition to accompany me. I permitted it to do so; occasionally stooping and patting it as I proceeded. When it reached the house it domesticated itself at once, and became immediately a great favorite with my wife.

For my own part, I soon found a dislike to it arising within me. This was just the reverse of what I had anticipated; but I know not how or why it was—its evident fondness for myself rather disgusted and annoyed. By slow degrees, these feelings of disgust and annoyance rose into the bitterness of hatred. I avoided the creature; a certain sense of shame, and the remembrance of my former deed of cruelty, preventing me from physically abusing it. I did not, for some weeks, strike, or otherwise violently ill use it; but gradually—very gradually—I came to look upon it with unutterable loathing, and to flee silently from its odious presence, as from the breath of a pestilence.

What added, no doubt, to my hatred of the beast, was the discovery, on the morning after I brought it home, that, like Pluto, it also had been deprived of one of its eyes. This circumstance, however, only endeared it to my wife, who, as I have already said, possessed, in a high degree, that humanity of feeling which had once been my distinguishing trait, and the source of many of my simplest and purest pleasures.

With my aversion to this cat, however, its partiality for myself seemed to increase. It followed my footsteps with a pertinacity which it would be difficult to make the reader comprehend. Whenever I sat, it would crouch beneath my chair, or spring upon my knees, covering me with its loathsome caresses. If I arose to walk it would get between my feet and thus nearly throw me down, or, fastening its long and sharp claws in my dress, clamber, in this manner, to my breast. At such times, although I longed to destroy it with a blow, I was yet withheld from so doing, partly by a memory of my former crime, but chiefly—let me confess it at once—by absolute *dread* of the beast.

This dread was not exactly a dread of physical evil—and yet I should be at a loss how otherwise to define it. I am almost ashamed to own—yes, even in this felon's cell, I am almost ashamed to own—that the terror and horror with which the animal inspired me, had been heightened by one of the merest chimæras it would be possible to conceive. My wife had called my attention, more than once, to the character of the mark of white hair, of which I have spoken, and which constituted the sole visible difference between the strange beast and the one I had destroyed. The reader will remember that this mark, although large, had been originally very indefinite; but, by slow degrees—degrees nearly imperceptible, and which for a long time my Reason struggled to reject as fanciful—it had, at length, assumed a rigorous distinctness of outline. It was now the representation of an object that I shudder to name—and for this, above all, I loathed, and dreaded, and would have rid myself of the monster *had I dared*— it was now, I say, the image of a hideous—of a ghastly thing—of the GALLOWS!—oh, mournful and terrible engine of Horror and of Crime—of Agony and of Death!

And now was I indeed wretched beyond the wretchedness of mere Humanity. And *a brute beast*—whose fellow I had contemptuously destroyed—*a brute beast* to work out for *me*—for me a man, fashioned in the image of the High God—so much of insufferable wo! Alas! neither by day nor by night knew I the blessing of Rest any more! During the former the creature left me no moment alone; and, in the latter, I started, hourly, from dreams of unutterable fear, to find the hot breath of *the thing* upon my face, and its vast weight—an incarnate Night-Mare that I had no power to shake off—incumbent eternally upon my *heart!*

Beneath the pressure of torments such as these, the feeble remnant of the good within me succumbed. Evil thoughts became my sole intimates—the darkest and most evil of thoughts. The moodiness of my usual temper increased to hatred of all things and of all mankind;

while, from the sudden, frequent, and ungovernable outbursts of a fury to which I now blindly abandoned myself, my uncomplaining wife, alas! was the most usual and the most patient of sufferers.

One day she accompanied me, upon some household errand, into the cellar of the old building which our poverty compelled us to inhabit. The cat followed me down the steep stairs, and, nearly throwing me headlong, exasperated me to madness. Uplifting an axe, and forgetting, in my wrath, the childish dread which had hitherto stayed my hand, I aimed a blow at the animal which, of course, would have proved instantly fatal had it descended as I wished. But this blow was arrested by the hand of my wife. Goaded, by the interference, into a rage more than demoniacal, I withdrew my arm from her grasp and buried the axe in her brain. She fell dead upon the spot, without a groan.

This hideous murder accomplished, I set myself forthwith, and with entire deliberation, to the task of concealing the body. I knew that I could not remove it from the house, either by day or by night, without the risk of being observed by the neighbors. Many projects entered my mind. At one period I thought of cutting the corpse into minute fragments, and destroying them by fire. At another, I resolved to dig a grave for it in the floor of the cellar. Again, I deliberated about casting it in the well in the yard—about packing it in a box, as if merchandise, with the usual arrangements, and so getting a porter to take it from the house. Finally I hit upon what I considered a far better expedient than either of these. I determined to wall it up in the cellar—as the monks of the middle ages are recorded to have walled up their victims.

For a purpose such as this the cellar was well adapted. Its walls were loosely constructed, and had lately been plastered throughout with a rough plaster, which the dampness of the atmosphere had prevented from hardening. Moreover, in one of the walls was a projection, caused by a false chimney, or fireplace, that had been filled up, and made to resemble the rest of the cellar. I made no doubt that I could readily displace the bricks at this point, insert the corpse, and wall the whole up as before, so that no eye could detect anything suspicious.

And in this calculation I was not deceived. By means of a crow-bar I easily dislodged the bricks, and, having carefully deposited the body against the inner wall, I propped it in that position, while, with little trouble, I relaid the whole structure as it originally stood. Having procured mortar, sand, and hair, with every possible precaution, I prepared a plaster which could not be distinguished from the old, and with this I very carefully went over the new brick-work. When I had finished, I felt satisfied that all was right. The wall did not present the slightest appearance of having been disturbed. The rubbish on the floor was picked up with the minutest care. I looked around triumphantly, and said to myself—"Here at least, then, my labor has not been in vain."

My next step was to look for the beast which had been the cause of so much wretchedness; for I had, at length, firmly resolved to put it to death. Had I been able to meet with it, at the moment, there could have been no doubt of its fate; but it appeared that the crafty animal had been alarmed at the violence of my previous anger, and forebore to present itself in my present mood. It is impossible to describe, or to imagine, the deep, the blissful sense of relief which the absence of the detested creature occasioned in my bosom. It did not make its appearance during the night—and thus for one night at least, since its introduction into the house, I soundly and tranquilly slept; aye, *slept* even with the burden of murder upon my soul!

The second and the third day passed, and still my tormentor came not. Once again I breathed as a freeman. The monster, in terror, had fled the premises forever! I should behold it no more! My happiness was supreme! The guilt of my dark deed disturbed me but little. Some few inquiries had been made, but these had been readily answered. Even a search had been instituted—but of course nothing was to be discovered. I looked upon my future felicity as secured.

Upon the fourth day of the assassination, a party of the police came, very unexpectedly, into the house, and proceeded again to make rigorous investigation of the premises. Secure, however, in the inscrutability of my place of concealment, I felt no embarrassment whatever. The officers bade me accompany them in their search. They left no nook or corner unexplored. At length, for the third or fourth time, they descended into the cellar. I quivered not in a muscle. My heart beat calmly as that of one who slumbers in innocence. I walked the cellar from end to end. I folded my arms upon my bosom, and roamed easily to and fro. The police were thoroughly satisfied and prepared to depart. The glee at my heart was too strong to be restrained. I burned to say if but one word, by way of triumph, and to render doubly sure their assurance of my guiltlessness.

"Gentlemen," I said at last, as the party ascended the steps, "I delight to have allayed your suspicions. I wish you all health, and a little more courtesy. By the bye, gentlemen, this—this is a very well constructed house." [In the rabid desire to say something easily, I scarcely knew what I uttered at all ]—"I may say an *excellently* well constructed house. These walls—are you going, gentlemen?—these walls are solidly put together"; and here, through the mere phrenzy of bravado I rapped heavily, with a cane which I held in my hand, upon that very portion of the brick-work behind which stood the corpse of the wife of my bosom.

But may God shield and deliver me from the fangs of the Arch-Fiend! No sooner had the reverberation of my blows sunk into silence, than I was answered by a voice from within the tomb!—by a cry, at first muffled and broken, like the sobbing of a child, and then quickly swelling into one long, loud, and continuous scream, utterly anomalous and inhuman—a howl—a wailing shriek, half of horror and half of triumph, such as might have arisen only out of hell, conjointly from the throats of the damned in their agony and of the demons that exult in the damnation.

Of my own thoughts it is folly to speak. Swooning, I staggered to the opposite wall. For one instant the party upon the stairs remained motionless, through extremity of terror and of awe. In the next, a dozen stout arms were toiling at the wall. It fell bodily. The corpse, already greatly decayed and clotted with gore, stood erect before the eyes of the spectators. Upon its head, with red extended mouth and solitary eye of fire, sat the hideous beast whose craft had seduced me into murder, and whose informing voice had consigned me to the hangman. I had walled the monster up within the tomb!

# THE PIT AND THE PENDULUM

## Edgar Allan Poe

*Impia tortorum longos hic turba furores*
*Sanguinis innocui, non satiata, aluit.*
*Sospite nunc patriâ fracto nunc funeris antro,*
*Mors ubi dira fuit vita salusque patent[1].*

[QUATRAIN COMPOSED FOR THE GATES OF A MARKET TO BE ERECTED UPON THE SITE OF THE JACOBIN CLUB HOUSE AT PARIS.]

I WAS SICK—sick unto death with that long agony; and when they at length unbound me, and I was permitted to sit, I felt that my senses were leaving me. The sentence—the dread sentence of death—was the last of distinct accentuation which reached my ears. After that, the sound of the inquisitorial voices seemed merged in one dreamy indeterminate hum. It conveyed to my soul the idea of *revolution*—perhaps from its association in fancy with the burr of a millwheel. This only for a brief period; for presently I heard no more. Yet, for a while, I saw; but with how terrible an exaggeration! I saw the lips of the black-robed judges. They appeared to me white—whiter than the sheet upon which I trace these words—and thin even to grotesqueness; thin with the intensity of their expression of firmness—of immoveable resolution—of stern contempt of human torture. I saw that the decrees of what to me was Fate, were still issuing from those lips. I saw them writhe with a deadly locution. I saw them

---

[1] *Impia . . . patent*; Latin: Here an unholy mob of torturers, with an unquenchable thirst for innocent blood, once fed its long frenzy. We are now safe because the funeral cave has been destroyed, and life and health exist where death once was.

fashion the syllables of my name; and I shuddered because no sound succeeded. I saw, too, for a few moments of delirious horror, the soft and nearly imperceptible waving of the sable draperies which enwrapped the walls of the apartment. And then my vision fell upon the seven tall candles upon the table. At first they wore the aspect of charity, and seemed white slender angels who would save me; but then, all at once, there came a most deadly nausea over my spirit, and I felt every fibre in my frame thrill as if I had touched the wire of a galvanic battery, while the angel forms became meaningless spectres, with heads of flame, and I saw that from them there would be no help. And then there stole into my fancy, like a rich musical note, the thought of what sweet rest there must be in the grave. The thought came gently and stealthily, and it seemed long before it attained full appreciation; but just as my spirit came at length properly to feel and entertain it, the figures of the judges vanished, as if magically, from before me; the tall candles sank into nothingness; their flames went out utterly; the blackness of darkness supervened; all sensations appeared swallowed up in a mad rushing descent as of the soul into Hades. Then silence, and stillness, and night were the universe.

I had swooned; but still will not say that all of consciousness was lost. What of it there remained I will not attempt to define, or even to describe; yet all was not lost. In the deepest slumber—no! In delirium—no! In a swoon—no! In death—no! even in the grave all *is not* lost. Else there is no immortality for man. Arousing from the most profound of slumbers, we break the gossamer web of *some* dream. Yet in a second afterward (so frail may that web have been), we remember not that we have dreamed. In the return to life from the swoon there are two stages; first, that of the sense of mental or spiritual; secondly, that of the sense of physical, existence. It seems probable that if, upon reaching the second stage, we could recall the impressions of the first, we should find these impressions eloquent in memories of the gulf beyond. And that gulf is—what? How at least shall we distinguish its shadows from those of the tomb? But if the impressions of what I have termed the first stage, are not, at will, recalled, yet, after long interval, do they not come unbidden, while we marvel whence they come? He who has never swooned, is not he who finds strange palaces and wildly familiar faces in coals that glow; is not he who beholds floating in mid-air the sad visions that the many may not view; is not he who ponders over the perfume of some novel flower—is not he whose brain grows bewildered with the meaning of some musical cadence which has never before arrested his attention.

Amid frequent and thoughtful endeavors to remember; amid earnest struggles to regather some token of the state of seeming nothingness into which my soul had lapsed, there have been moments when I have dreamed of success; there have been brief, very brief periods when I have conjured up remembrances which the lucid reason of a later epoch assures me could have had reference only to that condition of seeming unconsciousness. These shadows of memory tell, indistinctly, of tall figures that lifted and bore me in silence down—down—still down—till a hideous dizziness oppressed me at the mere idea of the interminableness of the descent. They tell also of a vague horror at my heart, on account of that heart's unnatural stillness. Then comes a sense of sudden motionlessness throughout all things; as if those who bore me (a ghastly train!) had outrun, in their descent, the limits of the limitless, and paused from the wearisomeness of their toil. After this I call to mind flatness and dampness; and then all is *madness*—the madness of a memory which busies itself among forbidden things.

Very suddenly there came back to my soul motion and sound—the tumultuous motion of the heart, and, in my ears, the sound of its beating. Then a pause in which all is blank. Then again sound, and motion, and touch—a tingling sensation pervading my frame. Then the mere consciousness of existence, without thought—a condition which lasted long. Then, very suddenly, *thought,* and shuddering terror, and earnest endeavor to comprehend my true state. Then a strong desire to lapse into insensibility. Then a rushing revival of soul and a successful effort to move. And now a full memory of the trial, of the judges, of the sable draperies, of the sentence, of the sickness, of the swoon. Then entire forgetfulness of all that followed; of all that a later day and much earnestness of endeavor have enabled me vaguely to recall.

So far, I had not opened my eyes. I felt that I lay upon my back, unbound. I reached out my hand, and it fell heavily upon something damp and hard. There I suffered it to remain for many minutes, while I strove to imagine where and *what* I could be. I longed, yet dared not to employ my vision. I dreaded the first glance at objects around me. It was not that I feared to look upon things horrible, but that I grew aghast lest there should be *nothing* to see. At length, with a wild desperation at heart, I quickly unclosed my eyes. My worst thoughts, then, were confirmed. The blackness of eternal night encompassed me. I struggled for breath. The intensity of the darkness seemed to oppress and stifle me. The atmosphere was intolerably close. I still lay quietly, and made effort to exercise my reason. I brought to mind the inquisitorial proceedings, and attempted from that point to deduce my real condition. The sentence had passed; and it appeared to me that a very long interval of time had since elapsed. Yet not for a moment did I suppose myself actually dead. Such a supposition, notwithstanding what we read in fiction, is altogether inconsistent with real existence;—but where and in what state was I? The condemned to death, I knew, perished usually at the *autos-da-fé*[2], and one of these had been held on the very night of the day of my trial. Had I been remanded to my dungeon, to await the next sacrifice, which would not take place for many months? This I at once saw could not be. Victims had been in immediate demand. Moreover, my dungeon, as well as all the condemned cells at Toledo, had stone floors, and light was not altogether excluded.

A fearful idea now suddenly drove the blood in torrents upon my heart, and for a brief period, I once more relapsed into insensibility. Upon recovering, I at once started to my feet, trembling convulsively in every fibre. I thrust my arms wildly above and around me in all directions. I felt nothing; yet dreaded to move a step, lest I should be impeded by the walls of a *tomb*. Perspiration burst from every pore, and stood in cold big beads upon my forehead. The agony of suspense grew at length intolerable, and I cautiously moved forward, with my arms extended, and my eyes straining from their sockets, in the hope of catching some faint ray of light. I proceeded for many paces; but still all was blackness and vacancy. I breathed more freely. It seemed evident that mine was not, at least, the most hideous of fates.

And now, as I still continued to step cautiously onward, there came thronging upon my recollection a thousand vague rumors of the horrors of Toledo. Of the dungeons there had been strange things narrated—fables I had always deemed them—but yet strange, and too ghastly to repeat, save in a whisper. Was I left to perish of starvation in this subterranean world of darkness; or what fate, perhaps even more fearful, awaited me? That the result would be death, and a death of more than customary bitterness, I knew too well the character of my judges to doubt. The mode and the hour were all that occupied or distracted me.

My outstretched hands at length encountered some solid obstruction. It was a wall, seemingly of stone masonry—very smooth, slimy, and

---

2  *autos-da-fé*; Portuguese: a ritual of public penance.

cold. I followed it up; stepping with all the careful distrust with which certain antique narratives had inspired me. This process, however, afforded me no means of ascertaining the dimensions of my dungeon; as I might make its circuit, and return to the point whence I set out, without being aware of the fact; so perfectly uniform seemed the wall. I therefore sought the knife which had been in my pocket, when led into the inquisitorial chamber; but it was gone; my clothes had been exchanged for a wrapper of coarse serge. I had thought of forcing the blade in some minute crevice of the masonry, so as to identify my point of departure. The difficulty, nevertheless, was but trivial; although, in the disorder of my fancy, it seemed at first insuperable. I tore a part of the hem from the robe and placed the fragment at full length, and at right angles to the wall. In groping my way around the prison, I could not fail to encounter this rag upon completing the circuit. So, at least I thought: but I had not counted upon the extent of the dungeon, or upon my own weakness. The ground was moist and slippery. I staggered onward for some time, when I stumbled and fell. My excessive fatigue induced me to remain prostrate; and sleep soon overtook me as I lay.

Upon awaking, and stretching forth an arm, I found beside me a loaf and a pitcher with water. I was too much exhausted to reflect upon this circumstance, but ate and drank with avidity. Shortly afterward, I resumed my tour around the prison, and with much toil, came at last upon the fragment of the serge. Up to the period when I fell I had counted fifty-two paces, and upon resuming my walk, I had counted forty-eight more;—when I arrived at the rag. There were in all, then, a hundred paces; and, admitting two paces to the yard, I presumed the dungeon to be fifty yards in circuit. I had met, however, with many angles in the wall, and thus I could form no guess at the shape of the vault; for vault I could not help supposing it to be.

I had little object—certainly no hope—in these researches; but a vague curiosity prompted me to continue them. Quitting the wall, I resolved to cross the area of the enclosure. At first I proceeded with extreme caution, for the floor, although seemingly of solid material, was treacherous with slime. At length, however, I took courage, and did not hesitate to step firmly; endeavoring to cross in as direct a line as possible. I had advanced some ten or twelve paces in this manner, when the remnant of the torn hem of my robe became entangled between my legs. I stepped on it, and fell violently on my face.

In the confusion attending my fall, I did not immediately apprehend a somewhat startling circumstance, which yet, in a few seconds afterward, and while I still lay prostrate, arrested my attention. It was this—my chin rested upon the floor of the prison, but my lips and the upper portion of my head, although seemingly at a less elevation than the chin, touched nothing. At the same time my forehead seemed bathed in a clammy vapor, and the peculiar smell of decayed fungus arose to my nostrils. I put forward my arm, and shuddered to find that I had fallen at the very brink of a circular pit, whose extent, of course, I had no means of ascertaining at the moment. Groping about the masonry just below the margin, I succeeded in dislodging a small fragment, and let it fall into the abyss. For many seconds I hearkened to its reverberations as it dashed against the sides of the chasm in its descent; at length there was a sullen plunge into water, succeeded by loud echoes. At the same moment there came a sound resembling the quick opening, and as rapid closing of a door overhead, while a faint gleam of light flashed suddenly through the gloom, and as suddenly faded away.

I saw clearly the doom which had been prepared for me, and congratulated myself upon the timely accident by which I had escaped. Another step before my fall, and the world had seen me no more. And the death just avoided, was of that very character which I had regarded as fabulous and frivolous in the tales respecting the Inquisition. To the victims of its tyranny, there was the choice of death with its direst physical agonies, or death with its most hideous moral horrors. I had been reserved for the latter. By long suffering my nerves had been unstrung, until I trembled at the sound of my own voice, and had become in every respect a fitting subject for the species of torture which awaited me.

Shaking in every limb, I groped my way back to the wall; resolving there to perish rather than risk the terrors of the wells, of which my imagination now pictured many in various positions about the dungeon. In other conditions of mind I might have had courage to end my misery at once by a plunge into one of these abysses; but now I was the veriest of cowards. Neither could I forget what I had read of these pits—that the *sudden* extinction of life formed no part of their most horrible plan.

Agitation of spirit kept me awake for many long hours; but at length I again slumbered. Upon arousing, I found by my side, as before, a loaf and a pitcher of water. A burning thirst consumed me, and I emptied the vessel at a draught. It must have been drugged; for scarcely had I drunk, before I became irresistibly drowsy. A deep sleep fell upon me—a sleep like that of death. How long it lasted of course I know not; but when, once again, I unclosed my eyes, the objects around me were visible. By a wild sulphurous lustre, the origin of which I could not at first determine, I was enabled to see the extent and aspect of the prison.

In its size I had been greatly mistaken. The whole circuit of its walls did not exceed twenty-five yards. For some minutes this fact occasioned me a world of vain trouble; vain indeed! for what could be of less importance, under the terrible circumstances which environed me, than the mere dimensions of my dungeon? But my soul took a wild interest in trifles, and I busied myself in endeavors to account for the error I had committed in my measurement. The truth at length flashed upon me. In my first attempt at exploration I had counted fifty-two paces, up to the period when I fell; I must then have been within a pace or two of the fragment of serge; in fact, I had nearly performed the circuit of the vault. I then slept, and upon awaking, I must have returned upon my steps—thus supposing the circuit nearly double what it actually was. My confusion of mind prevented me from observing that I began my tour with the wall to the left, and ended it with the wall to the right.

I had been deceived, too, in respect to the shape of the enclosure. In feeling my way I had found many angles, and thus deduced an idea of great irregularity; so potent is the effect of total darkness upon one arousing from lethargy or sleep! The angles were simply those of a few slight depressions, or niches, at odd intervals. The general shape of the prison was square. What I had taken for masonry seemed now to be iron, or some other metal, in huge plates, whose sutures or joints occasioned the depression. The entire surface of this metallic enclosure was rudely daubed in all the hideous and repulsive devices to which the charnel superstition of the monks has given rise. The figures of fiends in aspects of menace, with skeleton forms, and other more really fearful images, overspread and disfigured the walls. I observed that the outlines of these monstrosities were sufficiently distinct, but that the colors seemed faded and blurred, as if from the effects of a damp atmosphere. I now noticed the floor, too, which was of stone. In the centre yawned the circular pit from whose jaws I had escaped; but it was the only one in the dungeon.

All this I saw indistinctly and by much effort: for my personal condition had been greatly changed during slumber. I now lay upon my back, and at full length, on a species of low framework of wood. To this I was securely bound by a long strap resembling a surcingle. It passed in many convolutions about my limbs and body, leaving at liberty only my head, and my left arm to such extent that I could, by dint of much exertion, supply myself with food from an earthen dish which lay by my side on the floor. I saw, to my horror, that the pitcher had been removed. I say to my horror; for I was consumed with intolerable thirst. This thirst it appeared to be the design of my persecutors to stimulate: for the food in the dish was meat pungently seasoned.

Looking upward, I surveyed the ceiling of my prison. It was some thirty or forty feet overhead, and constructed much as the side walls. In one of its panels a very singular figure riveted my whole attention. It was the painted picture of Time as he is commonly represented, save that, in lieu of a scythe, he held what, at a casual glance, I supposed to be the pictured image of a huge pendulum such as we see on antique clocks. There was something, however, in the appearance of this machine which caused me to regard it more attentively. While I gazed directly upward at it (for its position was immediately over my own) I fancied that I saw it in motion. In an instant afterward the fancy was confirmed. Its sweep was brief, and of course slow. I watched it for some minutes, somewhat in fear, but more in wonder. Wearied at length with observing its dull movement, I turned my eyes upon the other objects in the cell.

A slight noise attracted my notice, and, looking to the floor, I saw several enormous rats traversing it. They had issued from the well, which lay just within view to my right. Even then, while I gazed, they came up in troops, hurriedly, with ravenous eyes, allured by the scent of the meat. From this it required much effort and attention to scare them away.

It might have been half an hour, perhaps even an hour, (for I could take but imperfect note of time) before I again cast my eyes upward. What I then saw confounded and amazed me. The sweep of the pendulum had increased in extent by nearly a yard. As a natural consequence, its velocity was also much greater. But what mainly disturbed me was the idea that it had perceptibly *descended*. I now observed—with what horror it is needless to say—that its nether extremity was formed of a crescent of glittering steel, about a foot in length from horn to horn; the horns upward, and the under edge evidently as keen as that of a razor. Like a razor also, it seemed massy and heavy, tapering from the edge into a solid and broad structure above. It was appended to a weighty rod of brass, and the whole *hissed* as it swung through the air.

I could no longer doubt the doom prepared for me by monkish ingenuity in torture. My cognizance of the pit had become known to the inquisitorial agents—*the pit* whose horrors had been destined for so bold a recusant as myself—*the pit,* typical of hell, and regarded by rumor as the Ultima Thule of all their punishments. The plunge into this pit I had avoided by the merest of accidents, and I knew that surprise, or entrapment into torment, formed an important portion of all the grotesquerie of these dungeon deaths. Having failed to fall, it was no part of the demon plan to hurl me into the abyss; and thus (there being no alternative) a different and a milder destruction awaited me. Milder! I half smiled in my agony as I thought of such application of such a term.

What boots it to tell of the long, long hours of horror more than mortal, during which I counted the rushing vibrations of the steel! Inch by inch—line by line—with a descent only appreciable at intervals that seemed ages—down and still down it came! Days passed—it might have been that many days passed—ere it swept so closely over me as to fan me with its acrid breath. The odor of the sharp steel forced itself into my nostrils. I prayed—I wearied heaven with my prayer for its more speedy descent. I grew frantically mad, and struggled to force myself upward against the sweep of the fearful scimitar. And then I fell suddenly calm, and lay smiling at the glittering death, as a child at some rare bauble.

There was another interval of utter insensibility; it was brief; for, upon again lapsing into life there had been no perceptible descent in the pendulum. But it might have been long; for I knew there were demons who took note of my swoon, and who could have arrested the vibration at pleasure. Upon my recovery, too, I felt very—oh, inexpressibly sick and weak, as if through long inanition. Even amid the agonies of that period, the human nature craved food. With painful effort I outstretched my left arm as far as my bonds permitted, and took possession of the small remnant which had been spared me by the rats. As I put a portion of it within my lips, there rushed to my mind a half formed thought of joy—of hope. Yet what business had *I* with hope? It was, as I say, a half formed thought—man has many such which are never completed. I felt that it was of joy—of hope; but I felt also that it had perished in its formation. In vain I struggled to perfect—to regain it. Long suffering had nearly annihilated all my ordinary powers of mind. I was an imbecile—an idiot.

The vibration of the pendulum was at right angles to my length. I saw that the crescent was designed to cross the region of the heart. It would fray the serge of my robe—it would return and repeat its operation—again—and again. Notwithstanding its terrifically wide sweep (some thirty feet or more) and the hissing vigor of its descent, sufficient to sunder these very walls of iron, still the fraying of my robe would be all that, for several minutes, it would accomplish. And at this thought I paused. I dared not go farther than this reflection. I dwelt upon it with a pertinacity of attention—as if, in so dwelling, I could arrest *here* the descent of the steel. I forced myself to ponder upon the sound of the crescent as it should pass across the garment— upon the peculiar thrilling sensation which the friction of cloth produces on the nerves. I pondered upon all this frivolity until my teeth were on edge.

Down—steadily down it crept. I took a frenzied pleasure in contrasting its downward with its lateral velocity. To the right—to the left—far and wide—with the shriek of a damned spirit; to my heart with the stealthy pace of the tiger! I alternately laughed and howled as the one or the other idea grew predominant.

Down—certainly, relentlessly down! It vibrated within three inches of my bosom! I struggled violently, furiously, to free my left arm. This was free only from the elbow to the hand. I could reach the latter, from the platter beside me, to my mouth, with great effort, but no farther. Could I have broken the fastenings above the elbow, I would have seized and attempted to arrest the pendulum. I might as well have attempted to arrest an avalanche!

Down—still unceasingly—still inevitably down! I gasped and struggled at each vibration. I shrunk convulsively at its every sweep. My eyes followed its outward or upward whirls with the eagerness of the most unmeaning despair; they closed themselves spasmodically at the descent, although death would have been a relief, oh! how unspeakable! Still I quivered in every nerve to think how slight a sinking of the machinery would precipitate that keen, glistening axe upon my bosom. It was *hope* that prompted the nerve to quiver—the frame to shrink. It was *hope*—the hope that triumphs on the rack— that whispers to the death-condemned even in the dungeon of the Inquisition.

I saw that some ten or twelve vibrations would bring the steel in actual contact with my robe, and with this observation there suddenly came over my spirit all the keen, collected calmness of despair. For the first time during many hours—or perhaps days—I *thought*. It now occurred to me that the bandage, or surcingle, which enveloped me, was *unique*. I was tied by no separate cord. The first stroke of the razor-like crescent athwart any portion of the band, would so detach it that it might be unwound from my person by means of my left hand. But how fearful, in that case, the proximity of the steel! The result of the slightest struggle how deadly! Was it likely, moreover, that the minions of the torturer had not foreseen and provided for this possibility? Was it probable that the bandage crossed my bosom in the track of the pendulum? Dreading to find my faint, and, as it seemed, my last hope frustrated, I so far elevated my head as to obtain a distinct view of my breast. The surcingle enveloped my limbs and body close in all directions—*save in the path of the destroying crescent*.

Scarcely had I dropped my head back into its original position, when there flashed upon my mind what I cannot better describe than as the unformed half of that idea of deliverance to which I have previously alluded, and of which a moiety only floated indeterminately through my brain when I raised food to my burning lips. The whole thought was now present—feeble, scarcely sane, scarcely definite—but still entire. I proceeded at once, with the nervous energy of despair, to attempt its execution.

For many hours the immediate vicinity of the low framework upon which I lay, had been literally swarming with rats. They were wild, bold, ravenous; their red eyes glaring upon me as if they waited but for motionlessness on my part to make me their prey. "To what food," I thought, "have they been accustomed in the well?"

They had devoured, in spite of all my efforts to prevent them, all but a small remnant of the contents of the dish. I had fallen into an habitual seesaw, or wave of the hand about the platter: and, at length, the unconscious uniformity of the movement deprived it of effect. In their voracity the vermin frequently fastened their sharp fangs in my fingers. With the particles of the oily and spicy viand which now remained, I thoroughly rubbed the bandage wherever I could reach it; then, raising my hand from the floor, I lay breathlessly still.

At first the ravenous animals were startled and terrified at the change—at the cessation of movement. They shrank alarmedly back; many sought the well. But this was only for a moment. I had not counted in vain upon their voracity. Observing that I remained without motion, one or two of the boldest leaped upon the framework, and smelt at the surcingle. This seemed the signal for a general rush. Forth from the well they hurried in fresh troops. They clung to the wood—they overran it, and leaped in hundreds upon my person. The measured movement of the pendulum disturbed them not at all. Avoiding its strokes they busied themselves with the anointed bandage. They pressed—they swarmed upon me in ever accumulating heaps. They writhed upon my throat; their cold lips sought my own;

I was half stifled by their thronging pressure; disgust, for which the world had no name, swelled my bosom, and chilled, with a heavy clamminess, my heart. Yet one minute, and I felt that the struggle would be over. Plainly I perceived the loosening of the bandage. I knew that in more than one place it must be already severed. With a more than human resolution I lay *still*.

Nor had I erred in my calculations—nor had I endured in vain. I at length felt that I *was free*. The surcingle hung in ribands from my body. But the stroke of the pendulum already pressed upon my bosom. It had divided the serge of the robe. It had cut through the linen beneath. Twice again it swung, and a sharp sense of pain shot through every nerve. But the moment of escape had arrived. At a wave of my hand my deliverers hurried tumultuously away. With a steady movement—cautious, sidelong, shrinking, and slow—I slid from the embrace of the bandage and beyond the reach of the scimitar. For the moment, at least, *I was free*.

Free!—and in the grasp of the Inquisition! I had scarcely stepped from my wooden bed of horror upon the stone floor of the prison, when the motion of the hellish machine ceased and I beheld it drawn up, by some invisible force, through the ceiling. This was a lesson which I took desperately to heart. My every motion was undoubtedly watched. Free!—I had but escaped death in one form of agony, to be delivered unto worse than death in some other. With that thought I rolled my eyes nervously around on the barriers of iron that hemmed me in. Something unusual—some change which, at first, I could not appreciate distinctly—it was obvious, had taken place in the apartment. For many minutes of a dreamy and trembling abstraction, I busied myself in vain, unconnected conjecture. During this period, I became aware, for the first time, of the origin of the sulphurous light which illumined the cell. It proceeded from a fissure, about half an inch in width, extending entirely around the prison at the base of the walls, which thus appeared, and were, completely separated from the floor. I endeavored, but of course in vain, to look through the aperture.

As I arose from the attempt, the mystery of the alteration in the chamber broke at once upon my understanding. I had observed that, although the outlines of the figures upon the walls were sufficiently distinct, yet the colors seemed blurred and indefinite. These colors had now assumed, and were momentarily assuming, a startling and most intense brilliancy, that gave to the spectral and fiendish portraitures an aspect that might have thrilled even firmer nerves than my own. Demon eyes, of a wild and ghastly vivacity, glared upon me in a thousand directions, where none had been visible before, and gleamed with the lurid lustre of a fire that I could not force my imagination to regard as unreal.

*Unreal!*—Even while I breathed there came to my nostrils the breath of the vapour of heated iron! A suffocating odour pervaded the prison! A deeper glow settled each moment in the eyes that glared at my agonies! A richer tint of crimson diffused itself over the pictured horrors of blood. I panted! I gasped for breath! There could be no doubt of the design of my tormentors—oh! most unrelenting! oh! most demoniac of men! I shrank from the glowing metal to the centre of the cell. Amid the thought of the fiery destruction that impended, the idea of the coolness of the well came over my soul like balm. I rushed to its deadly brink. I threw my straining vision below. The glare from the enkindled roof illumined its inmost recesses. Yet, for a wild moment, did my spirit refuse to comprehend the meaning of what I saw. At length it forced—it wrestled its way into my soul—it burned itself in upon my shuddering reason.—Oh! for a voice to speak!—oh! horror!—oh! any horror but this! With a shriek, I rushed from the margin, and buried my face in my hands—weeping bitterly.

The heat rapidly increased, and once again I looked up, shuddering as with a fit of the ague. There had been a second change in the cell—and now the change was obviously in the *form*. As before, it was in vain that I, at first, endeavored to appreciate or understand what was taking place. But not long was I left in doubt. The Inquisitorial vengeance had been hurried by my two-fold escape, and there was to be no more dallying with the King of Terrors. The room had been square. I saw that two of its iron angles were now acute—two, consequently, obtuse. The fearful difference quickly increased with a low rumbling or moaning sound. In an instant the apartment had shifted its form into that of a lozenge. But the alteration stopped not here—I neither hoped nor desired it to stop. I could have clasped the red walls to my bosom as a garment of eternal peace. "Death," I said, "any death but that of the pit!" Fool! might I have not known that *into the pit* it was the object of the burning iron to urge me? Could I resist its glow? or, if even that, could I withstand its pressure? And now, flatter and flatter grew the lozenge, with a rapidity that left me no time for contemplation. Its centre, and of course, its greatest width, came just over the yawning gulf. I shrank back—but the closing walls pressed me resistlessly onward. At length for my seared and writhing body there was no longer an inch of foothold on the firm floor of the prison. I struggled no more, but the agony of my soul found vent in one loud, long, and final scream of despair. I felt that I tottered upon the brink—I averted my eyes—

There was a discordant hum of human voices! There was a loud blast as of many trumpets! There was a harsh grating as of a thousand thunders! The fiery walls rushed back! An outstretched arm caught my own as I fell, fainting, into the abyss. It was that of General Lasalle. The French army had entered Toledo. The Inquisition was in the hands of its enemies.

# THE MURDERS IN THE RUE MORGUE

### Edgar Allan Poe

> *What song the Syrens sang, or what name Achilles assumed when he hid*
> *himself among women, although puzzling questions are not beyond all conjecture.*
> —SIR THOMAS BROWNE, "Urn-Burial."

THE MENTAL FEATURES discoursed of as the analytical, are, in themselves, but little susceptible of analysis. We appreciate them only in their effects. We know of them, among other things, that they are always to their possessor, when inordinately possessed, a source of the liveliest enjoyment. As the strong man exults in his physical ability, delighting in such exercises as call his muscles into action, so glories the analyst in that moral activity which *disentangles*. He derives pleasure from even the most trivial occupations bringing his talents into play. He is fond of enigmas, of conundrums, of hieroglyphics; exhibiting in his solutions of each a degree of *acumen* which appears to the ordinary apprehension preternatural. His results, brought about by the very soul and essence of method, have, in truth, the whole air of intuition. The faculty of re-solution is possibly much invigorated by mathematical study, and especially by that highest branch of it which, unjustly, and merely on account of its retrograde operations, has been called, as if *par excellence*[1], analysis. Yet to calculate is not in itself to analyze. A chess-player, for example, does the one without effort at the other. It follows that the game of chess, in its effects upon mental character, is greatly misunderstood. I am not now writing a treatise, but simply prefacing a somewhat

---

[1] *par excellence*; French: superior, outstanding.

peculiar narrative by observations very much at random; I will, therefore, take occasion to assert that the higher powers of the reflective intellect are more decidedly and more usefully tasked by the unostentatious game of draughts than by all the elaborate frivolity of chess. In this latter, where the pieces have different and *bizarre* motions, with various and variable values, what is only complex is mistaken (a not unusual error) for what is profound. The *attention* is here called powerfully into play. If it flag for an instant, an oversight is committed, resulting in injury or defeat. The possible moves being not only manifold but involute, the chances of such oversights are multiplied; and in nine cases out of ten it is the more concentrative rather than the more acute player who conquers. In draughts, on the contrary, where the moves are *unique* and have but little variation, the probabilities of inadvertence are diminished, and the mere attention being left comparatively unemployed, what advantages are obtained by either party are obtained by superior *acumen*. To be less abstract—Let us suppose a game of draughts where the pieces are reduced to four kings, and where, of course, no oversight is to be expected. It is obvious that here the victory can be decided (the players being at all equal) only by some *recherché*[2] movement, the result of some strong exertion of the intellect. Deprived of ordinary resources, the analyst throws himself into the spirit of his opponent, identifies himself therewith, and not unfrequently sees thus, at a glance, the sole methods (sometimes indeed absurdly simple ones) by which he may seduce into error or hurry into miscalculation.

Whist has long been noted for its influence upon what is termed calculating power; and men of the highest order of intellect have been known to take an apparently unaccountable delight in it, while eschewing chess as frivolous. Beyond doubt there is nothing of a similar nature so greatly tasking the faculty of analysis. The best chess-player in Christendom *may* be little more than the best player of chess; but proficiency in whist implies capacity for success in all these more important undertakings where mind struggles with mind. When I say proficiency, I mean that perfection in the game which includes a comprehension of *all* the sources whence legitimate advantage may be derived. These are not only manifold but multiform, and lie frequently among recesses of thought altogether inaccessible to the ordinary understanding. To observe attentively is to

---

[2]  *recherché*; French: unique, original.

remember distinctly; and, so far, the concentrative chess-player will do very well at whist; while the rules of Hoyle (themselves based upon the mere mechanism of the game) are sufficiently and generally comprehensible. Thus to have a retentive memory, and to proceed by "the book," are points commonly regarded as the sum total of good playing. But it is in matters beyond the limits of mere rule that the skill of the analyst is evinced. He makes, in silence, a host of observations and inferences. So, perhaps, do his companions; and the difference in the extent of the information obtained, lies not so much in the validity of the inference as in the quality of the observation. The necessary knowledge is that of *what* to observe. Our player confines himself not at all; nor, because the game is the object, does he reject deductions from things external to the game. He examines the countenance of his partner, comparing it carefully with that of each of his opponents. He considers the mode of assorting the cards in each hand; often counting trump by trump, and honor by honor, through the glances bestowed by their holders upon each. He notes every variation of face as the play progresses, gathering a fund of thought from the differences in the expression of certainty, of surprise, of triumph, or chagrin. From the manner of gathering up a trick he judges whether the person taking it can make another in the suit. He recognizes what is played through feint, by the air with which it is thrown upon the table. A casual or inadvertent word; the accidental dropping or turning of a card, with the accompanying anxiety or carelessness in regard to its concealment; the counting of the tricks, with the order of their arrangement; embarrassment, hesitation, eagerness or trepidation—all afford, to his apparently intuitive perception, indications of the true state of affairs. The first two or three rounds having been played, he is in full possession of the contents of each hand, and thenceforward puts down his cards with as absolute a precision of purpose as if the rest of the party had turned outward the faces of their own.

The analytical power should not be confounded with simple ingenuity; for while the analyst is necessarily ingenious, the ingenious man is often remarkably incapable of analysis. The constructive or combining power, by which ingenuity is usually manifested, and to which the phrenologists (I believe erroneously) have assigned a separate organ, supposing it a primitive faculty, has been so frequently seen in those whose intellect bordered otherwise upon idiocy, as to have attracted general observation among writers on morals. Between ingenuity and the analytic ability there exists a difference far greater, indeed, than that between the fancy and the imagination, but of a character very strictly analogous. It will be found, in fact, that the ingenious are always fanciful, and the *truly* imaginative never otherwise than analytic.

The narrative which follows will appear to the reader somewhat in the light of a commentary upon the propositions just advanced.

Residing in Paris during the spring and part of the summer of 18—, I there became acquainted with a Monsieur C. Auguste Dupin. This young gentleman was of an excellent—indeed of an illustrious family, but, by a variety of untoward events, had been reduced to such poverty that the energy of his character succumbed beneath it, and he ceased to bestir himself in the world, or to care for the retrieval of his fortunes. By courtesy of his creditors, there still remained in his possession a small remnant of his patrimony; and, upon the income arising from this, he managed, by means of rigorous economy, to procure the necessaries of life, without troubling himself about its superfluities. Books, indeed, were his sole luxuries, and in Paris these are easily obtained.

Our first meeting was at an obscure library in the Rue Montmartre, where the accident of our both being in search of the same very rare and very remarkable volume, brought us into closer communion. We saw each other again and again. I was deeply interested in the little family history which he detailed to me with all that candour which a Frenchman indulges whenever mere self is the theme. I was astonished, too, at the vast extent of his reading; and, above all, I felt my soul enkindled within me by the wild fervor, and the vivid freshness of his imagination. Seeking in Paris the objects I then sought, I felt that the society of such a man would be to me a treasure beyond price; and this feeling I frankly confided to him. It was at length arranged that we should live together during my stay in the city; and as my worldly circumstances were somewhat less embarrassed than his own, I was permitted to be at the expense of renting, and furnishing in a style which suited the rather fantastic gloom of our common temper, a time-eaten and grotesque mansion, long deserted through superstitions into which we did not inquire, and tottering to its fall in a retired and desolate portion of the Faubourg St. Germain.

Had the routine of our life at this place been known to the world, we should have been regarded as madmen—although, perhaps, as madmen of a harmless nature. Our seclusion was perfect. We admitted no visitors. Indeed the locality of our retirement had been carefully kept a secret from my own former associates; and it had been many years since Dupin had ceased to know or be known in Paris. We existed within ourselves alone.

It was a freak of fancy in my friend (for what else shall I call it?) to be enamored of the Night for her own sake; and into this *bizarrerie*[3], as into all his others, I quietly fell; giving myself up to his wild whims with a perfect *abandon*. The sable divinity would not herself dwell with us always; but we could counterfeit her presence. At the first dawn of the morning we closed all the massy shutters of our old building; lighted a couple of tapers which, strongly perfumed, threw out only the ghastliest and feeblest of rays. By the aid of these we then busied our souls in dreams—reading, writing, or conversing, until warned by the clock of the advent of the true Darkness. Then we sallied forth into the streets, arm in arm, continuing the topics of the day, or roaming far and wide until a late hour, seeking, amid the wild lights and shadows of the populous city, that infinity of mental excitement which quiet observation can afford.

At such times I could not help remarking and admiring (although from his rich ideality I had been prepared to expect it) a peculiar analytic ability in Dupin. He seemed, too, to take an eager delight in its exercise—if not exactly in its display—and did not hesitate to confess the pleasure thus derived. He boasted to me, with a low chuckling laugh, that most men, in respect to himself, wore windows in their bosoms, and was wont to follow up such assertions by direct and very startling proofs of his intimate knowledge of my own. His manner at these moments was frigid and abstract; his eyes were vacant in expression; while his voice, usually a rich tenor, rose into a treble which would have sounded petulantly but for the deliberateness and entire distinctness of the enunciation. Observing him in these moods, I often dwelt meditatively upon the old philosophy of the Bi-Part Soul, and amused myself with the fancy of a double Dupin—the creative and the resolvent.

Let it not be supposed, from what I have just said, that I am detailing any mystery, or penning any romance. What I have described in the Frenchman was merely the result of an excited, or perhaps of a diseased intelligence. But of the character of his remarks at the periods in question an example will best convey the idea.

We were strolling one night down a long dirty street, in the vicinity of the Palais Royal. Being both, apparently, occupied with thought, neither of us had spoken a syllable for fifteen minutes at least. All at once Dupin broke forth with these words:

"He is a very little fellow, that's true, and would do better for the *Théâtre des Variétés*."

---

[3] *bizarrerie*; French: odd place.

"There can be no doubt of that," I replied unwittingly, and not at first observing (so much had I been absorbed in reflection) the extraordinary manner in which the speaker had chimed in with my meditations. In an instant afterward I recollected myself, and my astonishment was profound.

"Dupin," said I, gravely, "this is beyond my comprehension. I do not hesitate to say that I am amazed, and can scarcely credit my senses. How was *it* possible you should know I was thinking of—?" Here I paused, to ascertain beyond a doubt whether he really knew of whom I thought.

"—of Chantilly," said he, "why do you pause? You were remarking to yourself that his diminutive figure unfitted him for tragedy."

This was precisely what had formed the subject of my reflections. Chantilly was a *quondam*[4] cobbler of the Rue St. Denis, who, becoming stage-mad, had attempted the role of Xerxes, in Crébillon's tragedy so called, and been notoriously Pasquinaded for his pains.

"Tell me, for Heaven's sake," I exclaimed, "the method—if method there is—by which you have been enabled to fathom my soul in this matter." In fact I was even more startled than I would have been willing to express.

"It was the fruiterer," replied my friend, "who brought you to the conclusion that the mender of soles was not of sufficient height for Xerxes *et id genus omne*[5]."

"The fruiterer!—you astonish me—I know no fruiterer whomsoever."

"The man who ran up against you as we entered the street—it may have been fifteen minutes ago."

I now remembered that, in fact, a fruiterer, carrying upon his head a large basket of apples, had nearly thrown me down, by accident, as we passed from the Rue C—into the thoroughfare where we stood; but what this had to do with Chantilly I could not possibly understand.

There was not a particle of *charlatanerie*[6] about Dupin. "I will explain," he said, "and that you may comprehend all clearly, we will first retrace the course of your meditations, from the moment in which I spoke to you until that of the *rencontre*[7] with the fruiterer

---

[4]  *quondam*; borrowed from the Latin: former, onetime.
[5]  *et id genus omne*; Latin: and all of that kind.
[6]  *charlatanerie*; French: trickery, deception.
[7]  *rencontre*; French: a hostile meeting.

in question. The larger links of the chain run thus—Chantilly, Orion, Dr. Nicholas, Epicurus, Stereotomy, the street stones, the fruiterer."

There are few persons who have not, at some period of their lives, amused themselves in retracing the steps by which particular conclusions of their own minds have been attained. The occupation is often full of interest; and he who attempts it for the first time is astonished by the apparently illimitable distance and incoherence between the starting-point and the goal. What, then, must have been my amazement when I heard the Frenchman speak what he had just spoken? And when I could not help acknowledging that he had spoken the truth. He continued:

"We had been talking of horses, if I remember aright, just before leaving the Rue C—. This was the last subject we discussed. As we crossed into this street, a fruiterer, with a large basket upon his head, brushing quickly past us, thrust you upon a pile of paving-stones collected at a spot where the causeway is undergoing repair. You stepped upon one of the loose fragments, slipped, slightly strained your ankle, appeared vexed or sulky, muttered a few words, turned to look at the pile, and then proceeded in silence. I was not particularly attentive to what you did; but observation has become with me, of late, a species of necessity.

"You kept your eyes upon the ground—glancing, with a petulant expression, at the holes and ruts in the pavement (so that I saw you were still thinking of the stones), until we reached the little alley called Lamartine, which has been paved, by way of experiment, with the overlapping and riveted blocks. Here your countenance brightened up, and, perceiving your lips move, I could not doubt that you murmured the word 'stereotomy,' a term very affectedly applied to this species of pavement. I knew that you could not say to yourself 'stereotomy' without being brought to think of atomies, and thus of the theories of Epicurus; and since, when we discussed this subject not very long ago, I mentioned to you how singularly, yet with how little notice, the vague guesses of that noble Greek had met with confirmation in the late nebular cosmogony, I felt that you could not avoid casting your eyes upward to the great *nebula* in Orion, and I certainly expected that you would do so. You did look up; and I was now assured that I had correctly followed your steps. But in that bitter *tirade* upon Chantilly, which appeared in yesterday's *'Musée,'* the satirist, making some disgraceful allusions to the cobbler's change of name upon assuming the buskin, quoted a Latin line about which we have often conversed. I mean the line

*Perdidit antiquum litera prima sonum.*[8]

I had told you that this was in reference to Orion, formerly written Urion; and, from certain pungencies connected with this explanation, I was aware that you could not have forgotten it. It was clear, therefore, that you would not fail to combine the two ideas of Orion and Chantilly. That you did combine them I saw by the character of the smile which passed over your lips. You thought of the poor cobbler's immolation. So far, you had been stooping in your gait; but now I saw you draw yourself up to your full height. I was then sure that you reflected upon the diminutive figure of Chantilly. At this point I interrupted your meditations to remark that as, in fact, he *was* a very little fellow—that Chantilly—he would do better at the *Théâtre des Variétés*[9]."

Not long after this, we were looking over an evening edition of the "Gazette des Tribunaux," when the following paragraphs arrested our attention.

"EXTRAORDINARY MURDERS.—This morning, about three o'clock, the inhabitants of the Quartier St. Roch were aroused from sleep by a succession of terrific shrieks, issuing, apparently, from the fourth story of a house in the Rue Morgue, known to be in the sole occupancy of one Madame L'Espanaye, and her daughter, Mademoiselle Camille L'Espanaye. After some delay, occasioned by a fruitless attempt to procure admission in the usual manner, the gateway was broken in with a crowbar, and eight or ten of the neighbors entered, accompanied by two *gendarmes*[10]. By this time the cries had ceased; but, as the party rushed up the first flight of stairs, two or more rough voices, in angry contention, were distinguished, and seemed to proceed from the upper part of the house. As the second landing was reached, these sounds, also, had ceased, and everything remained perfectly quiet. The party spread themselves, and hurried from room to room. Upon arriving at a large back chamber in the fourth story (the door of which, being found locked, with the key inside, was forced open), a spectacle presented itself which struck everyone present not less with horror than with astonishment.

---

[8]   *Perdidit . . . sonum*; Latin: the first blast destroyed the old version.
[9]   *Théâtre des Variétés*; French: Variety Theater.
[10]  *gendarmes*; French: armed police officers.

"The apartment was in the wildest disorder—the furniture broken and thrown about in all directions. There was only one bedstead; and from this the bed had been removed, and thrown into the middle of the floor. On a chair lay a razor, besmeared with blood. On the hearth were two or three long and thick tresses of grey human hair, also dabbled in blood, and seeming to have been pulled out by the roots. Upon the floor were found four Napoleons, an ear-ring of topaz, three large silver spoons, three smaller of *métal d'Alger*[11], and two bags containing nearly four thousand francs in gold. The drawers of a *bureau*, which stood in one corner, were open, and had been, apparently, rifled, although many articles still remained in them. A small iron safe was discovered under the *bed* (not under the bedstead). It was open, with the key still in the door. It had no contents beyond a few old letters, and other papers of little consequence.

"Of Madame L'Espanaye no traces were here seen; but an unusual quantity of soot being observed in the fireplace, a search was made in the chimney and (horrible to relate!) the corpse of the daughter, head downward, was dragged therefrom; it having been thus forced up the narrow aperture for a considerable distance. The body was quite warm. Upon examining it, many excoriations were perceived, no doubt occasioned by the violence with which it had been thrust up and disengaged. Upon the face were many severe scratches, and, upon the throat, dark bruises, and deep indentations of finger nails, as if the deceased had been throttled to death.

"After a thorough investigation of every portion of the house, without farther discovery, the party made its way into a small paved yard in the rear of the building, where lay the corpse of the old lady, with her throat so entirely cut that, upon an attempt to raise her, the head fell off. The body, as well as the head, was fearfully mutilated—the former so much so as scarcely to retain any semblance of humanity.

"To this horrible mystery there is not as yet, we believe, the slightest clew."

The next day's paper had these additional particulars.

"*The Tragedy in the Rue Morgue.* Many individuals have been examined in relation to this most extraordinary and frightful affair." [The word *'affaire'* has not yet, in France, that levity of import which it conveys

---

[11] *métal d'Alger*, French: metal of Algiers.

with us], "but nothing whatever has transpired to throw light upon it. We give below all the material testimony elicited.

"*Pauline Dubourg,* laundress, deposes that she has known both the deceased for three years, having washed for them during that period. The old lady and her daughter seemed on good terms—very affectionate toward each other. They were excellent pay. Could not speak in regard to their mode or means of living. Believed that Madame L. told fortunes for a living. Was reputed to have money put by. Never met any persons in the house when she called for the clothes or took them home. Was sure that they had no servant in employ. There appeared to be no furniture in any part of the building except in the fourth story.

"*Pierre Moreau,* tobacconist, deposes that he has been in the habit of selling small quantities of tobacco and snuff to Madame L'Espanaye for nearly four years. Was born in the neighborhood, and has always resided there. The deceased and her daughter had occupied the house in which the corpses were found, for more than six years. It was formerly occupied by a jeweller, who under-let the upper rooms to various persons. The house was the property of Madame L. She became dissatisfied with the abuse of the premises by her tenant, and moved into them herself, refusing to let any portion. The old lady was childish. Witness had seen the daughter some five or six times during the six years. The two lived an exceedingly retired life—were reputed to have money. Had heard it said among the neighbors that Madame L. told fortunes—did not believe it. Had never seen any person enter the door except the old lady and her daughter, a porter once or twice, and a physician some eight or ten times.

"Many other persons, neighbors, gave evidence to the same effect. No one was spoken of as frequenting the house. It was not known whether there were any living connexions of Madame L. and her daughter. The shutters of the front windows were seldom opened. Those in the rear were always closed, with the exception of the large back room, fourth story. The house was a good house—not very old.

"*Isidore Muset, gendarme,* deposes that he was called to the house about three o'clock in the morning, and found some twenty or thirty persons at the gateway, endeavoring to gain admittance. Forced it open, at length, with a bayonet—not with a crowbar. Had but little difficulty in getting it open, on account of its being a double or folding gate, and bolted neither at bottom nor top. The shrieks were continued until the gate was forced—and then suddenly ceased. They seemed to be screams of some person (or persons) in great agony—were loud and drawn out, not short and quick. Witness led the way upstairs. Upon reaching the first landing, heard two voices in loud and angry contention—the one a gruff voice, the other much shriller—a very strange voice. Could distinguish some words of the former, which was that of a Frenchman. Was positive that it was not a woman's voice. Could distinguish the words *'sacré'*[12] and *'diable.'*[13] The shrill voice was that of a foreigner. Could not be sure whether it was the voice of a man or of a woman. Could not make out what was said, but believed the language to be Spanish. The state of the room and of the bodies was described by this witness as we described them yesterday.

"*Henri Duval,* a neighbor, and by trade a silversmith, deposes that he was one of the party who first entered the house. Corroborates the testimony of Muset in general. As soon as they forced an entrance, they reclosed the door, to keep out the crowd, which collected very fast, notwithstanding the lateness of the hour. The shrill voice, the witness thinks, was that of an Italian. Was certain it was not French. Could not be sure that it was a man's voice. It might have been a woman's. Was not acquainted with the Italian language. Could not distinguish words, but was convinced by the intonation that the speaker was an Italian. Knew Madame L. and her daughter. Had conversed with both frequently. Was sure that the shrill voice was not that of either of the deceased.

"—*Odenheimer, restaurateur.* This witness volunteered his testimony. Not speaking French, was examined through an interpreter. Is a native of Amsterdam. Was passing the house at the time of the shrieks. They lasted for several minutes—probably ten. They were long and loud—very awful and distressing. Was one of those who entered the building. Corroborated the previous evidence in every respect but one. Was sure the shrill voice was that of a man—of a Frenchman. Could not distinguish the words uttered. They were loud and quick—unequal—spoken apparently in fear as well as in anger. The voice was harsh—not so much shrill as harsh. Could not call it a shrill voice. The gruff voice said repeatedly *'sacré,'* *'diable'* and once *'mon Dieu.'*[14]

"*Jules Mignaud,* banker, of the firm of Mignaud et Fils, Rue Deloraine. Is the elder Mignaud. Madame L'Espanaye had some property. Had opened an account with his banking house in the spring of the year—(eight years previously). Made frequent deposits in small sums. Had checked for nothing until the third day before

---

[12] *sacré*; French: sacred.
[13] *diable*; French: devil.
[14] *mon Dieu*; French: my God.

her death, when she took out in person the sum of 4000 francs. This sum was paid in gold, and a clerk sent home with the money.

"*Adolphe Le Bon,* clerk to Mignaud et Fils, deposes that on the day in question, about noon, he accompanied Madame L'Espanaye to her residence with the 4000 francs, put up in two bags. Upon the door being opened, Mademoiselle L. appeared and took from his hands one of the bags, while the old lady relieved him of the other. He then bowed and departed. Did not see any person in the street at the time. It is a bye-street—very lonely.

"*William Bird,* tailor, deposes that he was one of the party who entered the house. Is an Englishman. Has lived in Paris two years. Was one of the first to ascend the stairs. Heard the voices in contention. The gruff voice was that of a Frenchman. Could make out several words, but cannot now remember all. Heard distinctly '*sacré*' and '*mon Dieu.*' There was a sound at the moment as if of several persons struggling—a scraping and scuffling sound. The shrill voice was very loud—louder than the gruff one. Is sure that it was not the voice of an Englishman. Appeared to be that of a German. Might have been a woman's voice. Does not understand German.

"Four of the above-named witnesses, being recalled, deposed that the door of the chamber in which was found the body of Mademoiselle L. was locked on the inside when the party reached it. Every thing was perfectly silent—no groans or noises of any kind. Upon forcing the door no person was seen. The windows, both of the back and front room, were down and firmly fastened from within. A door between the two rooms was closed, but not locked. The door leading from the front room into the passage was locked, with the key on the inside. A small room in the front of the house, on the fourth story, at the head of the passage, was open, the door being ajar. This room was crowded with old beds, boxes, and so forth. These were carefully removed and searched. There was not an inch of any portion of the house which was not carefully searched. Sweeps were sent up and down the chimneys. The house was a four story one, with garrets *(mansardes)*. A trapdoor on the roof was nailed down very securely— did not appear to have been opened for years. The time elapsing between the hearing of the voices in contention and the breaking open of the room door, was variously stated by the witnesses. Some made it as short as three minutes—some as long as five. The door was opened with difficulty.

"*Alfonzo Garcio,* undertaker, deposes that he resides in the Rue Morgue. Is a native of Spain. Was one of the party who entered the house. Did not proceed upstairs. Is nervous, and was apprehensive of the consequences of agitation. Heard the voices in contention. The gruff voice was that of a Frenchman. Could not distinguish what was said. The shrill voice was that of an Englishman—is sure of this. Does not understand the English language, but judges by the intonation.

"*Alberto Montani,* confectioner, deposes that he was among the first to ascend the stairs. Heard the voices in question. The gruff voice was that of a Frenchman. Distinguished several words. The speaker appeared to be expostulating. Could not make out the words of the shrill voice. Spoke quick and unevenly. Thinks it the voice of a Russian. Corroborates the general testimony. Is an Italian. Never conversed with a native of Russia.

"Several witnesses, recalled, here testified that the chimneys of all the rooms on the fourth story were too narrow to admit the passage of a human being. By 'sweeps' were meant cylindrical sweeping-brushes, such as are employed by those who clean chimneys. These brushes were passed up and down every flue in the house. There is no back passage by which anyone could have descended while the party proceeded upstairs. The body of Mademoiselle L'Espanaye was so firmly wedged in the chimney that it could not be got down until four or five of the party united their strength.

"*Paul Dumas,* physician, deposes that he was called to view the bodies about day-break. They were both then lying on the sacking of the bedstead in the chamber where Mademoiselle L. was found. The corpse of the young lady was much bruised and excoriated. The fact that it had been thrust up the chimney would sufficiently account for these appearances. The throat was greatly chafed. There were several deep scratches just below the chin, together with a series of livid spots which were evidently the impression of fingers. The face was fearfully discolored, and the eye-balls protruded. The tongue had been partially bitten through. A large bruise was discovered upon the pit of the stomach, produced, apparently, by the pressure of a knee. In the opinion of M. Dumas, Mademoiselle L'Espanaye had been throttled to death by some person or persons unknown. The corpse of the mother was horribly mutilated. All the bones of the right leg and arm were more or less shattered. The left *tibia* much splintered, as well as all the ribs of the left side. Whole body dreadfully bruised and discolored. It was not possible to say how the injuries had been inflicted. A heavy club of wood, or a broad bar of iron—a chair—any large, heavy, and obtuse weapon would have produced such results, if wielded by the hands of a very powerful man. No woman could have inflicted the blows with any weapon. The head of the deceased, when seen by witness, was entirely separated from the body, and was also greatly shattered. The throat had evidently been cut with some very sharp instrument—probably with a razor.

"*Alexandre Etienne,* surgeon, was called with M. Dumas to view the bodies. Corroborated the testimony, and the opinions of M. Dumas.

"Nothing farther of importance was elicited, although several other persons were examined. A murder so mysterious, and so perplexing in all its particulars, was never before committed in Paris—if indeed a murder has been committed at all. The police are entirely at fault— an unusual occurrence in affairs of this nature. There is not, however, the shadow of a clew apparent."

The evening edition of the paper stated that the greatest excitement still continued in the Quartier St. Roch—that the premises in question had been carefully re-searched, and fresh examinations of witnesses instituted, but all to no purpose. A postscript, however, mentioned that Adolphe Le Bon had been arrested and imprisoned— although nothing appeared to criminate him, beyond the facts already detailed.

Dupin seemed singularly interested in the progress of this affair— at least so I judged from his manner, for he made no comments. It was only after the announcement that Le Bon had been imprisoned that he asked me my opinion respecting the murders.

I could merely agree with all Paris in considering them an insoluble mystery. I saw no means by which it would be possible to trace the murderer.

"We must not judge of the means," said Dupin, "by this shell of an examination. The Parisian police, so much extolled for *acumen,* are cunning, but no more. There is no method in their proceedings, beyond the method of the moment. They make a vast parade of measures; but, not unfrequently, these are so ill adapted to the objects proposed, as to put us in mind of Monsieur Jourdain's calling for his *robe-de-chambre—pour mieux entendre la musique.*[15] The results attained by them are not infrequently surprising, but, for the most part, are brought about by simple diligence and activity. When these qualities are unavailing, their schemes fail. Vidocq, for example, was a good guesser, and a persevering man. But, without educated thought, he erred continually by the very intensity of his investigations. He

---

[15] *robe-de-chambre . . . musique*; French: dressing gown to better hear the music.

impaired his vision by holding the object too close. He might see, perhaps, one or two points with unusual clearness, but in so doing he, necessarily, lost sight of the matter as a whole. Thus there is such a thing as being too profound. Truth is not always in a well. In fact, as regards the more important knowledge, I do believe that she is invariably superficial. The depth lies in the valleys where we seek her, and not upon the mountain-tops where she is found. The modes and sources of this kind of error are well typified in the contemplation of the heavenly bodies. To look at a star by glances—to view it in a sidelong way, by turning toward it the exterior portions of the *retina* (more susceptible of feeble impressions of light than the interior), is to behold the star distinctly—is to have the best appreciation of its lustre—a lustre which grows dim just in proportion as we turn our vision *fully* upon it. A greater number of rays actually fall upon the eye in the latter case, but, in the former, there is the more refined capacity for comprehension. By undue profundity we perplex and enfeeble thought; and it is possible to make even Venus herself vanish from the firmament by a scrutiny too sustained, too concentrated, or too direct.

"As for these murders, let us enter into some examinations for ourselves, before we make up an opinion respecting them. An inquiry will afford us amusement" [I thought this an odd term, so applied, but said nothing], "and, besides, Le Bon once rendered me a service for which I am not ungrateful. We will go and see the premises with our own eyes. I know G——, the Prefect of Police, and shall have no difficulty in obtaining the necessary permission."

The permission was obtained, and we proceeded at once to the Rue Morgue. This is one of those miserable thoroughfares which intervene between the Rue Richelieu and the Rue St. Roch. It was late in the afternoon when we reached it; as this quarter is at a great distance from that in which we resided. The house was readily found; for there were still many persons gazing up at the closed shutters, with an objectless curiosity, from the opposite side of the way. It was an ordinary Parisian house, with a gateway, on one side of which was a glazed watch-box, with a sliding panel in the window, indicating a *loge de concierge*.[16] Before going in we walked up the street, turned down an alley, and then, again turning, passed in the rear of the building—Dupin, meanwhile, examining the whole neighborhood, as well as the house, with a minuteness of attention for which I could see no possible object.

---

[16] *loge de concierge*; French: concierge's lodge.

Retracing our steps, we came again to the front of the dwelling, rang, and, having shown our credentials, were admitted by the agents in charge. We went upstairs—into the chamber where the body of Mademoiselle L'Espanaye had been found, and where both the deceased still lay. The disorders of the room had, as usual, been suffered to exist. I saw nothing beyond what had been stated in the "Gazette des Tribunaux." Dupin scrutinized everything—not excepting the bodies of the victims. We then went into the other rooms, and into the yard; a *gendarme* accompanying us throughout. The examination occupied us until dark, when we took our departure. On our way home my companion stopped in for a moment at the office of one of the daily papers.

I have said that the whims of my friend were manifold, and that *je les ménageais:*[17]—for this phrase there is no English equivalent. It was his humor, now, to decline all conversation on the subject of the murder, until about noon the next day. He then asked me, suddenly, if I had observed anything *peculiar* at the scene of the atrocity.

There was something in his manner of emphasizing the word "peculiar" which caused me to shudder, without knowing why.

"No, nothing *peculiar,*" I said; "nothing more, at least, than we both saw stated in the paper."

"The 'Gazette,'" he replied, "has not entered, I fear, into the unusual horror of the thing. But dismiss the idle opinions of this print. It appears to me that this mystery is considered insoluble, for the very reason which should cause it to be regarded as easy of solution—I mean for the *outré*[18] character of its features. The police are confounded by the seeming absence of motive—not for the murder itself—but for the atrocity of the murder. They are puzzled, too, by the seeming impossibility of reconciling the voices heard in contention with the facts that no one was discovered upstairs but the assassinated Mademoiselle L'Espanaye, and that there were no means of egress without the notice of the party ascending. The wild disorder of the room; the corpse thrust, with the head downward, up the chimney; the frightful mutilation of the body of the old lady; these considerations, with those just mentioned, and others which I need not mention, have sufficed to paralyze the powers, by putting completely at fault the boasted *acumen,* of the government agents. They have fallen into the gross but common error of confounding the unusual

---

[17] *je les ménageais*; French: I put up with them.
[18] *outré*; French: outrageous.

with the abstruse. But it is by these deviations from the plane of the ordinary that reason feels its way, if at all, in its search for the true. In investigations such as we are now pursuing, it should not be so much asked 'what has occurred,' as 'what has occurred that has never occurred before.' In fact, the facility with which I shall arrive, or have arrived, at the solution of this mystery is in the direct ratio of its apparent insolubility in the eyes of the police."

I stared at the speaker in mute astonishment.

"I am now awaiting," continued he, looking toward the door of our apartment—"I am now awaiting a person who, although perhaps not the perpetrator of these butcheries, must have been in some measure implicated in their perpetration. Of the worst portion of the crimes committed, it is probable that he is innocent. I hope that I am right in this supposition; for upon it I build my expectation of reading the entire riddle. I look for the man here—in this room— every moment. It is true that he may not arrive; but the probability is that he will. Should he come, it will be necessary to detain him. Here are pistols; and we both know how to use them when occasion demands their use."

I took the pistols, scarcely knowing what I did, or believing what I heard, while Dupin went on, very much as if in a soliloquy. I have already spoken of his abstract manner at such times. His discourse was addressed to myself; but his voice, although by no means loud, had that intonation which is commonly employed in speaking to someone at a great distance. His eyes, vacant in expression, regarded only the wall.

"That the voices heard in contention," he said, "by the party upon the stairs, were not the voices of the women themselves, was fully proved by the evidence. This relieves us of all doubt upon the question whether the old lady could have first destroyed the daughter, and afterward have committed suicide. I speak of this point chiefly for the sake of method; for the strength of Madame L'Espanaye would have been utterly unequal to the task of thrusting her daughter's corpse up the chimney as it was found; and the nature of the wounds upon her own person entirely preclude the idea of self-destruction. Murder, then, has been committed by some third party; and the voices of this third party were those heard in contention. Let me now advert—not to the whole testimony respecting these voices—but to what was *peculiar* in that testimony. Did you observe anything peculiar about it?"

I remarked that, while all the witnesses agreed in supposing the gruff voice to be that of a Frenchman, there was much disagreement in regard to the shrill, or, as one individual termed it, the harsh voice.

"That was the evidence itself," said Dupin, "but it was not the peculiarity of the evidence. You have observed nothing distinctive. Yet there *was* something to be observed. The witnesses, as you remark, agreed about the gruff voice; they were here unanimous. But in regard to the shrill voice, the peculiarity is—not that they disagreed—but that, while an Italian, an Englishman, a Spaniard, a Hollander, and a Frenchman attempted to describe it, each one spoke of it as that *of a foreigner*. Each is sure that it was not the voice of one of his own countrymen. Each likens it—not to the voice of an individual of any nation with whose language he is conversant—but the converse. The Frenchman supposes it the voice of a Spaniard, and 'might have distinguished some words *had he been acquainted with the Spanish.*' The Dutchman maintains it to have been that of a Frenchman; but we find it stated that '*not understanding French this witness was examined through an interpreter.*' The Englishman thinks it the voice of a German, and '*does not understand German.*' The Spaniard 'is sure' that it was that of an Englishman, but 'judges by the intonation' altogether, '*as he has no knowledge of the English.*' The Italian believes it the voice of a Russian, but '*has never conversed with a native of Russia.*' A second Frenchman differs, moreover, with the first, and is positive that the voice was that of an Italian; but, *not being cognizant of that tongue,* is, like the Spaniard, 'convinced by the intonation.' Now, how strangely unusual must that voice have really been, about which such testimony as this *could* have been elicited!—in whose *tones,* even, denizens of the five great divisions of Europe could recognize nothing familiar! You will say that it might have been the voice of an Asiatic—of an African. Neither Asiatics nor Africans abound in Paris; but, without denying the inference, I will now merely call your attention to three points. The voice is termed by one witness 'harsh rather than shrill.' It is represented by two others to have been 'quick and *unequal.*' No words—no sounds resembling words—were by any witness mentioned as distinguishable.

"I know not," continued Dupin, "what impression I may have made, so far, upon your own understanding; but I do not hesitate to say that legitimate deductions even from this portion of the testimony—the portion respecting the gruff and shrill voices— are in themselves sufficient to engender a suspicion which should give direction to all farther progress in the investigation of the mystery. I said 'legitimate deductions': but my meaning is not thus fully expressed. I designed to imply that the deductions are the *sole* proper ones, and that the suspicion arises *inevitably* from them as the single result. What the suspicion is, however, I will not say just yet. I merely wish you to bear in mind that, with myself, it was sufficiently forcible to give a definite form—a certain tendency—to my inquiries in the chamber.

"Let us now transport ourselves, in fancy, to this chamber. What shall we first seek here? The means of egress employed by the murderers. It is not too much to say that neither of us believe in præternatural events. Madame and Mademoiselle L'Espanaye were not destroyed by spirits. The doers of the deed were material and escaped materially. Then how? Fortunately, there is but one mode of reasoning upon the point, and that mode *must* lead us to a definite decision. Let us examine, each by each, the possible means of egress. It is clear that the assassins were in the room where Mademoiselle L'Espanaye was found, or at least in the room adjoining, when the party ascended the stairs. It is then only from these two apartments that we have to seek issues. The police have laid bare the floors, the ceilings, and the masonry of the walls, in every direction. No *secret* issues could have escaped their vigilance. But, not trusting to *their* eyes, I examined with my own. There were, then, *no* secret issues. Both doors leading from the rooms into the passage were securely locked, with the keys inside. Let us turn to the chimneys. These, although of ordinary width for some eight or ten feet above the hearths, will not admit, throughout their extent, the body of a large cat. The impossibility of egress, by means already stated, being thus absolute, we are reduced to the windows. Through those of the front room no one could have escaped without notice from the crowd in the street. The murderers *must* have passed, then, through those of the back room. Now, brought to this conclusion in so unequivocal a manner as we are, it is not our part, as reasoners, to reject it on account of apparent impossibilities. It is only left for us to prove that these apparent 'impossibilities' are, in reality, not such.

"There are two windows in the chamber. One of them is unobstructed by furniture, and is wholly visible. The lower portion of the other is hidden from view by the head of the unwieldy bedstead which is thrust close up against it. The former was found securely fastened from within. It resisted the utmost force of those who endeavored to raise it. A large gimlet-hole had been pierced in its frame to the left, and a very stout nail was found fitted therein, nearly to the head. Upon examining the other window, a similar nail was seen similarly fitted in it; and a vigorous attempt to raise this sash, failed also. The police were now entirely satisfied that egress had not been in these directions. And, therefore, it was thought a matter of supererogation to withdraw the nails and open the windows.

"My own examination was somewhat more particular, and was so for the reason I have just given—because here it was, I knew, that all apparent impossibilities *must* be proved to be not such in reality.

"I proceed to think thus—*à posteriori*.[19] The murderers *did* escape from one of these windows. This being so, they could not have re-fastened the sashes from the inside, as they were found fastened;—the consideration which put a stop, through its obviousness, to the scrutiny of the police in this quarter. Yet the sashes *were* fastened. They *must,* then, have the power of fastening themselves. There was no escape from this conclusion. I stepped to the unobstructed casement, withdrew the nail with some difficulty, and attempted to raise the sash. It resisted all my efforts, as I had anticipated. A concealed spring must, I now knew, exist; and this corroboration of my idea convinced me that my premises, at least, were correct, however mysterious still appeared the circumstances attending the nails. A careful search soon brought to light the hidden spring. I pressed it, and, satisfied with the discovery, forebore to upraise the sash.

"I now replaced the nail and regarded it attentively. A person passing out through this window might have reclosed it, and the spring would have caught—but the nail could not have been replaced. The conclusion was plain, and again narrowed in the field of my investigations. The assassins *must* have escaped through the other window. Supposing, then, the springs upon each sash to be the same, as was probable, there *must* be found a difference between the nails, or at least between the modes of their fixture. Getting upon the sacking of the bedstead, I looked over the head-board minutely at the second casement. Passing my hand down behind the board, I readily discovered and pressed the spring, which was, as I had supposed, identical in character with its neighbor. I now looked at the nail. It was as stout as the other, and apparently fitted in the same manner—driven in nearly up to the head.

"You will say that I was puzzled; but, if you think so, you must have misunderstood the nature of the inductions. To use a sporting phrase, I had not been once 'at fault.' The scent had never for an instant been lost. There was no flaw in any link of the chain. I had traced the secret to its ultimate result—and that result was *the nail.*

---

[19] *à posteriori*; Latin: inductively.

It had, I say, in every respect, the appearance of its fellow in the other window; but this fact was an absolute nullity (conclusive as it might seem to be) when compared with the consideration that here, at this point, terminated the clew. 'There *must* be something wrong,' I said, 'about the nail.' I touched it; and the head, with about a quarter of an inch of the shank, came off in my fingers. The rest of the shank was in the gimlet-hole, where it had been broken off. The fracture was an old one (for its edges were incrusted with rust), and had apparently been accomplished by the blow of a hammer, which had partially imbedded, in the top of the bottom sash, the head portion of the nail. I now carefully replaced this head portion in the indentation whence I had taken it, and the resemblance to a perfect nail was complete—the fissure was invisible. Pressing the spring, I gently raised the sash for a few inches; the head went up with it, remaining firm in its bed. I closed the window, and the semblance of the whole nail was again perfect.

"The riddle, so far, was now unriddled. The assassin had escaped through the window which looked upon the bed. Dropping of its own accord upon his exit (or perhaps purposely closed), it had become fastened by the spring; and it was the retention of this spring which had been mistaken by the police for that of the nail—farther inquiry being thus considered unnecessary.

"The next question is that of the mode of descent. Upon this point I had been satisfied in my walk with you around the building. About five feet and a half from the casement in question there runs a lightning-rod. From this rod it would have been impossible for anyone to reach the window itself, to say nothing of entering it. I observed, however, that the shutters of the fourth story were of the peculiar kind called by Parisian carpenters *ferrades*—a kind rarely employed at the present day, but frequently seen upon very old mansions at Lyons and Bordeaux. They are in the form of an ordinary door, (a single, not a folding door) except that the upper half is latticed or worked in open trellis—thus affording an excellent hold for the hands. In the present instance these shutters are fully three feet and a half broad. When we saw them from the rear of the house, they were both about half open—that is to say, they stood off at right angles from the wall. It is probable that the police, as well as myself, examined the back of the tenement; but, if so, in looking at these *ferrades* in the line of their breadth (as they must have done), they did not perceive this great breadth itself, or, at all events, failed to take it into due consideration. In fact, having once satisfied themselves that no egress could have been made in this quarter, they would naturally bestow here a very cursory examination. It was clear to me, however, that the shutter belonging to the window at the head of the bed, would, if swung fully back to the wall, reach to within two feet of the lightning-rod. It was also evident that, by exertion of a very unusual degree of activity and courage, an entrance into the window, from the rod, might have been thus effected.—By reaching to the distance of two feet and a half (we now suppose the shutter open to its whole extent) a robber might have taken a firm grasp upon the trellis-work. Letting go, then, his hold upon the rod, placing his feet securely against the wall, and springing boldly from it, he might have swung the shutter so as to close it, and, if we imagine the window open at the time, might even have swung himself into the room.

"I wish you to bear especially in mind that I have spoken of a *very* unusual degree of activity as requisite to success in so hazardous and so difficult a feat. It is my design to show you, first, that the thing might possibly have been accomplished:—but, secondly and *chiefly*, I wish to impress upon your understanding the *very extraordinary*—the almost præternatural character of that agility which could have accomplished it.

"You will say, no doubt, using the language of the law, that 'to make out my case' I should rather undervalue, than insist upon a full estimation of the activity required in this matter. This may be the practice in law, but it is not the usage of reason. My ultimate object is only the truth. My immediate purpose is to lead you to place in juxtaposition that *very unusual* activity of which I have just spoken, with that *very peculiar* shrill (or harsh) and *unequal* voice, about whose nationality no two persons could be found to agree, and in whose utterance no syllabification could be detected."

At these words a vague and half-formed conception of the meaning of Dupin flitted over my mind. I seemed to be upon the verge of comprehension, without power to comprehend—as men, at times, find themselves upon the brink of remembrance, without being able, in the end, to remember. My friend went on with his discourse.

"You will see," he said, "that I have shifted the question from the mode of egress to that of ingress. It was my design to suggest that both were effected in the same manner, at the same point. Let us now revert to the interior of the room. Let us survey the appearances here. The drawers of the bureau, it is said, had been rifled, although many articles of apparel still remained within them. The conclusion here is absurd. It is a mere guess—a very silly one—and no more. How are we to know that the articles found in the drawers were not all these drawers had originally contained? Madame L'Espanaye and her daughter lived an exceedingly retired life—saw no company—seldom went out—had little use for numerous changes of habiliment. Those found were at least of as good quality as any likely to be possessed by these ladies. If a thief had taken any, why did he not take the best—why did he not take all? In a word, why did he abandon four thousand francs in gold to encumber himself with a bundle of linen? The gold *was* abandoned. Nearly the whole sum mentioned by Monsieur Mignaud, the banker, was discovered, in bags, upon the floor. I wish you, therefore, to discard from your thoughts the blundering idea of *motive*, engendered in the brains of the police by that portion of the evidence which speaks of money delivered at the door of the house. Coincidences ten times as remarkable as this (the delivery of the money, and murder committed within three days upon the party receiving it), happen to all of us every hour of our lives, without attracting even momentary notice. Coincidences, in general, are great stumbling-blocks in the way of that class of thinkers who have been educated to know nothing of the theory of probabilities—that theory to which the most glorious objects of human research are indebted for the most glorious of illustration. In the present instance, had the gold been gone, the fact of its delivery three days before would have formed something more than a coincidence. It would have been corroborative of this idea of motive. But, under the real circumstances of the case, if we are to suppose gold the motive of this outrage, we must also imagine the perpetrator so vacillating an idiot as to have abandoned his gold and his motive together.

"Keeping now steadily in mind the points to which I have drawn your attention—that peculiar voice, that unusual agility, and that startling absence of motive in a murder so singularly atrocious as this—let us glance at the butchery itself. Here is a woman strangled to death by manual strength, and thrust up a chimney, head downward. Ordinary assassins employ no such modes of murder as this. Least of all, do they thus dispose of the murdered. In the manner of thrusting the corpse up the chimney, you will admit that there was something *excessively outré*—something altogether irreconcilable with our common notions of human action, even when we suppose the actors the most depraved of men. Think, too, how great must have been that strength which could have thrust the body *up* such an aperture so forcibly that the united vigor of several persons was found barely sufficient to drag it *down!*

"Turn, now, to other indications of the employment of a vigor most marvellous. On the hearth were thick tresses—very thick tresses—of grey human hair. These had been torn out by the roots. You are aware of the great force necessary in tearing thus from the head even twenty or thirty hairs together. You saw the locks in question as well as myself. Their roots (a hideous sight!) were clotted with fragments of the flesh of the scalp—sure token of the prodigious power which had been exerted in uprooting perhaps half a million of hairs at a time. The throat of the old lady was not merely cut, but the head absolutely severed from the body: the instrument was a mere razor. I wish you also to look at the *brutal* ferocity of these deeds. Of the bruises upon the body of Madame L'Espanaye I do not speak. Monsieur Dumas, and his worthy coadjutor Monsieur Etienne, have pronounced that they were inflicted by some obtuse instrument; and so far these gentlemen are very correct. The obtuse instrument was clearly the stone pavement in the yard, upon which the victim had fallen from the window which looked in upon the bed. This idea, however simple it may now seem, escaped the police for the same reason that the breadth of the shutters escaped them— because, by the affair of the nails, their perceptions had been hermetically sealed against the possibility of the windows having ever been opened at all.

"If now, in addition to all these things, you have properly reflected upon the odd disorder of the chamber, we have gone so far as to combine the ideas of an agility astounding, a strength superhuman, a ferocity brutal, a butchery without motive, a *grotesquerie* in horror absolutely alien from humanity, and a voice foreign in tone to the ears of men of many nations, and devoid of all distinct or intelligible syllabification. What result, then, has ensued? What impression have I made upon your fancy?"

I felt a creeping of the flesh as Dupin asked me the question. "A madman," I said, "has done this deed—some raving maniac, escaped from a neighboring *Maison de Santé*."[20]

"In some respects," he replied, "your idea is not irrelevant. But the voices of madmen, even in their wildest paroxysms, are never found to tally with that peculiar voice heard upon the stairs. Madmen are of some nation, and their language, however incoherent in its

---

[20] *Maison de Santé*; French: insane asylum.

words, has always the coherence of syllabification. Besides, the hair of a madman is not such as I now hold in my hand. I disentangled this little tuft from the rigidly clutched fingers of Madame L'Espanaye. Tell me what you can make of it."

"Dupin!" I said, completely unnerved; "this hair is most unusual—this is no *human* hair."

"I have not asserted that it is," said he, "but, before we decide this point, I wish you to glance at the little sketch I have here traced upon this paper. It is a facsimile drawing of what has been described in one portion of the testimony as 'dark bruises, and deep indentations of finger nails,' upon the throat of Mademoiselle L'Espanaye, and in another (by Messrs. Dumas and Etienne), as a 'series of livid spots, evidently the impression of fingers.'

"You will perceive," continued my friend, spreading out the paper upon the table before us, "that this drawing gives the idea of a firm and fixed hold. There is no *slipping* apparent. Each finger has retained—possibly until the death of the victim—the fearful grasp by which it originally imbedded itself. Attempt, now, to place all your fingers, at the same time, in the respective impressions as you see them."

I made the attempt in vain.

"We are possibly not giving this matter a fair trial," he said. "The paper is spread out upon a plane surface; but the human throat is cylindrical. Here is a billet of wood, the circumference of which is about that of the throat. Wrap the drawing around it, and try the experiment again."

I did so; but the difficulty was even more obvious than before.

"This," I said, "is the mark of no human hand."

"Read now," replied Dupin, "this passage from Cuvier."

It was a minute anatomical and generally descriptive account of the large fulvous Ourang-Outang of the East Indian Islands. The gigantic stature, the prodigious strength and activity, the wild ferocity, and the imitative propensities of these mammalia are sufficiently well known to all. I understood the full horrors of the murder at once.

"The description of the digits," said I, as I made an end of the reading, "is in exact accordance with this drawing. I see that no animal but an Ourang-Outang, of the species here mentioned, could have impressed the indentations as you have traced them. This tuft of tawny hair, too, is identical in character with that of the beast of Cuvier. But I cannot possibly comprehend the particulars of this frightful mystery. Besides, there were *two* voices heard in contention, and one of them was unquestionably the voice of a Frenchman."

"True; and you will remember an expression attributed almost unanimously, by the evidence, to this voice—the expression, '*mon Dieu!*' This, under the circumstances, has been justly characterized by one of the witnesses (Montani, the confectioner), as an expression of remonstrance or expostulation. Upon these two words, therefore, I have mainly built my hopes of a full solution of the riddle. A Frenchman was cognizant of the murder. It is possible—indeed it is far more than probable—that he was innocent of all participation in the bloody transactions which took place. The Ourang-Outang may have escaped from him. He may have traced it to the chamber; but, under the agitating circumstances which ensued, he could never have re-captured it. It is still at large. I will not pursue these guesses—for I have no right to call them more—since the shades of reflection upon which they are based are scarcely of sufficient depth to be appreciable by my own intellect, and since I could not pretend to make them intelligible to the understanding of another. We will call them guesses then, and speak of them as such. If the Frenchman in question is indeed, as I suppose, innocent of this atrocity, this adver-tisement, which I left last night, upon our return home, at the office of 'Le Monde,' (a paper devoted to the shipping interest, and much sought by sailors), will bring him to our residence."

He handed me a paper, and I read thus:

> CAUGHT—*In the Bois de Boulogne, early in the morning of the—inst. (the morning of the murder), a very large, tawny Ourang-Outang of the Bornese species. The owner, (who is ascertained to be a sailor, belonging to a Maltese vessel), may have the animal again, upon identifying it satisfactorily, and paying a few charges arising from its capture and keeping. Call at No.—, Rue—, Faubourg St. Germain—au troisième.*[21]

"How was it possible," I asked, "that you should know the man to be a sailor, and belonging to a Maltese vessel?"

"I do *not* know it," said Dupin. "I am not *sure* of it. Here, however, is a small piece of ribbon, which from its form, and from its greasy appearance, has evidently been used in tying the hair in one of those long queues of which sailors are so fond. Moreover, this knot is one which few besides sailors can tie, and is peculiar to the Maltese. I picked the ribbon up at the foot of the lightning-rod. It could not have belonged to either of the deceased. Now if, after all, I am wrong

---

[21] *au troisième*; French: on the third floor.

in my induction from this ribbon, that the Frenchman was a sailor belonging to a Maltese vessel, still I can have done no harm in saying what I did in the advertisement. If I am in error, he will merely suppose that I have been misled by some circumstance into which he will not take the trouble to inquire. But if I am right, a great point is gained. Cognizant although innocent of the murder, the Frenchman will naturally hesitate about replying to the advertisement—about demanding the Ourang-Outang. He will reason thus:—'I am innocent; I am poor; my Ourang-Outang is of great value—to one in my circumstances a fortune of itself—why should I lose it through idle apprehensions of danger? Here it is, within my grasp. It was found in the Bois de Boulogne—at a vast distance from the scene of that butchery. How can it ever be suspected that a brute beast should have done the deed? The police are at fault—they have failed to procure the slightest clew. Should they even trace the animal, it would be impossible to prove me cognizant of the murder, or to implicate me in guilt on account of that cognizance. Above all, *I am known*. The advertiser designates me as the possessor of the beast. I am not sure to what limit his knowledge may extend. Should I avoid claiming a property of so great value, which it is known that I possess, I will render the animal, at least, liable to suspicion. It is not my policy to attract attention either to myself or to the beast. I will answer the advertisement, get the Ourang-Outang, and keep it close until this matter has blown over.'"

At this moment we heard a step upon the stairs.

"Be ready," said Dupin, "with your pistols, but neither use them nor show them until at a signal from myself."

The front door of the house had been left open, and the visitor had entered, without ringing, and advanced several steps upon the staircase. Now, however, he seemed to hesitate. Presently we heard him descending. Dupin was moving quickly to the door, when we again heard him coming up. He did not turn back a second time, but stepped up with decision and rapped at the door of our chamber.

"Come in," said Dupin, in a cheerful and hearty tone.

A man entered. He was a sailor, evidently—a tall, stout, and muscular-looking person, with a certain dare-devil expression of countenance, not altogether unprepossessing. His face, greatly sun-burnt, was more than half hidden by whisker and *mustachio*. He had with him a huge oaken cudgel, but appeared to be otherwise unarmed. He bowed awkwardly, and bade us "good evening," in French

accents, which, although somewhat Neufchatelish, were still sufficiently indicative of a Parisian origin.

"Sit down, my friend," said Dupin. "I suppose you have called
about the Ourang-Outang. Upon my word, I almost envy you the
possession of him; a remarkably fine, and no doubt a very valuable
animal. How old do you suppose him to be?"

The sailor drew a long breath, with the air of a man relieved of
some intolerable burden, and then replied, in an assured tone:

"I have no way of telling—but he can't be more than four or five
years old. Have you got him here?"

"Oh no; we had no conveniences for keeping him here. He is at
a livery stable in the Rue Dubourg, just by. You can get him in the
morning. Of course you are prepared to identify the property?"

"To be sure I am, sir."

"I shall be sorry to part with him," said Dupin.

"I don't mean that you should be at all this trouble for nothing,
sir," said the man. "Couldn't expect it. Am very willing to pay a reward
for the finding of the animal—that is to say, any thing in reason."

"Well," replied my friend, "that is all very fair, to be sure. Let
me think!—what should I have? Oh! I will tell you. My reward
shall be this. You shall give me all the information in your power
about these murders in the Rue Morgue."

Dupin said the last words in a very low tone, and very quietly.
Just as quietly, too, he walked toward the door, locked it, and put
the key in his pocket. He then drew a pistol from his bosom and
placed it, without the least flurry, upon the table.

The sailor's face flushed up as if he were struggling with suffocation.
He started to his feet and grasped his cudgel; but the next moment
he fell back into his seat, trembling violently, and with the countenance
of death itself. He spoke not a word. I pitied him from the bottom
of my heart.

"My friend," said Dupin, in a kind tone, "you are alarming yourself
unnecessarily—you are indeed. We mean you no harm whatever. I
pledge you the honor of a gentleman, and of a Frenchman, that we
intend you no injury. I perfectly well know that you are innocent
of the atrocities in the Rue Morgue. It will not do, however, to deny
that you are in some measure implicated in them. From what I have
already said, you must know that I have had means of information
about this matter—means of which you could never have dreamed.
Now the thing stands thus. You have done nothing which you could
have avoided—nothing, certainly, which renders you culpable. You

were not even guilty of robbery, when you might have robbed with impunity. You have nothing to conceal. You have no reason for concealment. On the other hand, you are bound by every principle of honor to confess all you know. An innocent man is now imprisoned, charged with that crime of which you can point out the perpetrator."

The sailor had recovered his presence of mind, in a great measure, while Dupin uttered these words; but his original boldness of bearing was all gone.

"So help me God," said he, after a brief pause, "I *will* tell you all I know about this affair;—but I do not expect you to believe one half I say—I would be a fool indeed if I did. Still, I *am* innocent, and I will make a clean breast if I die for it."

What he stated was, in substance, this. He had lately made a voyage to the Indian Archipelago. A party, of which he formed one, landed at Borneo, and passed into the interior on an excursion of pleasure. Himself and a companion had captured the Ourang-Outang. This companion dying, the animal fell into his own exclusive possession. After great trouble, occasioned by the intractable ferocity of his captive during the home voyage, he at length succeeded in lodging it safely at his own residence in Paris, where, not to attract toward himself the unpleasant curiosity of his neighbors, he kept it carefully secluded, until such time as it should recover from a wound in the foot, received from a splinter on board ship. His ultimate design was to sell it.

Returning home from some sailors' frolic on the night, or rather in the morning of the murder, he found the beast occupying his own bed-room, into which it had broken from a closet adjoining, where it had been, as was thought, securely confined. Razor in hand, and fully lathered, it was sitting before a looking-glass, attempting the operation of shaving, in which it had no doubt previously watched its master through the keyhole of the closet. Terrified at the sight of so dangerous a weapon in the possession of an animal so ferocious, and so well able to use it, the man, for some moments, was at a loss what to do. He had been accustomed, however, to quiet the creature, even in its fiercest moods, by the use of a whip, and to this he now resorted. Upon sight of it, the Ourang-Outang sprang at once through the door of the chamber, down the stairs, and thence, through a window, unfortunately open, into the street.

The Frenchman followed in despair; the ape, razor still in hand, occasionally stopping to look back and gesticulate at its pursuer, until the latter had nearly come up with it. It then again made off. In this manner the chase continued for a long time. The streets were profoundly quiet, as it was nearly three o'clock in the morning. In passing down an alley in the rear of the Rue Morgue, the fugitive's attention was arrested by a light gleaming from the open window of Madame L'Espanaye's chamber, in the fourth story of her house. Rushing to the building, it perceived the lightning-rod, clambered up with inconceivable agility, grasped the shutter, which was thrown fully back against the wall, and, by its means, swung itself directly upon the head-board of the bed. The whole feat did not occupy a minute. The shutter was kicked open again by the Ourang-Outang as it entered the room.

The sailor, in the meantime, was both rejoiced and perplexed. He had strong hopes of now recapturing the brute, as it could scarcely escape from the trap into which it had ventured, except by the rod, where it might be intercepted as it came down. On the other hand, there was much cause for anxiety as to what it might do in the house. This latter reflection urged the man still to follow the fugitive. A lightning-rod is ascended without difficulty, especially by a sailor; but, when he had arrived as high as the window, which lay far to his left, his career was stopped; the most that he could accomplish was to reach over so as to obtain a glimpse of the interior of the room. At this glimpse he nearly fell from his hold through excess of horror. Now it was that those hideous shrieks arose upon the night, which had startled from slumber the inmates of the Rue Morgue. Madame L'Espanaye and her daughter, habited in their night clothes, had apparently been arranging some papers in the iron chest already mentioned, which had been wheeled into the middle of the room. It was open, and its contents lay beside it on the floor. The victims must have been sitting with their backs toward the window; and, from the time elapsing between the ingress of the beast and the screams, it seems probable that it was not immediately perceived. The flapping-to of the shutter would naturally have been attributed to the wind.

As the sailor looked in, the gigantic animal had seized Madame L'Espanaye by the hair (which was loose, as she had been combing it), and was flourishing the razor about her face, in imitation of the motions of a barber. The daughter lay prostrate and motionless; she had swooned. The screams and struggles of the old lady (during which the hair was torn from her head) had the effect of changing the probably pacific purposes of the Ourang-Outang into those of wrath. With one determined sweep of its muscular arm it nearly severed her head from her body. The sight of blood inflamed its anger into phrenzy. Gnashing its teeth, and flashing fire from its eyes, it flew upon the body of the girl, and imbedded its fearful talons in her throat, retaining its grasp until she expired. Its wandering and wild glances fell at this moment upon the head of the bed, over which the face of its master, rigid with horror, was just discernible. The fury of the beast, who no doubt bore still in mind the dreaded whip, was instantly converted into fear. Conscious of having deserved punishment, it seemed desirous of concealing its bloody deeds, and skipped about the chamber in an agony of nervous agitation; throwing down and breaking the furniture as it moved, and dragging the bed from the bedstead. In conclusion, it seized first the corpse of the daughter, and thrust it up the chimney, as it was found; then that of the old lady, which it immediately hurled through the window headlong.

As the ape approached the casement with its mutilated burden, the sailor shrank aghast to the rod, and, rather gliding than clambering down it, hurried at once home—dreading the consequences of the butchery, and gladly abandoning, in his terror, all solicitude about the fate of the Ourang Outang. The words heard by the party upon the staircase were the Frenchman's exclamations of horror and affright, commingled with the fiendish jabberings of the brute.

I have scarcely anything to add. The Ourang-Outang must have escaped from the chamber, by the rod, just before the breaking of the door. It must have closed the window as it passed through it. It was subsequently caught by the owner himself, who obtained for it a very large sum at the *Jardin des Plantes*. Le Bon was instantly released, upon our narration of the circumstances (with some comments from Dupin) at the *bureau* of the Prefect of Police. This functionary, however well disposed to my friend, could not altogether conceal his chagrin at the turn which affairs had taken, and was fain to indulge in a sarcasm or two, about the propriety of every person minding his own business.

"Let them talk," said Dupin, who had not thought it necessary to reply. "Let him discourse; it will ease his conscience. I am satisfied with having defeated him in his own castle. Nevertheless, that he failed in the solution of this mystery, is by no means that matter for wonder which he supposes it; for, in truth, our friend the Prefect is somewhat too cunning to be profound. In his wisdom is no *stamen*. It is all head and no body, like the pictures of the Goddess Laverna—or, at best, all head and shoulders, like a codfish. But he is a good creature after all. I like him especially for one master stroke of cant, by which he has attained his reputation for ingenuity. I mean the way he has *'de nier ce qui est, et d'expliquer ce qui n'est pas.'*" ("To deny what exists, and to explain what doesn't.")

# THE GOLD-BUG

## Edgar Allan Poe

*What ho! what ho! this fellow is dancing mad!*
*He hath been bitten by the Tarantula.*
*—All in the Wrong*

MANY YEARS AGO, I contracted an intimacy with a Mr. William
Legrand. He was of an ancient Huguenot family, and had once been
wealthy; but a series of misfortunes had reduced him to want. To
avoid the mortification consequent upon his disasters, he left New
Orleans, the city of his forefathers, and took up his residence at
Sullivan's Island, near Charleston, South Carolina.

This Island is a very singular one. It consists of little else than the
sea sand, and is about three miles long. Its breadth at no point
exceeds a quarter of a mile. It is separated from the mainland by a
scarcely perceptible creek, oozing its way through a wilderness of
reeds and slime, a favorite resort of the marsh-hen. The vegetation,
as might be supposed, is scant, or at least dwarfish. No trees of any
magnitude are to be seen. Near the western extremity, where Fort
Moultrie stands, and where are some miserable frame buildings,
tenanted, during the summer, by the fugitives from Charleston dust
and fever, may be found, indeed, the bristly palmetto; but the whole
island, with the exception of this western point, and a line of hard,
white beach on the seacoast, is covered with a dense undergrowth
of the sweet myrtle, so much prized by the horticulturists of England.
The shrub here often attains the height of fifteen or twenty feet,
and forms an almost impenetrable coppice, burthening the air with
its fragrance.

In the inmost recesses of this coppice, not far from the eastern or more remote end of the island, Legrand had built himself a small hut, which he occupied when I first, by mere accident, made his acquaintance. This soon ripened into friendship—for there was much in the recluse to excite interest and esteem. I found him well educated, with unusual powers of mind, but infected with misanthropy, and subject to perverse moods of alternate enthusiasm and melancholy. He had with him many books, but rarely employed them. His chief amusements were gunning and fishing, or sauntering along the beach and through the myrtles, in quest of shells or entomological specimens;—his collection of the latter might have been envied by a Swammerdamm. In these excursions he was usually accompanied by an old negro, called Jupiter, who had been manumitted before the reverses of the family, but who could be induced, neither by threats nor by promises, to abandon what he considered his right of attendance upon the footsteps of his young "Massa Will." It is not improbable that the relatives of Legrand, conceiving him to be somewhat unsettled in intellect, had contrived to instil this obstinacy into Jupiter, with a view to the supervision and guardianship of the wanderer.

The winters in the latitude of Sullivan's Island are seldom very severe, and in the fall of the year it is a rare event indeed when a fire is considered necessary. About the middle of October, 18—, there occurred, however, a day of remarkable chilliness. Just before sunset I scrambled my way through the evergreens to the hut of my friend, whom I had not visited for several weeks—my residence being, at that time, in Charleston, a distance of nine miles from the Island, while the facilities of passage and repassage were very far behind those of the present day. Upon reaching the hut I rapped, as was my custom, and getting no reply, sought for the key where I knew it was secreted, unlocked the door and went in. A fine fire was blazing upon the hearth. It was a novelty, and by no means an ungrateful one. I threw off an overcoat, took an arm-chair by the crackling logs, and awaited patiently the arrival of my hosts.

Soon after dark they arrived, and gave me a most cordial welcome. Jupiter, grinning from ear to ear, bustled about to prepare some marsh-hens for supper. Legrand was in one of his fits—how else shall I term them?—of enthusiasm. He had found an unknown bivalve, forming a new genus, and, more than this, he had hunted down and secured, with Jupiter's assistance, a *scarabæus* which he believed to be totally new, but in respect to which he wished to have my opinion on the morrow.

"And why not tonight?" I asked, rubbing my hands over the blaze, and wishing the whole tribe of *scarabæi* at the devil.

"Ah, if I had only known you were here!" said Legrand, "but it's so long since I saw you; and how could I foresee that you would pay me a visit this very night of all others? As I was coming home I met Lieutenant G——, from the fort, and, very foolishly, I lent him the bug; so it will be impossible for you to see it until morning. Stay here tonight, and I will send Jup down for it at sunrise. It is the loveliest thing in creation!"

"What?—sunrise?"

"Nonsense! no!—the bug. It is of a brilliant gold color—about the size of a large hickory-nut—with two jet black spots near one extremity of the back, and another, somewhat longer, at the other. The *antennæ* are——"

"Dey ain't *no* tin in him, Massa Will, I keep a tellin on you," here interrupted Jupiter; "de bug is a goole bug, solid, ebery bit of him, inside and all, sep him wing—neber feel half so hebby a bug in my life."

"Well, suppose it is, Jup," replied Legrand, somewhat more earnestly, it seemed to me, than the case demanded, "is that any reason for your letting the birds burn? The color"——here he turned to me——"is really almost enough to warrant Jupiter's idea. You never saw a more brilliant metallic lustre than the scales emit—but of this you cannot judge till tomorrow. In the mean time I can give you some idea of the shape." Saying this, he seated himself at a small table, on which were a pen and ink, but no paper. He looked for some in a drawer, but found none.

"Never mind," said he at length, "this will answer"; and he drew from his waistcoat pocket a scrap of what I took to be very dirty foolscap, and made upon it a rough drawing with the pen. While he did this, I retained my seat by the fire, for I was still chilly. When the design was complete, he handed it to me without rising. As I received it, a loud growl was heard, succeeded by a scratching at the door. Jupiter opened it, and a large Newfoundland, belonging to Legrand, rushed in, leaped upon my shoulders, and loaded me with caresses; for I had shown him much attention during previous visits. When his gambols were over, I looked at the paper, and, to speak the truth, found myself not a little puzzled at what my friend had depicted.

"Well!" I said, after contemplating it for some minutes, "this *is* a strange *scarabœus*, I must confess: new to me: never saw anything like it before—unless it was a skull, or a death's-head—which it more nearly resembles than anything else that has come under *my* observation."

"A death's-head!" echoed Legrand—"Oh—yes—well, it has something of that appearance upon paper, no doubt. The two upper black spots look like eyes, eh? and the longer one at the bottom like a mouth—and then the shape of the whole is oval."

"Perhaps so," said I; "but, Legrand, I fear you are no artist. I must wait until I see the beetle itself, if I am to form any idea of its personal appearance."

"Well, I don't know," said he, a little nettled, "I draw tolerably— *should* do it at least—have had good masters, and flatter myself that I am not quite a blockhead."

"But, my dear fellow, you are joking then," said I, "this is a very passable *skull*—indeed, I may say that it is a very excellent skull, according to the vulgar notions about such specimens of physiology— and your *scarabœus* must be the queerest *scarabœus* in the world if it resembles it. Why, we may get up a very thrilling bit of superstition upon this hint. I presume you will call the bug *scarabœus caput hominis*, or something of that kind—there are many similar titles in the Natural Histories. But where are the *antennœ* you spoke of?"

"The *antennœ*!" said Legrand, who seemed to be getting unaccountably warm upon the subject; "I am sure you must see the *antennœ*. I made them as distinct as they are in the original insect, and I presume that is sufficient."

"Well, well," I said, "perhaps you have—still I don't see them"; and I handed him the paper without additional remark, not wishing to ruffle his temper; but I was much surprised at the turn affairs had taken; his ill humor puzzled me—and, as for the drawing of the beetle, there were positively *no antennœ* visible, and the whole *did* bear a very close resemblance to the ordinary cuts of a death's-head.

He received the paper very peevishly, and was about to crumple it, apparently to throw it in the fire, when a casual glance at the design seemed suddenly to rivet his attention. In an instant his face grew violently red—in another as excessively pale. For some minutes he continued to scrutinize the drawing minutely where he sat. At length he arose, took a candle from the table, and proceeded to seat himself upon a sea chest in the farthest corner of the room. Here again he made an anxious examination of the paper; turning it in all directions. He said nothing, however, and his conduct greatly astonished me; yet I thought it prudent not to exacerbate the growing moodiness of his temper by any comment. Presently he took from his coat pocket a wallet, placed the paper carefully in it, and deposited both in a writing-desk, which he locked. He now grew more composed in his demeanor; but his original air of enthusiasm had quite disappeared. Yet he seemed not so much sulky as abstracted. As the evening wore away he became more and more absorbed in reverie, from which no sallies of mine could arouse him. It had been my intention to pass the night at the hut, as I had frequently done before, but, seeing my host in this mood, I deemed it proper to take leave. He did not press me to remain, but, as I departed, he shook my hand with even more than his usual cordiality.

It was about a month after this (and during the interval I had seen nothing of Legrand) when I received a visit, at Charleston, from his man, Jupiter. I had never seen the good old negro look so dispirited, and I feared that some serious disaster had befallen my friend.

"Well, Jup," said I, "what is the matter now?—how is your master?"

"Why, to speak de troof, massa, him not so berry well as mought be."

"Not well! I am truly sorry to hear it. What does he complain of?"

"Dar! dat's it!—him neber plain of notin—but him berry sick for all dat."

"*Very* sick, Jupiter!—why didn't you say so at once? Is he confined to bed?"

"No, dat he ain't!—he ain't find nowhar—dat's just whar de shoe pinch—my mind is got to be berry hebby bout poor Massa Will."

"Jupiter, I should like to understand what it is you are talking about. You say your master is sick. Hasn't he told you what ails him?"

"Why, massa, 'tain't worf while for to git mad bout de matter— Massa Will say noffin at all ain't de matter wid him—but den what make him go about looking dis here way, wid he head down and he soldiers up, and as white as a gose? And den he keep a syphon all de time—"

"Keeps a what, Jupiter?"

"Keeps a syphon wid de figgurs on de slate—de queerest figgurs I ebber did see. Ise gittin to be skeered, I tell you. Hab for to keep mighty tight eye pon him noovers. Todder day he gib me slip fore de sun up and was gone de whole ob de blessed day. I had a big stick ready cut for to gib him d—d good beating when he did come—but Ise sich a fool dat I hadn't de heart arter all—he look so berry poorly."

"Eh?—what?—ah yes!—upon the whole I think you had better not be too severe with the poor fellow—don't flog him, Jupiter—he can't very well stand it—but can you form no idea of what has occasioned this illness, or rather this change of conduct? Has anything unpleasant happened since I saw you?"

"No, massa, dey ain't bin noffin onpleasant *since* den—'t was *fore* den I'm feared—'t was de berry day you was dare."

"How? what do you mean?"

"Why, massa, I mean de bug—dare now."

"The what?"

"De bug—I'm berry sartain dat Massa Will bin bit somewhere bout de head by dat goole-bug."

"And what cause have you, Jupiter, for such a supposition?"

"Claws enuff, massa, and mouff too. I nebber did see sich a d—d bug—he kick and he bite ebery ting what cum near him. Massa Will cotch him fuss, but had for to let him go gin mighty quick, I tell you—den was de time he must ha got de bite. I didn't like de look ob de bug mouff, myself, no how, so I wouldn't take hold ob him wid my finger, but I cotch him wid a piece ob paper dat I found. I rap him up in de paper and stuff piece ob it in he mouff—dat was de way."

"And you think, then, that your master was really bitten by the beetle, and that the bite made him sick?"

"I don't tink noffin about it—I nose it. What make him dream bout de goole so much, if 'tain't cause he bit by de goole-bug? Ise heerd bout dem goole-bugs fore dis."

"But how do you know he dreams about gold?"

"How I know? why cause he talk about it in he sleep—dat's how I nose."

"Well, Jup, perhaps you are right; but to what fortunate circumstance am I to attribute the honor of a visit from you today?"

"What de matter, massa?"

"Did you bring any message from Mr. Legrand?"

"No, massa, I bring dis here pissel"; and here Jupiter handed me a note which ran thus:

MY DEAR—

Why have I not seen you for so long a time? I hope you have not been so foolish as to take offence at any little *brusquerie* of mine; but no, that is improbable.

Since I saw you I have had great cause for anxiety. I have something to tell you, yet scarcely know how to tell it, or whether I should tell it at all.

I have not been quite well for some days past, and poor old Jup annoys me, almost beyond endurance, by his well-meant attentions. Would you believe it?—he had prepared a huge stick, the other day, with which to chastise me for giving him the slip, and spending the day, *solus*, among the hills on the main land. I verily believe that my ill looks alone saved me a flogging.

I have made no addition to my cabinet since we met.

If you can, in any way, make it convenient, come over with Jupiter. *Do* come. I wish to see you *tonight*, upon business of importance. I assure you that it is of the *highest* importance.

Ever yours,

WILLIAM LEGRAND.

There was something in the tone of this note which gave me great uneasiness. Its whole style differed materially from that of Legrand. What could he be dreaming of? What new crotchet possessed his excitable brain? What "business of the highest importance" could *he* possibly have to transact? Jupiter's account of him boded no good. I dreaded lest the continued pressure of misfortune had, at length, fairly unsettled the reason of my friend. Without a moment's hesitation, therefore, I prepared to accompany the negro.

Upon reaching the wharf, I noticed a scythe and three spades, all apparently new, lying in the bottom of the boat in which we were to embark.

"What is the meaning of all this, Jup?" I inquired.

"Him syfe, massa, and spade."

"Very true; but what are they doing here?"

"Him de syfe and de spade what Massa Will sis pon my buying for him in de town, and de debbil's own lot of money I had to gib for em."

"But what, in the name of all that is mysterious, is your 'Massa Will' going to do with scythes and spades?"

"Dat's more dan *I* know, and debbil take me if I don't believe 't is more dan he know, too. But it's all cum ob de bug."

Finding that no satisfaction was to be obtained of Jupiter, whose whole intellect seemed to be absorbed by "de bug," I now stepped into the boat and made sail. With a fair and strong breeze we soon ran into the little cove to the northward of Fort Moultrie, and a walk of some two miles brought us to the hut. It was about three in the afternoon when we arrived. Legrand had been awaiting us in eager expectation. He grasped my hand with a nervous *empressement* which alarmed me and strengthened the suspicions already entertained. His countenance was pale even to ghastliness, and his deep-set eyes glared with unnatural lustre. After some inquiries respecting his health, I asked him, not knowing what better to say, if he had yet obtained the *scarabæus* from Lieutenant G——.

"Oh, yes," he replied, coloring violently, "I got it from him the next morning. Nothing should tempt me to part with that *scarabæus*. Do you know that Jupiter is quite right about it?"

"In what way?" I asked, with a sad foreboding at heart.

"In supposing it to be a bug of *real gold*." He said this with an air of profound seriousness, and I felt inexpressibly shocked.

"This bug is to make my fortune," he continued, with a triumphant smile, "to reinstate me in my family possessions. Is it any wonder, then, that I prize it? Since Fortune has thought fit to bestow it upon me, I have only to use it properly and I shall arrive at the gold of which it is the index. Jupiter, bring me that *scarabæus*!"

"What! de bug, massa? I'd rudder not go fer trubble dat bug—you mus git him for your own self." Hereupon Legrand arose, with a grave and stately air, and brought me the beetle from a glass case in which it was enclosed. It was a beautiful *scarabæus* and, at that time, unknown to naturalists—of course a great prize in a scientific point of view. There were two round, black spots near one extremity of the back and a long one near the other. The scales were exceedingly hard and glossy, with all the appearance of burnished gold. The weight of the insect was very remarkable, and, taking all things into consideration, I could hardly blame Jupiter for his opinion respecting it; but what to make of Legrand's agreement with that opinion, I could not, for the life of me, tell.

"I sent for you," said he, in a grandiloquent tone, when I had completed my examination of the beetle, "I sent for you, that I might have your counsel and assistance in furthering the views of Fate and of the bug"——

"My dear Legrand," I cried, interrupting him, "you are certainly unwell, and had better use some precautions. You shall go to bed, and I will remain with you a few days, until you get over this. You are feverish and"——

"Feel my pulse," said he.

I felt it, and, to say the truth, found not the slightest indication of fever.

"But you may be ill and yet have no fever. Allow me this once to prescribe for you. In the first place, go to bed. In the next"—

"You are mistaken," he interposed, "I am as well as I can expect to be under the excitement which I suffer. If you really wish me well, you will relieve this excitement."

"And how is this to be done?"

"Very easily. Jupiter and myself are going upon an expedition into the hills, upon the main land, and, in this expedition, we shall need the aid of some person in whom we can confide. You are the only one we can trust. Whether we succeed or fail, the excitement which you now perceive in me will be equally allayed."

"I am anxious to oblige you in any way," I replied; "but do you mean to say that this infernal beetle has any connection with your expedition into the hills?"

"It has."

"Then, Legrand, I can become a party to no such absurd proceeding."

"I am sorry—very sorry—for we shall have to try it by ourselves."

"Try it by yourselves! The man is surely mad!—but stay!—how long do you propose to be absent?"

"Probably all night. We shall start immediately, and be back, at all events, by sunrise."

"And you will promise me, upon your honor, that when this freak of yours is over, and the bug business (good God!) settled to your satisfaction, you will then return home and follow my advice implicitly, as that of your physician?"

"Yes; I promise; and now let us be off, for we have no time to lose."

With a heavy heart I accompanied my friend. We started about four o'clock—Legrand, Jupiter, the dog, and myself. Jupiter had with him the scythe and spades—the whole of which he insisted upon carrying—more through fear, it seemed to me, of trusting either of the implements within reach of his master, than from any excess of industry or complaisance. His demeanor was dogged in the extreme, and "dat d—d bug" were the sole words which escaped his lips during the journey. For my own part, I had charge of a couple of dark lanterns, while Legrand contented himself with the *scarabœus*, which he carried attached to the end of a bit of whip-cord; twirling it to and fro, with the air of a conjuror, as he went. When I observed this last, plain evidence of my friend's aberration of mind, I could scarcely refrain from tears. I thought it best, however, to humor his fancy, at least for the present, or until I could adopt some more energetic measures with a chance of success. In the mean time I endeavored, but all in vain, to sound him in regard to the object of the expedition. Having succeeded in inducing me to accompany him, he seemed unwilling to hold conversation upon any topic of minor importance, and to all my questions vouchsafed no other reply than "we shall see!"

We crossed the creek at the head of the island by means of a skiff, and, ascending the high grounds on the shore of the main land, proceeded in a northwesterly direction, through a tract of country excessively wild and desolate, where no trace of a human footstep was to be seen. Legrand led the way with decision; pausing only for an instant, here and there, to consult what appeared to be certain landmarks of his own contrivance upon a former occasion.

In this manner we journeyed for about two hours, and the sun was just setting when we entered a region infinitely more dreary than any yet seen. It was a species of table land, near the summit of an almost inaccessible hill, densely wooded from base to pinnacle, and interspersed with huge crags that appeared to lie loosely upon the soil, and in many cases were prevented from precipitating themselves into the valleys below, merely by the support of the trees against which they reclined. Deep ravines, in various directions, gave an air of still sterner solemnity to the scene.

The natural platform to which we had clambered was thickly overgrown with brambles, through which we soon discovered that it would have been impossible to force our way but for the scythe; and Jupiter, by direction of his master, proceeded to clear for us a path to the foot of an enormously tall tulip-tree, which stood, with some eight or ten oaks, upon the level, and far surpassed them all, and all other trees which I had then ever seen, in the beauty of its foliage and form, in the wide spread of its branches, and in the general majesty of its appearance. When we reached this tree, Legrand turned to Jupiter, and asked him if he thought he could climb it. The old man seemed a little staggered by the question, and for some moments made no reply. At length he approached the huge trunk, walked slowly around it, and examined it with minute attention. When he had completed his scrutiny, he merely said,

"Yes, massa, Jup climb any tree he ebber see in he life."

"Then up with you as soon as possible, for it will soon be too dark to see what we are about."

"How far mus go up, massa?" inquired Jupiter.

"Get up the main trunk first, and then I will tell you which way to go—and here—stop! take this beetle with you."

"De bug, Massa Will!—de goole bug!" cried the negro, drawing back in dismay—"what for mus tote de bug way up de tree?—d—n if I do!"

"If you are afraid, Jup, a great big negro like you, to take hold of a harmless little dead beetle, why you can carry it up by this string—but, if you do not take it up with you in some way, I shall be under the necessity of breaking your head with this shovel."

"What de matter now, massa?" said Jup, evidently shamed into compliance; "always want for to raise fuss wid old nigger. Was only funnin any how. *Me* feered de bug! what I keer for de bug?" Here he took cautiously hold of the extreme end of the string, and, maintaining the insect as far from his person as circumstances would permit, prepared to ascend the tree.

In youth, the tulip-tree, or *Liriodendron Tulipiferum,* the most magnificent of American foresters, has a trunk peculiarly smooth, and often rises to a great height without lateral branches; but, in its riper age, the bark becomes gnarled and uneven, while many short limbs make their appearance on the stem. Thus the difficulty of ascension, in the present case, lay more in semblance than in reality. Embracing the huge cylinder, as closely as possible, with his arms and knees, seizing with his hands some projections, and resting his naked toes upon others, Jupiter, after one or two narrow escapes from falling, at length wriggled himself into the first great fork, and seemed to consider the whole business as virtually accomplished. The *risk* of the achievement was, in fact, now over, although the climber was some sixty or seventy feet from the ground.

"Which way mus go now, Massa Will?" he asked.

"Keep up the largest branch—the one on this side," said Legrand. The negro obeyed him promptly, and apparently with but little trouble; ascending higher and higher, until no glimpse of his squat figure could be obtained through the dense foliage which enveloped it. Presently his voice was heard in a sort of halloo.

"How much fudder is got for go?"

"How high up are you?" asked Legrand.

"Ebber so fur," replied the negro; "can see de sky fru de top ob de tree."

"Never mind the sky, but attend to what I say. Look down the trunk and count the limbs below you on this side. How many limbs have you passed?"

"One, two, tree, four, fibe—I done pass fibe big limb, massa, pon dis side."

"Then go one limb higher."

In a few minutes the voice was heard again, announcing that the seventh limb was attained.

"Now, Jup," cried Legrand, evidently much excited, "I want you to work your way out upon that limb as far as you can. If you see anything strange, let me know."

By this time what little doubt I might have entertained of my poor friend's insanity, was put finally at rest. I had no alternative but to conclude him stricken with lunacy, and I became seriously anxious about getting him home. While I was pondering upon what was best to be done, Jupiter's voice was again heard.

"Mos feered for to venture pon dis limb berry far—tis dead limb putty much all de way."

"Did you say it was a *dead* limb, Jupiter?" cried Legrand in a quavering voice.

"Yes, massa, him dead as de door-nail—done up for sartain—done departed dis here life."

"What in the name of heaven shall I do?" asked Legrand, seemingly in the greatest distress.

"Do!" said I, glad of an opportunity to interpose a word, "why come home and go to bed. Come now!—that's a fine fellow. It's getting late, and, besides, you remember your promise."

"Jupiter," cried he, without heeding me in the least, "do you hear me?"

"Yes, Massa Will, hear you ebber so plain."

"Try the wood well, then, with your knife, and see if you think it *very* rotten."

"Him rotten, massa, sure nuff," replied the negro in a few moments, "but not so berry rotten as mought be. Mought ventur out leetle way pon de limb by myself, dat's true."

"By yourself!—what do you mean?"

"Why I mean de bug. 'T is *berry* hebby bug. Spose I drop him down fuss, and den de limb won't break wid just de weight ob one nigger."

"You infernal scoundrel!" cried Legrand, apparently much relieved, "what do you mean by telling me such nonsense as that? As sure as you let that beetle fall!—I'll break your neck. Look here, Jupiter! do you hear me?"

"Yes, massa, needn't hollo at poor nigger dat style."

"Well! now listen!—if you will venture out on the limb as far as you think safe, and not let go the beetle, I'll make you a present of a silver dollar as soon as you get down."

"I'm gwine, Massa Will—deed I is," replied the negro very promptly—"mos out to the eend now."

"*Out to the end!*" here fairly screamed Legrand, "do you say you are out to the end of that limb?"

"Soon be to de eend, massa—o-o-o-o-oh! Lor-gol-a-marcy! what *is* dis here pon de tree?"

"Well!" cried Legrand, highly delighted, "what is it?"

"Why 'tain't noffin but a skull—somebody bin lef him head up de tree, and de crows done gobble ebery bit ob de meat off."

"A skull, you say!—very well!—how is it fastened to the limb?— what holds it on?"

"Sure nuff, massa; mus look. Why dis berry curous sarcumstance, pon my word—dare's a great big nail in de skull, what fastens ob it on to de tree."

"Well now, Jupiter, do exactly as I tell you—do you hear?"

"Yes, massa."

"Pay attention, then!—find the left eye of the skull."

"Hum! hoo! dat's good! why dar ain't no eye lef at all."

"Curse your stupidity! do you know your right hand from your left?"

"Yes, I nose dat—nose all bout dat—tis my left hand what I chops de wood wid."

"To be sure! you are left-handed; and your left eye is on the same side as your left hand. Now, I suppose, you can find the left eye of the skull, or the place where the left eye has been. Have you found it?"

Here was a long pause. At length the negro asked,

"Is de lef eye of de skull pon de same side as de lef hand of de skull, too?—cause de skull ain't got not a bit ob a hand at all—nebber mind! I got de lef eye now—here the lef eye! what mus do wid it?"

"Let the beetle drop through it, as far as the string will reach—but be careful and not let go your hold of the string."

"All dat done, Massa Will; mighty easy ting for to put de bug fru de hole—look out for him dar below!"

During this colloquy no portion of Jupiter's person could be seen; but the beetle, which he had suffered to descend, was now visible at the end of the string, and glistened, like a globe of burnished gold, in the last rays of the setting sun, some of which still faintly illumined the eminence upon which we stood. The *scarabæus* hung quite clear of any branches, and, if allowed to fall, would have fallen at our feet. Legrand immediately took the scythe, and cleared with it a circular space, three or four yards in diameter, just beneath the insect, and, having accomplished this, ordered Jupiter to let go the string and come down from the tree.

Driving a peg, with great nicety, into the ground, at the precise spot where the beetle fell, my friend now produced from his pocket a tape-measure. Fastening one end of this at that point of the trunk of the tree which was nearest the peg, he unrolled it till it reached the peg, and thence farther unrolled it, in the direction already established by the two points of the tree and the peg, for the distance of fifty feet—Jupiter clearing away the brambles with the scythe. At the spot thus attained a second peg was driven, and about this, as a centre, a rude circle, about four feet in diameter, described. Taking now a spade himself, and giving one to Jupiter and one to me, Legrand begged us to set about digging as quickly as possible.

To speak the truth, I had no especial relish for such amusement at any time, and, at that particular moment, would most willingly have declined it; for the night was coming on, and I felt much fatigued with the exercise already taken; but I saw no mode of escape, and was fearful of disturbing my poor friend's equanimity by a refusal. Could I have depended, indeed, upon Jupiter's aid, I would have had no hesitation in attempting to get the lunatic home by force; but I was too well assured of the old negro's disposition, to hope that he would assist me under any circumstances, in a personal contest with his master. I made no doubt that the latter had been infected with some of the innumerable Southern superstitions about money buried, and that his phantasy had received confirmation by the finding of the *scarabæus,* or, perhaps, by Jupiter's obstinacy in maintaining it to be "a bug of real gold." A mind disposed to lunacy would readily be led away by such suggestions—especially if chiming in with favorite preconceived ideas—and then I called to mind the poor fellow's speech about the beetle's being "the index of his fortune." Upon the whole, I was sadly vexed and puzzled, but, at length, I concluded to make a virtue of necessity—to dig with a good will, and thus the sooner to convince the visionary, by ocular demonstration, of the fallacy of the opinions he entertained.

The lanterns having been lit, we all fell to work with a zeal worthy a more rational cause; and, as the glare fell upon our persons and implements, I could not help thinking how picturesque a group we composed, and how strange and suspicious our labors must have appeared to any interloper who, by chance, might have stumbled upon our whereabouts.

We dug very steadily for two hours. Little was said; and our chief embarrassment lay in the yelpings of the dog, who took exceeding interest in our proceedings. He, at length, became so obstreperous that we grew fearful of his giving the alarm to some stragglers in the vicinity;—or, rather, this was the apprehension of Legrand;—for myself, I should have rejoiced at any interruption which might have enabled me to get the wanderer home. The noise was, at length, very effectually silenced by Jupiter, who, getting out of the hole with a dogged air of deliberation, tied the brute's mouth up with one of his suspenders, and then returned, with a grave chuckle, to his task.

When the time mentioned had expired, we had reached a depth of five feet, and yet no signs of any treasure became manifest. A general pause ensued, and I began to hope that the farce was at an end. Legrand, however, although evidently much disconcerted, wiped his brow thoughtfully and recommenced. We had excavated the entire circle of four feet diameter, and now we slightly enlarged the limit, and went to the farther depth of two feet. Still nothing appeared. The goldseeker, whom I sincerely pitied, at length clambered from the pit, with the bitterest disappointment imprinted upon every feature, and proceeded, slowly and reluctantly, to put on his coat, which he had thrown off at the beginning of his labor. In the mean time I made no remark. Jupiter, at a signal from his master, began to gather up his tools. This done, and the dog having been unmuzzled, we turned in profound silence towards home.

We had taken, perhaps, a dozen steps in this direction, when, with a loud oath, Legrand strode up to Jupiter, and seized him by the collar. The astonished negro opened his eyes and mouth to the fullest extent, let fall the spades, and fell upon his knees.

"You scoundrel," said Legrand, hissing out the syllables from between his clenched teeth—"you infernal black villain!—speak, I tell you!—answer me this instant, without prevarication!—which— which is your left eye?"

"Oh, my golly, Massa Will! ain't dis here my lef eye for sartin?" roared the terrified Jupiter, placing his hand upon his *right* organ of vision, and holding it there with a desperate pertinacity, as if in immediate dread of his master's attempt at a gouge.

"I thought so!—I knew it!—hurrah!" vociferated Legrand, letting the negro go, and executing a series of curvets and caracols, much to the astonishment of his valet, who, arising from his knees, looked, mutely, from his master to myself, and then from myself to his master.

"Come! we must go back," said the latter, "the game's not up yet"; and he again led the way to the tulip-tree.

"Jupiter," said he, when we reached its foot, "come here! was the skull nailed to the limb with the face outward or with the face to the limb?"

"De face was out, massa, so dat de crows could get at de eyes good, widout any trouble."

"Well, then, was it this eye or that through which you let the beetle fall?"—here Legrand touched each of Jupiter's eyes.

"'twas dis eye, massa—de lef eye—jis as you tell me," and here it was his right eye that the negro indicated.

"That will do—we must try again."

Here my friend, about whose madness I now saw, or fancied that I saw, certain indications of method, removed the peg which marked the spot where the beetle fell, to a spot about three inches to the west-ward of its former position. Taking, now, the tape-measure from the nearest point of the trunk to the peg, as before, and continuing the extension in a straight line to the distance of fifty feet, a spot was indicated, removed, by several yards, from the point at which we had been digging.

Around the new position a circle, somewhat larger than in the former instance, was now described, and we again set to work with the spades. I was dreadfully weary, but, scarcely understanding what had occasioned the change in my thoughts, I felt no longer any great aversion from the labor imposed. I had become most unaccountably interested—nay, even excited. Perhaps there was something, amid all the extravagant demeanor of Legrand—some air of forethought, or of deliberation, which impressed me. I dug eagerly, and now and then caught myself actually looking, with something that very much resembled expectation, for the fancied treasure, the vision of which had demented my unfortunate companion. At a period when such vagaries of thought most fully possessed me, and when we had been at work perhaps an hour and a half, we were again interrupted by the violent howlings of the dog. His uneasiness, in the first instance, had been, evidently, but the result of playfulness or caprice, but he now assumed a bitter and serious tone. Upon Jupiter's again attempting to muzzle him, he made furious resistance, and, leaping into the hole, tore up the mould frantically with his claws. In a few seconds he had uncovered a mass of human bones, forming two complete skeletons, inter-mingled with several buttons ot metal, and what appeared to be the dust of decayed woolen. One or two strokes of a spade upturned the blade of a large Spanish knife, and, as we dug farther, three or four loose pieces of gold and silver coin came to light.

At sight of these the joy of Jupiter could scarcely be restrained, but the countenance of his master wore an air of extreme disappointment. He urged us, however, to continue our exertions, and the words were hardly uttered when I stumbled and fell forward, having caught the toe of my boot in a large ring of iron that lay half buried in the loose earth.

We now worked in earnest, and never did I pass ten minutes of more intense excitement. During this interval we had fairly unearthed an oblong chest of wood, which, from its perfect preservation, and wonderful hardness, had plainly been subjected to some mineralizing process—perhaps that of the Bi-chloride of Mercury. This box was three feet and a half long, three feet broad, and two and a half feet deep. It was firmly secured by bands of wrought iron, riveted, and forming a kind of trellis-work over the whole. On each side of the chest, near the top, were three rings of iron—six in all—by means of which a firm hold could be obtained by six persons. Our utmost united endeavors served only to disturb the coffer very slightly in its bed. We at once saw the impossibility of removing so great a weight. Luckily, the sole fastenings of the lid consisted of two sliding bolts. These we drew back—trembling and panting with anxiety. In an instant, a treasure of incalculable value lay gleaming before us. As the rays of the lanterns fell within the pit, there flashed upwards, from a confused heap of gold and of jewels, a glow and a glare that absolutely dazzled our eyes.

I shall not pretend to describe the feelings with which I gazed. Amazement was, of course, predominant. Legrand appeared exhausted with excitement, and spoke very few words. Jupiter's countenance wore, for some minutes, as deadly a pallor as it is possible, in the nature of things, for any negro's visage to assume. He seemed stupefied—thunderstricken. Presently he fell upon his knees in the pit, and, burying his naked arms up to the elbows in gold, let them there remain, as if enjoying the luxury of a bath. At length, with a deep sigh, he exclaimed, as if in a soliloquy,

"And dis all cum ob de goole-bug! de putty goole-bug! de poor little goole-bug, what I boosed in dat sabage kind ob style! Ain't you shamed ob yourself, nigger?—answer me dat!"

It became necessary, at last, that I should arouse both master and valet to the expediency of removing the treasure. It was growing late, and it behooved us to make exertion, that we might get every thing housed before daylight. It was difficult to say what should be done; and much time was spent in deliberation—so confused were the ideas of all. We, finally, lightened the box by removing two thirds of its contents, when we were enabled, with some trouble, to raise it from the hole. The articles taken out were deposited among the brambles, and the dog left to guard them, with strict orders from Jupiter neither, upon any pretence, to stir from the spot, nor to open his mouth until our return. We then hurriedly made for home with the chest; reaching the hut in safety, but after excessive toil, at one o'clock in the morning. Worn out as we were, it was not in human nature to do more just then. We rested until two, and had supper; starting for the hills immediately afterwards, armed with three stout sacks, which, by good luck, were upon the premises. A little before four we arrived at the pit, divided the remainder of the booty, as equally as might be, among us, and, leaving the holes unfilled, again set out for the hut, at which, for the second time, we deposited our golden burthens, just as the first streaks of the dawn gleamed from over the tree-tops in the East.

We were now thoroughly broken down; but the intense excitement of the time denied us repose. After an unquiet slumber of some three or four hours' duration, we arose, as if by preconcert, to make examination of our treasure.

The chest had been full to the brim, and we spent the whole day, and the greater part of the next night, in a scrutiny of its contents. There had been nothing like order or arrangement. Every thing had been heaped in promiscuously. Having assorted all with care, we found ourselves possessed of even vaster wealth than we had at first supposed. In coin there was rather more than four hundred and fifty thousand dollars—estimating the value of the pieces, as accurately as we could, by the tables of the period. There was not a particle of silver. All was gold of antique date and of great variety—French, Spanish, and German money, with a few English guineas, and some counters, of which we had never seen specimens before. There were several very large and heavy coins, so worn that we could make nothing of their inscriptions. There was no American money. The value of the jewels we found more difficulty in estimating. There were diamonds  some of them exceedingly large and fine—a hundred and ten in all, and not one of them small;

eighteen rubies of remarkable brilliancy;—three hundred and ten emeralds, all very beautiful; and twenty-one sapphires, with an opal. These stones had all been broken from their settings and thrown loose in the chest. The settings themselves, which we picked out from among the other gold, appeared to have been beaten up with hammers, as if to prevent identification. Besides all this, there was a vast quantity of solid gold ornaments;—nearly two hundred massive finger and ear rings;—rich chains—thirty of these, if I remember;—eighty-three very large and heavy crucifixes;—five gold censers of great value;—a prodigious golden punch-bowl, ornamented with richly chased vine-leaves and Bacchanalian figures; with two sword-handles exquisitely embossed, and many other smaller articles which I cannot recollect. The weight of these valuables exceeded three hundred and fifty pounds avoirdupois; and in this estimate I have not included one hundred and ninety-seven superb gold watches; three of the number being worth each five hundred dollars, if one. Many of them were very old, and as time keepers valueless; the works having suffered, more or less, from corrosion—but all were richly jewelled and in cases of great worth. We estimated the entire contents of the chest, that night, at a million and a half of dollars; and, upon the subsequent disposal of the trinkets and jewels (a few being retained for our own use), it was found that we had greatly undervalued the treasure.

When, at length, we had concluded our examination, and the intense excitement of the time had, in some measure, subsided, Legrand, who saw that I was dying with impatience for a solution of this most extraordinary riddle, entered into a full detail of all the circumstances connected with it.

"You remember," said he, "the night when I handed you the rough sketch I had made of the *scarabœus*. You recollect also, that I became quite vexed at you for insisting that my drawing resembled a death's-head. When you first made this assertion I thought you were jesting; but afterwards I called to mind the peculiar spots on the back of the insect, and admitted to myself that your remark had some little foundation in fact. Still, the sneer at my graphic powers irritated me—for I am considered a good artist—and, therefore, when you handed me the scrap of parchment, I was about to crumple it up and throw it angrily into the fire."

"The scrap of paper, you mean," said I.

"No; it had much of the appearance of paper, and at first I supposed it to be such, but when I came to draw upon it, I discovered it, at once, to be a piece of very thin parchment. It was quite dirty, you remember. Well, as I was in the very act of crumpling it up, my glance fell upon the sketch at which you had been looking, and you may imagine my astonishment when I perceived, in fact, the figure of a death's-head just where, it seemed to me, I had made the drawing of the beetle. For a moment I was too much amazed to think with accuracy. I knew that my design was very different in detail from this—although there was a certain similarity in general outline. Presently I took a candle, and seating myself at the other end of the room, proceeded to scrutinize the parchment more closely. Upon turning it over, I saw my own sketch upon the reverse, just as I had made it. My first idea, now, was mere surprise at the really remarkable similarity of outline—at the singular coincidence involved in the fact, that unknown to me, there should have been a skull upon the other side of the parchment, immediately beneath my figure of the *scarabœus,* and that this skull, not only in outline, but in size, should so closely resemble my drawing. I say the singularity of this coincidence absolutely stupefied me for a time. This is the usual effect of such coincidences. The mind struggles to establish a connection—a sequence of cause and effect—and, being unable to do so, suffers a species of temporary paralysis. But, when I recovered from this stupor, there dawned upon me gradually a conviction which startled me even far more than the coincidence. I began distinctly, positively, to remember that there had been *no* drawing on the parchment when I made my sketch of the *scarabœus.* I became perfectly certain of this; for I recollected turning up first one side and then the other, in search of the cleanest spot. Had the skull been then there, of course I could not have failed to notice it. Here was indeed a mystery which I felt it impossible to explain; but, even at that early moment, there seemed to glimmer, faintly, within the most remote and secret chambers of my intellect, a glow-wormlike conception of that truth which last night's adventure brought to so magnificent a demonstration. I arose at once, and putting the parchment securely away, dismissed all farther reflection until I should be alone.

"When you had gone, and when Jupiter was fast asleep, I betook myself to a more methodical investigation of the affair. In the first place I considered the manner in which the parchment had come into my possession. The spot where we discovered the *scarabœus* was on the coast of the main land, about a mile eastward of the island, and but a short distance above high water mark. Upon my taking hold of it, it gave me a sharp bite, which caused me to let it drop.

Jupiter, with his accustomed caution, before seizing the insect, which had flown towards him, looked about him for a leaf, or something of that nature, by which to take hold of it. It was at this moment that his eyes, and mine also, fell upon the scrap of parchment, which I then supposed to be paper. It was lying half buried in the sand, a corner sticking up. Near the spot where we found it, I observed the remnants of the hull of what appeared to have been a ship's long boat. The wreck seemed to have been there for a very great while; for the resemblance to boat timbers could scarcely be traced.

"Well, Jupiter picked up the parchment, wrapped the beetle in it, and gave it to me. Soon afterwards we turned to go home, and on the way met Lieutenant G——. I showed him the insect, and he begged me to let him take it to the fort. On my consenting, he thrust it forthwith into his waistcoat pocket, without the parchment in which it had been wrapped, and which I had continued to hold in my hand during his inspection. Perhaps he dreaded my changing my mind, and thought it best to make sure of the prize at once—you know how enthusiastic he is on all subjects connected with Natural History. At the same time, without being conscious of it, I must have deposited the parchment in my own pocket.

"You remember that when I went to the table, for the purpose of making a sketch of the beetle, I found no paper where it was usually kept. I looked in the drawer, and found none there. I searched my pockets, hoping to find an old letter—and then my hand fell upon the parchment. I thus detail the precise mode in which it came into my possession; for the circumstances impressed me with peculiar force.

"No doubt you will think me fanciful—but I had already established a kind of *connection*. I had put together two links of a great chain. There was a boat lying on a sea-coast, and not far from the boat was a parchment—*not a paper*—with a skull depicted on it. You will, of course, ask 'where is the connection?' I reply that the skull, or death's-head, is the well-known emblem of the pirate. The flag of the death's-head is hoisted in all engagements.

"I have said that the scrap was parchment, and not paper. Parchment is durable—almost imperishable. Matters of little moment are rarely consigned to parchment; since, for the mere ordinary purposes of drawing or writing, it is not nearly so well adapted as paper. This reflection suggested some meaning—some relevancy—in the death's-head. I did not fail to observe, also, the *form* of the parchment. Although one of its corners had been, by some accident, destroyed, it could be seen that the original form was oblong. It was just such a slip, indeed, as might have been chosen for a memorandum—for a record of something to be long remembered and carefully preserved."

"But," I interposed, "you say that the skull was *not* upon the parchment when you made the drawing of the beetle. How then do you trace any connection between the boat and the skull—since this latter, according to your own admission, must have been designed (God only knows how or by whom) at some period subsequent to your sketching the *scarabæus?*"

"Ah, hereupon turns the whole mystery; although the secret, at this point, I had comparatively little difficulty in solving. My steps were sure, and could afford but a single result. I reasoned, for example, thus: When I drew the *scarabæus,* there was no skull apparent on the parchment. When I had completed the drawing, I gave it to you, and observed you narrowly until you returned it. *You,* therefore, did not design the skull, and no one else was present to do it. Then it was not done by human agency. And nevertheless it was done.

"At this stage of my reflections I endeavored to remember, and *did* remember, with entire distinctness, every incident which occurred about the period in question. The weather was chilly (oh rare and happy accident!), and a fire was blazing on the hearth. I was heated with exercise and sat near the table. You, however, had drawn a chair close to the chimney. Just as I placed the parchment in your hand, and as you were in the act of inspecting it, Wolf, the Newfoundland, entered, and leaped upon your shoulders. With your left hand you caressed him and kept him off, while your right, holding the parchment, was permitted to fall listlessly between your knees, and in close proximity to the fire. At one moment I thought the blaze had caught it, and was about to caution you, but, before I could speak, you had withdrawn it, and were engaged in its examination. When I considered all these particulars, I doubted not for a moment that *heat* had been the agent in bringing to light, on the parchment, the skull which I saw designed on it. You are well aware that chemical preparations exist, and have existed time out of mind, by means of which it is possible to write on either paper or vellum, so that the characters shall become visible only when subjected to the action of fire. Zaffre, digested in *aqua regia,* and diluted with four times its weight of water, is sometimes employed; a green tint results. The regulus of cobalt, dissolved in spirit of nitre, gives a red. These colors disappear at longer or shorter intervals after the material written on cools, but again become apparent upon the reapplication of heat.

"I now scrutinized the death's-head with care. Its outer edges—the edges of the drawing nearest the edge of the vellum—were far more *distinct* than the others. It was clear that the action of the caloric had been imperfect or unequal. I immediately kindled a fire, and subjected every portion of the parchment to a glowing heat. At first, the only effect was the strengthening of the faint lines in the skull; but, on persevering in the experiment, there became visible, at the corner of the slip, diagonally opposite to the spot in which the death's-head was delineated, the figure of what I at first supposed to be a goat. A closer scrutiny, however, satisfied me that it was intended for a kid."

"Ha! ha!" said I, "to be sure I have no right to laugh at you—a million and a half of money is too serious a matter for mirth—but you are not about to establish a third link in your chain—you will not find any especial connexion between your pirates and a goat— pirates, you know, have nothing to do with goats; they appertain to the farming interest."

"But I have just said that the figure was *not* that of a goat."

"Well, a kid then—pretty much the same thing."

"Pretty much, but not altogether," said Legrand. "You may have heard of one *Captain* Kidd. I at once looked on the figure of the animal as a kind of punning or hieroglyphical signature. I say signature; because its position on the vellum suggested this idea. The death's-head at the corner diagonally opposite, had, in the same manner, the air of a stamp, or seal. But I was sorely put out by the absence of all else—of the body to my imagined instrument—of the text for my context."

"I presume you expected to find a letter between the stamp and the signature."

"Something of that kind. The fact is, I felt irresistibly impressed with a presentiment of some vast good fortune impending. I can scarcely say why. Perhaps, after all, it was rather a desire than an actual belief;—but do you know that Jupiter's silly words, about the bug being of solid gold, had a remarkable effect on my fancy? And then the series of accidents and coincidences—these were so *very* extraordinary. Do you observe how mere an accident it was that these events should have occurred on the *sole* day of all the year in which it has been, or may be, sufficiently cool for fire, and that without the fire, or without the intervention of the dog at the precise moment in which he appeared, I should never have become aware of the death's-head, and so never the possessor of the treasure?"

"But proceed—I am all impatience."

"Well, you have heard, of course, the many stories current—the thousand vague rumors afloat about money buried, somewhere on the Atlantic coast, by Kidd and his associates. These rumors must have had some foundation in fact. And that the rumors have existed so long and so continuously could have resulted, it appeared to me, only from the circumstance of the buried treasure still *remaining* entombed. Had Kidd concealed his plunder for a time, and afterwards reclaimed it, the rumors would scarcely have reached us in their present unvarying form. You will observe that the stories told are all about money-seekers, not about money-finders. Had the pirate recovered his money, there the affair would have dropped. It seemed to me that some accident—say the loss of a memorandum indicating its locality—had deprived him of the means of recovering it, and that this accident had become known to his followers, who otherwise might never have heard that treasure had been concealed at all, and who, busying themselves in vain, because unguided attempts, to regain it, had given first birth, and then universal currency, to the reports which are now so common. Have you ever heard of any important treasure being unearthed along the coast?"

"Never."

"But that Kidd's accumulations were immense, is well known. I took it for granted, therefore, that the earth still held them; and you will scarcely be surprised when I tell you that I felt a hope, nearly amounting to certainty, that the parchment so strangely found, involved a lost record of the place of deposit."

"But how did you proceed?"

"I held the vellum again to the fire, after increasing the heat; but nothing appeared. I now thought it possible that the coating of dirt might have something to do with the failure; so I carefully rinsed the parchment by pouring warm water over it, and, having done this, I placed it in a tin pan, with the skull downwards, and put the pan upon a furnace of lighted charcoal. In a few minutes, the pan having become thoroughly heated, I removed the slip, and, to my inexpressible joy, found it spotted, in several places, with what appeared to be figures arranged in lines. Again I placed it in the pan, and suffered it to remain another minute. On taking it off, the whole was just as you see it now."

Here Legrand, having re-heated the parchment, submitted it to my inspection. The following characters were rudely traced, in a red tint, between the death's-head and the goat:

53‡‡†305))6★;4826)4‡.)4‡);806★;48†8¶60))85;;]8★;:‡★8†83
(88)5★†;46(;88★96★?;8)★ ‡ (;485);5★†2:★ ‡ (;4956★2(5★—4)8¶8★
;4069285);)6†8)4‡‡;l(‡9;48081;8:8‡l;48†85;4)485†528806★81
(‡9;48;(88;4(‡?34;48)4‡;161;:188;‡?;

"But," said I, returning him the slip, "I am as much in the dark as ever. Were all the jewels of Golconda awaiting me on my solution of this enigma, I am quite sure that I should be unable to earn them."

"And yet," said Legrand, "the solution is by no means so difficult as you might be led to imagine from the first hasty inspection of the characters. These characters, as anyone might readily guess, form a cipher—that is to say, they convey a meaning; but then, from what is known of Kidd, I could not suppose him capable of constructing any of the more abstruse cryptographs. I made up my mind, at once, that this was of a simple species—such, however, as would appear, to the crude intellect of the sailor, absolutely insoluble without the key."

"And you really solved it?"

"Readily; I have solved others of an abstruseness ten thousand times greater. Circumstances, and a certain bias of mind, have led me to take interest in such riddles, and it may well be doubted whether human ingenuity can construct an enigma of the kind which human ingenuity may not, by proper application, resolve. In fact, having once established connected and legible characters, I scarcely gave a thought to the mere difficulty of developing their import.

"In the present case—indeed in all cases of secret writing—the first question regards the *language* of the cipher; for the principles of solution, so far, especially, as the more simple ciphers are concerned, depend on, and are varied by, the genius of the particular idiom. In general, there is no alternative but experiment (directed by probabilities) of every tongue known to him who attempts the solution, until the true one be attained. But, with the cipher now before us, all difficulty is removed by the signature. The pun on the word 'Kidd' is appreciable in no other language than the English. But for this consideration I should have begun my attempts with the Spanish and French, as the tongues in which a secret of this kind would most naturally have been written by a pirate of the Spanish main. As it was, I assumed the cryptograph to be English.

"You observe there are no divisions between the words. Had there been divisions, the task would have been comparatively easy. In such case I should have commenced with a collation and analysis of the shorter words, and, had a word of a single letter occurred, as is most likely (*a* or *I*, for example), I should have considered the solution as assured. But, there being no division, my first step was to ascertain the predominant letters, as well as the least frequent. Counting all, I constructed a table, thus:

Of the character 8 there are 33.

|        |    |     |
|-------:|----|-----|
| ;      | "  | 26. |
| 4      | "  | 19. |
| ‡ )    | "  | 16. |
| ★      | "  | 13. |
| 5      | "  | 12. |
| 6      | "  | 11. |
| † 1    | "  | 8.  |
| 0      | "  | 6.  |
| 9 2    | "  | 5.  |
| : 3    | "  | 4.  |
| ?      | "  | 3.  |
| ¶      | "  | 2.  |
| ] —.   | "  | 1.  |

"Now, in English, the letter which most frequently occurs is *e*. Afterwards, the succession runs thus: *a o i d h n r s t u y c f g l m w b k p q x z*. E however predominates so remarkably that an individual sentence of any length is rarely seen, in which it is not the prevailing character.

"Here, then, we have, in the very beginning, the groundwork for something more than a mere guess. The general use which may be made of the table is obvious—but, in this particular cipher, we shall only very partially require its aid. As our predominant character is 8, we will commence by assuming it as the *e* of the natural alphabet. To verify the supposition, let us observe if the 8 be seen often in couples—for *e* is doubled with great frequency in English—in such words, for example, as 'meet,' 'fleet,' 'speed,' 'seen,' 'been,' 'agree,' &c. In the present instance we see it doubled no less than five times, although the cryptograph is brief.

"Let us assume 8, then, as *e*. Now, of all *words* in the language, 'the' is most usual; let us see, therefore, whether there are not repetitions of any three characters, in the same order of collocation, the last of them being 8. If we discover repetitions of such letters, so arranged, they will most probably represent the word 'the.' On inspection we find no less than seven such arrangements, the characters being ;48. We may, therefore, assume that the semicolon represents *t,* that 4 represents *h,* and that 8 represents *e*—the last being now well confirmed. Thus a great step has been taken.

"But, having established a single word, we are enabled to establish a vastly important point; that is to say, several commencements and terminations of other words. Let us refer, for example, to the last instance but one, in which the combination ;48 occurs—not far from the end of the cipher. We know that the semicolon immediately ensuing is the commencement of a word, and, of the six characters succeeding this 'the,' we are cognizant of no less than five. Let us set these characters down, thus, by the letters we know them to represent, leaving a space for the unknown—

t eeth.

"Here we are enabled, at once, to discard the '*th*,' as forming no portion of the word commencing with the first *t;* since, by experiment of the entire alphabet for a letter adapted to the vacancy we perceive that no word can be formed of which this *th* can be a part. We are thus narrowed into

t ee,

and, going through the alphabet, if necessary, as before, we arrive at the word 'tree,' as the sole possible reading. We thus gain another letter, *r*, represented by (, with the words 'the tree' in juxtaposition.

"Looking beyond these words, for a short distance, we again see the combination of ;48, and employ it by way of *termination* to what immediately precedes. We have thus this arrangement:

the tree;4 (‡?34 the,

or, substituting the natural letters, where known, it reads thus:

the tree thr ‡?3h the.

"Now, if, in place of the unknown characters, we leave blank spaces, or substitute dots, we read thus:

the tree thr . . . h the,

when the word '*through*' makes itself evident at once. But this discovery gives us three new letters, *o, u* and *g,* represented by ‡ ? and 3.

"Looking now, narrowly, through the cipher for combinations of known characters, we find, not very far from the beginning, this arrangement,

83(88, or egree,

which, plainly, is the conclusion of the word 'degree,' and gives us another letter, *d,* represented by †.

"Four letters beyond the word 'degree,' we perceive the combination
;46(;88*.

"Translating the known characters, and representing the unknown by dots, as before, we read thus:

th.rtee.

an arrangement immediately suggestive of the word 'thirteen,' and again furnishing us with two new characters, *i* and *n,* represented by 6 and *.

"Referring, now, to the beginning of the cryptograph, we find the combination,

53‡‡†.

"Translating, as before, we obtain

.good,

which assures us that the first letter is A, and that the first two words are 'A good.'

"To avoid confusion, it is now time that we arrange our key, as far as discovered, in a tabular form. It will stand thus:

| 5 | represents | a |
|---|------------|---|
| † | " | d |
| 8 | " | e |
| 3 | " | g |
| 4 | " | h |
| 6 | " | i |
| * | " | n |
| ‡ | " | o |
| ( | " | r |
| ; | " | t |

"We have, therefore, no less than ten of the most important letters represented, and it will be unnecessary to proceed with the details of the solution. I have said enough to convince you that ciphers of this nature are readily soluble, and to give you some insight into the *rationale* of their development. But be assured that the specimen before us appertains to the very simplest species of cryptograph. It now only remains to give you the full translation of the characters upon the parchment, as unriddled. Here it is:

" '*A good glass in the bishop's hostel in the devil's seat twenty-one degrees and thirteen minutes northeast and by north main branch seventh limb east side shoot from the left eye of the death's-head a bee line from the tree through the shot fifty feet out.'"*

"But," said I, "the enigma seems still in as bad a condition as ever. How is it possible to extort a meaning from all this jargon about 'devil's seats,' 'death's-heads,' and 'bishop's hostels?'"

"I confess," replied Legrand, "that the matter still wears a serious aspect, when regarded with a casual glance. My first endeavor was to divide the sentence into the natural division intended by the cryptographist."

"You mean, to punctuate it?"

"Something of that kind."

"But how was it possible to effect this?"

"I reflected that it had been a *point* with the writer to run his words together without division, so as to increase the difficulty of solution. Now, a not over-acute man, in pursuing such an object, would be nearly certain to overdo the matter. When, in the course of his composition, he arrived at a break in his subject which would naturally require a pause, or a point, he would be exceedingly apt to run his characters, at this place, more than usually close together. If you will observe the MS., in the present instance, you will easily detect five such cases of unusual crowding. Acting on this hint, I made the division thus:

"'*A good glass in the Bishop's hostel in the Devil's seat—twenty-one degrees and thirteen minutes—northeast and by north—main branch seventh limb east side—shoot from the left eye of the death's-head—a beeline from the tree through the shot fifty feet out.'*'"

"Even this division," said I, "leaves me still in the dark."

"It left me also in the dark," replied Legrand, "for a few days; during which I made diligent inquiry, in the neighborhood of Sullivan's Island, for any building which went by the name of the 'Bishop's Hotel;' for, of course, I dropped the obsolete word 'hostel.' Gaining no information on the subject, I was on the point of extending my sphere of search, and proceeding in a more systematic manner, when, one morning, it entered into my head, quite suddenly, that this 'Bishop's Hostel' might have some reference to an old family, of the name of Bessop, which, time out of mind, had held possession of an ancient manor-house, about four miles to the northward of the Island. I accordingly went over to the plantation, and reinstituted my inquiries among the older negroes of the place. At length one of the most aged of the women said that she had heard of such a place as *Bessop's Castle,* and thought that she could guide me to it, but that it was not a castle, nor a tavern, but a high rock.

"I offered to pay her well for her trouble, and, after some demur, she consented to accompany me to the spot. We found it without much difficulty, when, dismissing her, I proceeded to examine the place. The 'castle' consisted of an irregular assemblage of cliffs and rocks—one of the latter being quite remarkable for its height as well as for its insulated and artificial appearance. I clambered to its apex, and then felt much at a loss as to what should be next done.

"While I was busied in reflection, my eyes fell upon a narrow ledge in the eastern face of the rock, perhaps a yard below the summit on which I stood. This ledge projected about eighteen inches, and was not more than a foot wide, while a niche in the cliff just above it, gave it a rude resemblance to one of the hollow-backed chairs used by our ancestors. I made no doubt that here was the 'devil's seat' alluded to in the MS., and now I seemed to grasp the full secret of the riddle.

"The 'good glass,' I knew, could have reference to nothing but a telescope; for the word 'glass' is rarely employed in any other sense by seamen. Now here, I at once saw, was a telescope to be used, and a definite point of view, *admitting no variation,* from which to use it. Nor did I hesitate to believe that the phrases, 'twenty-one degrees and thirteen minutes,' and 'northeast and by north,' were intended as directions for the levelling of the glass. Greatly excited by these discoveries, I hurried home, procured a telescope, and returned to the rock.

"I let myself down to the ledge, and found that it was impossible to retain a seat on it unless in one particular position. This fact confirmed my preconceived idea. I proceeded to use the glass. Of course, the 'twenty-one degrees and thirteen minutes' could allude to nothing but elevation above the visible horizon, since the horizontal direction was clearly indicated by the words, 'northeast and by north.' This latter direction I at once established by means of a pocket-compass; then, pointing the glass as nearly at an angle of twenty-one degrees of elevation as I could do it by guess, I moved it cautiously up or down, until my attention was arrested by a circular rift or opening in the foliage of a large tree that overtopped its fellows in the distance. In the centre of this rift I perceived a white spot, but could not, at first, distinguish what it was. Adjusting the focus of the telescope, I again looked, and now made it out to be a human skull.

"On this discovery I was so sanguine as to consider the enigma solved for the phrase 'main branch, seventh limb, east side,' could refer only to the position of the skull on the tree, while 'shoot from the left eye of the death's-head' admitted, also, of but one interpretation, in regard to a search for buried treasure. I perceived that the design was to drop a bullet from the left eye of the skull, and that a bee-line, or, in other words, a straight line, drawn from the nearest point of the trunk through 'the shot,' (or the spot where the bullet fell,) and thence extended to a distance of fifty feet, would indicate a definite point—and beneath this point I thought it at least possible that a deposit of value lay concealed."

"All this," I said, "is exceedingly clear, and, although ingenious, still simple and explicit. When you left the Bishop's Hotel, what then?"

"Why, having carefully taken the bearings of the tree, I turned homewards. The instant that I left 'the devil's seat,' however, the circular rift vanished; nor could I get a glimpse of it afterwards, turn as I would. What seems to me the chief ingenuity in this whole business, is the fact (for repeated experiment has convinced me it *is* a fact) that the circular opening in question is visible from no other attainable point of view than that afforded by the narrow ledge on the face of the rock.

"In this expedition to the 'Bishop's Hotel' I had been attended by Jupiter, who had, no doubt, observed, for some weeks past, the abstraction of my demeanor, and took especial care not to leave me alone. But, on the next day, getting up very early, I contrived to give him the slip, and went into the hills in search of the tree. After much toil I found it. When I came home at night my valet proposed to give me a flogging. With the rest of the adventure I believe you are as well acquainted as myself."

"I suppose," said I, "you missed the spot, in the first attempt at digging, through Jupiter's stupidity in letting the bug fall through the right instead of through the left eye of the skull."

"Precisely. This mistake made a difference of about two inches and a half in the 'shot'—that is to say, in the position of the peg nearest the tree; and had the treasure been *beneath* the 'shot,' the error would have been of little moment; but 'the shot,' together with the nearest point of the tree, were merely two points for the establishment of a line of direction; of course the error, however trivial in the beginning, increased as we proceeded with the line, and by the time we had gone fifty feet, threw us quite off the scent. But for my deep-seated convictions that treasure was here somewhere actually buried, we might have had all our labor in vain."

"I presume the fancy of *the skull,* of letting fall a bullet through the skull's eye—was suggested to Kidd by the piratical flag. No doubt he felt a kind of poetical consistency in recovering his money through this ominous insignium."

"Perhaps so; still I cannot help thinking that common-sense had quite as much to do with the matter as poetical consistency. To be visible from the devil's seat, it was necessary that the object, if small, should be white; and there is nothing like your human skull for retaining and even increasing its whiteness under exposure to all vicissitudes of weather."

"But your grandiloquence, and your conduct in swinging the beetle—how excessively odd! I was sure you were mad. And why did you insist on letting fall the bug, instead of a bullet, from the skull?"

"Why, to be frank, I felt somewhat annoyed by your evident suspicions touching my sanity, and so resolved to punish you quietly, in my own way, by a little bit of sober mystification. For this reason I swung the beetle, and for this reason I let it fall from the tree. An observation of yours about its great weight suggested the latter idea."

"Yes, I perceive; and now there is only one point which puzzles me. What are we to make of the skeletons found in the hole?"

"That is a question I am no more able to answer than yourself. There seems, however, only one plausible way of accounting for them—and yet it is dreadful to believe in such atrocity as my suggestion would imply. It is clear that Kidd—if Kidd indeed secreted this treasure, which I doubt not—it is clear that he must have had assistance in the labor. But, the worst of this labor concluded, he may have thought it expedient to remove all participants in his secret. Perhaps a couple of blows with a mattock were sufficient, while his coadjutors were busy in the pit; perhaps it required a dozen—who shall tell?"

# ZELIG

## Benjamin Rosenblatt

OLD ZELIG WAS eyed askance by his brethren. No one deigned to call him "Reb" Zelig, nor to prefix to his name the American equivalent—"Mr." "The old one is a barrel with a stave missing," knowingly declared his neighbors. "He never spends a cent; and he belongs nowheres." For "to belong," on New York's East Side, is of no slight importance. It means being a member in one of the numberless congregations. Every decent Jew must join "A Society for Burying Its Members," to be provided at least with a narrow cell at the end of the long road. Zelig was not even a member of one of these. "Alone, like a stone," his wife often sighed.

In the cloakshop where Zelig worked he stood daily, brandishing his heavy iron on the sizzling cloth, hardly ever glancing about him. The workmen despised him, for during a strike he returned to work after two days' absence. He could not be idle, and thought with dread of the Saturday that would bring him no pay envelope.

His very appearance seemed alien to his brethren. His figure was tall, and of cast-iron mold. When he stared stupidly at something, he looked like a blind Samson. His gray hair was long, and it fell in disheveled curls on gigantic shoulders somewhat inclined to stoop. His shabby clothes hung loosely on him; and, both summer and winter, the same old cap covered his massive head.

He had spent most of his life in a sequestered village in Little Russia, where he tilled the soil and even wore the national peasant costume. When his son and only child, a poor widower with a boy of twelve on his hands, emigrated to America, the father's heart bled. Yet he chose to stay in his native village at all hazards, and to die

920

there. One day, however, a letter arrived from the son that he was sick; this sad news was followed by words of a more cheerful nature— "and your grandson Moses goes to public school. He is almost an American; and he is not forced to forget the God of Israel. He will soon be confirmed. His Bar Mitsva is near." Zelig's wife wept three days and nights upon the receipt of this letter. The old man said little; but he began to sell his few possessions.

To face the world outside his village spelled agony to the poor rustic. Still he thought he would get used to the new home which his son had chosen. But the strange journey with locomotive and steamship bewildered him dreadfully; and the clamor of the metropolis, into which he was flung pell-mell, altogether stupefied him. With a vacant air he regarded the Pandemonium, and a petrifaction of his inner being seemed to take place. He became "a barrel with a stave missing." No spark of animation visited his eye. Only one thought survived in his brain, and one desire pulsed in his heart. to save money enough for himself and family to hurry back to his native village. Blind and dead to everything, he moved about with a dumb, lacerating pain in his heart—he longed for home. Before he found steady employment, he walked daily with titanic strides through the entire length of Manhattan, while children and even adults often slunk into byways to let him pass. Like a huge monster he seemed, with an arrow in his vitals.

In the shop where he found a job at last, the workmen feared him at first; but, ultimately finding him a harmless giant, they more than once hurled their sarcasms at his head. Of the many men and women employed there, only one person had the distinction of getting fellowship from old Zelig. That person was the Gentile watchman or janitor of the shop, a little blond Pole with an open mouth and frightened eyes. And many were the witticisms aimed at this uncouth pair. "The big one looks like an elephant," the joker of the shop would say; "only he likes to be fed on pennies instead of peanuts."

"Oi, oi, his nose would betray him," the "philosopher" of the shop chimed in; and during the dinner hour he would expatiate thus: "You see, money is his blood. He starves himself to have enough dollars to go back to his home; the Pole told me all about it. And why should he stay here? Freedom of religion means nothing to him, he never goes to synagogue; and freedom of the press? Bah—he never even reads the conservative Tageblatt!"

Old Zelig met such gibes with stoicism. Only rarely would he turn up the whites of his eyes, as if in the act of ejaculation; but he would soon contract his heavy brows into a scowl and emphasize the last with a heavy thump of his sizzling iron.

When the frightful cry of the massacred Jews in Russia rang across the Atlantic, and the Ghetto of Manhattan paraded one day through the narrow streets draped in black, through the erstwhile clamorous thoroughfares steeped in silence, stores and shops bolted, a wail of anguish issuing from every door and window—the only one remaining in his shop that day was old Zelig. His fellow-workmen did not call upon him to join the procession. They felt the incongruity of "this brute" in line with mourners in muffled tread. And the Gentile watchman reported the next day that the moment the funeral dirge of the music echoed from a distant street, Zelig snatched off the greasy cap he always wore, and in confusion instantly put it on again. "All the rest of the day," the Pole related with awe, "he looked wilder than ever, and so thumped with his iron on the cloth that I feared the building would come down."

But Zelig paid little heed to what was said about him. He dedicated his existence to the saving of his earnings, and only feared that he might be compelled to spend some of them. More than once his wife would be appalled in the dark of night by the silhouette of old Zelig in nightdress, sitting up in bed and counting a bundle of bank notes which he always replaced under his pillow. She frequently upbraided him for his niggardly nature, for his warding off all requests outside the pittance for household expense. She pleaded, exhorted, wailed. He invariably answered: "I haven't a cent by my soul." She pointed to the bare walls, the broken furniture, their beggarly attire.

"Our son is ill," she moaned. "He needs special food and rest; and our grandson is no more a baby; he'll soon need money for his studies. Dark is my world; you are killing both of them."

Zelig's color vanished; his old hands shook with emotion. The poor woman thought herself successful, but the next moment he would gasp: "Not a cent by my soul."

One day old Zelig was called from his shop, because his son had a sudden severe attack; and, as he ascended the stairs of his home, a neighbor shouted: "Run for a doctor; the patient cannot be revived." A voice as if from a tomb suddenly sounded in reply, "I haven't a cent by my soul."

The hallway was crowded with the ragged tenants of the house, mostly women and children; from far off were heard the rhythmic cries of the mother. The old man stood for a moment as if chilled from the roots of his hair to the tips of his fingers. Then the neighbors heard his sepulchral mumble: "I'll have to borrow somewheres, beg someone," as he retreated down the stairs. He brought a physician; and when the grandson asked for money to go for the medicine, Zelig snatched the prescription and hurried away, still murmuring: "I'll have to borrow, I'll have to beg."

Late that night, the neighbors heard a wail issuing from old Zelig's apartment; and they understood that the son was no more.

Zelig's purse was considerably thinned. He drew from it with palsied fingers for all burial expenses, looking about him in a dazed way. Mechanically he performed the Hebrew rites for the dead, which his neighbors taught him. He took a knife and made a deep gash in his shabby coat; then he removed his shoes, seated himself on the floor, and bowed his poor old head, tearless, benumbed.

The shop stared when the old man appeared after the prescribed three days' absence. Even the Pole dared not come near him. A film seemed to coat his glaring eye; deep wrinkles contracted his features, and his muscular frame appeared to shrink even as one looked. From that day on, he began to starve himself more than ever. The passion for sailing back to Russia, "to die at home at last," lost but little of its original intensity. Yet there was something now which by a feeble thread bound him to the New World.

In a little mound on the Base Achaim, the "House of Life," under a tombstone engraved with old Hebrew script, a part of himself lay buried. But he kept his thoughts away from that mound. How long and untiringly he kept on saving! Age gained on him with rapid strides. He had little strength left for work, but his dream of home seemed nearing its realization. Only a few more weeks, a few more months! And the thought sent a glow of warmth to his frozen frame. He would even condescend now to speak to his wife concerning the plans he had formed for their future welfare, more especially when she revived her pecuniary complaints.

"See what you have made of us, of the poor child," she often argued, pointing to the almost grown grandson. "Since he left school, he works for you, and what will be the end?"

At this, Zelig's heart would suddenly clutch, as if conscious of some indistinct, remote fear. His answers touching the grandson were abrupt, incoherent, as of one who replies to a question unintelligible to him, and is in constant dread lest his interlocutor should detect it.

Bitter misgivings concerning the boy began to mingle with the reveries of the old man. At first, he hardly gave a thought to him. The boy grew noiselessly. The ever-surging tide of secular studies that runs so high on the East Side caught this boy in its wave. He was quietly preparing himself for college. In his eagerness to accumulate the required sum, Zelig paid little heed to what was going on around him; and now, on the point of victory, he became aware with growing dread of something abrewing out of the common. He sniffed suspiciously; and one evening he overheard the boy talking to grandma about his hatred of Russian despotism, about his determination to remain in the States. He ended by entreating her to plead with grandpa to promise him the money necessary for a college education.

Old Zelig swooped down upon them with wild eyes. "Much you need it, you stupid," he thundered at the youngster in unrestrained fury. "You will continue your studies in Russia, durak, stupid." His timid wife, however, seemed suddenly to gather courage and she exploded: "Yes, you should give your savings for the child's education here. Woe is me, in the Russian universities no Jewish children are taken."

Old Zelig's face grew purple. He rose, and abruptly seated himself again. Then he rushed madly, with a raised, menacing arm, at the boy in whom he saw the formidable foe—the foe he had so long been dreading.

But the old woman was quick to interpose with a piercing shriek: "You madman, look at the sick child; you forget from what our son died, going out like a flickering candle."

That night Zelig tossed feverishly on his bed. He could not sleep. For the first time, it dawned upon him what his wife meant by pointing to the sickly appearance of the child. When the boy's father died, the physician declared that the cause was tuberculosis.

He rose to his feet. Beads of cold sweat glistened on his forehead, trickled down his cheeks, his beard. He stood pale and panting. Like a startling sound, the thought entered his mind—the boy, what should be done with the boy?

The dim, blue night gleamed in through the windows. All was shrouded in the city silence, which yet has a peculiar, monotonous ring in it. Somewhere, an infant awoke with a sickly cry which ended in a suffocating cough. The grizzled old man bestirred himself, and with hasty steps he tiptoed to the place where the boy lay. For a time he stood gazing on the pinched features, the under-sized body of the lad; then he raised one hand, passed it lightly over the boy's hair, stroking his cheeks and chin. The boy opened his eyes, looked for a moment at the shriveled form bending over him, then he petulantly closed them again.

"You hate to look at granpa, he is your enemy, eh?" The aged man's voice shook, and sounded like that of the child's awaking in the night. The boy made no answer; but the old man noticed how the frail body shook, how the tears rolled, washing the sunken cheeks.

For some moments he stood mute, then his form literally shrank to that of a child's as he bent over the ear of the boy and whispered hoarsely: "You are weeping, eh? Granpa is your enemy, you stupid! Tomorrow I will give you the money for the college. You hate to look at granpa; he is your enemy, eh?"

# THE PHILOSOPHY OF RELATIVE EXISTENCES

### Frank R. Stockton

IN A CERTAIN summer, not long gone, my friend Bentley and I found ourselves in a little hamlet which overlooked a placid valley, through which a river gently moved, winding its way through green stretches until it turned the end of a line of low hills and was lost to view. Beyond this river, far away, but visible from the door of the cottage where we dwelt, there lay a city. Through the mists which floated over the valley we could see the outlines of steeples and tall roofs; and buildings of a character which indicated thrift and business stretched themselves down to the opposite edge of the river. The more distant parts of the city, evidently a small one, lost themselves in the hazy summer atmosphere.

Bentley was young, fair-haired, and a poet; I was a philosopher, or trying to be one. We were good friends, and had come down into this peaceful region to work together. Although we had fled from the bustle and distractions of the town, the appearance in this rural region of a city, which, so far as we could observe, exerted no influence on the quiet character of the valley in which it lay, aroused our interest. No craft plied up and down the river; there were no bridges from shore to shore; there were none of those scattered and half-squalid habitations which generally are found on the outskirts of a city; there came to us no distant sound of bells; and not the smallest wreath of smoke rose from any of the buildings.

In answer to our inquiries our landlord told us that the city over the river had been built by one man, who was a visionary, and who had a great deal more money than common sense. "It is not as big a town as you would think, sirs," he said, "because the general mistiness of things in this valley makes them look larger than they are. Those hills, for instance, when you get to them are not as high as they look to be from here. But the town is big enough, and a good deal too big; for it ruined its builder and owner, who when he came to die had not money enough left to put up a decent tombstone at the head of his grave. He had a queer idea that he would like to have his town all finished before anybody lived in it, and so he kept on working and spending money year after year and year after year until the city was done and he had not a cent left. During all the time that the place was building hundreds of people came to him to buy houses or to hire them, but he would not listen to anything of the kind. No one must live in his town until it was all done. Even his workmen were obliged to go away at night to lodge. It is a town, sirs, I am told, in which nobody has slept for even a night. There are streets there, and places of business, and churches, and public halls, and everything that a town full of inhabitants could need; but it is all empty and deserted, and has been so as far back as I can remember, and I came to this region when I was a little boy."

"And is there no one to guard the place?" we asked; "no one to protect it from wandering vagrants who might choose to take possession of the buildings?"

"There are not many vagrants in this part of the country," he said; "and if there were, they would not go over to that city. It is haunted."

"By what?" we asked.

"Well, sirs, I scarcely can tell you; queer beings that are not flesh and blood, and that is all I know about it. A good many people living hereabouts have visited that place once in their lives, but I know of no one who has gone there a second time."

"And travelers," I said; "are they not excited by curiosity to explore that strange uninhabited city?"

"Oh, yes," our host replied; "almost all visitors to the valley go over to that queer city—generally in small parties, for it is not a place in which one wishes to walk about alone. Sometimes they see things, and sometimes they don't. But I never knew any man or woman to show a fancy for living there, although it is a very-good town."

This was said at supper-time, and, as it was the period of full moon, Bentley and I decided that we would visit the haunted city that evening. Our host endeavored to dissuade us, saying that no one ever went over there at night; but as we were not to be deterred, he told us where we would find his small boat tied to a stake on the river-bank. We soon crossed the river, and landed at a broad, but low, stone pier, at the land end of which a line of tall grasses waved in the gentle night wind as if they were sentinels warning us from entering the silent city. We pushed through these, and walked up a street fairly wide, and so well paved that we noticed none of the weeds and other growths which generally denote desertion or little use. By the bright light of the moon we could see that the architecture was simple, and of a character highly gratifying to the eye. All the buildings were of stone and of good size. We were greatly excited and interested, and proposed to continue our walks until the moon should set, and to return on the following morning—"to live here, perhaps," said Bentley. "What could be so romantic and yet so real? What could conduce better to the marriage of verse and philosophy?" But as he said this we saw around the corner of a cross-street some forms as of people hurrying away.

"The specters," said my companion, laying his hand on my arm.

"Vagrants, more likely," I answered, "who have taken advantage of the superstition of the region to appropriate this comfort and beauty to themselves."

"If that be so," said Bentley, "we must have a care for our lives."

We proceeded cautiously, and soon saw other forms fleeing before us and disappearing, as we supposed, around corners and into houses. And now suddenly finding ourselves upon the edge of a wide, open public square, we saw in the dim light—for a tall steeple obscured the moon—the forms of vehicles, horses, and men moving here and there. But before, in our astonishment, we could say a word one to the other, the moon moved past the steeple, and in its bright light we could see none of the signs of life and traffic which had just astonished us.

Timidly, with hearts beating fast, but with not one thought of turning back, nor any fear of vagrants—for we were now sure that what we had seen was not flesh and blood, and therefore harmless—we crossed the open space and entered a street down which the moon shone clearly. Here and there we saw dim figures, which quickly disappeared; but, approaching a low stone balcony in front of one of the houses, we were surprised to see, sitting thereon and leaning over a book which lay open upon the top of the carved parapet, the figure of a woman who did not appear to notice us.

"That is a real person," whispered Bentley, "and it does not see us."

"No," I replied; "it is like the others. Let us go near it."

We drew near to the balcony and stood before it. At this the figure raised its head and looked at us. It was beautiful, it was young; but its substance seemed to be of an ethereal quality which we had never seen or known of. With its full, soft eyes fixed upon us, it spoke:

"Why are you here?" it asked. "I have said to myself that the next time I saw any of you I would ask you why you come to trouble us. Cannot you live content in your own realms and spheres, knowing, as you must know, how timid we are, and how you frighten us and make us unhappy? In all this city there is, I believe, not one of us except myself who does not flee and hide from you whenever you cruelly come here. Even I would do that, had not I declared to myself that I would see you and speak to you, and endeavor to prevail upon you to leave us in peace."

The clear, frank tones of the speaker gave me courage. "We are two men," I answered, "strangers in this region, and living for the time in the beautiful country on the other side of the river. Having heard of this quiet city, we have come to see it for ourselves. We had supposed it to be uninhabited, but now that we find that this is not the case, we would assure you from our hearts that we do not wish to disturb or annoy anyone who lives here. We simply came as honest travelers to view the city."

The figure now seated herself again, and as her countenance was nearer to us, we could see that it was filled with pensive thought. For a moment she looked at us without speaking. "Men!" she said. "And so I have been right. For a long time I have believed that the beings who sometimes come here, filling us with dread and awe, are men."

"And you," I exclaimed—"who are you, and who are these forms that we have seen, these strange inhabitants of this city?"

She gently smiled as she answered: "We are the ghosts of the future. We are the people who are to live in this city generations hence. But all of us do not know that, principally because we do not think about it and study about it enough to know it. And it is generally believed that the men and women who sometimes come here are ghosts who haunt the place."

"And that is why you are terrified and flee from us?" I exclaimed. "You think we are ghosts from another world?"

"Yes," she replied; "that is what is thought, and what I used to think."

"And you," I asked, "are spirits of human beings yet to be?"

"Yes," she answered; "but not for a long time. Generations of men, I know not how many, must pass away before we are men and women."

"Heavens!" exclaimed Bentley, clasping his hands and raising his eyes to the sky, "I shall be a spirit before you are a woman."

"Perhaps," she said again, with a sweet smile upon her face, "you may live to be very, very old."

But Bentley shook his head. This did not console him. For some minutes I stood in contemplation, gazing upon the stone pavement beneath my feet. "And this," I ejaculated, "is a city inhabited by the ghosts of the future, who believe men and women to be phantoms and specters?"

She bowed her head.

"But how is it," I asked, "that you discovered that you are spirits and we mortal men?"

"There are so few of us who think of such things," she answered, "so few who study, ponder, and reflect. I am fond of study, and I love philosophy; and from the reading of many books I have learned much. From the book which I have here I have learned most; and from its teachings I have gradually come to the belief, which you tell me is the true one, that we are spirits and you men."

"And what book is that?" I asked.

"It is 'The Philosophy of Relative Existences,' by Rupert Vance."

"Ye gods!" I exclaimed, springing upon the balcony, "that is my book, and I am Rupert Vance." I stepped toward the volume to seize it, but she raised her hand.

"You cannot touch it," she said. "It is the ghost of a book. And did you write it?"

"Write it? No," I said; "I am writing it. It is not yet finished."

"But here it is," she said, turning over the last pages. "As a spirit book it is finished. It is very successful; it is held in high estimation by intelligent thinkers; it is a standard work."

I stood trembling with emotion. "High estimation!" I said. "A standard work!"

"Oh, yes," she replied with animation; "and it well deserves its great success, especially in its conclusion. I have read it twice."

"But let me see these concluding pages," I exclaimed. "Let me look upon what I am to write."

She smiled, and shook her head, and closed the book. "I would like to do that," she said, "but if you are really a man you must not know what you are going to do."

"Oh, tell me, tell me," cried Bentley from below, "do you know a book called 'Stellar Studies,' by Arthur Bentley? It is a book of poems."

The figure gazed at him. "No," it said presently; "I never heard of it."

I stood trembling. Had the youthful figure before me been flesh and blood, had the book been a real one, I would have torn it from her.

"O wise and lovely being!" I exclaimed, falling on my knees before her, "be also benign and generous. Let me but see the last page of my book. If I have been of benefit to your world; more than all, if I have been of benefit to you, let me see, I implore you—let me see how it is that I have done it."

She rose with the book in her hand. "You have only to wait until you have done it," she said, "and then you will know all that you could see here." I started to my feet, and stood alone upon the balcony.

"I am sorry," said Bentley, as we walked toward the pier where we had left our boat, "that we talked only to that ghost girl, and that the other spirits were all afraid of us. Persons whose souls are choked up with philosophy are not apt to care much for poetry; and even if my book is to be widely known, it is easy to see that she may not have heard of it."

I walked triumphant. The moon, almost touching the horizon, beamed like red gold. "My dear friend," said I, "I have always told you that you should put more philosophy into your poetry. That would make it live."

"And I have always told you," said he, "that you should not put so much poetry into your philosophy. It misleads people."

"It didn't mislead that ghost girl," said I.

"How do you know?" said he. "Perhaps she is wrong, and the other inhabitants of the city are right, and we may be the ghosts after all. Such things, you know, are only relative. Anyway," he continued, after a little pause, "I wish I knew that those ghosts were now reading the poem I am going to begin tomorrow."

# THE GHOST IN THE MILL

### Harriet Beecher Stowe

"Come, Sam, tell us a story," said I, as Harry and I crept to his knees, in the glow of the bright evening firelight; while Aunt Lois was busily rattling the tea-things, and grandmamma, at the other end of the fireplace, was quietly setting the heel of a blue-mixed yarn stocking.

In those days we had no magazines and daily papers, each reeling off a serial story. Once a week, *The Columbian Sentinel* came from Boston with its slender stock of news and editorial; but all the multiform devices—pictorial, narrative, and poetical—which keep the mind of the present generation ablaze with excitement, had not then even an existence. There was no theatre, no opera; there were in Oldtown no parties or balls, except, perhaps, the annual election, or Thanksgiving festival; and when winter came, and the sun went down at half-past four o'clock, and left the long, dark hours of evening to be provided for, the necessity of amusement became urgent. Hence, in those days, chimney-corner storytelling became an art and an accomplishment. Society then was full of traditions and narratives which had all the uncertain glow and shifting mystery of the firelit hearth upon them. They were told to sympathetic audiences, by the rising and falling light of the solemn embers, with the hearth-crickets filling up every pause. Then the aged told their stories to the young—tales of early life; tales of war and adventure, of forest-days, of Indian captivities and escapes, of bears and wild-cats and panthers, of rattlesnakes, of witches and wizards, and strange and wonderful dreams and appearances and providences.

In those days of early Massachusetts, faith and credence were in the very air. Two-thirds of New England was then dark, unbroken forests, through whose tangled paths the mysterious winter wind groaned and shrieked and howled with weird noises and unaccountable clamors. Along the iron-bound shore, the stormful Atlantic raved and thundered, and dashed its moaning waters, as if to deaden and deafen any voice that might tell of the settled life of the old civilized world, and shut us forever into the wilderness. A good story-teller, in those days, was always sure of a warm seat at the hearth-stone, and the delighted homage of children; and in all Oldtown there was no better story-teller than Sam Lawson.

"Do, do, tell us a story," said Harry, pressing upon him, and opening very wide blue eyes, in which undoubting faith shone as in a mirror; "and let it be something strange, and different from common."

"Wal, I know lots o' strange things," said Sam, looking mysteriously into the fire. "Why, I know things, that ef I should tell—why, people might say they wa'n't so; but then they *is* so for all that."

"Oh, *do,* do, tell us!"

"Why, I should scare ye to death, mebbe," said Sam doubtingly.

"Oh, pooh! no, you wouldn't," we both burst out at once.

But Sam was possessed by a reticent spirit, and loved dearly to be wooed and importuned; and so he only took up the great kitchen-tongs, and smote on the hickory forestick, when it flew apart in the middle, and scattered a shower of clear bright coals all over the hearth.

"Mercy on us, Sam Lawson!" said Aunt Lois in an indignant voice, spinning round from her dish-washing.

"Don't you worry a grain. Miss Lois," said Sam composedly. "I see that are stick was e'en a'most in two, and I thought I'd jest settle it. I'll sweep up the coals now," he added, vigorously applying a turkey-wing to the purpose, as he knelt on the hearth, his spare, lean figure glowing in the blaze of the firelight, and getting quite flushed with exertion.

"There, now!" he said, when he had brushed over and under and between the fire-irons, and pursued the retreating ashes so far into the red, fiery citadel, that his finger-ends were burning and tingling, "that are's done now as well as Hepsy herself could 'a' done it. I allers sweeps up the haarth: I think it's part o' the man's bisness when he makes the fire. But Hepsy's so used to seein' me a doin' on't, that she don't see no kind o' merit in't. It's just as Parson Lothrop said in his sermon—folks allers overlook their common marcies"—

"But come, Sam, that story," said Harry and I coaxingly, pressing upon him, and pulling him down into his seat in the corner.

"Lordy massy, these 'ere young uns!" said Sam. "There's never no contentin' on em: ye tell 'em one story, and they jest swallows it as a dog does a gob o' meat; and they're all ready for another. What do ye want to hear now?"

Now, the fact was, that Sam's stories had been told us so often, that they were all arranged and ticketed in our minds. We knew every word in them, and could set him right if he varied a hair from the usual track; and still the interest in them was unabated. Still we shivered, and clung to his knee, at the mysterious parts, and felt gentle, cold chills run down our spines at appropriate places. We were always in the most receptive and sympathetic condition. Tonight, in particular, was one of those thundering stormy ones, when the winds appeared to be holding a perfect mad carnival over my grandfather's house. They yelled and squealed round the corners; they collected in troops, and came tumbling and roaring down chimney; they shook and rattled the buttery-door and the sinkroom-door and the cellar-door and the chamber-door, with a constant undertone of squeak and clatter, as if at every door were a cold, discontented spirit, tired of the chill outside, and longing for the warmth and comfort within.

"Wal, boys," said Sam confidentially, "what'll ye have?"

"Tell us 'Come down, come down!'" we both shouted with one voice. This was, in our mind, an "A No. 1" among Sam's stories.

"Ye mus'n't be frightened now," said Sam paternally.

"Oh, no! we ar'n't frightened *ever*," said we both in one breath.

"Not when ye go down the cellar arter cider?" said Sam with severe scrutiny. "Efye should be down cellar, and the candle should go out, now?"

"I ain't," said I: "I ain't afraid of any thing. I never knew what it was to be afraid in my life."

"Wal, then," said Sam, "I'll tell ye. This 'ere's what Cap'n Eb Sawin told me when I was a boy about your bigness, I reckon.

"Cap'n Eb Sawin was a most respectable man. Your gran'ther knew him very well; and he was a deacon in the church in Dedham afore he died. He was at Lexington when the fust gun was fired agin the British. He was a dreffle smart man, Cap'n Eb was, and driv team a good many years atween here and Boston. He married Lois Peabody, that was cousin to your gran'ther then. Lois was a real sensible woman; and I've heard her tell the story as he told her, and it was jest as he told it to me—jest exactly; and I shall never forget it if I live to be nine hundred years old, like Mathuselah.

"Ye see, along back in them times, there used to be a fellow come round these 'ere parts, spring and fall, a-peddlin' goods, with his pack on his back; and his name was Jehiel Lommedieu. Nobody rightly knew where he come from. He wasn't much of a talker; but the women rather liked him, and kind o' liked to have him round. Women will like some fellows, when men can't see no sort o' reason why they should; and they liked this 'ere Lommedieu, though he was kind o' mournful and thin and shad-bellied, and hadn't nothin' to say for himself. But it got to be so, that the women would count and calculate so many weeks afore 'twas time for Lommedieu to be along; and they'd make up ginger-snaps and preserves and pies, and make him stay to tea at the houses, and feed him up on the best there was: and the story went round, that he was a-courtin' Phebe Ann Parker, or Phebe Ann was a-courtin' him—folks didn't rightly know which. Wal, all of a sudden, Lommedieu stopped comin' round; and nobody knew why—only jest he didn't come. It turned out that Phebe Ann Parker had got a letter from him, sayin' he'd be along afore Thanksgiving; but he didn't come, neither afore nor at Thanksgiving time, nor arter, nor next spring: and finally the women they gin up lookin' for him. Some said he was dead; some said he was gone to Canada; and some said he hed gone over to the Old Country.

"Wal, as to Phebe Ann, she acted like a gal o' sense, and married 'Bijah Moss, and thought no more 'bout it. She took the right view on't, and said she was sartin that all things was ordered out for the best; and it was jest as well folks couldn't always have their own way. And so, in time, Lommedieu was gone out o' folks's minds, much as a last year's apple-blossom.

"It's relly affectin' to think how little these 'ere folks is missed that's so much sot by. There ain't nobody, ef they's ever so important, but what the world gets to goin' on without 'em, pretty much as it did with 'em, though there's some little flurry at fust. Wal, the last thing that was in anybody's mind was, that they ever should hear from Lommedieu agin. But there ain't nothin' but what has its time o' turnin' up; and it seems his turn was to come.

"Wal, ye see, 'twas the 19th o' March, when Cap'n Eb Sawin started with a team for Boston. That day, there come on about the biggest snow-storm that there'd been in them parts sence the oldest man could remember. "'Twas this ere fine, siftin' snow, that drives in your face like needles, with a wind to cut your nose off: it made teamin' pretty tedious work. Cap'n Eb was about the toughest man in them parts. He'd spent days in the woods a-loggin', and he'd been up to the deestrict o' Maine a-lumberin', and was about up to any sort o' thing a man gen'ally could be up to; but these 'ere March winds sometimes does set on a fellow so, that neither natur' nor grace can stan' em. The cap'n used to say he could stan' any wind that blew one way 't time for five minutes; but come to winds that blew all four p'ints at the same minit—why, they flustered him.

"Wal, that was the sort o' weather it was all day: and by sundown Cap'n Eb he got clean bewildered, so that he lost his road; and, when night came on, he didn't know nothin' where he was. Ye see the country was all under drift, and the air so thick with snow, that he couldn't see a foot afore him; and the fact was, he got off the Boston road without knowin' it, and came out at a pair o' bars nigh upon Sherburn, where old Cack Sparrock's mill is.

"Your gran'ther used to know old Cack, boys. He was a drefful drinkin' old crittur, that lived there all alone in the woods by himself a-tendin' saw and grist mill. He wa'nt allers jest what he was then. Time was that Cack was a pretty consid'ably likely young man, and his wife was a very respectable woman—Deacon Amos Petengall's dater from Sherburn.

"But ye see, the year arter his wife died, Cack he gin up goin' to meetin' Sundays, and, all the tithing-men and selectmen could do, they couldn't get him out to meetin'; and, when a man neglects means o' grace and sanctuary privileges, there ain't no sayin' *what* he'll do next. Why, boys, jist think on't!—an immortal crittur lyin' round loose all day Sunday, and not puttin' on so much as a clean shirt, when all 'spectable folks has on their best close, and is to meetin' worshippin' the Lord! What can you spect to come of it, when he lies idlin' round in his old week-day close, fishing, or some sich, but what the Devil should be arter him at last, as he was arter old Cack?"

Here Sam winked impressively to my grandfather in the opposite corner, to call his attention to the moral which he was interweaving with his narrative.

"Wal, ye see, Cap'n Eb he told me, that when he come to them bars and looked up, and saw the dark a-comin' down, and the storm a-thickenin' up, he felt that things was gettin' pretty consid'able serious. There was a dark piece o' woods on ahead of him inside the bars; and he knew, come to get in there, the light would give out clean. So he jest thought he'd take the hoss out o' the team, and go ahead a little, and see where he was. So he driv his oxen up ag'in the fence, and took out the hoss, and got on him, and pushed along through the woods, not rightly knowin' where he was goin'.

"Wal, afore long he see a light through the trees and, sure enough, he come out to Cack Sparrock's old mill.

"It was a pretty consid'able gloomy sort of a place, that are old mill was. There was a great fall of water that come rushin' down the rocks, and fell in a deep pool; and it sounded sort o' wild and lonesome; but Cap'n Eb he knocked on the door with his whip-handle, and got in.

"There, to be sure, sot old Cack beside a great blazin' fire, with his rum-jug at his elbow. He was a dreful fellow to drink, Cack was! For all that, there was some good in him, for he was pleasant-spoken and 'blig-ing; and he made the cap'n welcome.

"'Ye see, Cack,' said Cap'n Eb, 'I'm off my road and got snowed up down by your bars,' says he.

"'Want ter know!' says Cack. 'Calculate you'll jest have to camp down here till mornin',' says he.

"Wal, so old Cack he got out his tin lantern, and went with Cap'n Eb back to the bars to help him fetch along his critturs. He told him he could put 'em under the mill-shed. So they got the critturs up to the shed, and got the cart under; and by that time the storm was awful.

"But Cack he made a great roarin' fire, 'cause, ye see, Cack allers had slab-wood a plenty from his mill; and a roarin' fire is jest so much company. It sort o' keeps a fellow's spirits up, a good fire does. So Cack he sot on his old teakettle, and made a swingeing lot o' toddy; and he and Cap'n Eb were havin' a tol'able comfortable time there. Cack was a pretty good hand to tell stories; and Cap'n Eb warn't no way backward in that line, and kep' up his end pretty well: and pretty soon they was a-roarin' and haw-hawin' inside about as loud as the storm outside; when all of a sudden, bout midnight, there come a loud rap on the door.

"'Lordy massy! what's that?' says Cack. Folks is rather startled allers to be checked up sudden when they are a-carryin' on and laughin'; and it was such an awful blowy night, it was a little scary to have a rap on the door.

"Wal, they waited a minit, and didn't hear nothin' but the wind a-screechin' round the chimbley; and old Cack was jest goin' on with his story, when the rap come ag'in, harder'n ever, as if it'd shook the door open.

" 'Wal,' says old Cack, 'if 'tis the Devil, we'd jest as good's open, and have it out with him to onst,' says he; and so he got up and opened the door, and, sure enough, there was old Ketury there. Expect you've heard your grandma tell about old Ketury. She used to come to meetin's sometimes, and her husband was one o' the prayin' Indians; but Ketury was one of the real wild sort, and you couldn't no more convert *her* than you could convert a wild-cat or a panth'a. Lordy massy! Ketury used to come to meetin', and sit there on them Indian benches; and when the second bell was a-tollin', and when Parson Lothrop and his wife was comin' up the broad aisle, and everybody in the house ris' up and stood, Ketury would sit there, and look at 'em out o' the corner o' her eyes; and folks used to say she rattled them necklaces o' rattlesnakes' tails and wild-cat teeth, and sich like heathen trumpery, and looked for all the world as if the spirit of the old Sarpent himself was in her. I've seen her sit and look at Lady Lothrop out o' the corner o' her eyes; and her old brown baggy neck would kind o' twist and work; and her eyes they looked so, that 'twas enough to scare a body. For all the world, she looked jest as if she was a-workin' up to spring at her. Lady Lothrop was jest as kind to Ketury as she always was to every poor crittur. She'd bow and smile as gracious to her when meetin was over, and she come down the aisle, passin' out o' meetin'; but Ketury never took no notice. Ye see, Ketury's father was one o' them great powwows down to Martha's Vineyard; and people used to say she was set apart, when she was a child, to the sarvice o' the Devil: any way, she never could be made nothin' of in a Christian way. She come down to Parson Lothrop's study once or twice to be catechised; but he couldn't get a word out o' her, and she kind o' seemed to sit scornful while he was a-talkin'. Folks said, if it was in old times, Ketury wouldn't have been allowed to go on so; but Parson Lothrop's so sort o' mild, he let her take pretty much her own way. Everybody thought that Ketury was a witch: at least, she knew consid'able more'n she ought to know, and so they was kind o' 'fraid on her. Cap'n Eb says he never see a fellow seem scareder than Cack did when he see Ketury a-standin' there.

"Why, ye see, boys, she was as withered and wrinkled and brown as an old frosted punkin-vine; and her little snaky eyes sparkled and snapped, and it made yer head kind o' dizzy to look at 'em; and folks used to say that anybody that Ketury got mad at was sure to get the worst of it fust or last. And so, no matter what day or hour Ketury had a mind to rap at anybody's door, folks gen'lly thought it was best to let her in; but then, they never thought her coming was for any good, for she was just like the wind—she came when the fit was on her, she staid jest so long as it pleased her, and went when she got ready, and not before. Ketury understood English, and could talk it well enough, but always seemed to scorn it, and was allers mowin' and mutterin' to herself in Indian, and winkin' and blinkin' as if she saw more folks round than you did, so that she wa'n't no way pleasant company: and yet everybody took good care to be polite to her.

So old Cack asked her to come in, and didn't make no question where she come from, or what she come on; but he knew it was twelve good miles from where she lived to his hut, and the snow was drifted above her middle: and Cap'n Eb declared that there wa'n't no track, nor sign o' a track, of anybody's coming through that snow next morning."

"How did she get there, then?" said I.

"Didn't ye never see brown leaves a-ridin' on the wind? 'Well,' Cap'n Eb he says, 'she came on the wind,' and I'm sure it was strong enough to fetch her. But Cack he got her down into the warm corner, and he poured her out a mug o' hot toddy, and give her: but ye see her bein' there sort o' stopped the conversation; for she sot there a-rockin' back'ards and for'ards, a-sippin her toddy, and a-mutterin', and lookin' up chimbley.

"Cap'n Eb says in all his born days he never hearn such screeches and yells as the wind give over that chimbley; and old Cack got so frightened, you could fairly hear his teeth chatter.

"But Cap'n Eb he was a putty brave man, and he wa'n't goin' to have conversation stopped by no woman, witch or no witch; and so, when he see her mutterin', and lookin' up chimbley, he spoke up, and says he, 'Well, Ketury, what do you see?' says he. 'Come, out with it; don't keep it to yourself.' Ye see Cap'n Eb was a hearty fellow, and then he was a leetle warmed up with the toddy.

"Then he said he see an evil kind o' smile on Ketury's face, and she rattled her necklace o' bones and snakes' tails; and her eyes seemed to snap; and she looked up the chimbley, and called out, 'Come down, come down! let's see who ye be.'

"Then there was a scratchin' and a rumblin' and a groan; and a pair of feet come down the chimbley, and stood right in the middle of the haarth, the toes pi'ntin' out'rds, with shoes and silver buckles a-shinin' in the firelight. Cap'n Eb says he never come so near bein' scared in his life; and, as to old Cack, he jest wilted right down in his chair.

"Then old Ketury got up, and reached her stick up chimbley, and called out louder, 'Come down, come down! Let's see who ye be.' And, sure enough, down came a pair o' legs, and j'ined right on to the feet: good fair legs they was, with ribbed stockings and leather breeches.

"'Wal, we're in for it now,' says Cap'n Eb. 'Go it, Ketury, and let's have the rest on him.'

"Ketury didn't seem to mind him: she stood there as stiff as a stake, and kep' callin' out, 'Come down, come down! Let's see who ye be.' And then come down the body of a man with a brown coat and yellow vest, and j'ined right on to the legs; but there wa'n't no arms to it. Then Ketury shook her stick up chimbley, and called, *'Come down, come down!'* And there came down a pair o' arms, and went on each side o' the body; and there stood a man all finished, only there wa'n't no head on him.

"'Wal, Ketury,' says Cap'n Eb, 'this 'ere's getting serious. I 'spec' you must finish him up, and let's see what he wants of us.'

"Then Ketury called out once more, louder'n ever, 'Come down, come down! let's see who ye be.' And, sure enough, down comes a man's head, and settled on the shoulders straight enough; and Cap'n Eb, the minit he sot eyes on him, knew he was Jehiel Lommedieu.

"Old Cack knew him too; and he fell flat on his face, and prayed the Lord to have mercy on his soul: but Cap'n Eb he was for gettin' to the bottom of matters, and not have his scare for nothin'; so he says to him, 'What do you want, now you hev come?'

"The man he didn't speak; he only sort o' moaned, and p'inted to the chimbley. He seemed to try to speak, but couldn't; for ye see it isn't often that his sort o' folks is permitted to speak: but just then there came a screechin' blast o' wind, and blowed the door open, and blowed the smoke and fire all out into the room, and there seemed to be a whirlwind and darkness and moans and screeches; and, when it all cleared up, Ketury and the man was both gone, and only old Cack lay on the ground, rolling and moaning as if he'd die.

"Wal, Cap'n Eb he picked him up, and built up the fire, and sort o' comforted him up, 'cause the crittur was in distress o' mind that was drefful. The awful Providence, ye see, had awakened him, and his sin had been set home to his soul; and he was under such conviction, that it all had to come out—how old Cack's father had murdered poor Lommedieu for his money, and Cack had been privy to it, and helped his father build the body up in that very chimbley; and he said that he hadn't had neither peace nor rest since then, and that was what had driv' him away from ordinances; for ye know sinnin' will always make a man leave prayin'. Wal, Cack didn't live but a day or two. Cap'n Eb he got the minister o' Sherburn and one o' the selectmen down to see him, and they took his deposition. He seemed railly quite penitent; and Parson Carryl he prayed with him, and was faithful in settin' home the providence to his soul: and so, at the eleventh hour, poor old Cack might have got in; at least it looks a leetle like it. He was distressed to think he couldn't live to be hung. He sort o' seemed to think, that if he was fairly tried, and hung, it would make it all square. He made Parson Carryl promise to have the old mill pulled down, and bury the body; and, after he was dead, they did it.

"Cap'n Eb he was one of a party o' eight that pulled down the chimbley; and there, sure enough, was the skeleton of poor Lommedieu.

"So there you see, boys, there can't be no iniquity so hid but what it'll come out. The wild Indians of the forest, and the stormy winds and tempests, j'ined together to bring out this 'ere."

"For my part," said Aunt Lois sharply, "I never believed that story."

"Why, Lois," said my grandmother, "Cap'n Eb Sawin was a regular church-member, and a most respectable man."

"Law, mother! I don't doubt he thought so. I suppose he and Cack got drinking toddy together, till he got asleep, and dreamed it. I wouldn't believe such a thing if it did happen right before my face and eyes. I should only think I was crazy, that's all."

"Come, Lois, if I was you, I wouldn't talk so like a Sadducee," said my grandmother. "What would become of all the accounts in Dr. Cotton Mather's 'Magnilly' if folks were like you?"

"Wal," said Sam Lawson, drooping contemplatively over the coals, and gazing into the fire, "there's a putty consid'able sight o' things in this world that's true; and then ag'in there's a sight o' things that ain't true. Now, my old gran'ther used to say, 'Boys,' says he, 'if ye want to lead a pleasant and prosperous life, ye must contrive allers to keep jest the *happy medium* between truth and falsehood.' Now, that are's my doctrine."

Aunt Lois knit severely.

"Boys," said Sam, "don't you want ter go down with me and get a mug o' cider?"

Of course we did, and took down a basket to bring up some apples to roast.

"Boys," says Sam mysteriously, while he was drawing the cider, "you jest ask your Aunt Lois to tell you what she knows 'bout Ruth Sullivan."

"Why, what is it?"

"Oh! you must ask *her*. These 'ere folks that's so kind o' toppin' about sperits and sich, come sift 'em down, you gen'lly find they knows one story that kind o' puzzles 'em. Now you mind, and jist ask your Aunt Lois about Ruth Sullivan."

# BLOOD-BURNING MOON

## Jean Toomer

### 1

UP FROM THE skeleton stone walls, up from the rotting floorboards and the solid hand-hewn beams of oak of the pre-war cotton factory, dusk came. Up from the dusk the full moon came. Glowing like a fired pine-knot it illumined the great door and soft showered the Negro shanties aligned along the single street of factory town. The full moon in the great door was an omen. Negro women improvised songs against its spell.

Louisa sang as she came over the crest of the hill from the white folk's kitchen. Her skin was the color of oak leaves on young trees in fall. Her breasts, firm and up-pointed like ripe acorns. And her singing had the low murmur of winds in fig trees. Bob Stone, younger son of the people she worked for, loved her. By the way the world reckons things he had won her. By measure of that warm glow which came into her mind at thought of him, he had won her. Tom Burwell, whom the whole town called Big Boy, also loved her. But working in the fields all day, and far away from her, gave him no chance to show it. Though often enough of evenings he had tried to. Somehow, he never got along. Strong as he was with hands upon the axe or plow, he found it difficult to hold her. Or so he thought. But the fact was that he held her to factory town more firmly than he thought for. His black balanced, and pulled against the white of Stone, when she thought of them. And her mind was vaguely upon them as she came over the crest of the hill, coming from the white folk's kitchen. As she sang softly at the veil face of the full moon.

A strange stir was in her. Indolently she tried to fix upon Bob or Tom as the cause of it. To meet Bob in the canebrake as she was going to do an hour or so later, was nothing new. And Tom's proposal which she felt on its way to her could be indefinitely put off. Separately, there was no unusual significance to either one. But for some reason they jumbled when her eyes gazed vacantly at the rising moon. And from the jumble came the stir that was strangely within her. Her lips trembled. The slow rhythm of her song grew agitant and restless. Rusty black and tan spotted hounds, lying in the dark corners of porches or prowling around back yards, put their noses in the air and caught its tremor. They began to plaintively yelp and howl. Chickens woke up, and cackled. Intermittently, all over the country-side dogs barked and roosters crowed as if heralding a weird dawn or some ungodly awakening. The women sang lustily. Their songs were cottonwads to stop their ears. Louisa came down into factory town and sank wearily upon the step before her home. The moon was rising towards a thick cloud-bank which soon would hide it.

> *Red nigger moon. Sinner!*
> *Blood-burning moon. Sinner!*
> *Come out that fact'ry door.*

## 2

Up from the deep dusk of a cleared spot on the edge of the forest a mellow glow arose and spread fan-wise into the low-hanging heavens. And all around the air was heavy with the scent of boiling cane. A large pile of cane-stalks lay like ribboned shadows upon the ground. A mule, harnessed to a pole, trudged lazily round and round the pivot of the grinder. Beneath a swaying oil lamp, a Negro alternately whipped out at the mule, and fed cane-stalks to the grinder. A fat boy waddled pails of fresh ground juice between the grinder and the boiling stove. Steam came from the copper boiling pan. The scent of cane came from the copper pan and drenched the forest and the hill that sloped to factory town, beneath its fragrance. It drenched the men in circle seated round the stove. Some of them chewed at the white pulp of stalks, but there was no need for them to, if all they wanted was to taste the cane. One tasted it in factory town. And from factory town one could see the soft haze thrown by the glowing stove upon the low-hanging heavens.

Old David Georgia stirred the thickening syrup with a long ladle, and ever so often drew it off. Old David Georgia tended his stove and told tales about the white folks, about moonshining and cotton picking and about sweet nigger gals, to the men who sat there about his stove to listen to him. Tom Burwell chewed cane-stalk and laughed with the others till someone mentioned Louisa. Till someone said something about Louisa and Bob Stone, about the silk stockings she must have gotten from him. Blood ran up Tom's neck hotter than the glow that flooded from the stove. He sprang up. Glared at the men and said, "She's my gal." Will Manning laughed. Tom strode over to him. Yanked him up, and knocked him to the ground. Several of Manning's friends got up to fight for him. Tom whipped out a long knife and would have cut them to shreds if they hadn't ducked into the woods. Tom had had enough. He nodded to old David Georgia and swung down the path to factory town. Just then, the dogs started barking and the roosters began to crow. Tom felt funny. Away from the fight, away from the stove, chill got to him. He shivered. He shuddered when he saw the full moon rising towards the cloud-bank. He who didn't give a godam for the fears of old women. He forced his mind to fasten on Louisa. Bob Stone. Better not be. He turned into the street and saw Louisa sitting before her home. He went towards her, ambling, touched the brim of a marvelously shaped, spotted, felt hat, said he wanted to say something to her, and then found that he didn't know what he had to say, or if he did, that he couldn't say it. He shoved his big fists in his overalls, grinned, and started to move off.

"Youall want me, Tom?"

"That's what us wants sho, Louisa."

"Well, here I am—"

"An' here I is, but that ain't ahelpin' none, all th' same."

"You wanted to say something . . . ?"

"I did that, sho. But words is like th' spots on dice; no matter how y' fumbles 'em there's times when they jes won't come. I dunno why. Seems like th' love I feels fo' yo' done stole m' tongue. I got it now. Wheel Louisa, honey, I oughtn't tell y', I feel I oughtn't cause yo' is young an' goes t' church an' I has had other gals, but Louisa I sho do love y'. Lil' gal I'se watched y' from them first days wen youall sat right here befo' yo' door befo' th' well an' sang sometimes in a way that like t' broke m' heart. I'se carried y' with me into th' fields, day after day, an' after that, an' I sho can plow when yo' is ther, an'

I can pick cotton. Yassur! Come near beatin' Barlo yesterday. I sho did. Yassur! An' next year if ol'e Stone'll trust me, I'll have a farm. My own. My bales will buy yo' what y' gets from white folks now. Silk stockings, an' purple dresses—course I don't believe what some folks been whisperin' as t'how y' gets them things now. White folks always did do for niggers what they likes. An' they jes can't help alikin' yo, Louisa. Bob Stone like y'. Course he does. But not th' way folks is awhisperin'. Does he, hon?"

"I don't know what you mean, Tom."

"Course y' don't. I'se already cut two niggers. Had t' hon, t' tell 'em so. Niggers always tryin' t' make somethin' out a'nothin'. An' then besides, white folks ain't up t' them tricks so much nowadays. Godam better not be. Leastwise not with yo'. Cause I wouldn't stand f' it. Nassur."

"What would you do, Tom?"

"Cut him jes like I cut a nigger."

"No, Tom—"

"I said I would an' there ain't no mo' to it. But that ain't th' talk f' now. Sing, honey Louisa, an' while I'm listenin' t' y' I'll be makin' love."

Tom took her hand in his. Against the tough thickness of his own, hers felt soft and small. His huge body slipped down to the step beside her. The full moon sank upward into the deep purple of the cloud-bank. An old woman brought a lighted lamp and hung it on the common well whose bulky shadow squatted in the middle of the road, opposite Tom and Louisa. The old woman lifted the well-lid, took hold of the chain, and began drawing up the heavy bucket. As she did so, she sang. Figures shifted, restless-like, between lamp and window in the front rooms of the shanties. Shadows of the figures fought each other on the grey dust of the road. Figures raised the windows and joined the old woman in song. Louisa and Tom, the whole street, singing:

> *Red nigger moon. Sinner!*
> *Blood-burning moon. Sinner!*
> *Come out that fact'ry door.*

Bob Stone sauntered from his veranda out into the gloom of fir trees and magnolias. The clear white of his skin paled, and the flush of his cheeks turned purple. As if to balance this outer change, his mind became consciously a white man's. He passed the house with its huge open hearth which in the days of slavery was the plantation cookery. He saw Louisa bent over that hearth. He went in as a master should, and took her. Direct, honest, bold. None of this sneaking that he had to go through now. The contrast was repulsive to him. His family had lost ground. Hell no, his family still owned the niggers, practically. Damned if they did, or he wouldn't have to duck around so. What would they think if they knew? His mother? His sister? He shouldn't mention them, shouldn't think of them in this connection. There in the dusk he blushed at doing so. Fellows about town were all right, but how about his friends up north? He could see them incredible, repulsed. They didn't know. The thought first made him laugh. Then, with their eyes still upon him, he began to feel embarrassed. He felt the need of explaining things to them. Explain hell. They wouldn't understand, and moreover who ever heard of a Southerner getting on his knees to any Yankee, or anyone. No sir. He was going to see Louisa tonight, and love her. She was lovely—in her way. Nigger way. What way was that? Damned if he knew. Must know. He'd known her long enough to know. Was there something about niggers that you couldn't know? Listening to them at church didn't tell you anything. Looking at them didn't tell you anything. Talking to them didn't tell you anything—unless it was gossip, unless they wanted to talk. Of course about farming, and licker, and craps—but those weren't niggers. Nigger was something more. How much more? Something to be afraid of, more? Hell no. Who ever heard of being afraid of a nigger? Tom Burwell, Cartwell had told him that Tom went with Louisa after she reached home. No sir. No nigger had ever been with his girl. He'd like to see one try. Some position for him to be in. Him, Bob Stone, of the old Stone family, in a scrap with a nigger over a nigger girl. In the good old days . . . Ha! Those were the days. His family had lost ground. Not so much, though. Enough for him to have to cut through old Lemon's canefield by way of the woods, that he might meet her. She was worth it. Beautiful nigger gal. Why nigger? Why not, just gal? No, it was because she was nigger that he went to her. Sweet . . . The scent of boiling cane came to him. Then he saw the rich glow of the stove. He heard the voices of the men circled round it. He was about to skirt the clearing when he heard his own name mentioned. He stopped. Quivering. Leaning against a tree, he listened.

"Bad nigger. Yassur he sho' is one bad nigger when he gets started."

"Tom Burwell's been on th' gang three times fo' cuttin' men."

"What y' think he's agwine t' do t' Bob Stone?"

"Dunno yet. He ain't found out. When he does—Baby!"

"Ain't no tellin'."

"Young Stone ain't no quitter an' I ken tell y' that. Blood of th' old uns in his veins."

"That's right. He'll scrap sho."

"Be gettin' too hot f' niggers 'round this away."

"Shut up nigger. Y' don't know what y' talking 'bout."

Bob Stone's ears burnt like he had been holding them over the stove. Sizzling heat welled up within him. His feet felt as if they rested on red hot coals. They stung him to quick movement. He circled the fringe of the glowing. Not a twig cracked beneath his feet. He reached the path that led to factory town. Plunged furiously down it. Half way along, a blindness within him veered him aside. He crashed into the bordering canebrake. Cane leaves cut his face and lips. He tasted blood. He threw himself down and dug his fingers in the ground. The earth was cool. Cane-roots took the fever from his hands. After a long while, or so it seemed to him, the thought came to him that it must be time to see Louisa. He got to his feet, and walked calmly to their meeting place. No Louisa. Tom Burwell had her. Veins in his forehead bulged and distended. Saliva moistened the dried blood on his lips. He bit down on his lips. He tasted blood. Not his own blood; Tom Burwell's blood. Bob drove through the cane, and out again upon the road. A hound swung down the path before him towards factory town. Bob couldn't see it. The dog loped aside to let him pass. Bob's blind rushing made him stumble over it. He fell with a thud that dazed him. The hound yelped. Answering yelps came from all over the country-side. Chickens cackled. Roosters crowed, heralding the blood-shot eyes of southern awakening. Singers in the town were silenced. They shut their windows down. Palpitant between the rooster crows, a chill hush settled upon the huddled forms of Tom and Louisa. A figure rushed from the shadow and stood before them. Tom popped to his feet.

"What's y' want?"

"I'm Bob Stone."

"Yassur—an' I'm Tom Burwell. What's y' want?"

Bob lunged at him. Tom side stepped, caught him by the shoulder, and flung him to the ground. Straddled him.

Let me up.

"Yassur—but watch yo' doin's Bob Stone."

A few dark figures, drawn by the sound of scuffle, stood about them. Bob sprang to his feet.

"Fight like a man Tom Burwell an' I'll lick y'."

Again he lunged. Tom side stepped and flung him to the ground. Straddled him.

"Get off me you godam nigger you."

"Yo' sho has started somethin' now. Get up."

Tom yanked him up and began hammering at him. Each blow sounded as if it smashed into a precious, irreplacable soft something. Beneath them, Bob staggered back. He reached in his pocket and whipped out a knife.

"That's my game, sho."

Blue flashed, a steel blade slashed across Bob Stone's throat. He had a sweetish sick feeling. Blood began to flow. Then he felt a sharp twitch of pain. He let his knife drop. He slapped one hand against his neck. He pressed the other on top of his head as if to hold it down. He groaned. He turned, and staggered toward the crest of the hill in the direction of white town. Negroes who had seen the fight slunk into their homes and blew the lamps out. Louisa, dazed, hysterical, refused to go indoors. She slipped, crumbled, her body loosely propped against the wood-work of the well. Tom Burwell leaned against it. He seemed rooted there.

Bob reached Broad Street. White men rushed up to him. He collapsed in their arms.

"Tom Burwell . . ."

White men like ants upon a forage rushed about. Except for the taut hum of their moving, all was silent. Shotguns, revolvers, rope, kerosene, torches. Two high powered cars with glaring search lights. They came together. The taut hum rose to a low roar. Then nothing could be heard but the flop of their feet in the thick dust of the road. The moving body of their silence preceded them over the crest of the hill into factory town. It flattened the Negroes beneath it. It rolled to the wall of the factory, where it stopped. Tom knew that they were coming. He couldn't move. And then he saw the search lights of the two cars glaring down on him. A quick stock went through him. He stiffened. He started to run. A yell went up from the mob. Tom wheeled about and faced them. They poured on him. They swarmed. A large man with dead white face and flabby cheeks came to him and almost jabbed a gun-barrel through his guts.

"Hands behind y' nigger."

Tom's wrists were bound. The big man shoved him to the well. Burn him over it, and when the wood-work caved in, his body would drop to the bottom. Two deaths for a godam nigger. Louisa was driven back. The mob pushed in. Its pressure, its momentum was too great. Drag him to the factory. Tom moved in the direction indicated. But they had to drag him. They reached the great door. Too many to get in there. The mob divided, and flowed around the walls to either side. The big man shoved him through the door. The mob pressed in from the sides. Taut humming. No words. A stake was sunk into the ground. Rotting floor boards piled around it. Kerosene poured on the rotting floor boards. Tom bound to the stake. His breast was bare. Nail scratches let little lines of blood trickle down, and mat into the hair. His face, his eyes were set and stony. Except for irregular breathing, one would have thought him already dead. Torches were flung onto the pile. A great flare muffled in black smoke shot upward. The mob yelled. The mob was silent. Now Tom could be seen within the flames. Only his head, erect, like a blackened stone. Stench of burning flesh soaked the air. Tom's eyes popped. His head settled downward. The mob yelled. Its yell echoed against the skeleton stone walls and sounded like a hundred yells. Like a hundred mobs yelling. Its yell thudded against the thick front wall, and fell back. Ghost of a yell slipped through the flames, and out the great door of the factory. It fluttered like a dying thing down the single street of factory town. Louisa, upon the step before her home, did not hear it, but her eyes opened slowly. They saw the full moon glowing in the great door. The full moon, an evil thing, an omen, soft showering the homes of folks she knew. Where were they, these people? She'd sing, and perhaps they'd come out and join her. Perhaps Tom Burwell would come. At any rate, the full moon in the great door was an omen which she must sing to:

> Red nigger moon. Sinner!
> Blood-burning moon. Sinner!
> Come out that fact'ry door.

# BECKY

## Jean Toomer

Becky was the white woman who had two Negro sons. She's dead; they've gone away. The pines whisper to Jesus. The Bible flaps its leaves with an aimless rustle on her mound.

BECKY HAD ONE Negro son. Who gave it to her? Damn buck nigger, said the white folks' mouths. She wouldn't tell. Common, God-forsaken, insane white shameless wench, said the white folks' mouths. Her eyes were sunken, her neck stringy, her breasts fallen, till then. Taking their words, they filled her, like a bubble rising—then she broke. Mouth setting in a twist that held her eyes, harsh, vacant, staring . . . Who gave it to her? Low-down nigger with no self-respect, said the black folks' mouths. She wouldn't tell. Poor Catholic poor-white crazy woman, said the black folks' mouths. White folks and black folks built her cabin, fed her and her growing baby, prayed secretly to God who'd put His cross upon her and cast her out.

When the first was born, the white folks said they'd have no more to do with her. And black folks, they too joined hands to cast her out . . . The pines whispered to Jesus . . . The railroad boss said not to say he said it, but she could live, if she wanted to, on the narrow strip of land between the railroad and the road. John Stone, who owned the lumber and the bricks, would have shot the man who told he gave the stuff to Lonnie Deacon, who stole out there at night and built the cabin. A single room held down to earth . . . O fly away to Jesus . . . by a leaning chimney . . .

★ ★ ★

Six trains each day rumbled past and shook the ground under her cabin. Fords, and horse- and mule-drawn buggies went back and forth along the road. No one ever saw her. Trainmen, and passengers who'd heard about her, threw out papers and food. Threw out little crumpled slips of paper scribbled with prayers, as they passed her eye-shaped piece of sandy ground. Ground islandized between the road and railroad track. Pushed up where a blue-sheen God with listless eyes could look at it. Folks from the town took turns, unknown, of course, to each other, in bringing corn and meat and sweet potatoes. Even sometimes snuff . . . O thank y Jesus . . . Old David Georgia, grinding cane and boiling syrup, never went her way without some sugar sap. No one ever saw her. The boy grew up and ran around. When he was five years old as folks reckoned it, Hugh Jourdon saw him carrying a baby. "Becky has another son," was what the whole town knew. But nothing was said, for the part of man that says things to the likes of that had told itself that if there was a Becky, that Becky now was dead.

★   ★   ★

The two boys grew. Sullen and cunning . . . O pines, whisper to Jesus; tell Him to come and press sweet Jesus-lips against their lips and eyes . . . It seemed as though with those two big fellows there, there could be no room for Becky. The part that prayed wondered if perhaps she'd really died, and they had buried her. No one dared ask. They'd beat and cut a man who meant nothing at all in mentioning that they lived along the road. White or colored? No one knew, and least of all themselves. They drifted around from job to job. We, who had cast out their mother because of them, could we take them in? They answered black and white folks by shooting up two men and leaving town. "Godam the white folks; godam the niggers," they shouted as they left town. Becky? Smoke curled up from her chimney; she must be there. Trains passing shook the ground. The ground shook the leaning chimney. Nobody noticed it. A creepy feeling came over all who saw that thin wraith of smoke and felt the trembling of the ground. Folks began to take her food again. They quit it soon because they had a fear. Becky if dead might be a hant, and if alive—it took some nerve even to mention it . . . O pines, whisper to Jesus . . .

★   ★   ★

It was Sunday. Our congregation had been visiting at Pulverton, and were coming home. There was no wind. The autumn sun, the bell from Ebenezer Church, listless and heavy. Even the pines were stale, sticky, like the smell of food that makes you sick. Before we turned the bend of the road that would show us the Becky cabin, the horses stopped stock-still, pushed back their ears, and nervously whinnied. We urged, then whipped them on. Quarter of a mile away thin smoke curled up from the leaning chimney . . . O pines, whisper to Jesus . . . Goose-flesh came on my skin though there still was neither chill nor wind. Eyes left their sockets for the cabin. Ears burned and throbbed. Uncanny eclipse! fear closed my mind. We were just about to pass . . . Pines shout to Jesus! . . . the ground trembled as a ghost train rumbled by. The chimney fell into the cabin. Its thud was like a hollow report, ages having passed since it went off. Barlo and I were pulled out of our seats. Dragged to the door that had swung open. Through the dust we saw the bricks in a mound upon the floor. Becky, if she was there, lay under them. I thought I heard a groan. Barlo, mumbling something, threw his Bible on the pile. (No one has ever touched it.) Somehow we got away. My buggy was still on the road. The last thing that I remember was whipping old Dan like fury; I remember nothing after that—that is, until I reached town and folks crowded round to get the true word of it.

Becky was the white woman who had two Negro sons. She's dead; they've gone away. The pines whisper to Jesus. The Bible flaps its leaves with an aimless rustle on her mound.

# LUCK[1]

## Mark Twain

IT WAS AT a banquet in London in honor of one of the two or three conspicuously illustrious English military names of this generation. For reasons which will presently appear, I will withhold his real name and titles and call him Lieutenant-General Lord Arthur Scoresby, Y.C., K.C.B., etc., etc., etc. What a fascination there is in a renowned name! There sat the man, in actual flesh, whom I had heard of so many thousands of times since that day, thirty years before, when his name shot suddenly to the zenith from a Crimean battlefield, to remain forever celebrated. It was food and drink to me to look, and look, and look at that demi-god; scanning, searching, noting: the quietness, the reserve, the noble gravity of his countenance; the simple honesty that expressed itself all over him; the sweet unconsciousness of his greatness—unconsciousness of the hundreds of admiring eyes fastened upon him, unconsciousness of the deep, loving, sincere worship welling out of the breasts of those people and flowing toward him.

The clergyman at my left was an old acquaintance of mine—clergyman now, but had spent the first half of his life in the camp and field and as an instructor in the military school at Woolwich. Just at the moment I have been talking about a veiled and singular light glimmered in his eyes and he leaned down and muttered confidently to me—indicating the hero of the banquet with a gesture:

"Privately—he's an absolute fool."

---

[1] This is not a fancy sketch. I got it from a clergyman who was an instructor at Woolwich forty years ago, and who vouched for its truth, M.T.

This verdict was a great surprise to me. If its subject had been Napoleon, or Socrates, or Solomon, my astonishment could not have been greater. Two things I was well aware of: that the Reverend was a man of strict veracity and that his judgment of men was good. Therefore I knew, beyond doubt or question, that the world was mistaken about this hero: he *was* a fool. So I meant to find out, at a convenient moment, how the Reverend, all solitary and alone, had discovered the secret.

★   ★   ★

Some days later the opportunity came, and this is what the Reverend told me:

About forty years ago I was an instructor in the military academy at Woolwich. I was present in one of the sections when young Scoresby underwent his preliminary examination. I was touched to the quick with pity, for the rest of the class answered up brightly and handsomely, while he—why, dear me, he didn't know *anything,* so to speak. He was evidently good, and sweet, and lovable, and guileless; and so it was exceedingly painful to see him stand there, as serene as a graven image, and deliver himself of answers which were veritably miraculous for stupidity and ignorance. All the compassion in me was aroused in his behalf. I said to myself, when he comes to be examined again he will be flung over, of course; so it will be simply a harmless act of charity to ease his fall as much as I can. I took him aside and found that he knew a little of Cæsar's history; and as he didn't know anything else, I went to work and drilled him like a galley-slave on a certain line of stock questions concerning Cæsar which I knew would be used. If you'll believe me, he went through with flying colors on examination day! He went through on that purely superficial "cram," and got compliments too, while others, who knew a thousand times more than he, got plucked. By some strangely lucky accident—an accident not likely to happen twice in a century—he was asked no question outside of the narrow limits of his drill.

It was stupefying. Well, all through his course I stood by him, with something of the sentiment which a mother feels for a crippled child; and he always saved himself—just by miracle, apparently.

Now, of course, the thing that would expose him and kill him at last was mathematics. I resolved to make his death as easy as I could; so I drilled him and crammed him, and crammed him and drilled him, just on the line of questions which the examiners would be most likely to use, and then launched him on his fate. Well, sir, try to conceive of the result: to my consternation, he took the first prize! And with it he got a perfect ovation in the way of compliments.

Sleep? There was no more sleep for me for a week. My conscience tortured me day and night. What I had done I had done purely through charity, and only to ease the poor youth's fall. I never had dreamed of any such preposterous results as the thing that had happened. I felt as guilty and miserable as Frankenstein. Here was a wooden-head whom I had put in the way of glittering promotions and prodigious responsibilities and but one thing could happen: he and his responsibilities would all go to ruin together at the first opportunity.

The Crimean War had just broken out. Of course there had to be a war, I said to myself. We couldn't have peace and give this donkey a chance to die before he is found out. I waited for the earthquake. It came. And it made me reel when it did come. He was actually gazetted to a captaincy in a marching regiment! Better men grow old and gray in the service before they climb to a sublimity like that. And who could ever have foreseen that they would go and put such a load of responsibility on such green and inadequate shoulders? I could just barely have stood it if they had made him a cornet; but a captain—think of it! I thought my hair would turn white.

Consider what I did—I who so loved repose and inaction. I said to myself, I am responsible to the country for this, and I must go along with him and protect the country against him as far as I can. So I took my poor little capital that I had saved up through years of work and grinding economy, and went with a sigh and bought a cornetcy in his regiment, and away we went to the field.

And there—oh, dear, it was awful. Blunders?—why he never did anything *but* blunder. But, you see, nobody was in the fellow's secret. Everybody had him focused wrong, and necessarily misinterpreted his performance every time. Consequently they took his idiotic blunders for inspirations of genius. They did, honestly! His mildest blunders were enough to make a man in his right mind cry; and they did make me cry—and rage and rave, too, privately. And the thing that kept me always in a sweat of apprehension was the fact that every fresh blunder he made increased the luster of his reputation! I kept saying to myself, he'll get so high that when discovery does finally come it will be like the sun falling out of the sky.

He went right along, up from grade to grade, over the dead bodies of his superiors, until at last, in the hottest moment of the battle of down went our colonel, and my heart jumped into my mouth, for Scoresby was next in rank! Now for it, said I; we'll all land in Sheol in ten minutes, sure.

The battle was awfully hot; the allies were steadily giving way all over the field. Our regiment occupied a position that was vital; a blunder now must be destruction. At this crucial moment, what does this immortal fool do but detach the regiment from its place and order a charge over a neighboring hill where there wasn't a suggestion of an enemy! "There you go!" I said to myself; "this *is* the end at last."

And away we did go, and were over the shoulder of the hill before the insane movement could be discovered and stopped. And what did we find? An entire and unsuspected Russian army in reserve! And what happened? We were eaten up? That is necessarily what would have happened in ninety-nine cases out of a hundred. But no, those Russians argued that no single regiment would come browsing around there at such a time. It must be the entire English army, and that the sly Russian game was detected and blocked; so they turned tail, and away they went, pell-mell, over the hill and down into the field, in wild confusion, and we after them; they themselves broke the solid Russian center in the field, and tore through, and in no time there was the most tremendous rout you ever saw, and the defeat of the allies was turned into a sweeping and splendid victory! Marshal Canrobert looked on, dizzy with astonishment, admiration, and delight; and sent right off for Scoresby, and hugged him, and decorated him on the field in presence of all the armies!

And what was Scoresby's blunder that time? Merely the mistaking his right hand for his left—that was all. An order had come to him to fall back and support our right; and, instead, he fell *forward* and went over the hill to the left. But the name he won that day as a marvelous military genius filled the world with his glory, and that glory will never fade while history books last.

He is just as good and sweet and lovable and unpretending as a man can be, but he doesn't know enough to come in when it rains. Now that is absolutely true. He is the supremest ass in the universe; and until half an hour ago nobody knew it but himself and me. He has been pursued, day by day and year by year, by a most phenomenal and astonishing luckiness. He has been a shining soldier in all our wars for a generation; he has littered his whole military life with blunders, and yet has never committed one that didn't make him a knight or a baronet or a lord or something. Look at his breast; why, he is just clothed in domestic and foreign decorations. Well, sir, everyone of them is the record of some shouting stupidity or other; and, taken together, they are proof that the very best thing in all this world that can befall a man is to be born lucky. I say again, as I said at the banquet, Scoresby's an absolute fool.

# BAKER'S BLUEJAY YARN

## Mark Twain

ANIMALS TALK TO each other, of course. There can be no question about that; but I suppose there are very few people who can understand them. I never knew but one man who could. I knew he could, however, because he told me so himself. He was a middle-aged, simple-hearted miner who had lived in a lonely corner of California, among the woods and mountains, a good many years, and had studied the ways of his only neighbors, the beasts and the birds, until he believed he could accurately translate any remark which they made. This was Jim Baker. According to Jim Baker, some animals have only a limited education, and use only very simple words, and scarcely ever a comparison or a flowery figure, whereas, certain other animals have a large vocabulary, a fine command of language and a ready and fluent delivery; consequently these latter talk a great deal; they like it; they are conscious of their talent, and they enjoy "showing off." Baker said, that after long and careful observation, he had come to the conclusion that the bluejays were the best talkers he had found among birds and beasts. Said he:

"There's more *to* a bluejay than any other creature. He has got more moods, and more different kinds of feelings than other creatures; and, mind you, whatever a bluejay feels, he can put into language. And no mere commonplace language, either, but rattling, out-and-out book-talk—and bristling with metaphor, too—just bristling! And as for command of language—why *you* never see a bluejay get stuck for a word. No man ever did. They just boil out of him! And another thing: I've noticed a good deal, and there's no bird, or cow, or anything that uses as good grammar as a bluejay. You may say a cat uses good grammar. Well, a cat does—but you let a cat get excited once; you let a cat get to pulling fur with another cat on a shed, nights, and you'll hear grammar that will give you the lockjaw. Ignorant people think it's the *noise* which fighting cats make that is so aggravating, but it ain't so; it's the sickening grammar they use. Now I've never heard a jay use bad grammar but very seldom; and when they do, they are as ashamed as a human; they shut right down and leave.

"You may call a jay a bird. Well, so he is, in a measure—because he's got feathers on him, and don't belong to no church, perhaps; but otherwise he is just as much a human as you be. And I'll tell you for why. A jay's gifts, and instincts, and feelings, and interests, cover the whole ground. A jay hasn't got any more principle than a Congressman. A jay will lie, a jay will steal, a jay will deceive, a jay will betray; and four times out of five, a jay will go back on his solemnest promise. The sacredness of an obligation is a thing which you can't cram into no bluejay's head. Now, on top of all this, there's another thing; a jay can outswear any gentleman in the mines. You think a cat can swear. Well, a cat can; but you give a bluejay a subject that calls for his reserve-powers, and where is your cat? Don't talk to *me*—I know too much about this thing. And there's yet another thing; in the one little particular of scolding—just good, clean, out-and-out scolding—a bluejay can lay over anything, human or divine. Yes, sir, a jay is everything that a man is. A jay can cry, a jay can laugh, a jay can feel shame, a jay can reason and plan and discuss, a jay likes gossip and scandal, a jay has got a sense of humor, a jay knows when he is an ass just as well as you do—maybe better. If a jay ain't human, he better take in his sign, that's all. Now I'm going to tell you a perfectly true fact about some bluejays.

"When I first begun to understand jay language correctly, there was a little incident happened here. Seven years ago, the last man in this region but me moved away. There stands his house—been empty ever since; a log house, with a plank roof—just One big room, and no more; no ceiling—nothing between the rafters and the floor. Well, one Sunday morning I was sitting out here in front of my cabin, with my cat, taking the sun, and looking at the blue hills, and listening to the leaves rustling so lonely in the trees, and thinking of the home away yonder in the states, that I hadn't heard from in thirteen years, when a bluejay lit on that house, with an acorn in his mouth, and says, 'Hello, I reckon I've struck something.' When he spoke, the acorn dropped out of his mouth and rolled down the roof, of course, but he didn't care; his mind was all on the thing he had struck. It was a knot-hole in the roof. He cocked his head to one side, shut one eye and put the other one to the hole, like a 'possum looking down a jug; then he glanced up with his bright eyes, gave a wink or two with his wings—which signifies gratification, you understand—and says, 'It looks like a hole, it's located like a hole— blamed if I don't believe it *is* a hole!'

"Then he cocked his head down and took another look; he glances up perfectly joyful, this time; winks his wings and his tail both, and says, 'Oh, no, this ain't no fat thing, I reckon! If I ain't in luck!—why it's a perfectly elegant hole!' So he flew down and got that acorn, and fetched it up and dropped it in, and was just tilting his head back, with the heavenliest smile on his face, when all of a sudden he was paralyzed into a listening attitude and that smile faded gradually out of his countenance like breath off'n a razor, and the queerest look of surprise took its place. Then he says, 'Why, I didn't hear it fall!' He cocked his eye at the hole again, and took a long look; raised up and shook his head; stepped around to the other side of the hole and took another look from that side; shook his head again. He studied a while, then he just went into the *de*tails—walked round and round the hole and spied into it from every point of the compass. No use. Now he took a thinking attitude on the comb of the roof and scratched the back of his head with his right foot a minute, and finally says, 'Well, it's too many for *me*, that's certain; must be a mighty long hole; however, I ain't got no time to fool around here, I got to 'tend to business; I reckon it's all right—chance it, anyway.'

"So he flew off and fetched another acorn and dropped it in, and tried to flirt his eye to the hole quick enough to see what become of it, but he was too late. He held his eye there as much as a minute; then he raised up and sighed, and says, 'Confound it, I don't seem to understand this thing, no way; however, I'll tackle her again.' He fetched another acorn, and done his level best to see what become of it, but he couldn't. He says, 'Well, *I* never struck no such a hole as this before; I'm of the opinion it's a totally new kind of a hole.' Then he begun to get mad. He held in for a spell, walking up and down the comb of the roof and shaking his head and muttering to himself; but his feelings got the upper hand of him, presently, and he broke loose and cussed himself black in the face. I never see a bird take on so about a little thing. When he got through he walks to the hole and looks in again for half a minute; then he says, 'Well, you're a long hole, and a deep hole, and a mighty singular hole altogether— but I've started in to fill you, and I'm d—d if I *don't* fill you, if it takes a hundred years!'

"And with that, away he went. You never see a bird work so since you was born. He laid into his work like a nigger, and the way he hove acorns into that hole for about two hours and a half was one of the most exciting and astonishing spectacles I ever struck. He never stopped to take a look any more—he just hove 'em in and went for more. Well, at last he could hardly flop his wings, he was so tuckered out. He comes a–drooping down, once more, sweating like an ice-pitcher, drops his acorn in and says, '*Now* I guess I've got the bulge on you by this time!' So he bent down for a look. If you'll believe me, when his head come up again he was just pale with rage. He says, 'I've shoveled acorns enough in there to keep the family thirty years, and if I can see a sign of one of 'em I wish I may land in a museum with a belly full of sawdust in two minutes!'

"He just had strength enough to crawl up on to the comb and lean his back agin the chimbly, and then he collected his impressions and begun to free his mind. I see in a second that what I had mistook for profanity in the mines was only just the rudiments, as you may say.

"Another jay was going by, and heard him doing his devotions, and stops to inquire what was up. The sufferer told him the whole circumstance, and says, 'Now yonder's the hole, and if you don't believe me, go and look for yourself.' So this fellow went and looked, and comes back and says, 'How many did you say you put in there?' 'Not any less than two tons,' says the sufferer. The other jay went and looked again. He couldn't seem to make it out, so he raised a yell, and three more jays come. They all examined the hole, they all made the sufferer tell it over again, then they all discussed it, and got off as many leather-headed opinions about it as an average crowd of humans could have done.

"They called in more jays; then more and more, till pretty soon this whole region 'peared to have a blue flush about it. There must have been five thousand of them; and such another jawing and dis- puting and ripping and cussing, you never heard. Every jay in the whole lot put his eye to the hole and delivered a more chuckle-headed opinion about the mystery than the jay that went there before him. They examined the house all over, too. The door was standing half open, and at last one old jay happened to go and light on it and look in. Of course, that knocked the mystery galley-west in a second. There lay the acorns, scattered all over the floor. He flopped his wings and raised a whoop. 'Come here!' he says, 'Come here, everybody; hang'd if this fool hasn't been trying to fill up a house with acorns!' They all came a-swooping down like a blue cloud, and as each fellow lit on the door and took a glance, the whole absurdity of the contract that that first jay had tackled hit him home and he fell over backwards suffocating with laughter, and the next jay took his place and done the same.

"Well, sir, they roosted around here on the housetop and the trees for an hour, and guffawed over that thing like human beings. It ain't any use to tell me a bluejay hasn't got a sense of humor, because I know better. And memory, too. They brought jays here from all over the United States to look down that hole, every summer for three years. Other birds, too. And they could all see the point, except an owl that come from Nova Scotia to visit the Yo Semite, and he took this thing in on his way back. He said he couldn't see anything funny in it. But then he was a good deal disappointed about Yo Semite, too."

# THE OTHER TWO

## Edith Wharton

## I

WAYTHORN, ON THE drawing-room hearth, waited for his wife to come down to dinner.

It was their first night under his own roof, and he was surprised at his thrill of boyish agitation. He was not so old, to be sure—his glass gave him little more than the five-and-thirty years to which his wife confessed—but he had fancied himself already in the temperate zone; yet here he was listening for her step with a tender sense of all it symbolized, with some old trail of verse about the garlanded nuptial doorposts floating through his enjoyment of the pleasant room and the good dinner just beyond it.

They had been hastily recalled from their honeymoon by the illness of Lily Haskett, the child of Mrs. Waythorn's first marriage. The little girl, at Waythorn's desire, had been transferred to his house on the day of her mother's wedding, and the doctor, on their arrival, broke the news that she was ill with typhoid, but declared that all the symptoms were favorable. Lily could show twelve years of unblemished health, and the case promised to be a light one. The nurse spoke as reassuringly, and after a moment of alarm Mrs. Waythorn had adjusted herself to the situation. She was very fond of Lily—her affection for the child had perhaps been her decisive charm in Waythorn's eyes—but she had the perfectly balanced nerves which her little girl had inherited, and no woman ever wasted less tissue in unproductive worry. Waythorn was therefore quite prepared to see her come in presently, a little late because of a last look at Lily, but as serene and well-appointed as if her good-night kiss had been laid on the brow of health. Her composure was restful to him; it acted as ballast to his somewhat unstable sensibilities. As he pictured her bending over the child's bed he thought how soothing her presence must be in illness: her very step would prognosticate recovery.

His own life had been a gray one, from temperament rather than circumstance, and he had been drawn to her by the unperturbed gaiety which kept her fresh and elastic at an age when most women's activities are growing either slack or febrile. He knew what was said about her; for, popular as she was, there had always been a faint undercurrent of detraction. When she had appeared in New York, nine or ten years earlier, as the pretty Mrs. Haskett whom Gus Varick had unearthed somewhere—was it in Pittsburgh or Utica?—society, while promptly accepting her, had reserved the right to cast a doubt on its own indiscrimination. Inquiry, however, established her undoubted connection with a socially reigning family, and explained her recent divorce as the natural result of a runaway match at seventeen; and as nothing was known of Mr. Haskett it was easy to believe the worst of him.

Alice Haskett's remarriage with Gus Varick was a passport to the set whose recognition she coveted, and for a few years the Varicks were the most popular couple in town. Unfortunately the alliance was brief and stormy, and this time the husband had his champions. Still, even Varick's stanchest supporters admitted that he was not meant for matrimony, and Mrs. Varick's grievances were of a nature to bear the inspection of the New York courts. A New York divorce is in itself a diploma of virtue, and in the semiwidowhood of this second separation Mrs. Varick took on an air of sanctity, and was allowed to confide her wrongs to some of the most scrupulous ears in town. But when it was known that she was to marry Waythorn there was a momentary reaction. Her best friends would have preferred to see her remain in the role of the injured wife, which was as becoming to her as crepe to a rosy complexion. True, a decent time had elapsed, and it was not even suggested that Waythorn had supplanted his predecessor. People shook their heads over him, however, and one grudging friend, to whom he affirmed that he took the step with his eyes open, replied oracularly: "Yes—and with your ears shut."

Waythorn could afford to smile at these innuendoes. In the Wall Street phrase, he had "discounted" them. He knew that society has not yet adapted itself to the consequences of divorce, and that till the adaptation takes place every woman who uses the freedom the law accords her must be her own social justification. Waythorn had an amused confidence in his wife's ability to justify herself. His expectations were fulfilled, and before the wedding took place Alice Varick's group had rallied openly to her support. She took it all imperturbably: she had a way of surmounting obstacles without seeming to be aware of them, and Waythorn looked back with wonder at the trivialities over which he had worn his nerves thin. He had the sense of having found refuge in a richer, warmer nature than his own, and his satisfaction, at the moment, was humorously summed up in the thought that his wife, when she had done all she could for Lily, would not be ashamed to come down and enjoy a good dinner.

The anticipation of such enjoyment was not, however, the sentiment expressed by Mrs. Waythorn's charming face when she presently joined him. Though she had put on her most engaging tea gown she had neglected to assume the smile that went with it, and Waythorn thought he had never seen her look so nearly worried.

"What is it?" he asked. "Is anything wrong with Lily?"

"No; I've just been in and she's still sleeping." Mrs. Waythorn hesitated. "But something tiresome has happened."

He had taken her two hands, and now perceived that he was crushing a paper between them.

"This letter?"

"Yes—Mr. Haskett has written—I mean his lawyer has written."

Waythorn felt himself flush uncomfortably. He dropped his wife's hands.

"What about?"

"About seeing Lily. You know the courts—"

"Yes, yes," he interrupted nervously.

Nothing was known about Haskett in New York. He was vaguely supposed to have remained in the outer darkness from which his wife had been rescued, and Waythorn was one of the few who were aware that he had given up his business in Utica and followed her to New York in order to be near his little girl. In the days of his wooing, Waythorn had often met Lily on the doorstep, rosy and smiling, on her way "to see papa."

"I am so sorry," Mrs. Waythorn murmured.

He roused himself. "What does he want?"

"He wants to see her. You know she goes to him once a week."

"Well—he doesn't expect her to go to him now, does he?"

"No—he has heard of her illness; but he expects to come here."

"*Here?*"

Mrs. Waythorn reddened under his gaze. They looked away from each other.

"I'm afraid he has the right . . . You'll see. . . ." She made a proffer of the letter.

Waythorn moved away with a gesture of refusal. He stood staring about the softly-lighted room, which a moment before had seemed so full of bridal intimacy.

"I'm so sorry," she repeated. "If Lily could have been moved—"

"That's out of the question," he returned impatiently.

"I suppose so."

Her lip was beginning to tremble, and he felt himself a brute.

"He must come, of course," he said. "When is—his day?"

"I'm afraid—tomorrow."

"Very well. Send a note in the morning."

The butler entered to announce dinner.

Waythorn turned to his wife. "Come—you must be tired. It's beastly, but try to forget about it," he said, drawing her hand through his arm.

"You're so good, dear. I'll try," she whispered back.

Her face cleared at once, and as she looked at him across the flowers, between the rosy candleshades, he saw her lips waver back into a smile.

"How pretty everything is!" she sighed luxuriously.

He turned to the butler. "The champagne at once, please. Mrs. Waythorn is tired."

In a moment or two their eyes met above the sparkling glasses. Her own were quite clear and untroubled: he saw that she had obeyed his injunction and forgotten.

## II

Waythorn, the next morning, went downtown earlier than usual. Haskett was not likely to come till the afternoon, but the instinct of flight drove him forth. He meant to stay away all day—he had thoughts of dining at his club. As his door closed behind him he reflected that before he opened it again it would have admitted another man who had as much right to enter it as himself, and the thought filled him with a physical repugnance.

He caught the elevated at the employees' hour, and found himself crushed between two layers of pendulous humanity. At Eighth Street the man facing him wriggled out, and another took his place. Waythorn glanced up and saw that it was Gus Varick. The men were so close together that it was impossible to ignore the smile of recognition on Varick's handsome overblown face. And after all—why not? They had always been on good terms, and Varick had been divorced before Waythorn's attentions to his wife began. The two exchanged a word on the perennial grievance of the congested trains, and when a seat at their side was miraculously left empty the instinct of self-preservation made Waythorn slip into it after Varick.

The latter drew the stout man's breath of relief. "Lord—I was beginning to feel like a pressed flower." He leaned back, looking unconcernedly at Waythorn. "Sorry to hear that Sellers is knocked out again."

"Sellers?" echoed Waythorn, starting at his partner's name.

Varick looked surprised. "You didn't know he was laid up with the gout?"

"No. I've been away—I only got back last night." Waythorn felt himself reddening in anticipation of the other's smile.

"Ah—yes; to be sure. And Sellers' attack came on two days ago. I'm afraid he's pretty bad. Very awkward for me, as it happens, because he was just putting through a rather important thing for me."

"Ah?" Waythorn wondered vaguely since when Varick had been dealing in "important things." Hitherto he had dabbled only in the shallow pools of speculation, with which Waythorn's office did not usually concern itself.

It occurred to him that Varick might be talking at random, to relieve the strain of their propinquity. That strain was becoming momentarily more apparent to Waythorn, and when, at Cortlandt Street, he caught sight of an acquaintance and had a sudden vision of the picture he and Varick must present to an initiated eye, he jumped up with a muttered excuse.

"I hope you'll find Sellers better," said Varick civilly, and he stammered back: "If I can be of any use to you—" and let the departing crowd sweep him to the platform.

At his office he heard that Sellers was in fact ill with the gout, and would probably not be able to leave the house for some weeks.

"I'm sorry it should have happened so, Mr. Waythorn," the senior clerk said with affable significance. "Mr. Sellers was very much upset at the idea of giving you such a lot of extra work just now."

"Oh, that's no matter," said Waythorn hastily. He secretly welcomed the pressure of additional business, and was glad to think that, when the day's work was over, he would have to call at his partner's on the way home.

He was late for luncheon, and turned in at the nearest restaurant instead of going to his club. The place was full, and the waiter hurried him to the back of the room to capture the only vacant table. In the cloud of cigar smoke Waythorn did not at once distinguish his neighbors: but presently, looking about him, he saw Varick seated a few feet off. This time, luckily, they were too far apart for conversation, and Varick, who faced another way, had probably not even seen him; but there was an irony in their renewed nearness.

Varick was said to be fond of good living, and as Waythorn sat dispatching his hurried luncheon he looked across half enviously at the other's leisurely degustation of his meal. When Waythorn first saw him he had been helping himself with critical deliberation to a bit of Camembert at the ideal point of liquefaction, and now, the cheese removed, he was just pouring his *café double*[1] from its little two-storied earthen pot. He poured slowly, his ruddy profile bent over the task, and one beringed white hand steadying the lid of the coffeepot; then he streched his other hand to the decanter of cognac at his elbow, filled a liqueur glass, took a tentative sip, and poured the brandy into his coffee cup.

Waythorn watched him in a kind of fascination. What was he thinking of—only of the flavor of the coffee and the liqueur? Had the morning's meeting left no more trace in his thoughts than on his face? Had his wife so completely passed out of his life that even this odd encounter with her present husband, within a week after her remarriage, was no more than an incident in his day? And as Waythorn mused, another idea struck him: had Haskett ever met Varick as Varick and he had just met? The recollection of Haskett perturbed him, and he rose and left the restaurant, taking a circuitous way out to escape the placid irony of Varick's nod.

It was after seven when Waythorn reached home. He thought the footman who opened the door looked at him oddly.

"How is Miss Lily?" he asked in haste.

"Doing very well, sir. A gentleman—"

"Tell Barlow to put off dinner for half an hour," Waythorn cut him off, hurrying upstairs.

---

[1] *café double*; French: very strong coffee.

He went straight to his room and dressed without seeing his wife. When he reached the drawing room she was there, fresh and radiant. Lily's day had been good; the doctor was not coming back that evening.

At dinner Waythorn told her of Sellers' illness and of the resulting complications. She listened sympathetically, adjuring him not to let himself be overworked, and asking vague feminine questions about the routine of the office. Then she gave him the chronicle of Lily's day; quoted the nurse and doctor, and told him who had called to inquire. He had never seen her more serene and unruffled. It struck him with a curious pang, that she was very happy in being with him, so happy that she found a childish pleasure in rehearsing the trivial incidents of her day.

After dinner they went to the library, and the servant put the coffee and liqueurs on a low table before her and left the room. She looked singularly soft and girlish in her rosy-pale dress, against the dark leather of one of his bachelor armchairs. A day earlier the contrast would have charmed him.

He turned away now, choosing a cigar with affected deliberation.

"Did Haskett come?" he asked, with his back to her.

"Oh, yes—he came."

"You didn't see him, of course?"

She hesitated a moment. "I let the nurse see him."

That was all. There was nothing more to ask. He swung round toward her, applying a match to his cigar. Well, the thing was over for a week, at any rate. He would try not to think of it. She looked up at him, a trifle rosier than usual, with a smile in her eyes.

"Ready for your coffee, dear?"

He leaned against the mantelpiece, watching her as she lifted the coffeepot. The lamplight struck a gleam from her bracelets and tipped her soft hair with brightness. How light and slender she was, and how each gesture flowed into the next! She seemed a creature all compact of harmonies. As the thought of Haskett receded, Waythorn felt himself yielding again to the joy of possessorship. They were his, those white hands with their flitting motions, his the light haze of hair, the lips and eyes. . . .

She set down the coffeepot, and reaching for the decanter of cognac, measured off a liqueur glass and poured it into his cup.

Waythorn uttered a sudden exclamation.

"What is the matter?" she said, startled.

"Nothing; only—I don't take cognac in my coffee."

"Oh, how stupid of me," she cried.

Their eyes met, and she blushed a sudden agonized red.

### III

Ten days later, Mr. Sellers, still housebound, asked Waythorn to call on his way downtown.

The senior partner, with his swaddled foot propped up by the fire, greeted his associate with an air of embarrassment.

"I'm sorry, my dear fellow; I've got to ask you to do an awkward thing for me."

Waythorn waited, and the other went on, after a pause apparently given to the arrangement of his phrases: "The fact is, when I was knocked out I had just gone into a rather complicated piece of business for—Gus Varick."

"Well?" said Waythorn, with an attempt to put him at his ease.

"Well—it's this way: Varick came to me the day before my attack. He had evidently had an inside tip from somebody, and had made about a hundred thousand. He came to me for advice, and I suggested his going in with Vanderlyn."

"Oh, the deuce!" Waythorn exclaimed. He saw in a flash what had happened. The investment was an alluring one, but required negotiation. He listened quietly while Sellers put the case before him, and, the statement ended, he said: "You think I ought to see Varick?"

"I'm afraid I can't as yet. The doctor is obdurate. And this thing can't wait. I hate to ask you, but no one else in the office knows the ins and outs of it."

Waythorn stood silent. He did not care a farthing for the success of Varick's venture, but the honor of the office was to be considered, and he could hardly refuse to oblige his partner.

"Very well," he said, "I'll do it."

That afternoon, apprised by telephone, Varick called at the office. Waythorn, waiting in his private room, wondered what the others thought of it. The newspapers, at the time of Mrs. Waythorn's marriage, had acquainted their readers with every detail of her previous matrimonial ventures, and Waythorn could fancy the clerks smiling behind Varick's back as he was ushered in.

Varick bore himself admirably. He was easy without being undignified, and Waythorn was conscious of cutting a much less impressive figure. Varick had no experience of business, and the talk prolonged itself for nearly an hour while Waythorn set forth with scrupulous precision the details of the proposed transaction.

"I'm awfully obliged to you," Varick said as he rose. "The fact is I'm not used to having much money to look after, and I don't want to make an ass of myself—" He smiled, and Waythorn could not help noticing that there was something pleasant about his smile. "It feels uncommonly queer to have enough cash to pay one's bills. I'd have sold my soul for it a few years ago!"

Waythorn winced at the allusion. He had heard it rumored that a lack of funds had been one of the determining causes of the Varick separation, but it did not occur to him that Varick's words were intentional. It seemed more likely that the desire to keep clear of embarrassing topics had fatally drawn him into one. Waythorn did not wish to be outdone in civility.

"We'll do the best we can for you," he said. "I think this is a good thing you're in."

"Oh, I'm sure it's immense. It's awfully good of you—" Varick broke off, embarrassed. "I suppose the thing's settled now—but if—"

"If anything happens before Sellers is about, I'll see you again," said Waythorn quietly. He was glad, in the end, to appear the more self-possessed of the two.

The course of Lily's illness ran smooth, and as the days passed Waythorn grew used to the idea of Haskett's weekly visit. The first time the day came round, he stayed out late, and questioned his wife as to the visit on his return. She replied at once that Haskett had merely seen the nurse downstairs, as the doctor did not wish anyone in the child's sickroom till after the crisis.

The following week Waythorn was again conscious of the recurrence of the day, but had forgotten it by the time he came home to dinner. The crisis of the disease came a few days later, with a rapid decline of fever, and the little girl was pronounced out of danger. In the rejoicing which ensued the thought of Haskett passed out of Waythorn's mind, and one afternoon, letting himself into the house with a latchkey, he went straight to his library without noticing a shabby hat and umbrella in the hall.

In the library he found a small effaced-looking man with a thinnish gray beard sitting on the edge of a chair. The stranger might have been a piano tuner, or one of those mysteriously efficient persons who are summoned in emergencies to adjust some detail of the domestic machinery. He blinked at Waythorn through a pair of gold-rimmed spectacles and said mildly: "Mr. Waythorn, I presume? I am Lily's father."

Waythorn flushed. "Oh—" he stammered uncomfortably. He broke off, disliking to appear rude. Inwardly he was trying to adjust the actual Haskett to the image of him projected by his wife's reminiscences. Waythorn had been allowed to infer that Alice's first husband was a brute.

"I am sorry to intrude," said Haskett, with his over-the-counter politeness.

"Don't mention it," returned Waythorn, collecting himself. "I suppose the nurse has been told?"

"I presume so. I can wait," said Haskett. He had a resigned way of speaking, as though life had worn down his natural powers of resistance.

Waythorn stood on the threshold, nervously pulling off his gloves.

"I'm sorry you've been detained. I will send for the nurse," he said; and as he opened the door he added with an effort: "I'm glad we can give you a good report of Lily." He winced as the *we* slipped out, but Haskett seemed not to notice it.

"Thank you, Mr. Waythorn, it's been an anxious time for me."

"Ah, well, that's past. Soon she'll be able to go to you." Waythorn nodded and passed out.

In his own room he flung himself down with a groan. He hated the womanish sensibility which made him suffer so acutely from the grotesque chances of life. He had known when he married that his wife's former husbands were both living, and that amid the multiplied contacts of modern existence there were a thousand chances to one that he would run against one or the other, yet he found himself as much disturbed by his brief encounter with Haskett as though the law had not obligingly removed all difficulties in the way of their meeting.

Waythorn sprang up and began to pace the room nervously. He had not suffered half as much from his two meetings with Varick. It was Haskett's presence in his own house that made the situation so intolerable. He stood still, hearing steps in the passage.

"This way, please," he heard the nurse say. Haskett was being taken upstairs, then: not a corner of the house but was open to him. Waythorn dropped into another chair, staring vaguely ahead of him. On his dressing table stood a photograph of Alice, taken when he had first known her. She was Alice Varick then—how fine and exquisite he had thought her! Those were Varick's pearls about her neck. At Waythorn's instance they had been returned before her marriage. Had Haskett ever given her any trinkets— and what had become of them, Waythorn wondered? He realized suddenly that he knew very little of Haskett's past or present situation; but from the man's appearance and manner of speech he could reconstruct with curious precision the surroundings of Alice's first marriage. And it startled him to think that she had, in the background of her life, a phase of existence so different from any- thing with which he had connected her. Varick, whatever his faults, was a gentleman, in the conventional, traditional sense of the term: the sense which at that moment seemed, oddly enough, to have most meaning to Waythorn. He and Varick had the same social habits, spoke the same language, understood the same allusions. But this other man . . . it was grotesquely uppermost in Waythorn's mind that Haskett had worn a made-up tie attached with an elastic. Why should that ridiculous detail symbolize the whole man? Waythorn was exasperated by his own paltriness, but the fact of the tie expanded, forced itself on him, became as it were the key to Alice's past. He could see her, as Mrs. Haskett, sitting in a "front parlor" furnished in plush, with a pianola, and copy of *Ben Hur* on the center table. He could see her going to the theater with Haskett—or perhaps even to a "Church Sociable"—she in a "picture hat" and Haskett in a black frock coat, a little creased, with the made-up tie on an elastic. On the way home they would stop and look at the illuminated shop windows, lingering over the photographs of New York actresses. On Sunday afternoons Haskett would take her for a walk, pushing Lily ahead of them in a white enameled perambulator, and Waythorn had a vision of the people they would stop and talk to. He could fancy how pretty Alice must have looked, in a dress adroitly constructed from the hints of a New York fashion paper, and how she must have looked down on the other women, chafing at her life, and secretly feeling that she belonged in a bigger place.

For the moment his foremost thought was one of wonder at the way in which she had shed the phase of existence which her marriage with Haskett implied. It was as if her whole aspect, every gesture, every inflection, every allusion, were a studied negation of that period of her life. If she had denied being married to Haskett she could hardly have stood more convicted of duplicity than in this obliteration of the self which had been his wife.

Waythorn started up, checking himself in the analysis of her motives. What right had he to create a fantastic effigy of her and then pass judgment on it? She had spoken vaguely of her first marriage as unhappy, had hinted, with becoming reticence, that Haskett had wrought havoc among her young illusions. . . . It was a pity for Waythorn's peace of mind that Haskett's very inoffensiveness shed a new light on the nature of those illusions. A man would rather think that his wife has been brutalized by her first husband than that the process has been reversed.

## IV

"Mr. Waythorn, I don't like that French governess of Lily's."

Haskett, subdued and apologetic, stood before Waythorn in the library, revolving his shabby hat in his hand.

Waythorn, surprised in his armchair over the evening paper, stared back perplexedly at his visitor.

"You'll excuse my asking to see you," Haskett continued. "But this is my last visit, and I thought if I could have a word with you it would be a better way than writing to Mrs. Waythorn's lawyer."

Waythorn rose uneasily. He did not like the French governess either; but that was irrelevant.

"I am not so sure of that," he returned stiffly; "but since you wish it I will give your message to—my wife." He always hesitated over the possessive pronoun in addressing Haskett.

The latter sighed. "I don't know as that will help much. She didn't like it when I spoke to her."

Waythorn turned red. "When did you see her?" he asked.

"Not since the first day I came to see Lily—right after she was taken sick. I remarked to her then that I didn't like the governess."

Waythorn made no answer. He remembered distinctly that, after that first visit, he had asked his wife if she had seen Haskett. She had lied to him then, but she had respected his wishes since; and the incident cast a curious light on her character. He was sure she would not have seen Haskett that first day if she had divined that Waythorn would object, and the fact that she did not divine it was almost as disagreeable to the latter as the discovery that she had lied to him.

"I don't like the woman," Haskett was repeating with mild persistency. "She ain't straight, Mr. Waythorn—she'll teach the child to be underhand. I've noticed a change in Lily—she's too anxious to please—and she don't always tell the truth. She used to be the straightest child. Mr. Waythorn—" He broke off, his voice a little thick. "Not but what I want her to have a stylish education," he ended.

Waythorn was touched. "I'm sorry, Mr. Haskett; but frankly, I don't quite see what I can do."

Haskett hesitated. Then he laid his hat on the table, and advanced to the hearthrug, on which Waythorn was standing. There was nothing aggressive in his manner, but he had the solemnity of a timid man resolved on a decisive measure.

"There's just one thing you can do, Mr. Waythorn," he said. "You can remind Mrs. Waythorn that, by the decree of the courts, I am entitled to have a voice in Lily's bringing-up." He paused, and went on more deprecatingly: "I am not the kind to talk about enforcing my rights, Mr. Waythorn. I don't know as I think a man is entitled to rights he hasn't known how to hold on to; but this business of the child is different. I've never let go there—and I never mean to."

The scene left Waythorn deeply shaken. Shamefacedly, in indirect ways, he had been finding out about Haskett; and all that he had learned was favorable. The little man, in order to be near his daughter, had sold out his share in a profitable business in Utica, and accepted a modest clerkship in a New York manufacturing house. He boarded in a shabby street and had few acquaintances. His passion for Lily filled his life. Waythorn felt that this exploration of Haskett was like groping about with a dark lantern in his wife's past; but he saw now that there were recesses his lantern had not explored. He had never inquired into the exact circumstances of his wife's first matrimonial rupture. On the surface all had been fair. It was she who had obtained the divorce, and the court had given her the child. But Waythorn knew how many ambiguities such a verdict might cover. The mere fact that Haskett retained a right over his daughter implied an unsuspected compromise. Waythorn was an idealist. He always refused to recognize unpleasant contingencies till he found himself confronted with them, and then he saw them followed by a spectral train of consequences. His next days were thus haunted, and he determined to try to lay the ghosts by conjuring them up in his wife's presence.

When he repeated Haskett's request a flame of anger passed over her face; but she subdued it instantly and spoke with a slight quiver of outraged motherhood.

"It is very ungentlemanly of him," she said.

The word grated on Waythorn. "That is neither here nor there. It's a bare question of rights."

She murmured: "It's not as if he could ever be a help to Lily—"

Waythorn flushed. This was even less to his taste. "The question is," he repeated, "what authority has he over her?"

She looked downward, twisting herself a little in her seat. "I am willing to see him—I thought you objected," she faltered.

In a flash he understood that she knew the extent of Haskett's claims. Perhaps it was not the first time she had resisted them.

"My objecting has nothing to do with it," he said coldly; "if Haskett has a right to be consulted you must consult him."

She burst into tears, and he saw that she expected him to regard her as a victim.

Haskett did not abuse his rights. Waythorn had felt miserably sure that he would not. But the governess was dismissed, and from time to time the little man demanded an interview with Alice. After the first outburst she accepted the situation with her usual adaptability. Haskett had once reminded Waythorn of the piano tuner, and Mrs. Waythorn, after a month or two, appeared to class him with that domestic familiar. Waythorn could not but respect the father's tenacity. At first he had tried to cultivate the suspicion that Haskett might be "up to" something, that he had an object in securing a foothold in the house. But in his heart Waythorn was sure of Haskett's single-mindedness; he even guessed in the latter a mild contempt for such advantages as his relation with the Waythorns might offer. Haskett's sincerity of purpose made him invulnerable, and his successor had to accept him as a lien on the property.

Mr. Sellers was sent to Europe to recover from his gout, and Varick's affairs hung on Waythorn's hands. The negotiations were prolonged and complicated; they necessitated frequent conferences between the two men, and the interests of the firm forbade Waythorn's suggesting that his client should transfer his business to another office.

Varick appeared well in the transaction. In moments of relaxation his coarse streak appeared, and Waythorn dreaded his geniality; but in the office he was concise and clear-headed, with a flattering deference to Waythorn's judgment. Their business relations being so affably established, it would have been absurd for the two men to ignore each other in society. The first time they met in a drawing room, Varick took up their intercourse in the same easy key, and his hostess' grateful glance obliged Waythorn to respond to it. After that they ran across each other frequently, and one evening at a ball Waythorn, wandering through the remoter rooms, came upon Varick seated beside his wife. She colored a little, and faltered in what she was saying; but Varick nodded to Waythorn without rising, and the latter strolled on.

In the carriage, on the way home, he broke out nervously: "I didn't know you spoke to Varick."

Her voice trembled a little. "It's the first time—he happened to be standing near me; I didn't know what to do. It's so awkward, meeting everywhere—and he said you had been very kind about some business."

"That's different," said Waythorn.

She paused a moment. "I'll do just as you wish," she returned pliantly. "I thought it would be less awkward to speak to him when we meet."

Her pliancy was beginning to sicken him. Had she really no will of her own—no theory about her relation to these men? She had accepted Haskett—did she mean to accept Varick? It was "less awkward," as she had said, and her instinct was to evade difficulties or to circumvent them. With sudden vividness Waythorn saw how the instinct had developed. She was "as easy as an old shoe"—a shoe that too many feet had worn. Her elasticity was the result of tension in too many different directions. Alice Haskett—Alice Varick—Alice Waythorn—she had been each in turn, and had left hanging to each name a little of her privacy, a little of her personality, a little of the inmost self where the unknown god abides.

"Yes—it's better to speak to Varick," said Waythorn wearily.

## V

The winter wore on, and society took advantage of the Waythorns' acceptance of Varick. Harassed hostesses were grateful to them for bridging over a social difficulty, and Mrs. Waythorn was held up as a miracle of good taste. Some experimental spirits could not resist the diversion of throwing Varick and his former wife together, and there were those who thought he found a zest in the propinquity. But Mrs. Waythorn's conduct remained irreproachable. She neither avoided Varick nor sought him out. Even Waythorn could not but admit that she had discovered the solution of the newest social problem.

He had married her without giving much thought to that problem. He had fancied that a woman can shed her past like a man. But now he saw that Alice was bound to hers both by the circumstances which forced her into continued relation with it, and by the traces it had left on her nature. With grim irony Waythorn compared himself to a member of a syndicate. He held so many shares in his wife's personality and his predecessors were his partners in the business. If there had been any element of passion in the transaction he would have felt less deteriorated by it. The fact that Alice took her change of husbands like a change of weather reduced the situation to mediocrity. He could have forgiven her for blunders, for excesses: for resisting Haskett, for yielding to Varick; for anything but her acquiescence and her tact. She reminded him of a juggler tossing knives; but the knives were blunt and she knew they would never cut her.

And then, gradually, habit formed a protecting surface for his sensibilities. If he paid for each day's comfort with the small change of his illusions, he grew daily to value the comfort more and set less store upon the coin. He had drifted into a dulling propinquity with Haskett and Varick and he took refuge in the cheap revenge of satirizing the situation. He even began to reckon up the advantages which accrued from it, to ask himself if it were not better to own a third of a wife who knew how to make a man happy than a whole one who had lacked opportunity to acquire the art. For it *was* an art, and made up, like all others, of concessions, eliminations and embellishments; of lights judiciously thrown and shadows skillfully softened. His wife knew exactly how to manage the lights, and he knew exactly to what training she owed her skill. He even tried to trace the source of his obligations, to discriminate between the influences which had combined to produce his domestic happiness: he perceived that Haskett's commonness had made Alice worship good breeding, while Varick's liberal construction of the marriage bond had taught her to value the conjugal virtues; so that he was directly indebted to his predecessors for the devotion which made his life easy if not inspiring.

From this phase he passed into that of complete acceptance. He ceased to satirize himself because time dulled the irony of the situation and the joke lost its humor with its sting. Even the sight of Haskett's hat on the hall table had ceased to touch the springs of epigram. The hat was often seen there now, for it had been decided that it was better for Lily's father to visit her than for the little girl to go to his boardinghouse. Waythorn, having acquiesced in this arrangement, had been surprised to find how little difference it made. Haskett was never obtrusive, and the few visitors who met him on the stairs were unaware of his identity. Waythorn did not know how often he saw Alice, but with himself Haskett was seldom in contact.

One afternoon, however, he learned on entering that Lily's father was waiting to see him. In the library he found Haskett occupying a chair in his usual provisional way. Waythorn always felt grateful to him for not leaning back.

"I hope you'll excuse me, Mr. Waythorn," he said rising. "I wanted to see Mrs. Waythorn about Lily, and your man asked me to wait here till she came in."

"Of course," said Waythorn, remembering that a sudden leak had that morning given over the drawing room to the plumbers.

He opened his cigar case and held it out to his visitor, and Haskett's acceptance seemed to mark a fresh stage in their intercourse. The spring evening was chilly, and Waythorn invited his guest to draw up his chair to the fire. He meant to find an excuse to leave Haskett in a moment; but he was tired and cold, and after all the little man no longer jarred on him.

The two were enclosed in the intimacy of their blended cigar smoke when the door opened and Varick walked into the room. Waythorn rose abruptly. It was the first time that Varick had come to the house, and the surprise of seeing him, combined with the singular inopportuneness of his arrival, gave a new edge to Waythorn's blunted sensibilities. He stared at his visitor without speaking.

Varick seemed too preoccupied to notice his host's embarrassment. "My dear fellow," he exclaimed in his most expansive tone, "I must apologize for tumbling in on you in this way, but I was too late to catch you downtown, and so I thought—"

He stopped short, catching sight of Haskett, and his sanguine color deepened to a flush which spread vividly under his scant blond hair. But in a moment he recovered himself and nodded slightly. Haskett returned the bow in silence, and Waythorn was still groping for speech when the footman came in carrying a tca table.

The intrusion offered a welcome vent to Waythorn's nerves. "What the deuce are you bringing this here for?" he said sharply.

"I beg your pardon, sir, but the plumbers are still in the drawing room, and Mrs. Waythorn said she would have tea in the library."

The footman's perfectly respectful tone implied a reflection on Waythorn's reasonableness.

"Oh, very well," said the latter resignedly, and the footman proceeded to open the folding tea table and set out its complicated appointments. While this interminable process continued the three men stood motionless, watching it with a fascinated stare, till Waythorn, to break the silence, said to Varick, "Won't you have a cigar?"

He held out the case he had just tendered to Haskett, and Varick helped himself with a smile. Waythorn looked about for a match, and finding none, proffered a light from his own cigar. Haskett, in the background, held his ground mildly, examining his cigar tip now and then, and stepping forward at the right moment to knock its ashes into the fire.

The footman at last withdrew, and Varick immediately began: "If I could just say half a word to you about this business—"

"Certainly," stammered Waythorn; "in the dining room—"

But as he placed his hand on the door it opened from without, and his wife appeared on the threshold.

She came in fresh and smiling, in her street dress and hat, shedding a fragrance from the boa which she loosened in advancing.

"Shall we have tea in here, dear?" she began; and then she caught sight of Varick. Her smile deepened, veiling a slight tremor of surprise.

"Why, how do you do?" she said with a distinct note of pleasure.

As she shook hands with Varick she saw Haskett standing behind him. Her smile faded for a moment, but she recalled it quickly, with a scarcely perceptible side glance at Waythorn.

"How do you do, Mr. Haskett?" she said, and shook hands with him a shade less cordially.

The three men stood awkwardly before her, till Varick, always the most self-possessed, dashed into an explanatory phrase.

"We—I had to see Waythorn a moment on business," he stammered, brick-red from chin to nape.

Haskett stepped forward with his air of mild obstinacy. "I am sorry to intrude; but you appointed five o'clock—" he directed his resigned glance to the timepiece on the mantel.

She swept aside their embarrassment with a charming gesture of hospitality.

"I'm so sorry—I'm always late; but the afternoon was so lovely." She stood drawing off her gloves, propitiatory and graceful, diffusing about her a sense of ease and familiarity in which the situation lost its grotesqueness. "But before talking business," she added brightly, "I'm sure everyone wants a cup of tea."

She dropped into her low chair by the tea table, and the two visitors, as if drawn by her smile, advanced to receive the cups she held out.

She glanced about for Waythorn, and he took the third cup with a laugh.

# THE MUSE'S TRAGEDY

## Edith Wharton

## I

DANYERS AFTERWARDS LIKED to fancy that he had recognized Mrs. Anerton at once; but that, of course, was absurd, since he had seen no portrait of her—she affected a strict anonymity, refusing even her photograph to the most privileged—and from Mrs. Memorall, whom he revered and cultivated as her friend, he had extracted but the one impressionist phrase: "Oh, well, she's like one of those old prints where the lines have the value of color."

He was almost certain, at all events, that he had been thinking of Mrs. Anerton as he sat over his breakfast in the empty hotel restaurant, and that, looking up on the approach of the lady who seated herself at the table near the window, he had said to himself, *"That might be she."*

Ever since his Harvard days—he was still young enough to think of them as immensely remote—Danyers had dreamed of Mrs. Anerton, the Silvia of Vincent Rendle's immortal sonnet cycle, the Mrs. A. of the *Life and Letters*. Her name was enshrined in some of the noblest English verse of the nineteenth century—and of all past or future centuries, as Danyers, from the standpoint of a maturer judgment, still believed. The first reading of certain poems—of the *Antinous,* the *pia Tolomei,* the *Sonnets to Silvia*—had been epochs in Danyers' growth, and the verse seemed to gain in mellowness, in amplitude, in meaning as one brought to its interpretation more experience of life, a finer emotional sense. Where, in his boyhood, he had felt only the perfect, the almost austere beauty of form, the subtle interplay of vowel sounds, the rush and fullness of lyric emotion, he now thrilled to the close-packed significance of each line, the allusiveness of each word—his imagination lured hither and thither on fresh trails of thought, and perpetually spurred by the sense that, beyond what he had already discovered, more marvelous regions lay waiting to be explored. Danyers had written, at college, the prize essay on Rendle's poetry (it chanced to be the moment of the great man's death); he had fashioned the fugitive verse of his own Storm and Stress period on the forms which Rendle had first given to English meter, and when two years later the *Life and Letters* appeared, and the Silvia of the sonnets took substance as Mrs. A., he had included in his worship of Rendle the woman who had inspired not only such divine verse but such playful, tender, incomparable prose.

Danyers never forgot the day when Mrs. Memorall happened to mention that she knew Mrs. Anerton. He had known Mrs. Memorall for a year or more, and had somewhat contemptuously classified her as the kind of woman who runs cheap excursions to celebrities; when one afternoon she remarked, as she put a second lump of sugar in his tea:

"Is it right this time? You're almost as particular as Mary Anerton."

"Mary Anerton?"

"Yes, I never *can* remember how she likes her tea. Either it's lemon *with* sugar, or lemon without sugar, or cream without either, and whichever it is must be put into the cup before the tea is poured in; and if one hasn't remembered, one must begin all over again. I suppose it was Vincent Rendle's way of taking his tea and has become a sacred rite."

"Do you *know* Mrs. Anerton?" cried Danyers, disturbed by this careless familiarity with the habits of his divinity.

"'And did I once see Shelley plain?' Mercy, yes! She and I were at school together—she's an American, you know. We were at a *pension* near Tours for nearly a year; then she went back to New York, and I didn't see her again till after her marriage. She and Anerton spent a winter in Rome while my husband was attached to our Legation there, and she used to be with us a great deal." Mrs. Memorall smiled reminiscently. "It was *the* winter."

"The winter they first met?"

"Precisely—but unluckily I left Rome just before the meeting took place. Wasn't it too bad? I might have been in the *Life and Letters*. You know he mentions that stupid Madame Vodki, at whose house he first saw her."

"And did you see much of her after that?"

"Not during Rendle's life. You know she has lived in Europe almost entirely, and though I used to see her off and on when I went abroad, she was always so engrossed, so preoccupied, that one felt one wasn't wanted. The fact is, she cared only about his friend—she separated herself gradually from all her own people. Now, of course, it's different; she's desperately lonely; she's taken to writing to me now and then; and last year, when she heard I was going abroad, she asked me to meet her in Venice, and I spent a week with her there."

"And Rendle?"

Mrs. Memorall smiled and shook her head. "Oh, I never was allowed a peep at *him;* none of her old friends met him, except by accident. Ill-natured people say that was the reason she kept him so long. If one happened in while he was there, he was hustled into Anerton's study, and the husband mounted guard till the inopportune visitor had departed. Anerton, you know, was really much more ridiculous about it than his wife. Mary was too clever to lose her head, or at least to show she'd lost it—but Anerton couldn't conceal his pride in the conquest. I've seen Mary shiver when he spoke of Rendle as *our poet.* Rendle always had to have a certain seat at the dinner table, away from the draft and not too near the fire, and a box of cigars that no one else was allowed to touch, and a writing table of his own in Mary's sitting room—and Anerton was always telling one of the great man's idiosyncrasies: how he never would cut the ends of his cigars, though Anerton himself had given him a gold cutter set with a star sapphire, and how untidy his writing table was, and how the housemaid had orders always to bring the waste-paper basket to her mistress before emptying it, lest some immortal verse should be thrown into the dustbin."

"The Anertons never separated, did they?"

"Separated? Bless you, no. He never would have left Rendle! And besides, he was very fond of his wife."

"And she?"

"Oh, she saw he was the kind of man who was fated to make himself ridiculous, and she never interfered with his natural tendencies."

From Mrs. Memorall, Danyers further learned that Mrs. Anerton, whose husband had died some years before her poet, now divided her life between Rome, where she had a small apartment, and England, where she occasionally went to stay with those of her friends who had been Rendle's. She had been engaged, for some time after his death, in editing some juvenilia which he had bequeathed to her care; but that task being accomplished, she had been left without definite occupation, and Mrs. Memorall, on the occasion of their last meeting, had found her listless and out of spirits.

"She misses him too much—her life is too empty. I told her so—I told her she ought to marry."

"Oh!"

"Why not, pray? She's a young woman still—what many people would call young," Mrs. Memorall interjected, with a parenthetic glance at the mirror. "Why not accept the inevitable and begin over again? All the King's horses and all the King's men won't bring Rendle to life—and besides, she didn't marry *him* when she had the chance."

Danyers winced slightly at this rude fingering of his idol. Was it possible that Mrs. Memorall did not see what an anticlimax such a marriage would have been? Fancy Rendle "making an honest woman" of Silvia; for so society would have viewed it! How such a reparation would have vulgarized their past—it would have been like "restoring" a masterpiece; and how exquisite must have been the perceptions of the woman who, in defiance of appearances, and perhaps of her own secret inclination, chose to go down to posterity as Silvia rather than as Mrs. Vincent Rendle!

Mrs. Memorall, from this day forth, acquired an interest in Danyers' eyes. She was like a volume of unindexed and discursive memoirs, through which he patiently plodded in the hope of finding embedded amid layers of dusty twaddle some precious allusion to the subject of his thought. When, some months later, he brought out his first slim volume, in which the remodeled college essay on Rendle figured among a dozen somewhat overstudied "appreciations," he offered a copy to Mrs. Memorall; who surprised him, the next time they met, with the announcement that she had sent the book to Mrs. Anerton.

Mrs. Anerton in due time wrote to thank her friend. Danyers was privileged to read the few lines in which, in terms that suggested the habit of "acknowledging" similar tributes, she spoke of the author's "feeling and insight," and was "so glad of the opportunity," etc. He went away disappointed, without clearly knowing what else he had expected.

The following spring, when he went abroad, Mrs. Memorall offered him letters to everybody, from the Archbishop of Canterbury to Louise Michel. She did not include Mrs. Anerton, however, and Danyers knew, from a previous conversation, that Silvia objected to people who "brought letters." He knew also that she traveled during the summer, and was unlikely to return to Rome before the term of his holiday should be reached, and the hope of meeting her was not included among his anticipations.

The lady whose entrance broke upon his solitary repast in the restaurant of the Hotel Villa d'Este had seated herself in such a way that her profile was detached against the window, and thus viewed, her domed forehead, small arched nose, and fastidious lip suggested a silhouette of Marie Antoinette. In the lady's dress and movements—in the very turn of her wrist as she poured out her coffee—Danyers thought he detected the same fastidiousness, the same air of tacitly excluding the obvious and unexceptional. Here was a woman who had been much bored and keenly interested. The waiter brought her a *Secolo,* and as she bent above it Danyers noticed that the hair rolled back from her forehead was turning gray; but her figure was straight and slender, and she had the invaluable gift of a girlish back.

The rush of Anglo-Saxon travel had not set toward the lakes, and with the exception of an Italian family or two, and a hump-backed youth with an *abbé,* Danyers and the lady had the marble halls of the Villa d'Este to themselves.

When he returned from his morning ramble among the hills he saw her sitting at one of the little tables at the edge of the lake. She was writing, and a heap of books and newspapers lay on the table at her side. That evening they met again in the garden. He had strolled out to smoke a last cigarette before dinner, and under the black vaulting of ilexes, near the steps leading down to the boat landing, he found her leaning on the parapet above the lake. At the sound of his approach she turned and looked at him. She had thrown a black lace scarf over her head, and in this somber setting her face seemed thin and unhappy. He remembered afterwards that her eyes, as they met his, expressed not so much sorrow as profound discontent.

To his surprise she stepped toward him with a detaining gesture.

"Mr. Lewis Danyers, I believe?"

He bowed.

"I am Mrs. Anerton. I saw your name on the visitors' list and wished to thank you for an essay on Mr. Rendle's poetry—or rather to tell you how much I appreciated it. The book was sent to me last winter by Mrs. Memorall."

She spoke in even melancholy tones, as though the habit of perfunctory utterance had robbed her voice of more spontaneous accents; but her smile was charming.

They sat down on a stone bench under the ilexes, and she told him how much pleasure his essay had given her. She thought it the best in the book—she was sure he had put more of himself into it than into any other; was she not right in conjecturing that he had been very deeply influenced by Mr. Rendle's poetry? *Pour comprendre il faut aimer,*[1] and it seemed to her that, in some ways, he had penetrated the poet's inner meaning more completely than any other critic. There were certain problems, of course, that he had left untouched; certain aspects of that many-sided mind that he had perhaps failed to seize—

"But then you are young," she concluded gently, "and one could not wish you, as yet, the experience that a fuller understanding would imply."

## II

She stayed a month at Villa d'Este, and Danyers was with her daily. She showed an unaffected pleasure in his society; a pleasure so obviously founded on their common veneration of Rendle, that the young man could enjoy it without fear of fatuity. At first he was merely one more grain of frankincense on the altar of her insatiable divinity; but gradually a more personal note crept into their intercourse. If she still liked him only because he appreciated Rendle, she at least perceptibly distinguished him from the herd of Rendle's appreciators.

Her attitude toward the great man's memory struck Danyers as perfect. She neither proclaimed nor disavowed her identity. She was frankly Silvia to those who knew and cared; but there was no trace of the Egeria in her pose. She spoke often of Rendle's books, but seldom of himself; there was no posthumous conjugality, no use of the possessive tense, in her abounding reminiscences. Of the master's intellectual life, of his habits of thought and work, she never wearied of talking. She knew the history of each poem; by what scene or episode each image had been evoked; how many times the words in a certain line had been transposed; how long a certain adjective had been sought, and what had at last suggested it; she

---

[1] *Pour . . . aimer,* French: To understand, it is necessary to love.

could even explain that one impenetrable line, the torment of critics, the joy of detractors, the last line of *The Old Odysseus.*

Danyers felt that in talking of these things she was no mere echo of Rendle's thought. If her identity had appeared to be merged in his it was because they thought alike, not because he had thought for her. Posterity is apt to regard the women whom poets have sung as chance pegs on which they hung their garlands; but Mrs. Anerton's mind was like some fertile garden wherein, inevitably, Rendle's imagination had rooted itself and flowered. Danyers began to see how many threads of his complex mental tissue the poet had owed to the blending of her temperament with his; in a certain sense Silvia had herself created the *Sonnets to Silvia.*

To be the custodian of Rendle's inner self, the door, as it were, to the sanctuary, had at first seemed to Danyers so comprehensive a privilege that he had the sense, as his friendship with Mrs. Anerton advanced, of forcing his way into a life already crowded. What room was there, among such towering memories, for so small an actuality as his? Quite suddenly, after this, he discovered that Mrs. Memorall knew better: his fortunate friend was bored as well as lonely.

"You have had more than any other woman!" he had exclaimed to her one day: and her smile flashed a derisive light on his blunder. Fool that he was, not to have seen that she had not had enough! That she was young still—do years count?—tender, human, a woman; that the living have need of the living.

After that, when they climbed the alleys of the hanging park, resting in one of the little ruined temples, or watching, through a ripple of foliage, the remote blue flash of the lake, they did not always talk of Rendle or of literature. She encouraged Danyers to speak of himself; to confide his ambitions to her; she asked him the questions which are the wise woman's substitute for advice.

"You must write," she said, administering the most exquisite flattery that human lips could give.

Of course he meant to write—why not do something great in his turn? His best, at least; with the resolve, at the outset, that his best should be *the* best. Nothing less seemed possible with that mandate in his ears. How she had divined him; lifted and disentangled his groping ambitions; laid the awakening touch on his spirit with her creative *Let there be light!*

It was his last day with her, and he was feeling very hopeless and happy.

"You ought to write a book about *him*," she went on gently.

Danyers started; he was beginning to dislike Rendle's way of walking in unannounced.

"You ought to do it," she insisted. "A complete interpretation—a summing up of his style, his purpose, his theory of life and art. No one else could do it as well."

He sat looking at her perplexedly. Suddenly—dared he guess?

"I couldn't do it without you," he faltered.

"I could help you—I would help you, of course."

They sat silent, both looking at the lake.

It was agreed, when they parted, that he should rejoin her six weeks later in Venice. There they were to talk about the book.

### III

*Lago d'Iseo, August 14th.*

When I said good-bye to you yesterday I promised to come back to Venice in a week: I was to give you your answer then. I was not honest in saying that; I didn't mean to go back to Venice or to see you again. I was running away from you—and I mean to keep on running! If *you* won't, *I* must. Somebody must save you from marrying a disappointed woman of—well, you say years don't count, and why should they, after all, since you are not to marry me?

That is what I dare not go back to say. *You are not to marry me.* We have had our month together in Venice (such a good month, was it not?) and now you are to go home and write a book—any book but the one we—didn't talk of!—and I am to stay here, attitudinizing among my memories like a sort of female Tithonus. The dreariness of this enforced immortality!

But you shall know the truth. I care for you, or at least for your love, enough to owe you that.

You thought it was because Vincent Rendle had loved me that there was so little hope for you. I had had what I wanted to the full; wasn't that what you said? It is just when a man begins to think he understands a woman that he may be sure he doesn't! It is because Vincent Rendle *didn't love me* that there is no hope for you. I never had what I wanted, and never, never, never will I stoop to wanting anything else.

Do you begin to understand? It was all a sham then, you say? No, it was all real as far as it went. You are young—you haven't learned, as you will later, the thousand imperceptible signs by which one gropes one's way through the labyrinth of human nature; but didn't it strike you, sometimes, that I never told you any foolish little anecdotes about him? His trick, for instance, of twirling a paper knife round and round between his thumb and forefinger while he talked; his mania for saving the backs of notes; his greediness for wild strawberries, the little pungent Alpine ones; his childish delight in acrobats and jugglers; his way of always calling me *you—dear you,* every letter began—I never told you a word of all that, did I? Do you suppose I could have helped telling you, if he had loved me? These little things would have been mine, then, a part of my life—of our life—they would have slipped out in spite of me (it's only your unhappy woman who is always reticent and dignified). But there never was any "our life"; it was always "our lives" to the end. . . .

If you knew what a relief it is to tell someone at last, you would bear with me, you would let me hurt you! I shall never be quite so lonely again, now that someone knows.

Let me begin at the beginning. When I first met Vincent Rendle I was not twenty-five. That was twenty years ago. From that time until his death, five years ago, we were fast friends. He gave me fifteen years, perhaps the best fifteen years, of his life. The world, as you know, thinks that his greatest poems were written during those years; I am supposed to have "inspired" them, and in a sense I did. From the first, the intellectual sympathy between us was almost complete; my mind must have been to him (I fancy) like some perfectly tuned instrument on which he was never tired of playing. Someone told me of his once saying of me that I "always understood"; it is the only praise I ever heard of his giving me. I don't even know if he thought me pretty, though I hardly think my appearance could have been disagreeable to him, for he hated to be with ugly people. At all events he fell into the way of spending more and more of his time with me. He liked our house; our ways suited him. He was nervous, irritable; people bored him and yet he disliked solitude. He took sanctuary with us. When we traveled he went with us; in the winter he took rooms near us in Rome. In England or on the continent he was always with us for a good part of the year. In small ways I was able to help him in his work; he grew dependent on me. When we were apart he wrote to me continually—he liked to have me share in all he was doing or thinking; he was impatient for my criticism of every new book that interested him; I was a part of his intellectual life

The pity of it was that I wanted to be something more. I was a young woman and I was in love with him—not because he was Vincent Rendle, but just because he was himself!

People began to talk, of course—I was Vincent Rendle's Mrs. Anerton; when the *Sonnets to Silvia* appeared, it was whispered that I was Silvia. Wherever he went, I was invited; people made up to me in the hope of getting to know him; when I was in London my doorbell never stopped ringing. Elderly peeresses, aspiring hostesses, lovesick girls and struggling authors overwhelmed me with their assiduities. I hugged my success, for I knew what it meant—they thought that Rendle was in love with me! Do you know, at times, they almost made me think so too? Oh, there was no phase of folly I didn't go through. You can't imagine the excuses a woman will invent for a man's not telling her that he loves her—pitiable arguments that she would see through at a glance if any other woman used them! But all the while, deep down, I knew he had never cared. I should have known it if he had made love to me every day of his life. I could never guess whether he knew what people said about us—he listened so little to what people said; and cared still less, when he heard. He was always quite honest and straightforward with me; he treated me as one man treats another; and yet at times I felt he *must* see that with me it was different. If he did see, he made no sign. Perhaps he never noticed—I am sure he never meant to be cruel. He had never made love to me; it was no fault of his if I wanted more than he could give me. The *Sonnets to Silvia,* you say? But what are they? A cosmic philosophy, not a love poem; addressed to Woman, not to a woman!

But then, the letters? Ah, the letters! Well, I'll make a clean breast of it. You have noticed the breaks in the letters here and there, just as they seem to be on the point of growing a little—warmer? The critics, you may remember, praised the editor for his commendable delicacy and good taste (so rare in these days!) in omitting from the correspondence all personal allusions, all those *détails intimes*[2] which should be kept sacred from the public gaze. They referred, of course, to the asterisks in the letters to Mrs. A. Those letters I myself prepared for publication; that is to say, I copied them out for the editor, and every now and then I put in a line of asterisks to make it appear that something had been left out. You understand? The asterisks were a sham—*there was nothing to leave out.*

---

[2]  *détails intimes*; French: intimate details

No one but a woman could understand what I went through during those years—the moments of revolt, when I felt I must break away from it all, fling the truth in his face and never see him again; the inevitable reaction, when not to see him seemed the one unendurable thing, and I trembled lest a look or word of mine should disturb the poise of our friendship; the silly days when I hugged the delusion that he *must* love me, since everybody thought he did; the long periods of numbness, when I didn't seem to care whether he loved me or not. Between these wretched days came others when our intellectual accord was so perfect that I forgot everything else in the joy of feeling myself lifted up on the wings of his thought. Sometimes, then, the heavens seemed to be opened.

All this time he was so dear a friend! He had the genius of friendship, and he spent it all on me. Yes, you were right when you said that I have had more than any other woman. *Il faut de l'adresse pour aimer,*[3] Pascal says; and I was so quiet, so cheerful, so frankly affectionate with him, that in all those years I am almost sure I never bored him. Could I have hoped as much if he had loved me?

You mustn't think of him, though, as having been tied to my skirts. He came and went as he pleased, and so did his fancies. There was a girl once (I am telling you everything), a lovely being who called his poetry "deep" and gave him *Lucile* on his birthday. He followed her to Switzerland one summer, and all the time that he was dangling after her (a little too conspicuously, I always thought, for a Great Man), he was writing to *me* about his theory of vowel combinations—or was it his experiments in English hexameter? The letters were dated from the very places where I knew they went and sat by waterfalls together and he thought out adjectives for her hair. He talked to me about it quite frankly afterwards. She was perfectly beautiful and it had been a pure delight to watch her; but she *would* talk, and her mind, he said, was "all elbows." And yet, the next year, when her marriage was announced, he went away alone, quite suddenly . . . and it was just afterwards that he published *Love's Viaticum.* Men are queer!

After my husband died—I am putting things crudely, you see— I had a return of hope. It was because he loved me, I argued, that he had never spoken; because he had always hoped some day to make me his wife; because he wanted to spare me the "reproach." Rubbish!

---

[3]  *Il faut . . . aimer,* French: It takes skill to love.

I knew well enough, in my heart of hearts, that my one chance lay in the force of habit. He had grown used to me; he was no longer young; he dreaded new people and new ways; *il avait pris son pli.*[4] Would it not be easier to marry me?

I don't believe he ever thought of it. He wrote me what people call "a beautiful letter"; he was kind, considerate, decently commiserating; then, after a few weeks, he slipped into his old way of coming in every afternoon, and our interminable talks began again just where they had left off. I heard later that people thought I had shown "such good taste" in not marrying him.

So we jogged on for five years longer. Perhaps they were the best years, for I had given up hoping. Then he died.

After his death—this is curious—there came to me a kind of mirage of love. All the books and articles written about him, all the reviews of the *Life,* were full of discreet allusions to Silvia. I became again the Mrs. Anerton of the glorious days. Sentimental girls and dear lads like you turned pink when somebody whispered, "That was Silvia you were talking to." Idiots begged for my autograph—publishers urged me to write my reminiscences of him—critics consulted me about the reading of doubtful lines. And I knew that, to all these people, I was the woman Vincent Rendle had loved.

After a while that fire went out too and I was left alone with my past. Alone—quite alone; for he had never really been with me. The intellectual union counted for nothing now. It had been soul to soul, but never hand in hand, and there were no little things to remember him by.

Then there set in a kind of Arctic winter. I crawled into myself as into a snow hut. I hated my solitude and yet dreaded anyone who disturbed it. That phase, of course, passed like the others. I took up life again, and began to read the papers and consider the cut of my gowns. But here was one question that I could not be rid of, that haunted me night and day. Why had he never loved me? Why had I been so much to him, and no more? Was I so ugly, so essentially unlovable, that though a man might cherish me as his mind's comrade, he could not care for me as a woman? I can't tell you how that question tortured me. It became an obsession.

My poor friend, do you begin to see? I had to find out what some other man thought of me. Don't be too hard on me! Listen first—consider. When I first met Vincent Rendle I was a young woman,

---

[4] *il avait . . . pli*; French: he had formed the habit.

who had married early and led the quietest kind of life; I had had no "experiences." From the hour of our first meeting to the day of his death I never looked at any other man, and never noticed whether any other man looked at me. When he died, five years ago, I knew the extent of my powers no more than a baby. Was it too late to find out? Should I never know *why?*

Forgive me—forgive me. You are so young; it will be an episode, a mere "document," to you so soon! And, besides, it wasn't as deliberate, as cold-blooded as these disjointed lines have made it appear. I didn't plan it, like a woman in a book. Life is so much more complex than any rendering of it can be. I liked you from the first—I was drawn to you (you must have seen that)— I wanted you to like me; it was not a mere psychological experiment. And yet in a sense it was that, too—I must be honest. I had to have an answer to that question; it was a ghost that had to be laid.

At first I was afraid—oh, so much afraid—that you cared for me only because I was Silvia, that you loved me because you thought Rendle had loved me. I began to think there was no escaping my destiny.

How happy I was when I discovered that you were growing jealous of my past; that you actually hated Rendle! My heart beat like a girl's when you told me you meant to follow me to Venice.

After our parting at Villa d'Este my old doubts reasserted themselves. What did I know of your feeling for me, after all? Were you capable of analyzing it yourself? Was it not likely to be two-thirds vanity and curiosity, and one-third literary sentimentality? You might easily fancy that you cared for Mary Anerton when you were really in love with Silvia—the heart is such a hypocrite! Or you might be more calculating than I had supposed. Perhaps it was you who had been flattering *my* vanity in the hope (the pardonable hope!) of turning me, after a decent interval, into a pretty little essay with a margin.

When you arrived in Venice and we met again—do you remember the music on the lagoon, that evening, from my balcony?—I was so afraid you would begin to talk about the book—the book, you remember, was your ostensible reason for coming. You never spoke of it, and I soon saw your one fear was *I* might do so—might remind you of your object in being with me. Then I knew you cared for me! yes, at that moment really cared! We never mentioned the book once, did we, during that month in Venice?

I have read my letter over; and now I wish that I had said this to you instead of writing it. I could have felt my way then, watching your face and seeing if you understood. But, no, I could not go back to Venice; and I could not tell you (though I tried) while we were there together. I couldn't spoil that month—my one month. It was so good, for once in my life, to get away from literature.

You will be angry with me at first—but, alas! not for long. What I have done would have been cruel if I had been a younger woman; as it is, the experiment will hurt no one but myself. And it will hurt me horribly (as much as, in your first anger, you may perhaps wish), because it has shown me, for the first time, all that I have missed.

# A JOURNEY

### Edith Wharton

As SHE LAY in her berth, staring at the shadows overhead, the rush of the wheels was in her brain, driving her deeper and deeper into circles of wakeful lucidity. The sleeping car had sunk into its night silence. Through the wet windowpane she watched the sudden lights, the long stretches of hurrying blackness. Now and then she turned her head and looked through the opening in the hangings at her husband's curtains across the aisle. . . .

She wondered restlessly if he wanted anything and if she could hear him if he called. His voice had grown very weak within the last months and it irritated him when she did not hear. This irritability, this increasing childish petulance seemed to give expression to their imperceptible estrangement. Like two faces looking at one another through a sheet of glass they were close together, almost touching, but they could not hear or feel each other: the conductivity between them was broken. She, at least, had this sense of separation, and she fancied sometimes that she saw it reflected in the look with which he supplemented his failing words. Doubtless the fault was hers. She was too impenetrably healthy to be touched by the irrelevancies of disease. Her self-reproachful tenderness was tinged with the sense of his irrationality: she had a vague feeling that there was a purpose in his helpless tyrannies. The suddenness of the change had found her so unprepared. A year ago their pulses had beat to one robust measure; both had the same prodigal confidence in an exhaustless future. Now their energies no longer kept step: hers still bounded ahead of life, preempting unclaimed regions of hope and activity, while his lagged behind, vainly struggling to overtake her.

When they married, she had such arrears of living to make up: her days had been as bare as the whitewashed schoolroom where she forced innutritious facts upon reluctant children. His coming had broken in on the slumber of circumstance, widening the present till it became the encloser of remotest chances. But imperceptibly the horizon narrowed. Life had a grudge against her: she was never to be allowed to spread her wings.

At first the doctors had said that six weeks of mild air would set him right; but when he came back this assurance was explained as having of course included a winter in a dry climate. They gave up their pretty house, storing the wedding presents and new furniture, and went to Colorado. She had hated it there from the first. Nobody knew her or cared about her; there was no one to wonder at the good match she had made, or to envy her the new dresses and the visiting cards which were still a surprise to her. And he kept growing worse. She felt herself beset with difficulties too evasive to be fought by so direct a temperament. She still loved him, of course; but he was gradually, undefinably ceasing to be himself. The man she had married had been strong, active, gently masterful: the male whose pleasure it is to clear a way through the material obstructions of life; but now it was she who was the protector, he who must be shielded from importunities and given his drops or his beef juice though the skies were falling. The routine of the sickroom bewildered her; this punctual administering of medicine seemed as idle as some uncomprehended religious mummery.

There were moments, indeed, when warm gushes of pity swept away her instinctive resentment of his condition, when she still found his old self in his eyes as they groped for each other through the dense medium of his weakness. But these moments had grown rare. Sometimes he frightened her: his sunken expressionless face seemed that of a stranger; his voice was weak and hoarse; his thin-lipped smile a mere muscular contraction. Her hand avoided his damp soft skin, which had lost the familiar roughness of health: she caught herself furtively watching him as she might have watched a strange animal. It frightened her to feel that this was the man she loved; there were hours when to tell him what she suffered seemed the one escape from her fears. But in general she judged herself more leniently, reflecting that she had perhaps been too long alone with him, and that she would feel differently when they were at home again, surrounded by her robust and buoyant family. How she had rejoiced when the doctors at last gave their consent to his going home!

She knew, of course, what the decision meant; they both knew. It meant that he was to die; but they dressed the truth in hopeful euphemisms, and at times, in the joy of preparation, she really forgot the purpose of their journey, and slipped into an eager allusion to next year's plans.

At last the day of leaving came. She had a dreadful fear that they would never get away; that somehow at the last moment he would fail her; that the doctors held one of their accustomed treacheries in reserve; but nothing happened. They drove to the station, he was installed in a seat with a rug over his knees and a cushion at his back, and she hung out of the window waving unregretful farewells to the acquaintances she had really never liked till then.

The first twenty-four hours had passed off well. He revived a little and it amused him to look out of the window and to observe the humors of the car. The second day he began to grow weary and to chafe under the dispassionate stare of the freckled child with the lump of chewing gum. She had to explain to the child's mother that her husband was too ill to be disturbed: a statement received by that lady with a resentment visibly supported by the maternal sentiment of the whole car. . . .

That night he slept badly and the next morning his temperature frightened her: she was sure he was growing worse. The day passed slowly, punctuated by the small irritations of travel. Watching his tired face, she traced in its contractions every rattle and jolt of the train, till her own body vibrated with sympathetic fatigue. She felt the others observing him too, and hovered restlessly between him and the line of interrogative eyes. The freckled child hung about him like a fly; offers of candy and picture books failed to dislodge her: she twisted one leg around the other and watched him imperturbably. The porter, as he passed, lingered with vague proffers of help, probably inspired by philanthropic passengers swelling with the sense that "something ought to be done"; and one nervous man in a skull cap was audibly concerned as to the possible effect on his wife's health.

The hours dragged on in a dreary inoccupation. Towards dusk she sat down beside him and he laid his hand on hers. The touch startled her. He seemed to be calling her from far off. She looked at him helplessly and his smile went through her like a physical pang.

"Are you very tired?" she asked.

"No, not very."

"We'll be there soon now."

"Yes, very soon."

"This time tomorrow—"

He nodded and they sat silent. When she had put him to bed and crawled into her own berth she tried to cheer herself with the thought that in less than twenty-four hours they would be in New York. Her people would all be at the station to meet her—she pictured their round unanxious faces pressing through the crowd. She only hoped they would not tell him too loudly that he was looking splendidly and would be all right in no time: the subtler sympathies developed by long contact with suffering were making her aware of a certain coarseness of texture in the family sensibilities.

Suddenly she thought she heard him call. She parted the curtains and listened. No, it was only a man snoring at the other end of the car. His snores had a greasy sound, as though they passed through tallow. She lay down and tried to sleep. . . . Had she not heard him move? She started up trembling. . . . The silence frightened her more than any sound. He might not be able to make her hear—he might be calling her now. . . . What made her think of such things? It was merely the familiar tendency of an overtired mind to fasten itself on the most intolerable chance within the range of its forebodings. . . . Putting her head out, she listened: but she could not distinguish his breathing from that of the other pairs of lungs about her. She longed to get up and look at him, but she knew the impulse was a mere vent for her restlessness, and the fear of disturbing him restrained her. . . . The regular movement of his curtain reassured her, she knew not why; she remembered that he had wished her a cheerful good night; and the sheer inability to endure her fears a moment longer made her put them from her with an effort of her whole sound-tired body. She turned on her side and slept.

She sat up stiffly, staring out at the dawn. The train was rushing through a region of bare hillocks huddled against a lifeless sky. It looked like the first day of creation. The air of the car was close, and she pushed up her window to let in the keen wind. Then she looked at her watch: it was seven o'clock, and soon the people about her would be stirring. She slipped into her clothes, smoothed her disheveled hair and crept to the dressing room. When she had washed her face and adjusted her dress she felt more hopeful. It was always a struggle for her not to be cheerful in the morning. Her cheeks burned deliriously under the coarse towel and the wet hair about her temples broke into strong upward tendrils. Every inch of her was full of life and elasticity. And in ten hours they would be at home!

She stepped to her husband's berth: it was time for him to take his early glass of milk. The window shade was down, and in the dusk of the curtained enclosure she could just see that he lay sideways, with his face away from her. She leaned over him and drew up the shade. As she did so she touched one of his hands. It felt cold. . . .

She bent closer, laying her hand on his arm and calling him by name. He did not move. She spoke again more loudly; she grasped his shoulder and gently shook it. He lay motionless. She caught hold of his hand again: it slipped from her limply, like a dead thing. A dead thing?

Her breath caught. She must see his face. She leaned forward, and hurriedly, shrinkingly, with a sickening reluctance of the flesh, laid her hands on his shoulders and turned him over. His head fell back; his face looked small and smooth; he gazed at her with steady eyes.

She remained motionless for a long time, holding him thus; and they looked at each other. Suddenly she shrank back; the longing to scream, to call out, to fly from him, had almost overpowered her. But a strong hand arrested her. Good God! If it were known that he was dead they would be put off the train at the next station—

In a terrifying flash of remembrance there arose before her a scene she had once witnessed in traveling, when a husband and wife, whose child had died in the train, had been thrust out at some chance station. She saw them standing on the platform with the child's body between them; she had never forgotten the dazed look with which they followed the receding train. And this was what would happen to her. Within the next hour she might find herself on the platform of some strange station, alone with her husband's body. . . . Anything but that! It was too horrible—She quivered like a creature at bay.

As she cowered there, she felt the train moving more slowly. It was coming then—they were approaching a station! She saw again the husband and wife standing on the lonely platform; and with a violent gesture she drew down the shade to hide her husband's face.

Feeling dizzy, she sank down on the edge of the berth, keeping away from his outstretched body, and pulling the curtains close, so that he and she were shut into a kind of sepulchral twilight. She tried to think. At all costs she must conceal the fact that he was dead. But how? Her mind refused to act: she could not plan, combine. She could think of no way but to sit there, clutching the curtains, all day long. . . .

She heard the porter making up her bed; people were beginning to move about the car; the dressing-room door was being opened and shut. She tried to rouse herself. At length with a supreme effort she rose to her feet, stepping into the aisle of the car and drawing the curtains tight behind her. She noticed that they still parted slightly with the motion of the car, and finding a pin in her dress she fastened them together. Now she was safe. She looked round and saw the porter. She fancied he was watching her.

"Ain't he awake yet?" he inquired.

"No," she faltered.

"I got his milk all ready when he wants it. You know you told me to have it for him by seven."

She nodded silently and crept into her seat.

At half-past eight the train reached Buffalo. By this time the other passengers were dressed and the berths had been folded back for the day. The porter, moving to and fro under his burden of sheets and pillows, glanced at her as he passed. At length he said: "Ain't he going to get up? You know we're ordered to make up the berths as early as we can."

She turned cold with fear. They were just entering the station.

"Oh, not yet," she stammered. "Not till he's had his milk. Won't you get it, please?'

"All right. Soon as we start again."

When the train moved on he reappeared with the milk. She took it from him and sat vaguely looking at it: her brain moved slowly from one idea to another, as though they were stepping–stones set far apart across a whirling flood. At length she became aware that the porter still hovered expectantly.

"Will I give it to him?" he suggested.

"Oh, no," she cried, rising. "He—he's asleep yet, I think—"

She waited till the porter had passed on; then she unpinned the curtains and slipped behind them. In the semiobscurity her husband's face stared up at her like a marble mask with agate eyes. The eyes were dreadful. She put out her hand and drew down the lids. Then she remembered the glass of milk in her other hand: what was she to do with it? She thought of raising the window and throwing it out; but to do so she would have to lean across his body and bring her face close to his. She decided to drink the milk.

She returned to her seat with the empty glass and after a while the porter came back to get it.

"When'll I fold up his bed?" he asked.

"Oh, not now—not yet; he's ill—he's very ill. Can't you let him stay as he is? The doctor wants him to lie down as much as possible."

He scratched his head. "Well, if he's *really* sick—"

He took the empty glass and walked away, explaining to the passengers that the party behind the curtains was too sick to get up just yet.

She found herself the center of sympathetic eyes. A motherly woman with an intimate smile sat down beside her.

"I'm really sorry to hear your husband's sick. I've had a remarkable amount of sickness in my family and maybe I could assist you. Can I take a look at him?"

"Oh, no—no please! He mustn't be disturbed."

The lady accepted the rebuff indulgently.

"Well, it's just as you say, of course, but you don't look to me as if you'd had much experience in sickness and I'd have been glad to assist you. What do you generally do when your husband's taken this way?"

"I—I let him sleep."

"Too much sleep ain't any too healthful either. Don't you give him any medicine?"

"Y—yes."

"Don't you wake him to take it?"

"Yes."

"When does he take the next dose?"

"Not for—two hours—"

The lady looked disappointed. "Well, if I was you I'd try giving it oftener. That's what I do with my folks."

After that many faces seemed to press upon her. The passengers were on their way to the dining car, and she was conscious that as they passed down the aisle they glanced curiously at the closed curtains. One lantern-jawed man with prominent eyes stood still and tried to shoot his projecting glance through the division between the folds. The freckled child, returning from breakfast, waylaid the passers with a buttery clutch, saying in a loud whisper, "He's sick"; and once the conductor came by, asking for tickets. She shrank into her corner and looked out of the window at the flying trees and houses, meaningless hieroglyphs of an endlessly unrolled papyrus.

Now and then the train stopped, and the newcomers on entering the car stared in turn at the closed curtains. More and more people seemed to pass—their faces began to blend fantastically with the images surging in her brain. . . .

Later in the day a fat man detached himself from the mist of faces. He had a creased stomach and soft pale lips. As he pressed himself into the seat facing her she noticed that he was dressed in black broadcloth, with a soiled white tie.

"Husband's pretty bad this morning, is he?"

"Yes."

"Dear, dear! Now that's terribly distressing, ain't it?" An apostolic smile revealed his gold-filled teeth. "Of course you know there's no sech thing as sickness. Ain't that a lovely thought? Death itself is but a deloosion of our grosser senses. On'y lay yourself open to the influx of the sperrit, submit yourself passively to the action of the divine force, and disease and dissolution will cease to exist for you. If you could indooce your husband to read this little pamphlet—"

The faces about her again grew indistinct. She had a vague recollection of hearing the motherly lady and the parent of the freckled child ardently disputing the relative advantages of trying several medicines at once, or of taking each in turn; the motherly lady maintaining that the competitive system saved time; the other objecting that you couldn't tell which remedy had effected the cure; their voices went on and on, like bell buoys droning through a fog. . . . The porter came up now and then with questions that she did not understand, but somehow she must have answered since he went away again without repeating them; every two hours the motherly lady reminded her that her husband ought to have his drops; people left the car and others replaced them. . . .

Her head was spinning and she tried to steady herself by clutching at her thoughts as they swept by, but they slipped away from her like bushes on the side of a sheer precipice down which she seemed to be falling. Suddenly her mind grew clear again and she found herself vividly picturing what would happen when the train reached New York. She shuddered as it occurred to her that he would be quite cold and that someone might perceive he had been dead since morning.

She thought hurriedly: "If they see I am not surprised they will suspect something. They will ask questions, and if I tell them the truth they won't believe me—no one would believe me! It will be terrible"—and she kept repeating to herself—"I must pretend I don't know. I must pretend I don't know. When they open the curtains I must go up to him quite naturally—and then I must scream!" She had an idea that the scream would be very hard to do.

Gradually new thoughts crowded upon her, vivid and urgent: she tried to separate and restrain them, but they beset her clamorously, like her school children at the end of a hot day, when she was too tired to silence them. Her head grew confused, and she felt a sick fear of forgetting her part, of betraying herself by some unguarded word or look.

"I must pretend I don't know," she went on murmuring. The words had lost their significance, but she repeated them mechanically, as though they had been a magic formula, until suddenly she heard herself saying: "I can't remember, I can't remember!"

Her voice sounded very loud, and she looked about her in terror; but no one seemed to notice that she had spoken.

As she glanced down the car her eye caught the curtains of her husband's berth, and she began to examine the monotonous arabesques woven through their heavy folds. The pattern was intricate and difficult to trace; she gazed fixedly at the curtains and as she did so the thick stuff grew transparent and through it she saw her husband's face—his dead face. She struggled to avert her look, but her eyes refused to move and her head seemed to be held in vice. At last, with an effort that left her weak and shaking, she turned away; but it was of no use; close in front of her, small and smooth, was her husband's face. It seemed to be suspended in the air between her and the false braids of the woman who sat in front of her. With an uncontrollable gesture she stretched out her hand to push the face away, and suddenly she felt the touch of his smooth skin. She repressed a cry and half started from her seat. The woman with the false braids looked around, and feeling that she must justify her movement in some way she rose and lifted her traveling bag from the opposite seat. She unlocked the bag and looked into it; but the first object her hand met was a small flask of her husband's, thrust there at the last moment, in the haste of departure. She locked the bag and closed her eyes . . . his face was there again, hanging between her eyeballs and lids like a waxen mask against a red curtain. . . .

She roused herself with a shiver. Had she fainted or slept? Hours seemed to have elapsed; but it was still broad day, and the people about her were sitting in the same attitudes as before.

A sudden sense of hunger made her aware that she had eaten nothing since morning. The thought of food filled her with disgust, but she dreaded a return of faintness, and remembering that she had some biscuits in her bag she took one out and ate it. The dry crumbs choked her, and she hastily swallowed a little brandy from her husband's flask. The burning sensation in her throat acted as a counterirritant, momentarily relieving the dull ache of her nerves. Then she felt a gently-stealing warmth, as though a soft air fanned her, and the swarming fears relaxed their clutch, receding through the stillness that enclosed her, a stillness soothing as the spacious quietude of a summer day. She slept.

Through her sleep she felt the impetuous rush of the train. It seemed to be life itself that was sweeping her on with headlong inexorable force—sweeping her into darkness and terror, and the awe of unknown days.—Now all at once everything was still—not a sound, not a pulsation. . . . She was dead in her turn, and lay beside him with smooth upstaring face. How quiet it was!—and yet she heard feet coming, the feet of the men who were to carry them away. . . . She could feel too—she felt a sudden prolonged vibration, a series of hard shocks, and then another plunge into darkness, the darkness of death this time—a black whirlwind on which they were both spinning like leaves, in wild uncoiling spirals, with millions and millions of the dead. . . .

She sprang up in terror. Her sleep must have lasted a long time, for the winter day had paled and the lights had been lit. The car was in confusion, and as she regained her self-possession she saw that the passengers were gathering up their wraps and bags. The woman with the false braids had brought from the dressing room a sickly ivy plant in a bottle, and the Christian Scientist was reversing his cuffs. The porter passed down the aisle with his impartial brush. An impersonal figure with a gold-banded cap asked for her husband's ticket. A voice shouted "Baig-gage express!" and she heard the clicking of metal as the passengers handed over their checks.

Presently her window was blocked by an expanse of sooty wall, and the train passed into the Harlem tunnel. The journey was over; in a few minutes she would see her family pushing their joyous way through the throng at the station. Her heart dilated. The worst terror was past. . . .

"We'd better get him up now, hadn't we?" asked the porter, touching her arm.

He had her husband's hat in his hand and was meditatively revolving it under his brush.

She looked at the hat and tried to speak; but suddenly the car grew dark. She flung up her arms, struggling to catch at something, and fell face downward, striking her head against the dead man's berth.

# THE DILETTANTE

## Edith Wharton

IT WAS ON an impulse hardly needing the arguments he found himself advancing in its favor, that Thursdale, on his way to the club, turned as usual into Mrs. Vervain's street.

The "as usual" was his own qualification of the act; a convenient way of bridging the interval—in days and other sequences—that lay between this visit and the last. It was characteristic of him that he instinctively excluded his call two days earlier, with Ruth Gaynor, from the list of his visits to Mrs. Vervain: the special conditions attending it had made it no more like a visit to Mrs. Vervain than an engraved dinner invitation is like a personal letter. Yet it was to talk over his call with Miss Gaynor that he was now returning to the scene of that episode; and it was because Mrs. Vervain could be trusted to handle the talking over as skillfully as the interview itself that, at her corner, he had felt the dilettante's irresistible craving to take a last look at a work of art that was passing out of his possession.

On the whole, he knew no one better fitted to deal with the unexpected than Mrs. Vervain. She excelled in the rare art of taking things for granted, and Thursdale felt a pardonable pride in the thought that she owed her excellence to his training. Early in his career, Thursdale had made the mistake, at the outset of his acquaintance with a lady, of telling her that he loved her, and exacting the same avowal in return. The latter part of that episode had been like the long walk back from a picnic, when one has to carry all the crockery one has finished using: it was the last time Thursdale ever allowed himself to be encumbered with the debris of a feast. He thus incidentally learned that the privilege of loving her is one of the least favors that a charming woman can accord; and in seeking to avoid the pitfalls of sentiment he had developed a science of evasion in which the woman of the moment became a mere implement of the game. He owed a great deal of delicate enjoyment to the cultivation of this art. The perils from which it had been his refuge became naively harmless: was it possible that he who now took his easy way along the levels had once preferred to gasp on the raw heights of emotion? Youth is a high-colored season; but he had the satisfaction of feeling that he had entered earlier than most into that chiaroscuro of sensation where every half-tone has its value.

As a promoter of this pleasure no one he had known was comparable to Mrs. Vervain. He had taught a good many women not to betray their feelings, but he had never before had such fine material to work with. She had been surprisingly crude when he first knew her; capable of making the most awkward inferences, of plunging through thin ice, of recklessly undressing her emotions; but she had acquired, under the discipline of his reticences and evasions, a skill almost equal to his own, and perhaps more remarkable in that it involved keeping time with any tune he played and reading at sight some uncommonly difficult passages.

It had taken Thursdale seven years to form this fine talent; but the result justified the effort. At the crucial moment she had been perfect: her way of greeting Miss Gaynor had made him regret that he had announced his engagement by letter. It was an evasion that confessed a difficulty; a deviation implying an obstacle, where, by common consent, it was agreed to see none; it betrayed, in short, a lack of confidence in the completeness of his method. It had been his pride never to put himself in a position which had to be quitted, as it were, by the back door; but here, as he perceived, the main portals would have opened for him of their own accord. All this, and much more, he read in the finished naturalness with which Mrs. Vervain had met Miss Gaynor. He had never seen a better piece of work: there was no overeagerness, no suspicious warmth, above all (and this gave her art the grace of a natural quality) there were none of those damnable implications whereby a woman, in welcoming her friend's betrothed, may keep him on pins and needles while she laps the lady in complacency. So masterly a performance, indeed, hardly needed the offset of Miss Gaynor's doorstep words—"To be so kind to me, how she must have liked you!"—though he caught himself wishing it lay within the bounds of fitness to transmit them, as a final tribute, to the one woman he knew who was unfailingly certain to enjoy a good thing. It was perhaps the one drawback to his new situation that it might develop good things which it would be impossible to hand on to Margaret Vervain.

The fact that he had made the mistake of underrating his friend's powers, the consciousness that his writing must have betrayed his distrust of her efficiency, seemed an added reason for turning down her street instead of going on to the club. He would show her that he knew how to value her; he would ask her to achieve with him a feat infinitely rarer and more delicate than the one he had appeared to avoid. Incidentally, he would also dispose of the interval of time before dinner: ever since he had seen Miss Gaynor off, an hour earlier, on her return journey to Buffalo, he had been wondering how he should put in the rest of the afternoon. It was absurd, how he missed the girl. . . . Yes, that was it: the desire to talk about her was, after all, at the bottom of his impulse to call on Mrs. Vervain! It was absurd, if you like—but it was delightfully rejuvenating. He could recall the time when he had been afraid of being obvious: now he felt that his return to the primitive emotions might be as restorative as a holiday in the Canadian woods. And it was precisely by the girl's candor, her directness, her lack of complications, that he was taken. The sense that she might say something rash at any moment was positively exhilarating: if she had thrown her arms about him at the station he would not have given a thought to his crumpled dignity. It surprised Thursdale to find what freshness of heart he brought to the adventure; and though his sense of irony prevented his ascribing his intactness to any conscious purpose, he could but rejoice in the fact that his sentimental economies had left him such a large surplus to draw upon.

Mrs. Vervain was at home—as usual. When one visits the cemetery one expects to find the angel on the tombstone, and it struck Thursdale as another proof of his friend's good taste that she had been in no undue haste to change her habits. The whole house appeared to count on his coming; the footman took his hat and overcoat as naturally as though there had been no lapse in his visits; and the drawing room at once enveloped him in that atmosphere of tacit intelligence which Mrs. Vervain imparted to her very furniture.

It was a surprise that, in this general harmony of circumstances, Mrs. Vervain should herself sound the first false note.

"You?" she exclaimed; and the book she held slipped from her hand.

It was crude, certainly; unless it were a touch of the finest art. The difficulty of classifying it disturbed Thursdale's balance.

"Why not?" he said, restoring the book. "Isn't it my hour?" And as she made no answer, he added gently, "Unless it's someone else's?"

She laid the book aside and sank back into her chair. "Mine, merely," she said.

"I hope that doesn't mean that you're unwilling to share it?"

"With you? By no means. You're welcome to my last crust."

He looked at her reproachfully. "Do you call this the last?"

She smiled as he dropped into the seat across the hearth. "It's a way of giving it more flavor!"

He returned the smile. "A visit to you doesn't need such condiments."

She took this with just the right measure of retrospective amusement.

"Ah, but I want to put into this one a very special taste," she confessed.

Her smile was so confident, so reassuring, that it lulled him into the imprudence of saying: "Why should you want it to be different from what was always so perfectly right?"

She hesitated. "Doesn't the fact that it's the last constitute a difference?"

"The last—my last visit to you?"

"Oh, metaphorically, I mean—there's a break in the continuity."

Decidedly, she was pressing too hard: unlearning his arts already!

"I don't recognize it," he said. "Unless you make me—" he added, with a note that slightly stirred her attitude of languid attention.

She turned to him with grave eyes. "You recognize no difference whatever?"

"None—except an added link in the chain."

"An added link?"

"In having one more thing to like you for—your letting Miss Gaynor see why I had already so many." He flattered himself that this turn had taken the least hint of fatuity from the phrase.

Mrs. Vervain sank into her former easy pose. "Was it that you came for?" she asked, almost gaily.

"If it is necessary to have a reason—that was one."

"To talk to me about Miss Gaynor?"

"To tell you how she talks about you."

"That will be very interesting—especially if you have seen her since her second visit to me."

"Her second visit?" Thursdale pushed his chair back with a start and moved to another. "She came to see you again?"

"This morning, yes—by appointment."

He continued to look at her blankly. "You sent for her?"

"I didn't have to—she wrote and asked me last night. But no doubt you have seen her since."

Thursdale sat silent. He was trying to separate his words from his thoughts, but they still clung together inextricably. "I saw her off just now at the station."

"And she didn't tell you that she had been here again?"

"There was hardly time, I suppose—there were people about—" he floundered.

"Ah, she'll write, then."

He regained his composure. "Of course she'll write: very often, I hope. You know I'm absurdly in love," he cried audaciously.

She tilted her head back, looking up at him as he leaned against the chimney piece. He had leaned there so often that the attitude touched a pulse which set up a throbbing in her throat. "Oh, my poor Thursdale!" she murmured.

"I suppose it's rather ridiculous," he owned; and as she remained silent, he added, with a sudden break—"Or have you another reason for pitying me?"

Her answer was another question. "Have you been back to your rooms since you left her?"

"Since I left her at the station? I came straight here."

"Ah, yes—you *could:* there was no reason—" Her words passed into a silent musing.

Thursdale moved nervously nearer. "You said you had something to tell me?"

"Perhaps I had better let her do so. There may be a letter at your rooms."

"A letter? What do you mean? A letter from *her?* What has happened?"

His paleness shook her, and she raised a hand of reassurance. "Nothing has happened—perhaps that is just the worst of it. You always *hated,* you know," she added incoherently, "to have things happen: you never would let them."

"And now—"

"Well, that was what she came here for: I supposed you had guessed. To know if anything had happened."

"Had happened?" He gazed at her slowly. "Between you and me?" he said with a rush of light.

The words were so much cruder than any that had ever passed between them, that the color rose to her face; but she held his startled gaze.

"You know girls are not quite as unsophisticated as they used to be. Are you surprised that such an idea should occur to her?"

His own color answered hers: it was the only reply that came to him.

Mrs. Vervain went on smoothly: "I supposed it might have struck you that there were times when we presented that appearance."

He made an impatient gesture. "A man's past is his own!"

"Perhaps—it certainly never belongs to the woman who has shared it. But one learns such truths only by experience; and Miss Gaynor is naturally inexperienced."

"Of course—but—supposing her act a natural one—" he floundered lamentably among his innuendoes "—I still don't see—how there was anything—"

"Anything to take hold of? There wasn't—"

"Well, then—?" escaped him, in undisguised satisfaction; but as she did not complete the sentence he went on with a faltering laugh: "She can hardly object to the existence of a mere friendship between us!"

"But she does," said Mrs. Vervain.

Thursdale stood perplexed. He had seen, on the previous day, no trace of jealousy or resentment in his betrothed: he could still hear the candid ring of the girl's praise of Mrs. Vervain. If she were such an abyss of insincerity as to dissemble distrust under such frankness, she must at least be more subtle than to bring her doubts to her rival for solution. The situation seemed one through which one could no longer move in a penumbra, and he let in a burst of light with the direct query: "Won't you explain what you mean?"

Mrs. Vervain sat silent, not provokingly, as though to prolong his distress, but as if, in the attenuated phraseology he had taught her, it was difficult to find words robust enough to meet his challenge. It was the first time he had ever asked her to explain anything; and she had lived so long in dread of offering elucidations which were not wanted, that she seemed unable to produce one on the spot.

At last she said slowly: "She came to find out if you were really free."

Thursdale colored again. "Free?" he stammered, with a sense of physical disgust at contact with such crassness.

"Yes—if I had quite done with you." She smiled in recovered security. "It seems she likes clear outlines; she has a passion for definitions."

"Yes—well?" he said, wincing at the echo of his own subtlety.

"Well—and when I told her that you had never belonged to me, she wanted me to define *my* status—to know exactly where I had stood all along."

Thursdale sat gazing at her intently; his hand was not yet on the clue. "And even when you had told her that—"

"Even when I had told her that I had had no status—that I had never stood anywhere, in any sense she meant," said Mrs. Vervain, slowly, "even then she wasn't satisfied, it seems."

He uttered an uneasy exclamation. "She didn't believe you, you mean?"

"I mean that she *did* believe me: too thoroughly."

"Well, then—in God's name, what did she want?"

"Something more—those were the words she used."

"Something more? Between—between you and me? Is it a conundrum?" He laughed awkwardly.

"Girls are not what they were in my day; they are no longer forbidden to contemplate the relation of the sexes."

"So it seems!" he commented. "But since, in this case, there wasn't any—" he broke off, catching the dawn of a revelation in her gaze.

"That's just it. The unpardonable offence has been—in our not offending."

He flung himself down despairingly. "I give up! What did you tell her?" he burst out with sudden crudeness.

"The exact truth. If I had only known," she broke off with a beseeching tenderness, "won't you believe that I would still have lied for you?"

"Lied for me? Why on earth should you have lied for either of us?"

"To save you—to hide you from her to the last! As I've hidden you from myself all these years!" She stood up with a sudden tragic import in her movement. "You believe me capable of that, don't you? If I had only guessed—but I have never known a girl like her; she had the truth out of me with a spring."

"The truth that you and I had never—"

"Had never—never in all these years! Oh, she knew why—she measured us both in a flash. She didn't suspect me of having haggled with you—her words pelted me like hail. 'He just took what he wanted—sifted and sorted you to suit his taste. Burnt out the gold and left a heap of cinders. And you let him—you let yourself be cut in bits'—she mixed her metaphors a little—'be cut in bits, and used or discarded, while all the while every drop of blood in you belonged to him! But he's Shylock—he's Shylock—and you have bled to death of the pound of flesh he has cut off you.' But she despises me the most, you know—far, far the most—" Mrs. Vervain ended.

The words fell strangely on the scented stillness of the room: they seemed out of harmony with its setting of afternoon intimacy, the kind of intimacy on which, at any moment, a visitor might intrude without perceptibly lowering the atmosphere. It was as though a grand opera singer had strained the acoustics of a private music room.

Thursdale stood up, facing his hostess. Half the room was between them, but they seemed to stare close at each other now that the veils of reticence and ambiguity had fallen.

His first words were characteristic: "She *does* despise me, then?" he exclaimed.

"She thinks the pound of flesh you took was a little too near the heart."

He was excessively pale. "Please tell me exactly what she said of me."

"She did not speak much of you: she is proud. But I gather that while she understands love or indifference, her eyes have never been opened to the many intermediate shades of feeling. At any rate, she expressed an unwillingness to be taken with reservations—she thinks you would have loved her better if you had loved someone else first. The point of view is original—she insists on a man with a past!"

"Oh, a past—if she's serious—I could rake up a past!" he said with a laugh.

"So I suggested: but she has her eyes on this particular portion of it. She insists on making it a test case. She wanted to know what you had done to me; and before I could guess her drift I blundered into telling her."

Thursdale drew a difficult breath. "I never supposed—your revenge is complete," he said slowly.

He heard a little gasp in her throat. "My revenge? When I sent for you to warn you—to save you from being surprised as *I* was surprised?"

"You're very good—but it's rather late to talk of saving me." He held out his hand in the mechanical gesture of leave-taking.

"How you must care!—for I never saw you so dull," was her answer. "Don't you see that it's not too late for me to help you?" And as he continued to stare, she brought out sublimely: "Take the rest—in imagination! Let it at least be of that much use to you. Tell her I lied to her—she's too ready to believe it! And so, after all, in a sense, I shan't have been wasted."

His stare hung on her, widening to a kind of wonder. She gave the look back brightly, unblushingly, as though the expedient were too simple to need oblique approaches. It was extraordinary how a few words had swept them from an atmosphere of the most complex dissimulations to this contact of naked souls.

It was not in Thursdale to expand with the pressure of fate; but something in him cracked with it, and the rift let in new light. He went up to his friend and took her hand.

"You would do it—you would do it!"

She looked at him, smiling, but her hand shook.

"Good-bye," he said, kissing it.

"Good-bye? You are going—?"

"To get my letter."

"Your letter? The letter won't matter, if you will only do what I ask."

He returned her gaze. "I might, I suppose, without being out of character. Only, don't you see that if your plan helped me it could only harm her?"

"Harm *her?*"

"To sacrifice you wouldn't make me different. I shall go on being what I have always been—sifting and sorting, as she calls it. Do you want my punishment to fall on *her?*"

She looked at him long and deeply. "Ah, if I had to choose between you—!"

"You would let her take her chance? But I can't, you see, I must take my punishment alone."

She drew her hand away, sighing. "Oh, there will be no punishment for either of you."

"For either of us? There will be the reading of her letter for me."

She shook her head with a slight laugh. "There will be no letter."

Thursdale faced about from the threshold with fresh life in his look. "No letter? You don't mean—"

"I mean that she's been with you since I saw her—she's seen you and heard your voice. If there *is* a letter, she has recalled it—from the first station, by telegraph."

He turned back to the door, forcing an answer to her smile. "But in the meanwhile I shall have read it," he said.

The door closed on him, and she hid her eyes from the dreadful emptiness of the room.

# DOVER THRIFT EDITIONS

## POETRY

101 GREAT AMERICAN POEMS, Edited by The American Poetry & Literacy Project. (0-486-40158-8)

100 BEST-LOVED POEMS, Edited by Philip Smith. (0-486-28553-7)

ENGLISH ROMANTIC POETRY: An Anthology, Edited by Stanley Appelbaum. (0-486-29282-7)

THE INFERNO, Dante Alighieri. Translated and with notes by Henry Wadsworth Longfellow. (0-486-44288-8)

PARADISE LOST, John Milton. Introduction and Notes by John A. Himes. (0-486-44287-X)

SPOON RIVER ANTHOLOGY, Edgar Lee Masters. (0-486-27275-3)

SELECTED CANTERBURY TALES, Geoffrey Chaucer. (0-486-28241-4)

SELECTED POEMS, Emily Dickinson. (0-486-26466-1)

LEAVES OF GRASS: The Original 1855 Edition, Walt Whitman. (0-486-45676-5)

COMPLETE SONNETS, William Shakespeare. (0-486-26686-9)

THE RAVEN AND OTHER FAVORITE POEMS, Edgar Allan Poe. (0-486-26685-0)

ENGLISH VICTORIAN POETRY: An Anthology, Edited by Paul Negri. (0-486-40425-0)

SELECTED POEMS, Walt Whitman. (0-486-26878-0)

THE ROAD NOT TAKEN AND OTHER POEMS, Robert Frost. (0-486-27550-7)

AFRICAN-AMERICAN POETRY: An Anthology, 1773-1927, Edited by Joan R. Sherman. (0-486-29604-0)

GREAT SHORT POEMS, Edited by Paul Negri. (0-486-41105-2)

THE RIME OF THE ANCIENT MARINER, Samuel Taylor Coleridge. (0-486-27266-4)

THE WASTE LAND, PRUFROCK AND OTHER POEMS, T. S. Eliot. (0-486-40061-1)

SONG OF MYSELF, Walt Whitman. (0-486-41410-8)

AENEID, Vergil. (0-486-28749-1)

SONGS FOR THE OPEN ROAD: Poems of Travel and Adventure, Edited by The American Poetry & Literacy Project. (0-486-40646-6)

SONGS OF INNOCENCE AND SONGS OF EXPERIENCE, William Blake. (0-486-27051-3)

WORLD WAR ONE BRITISH POETS: Brooke, Owen, Sassoon, Rosenberg and Others, Edited by Candace Ward. (0-486-29568-0)

GREAT SONNETS, Edited by Paul Negri. (0-486-28052-7)

CHRISTMAS CAROLS: Complete Verses, Edited by Shane Weller. (0-486-27397-0)

## POETRY

GREAT POEMS BY AMERICAN WOMEN: An Anthology, Edited by Susan L. Rattiner. (0-486-40164-2)

FAVORITE POEMS, Henry Wadsworth Longfellow. (0-486-27273-7)

BHAGAVADGITA, Translated by Sir Edwin Arnold. (0-486-27782-8)

ESSAY ON MAN AND OTHER POEMS, Alexander Pope. (0-486-28053-5)

GREAT LOVE POEMS, Edited by Shane Weller. (0-486-27284-2)

DOVER BEACH AND OTHER POEMS, Matthew Arnold. (0-486-28037-3)

THE SHOOTING OF DAN MCGREW AND OTHER POEMS, Robert Service. (0-486-27556-6)

THE BALLAD OF READING GAOL AND OTHER POEMS, Oscar Wilde. (0-486-27072-6)

SELECTED POEMS OF RUMI, Jalalu'l-Din Rumi. (0-486-41583-X)

SELECTED POEMS OF GERARD MANLEY HOPKINS, Gerard Manley Hopkins. Edited and with an Introduction by Bob Blaisdell. (0-486-47867-X)

RENASCENCE AND OTHER POEMS, Edna St. Vincent Millay. (0-486-26873-X)

THE RUBÁIYÁT OF OMAR KHAYYÁM: First and Fifth Editions, Edward FitzGerald. (0-486-26467-X)

TO MY HUSBAND AND OTHER POEMS, Anne Bradstreet. (0-486-41408-6)

LITTLE ORPHANT ANNIE AND OTHER POEMS, James Whitcomb Riley. (0-486-28260-0)

IMAGIST POETRY: AN ANTHOLOGY, Edited by Bob Blaisdell. (0-486-40875-2)

FIRST FIG AND OTHER POEMS, Edna St. Vincent Millay. (0-486-41104-4)

GREAT SHORT POEMS FROM ANTIQUITY TO THE TWENTIETH CENTURY, Edited by Dorothy Belle Pollack. (0-486-47876-9)

THE FLOWERS OF EVIL & PARIS SPLEEN: Selected Poems, Charles Baudelaire. Translated by Wallace Fowlie. (0-486-47545-X)

CIVIL WAR SHORT STORIES AND POEMS, Edited by Bob Blaisdell. (0-486-48226-X)

EARLY POEMS, Edna St. Vincent Millay. (0-486-43672-1)

JABBERWOCKY AND OTHER POEMS, Lewis Carroll. (0-486-41582-1)

THE METAMORPHOSES: Selected Stories in Verse, Ovid. (0-486-42758-7)

IDYLLS OF THE KING, Alfred, Lord Tennyson. Edited by W. J. Rolfe. (0-486-43795-7)

A BOY'S WILL AND NORTH OF BOSTON, Robert Frost. (0-486-26866-7)

100 FAVORITE ENGLISH AND IRISH POEMS, Edited by Clarence C. Strowbridge. (0-486-44429-5)

## FICTION

FLATLAND: A ROMANCE OF MANY DIMENSIONS, Edwin A. Abbott. (0-486-27263-X)

PRIDE AND PREJUDICE, Jane Austen. (0-486-28473-5)

CIVIL WAR SHORT STORIES AND POEMS, Edited by Bob Blaisdell. (0-486-48226-X)

THE DECAMERON: Selected Tales, Giovanni Boccaccio. Edited by Bob Blaisdell. (0-486-41113-3)

JANE EYRE, Charlotte Brontë. (0-486-42449-9)

WUTHERING HEIGHTS, Emily Brontë. (0-486-29256-8)

THE THIRTY-NINE STEPS, John Buchan. (0-486-28201-5)

ALICE'S ADVENTURES IN WONDERLAND, Lewis Carroll. (0-486-27543-4)

MY ÁNTONIA, Willa Cather. (0-486-28240-6)

THE AWAKENING, Kate Chopin. (0-486-27786-0)

HEART OF DARKNESS, Joseph Conrad. (0-486-26464-5)

LORD JIM, Joseph Conrad. (0-486-40650-4)

THE RED BADGE OF COURAGE, Stephen Crane. (0-486-26465-3)

THE WORLD'S GREATEST SHORT STORIES, Edited by James Daley. (0-486-44716-2)

A CHRISTMAS CAROL, Charles Dickens. (0-486-26865-9)

GREAT EXPECTATIONS, Charles Dickens. (0-486-41586-4)

A TALE OF TWO CITIES, Charles Dickens. (0-486-40651-2)

CRIME AND PUNISHMENT, Fyodor Dostoyevsky. Translated by Constance Garnett. (0-486-41587-2)

THE ADVENTURES OF SHERLOCK HOLMES, Sir Arthur Conan Doyle. (0-486-47491-7)

THE HOUND OF THE BASKERVILLES, Sir Arthur Conan Doyle. (0-486-28214-7)

BLAKE: PROPHET AGAINST EMPIRE, David V. Erdman. (0-486-26719-9)

WHERE ANGELS FEAR TO TREAD, E. M. Forster. (0-486-27791-7)

BEOWULF, Translated by R. K. Gordon. (0-486-27264-8)

THE RETURN OF THE NATIVE, Thomas Hardy. (0-486-43165-7)

THE SCARLET LETTER, Nathaniel Hawthorne. (0-486-28048-9)

SIDDHARTHA, Hermann Hesse. (0-486-40653-9)

THE ODYSSEY, Homer. (0-486-40654-7)

THE TURN OF THE SCREW, Henry James. (0-486-26684-2)

DUBLINERS, James Joyce. (0-486-26870-5)

## FICTION

THE METAMORPHOSIS AND OTHER STORIES, Franz Kafka. (0-486-29030-1)

SONS AND LOVERS, D. H. Lawrence. (0-486-42121-X)

THE CALL OF THE WILD, Jack London. (0-486-26472-6)

GREAT AMERICAN SHORT STORIES, Edited by Paul Negri. (0-486-42119-8)

THE GOLD-BUG AND OTHER TALES, Edgar Allan Poe. (0-486-26875-6)

ANTHEM, Ayn Rand. (0-486-49277-X)

FRANKENSTEIN, Mary Shelley. (0-486-28211-2)

THE JUNGLE, Upton Sinclair. (0-486-41923-1)

THREE LIVES, Gertrude Stein. (0-486-28059-4)

THE STRANGE CASE OF DR. JEKYLL AND MR. HYDE, Robert Louis Stevenson. (0-486-26688-5)

DRACULA, Bram Stoker. (0-486-41109-5)

UNCLE TOM'S CABIN, Harriet Beecher Stowe. (0-486-44028-1)

ADVENTURES OF HUCKLEBERRY FINN, Mark Twain. (0-486-28061-6)

THE ADVENTURES OF TOM SAWYER, Mark Twain. (0-486-40077-8)

CANDIDE, Voltaire. Edited by Francois-Marie Arouet. (0-486-26689-3)

THE COUNTRY OF THE BLIND: and Other Science-Fiction Stories, H. G. Wells. Edited by Martin Gardner. (0-486-48289-8)

THE WAR OF THE WORLDS, H. G. Wells. (0-486-29506-0)

ETHAN FROME, Edith Wharton. (0-486-26690-7)

THE PICTURE OF DORIAN GRAY, Oscar Wilde. (0-486-27807-7)

MONDAY OR TUESDAY: Eight Stories, Virginia Woolf. (0-486-29453-6)

## NONFICTION

POETICS, Aristotle. (0-486-29577-X)

MEDITATIONS, Marcus Aurelius. (0-486-29823-X)

THE WAY OF PERFECTION, St. Teresa of Avila. Edited and Translated by
E. Allison Peers. (0-486-48451-3)

THE DEVIL'S DICTIONARY, Ambrose Bierce. (0-486-27542-6)

GREAT SPEECHES OF THE 20TH CENTURY, Edited by Bob Blaisdell.
(0-486-47467-4)

THE COMMUNIST MANIFESTO AND OTHER REVOLUTIONARY WRITINGS:
Marx, Marat, Paine, Mao Tse-Tung, Gandhi and Others, Edited by Bob Blaisdell.
(0-486-42465-0)

INFAMOUS SPEECHES: From Robespierre to Osama bin Laden, Edited by Bob
Blaisdell. (0-486-47849-1)

GREAT ENGLISH ESSAYS: From Bacon to Chesterton, Edited by Bob Blaisdell.
(0-486-44082-6)

GREEK AND ROMAN ORATORY, Edited by Bob Blaisdell. (0-486-49622-8)

THE UNITED STATES CONSTITUTION: The Full Text with Supplementary
Materials, Edited and with supplementary materials by Bob Blaisdell.
(0-486-47166-7)

GREAT SPEECHES BY NATIVE AMERICANS, Edited by Bob Blaisdell.
(0-486-41122-2)

GREAT SPEECHES BY AFRICAN AMERICANS: Frederick Douglass, Sojourner
Truth, Dr. Martin Luther King, Jr., Barack Obama, and Others, Edited by
James Daley. (0-486-44761-8)

GREAT SPEECHES BY AMERICAN WOMEN, Edited by James Daley.
(0-486-46141-6)

HISTORY'S GREATEST SPEECHES, Edited by James Daley. (0-486-49739-9)

GREAT INAUGURAL ADDRESSES, Edited by James Daley. (0-486-44577-1)

GREAT SPEECHES ON GAY RIGHTS, Edited by James Daley. (0-486-47512-3)

ON THE ORIGIN OF SPECIES: By Means of Natural Selection, Charles Darwin.
(0-486-45006-6)

NARRATIVE OF THE LIFE OF FREDERICK DOUGLASS, Frederick Douglass.
(0-486-28499-9)

THE SOULS OF BLACK FOLK, W. E. B. Du Bois. (0-486-28041-1)

NATURE AND OTHER ESSAYS, Ralph Waldo Emerson. (0-486-46947-6)

SELF-RELIANCE AND OTHER ESSAYS, Ralph Waldo Emerson. (0-486-27790-9)

THE LIFE OF OLAUDAH EQUIANO, Olaudah Equiano. (0-486-40661-X)

WIT AND WISDOM FROM POOR RICHARD'S ALMANACK, Benjamin Franklin.
(0-486-40891-4)

THE AUTOBIOGRAPHY OF BENJAMIN FRANKLIN, Benjamin Franklin.
(0-486-29073-5)

## NONFICTION

THE DECLARATION OF INDEPENDENCE AND OTHER GREAT DOCUMENTS OF AMERICAN HISTORY: 1775-1865, Edited by John Grafton. (0-486-41124-9)

INCIDENTS IN THE LIFE OF A SLAVE GIRL, Harriet Jacobs. (0-486-41931-2)

GREAT SPEECHES, Abraham Lincoln. (0-486-26872-1)

THE WIT AND WISDOM OF ABRAHAM LINCOLN: A Book of Quotations, Abraham Lincoln. Edited by Bob Blaisdell. (0-486-44097-4)

THE SECOND TREATISE OF GOVERNMENT AND A LETTER CONCERNING TOLERATION, John Locke. (0-486-42464-2)

THE PRINCE, Niccolò Machiavelli. (0-486-27274-5)

MICHEL DE MONTAIGNE: Selected Essays, Michel de Montaigne. Translated by Charles Cotton. Edited by William Carew Hazlitt. (0-486-48603-6)

UTOPIA, Sir Thomas More. (0-486-29583-4)

BEYOND GOOD AND EVIL: Prelude to a Philosophy of the Future, Friedrich Nietzsche. (0-486-29868-X)

TWELVE YEARS A SLAVE, Solomon Northup. (0-486-78962-4)

COMMON SENSE, Thomas Paine. (0-486-29602-4)

BOOK OF AFRICAN-AMERICAN QUOTATIONS, Edited by Joslyn Pine. (0-486-47589-1)

THE TRIAL AND DEATH OF SOCRATES: Four Dialogues, Plato. (0-486-27066-1)

THE REPUBLIC, Plato. (0-486-41121-4)

SIX GREAT DIALOGUES: Apology, Crito, Phaedo, Phaedrus, Symposium, The Republic, Plato. Translated by Benjamin Jowett. (0-486-45465-7)

WOMEN'S WIT AND WISDOM: A Book of Quotations, Edited by Susan L. Rattiner. (0-486-41123-0)

GREAT SPEECHES, Franklin Delano Roosevelt. (0-486-40894-9)

THE CONFESSIONS OF ST. AUGUSTINE, St. Augustine. (0-486-42466-9)

A MODEST PROPOSAL AND OTHER SATIRICAL WORKS, Jonathan Swift. (0-486-28759-9)

THE IMITATION OF CHRIST, Thomas à Kempis. Translated by Aloysius Croft and Harold Bolton. (0-486-43185-1)

CIVIL DISOBEDIENCE AND OTHER ESSAYS, Henry David Thoreau. (0-486-27563-9)

WALDEN; OR, LIFE IN THE WOODS, Henry David Thoreau. (0-486-28495-6)

NARRATIVE OF SOJOURNER TRUTH, Sojourner Truth. (0-486-29899-X)

THE WIT AND WISDOM OF MARK TWAIN: A Book of Quotations, Mark Twain. (0-486-40664-4)

UP FROM SLAVERY, Booker T. Washington. (0-486-28738-6)

A VINDICATION OF THE RIGHTS OF WOMAN, Mary Wollstonecraft. (0-486-29036-0)

## PLAYS

THE ORESTEIA TRILOGY: Agamemnon, the Libation-Bearers and the Furies, Aeschylus. (0-486-29242-8)

EVERYMAN, Anonymous. (0-486-28726-2)

THE BIRDS, Aristophanes. (0-486-40886-8)

LYSISTRATA, Aristophanes. (0-486-28225-2)

THE CHERRY ORCHARD, Anton Chekhov. (0-486-26682-6)

THE SEA GULL, Anton Chekhov. (0-486-40656-3)

MEDEA, Euripides. (0-486-27548-5)

FAUST, PART ONE, Johann Wolfgang von Goethe. (0-486-28046-2)

THE INSPECTOR GENERAL, Nikolai Gogol. (0-486-28500-6)

SHE STOOPS TO CONQUER, Oliver Goldsmith. (0-486-26867-5)

GHOSTS, Henrik Ibsen. (0-486-29852-3)

A DOLL'S HOUSE, Henrik Ibsen. (0-486-27062-9)

HEDDA GABLER, Henrik Ibsen. (0-486-26469-6)

DR. FAUSTUS, Christopher Marlowe. (0-486-28208-2)

TARTUFFE, Molière. (0-486-41117-6)

BEYOND THE HORIZON, Eugene O'Neill. (0-486-29085-9)

THE EMPEROR JONES, Eugene O'Neill. (0-486-29268-1)

CYRANO DE BERGERAC, Edmond Rostand. (0-486-41119-2)

MEASURE FOR MEASURE: Unabridged, William Shakespeare. (0-486-40889-2)

FOUR GREAT TRAGEDIES: Hamlet, Macbeth, Othello, and Romeo and Juliet, William Shakespeare. (0-486-44083-4)

THE COMEDY OF ERRORS, William Shakespeare. (0-486-42461-8)

HENRY V, William Shakespeare. (0-486-42887-7)

MUCH ADO ABOUT NOTHING, William Shakespeare. (0-486-28272-4)

FIVE GREAT COMEDIES: Much Ado About Nothing, Twelfth Night, A Midsummer Night's Dream, As You Like It and The Merry Wives of Windsor, William Shakespeare. (0-486-44086-9)

OTHELLO, William Shakespeare. (0-486-29097-2)

AS YOU LIKE IT, William Shakespeare. (0-486-40432-3)

ROMEO AND JULIET, William Shakespeare. (0-486-27557-4)

A MIDSUMMER NIGHT'S DREAM, William Shakespeare. (0-486-27067-X)

THE MERCHANT OF VENICE, William Shakespeare. (0-486-28492-1)

HAMLET, William Shakespeare. (0-486-27278-8)

RICHARD III, William Shakespeare. (0-486-28747-5)

## PLAYS

THE TAMING OF THE SHREW, William Shakespeare. (0-486-29765-9)

MACBETH, William Shakespeare. (0-486-27802-6)

KING LEAR, William Shakespeare. (0-486-28058-6)

FOUR GREAT HISTORIES: Henry IV Part I, Henry IV Part II, Henry V, and Richard III, William Shakespeare. (0-486-44629-8)

THE TEMPEST, William Shakespeare. (0-486-40658-X)

JULIUS CAESAR, William Shakespeare. (0-486-26876-4)

TWELFTH NIGHT; OR, WHAT YOU WILL, William Shakespeare. (0-486-29290-8)

HEARTBREAK HOUSE, George Bernard Shaw. (0-486-29291-6)

PYGMALION, George Bernard Shaw. (0-486-28222-8)

ARMS AND THE MAN, George Bernard Shaw. (0-486-26476-9)

OEDIPUS REX, Sophocles. (0-486-26877-2)

ANTIGONE, Sophocles. (0-486-27804-2)

FIVE GREAT GREEK TRAGEDIES, Sophocles, Euripides and Aeschylus. (0-486-43620-9)

THE FATHER, August Strindberg. (0-486-43217-3)

THE PLAYBOY OF THE WESTERN WORLD AND RIDERS TO THE SEA, J. M. Synge. (0-486-27562-0)

TWELVE CLASSIC ONE-ACT PLAYS, Edited by Mary Carolyn Waldrep. (0-486-47490-9)

LADY WINDERMERE'S FAN, Oscar Wilde. (0-486-40078-6)

AN IDEAL HUSBAND, Oscar Wilde. (0-486-41423-X)

THE IMPORTANCE OF BEING EARNEST, Oscar Wilde. (0-486-26478-5)